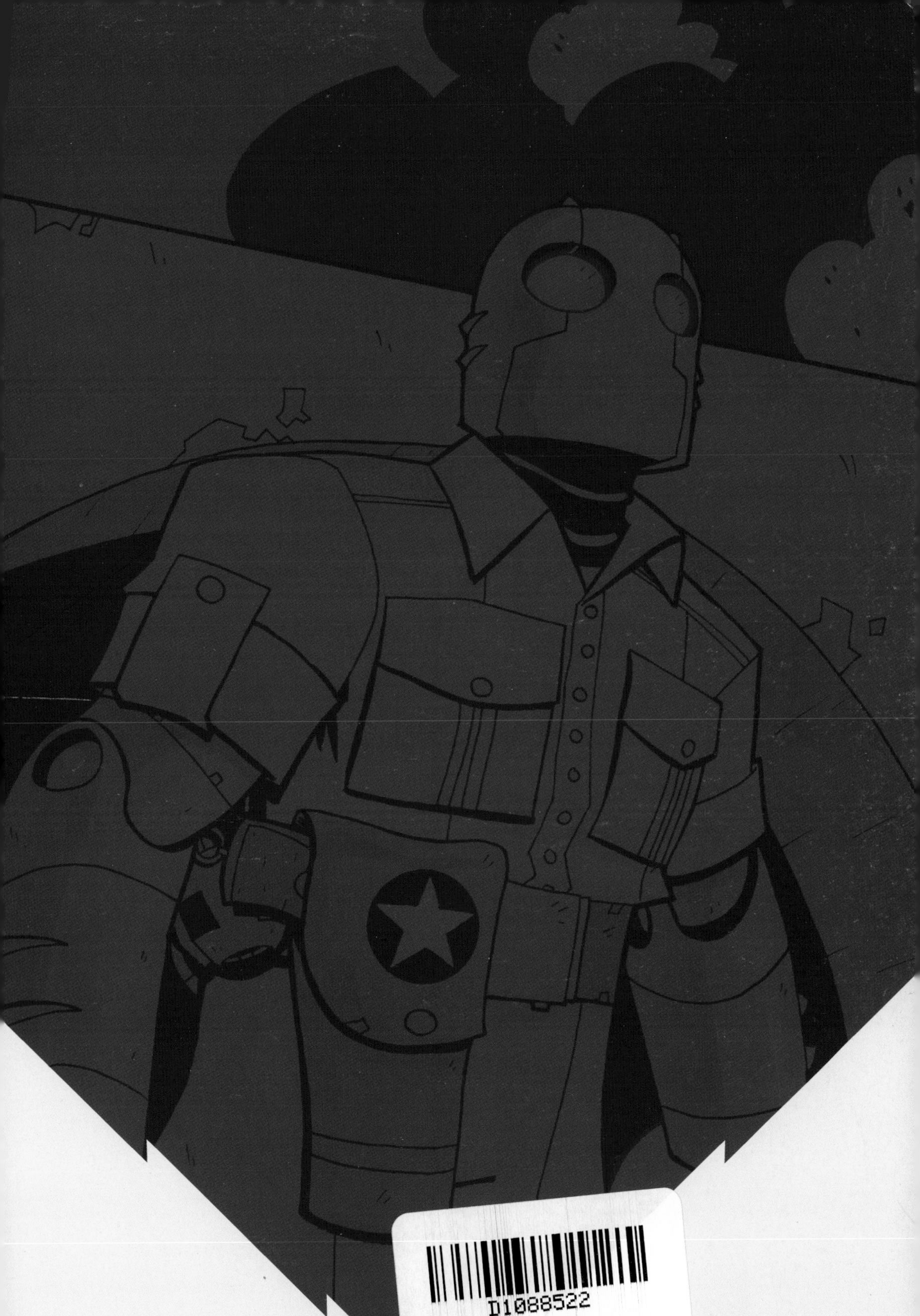

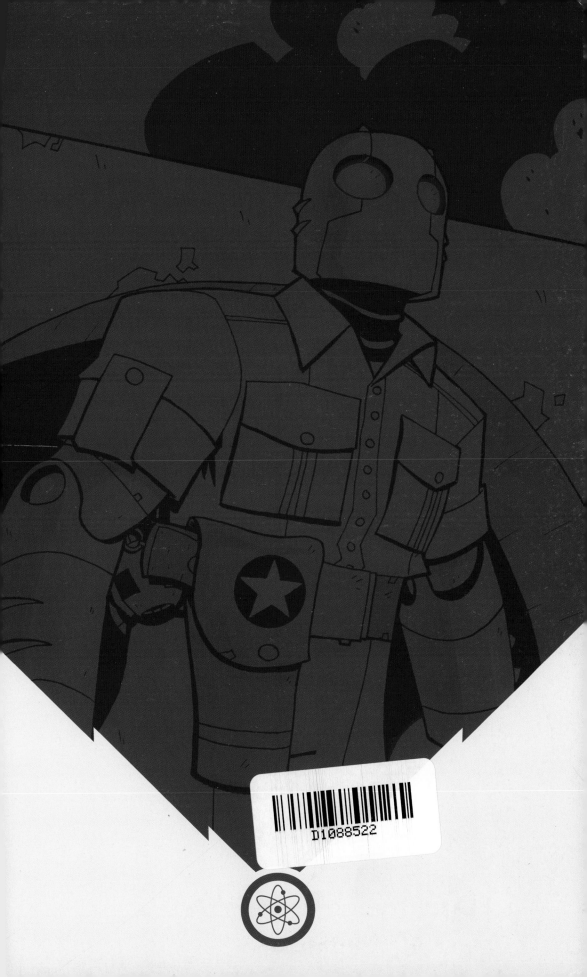

Facebook: **facebook.com/idwpublishing**
Twitter: **@idwpublishing**
YouTube: **youtube.com/idwpublishing**
Tumblr: **tumblr.idwpublishing.com**
Instagram: **instagram.com/idwpublishing**

COVER ART BY
SCOTT WEGENER
AND ANTHONY CLARK

COLLECTION EDITS BY
JUSTIN EISINGER
AND ALONZO SIMON

COLLECTION DESIGN BY
JEFF POWELL

978-1-63140-423-8   19 18 17 16   2 3 4 5

Ted Adams, CEO & Publisher

Greg Goldstein, President & COO

Robbie Robbins, EVP/Sr. Graphic Artist

Chris Ryall, Chief Creative Officer/Editor-in-Chief

Matthew Ruzicka, CPA, Chief Financial Officer

Alan Payne, VP of Sales

Dirk Wood, VP of Marketing

Lorelei Bunjes, VP of Digital Services

Jeff Webber, VP of Digital Publishing & Business Development

IDW founded by Ted Adams, Alex Garner,
Kris Oprisko, and Robbie Robbins

TESLADYNE LLC

Atomic Robo

The Everything Explodes Collection

WORDS
BRIAN CLEVINGER

ART
SCOTT WEGENER

— CREATORS —

COLORS
RONDA PATTISON

LETTERS
JEFF POWELL

EDITS
LEE BLACK

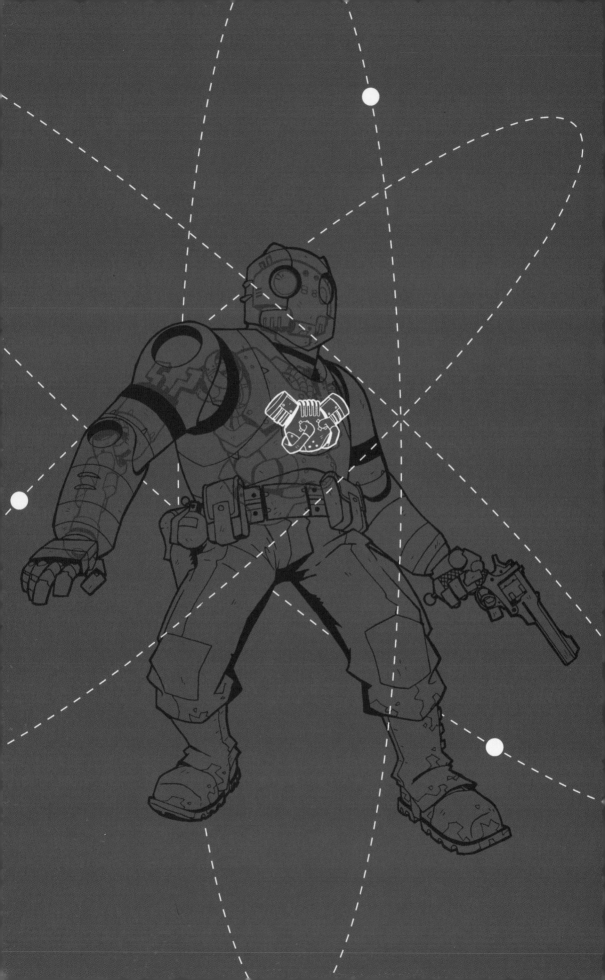

THE VRIL TO POWER

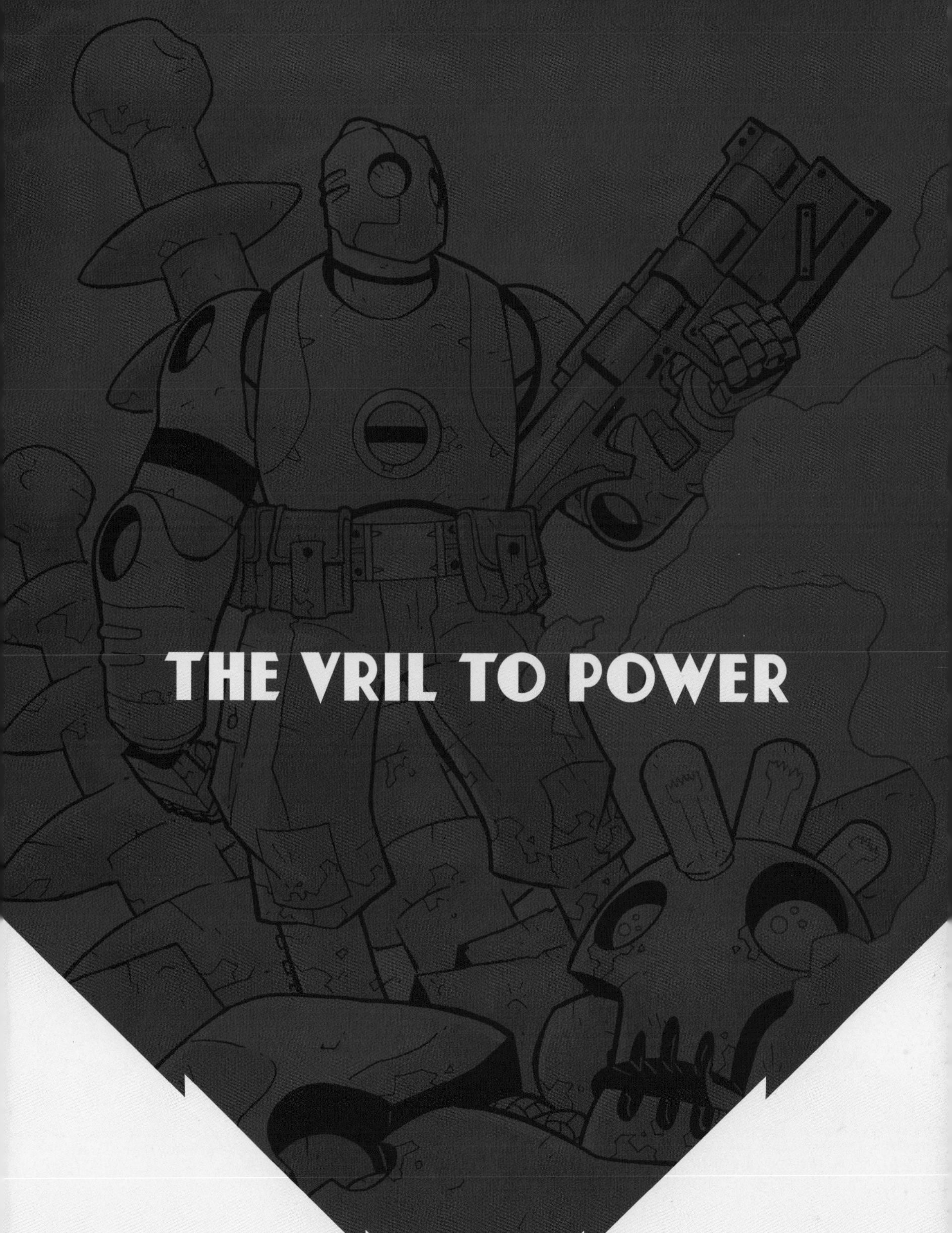

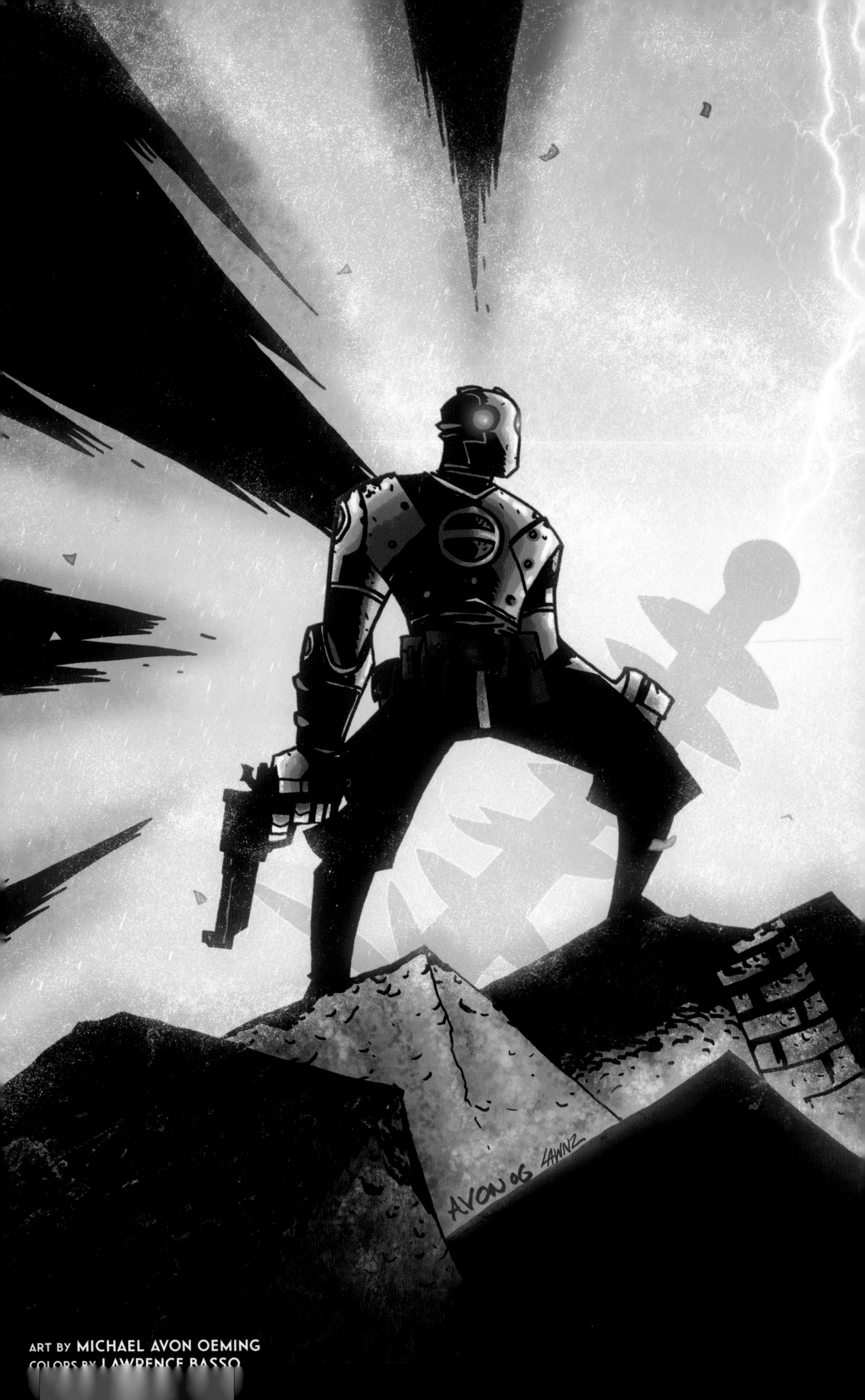
AVON 06
LAWNZ

ART BY MICHAEL AVON OEMING
COLORS BY LAWRENCE BASSO

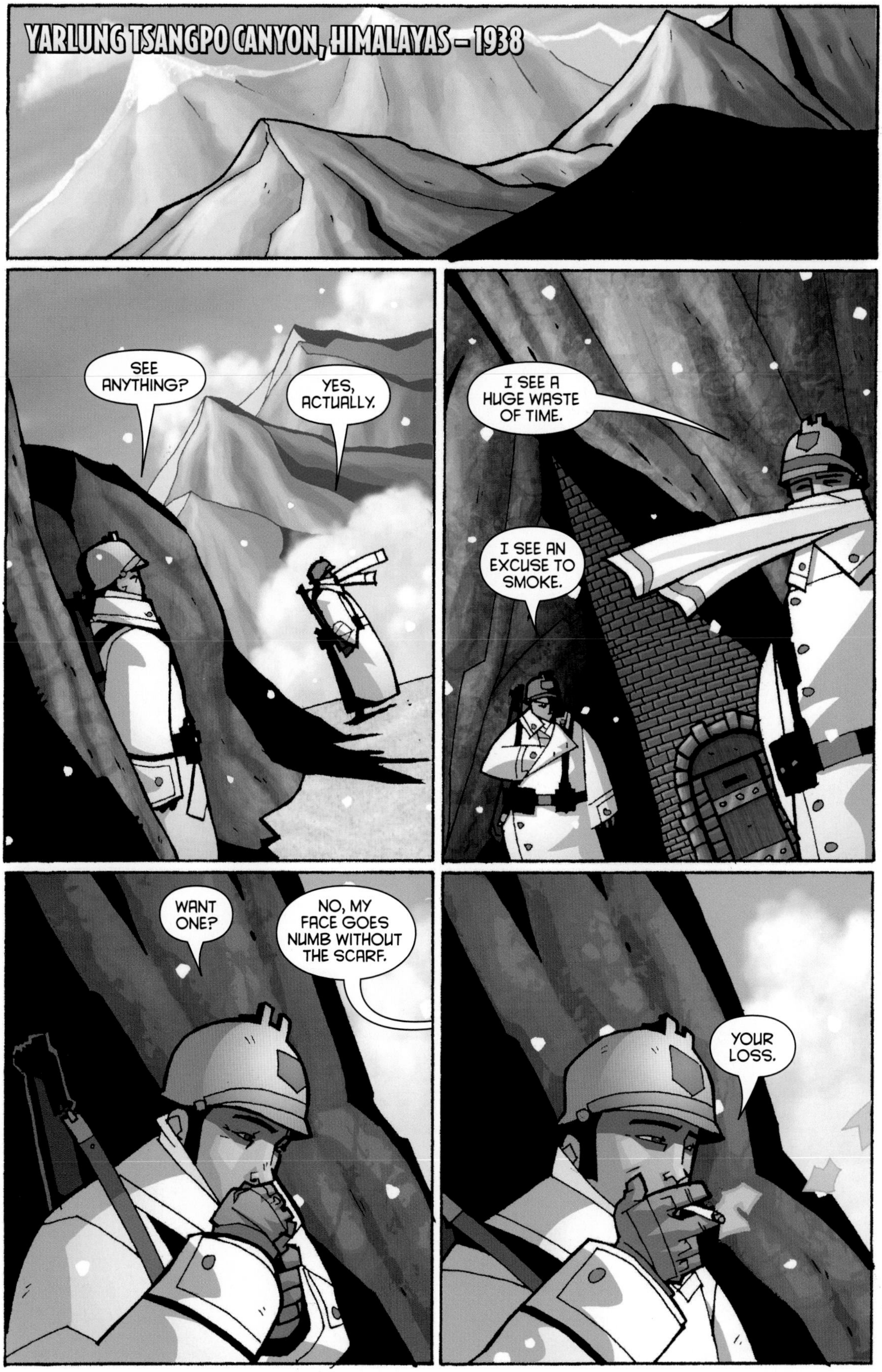
YARLUNG TSANGPO CANYON, HIMALAYAS – 1938
SEE ANYTHING?
YES, ACTUALLY.
I SEE A HUGE WASTE OF TIME.
I SEE AN EXCUSE TO SMOKE.
WANT ONE?
NO, MY FACE GOES NUMB WITHOUT THE SCARF.
YOUR LOSS.

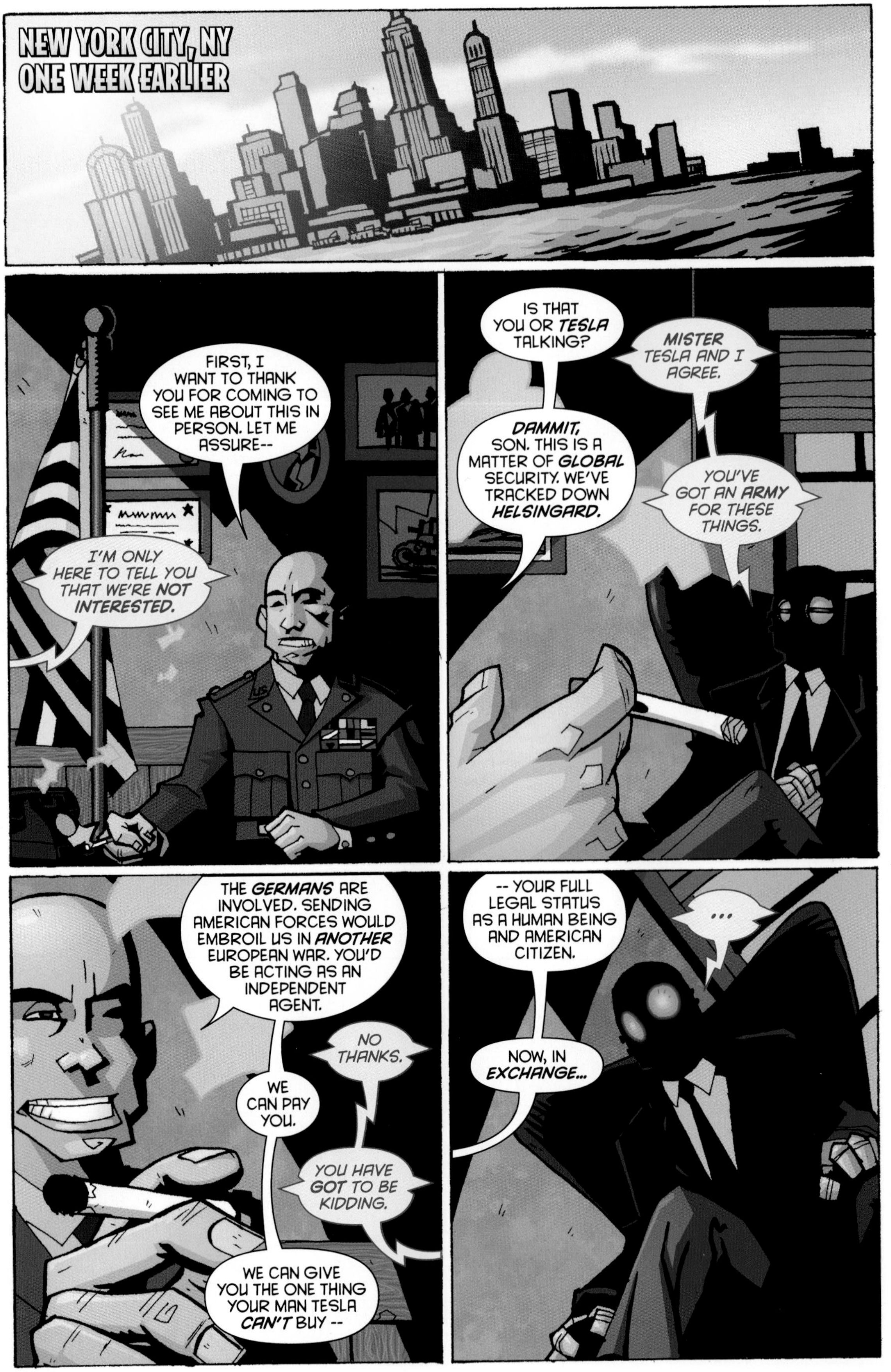
NEW YORK CITY, NY
ONE WEEK EARLIER
FIRST, I WANT TO THANK YOU FOR COMING TO SEE ME ABOUT THIS IN PERSON. LET ME ASSURE--
I'M ONLY HERE TO TELL YOU THAT WE'RE NOT INTERESTED.
IS THAT YOU OR TESLA TALKING?
MISTER TESLA AND I AGREE.
DAMMIT, SON. THIS IS A MATTER OF GLOBAL SECURITY. WE'VE TRACKED DOWN HELSINGARD.
YOU'VE GOT AN ARMY FOR THESE THINGS.
THE GERMANS ARE INVOLVED. SENDING AMERICAN FORCES WOULD EMBROIL US IN ANOTHER EUROPEAN WAR. YOU'D BE ACTING AS AN INDEPENDENT AGENT.
NO THANKS.
WE CAN PAY YOU.
YOU HAVE GOT TO BE KIDDING.
WE CAN GIVE YOU THE ONE THING YOUR MAN TESLA CAN'T BUY --
-- YOUR FULL LEGAL STATUS AS A HUMAN BEING AND AMERICAN CITIZEN.
...
NOW, IN EXCHANGE...

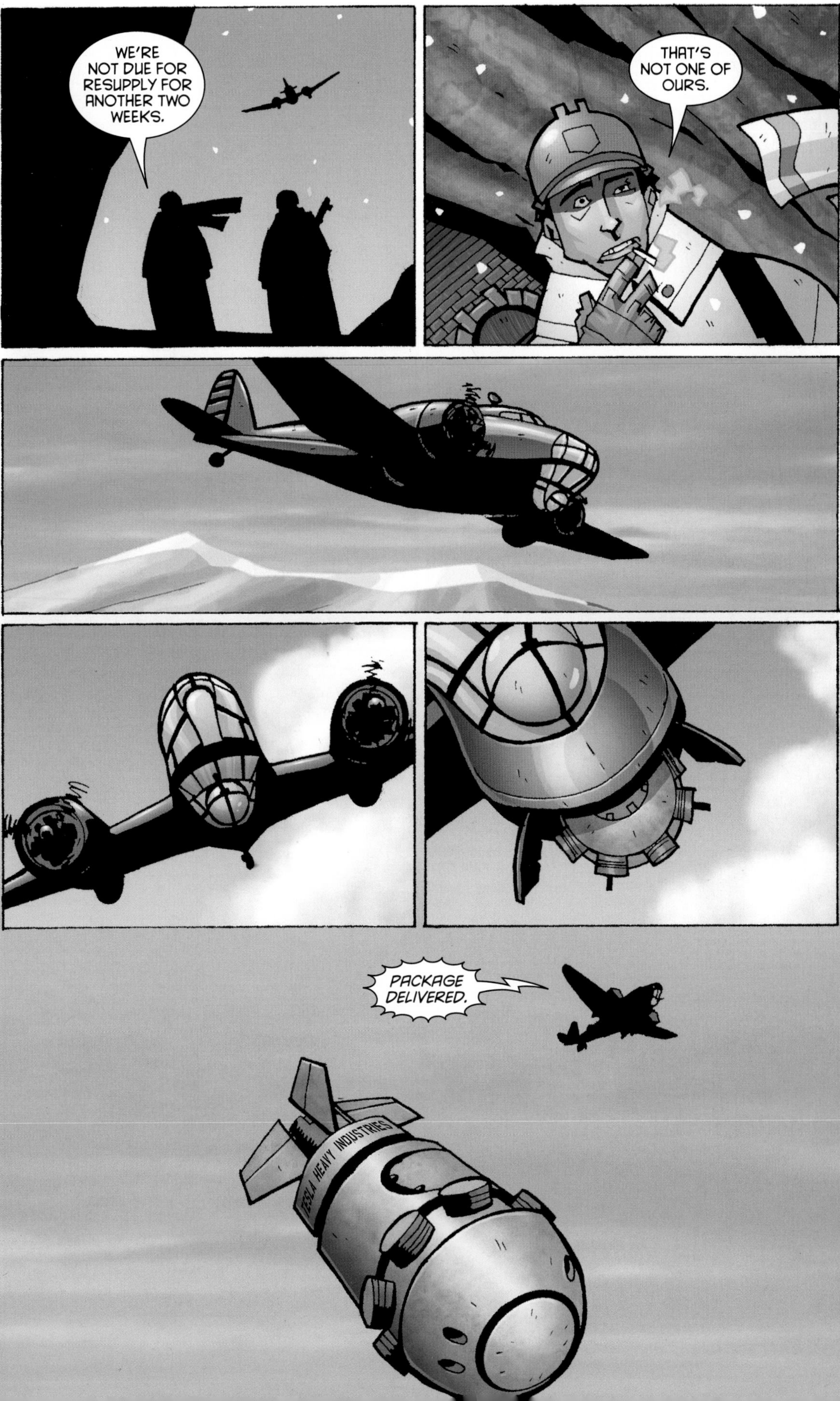
WE'RE NOT DUE FOR RESUPPLY FOR ANOTHER TWO WEEKS.
THAT'S NOT ONE OF OURS.
PACKAGE DELIVERED.
TESLA HEAVY INDUSTRIES

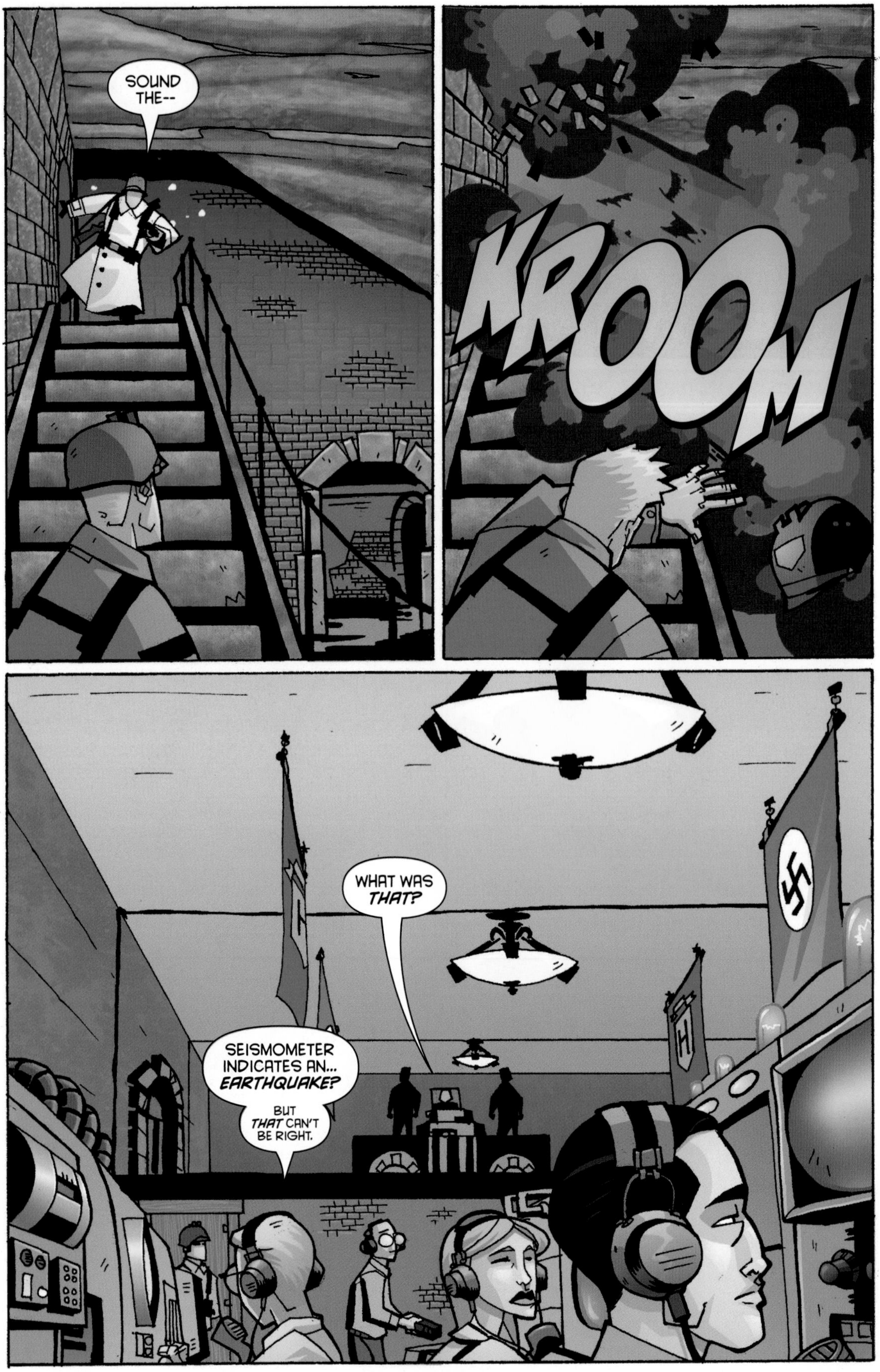
SOUND THE--
KROOM
WHAT WAS THAT?
SEISMOMETER INDICATES AN... EARTHQUAKE?
BUT THAT CAN'T BE RIGHT.

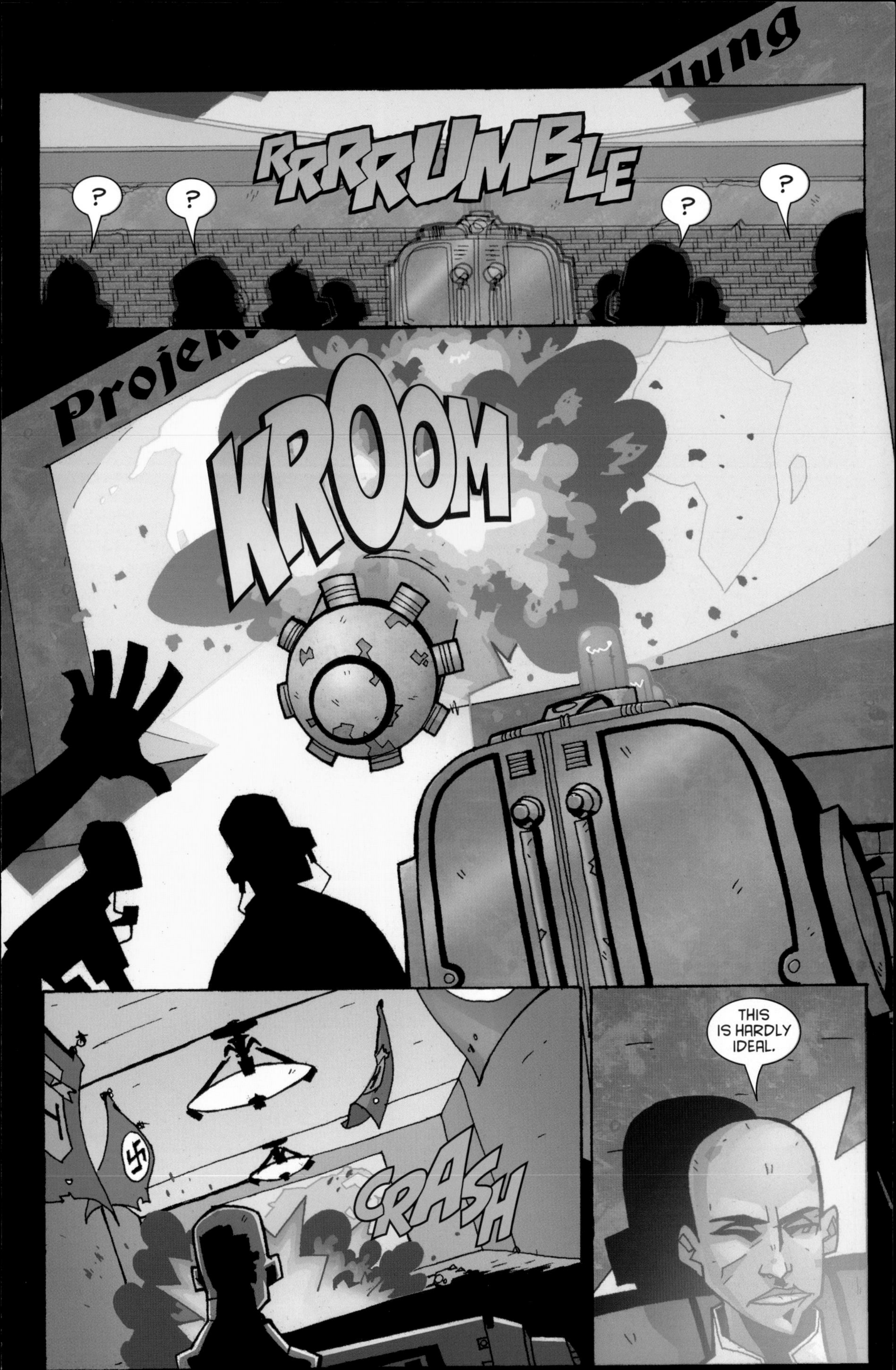
llung
RRRRUMBLE
?
?
?
?
Projek
KROOM
CRASH
THIS IS HARDLY IDEAL.

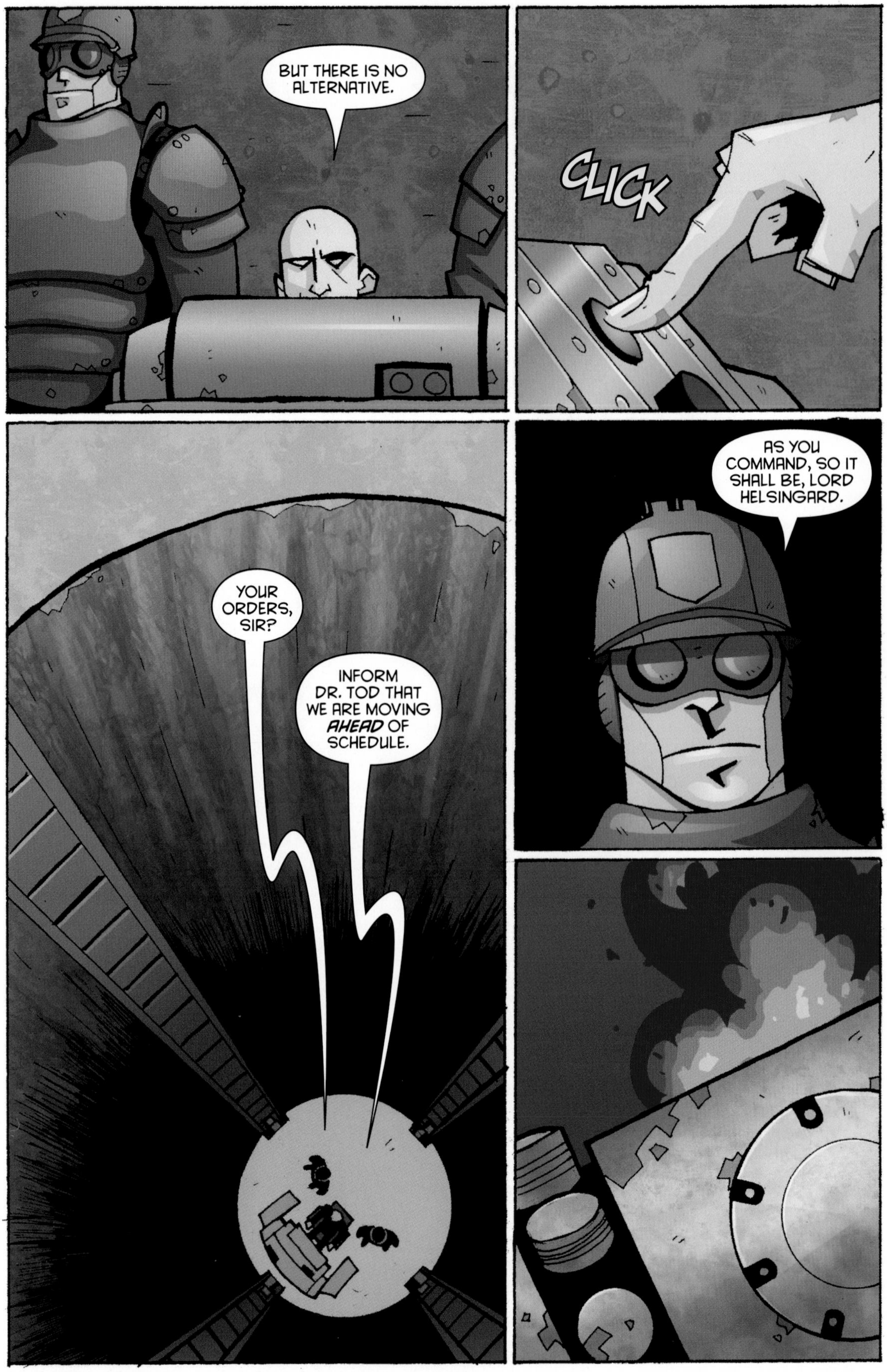

BUT THERE IS NO ALTERNATIVE.
CLICK
YOUR ORDERS, SIR?
INFORM DR. TOD THAT WE ARE MOVING AHEAD OF SCHEDULE.
AS YOU COMMAND, SO IT SHALL BE, LORD HELSINGARD.

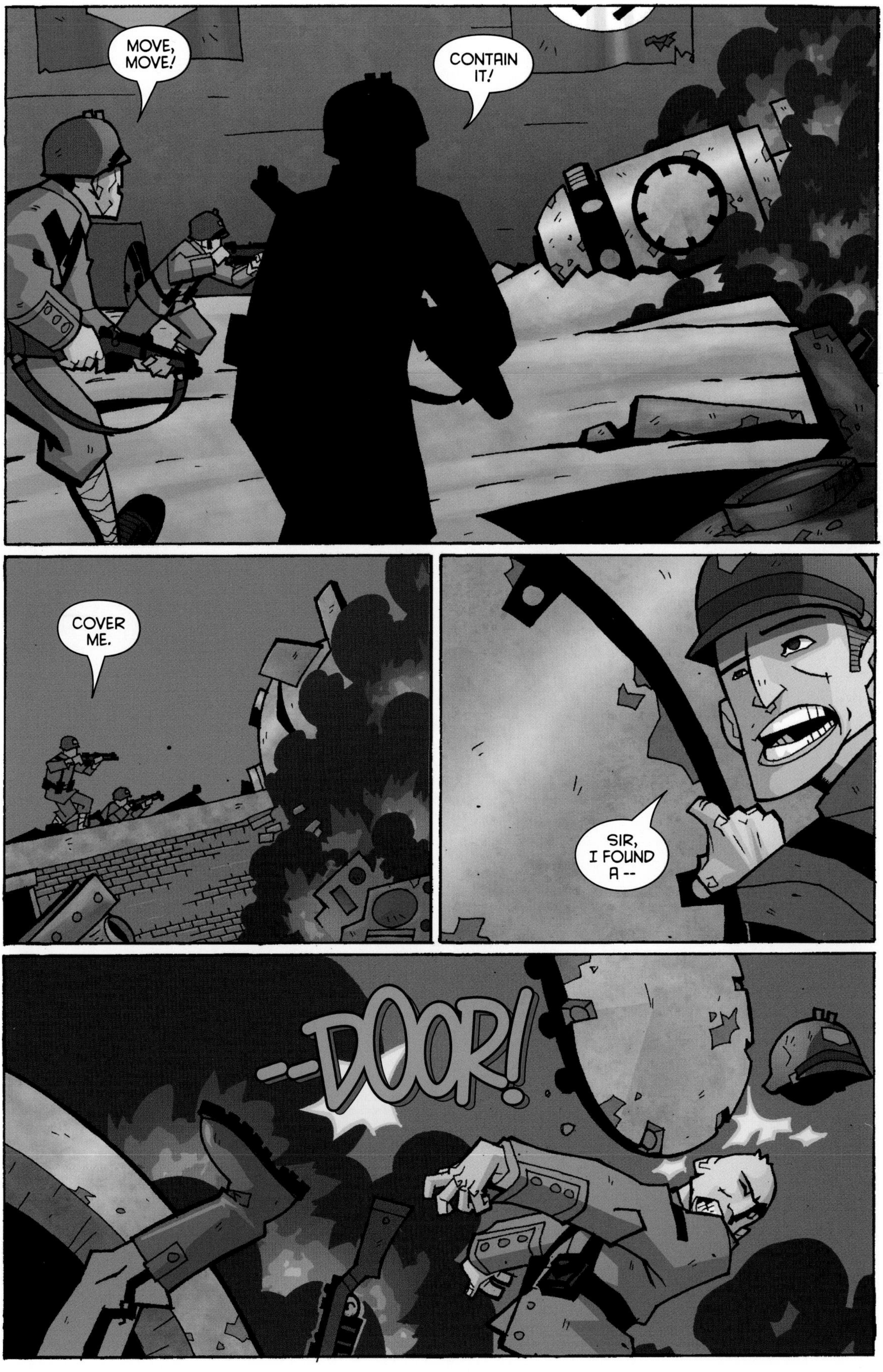
MOVE, MOVE!
CONTAIN IT!
COVER ME.
SIR, I FOUND A --
--DOOR!

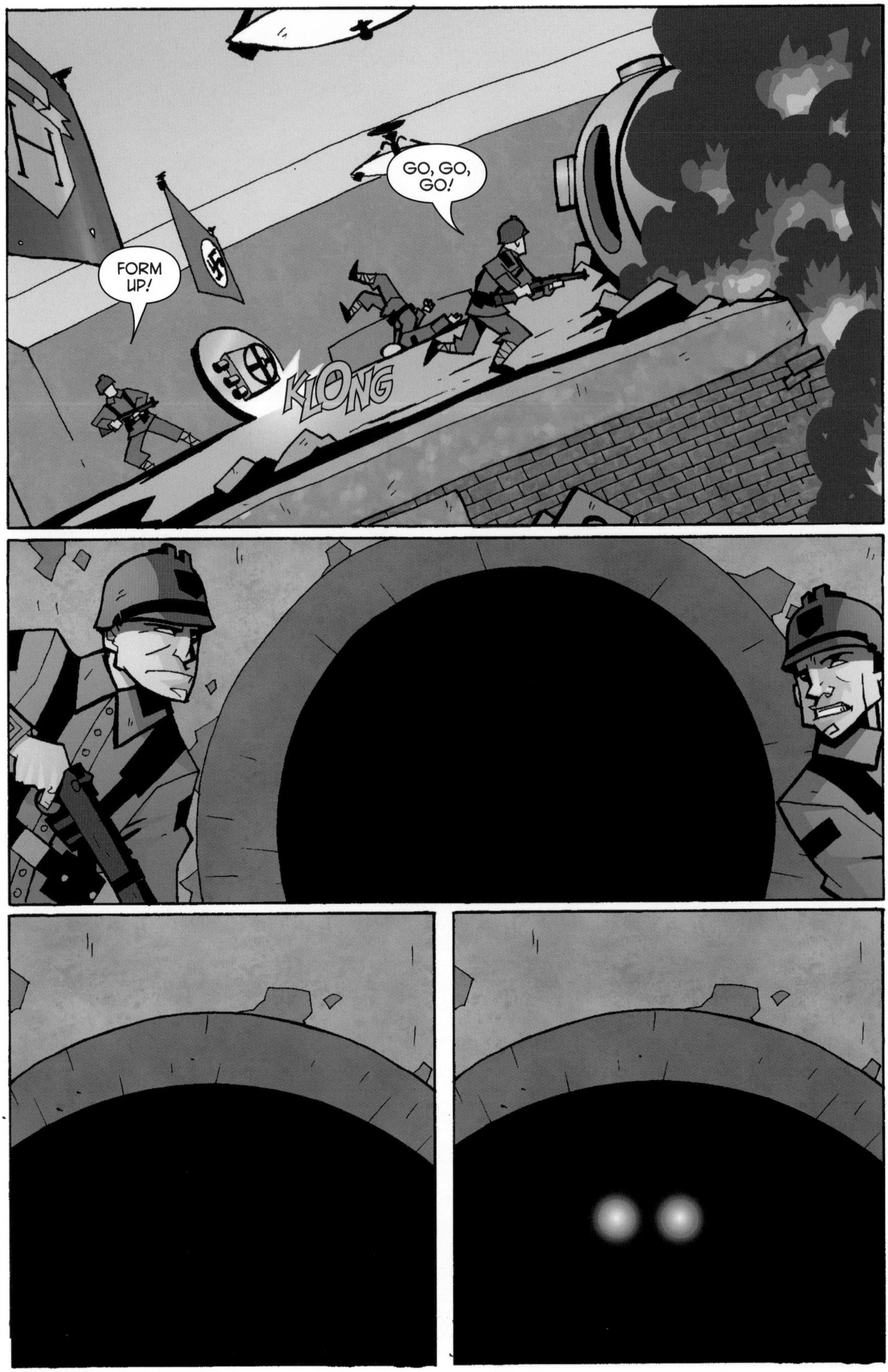
FORM UP!
KLONG
GO, GO, GO!

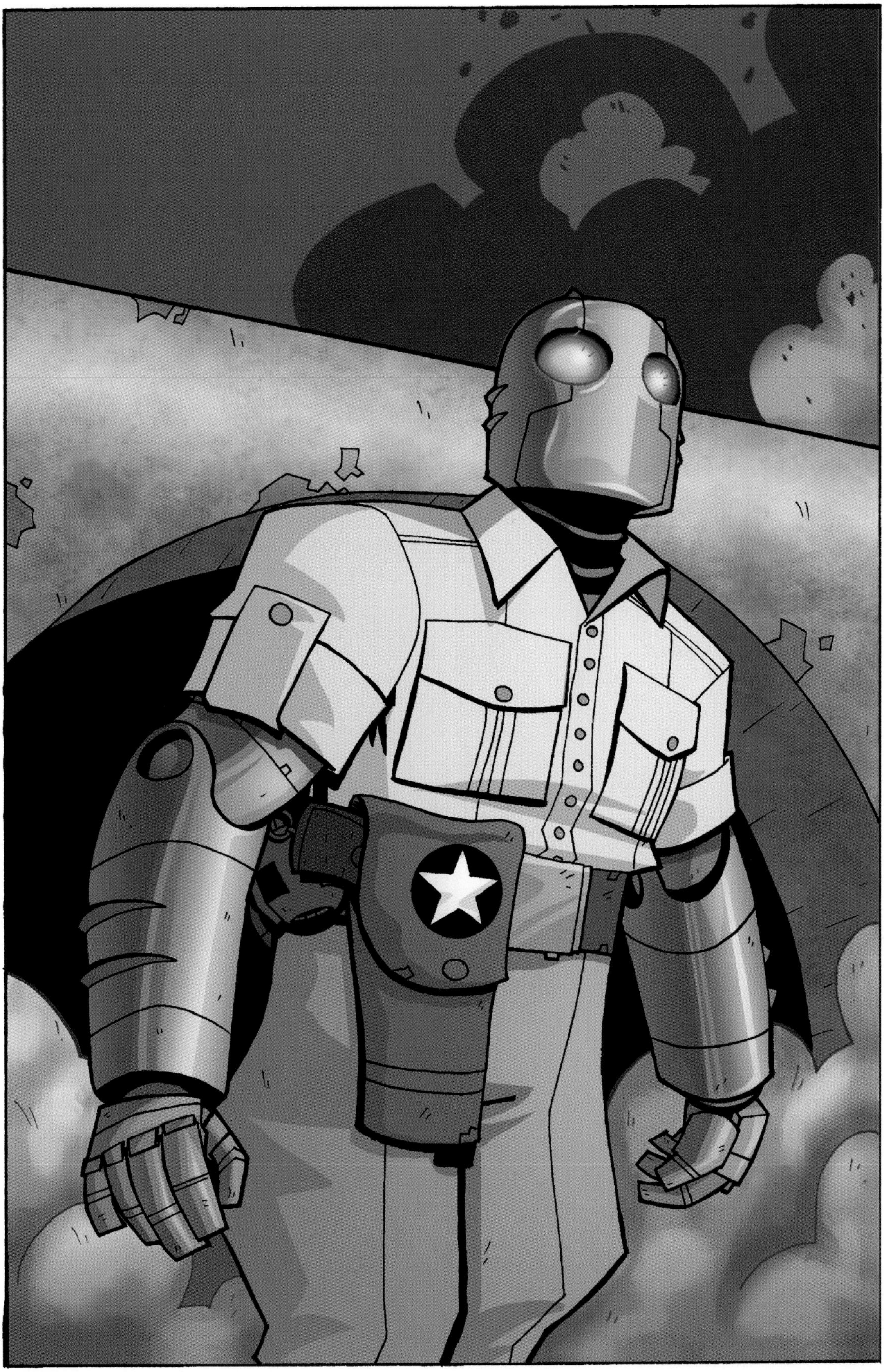

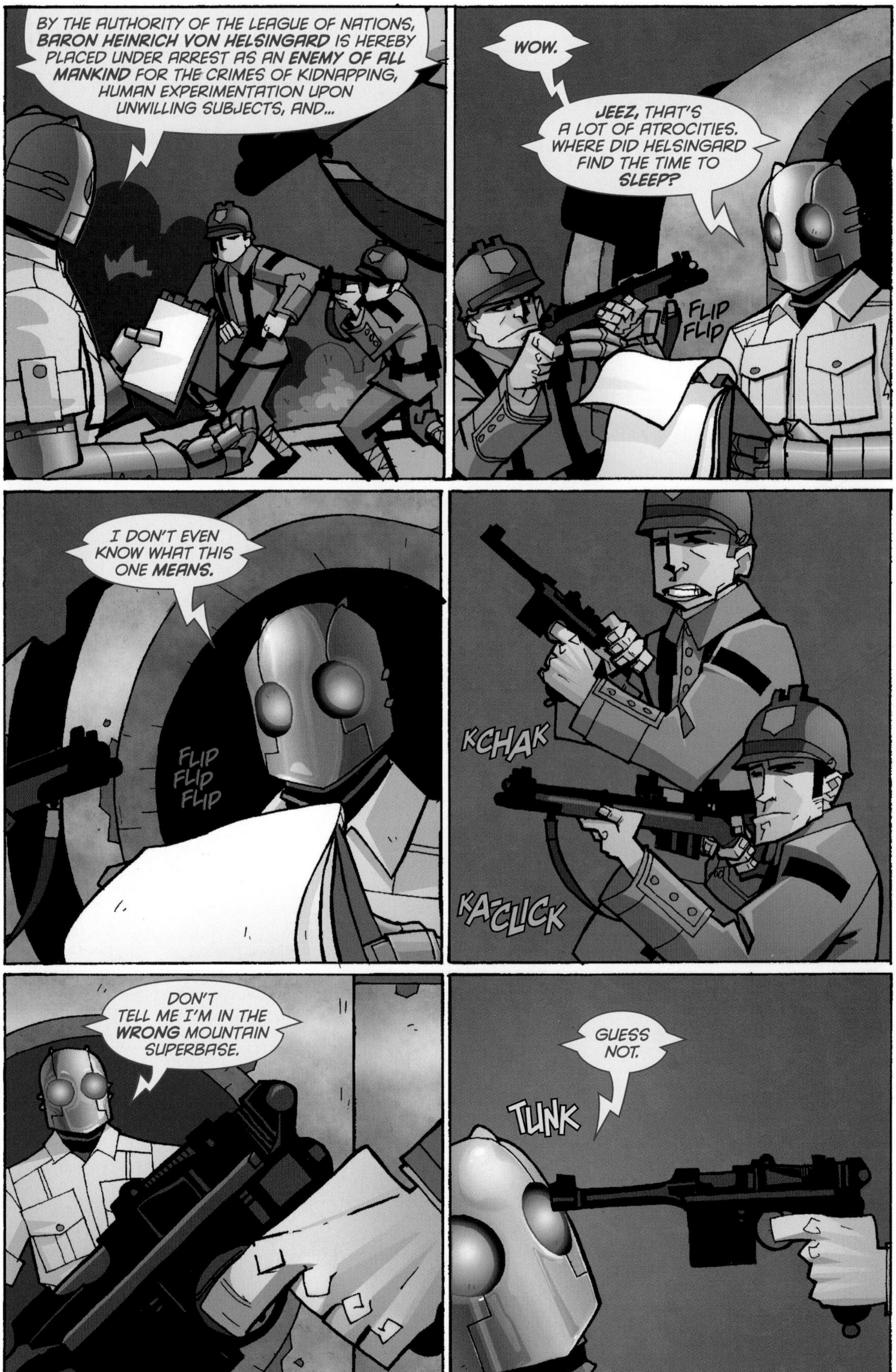
BY THE AUTHORITY OF THE LEAGUE OF NATIONS, BARON HEINRICH VON HELSINGARD IS HEREBY PLACED UNDER ARREST AS AN ENEMY OF ALL MANKIND FOR THE CRIMES OF KIDNAPPING, HUMAN EXPERIMENTATION UPON UNWILLING SUBJECTS, AND...
WOW.
JEEZ, THAT'S A LOT OF ATROCITIES. WHERE DID HELSINGARD FIND THE TIME TO SLEEP?
FLIP FLIP
I DON'T EVEN KNOW WHAT THIS ONE MEANS.
FLIP FLIP FLIP
KCHAK
KA-CLICK
DON'T TELL ME I'M IN THE WRONG MOUNTAIN SUPERBASE.
GUESS NOT.
TUNK

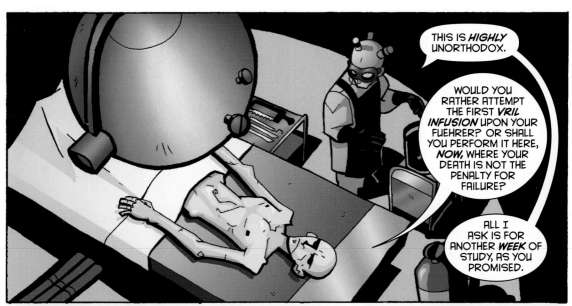

THIS IS *HIGHLY* UNORTHODOX.

WOULD YOU RATHER ATTEMPT THE FIRST *VRIL INFUSION* UPON YOUR FUEHRER? OR SHALL YOU PERFORM IT HERE, *NOW,* WHERE YOUR DEATH IS NOT THE PENALTY FOR FAILURE?

ALL I ASK IS FOR ANOTHER *WEEK* OF STUDY, AS YOU PROMISED.

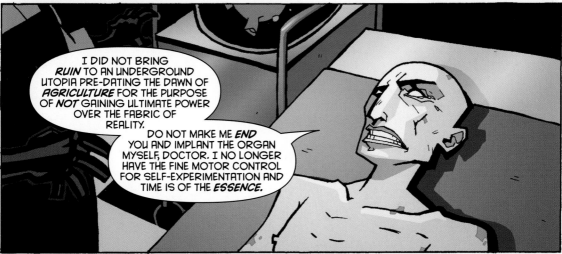

I DID NOT BRING *RUIN* TO AN UNDERGROUND UTOPIA PRE-DATING THE DAWN OF *AGRICULTURE* FOR THE PURPOSE OF *NOT* GAINING ULTIMATE POWER OVER THE FABRIC OF REALITY.

DO NOT MAKE ME *END* YOU AND IMPLANT THE ORGAN MYSELF, DOCTOR. I NO LONGER HAVE THE FINE MOTOR CONTROL FOR SELF-EXPERIMENTATION AND TIME IS OF THE *ESSENCE.*

BLUB

LOOK, GUYS? JUST PUT THE GUNS DOWN. I'M BUILT LIKE A TANK.

BLAM
BA-BLAM
BLAM
BLAM
BLAM

STOP THAT.

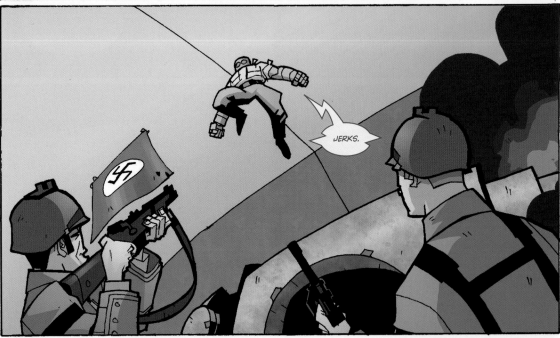

JERKS.

WHUD

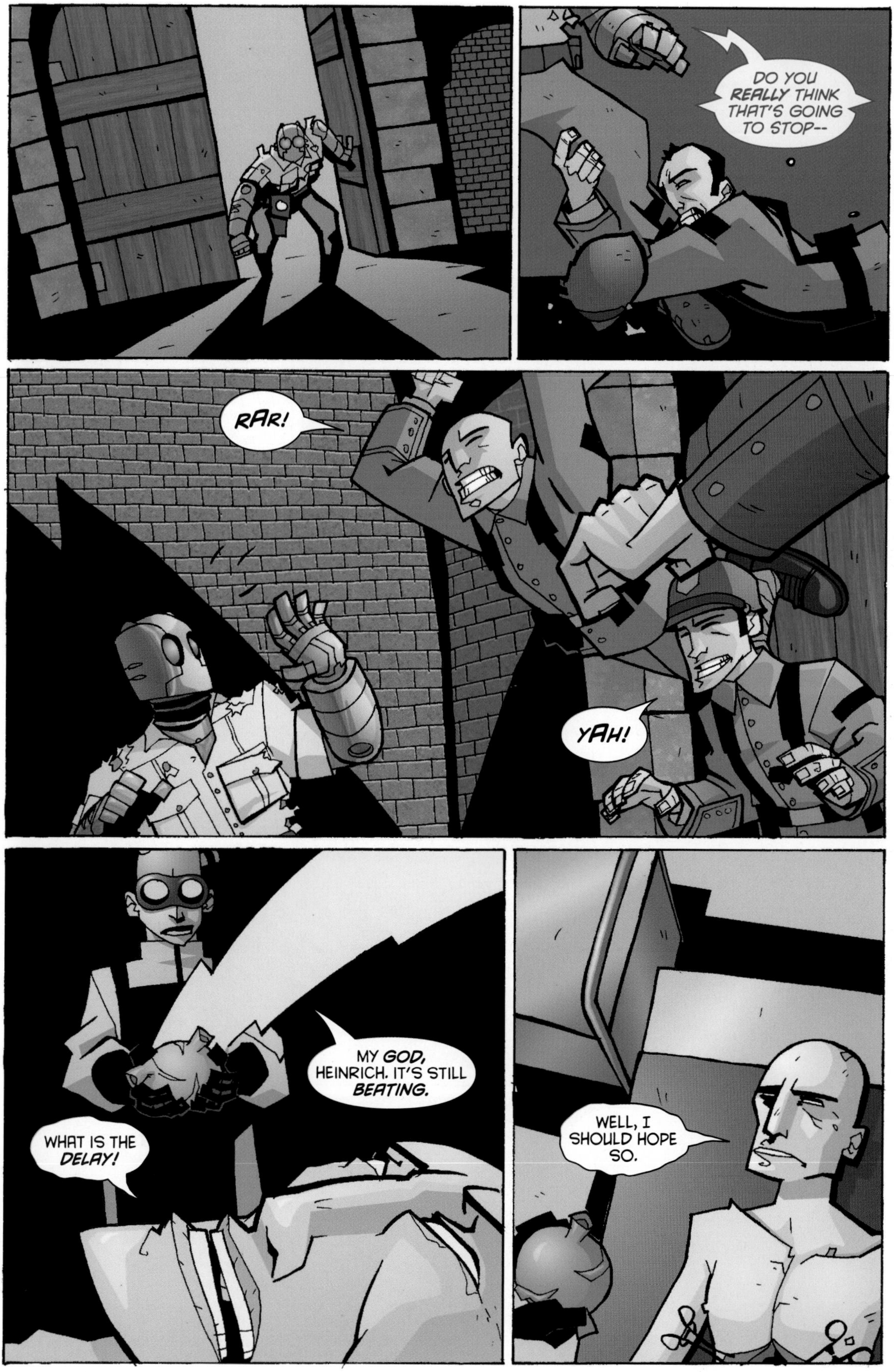
DO YOU *REALLY* THINK THAT'S GOING TO STOP--
RAR!
YAH!
MY *GOD,* HEINRICH. IT'S STILL *BEATING.*
WHAT IS THE *DELAY!*
WELL, I SHOULD HOPE SO.

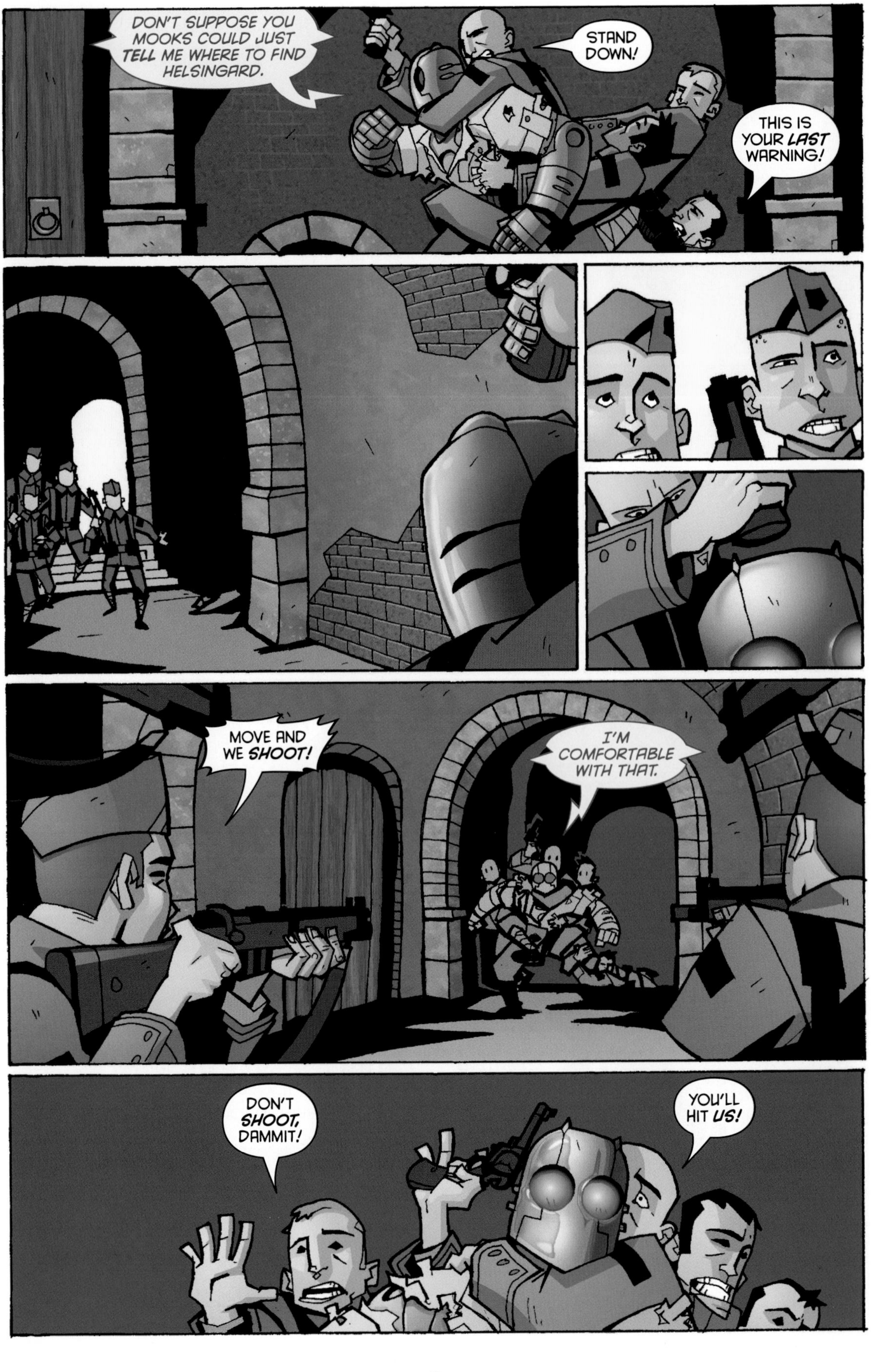

DON'T SUPPOSE YOU MOOKS COULD JUST TELL ME WHERE TO FIND HELSINGARD.
STAND DOWN!
THIS IS YOUR LAST WARNING!
MOVE AND WE SHOOT!
I'M COMFORTABLE WITH THAT.
DON'T SHOOT, DAMMIT!
YOU'LL HIT US!

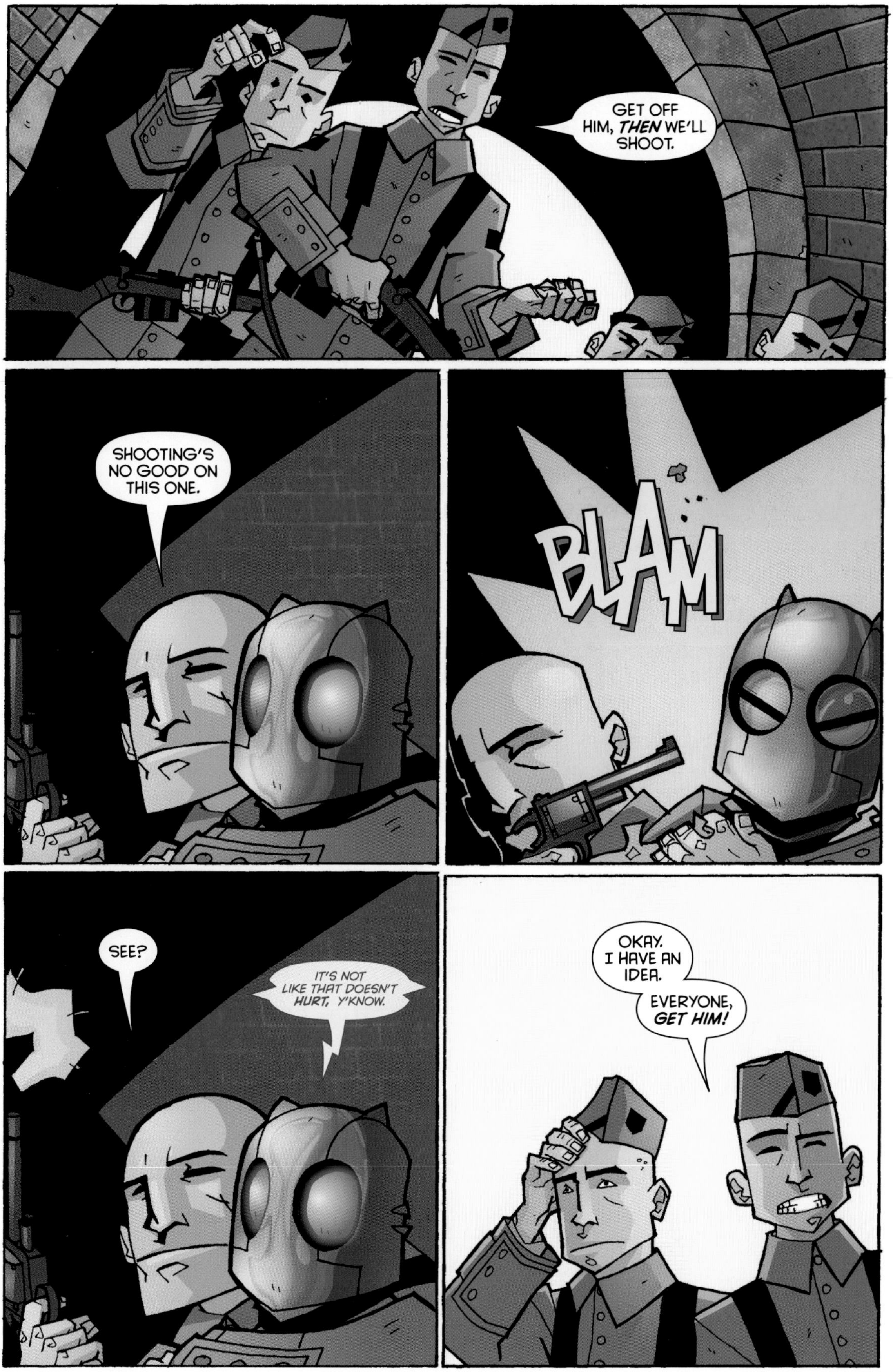
GET OFF HIM, *THEN* WE'LL SHOOT.
SHOOTING'S NO GOOD ON THIS ONE.
BLAM
SEE?
IT'S NOT LIKE THAT DOESN'T *HURT,* Y'KNOW.
OKAY. I HAVE AN IDEA.
EVERYONE, *GET HIM!*

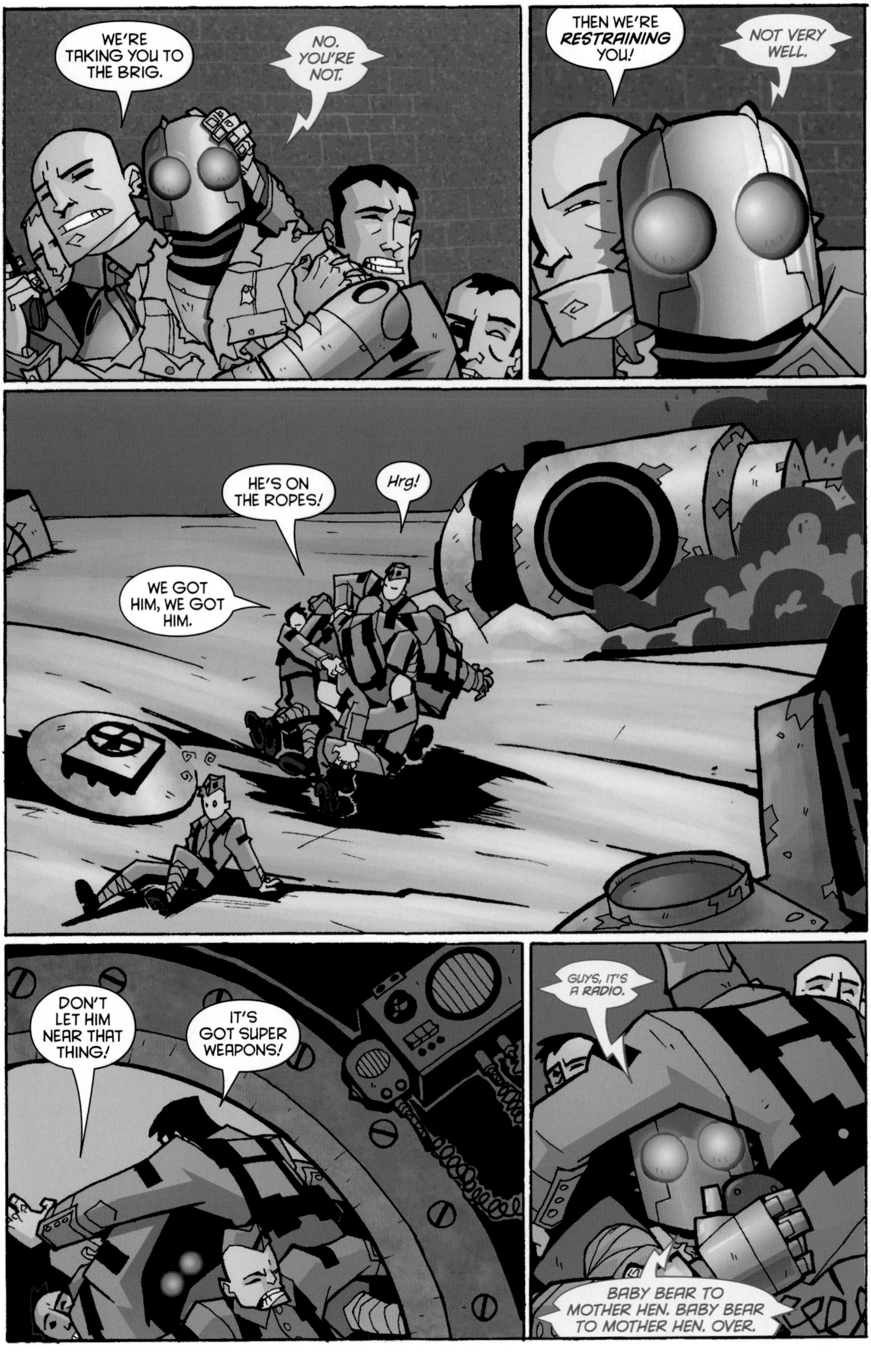
WE'RE TAKING YOU TO THE BRIG.
NO. YOU'RE NOT.
THEN WE'RE *RESTRAINING* YOU!
NOT VERY WELL.
HE'S ON THE ROPES!
Hrg!
WE GOT HIM, WE GOT HIM.
DON'T LET HIM NEAR THAT THING!
IT'S GOT SUPER WEAPONS!
GUYS, IT'S A RADIO.
BABY BEAR TO MOTHER HEN. BABY BEAR TO MOTHER HEN. OVER.

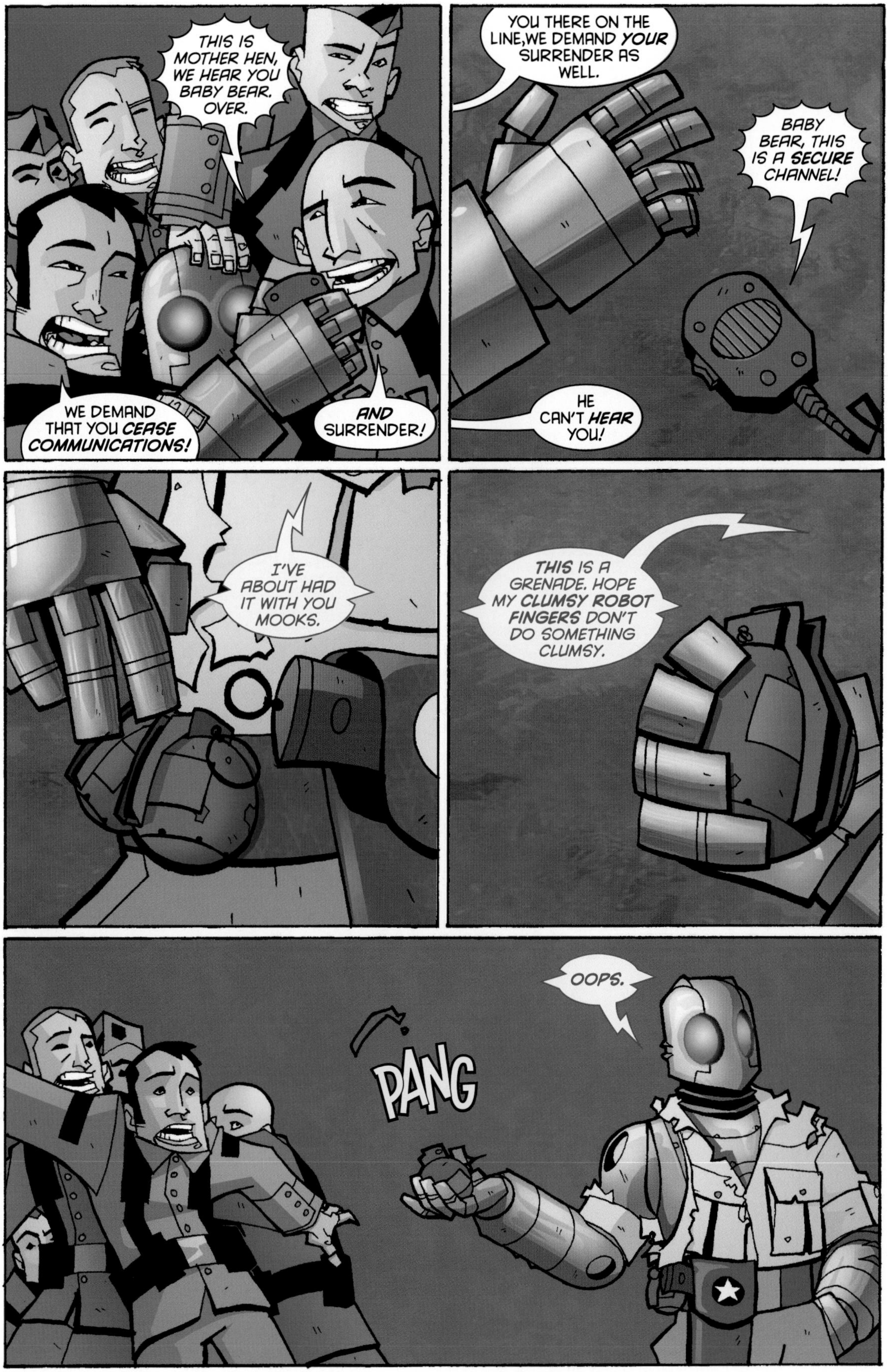
THIS IS MOTHER HEN, WE HEAR YOU BABY BEAR. OVER.
WE DEMAND THAT YOU CEASE COMMUNICATIONS!
AND SURRENDER!
YOU THERE ON THE LINE,WE DEMAND YOUR SURRENDER AS WELL.
BABY BEAR, THIS IS A SECURE CHANNEL!
HE CAN'T HEAR YOU!
I'VE ABOUT HAD IT WITH YOU MOOKS.
THIS IS A GRENADE. HOPE MY CLUMSY ROBOT FINGERS DON'T DO SOMETHING CLUMSY.
OOPS.
PANG

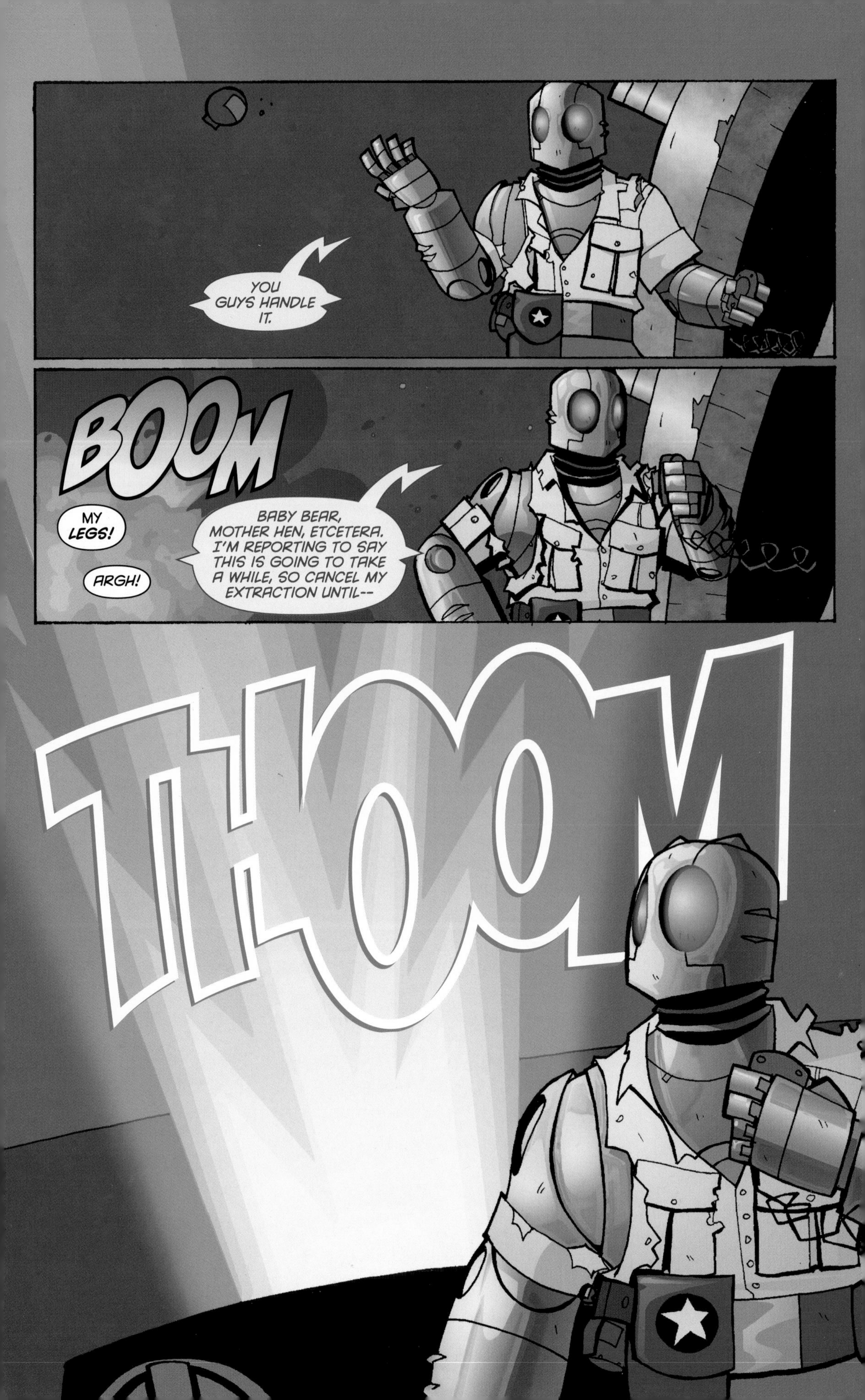
YOU GUYS HANDLE IT.
BOOM
MY LEGS!
ARGH!
BABY BEAR, MOTHER HEN, ETCETERA. I'M REPORTING TO SAY THIS IS GOING TO TAKE A WHILE, SO CANCEL MY EXTRACTION UNTIL--
THOOM

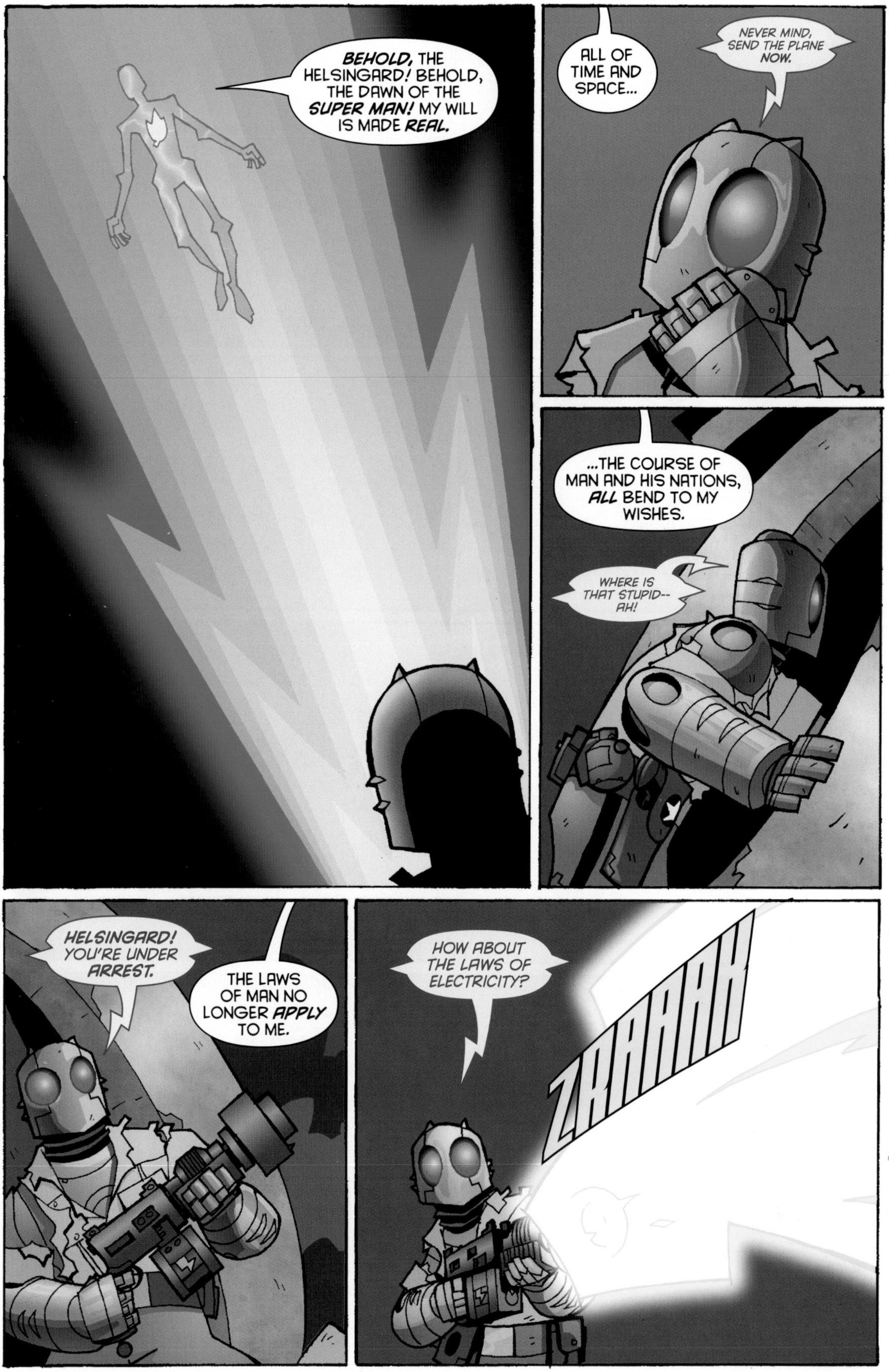
BEHOLD, THE HELSINGARD! BEHOLD, THE DAWN OF THE SUPER MAN! MY WILL IS MADE REAL.
ALL OF TIME AND SPACE...
NEVER MIND, SEND THE PLANE NOW.
...THE COURSE OF MAN AND HIS NATIONS, ALL BEND TO MY WISHES.
WHERE IS THAT STUPID-- AH!
HELSINGARD! YOU'RE UNDER ARREST.
THE LAWS OF MAN NO LONGER APPLY TO ME.
HOW ABOUT THE LAWS OF ELECTRICITY?
ZRAAAK

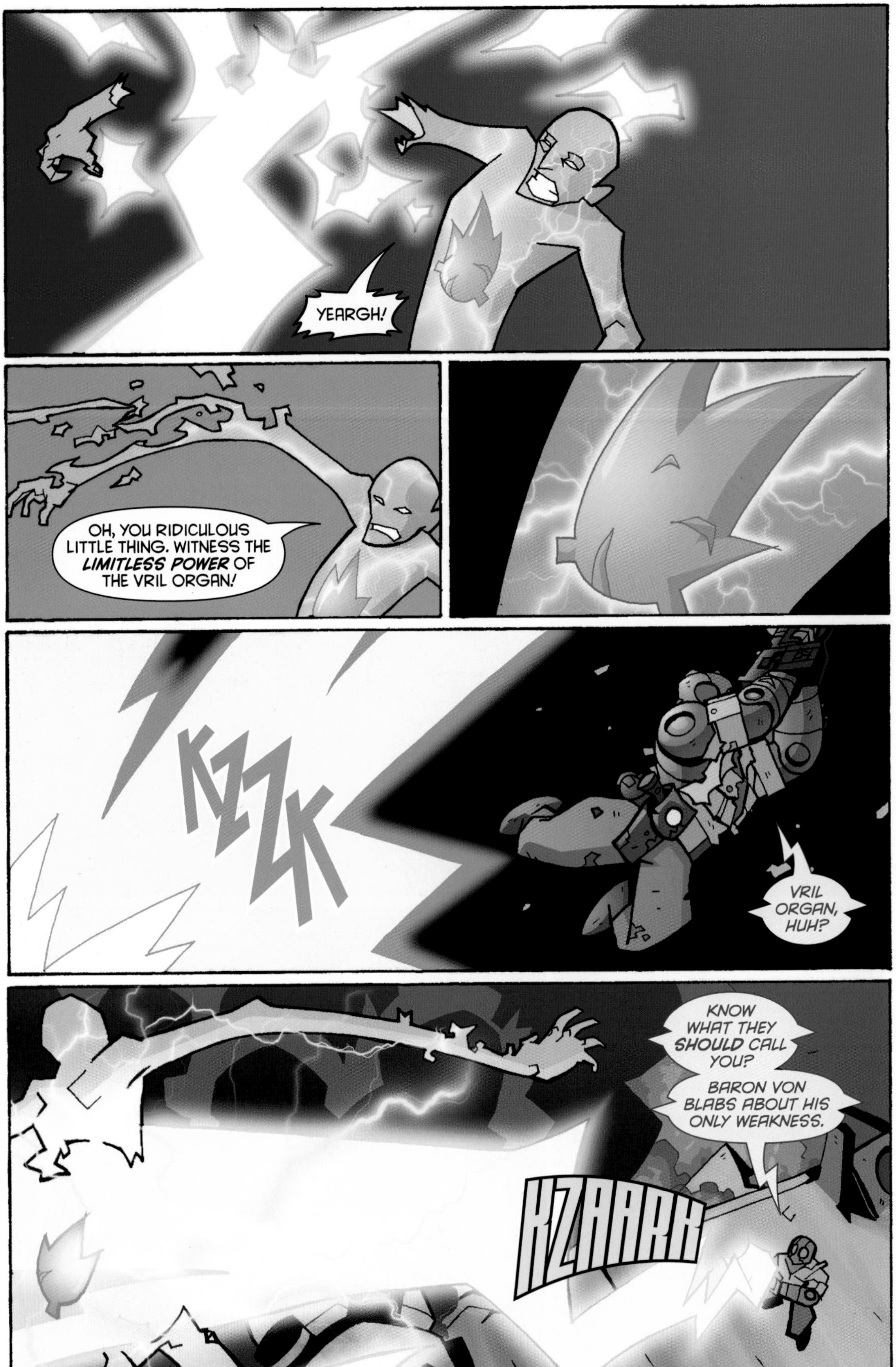
YEARGH!
OH, YOU RIDICULOUS LITTLE THING. WITNESS THE *LIMITLESS POWER* OF THE VRIL ORGAN!
KZZZK
VRIL ORGAN, HUH?
KNOW WHAT THEY *SHOULD* CALL YOU?
BARON VON BLABS ABOUT HIS ONLY WEAKNESS.
KZAARK

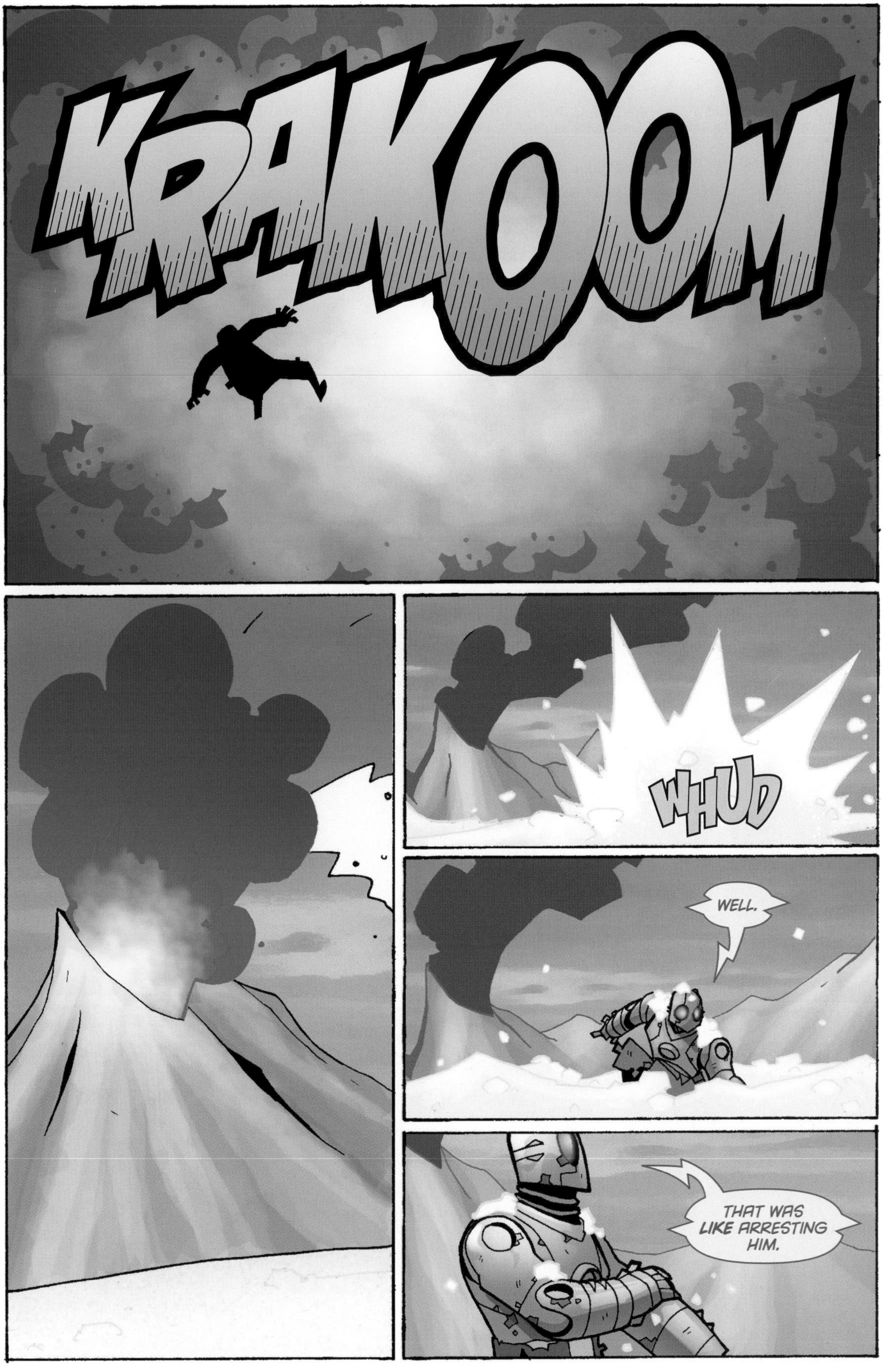
KRAKOOM
WHUD
WELL.
THAT WAS LIKE ARRESTING HIM.

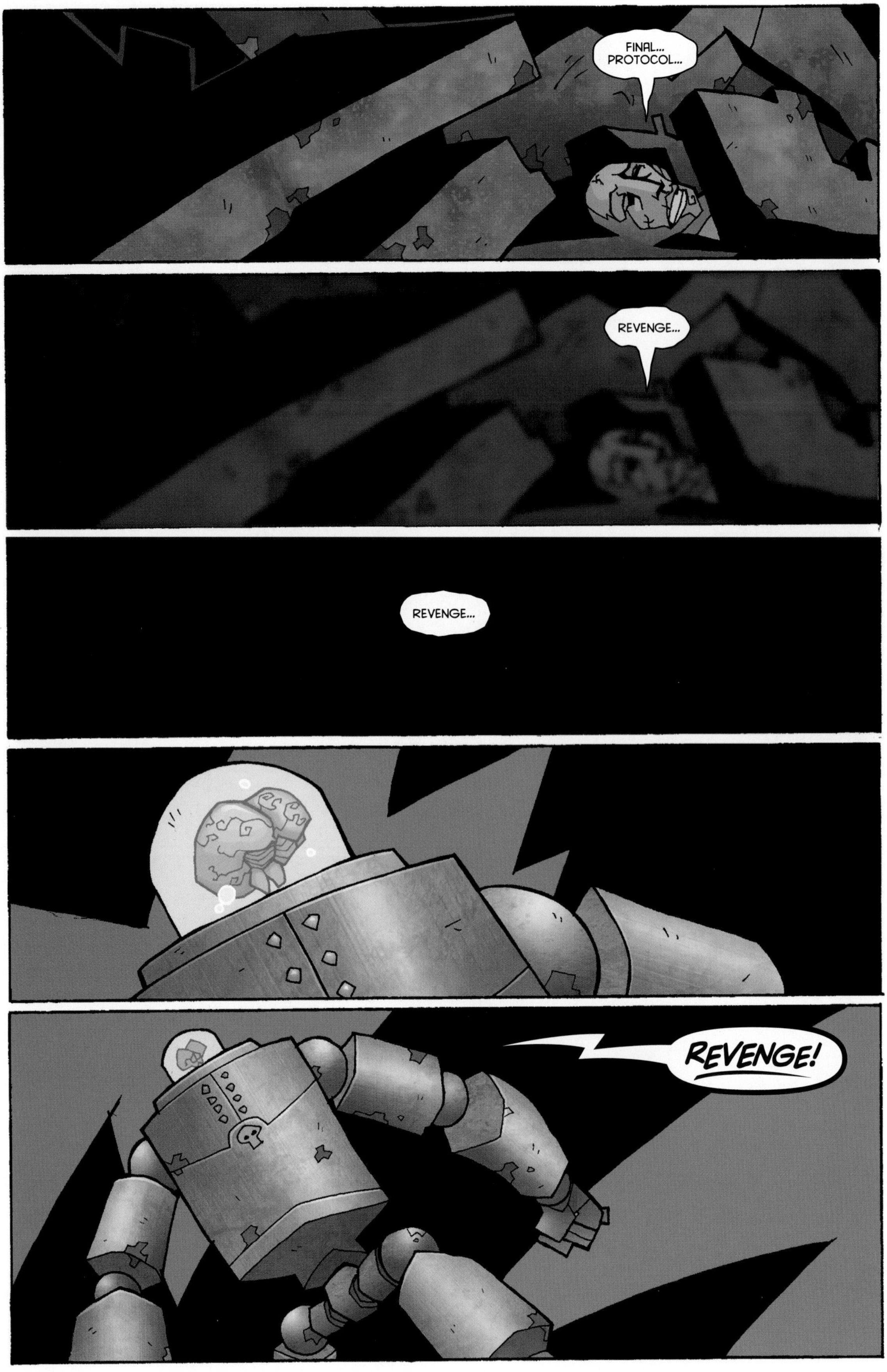
FINAL...
PROTOCOL...
REVENGE...
REVENGE...
REVENGE!

PEST CONTROL

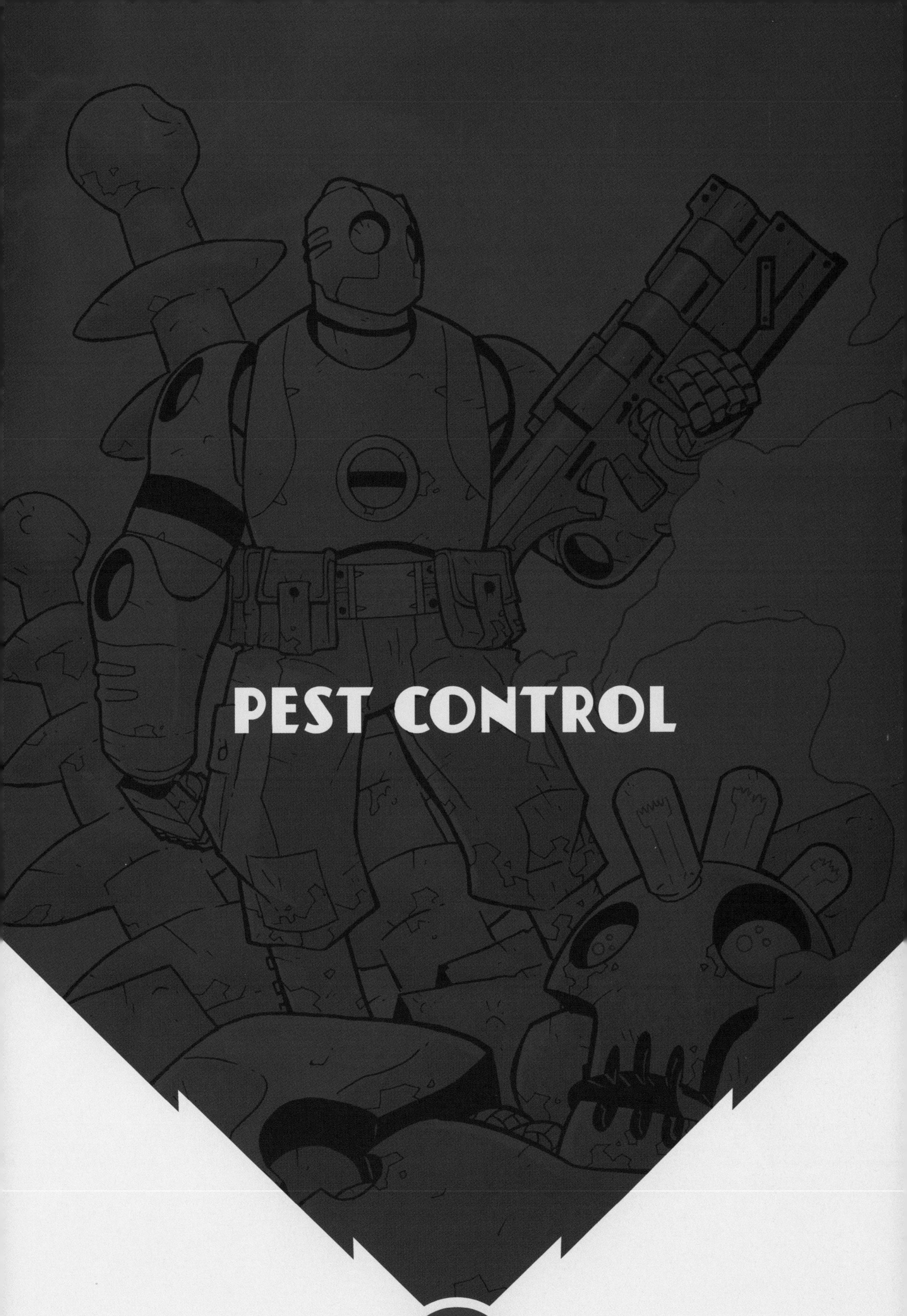

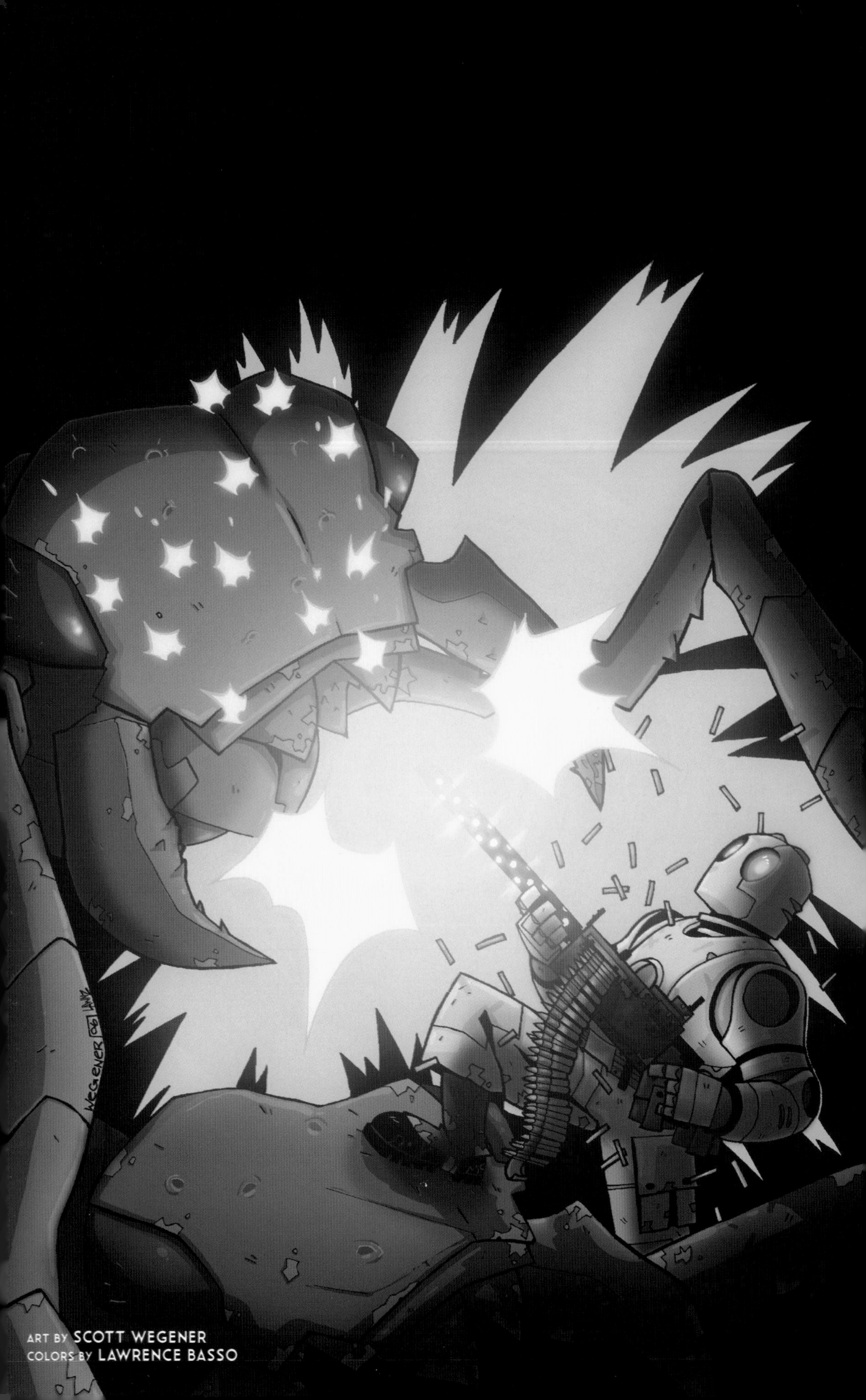

ART BY SCOTT WEGENER
COLORS BY LAWRENCE BASSO

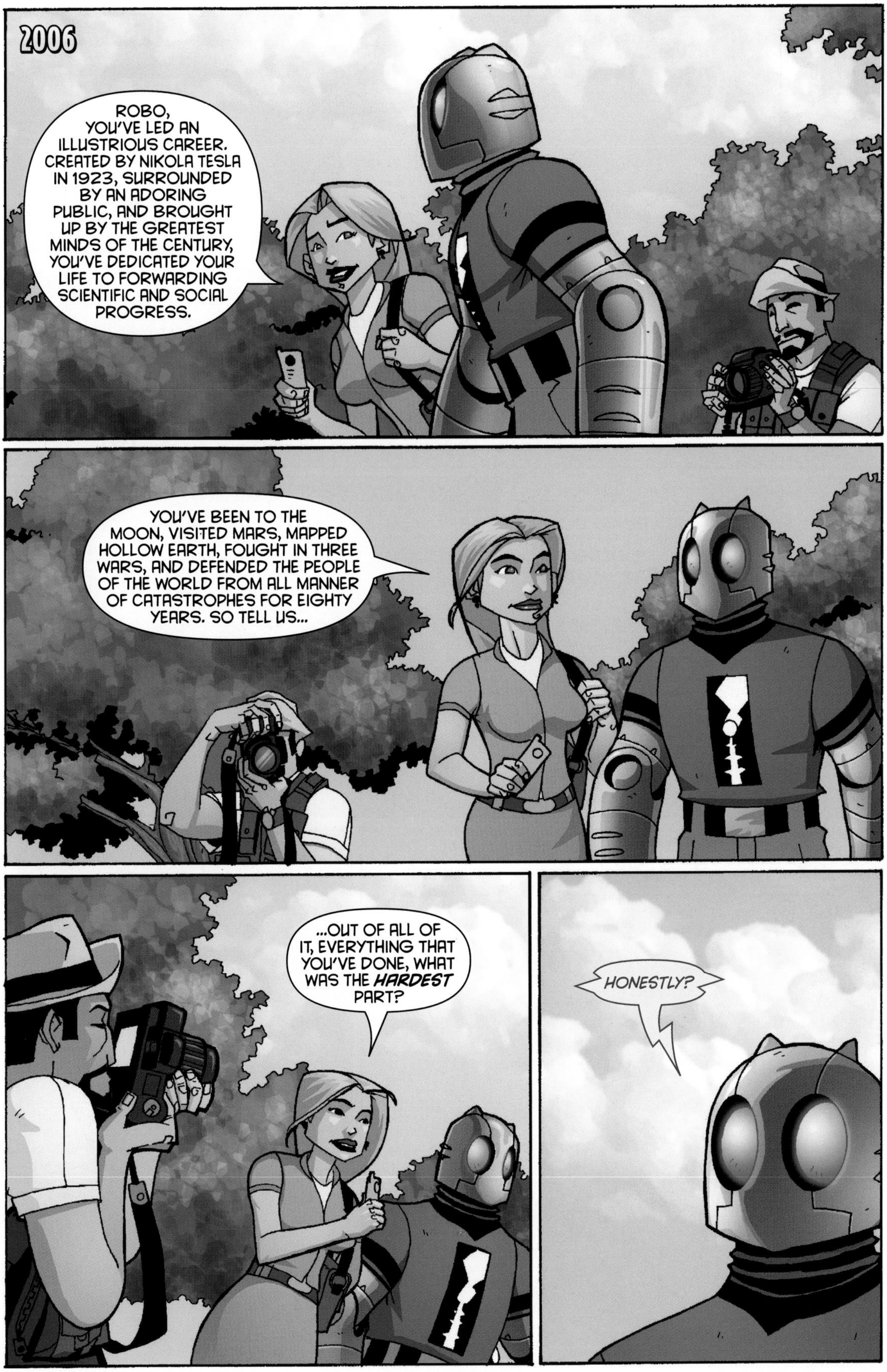
2006
ROBO, YOU'VE LED AN ILLUSTRIOUS CAREER. CREATED BY NIKOLA TESLA IN 1923, SURROUNDED BY AN ADORING PUBLIC, AND BROUGHT UP BY THE GREATEST MINDS OF THE CENTURY, YOU'VE DEDICATED YOUR LIFE TO FORWARDING SCIENTIFIC AND SOCIAL PROGRESS.
YOU'VE BEEN TO THE MOON, VISITED MARS, MAPPED HOLLOW EARTH, FOUGHT IN THREE WARS, AND DEFENDED THE PEOPLE OF THE WORLD FROM ALL MANNER OF CATASTROPHES FOR EIGHTY YEARS. SO TELL US...
...OUT OF ALL OF IT, EVERYTHING THAT YOU'VE DONE, WHAT WAS THE HARDEST PART?
HONESTLY?

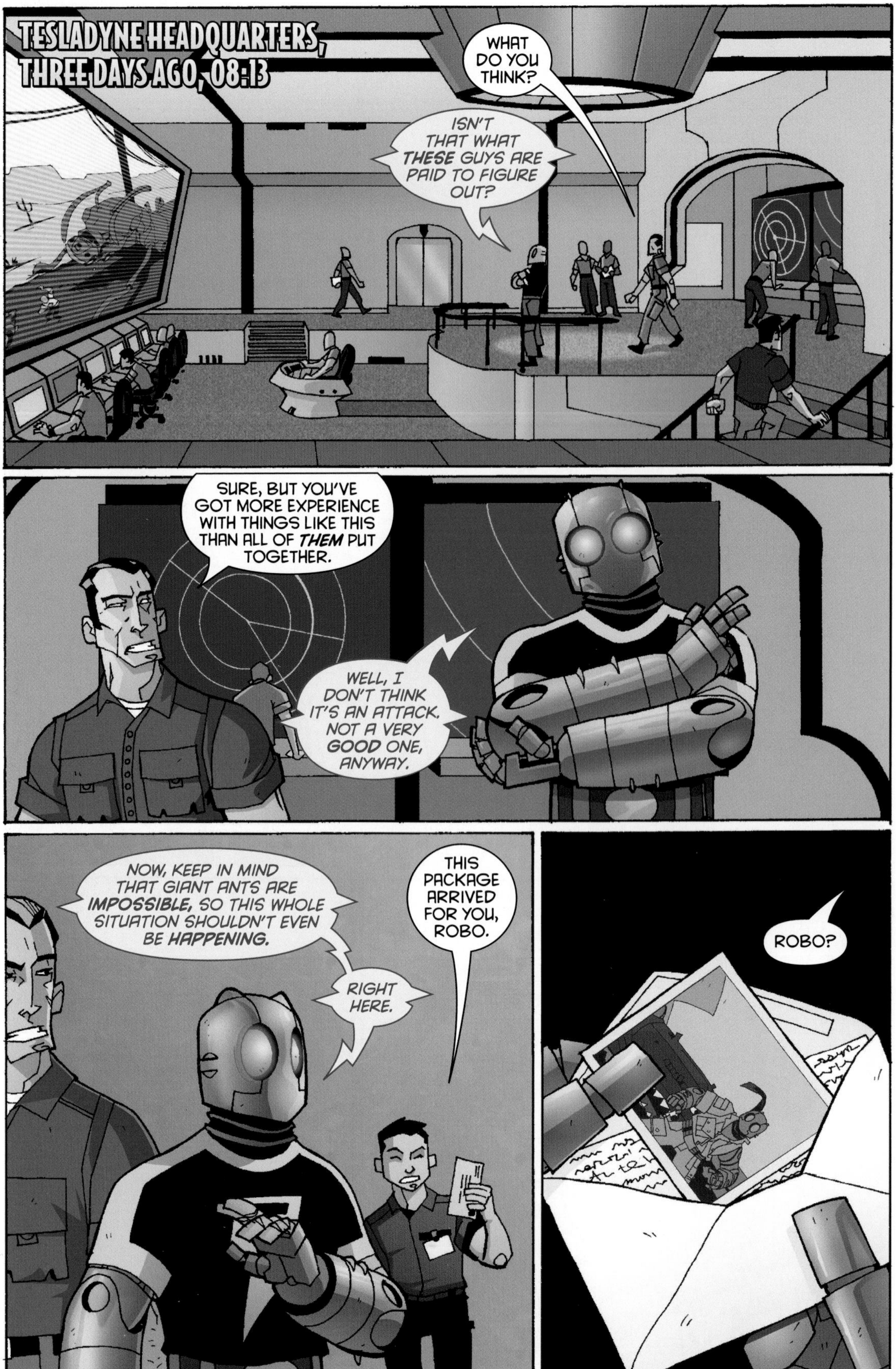
TESLADYNE HEADQUARTERS, THREE DAYS AGO, 08:13
WHAT DO YOU THINK?
ISN'T THAT WHAT THESE GUYS ARE PAID TO FIGURE OUT?
SURE, BUT YOU'VE GOT MORE EXPERIENCE WITH THINGS LIKE THIS THAN ALL OF THEM PUT TOGETHER.
WELL, I DON'T THINK IT'S AN ATTACK. NOT A VERY GOOD ONE, ANYWAY.
NOW, KEEP IN MIND THAT GIANT ANTS ARE IMPOSSIBLE, SO THIS WHOLE SITUATION SHOULDN'T EVEN BE HAPPENING.
RIGHT HERE.
THIS PACKAGE ARRIVED FOR YOU, ROBO.
ROBO?

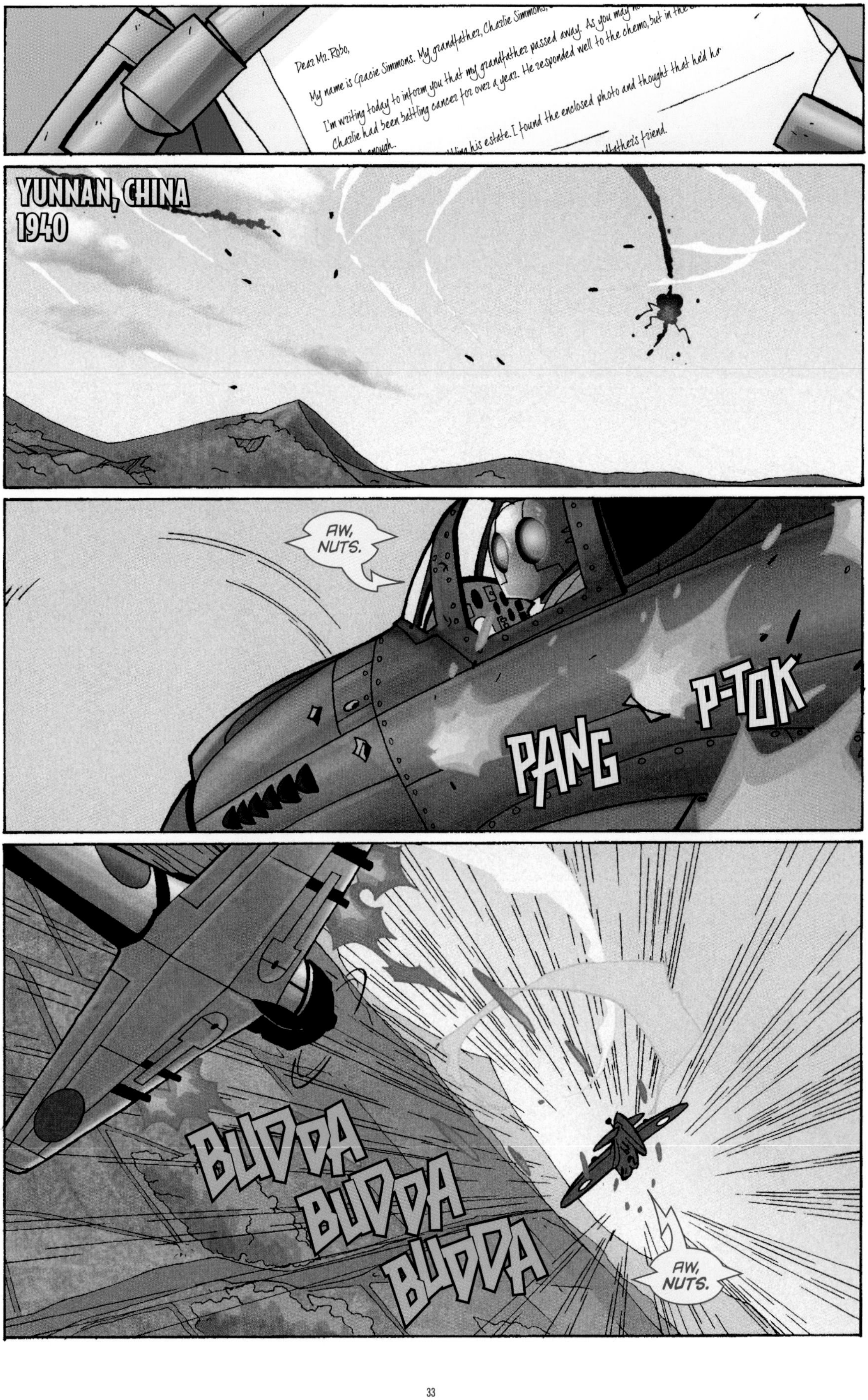
Dear Mr. Robo,
My name is Gracie Simmons. My grandfather, Charlie Simmons,
I'm writing today to inform you that my grandfather passed away. As you may
Charlie had been battling cancer for over a year. He responded well to the chemo, but in the
enough.
his estate. I found the enclosed photo and thought that he'd
friend.
YUNNAN, CHINA
1940
AW, NUTS.
P-TOK
PANG
BUDDA
BUDDA
BUDDA
AW, NUTS.

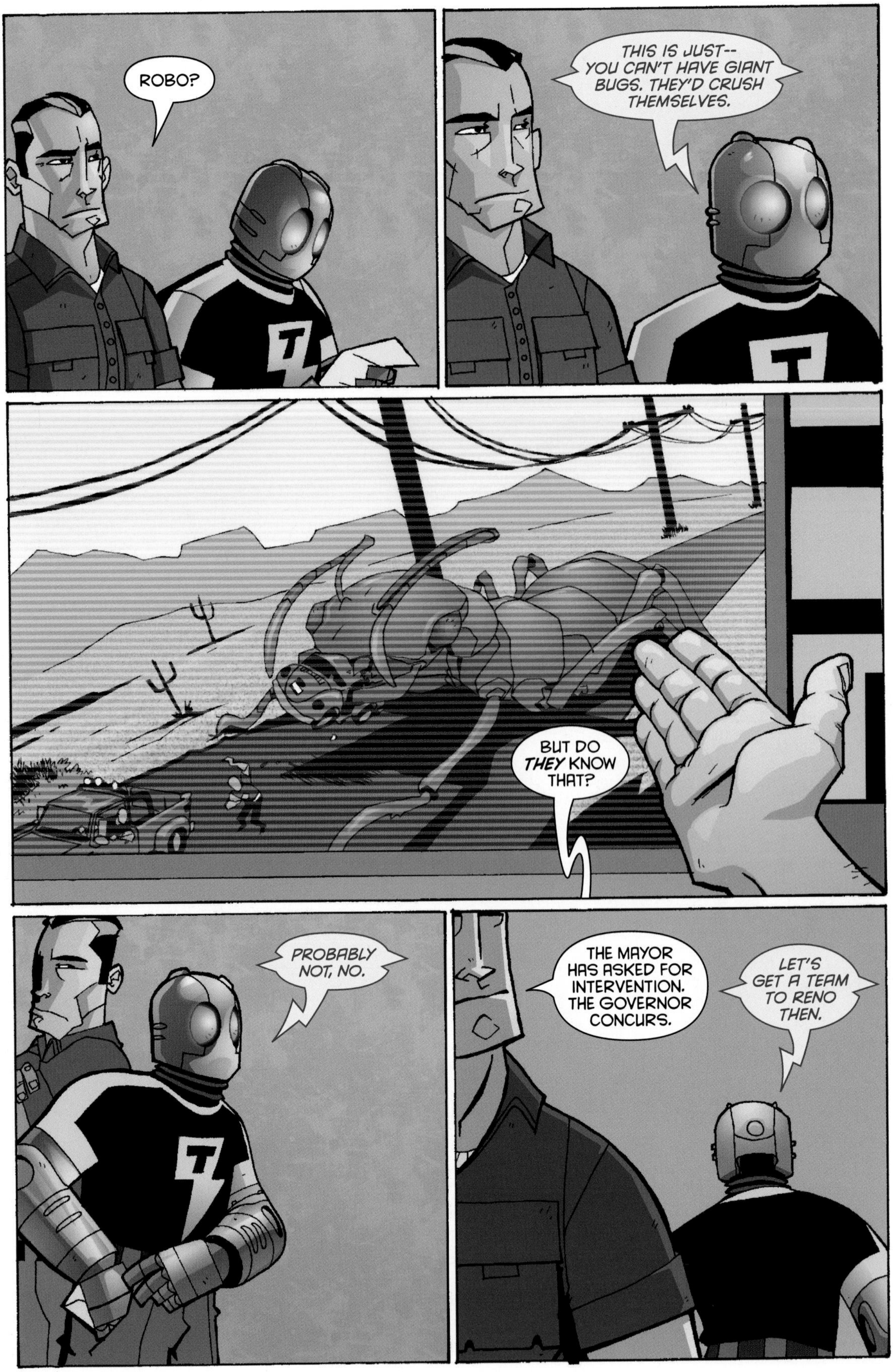
ROBO?
THIS IS JUST-- YOU CAN'T HAVE GIANT BUGS. THEY'D CRUSH THEMSELVES.
BUT DO THEY KNOW THAT?
PROBABLY NOT, NO.
THE MAYOR HAS ASKED FOR INTERVENTION. THE GOVERNOR CONCURS.
LET'S GET A TEAM TO RENO THEN.

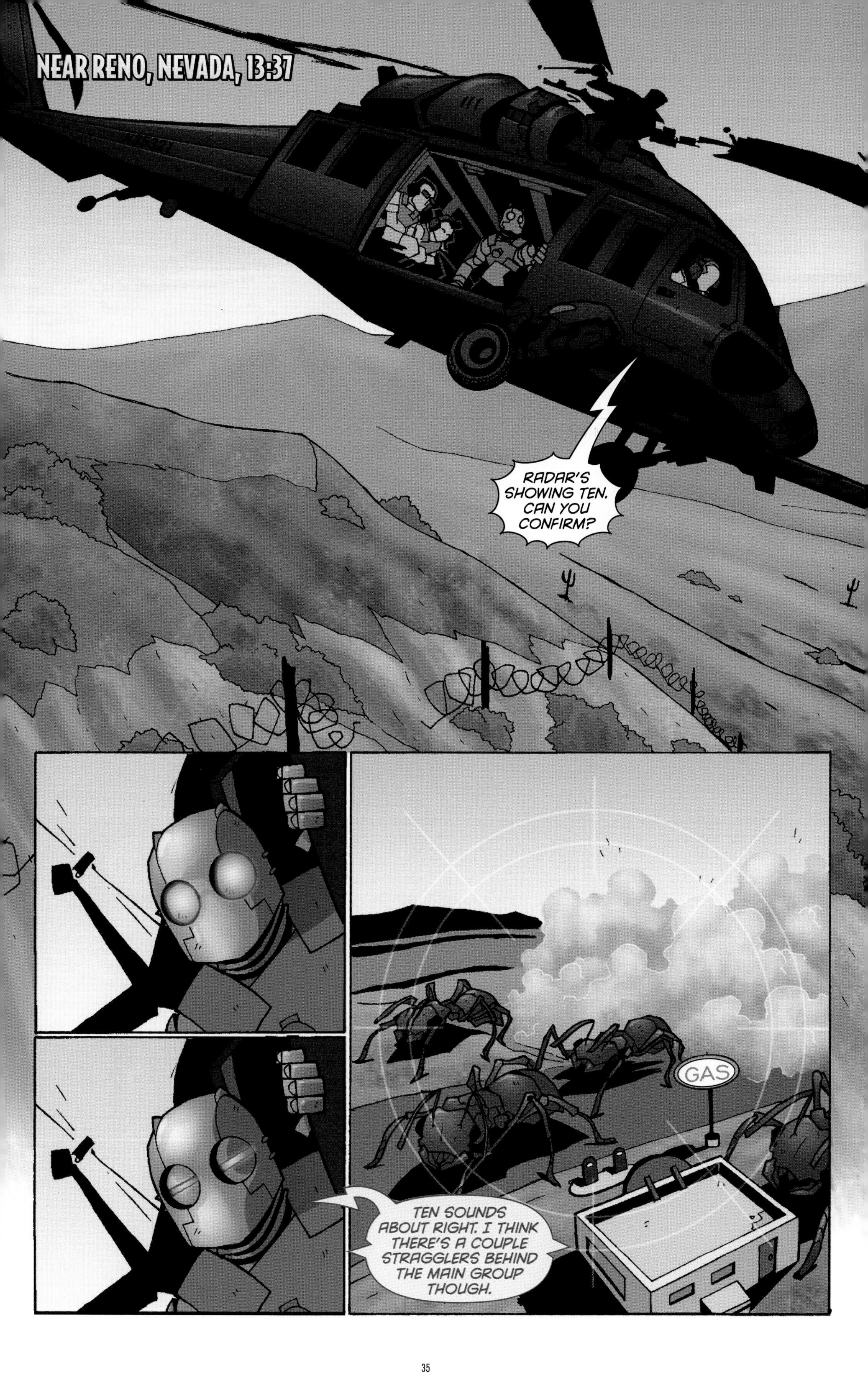
NEAR RENO, NEVADA, 13:37
RADAR'S SHOWING TEN. CAN YOU CONFIRM?
GAS
TEN SOUNDS ABOUT RIGHT. I THINK THERE'S A COUPLE STRAGGLERS BEHIND THE MAIN GROUP THOUGH.

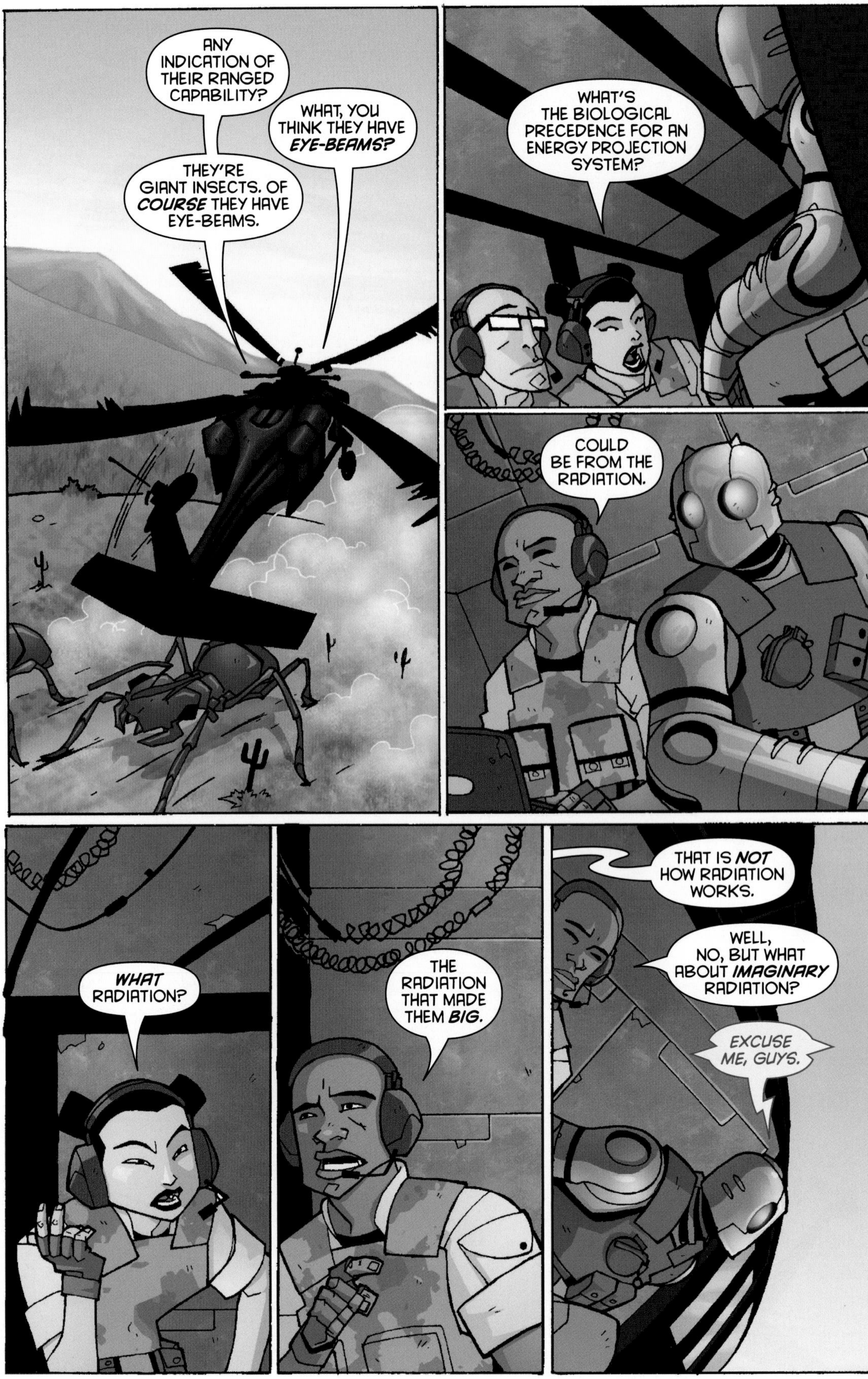
ANY INDICATION OF THEIR RANGED CAPABILITY?
THEY'RE GIANT INSECTS. OF *COURSE* THEY HAVE EYE-BEAMS.
WHAT, YOU THINK THEY HAVE *EYE-BEAMS?*
WHAT'S THE BIOLOGICAL PRECEDENCE FOR AN ENERGY PROJECTION SYSTEM?
COULD BE FROM THE RADIATION.
WHAT RADIATION?
THE RADIATION THAT MADE THEM *BIG.*
THAT IS *NOT* HOW RADIATION WORKS.
WELL, NO, BUT WHAT ABOUT *IMAGINARY* RADIATION?
EXCUSE ME, GUYS.

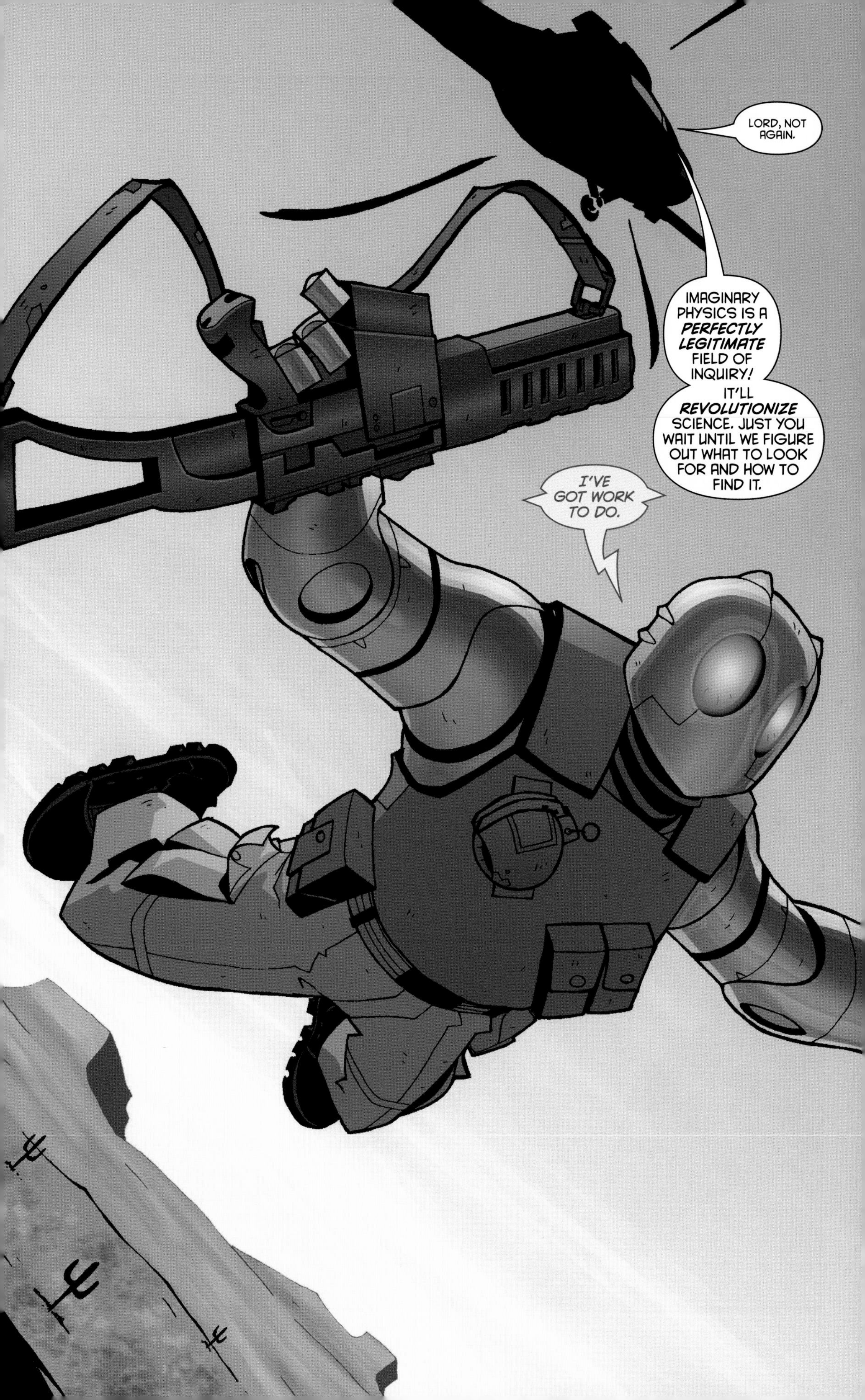
LORD, NOT AGAIN.
IMAGINARY PHYSICS IS A *PERFECTLY LEGITIMATE* FIELD OF INQUIRY!
IT'LL *REVOLUTIONIZE* SCIENCE. JUST YOU WAIT UNTIL WE FIGURE OUT WHAT TO LOOK FOR AND HOW TO FIND IT.
I'VE GOT WORK TO DO.

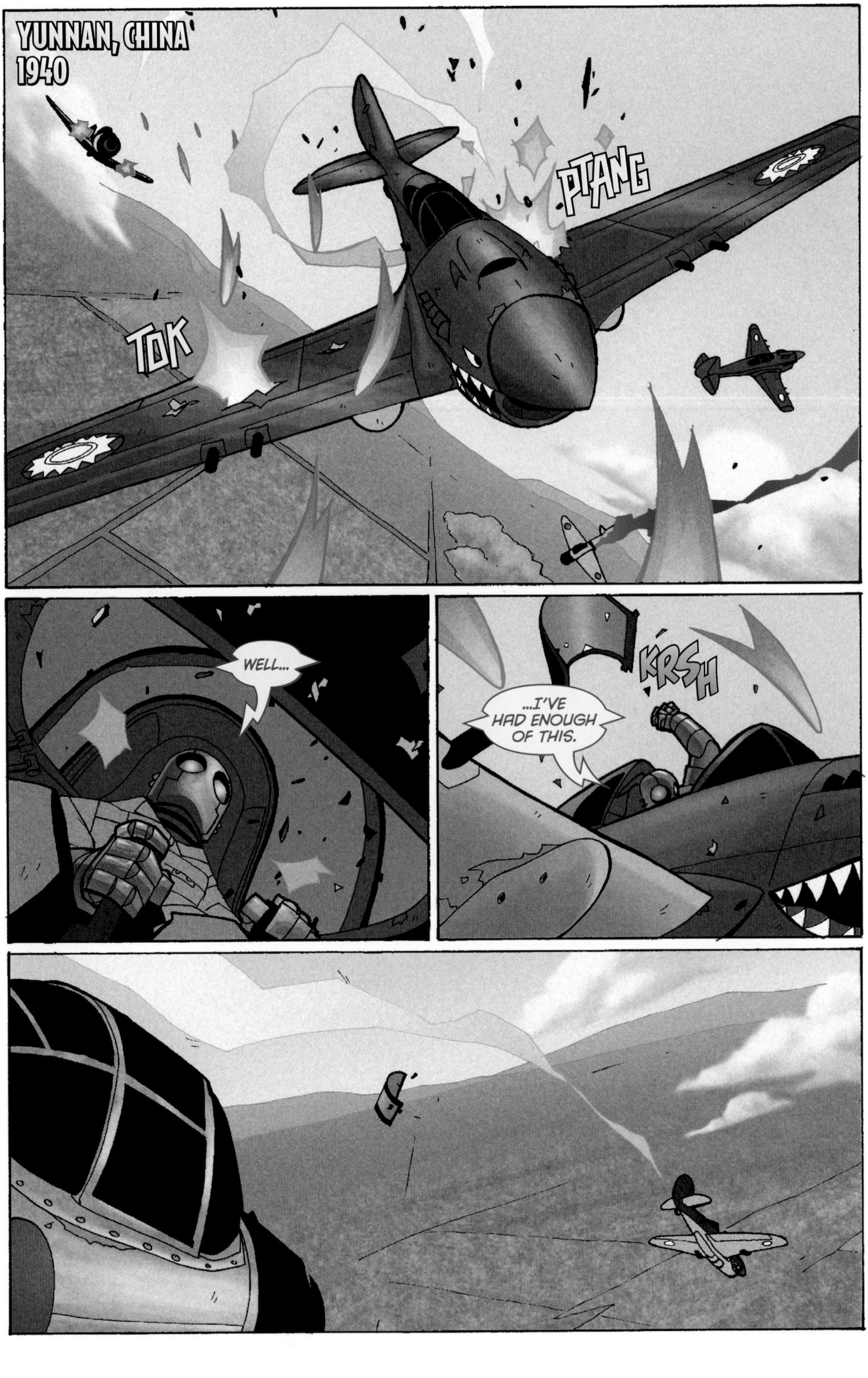
YUNNAN, CHINA
1940
PTANG
TOK
WELL...
KRSH
...I'VE HAD ENOUGH OF THIS.

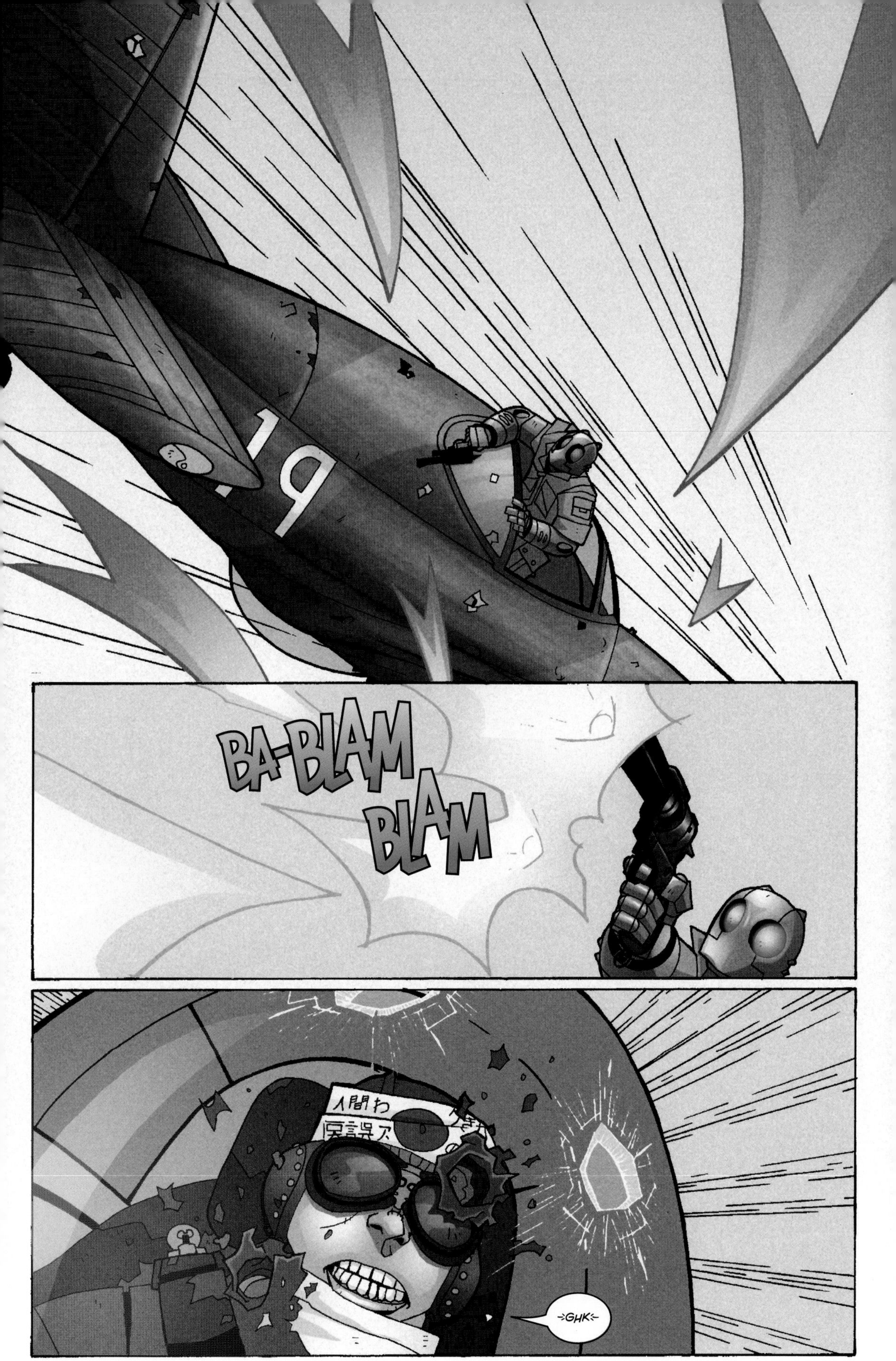
BA-BLAM
BLAM
人間わ
GHK

AND HERE'S ONE MORE, Y'MEATBALL!
KA-BLAM
AW, NUTS.

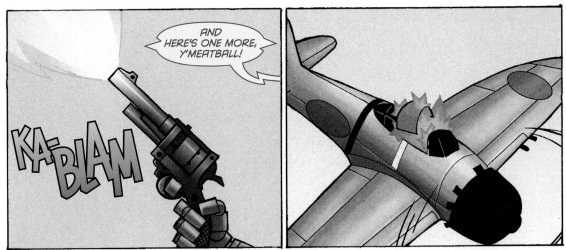

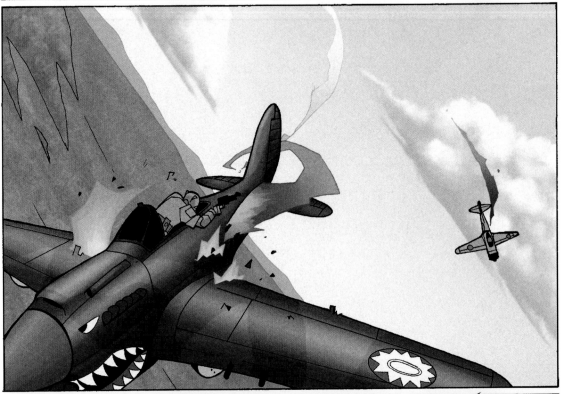

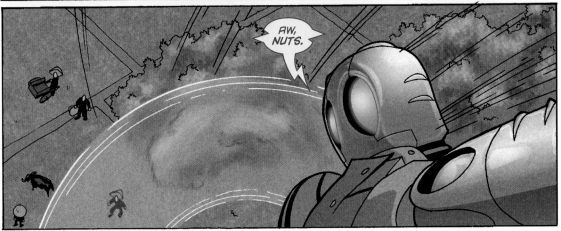

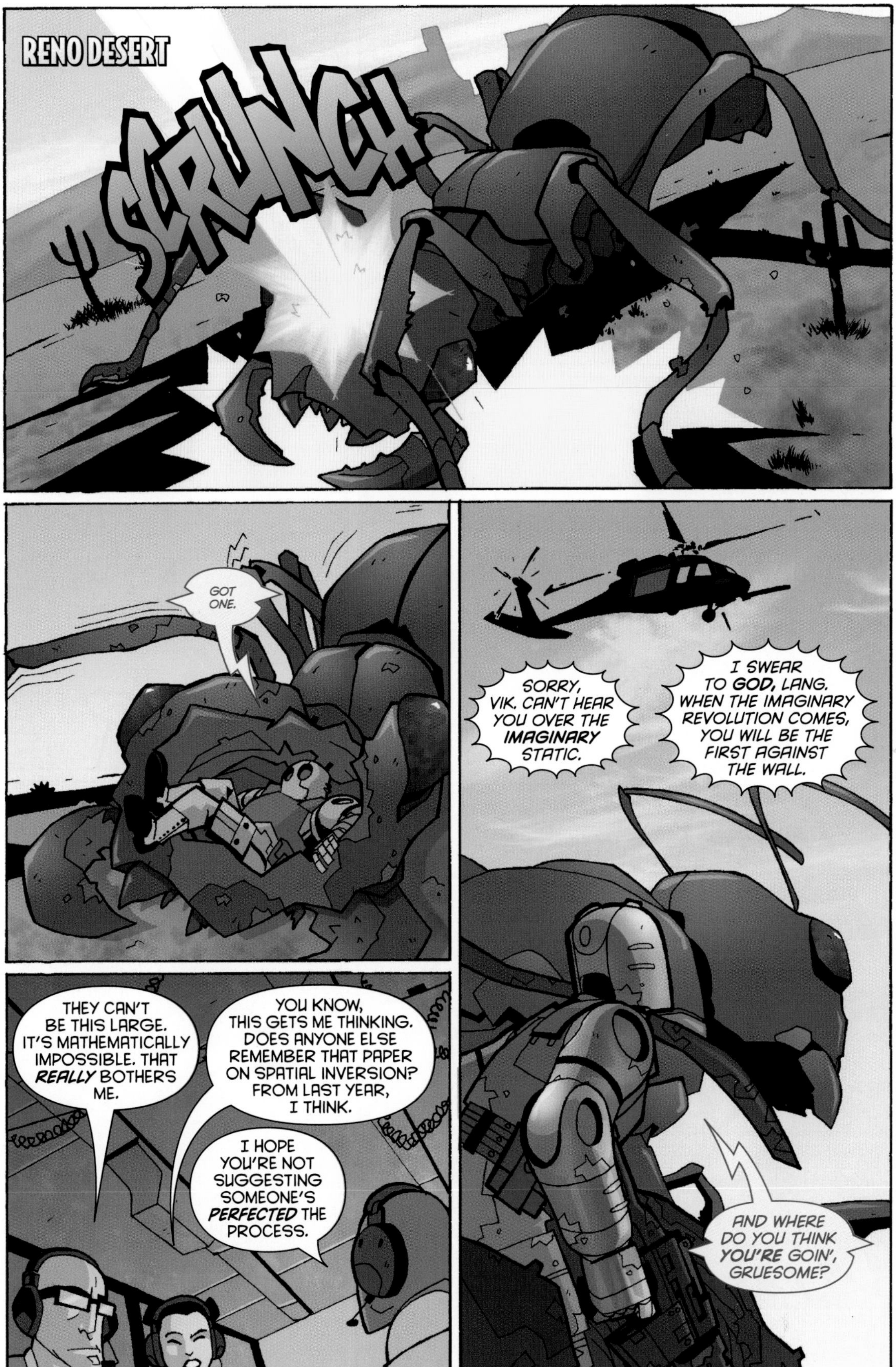
RENO DESERT
SCRUNCH
GOT ONE.
SORRY, VIK. CAN'T HEAR YOU OVER THE IMAGINARY STATIC.
I SWEAR TO GOD, LANG. WHEN THE IMAGINARY REVOLUTION COMES, YOU WILL BE THE FIRST AGAINST THE WALL.
THEY CAN'T BE THIS LARGE. IT'S MATHEMATICALLY IMPOSSIBLE. THAT REALLY BOTHERS ME.
YOU KNOW, THIS GETS ME THINKING. DOES ANYONE ELSE REMEMBER THAT PAPER ON SPATIAL INVERSION? FROM LAST YEAR, I THINK.
I HOPE YOU'RE NOT SUGGESTING SOMEONE'S PERFECTED THE PROCESS.
AND WHERE DO YOU THINK YOU'RE GOIN', GRUESOME?

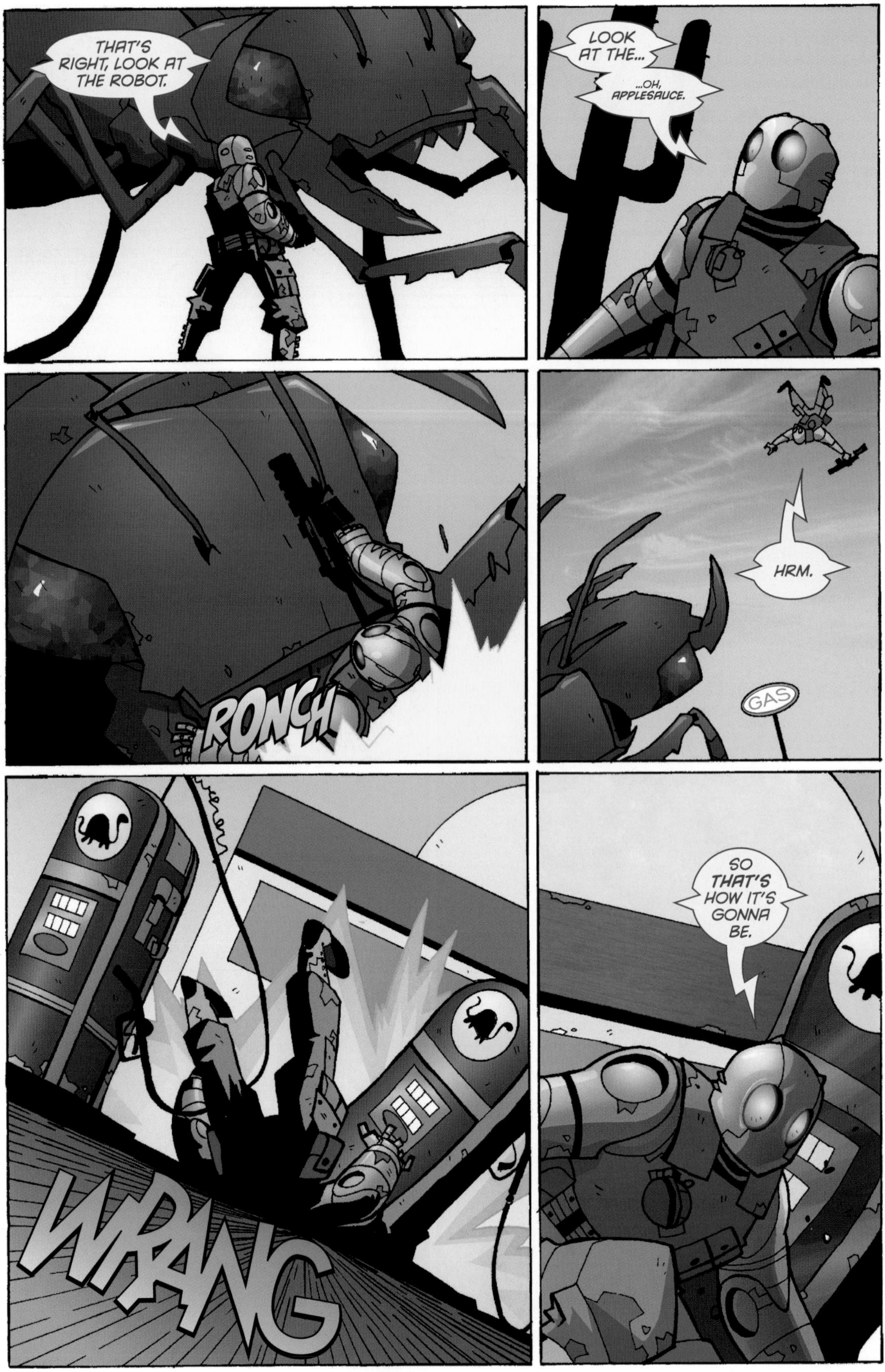
THAT'S RIGHT, LOOK AT THE ROBOT.
LOOK AT THE...
...OH, APPLESAUCE.
RONCH
HRM.
GAS
WRANG
SO THAT'S HOW IT'S GONNA BE.

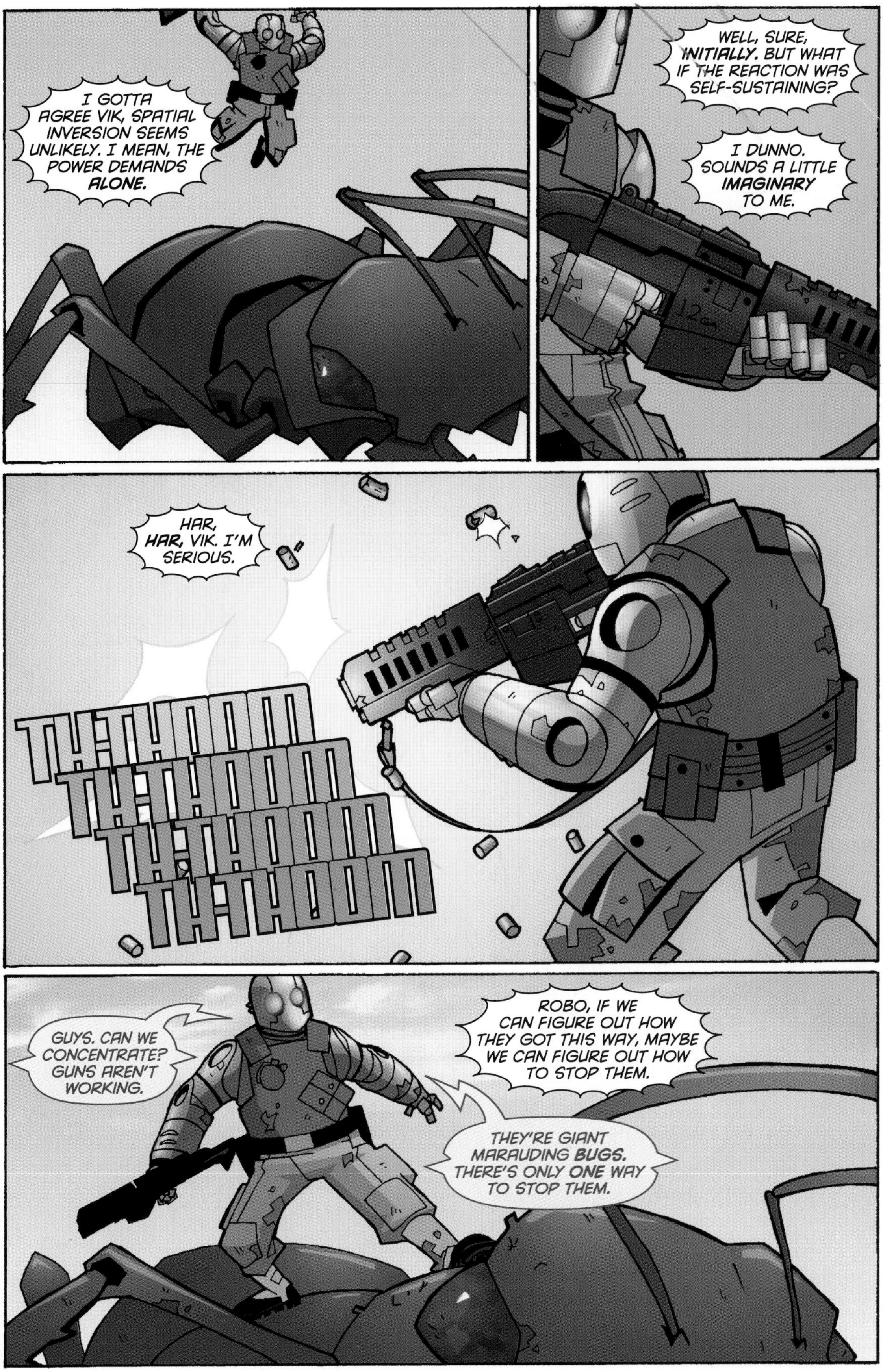
I GOTTA AGREE VIK, SPATIAL INVERSION SEEMS UNLIKELY. I MEAN, THE POWER DEMANDS ALONE.
WELL, SURE, INITIALLY. BUT WHAT IF THE REACTION WAS SELF-SUSTAINING?
I DUNNO. SOUNDS A LITTLE IMAGINARY TO ME.
12 GA.
HAR, HAR, VIK. I'M SERIOUS.
TH-THOOM
TH-THOOM
TH-THOOM
TH-THOOM
GUYS. CAN WE CONCENTRATE? GUNS AREN'T WORKING.
ROBO, IF WE CAN FIGURE OUT HOW THEY GOT THIS WAY, MAYBE WE CAN FIGURE OUT HOW TO STOP THEM.
THEY'RE GIANT MARAUDING BUGS. THERE'S ONLY ONE WAY TO STOP THEM.

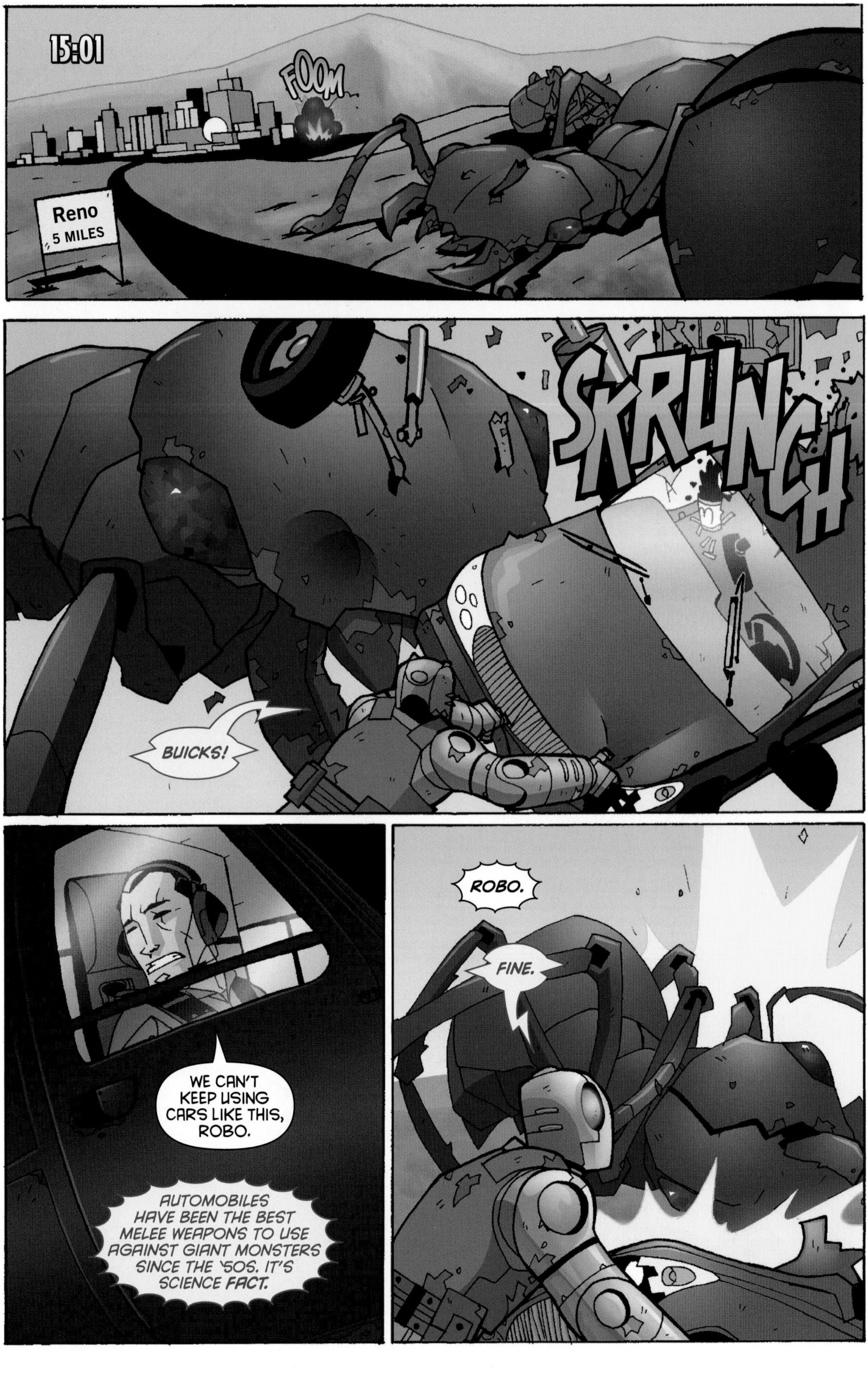
15:01
FOOM
Reno
5 MILES
SKRUNCH
BUICKS!
WE CAN'T KEEP USING CARS LIKE THIS, ROBO.
AUTOMOBILES HAVE BEEN THE BEST MELEE WEAPONS TO USE AGAINST GIANT MONSTERS SINCE THE '50S. IT'S SCIENCE FACT.
ROBO.
FINE.

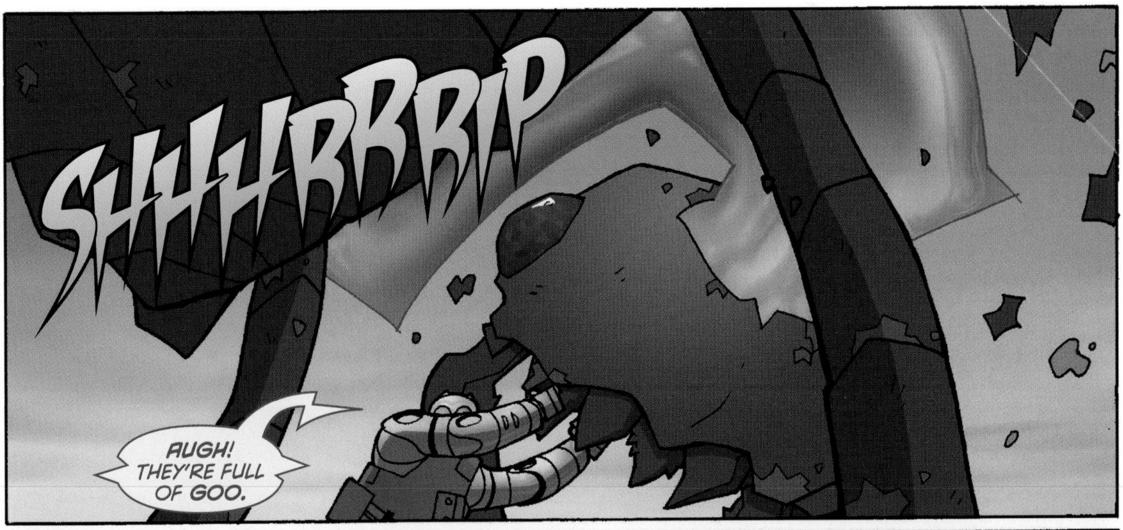
SHHHBBRIP
AUGH! THEY'RE FULL OF GOO.

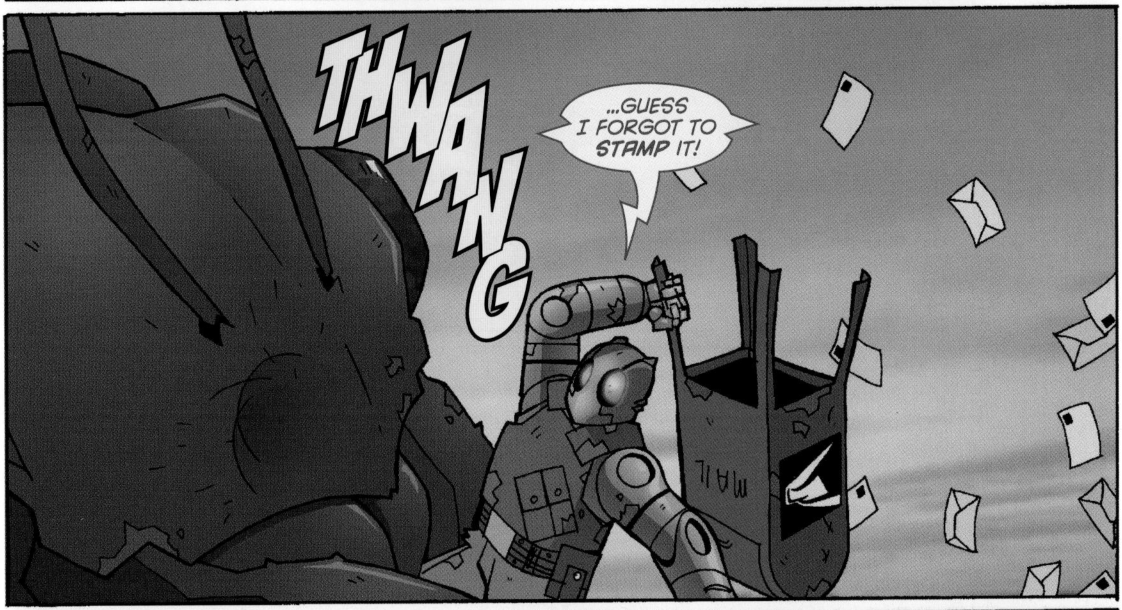
THWANG
...GUESS I FORGOT TO STAMP IT!
MAIL

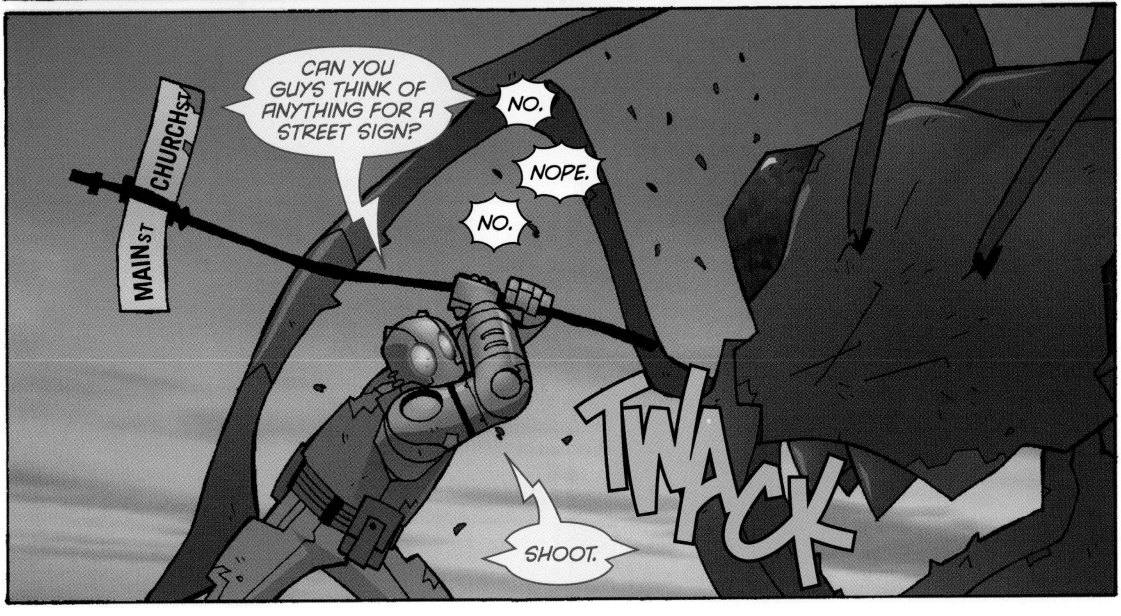
CHURCH ST
MAIN ST
CAN YOU GUYS THINK OF ANYTHING FOR A STREET SIGN?
NO.
NOPE.
NO.
TWACK
SHOOT.

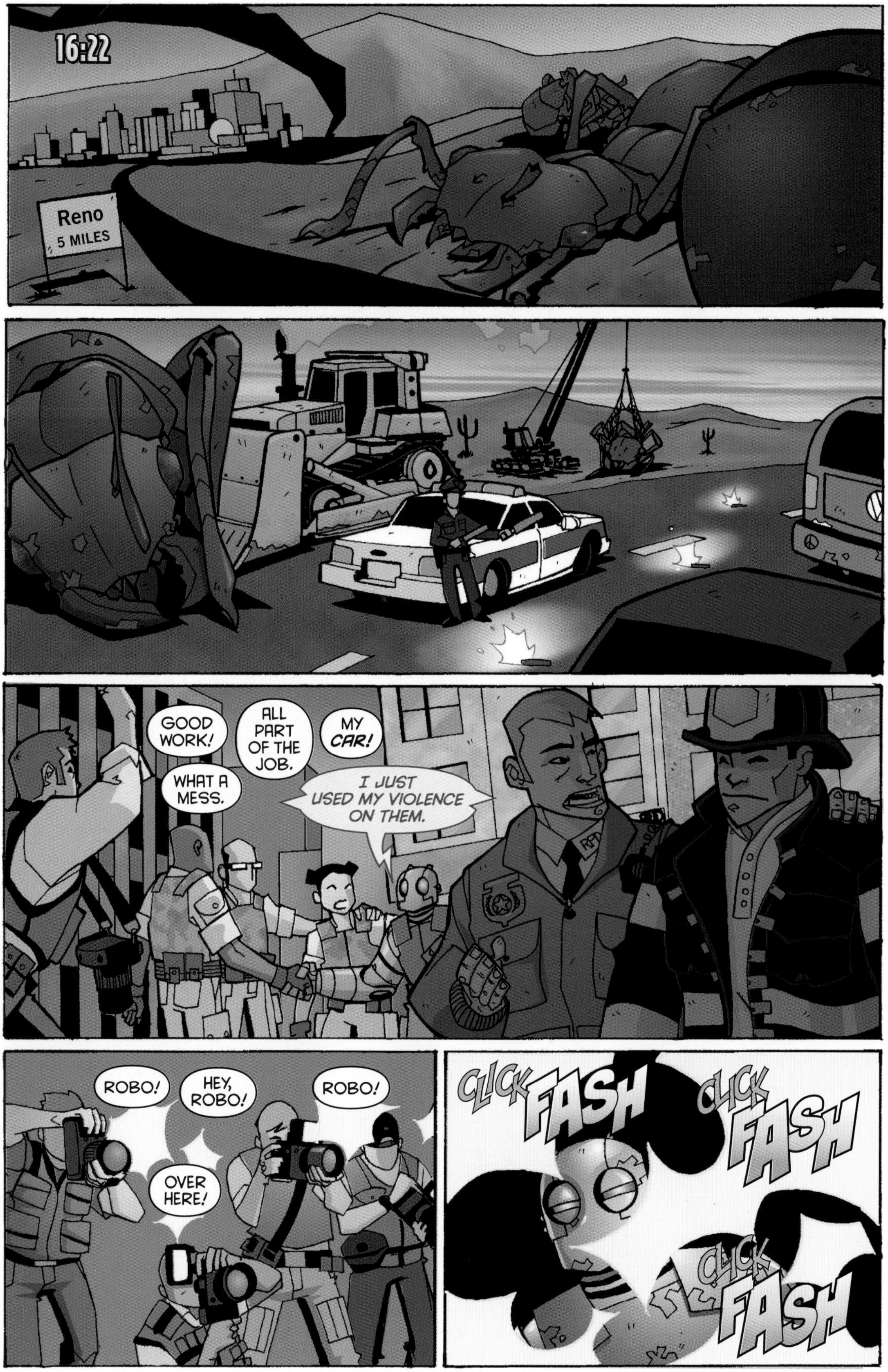
16:22
Reno
5 MILES
GOOD WORK!
ALL PART OF THE JOB.
MY CAR!
WHAT A MESS.
I JUST USED MY VIOLENCE ON THEM.
ROBO!
HEY, ROBO!
ROBO!
OVER HERE!
CLICK
FASH
CLICK
FASH
CLICK
FASH

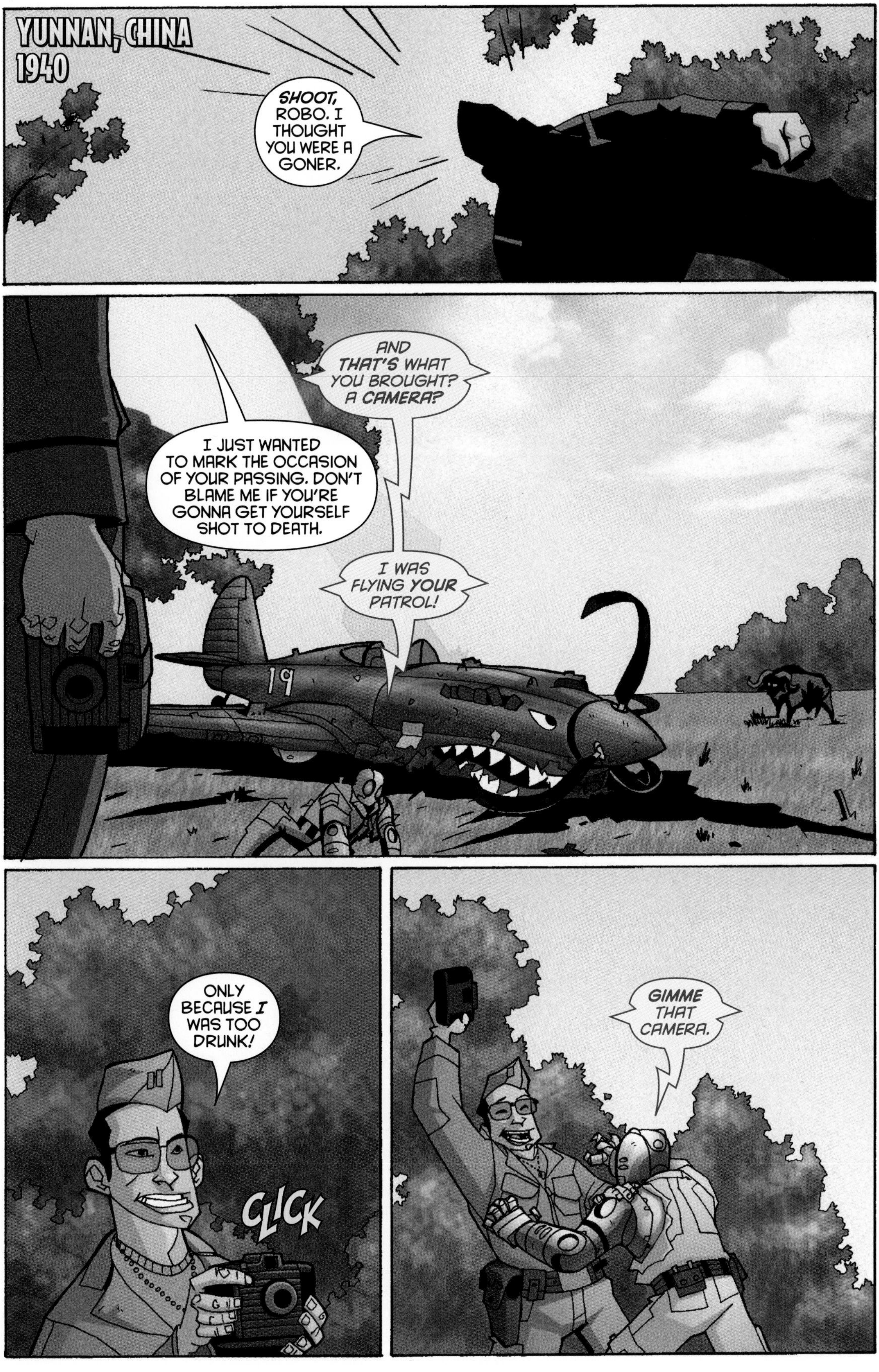
YUNNAN, CHINA
1940
SHOOT, ROBO. I THOUGHT YOU WERE A GONER.
AND THAT'S WHAT YOU BROUGHT? A CAMERA?
I JUST WANTED TO MARK THE OCCASION OF YOUR PASSING. DON'T BLAME ME IF YOU'RE GONNA GET YOURSELF SHOT TO DEATH.
I WAS FLYING YOUR PATROL!
19
ONLY BECAUSE I WAS TOO DRUNK!
CLICK
GIMME THAT CAMERA.

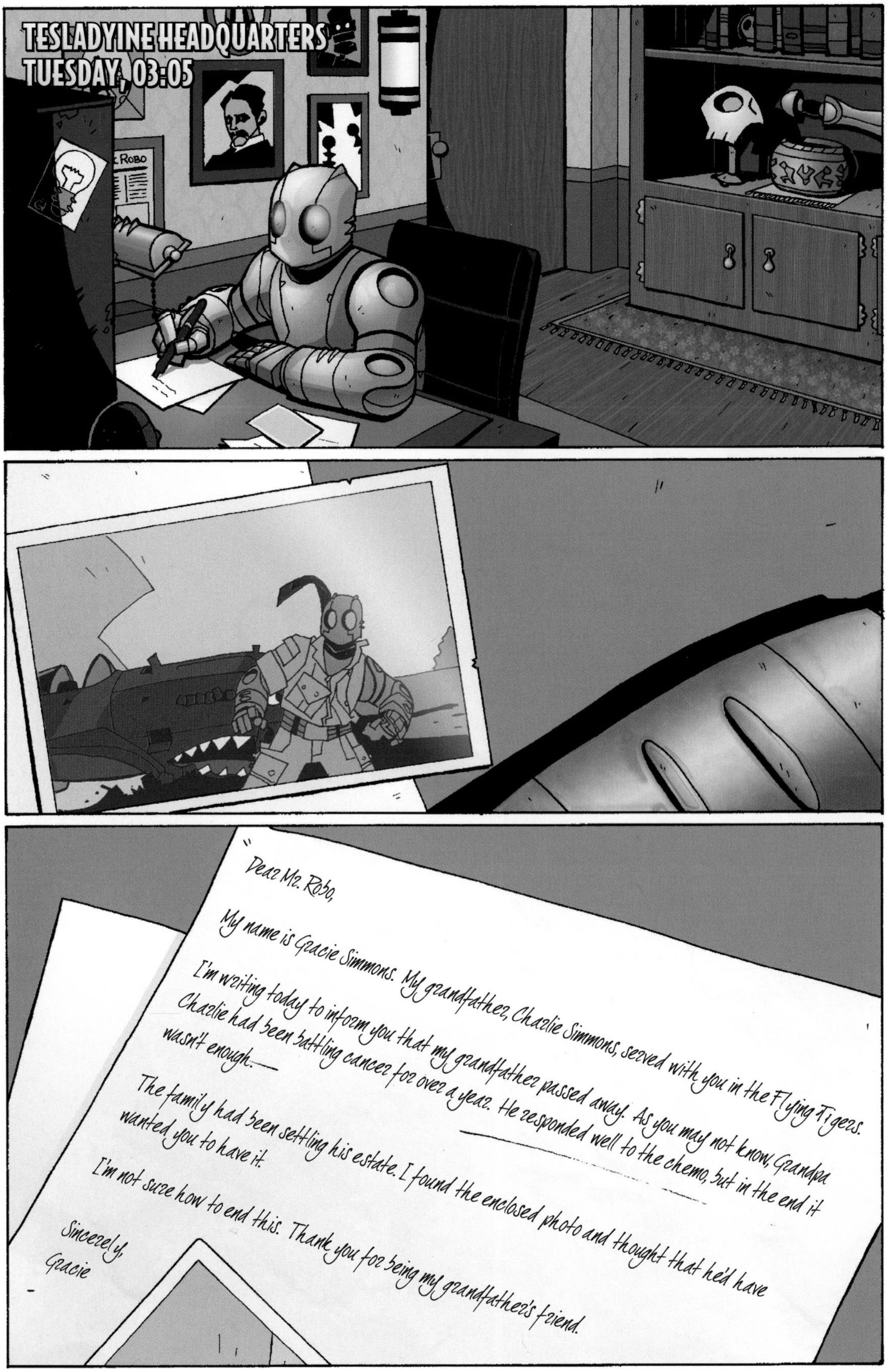
TESLADYINE HEADQUARTERS
TUESDAY, 03:05
ROBO
Dear Mr. Robo,
My name is Gracie Simmons. My grandfather, Charlie Simmons, served with you in the Flying Tigers.
I'm writing today to inform you that my grandfather passed away. As you may not know, Grandpa Charlie had been battling cancer for over a year. He responded well to the chemo, but in the end it wasn't enough.
The family had been settling his estate. I found the enclosed photo and thought that he'd have wanted you to have it.
I'm not sure how to end this. Thank you for being my grandfather's friend.
Sincerely,
Gracie

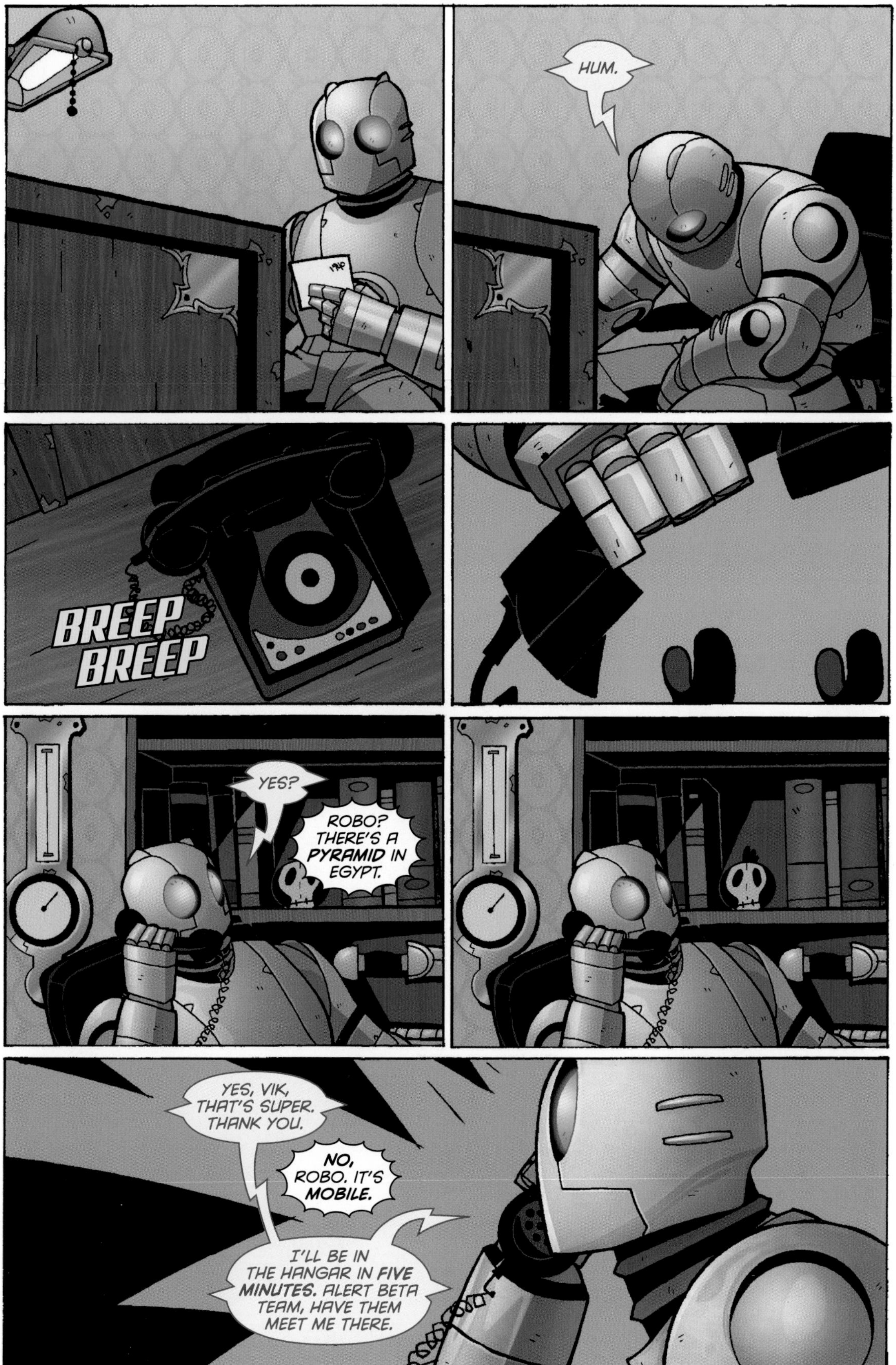
HUM.
BREEP
BREEP
YES?
ROBO? THERE'S A PYRAMID IN EGYPT.
YES, VIK, THAT'S SUPER. THANK YOU.
NO, ROBO. IT'S MOBILE.
I'LL BE IN THE HANGAR IN FIVE MINUTES. ALERT BETA TEAM, HAVE THEM MEET ME THERE.

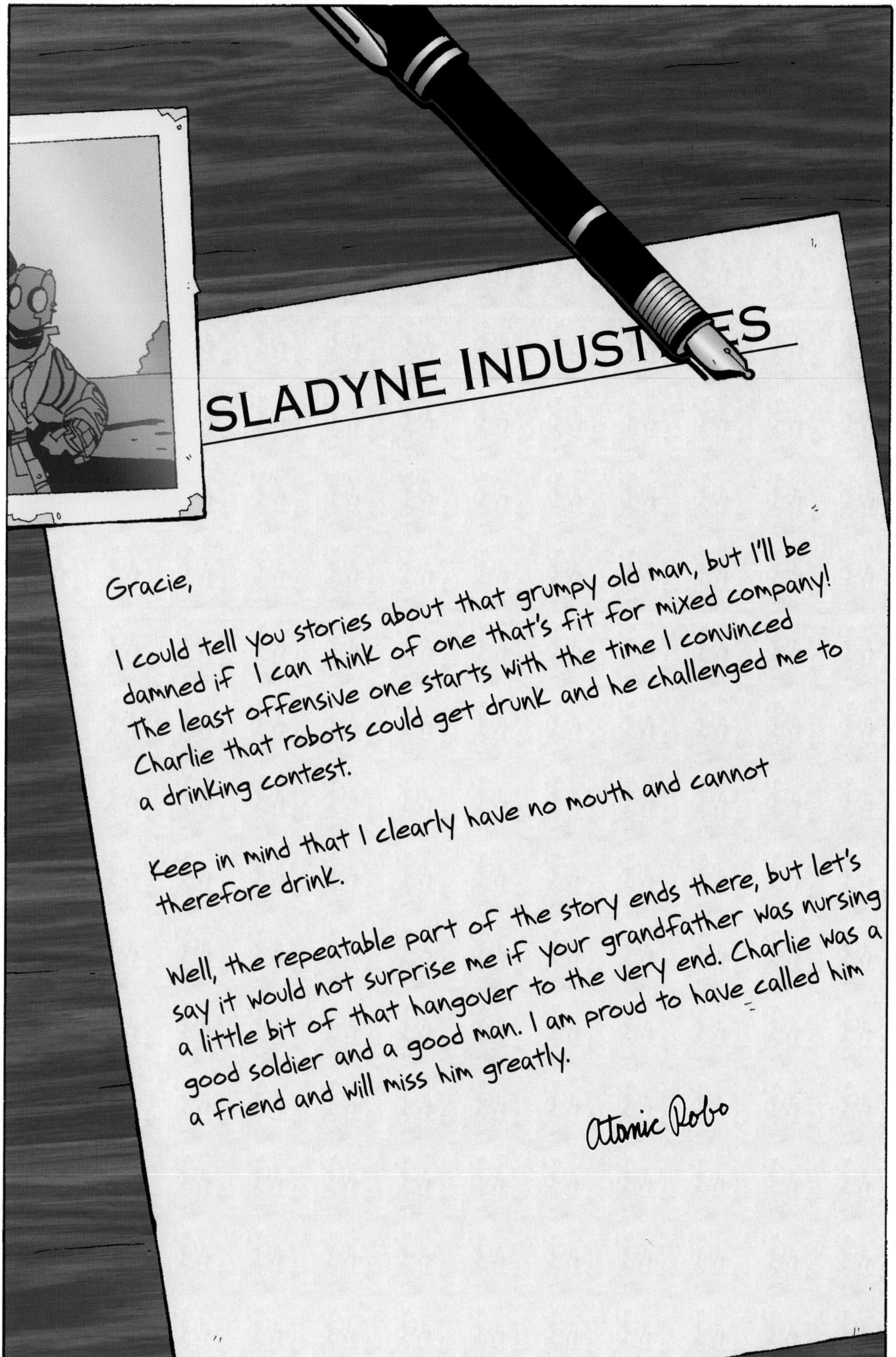
SLADYNE INDUSTRIES
Gracie,
I could tell you stories about that grumpy old man, but I'll be damned if I can think of one that's fit for mixed company! The least offensive one starts with the time I convinced Charlie that robots could get drunk and he challenged me to a drinking contest.
Keep in mind that I clearly have no mouth and cannot therefore drink.
Well, the repeatable part of the story ends there, but let's say it would not surprise me if your grandfather was nursing a little bit of that hangover to the very end. Charlie was a good soldier and a good man. I am proud to have called him a friend and will miss him greatly.
Atomic Robo

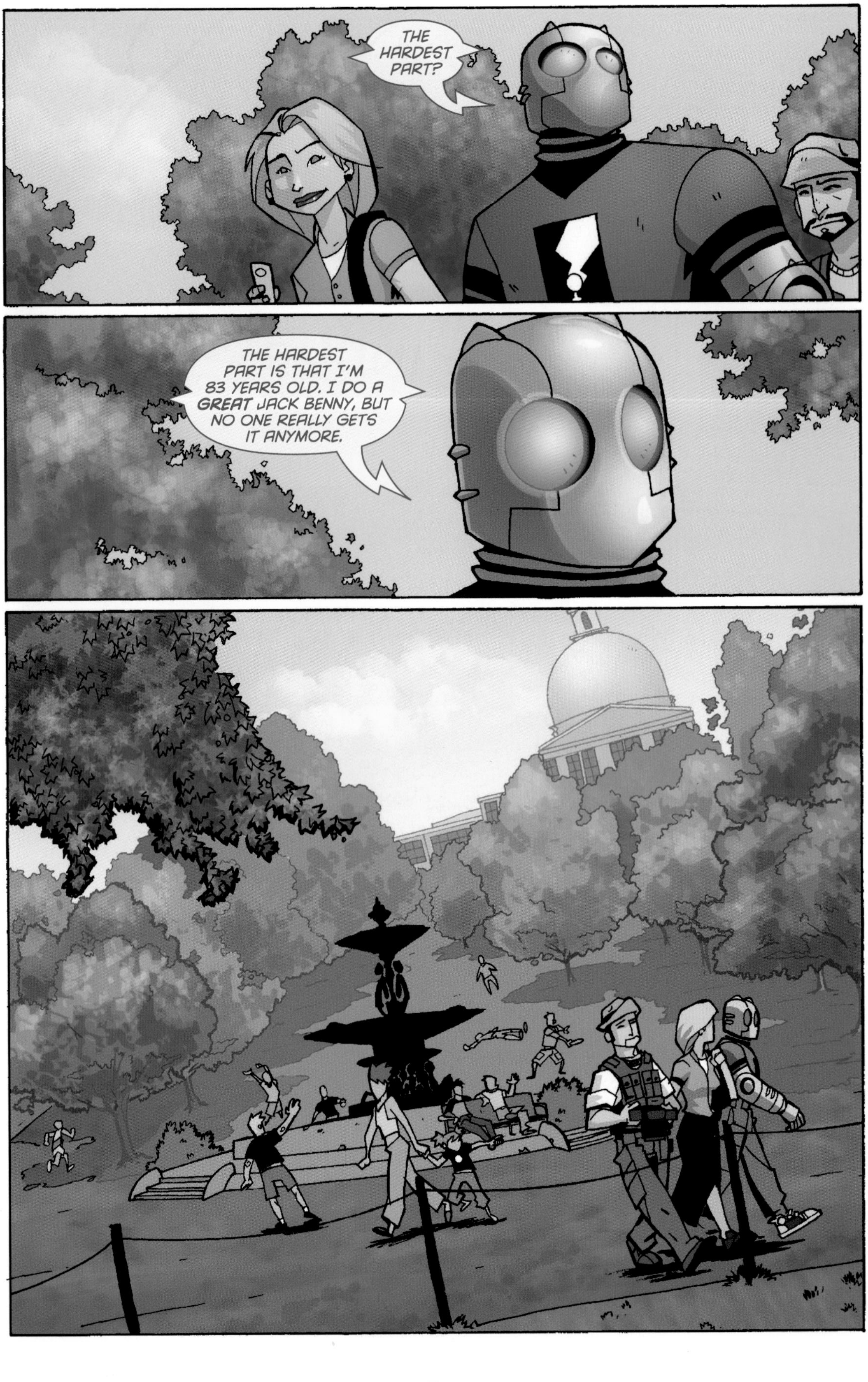
THE HARDEST PART?
THE HARDEST PART IS THAT I'M 83 YEARS OLD. I DO A GREAT JACK BENNY, BUT NO ONE REALLY GETS IT ANYMORE.

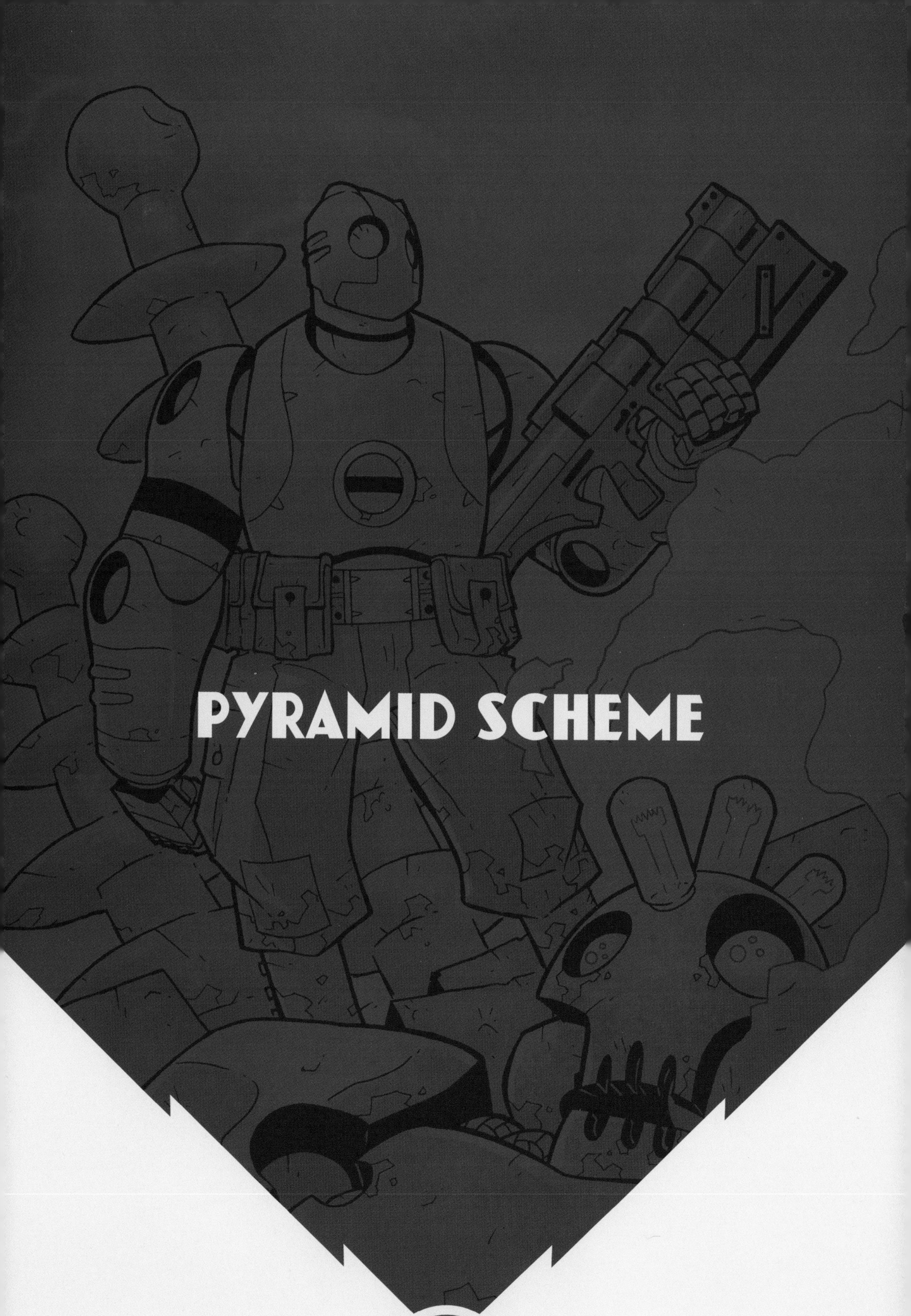

PYRAMID SCHEME

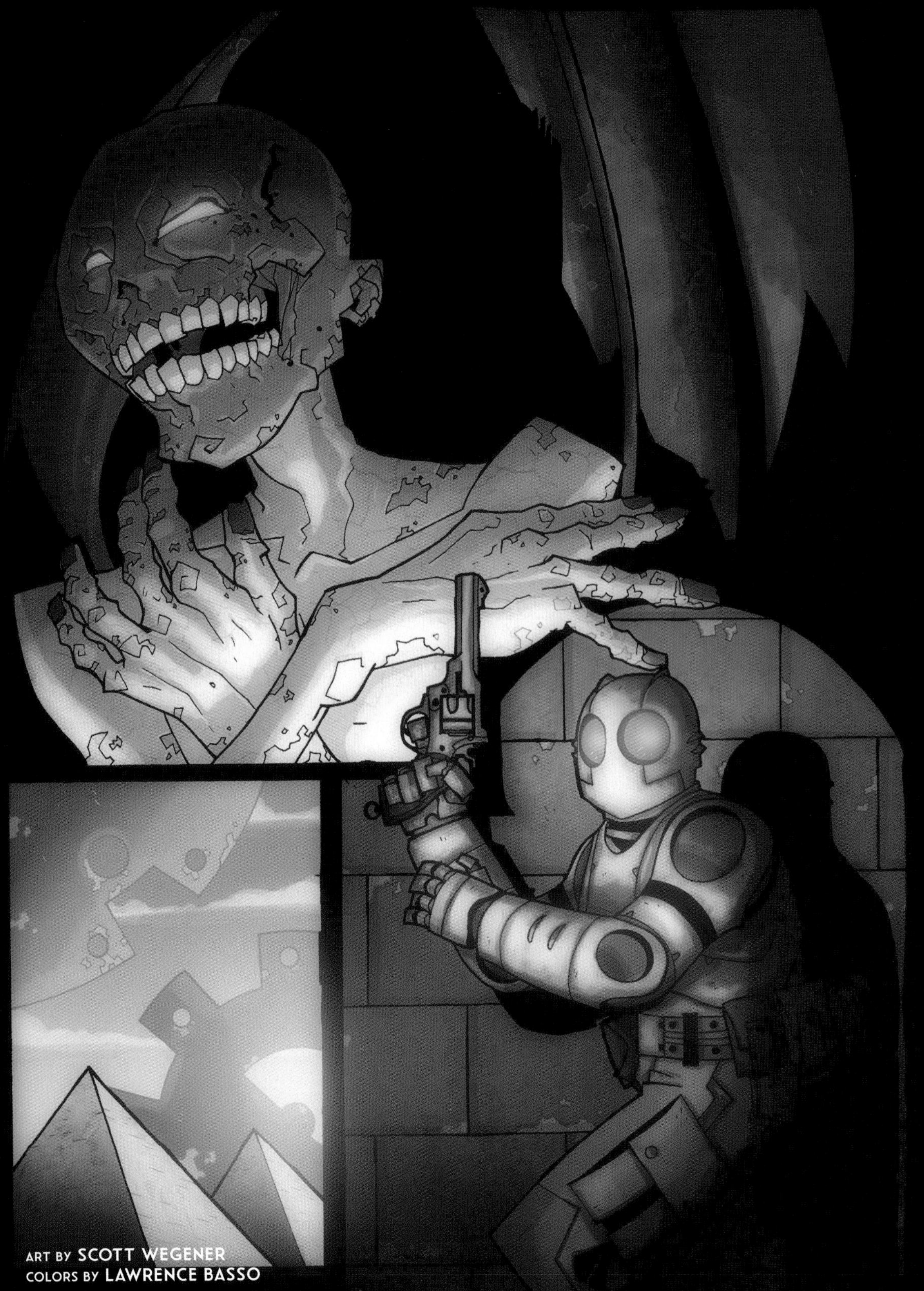

ART BY **SCOTT WEGENER**
COLORS BY **LAWRENCE BASSO**

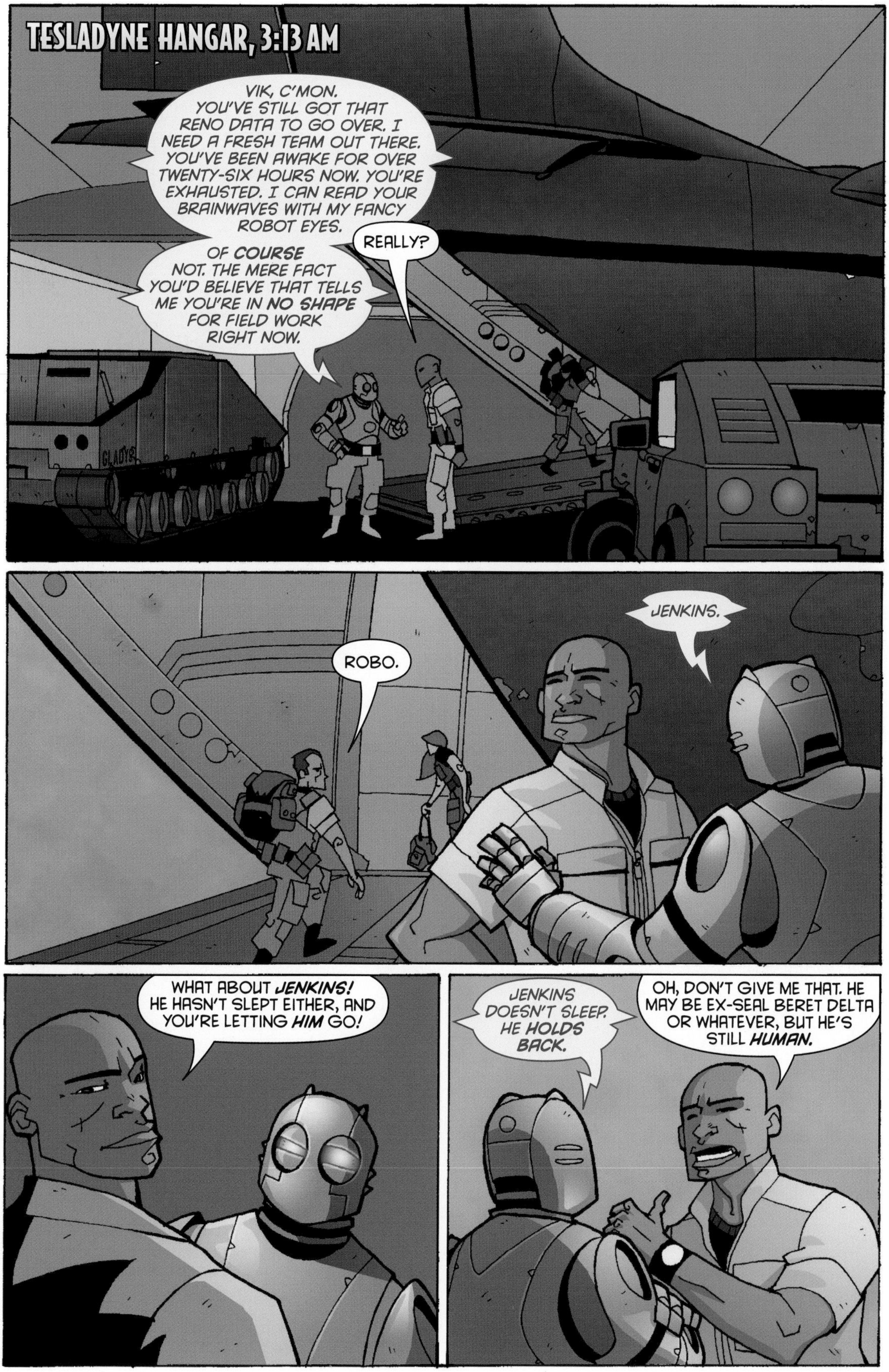
TESLADYNE HANGAR, 3:13 AM
VIK, C'MON. YOU'VE STILL GOT THAT RENO DATA TO GO OVER. I NEED A FRESH TEAM OUT THERE. YOU'VE BEEN AWAKE FOR OVER TWENTY-SIX HOURS NOW. YOU'RE EXHAUSTED. I CAN READ YOUR BRAINWAVES WITH MY FANCY ROBOT EYES.
REALLY?
OF COURSE NOT. THE MERE FACT YOU'D BELIEVE THAT TELLS ME YOU'RE IN NO SHAPE FOR FIELD WORK RIGHT NOW.
GLADYS
ROBO.
JENKINS.
WHAT ABOUT JENKINS! HE HASN'T SLEPT EITHER, AND YOU'RE LETTING HIM GO!
JENKINS DOESN'T SLEEP. HE HOLDS BACK.
OH, DON'T GIVE ME THAT. HE MAY BE EX-SEAL BERET DELTA OR WHATEVER, BUT HE'S STILL HUMAN.

HIT THE RENO DATA WITH THE REST OF ALPHA TEAM WHEN YOU WAKE UP. SOMETHING MADE THOSE ANTS GIGANTIC, AND I WANT A FULL REPORT ON IT WHEN I GET BACK.

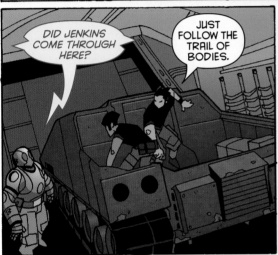

DID JENKINS COME THROUGH HERE?

JUST FOLLOW THE TRAIL OF BODIES.

YOU REALLY ENJOY CULTIVATING AN AIR OF TERROR, DON'T YOU?

"HERE'S WHAT WE KNOW SO FAR..."

CAIRO, EGYPT
FOURTEEN HOURS LATER

THERE'S A MOBILE PYRAMID WANDERING THE EGYPTIAN DESERT.

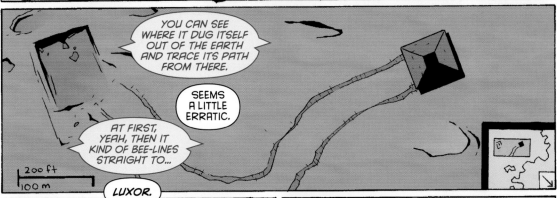

YOU CAN SEE WHERE IT DUG ITSELF OUT OF THE EARTH AND TRACE ITS PATH FROM THERE.

SEEMS A LITTLE ERRATIC.

AT FIRST, YEAH, THEN IT KIND OF BEE-LINES STRAIGHT TO...

200 ft
100 m

LUXOR.

ASSUMING IT KEEPS CURRENT COURSE AND SPEED, IT'LL HIT TOMORROW AT 20:00 LOCAL TIME AT BEST.

AND THEY WANT US TO FIGURE OUT HOW TO STOP IT WITHOUT BLOWING IT UP.

THE EGYPTIAN MILITARY'S BEEN ORDERED TO STAY CLEAR, BUT WE ARE ASSURED THEIR FULL COOPERATION.

EGYPT'S ENJOYED A LONG HISTORY OF NOT BLOWING UP PYRAMIDS, I THINK THEY AIM TO STICK TO THAT.

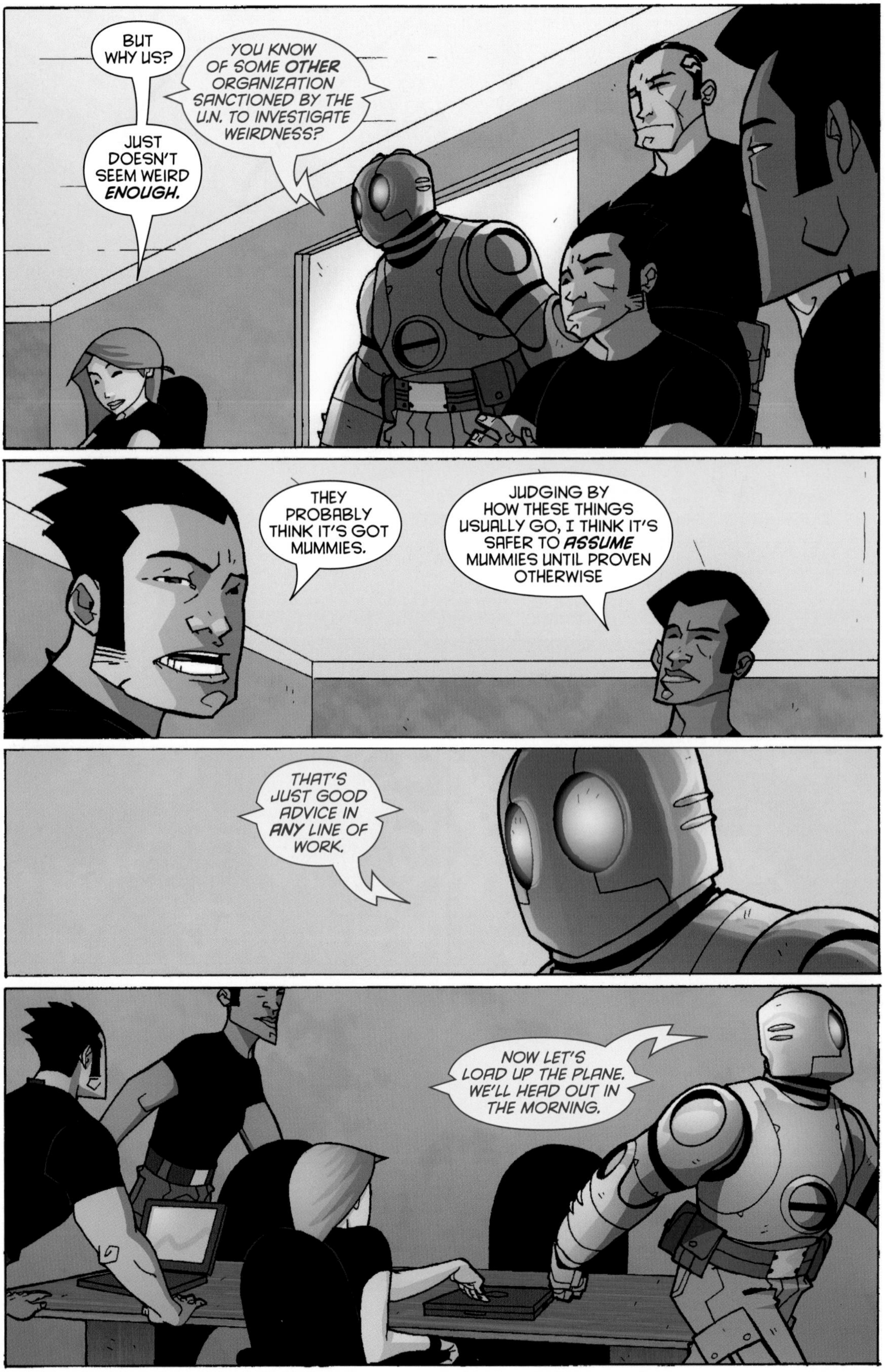

BUT WHY US?
YOU KNOW OF SOME OTHER ORGANIZATION SANCTIONED BY THE U.N. TO INVESTIGATE WEIRDNESS?
JUST DOESN'T SEEM WEIRD ENOUGH.
THEY PROBABLY THINK IT'S GOT MUMMIES.
JUDGING BY HOW THESE THINGS USUALLY GO, I THINK IT'S SAFER TO ASSUME MUMMIES UNTIL PROVEN OTHERWISE
THAT'S JUST GOOD ADVICE IN ANY LINE OF WORK.
NOW LET'S LOAD UP THE PLANE. WE'LL HEAD OUT IN THE MORNING.

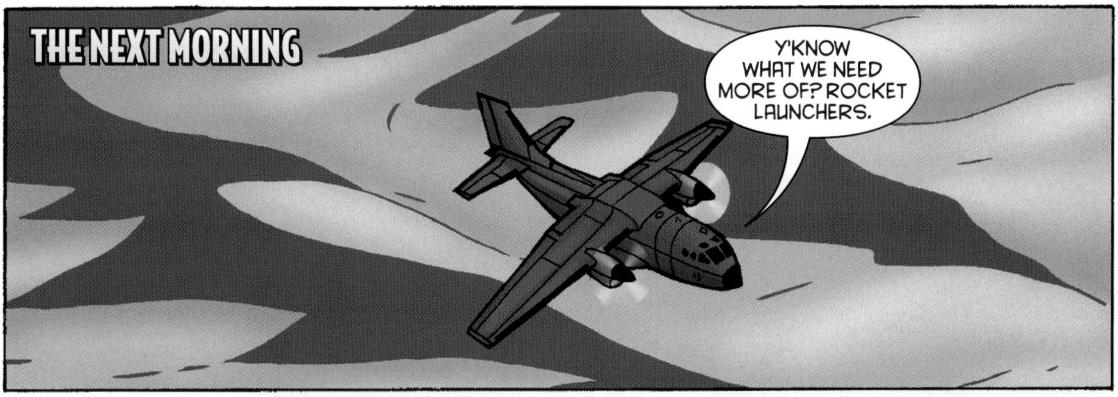
THE NEXT MORNING
Y'KNOW WHAT WE NEED MORE OF? ROCKET LAUNCHERS.

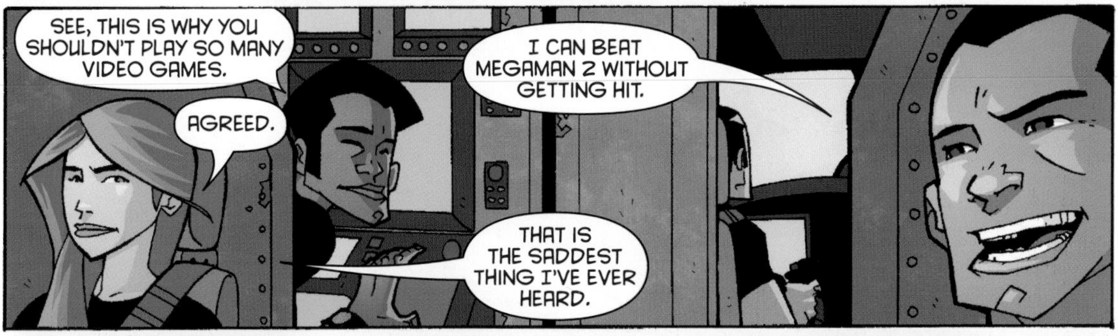
SEE, THIS IS WHY YOU SHOULDN'T PLAY SO MANY VIDEO GAMES.
AGREED.
I CAN BEAT MEGAMAN 2 WITHOUT GETTING HIT.
THAT IS THE SADDEST THING I'VE EVER HEARD.

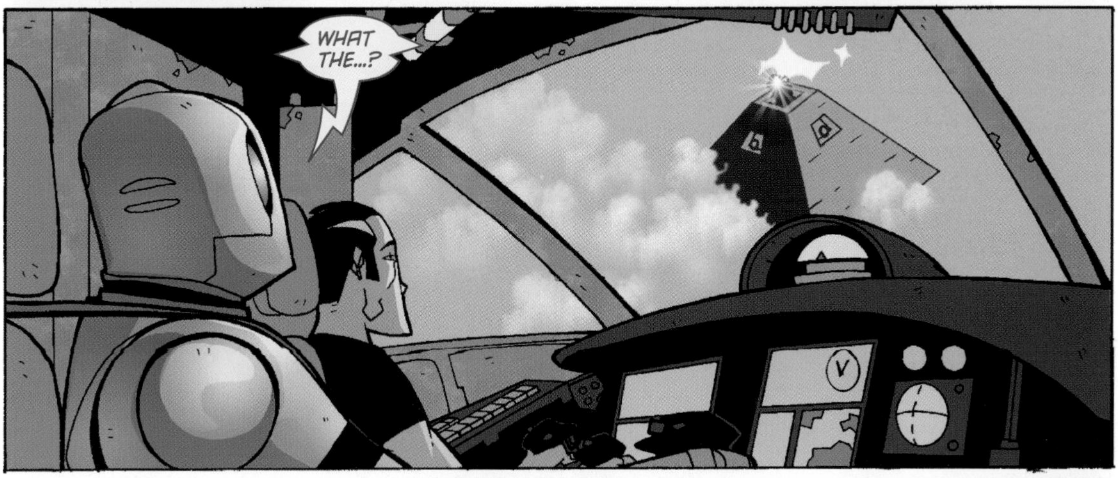
WHAT THE...?

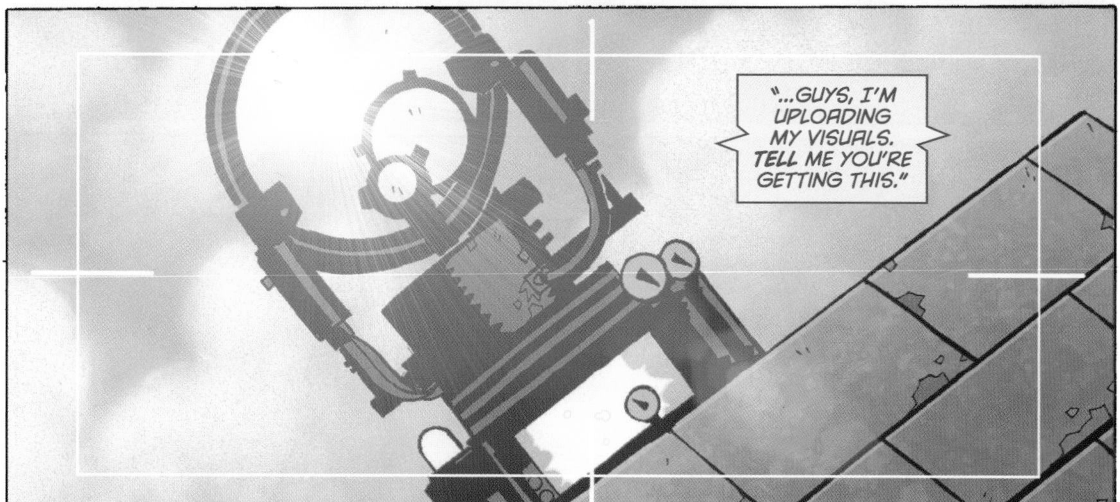
"...GUYS, I'M UPLOADING MY VISUALS. TELL ME YOU'RE GETTING THIS."

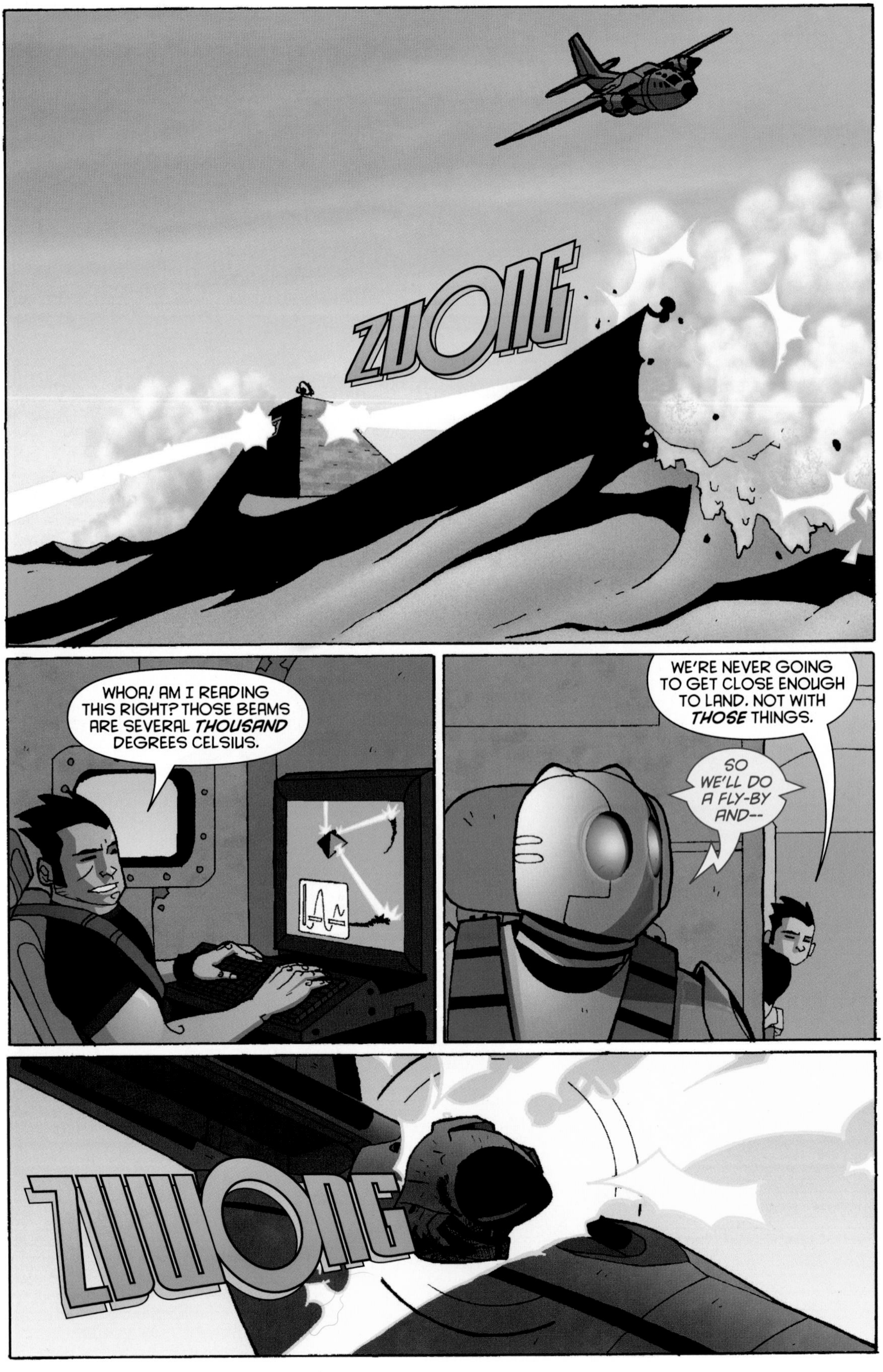
ZUONG
WHOA! AM I READING THIS RIGHT? THOSE BEAMS ARE SEVERAL *THOUSAND* DEGREES CELSIUS.
WE'RE NEVER GOING TO GET CLOSE ENOUGH TO LAND. NOT WITH *THOSE* THINGS.
SO WE'LL DO A FLY-BY AND--
ZUUONG

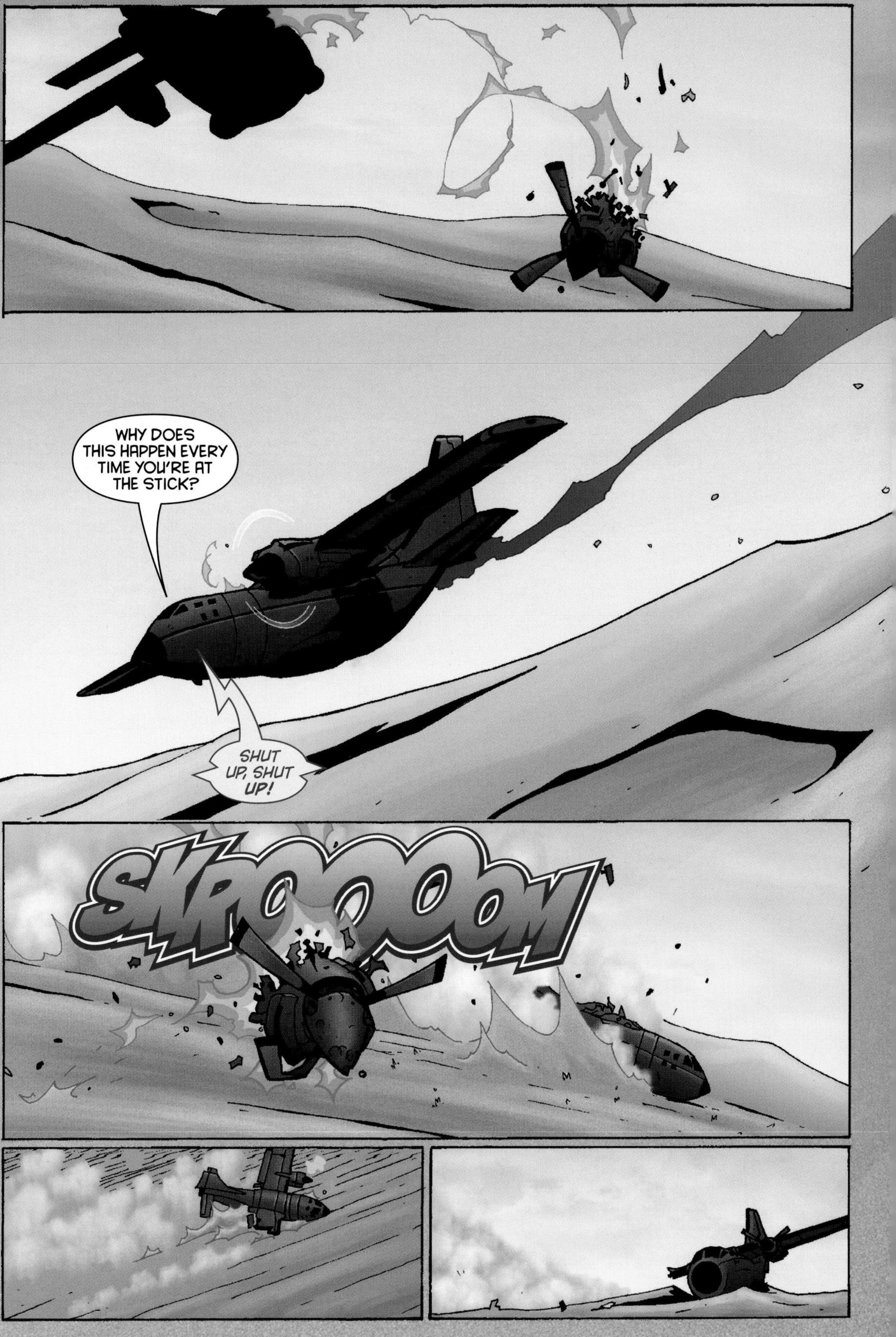
WHY DOES THIS HAPPEN EVERY TIME YOU'RE AT THE STICK?
SHUT UP, SHUT UP!
SKROOOOOM

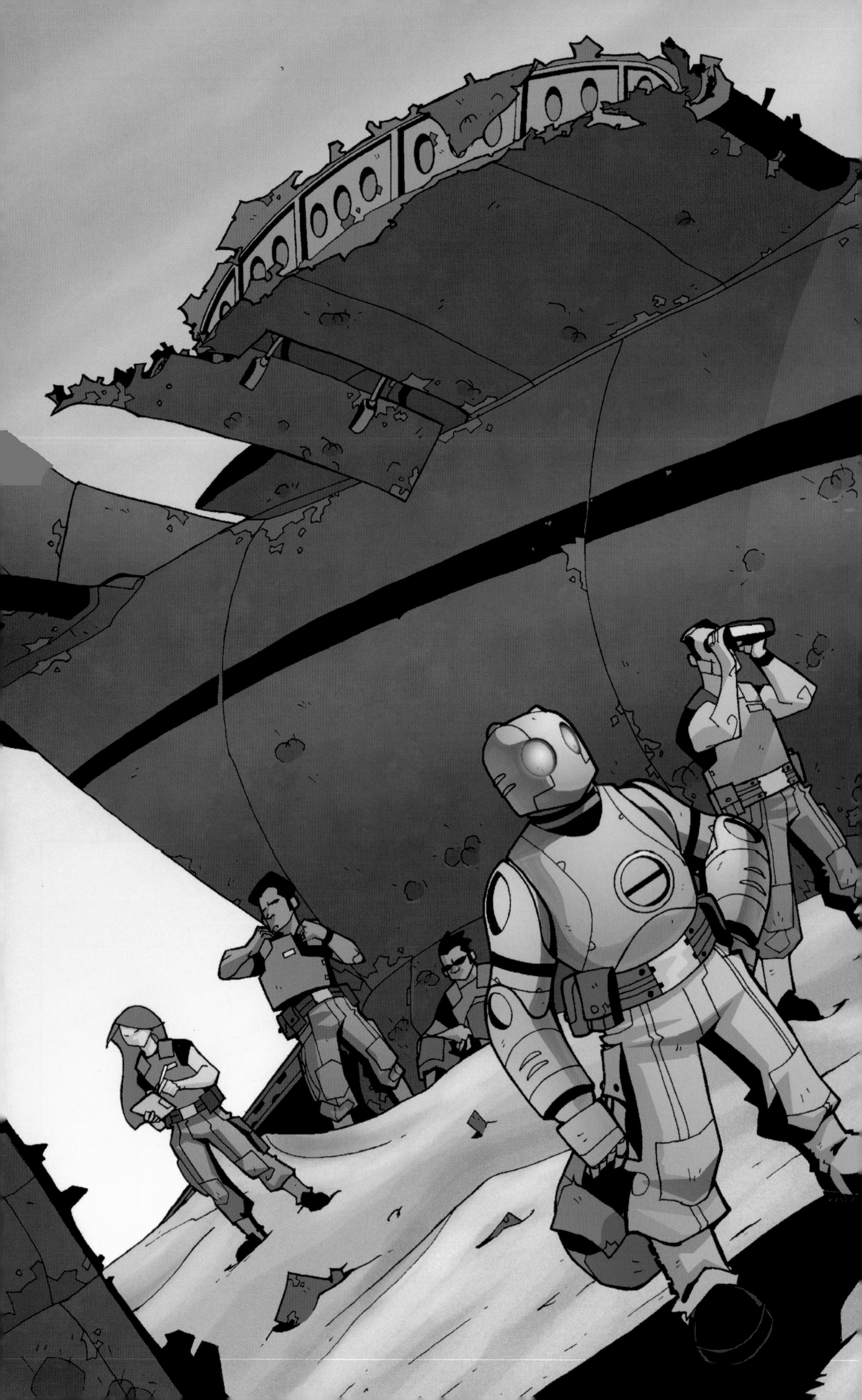

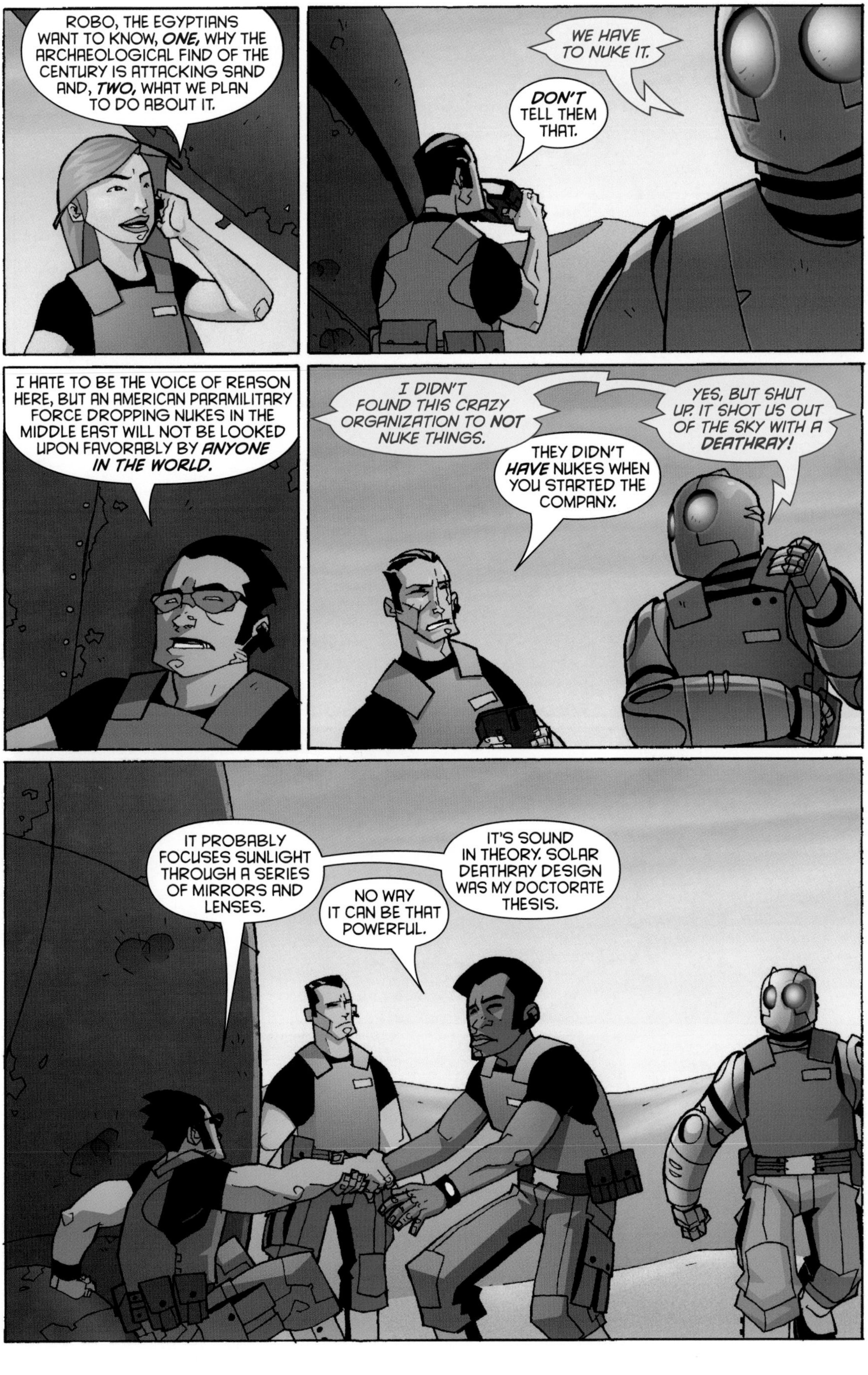
ROBO, THE EGYPTIANS WANT TO KNOW, ONE, WHY THE ARCHAEOLOGICAL FIND OF THE CENTURY IS ATTACKING SAND AND, TWO, WHAT WE PLAN TO DO ABOUT IT.
WE HAVE TO NUKE IT.
DON'T TELL THEM THAT.
I HATE TO BE THE VOICE OF REASON HERE, BUT AN AMERICAN PARAMILITARY FORCE DROPPING NUKES IN THE MIDDLE EAST WILL NOT BE LOOKED UPON FAVORABLY BY ANYONE IN THE WORLD.
I DIDN'T FOUND THIS CRAZY ORGANIZATION TO NOT NUKE THINGS.
THEY DIDN'T HAVE NUKES WHEN YOU STARTED THE COMPANY.
YES, BUT SHUT UP. IT SHOT US OUT OF THE SKY WITH A DEATHRAY!
IT PROBABLY FOCUSES SUNLIGHT THROUGH A SERIES OF MIRRORS AND LENSES.
NO WAY IT CAN BE THAT POWERFUL.
IT'S SOUND IN THEORY. SOLAR DEATHRAY DESIGN WAS MY DOCTORATE THESIS.

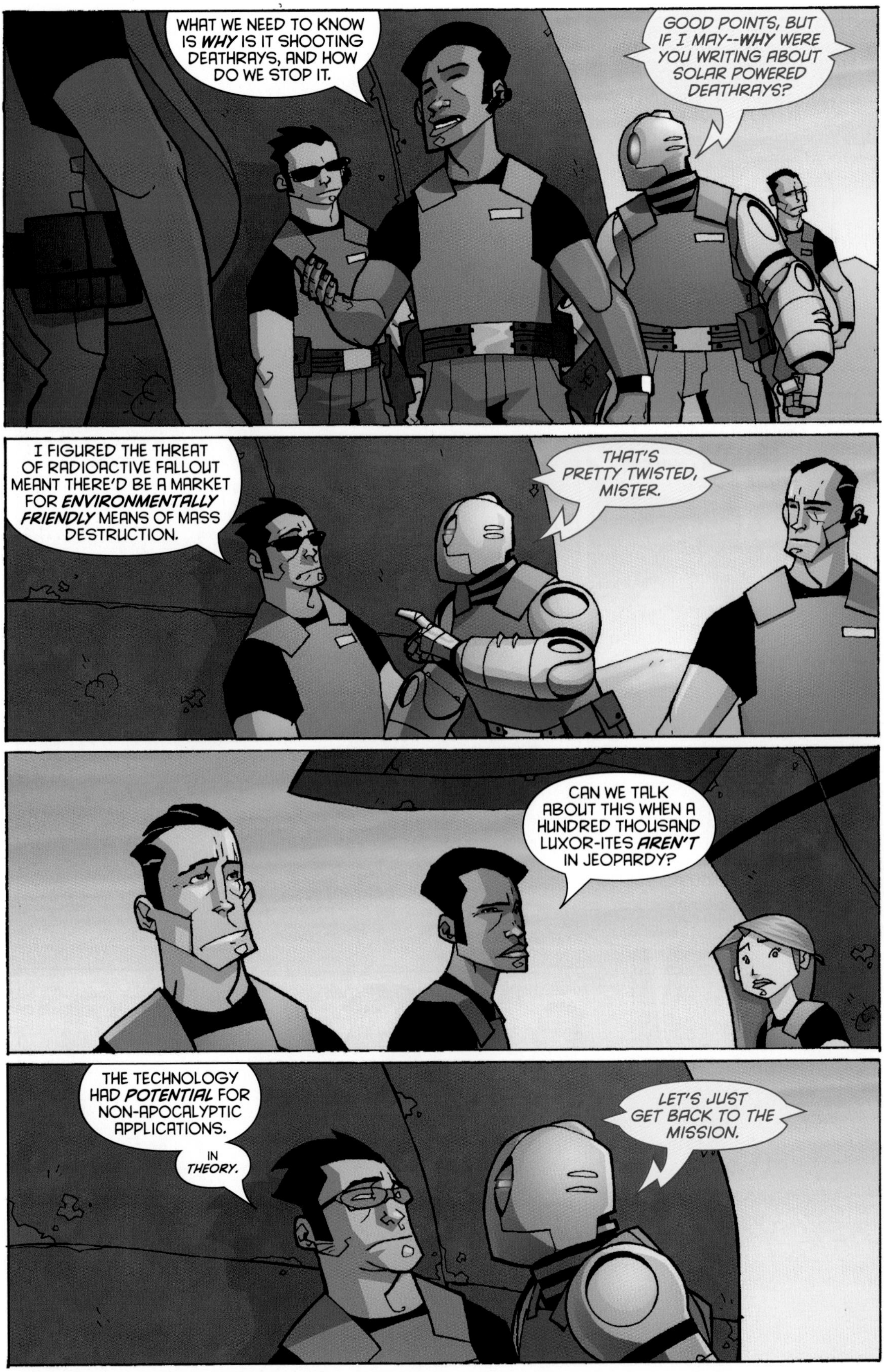
WHAT WE NEED TO KNOW IS ***WHY*** IS IT SHOOTING DEATHRAYS, AND HOW DO WE STOP IT.
*GOOD POINTS, BUT IF I MAY--**WHY** WERE YOU WRITING ABOUT SOLAR POWERED DEATHRAYS?*
I FIGURED THE THREAT OF RADIOACTIVE FALLOUT MEANT THERE'D BE A MARKET FOR ***ENVIRONMENTALLY FRIENDLY*** MEANS OF MASS DESTRUCTION.
THAT'S PRETTY TWISTED, MISTER.
CAN WE TALK ABOUT THIS WHEN A HUNDRED THOUSAND LUXOR-ITES ***AREN'T*** IN JEOPARDY?
THE TECHNOLOGY HAD ***POTENTIAL*** FOR NON-APOCALYPTIC APPLICATIONS.
IN *THEORY.*
LET'S JUST GET BACK TO THE MISSION.

CAREFUL WITH HER.

THIS AIN'T MY FIRST TIME AT THE RODEO.

WHAT DOES THAT *MEAN*?

SERIOUSLY, THOUGH, WHERE'S THE POWER BUTTON ON THIS THING?

THE EGYPTIANS ARE *STILL* WAITING FOR AN ANSWER, ROBO

RIGHT, OF COURSE. TELL THEM I HAVE A PLAN.

WHEN DO *WE* GET TO HEAR IT?

WE'RE USING GLADYS.

BRRRRUMMM

DIDN'T NEED YOU DUMB JERKS TO TELL ME HOW TO TURN IT ON ANYWAY, NYA.

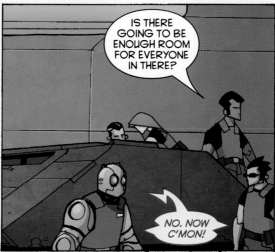

IS THERE GOING TO BE ENOUGH ROOM FOR EVERYONE IN THERE?

NO. NOW C'MON!

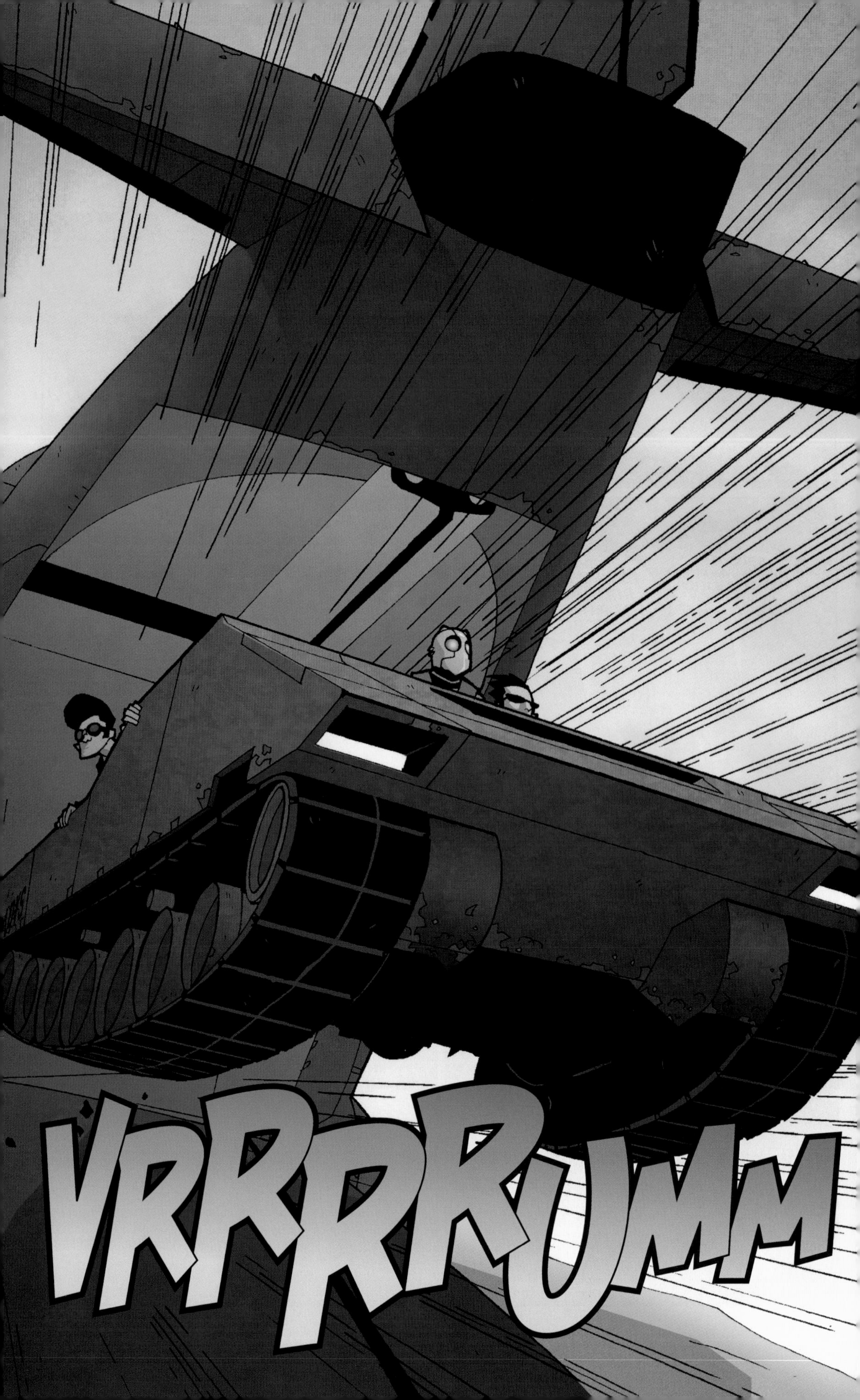
VRRRRUMM

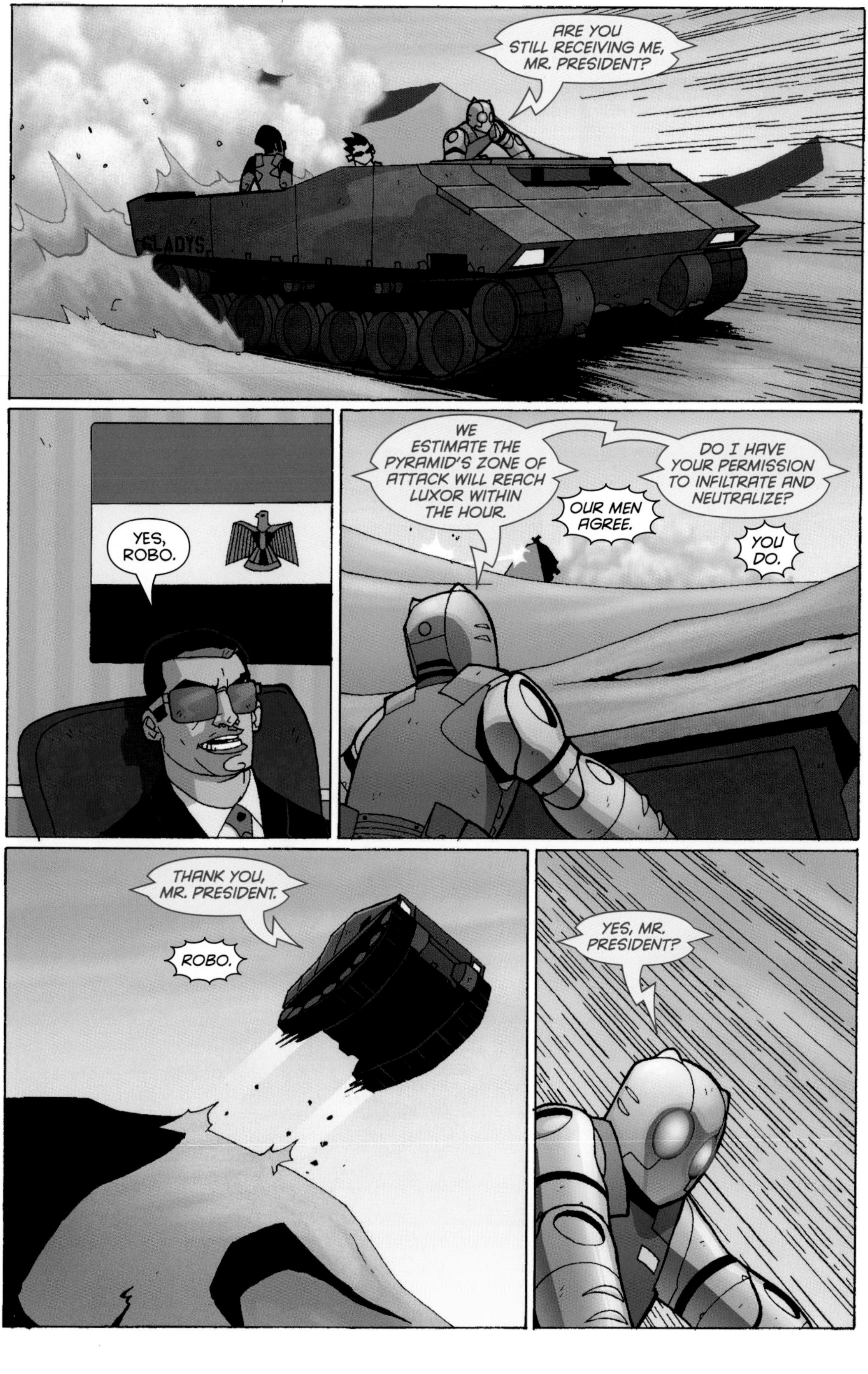
ARE YOU STILL RECEIVING ME, MR. PRESIDENT?
GLADYS
YES, ROBO.
WE ESTIMATE THE PYRAMID'S ZONE OF ATTACK WILL REACH LUXOR WITHIN THE HOUR.
OUR MEN AGREE.
DO I HAVE YOUR PERMISSION TO INFILTRATE AND NEUTRALIZE?
YOU DO.
THANK YOU, MR. PRESIDENT.
ROBO.
YES, MR. PRESIDENT?

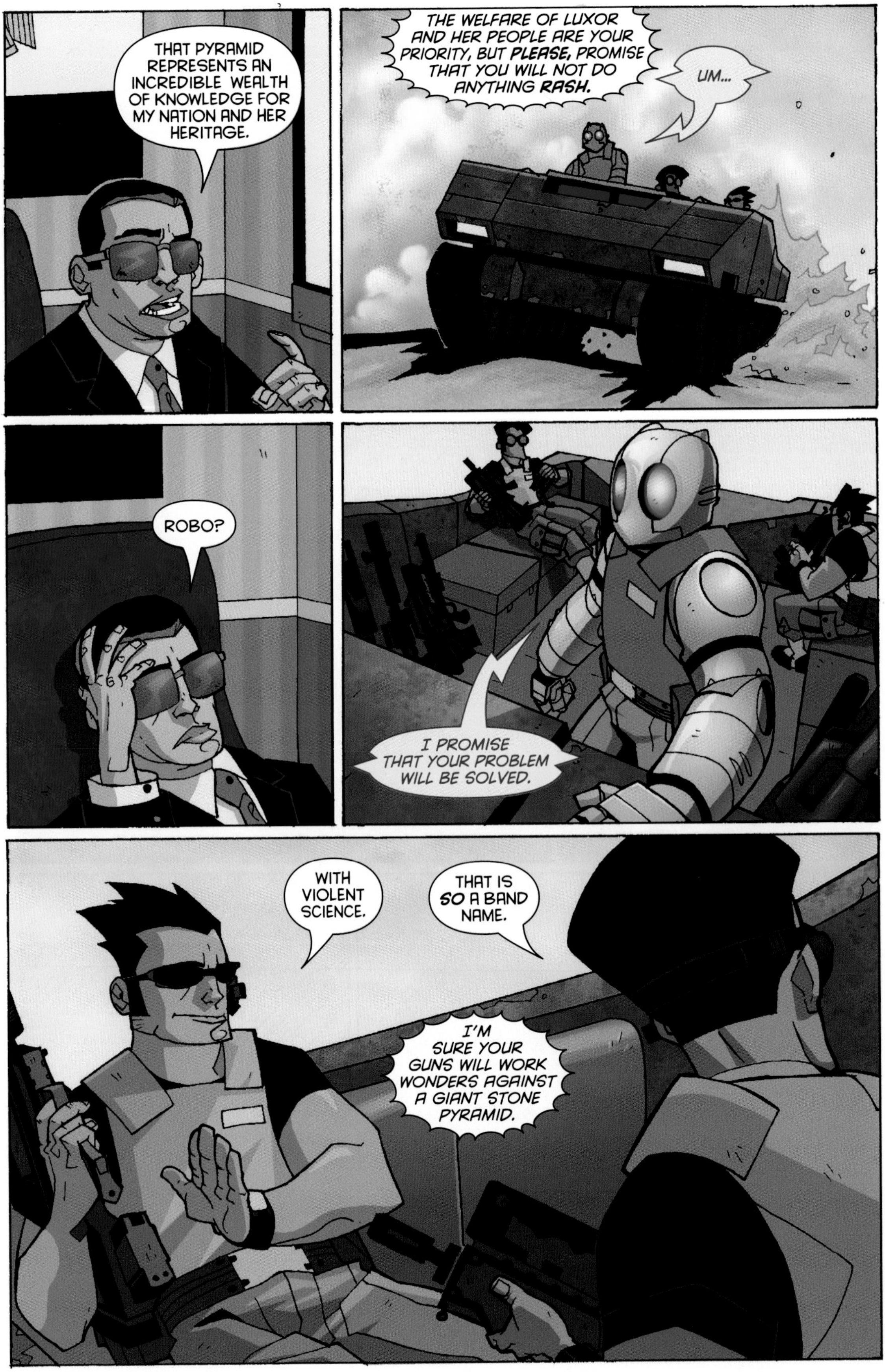
THAT PYRAMID REPRESENTS AN INCREDIBLE WEALTH OF KNOWLEDGE FOR MY NATION AND HER HERITAGE.
THE WELFARE OF LUXOR AND HER PEOPLE ARE YOUR PRIORITY, BUT PLEASE, PROMISE THAT YOU WILL NOT DO ANYTHING RASH.
UM...
ROBO?
I PROMISE THAT YOUR PROBLEM WILL BE SOLVED.
WITH VIOLENT SCIENCE.
THAT IS SO A BAND NAME.
I'M SURE YOUR GUNS WILL WORK WONDERS AGAINST A GIANT STONE PYRAMID.

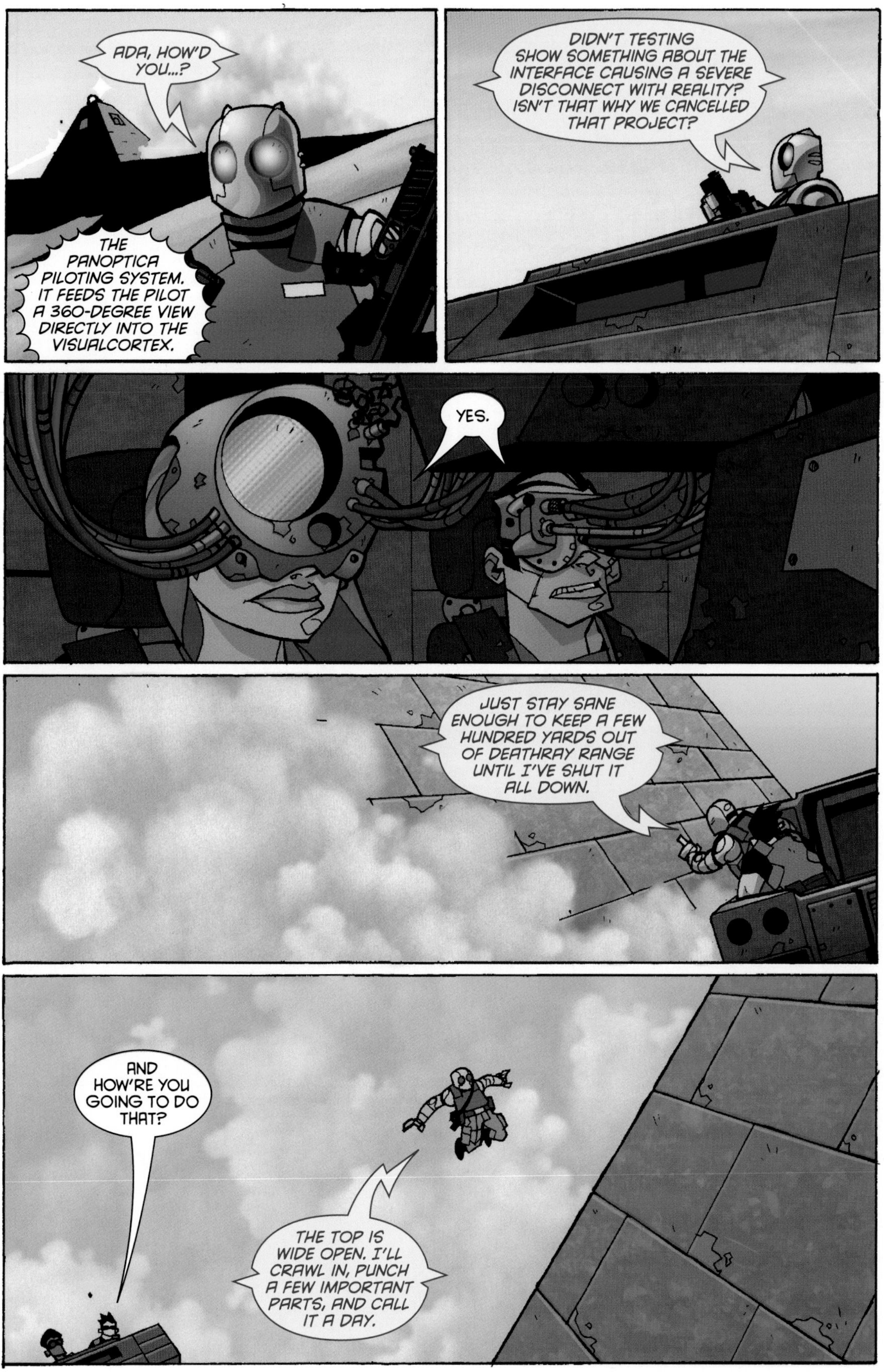
ADA, HOW'D YOU...?
THE PANOPTICA PILOTING SYSTEM. IT FEEDS THE PILOT A 360-DEGREE VIEW DIRECTLY INTO THE VISUALCORTEX.
DIDN'T TESTING SHOW SOMETHING ABOUT THE INTERFACE CAUSING A SEVERE DISCONNECT WITH REALITY? ISN'T THAT WHY WE CANCELLED THAT PROJECT?
YES.
JUST STAY SANE ENOUGH TO KEEP A FEW HUNDRED YARDS OUT OF DEATHRAY RANGE UNTIL I'VE SHUT IT ALL DOWN.
AND HOW'RE YOU GOING TO DO THAT?
THE TOP IS WIDE OPEN. I'LL CRAWL IN, PUNCH A FEW IMPORTANT PARTS, AND CALL IT A DAY.

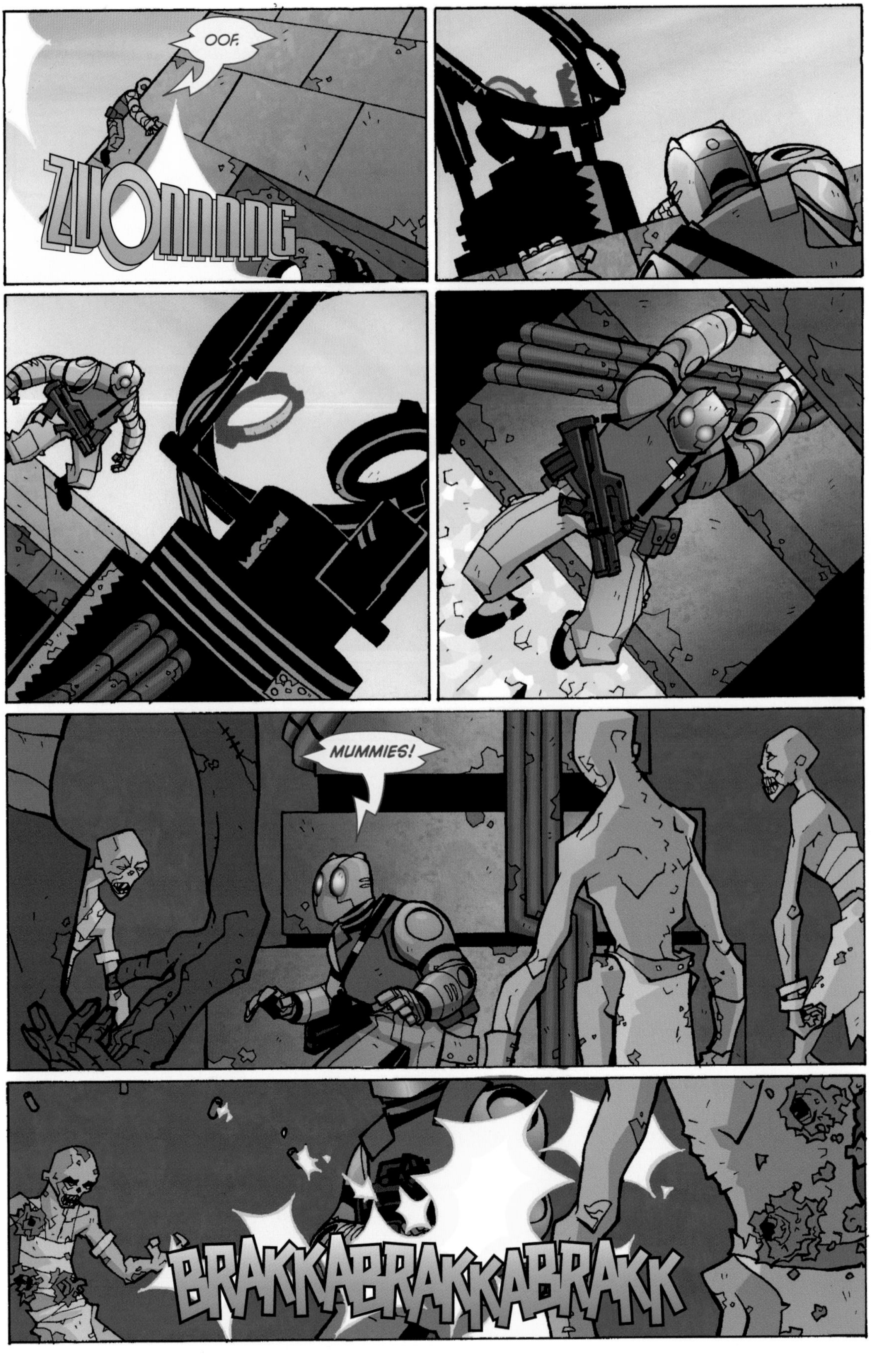
OOF.
ZUONNNNG
MUMMIES!
BRAKKABRAKKABRAKK

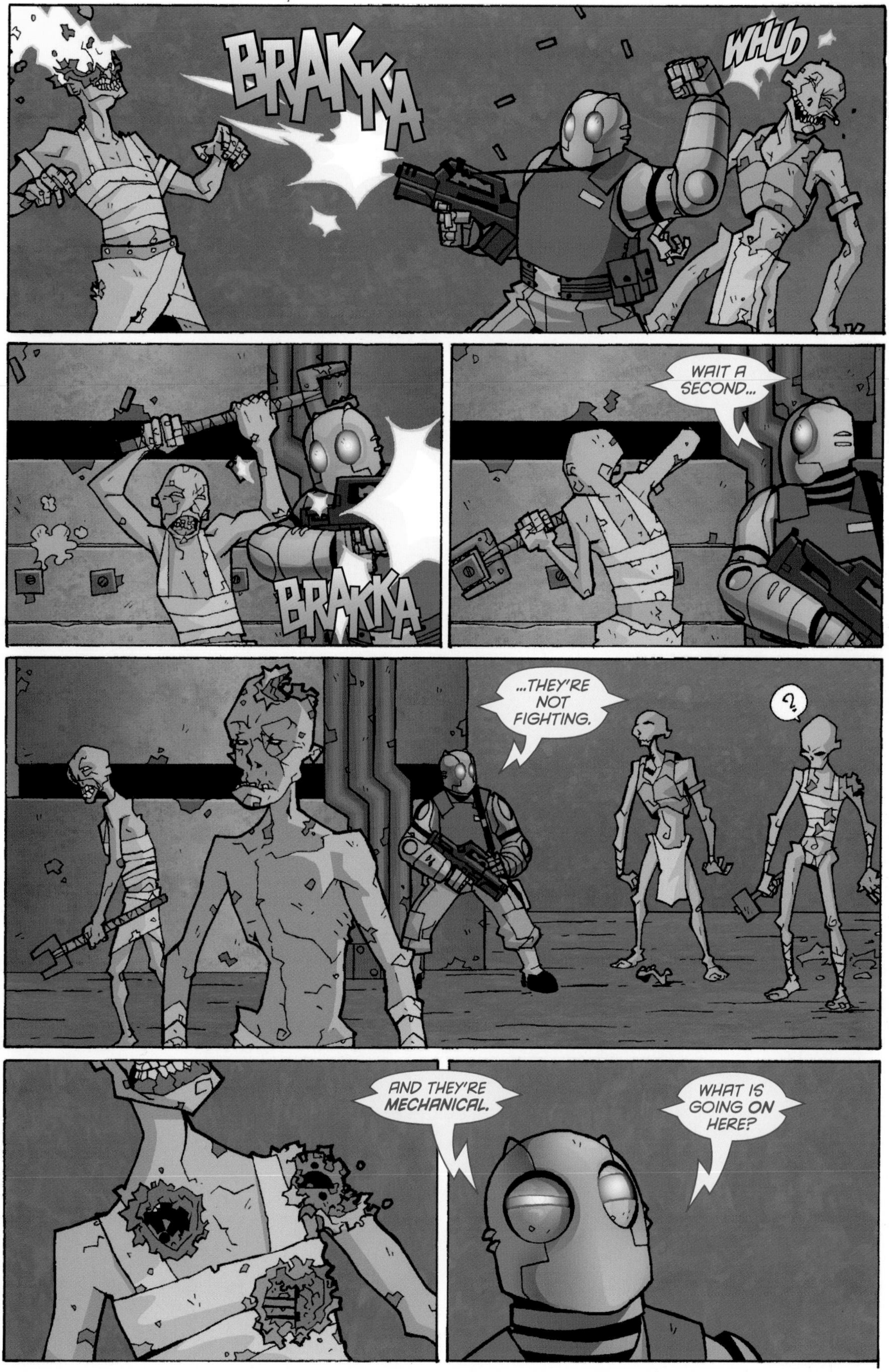
BRAKKA
WHUD
BRAKKA
WAIT A SECOND...
...THEY'RE NOT FIGHTING.
?
AND THEY'RE MECHANICAL.
WHAT IS GOING ON HERE?

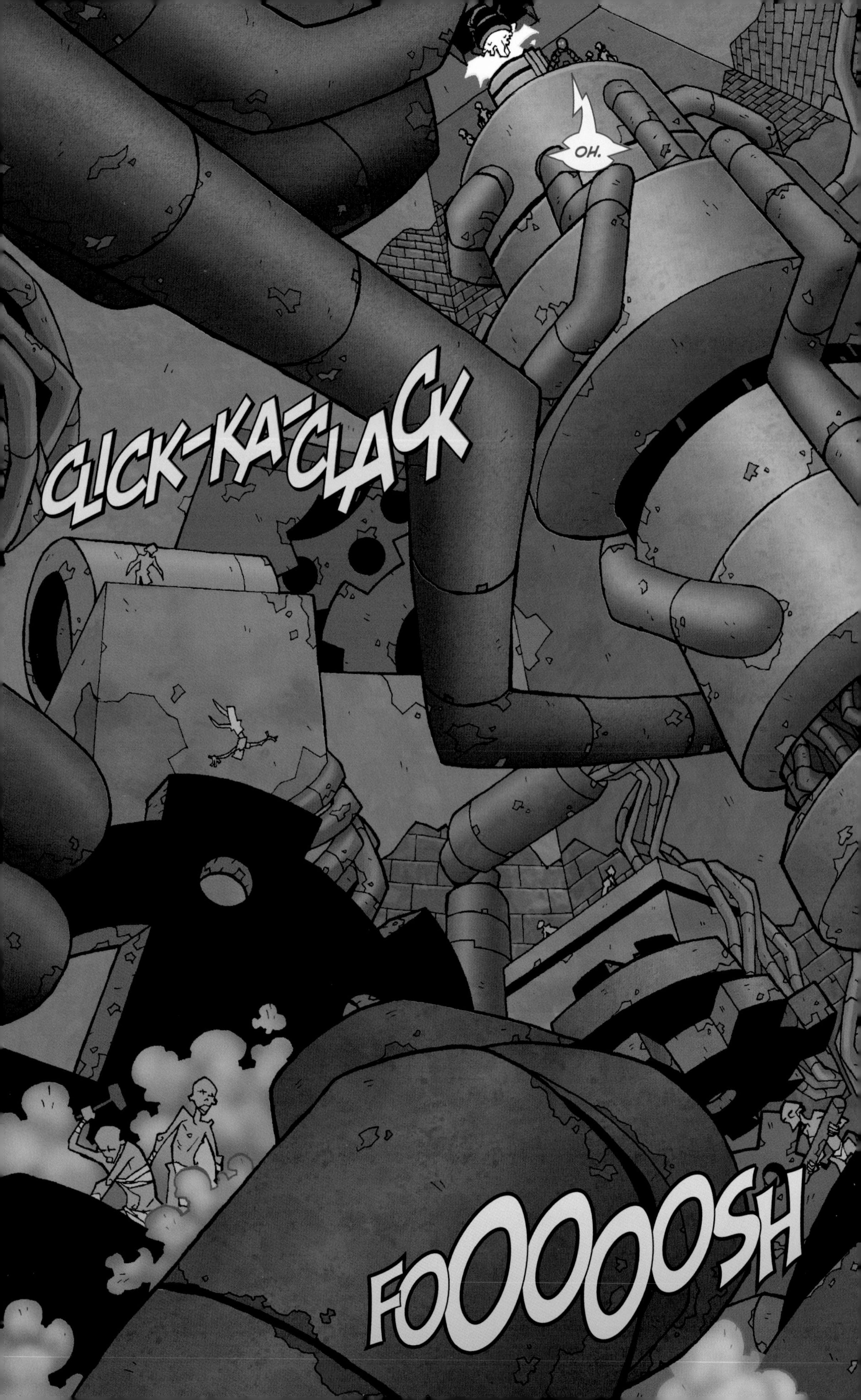
OH.
CLICK-KA-CLACK
FOOOOOOSH

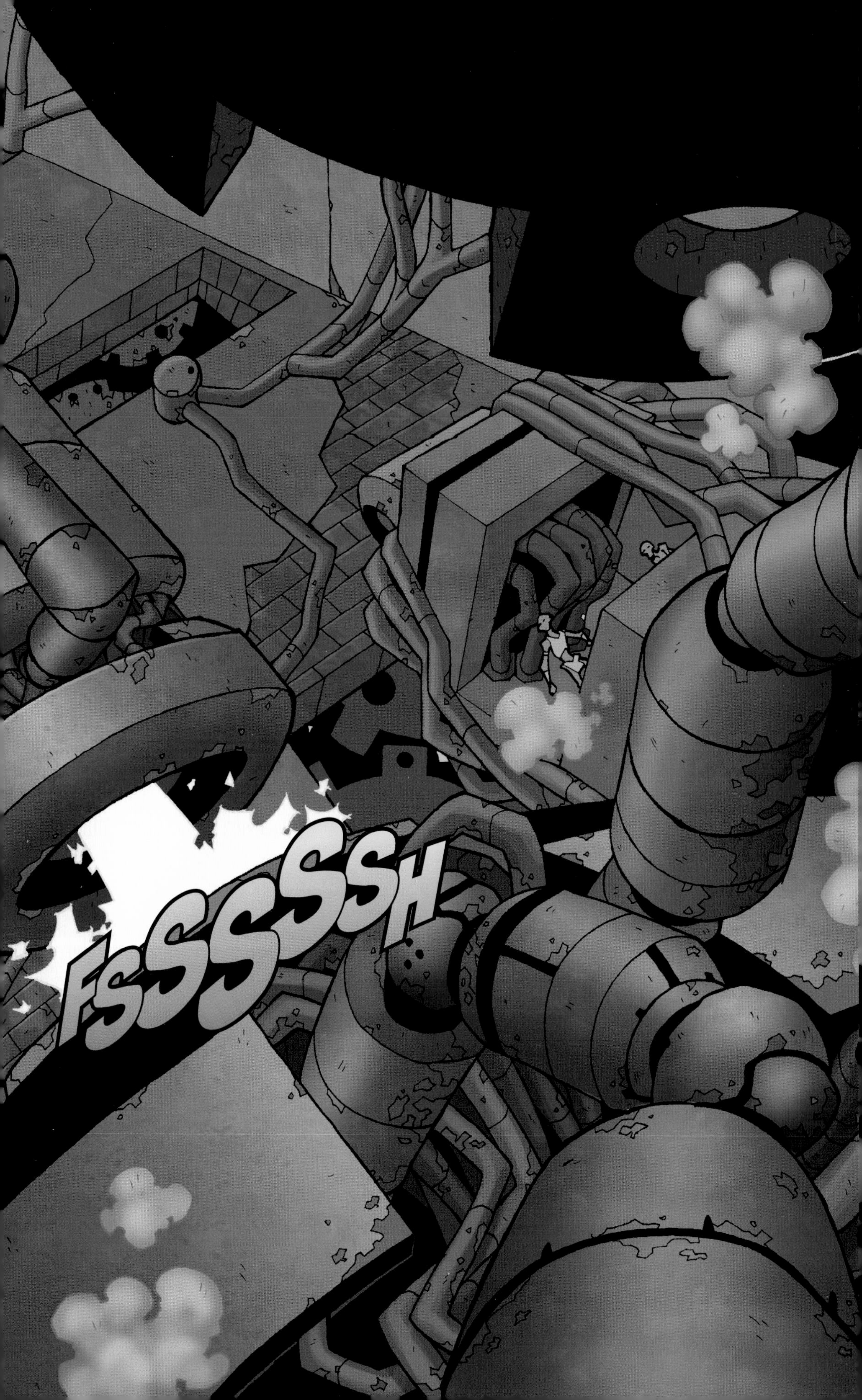
FSSSSSH

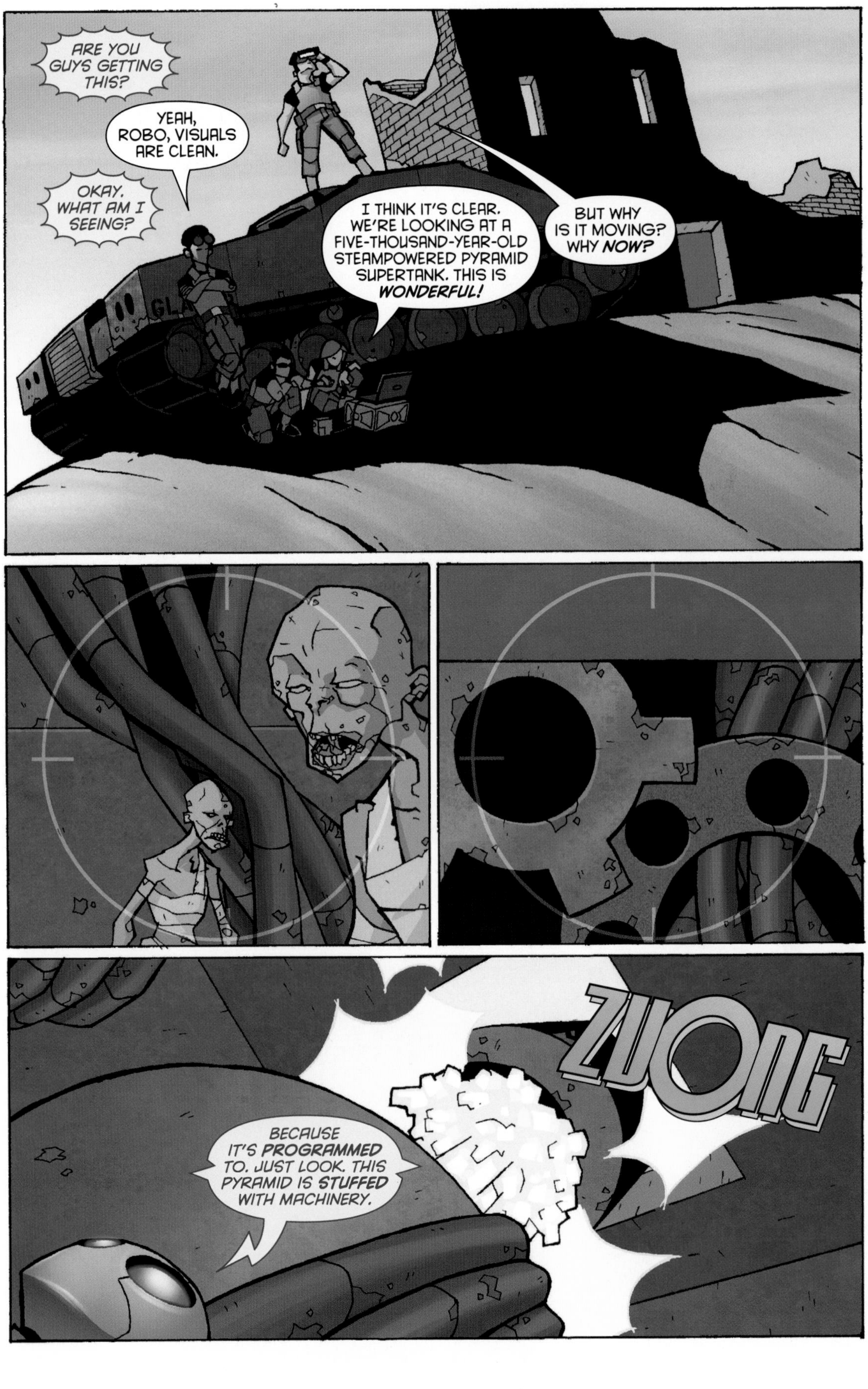

ARE YOU GUYS GETTING THIS?
YEAH, ROBO, VISUALS ARE CLEAN.
OKAY. WHAT AM I SEEING?
I THINK IT'S CLEAR. WE'RE LOOKING AT A FIVE-THOUSAND-YEAR-OLD STEAMPOWERED PYRAMID SUPERTANK. THIS IS WONDERFUL!
BUT WHY IS IT MOVING? WHY NOW?
ZUONG
BECAUSE IT'S PROGRAMMED TO. JUST LOOK. THIS PYRAMID IS STUFFED WITH MACHINERY.

A GIANT WATERCLOCK CARRYING OUT A PROGRAM THAT TOOK FIVE *THOUSAND* YEARS TO COMPUTE.

THE STEAM PROVIDES MOTIVE POWER WHILE CONDENSED WATER PROVIDES COMPUTATIONAL POWER! THE *ENTIRE INTERIOR* IS A HUGE MECHANICAL COMPUTER!

THE SHEER ENGINEERING *GENIUS* INVOLVED HERE IS *ASTOUNDING!*

ROBO, YOU'VE *GOT* TO STOP THE PYRAMID. THE EGYPTIANS HAVE A SQUAD OF TANKS AT THE CITY LIMITS WITH ORDERS TO REDUCE IT TO GRAVEL IF IT GETS TOO CLOSE TO LUXOR.

KEEP YOUR SHIRT ON.

IT'S AS SIMPLE AS BLASTING THE GIANT FOCUSING CRYSTAL OUTTA ALIGNMENT AND SITTING BACK WHILE THE WHOLE THING GRINDS TO A HALT.

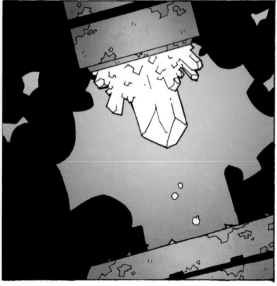

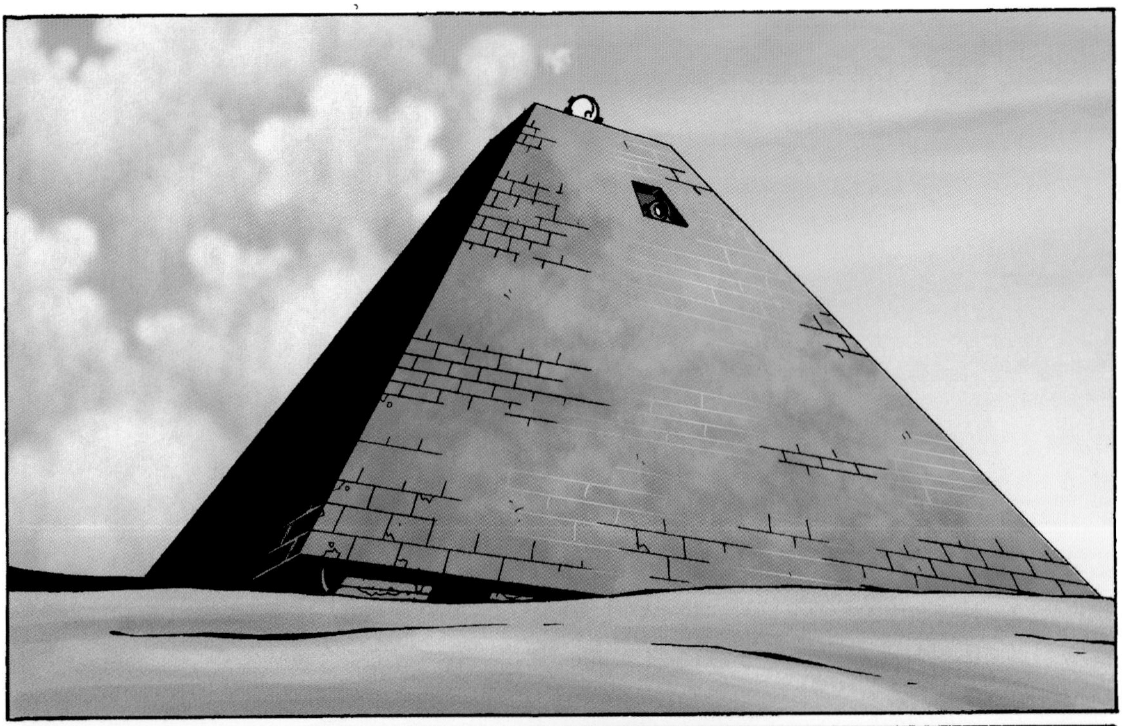

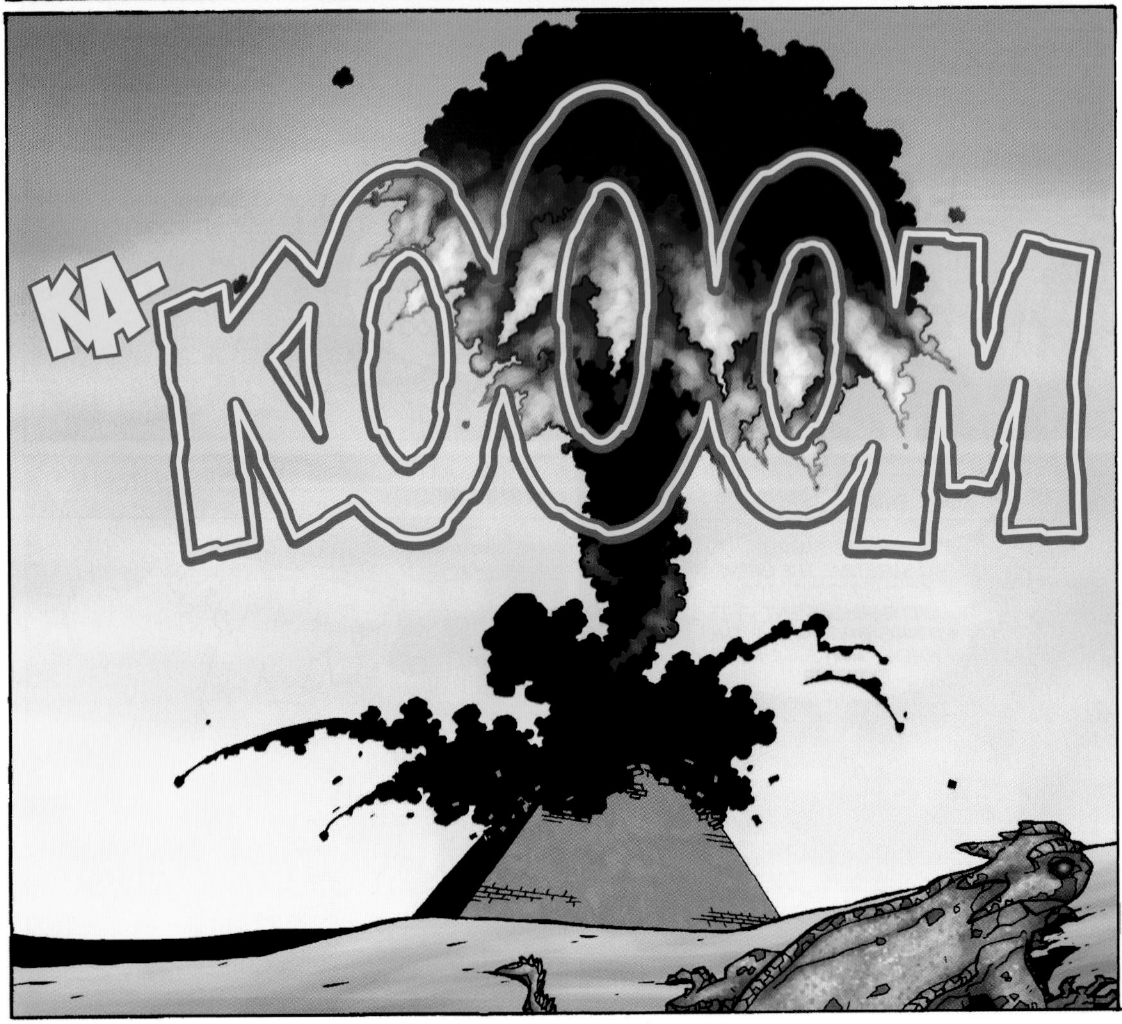
KA-
KOOOOM

ATOMIC ROBO OF MARS

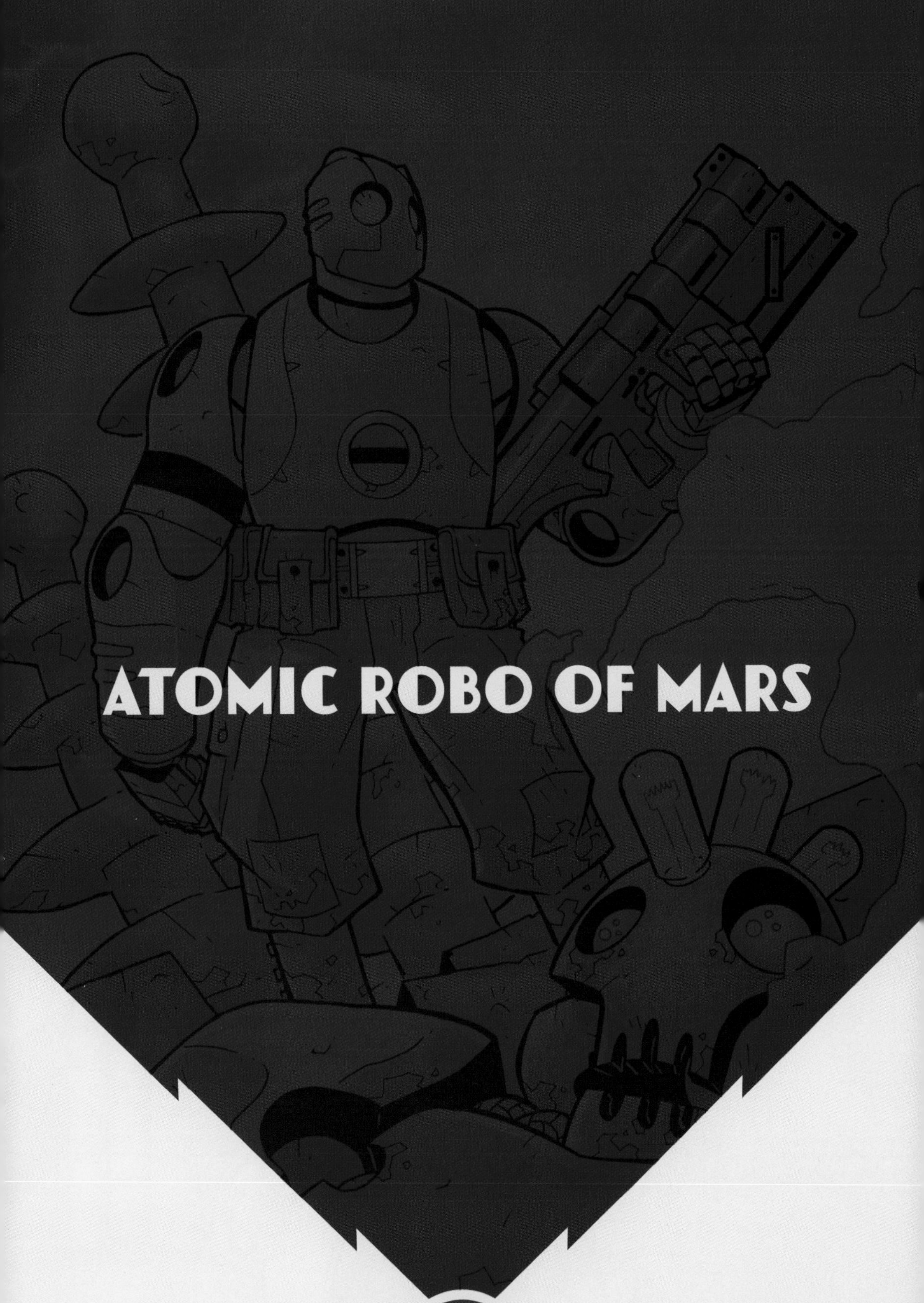

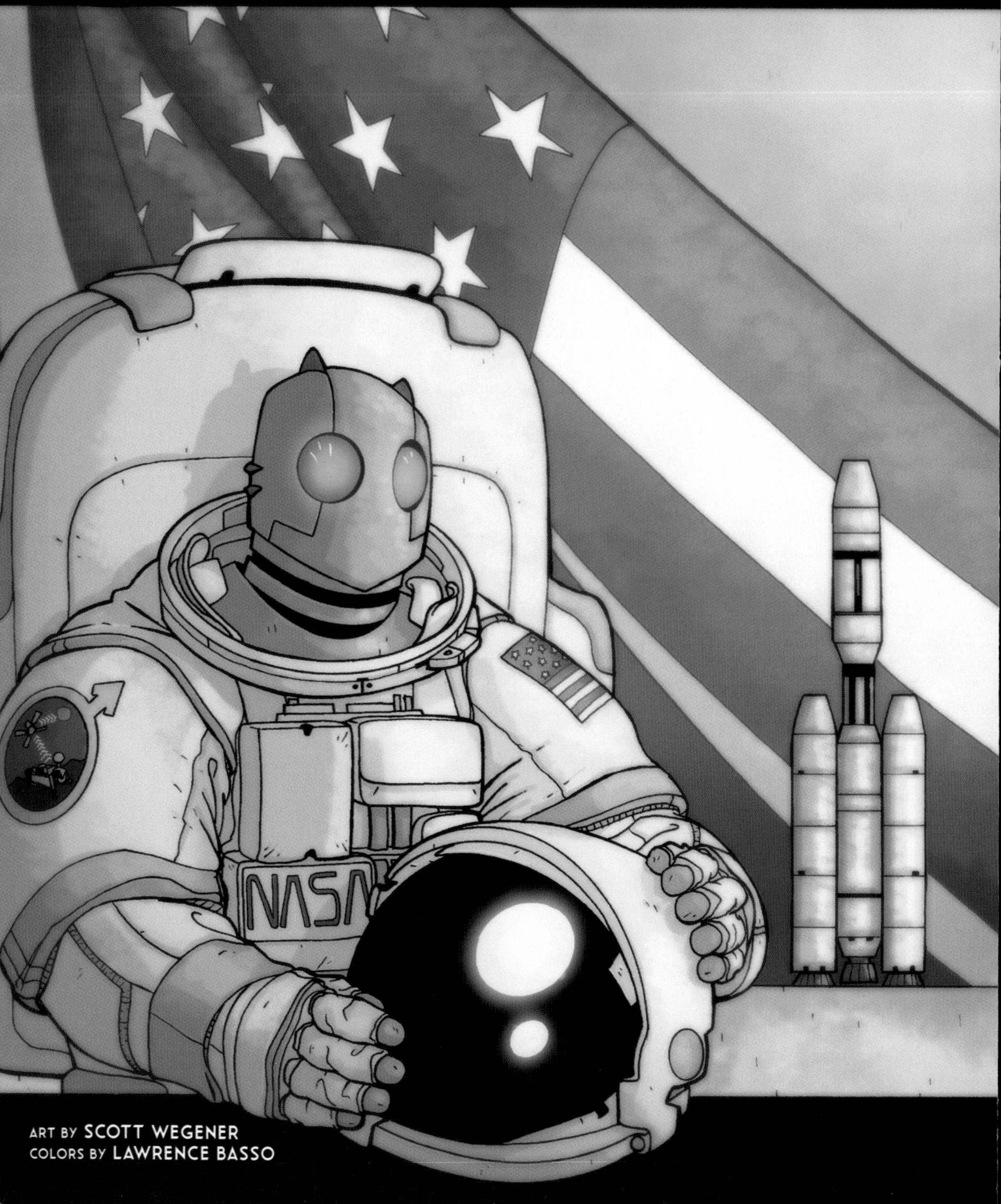
NASA

ART BY SCOTT WEGENER
COLORS BY LAWRENCE BASSO

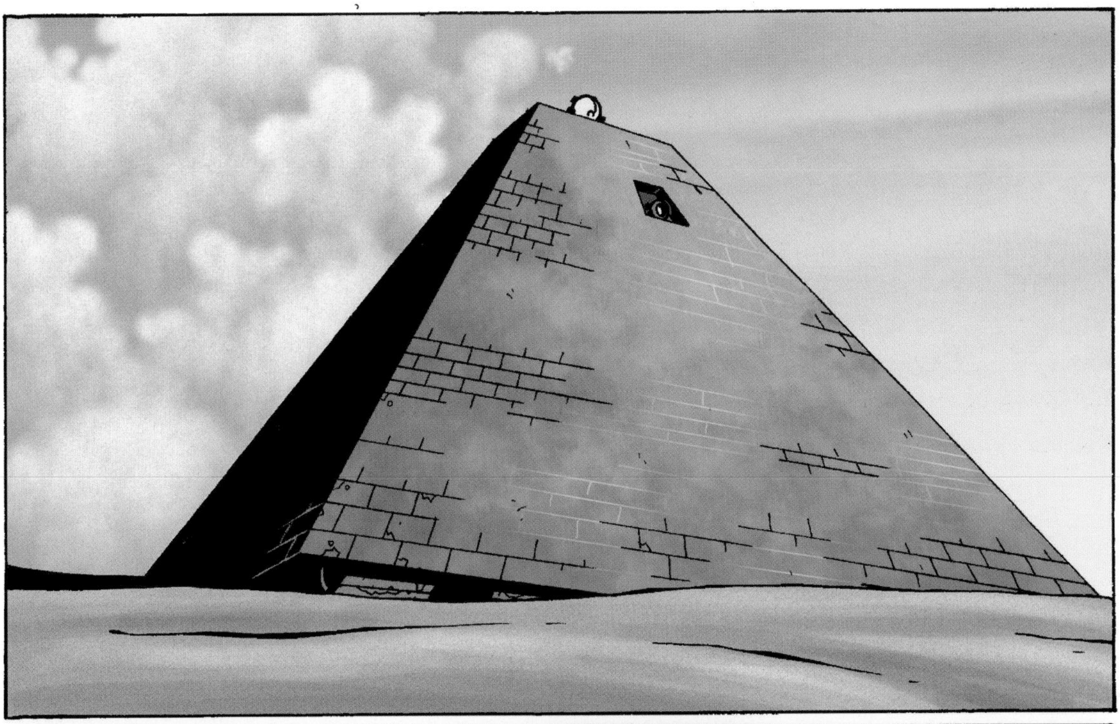

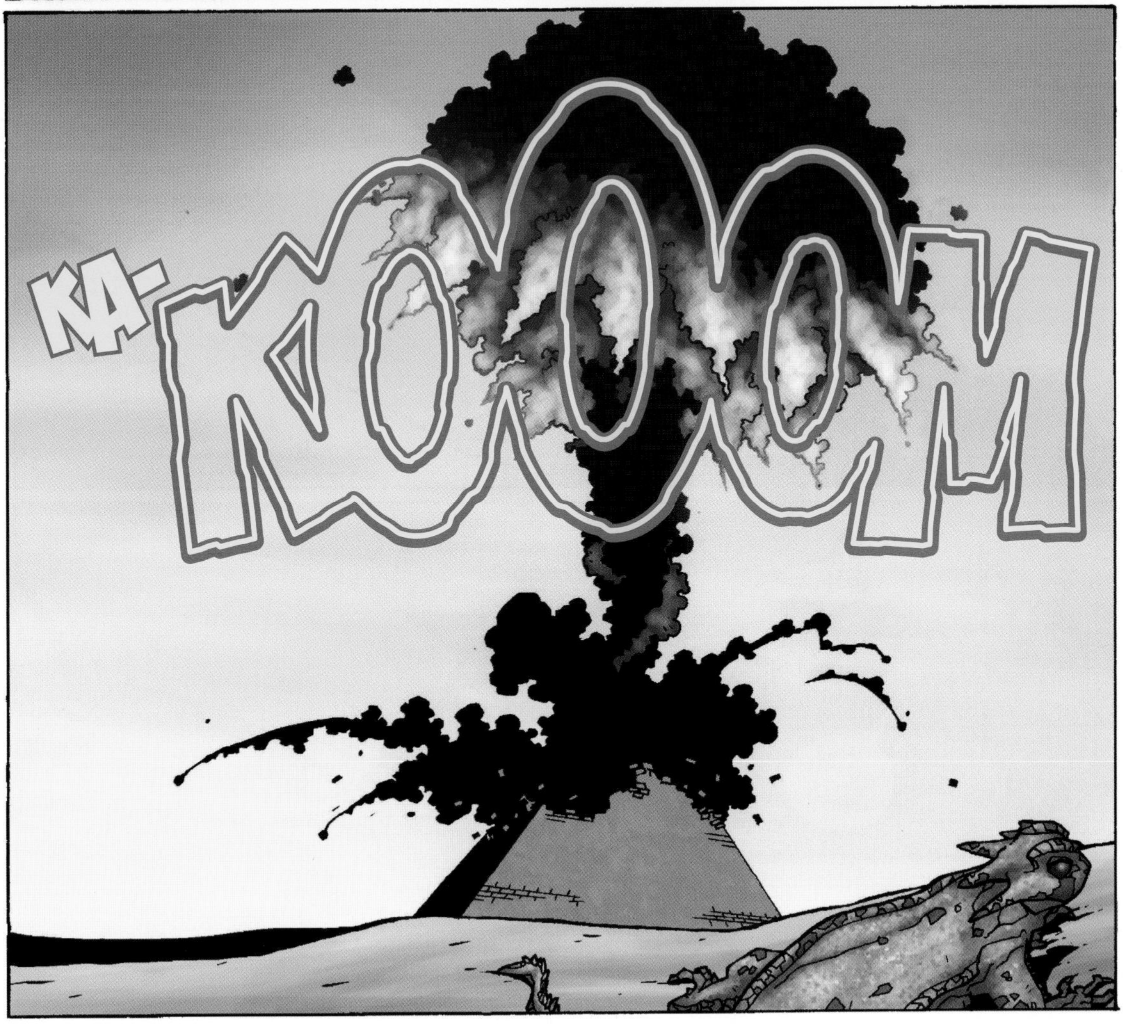
KA-KOOOOM

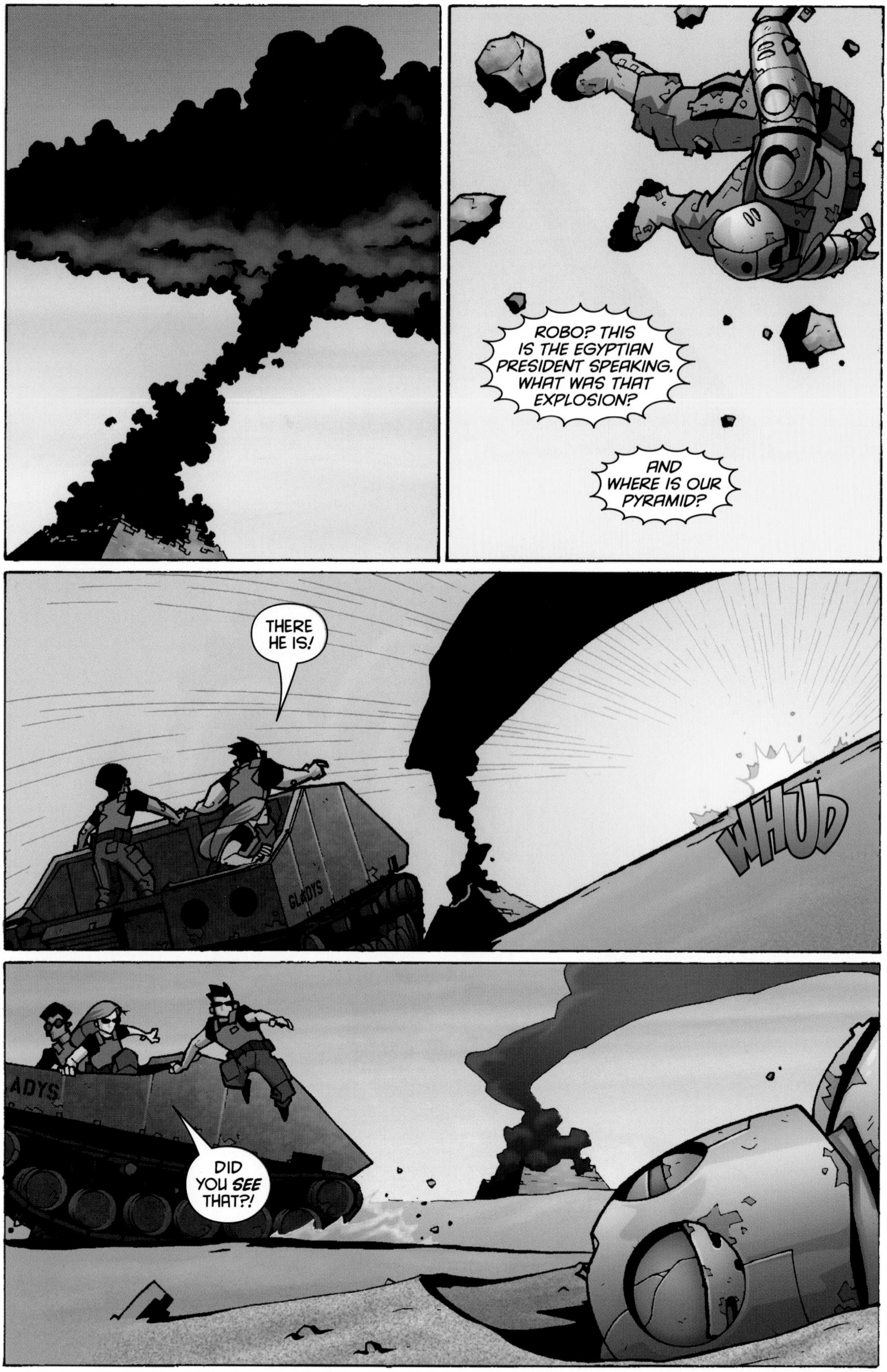
ROBO? THIS IS THE EGYPTIAN PRESIDENT SPEAKING. WHAT WAS THAT EXPLOSION?
AND WHERE IS OUR PYRAMID?
THERE HE IS!
WHUD
GLADYS
ADYS
DID YOU SEE THAT?!

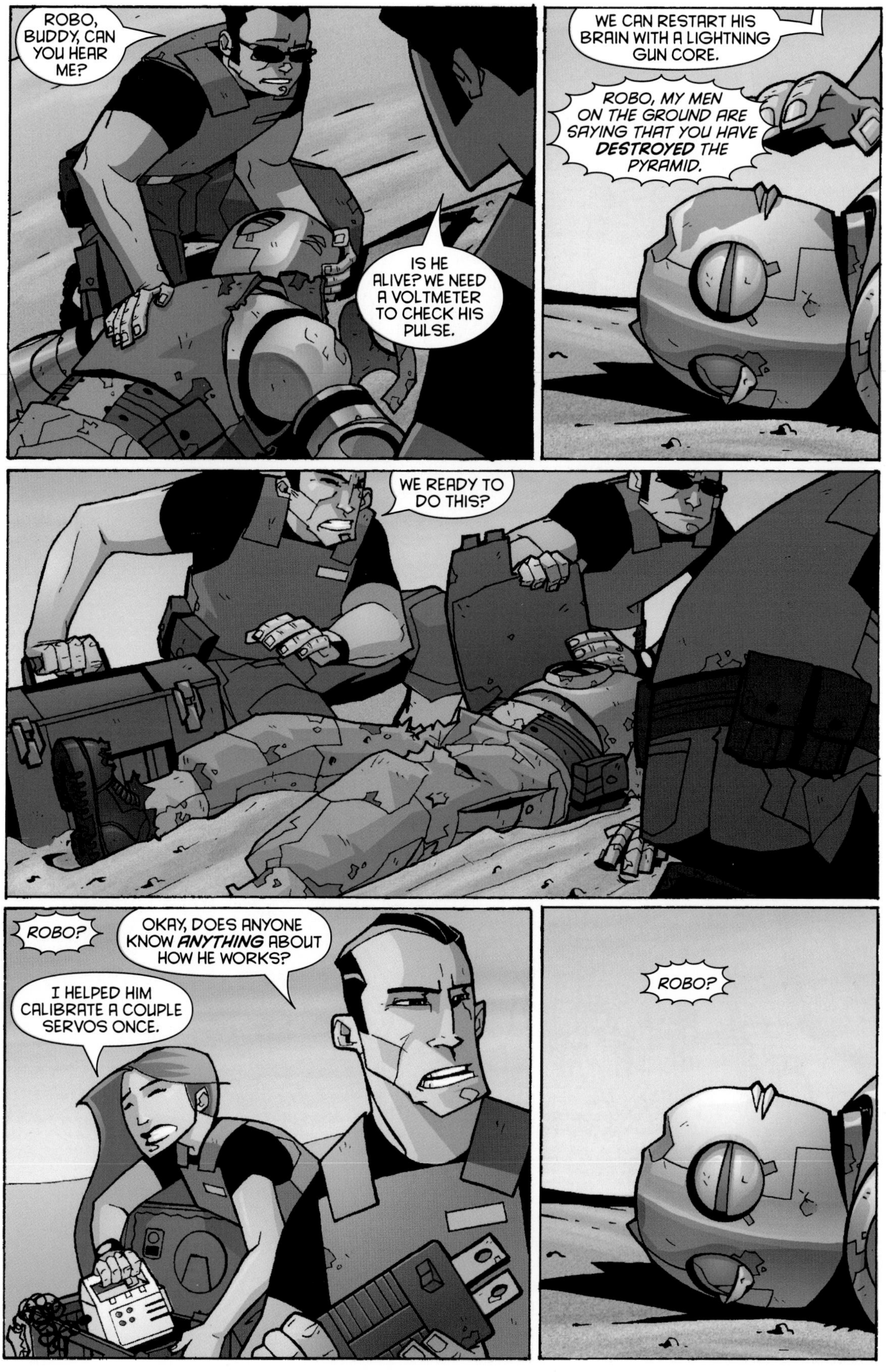
ROBO, BUDDY, CAN YOU HEAR ME?
IS HE ALIVE? WE NEED A VOLTMETER TO CHECK HIS PULSE.
WE CAN RESTART HIS BRAIN WITH A LIGHTNING GUN CORE.
ROBO, MY MEN ON THE GROUND ARE SAYING THAT YOU HAVE DESTROYED THE PYRAMID.
WE READY TO DO THIS?
ROBO?
OKAY, DOES ANYONE KNOW ANYTHING ABOUT HOW HE WORKS?
I HELPED HIM CALIBRATE A COUPLE SERVOS ONCE.
ROBO?

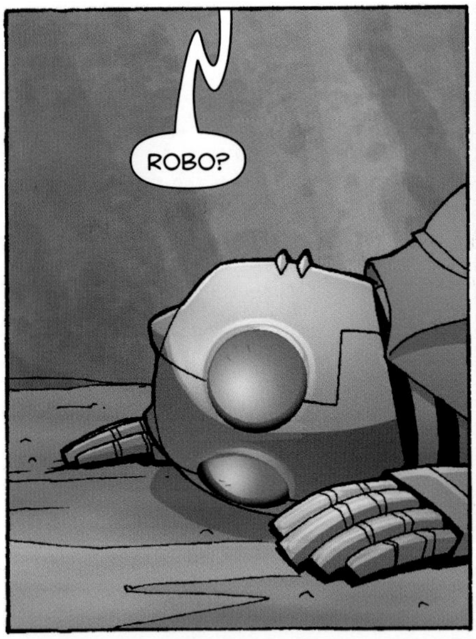
ROBO?

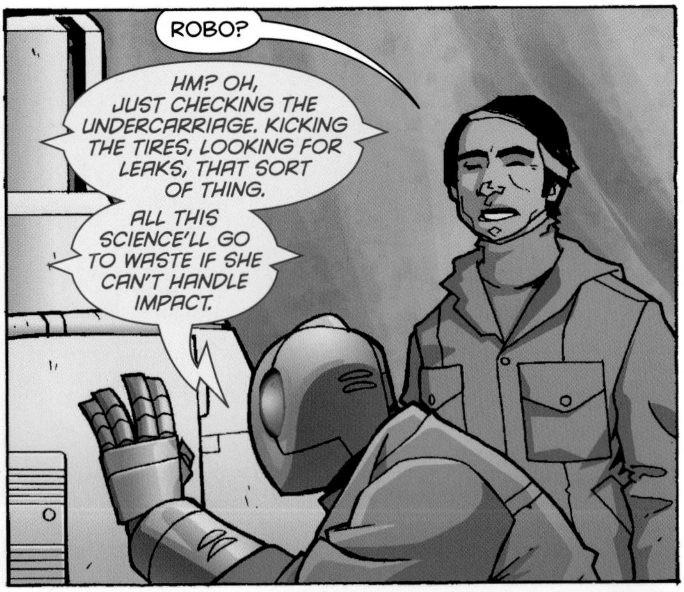
ROBO?
HM? OH, JUST CHECKING THE UNDERCARRIAGE. KICKING THE TIRES, LOOKING FOR LEAKS, THAT SORT OF THING.
ALL THIS SCIENCE'LL GO TO WASTE IF SHE CAN'T HANDLE IMPACT.

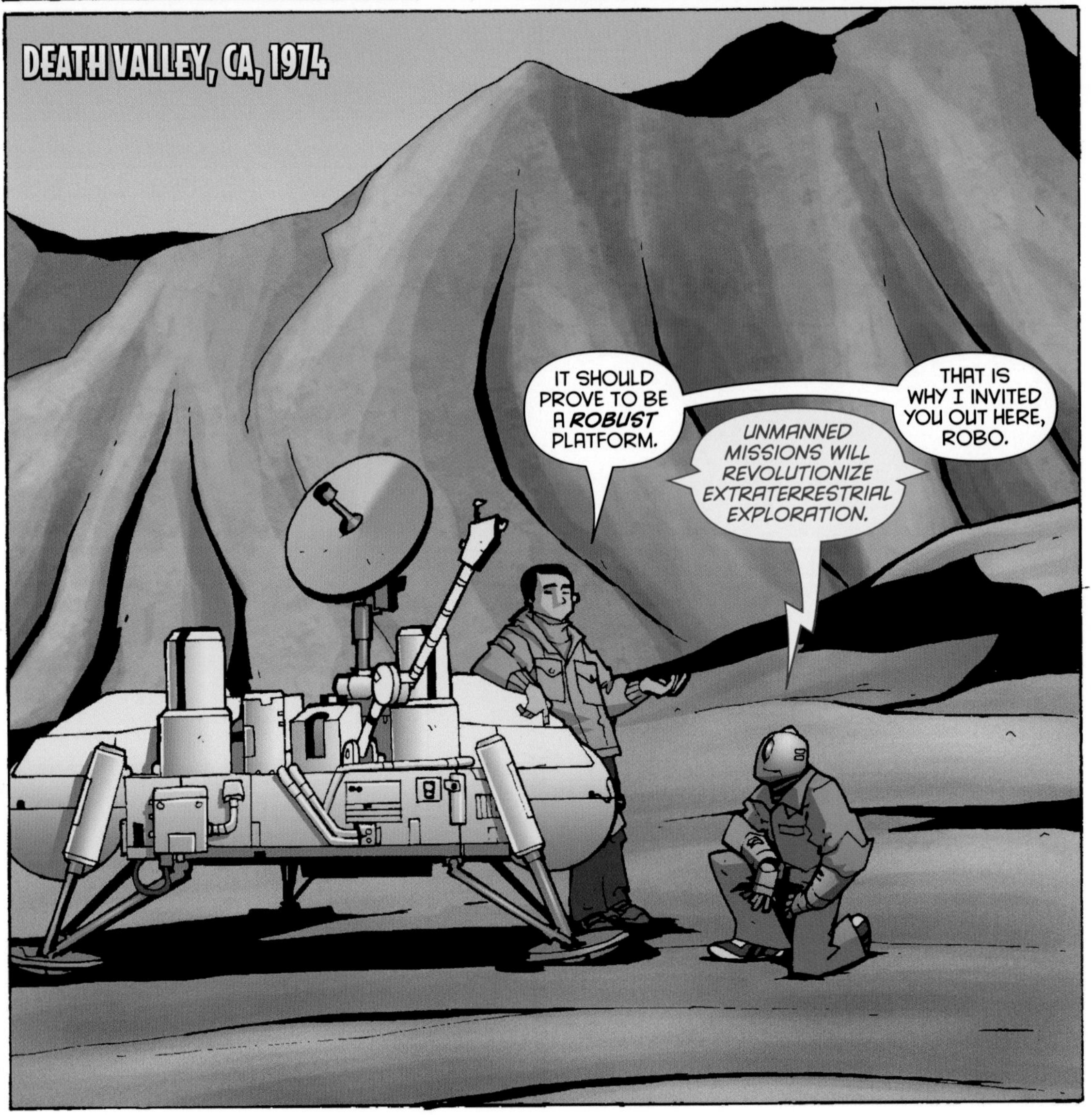
DEATH VALLEY, CA, 1974
IT SHOULD PROVE TO BE A ROBUST PLATFORM.
THAT IS WHY I INVITED YOU OUT HERE, ROBO.
UNMANNED MISSIONS WILL REVOLUTIONIZE EXTRATERRESTRIAL EXPLORATION.

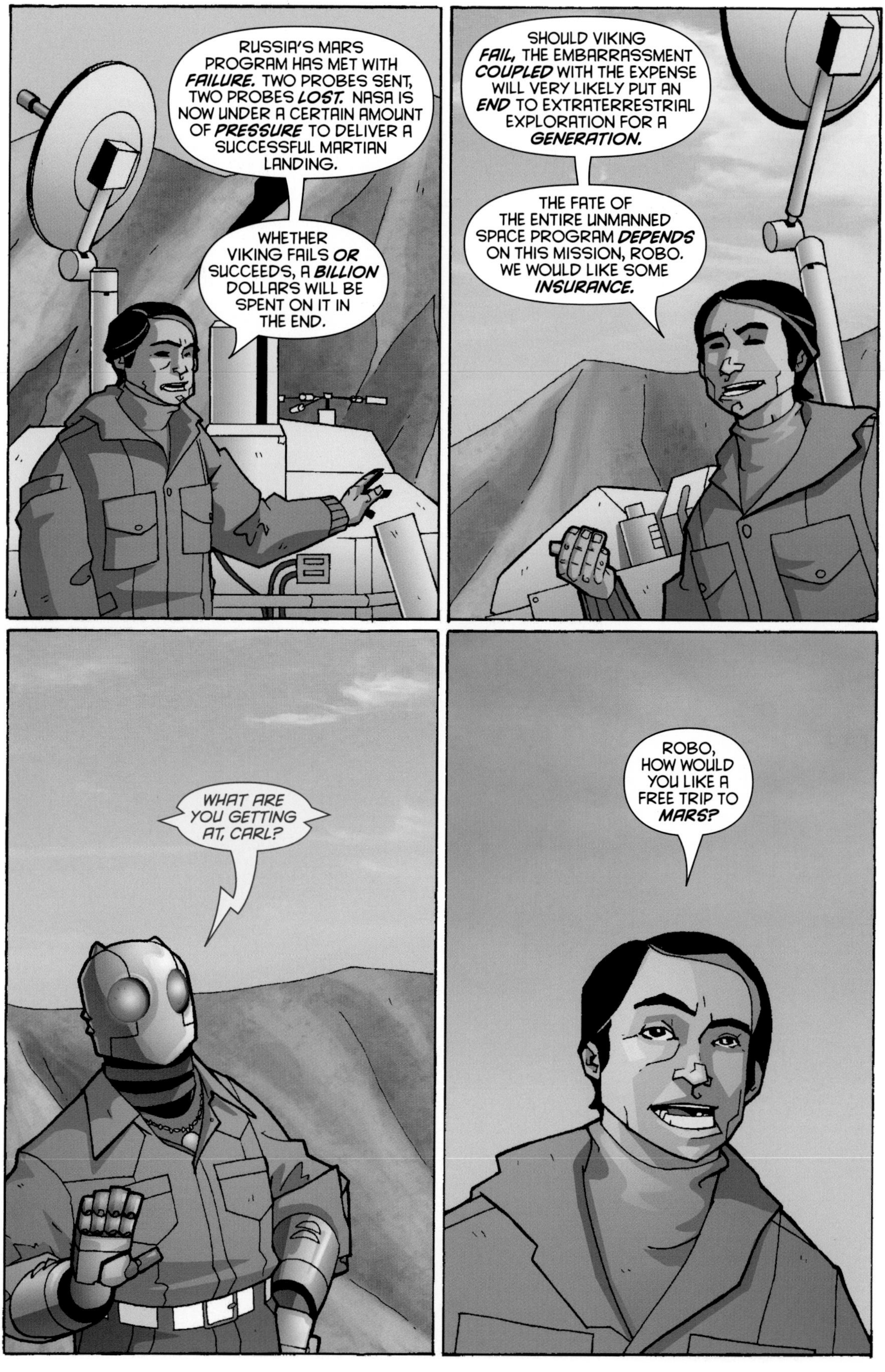
RUSSIA'S MARS PROGRAM HAS MET WITH FAILURE. TWO PROBES SENT, TWO PROBES LOST. NASA IS NOW UNDER A CERTAIN AMOUNT OF PRESSURE TO DELIVER A SUCCESSFUL MARTIAN LANDING.
WHETHER VIKING FAILS OR SUCCEEDS, A BILLION DOLLARS WILL BE SPENT ON IT IN THE END.
SHOULD VIKING FAIL, THE EMBARRASSMENT COUPLED WITH THE EXPENSE WILL VERY LIKELY PUT AN END TO EXTRATERRESTRIAL EXPLORATION FOR A GENERATION.
THE FATE OF THE ENTIRE UNMANNED SPACE PROGRAM DEPENDS ON THIS MISSION, ROBO. WE WOULD LIKE SOME INSURANCE.
WHAT ARE YOU GETTING AT, CARL?
ROBO, HOW WOULD YOU LIKE A FREE TRIP TO MARS?

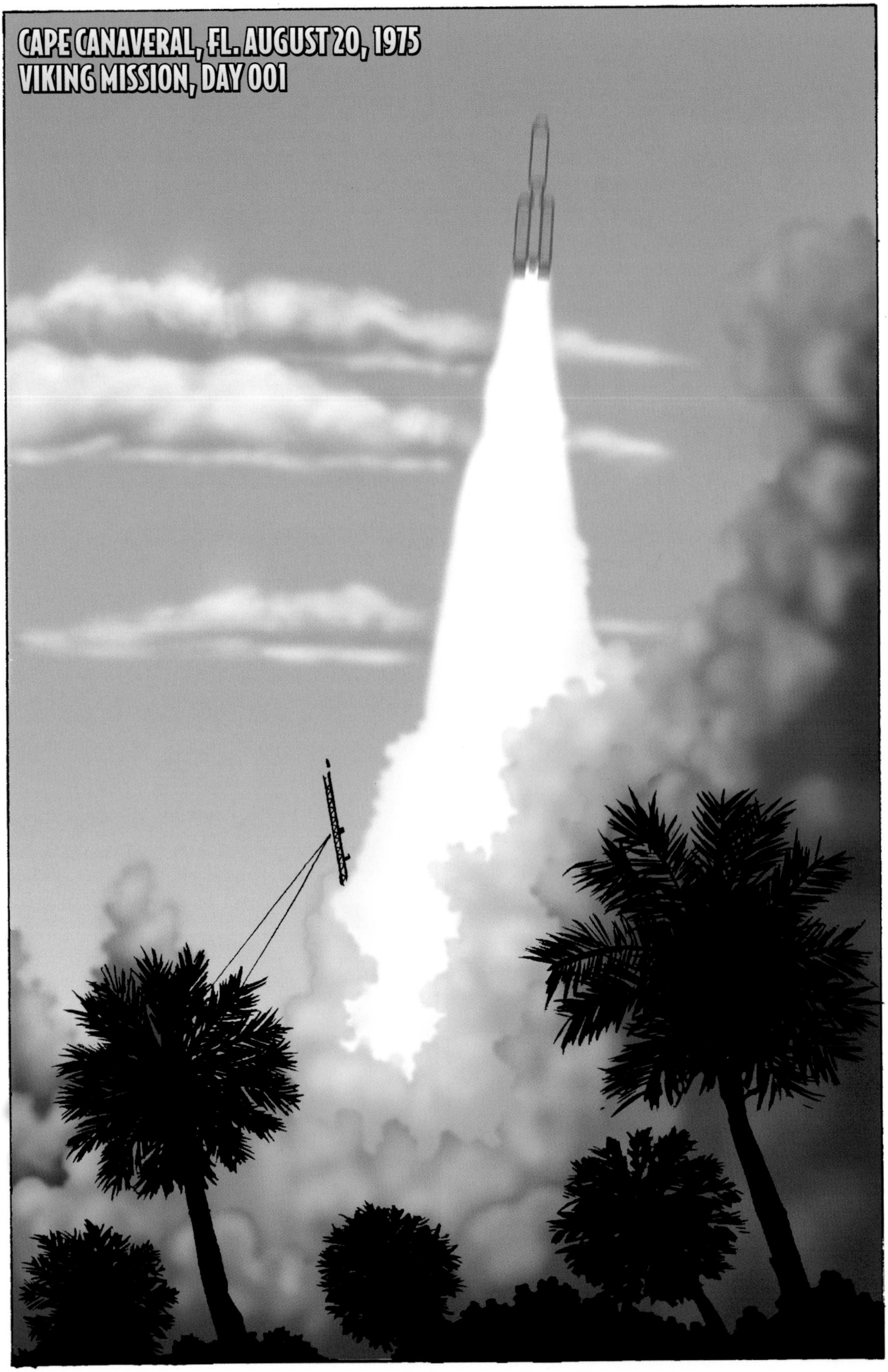
CAPE CANAVERAL, FL. AUGUST 20, 1975
VIKING MISSION, DAY 001

DAY 003

EMERALD CITY, THIS IS TIN MAN.

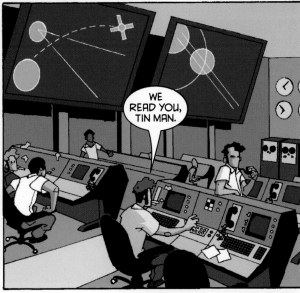

WE READ YOU, TIN MAN.

YEAH, SORRY TO BOTHER YOU GUYS WITH THIS, BUT I CAN'T FIND THE REST OF MY READING MATERIAL.

READING MATERIAL?

I WAS PROMISED BOOKS AND THINGS TO KEEP ME FROM LOSING MY MIND.

OKAY, YEAH. INVENTORY SHOWS TWO KILOGRAMS IN MAGAZINES. SHOULD BE LOCATED IN THE OVERHEAD COMPARTMENT.

RIGHT, FIVE MAGAZINES. I FOUND THOSE. WHERE'S THE REST?

THE REST?

THIS IS A TEN-MONTH TRIP.

GET SAGAN ON THE HORN.

UM, I'M NOT SHOWING ANY OTHER--

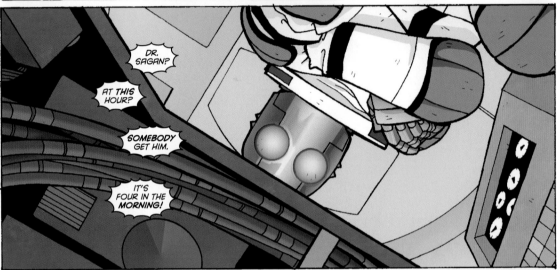

DR. SAGAN?

AT THIS HOUR?

SOMEBODY GET HIM.

IT'S FOUR IN THE MORNING!

SOMETHING ABOUT "READING MATERIAL."

WHAT, LIKE ROBOT PORNOGRAPHY?

WOULD THAT BE PICTURES OR EROTIC LITERATURE?

QUIET, PLEASE.

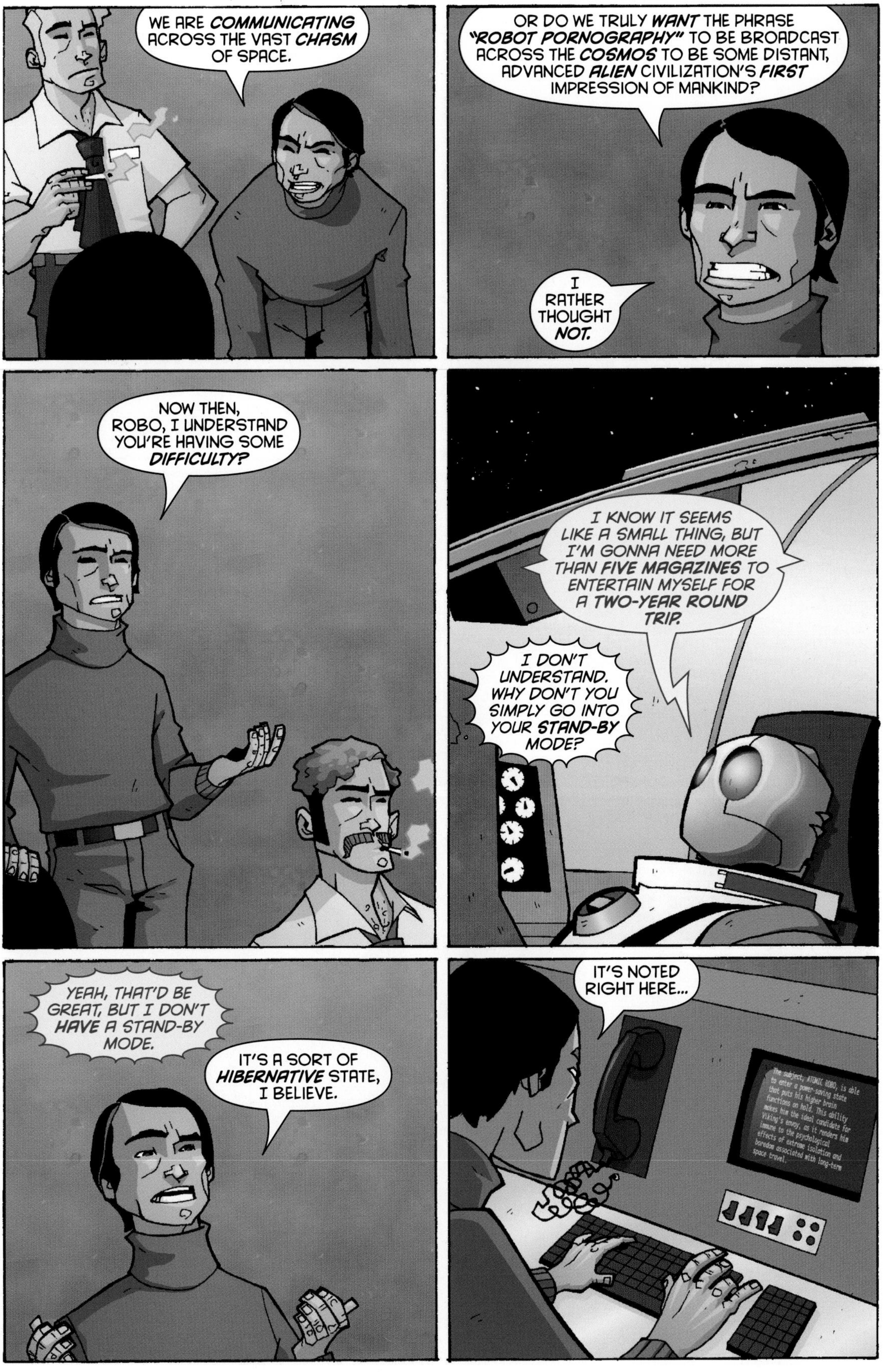
WE ARE COMMUNICATING ACROSS THE VAST CHASM OF SPACE.
OR DO WE TRULY WANT THE PHRASE "ROBOT PORNOGRAPHY" TO BE BROADCAST ACROSS THE COSMOS TO BE SOME DISTANT, ADVANCED ALIEN CIVILIZATION'S FIRST IMPRESSION OF MANKIND?
I RATHER THOUGHT NOT.
NOW THEN, ROBO, I UNDERSTAND YOU'RE HAVING SOME DIFFICULTY?
I KNOW IT SEEMS LIKE A SMALL THING, BUT I'M GONNA NEED MORE THAN FIVE MAGAZINES TO ENTERTAIN MYSELF FOR A TWO-YEAR ROUND TRIP.
I DON'T UNDERSTAND. WHY DON'T YOU SIMPLY GO INTO YOUR STAND-BY MODE?
YEAH, THAT'D BE GREAT, BUT I DON'T HAVE A STAND-BY MODE.
IT'S A SORT OF HIBERNATIVE STATE, I BELIEVE.
IT'S NOTED RIGHT HERE...
The subject, ATOMIC ROBO, is able to enter a power-saving state that puts his higher brain functions on hold. This ability makes him the ideal candidate for Viking's envoy, as it renders him immune to the psychological effects of extreme isolation and boredom associated with long-term space travel.

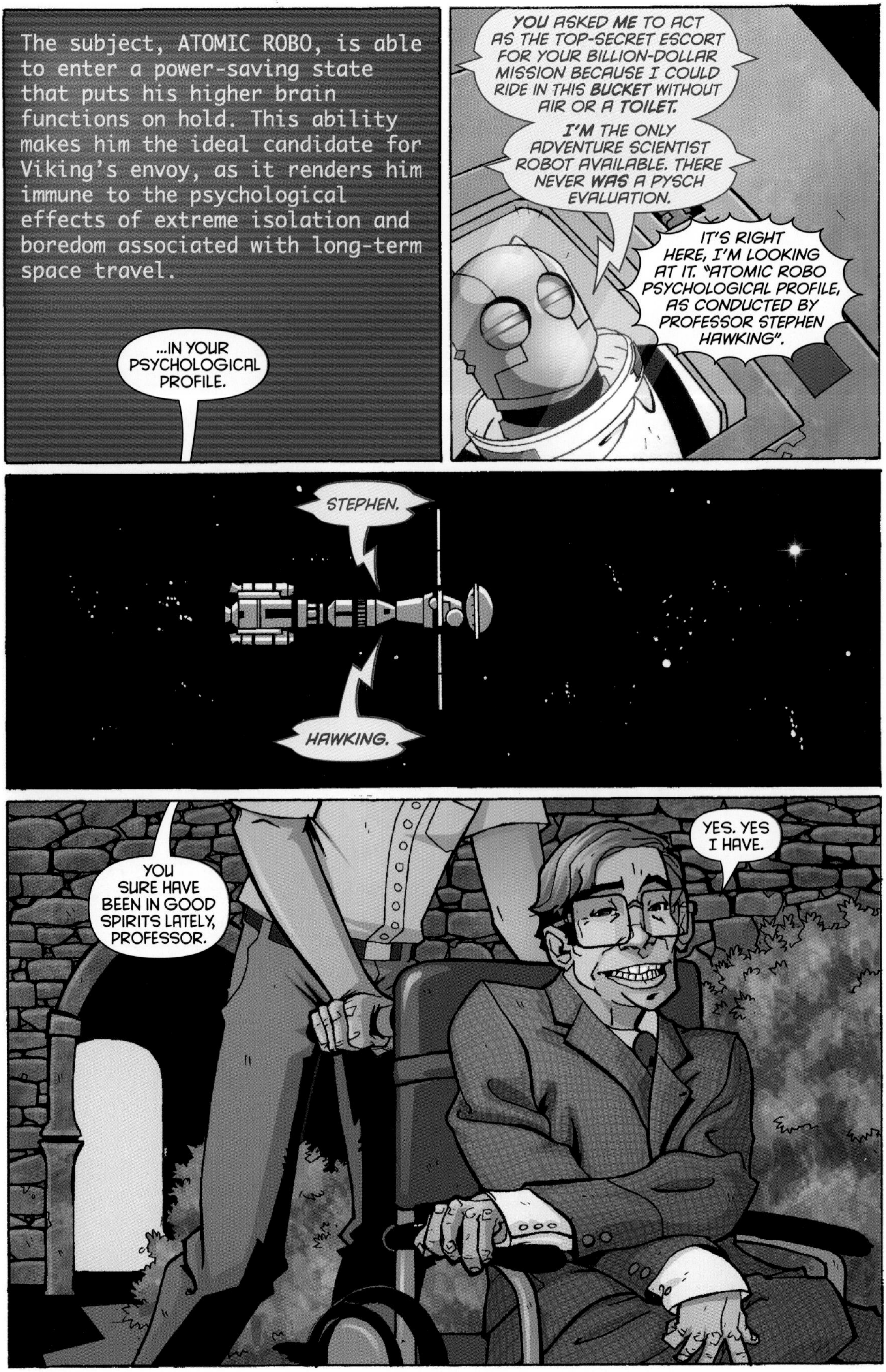
The subject, ATOMIC ROBO, is able to enter a power-saving state that puts his higher brain functions on hold. This ability makes him the ideal candidate for Viking's envoy, as it renders him immune to the psychological effects of extreme isolation and boredom associated with long-term space travel.
...IN YOUR PSYCHOLOGICAL PROFILE.
YOU ASKED ME TO ACT AS THE TOP-SECRET ESCORT FOR YOUR BILLION-DOLLAR MISSION BECAUSE I COULD RIDE IN THIS BUCKET WITHOUT AIR OR A TOILET.
I'M THE ONLY ADVENTURE SCIENTIST ROBOT AVAILABLE. THERE NEVER WAS A PYSCH EVALUATION.
IT'S RIGHT HERE, I'M LOOKING AT IT. "ATOMIC ROBO PSYCHOLOGICAL PROFILE, AS CONDUCTED BY PROFESSOR STEPHEN HAWKING".
STEPHEN.
HAWKING.
YOU SURE HAVE BEEN IN GOOD SPIRITS LATELY, PROFESSOR.
YES. YES I HAVE.

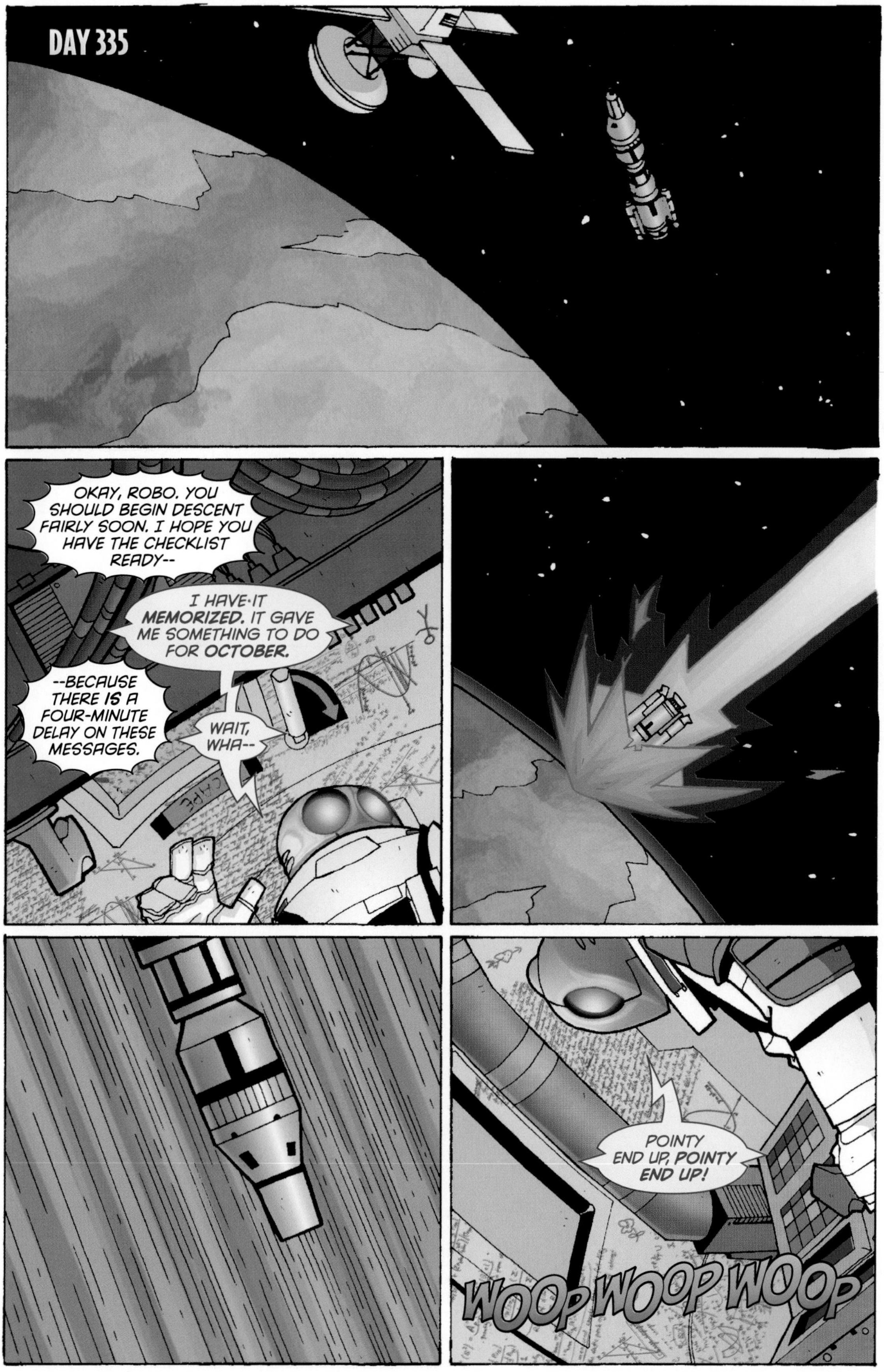
DAY 335
OKAY, ROBO. YOU SHOULD BEGIN DESCENT FAIRLY SOON. I HOPE YOU HAVE THE CHECKLIST READY--
I HAVE IT MEMORIZED. IT GAVE ME SOMETHING TO DO FOR OCTOBER.
--BECAUSE THERE IS A FOUR-MINUTE DELAY ON THESE MESSAGES.
WAIT, WHA--
POINTY END UP, POINTY END UP!
WOOP WOOP WOOP

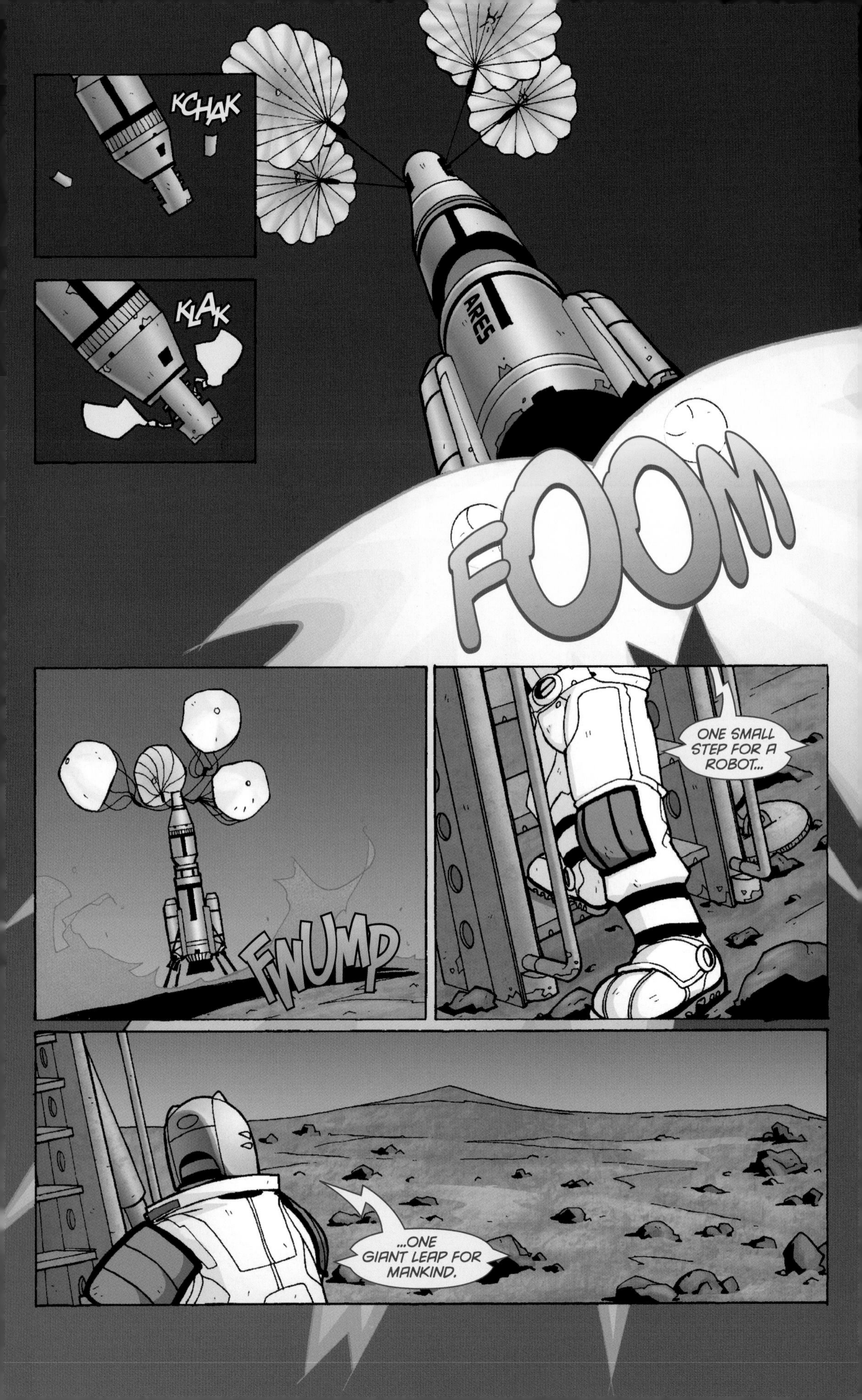
KCHAK
KLAK
ARES
FOOM
FWUMP
ONE SMALL STEP FOR A ROBOT...
...ONE GIANT LEAP FOR MANKIND.

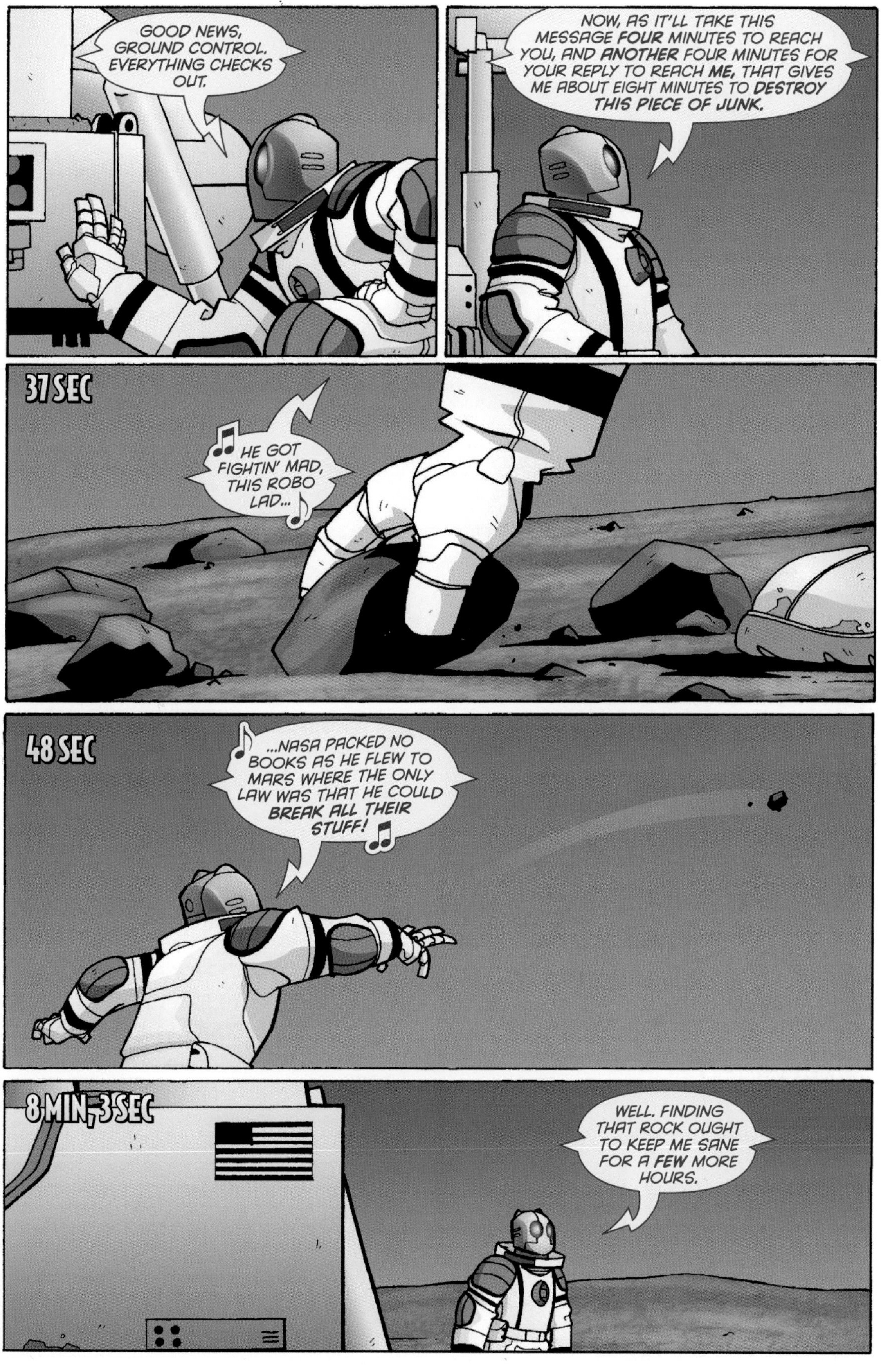
GOOD NEWS, GROUND CONTROL. EVERYTHING CHECKS OUT.
NOW, AS IT'LL TAKE THIS MESSAGE FOUR MINUTES TO REACH YOU, AND ANOTHER FOUR MINUTES FOR YOUR REPLY TO REACH ME, THAT GIVES ME ABOUT EIGHT MINUTES TO DESTROY THIS PIECE OF JUNK.
37 SEC
HE GOT FIGHTIN' MAD, THIS ROBO LAD...
48 SEC
...NASA PACKED NO BOOKS AS HE FLEW TO MARS WHERE THE ONLY LAW WAS THAT HE COULD BREAK ALL THEIR STUFF!
8 MIN, 3 SEC
WELL. FINDING THAT ROCK OUGHT TO KEEP ME SANE FOR A FEW MORE HOURS.

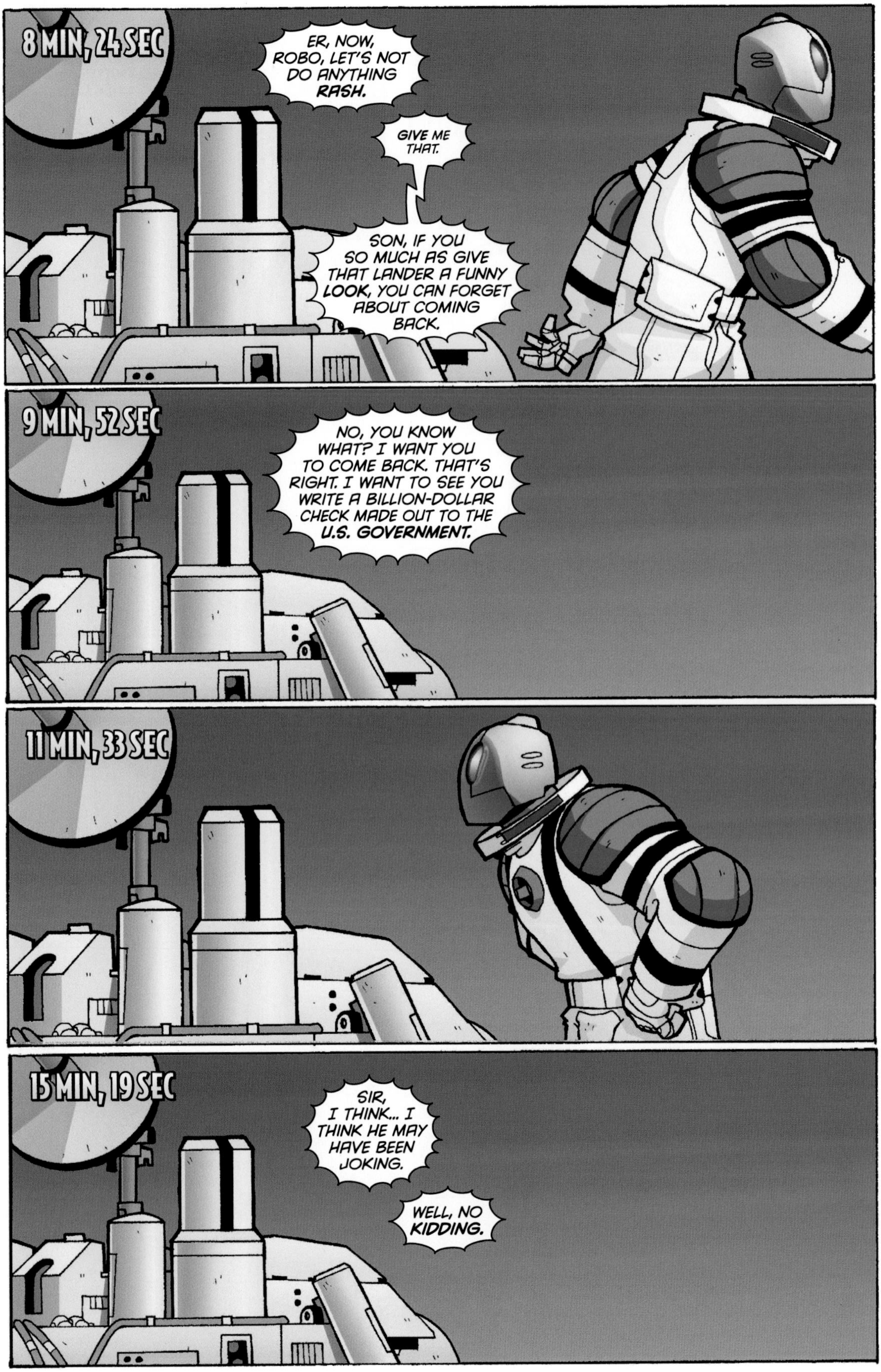
8 MIN, 24 SEC
ER, NOW, ROBO, LET'S NOT DO ANYTHING RASH.
GIVE ME THAT.
SON, IF YOU SO MUCH AS GIVE THAT LANDER A FUNNY LOOK, YOU CAN FORGET ABOUT COMING BACK.
9 MIN, 52 SEC
NO, YOU KNOW WHAT? I WANT YOU TO COME BACK. THAT'S RIGHT. I WANT TO SEE YOU WRITE A BILLION-DOLLAR CHECK MADE OUT TO THE U.S. GOVERNMENT.
11 MIN, 33 SEC
15 MIN, 19 SEC
SIR, I THINK... I THINK HE MAY HAVE BEEN JOKING.
WELL, NO KIDDING.

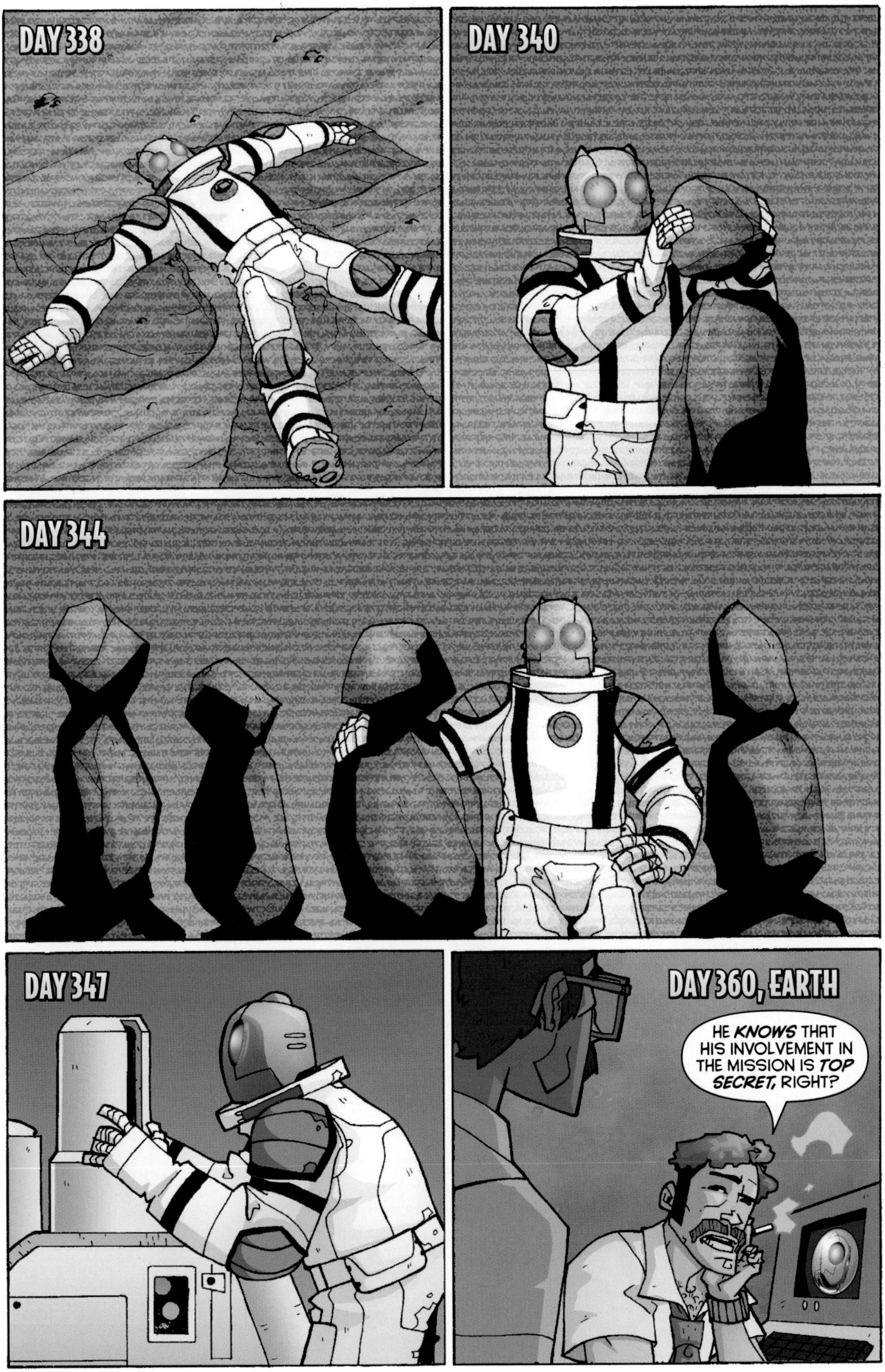
DAY 338
DAY 340
DAY 344
DAY 347
DAY 360, EARTH
HE *KNOWS* THAT HIS INVOLVEMENT IN THE MISSION IS *TOP SECRET,* RIGHT?

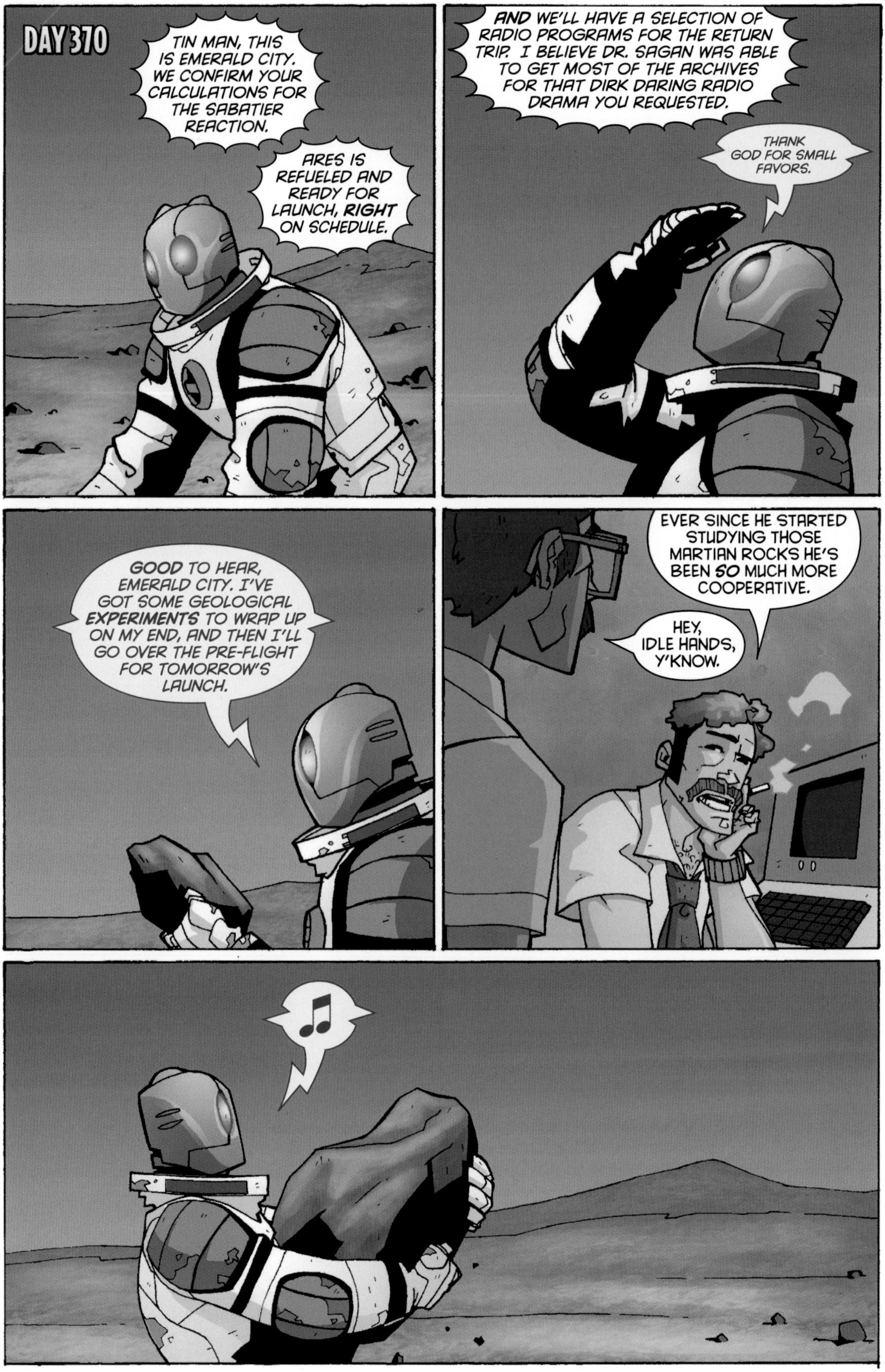
DAY 370
TIN MAN, THIS IS EMERALD CITY. WE CONFIRM YOUR CALCULATIONS FOR THE SABATIER REACTION.
ARES IS REFUELED AND READY FOR LAUNCH, RIGHT ON SCHEDULE.
AND WE'LL HAVE A SELECTION OF RADIO PROGRAMS FOR THE RETURN TRIP. I BELIEVE DR. SAGAN WAS ABLE TO GET MOST OF THE ARCHIVES FOR THAT DIRK DARING RADIO DRAMA YOU REQUESTED.
THANK GOD FOR SMALL FAVORS.
GOOD TO HEAR, EMERALD CITY. I'VE GOT SOME GEOLOGICAL EXPERIMENTS TO WRAP UP ON MY END, AND THEN I'LL GO OVER THE PRE-FLIGHT FOR TOMORROW'S LAUNCH.
EVER SINCE HE STARTED STUDYING THOSE MARTIAN ROCKS HE'S BEEN SO MUCH MORE COOPERATIVE.
HEY, IDLE HANDS, Y'KNOW.

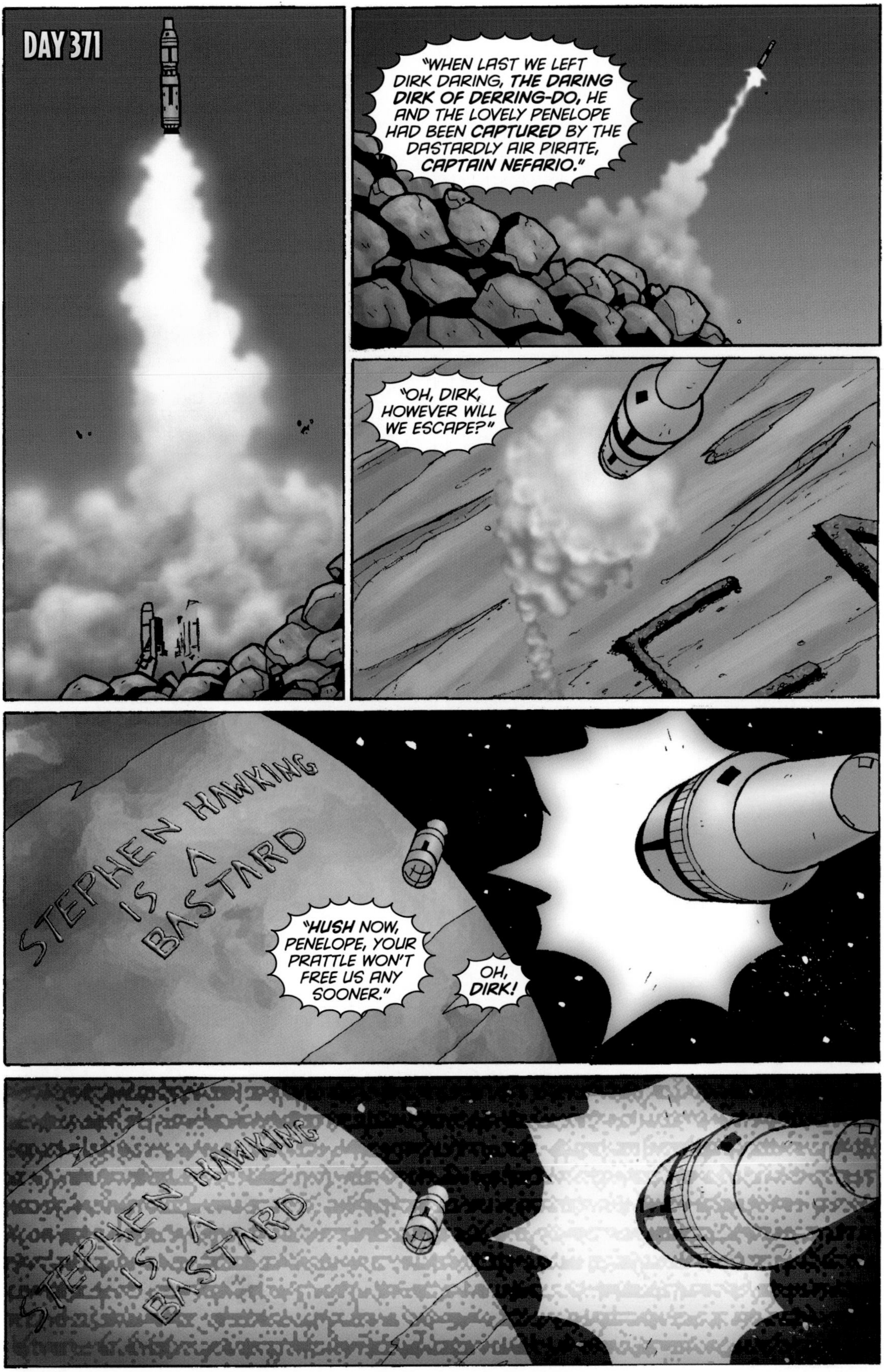
DAY 371
"WHEN LAST WE LEFT DIRK DARING, THE DARING DIRK OF DERRING-DO, HE AND THE LOVELY PENELOPE HAD BEEN CAPTURED BY THE DASTARDLY AIR PIRATE, CAPTAIN NEFARIO."
"OH, DIRK, HOWEVER WILL WE ESCAPE?"
STEPHEN HAWKING IS A BASTARD
"HUSH NOW, PENELOPE, YOUR PRATTLE WON'T FREE US ANY SOONER."
OH, DIRK!
STEPHEN HAWKING IS A BASTARD

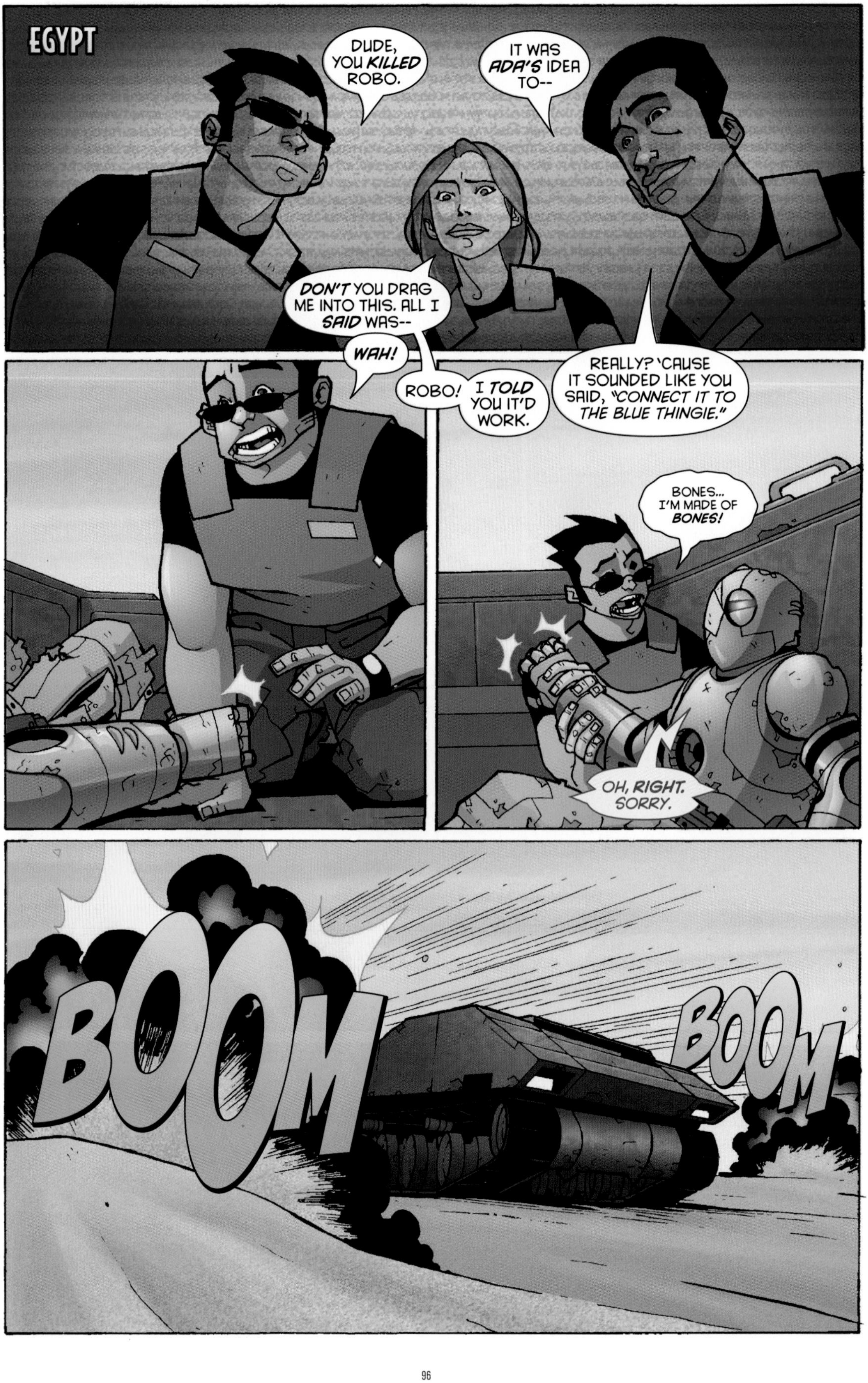
EGYPT
DUDE, YOU KILLED ROBO.
IT WAS ADA'S IDEA TO--
DON'T YOU DRAG ME INTO THIS. ALL I SAID WAS--
WAH!
ROBO!
I TOLD YOU IT'D WORK.
REALLY? 'CAUSE IT SOUNDED LIKE YOU SAID, "CONNECT IT TO THE BLUE THINGIE."
BONES... I'M MADE OF BONES!
OH, RIGHT. SORRY.
BOOM
BOOM

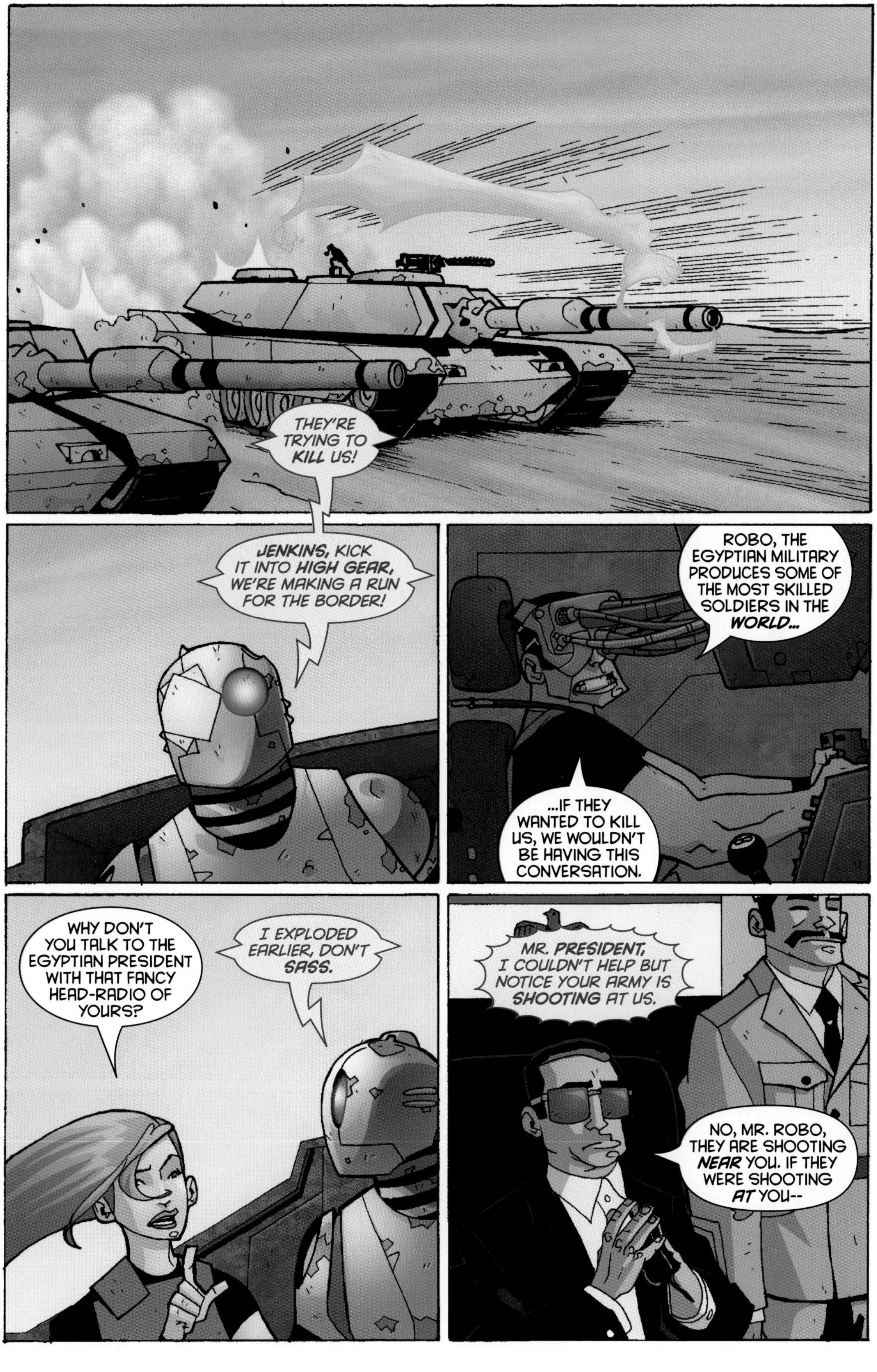
THEY'RE TRYING TO KILL US!
JENKINS, KICK IT INTO HIGH GEAR, WE'RE MAKING A RUN FOR THE BORDER!
ROBO, THE EGYPTIAN MILITARY PRODUCES SOME OF THE MOST SKILLED SOLDIERS IN THE WORLD...
...IF THEY WANTED TO KILL US, WE WOULDN'T BE HAVING THIS CONVERSATION.
WHY DON'T YOU TALK TO THE EGYPTIAN PRESIDENT WITH THAT FANCY HEAD-RADIO OF YOURS?
I EXPLODED EARLIER, DON'T SASS.
MR. PRESIDENT, I COULDN'T HELP BUT NOTICE YOUR ARMY IS SHOOTING AT US.
NO, MR. ROBO, THEY ARE SHOOTING NEAR YOU. IF THEY WERE SHOOTING AT YOU--

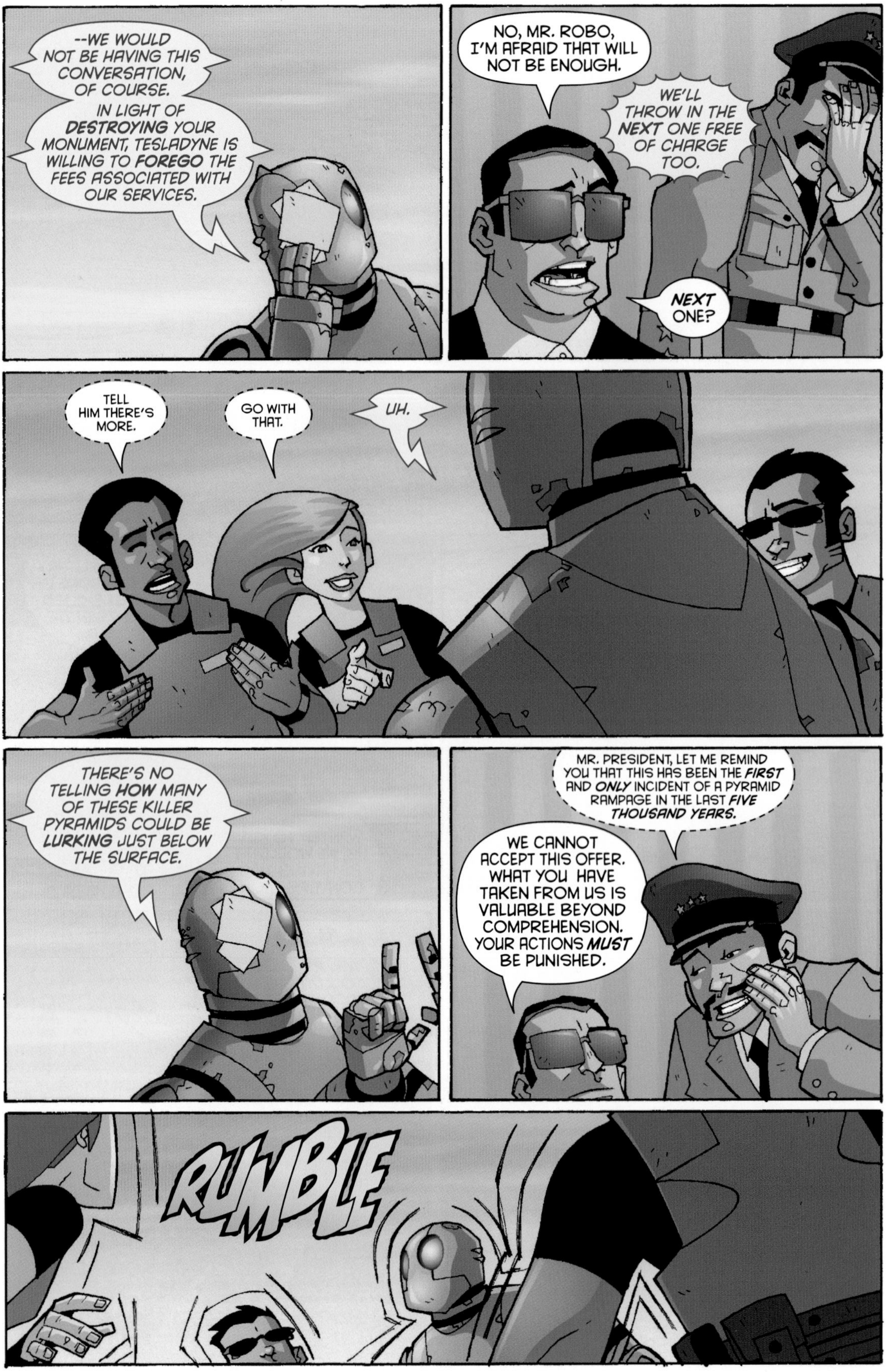
--WE WOULD NOT BE HAVING THIS CONVERSATION, OF COURSE.
IN LIGHT OF DESTROYING YOUR MONUMENT, TESLADYNE IS WILLING TO FOREGO THE FEES ASSOCIATED WITH OUR SERVICES.
NO, MR. ROBO, I'M AFRAID THAT WILL NOT BE ENOUGH.
WE'LL THROW IN THE NEXT ONE FREE OF CHARGE TOO.
NEXT ONE?
TELL HIM THERE'S MORE.
GO WITH THAT.
UH.
THERE'S NO TELLING HOW MANY OF THESE KILLER PYRAMIDS COULD BE LURKING JUST BELOW THE SURFACE.
MR. PRESIDENT, LET ME REMIND YOU THAT THIS HAS BEEN THE FIRST AND ONLY INCIDENT OF A PYRAMID RAMPAGE IN THE LAST FIVE THOUSAND YEARS.
WE CANNOT ACCEPT THIS OFFER. WHAT YOU HAVE TAKEN FROM US IS VALUABLE BEYOND COMPREHENSION. YOUR ACTIONS MUST BE PUNISHED.
RUMBLE

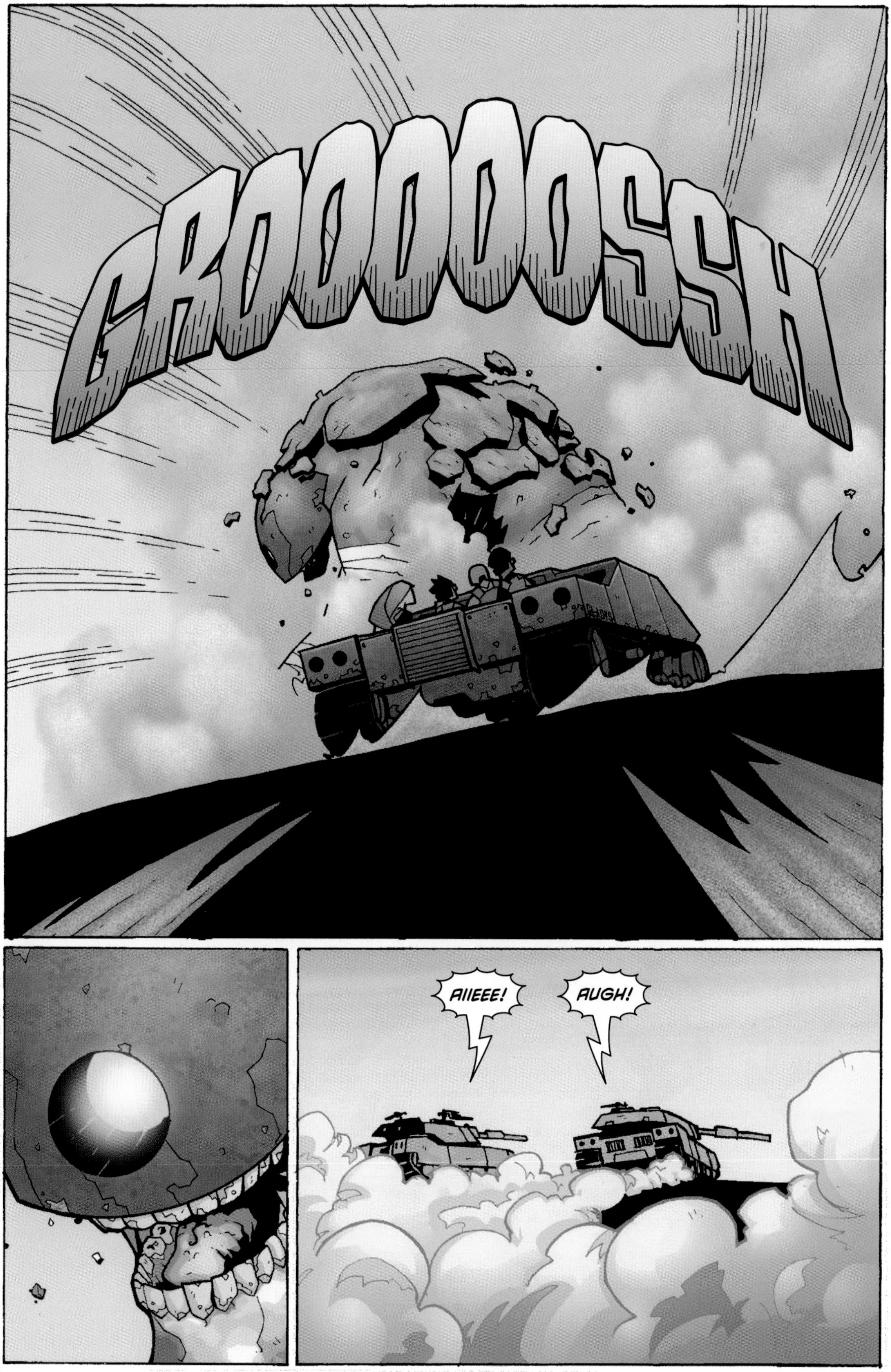
CROOOOOSSH
AIIEEE!
AUGH!

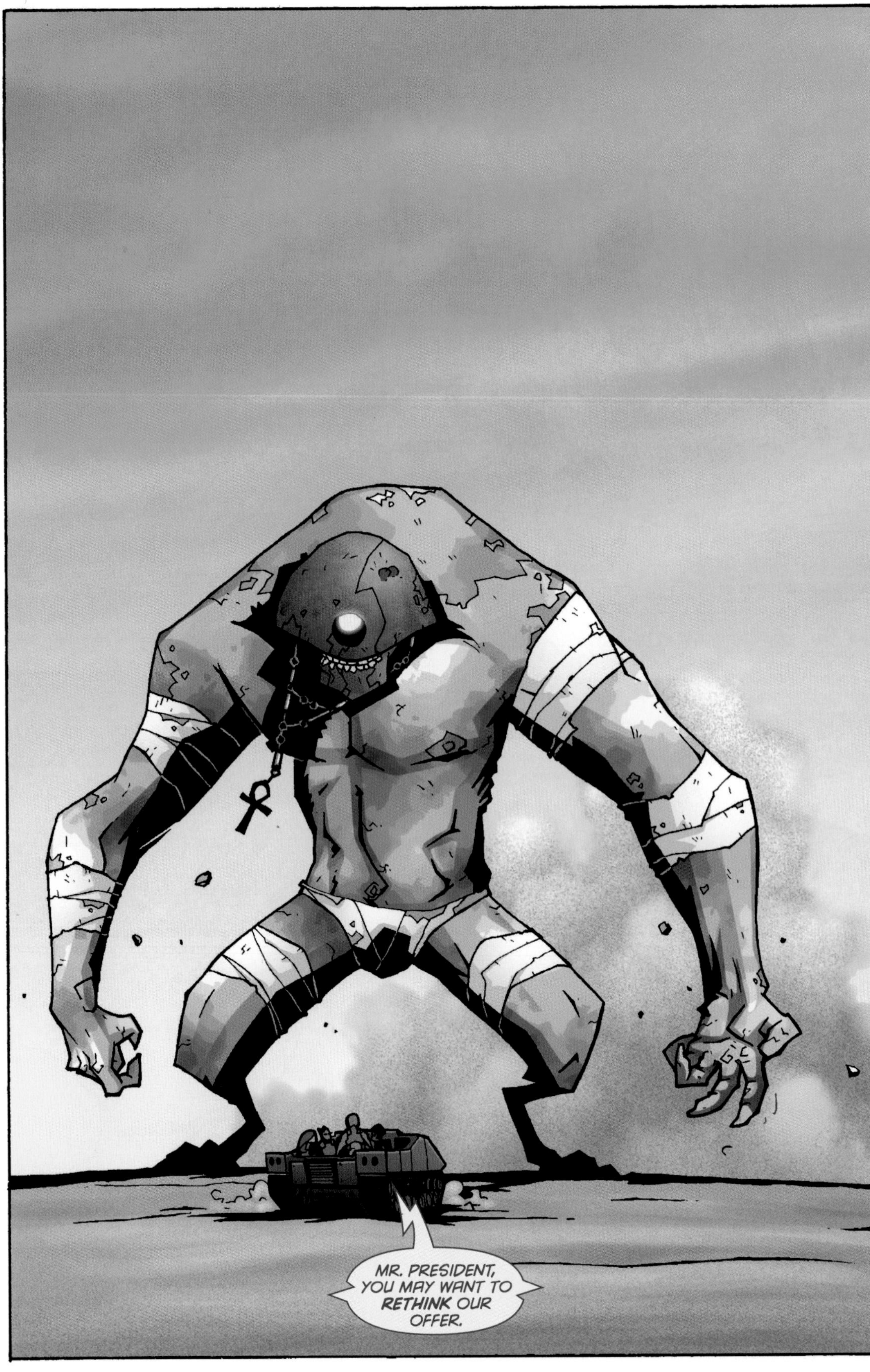
MR. PRESIDENT, YOU MAY WANT TO RETHINK OUR OFFER.

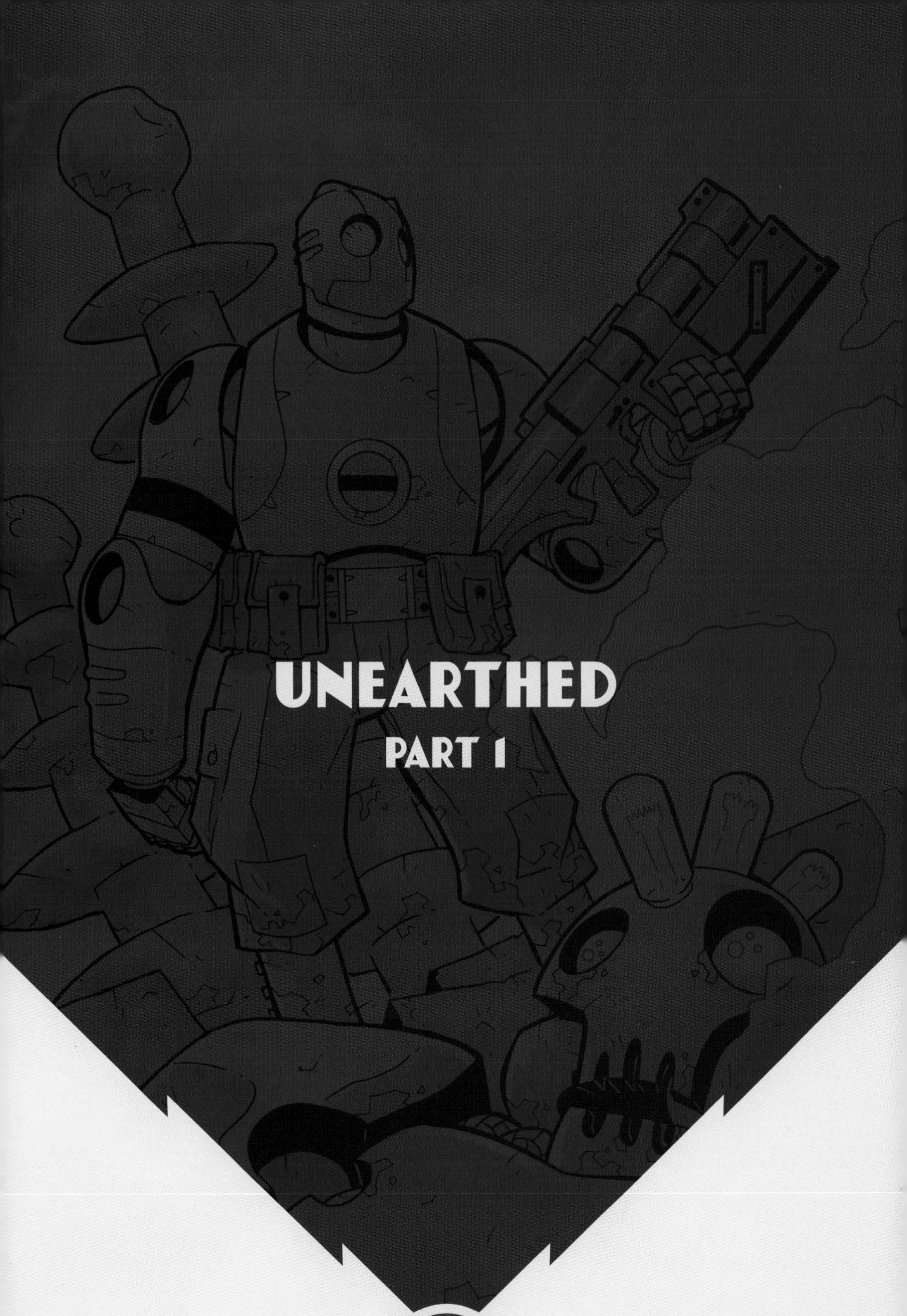

UNEARTHED

PART 1

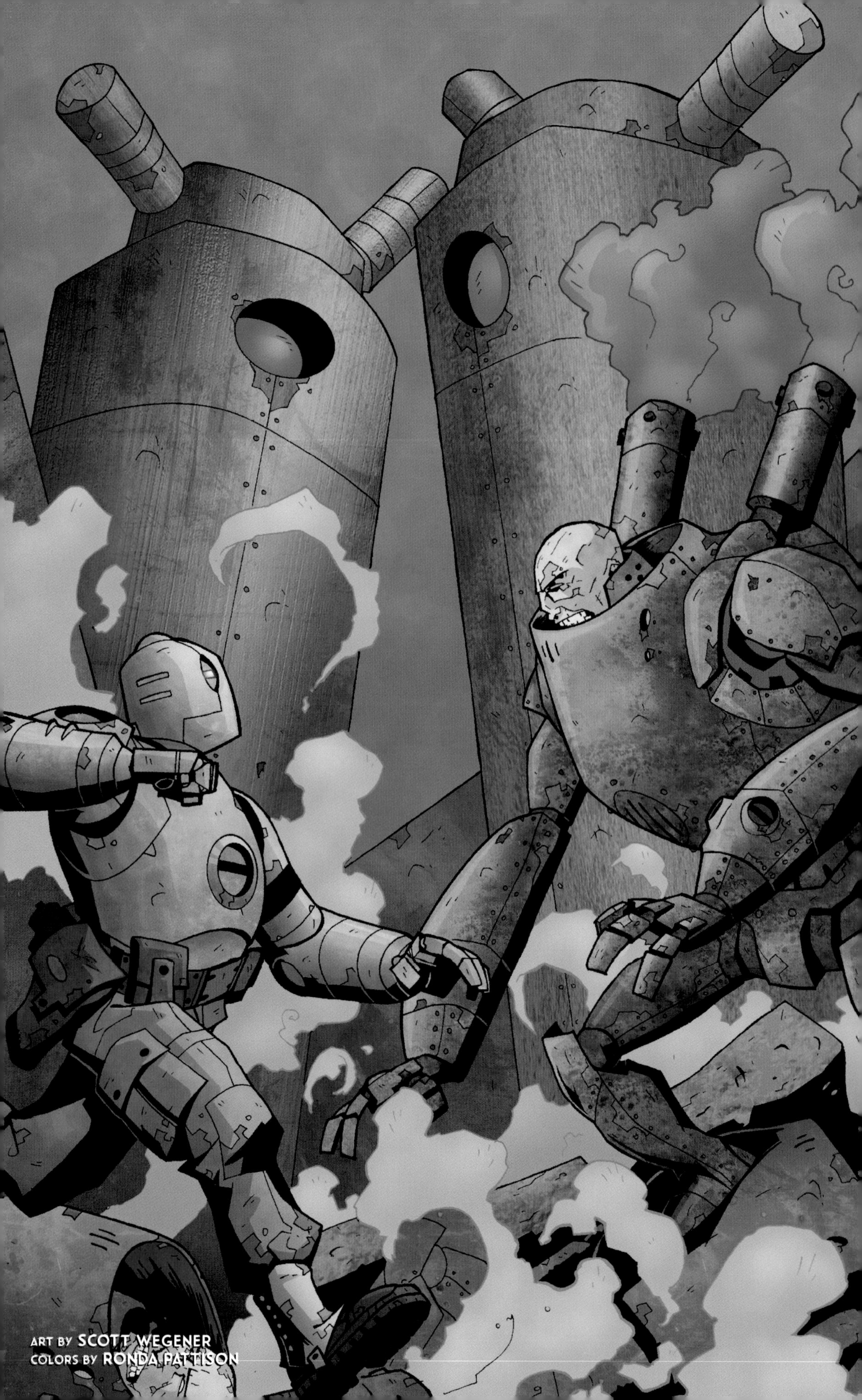

ART BY SCOTT WEGENER
COLORS BY RONDA PATTISON

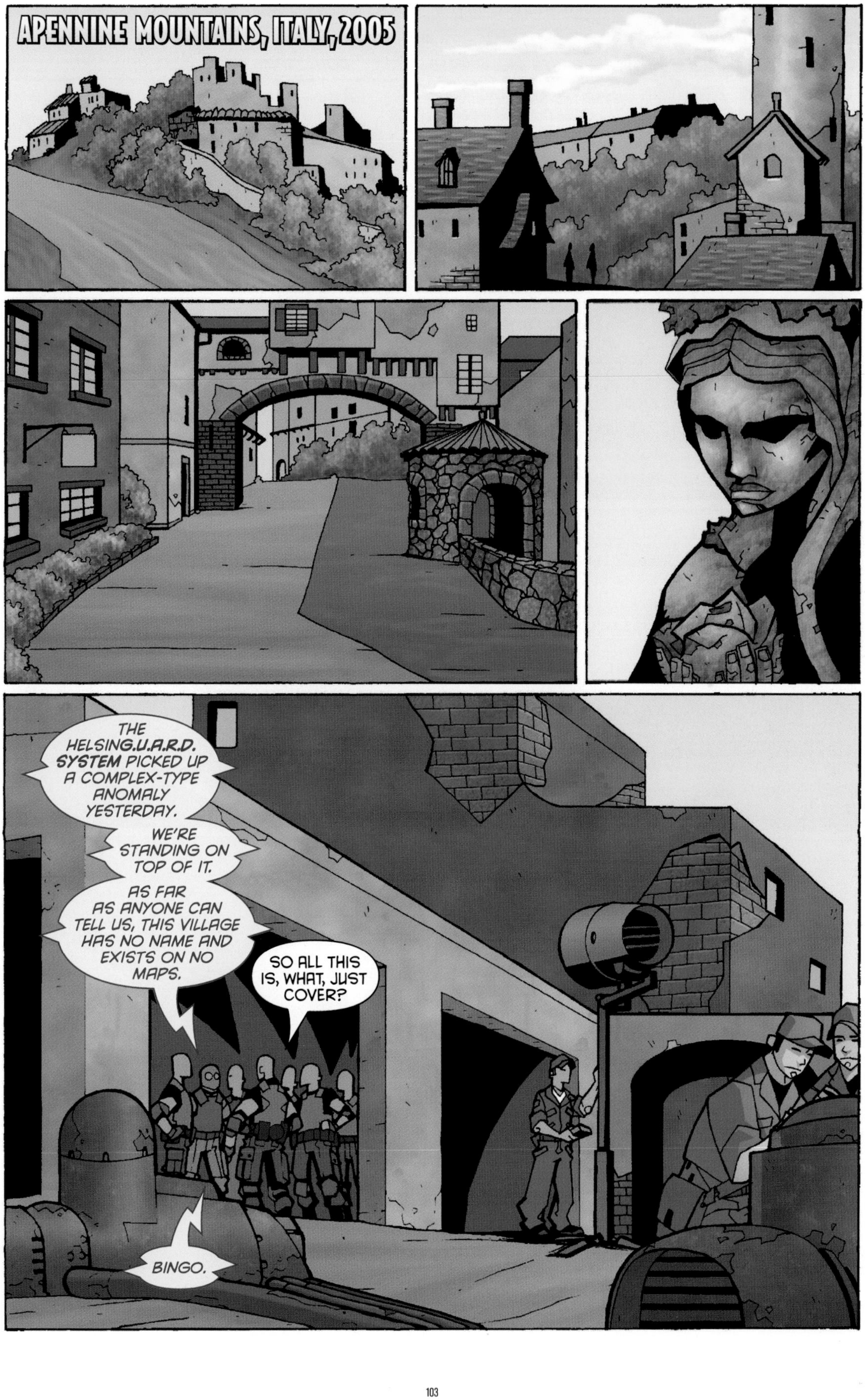
APENNINE MOUNTAINS, ITALY, 2005
THE HELSING.U.A.R.D. SYSTEM PICKED UP A COMPLEX-TYPE ANOMALY YESTERDAY.
WE'RE STANDING ON TOP OF IT.
AS FAR AS ANYONE CAN TELL US, THIS VILLAGE HAS NO NAME AND EXISTS ON NO MAPS.
SO ALL THIS IS, WHAT, JUST COVER?
BINGO.

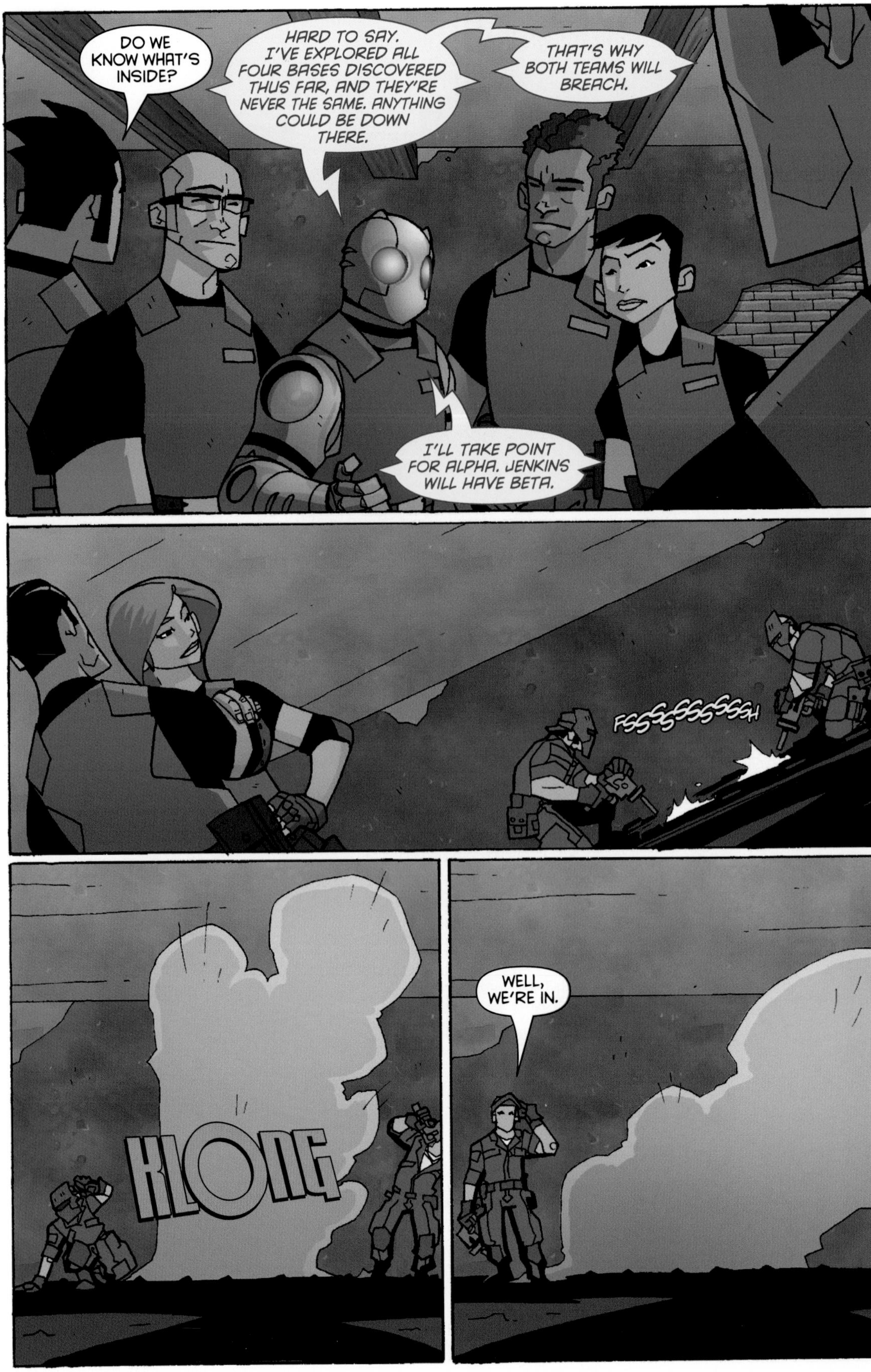
DO WE KNOW WHAT'S INSIDE?
HARD TO SAY. I'VE EXPLORED ALL FOUR BASES DISCOVERED THUS FAR, AND THEY'RE NEVER THE SAME. ANYTHING COULD BE DOWN THERE.
THAT'S WHY BOTH TEAMS WILL BREACH.
I'LL TAKE POINT FOR ALPHA. JENKINS WILL HAVE BETA.
FSSSSSSSSSSH
KLONG
WELL, WE'RE IN.

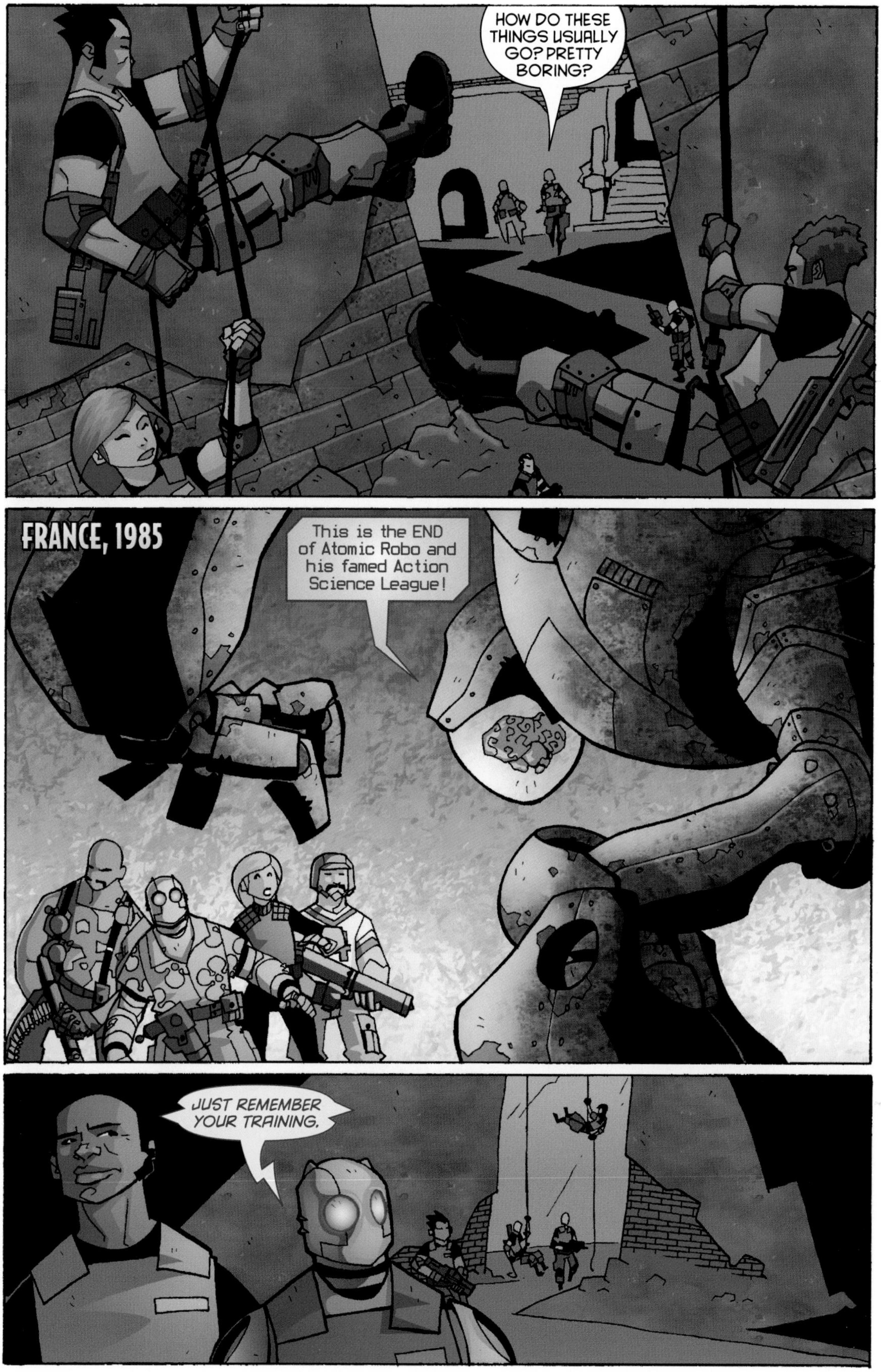

HOW DO THESE THINGS USUALLY GO? PRETTY BORING?
FRANCE, 1985
This is the END of Atomic Robo and his famed Action Science League!
JUST REMEMBER YOUR TRAINING.

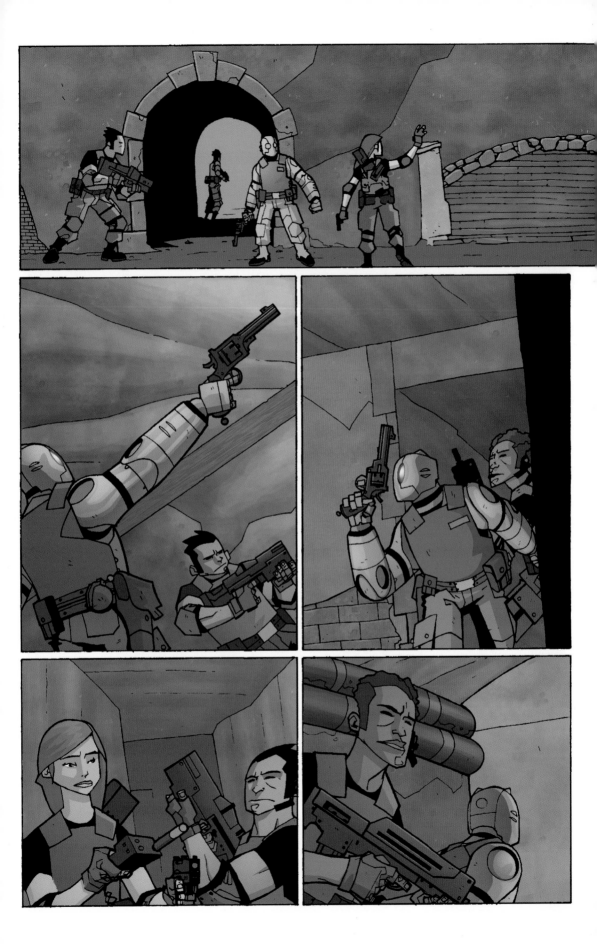

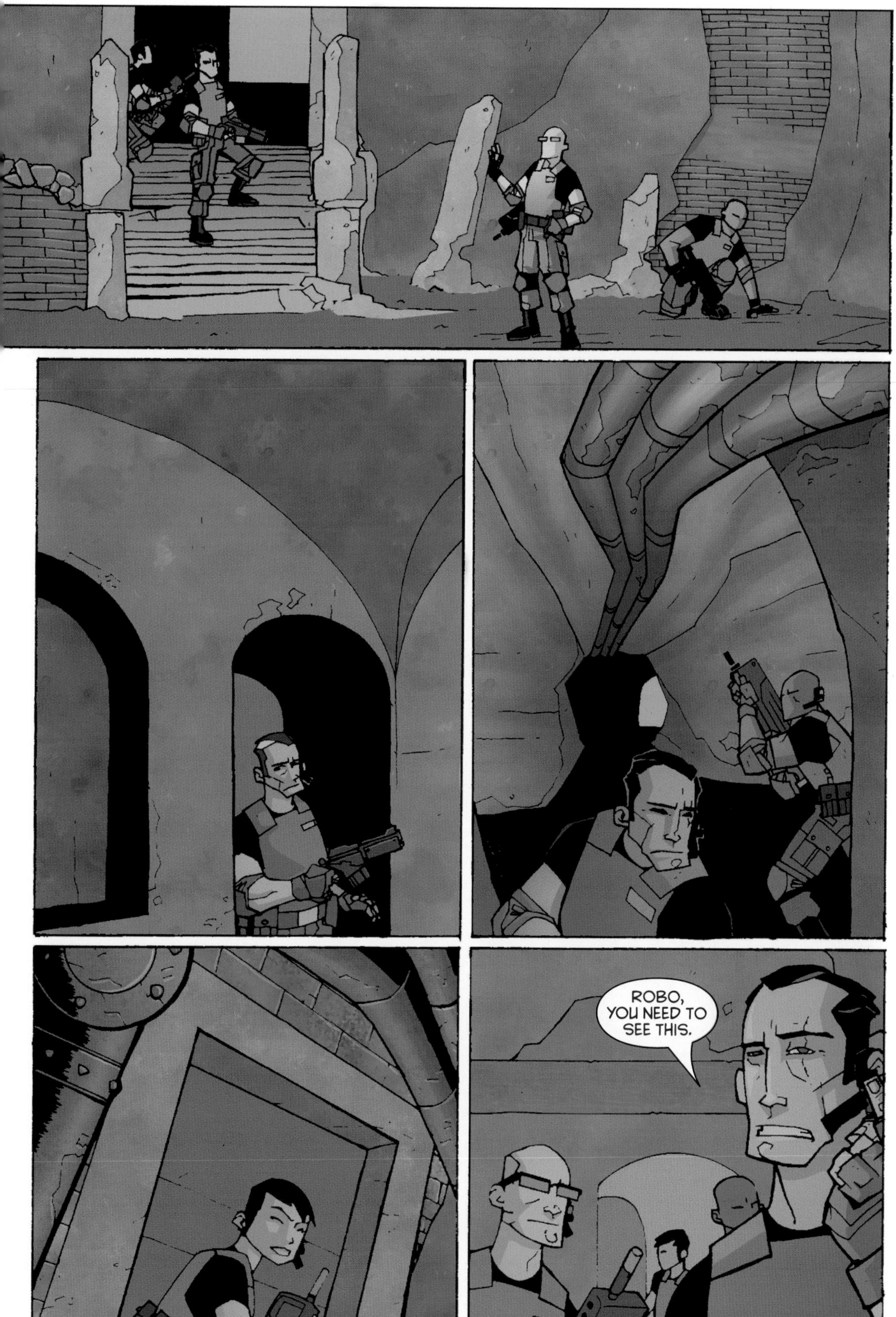
ROBO, YOU NEED TO SEE THIS.

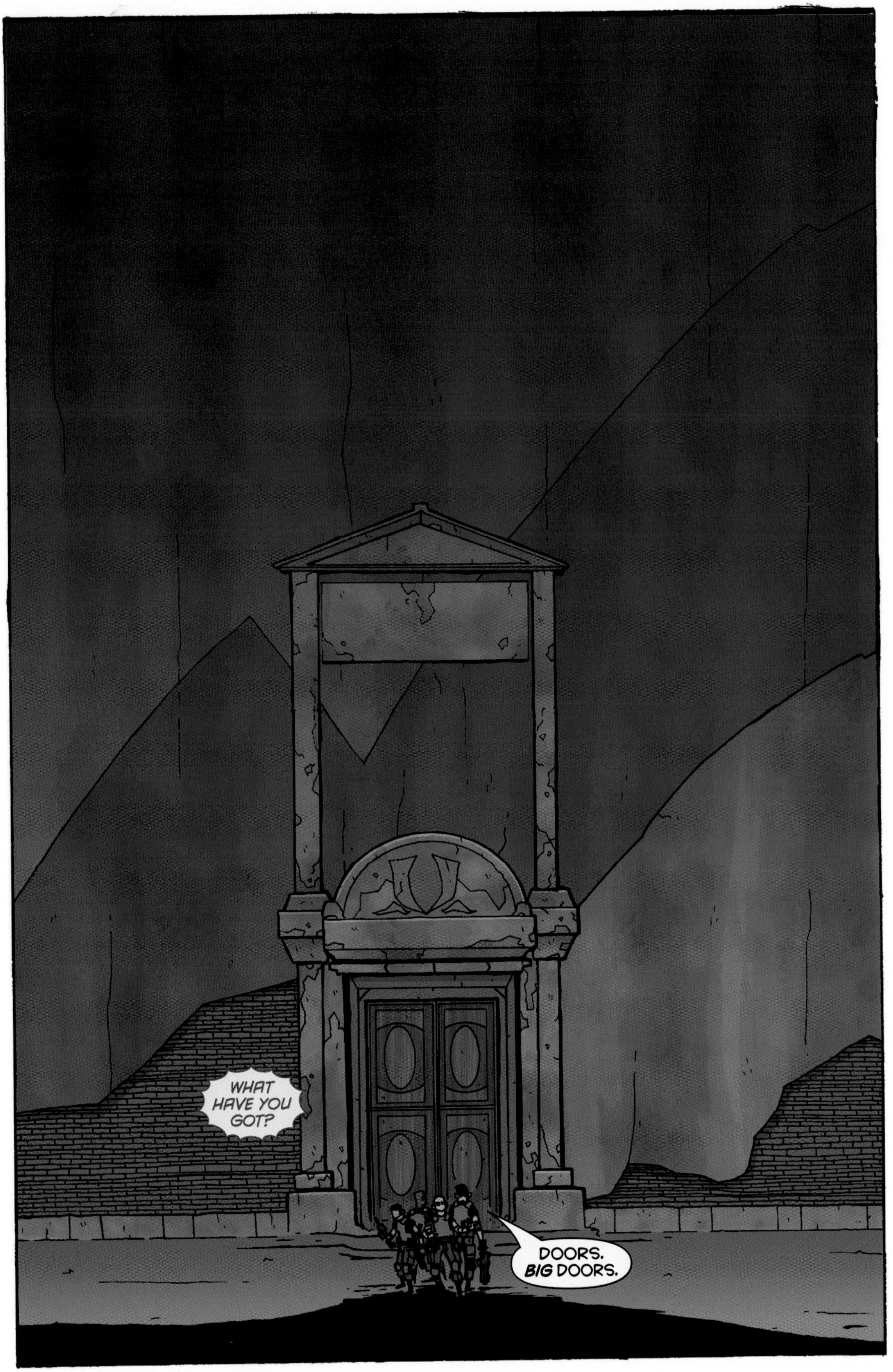
WHAT HAVE YOU GOT?
DOORS. BIG DOORS.

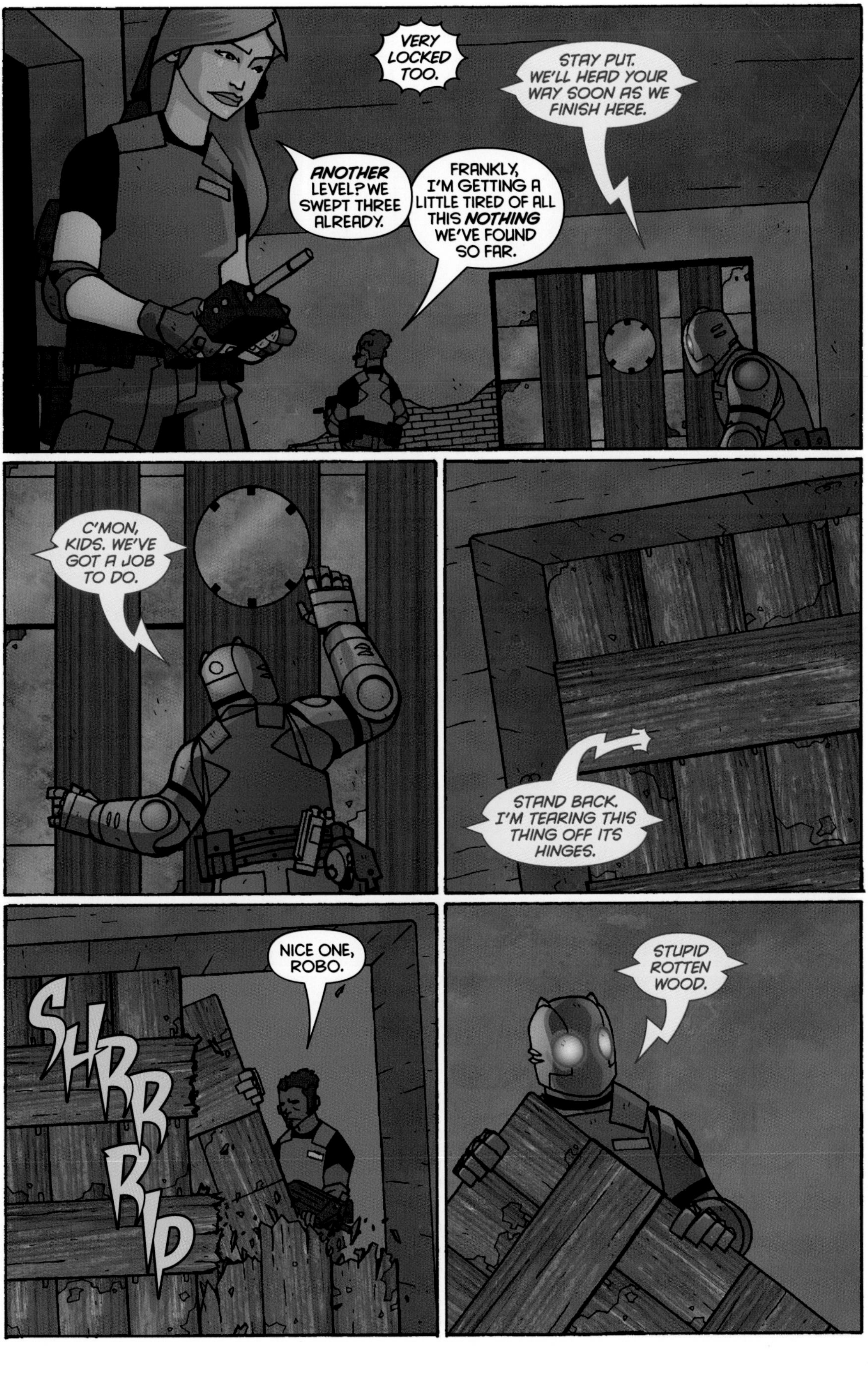
VERY LOCKED TOO.
ANOTHER LEVEL? WE SWEPT THREE ALREADY.
FRANKLY, I'M GETTING A LITTLE TIRED OF ALL THIS NOTHING WE'VE FOUND SO FAR.
STAY PUT. WE'LL HEAD YOUR WAY SOON AS WE FINISH HERE.
C'MON, KIDS. WE'VE GOT A JOB TO DO.
STAND BACK. I'M TEARING THIS THING OFF ITS HINGES.
SHRRRIP
NICE ONE, ROBO.
STUPID ROTTEN WOOD.

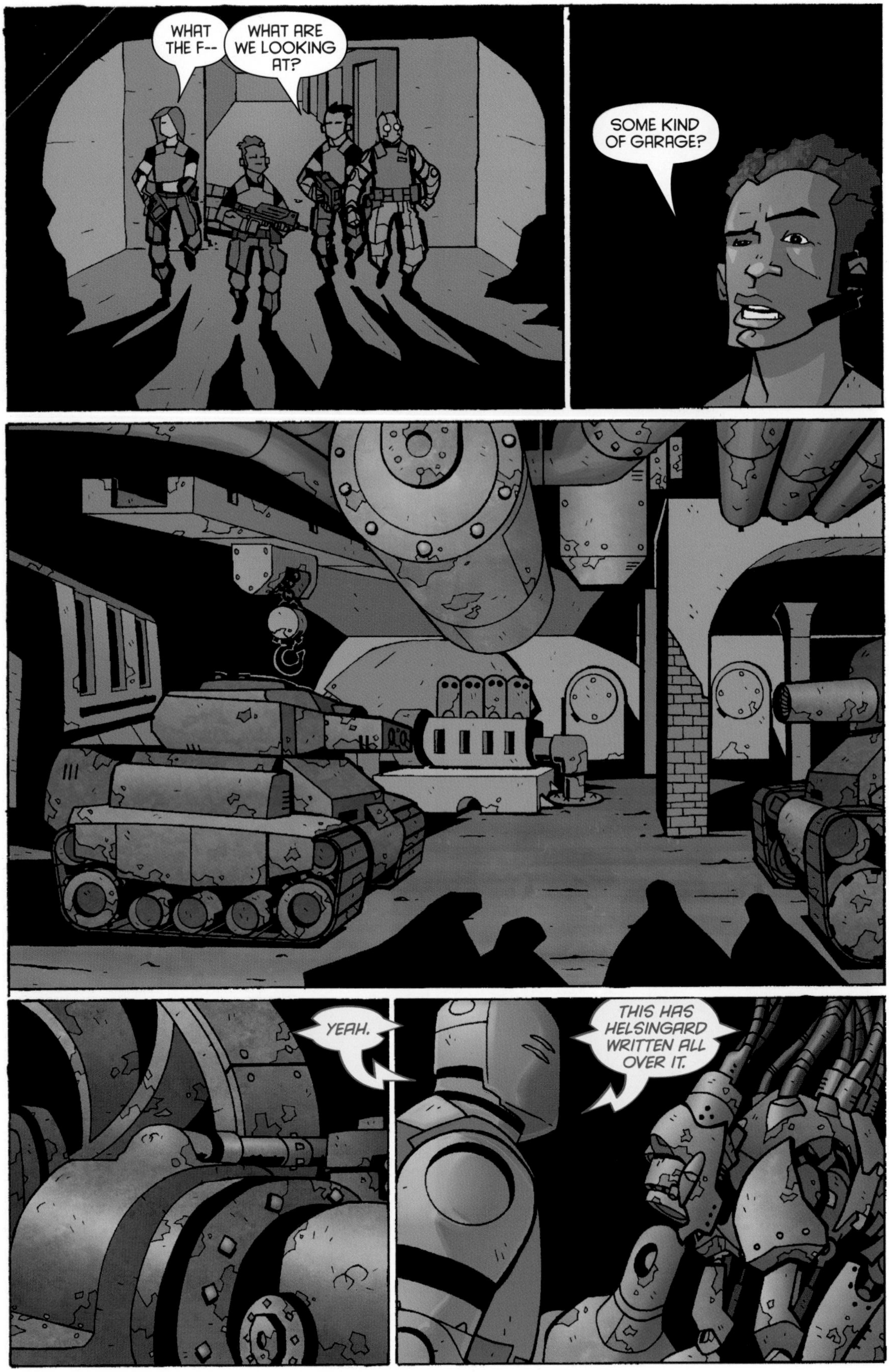
WHAT THE F--
WHAT ARE WE LOOKING AT?
SOME KIND OF GARAGE?
YEAH.
THIS HAS HELSINGARD WRITTEN ALL OVER IT.

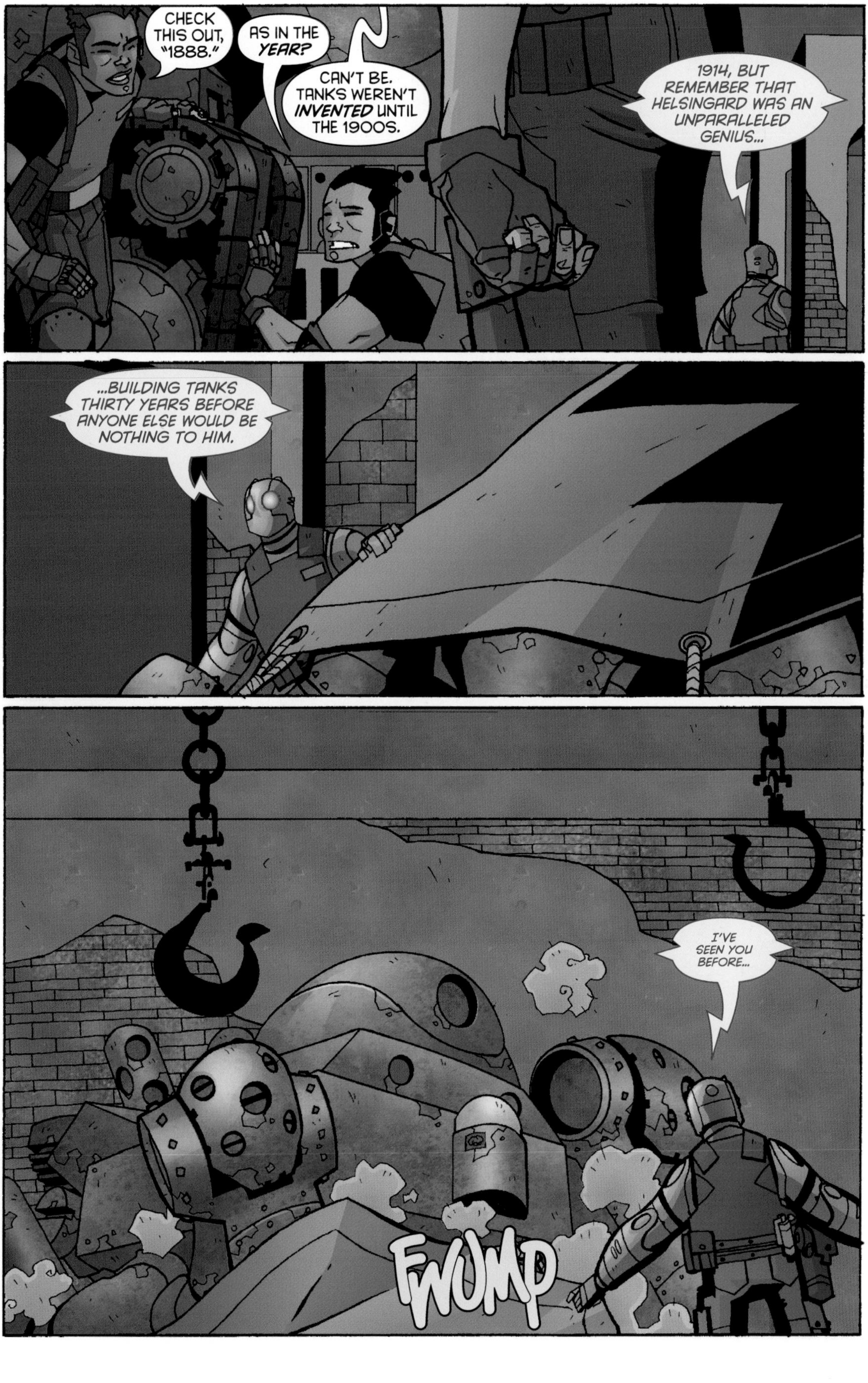

CHECK THIS OUT, "1888."
AS IN THE *YEAR?*
CAN'T BE. TANKS WEREN'T ***INVENTED*** UNTIL THE 1900S.
1914, BUT REMEMBER THAT HELSINGARD WAS AN UNPARALLELED GENIUS...
...BUILDING TANKS THIRTY YEARS BEFORE ANYONE ELSE WOULD BE NOTHING TO HIM.
I'VE SEEN YOU BEFORE...
FWUMP

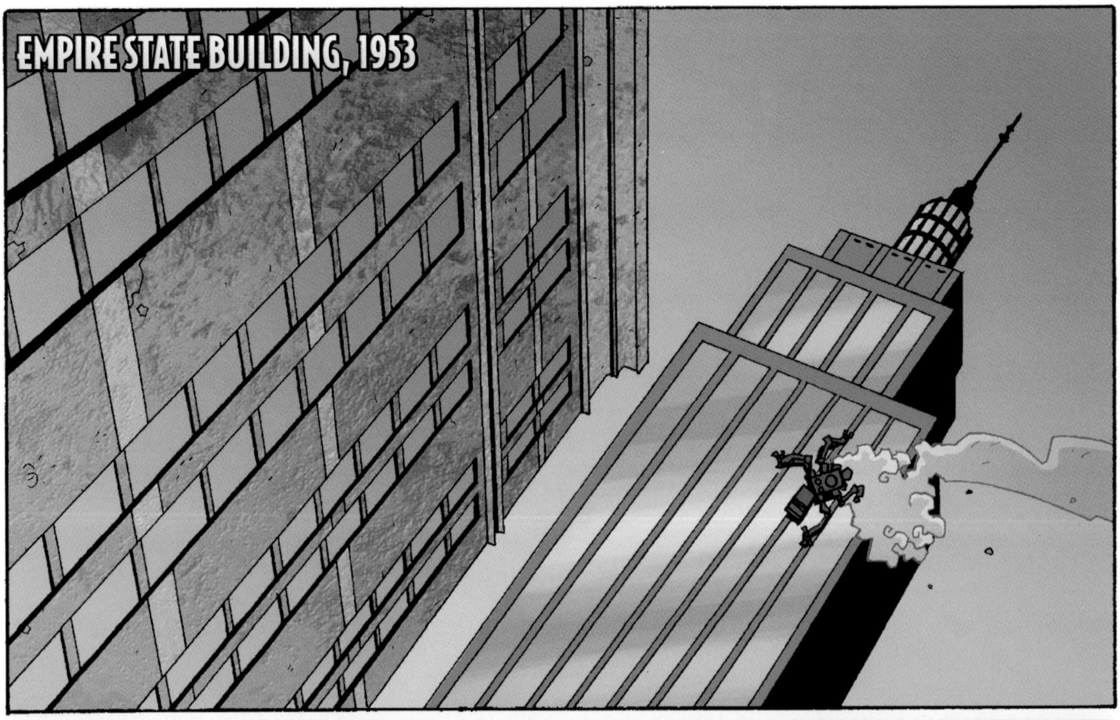
EMPIRE STATE BUILDING, 1953

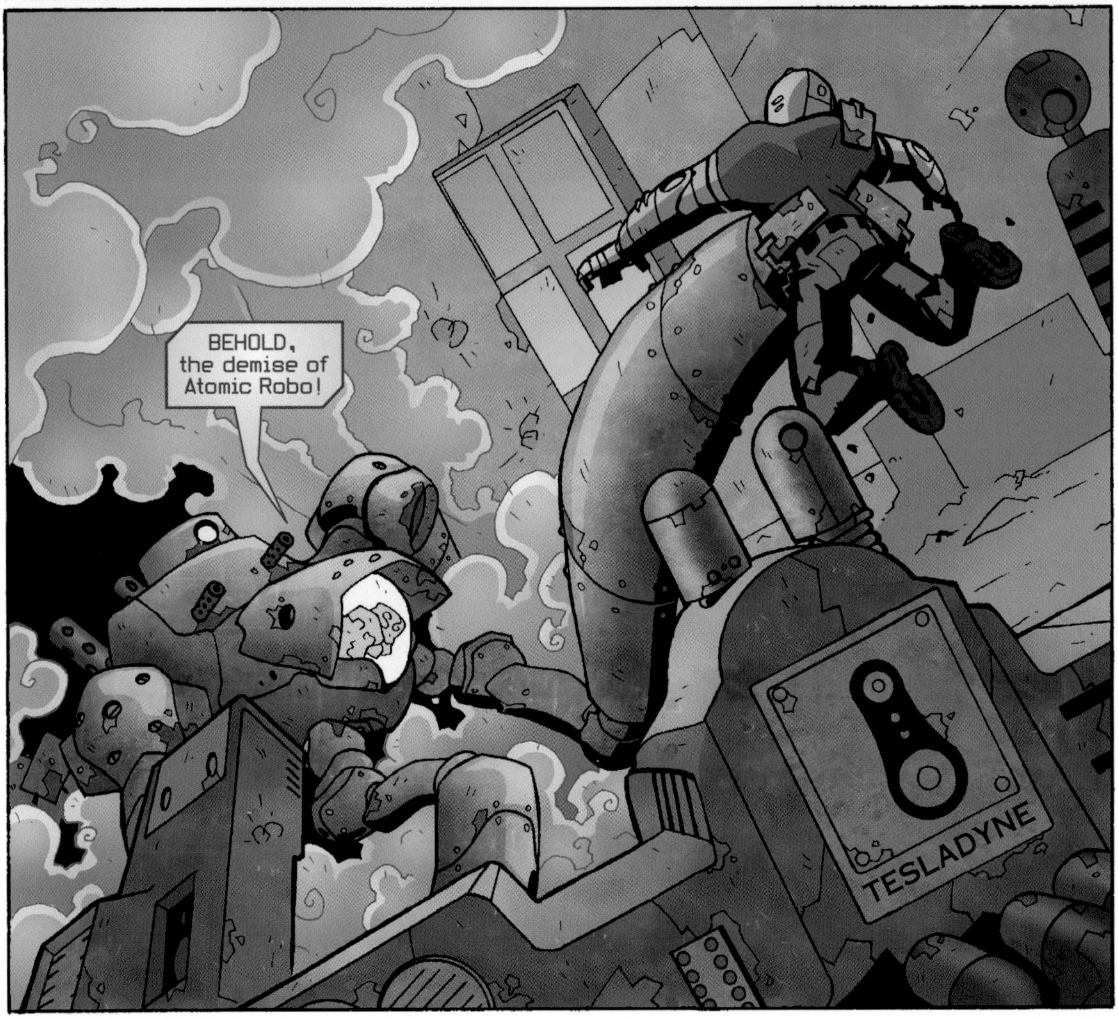
BEHOLD, the demise of Atomic Robo!
TESLADYNE

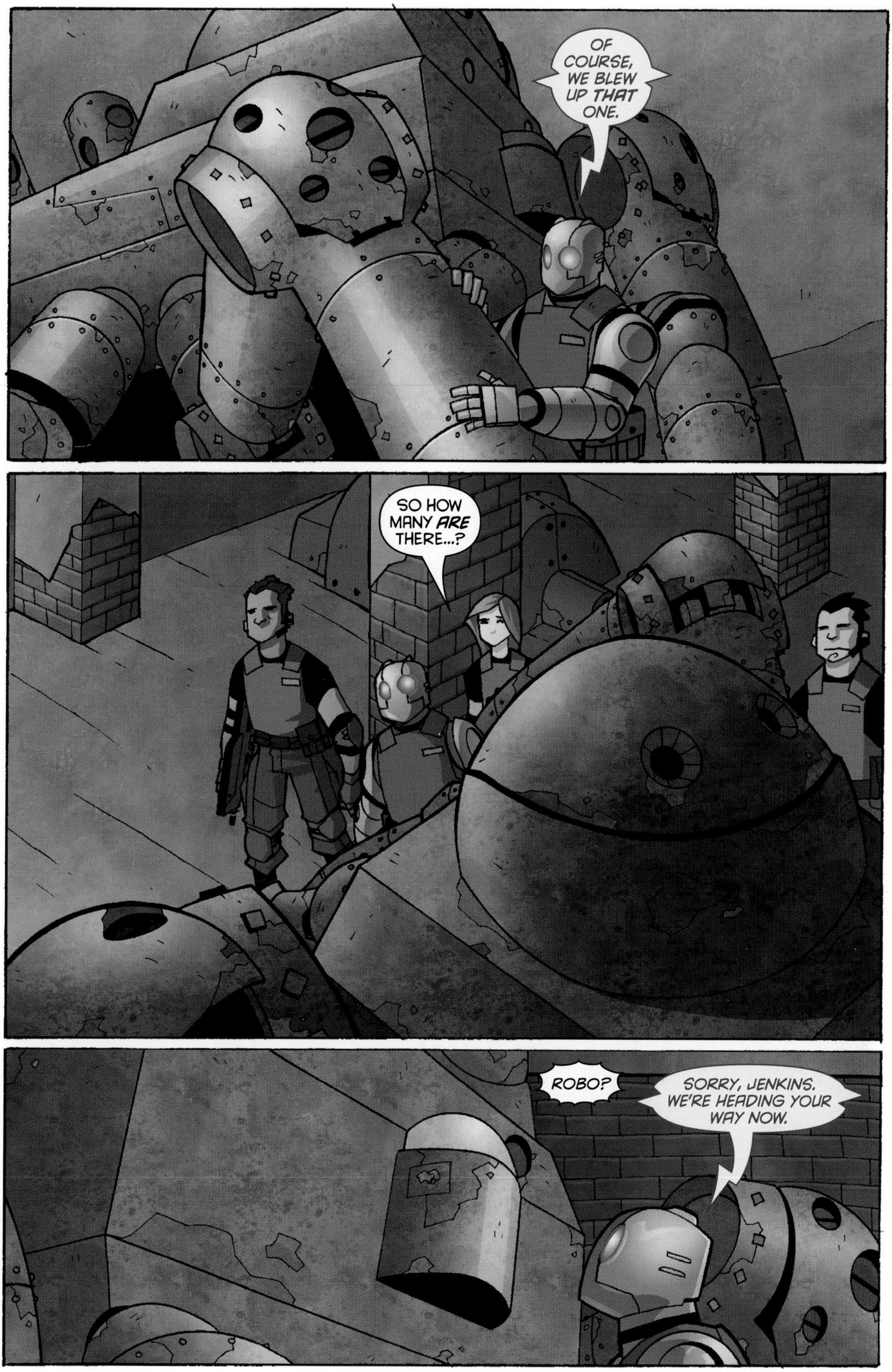
OF COURSE, WE BLEW UP THAT ONE.
SO HOW MANY ARE THERE...?
ROBO?
SORRY, JENKINS. WE'RE HEADING YOUR WAY NOW.

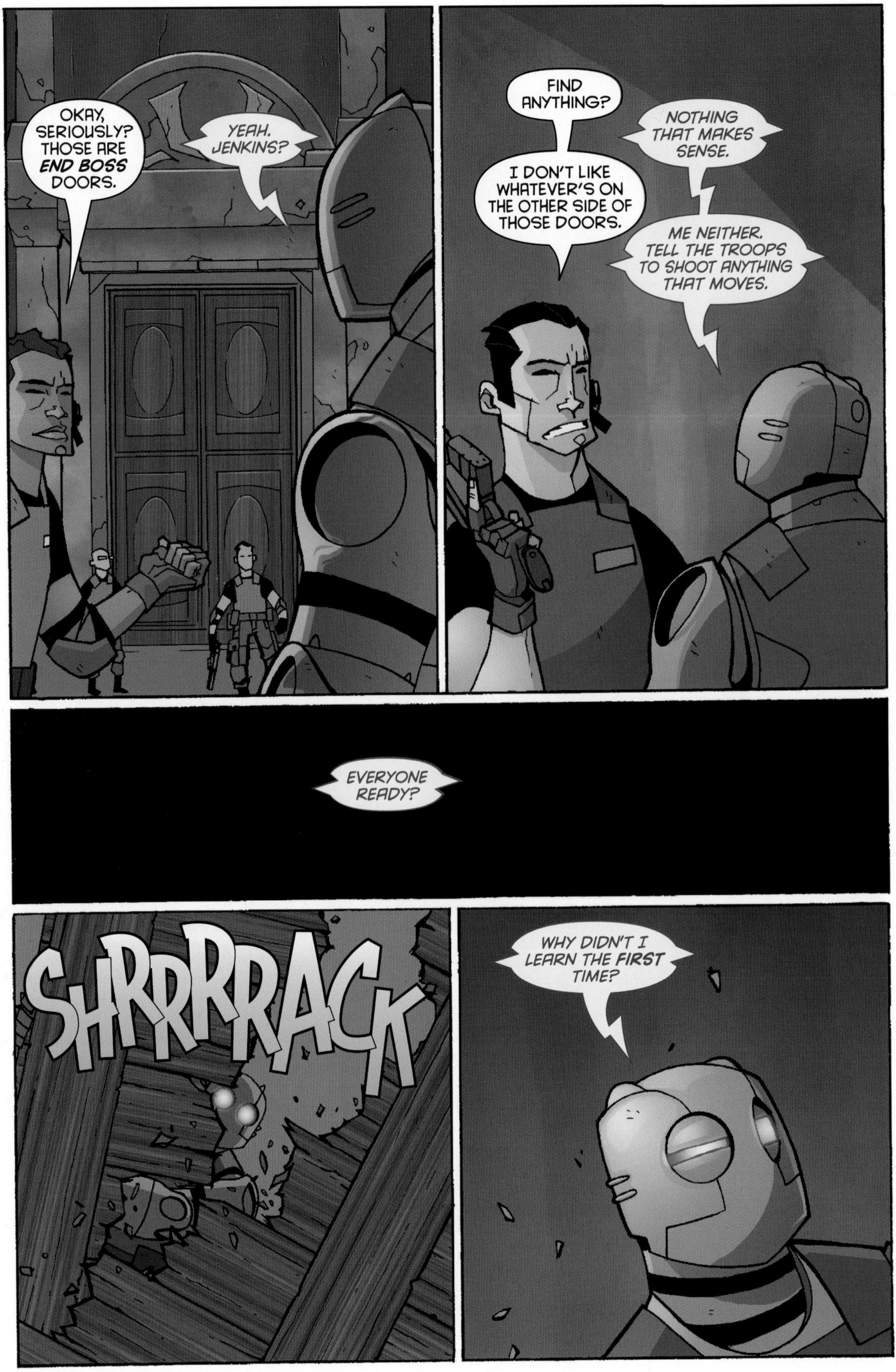
OKAY, SERIOUSLY? THOSE ARE **END BOSS** DOORS.
YEAH. JENKINS?
FIND ANYTHING?
NOTHING THAT MAKES SENSE.
I DON'T LIKE WHATEVER'S ON THE OTHER SIDE OF THOSE DOORS.
ME NEITHER. TELL THE TROOPS TO SHOOT ANYTHING THAT MOVES.
EVERYONE READY?
SHRRRRACK
WHY DIDN'T I LEARN THE **FIRST** TIME?

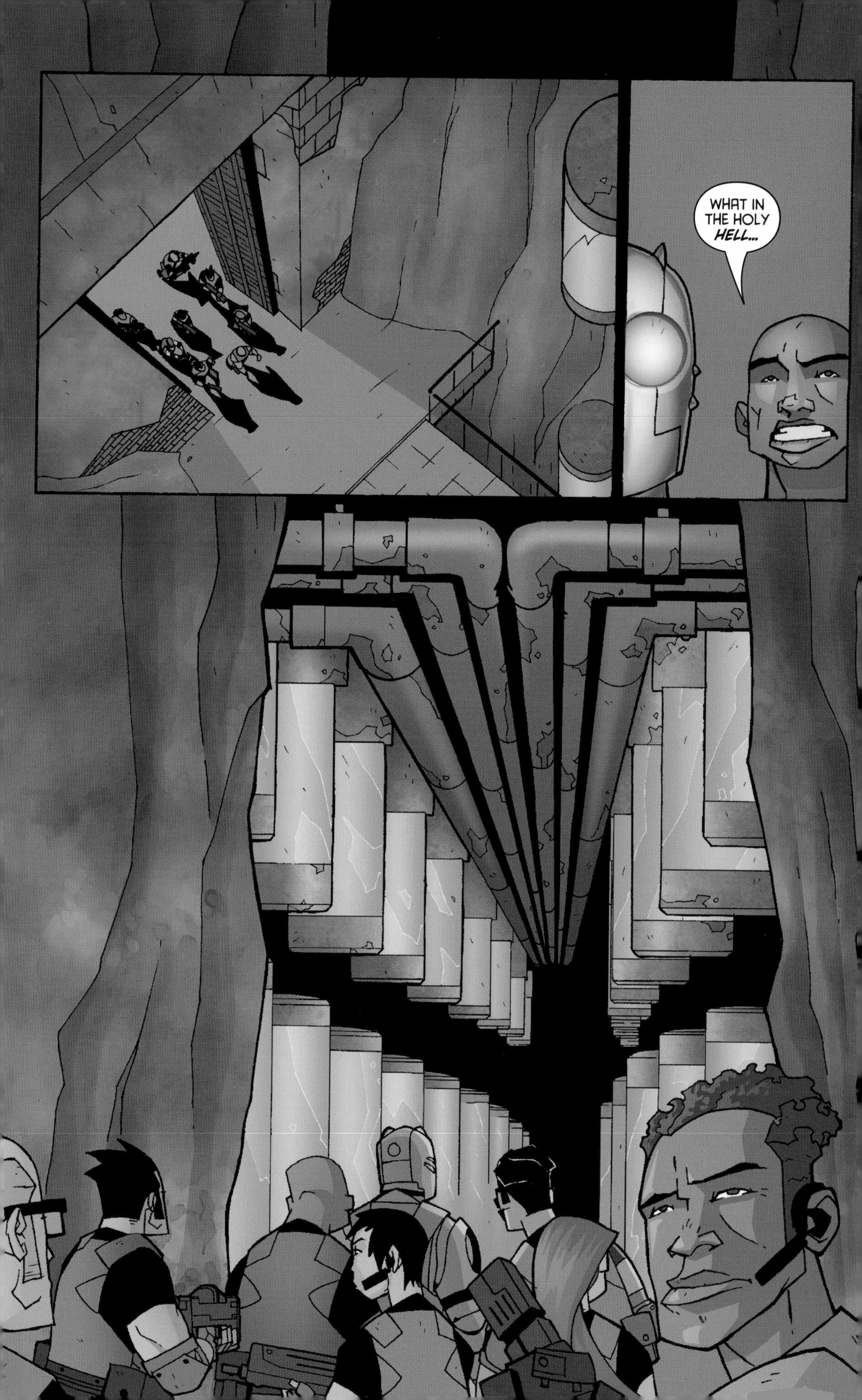
WHAT IN THE HOLY HELL...

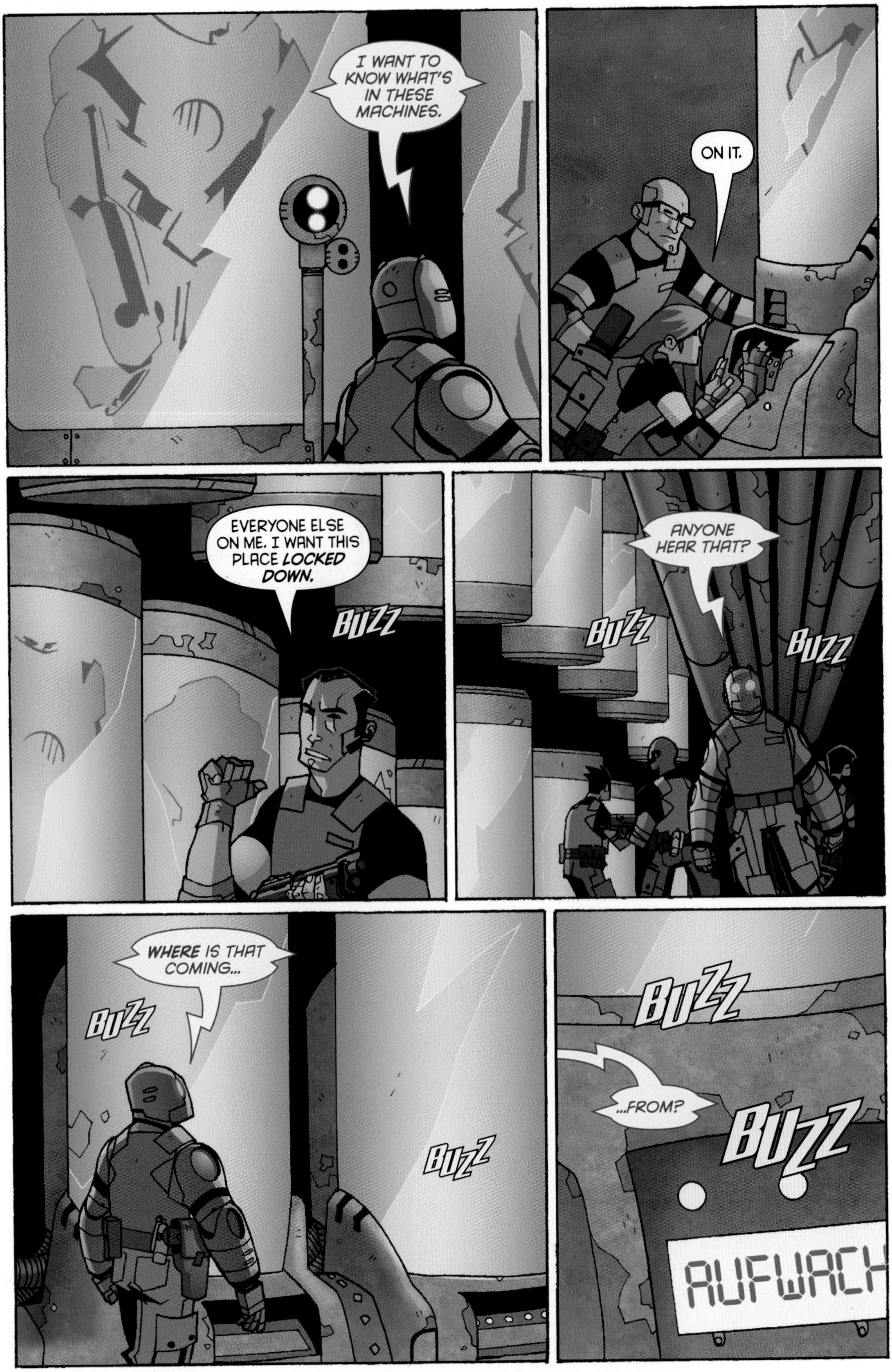
I WANT TO KNOW WHAT'S IN THESE MACHINES.
ON IT.
EVERYONE ELSE ON ME. I WANT THIS PLACE LOCKED DOWN.
BUZZ
ANYONE HEAR THAT?
BUZZ
BUZZ
WHERE IS THAT COMING...
BUZZ
BUZZ
BUZZ
...FROM?
BUZZ
AUFWACH

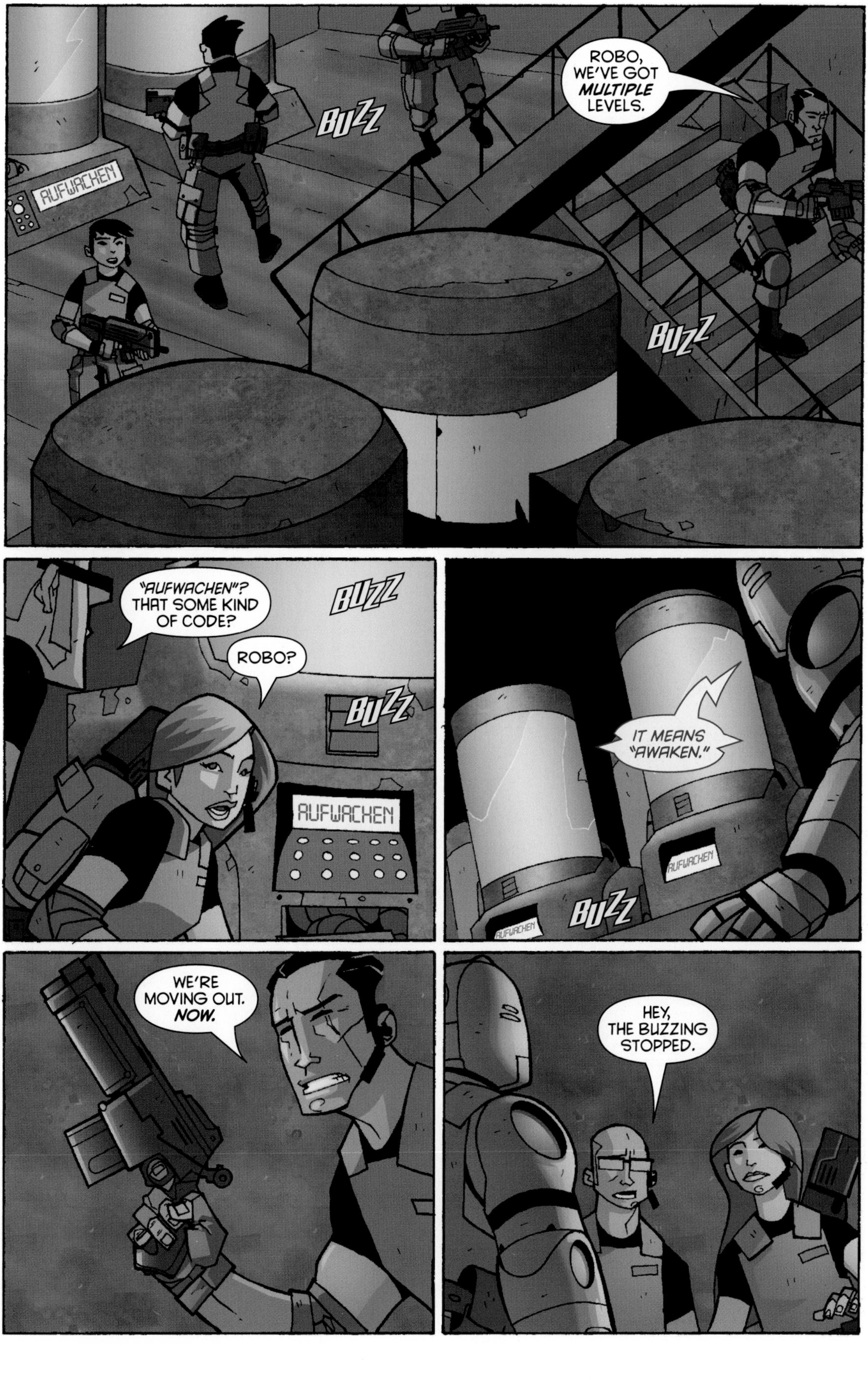
ROBO, WE'VE GOT MULTIPLE LEVELS.
BUZZ
AUFWACHEN
BUZZ
"AUFWACHEN"? THAT SOME KIND OF CODE?
ROBO?
BUZZ
BUZZ
AUFWACHEN
IT MEANS "AWAKEN."
AUFWACHEN
BUZZ
AUFWACHEN
WE'RE MOVING OUT. NOW.
HEY, THE BUZZING STOPPED.

CRKT

KRSH

KRSH

TELL ME IT'S NOT CYBORGS.

THEN I'LL HAVE TO LIE.

SECURE THE EXIT!

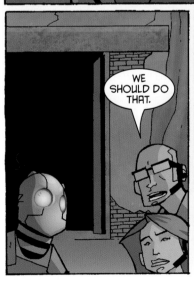

WE SHOULD DO THAT.

HEAD BACK TO THE ENTR--

BOOM

NEVERMIND.

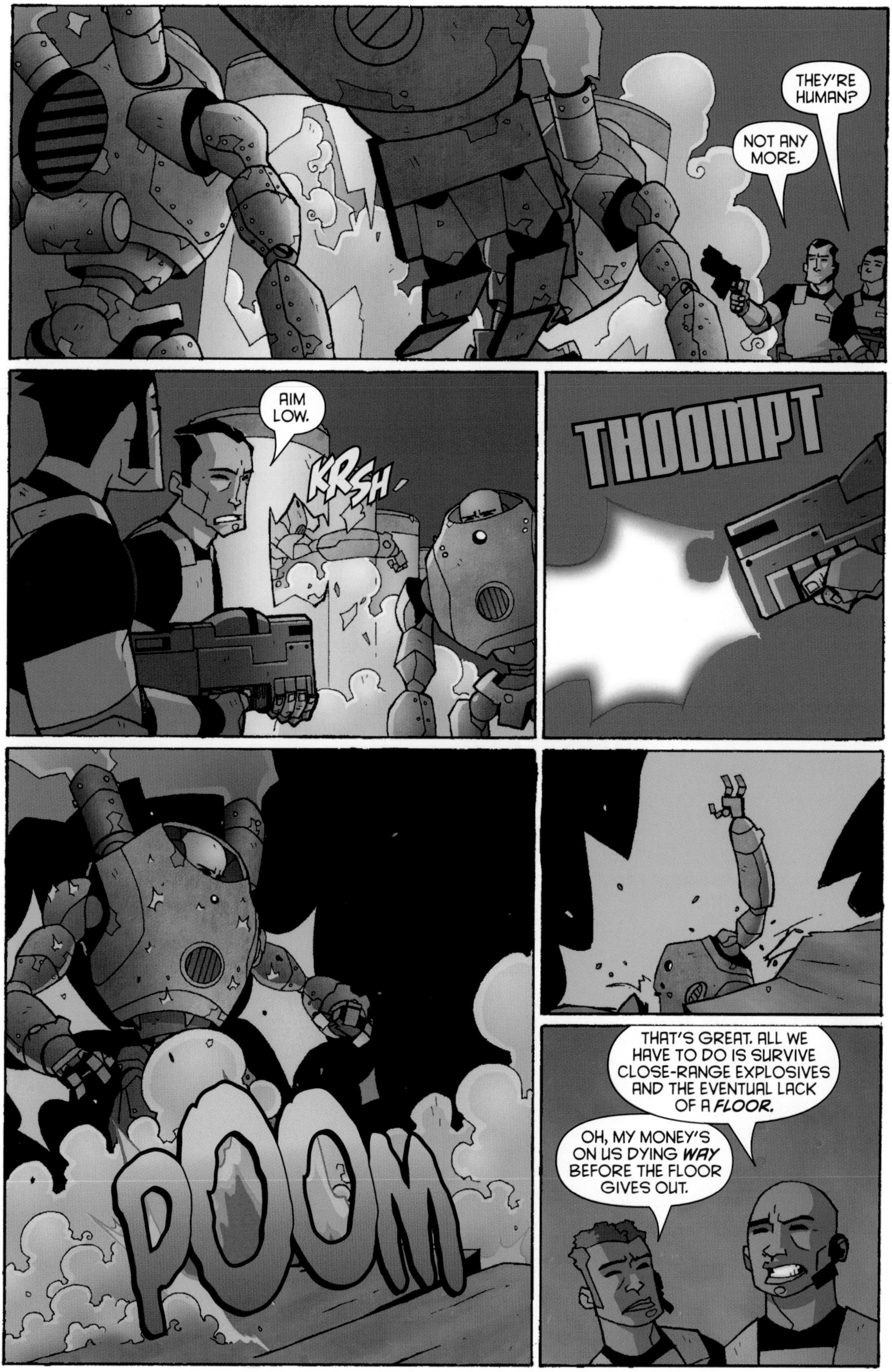
THEY'RE HUMAN?
NOT ANY MORE.
AIM LOW.
KRSH
THOOMPT
POOM
THAT'S GREAT. ALL WE HAVE TO DO IS SURVIVE CLOSE-RANGE EXPLOSIVES AND THE EVENTUAL LACK OF A FLOOR.
OH, MY MONEY'S ON US DYING WAY BEFORE THE FLOOR GIVES OUT.

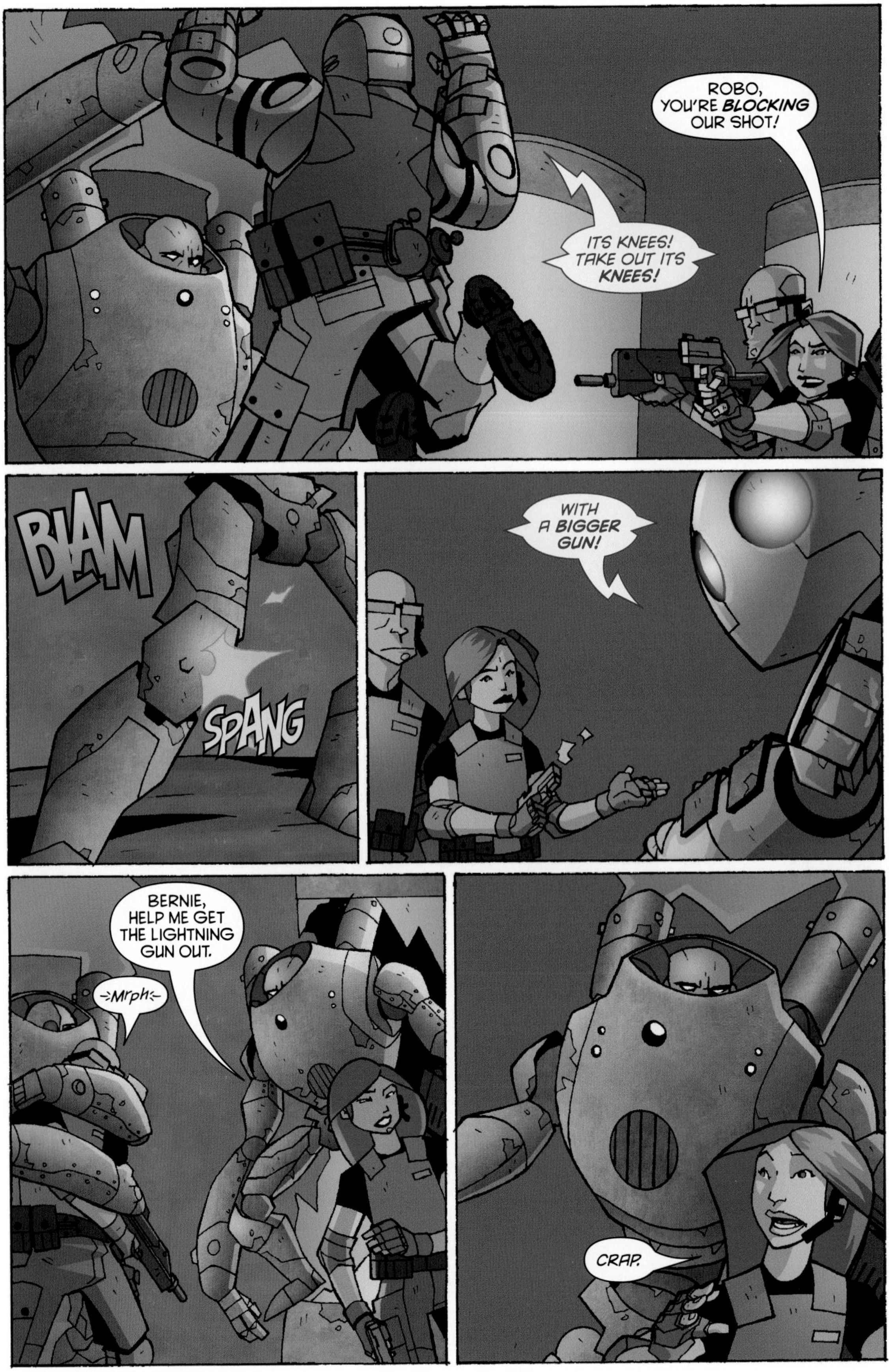
ROBO, YOU'RE BLOCKING OUR SHOT!
ITS KNEES! TAKE OUT ITS KNEES!
BLAM
SPANG
WITH A BIGGER GUN!
BERNIE, HELP ME GET THE LIGHTNING GUN OUT.
-Mrph-
CRAP.

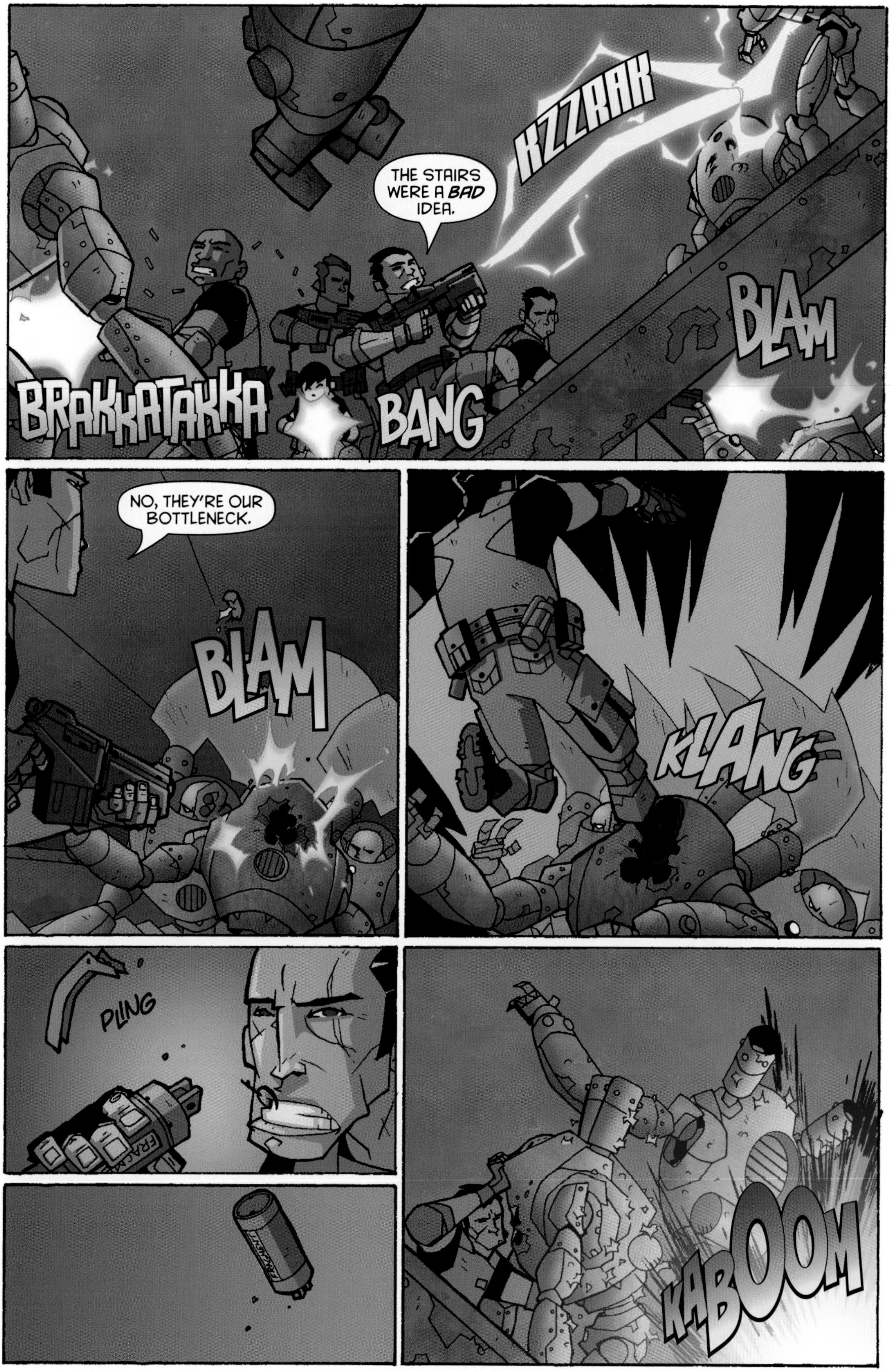
THE STAIRS WERE A *BAD* IDEA.
KZZRAK
BRAKKATAKKA
BANG
BLAM
NO, THEY'RE OUR BOTTLENECK.
BLAM
KLANG
PLING
KABOOM

KL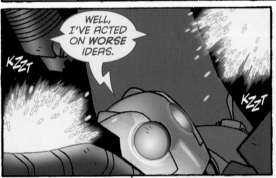

WELL, I'VE ACTED ON *WORSE* IDEAS.

KZZT

KZZT

KZZZZZZAK

ADA, DO *NOT* USE THAT LIGHTNING GUN ON MY DUDE!

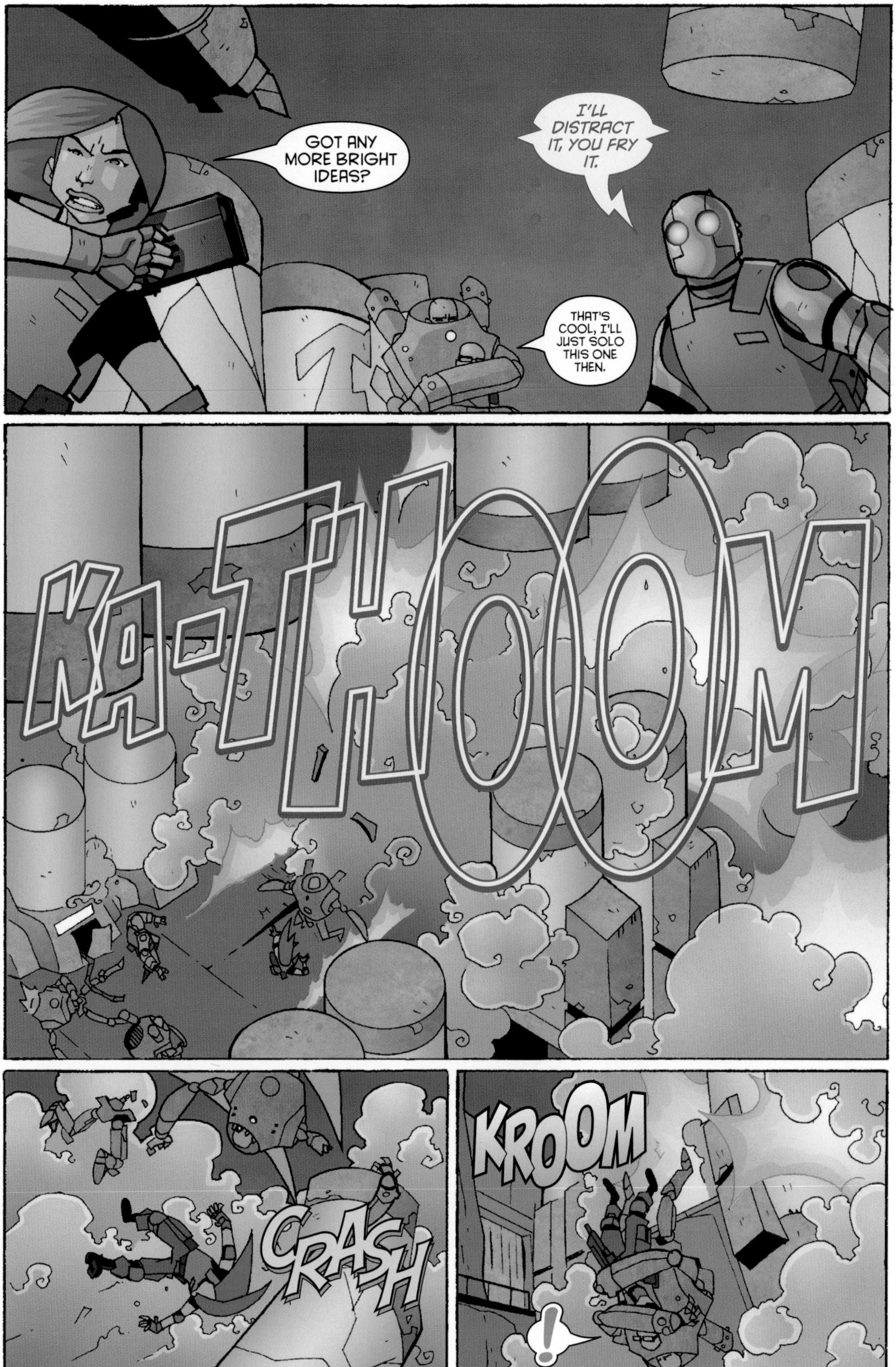

GOT ANY MORE BRIGHT IDEAS?
I'LL DISTRACT IT, YOU FRY IT.
THAT'S COOL, I'LL JUST SOLO THIS ONE THEN.
KA-THOOOM
CRASH
KROOM
!

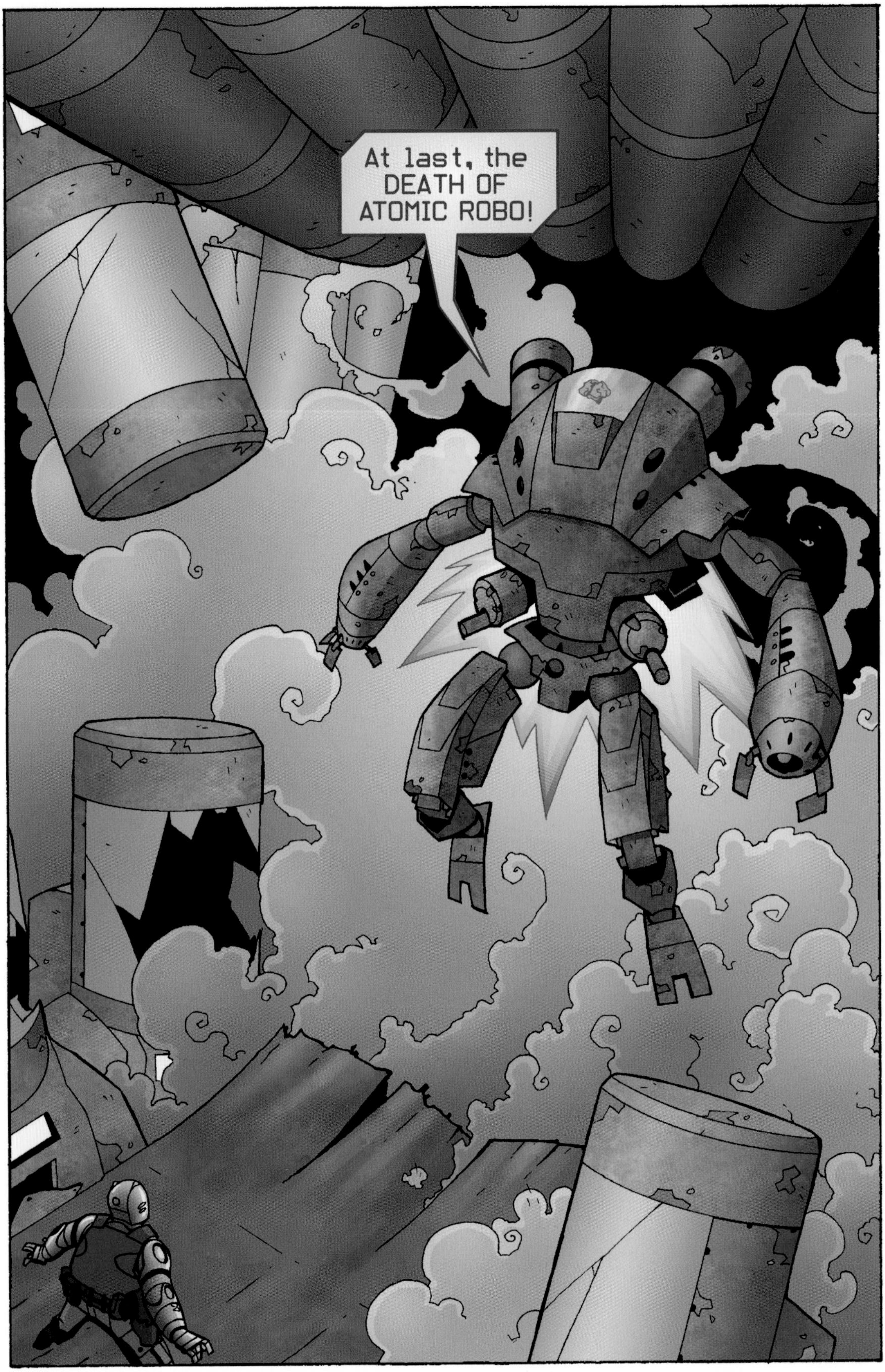
At last, the DEATH OF ATOMIC ROBO!

UNEARTHED

PART 2

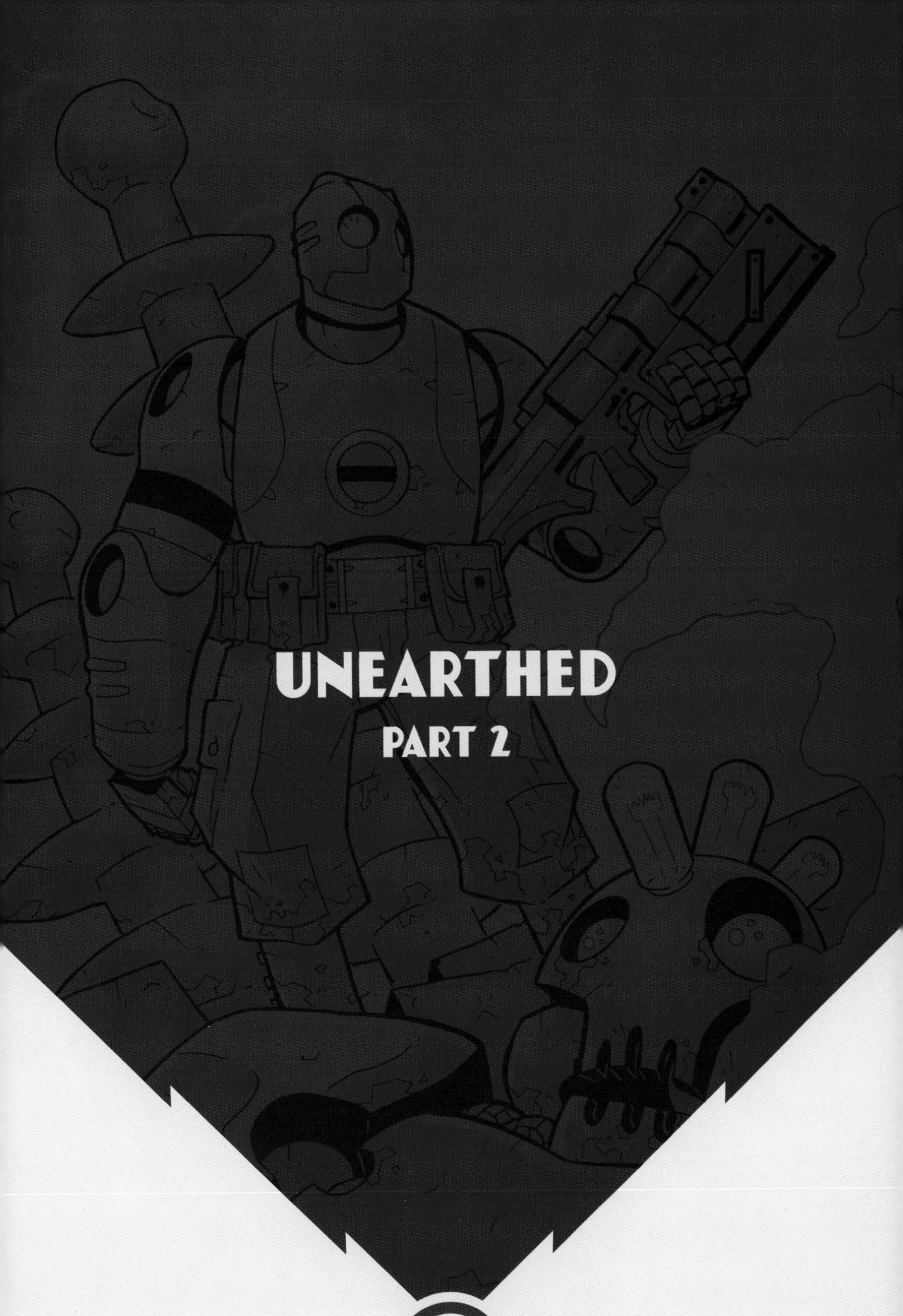

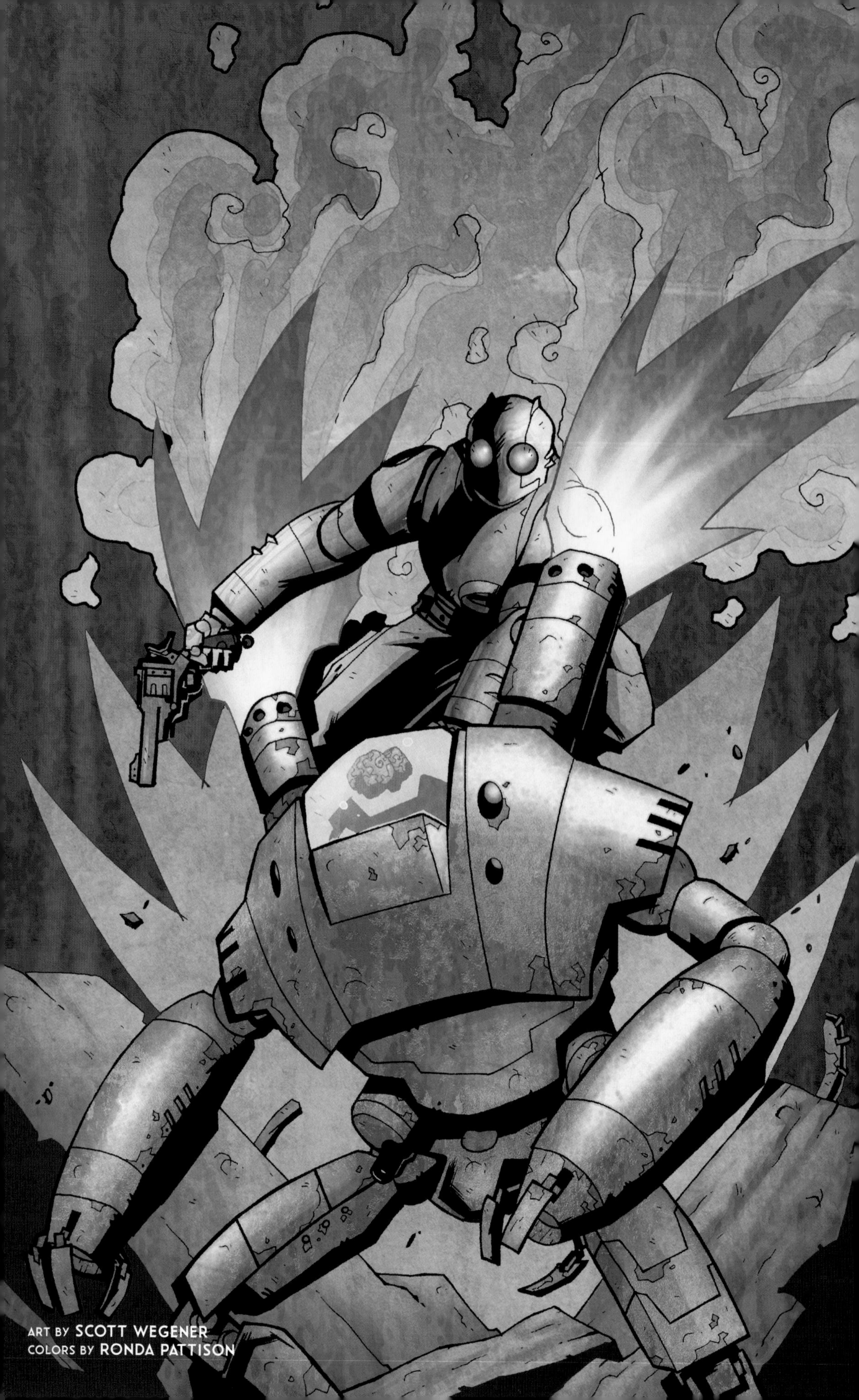
ART BY SCOTT WEGENER
COLORS BY RONDA PATTISON

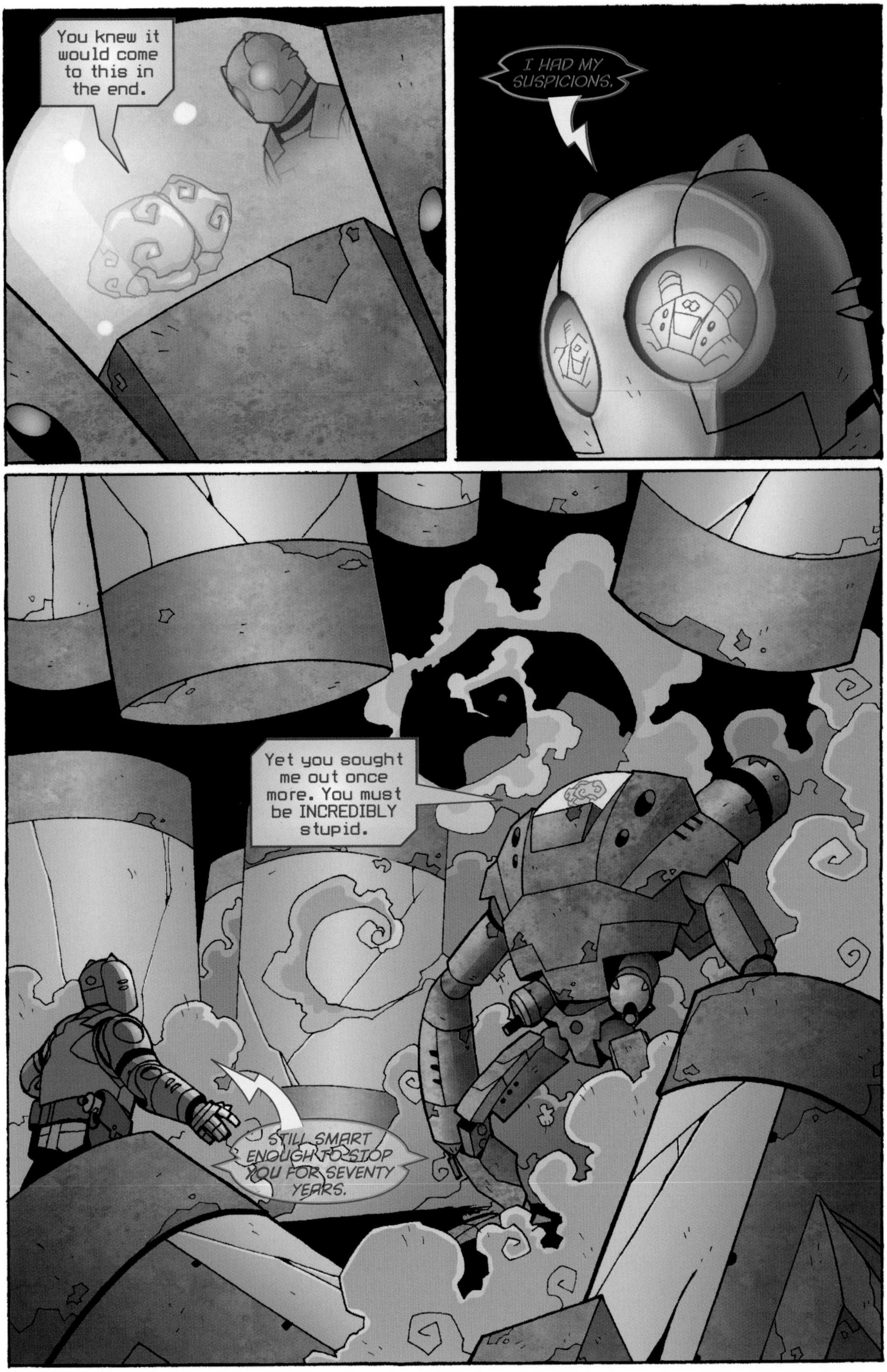
You knew it would come to this in the end.
I HAD MY SUSPICIONS.
Yet you sought me out once more. You must be INCREDIBLY stupid.
STILL SMART ENOUGH TO STOP YOU FOR SEVENTY YEARS.

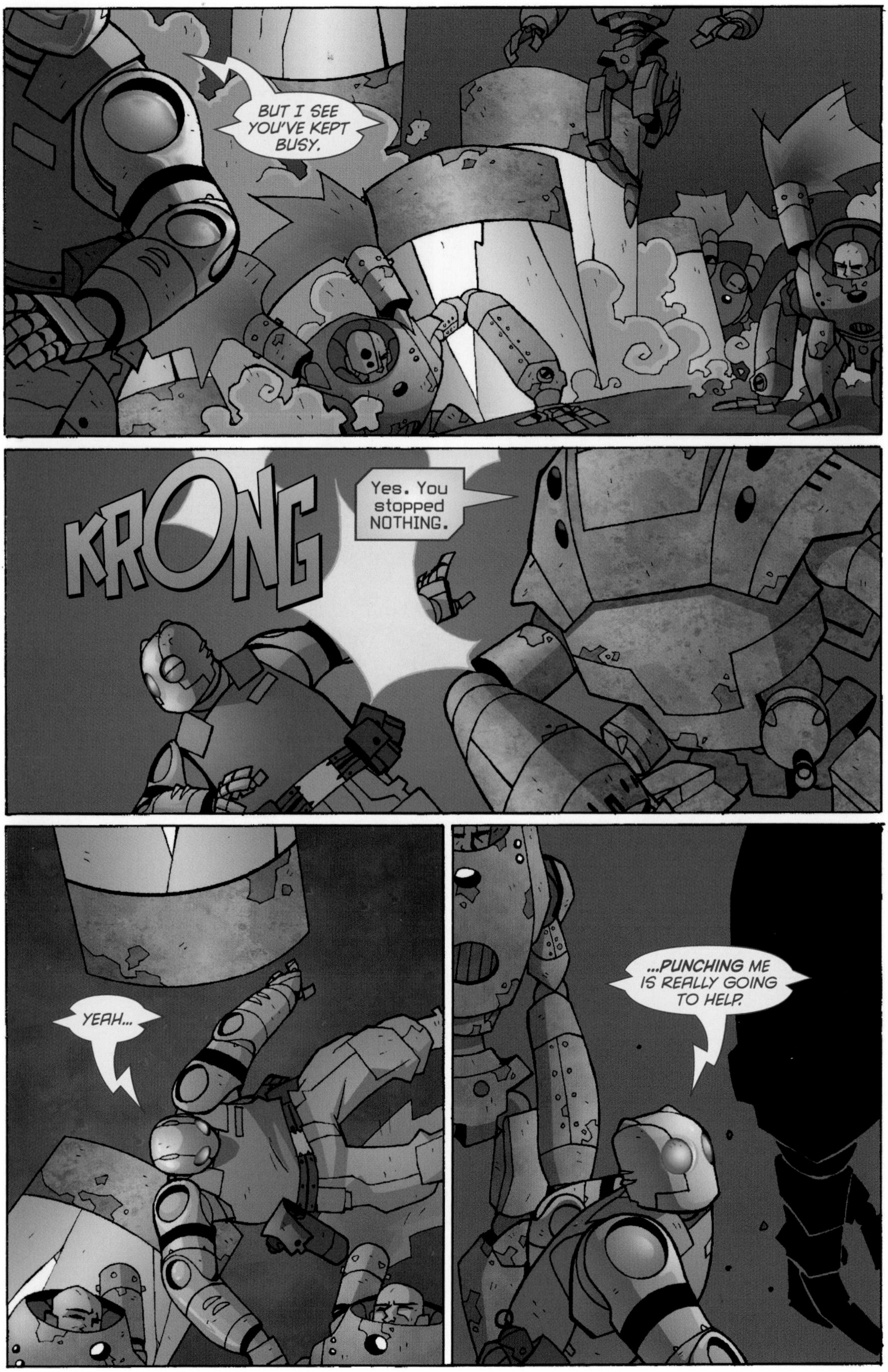
BUT I SEE YOU'VE KEPT BUSY.
KRONG
Yes. You stopped NOTHING.
YEAH...
...PUNCHING ME IS REALLY GOING TO HELP.

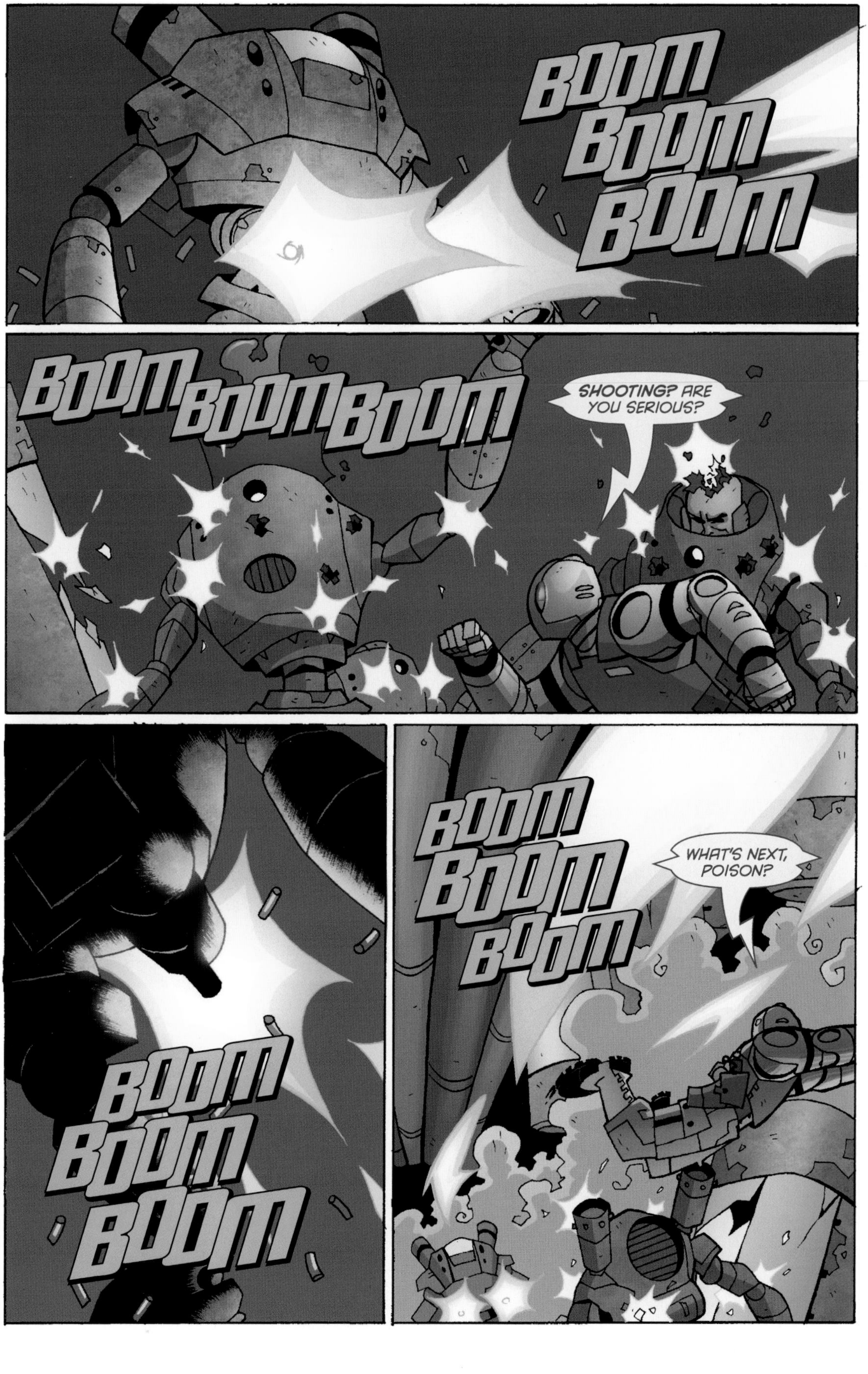
BOOM BOOM BOOM
BOOM BOOM BOOM
SHOOTING? ARE YOU SERIOUS?
BOOM BOOM BOOM
BOOM BOOM BOOM
WHAT'S NEXT, POISON?

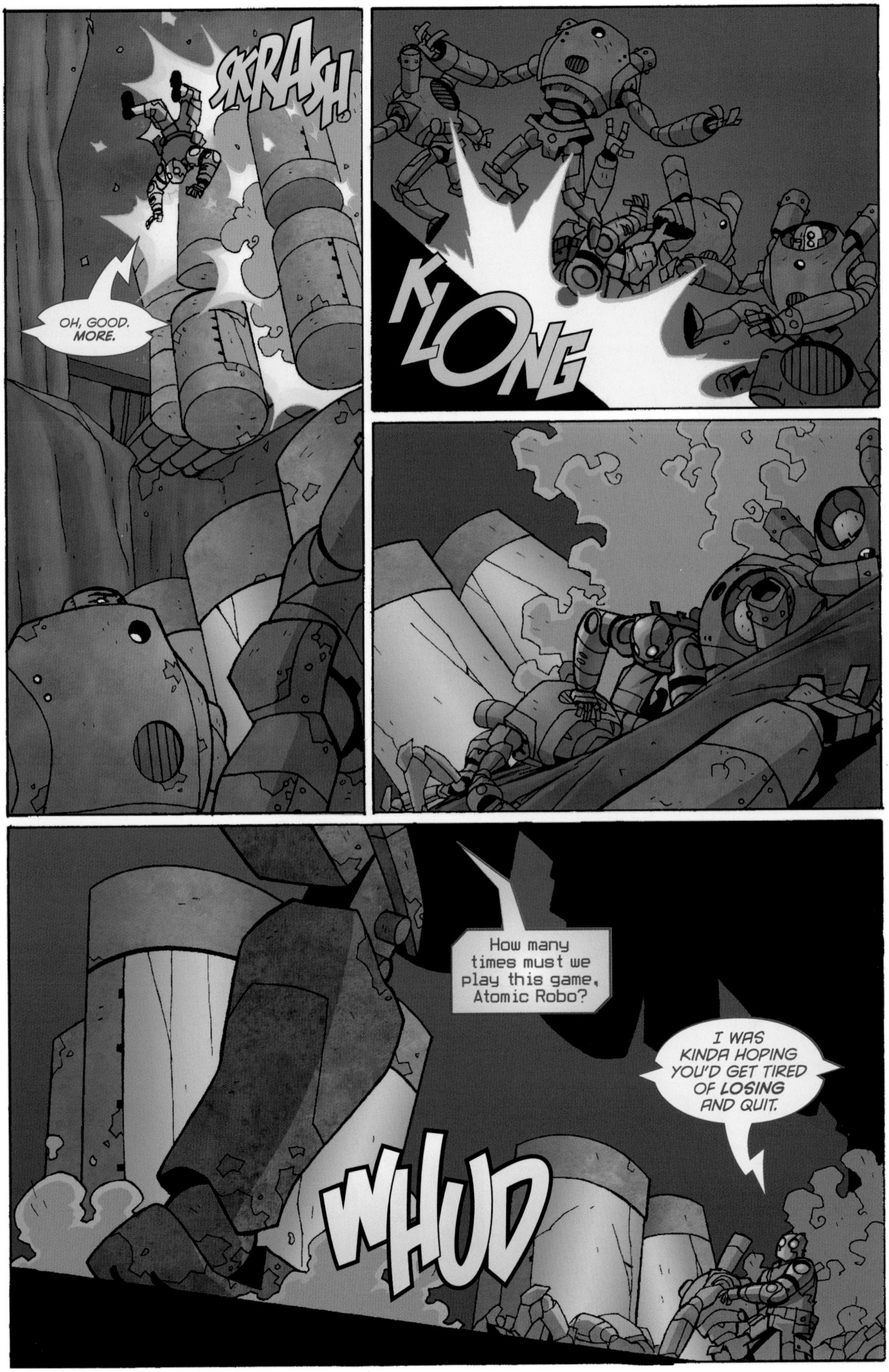
SKRASH
OH, GOOD. MORE.
KLONG
How many times must we play this game, Atomic Robo?
I WAS KINDA HOPING YOU'D GET TIRED OF **LOSING** AND QUIT.
WHUD

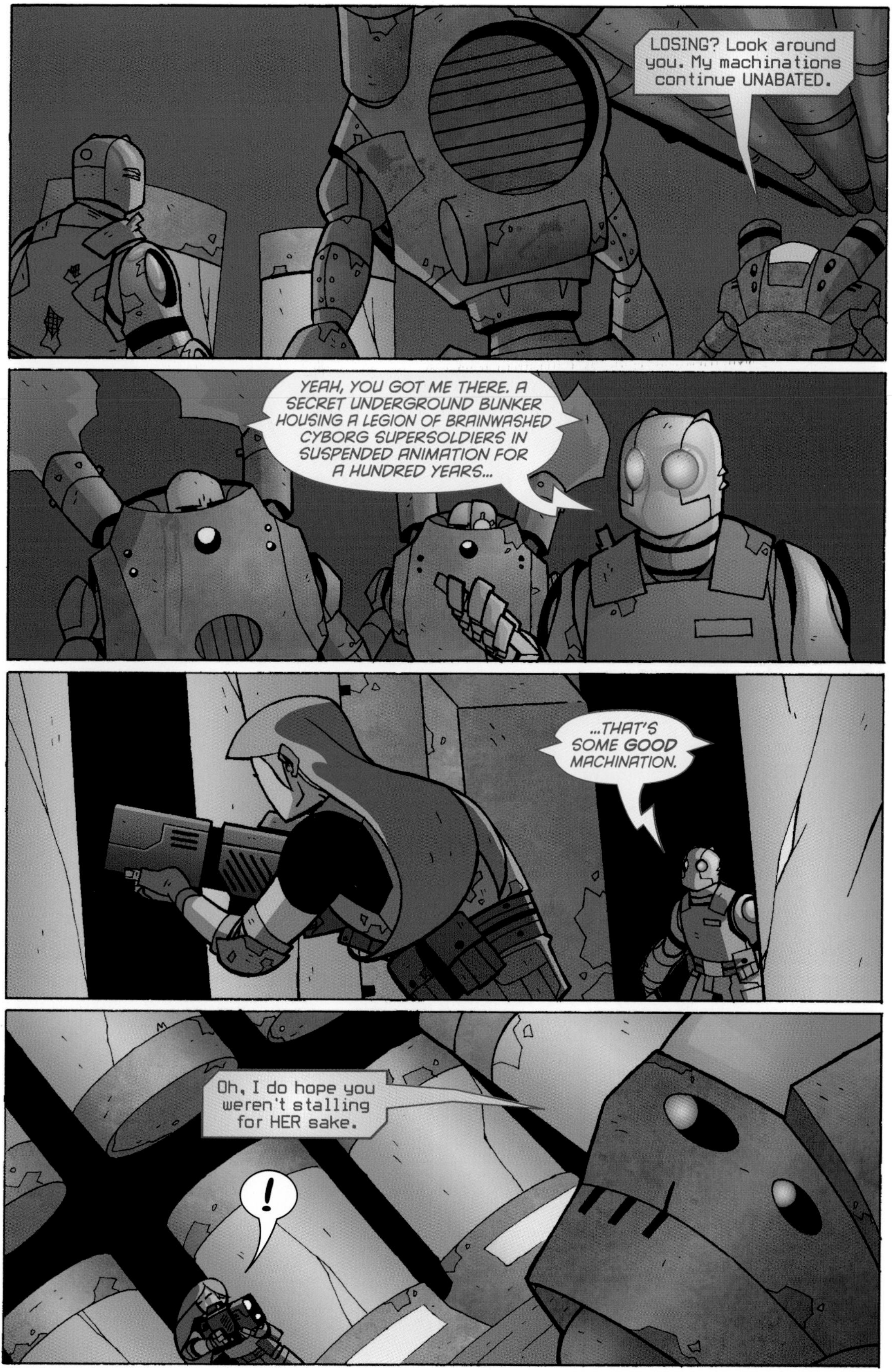
LOSING? Look around you. My machinations continue UNABATED.
YEAH, YOU GOT ME THERE. A SECRET UNDERGROUND BUNKER HOUSING A LEGION OF BRAINWASHED CYBORG SUPERSOLDIERS IN SUSPENDED ANIMATION FOR A HUNDRED YEARS...
...THAT'S SOME GOOD MACHINATION.
Oh, I do hope you weren't stalling for HER sake.
!

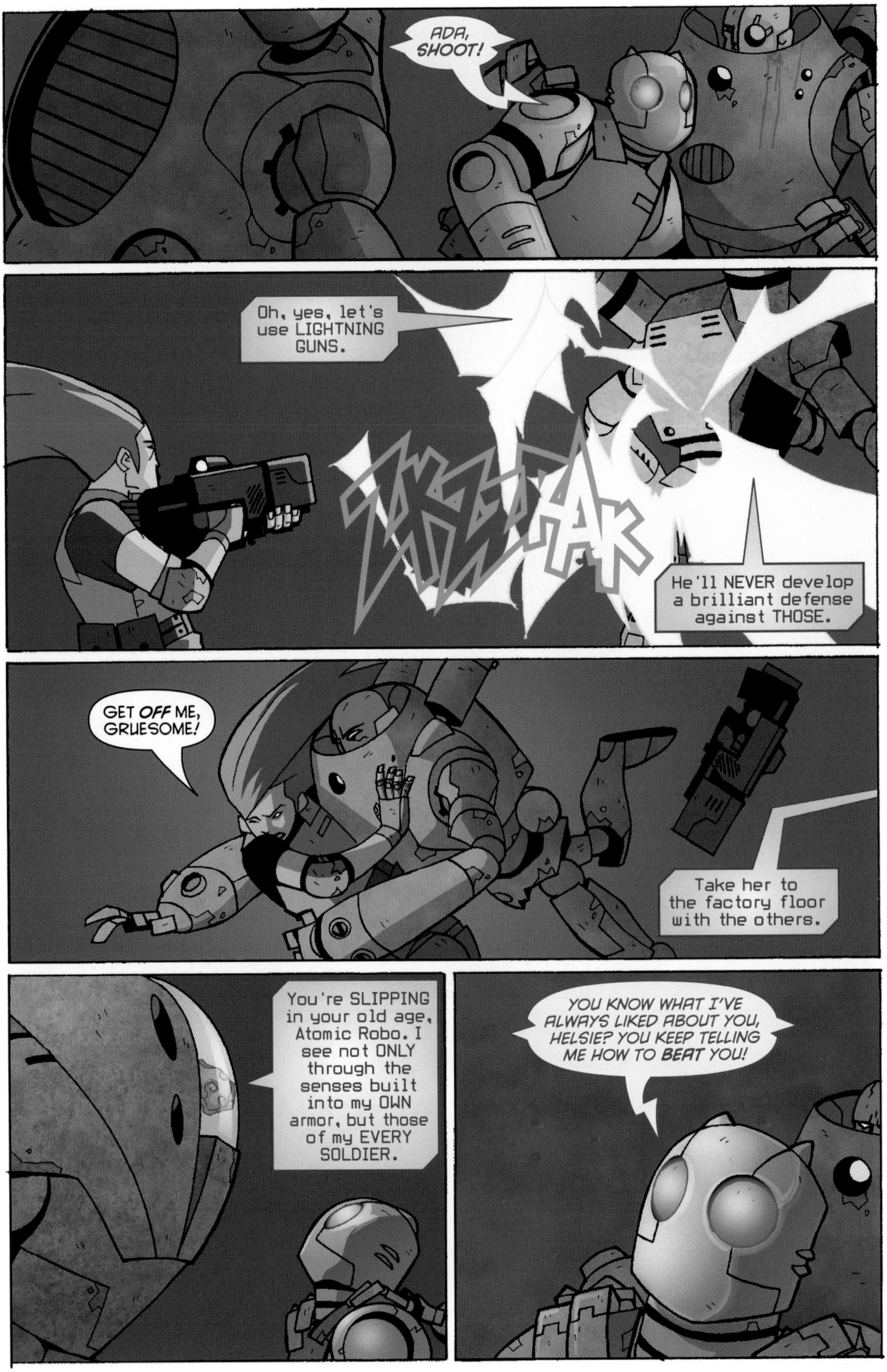
ADA, SHOOT!
Oh, yes, let's use LIGHTNING GUNS.
ZKZZZTAK
He'll NEVER develop a brilliant defense against THOSE.
GET OFF ME, GRUESOME!
Take her to the factory floor with the others.
You're SLIPPING in your old age, Atomic Robo. I see not ONLY through the senses built into my OWN armor, but those of my EVERY SOLDIER.
YOU KNOW WHAT I'VE ALWAYS LIKED ABOUT YOU, HELSIE? YOU KEEP TELLING ME HOW TO BEAT YOU!

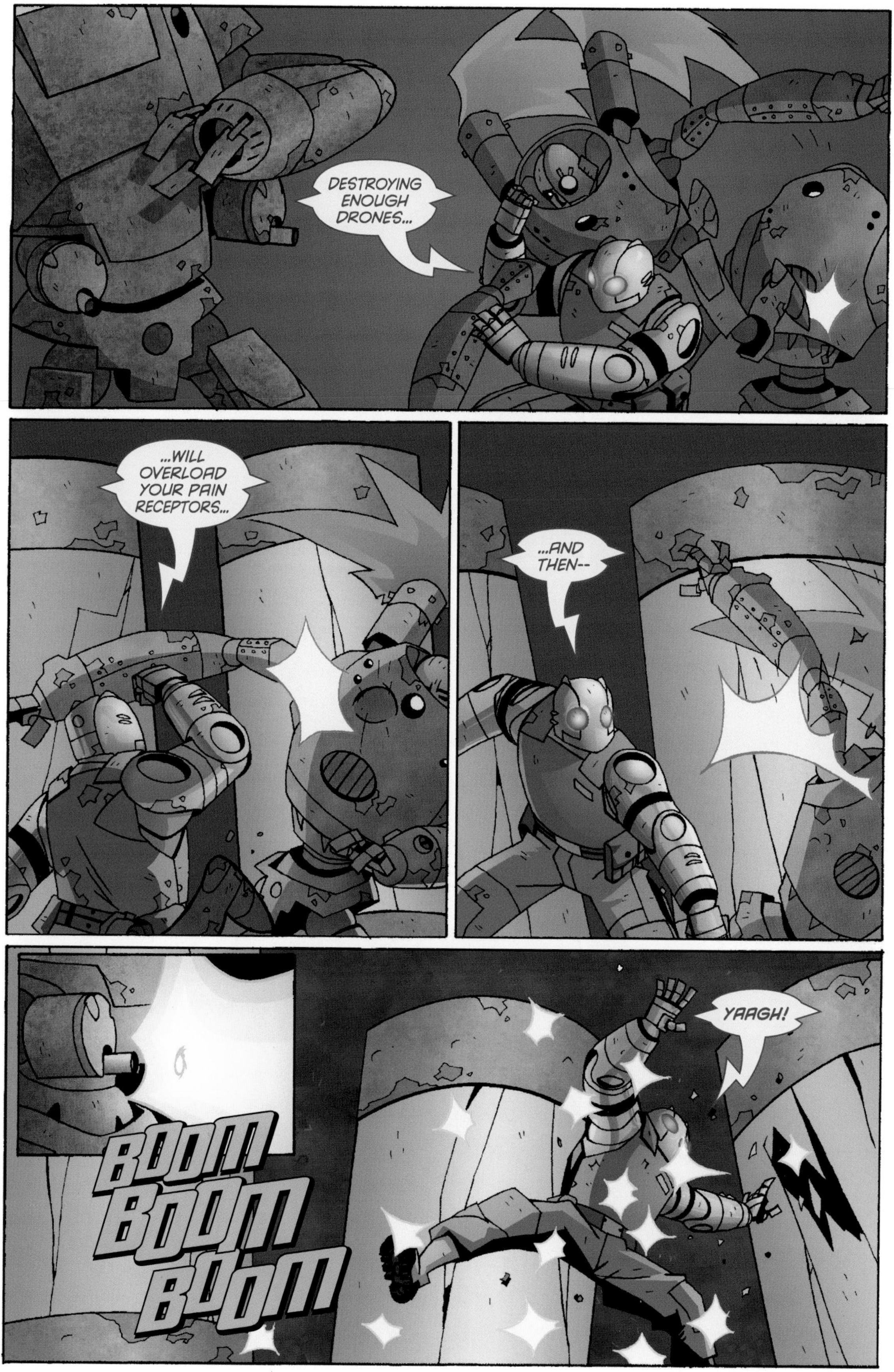
DESTROYING ENOUGH DRONES...
...WILL OVERLOAD YOUR PAIN RECEPTORS...
...AND THEN--
BOOM BOOM BOOM
YAAGH!

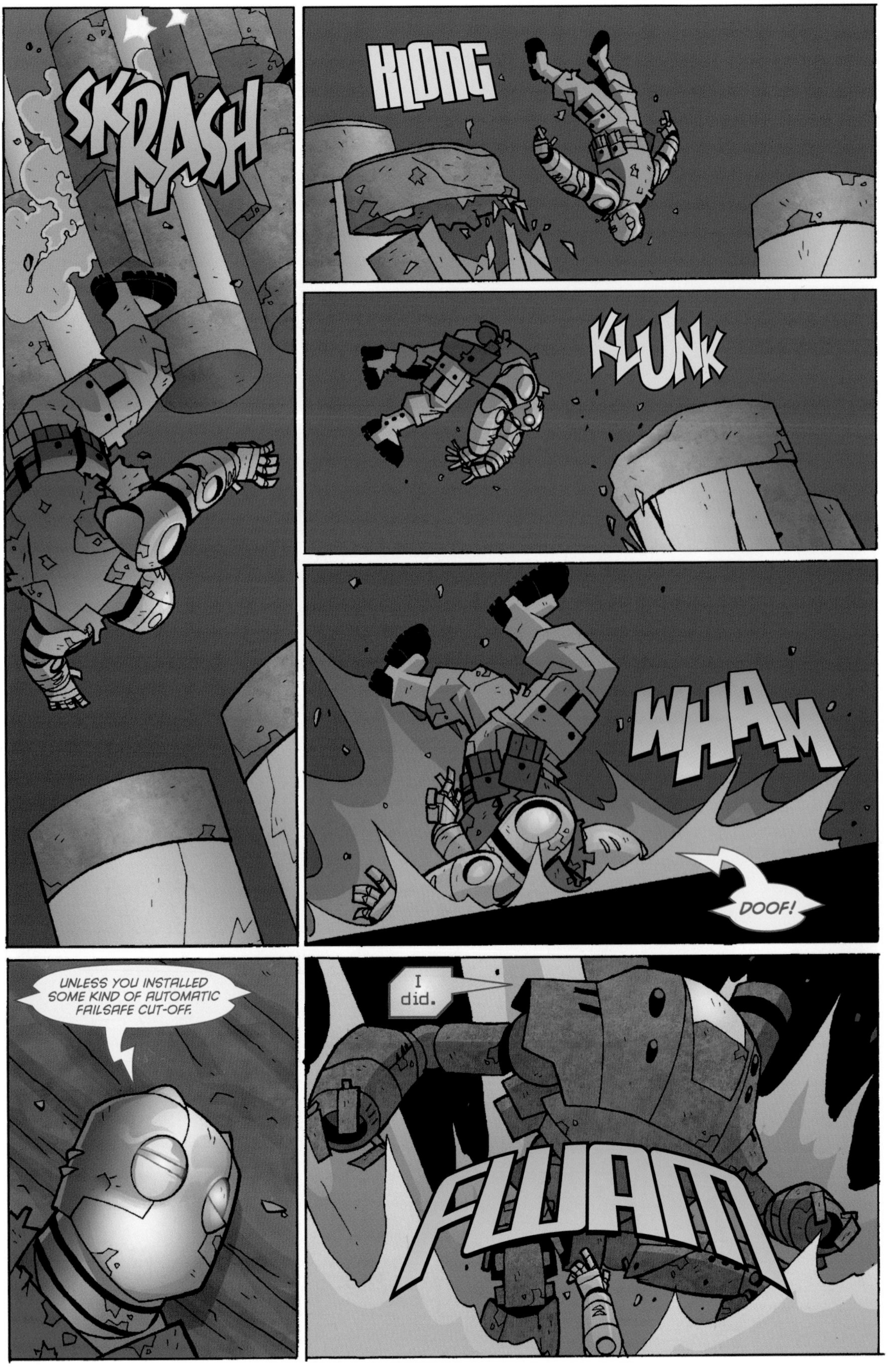
SKRASH
KLONG
KLUNK
WHAM
DOOF!
UNLESS YOU INSTALLED SOME KIND OF AUTOMATIC FAILSAFE CUT-OFF.
I did.
FWAM

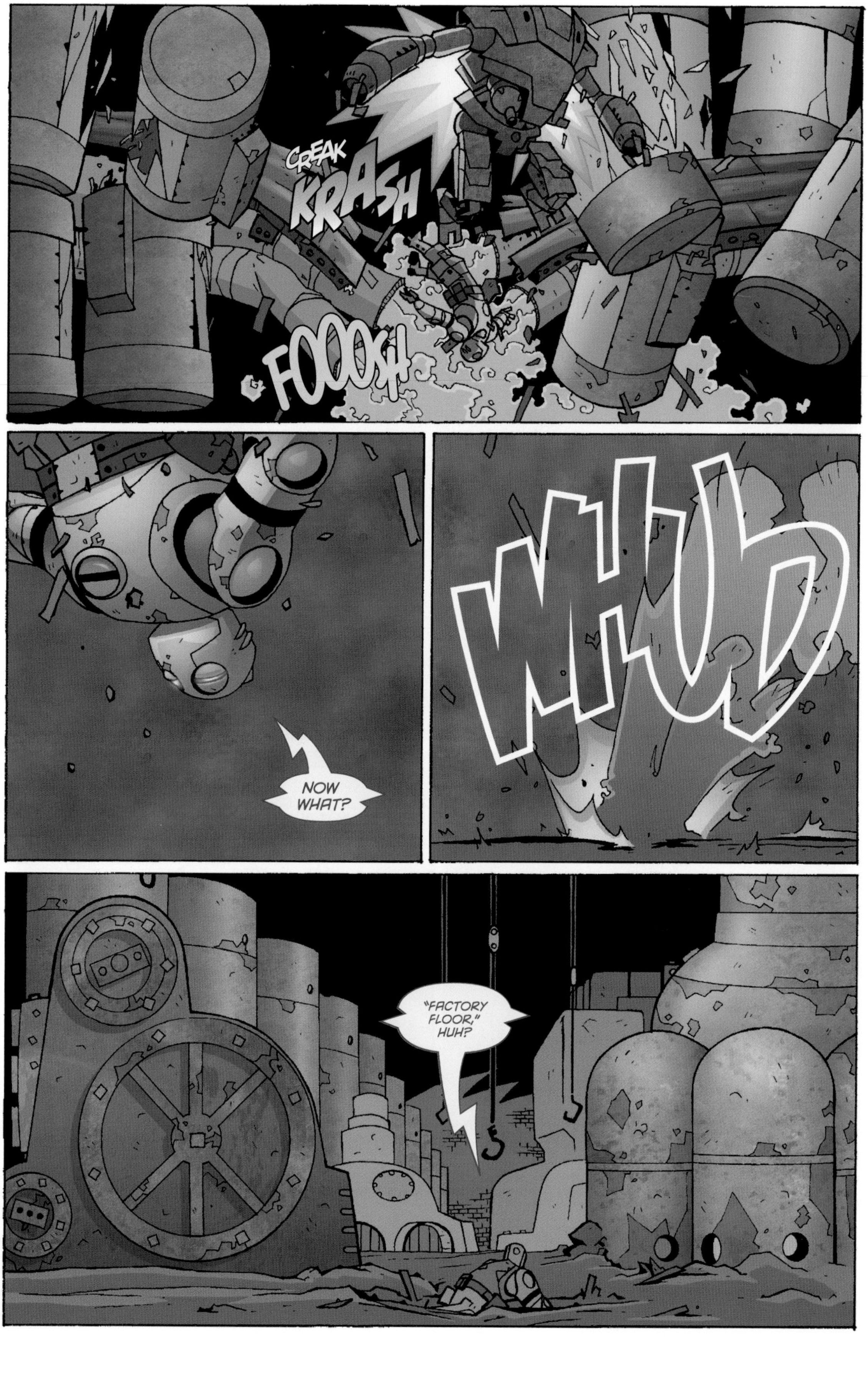
CREAK
KRASH
FOOOSH
NOW WHAT?
WHUD
"FACTORY FLOOR," HUH?

I had thought the last half century of FAILING to stop me would have taught you the meaning of futility. Perhaps removing your power core will ENLIGHTEN you on the subject in your final moments of electromatic consciousness.

GOOD LUCK WITH THAT.

KLANG

You are of course joking.

CRASH

NOPE.

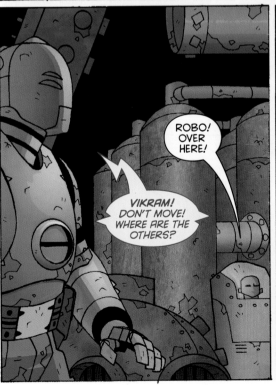

ROBO! OVER HERE!

VIKRAM! DON'T MOVE! WHERE ARE THE OTHERS?

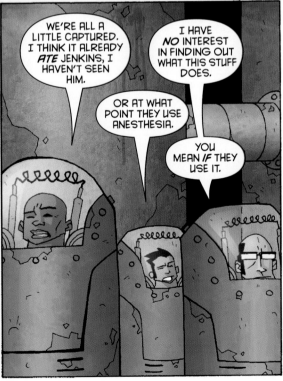

WE'RE ALL A LITTLE CAPTURED. I THINK IT ALREADY *ATE* JENKINS, I HAVEN'T SEEN HIM.

I HAVE *NO* INTEREST IN FINDING OUT WHAT THIS STUFF DOES.

OR AT WHAT POINT THEY USE ANESTHESIA.

YOU MEAN *IF* THEY USE IT.

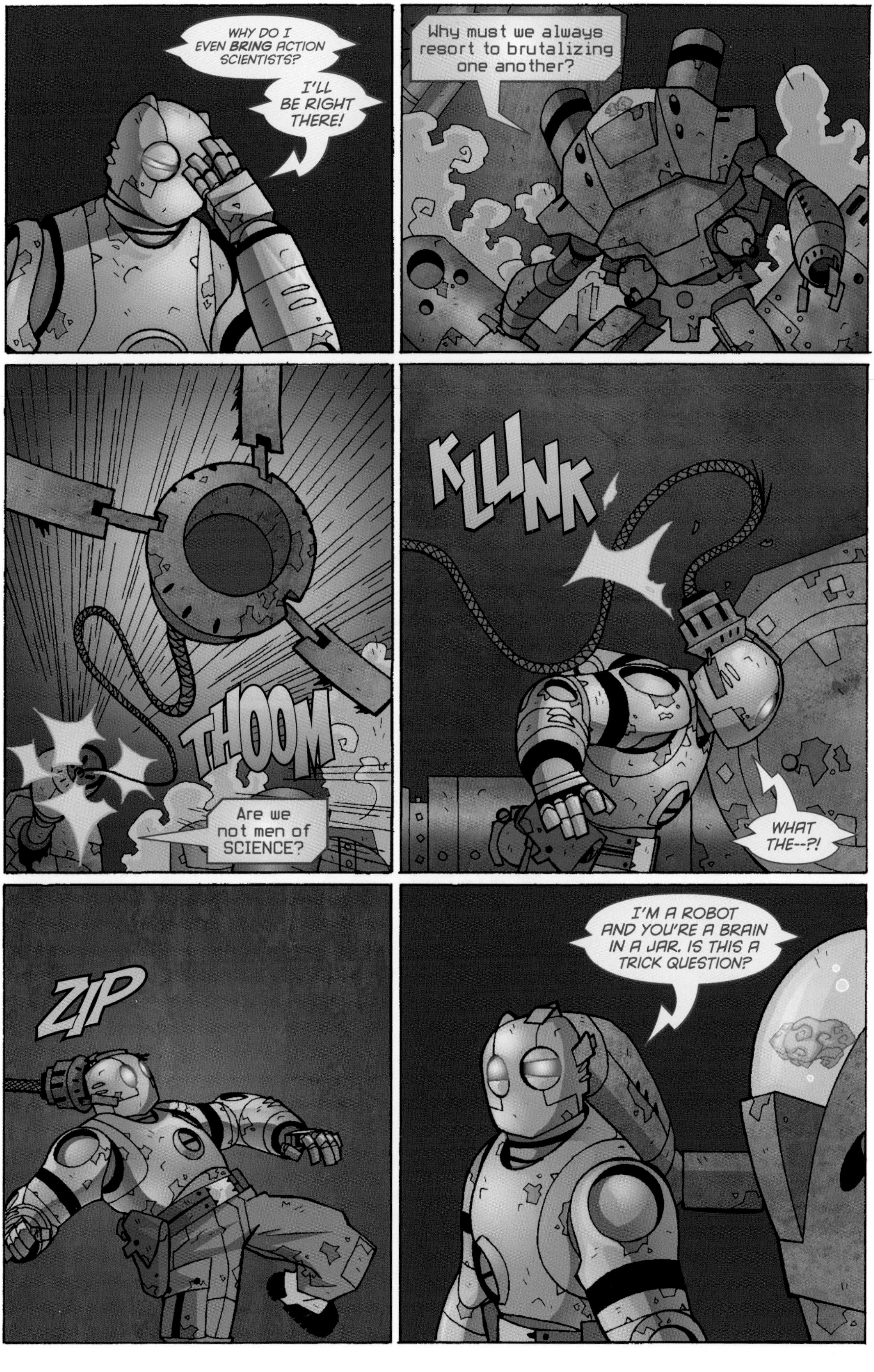
WHY DO I EVEN BRING ACTION SCIENTISTS?
I'LL BE RIGHT THERE!
Why must we always resort to brutalizing one another?
THOOM
Are we not men of SCIENCE?
KLUNK
WHAT THE--?!
ZIP
I'M A ROBOT AND YOU'RE A BRAIN IN A JAR. IS THIS A TRICK QUESTION?

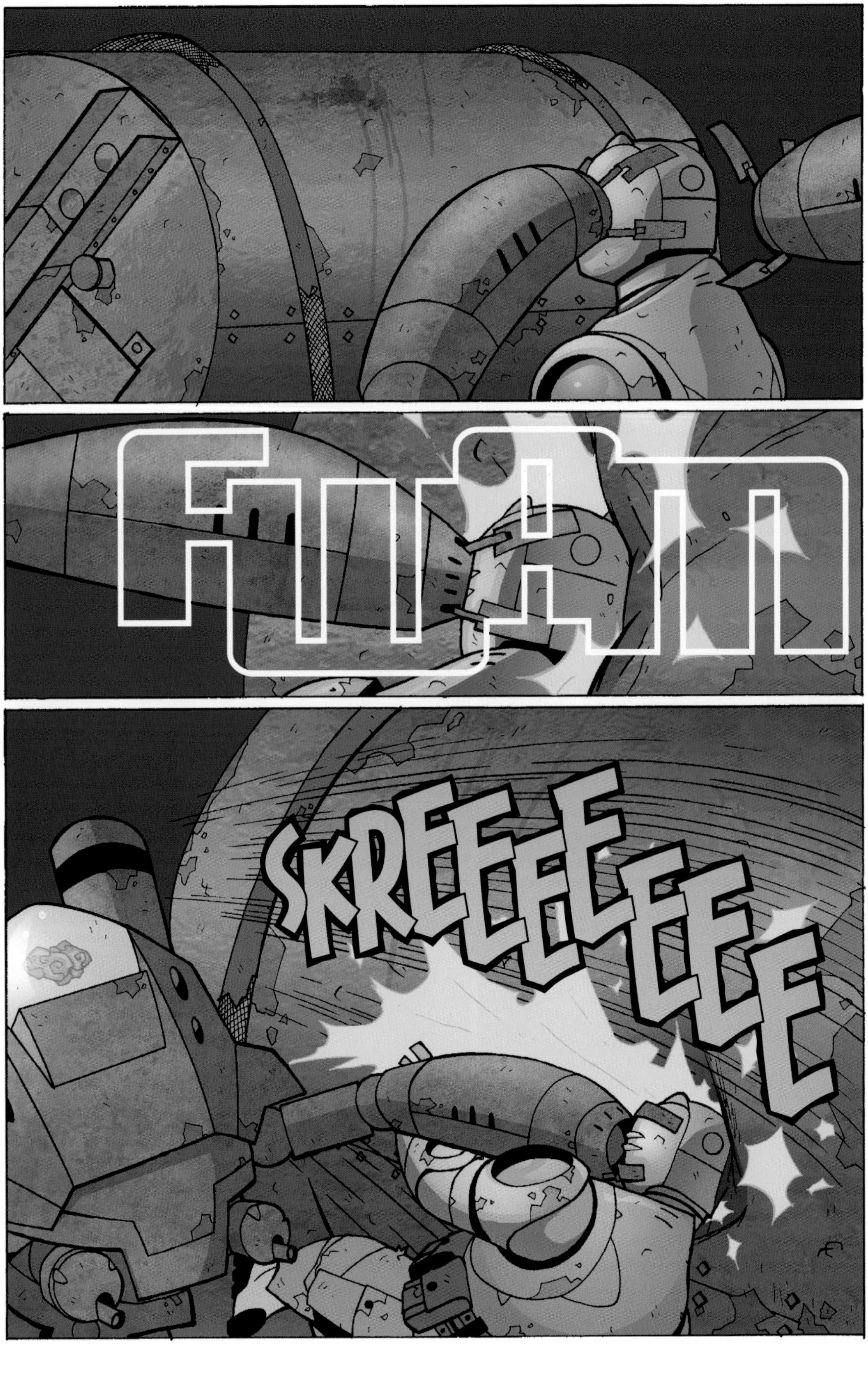
SKREEEEEEE

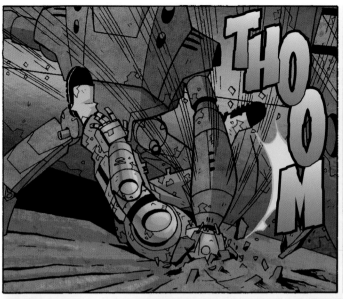

THO OOM

MY FLIPPANT REPLIES ARE SUPPOSED TO TRICK YOU INTO MAKING A MISTAKE, NOT TRICK YOU INTO BEATING ME SENSELESS.

And I was supposed to ascend to a state of GODHOOD over the nations of man!

OH, NOT THIS AGAIN.

LOOK, IF YOU WEREN'T SUCH AN EVIL MANIAC, I WOULDN'T HAVE DESTROYED YOUR BODY!

KLANK

You denied me the UNLIMITED power of the vril...

...but one does not enter into a gambit for world domination without taking precautions for EVERY contingency.

KLUD

AUGH!

And so your intervention in the Himalayas did little more than delay my INEVITABLE victory.

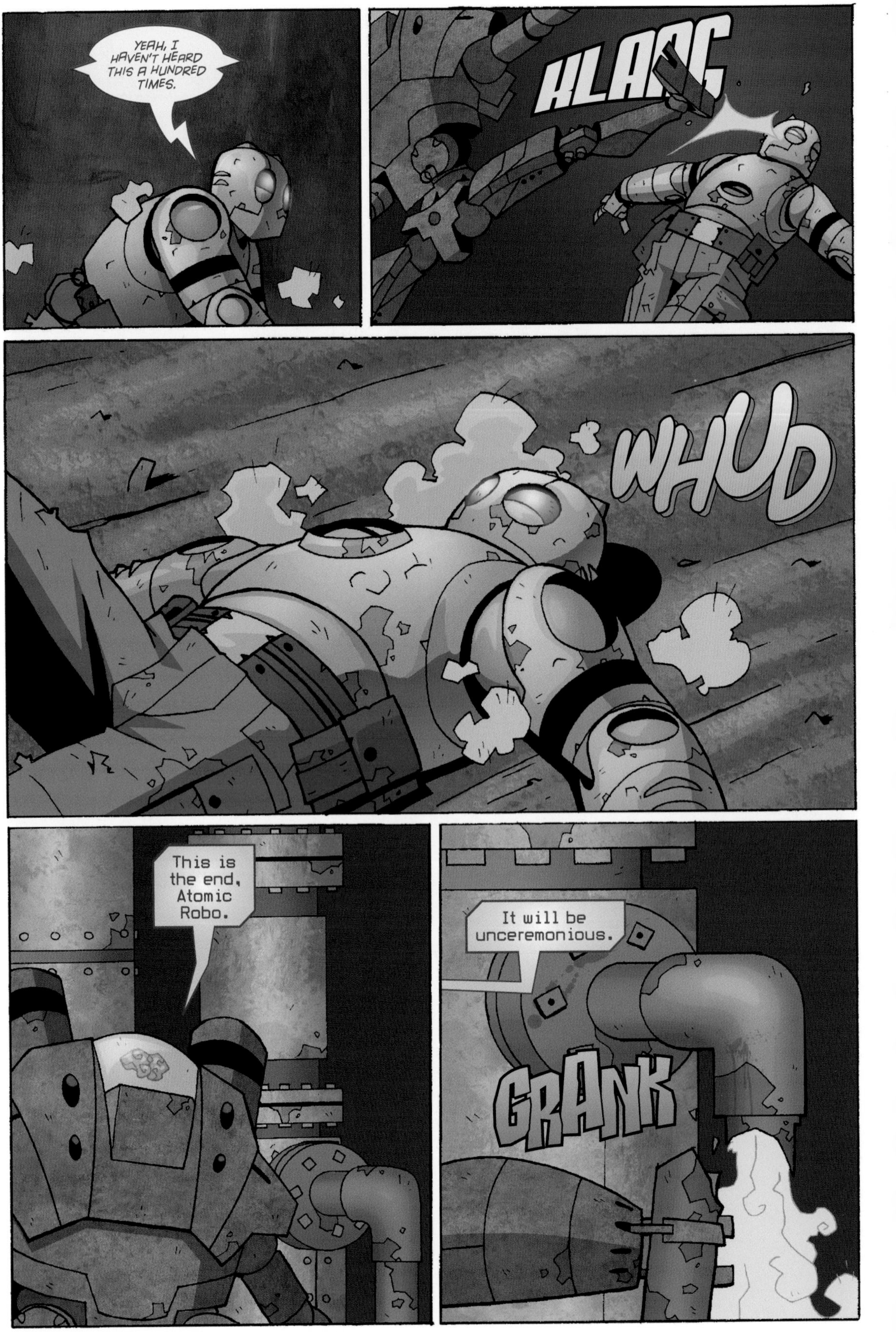
YEAH, I HAVEN'T HEARD THIS A HUNDRED TIMES.
KLANG
WHUD
This is the end, Atomic Robo.
It will be unceremonious.
GRANK

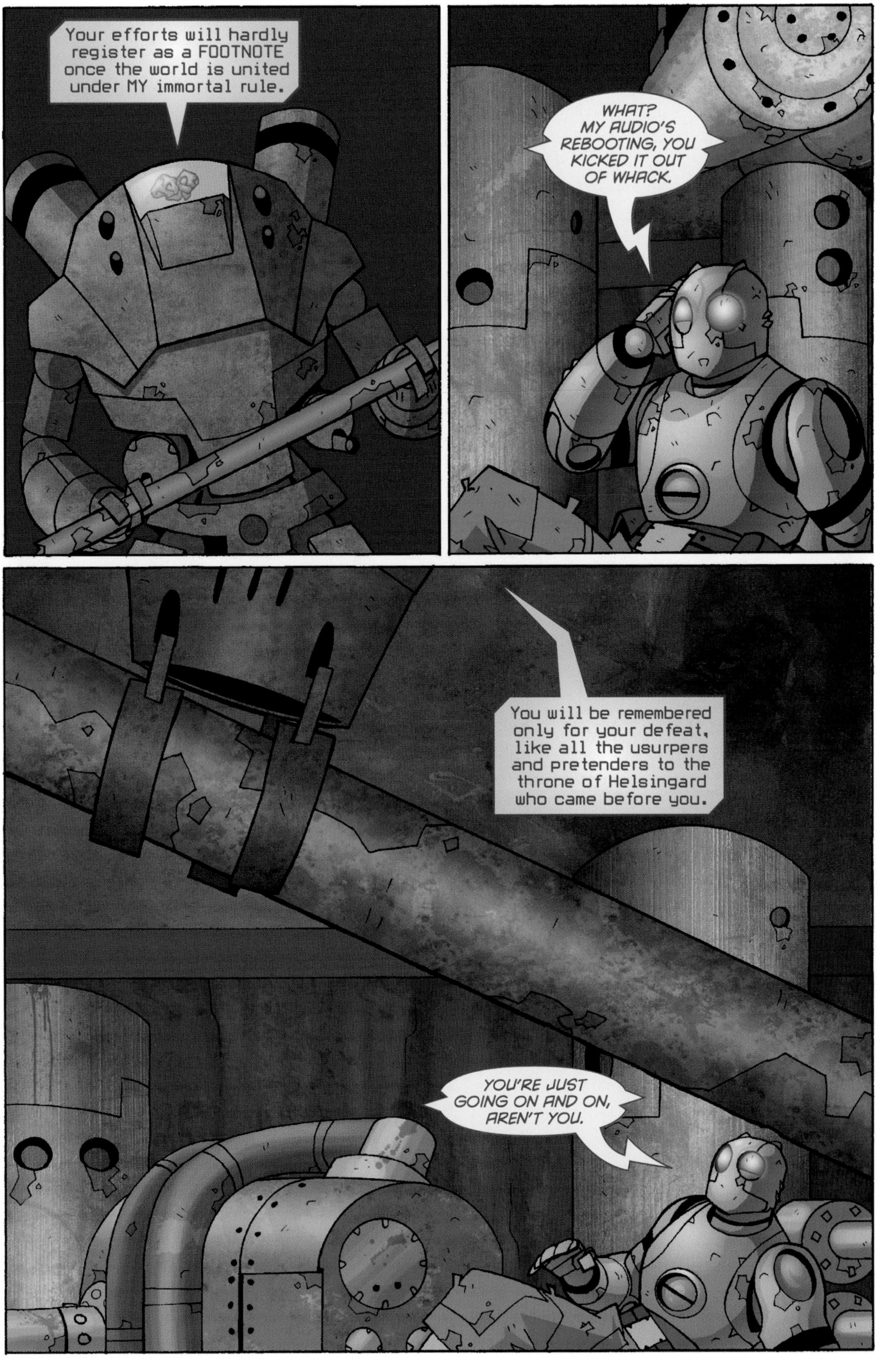
Your efforts will hardly register as a FOOTNOTE once the world is united under MY immortal rule.
WHAT? MY AUDIO'S REBOOTING, YOU KICKED IT OUT OF WHACK.
You will be remembered only for your defeat, like all the usurpers and pretenders to the throne of Helsingard who came before you.
YOU'RE JUST GOING ON AND ON, AREN'T YOU.

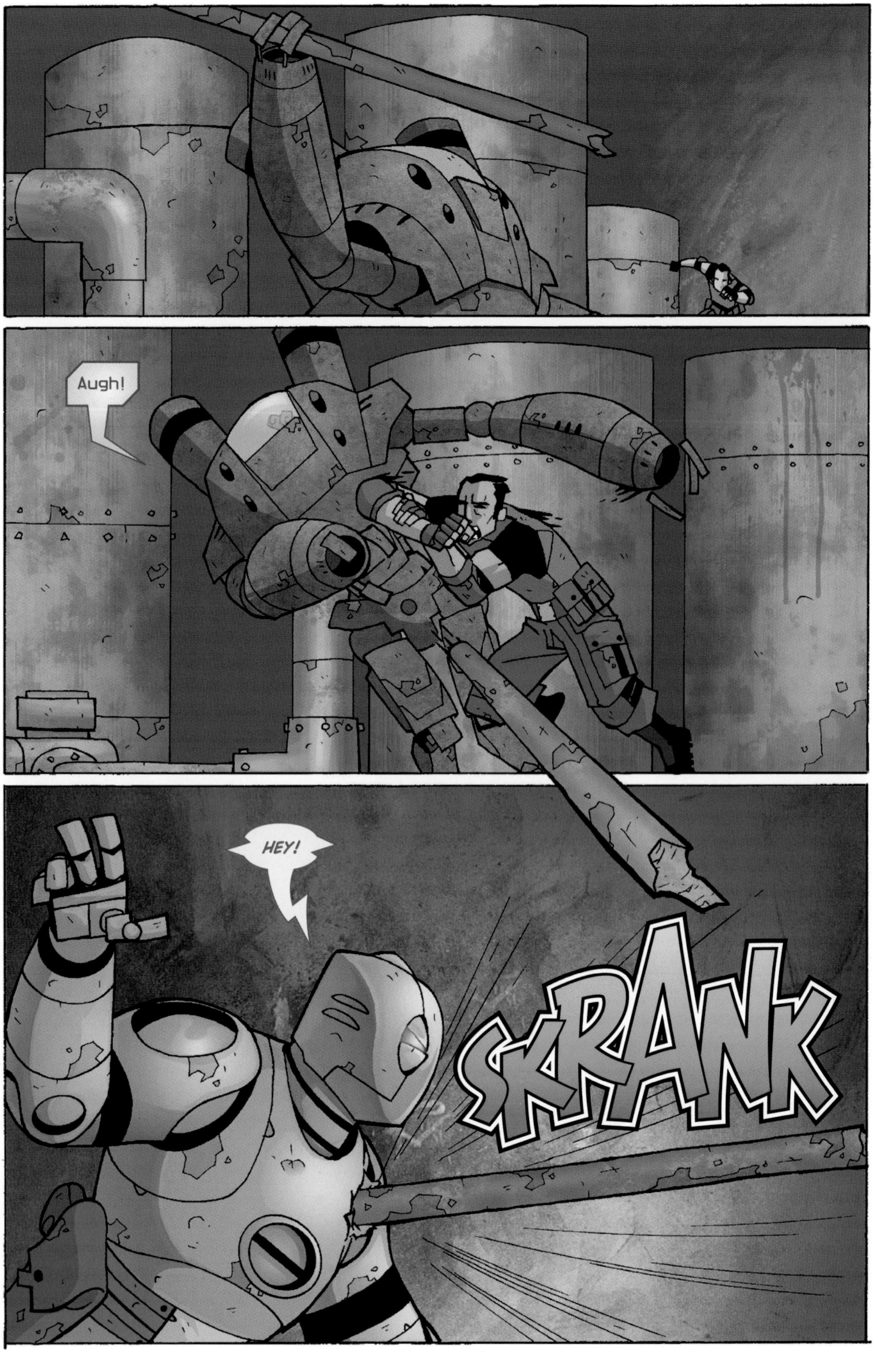
Augh!
HEY!
SKRANK

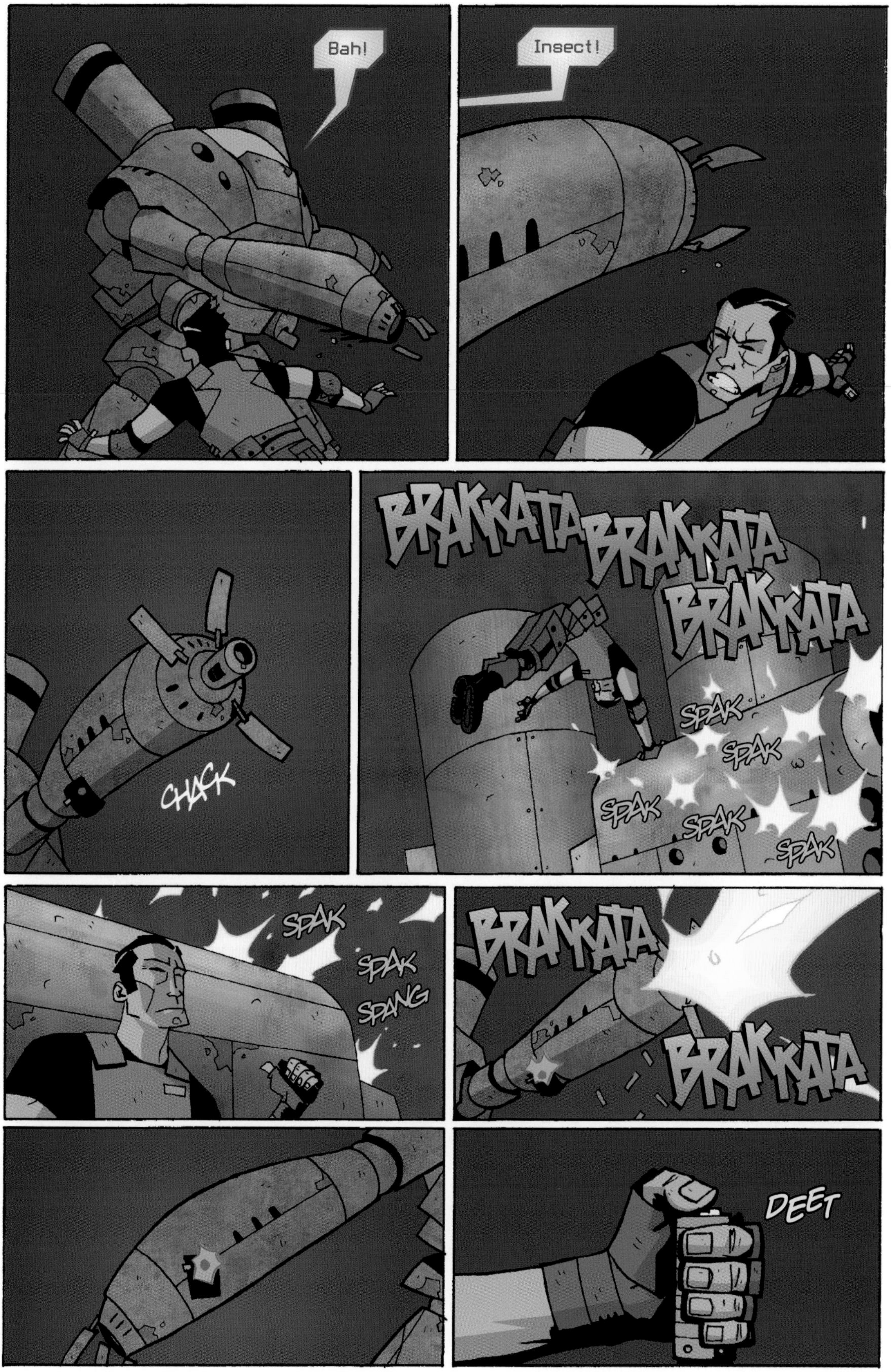
Bah!
Insect!
CHACK
BRAKKATA
BRAKKATA
BRAKKATA
SPAK
SPAK
SPAK
SPAK
SPAK
SPAK
SPAK
SPANG
BRAKKATA
BRAKKATA
DEET

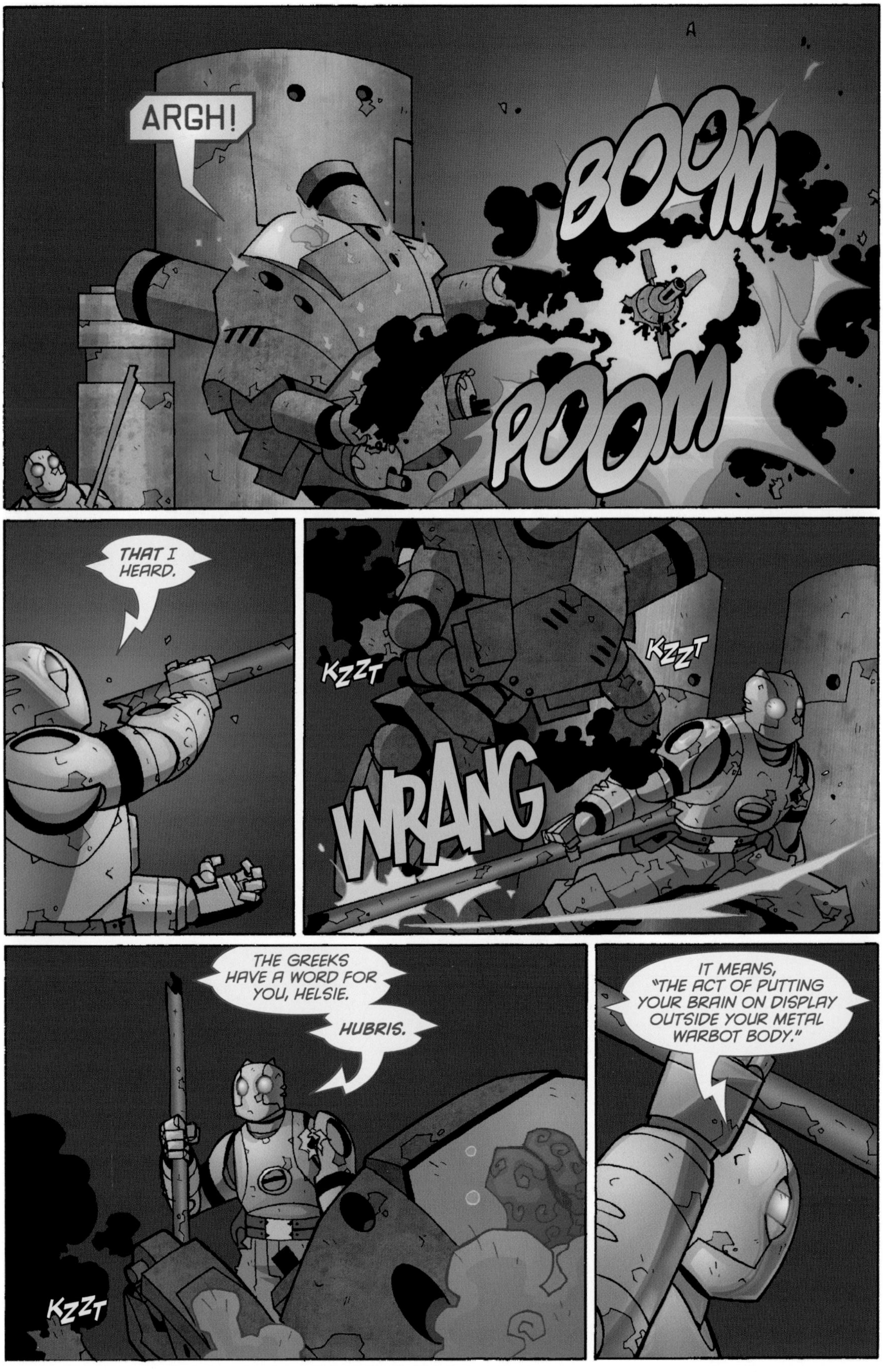
ARGH!
BOOM
POOM
THAT I HEARD.
KZZT
KZZT
WRANG
THE GREEKS HAVE A WORD FOR YOU, HELSIE.
HUBRIS.
KZZT
IT MEANS, "THE ACT OF PUTTING YOUR BRAIN ON DISPLAY OUTSIDE YOUR METAL WARBOT BODY."

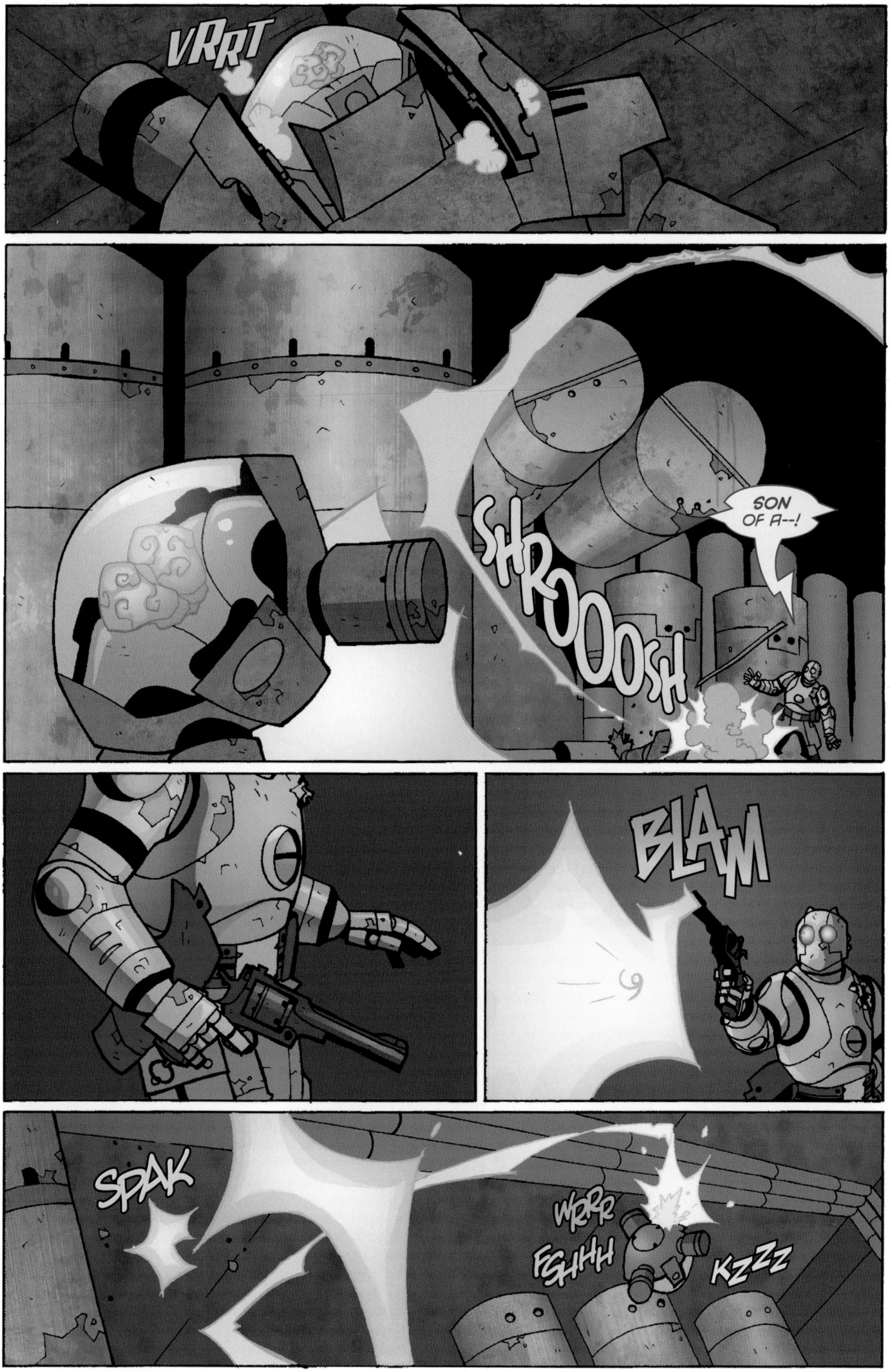
VRRT
SHROOOOSH
SON OF A--!
BLAM
SPAK
WRRR
FSHHH
KZZZ

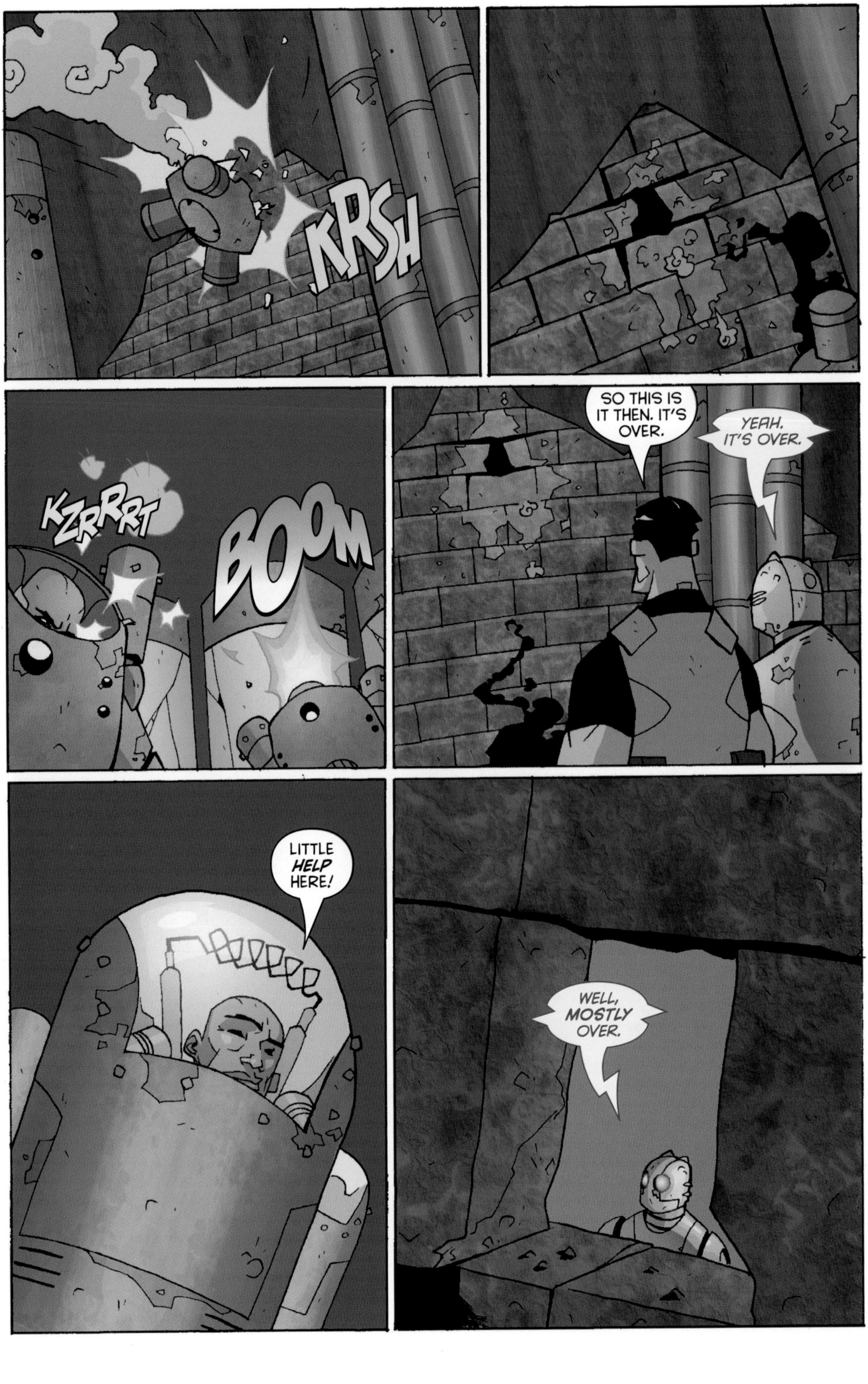
KRSH
KZRRRT
BOOM
SO THIS IS IT THEN. IT'S OVER.
YEAH. IT'S OVER.
LITTLE HELP HERE!
WELL, MOSTLY OVER.

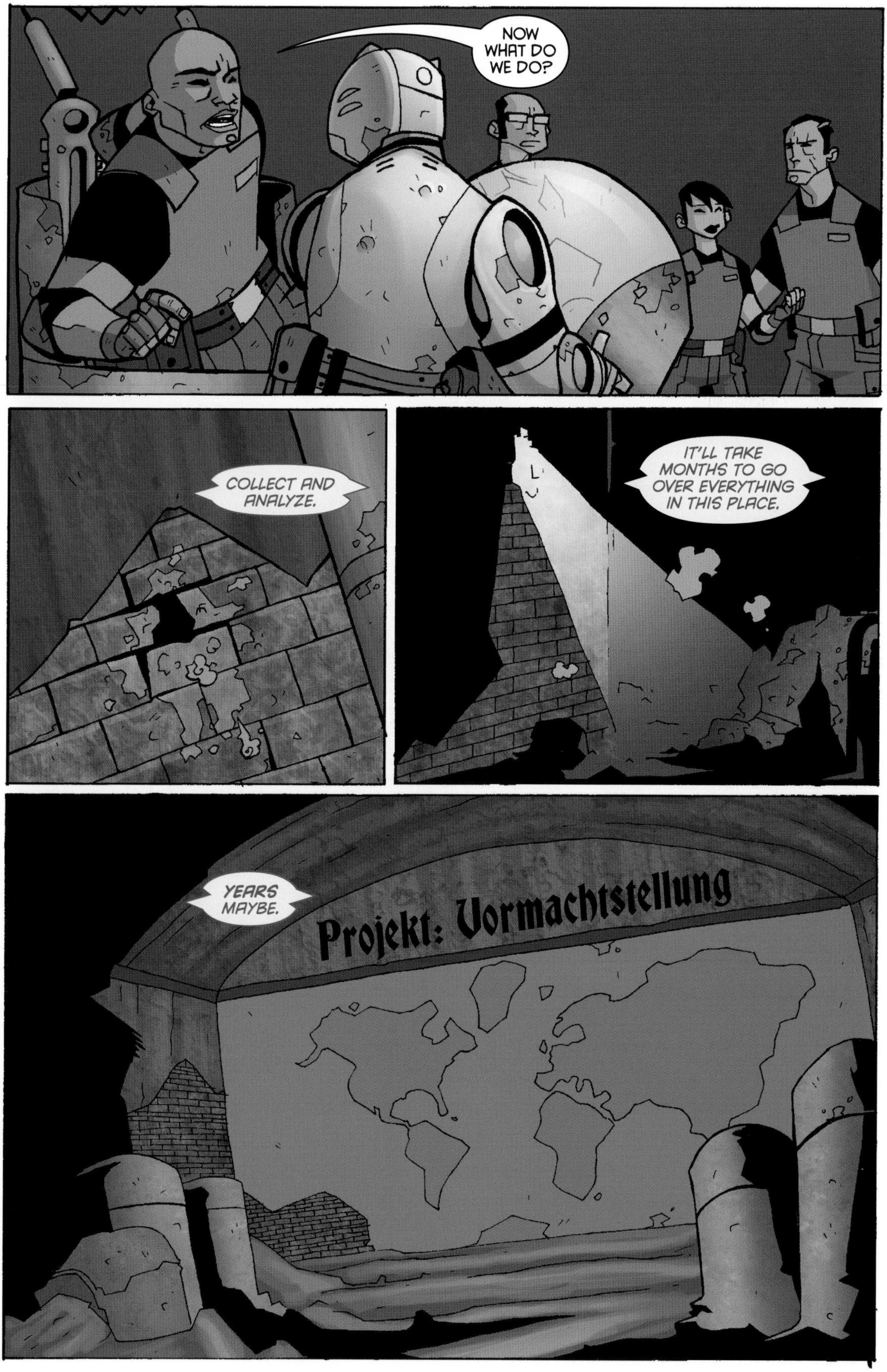
NOW WHAT DO WE DO?
COLLECT AND ANALYZE.
IT'LL TAKE MONTHS TO GO OVER EVERYTHING IN THIS PLACE.
YEARS MAYBE.
Projekt: Vormachtstellung

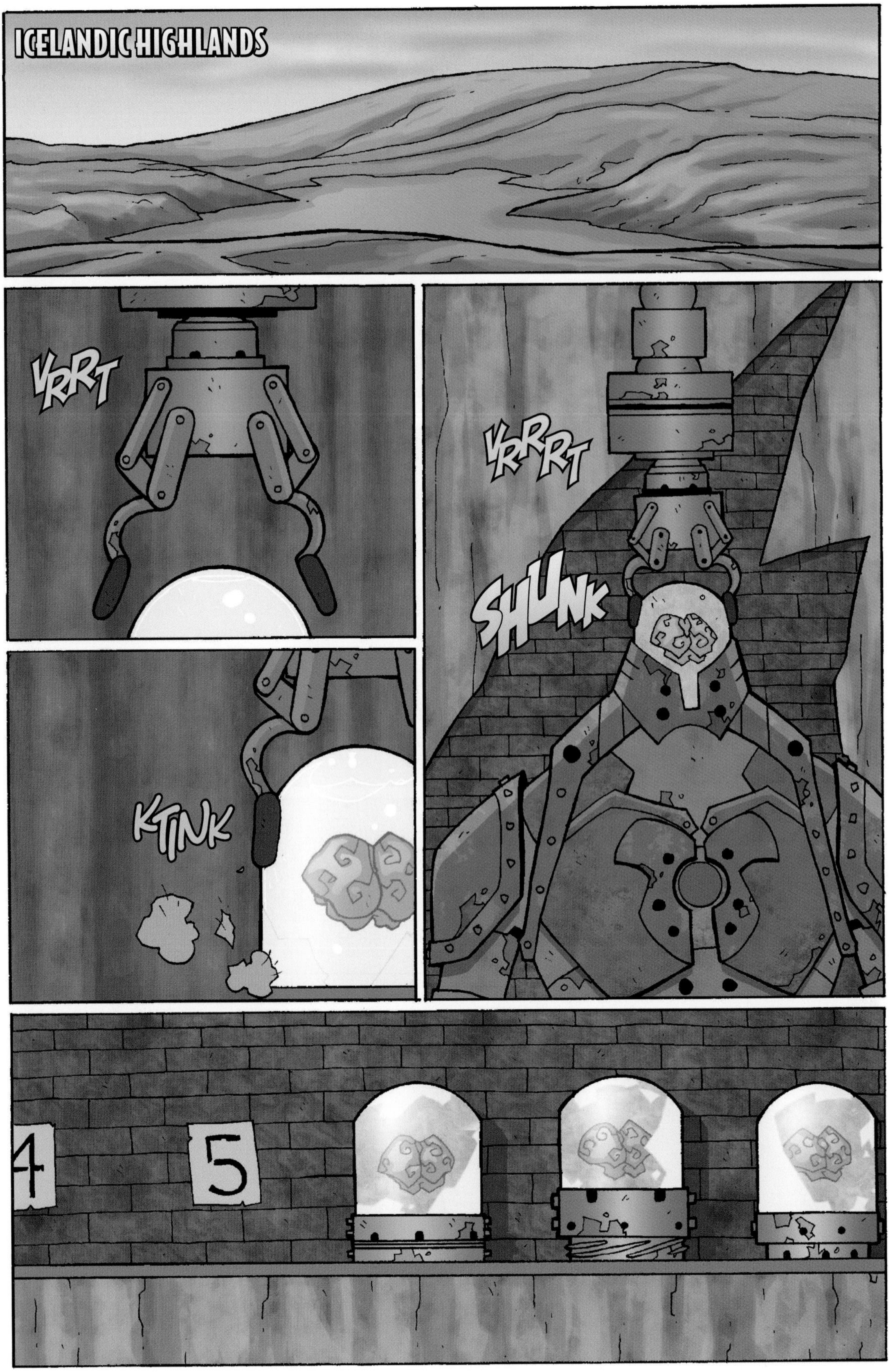
ICELANDIC HIGHLANDS
VRRT
VRRRT
SHUNK
KTINK
4
5

OPERATION HUSKY

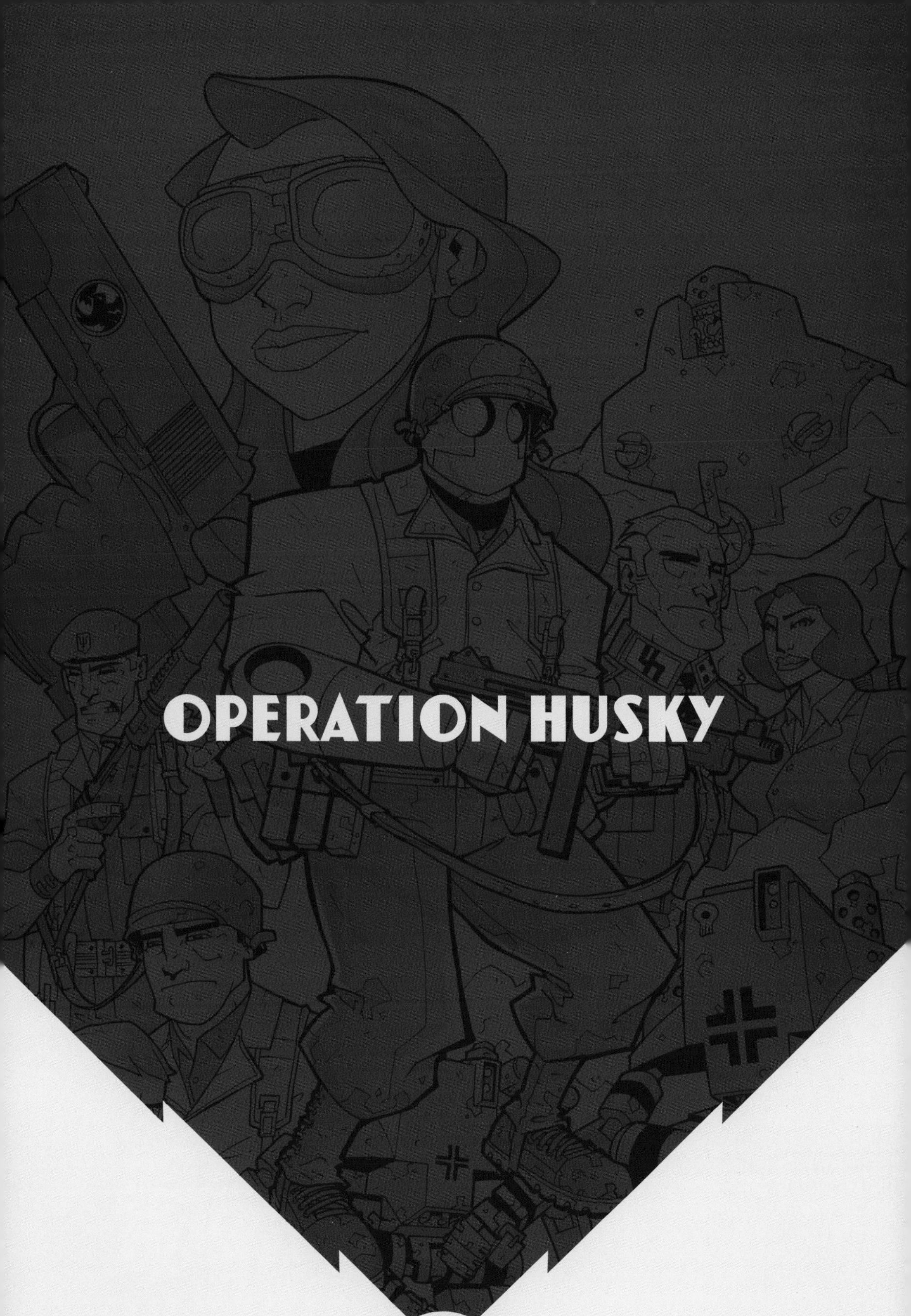

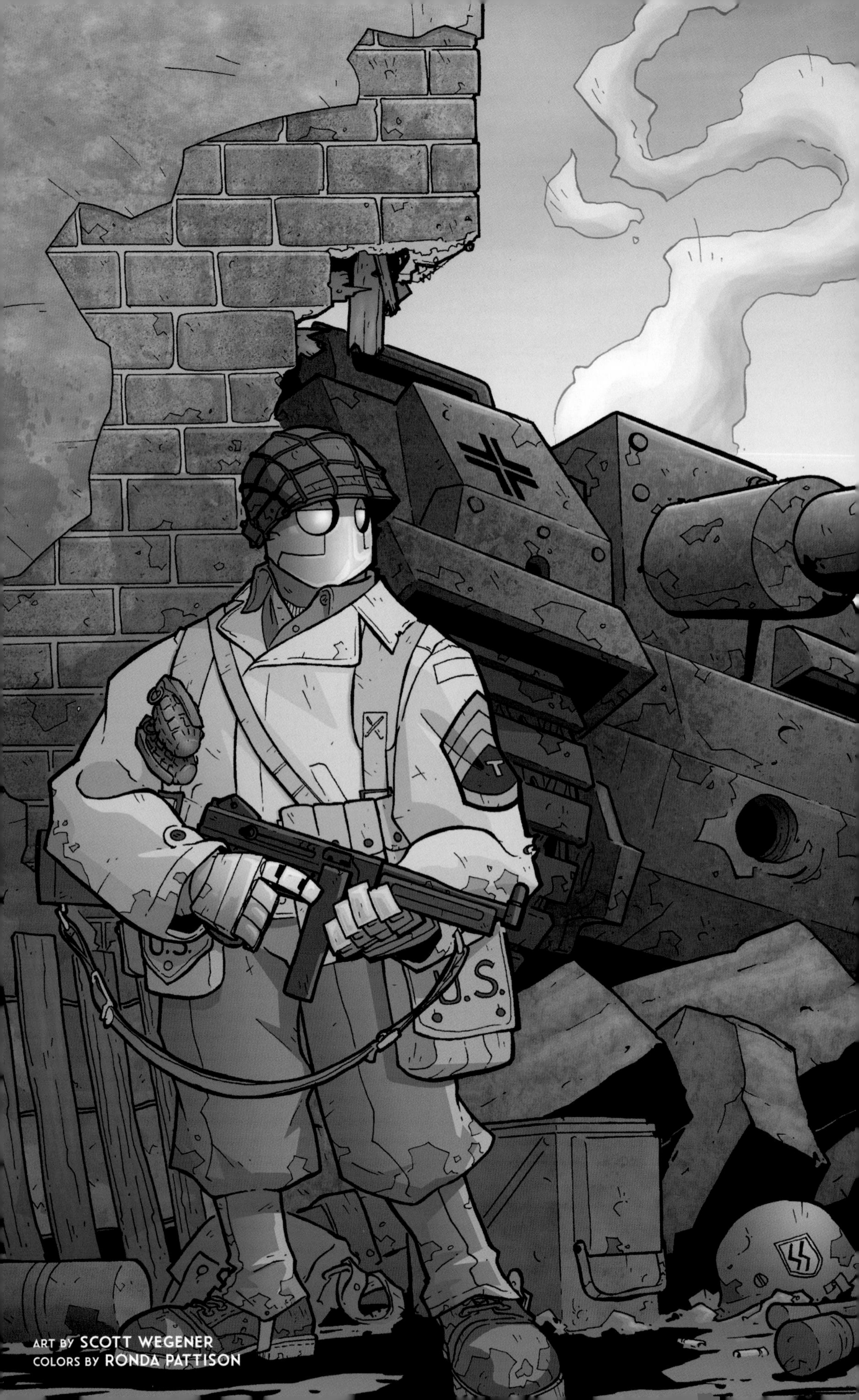
U.S.
U.S.

ART BY SCOTT WEGENER
COLORS BY RONDA PATTISON

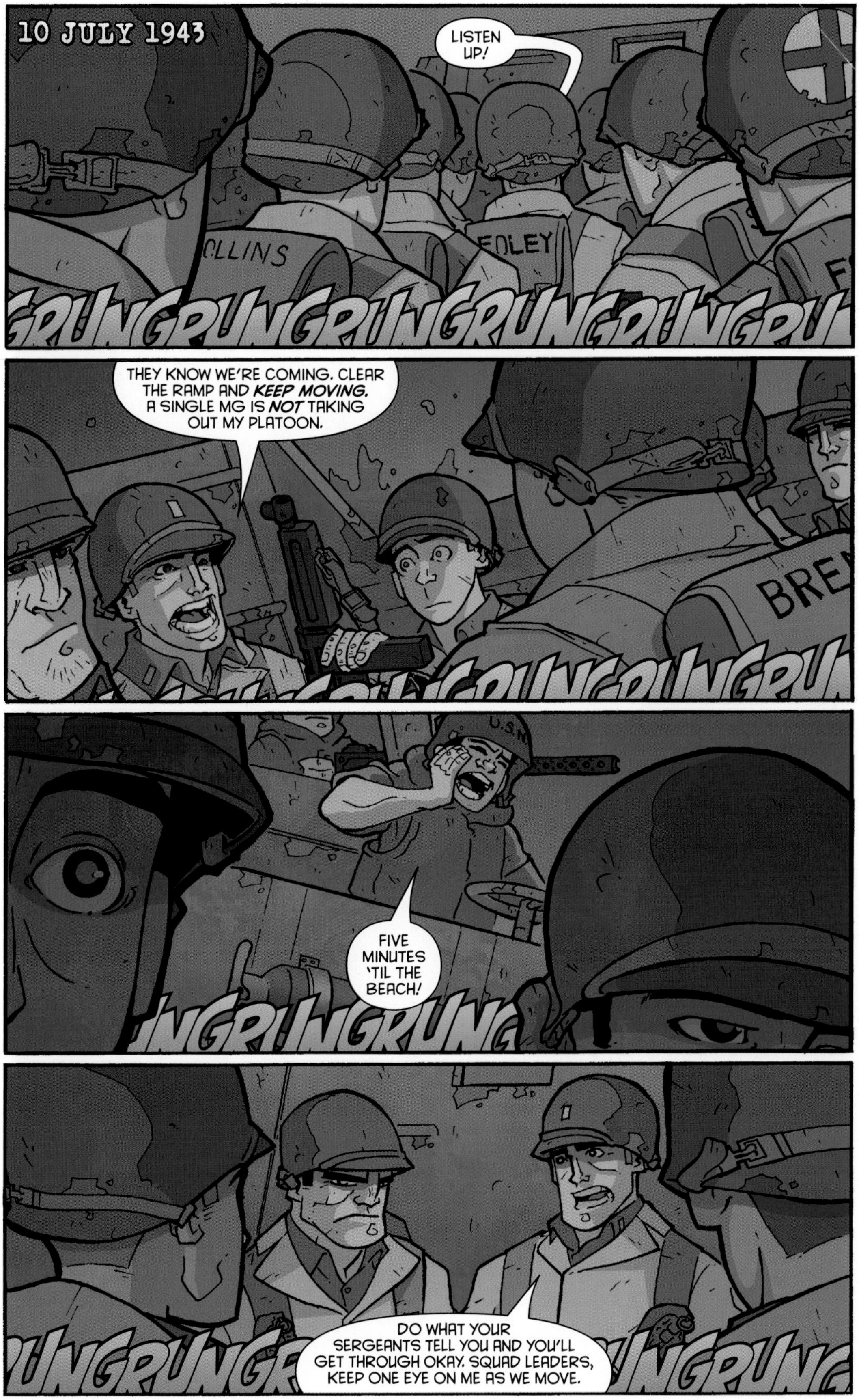
10 JULY 1943
LISTEN UP!
COLLINS
FOLEY
GRUNGRUNGRUNGRUNGRUNGRUNGRUN
THEY KNOW WE'RE COMING. CLEAR THE RAMP AND *KEEP MOVING.* A SINGLE MG IS *NOT* TAKING OUT MY PLATOON.
BRE
GRUNGRUN
U.S.N.
FIVE MINUTES 'TIL THE BEACH!
UNGRUNGRUNG
DO WHAT YOUR SERGEANTS TELL YOU AND YOU'LL GET THROUGH OKAY. SQUAD LEADERS, KEEP ONE EYE ON ME AS WE MOVE.
UNGRUNGR
UNGRUNG

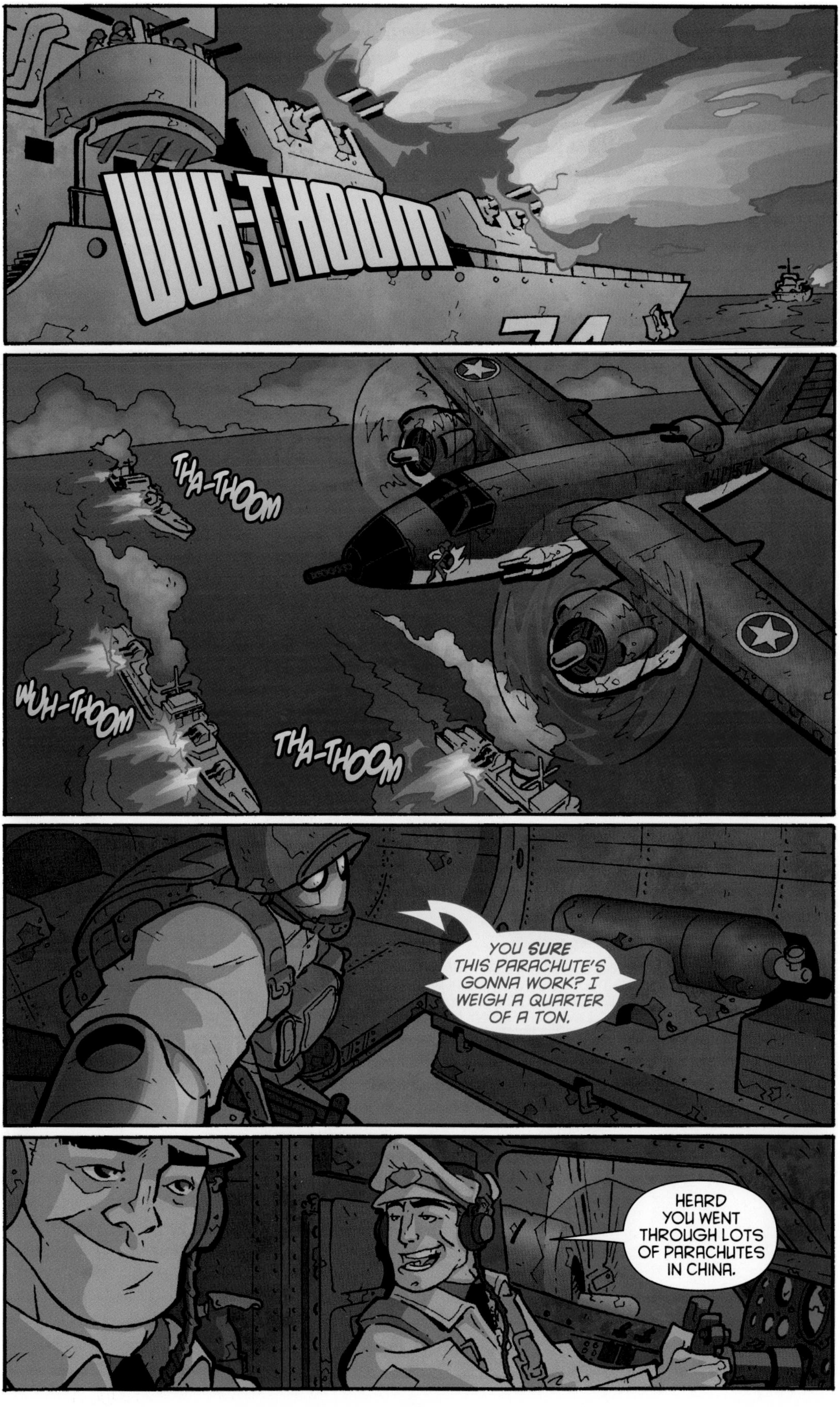
WUH-THOOM
THA-THOOM
WUH-THOOM
THA-THOOM
YOU SURE THIS PARACHUTE'S GONNA WORK? I WEIGH A QUARTER OF A TON.
HEARD YOU WENT THROUGH LOTS OF PARACHUTES IN CHINA.

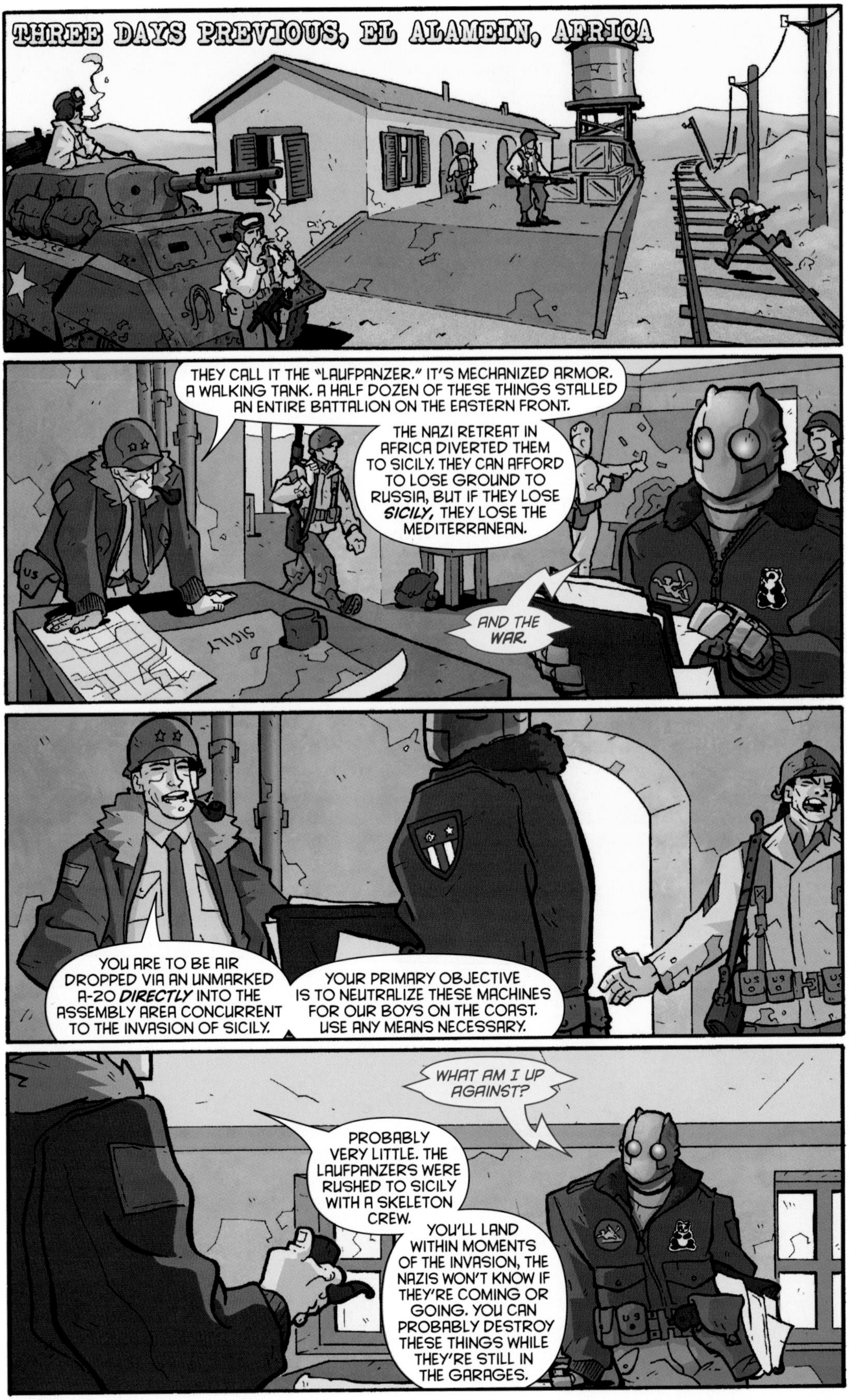
THREE DAYS PREVIOUS, EL ALAMEIN, AFRICA
THEY CALL IT THE "LAUFPANZER." IT'S MECHANIZED ARMOR. A WALKING TANK. A HALF DOZEN OF THESE THINGS STALLED AN ENTIRE BATTALION ON THE EASTERN FRONT.
THE NAZI RETREAT IN AFRICA DIVERTED THEM TO SICILY. THEY CAN AFFORD TO LOSE GROUND TO RUSSIA, BUT IF THEY LOSE *SICILY,* THEY LOSE THE MEDITERRANEAN.
AND THE *WAR.*
SICILY
YOU ARE TO BE AIR DROPPED VIA AN UNMARKED A-20 *DIRECTLY* INTO THE ASSEMBLY AREA CONCURRENT TO THE INVASION OF SICILY.
YOUR PRIMARY OBJECTIVE IS TO NEUTRALIZE THESE MACHINES FOR OUR BOYS ON THE COAST. USE ANY MEANS NECESSARY.
WHAT AM I UP AGAINST?
PROBABLY VERY LITTLE. THE LAUFPANZERS WERE RUSHED TO SICILY WITH A SKELETON CREW.
YOU'LL LAND WITHIN MOMENTS OF THE INVASION, THE NAZIS WON'T KNOW IF THEY'RE COMING OR GOING. YOU CAN PROBABLY DESTROY THESE THINGS WHILE THEY'RE STILL IN THE GARAGES.

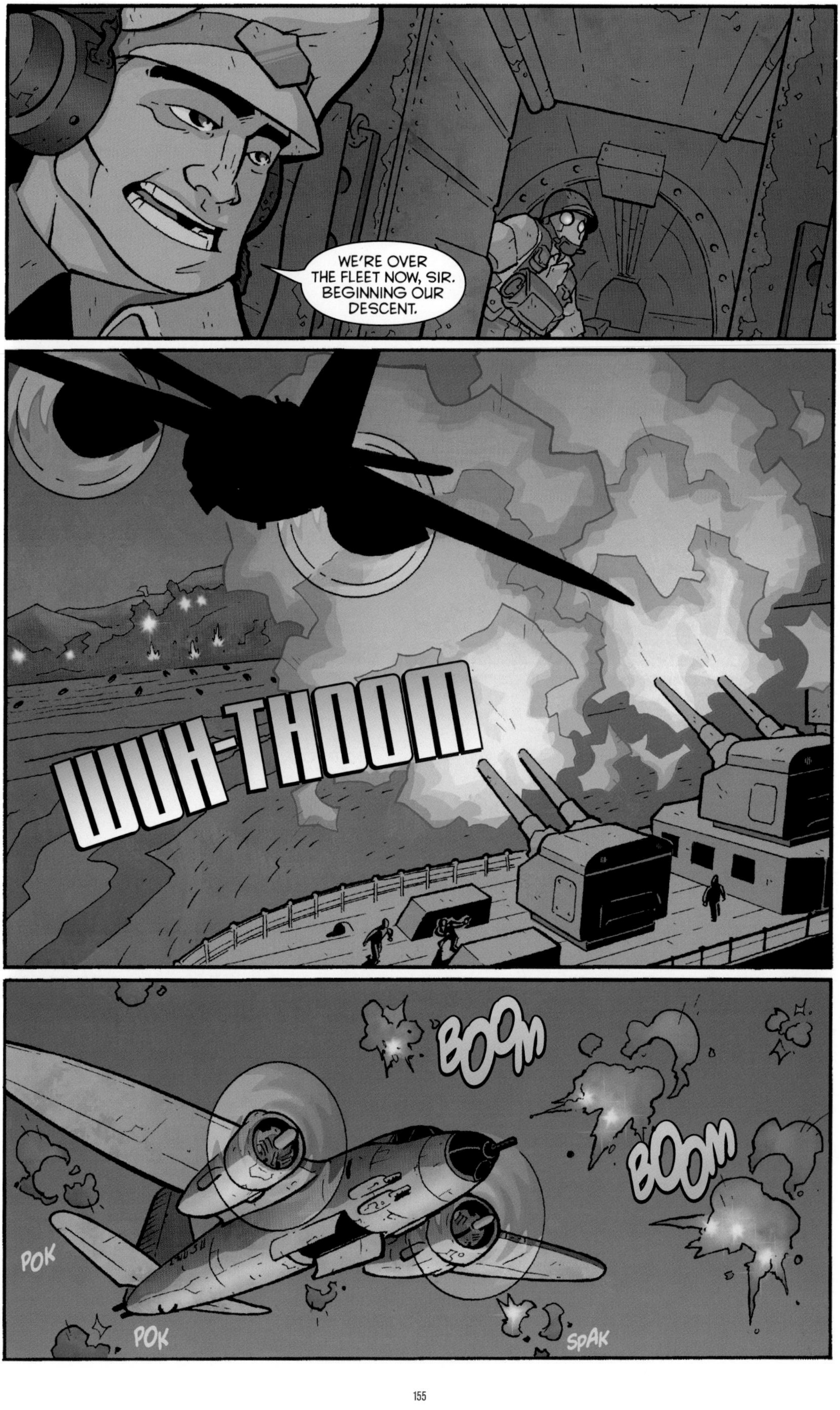
WE'RE OVER THE FLEET NOW, SIR. BEGINNING OUR DESCENT.
WUH-THOOM
BOOM
BOOM
POK
POK
SPAK

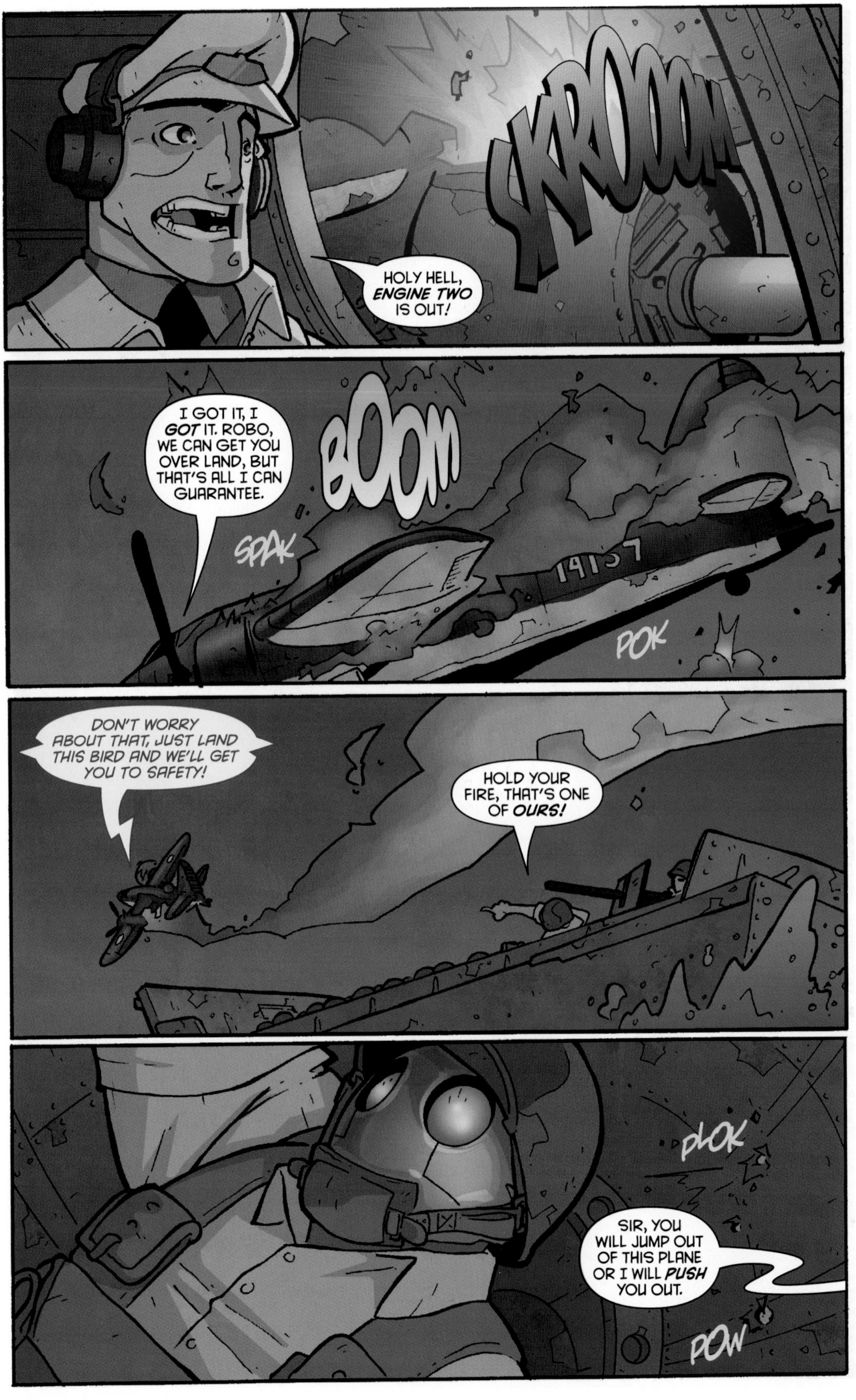
SKROOOM
HOLY HELL, ENGINE TWO IS OUT!
I GOT IT, I GOT IT. ROBO, WE CAN GET YOU OVER LAND, BUT THAT'S ALL I CAN GUARANTEE.
BOOM
SPAK
14157
POK
DON'T WORRY ABOUT THAT, JUST LAND THIS BIRD AND WE'LL GET YOU TO SAFETY!
HOLD YOUR FIRE, THAT'S ONE OF OURS!
PLOK
SIR, YOU WILL JUMP OUT OF THIS PLANE OR I WILL PUSH YOU OUT.
POW

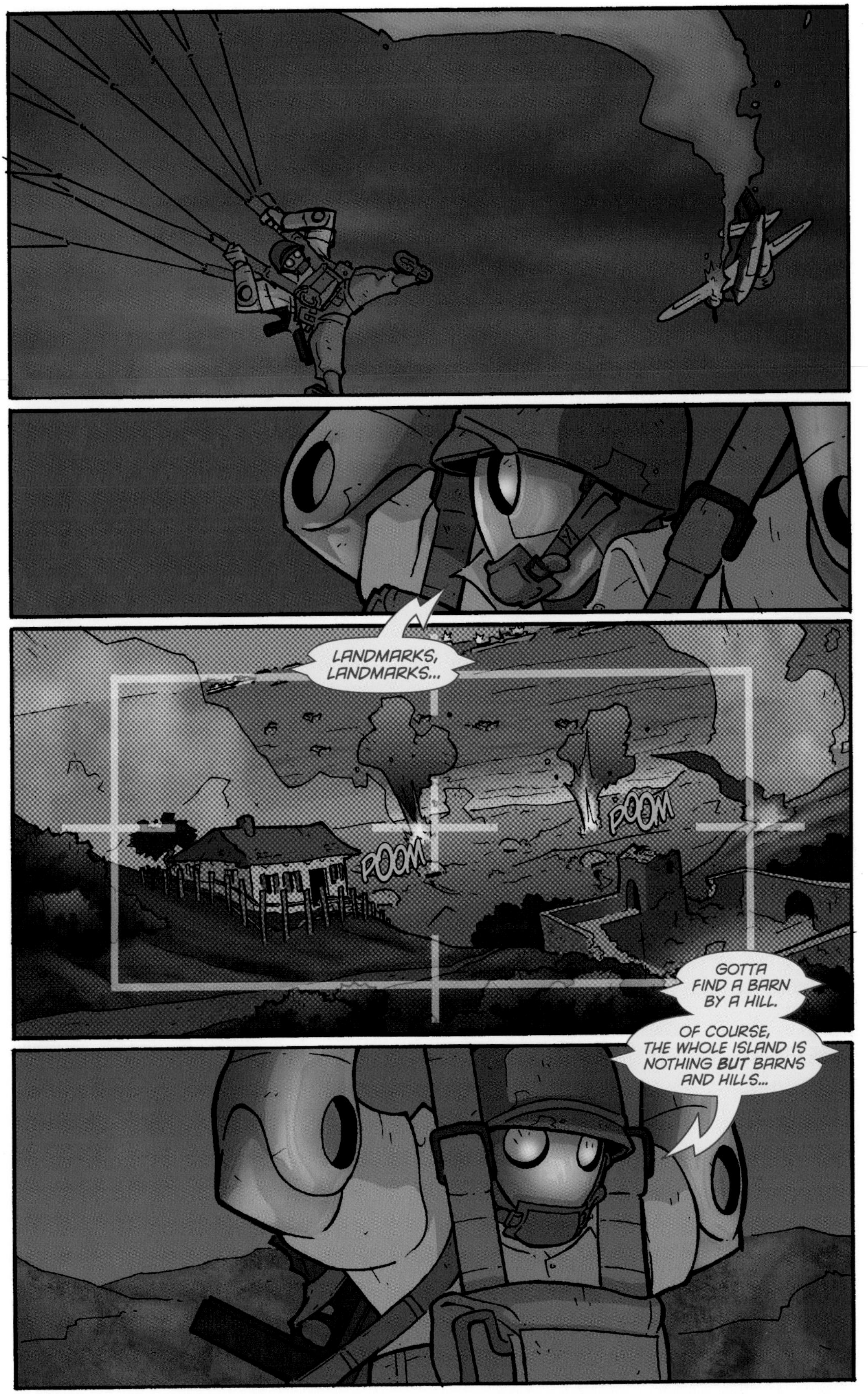
LANDMARKS, LANDMARKS...
POOM
POOM
GOTTA FIND A BARN BY A HILL.
OF COURSE, THE WHOLE ISLAND IS NOTHING BUT BARNS AND HILLS...

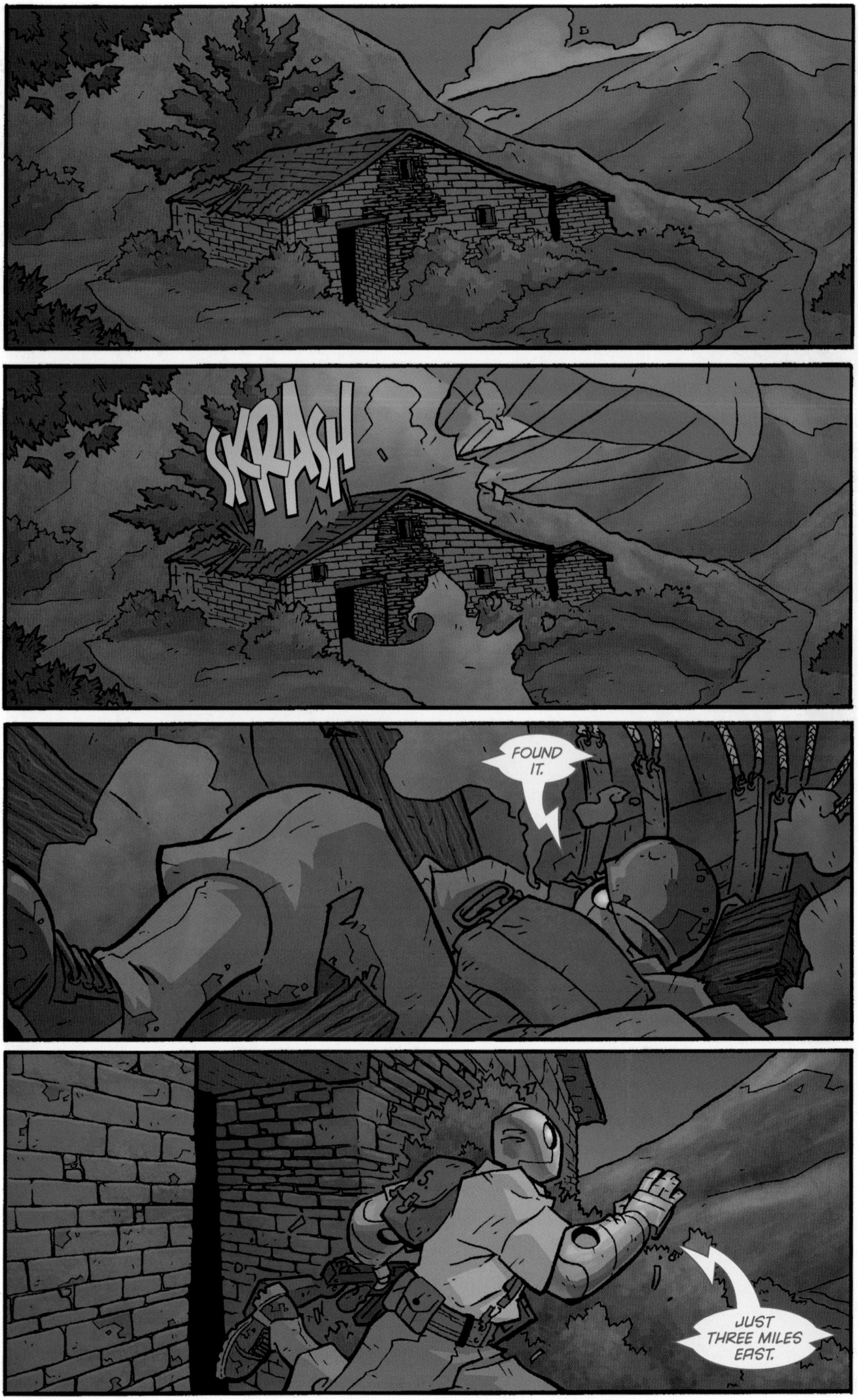
SKRASH
FOUND IT.
JUST THREE MILES EAST.

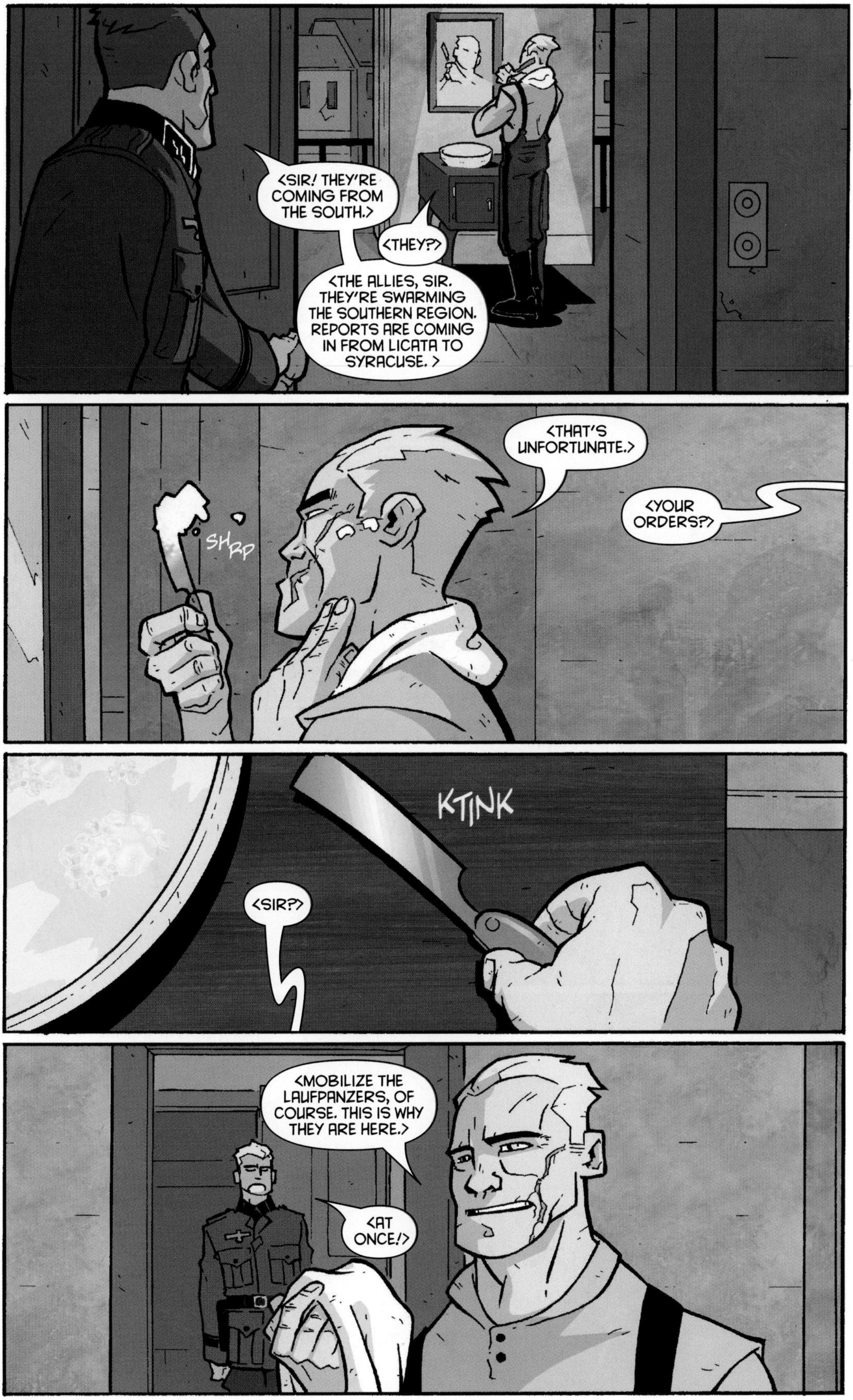
<SIR! THEY'RE COMING FROM THE SOUTH.>
<THEY?>
<THE ALLIES, SIR. THEY'RE SWARMING THE SOUTHERN REGION. REPORTS ARE COMING IN FROM LICATA TO SYRACUSE.>
SHRP
<THAT'S UNFORTUNATE.>
<YOUR ORDERS?>
KTINK
<SIR?>
<MOBILIZE THE LAUFPANZERS, OF COURSE. THIS IS WHY THEY ARE HERE.>
<AT ONCE!>

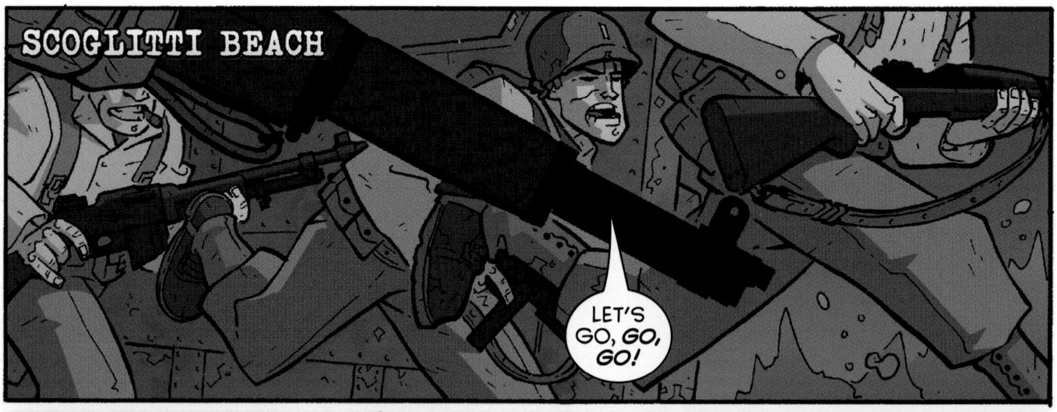
SCOGLITTI BEACH
LET'S GO, GO, GO!

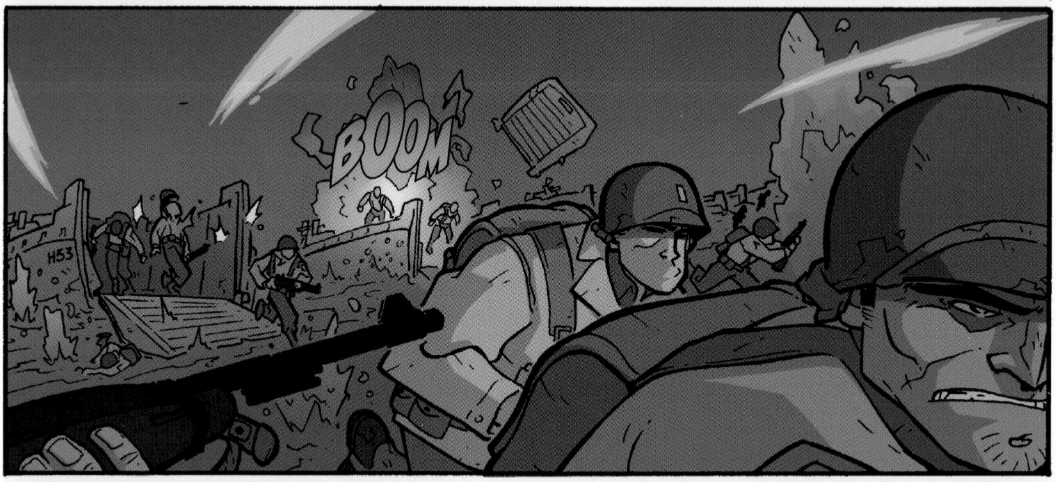
BOOM

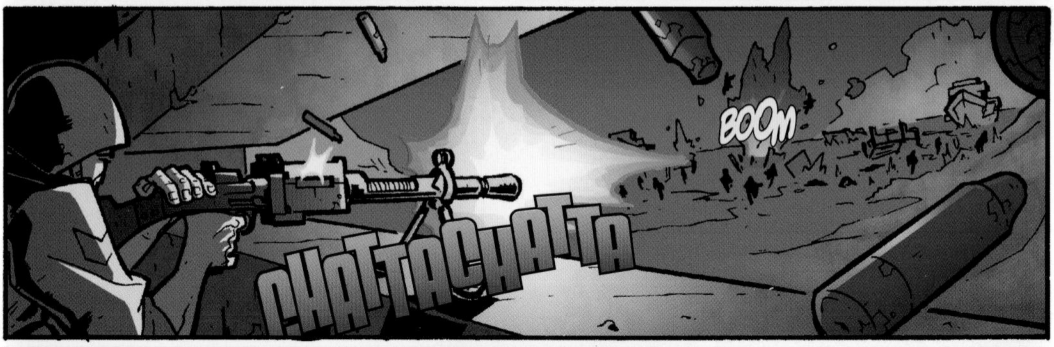
BOOM
CHATTACHATTA

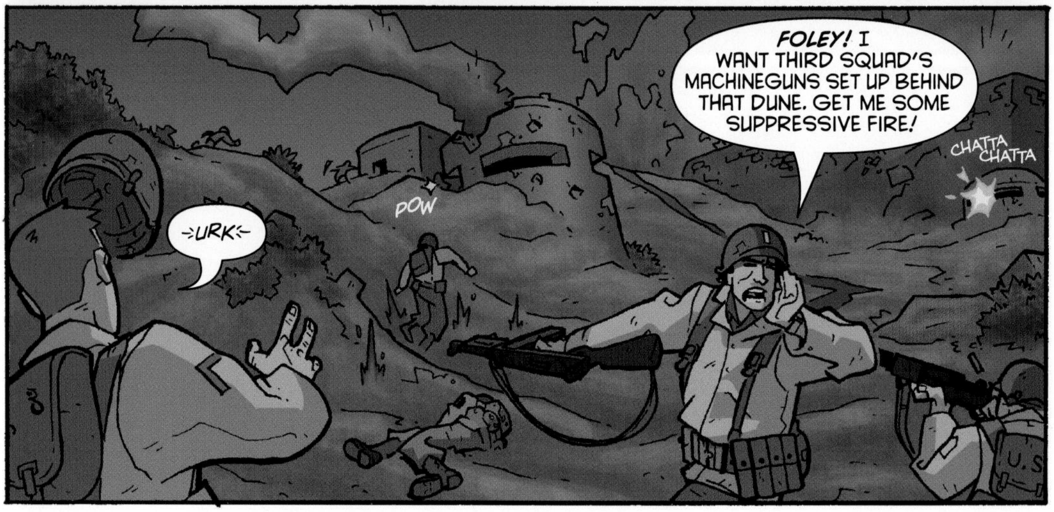
FOLEY! I WANT THIRD SQUAD'S MACHINEGUNS SET UP BEHIND THAT DUNE. GET ME SOME SUPPRESSIVE FIRE!
CHATTA CHATTA
POW
URK

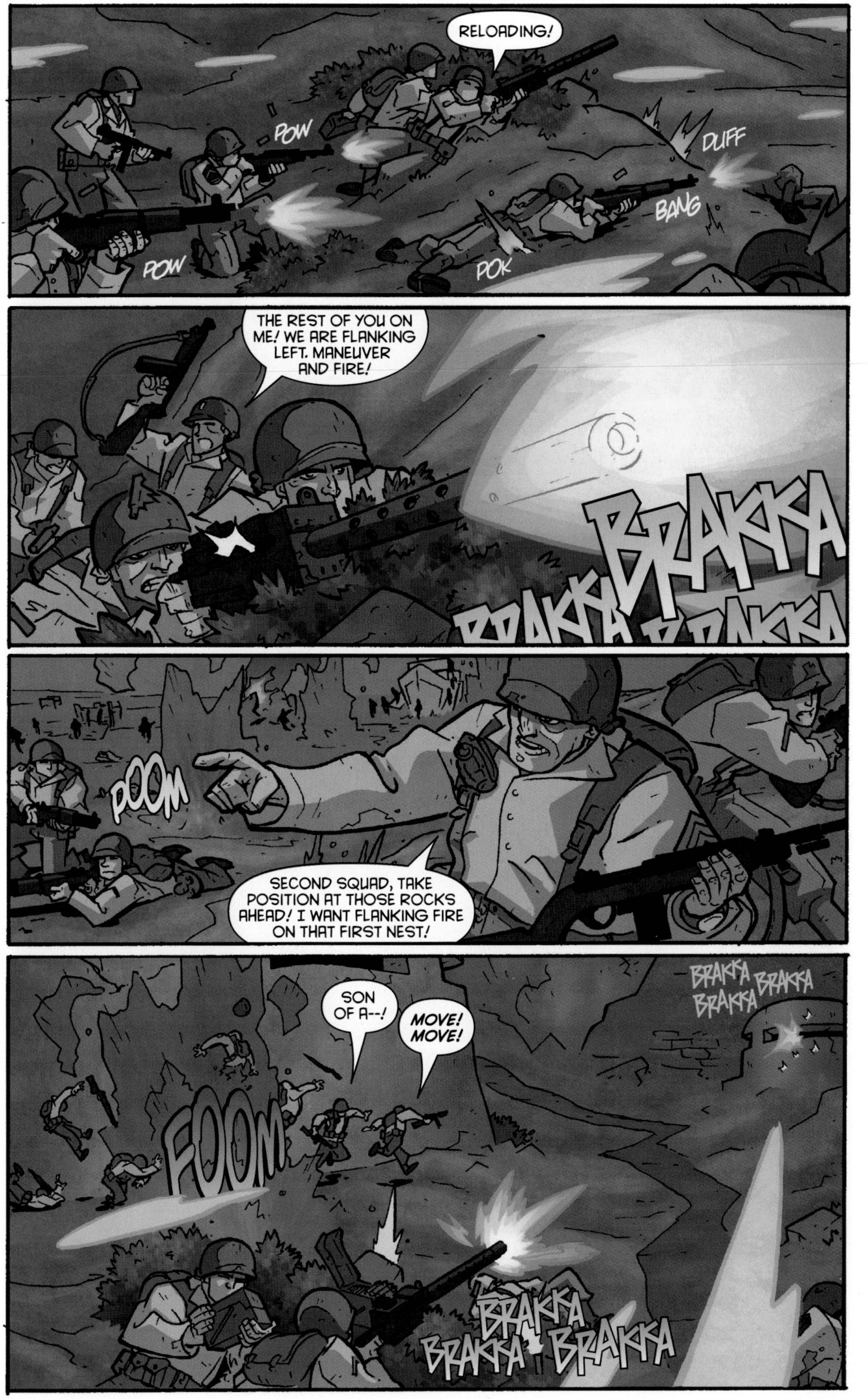
RELOADING!
POW
DUFF
BANG
POW
POK
THE REST OF YOU ON ME! WE ARE FLANKING LEFT. MANEUVER AND FIRE!
BRAKKA
POOM
SECOND SQUAD, TAKE POSITION AT THOSE ROCKS AHEAD! I WANT FLANKING FIRE ON THAT FIRST NEST!
BRAKKA BRAKKA BRAKKA
SON OF A--!
MOVE! MOVE!
FOOM
BRAKKA BRAKKA BRAKKA

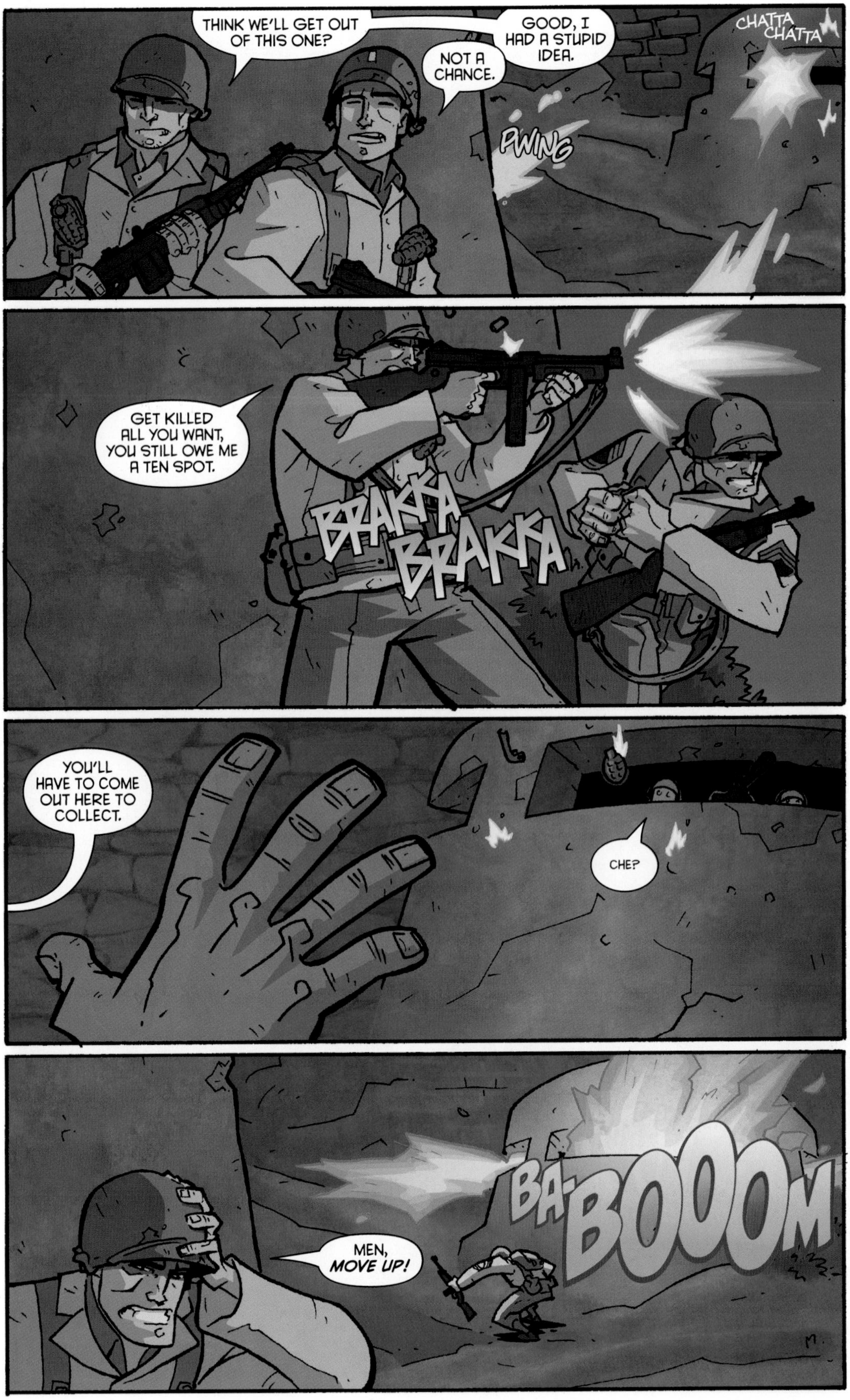
THINK WE'LL GET OUT OF THIS ONE?
NOT A CHANCE.
GOOD, I HAD A STUPID IDEA.
CHATTA CHATTA
PWING
GET KILLED ALL YOU WANT, YOU STILL OWE ME A TEN SPOT.
BRAKKA BRAKKA
YOU'LL HAVE TO COME OUT HERE TO COLLECT.
CHE?
MEN, *MOVE UP!*
BA-BOOOM

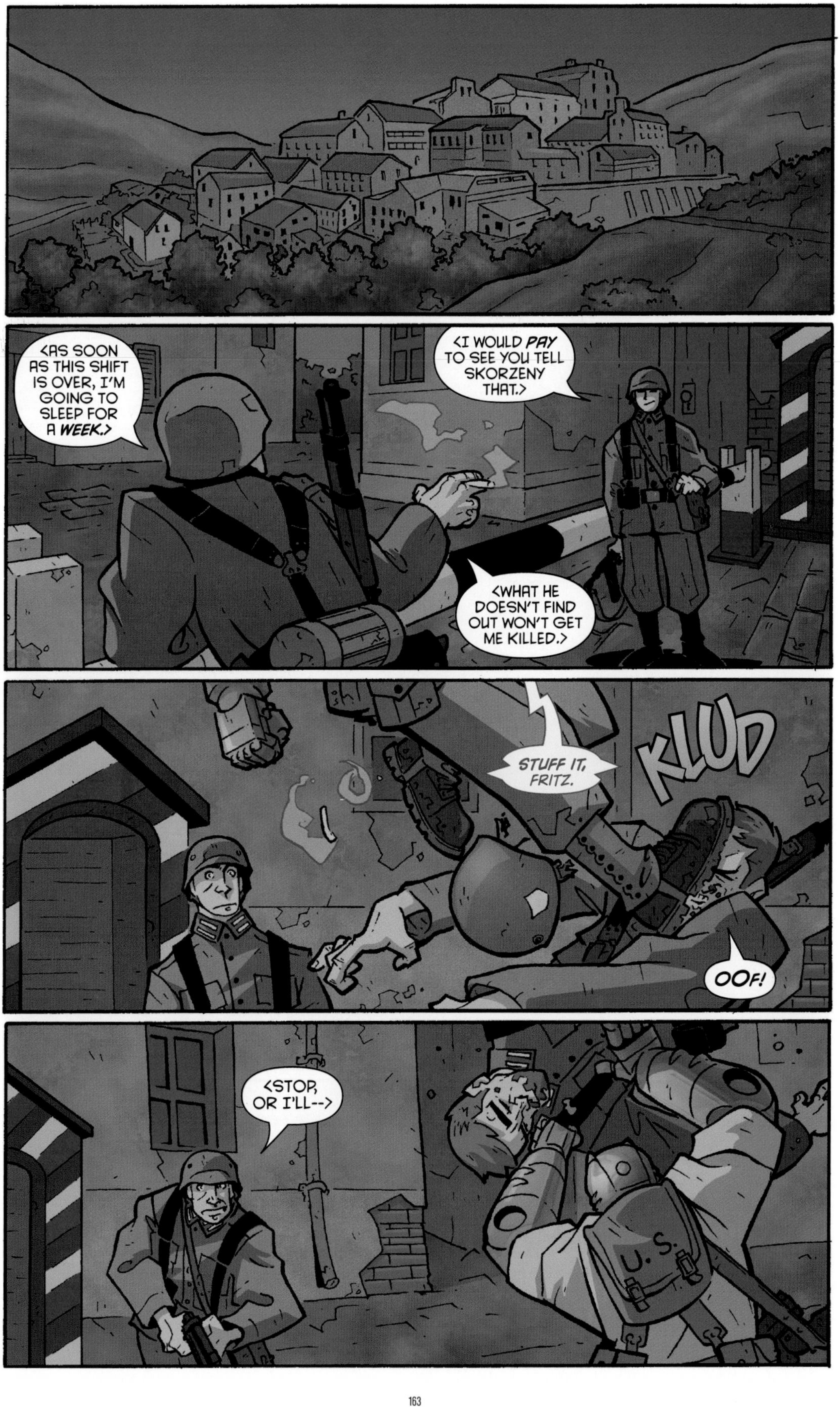
<AS SOON AS THIS SHIFT IS OVER, I'M GOING TO SLEEP FOR A WEEK.>
<I WOULD PAY TO SEE YOU TELL SKORZENY THAT.>
<WHAT HE DOESN'T FIND OUT WON'T GET ME KILLED.>
STUFF IT, FRITZ.
KLUD
OOF!
<STOP, OR I'LL-->
U.S.

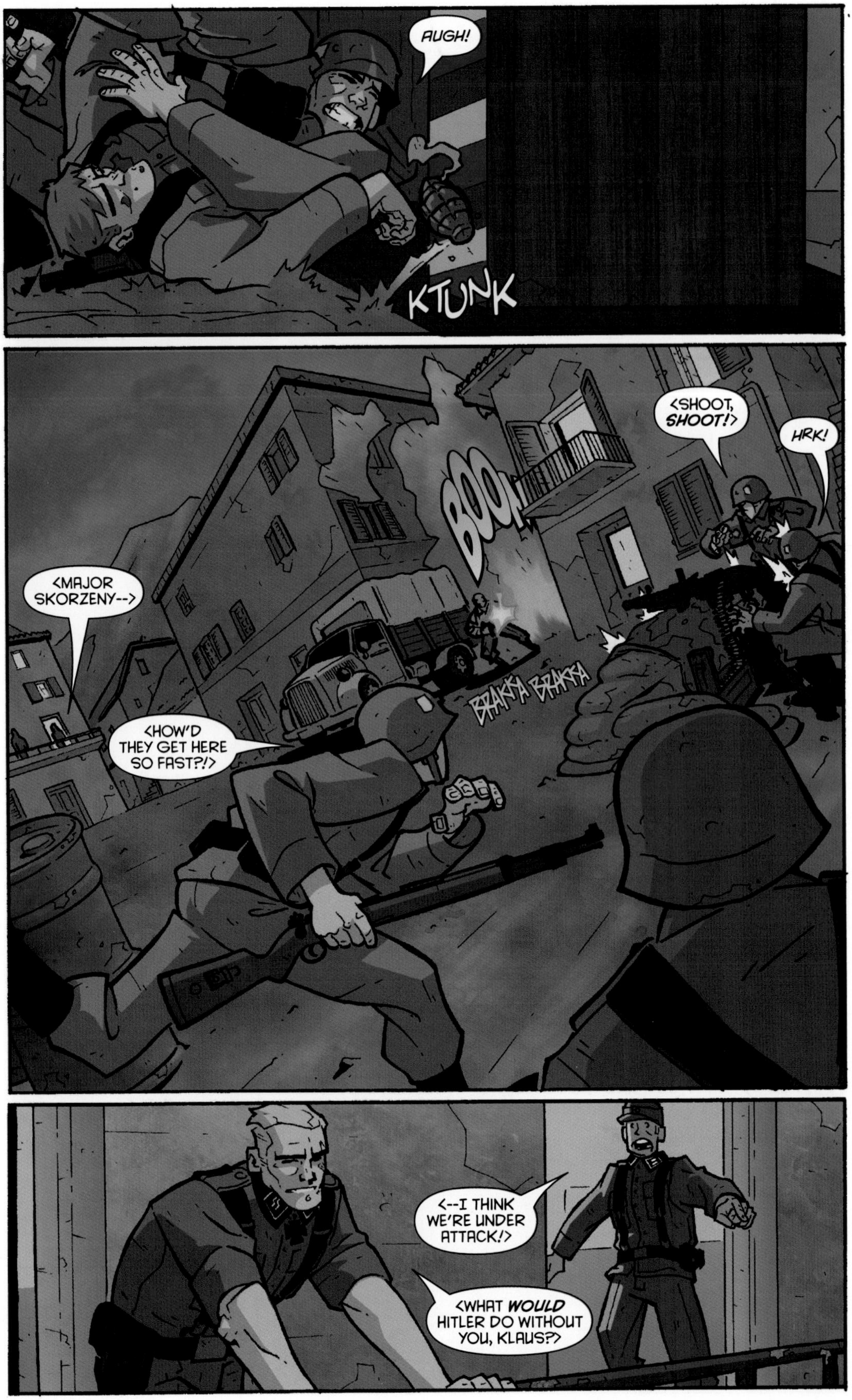
AUGH!
KTUNK
BOO
<SHOOT, SHOOT!>
HRK!
<MAJOR SKORZENY-->
<HOW'D THEY GET HERE SO FAST?!>
BRAKKA BRAKKA
<--I THINK WE'RE UNDER ATTACK!>
<WHAT *WOULD* HITLER DO WITHOUT YOU, KLAUS?>

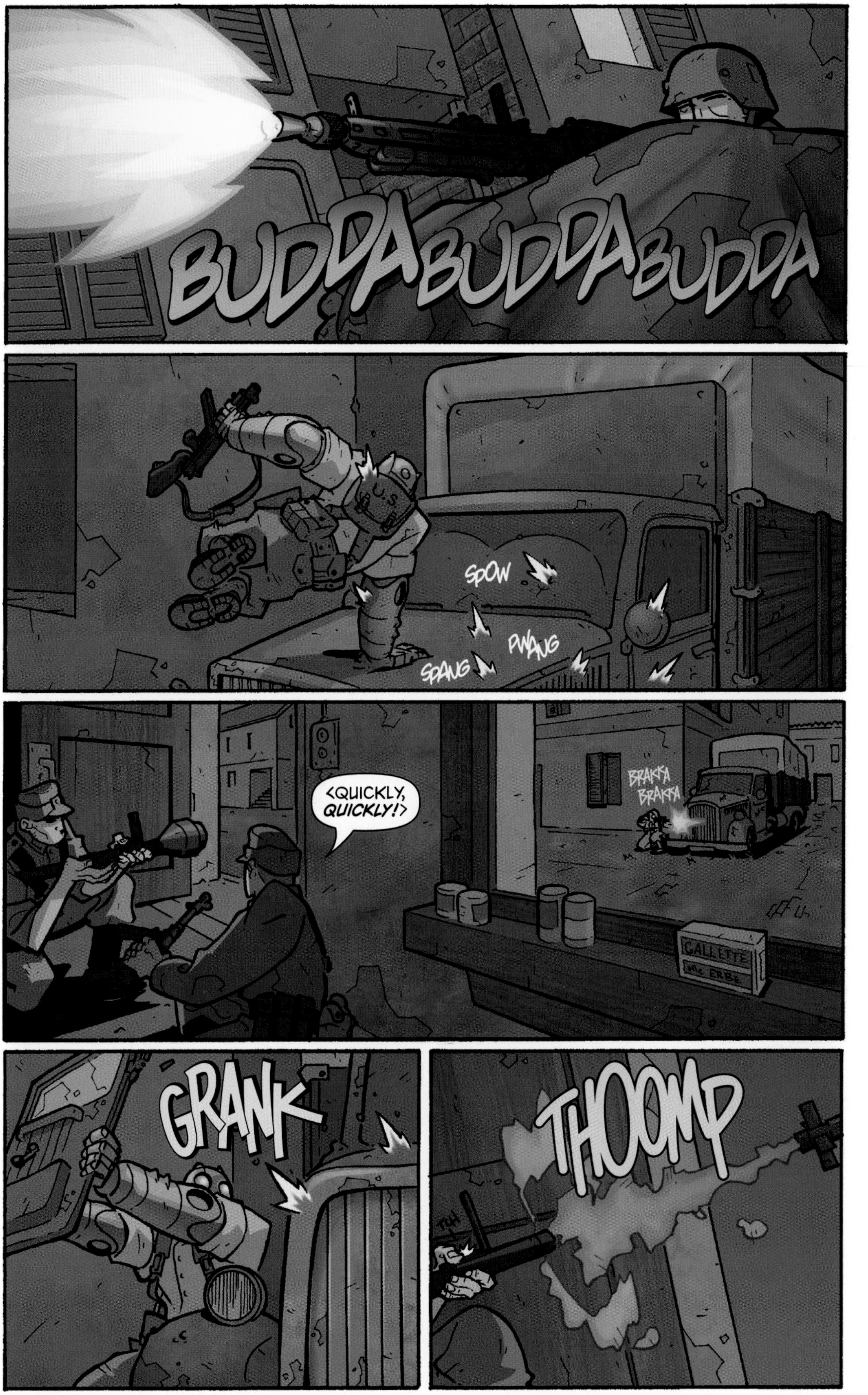
BUDDA BUDDA BUDDA
SPOW
PWANG
SPANG
<QUICKLY, QUICKLY!>
BRAKKA BRAKKA
GALLETTE
GRANK
THOOMP

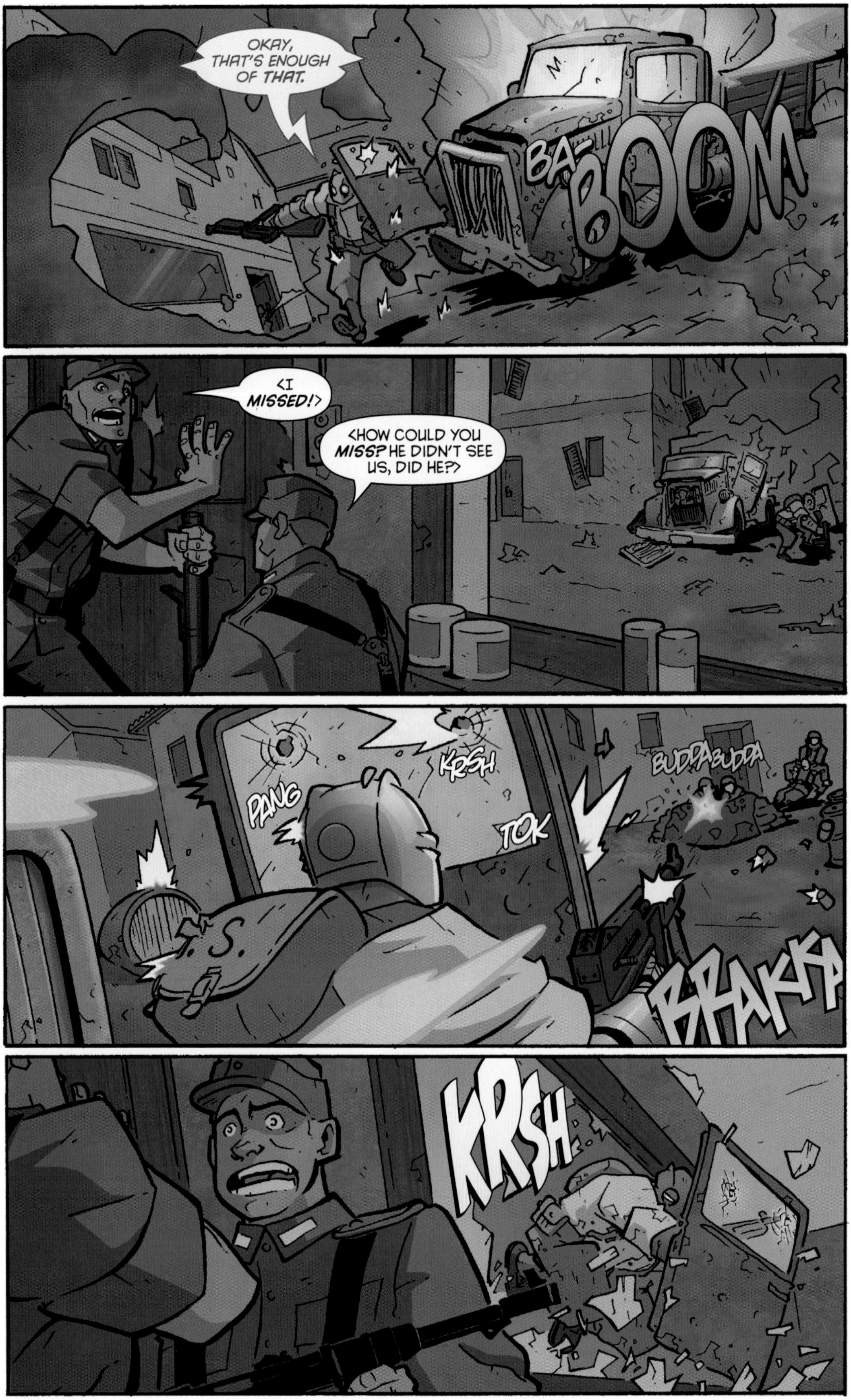
OKAY, THAT'S ENOUGH OF THAT.
BA-BOOM
<I MISSED!>
<HOW COULD YOU MISS? HE DIDN'T SEE US, DID HE?>
KRSH
PANG
BUDDABUDDA
TOK
KRSH

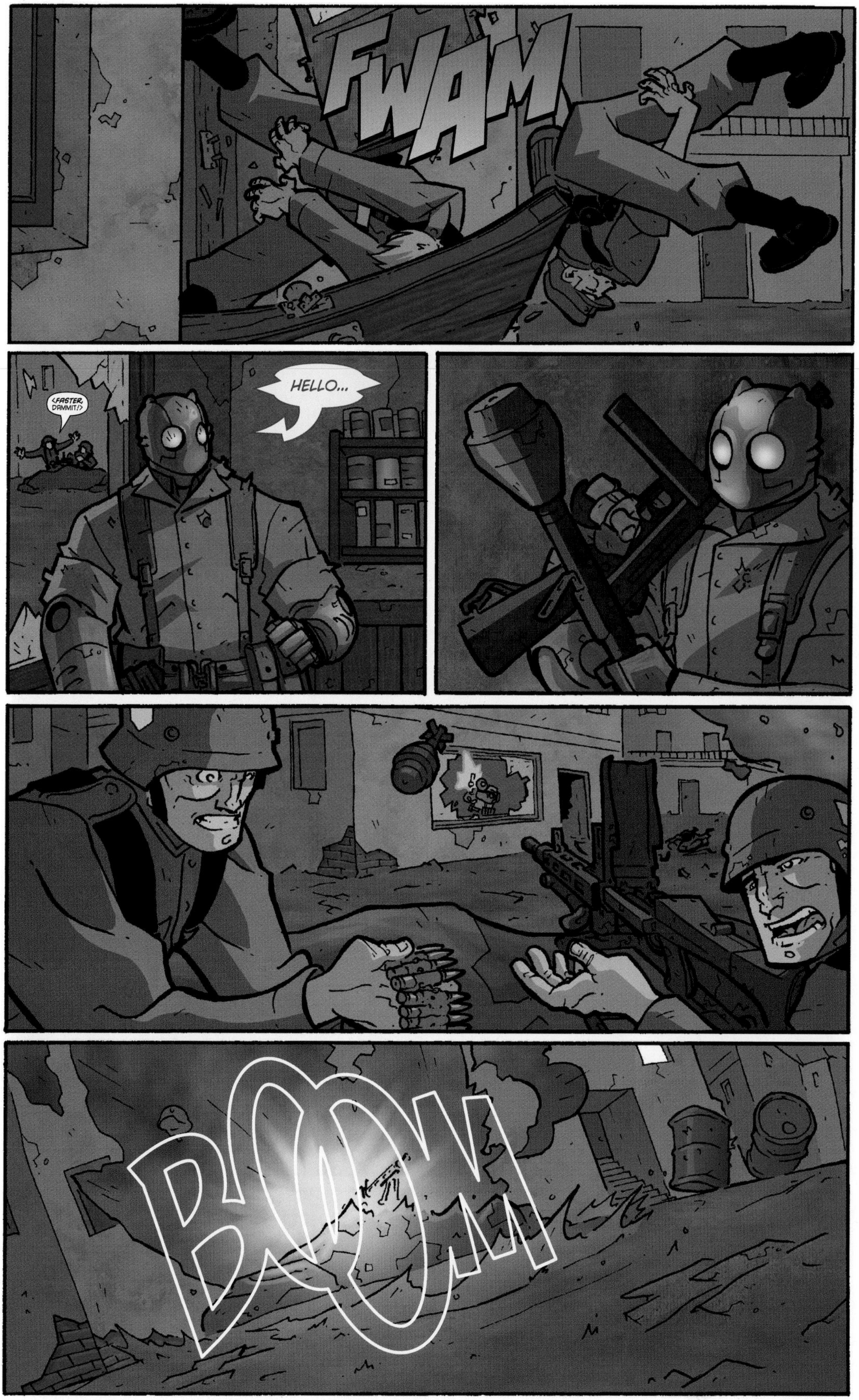
FWAM
<FASTER, DAMMIT!>
HELLO...
BOOM

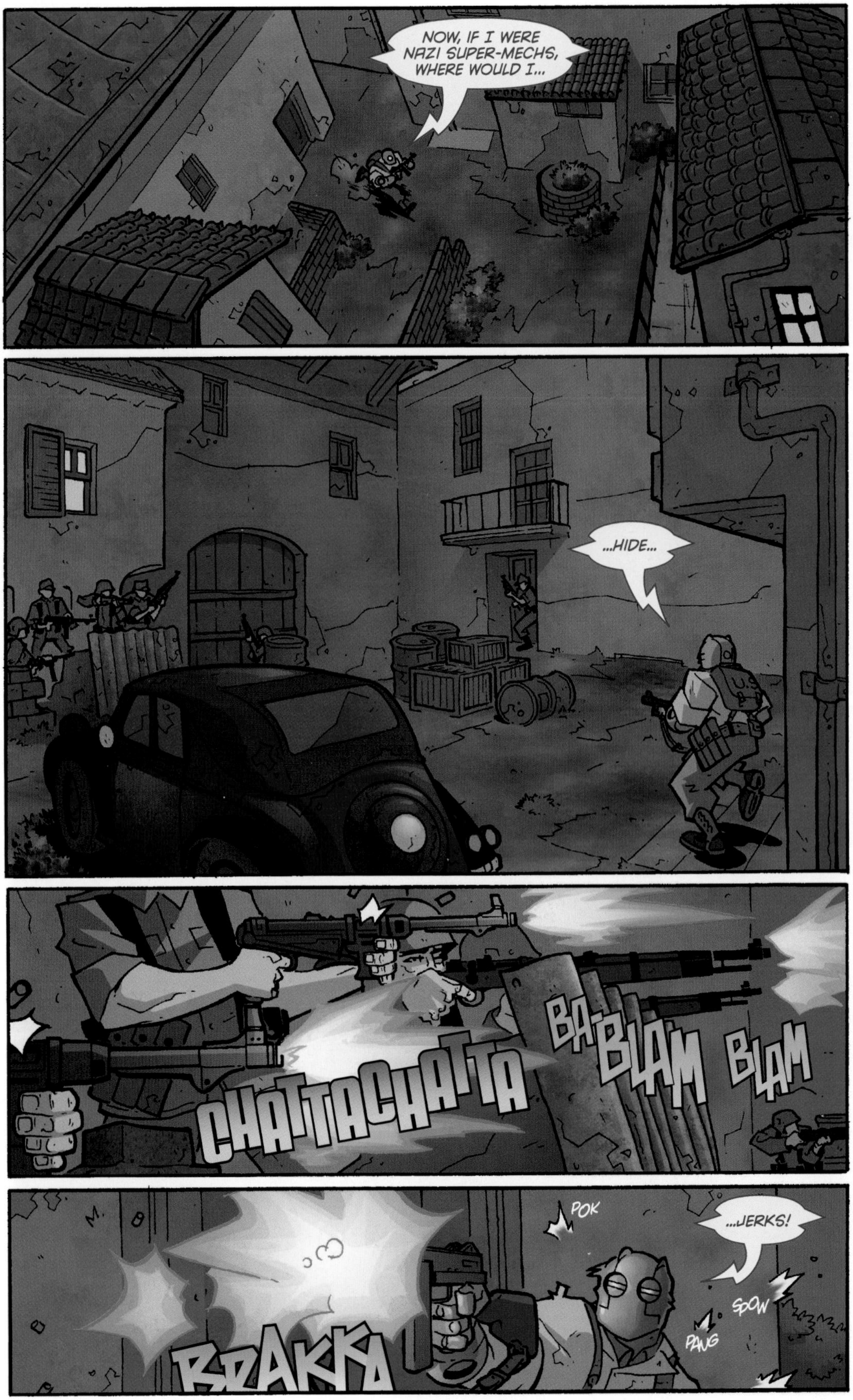
NOW, IF I WERE NAZI SUPER-MECHS, WHERE WOULD I...
...HIDE...
CHATTACHATTA
BA-BLAM
BLAM
POK
...JERKS!
SPOW
PANG
BRAKKA

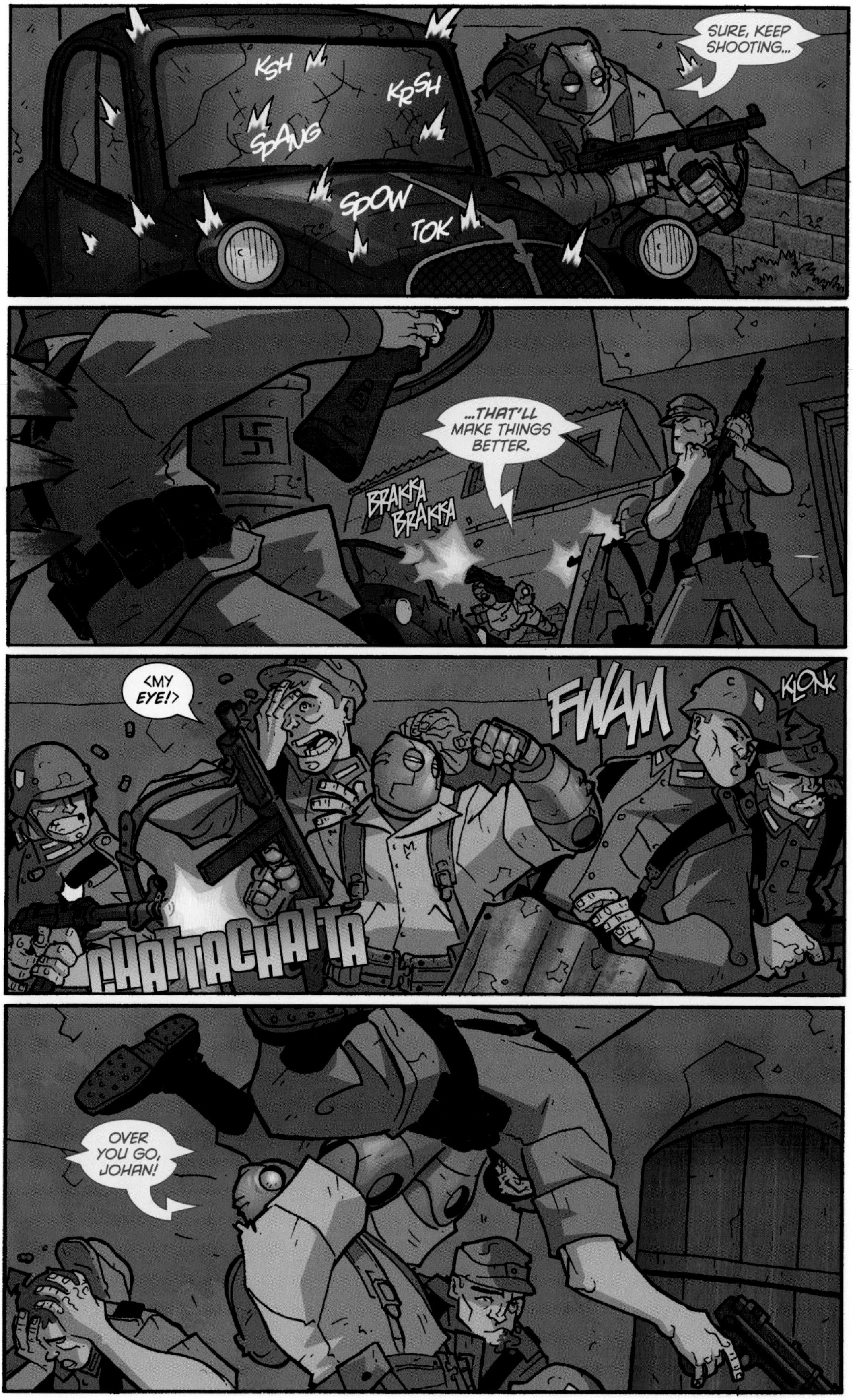
KSH
KRSH
SPANG
SPOW
TOK
SURE, KEEP SHOOTING...
...THAT'LL MAKE THINGS BETTER.
BRAKKA BRAKKA
<MY EYE!>
FWAM
KLONK
CHATTACHATTA
OVER YOU GO, JOHAN!

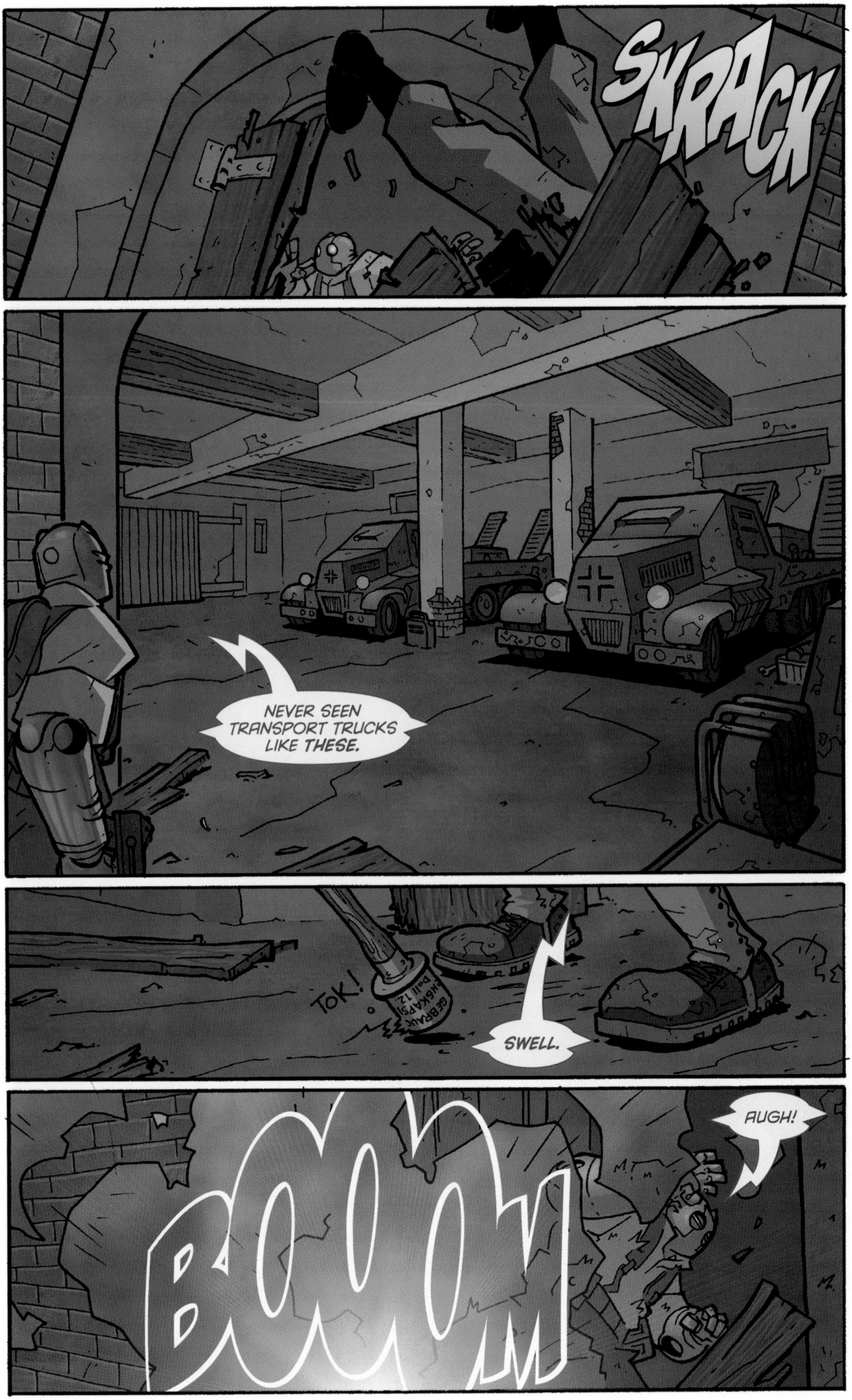
SKRACH
NEVER SEEN TRANSPORT TRUCKS LIKE THESE.
TOK!
SWELL.
BOOOM
AUGH!

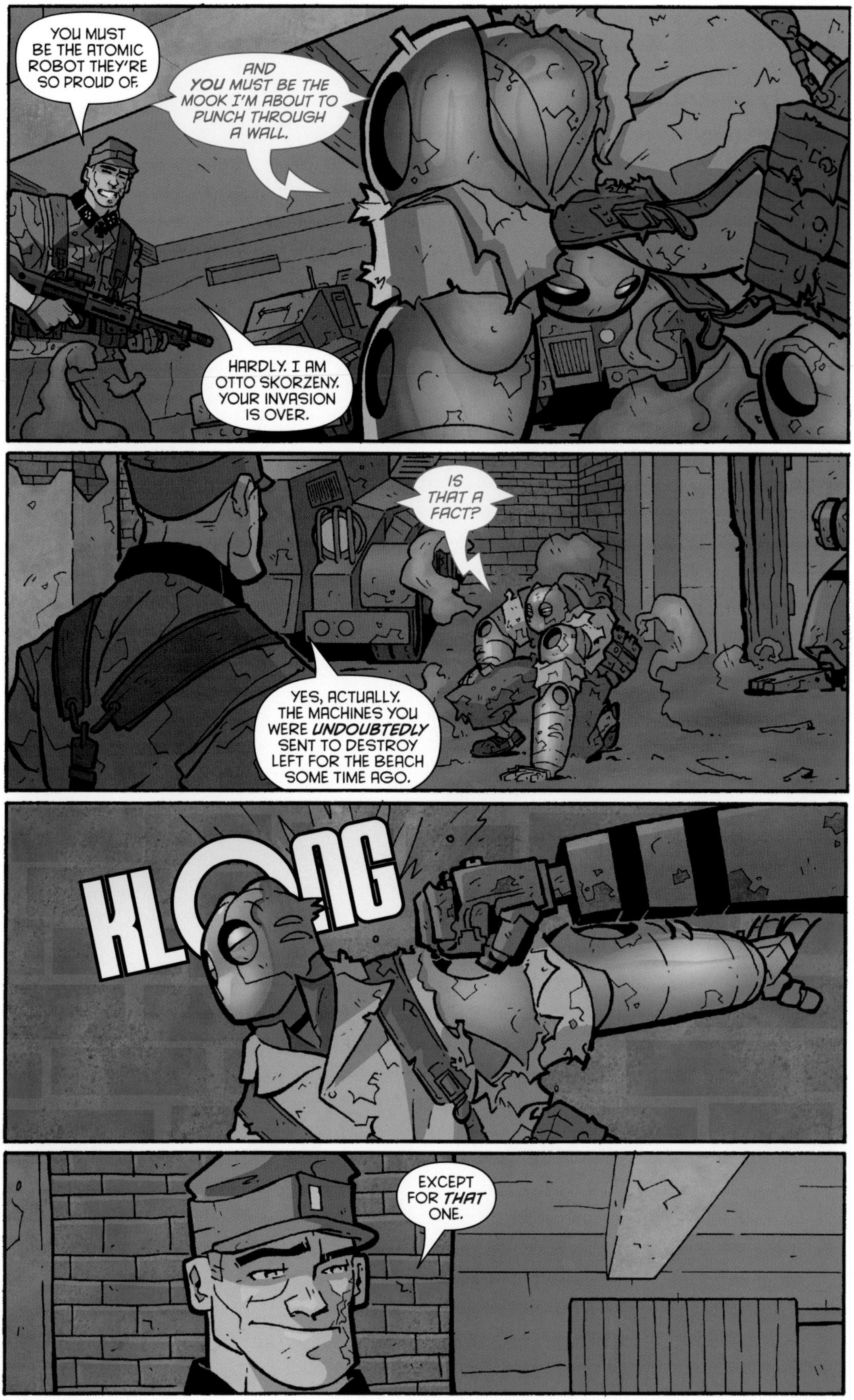
YOU MUST BE THE ATOMIC ROBOT THEY'RE SO PROUD OF.
AND *YOU* MUST BE THE MOOK I'M ABOUT TO PUNCH THROUGH A WALL.
HARDLY. I AM OTTO SKORZENY. YOUR INVASION IS OVER.
IS THAT A FACT?
YES, ACTUALLY. THE MACHINES YOU WERE *UNDOUBTEDLY* SENT TO DESTROY LEFT FOR THE BEACH SOME TIME AGO.
KLONG
EXCEPT FOR *THAT* ONE.

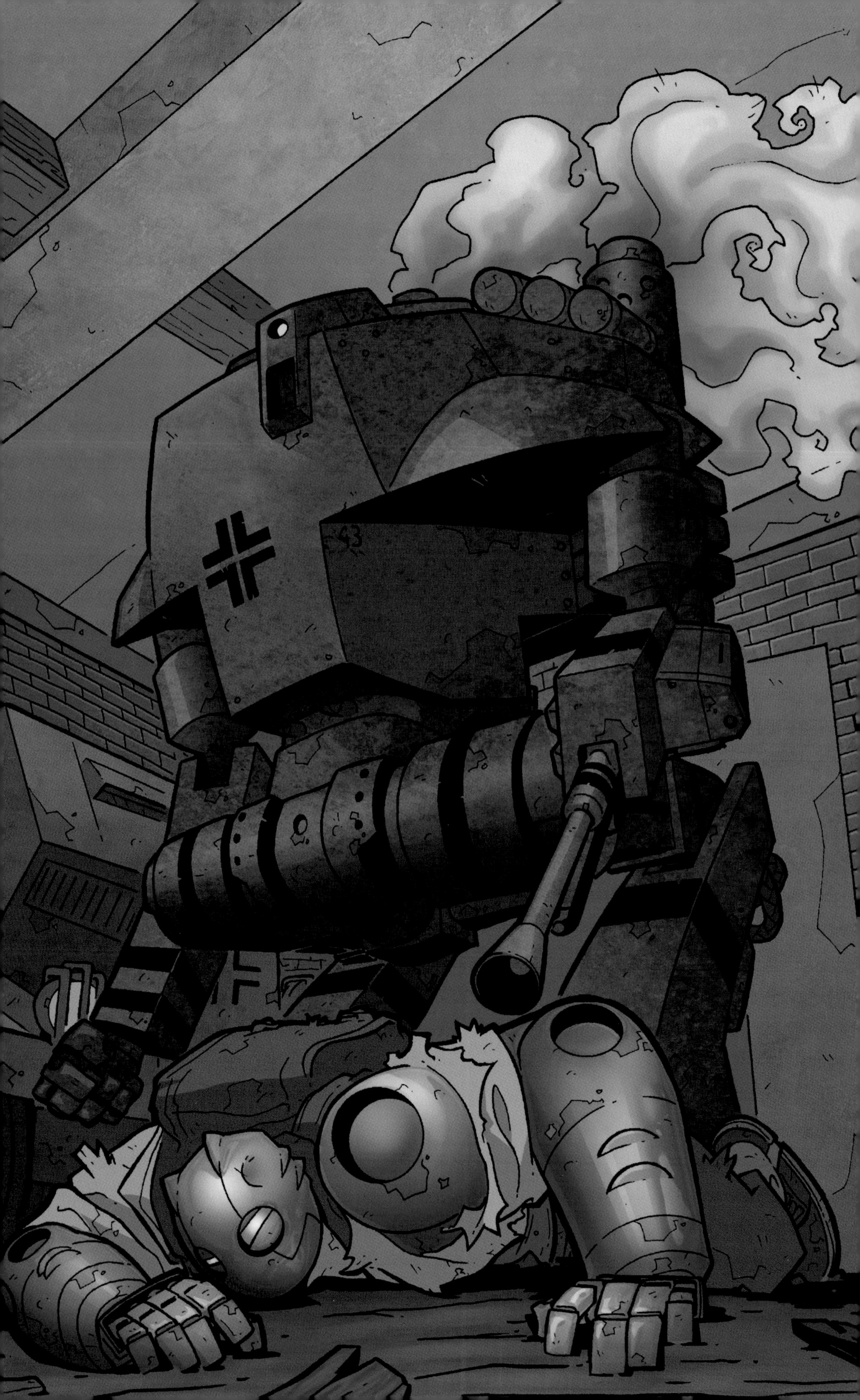
43

AND THEN THERE'S THE ROBOTS

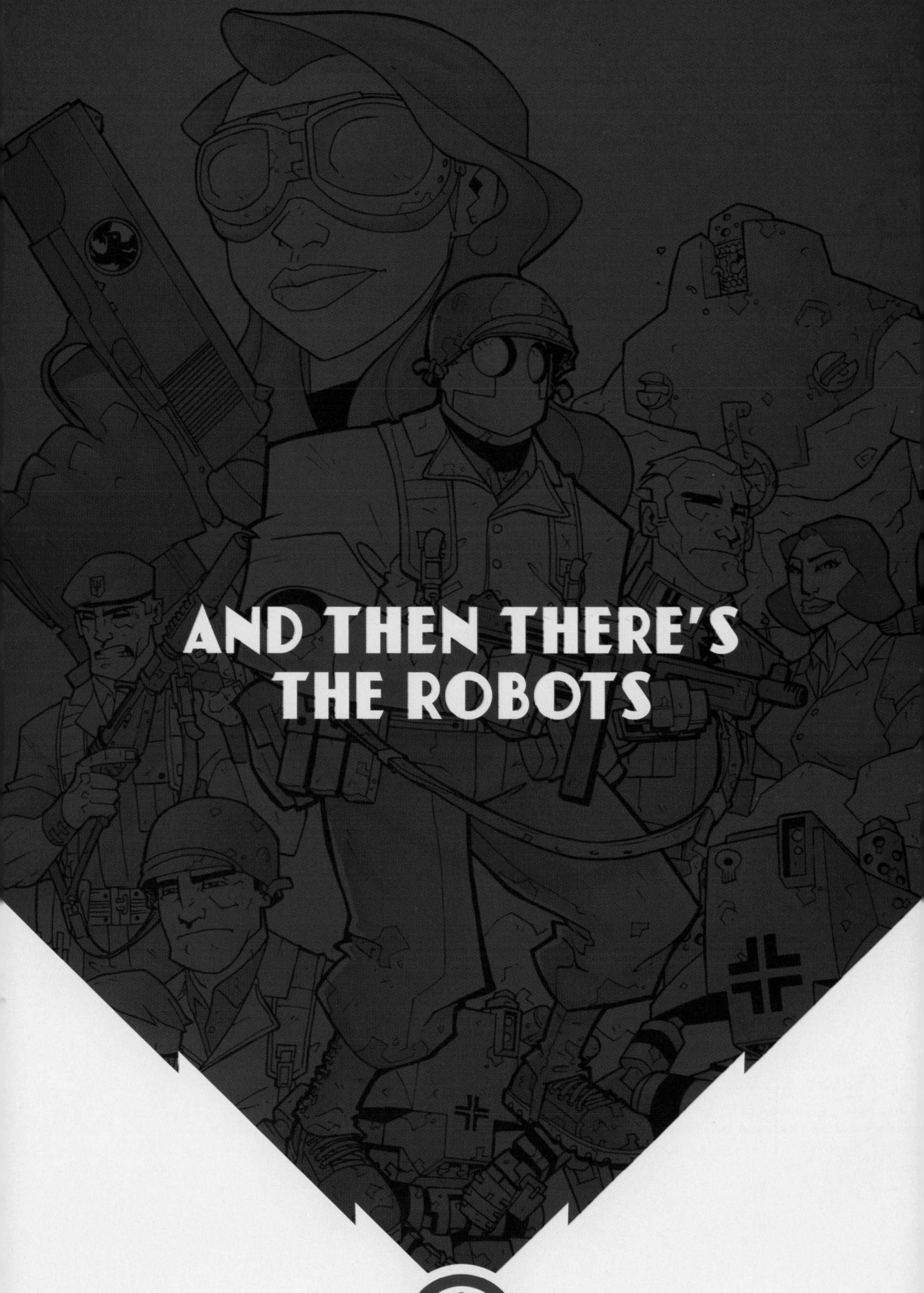

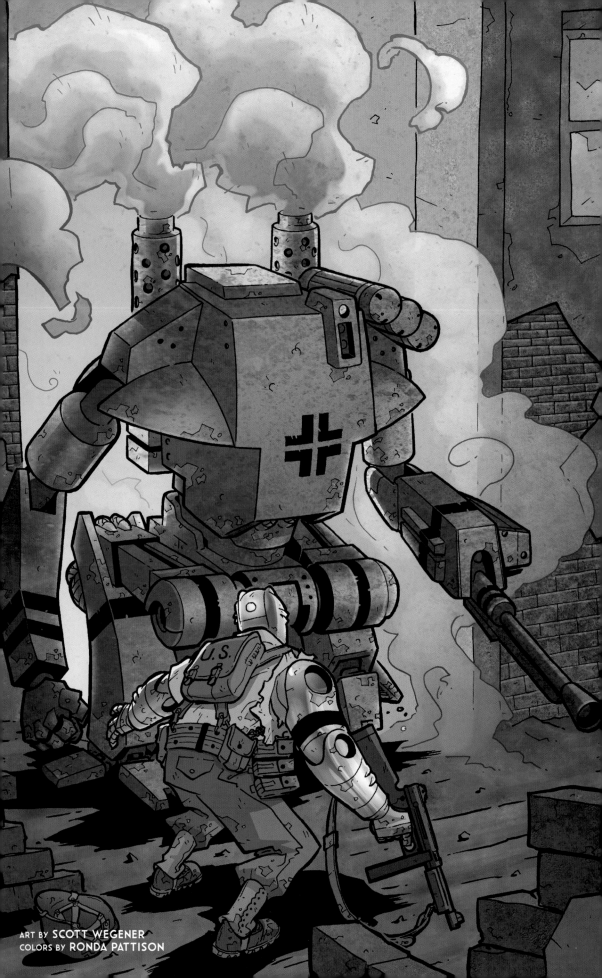

ART BY SCOTT WEGENER
COLORS BY RONDA PATTISON

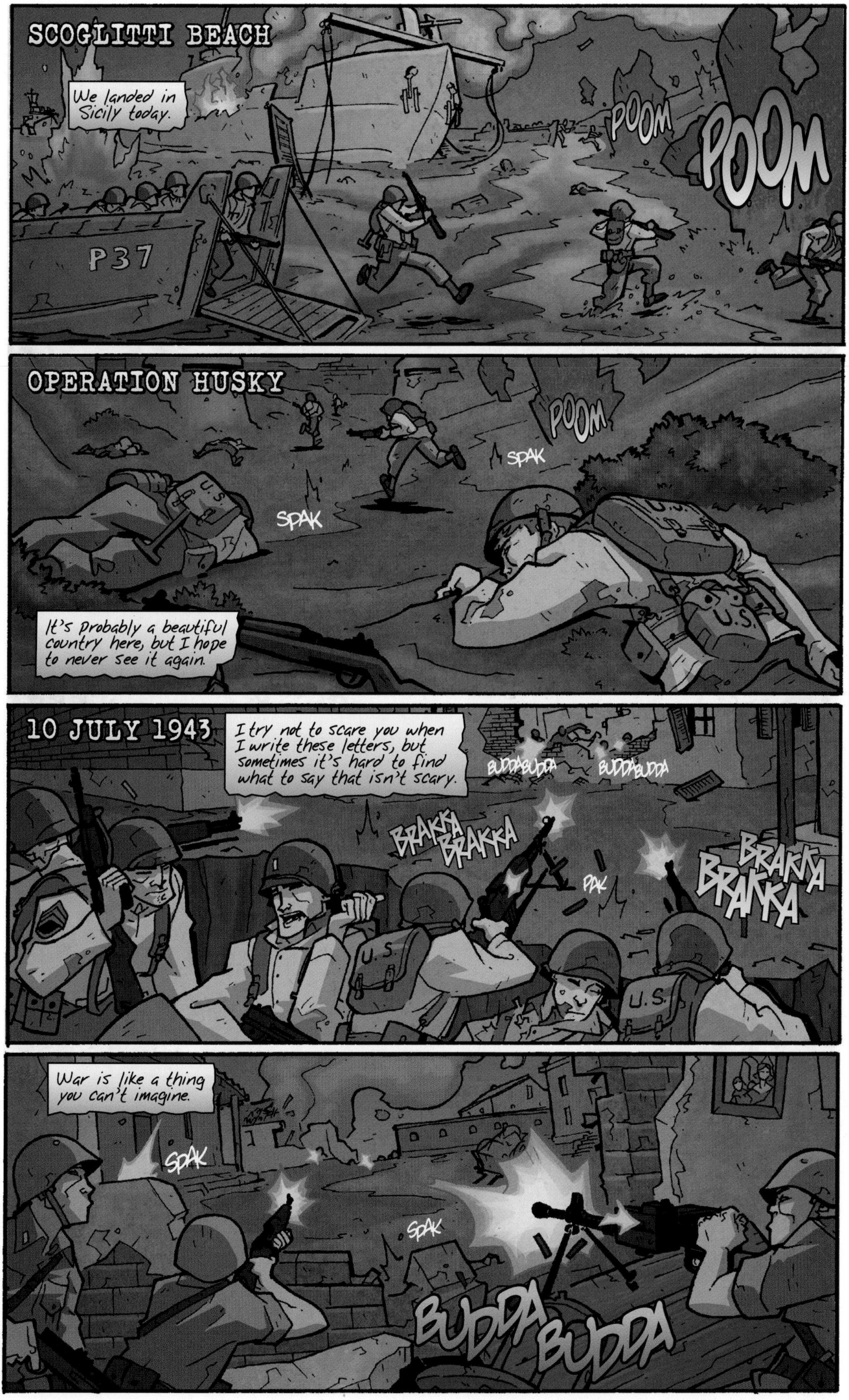
SCOGLITTI BEACH
We landed in Sicily today.
POOM
POOM
OPERATION HUSKY
POOM
SPAK
SPAK
It's probably a beautiful country here, but I hope to never see it again.
10 JULY 1943
I try not to scare you when I write these letters, but sometimes it's hard to find what to say that isn't scary.
BUDDABUDDA
BUDDABUDDA
BRAKKA BRAKKA
PAK
BRAKKA BRAKKA
War is like a thing you can't imagine.
SPAK
SPAK
BUDDA BUDDA

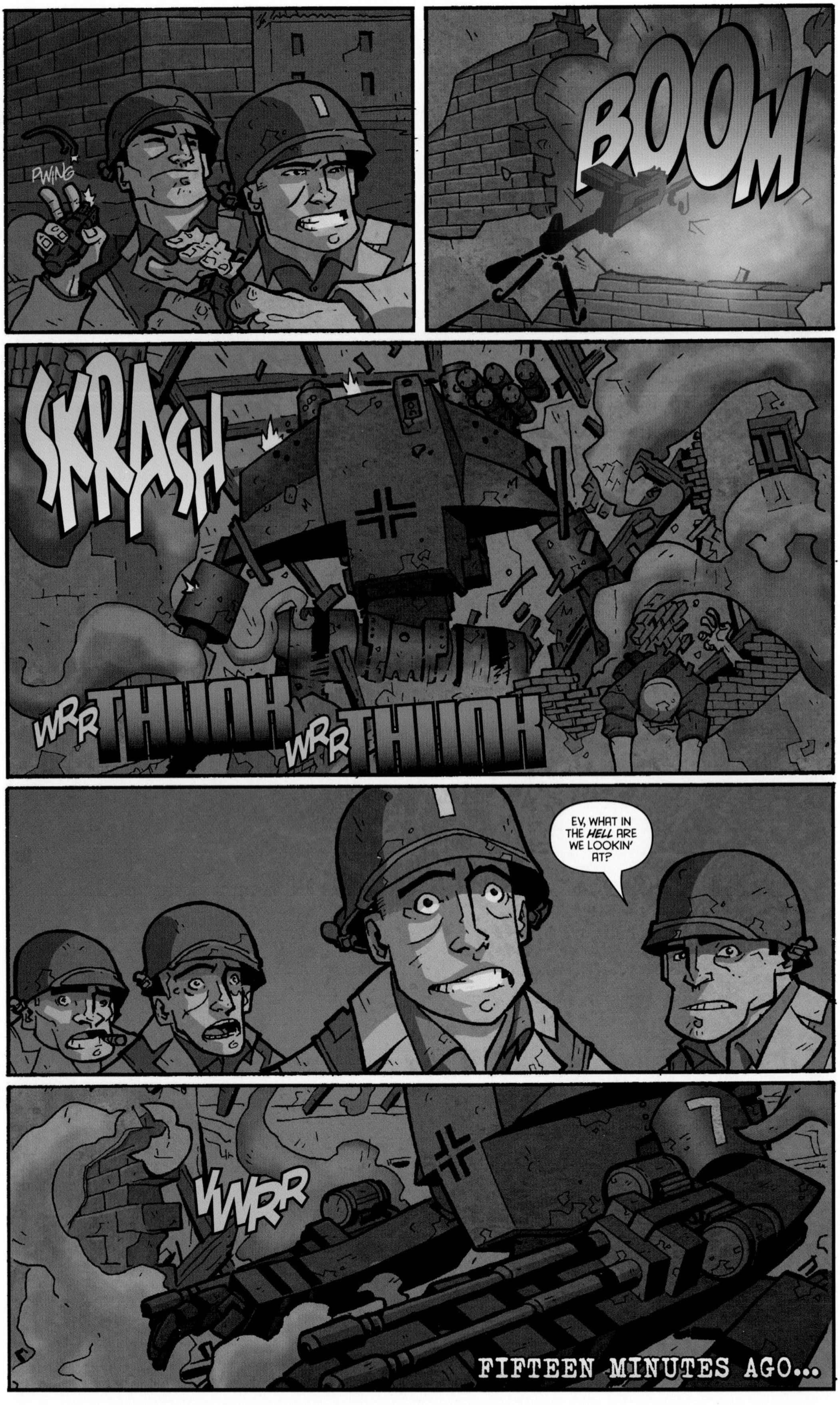
PWING
BOOM
SKRASH
WRR THUNK WRR THUNK
EV, WHAT IN THE *HELL* ARE WE LOOKIN' AT?
KWRR
FIFTEEN MINUTES AGO...

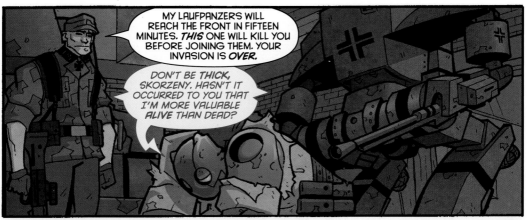

MY LAUFPANZERS WILL REACH THE FRONT IN FIFTEEN MINUTES. *THIS* ONE WILL KILL YOU BEFORE JOINING THEM. YOUR INVASION IS *OVER*.

DON'T BE *THICK*, SKORZENY. HASN'T IT OCCURRED TO YOU THAT I'M MORE VALUABLE *ALIVE* THAN DEAD?

NO, I QUITE DOUBT THAT.

DO YOU THINK THEY'D SEND ME HERE WITHOUT GIVING ME THE *BIG PICTURE*? HELL, I'M HERE AT FDR'S *PERSONAL* REQUEST. YOU COULD WIN THE WAR IN A *MONTH* USING WHAT I KNOW.

WENN ER NUR DIE *GERINGSTE* BEWEGUNG IN MEINE RICHTUNG MACHT, FEUERN SIE AUF IHN. HÖREN SIE *NICHT* AUF ZU FEUERN, BIS ICH DEN BEFEHL DAZU GEBE.

JAWOHL, OBERST!

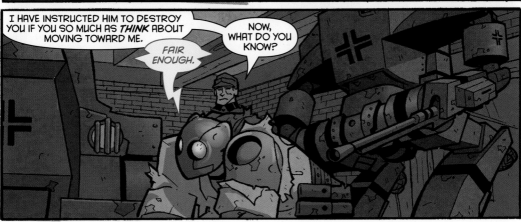

I HAVE INSTRUCTED HIM TO DESTROY YOU IF YOU SO MUCH AS *THINK* ABOUT MOVING TOWARD ME.

NOW, WHAT DO YOU KNOW?

FAIR ENOUGH.

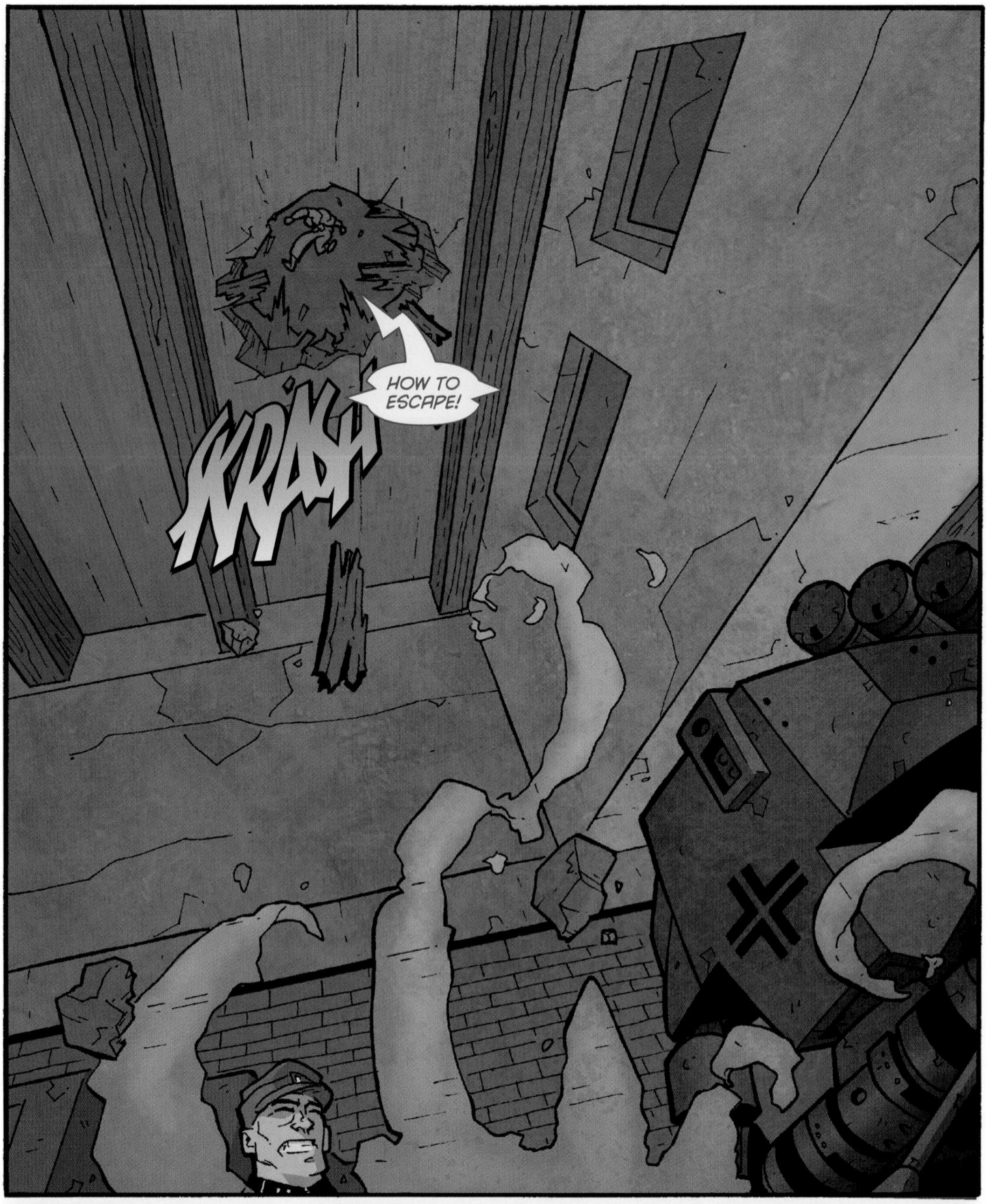
HOW TO ESCAPE!
KRASH

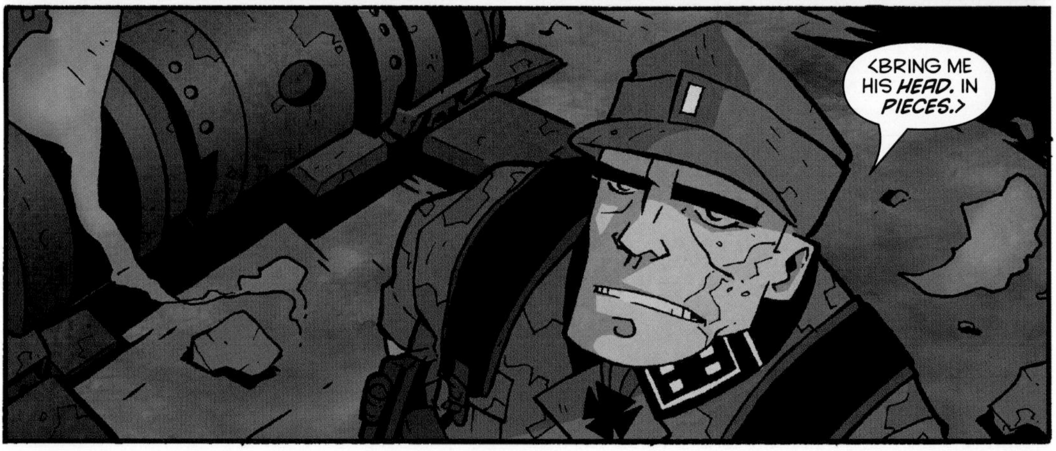
<BRING ME HIS HEAD. IN PIECES.>

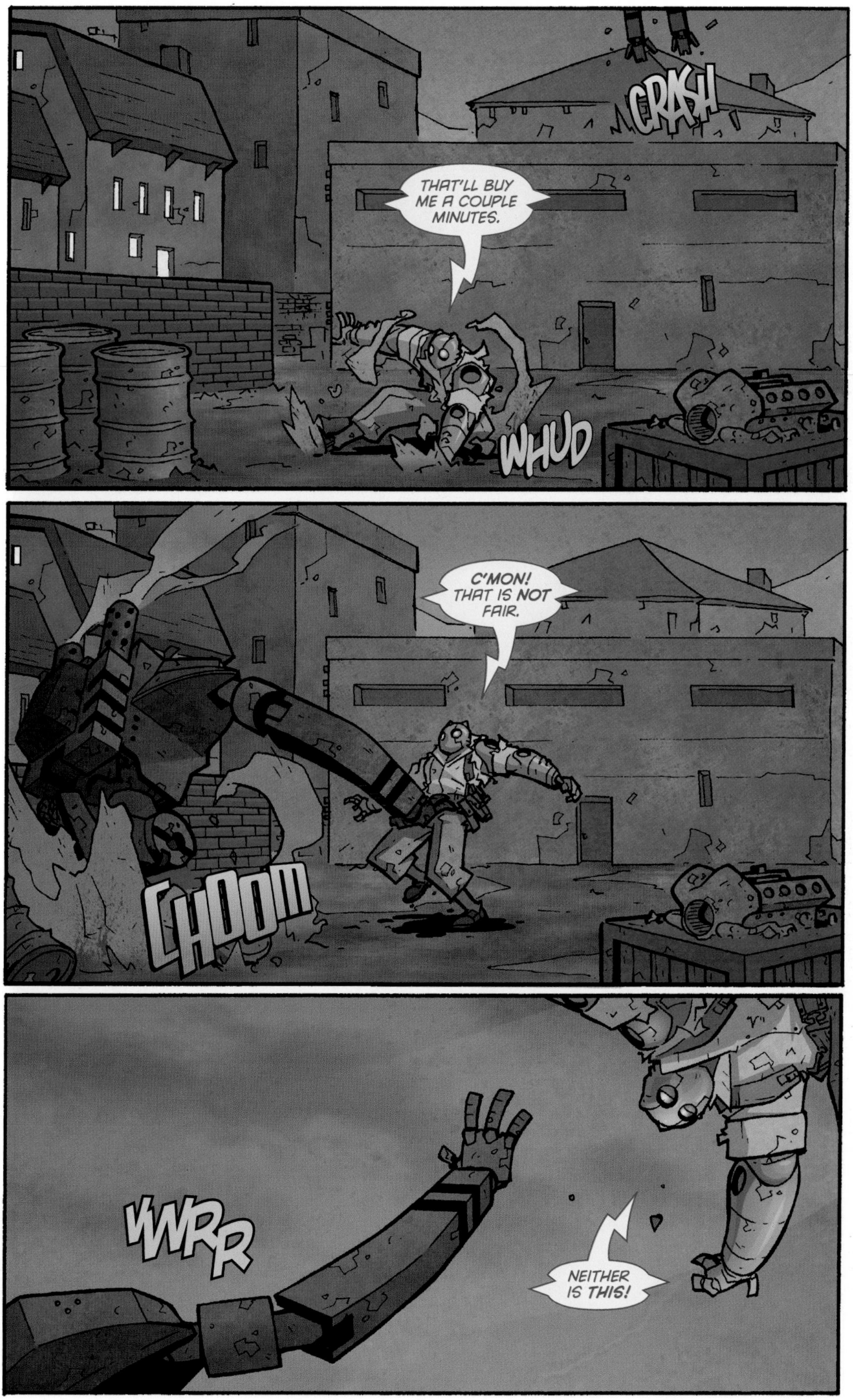
CRASH
THAT'LL BUY ME A COUPLE MINUTES.
WHUD
C'MON! THAT IS NOT FAIR.
CHOOM
WWRR
NEITHER IS THIS!

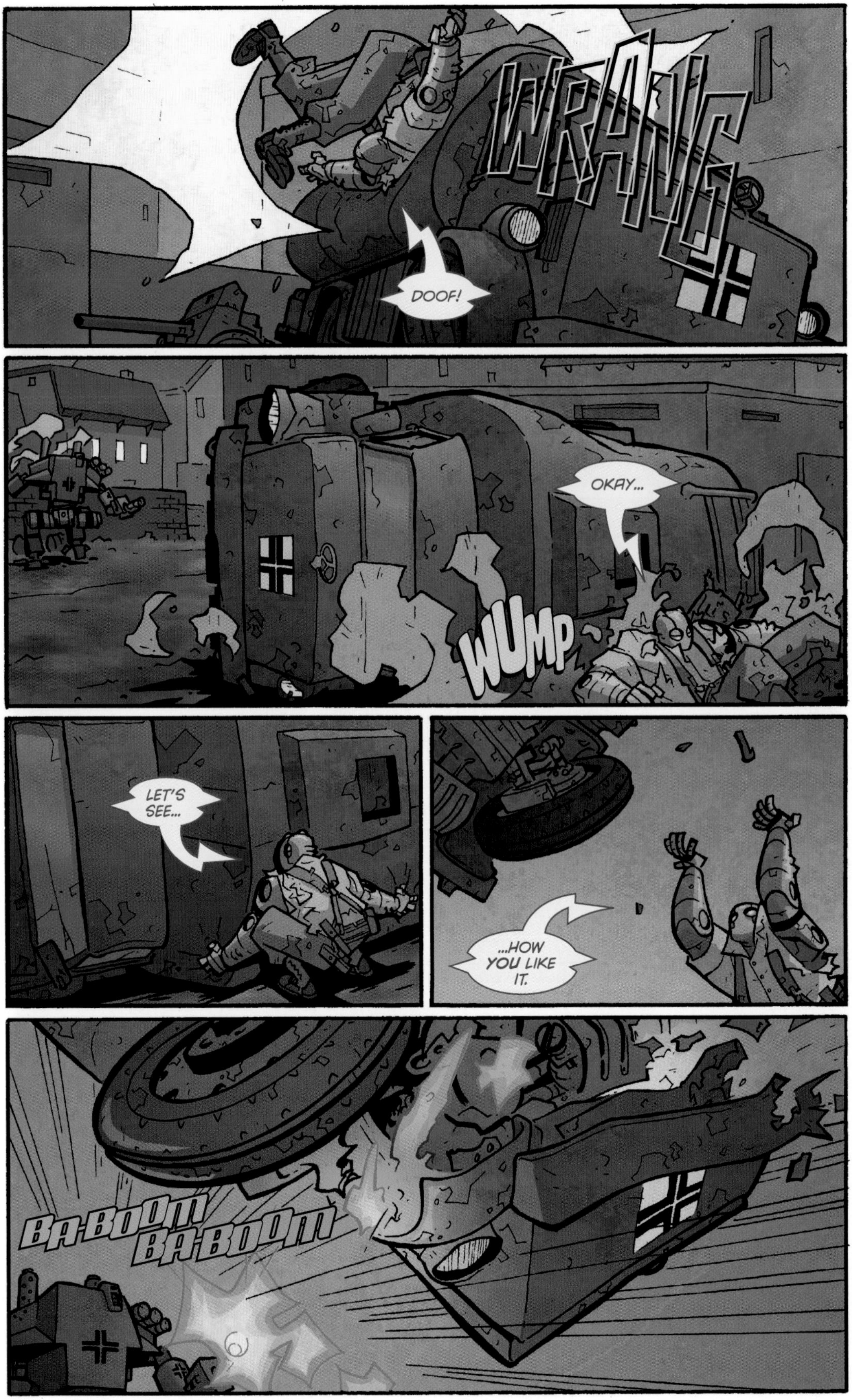
WRANG
DOOF!
OKAY...
WUMP
LET'S SEE...
...HOW YOU LIKE IT.
BA-BOOM BA-BOOM

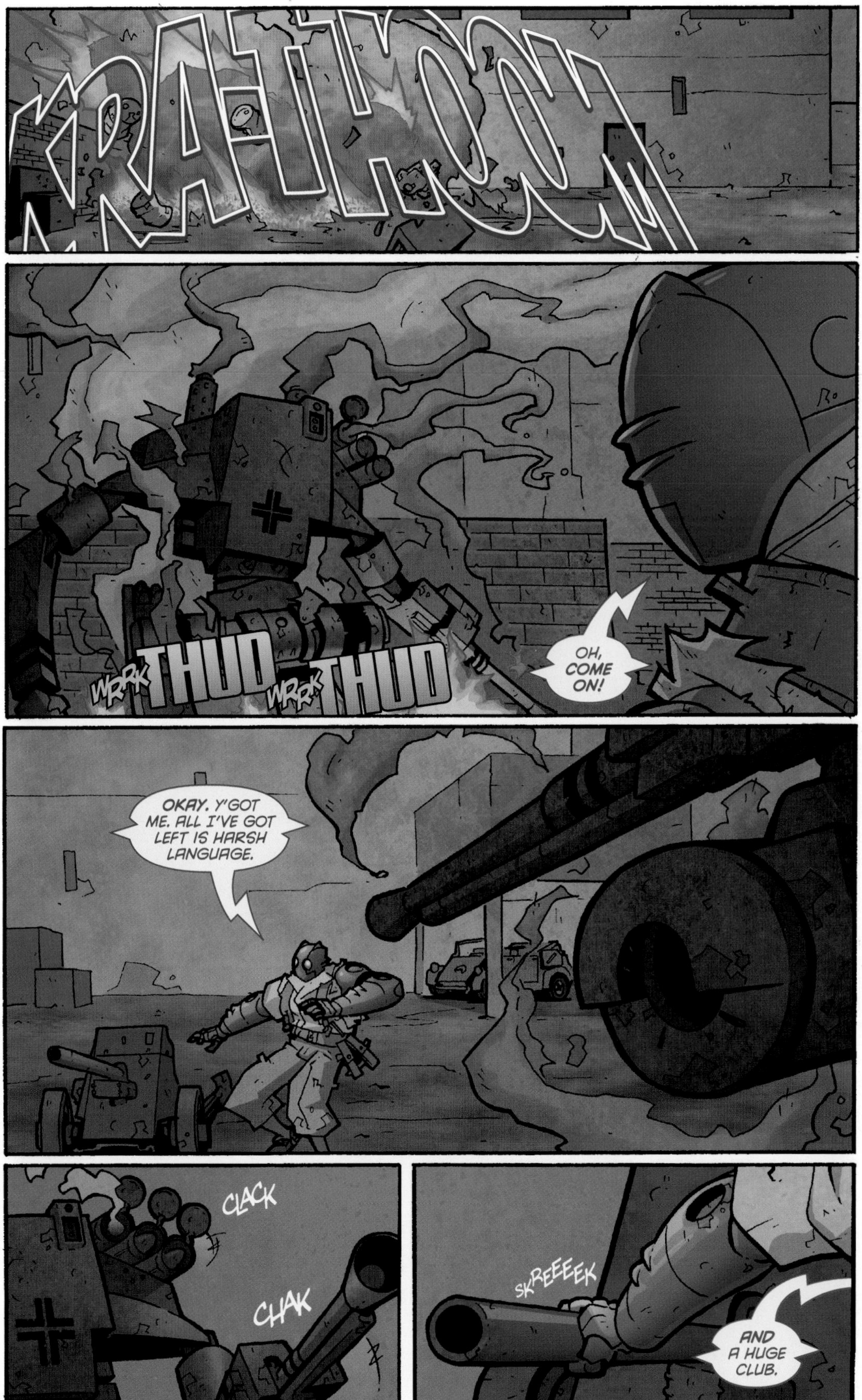
KRA-THOOM
WRRK THUD WRRK THUD
OH, COME ON!
OKAY. Y'GOT ME. ALL I'VE GOT LEFT IS HARSH LANGUAGE.
CLACK
CHAK
SKREEEEK
AND A HUGE CLUB.

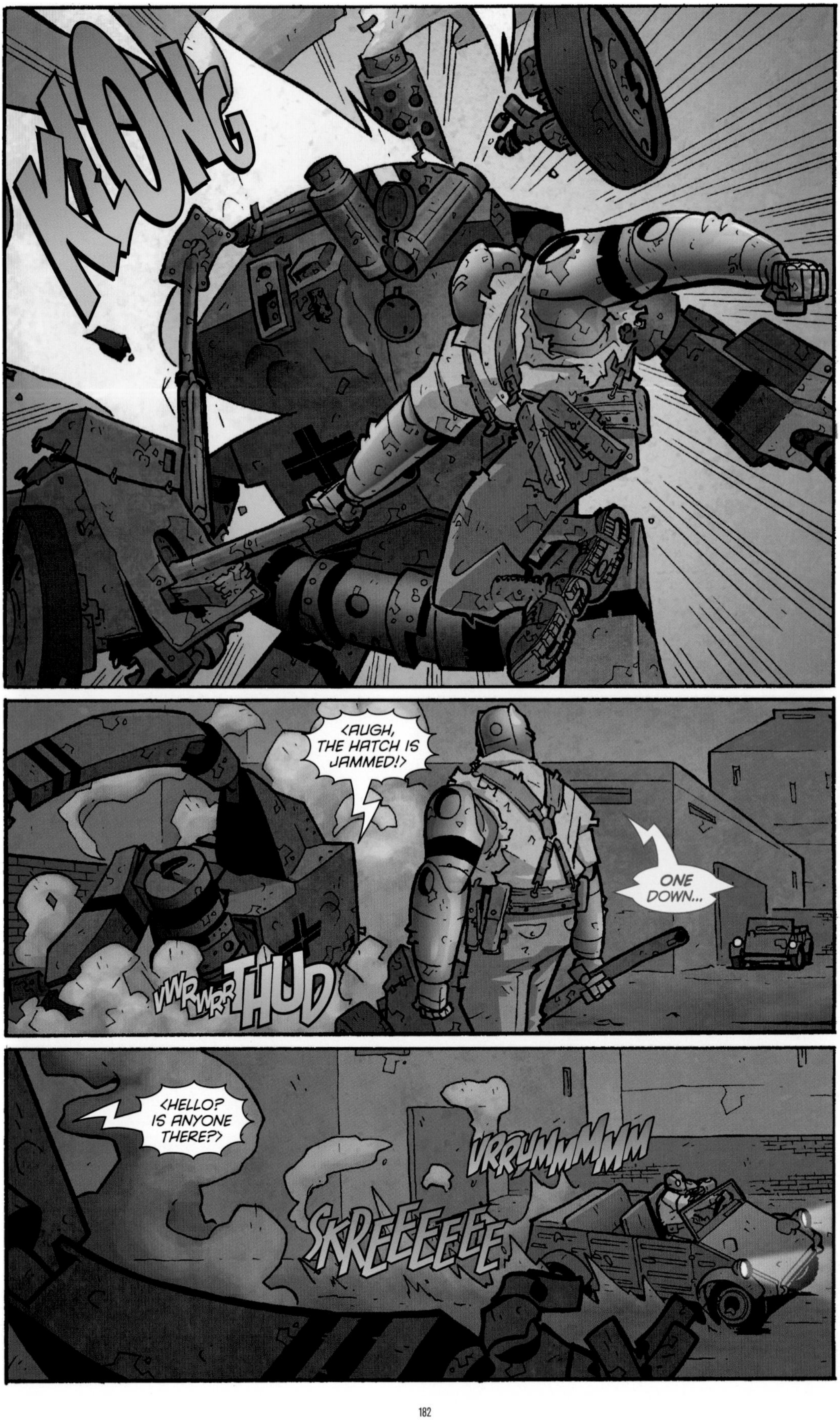
KLONG
<AUGH, THE HATCH IS JAMMED!>
ONE DOWN...
VWRWRR THUD
<HELLO? IS ANYONE THERE?>
URRUMMMMM
SKREEEEEE

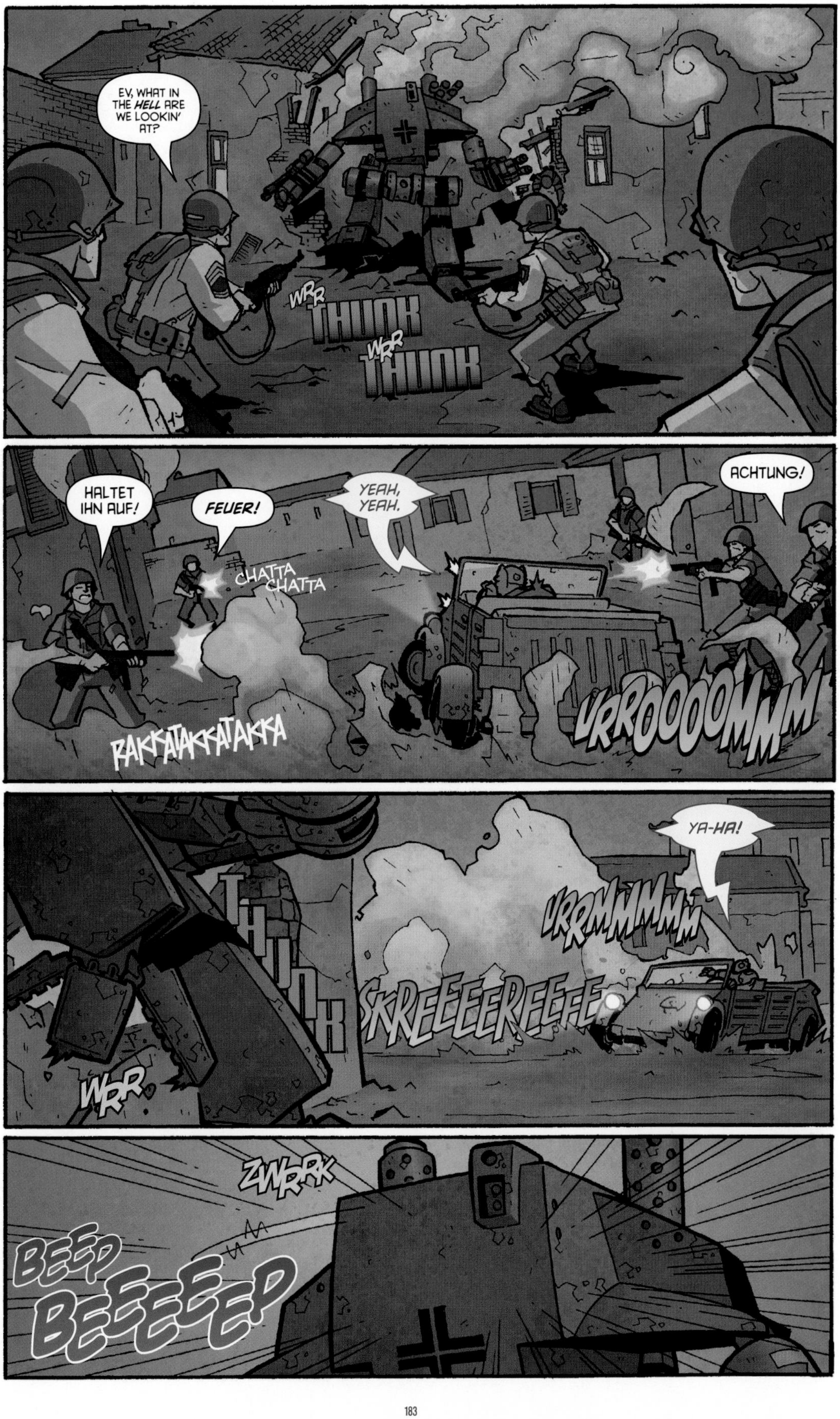
EV, WHAT IN THE HELL ARE WE LOOKIN' AT?
WRR THUNK
WRR THUNK
HALTET IHN AUF!
FEUER!
CHATTA CHATTA
YEAH, YEAH.
ACHTUNG!
RAKKATAKKATAKKA
URROOOOMMM
YA-HA!
URRMMMMMM
THUNK
SKREEEEREEEE
WRR
ZWRRK
BEEP BEEEEEP

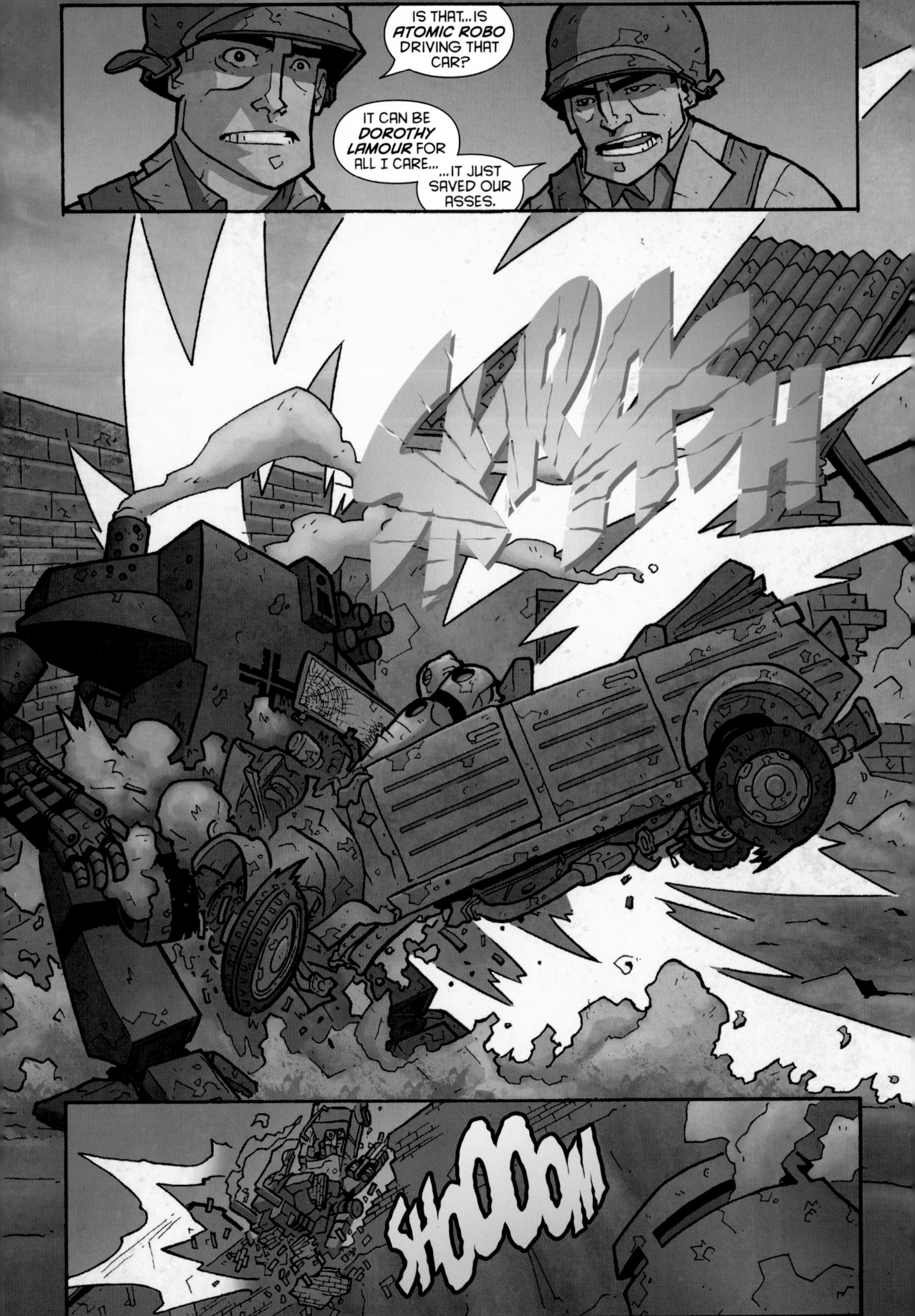
IS THAT...IS ATOMIC ROBO DRIVING THAT CAR?
IT CAN BE DOROTHY LAMOUR FOR ALL I CARE...
...IT JUST SAVED OUR ASSES.
SKRASH
SHOOOOM

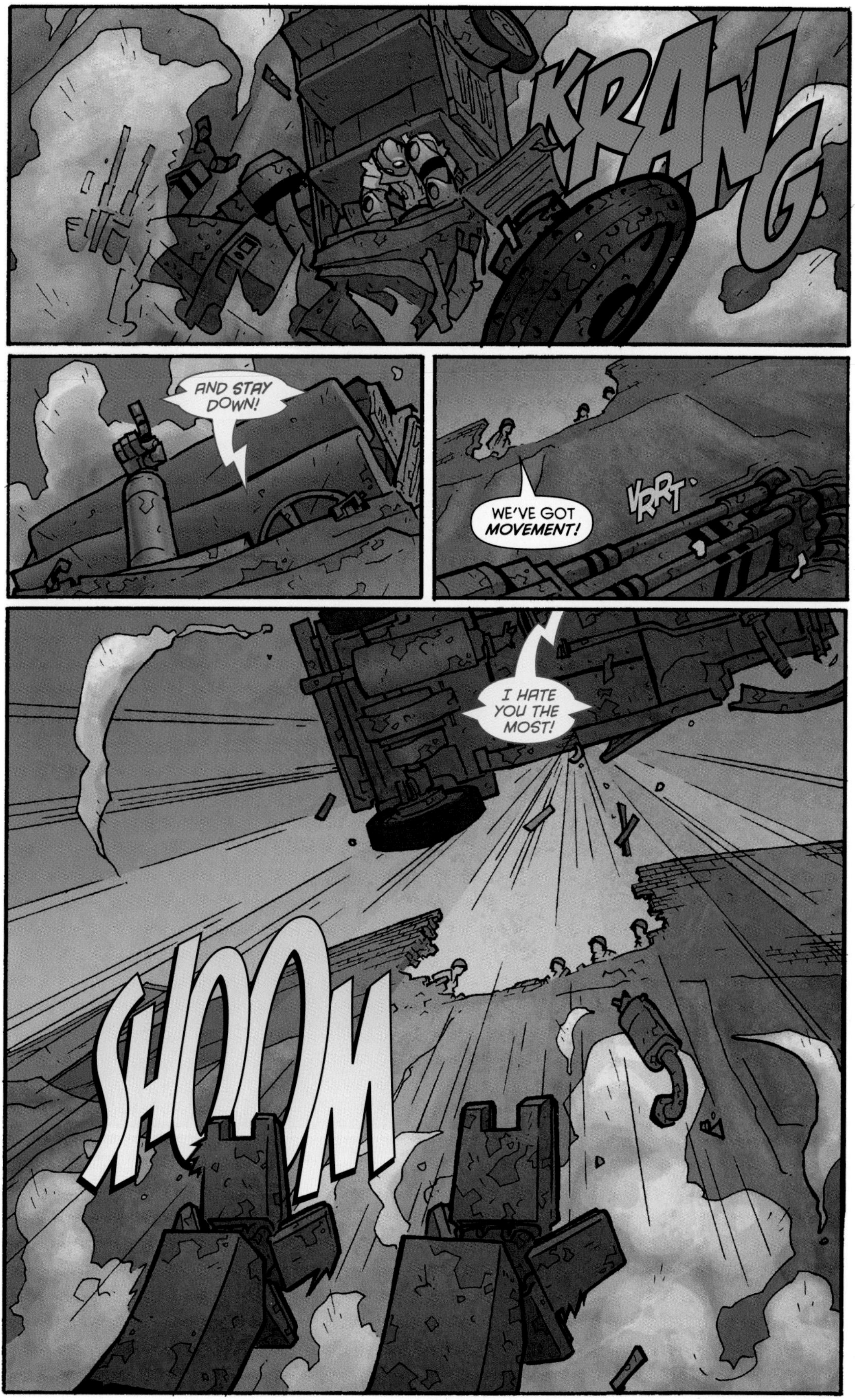
KRANG
AND STAY DOWN!
WE'VE GOT MOVEMENT!
VRRT
I HATE YOU THE MOST!
SHOOM

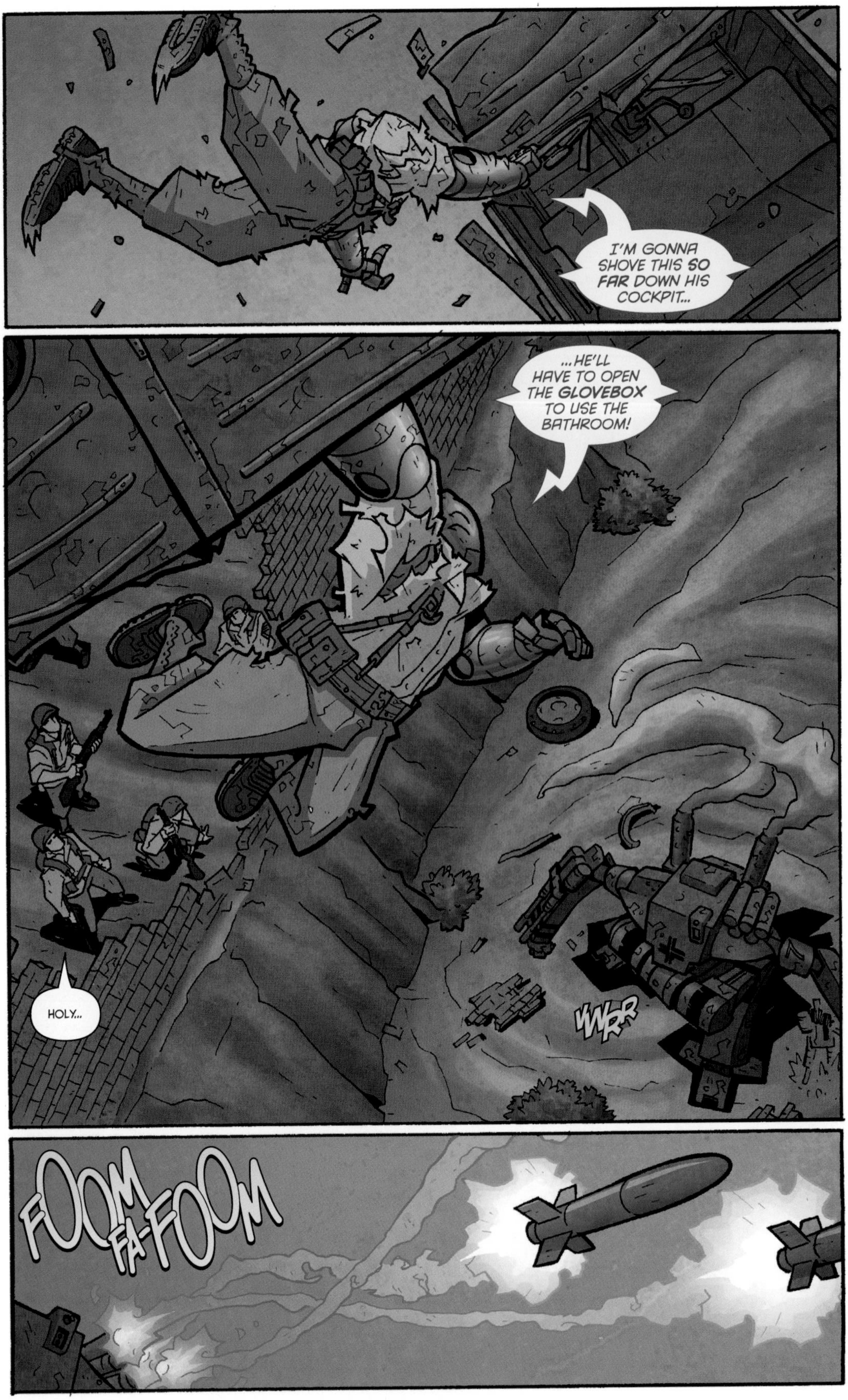
I'M GONNA SHOVE THIS **SO FAR** DOWN HIS COCKPIT...
...HE'LL HAVE TO OPEN THE **GLOVEBOX** TO USE THE BATHROOM!
HOLY...
WWRR
FOOM FA-FOOM

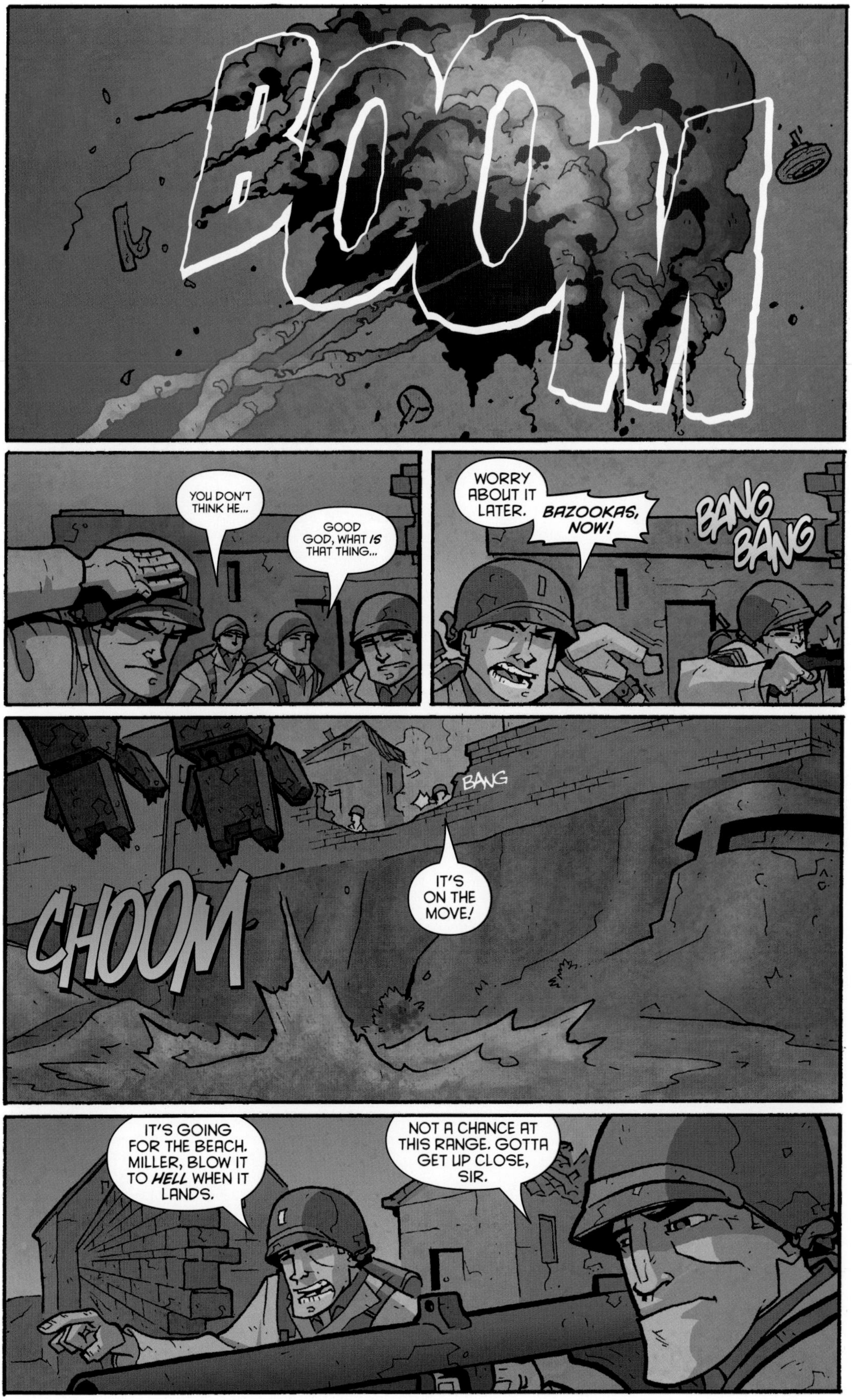
BOOM
YOU DON'T THINK HE...
GOOD GOD, WHAT *IS* THAT THING...
WORRY ABOUT IT LATER.
BAZOOKAS, NOW!
BANG BANG
BANG
IT'S ON THE MOVE!
CHOOM
IT'S GOING FOR THE BEACH. MILLER, BLOW IT TO *HELL* WHEN IT LANDS.
NOT A CHANCE AT THIS RANGE. GOTTA GET UP CLOSE, SIR.

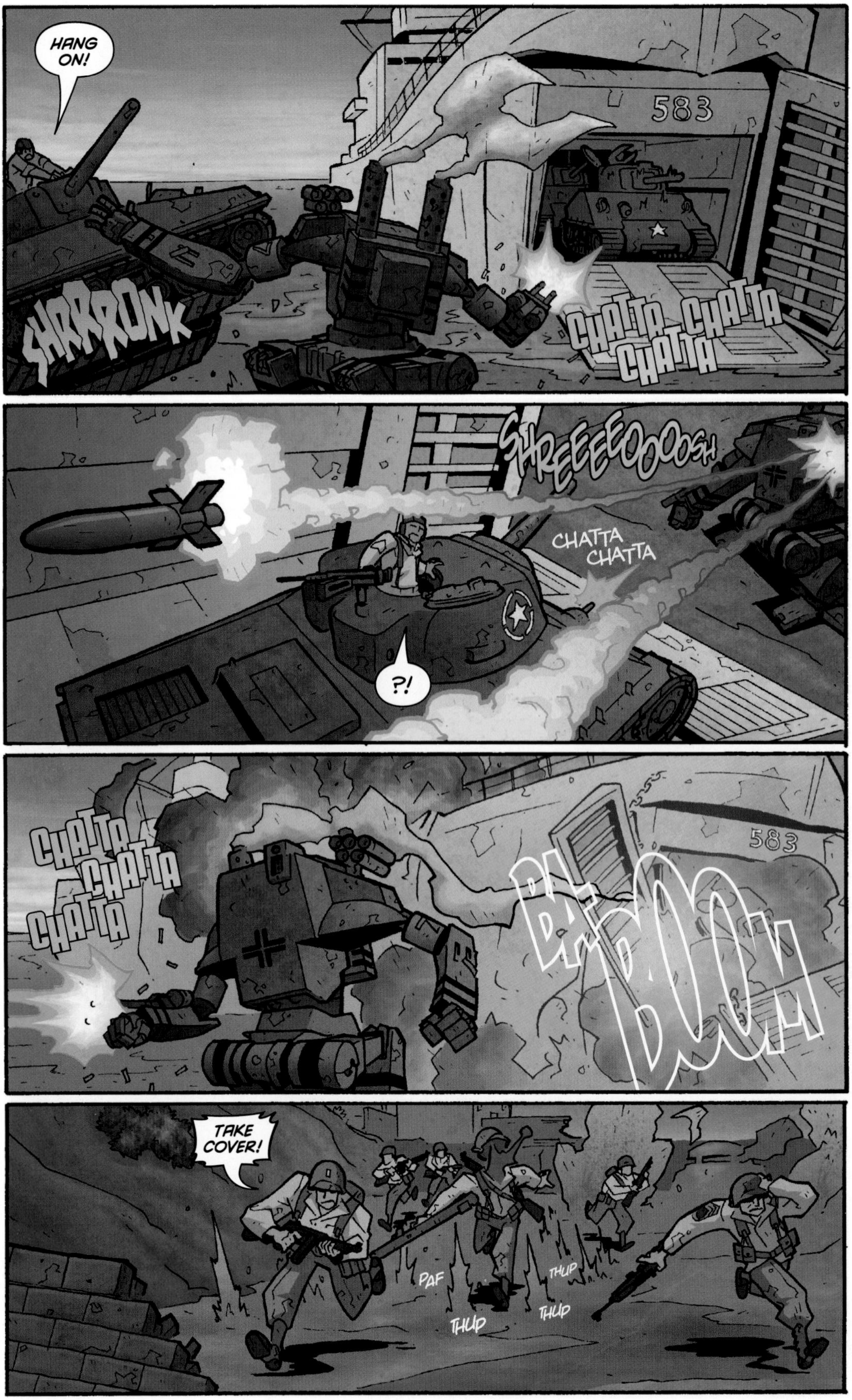
HANG ON!
583
SHRRONK
CHATTA CHATTA CHATTA
SHREEEEOOOOSH
CHATTA CHATTA
?!
CHATTA CHATTA CHATTA
583
BABOOM
TAKE COVER!
PAF
THUP
THUP
THUP

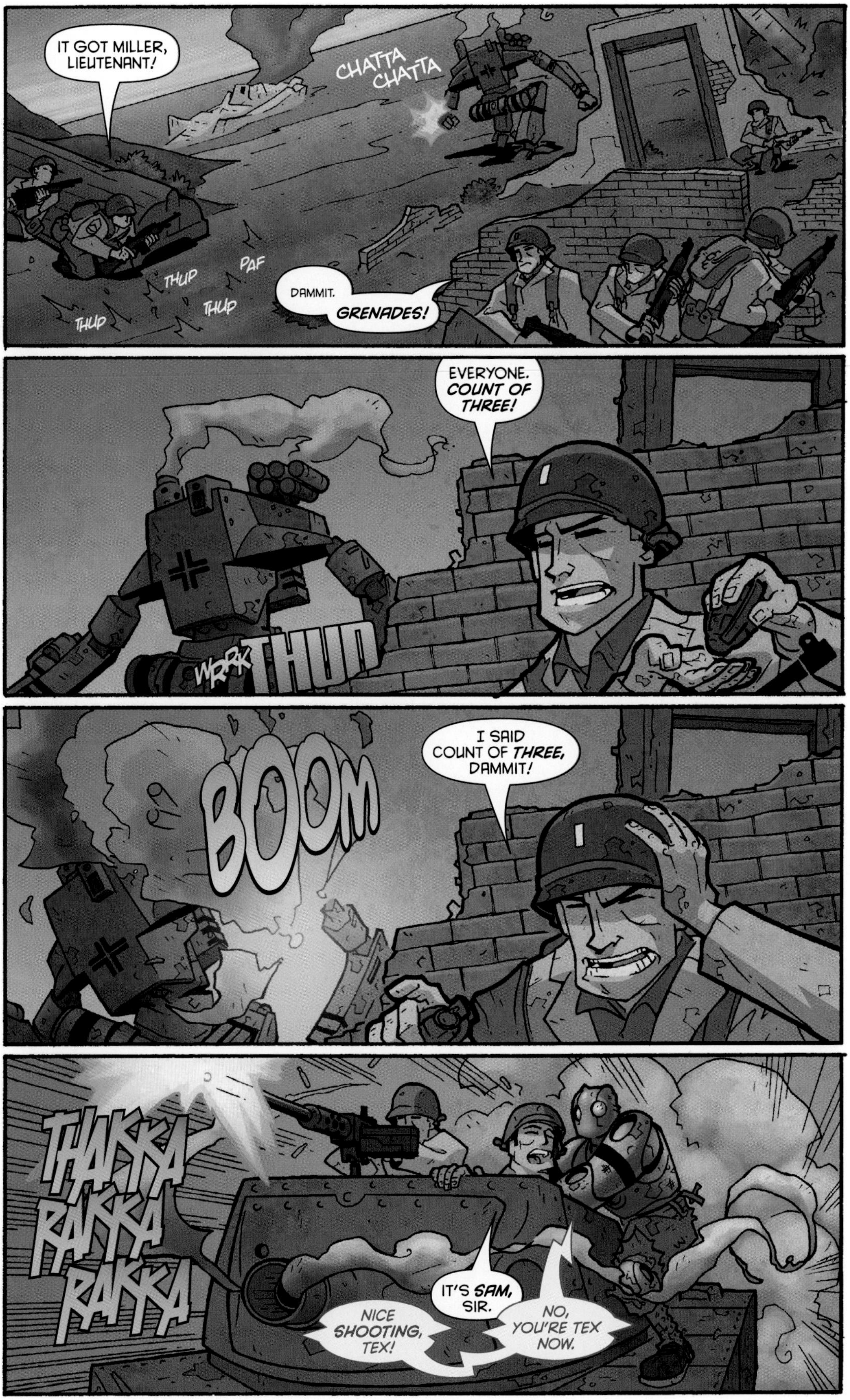
IT GOT MILLER, LIEUTENANT!
CHATTA CHATTA
THUP
THUP
PAF
THUP
DAMMIT. GRENADES!
EVERYONE. COUNT OF THREE!
WRRK THUD
BOOM
I SAID COUNT OF THREE, DAMMIT!
THAKKA RAKKA RAKKA
NICE SHOOTING, TEX!
IT'S SAM, SIR.
NO, YOU'RE TEX NOW.

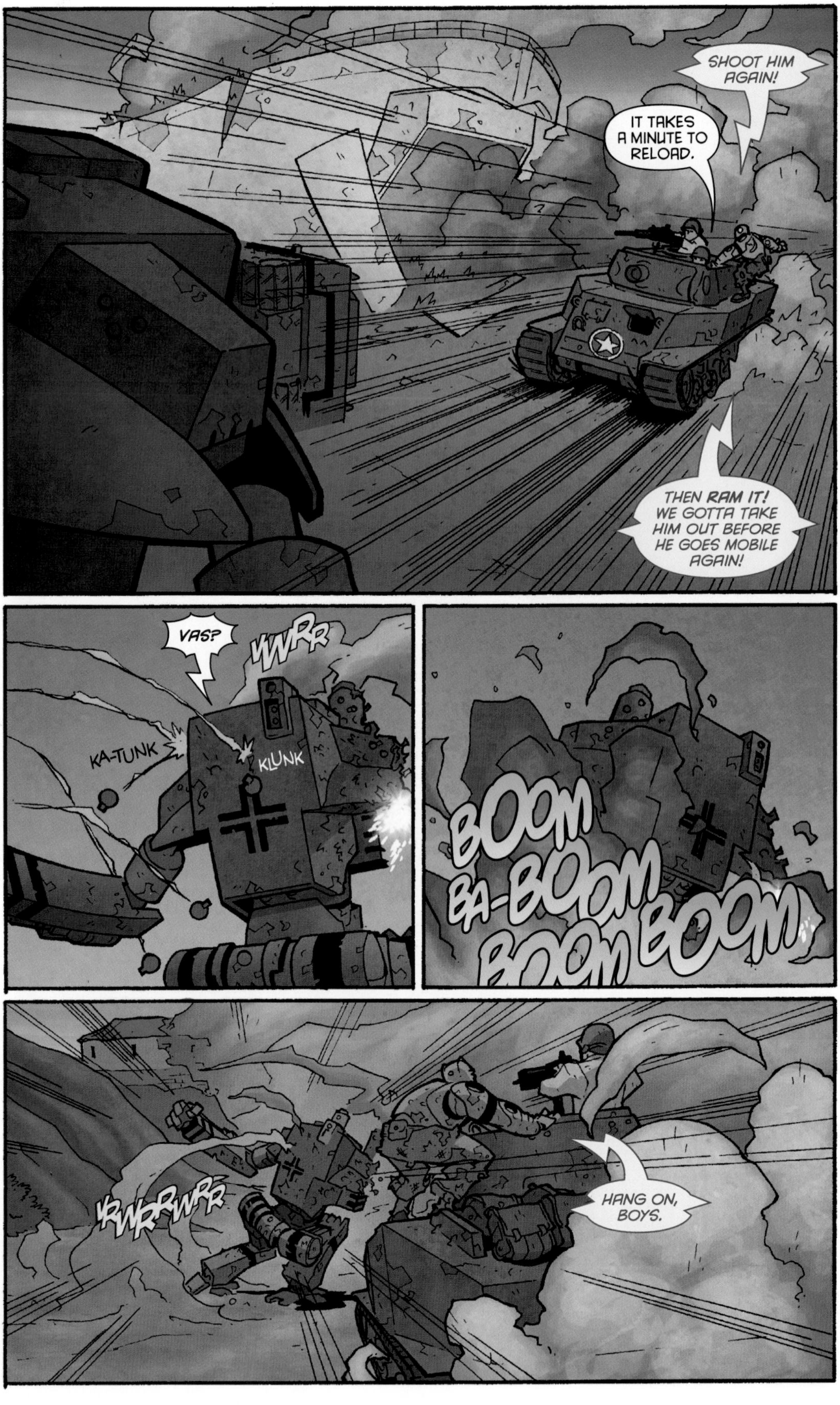

SHOOT HIM AGAIN!
IT TAKES A MINUTE TO RELOAD.
THEN **RAM IT!** WE GOTTA TAKE HIM OUT BEFORE HE GOES MOBILE AGAIN!
VAS?
WWRR
KA-TUNK
KLUNK
BOOM BA-BOOM BOOM BOOM
VRWRRWRR
HANG ON, BOYS.

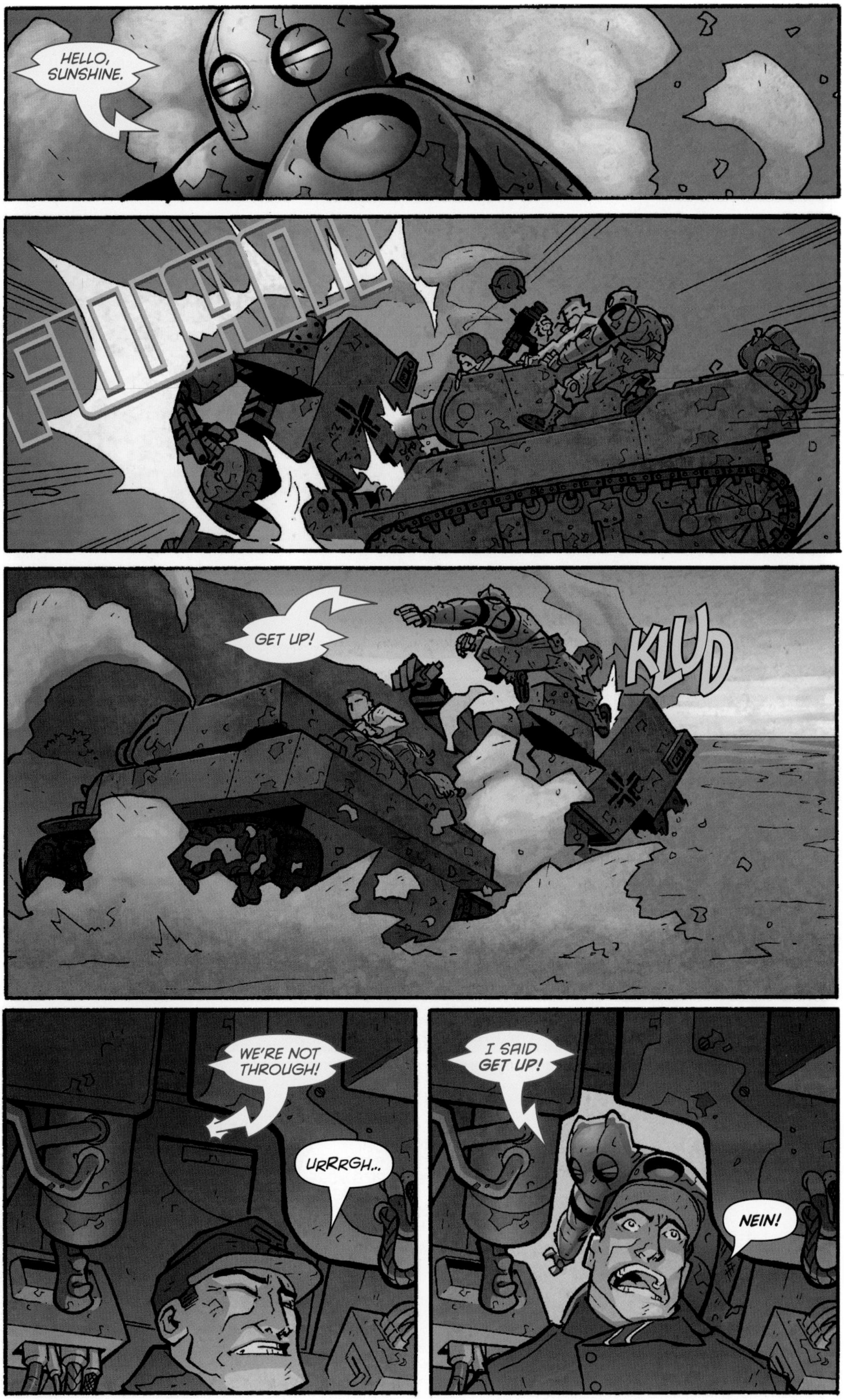
HELLO, SUNSHINE.
GET UP!
KLUD
WE'RE NOT THROUGH!
URRRGH...
I SAID GET UP!
NEIN!

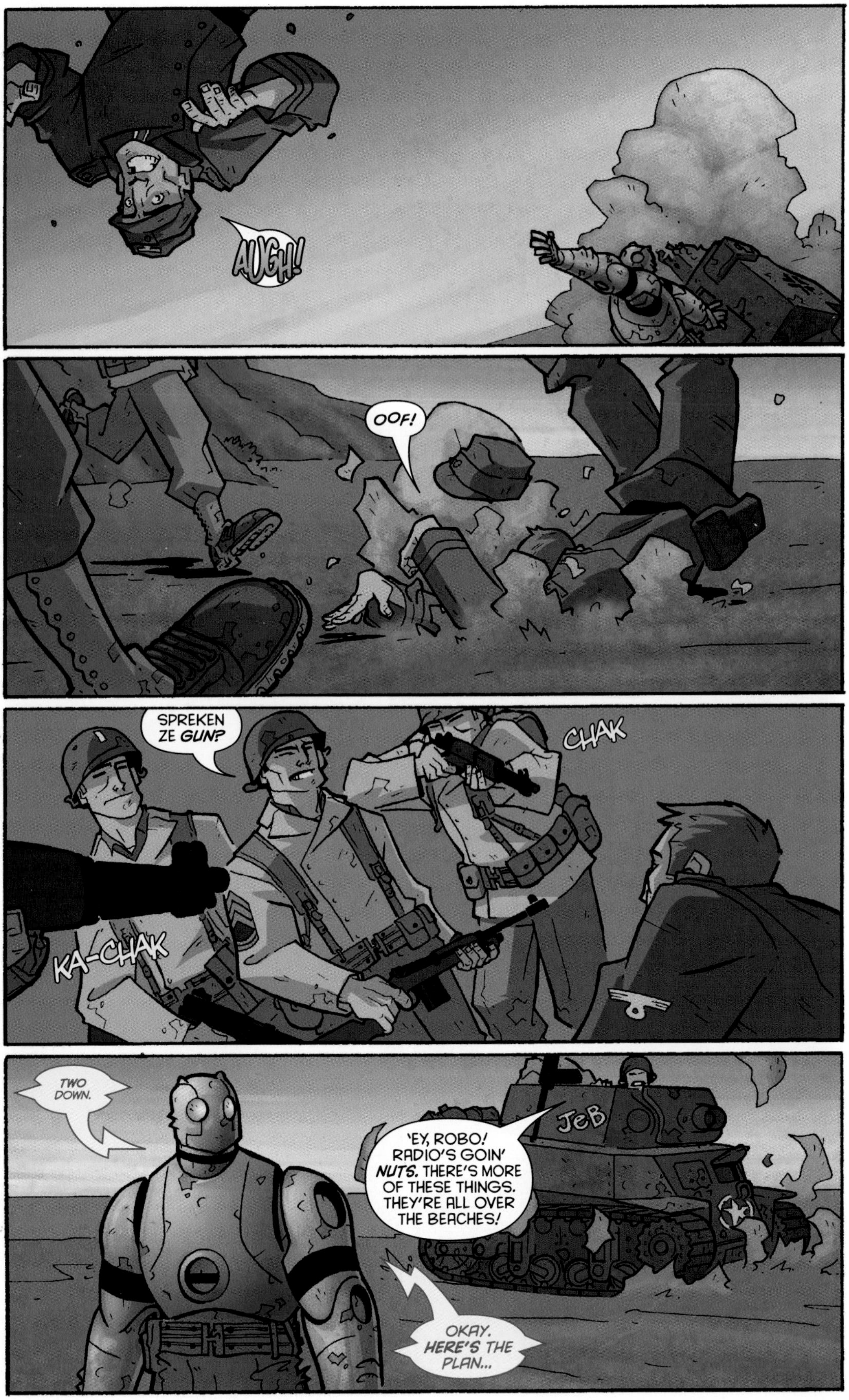
AUGH!
OOF!
SPREKEN ZE GUN?
CHAK
KA-CHAK
TWO DOWN.
'EY, ROBO! RADIO'S GOIN' NUTS. THERE'S MORE OF THESE THINGS. THEY'RE ALL OVER THE BEACHES!
JeB
OKAY. HERE'S THE PLAN...

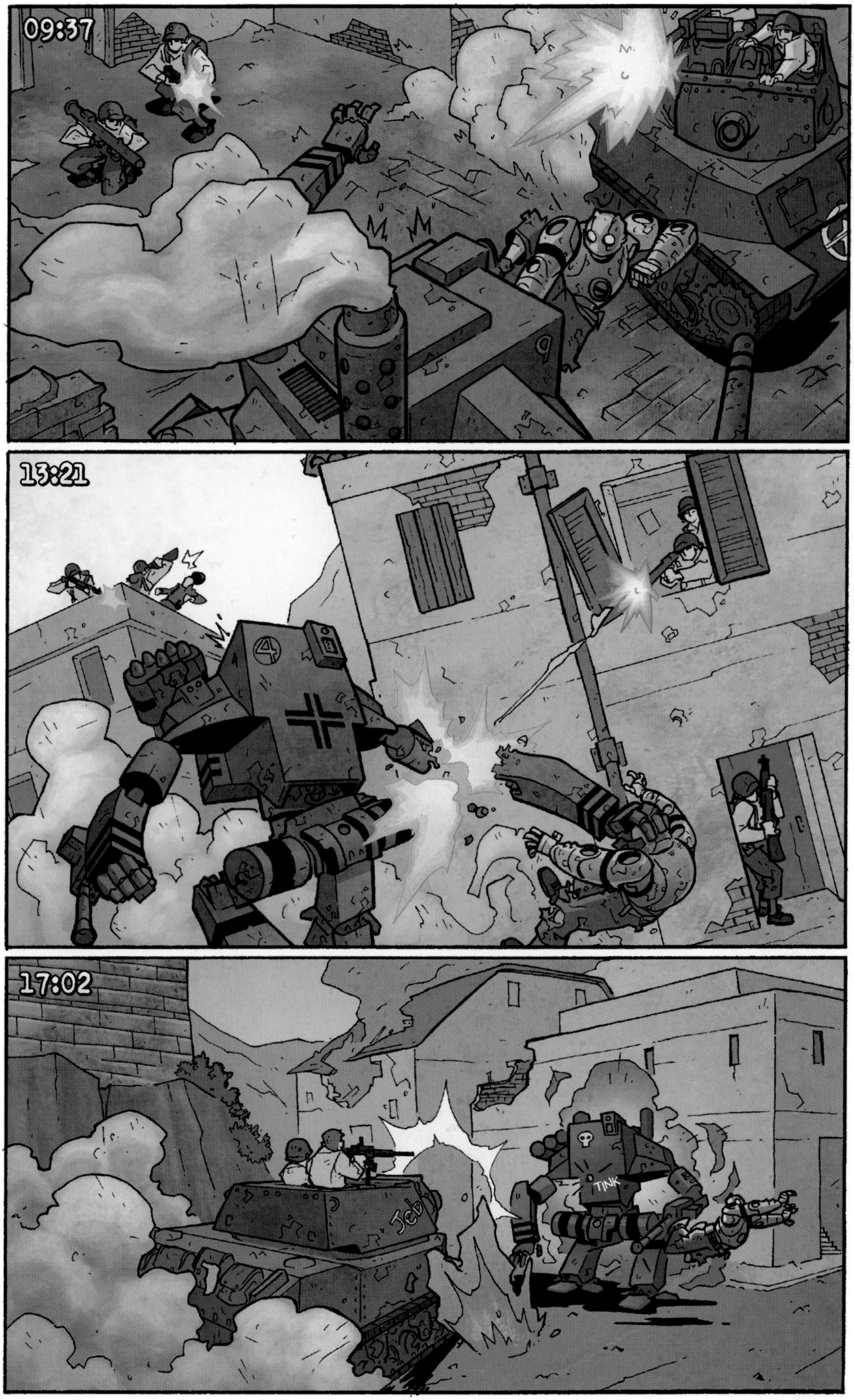
09:37
13:21
17:02
Jeb
TINK

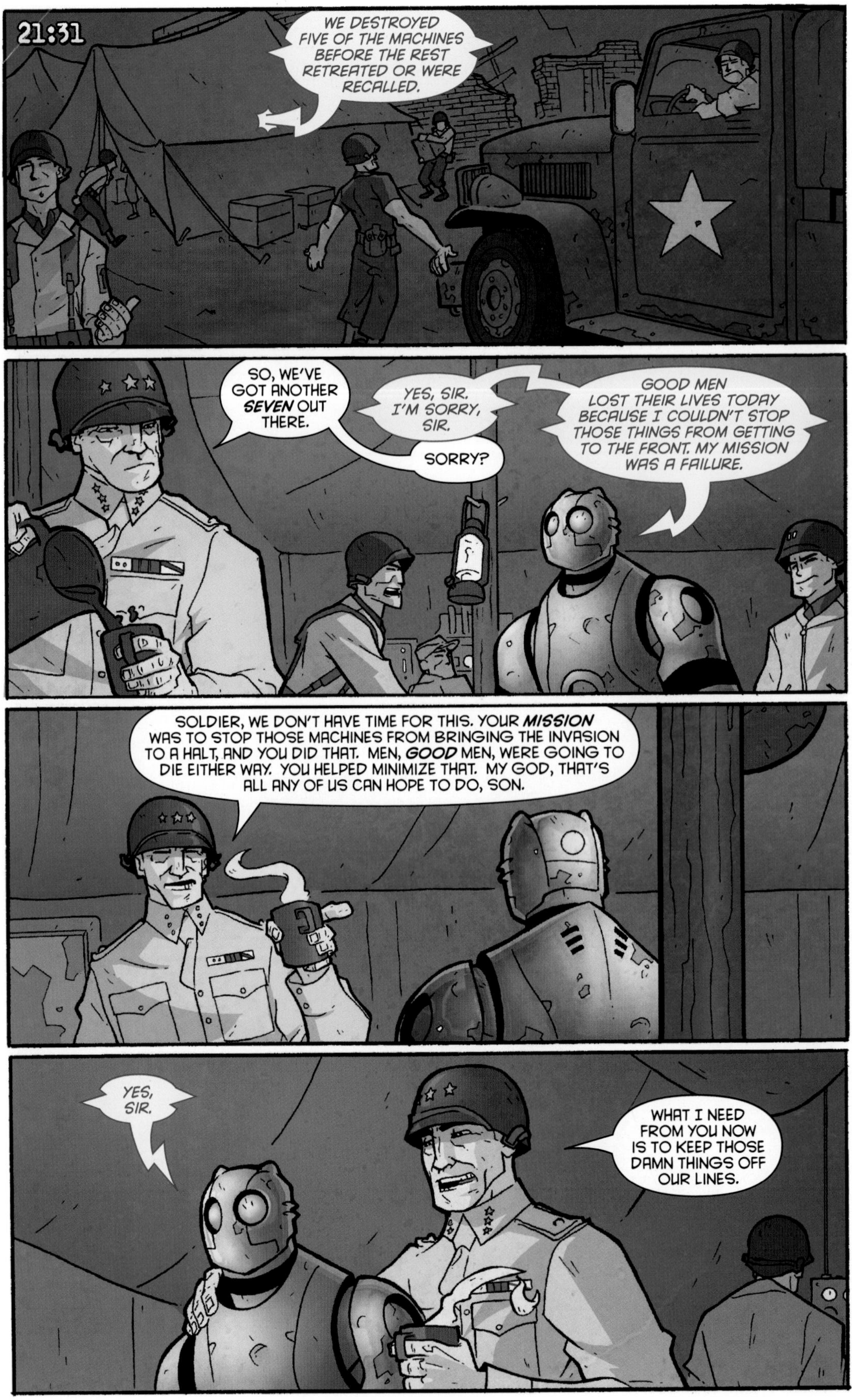
21:31
WE DESTROYED FIVE OF THE MACHINES BEFORE THE REST RETREATED OR WERE RECALLED.
SO, WE'VE GOT ANOTHER SEVEN OUT THERE.
YES, SIR. I'M SORRY, SIR.
SORRY?
GOOD MEN LOST THEIR LIVES TODAY BECAUSE I COULDN'T STOP THOSE THINGS FROM GETTING TO THE FRONT. MY MISSION WAS A FAILURE.
SOLDIER, WE DON'T HAVE TIME FOR THIS. YOUR MISSION WAS TO STOP THOSE MACHINES FROM BRINGING THE INVASION TO A HALT, AND YOU DID THAT. MEN, GOOD MEN, WERE GOING TO DIE EITHER WAY. YOU HELPED MINIMIZE THAT. MY GOD, THAT'S ALL ANY OF US CAN HOPE TO DO, SON.
YES, SIR.
WHAT I NEED FROM YOU NOW IS TO KEEP THOSE DAMN THINGS OFF OUR LINES.

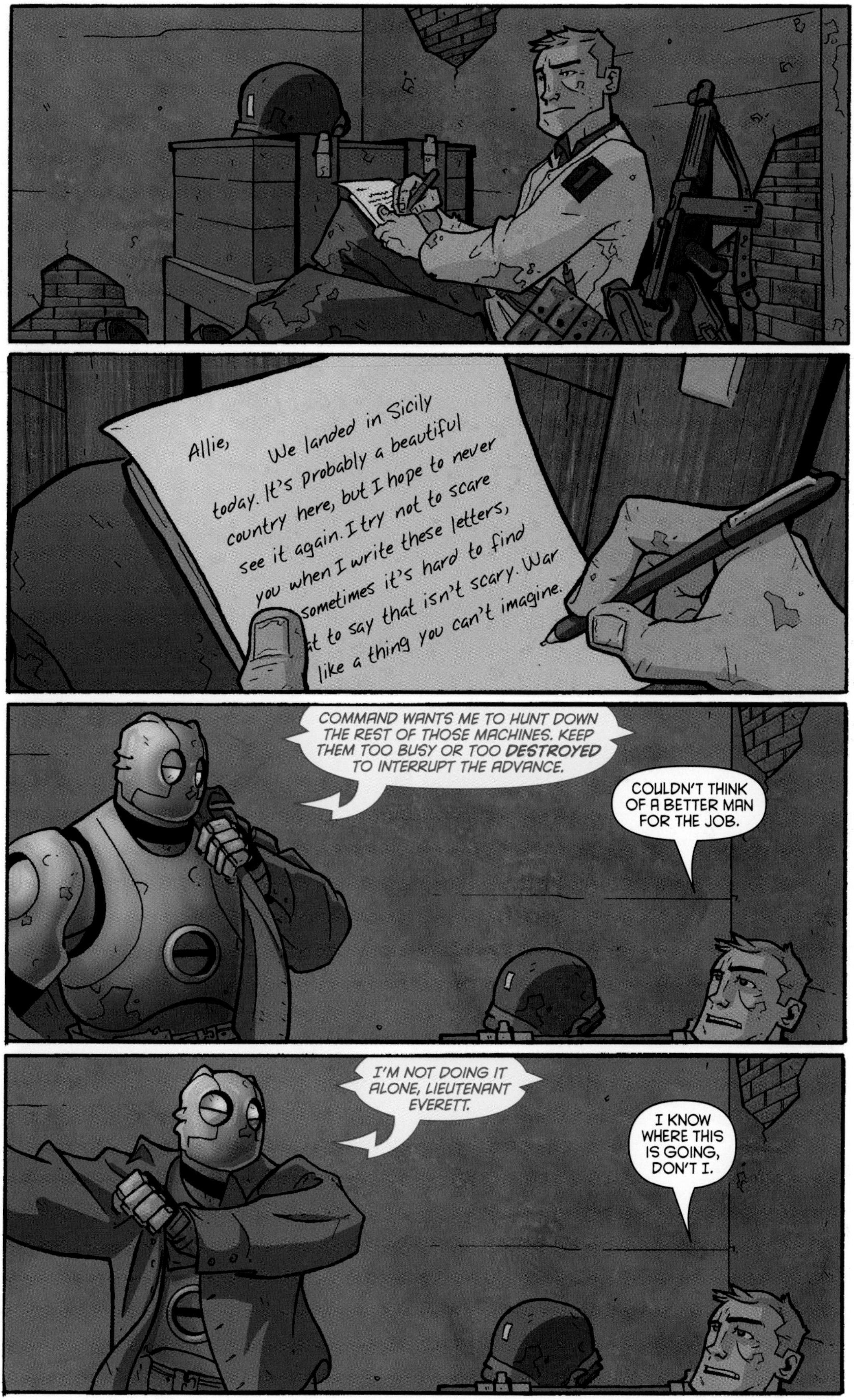
Allie,
We landed in Sicily today. It's probably a beautiful country here, but I hope to never see it again. I try not to scare you when I write these letters, sometimes it's hard to find
to say that isn't scary. War like a thing you can't imagine.
COMMAND WANTS ME TO HUNT DOWN THE REST OF THOSE MACHINES. KEEP THEM TOO BUSY OR TOO DESTROYED TO INTERRUPT THE ADVANCE.
COULDN'T THINK OF A BETTER MAN FOR THE JOB.
I'M NOT DOING IT ALONE, LIEUTENANT EVERETT.
I KNOW WHERE THIS IS GOING, DON'T I.

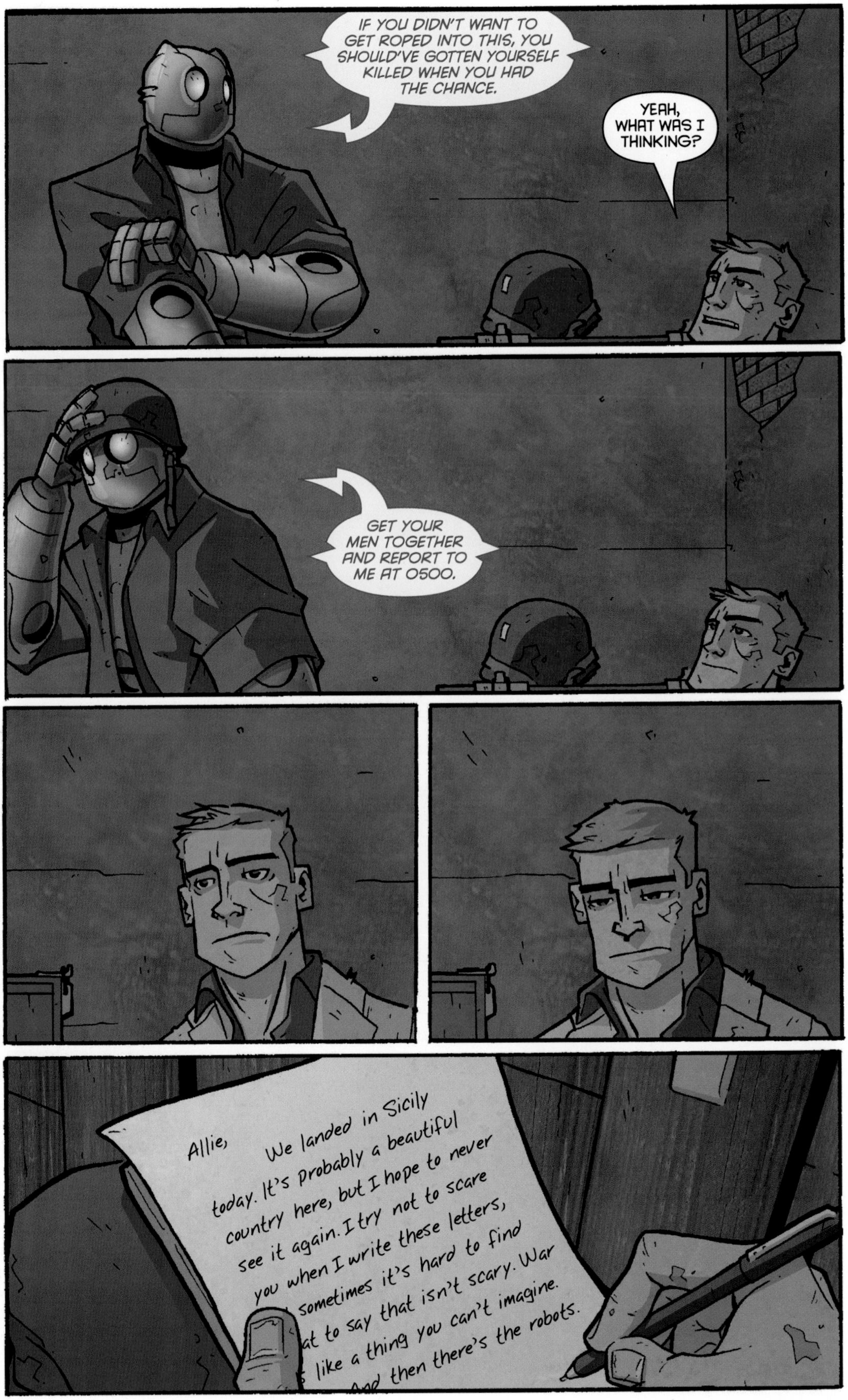
IF YOU DIDN'T WANT TO GET ROPED INTO THIS, YOU SHOULD'VE GOTTEN YOURSELF KILLED WHEN YOU HAD THE CHANCE.
YEAH, WHAT WAS I THINKING?
GET YOUR MEN TOGETHER AND REPORT TO ME AT 0500.
Allie,
We landed in Sicily
today. It's probably a beautiful
country here, but I hope to never
see it again. I try not to scare
you when I write these letters,
sometimes it's hard to find
at to say that isn't scary. War
like a thing you can't imagine.
then there's the robots.

GOING OFF TRACK

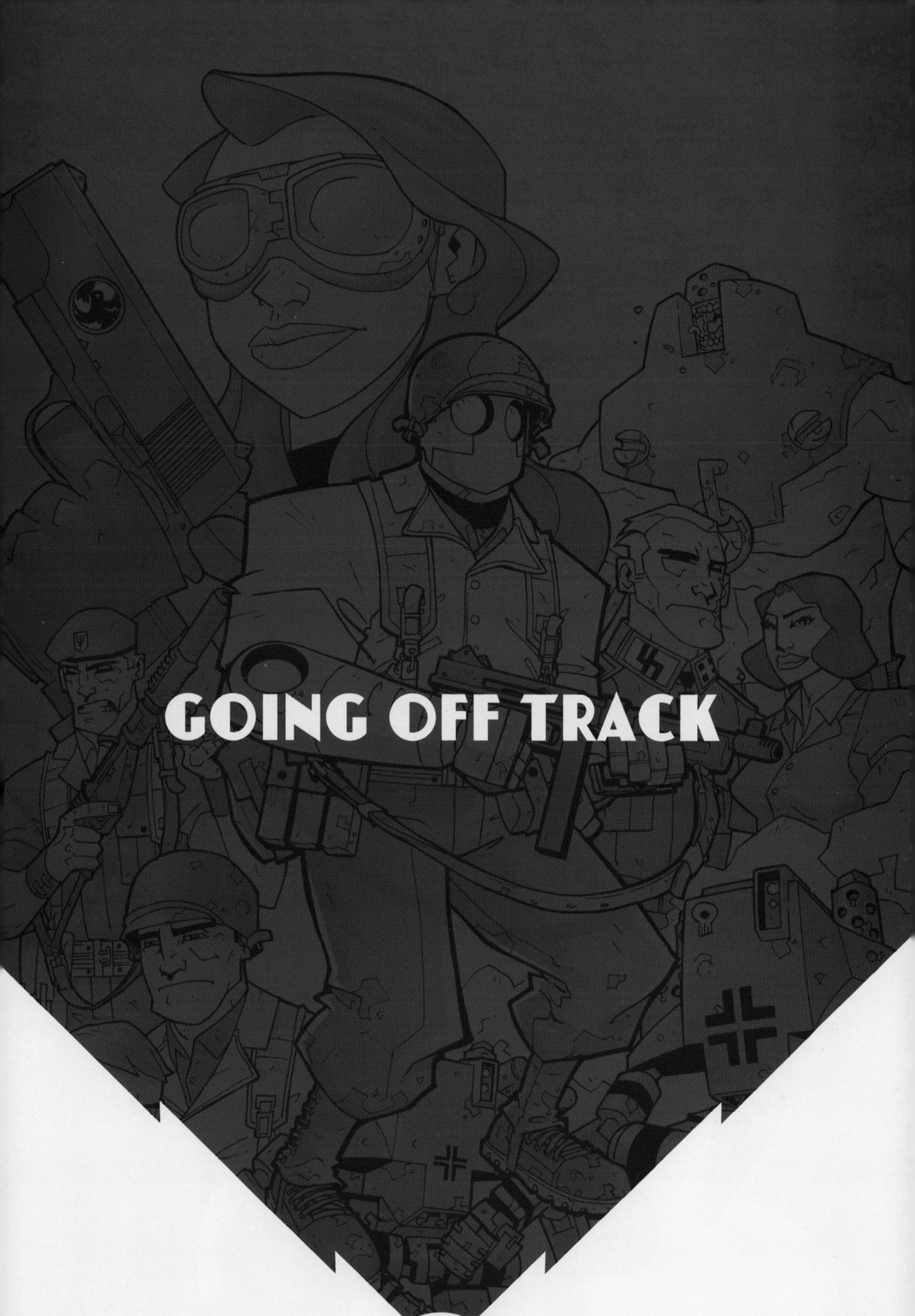

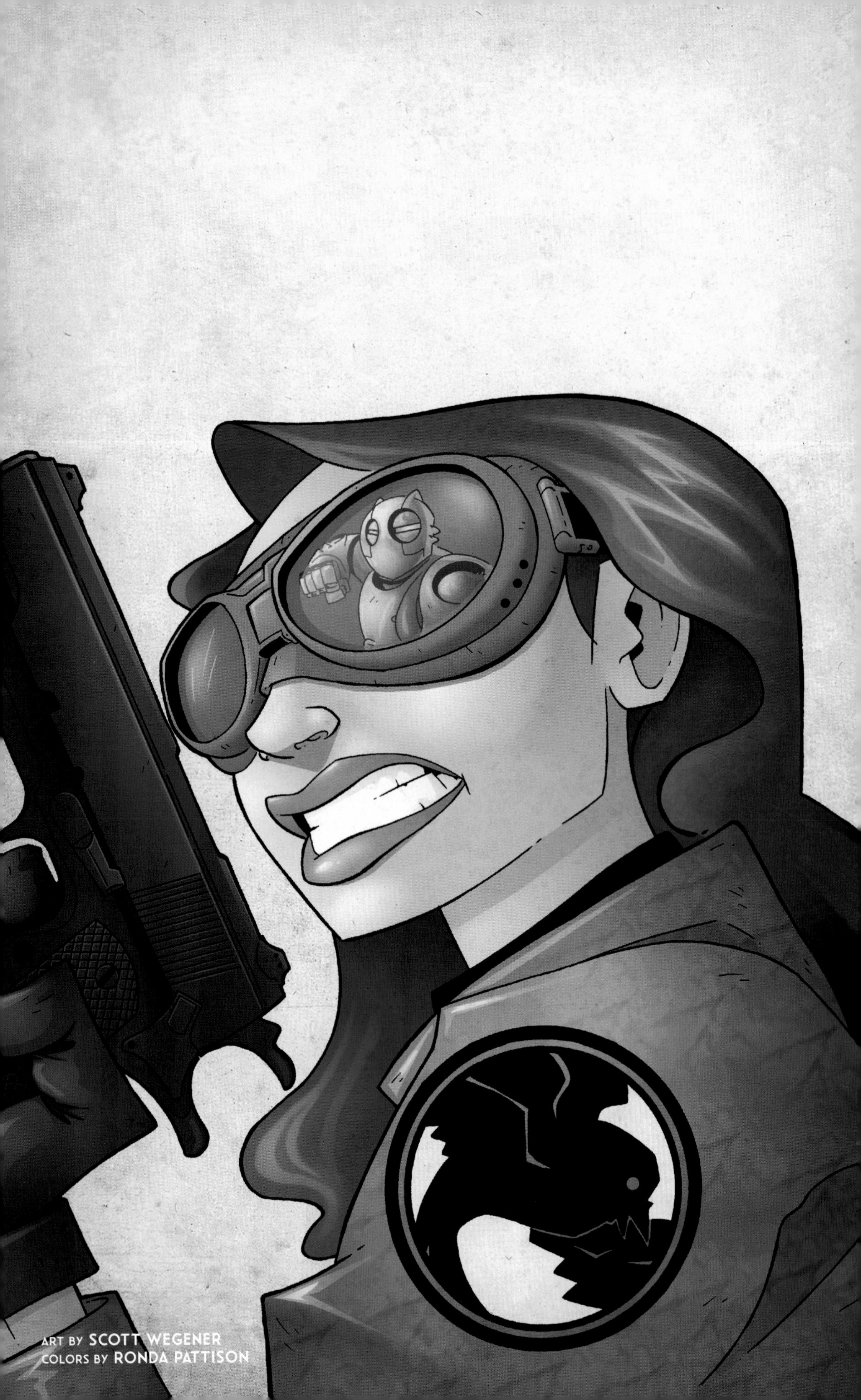
ART BY SCOTT WEGENER
COLORS BY RONDA PATTISON

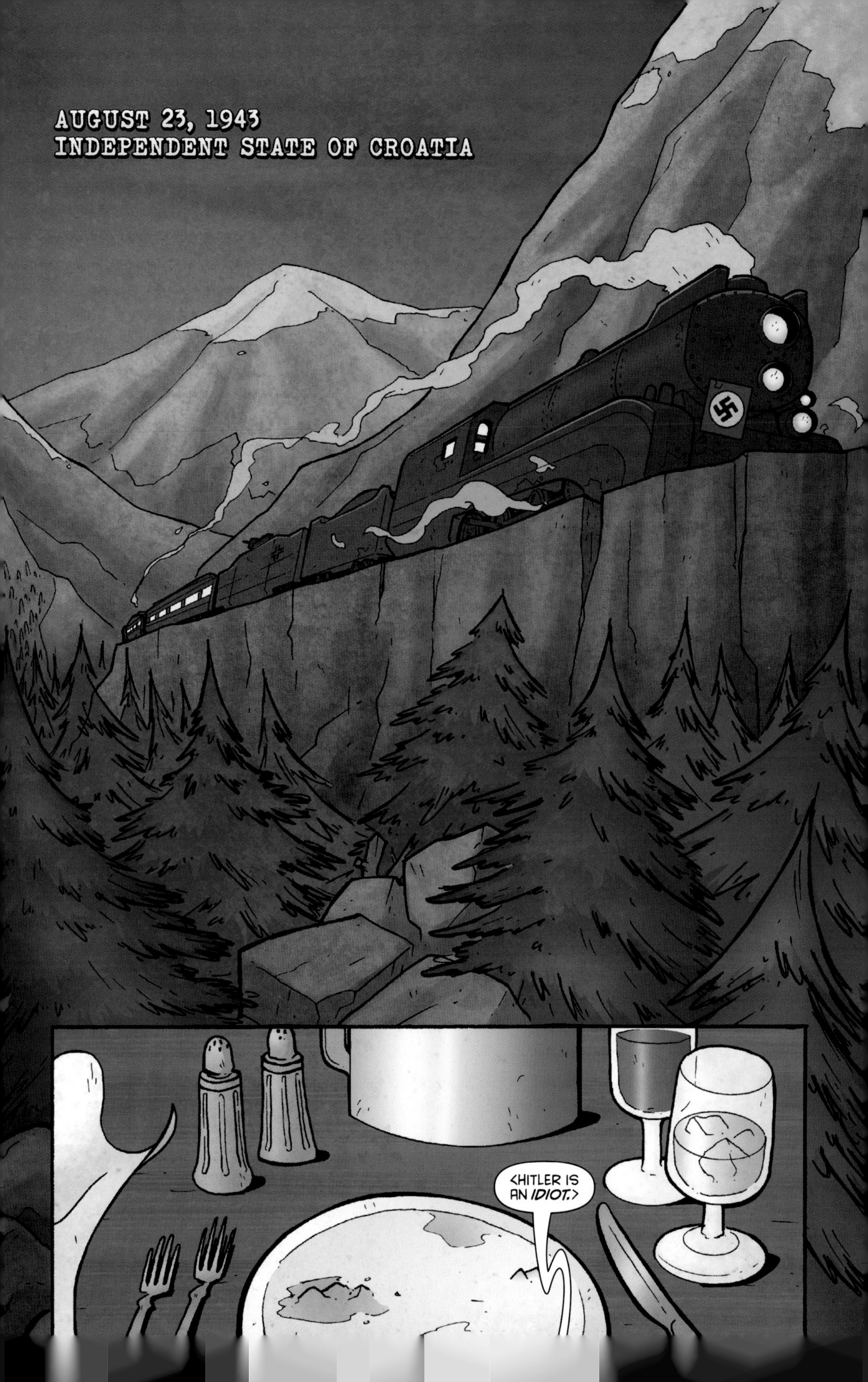
AUGUST 23, 1943
INDEPENDENT STATE OF CROATIA
<HITLER IS AN *IDIOT.*>

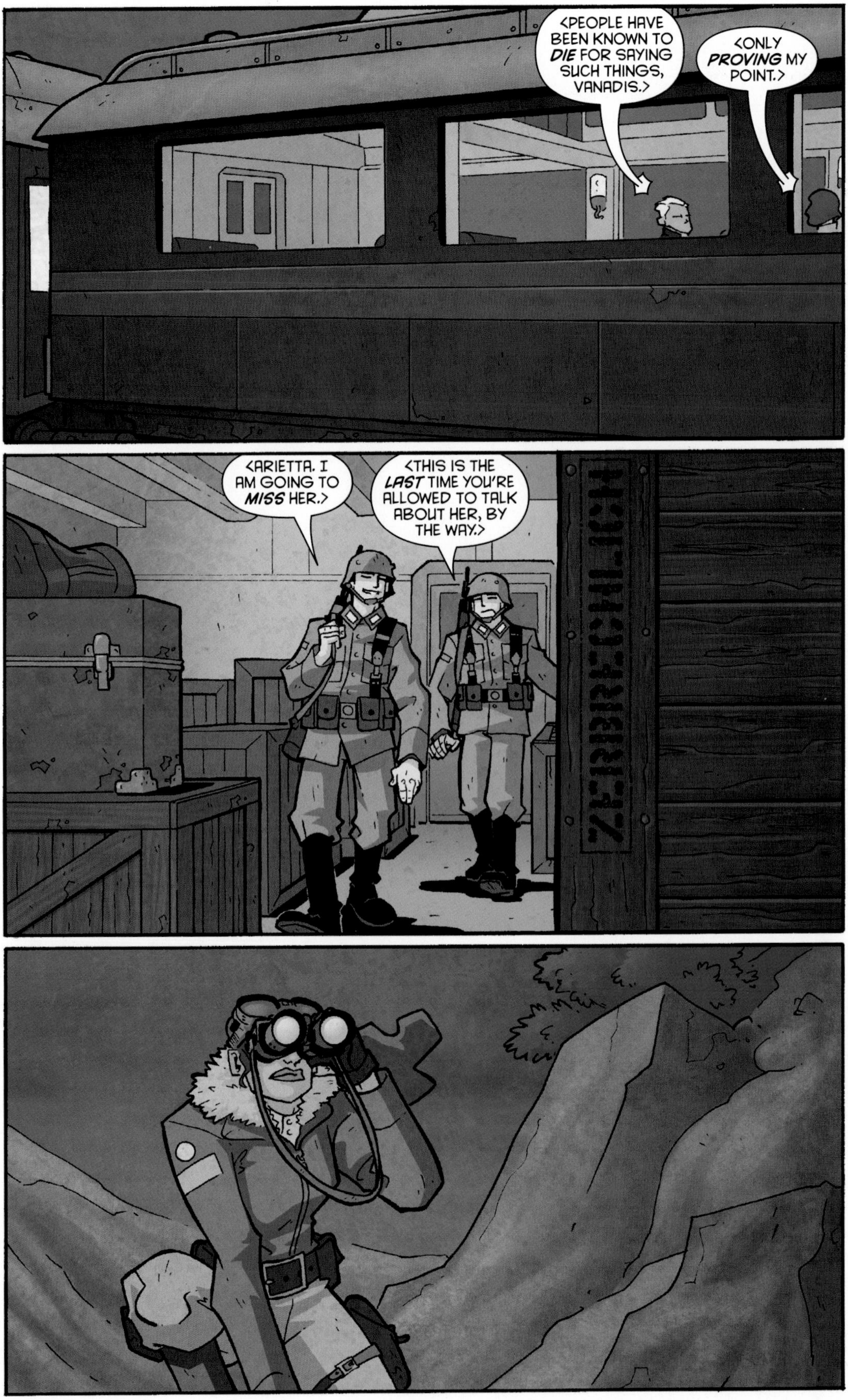
<PEOPLE HAVE BEEN KNOWN TO DIE FOR SAYING SUCH THINGS, VANADIS.>
<ONLY PROVING MY POINT.>
<ARIETTA. I AM GOING TO MISS HER.>
<THIS IS THE LAST TIME YOU'RE ALLOWED TO TALK ABOUT HER, BY THE WAY.>

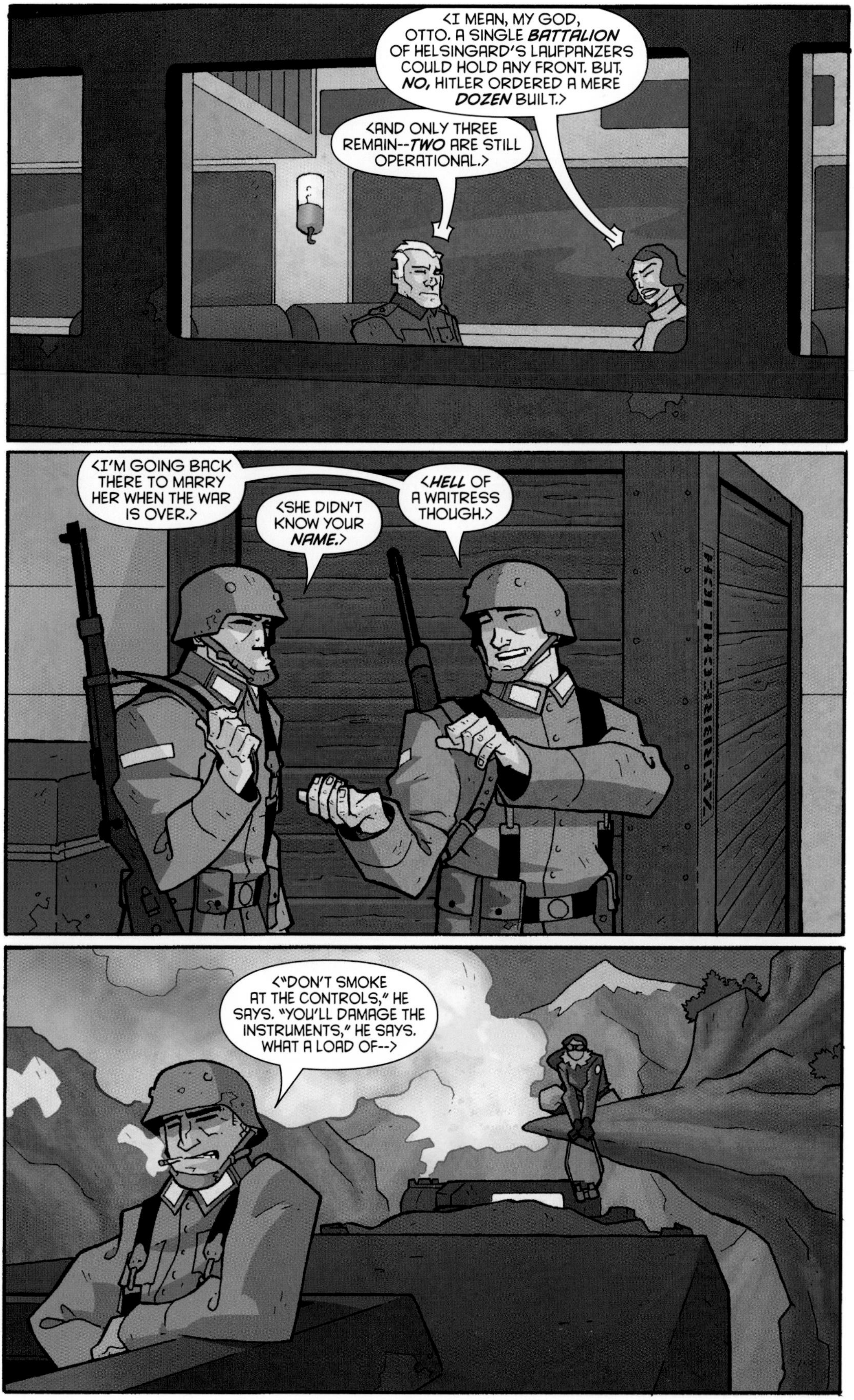
<I MEAN, MY GOD, OTTO. A SINGLE BATTALION OF HELSINGARD'S LAUFPANZERS COULD HOLD ANY FRONT. BUT, NO, HITLER ORDERED A MERE DOZEN BUILT.>
<AND ONLY THREE REMAIN--TWO ARE STILL OPERATIONAL.>
<I'M GOING BACK THERE TO MARRY HER WHEN THE WAR IS OVER.>
<SHE DIDN'T KNOW YOUR NAME.>
<HELL OF A WAITRESS THOUGH.>
<"DON'T SMOKE AT THE CONTROLS," HE SAYS. "YOU'LL DAMAGE THE INSTRUMENTS," HE SAYS. WHAT A LOAD OF-->

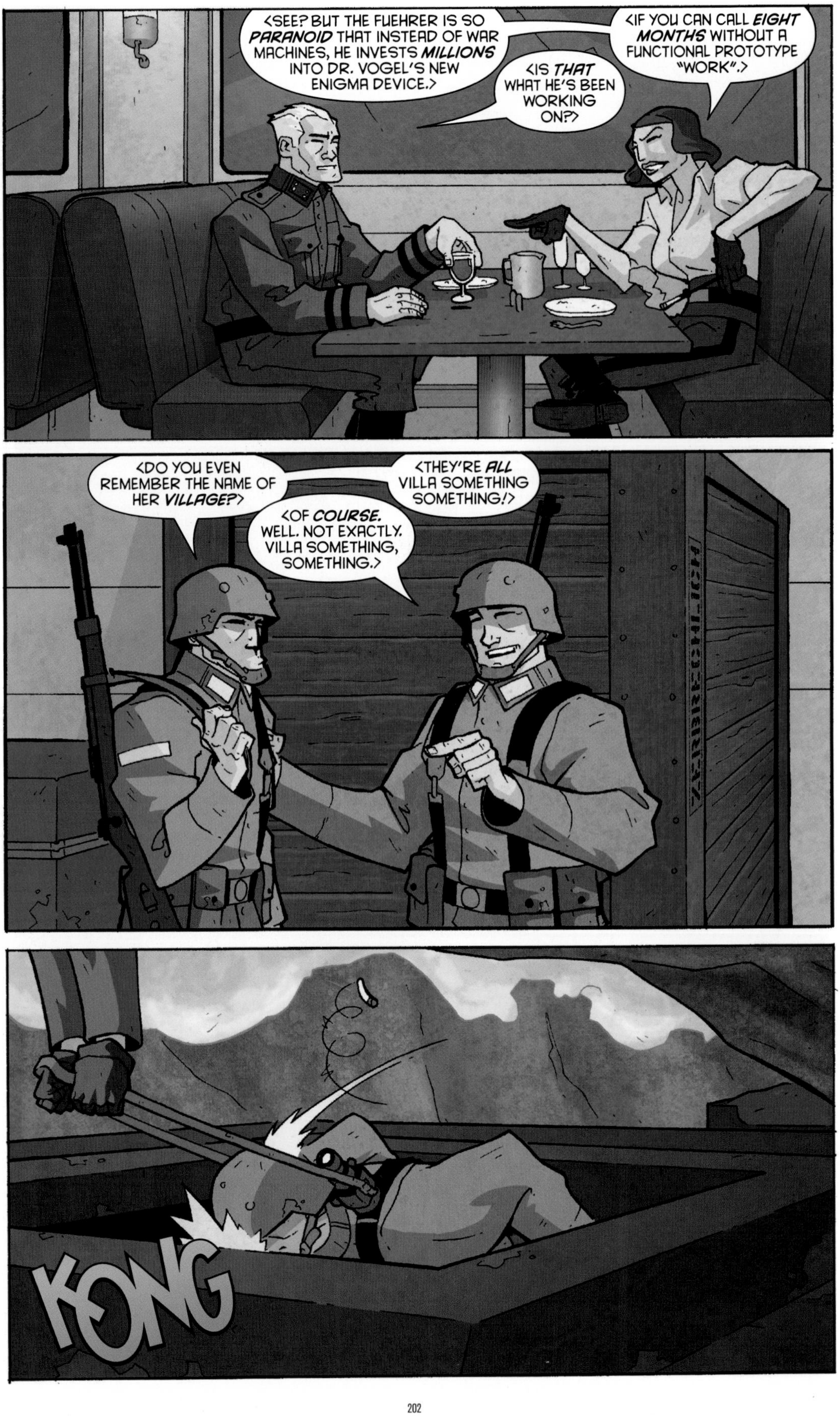
<SEE? BUT THE FUEHRER IS SO PARANOID THAT INSTEAD OF WAR MACHINES, HE INVESTS MILLIONS INTO DR. VOGEL'S NEW ENIGMA DEVICE.>
<IS THAT WHAT HE'S BEEN WORKING ON?>
<IF YOU CAN CALL EIGHT MONTHS WITHOUT A FUNCTIONAL PROTOTYPE "WORK".>
<DO YOU EVEN REMEMBER THE NAME OF HER VILLAGE?>
<OF COURSE. WELL. NOT EXACTLY. VILLA SOMETHING, SOMETHING.>
<THEY'RE ALL VILLA SOMETHING SOMETHING!>
KONG

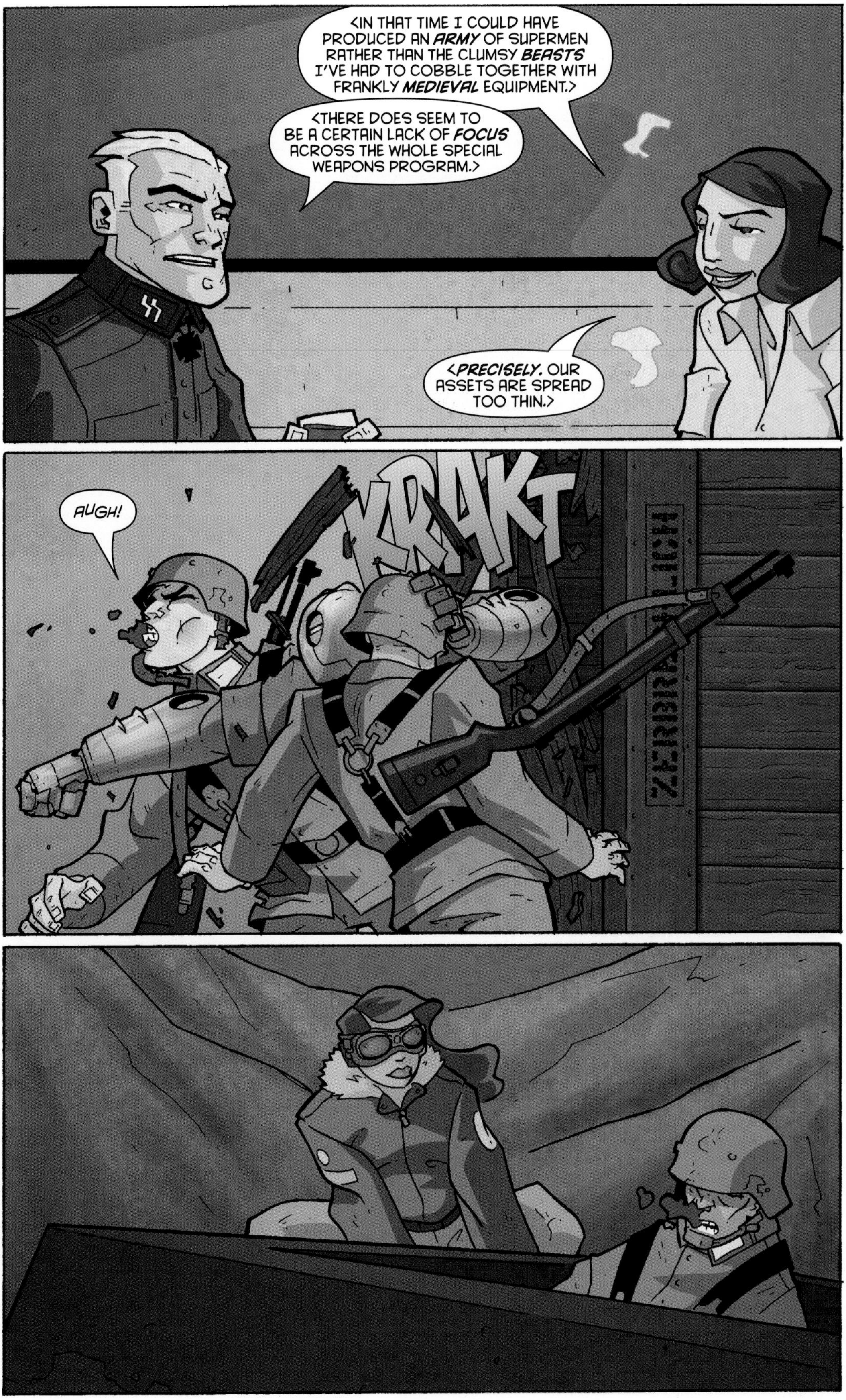
<IN THAT TIME I COULD HAVE PRODUCED AN ARMY OF SUPERMEN RATHER THAN THE CLUMSY BEASTS I'VE HAD TO COBBLE TOGETHER WITH FRANKLY MEDIEVAL EQUIPMENT.>
<THERE DOES SEEM TO BE A CERTAIN LACK OF FOCUS ACROSS THE WHOLE SPECIAL WEAPONS PROGRAM.>
<PRECISELY. OUR ASSETS ARE SPREAD TOO THIN.>
AUGH!
KRAKT

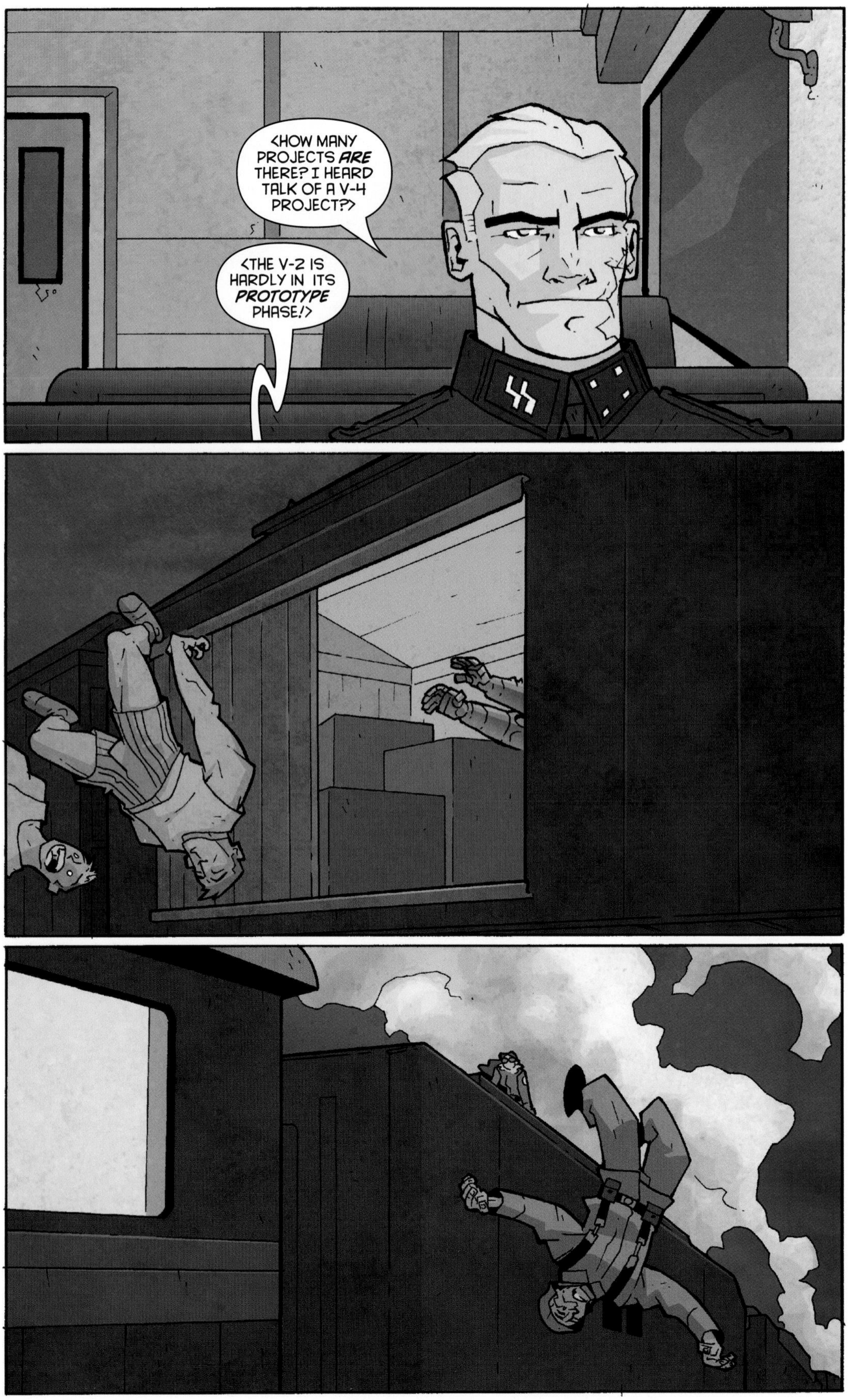
<HOW MANY PROJECTS ARE THERE? I HEARD TALK OF A V-4 PROJECT?>
<THE V-2 IS HARDLY IN ITS PROTOTYPE PHASE!>

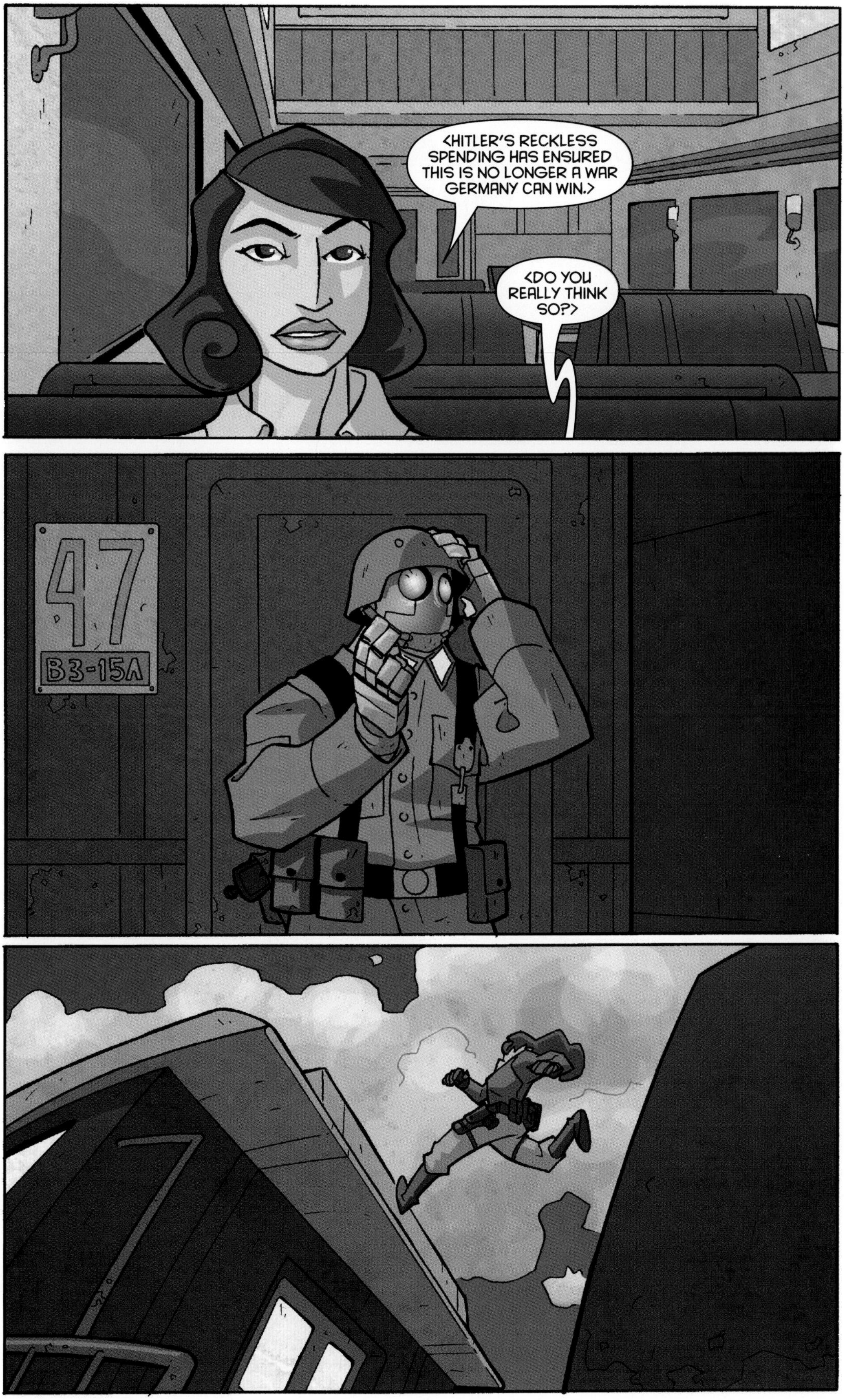
<HITLER'S RECKLESS SPENDING HAS ENSURED THIS IS NO LONGER A WAR GERMANY CAN WIN.>
<DO YOU REALLY THINK SO?>
47
B3-15A

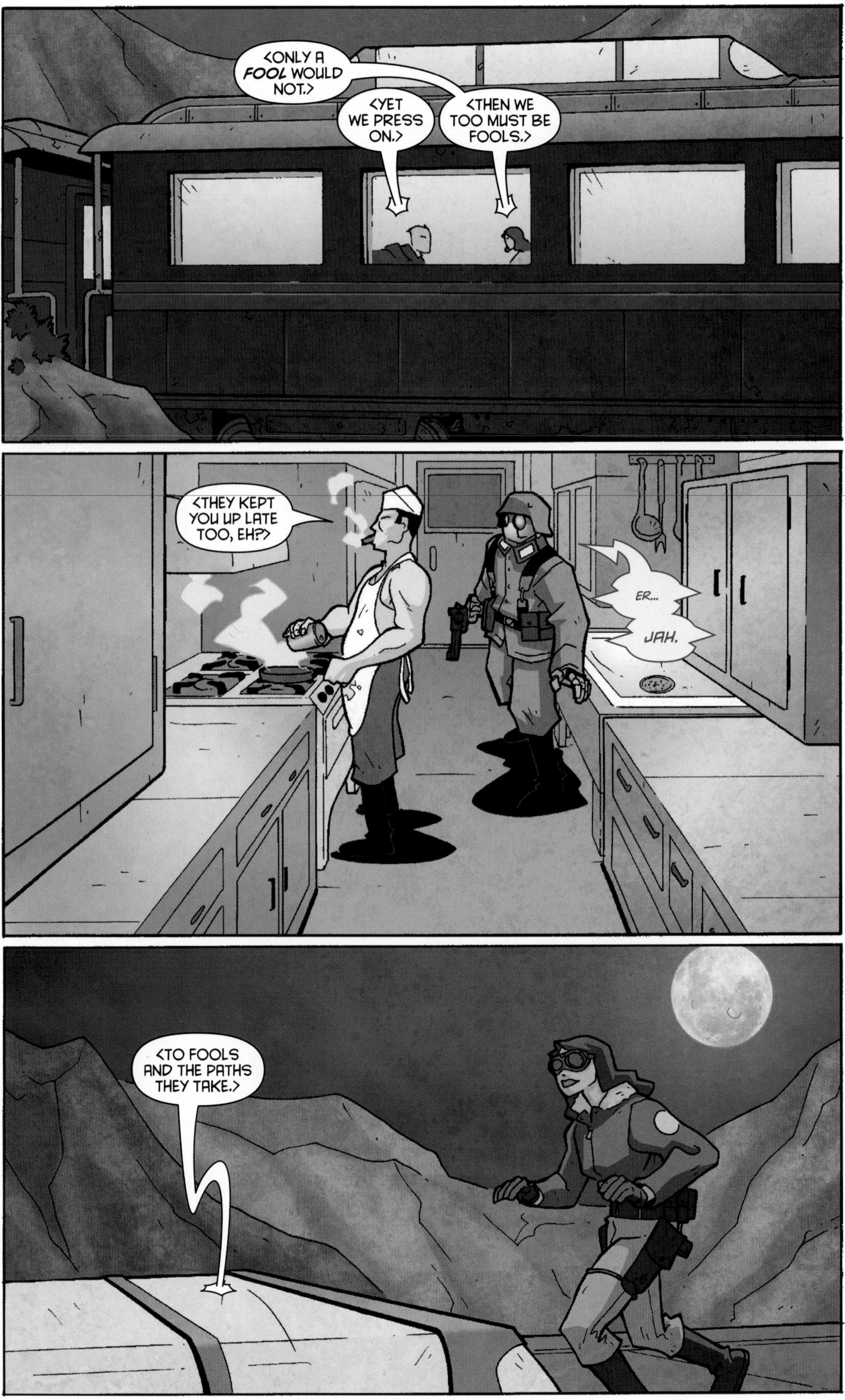
<ONLY A FOOL WOULD NOT.>
<YET WE PRESS ON.>
<THEN WE TOO MUST BE FOOLS.>
<THEY KEPT YOU UP LATE TOO, EH?>
ER...
JAH.
<TO FOOLS AND THE PATHS THEY TAKE.>

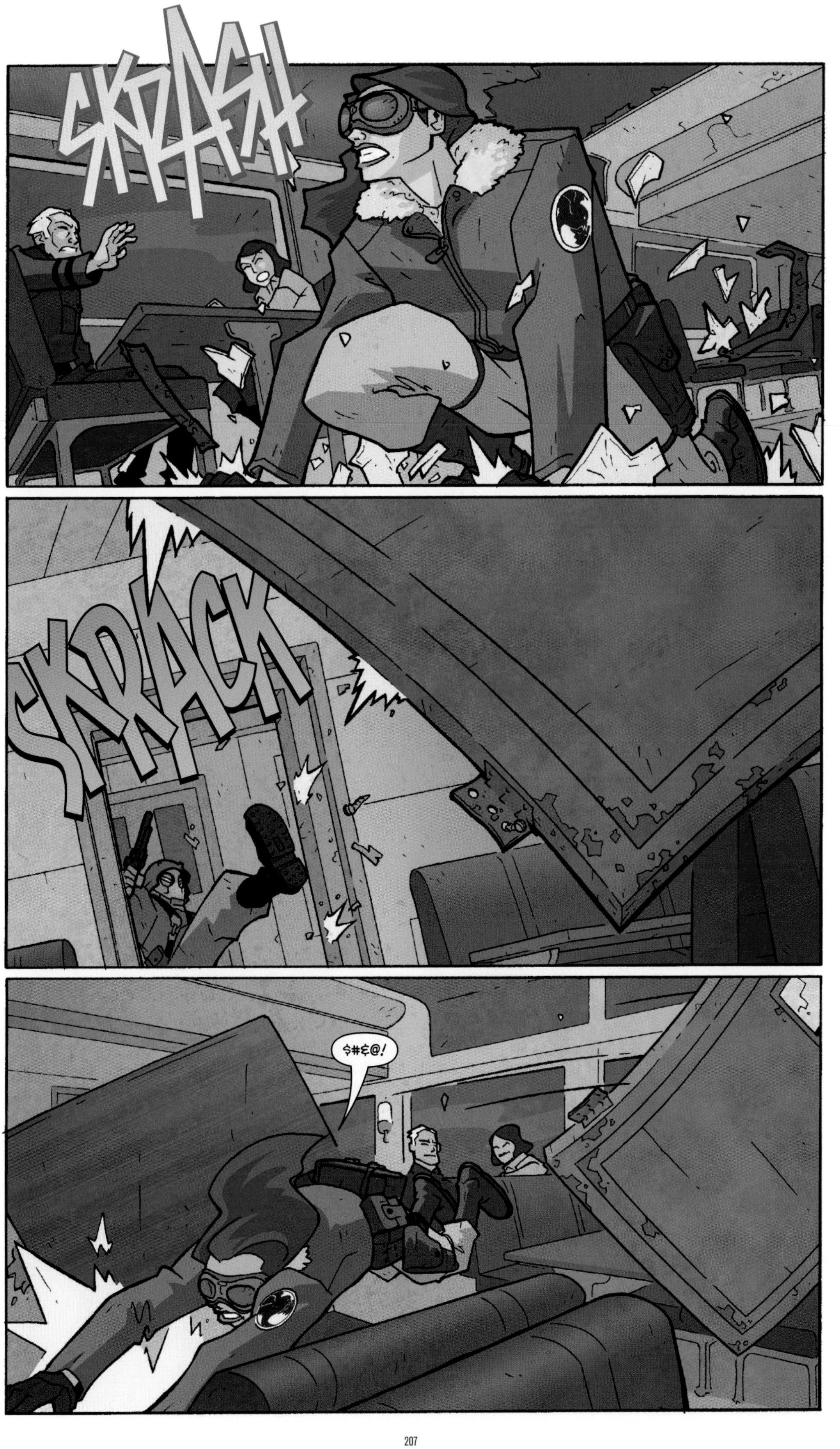
SKRASH
SKRACK
$#&@!

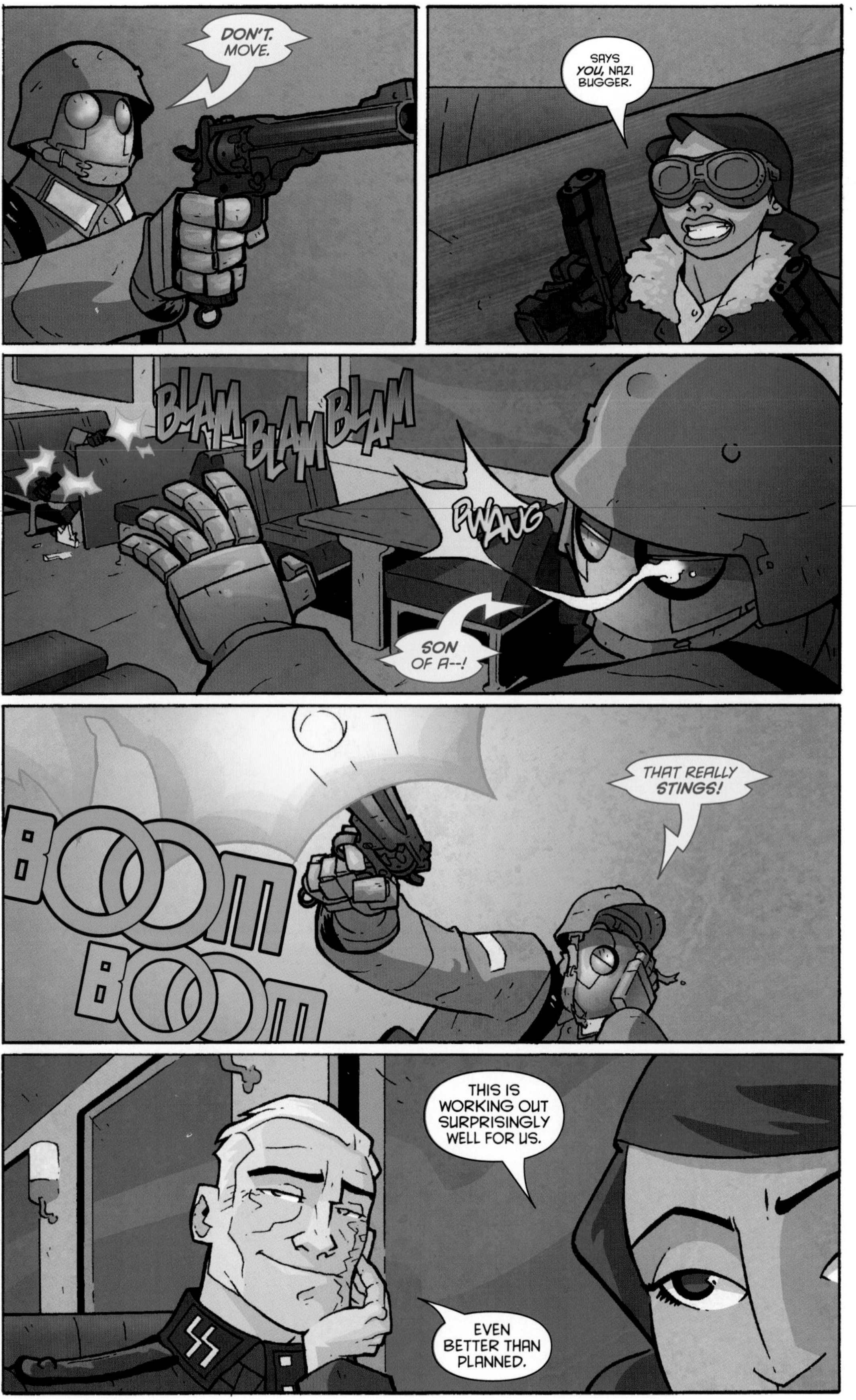
DON'T. MOVE.
SAYS YOU, NAZI BUGGER.
BLAM BLAM BLAM
PWANG
SON OF A--!
THAT REALLY STINGS!
BOOM BOOM
THIS IS WORKING OUT SURPRISINGLY WELL FOR US.
EVEN BETTER THAN PLANNED.

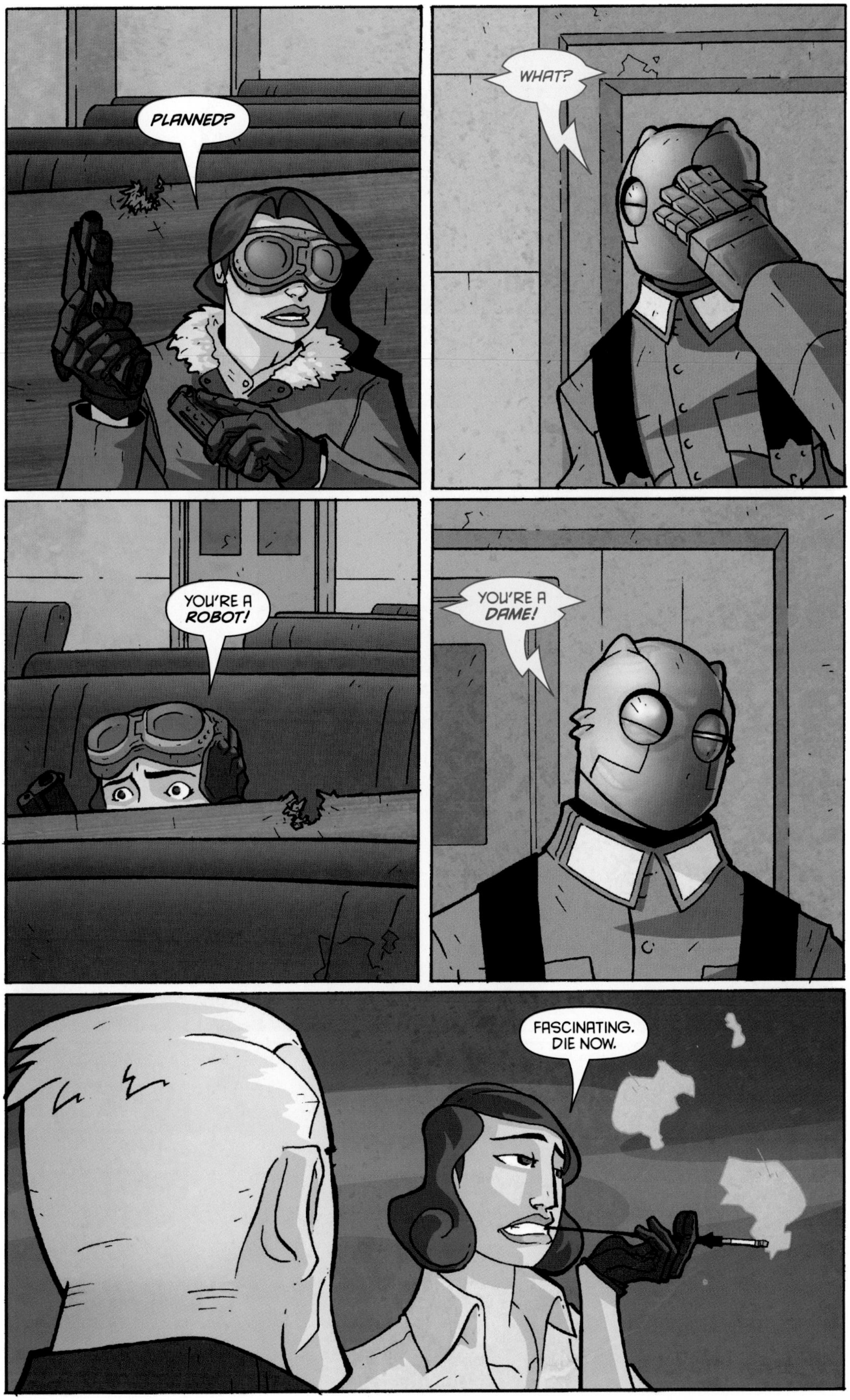
PLANNED?
WHAT?
YOU'RE A ROBOT!
YOU'RE A DAME!
FASCINATING. DIE NOW.

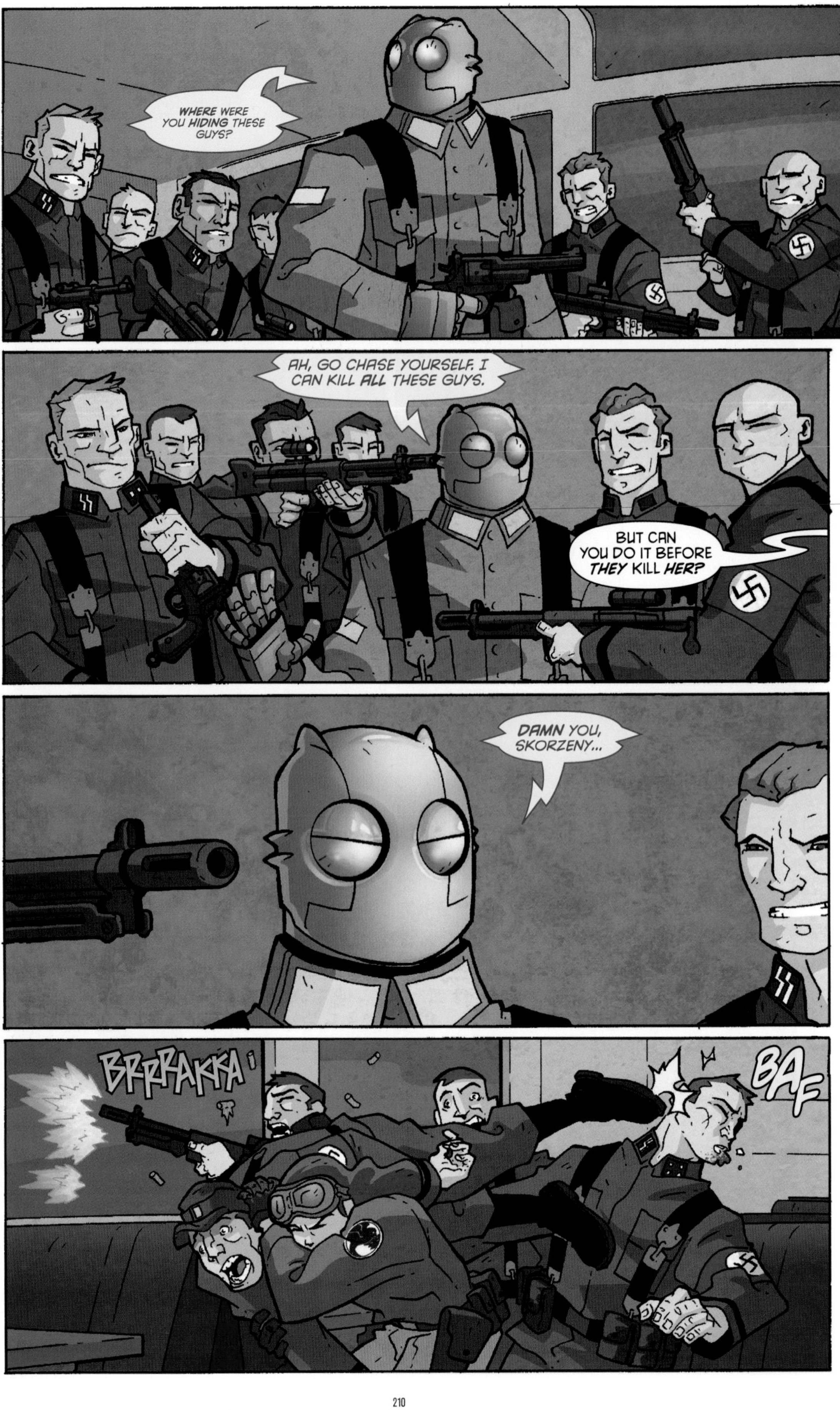
WHERE WERE YOU HIDING THESE GUYS?
AH, GO CHASE YOURSELF. I CAN KILL ALL THESE GUYS.
BUT CAN YOU DO IT BEFORE THEY KILL HER?
DAMN YOU, SKORZENY...
BRRRAKKA
BAF

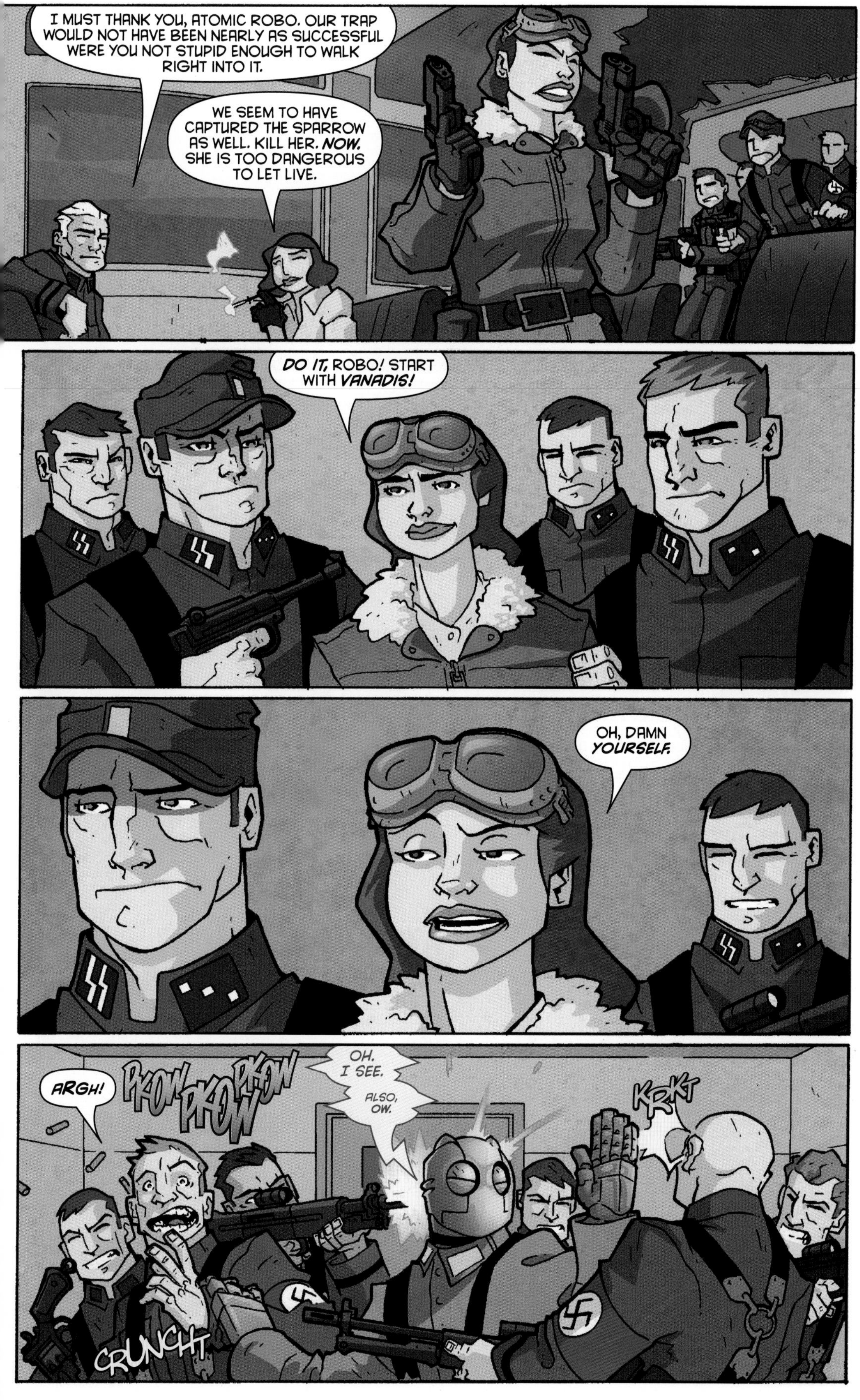
I MUST THANK YOU, ATOMIC ROBO. OUR TRAP WOULD NOT HAVE BEEN NEARLY AS SUCCESSFUL WERE YOU NOT STUPID ENOUGH TO WALK RIGHT INTO IT.
WE SEEM TO HAVE CAPTURED THE SPARROW AS WELL. KILL HER. NOW. SHE IS TOO DANGEROUS TO LET LIVE.
DO IT, ROBO! START WITH VANADIS!
OH, DAMN YOURSELF.
ARGH!
PKOW PKOW PKOW
OH. I SEE.
ALSO, OW.
KRAKT
CRUNCH

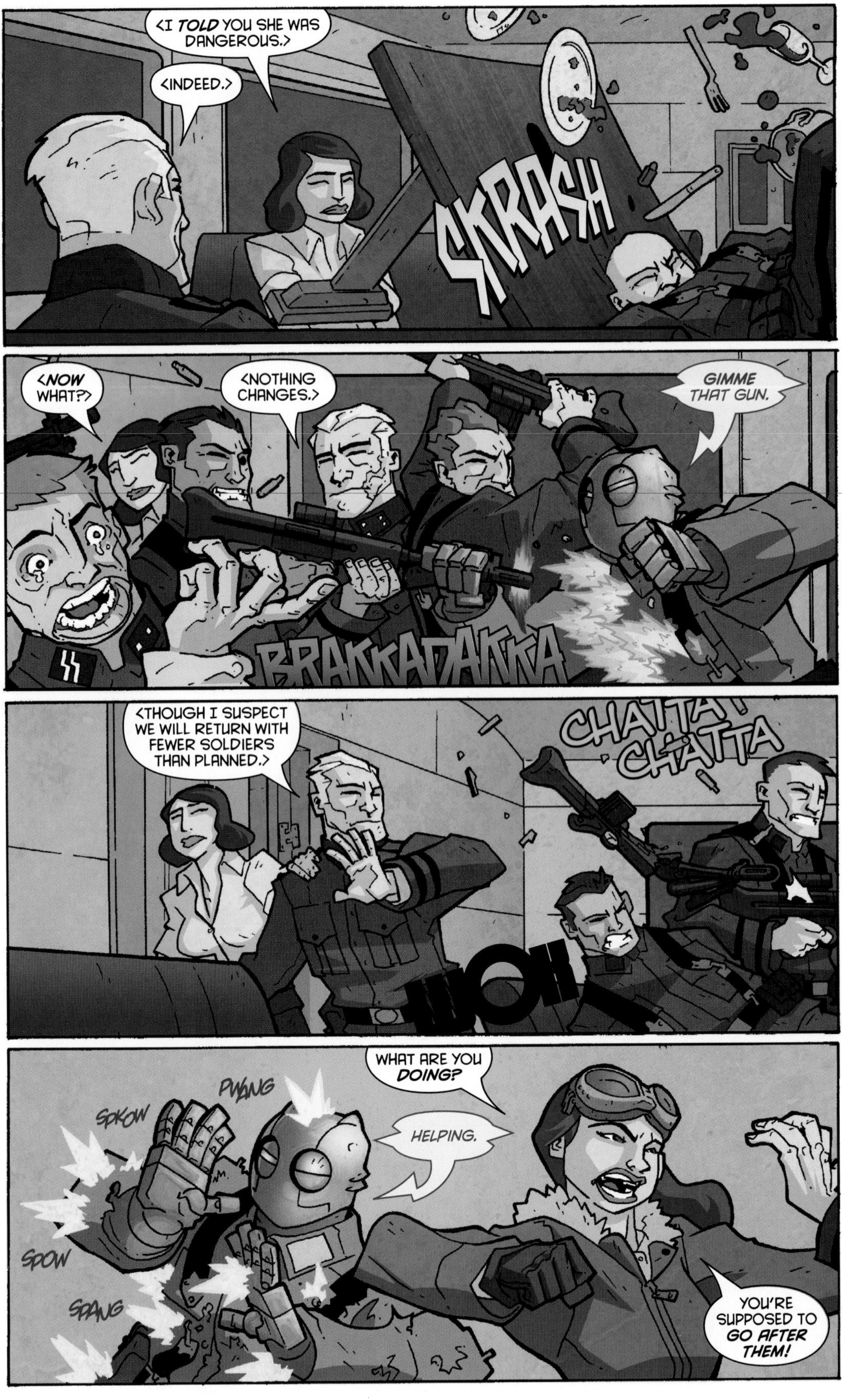
<I TOLD YOU SHE WAS DANGEROUS.>
<INDEED.>
SKRASH
<NOW WHAT?>
<NOTHING CHANGES.>
GIMME THAT GUN.
BRAKKADAKKA
<THOUGH I SUSPECT WE WILL RETURN WITH FEWER SOLDIERS THAN PLANNED.>
CHATTA CHATTA
WHAT ARE YOU DOING?
HELPING.
PWANG
SPKOW
SPOW
SPANG
YOU'RE SUPPOSED TO GO AFTER THEM!

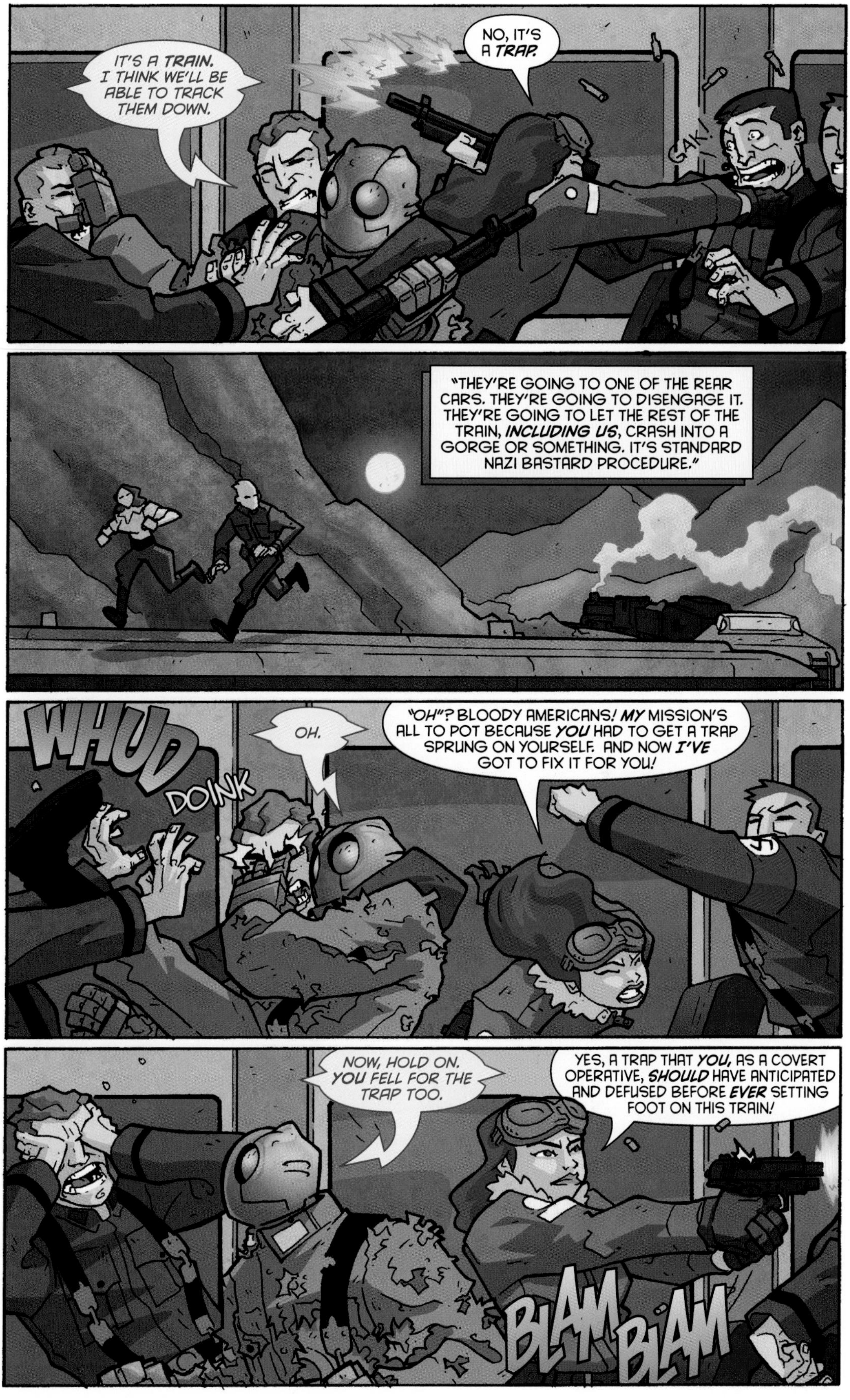
IT'S A TRAIN. I THINK WE'LL BE ABLE TO TRACK THEM DOWN.
NO, IT'S A TRAP.
GAK!
"THEY'RE GOING TO ONE OF THE REAR CARS. THEY'RE GOING TO DISENGAGE IT. THEY'RE GOING TO LET THE REST OF THE TRAIN, INCLUDING US, CRASH INTO A GORGE OR SOMETHING. IT'S STANDARD NAZI BASTARD PROCEDURE."
WHUD
DOINK
OH.
"OH"? BLOODY AMERICANS! MY MISSION'S ALL TO POT BECAUSE YOU HAD TO GET A TRAP SPRUNG ON YOURSELF. AND NOW I'VE GOT TO FIX IT FOR YOU!
NOW, HOLD ON. YOU FELL FOR THE TRAP TOO.
YES, A TRAP THAT YOU, AS A COVERT OPERATIVE, SHOULD HAVE ANTICIPATED AND DEFUSED BEFORE EVER SETTING FOOT ON THIS TRAIN!
BLAM BLAM

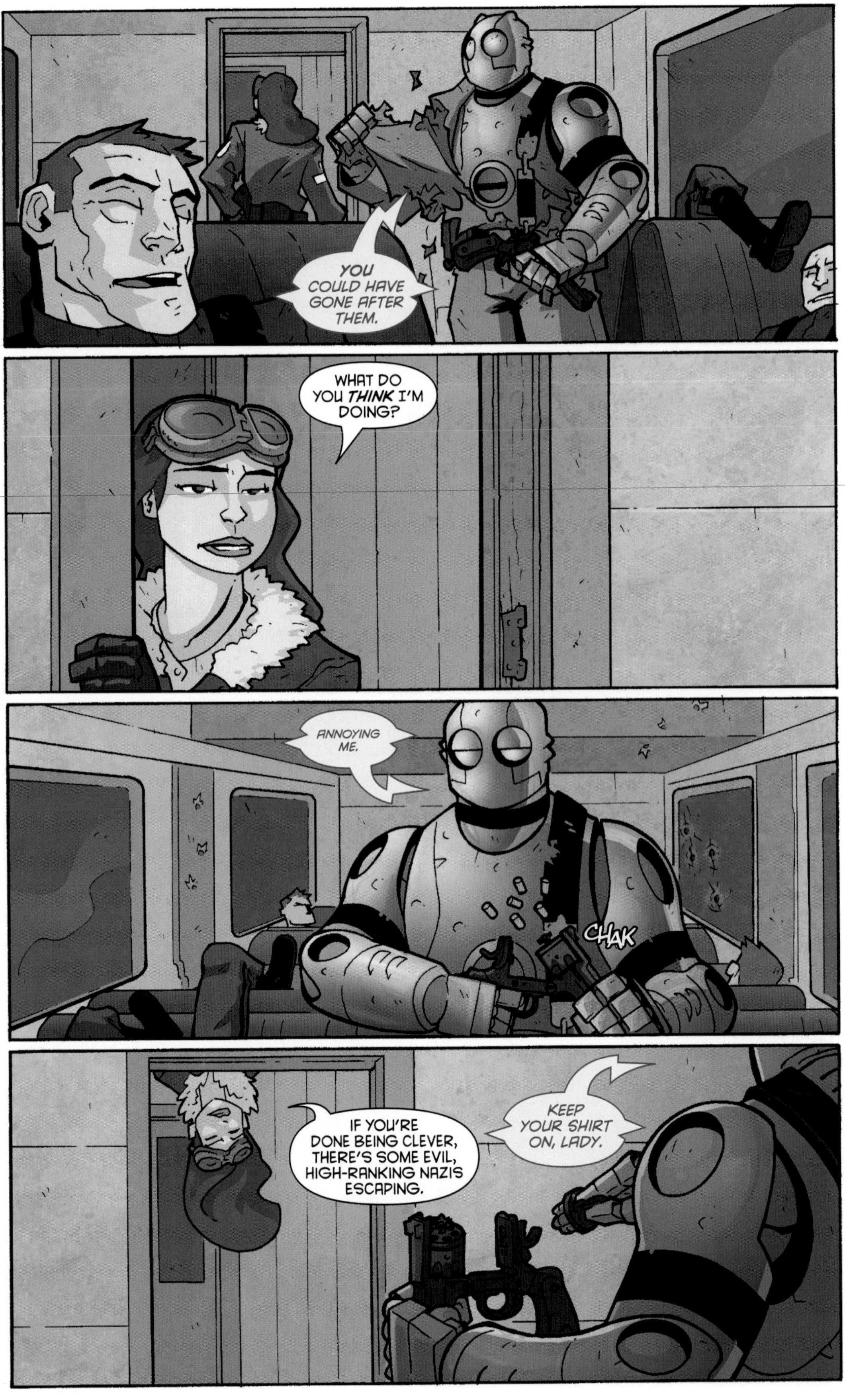
YOU COULD HAVE GONE AFTER THEM.
WHAT DO YOU THINK I'M DOING?
ANNOYING ME.
CHAK
IF YOU'RE DONE BEING CLEVER, THERE'S SOME EVIL, HIGH-RANKING NAZIS ESCAPING.
KEEP YOUR SHIRT ON, LADY.

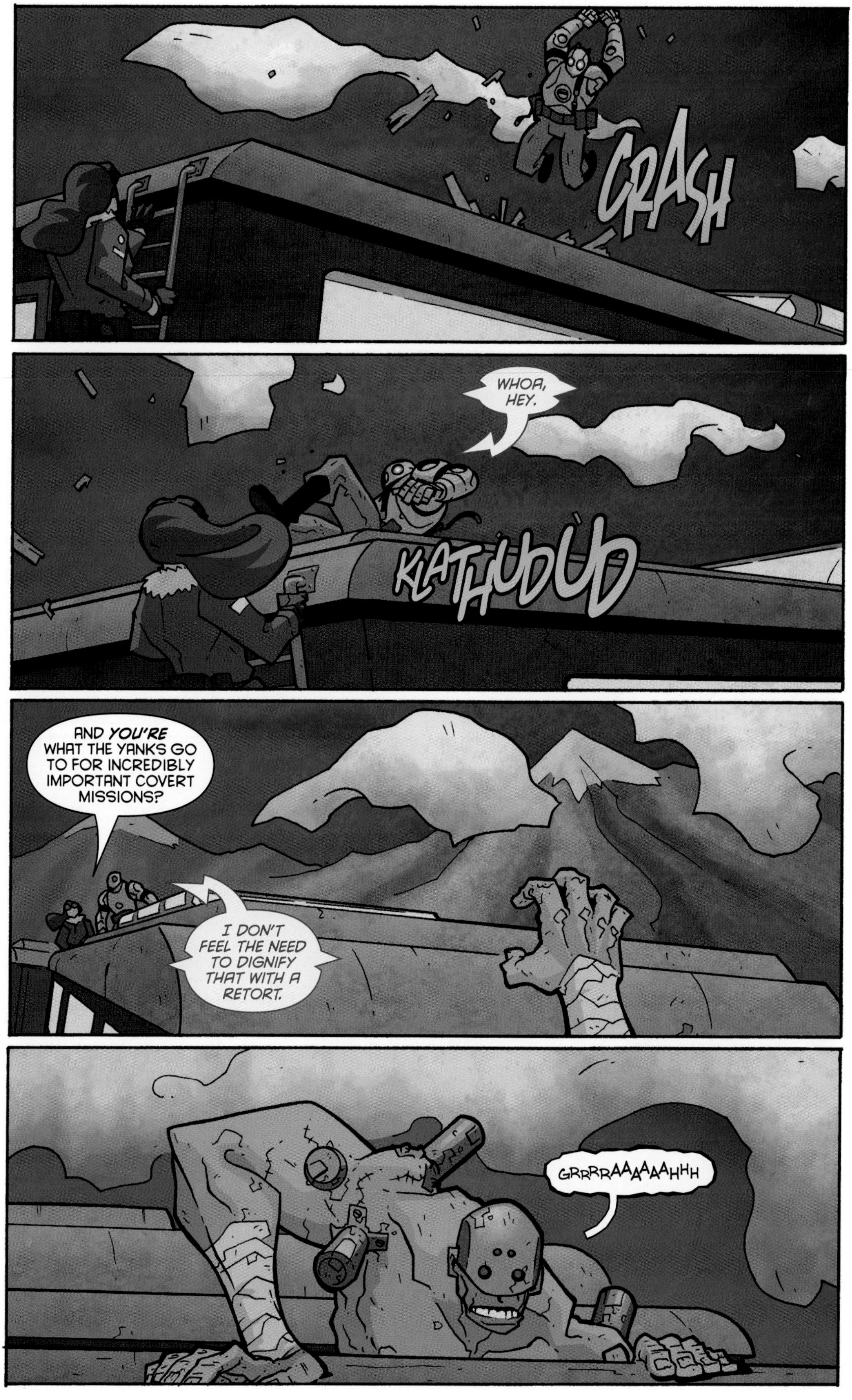
CRASH
WHOA, HEY.
KLATHUDUD
AND YOU'RE WHAT THE YANKS GO TO FOR INCREDIBLY IMPORTANT COVERT MISSIONS?
I DON'T FEEL THE NEED TO DIGNIFY THAT WITH A RETORT.
GRRRRAAAAAAHHH

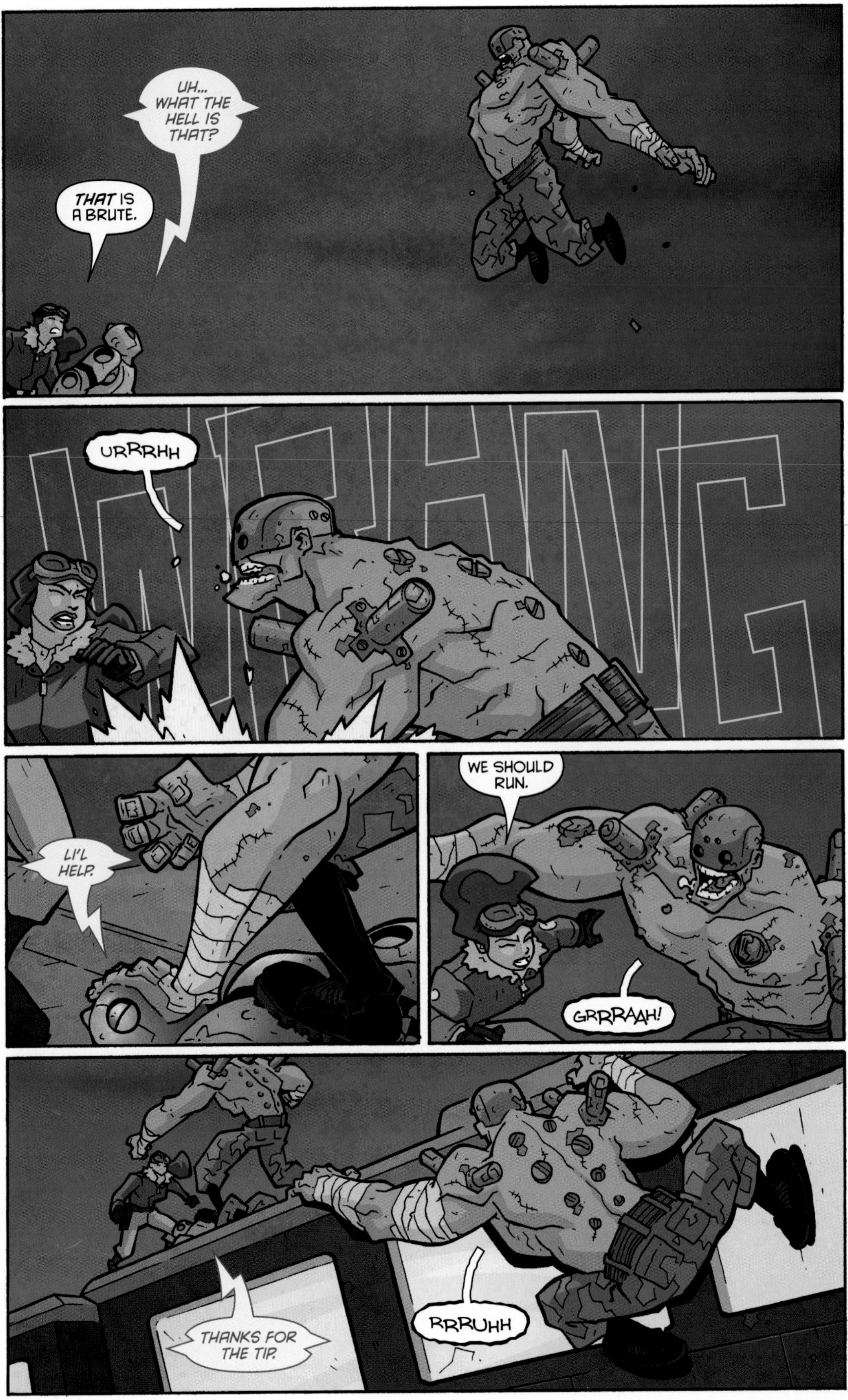
UH... WHAT THE HELL IS THAT?
THAT IS A BRUTE.
URRRHH
LI'L HELP.
WE SHOULD RUN.
GRRRAAH!
THANKS FOR THE TIP.
RRRUHH

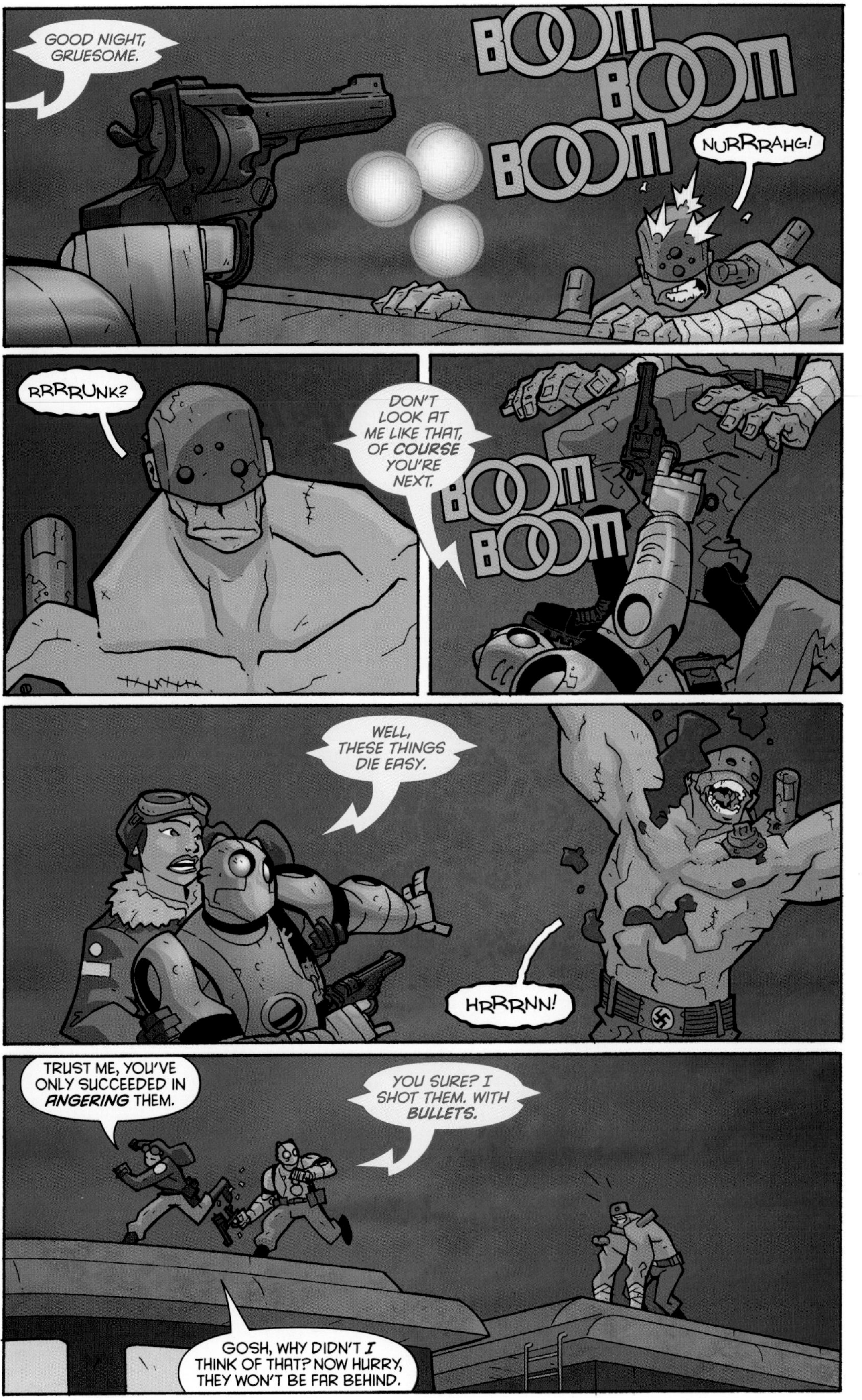

GOOD NIGHT, GRUESOME.
BOOM BOOM BOOM
NURRRAHG!
RRRRUNK?
DON'T LOOK AT ME LIKE THAT, OF COURSE YOU'RE NEXT.
BOOM BOOM
WELL, THESE THINGS DIE EASY.
HRRRNN!
TRUST ME, YOU'VE ONLY SUCCEEDED IN ANGERING THEM.
YOU SURE? I SHOT THEM. WITH BULLETS.
GOSH, WHY DIDN'T I THINK OF THAT? NOW HURRY, THEY WON'T BE FAR BEHIND.

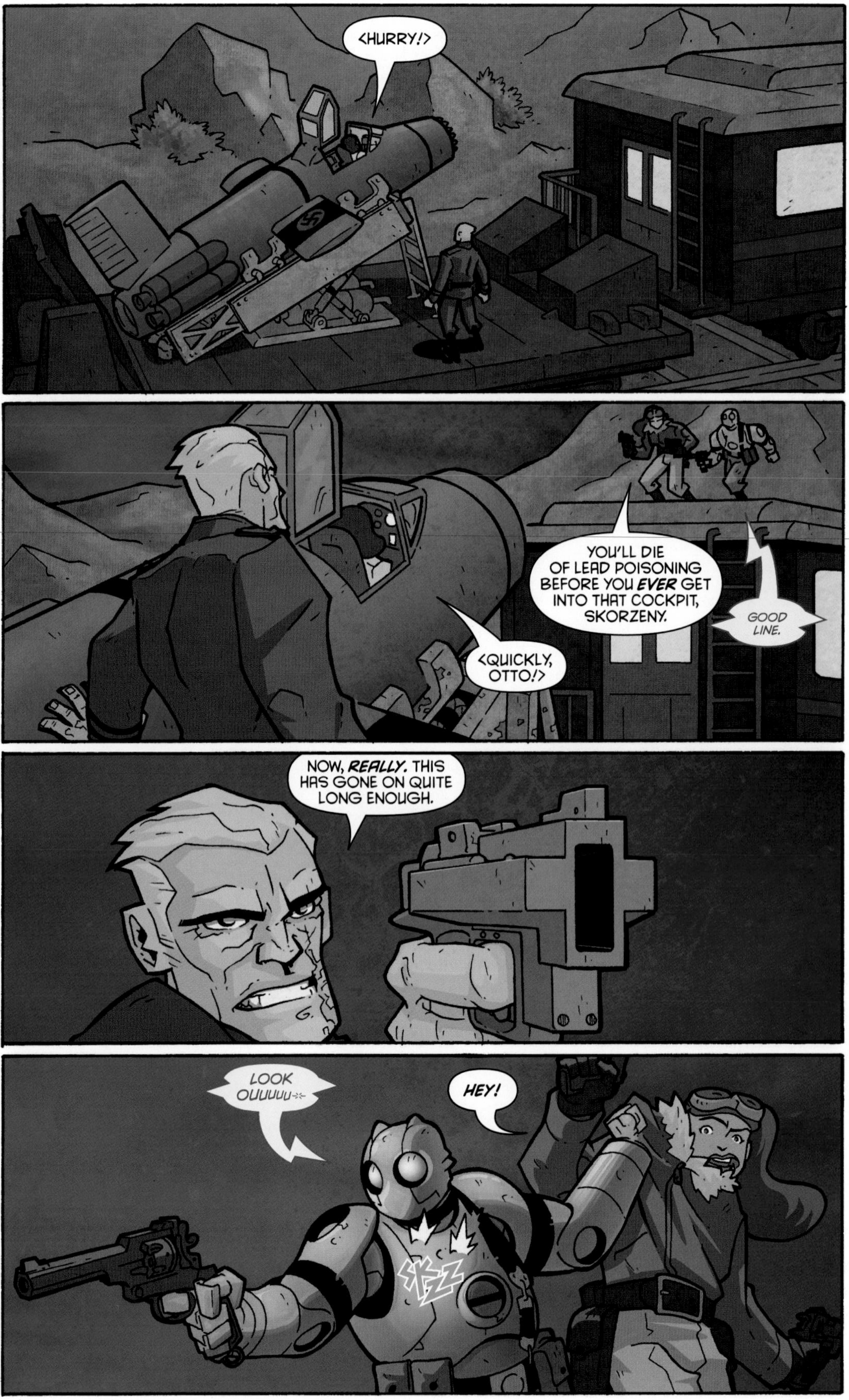
<HURRY!>
YOU'LL DIE OF LEAD POISONING BEFORE YOU EVER GET INTO THAT COCKPIT, SKORZENY.
GOOD LINE.
<QUICKLY, OTTO!>
NOW, REALLY. THIS HAS GONE ON QUITE LONG ENOUGH.
LOOK OUUUUU
HEY!
SKZZ

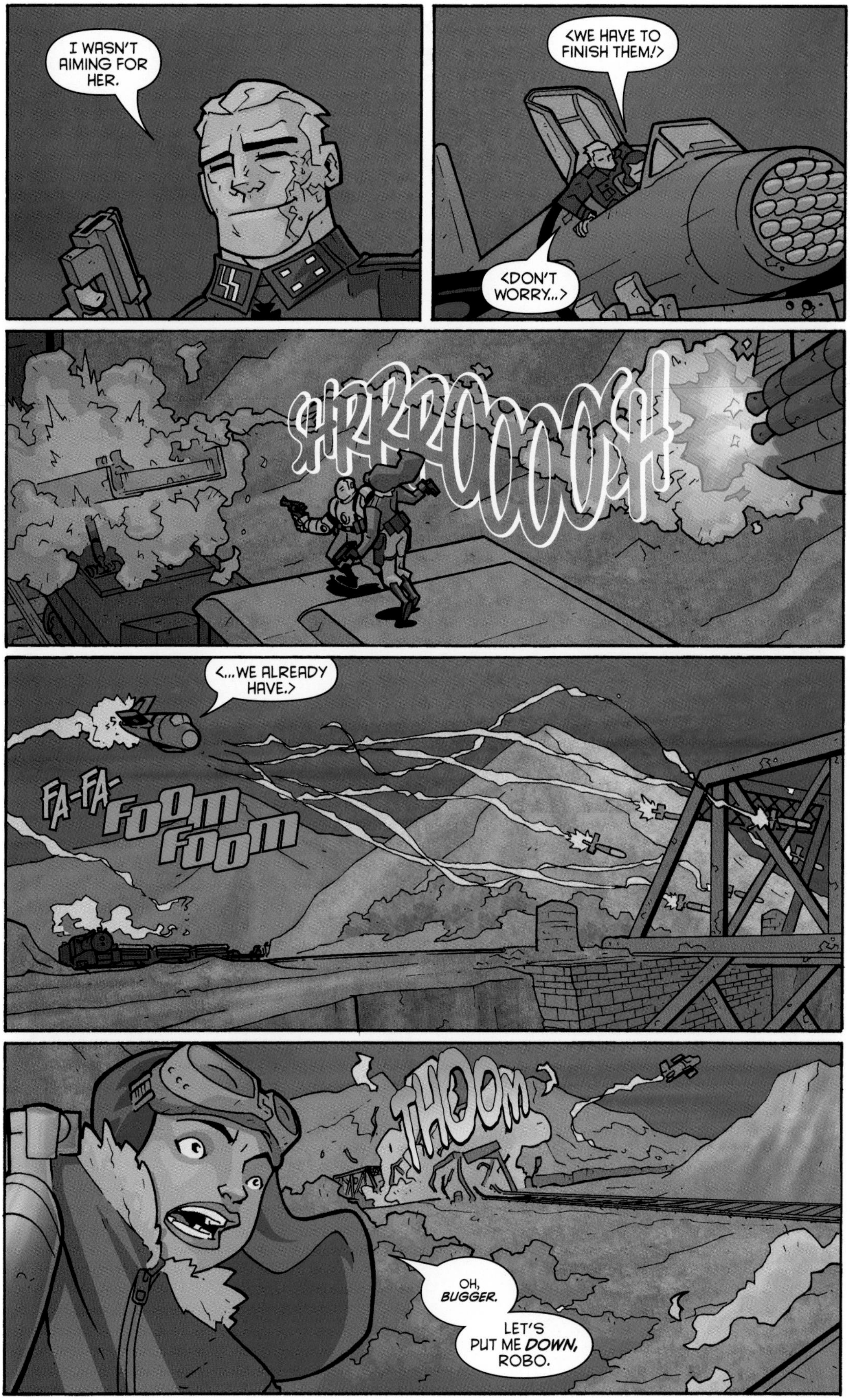
I WASN'T AIMING FOR HER.
<WE HAVE TO FINISH THEM!>
<DON'T WORRY...>
SHRRROOOOOSH
<...WE ALREADY HAVE.>
FA-FA-FOOM FOOM
THOOM
OH, *BUGGER.*
LET'S PUT ME *DOWN,* ROBO.

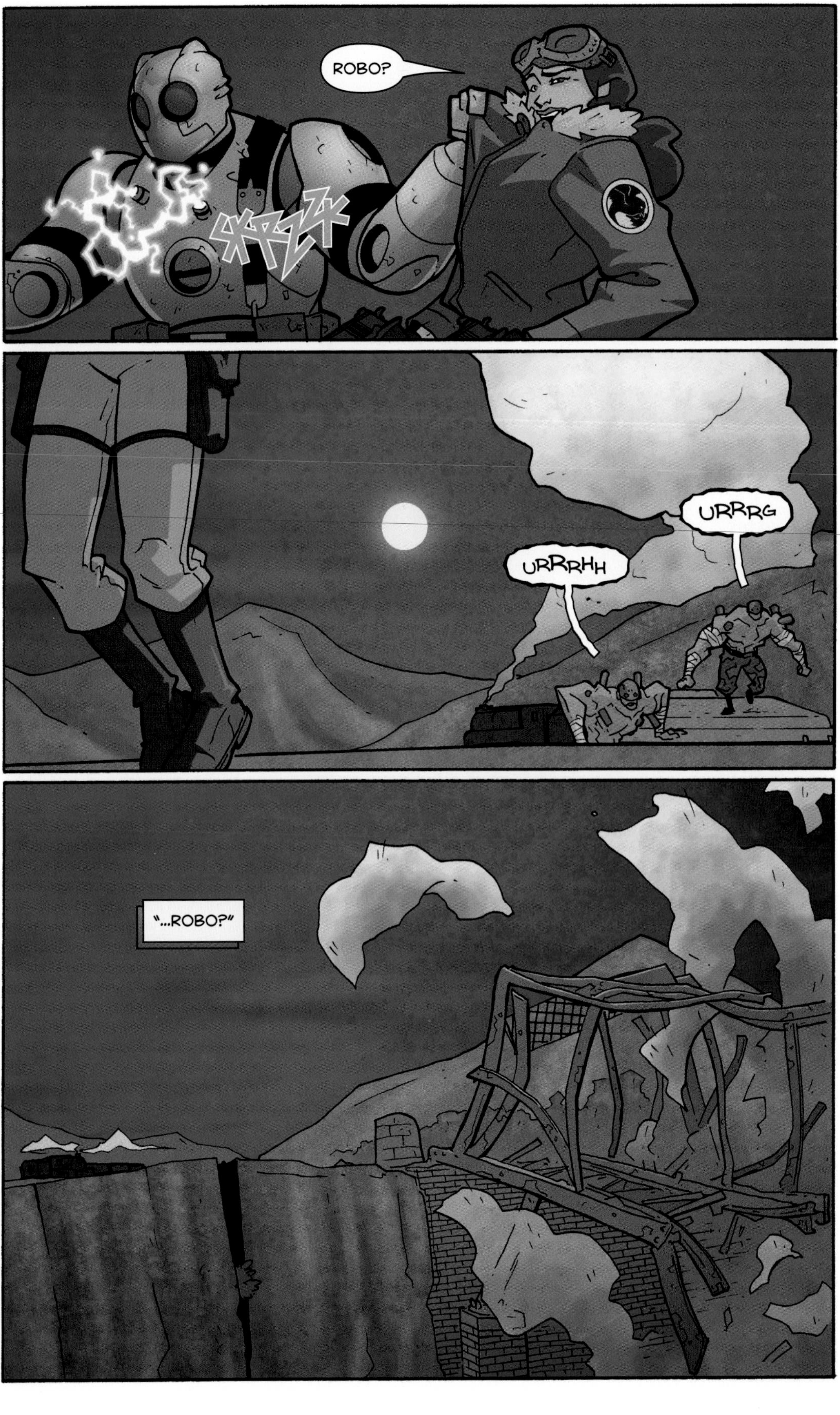
ROBO?
SKRZZK
URRRG
URRRHH
"...ROBO?"

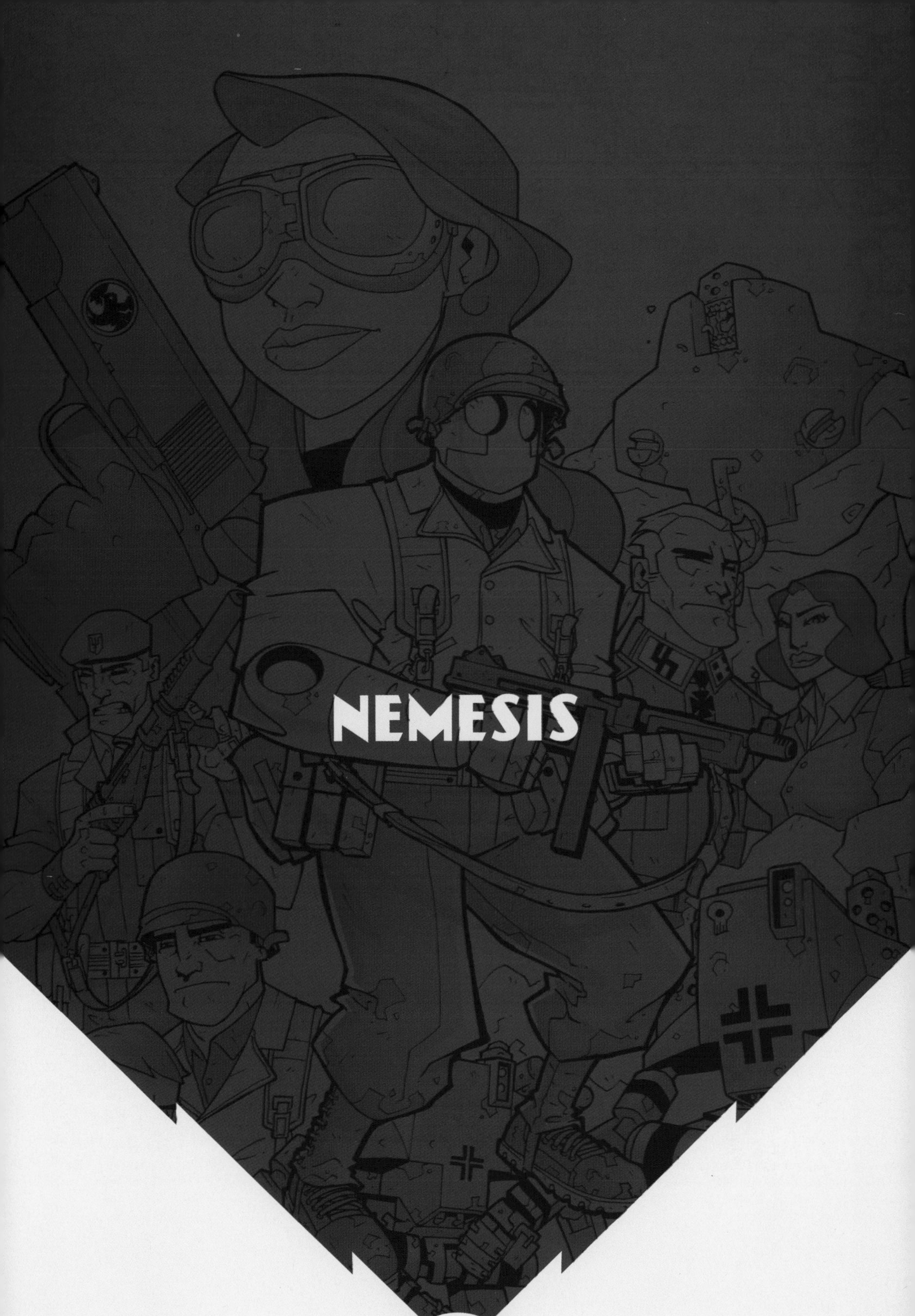

NEMESIS

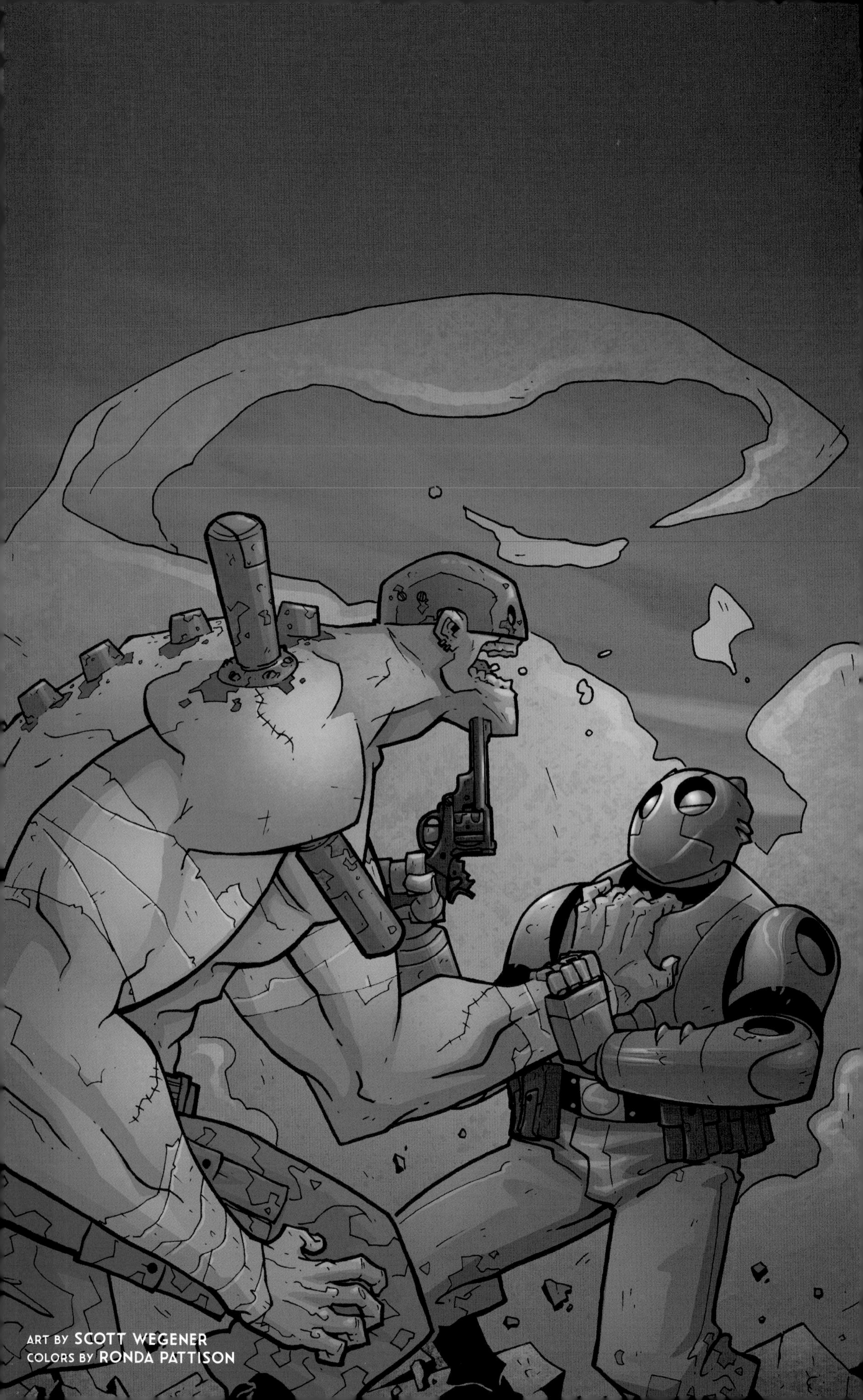

ART BY SCOTT WEGENER
COLORS BY RONDA PATTISON

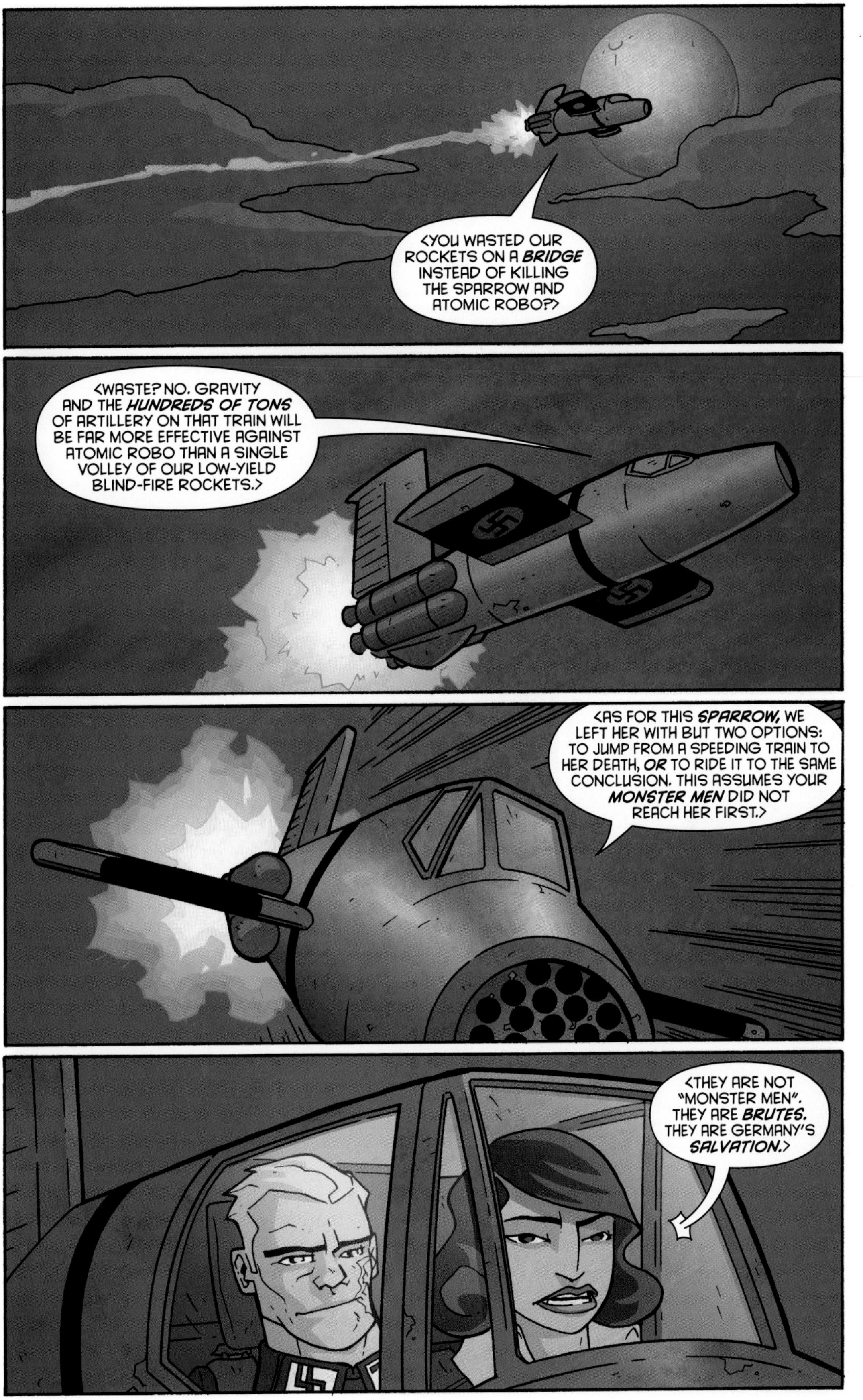
<YOU WASTED OUR ROCKETS ON A ***BRIDGE*** INSTEAD OF KILLING THE SPARROW AND ATOMIC ROBO?>
<WASTE? NO. GRAVITY AND THE ***HUNDREDS OF TONS*** OF ARTILLERY ON THAT TRAIN WILL BE FAR MORE EFFECTIVE AGAINST ATOMIC ROBO THAN A SINGLE VOLLEY OF OUR LOW-YIELD BLIND-FIRE ROCKETS.>
<AS FOR THIS ***SPARROW,*** WE LEFT HER WITH BUT TWO OPTIONS: TO JUMP FROM A SPEEDING TRAIN TO HER DEATH, ***OR*** TO RIDE IT TO THE SAME CONCLUSION. THIS ASSUMES YOUR ***MONSTER MEN*** DID NOT REACH HER FIRST.>
<THEY ARE NOT "MONSTER MEN". THEY ARE ***BRUTES.*** THEY ARE GERMANY'S ***SALVATION.***>

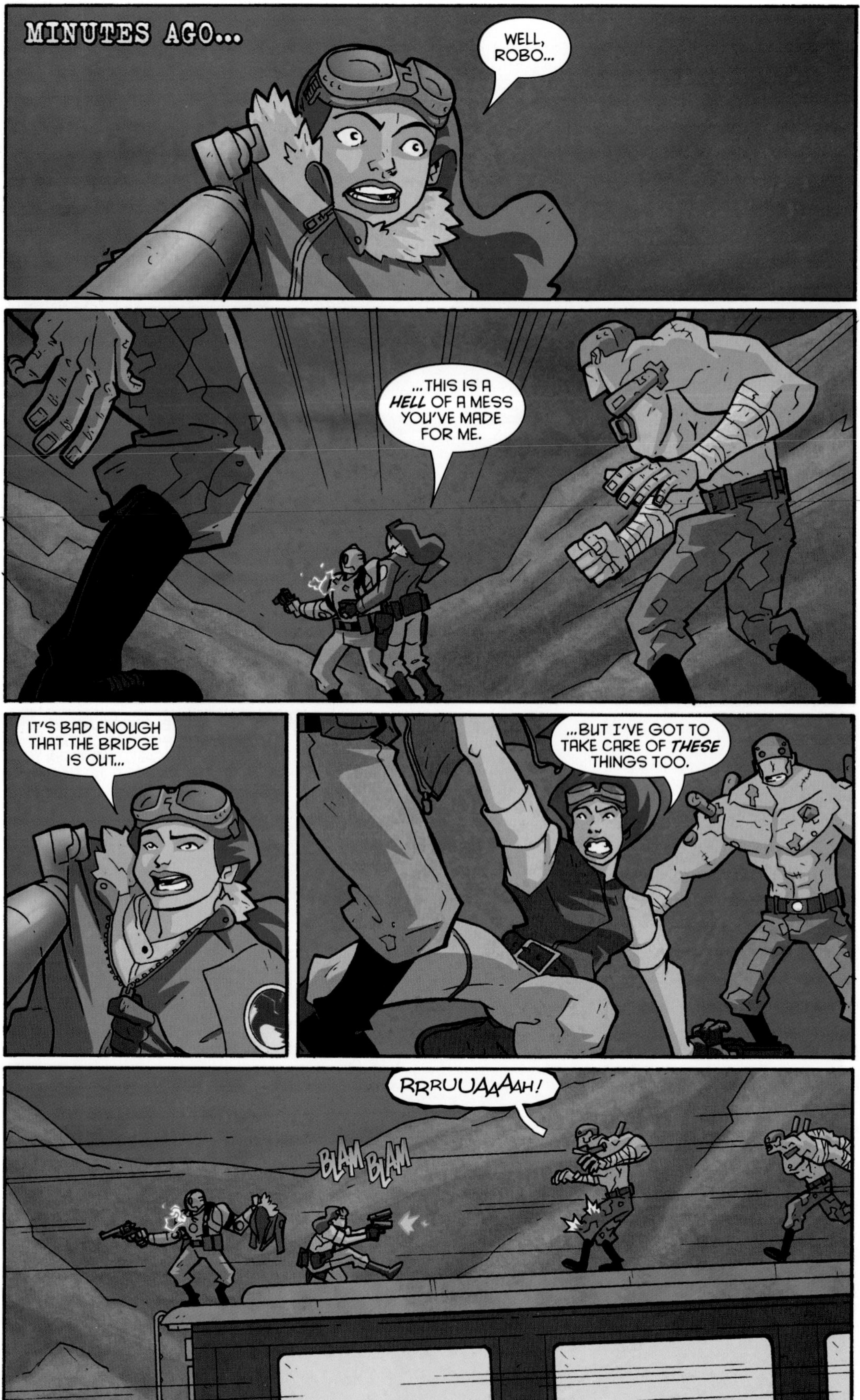
MINUTES AGO...
WELL, ROBO...
...THIS IS A HELL OF A MESS YOU'VE MADE FOR ME.
IT'S BAD ENOUGH THAT THE BRIDGE IS OUT...
...BUT I'VE GOT TO TAKE CARE OF THESE THINGS TOO.
RRRUUAAAAH!
BLAM BLAM

UAAAURGH!

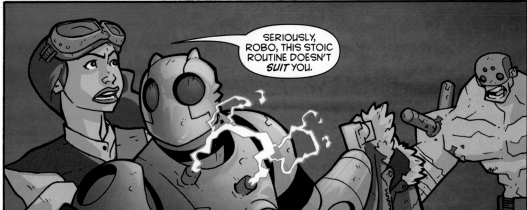

SERIOUSLY, ROBO, THIS STOIC ROUTINE DOESN'T *SUIT* YOU.

IT'S TOO DIGNIFIED.

KRUNCH

GRRRONK!

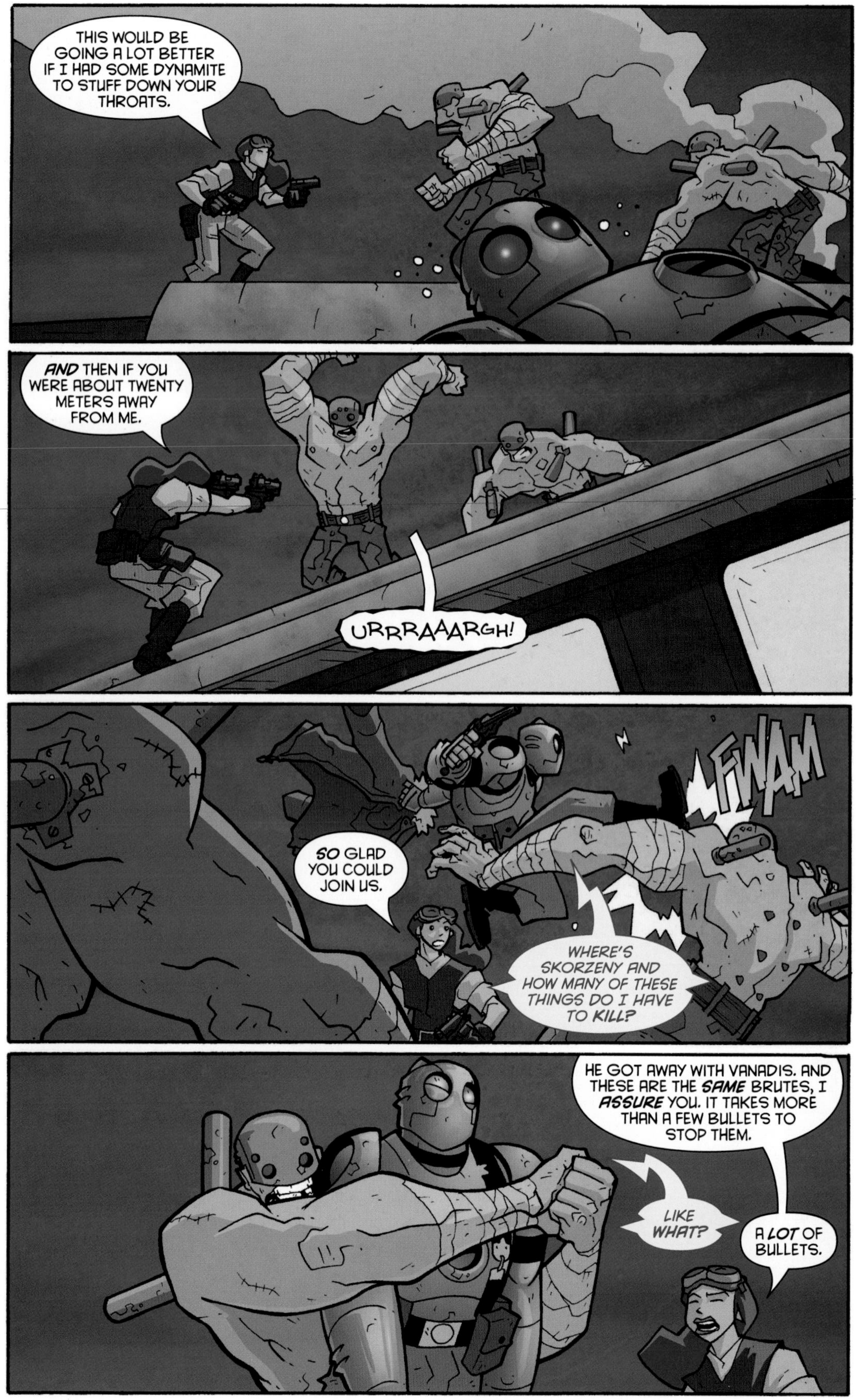

THIS WOULD BE GOING A LOT BETTER IF I HAD SOME DYNAMITE TO STUFF DOWN YOUR THROATS.
AND THEN IF YOU WERE ABOUT TWENTY METERS AWAY FROM ME.
URRRAAARGH!
FWAM
SO GLAD YOU COULD JOIN US.
WHERE'S SKORZENY AND HOW MANY OF THESE THINGS DO I HAVE TO KILL?
HE GOT AWAY WITH VANADIS. AND THESE ARE THE SAME BRUTES, I ASSURE YOU. IT TAKES MORE THAN A FEW BULLETS TO STOP THEM.
LIKE WHAT?
A LOT OF BULLETS.

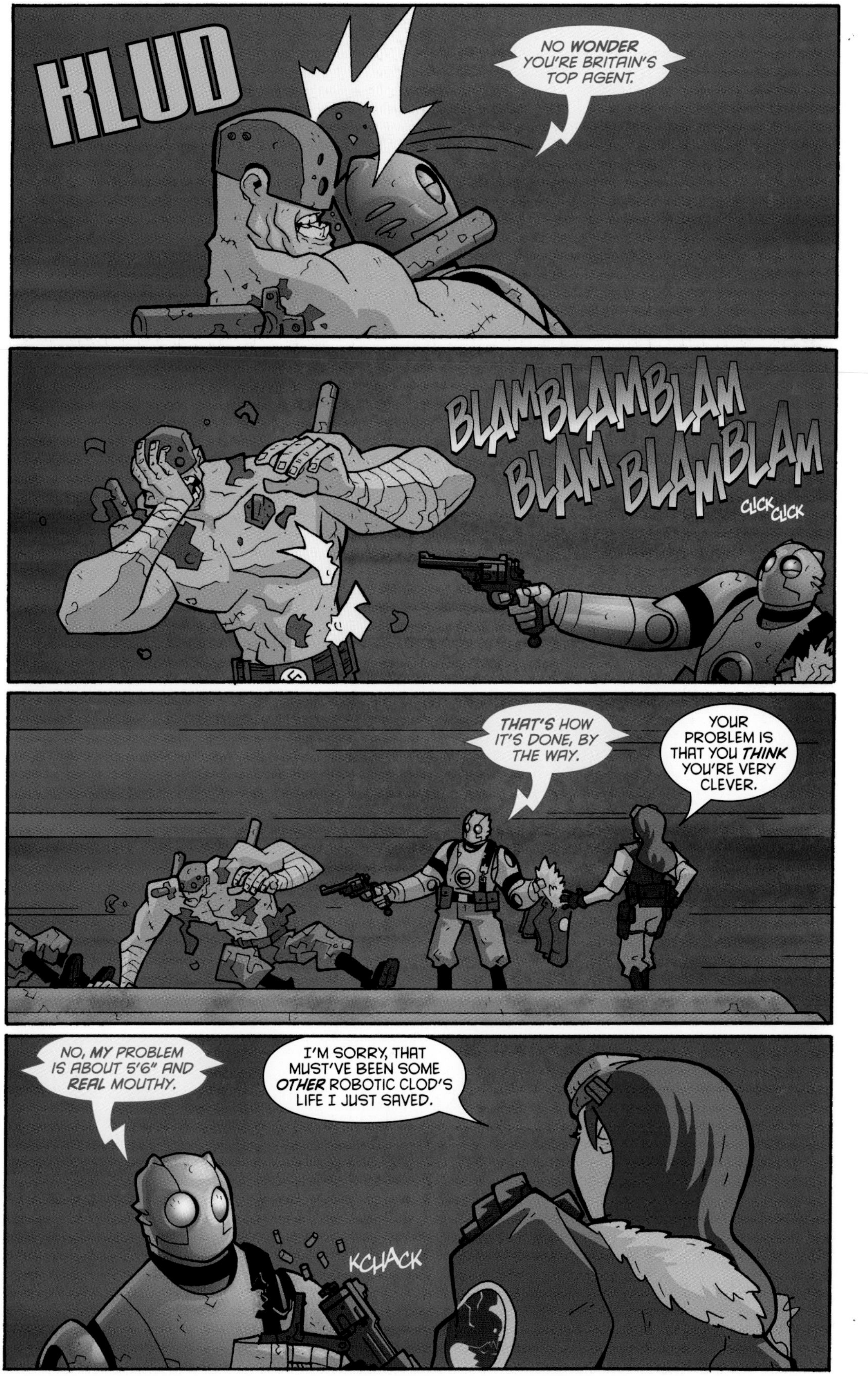
KLUD
NO WONDER YOU'RE BRITAIN'S TOP AGENT.
BLAMBLAMBLAM BLAM BLAMBLAM
CLICK CLICK
THAT'S HOW IT'S DONE, BY THE WAY.
YOUR PROBLEM IS THAT YOU THINK YOU'RE VERY CLEVER.
NO, MY PROBLEM IS ABOUT 5'6" AND REAL MOUTHY.
I'M SORRY, THAT MUST'VE BEEN SOME OTHER ROBOTIC CLOD'S LIFE I JUST SAVED.
KCHACK

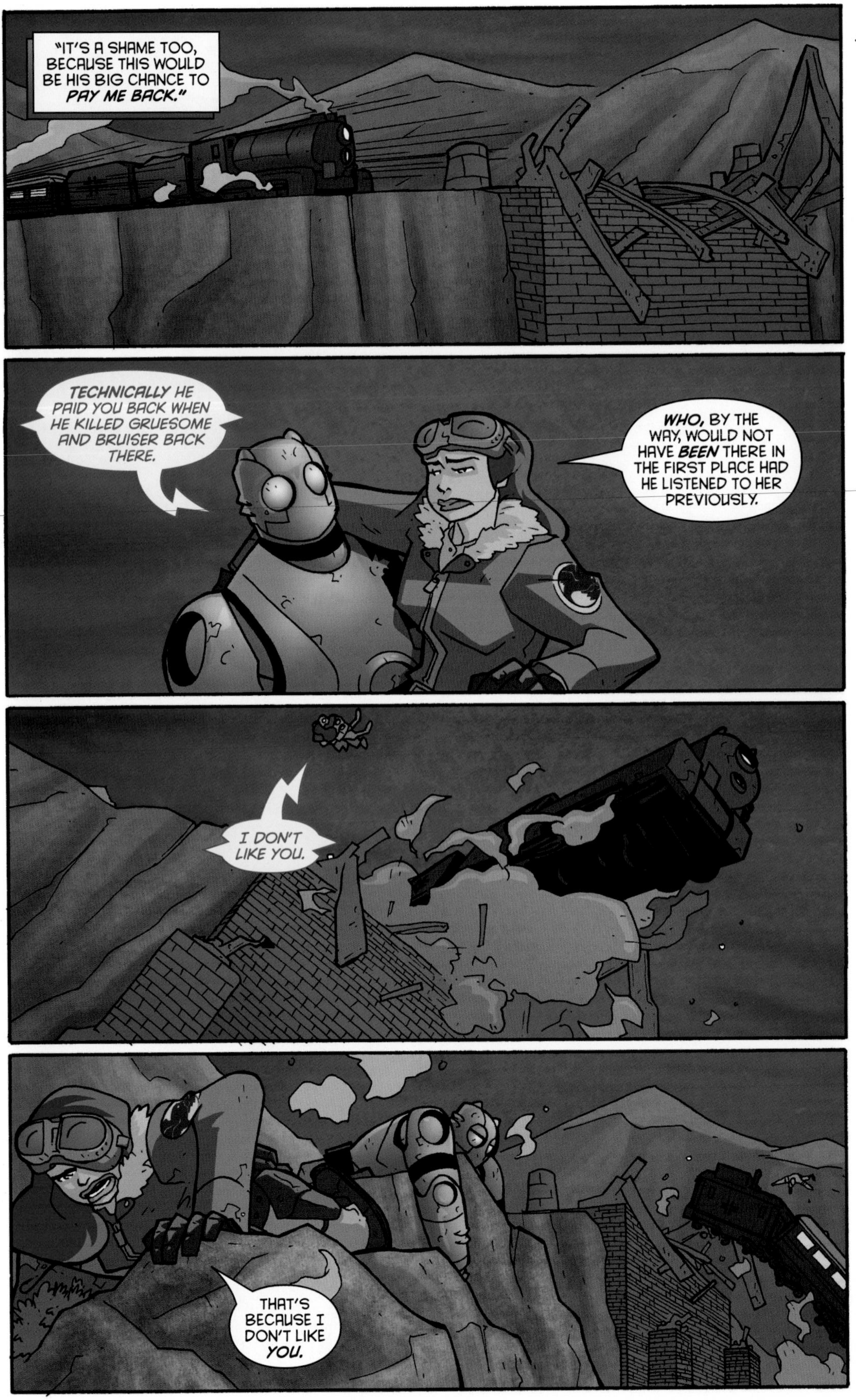
"IT'S A SHAME TOO, BECAUSE THIS WOULD BE HIS BIG CHANCE TO *PAY ME BACK.*"
TECHNICALLY HE PAID YOU BACK WHEN HE KILLED GRUESOME AND BRUISER BACK THERE.
WHO, BY THE WAY, WOULD NOT HAVE *BEEN* THERE IN THE FIRST PLACE HAD HE LISTENED TO HER PREVIOUSLY.
I DON'T LIKE YOU.
THAT'S BECAUSE I DON'T LIKE *YOU.*

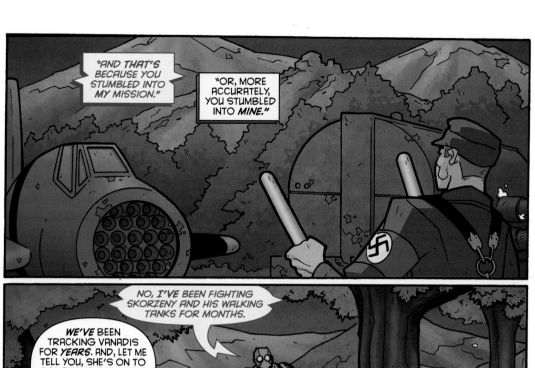

"AND *THAT'S* BECAUSE YOU STUMBLED INTO *MY* MISSION."

"OR, MORE ACCURATELY, YOU STUMBLED INTO *MINE.*"

NO, *I'VE* BEEN FIGHTING SKORZENY AND HIS WALKING TANKS FOR MONTHS.

WE'VE BEEN TRACKING VANADIS FOR *YEARS.* AND, LET ME TELL YOU, SHE'S ON TO SOMETHING FAR MORE DANGEROUS THAN A *HANDFUL* OF TANK PROTOTYPES.

"NO OFFENSE, BUT A *DOZEN* OF SKORZENY'S *LAUFPANZERS* NEARLY PUT A STOP TO SICILY ON DAY *ONE.* I THINK HE'S THE BIGGER FISH HERE."

"BLOODY YANKS. DON'T YOU KNOW *ANYTHING* ABOUT THE SPECIAL PROJECTS DIVISION? THOSE MACHINES YOU SPENT ALL THAT TIME HUNTING DOWN? THEY'RE ONLY THE *BEGINNING.*"

THE GERMANS CAN'T WIN A *CONVENTIONAL* WAR AT THIS POINT, AND THEY KNOW THAT.

THEY'VE GOT A BRAIN TRUST IN BERLIN LIKE NOTHING THE WORLD HAS *EVER* SEEN.

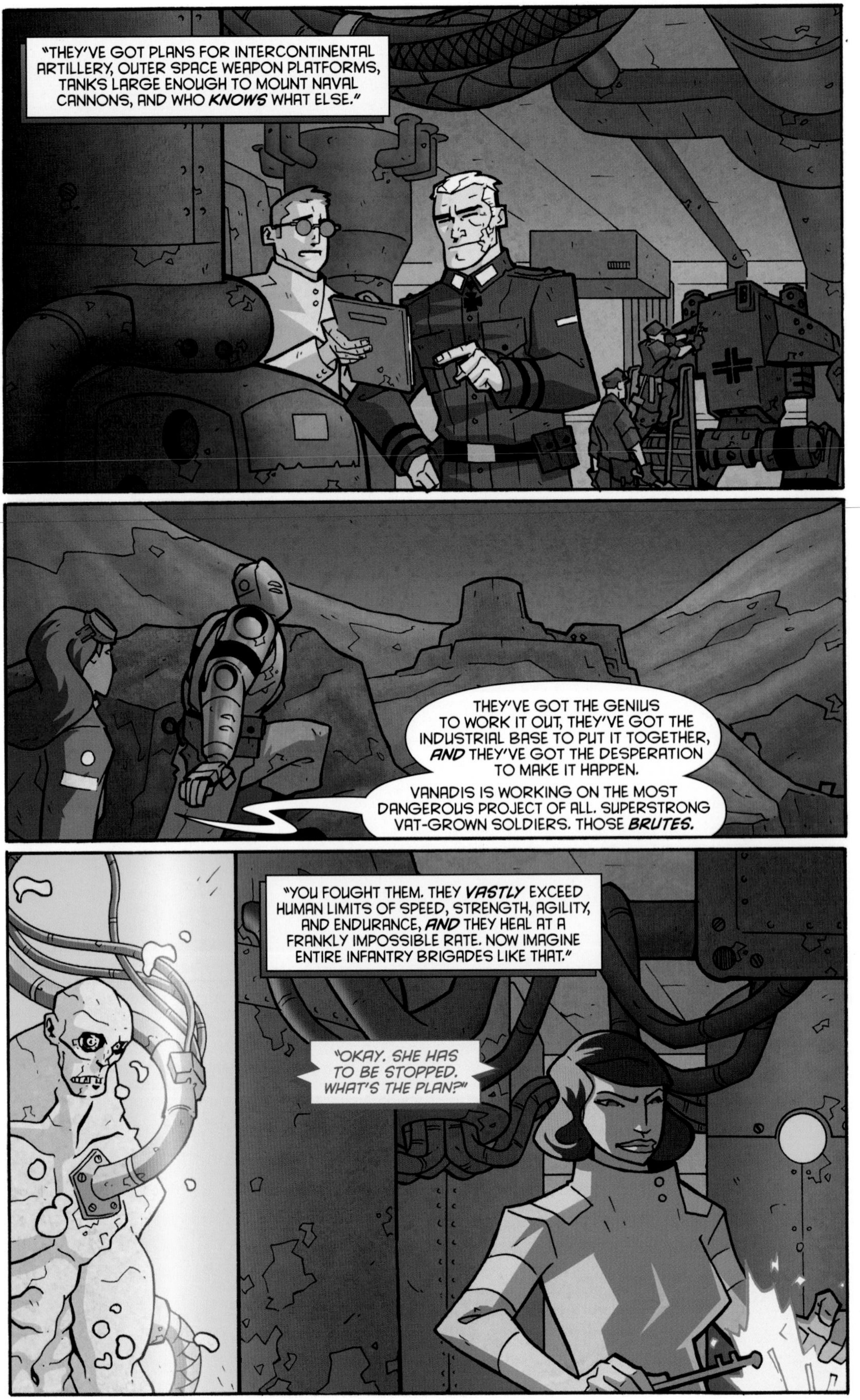
"THEY'VE GOT PLANS FOR INTERCONTINENTAL ARTILLERY, OUTER SPACE WEAPON PLATFORMS, TANKS LARGE ENOUGH TO MOUNT NAVAL CANNONS, AND WHO *KNOWS* WHAT ELSE."
THEY'VE GOT THE GENIUS TO WORK IT OUT, THEY'VE GOT THE INDUSTRIAL BASE TO PUT IT TOGETHER, *AND* THEY'VE GOT THE DESPERATION TO MAKE IT HAPPEN.
VANADIS IS WORKING ON THE MOST DANGEROUS PROJECT OF ALL. SUPERSTRONG VAT-GROWN SOLDIERS. THOSE *BRUTES.*
"YOU FOUGHT THEM. THEY *VASTLY* EXCEED HUMAN LIMITS OF SPEED, STRENGTH, AGILITY, AND ENDURANCE, *AND* THEY HEAL AT A FRANKLY IMPOSSIBLE RATE. NOW IMAGINE ENTIRE INFANTRY BRIGADES LIKE THAT."
"OKAY. SHE HAS TO BE STOPPED. WHAT'S THE PLAN?"

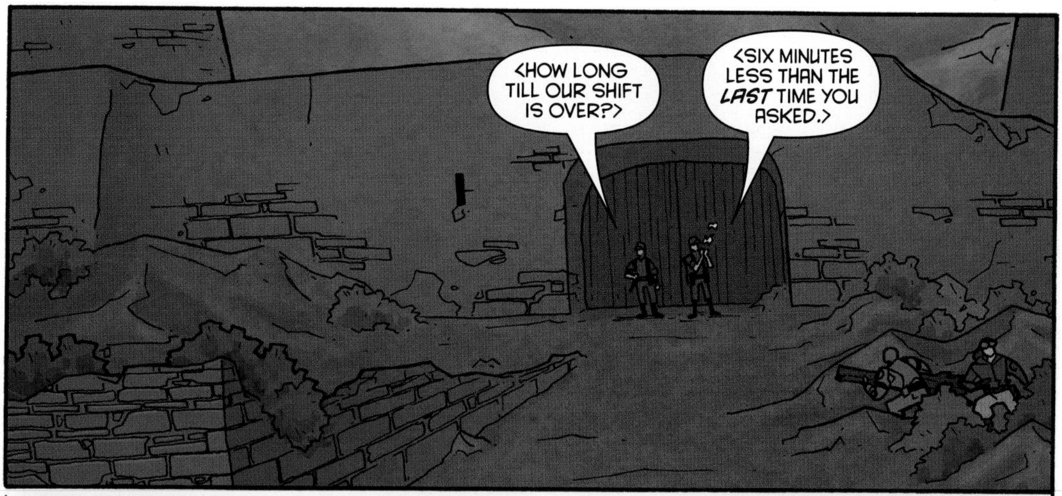
<HOW LONG TILL OUR SHIFT IS OVER?>
<SIX MINUTES LESS THAN THE LAST TIME YOU ASKED.>

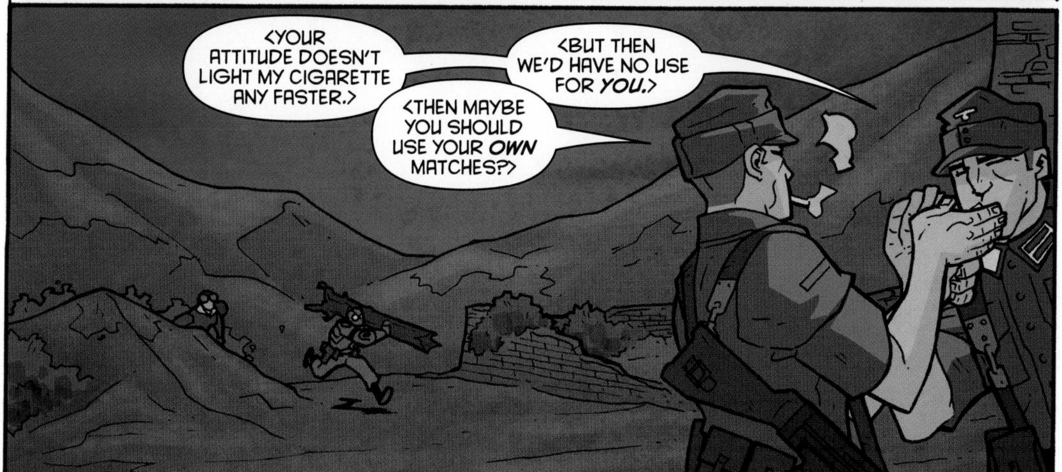
<YOUR ATTITUDE DOESN'T LIGHT MY CIGARETTE ANY FASTER.>
<THEN MAYBE YOU SHOULD USE YOUR OWN MATCHES?>
<BUT THEN WE'D HAVE NO USE FOR YOU.>

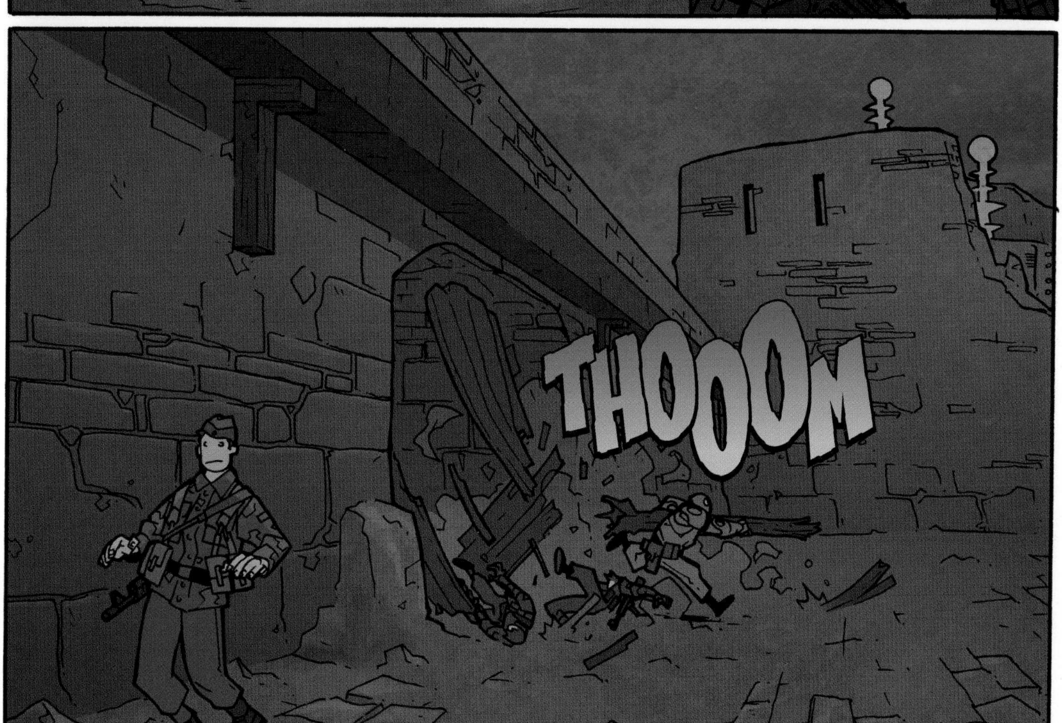
THOOOM

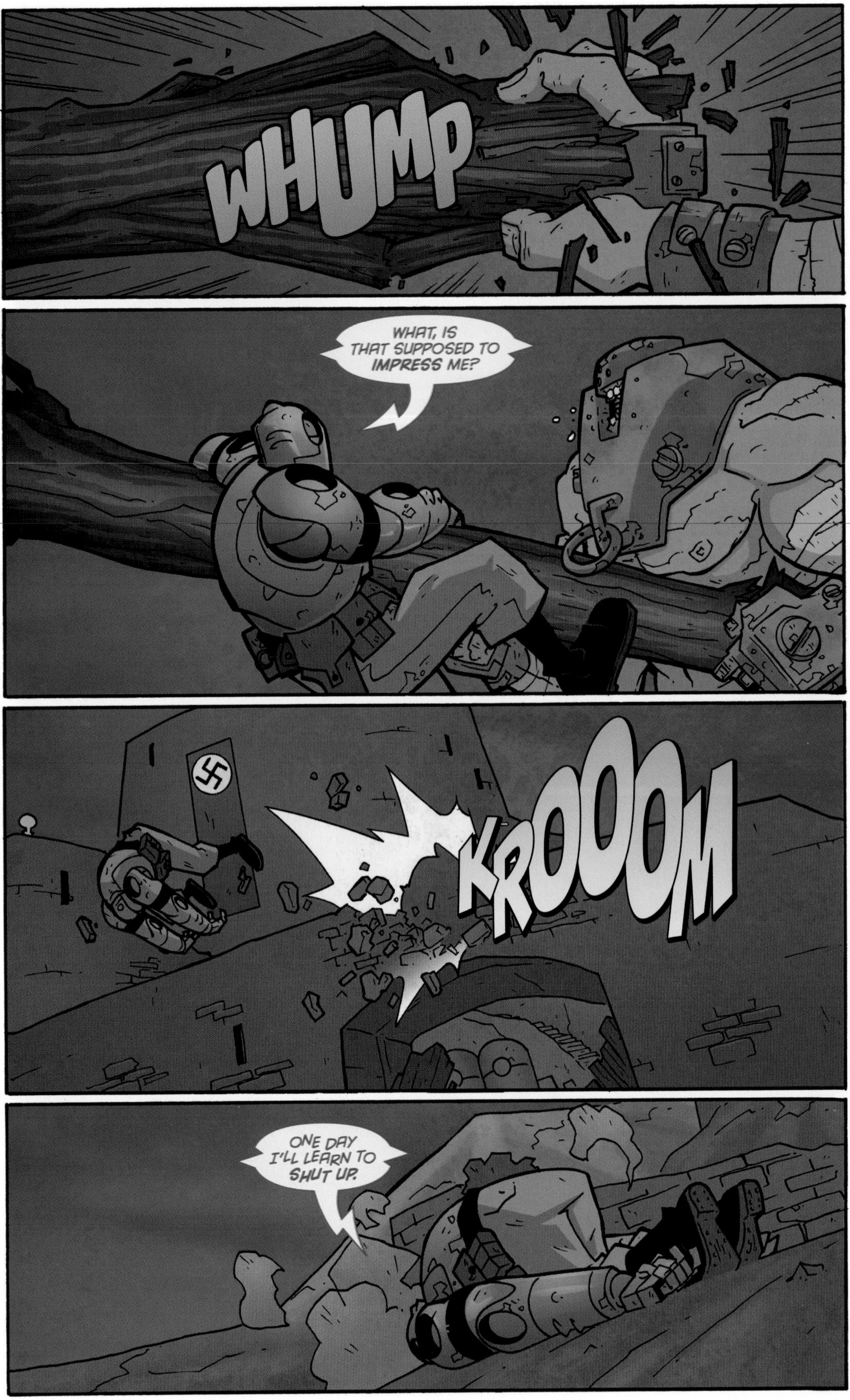
WHUMP
WHAT, IS THAT SUPPOSED TO IMPRESS ME?
KROOOM
ONE DAY I'LL LEARN TO SHUT UP.

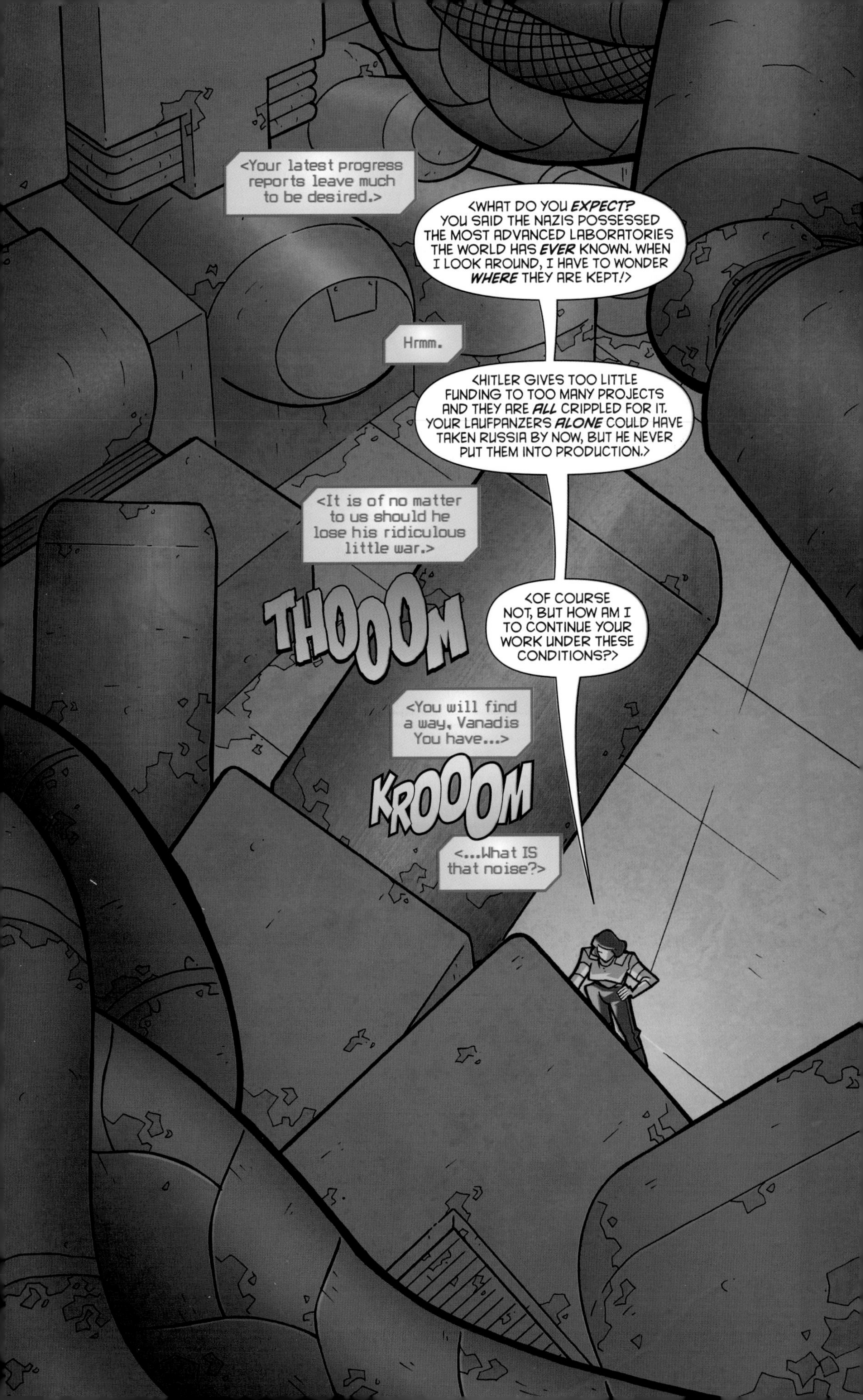

<Your latest progress reports leave much to be desired.>
<WHAT DO YOU EXPECT? YOU SAID THE NAZIS POSSESSED THE MOST ADVANCED LABORATORIES THE WORLD HAS EVER KNOWN. WHEN I LOOK AROUND, I HAVE TO WONDER WHERE THEY ARE KEPT!>
Hrmm.
<HITLER GIVES TOO LITTLE FUNDING TO TOO MANY PROJECTS AND THEY ARE ALL CRIPPLED FOR IT. YOUR LAUFPANZERS ALONE COULD HAVE TAKEN RUSSIA BY NOW, BUT HE NEVER PUT THEM INTO PRODUCTION.>
<It is of no matter to us should he lose his ridiculous little war.>
THOOOM
<OF COURSE NOT, BUT HOW AM I TO CONTINUE YOUR WORK UNDER THESE CONDITIONS?>
<You will find a way, Vanadis You have...>
KROOOM
<...What IS that noise?>

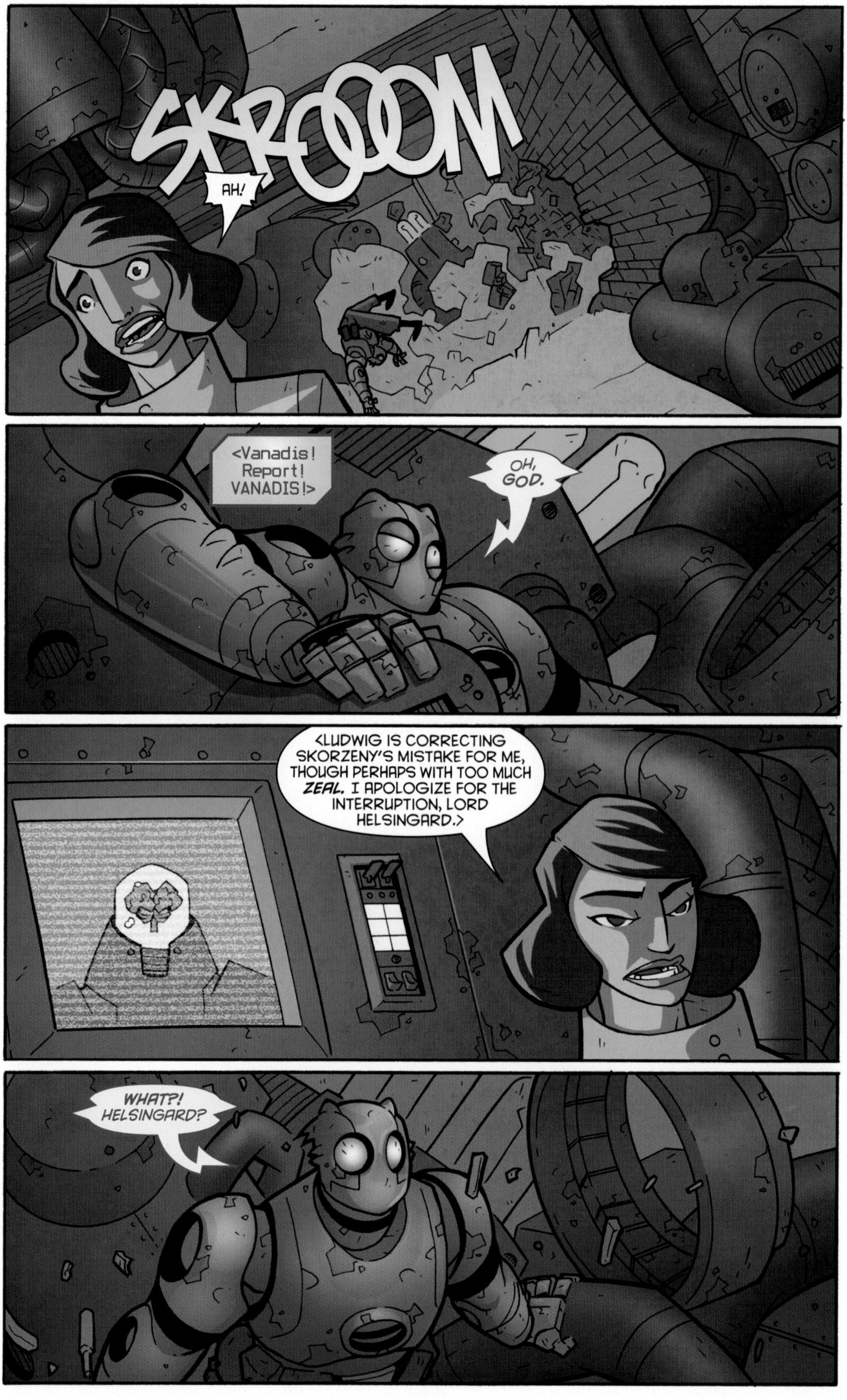

SKROOOM
AH!
<Vanadis! Report! VANADIS!>
OH, GOD.
<LUDWIG IS CORRECTING SKORZENY'S MISTAKE FOR ME, THOUGH PERHAPS WITH TOO MUCH ZEAL. I APOLOGIZE FOR THE INTERRUPTION, LORD HELSINGARD.>
WHAT?! HELSINGARD?

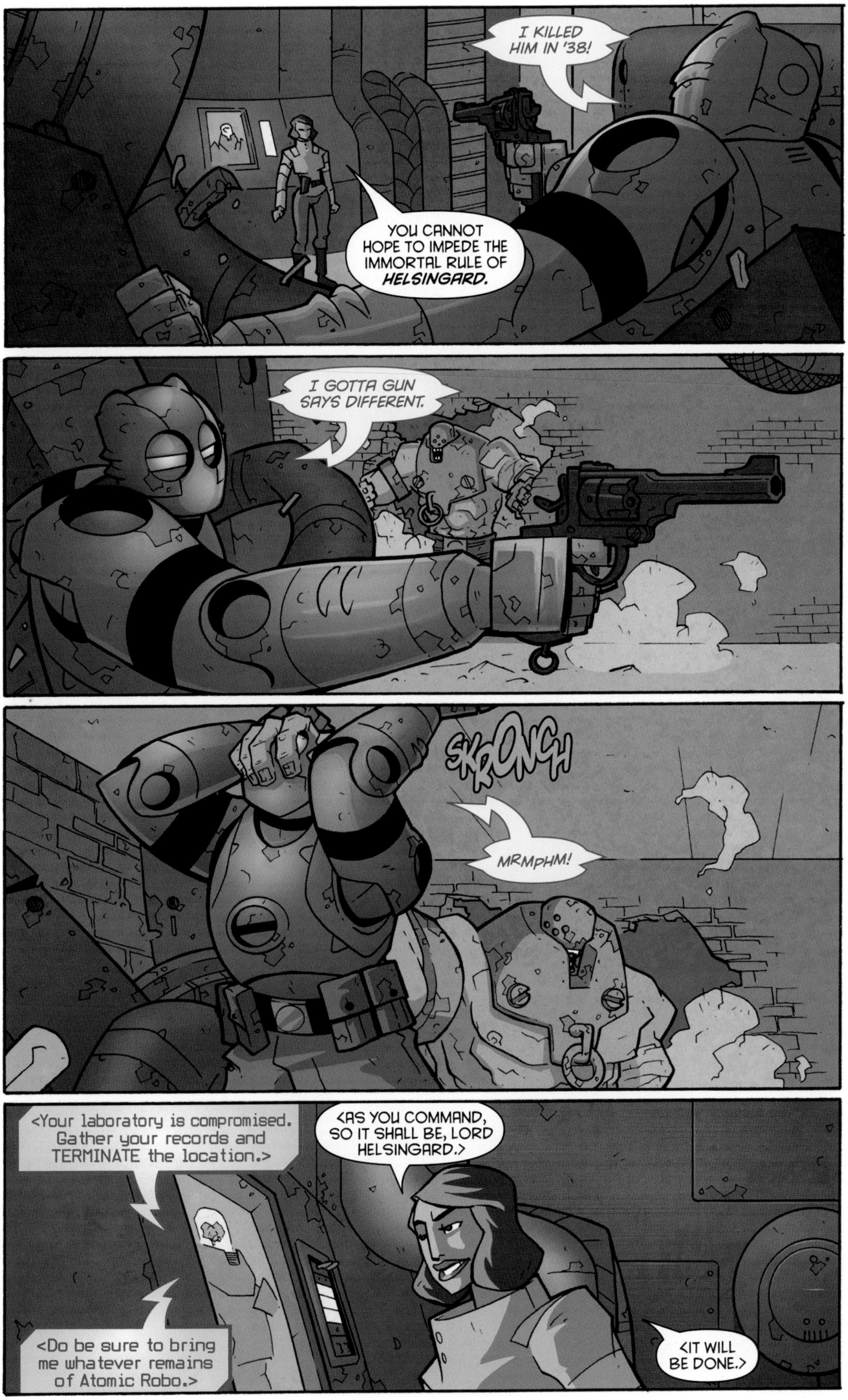
I KILLED HIM IN '38!
YOU CANNOT HOPE TO IMPEDE THE IMMORTAL RULE OF HELSINGARD.
I GOTTA GUN SAYS DIFFERENT.
SKRONCH
MRMPHM!
<Your laboratory is compromised. Gather your records and TERMINATE the location.>
<AS YOU COMMAND, SO IT SHALL BE, LORD HELSINGARD.>
<Do be sure to bring me whatever remains of Atomic Robo.>
<IT WILL BE DONE.>

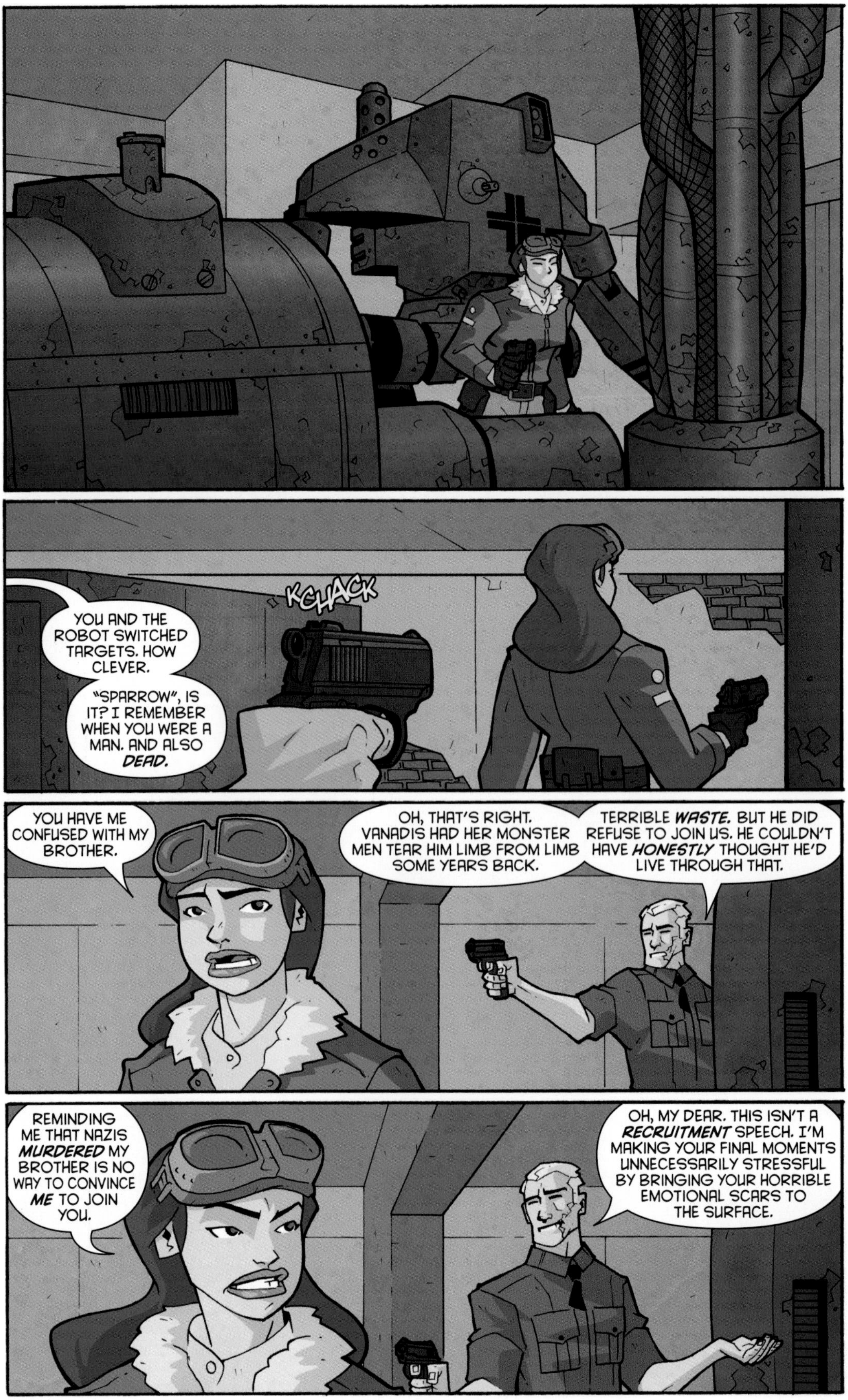
KCHACK
YOU AND THE ROBOT SWITCHED TARGETS. HOW CLEVER.
"SPARROW", IS IT? I REMEMBER WHEN YOU WERE A MAN. AND ALSO ***DEAD.***
YOU HAVE ME CONFUSED WITH MY BROTHER.
OH, THAT'S RIGHT. VANADIS HAD HER MONSTER MEN TEAR HIM LIMB FROM LIMB SOME YEARS BACK.
TERRIBLE ***WASTE.*** BUT HE DID REFUSE TO JOIN US. HE COULDN'T HAVE ***HONESTLY*** THOUGHT HE'D LIVE THROUGH THAT.
REMINDING ME THAT NAZIS ***MURDERED*** MY BROTHER IS NO WAY TO CONVINCE ***ME*** TO JOIN YOU.
OH, MY DEAR. THIS ISN'T A ***RECRUITMENT*** SPEECH. I'M MAKING YOUR FINAL MOMENTS UNNECESSARILY STRESSFUL BY BRINGING YOUR HORRIBLE EMOTIONAL SCARS TO THE SURFACE.

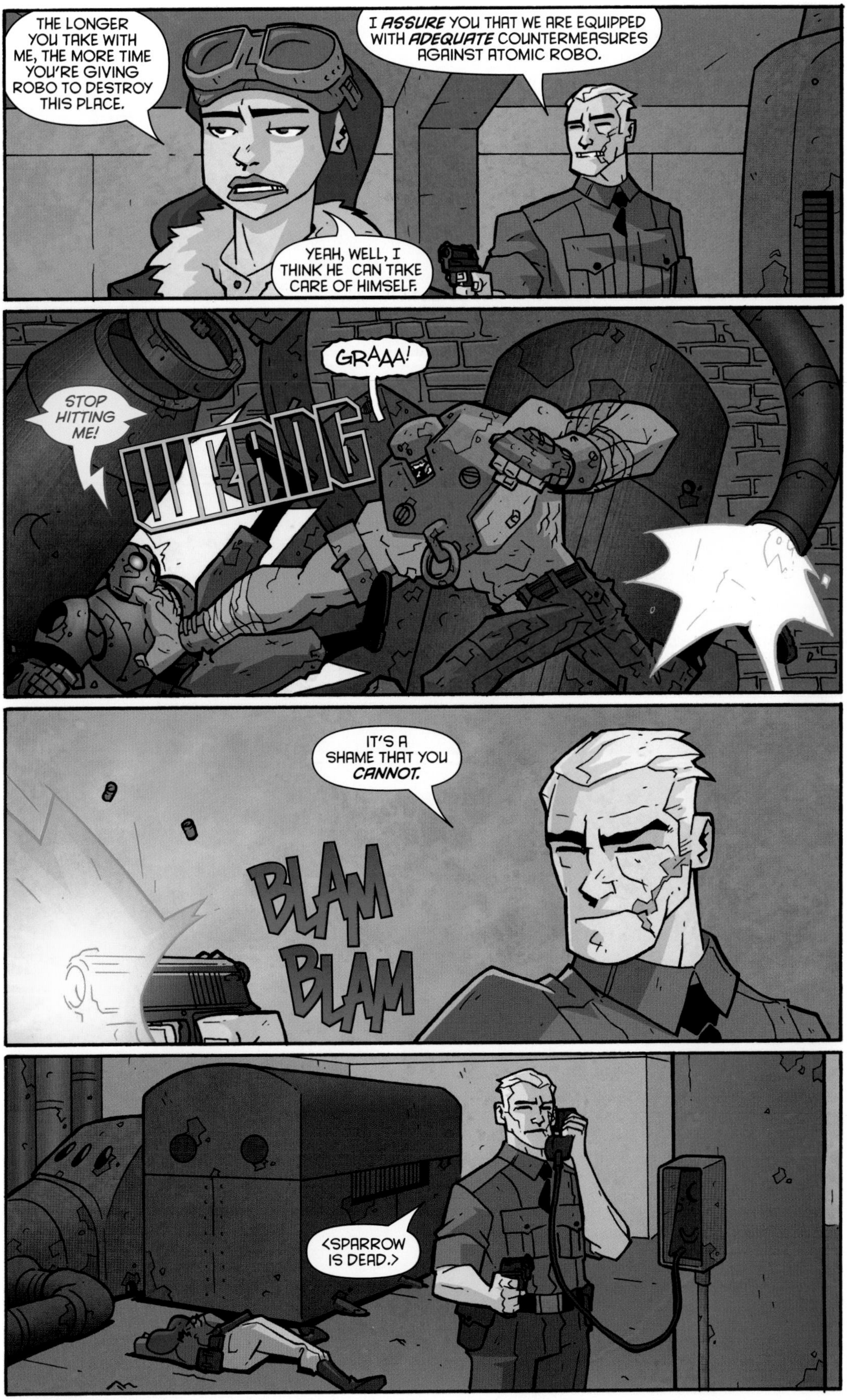
THE LONGER YOU TAKE WITH ME, THE MORE TIME YOU'RE GIVING ROBO TO DESTROY THIS PLACE.
I ASSURE YOU THAT WE ARE EQUIPPED WITH ADEQUATE COUNTERMEASURES AGAINST ATOMIC ROBO.
YEAH, WELL, I THINK HE CAN TAKE CARE OF HIMSELF.
STOP HITTING ME!
GRAAA!
WRANG
IT'S A SHAME THAT YOU CANNOT.
BLAM
BLAM
<SPARROW IS DEAD.>

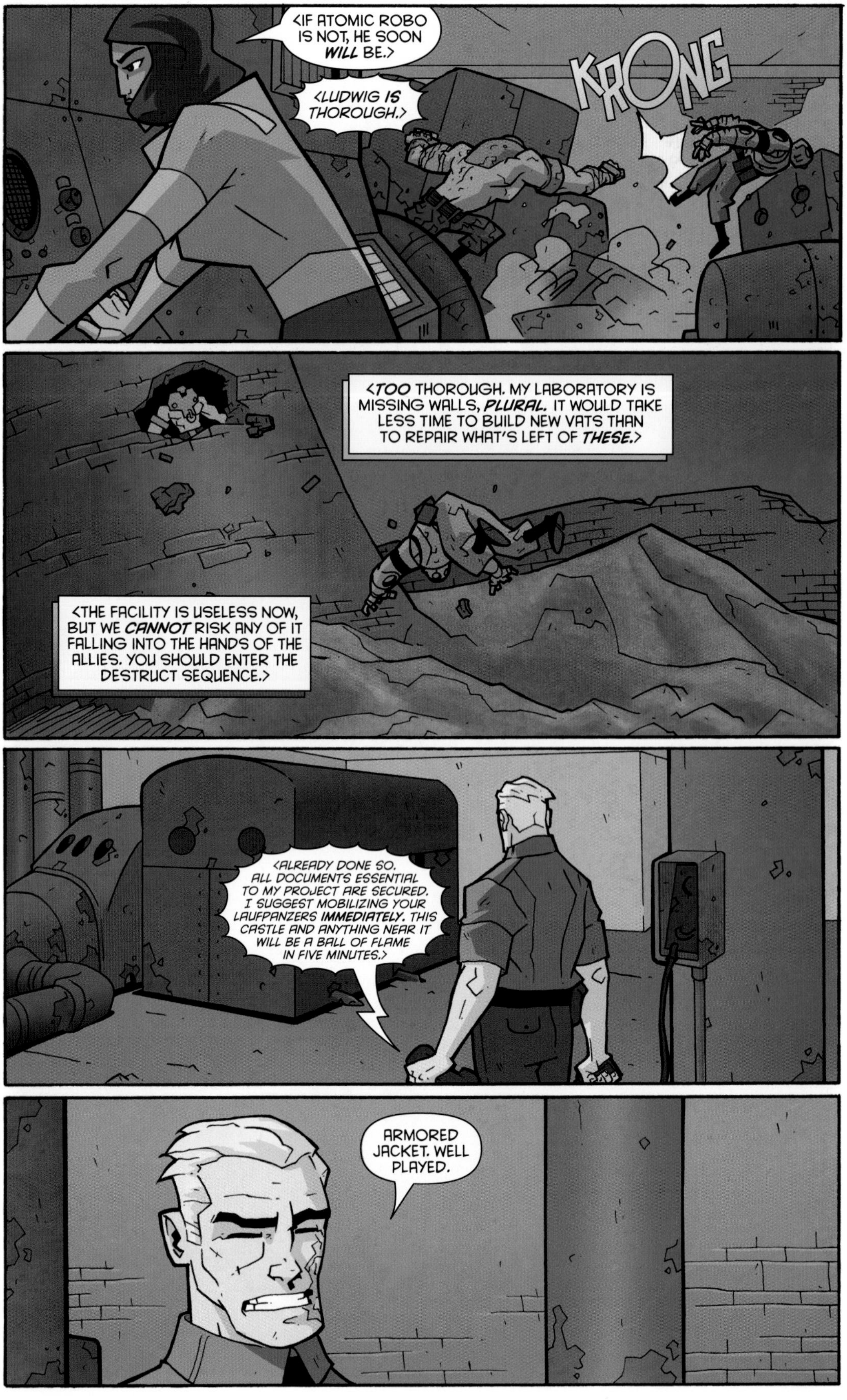

<IF ATOMIC ROBO IS NOT, HE SOON WILL BE.>
<LUDWIG IS THOROUGH.>
KRONG
<TOO THOROUGH. MY LABORATORY IS MISSING WALLS, PLURAL. IT WOULD TAKE LESS TIME TO BUILD NEW VATS THAN TO REPAIR WHAT'S LEFT OF THESE.>
<THE FACILITY IS USELESS NOW, BUT WE CANNOT RISK ANY OF IT FALLING INTO THE HANDS OF THE ALLIES. YOU SHOULD ENTER THE DESTRUCT SEQUENCE.>
<ALREADY DONE SO. ALL DOCUMENTS ESSENTIAL TO MY PROJECT ARE SECURED. I SUGGEST MOBILIZING YOUR LAUFPANZERS IMMEDIATELY. THIS CASTLE AND ANYTHING NEAR IT WILL BE A BALL OF FLAME IN FIVE MINUTES.>
ARMORED JACKET. WELL PLAYED.

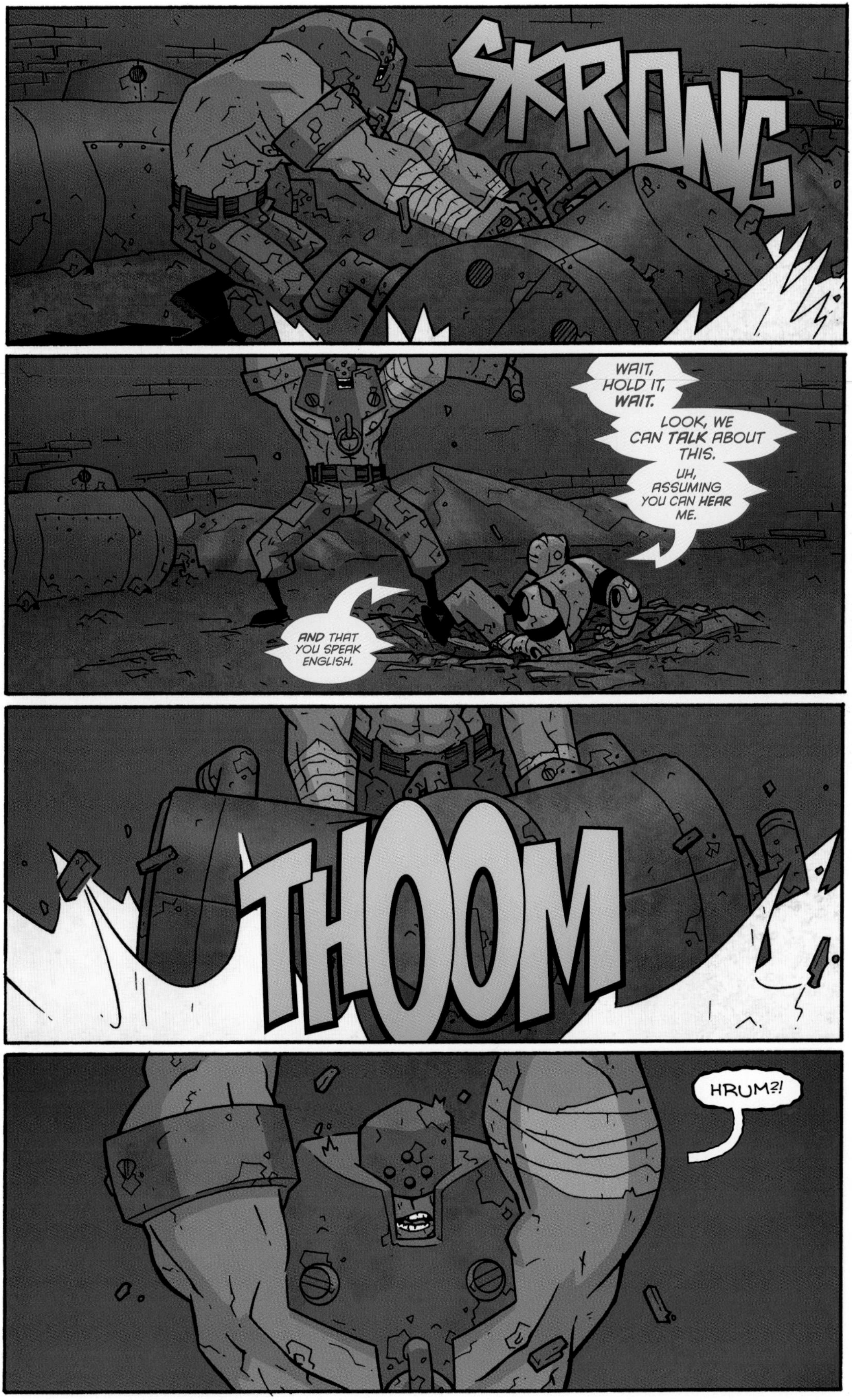
SKRONG
WAIT, HOLD IT, WAIT.
LOOK, WE CAN TALK ABOUT THIS.
UH, ASSUMING YOU CAN HEAR ME.
AND THAT YOU SPEAK ENGLISH.
THOOM
HRUM?!

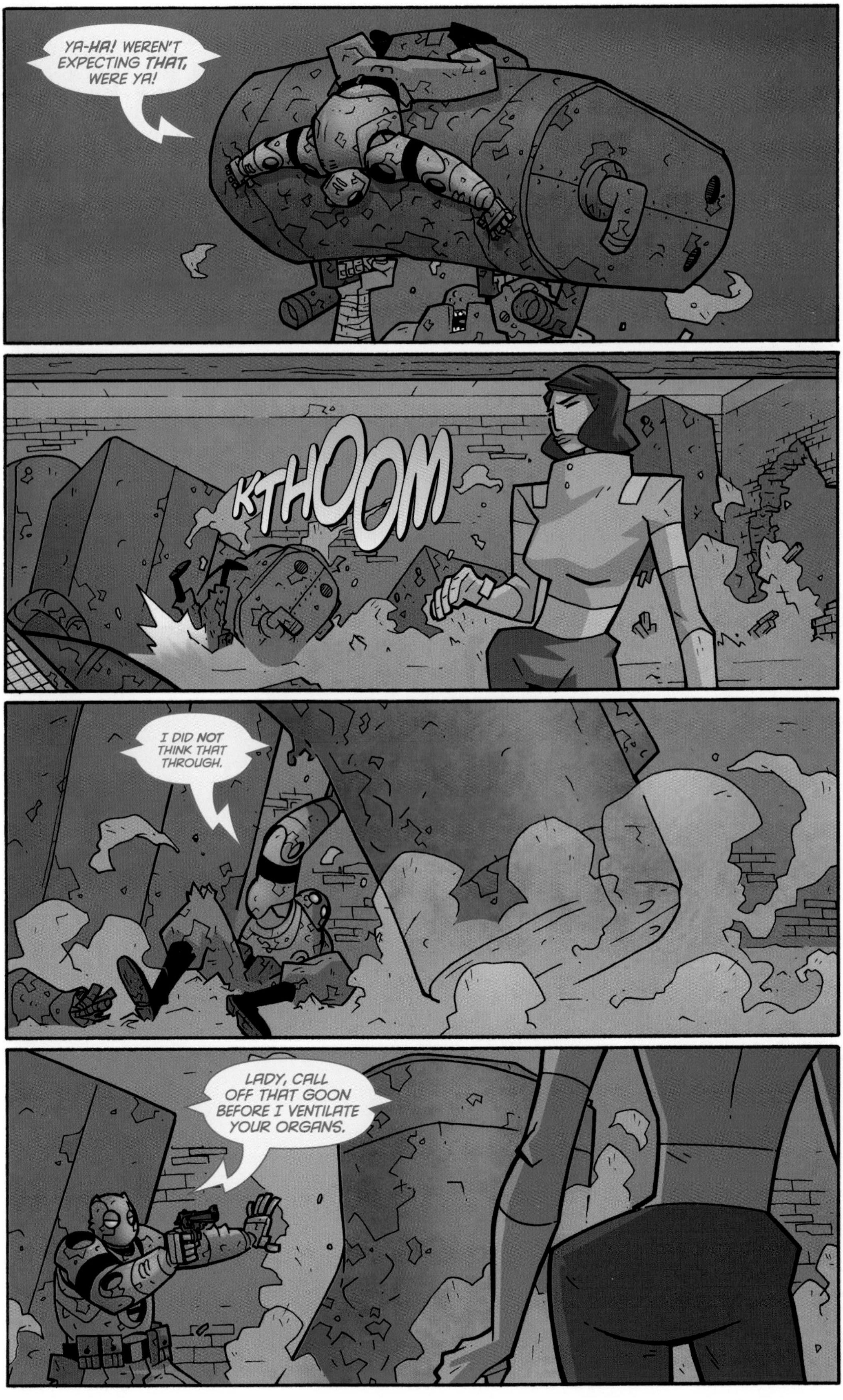
YA-HA! WEREN'T EXPECTING THAT, WERE YA!
KTHOOM
I DID NOT THINK THAT THROUGH.
LADY, CALL OFF THAT GOON BEFORE I VENTILATE YOUR ORGANS.

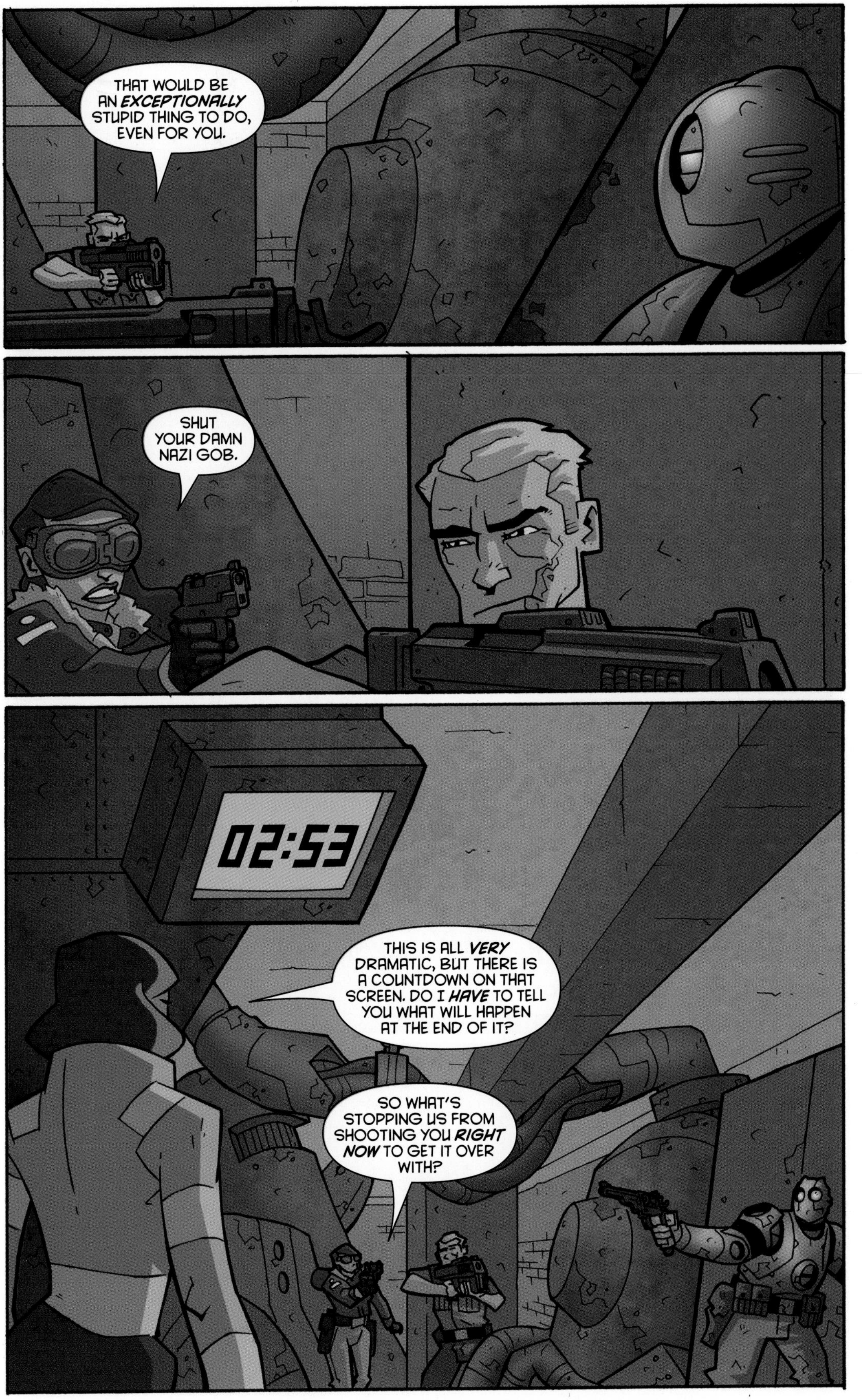
THAT WOULD BE AN EXCEPTIONALLY STUPID THING TO DO, EVEN FOR YOU.
SHUT YOUR DAMN NAZI GOB.
02:53
THIS IS ALL VERY DRAMATIC, BUT THERE IS A COUNTDOWN ON THAT SCREEN. DO I HAVE TO TELL YOU WHAT WILL HAPPEN AT THE END OF IT?
SO WHAT'S STOPPING US FROM SHOOTING YOU RIGHT NOW TO GET IT OVER WITH?

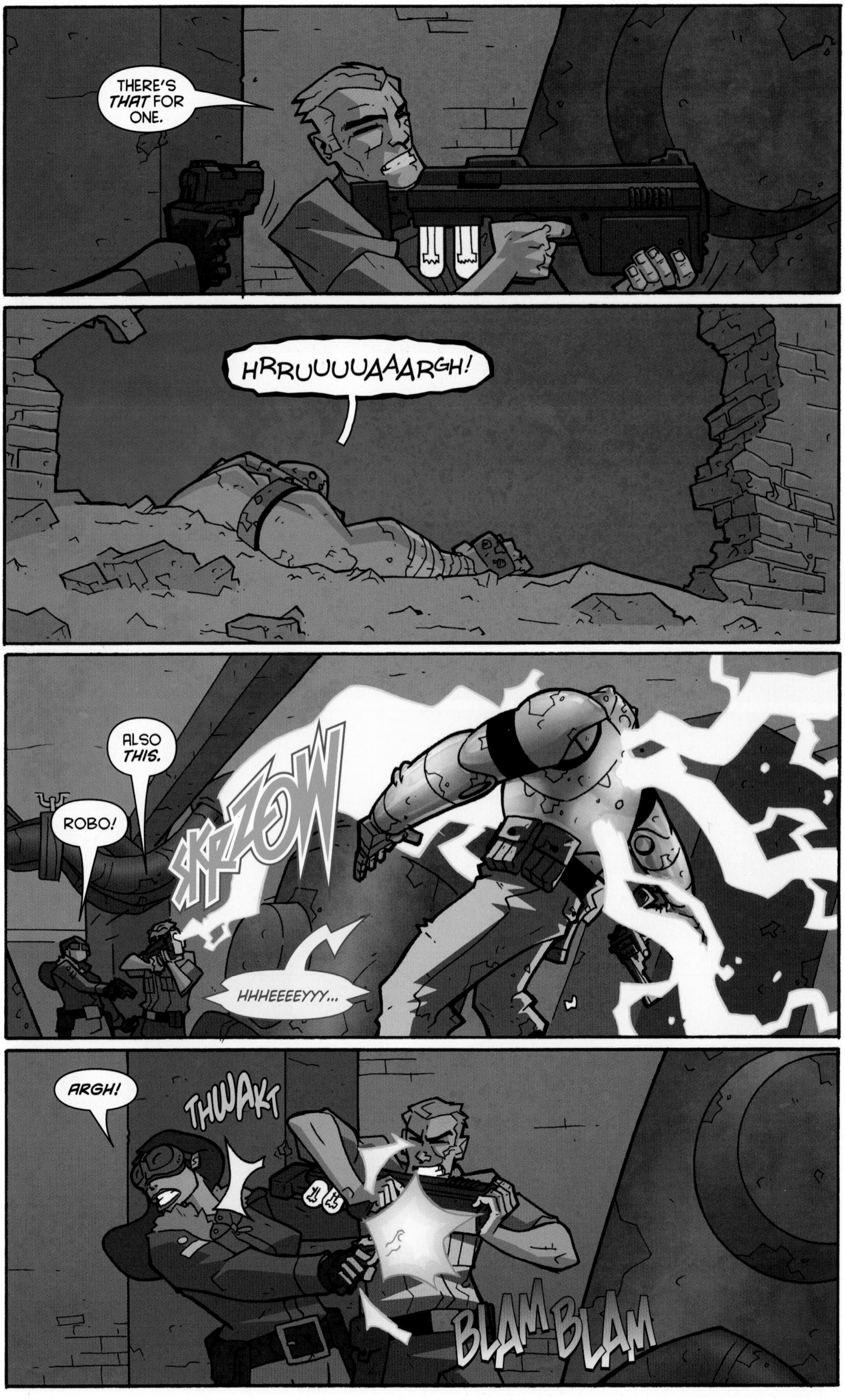
THERE'S *THAT* FOR ONE.
HRRUUUUAAARGH!
ALSO *THIS.*
ROBO!
SKRZOW
HHHEEEEYYY...
ARGH!
THWAKT
BLAM BLAM

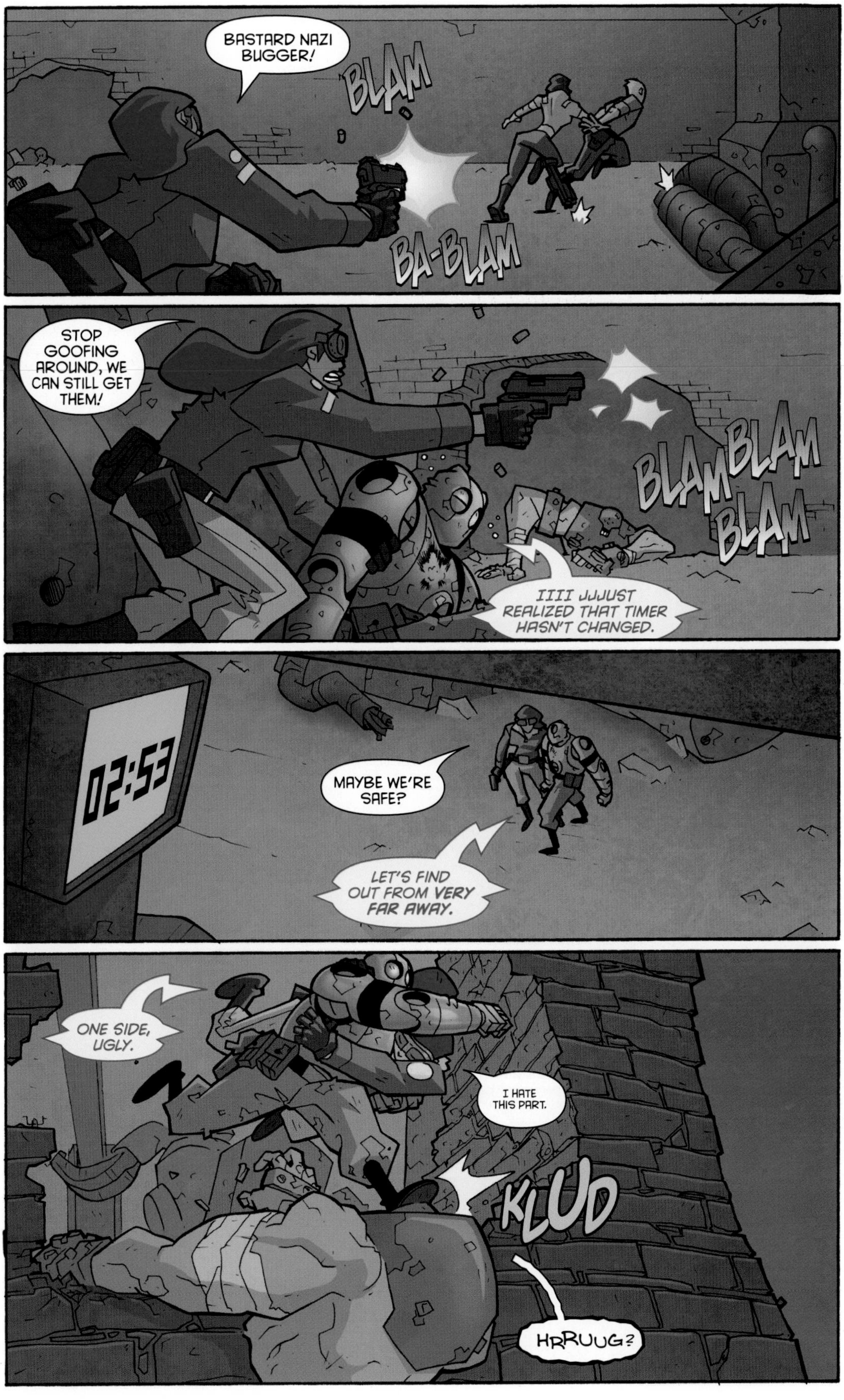
BASTARD NAZI BUGGER!
BLAM
BA-BLAM
STOP GOOFING AROUND, WE CAN STILL GET THEM!
BLAMBLAM BLAM
IIII JJJUST REALIZED THAT TIMER HASN'T CHANGED.
02:53
MAYBE WE'RE SAFE?
LET'S FIND OUT FROM VERY FAR AWAY.
ONE SIDE, UGLY.
I HATE THIS PART.
KLUD
HRRUUG?

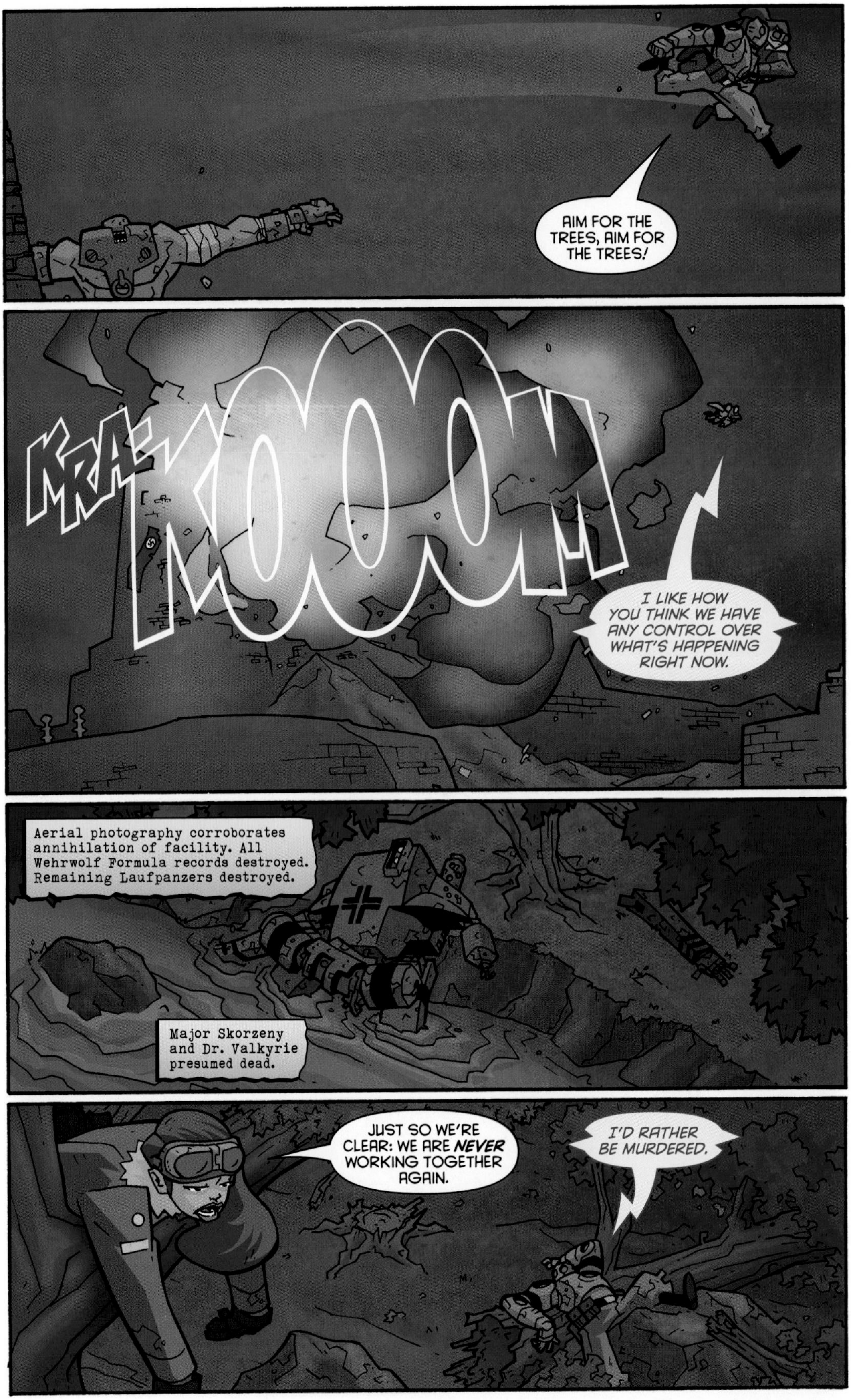
AIM FOR THE TREES, AIM FOR THE TREES!
KRA-KOOOM
I LIKE HOW YOU THINK WE HAVE ANY CONTROL OVER WHAT'S HAPPENING RIGHT NOW.
Aerial photography corroborates annihilation of facility. All Wehrwolf Formula records destroyed. Remaining Laufpanzers destroyed.
Major Skorzeny and Dr. Valkyrie presumed dead.
JUST SO WE'RE CLEAR: WE ARE NEVER WORKING TOGETHER AGAIN.
I'D RATHER BE MURDERED.

IT'S A LOVELY DAY TOMORROW

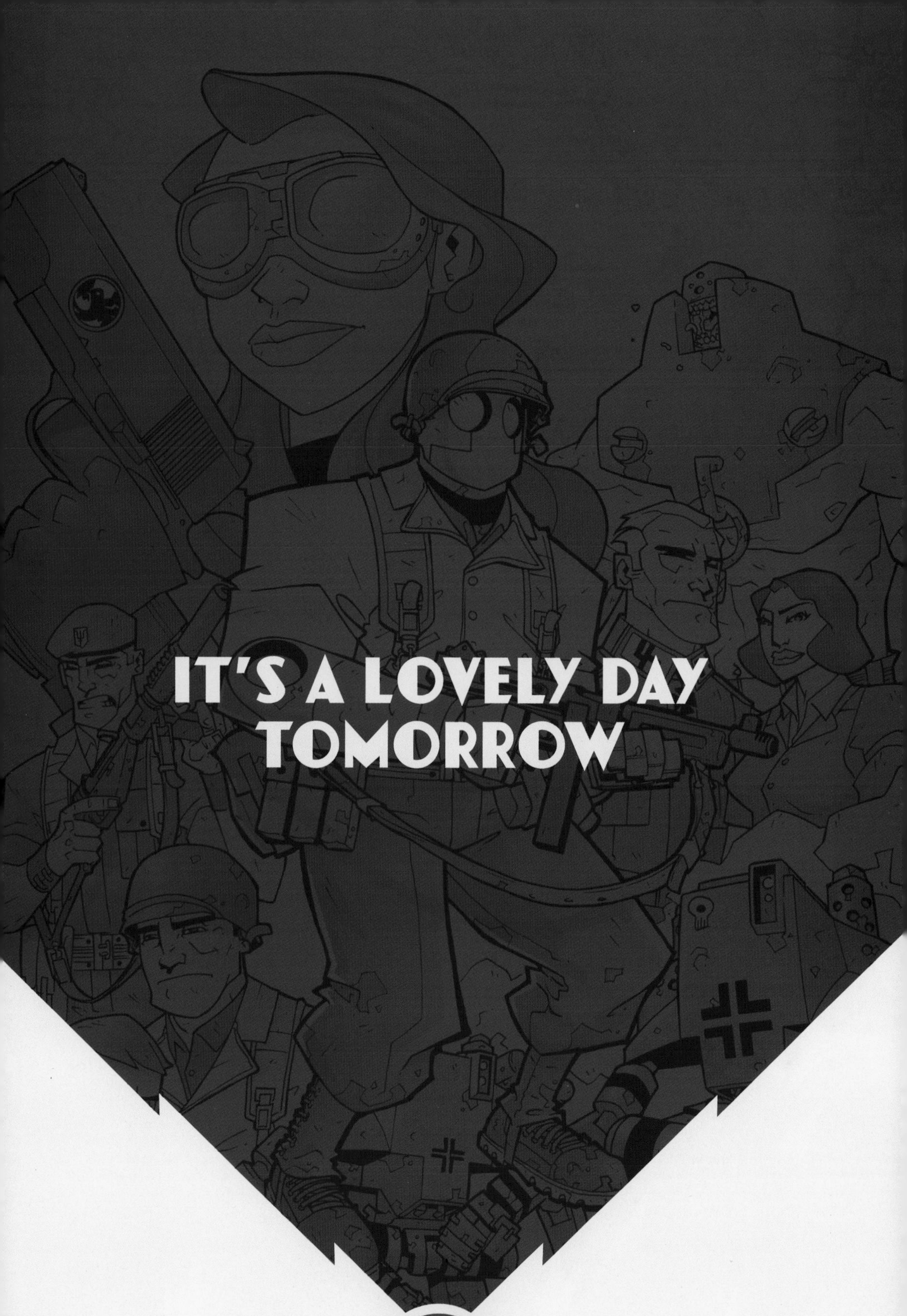

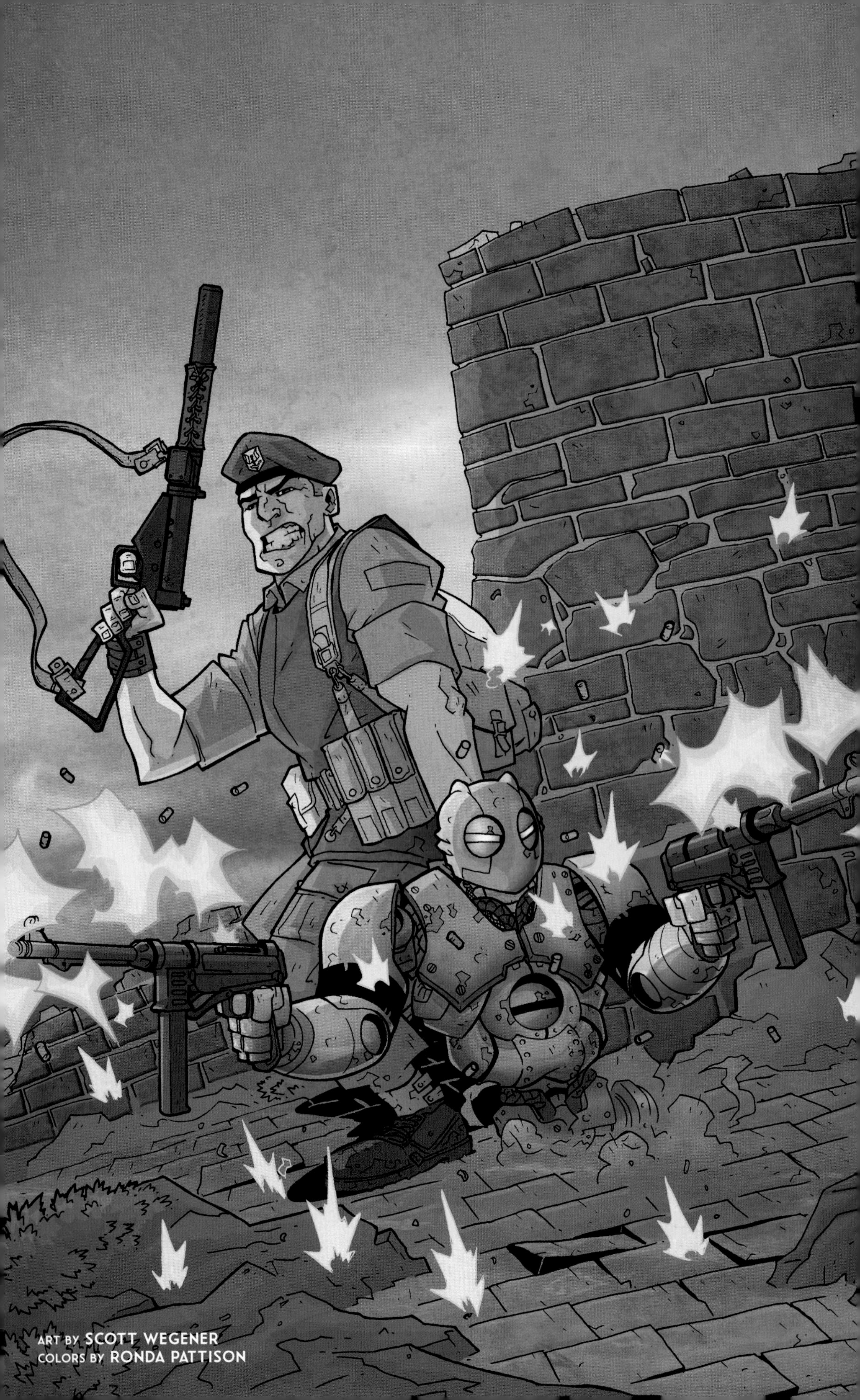
ART BY SCOTT WEGENER
COLORS BY RONDA PATTISON

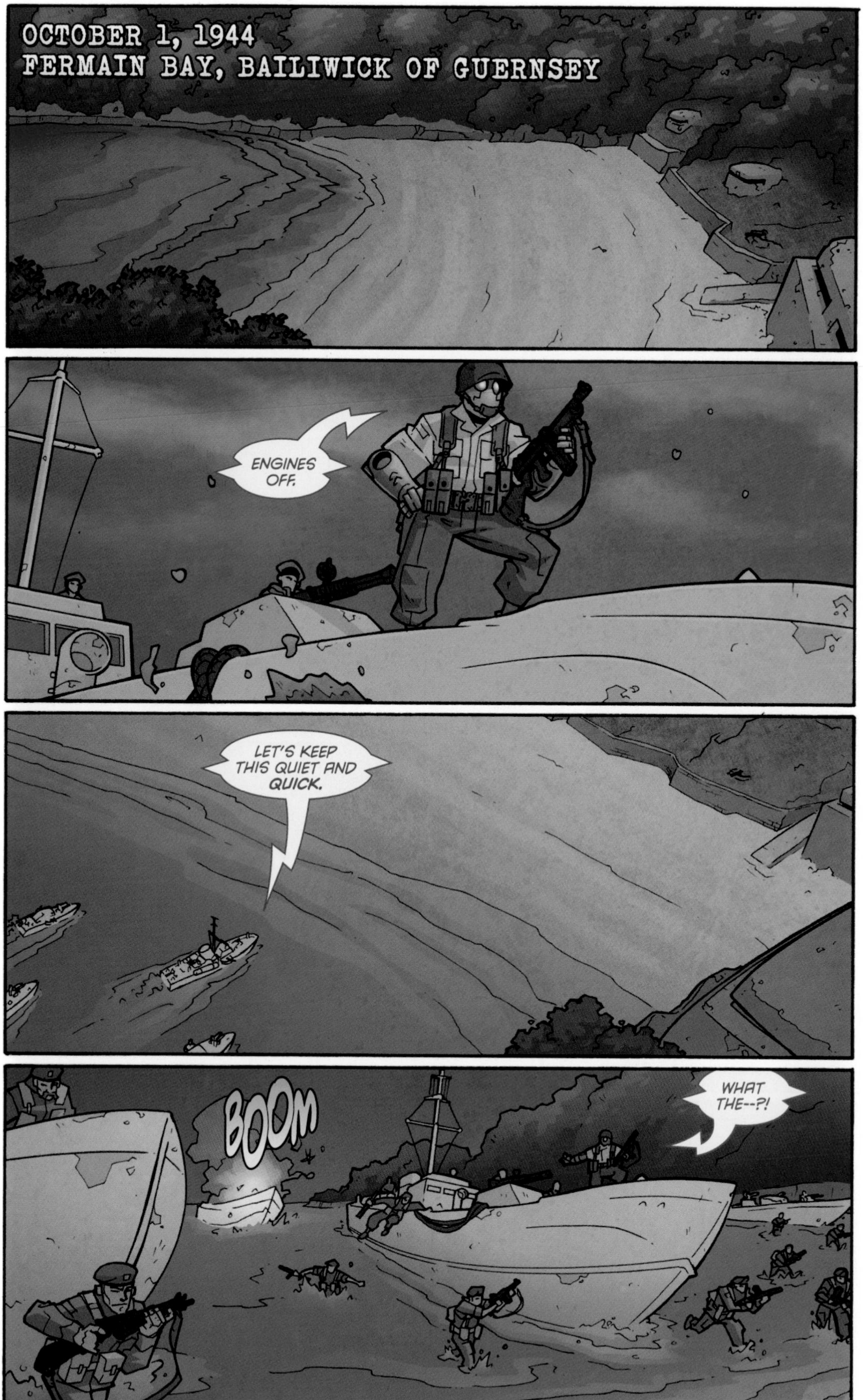
OCTOBER 1, 1944
FERMAIN BAY, BAILIWICK OF GUERNSEY
ENGINES OFF.
LET'S KEEP THIS QUIET AND QUICK.
BOOM
WHAT THE--?!

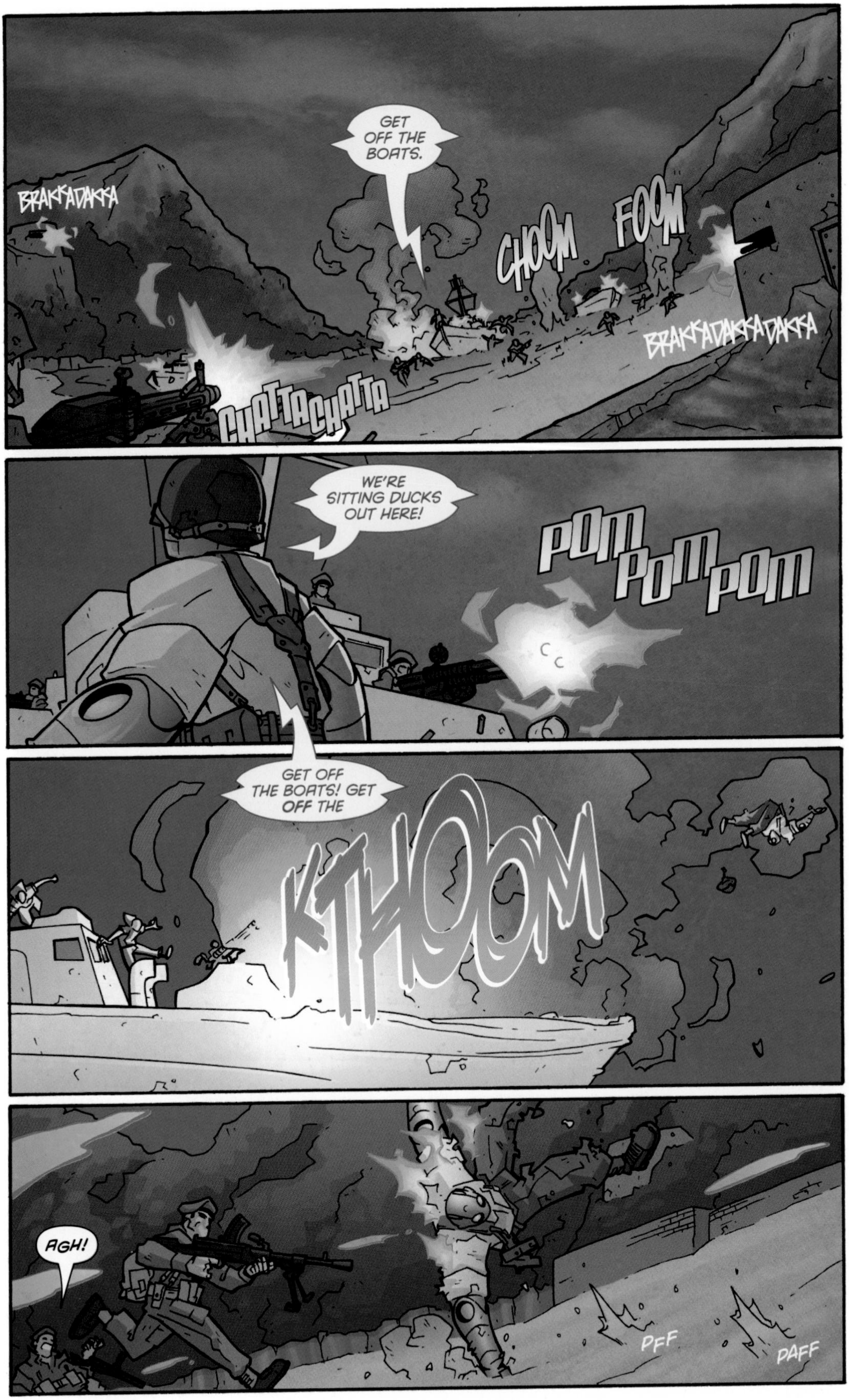
GET OFF THE BOATS.
BRAKKADAKKA
CHOOM
FOOM
BRAKKADAKKADAKKA
CHATTACHATTA
WE'RE SITTING DUCKS OUT HERE!
POM POM POM
GET OFF THE BOATS! GET OFF THE
KTHOOM
AGH!
PFF
PAFF

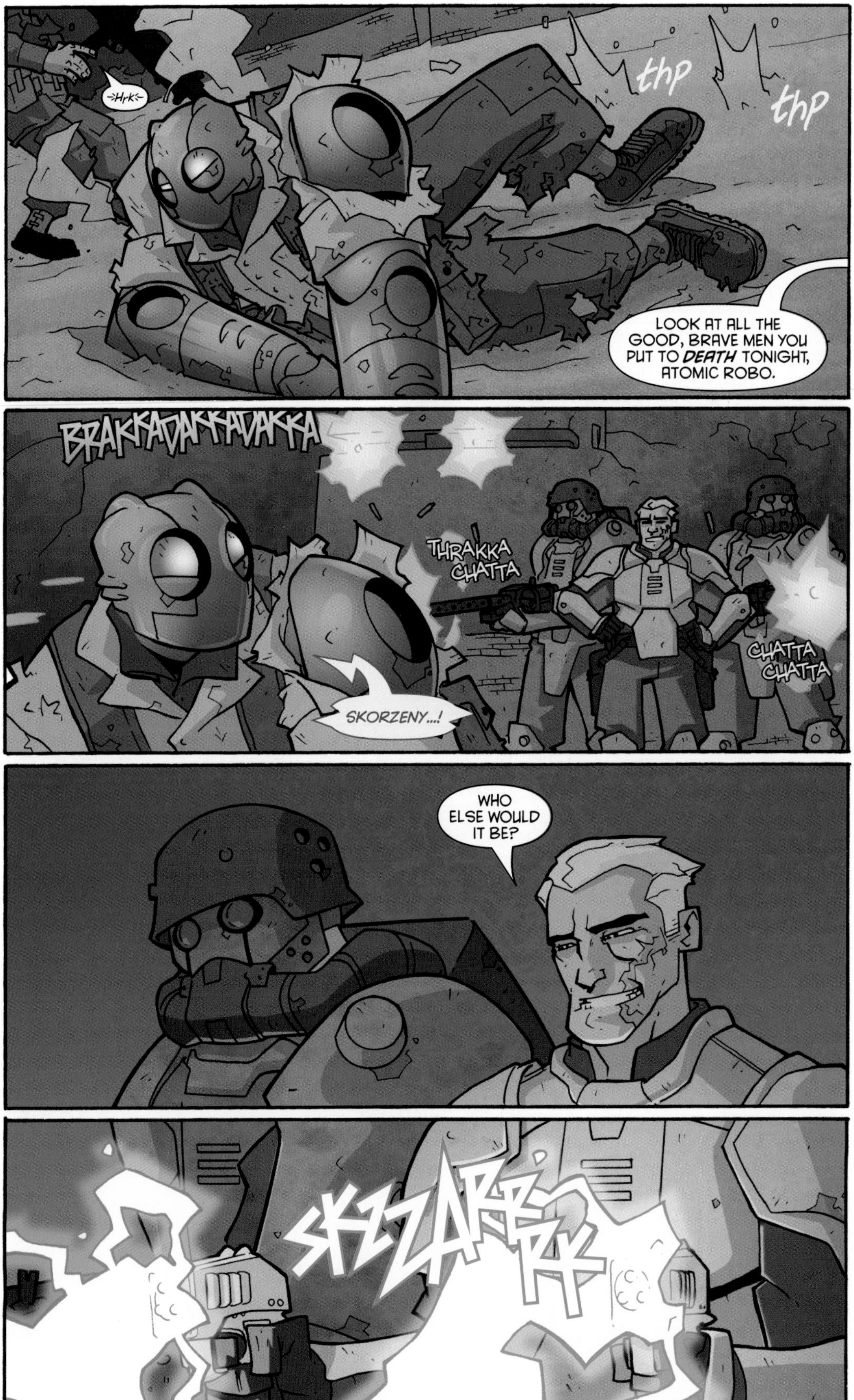

Hrk
thp
thp
LOOK AT ALL THE GOOD, BRAVE MEN YOU PUT TO *DEATH* TONIGHT, ATOMIC ROBO.
BRAKKADAKKADAKKA
THRAKKA CHATTA
CHATTA CHATTA
SKORZENY...!
WHO ELSE WOULD IT BE?
SKZZARRRK

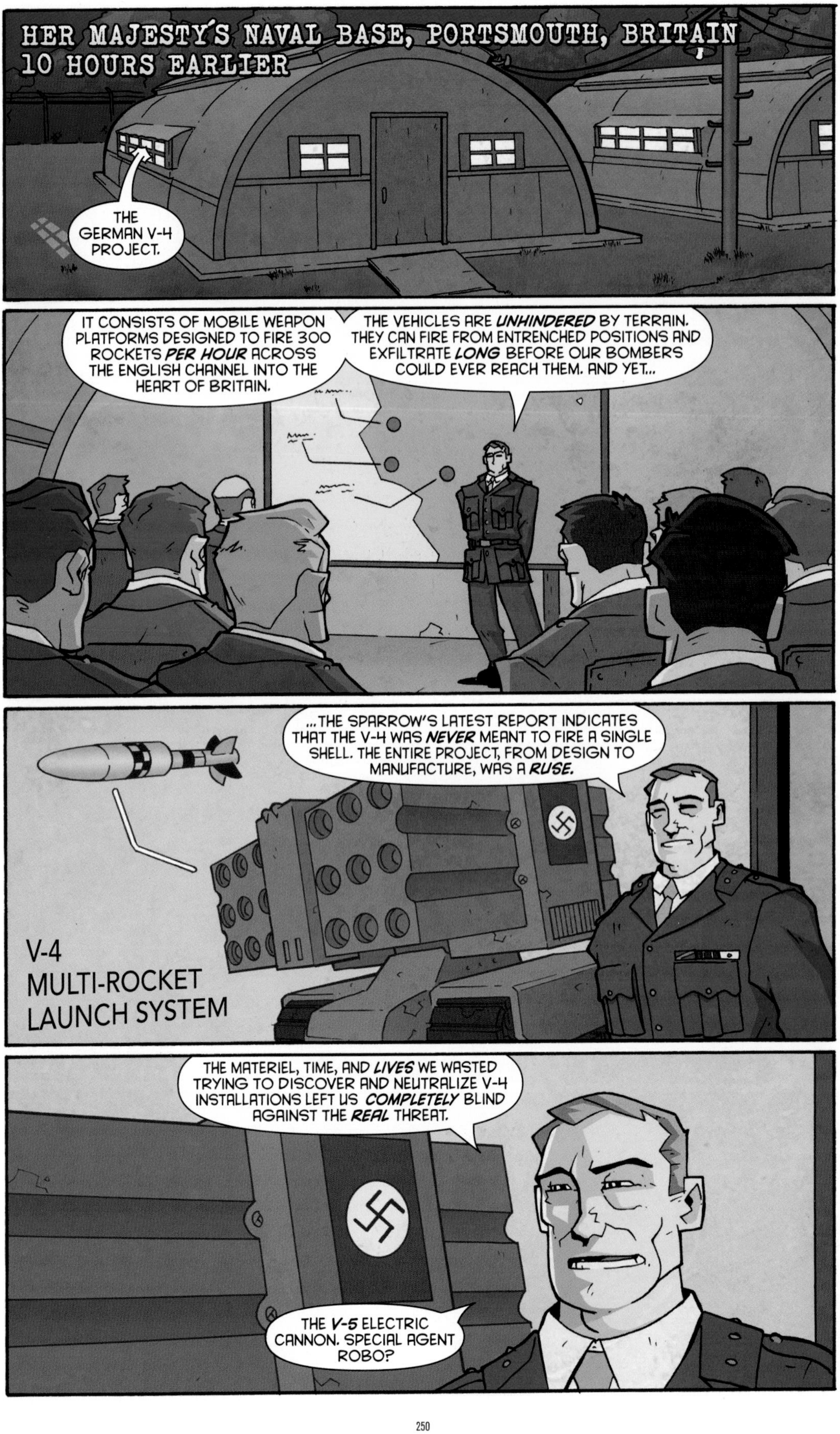
HER MAJESTY'S NAVAL BASE, PORTSMOUTH, BRITAIN
10 HOURS EARLIER
THE GERMAN V-4 PROJECT.
IT CONSISTS OF MOBILE WEAPON PLATFORMS DESIGNED TO FIRE 300 ROCKETS PER HOUR ACROSS THE ENGLISH CHANNEL INTO THE HEART OF BRITAIN.
THE VEHICLES ARE UNHINDERED BY TERRAIN. THEY CAN FIRE FROM ENTRENCHED POSITIONS AND EXFILTRATE LONG BEFORE OUR BOMBERS COULD EVER REACH THEM. AND YET...
...THE SPARROW'S LATEST REPORT INDICATES THAT THE V-4 WAS NEVER MEANT TO FIRE A SINGLE SHELL. THE ENTIRE PROJECT, FROM DESIGN TO MANUFACTURE, WAS A RUSE.
V-4 MULTI-ROCKET LAUNCH SYSTEM
THE MATERIEL, TIME, AND LIVES WE WASTED TRYING TO DISCOVER AND NEUTRALIZE V-4 INSTALLATIONS LEFT US COMPLETELY BLIND AGAINST THE REAL THREAT.
THE V-5 ELECTRIC CANNON. SPECIAL AGENT ROBO?

GUERNSEY ISLAND

THANK YOU, GENERAL. THE THEORY BEHIND THE V-4 WAS AT THE CUTTING EDGE OF WEAPONS TECHNOLOGY. THE *V-5* IS SOMETHING OUT OF SCIENCE FICTION.

YES, I RECOGNIZE THE IRONY.

BASED ON MY EXPERIENCE WITH ALTERNATIVE WEAPONS RESEARCH UNDER MR. TESLA, MY GUESS IS THAT THIS V-5 PROPELS *ENORMOUS* EXPLOSIVE SLUGS USING PRECISELY TIMED ELECTROMAGNETIC ARRAYS.

IMAGINE A BULLET FIRED WITH ALL THE FORCE OF A *HUNDRED* SEPARATE CHARGES. NOW APPLY THAT TO NAVAL ARTILLERY SHELLS.

GUERNSE

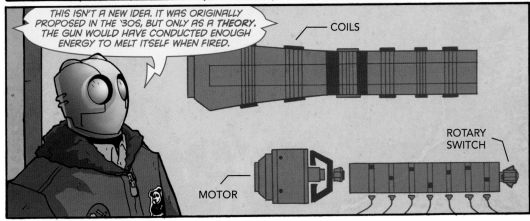

THIS ISN'T A NEW IDEA. IT WAS ORIGINALLY PROPOSED IN THE '30S, BUT ONLY AS A *THEORY.* THE GUN WOULD HAVE CONDUCTED ENOUGH ENERGY TO MELT ITSELF WHEN FIRED.

COILS

ROTARY SWITCH

MOTOR

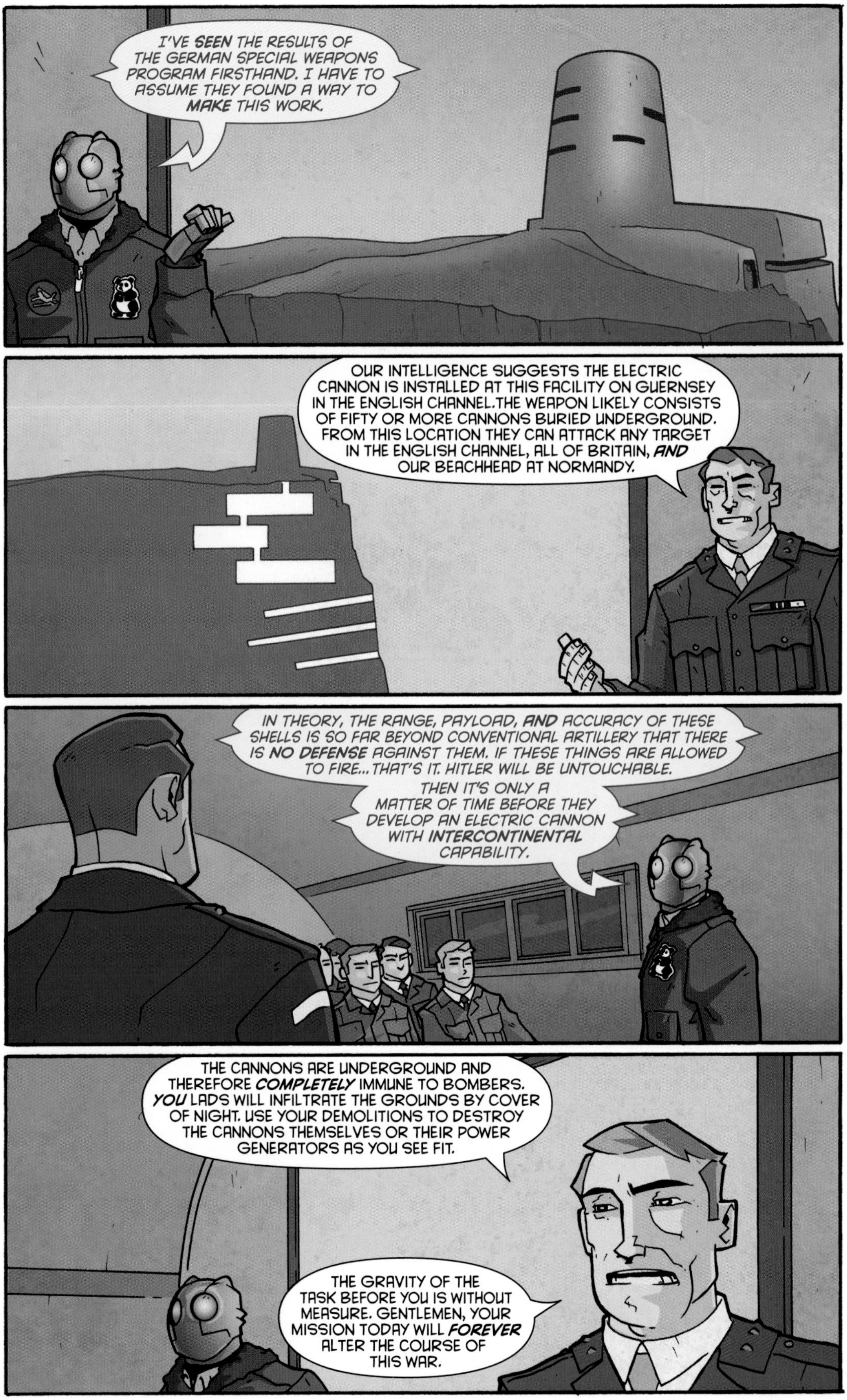
I'VE SEEN THE RESULTS OF THE GERMAN SPECIAL WEAPONS PROGRAM FIRSTHAND. I HAVE TO ASSUME THEY FOUND A WAY TO MAKE THIS WORK.
OUR INTELLIGENCE SUGGESTS THE ELECTRIC CANNON IS INSTALLED AT THIS FACILITY ON GUERNSEY IN THE ENGLISH CHANNEL. THE WEAPON LIKELY CONSISTS OF FIFTY OR MORE CANNONS BURIED UNDERGROUND. FROM THIS LOCATION THEY CAN ATTACK ANY TARGET IN THE ENGLISH CHANNEL, ALL OF BRITAIN, AND OUR BEACHHEAD AT NORMANDY.
IN THEORY, THE RANGE, PAYLOAD, AND ACCURACY OF THESE SHELLS IS SO FAR BEYOND CONVENTIONAL ARTILLERY THAT THERE IS NO DEFENSE AGAINST THEM. IF THESE THINGS ARE ALLOWED TO FIRE... THAT'S IT. HITLER WILL BE UNTOUCHABLE.
THEN IT'S ONLY A MATTER OF TIME BEFORE THEY DEVELOP AN ELECTRIC CANNON WITH INTERCONTINENTAL CAPABILITY.
THE CANNONS ARE UNDERGROUND AND THEREFORE COMPLETELY IMMUNE TO BOMBERS. YOU LADS WILL INFILTRATE THE GROUNDS BY COVER OF NIGHT. USE YOUR DEMOLITIONS TO DESTROY THE CANNONS THEMSELVES OR THEIR POWER GENERATORS AS YOU SEE FIT.
THE GRAVITY OF THE TASK BEFORE YOU IS WITHOUT MEASURE. GENTLEMEN, YOUR MISSION TODAY WILL FOREVER ALTER THE COURSE OF THIS WAR.

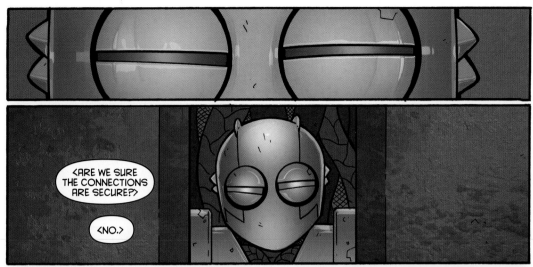

‹ARE WE SURE THE CONNECTIONS ARE SECURE?›

‹NO.›

‹FURTHER, WE HAVE NO IDEA WHAT THE TOLERANCES ARE, WHAT KIND OF OUTPUT TO EXPECT, OR HOW LONG HE'LL LAST.›

‹AND *THAT'S* ASSUMING THE CONNECTIONS *ARE* SECURE.›

‹IS HE... "ALIVE"?›

‹HE'D HAVE TO TELL US THAT. WE WOULDN'T EVEN KNOW WHAT TO LOOK FOR.›

ARE YOU IN THERE, ATOMIC ROBO? I HOPE SO. I WANT YOU TO KNOW WHAT YOU'VE DONE FOR US. I WANT YOU TO KNOW YOU'RE THE BEATING HEART OF OUR *WEATHER CANNON.*

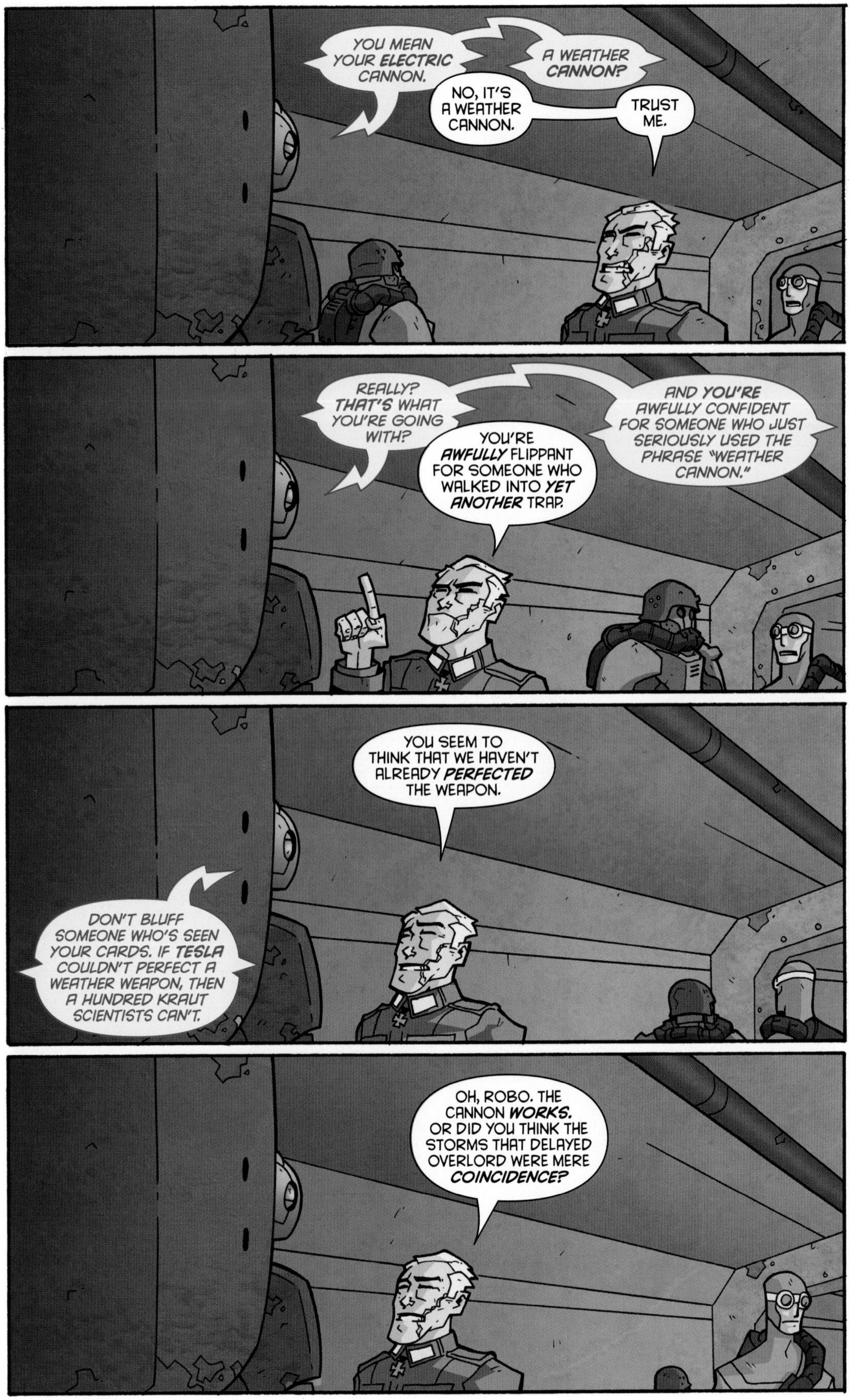
YOU MEAN YOUR ELECTRIC CANNON.
A WEATHER CANNON?
NO, IT'S A WEATHER CANNON.
TRUST ME.
REALLY? THAT'S WHAT YOU'RE GOING WITH?
AND YOU'RE AWFULLY CONFIDENT FOR SOMEONE WHO JUST SERIOUSLY USED THE PHRASE "WEATHER CANNON."
YOU'RE AWFULLY FLIPPANT FOR SOMEONE WHO WALKED INTO YET ANOTHER TRAP.
YOU SEEM TO THINK THAT WE HAVEN'T ALREADY PERFECTED THE WEAPON.
DON'T BLUFF SOMEONE WHO'S SEEN YOUR CARDS. IF TESLA COULDN'T PERFECT A WEATHER WEAPON, THEN A HUNDRED KRAUT SCIENTISTS CAN'T.
OH, ROBO. THE CANNON WORKS. OR DID YOU THINK THE STORMS THAT DELAYED OVERLORD WERE MERE COINCIDENCE?

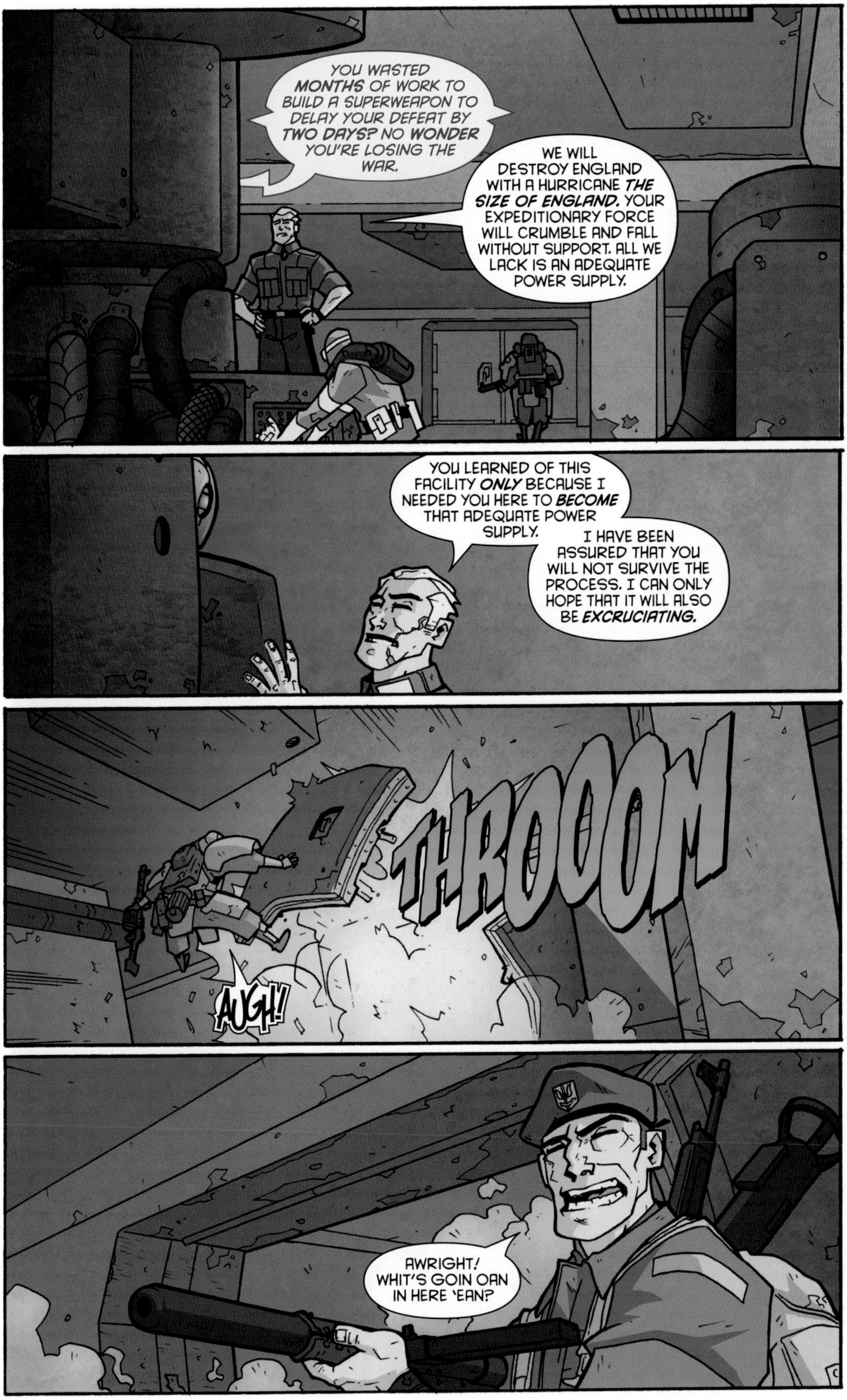
YOU WASTED **MONTHS** OF WORK TO BUILD A SUPERWEAPON TO DELAY YOUR DEFEAT BY **TWO DAYS?** NO **WONDER** YOU'RE LOSING THE WAR.
WE WILL DESTROY ENGLAND WITH A HURRICANE ***THE SIZE OF ENGLAND.*** YOUR EXPEDITIONARY FORCE WILL CRUMBLE AND FALL WITHOUT SUPPORT. ALL WE LACK IS AN ADEQUATE POWER SUPPLY.
YOU LEARNED OF THIS FACILITY ***ONLY*** BECAUSE I NEEDED YOU HERE TO ***BECOME*** THAT ADEQUATE POWER SUPPLY.
I HAVE BEEN ASSURED THAT YOU WILL NOT SURVIVE THE PROCESS. I CAN ONLY HOPE THAT IT WILL ALSO BE ***EXCRUCIATING.***
THROOOM
AUGH!
AWRIGHT! WHIT'S GOIN OAN IN HERE 'EAN?

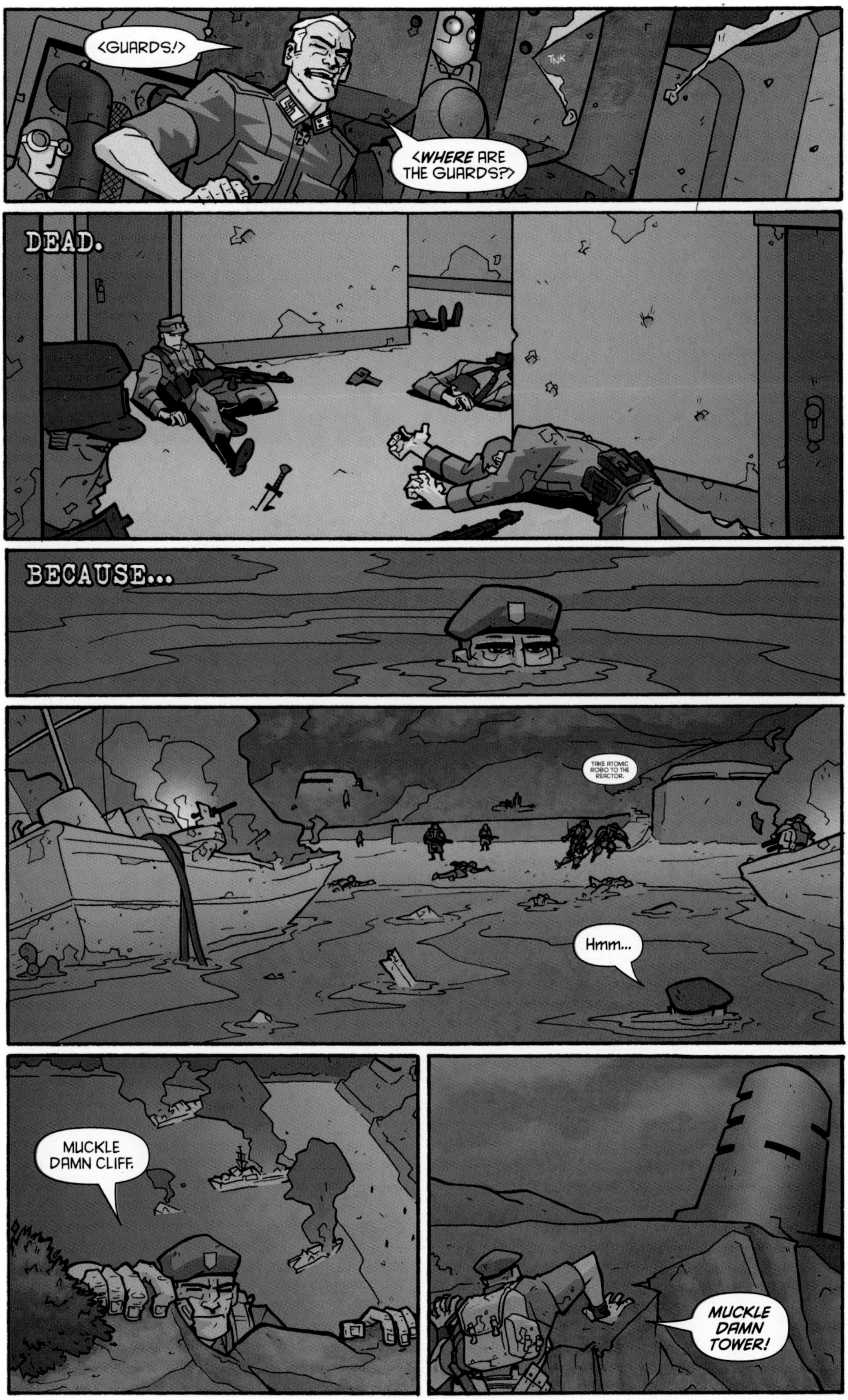
<GUARDS!>
TNK
<WHERE ARE THE GUARDS?>
DEAD.
BECAUSE...
TAKE ATOMIC ROBO TO THE REACTOR.
Hmm...
MUCKLE DAMN CLIFF.
MUCKLE DAMN TOWER!

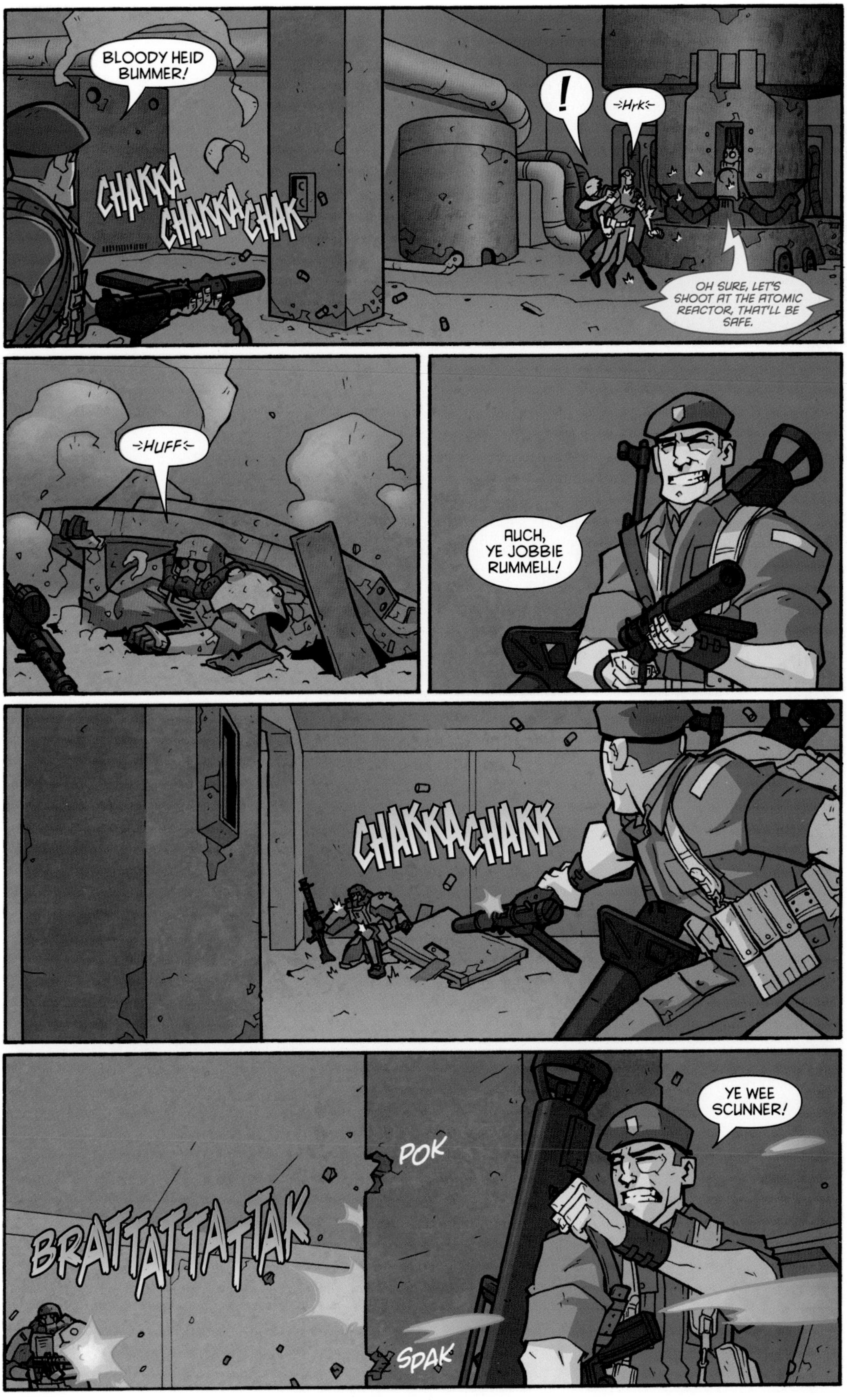
BLOODY HEID BUMMER!
CHAKKA CHAKKACHAK
!
Hrk
OH SURE, LET'S SHOOT AT THE ATOMIC REACTOR, THAT'LL BE SAFE.
HUFF
AUCH, YE JOBBIE RUMMELL!
CHAKKACHAKK
YE WEE SCUNNER!
POK
BRATTATTATTAK
SPAK

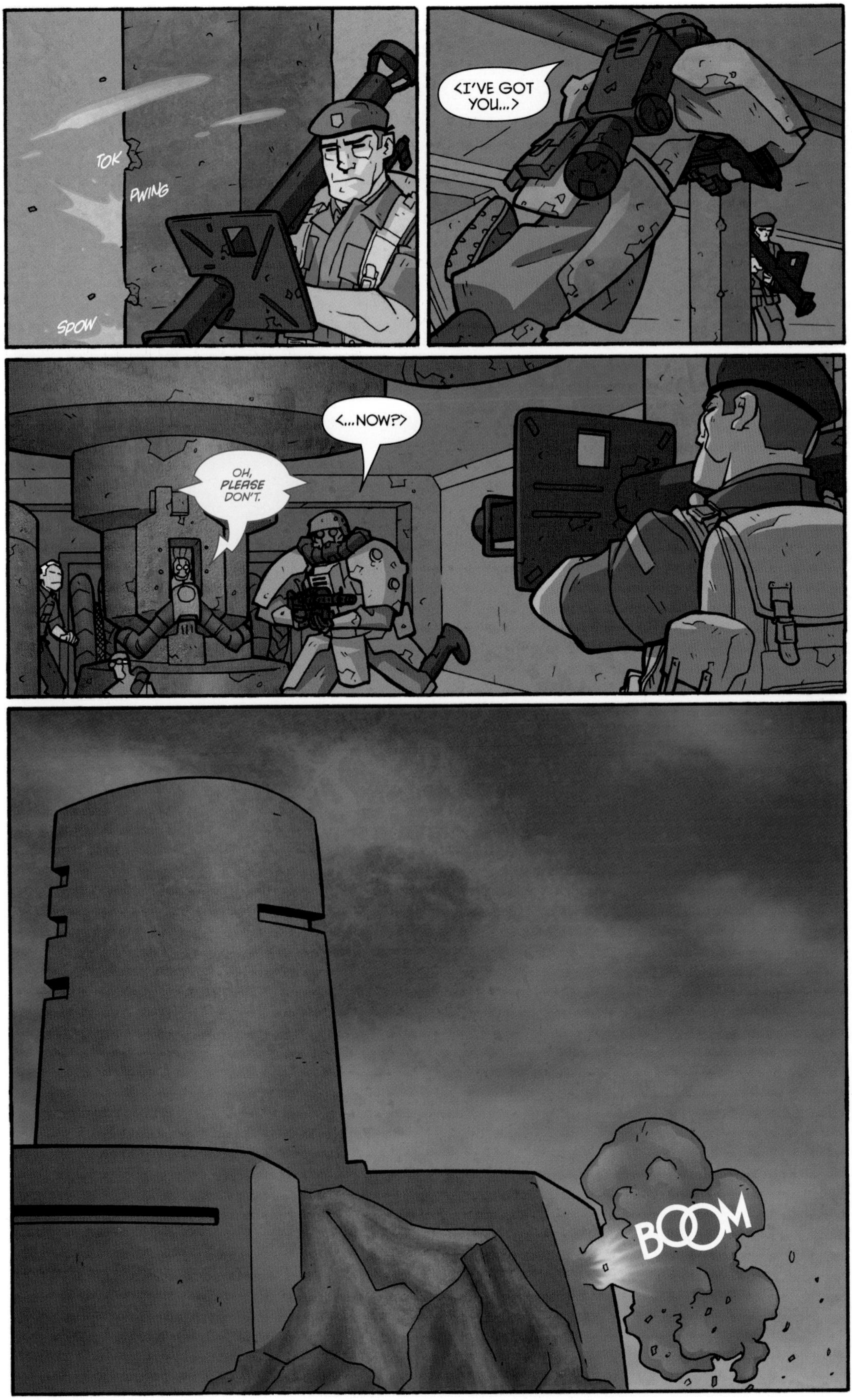
TOK
PWING
SPOW
<I'VE GOT YOU...>
<...NOW?>
OH, PLEASE DON'T.
BOOM

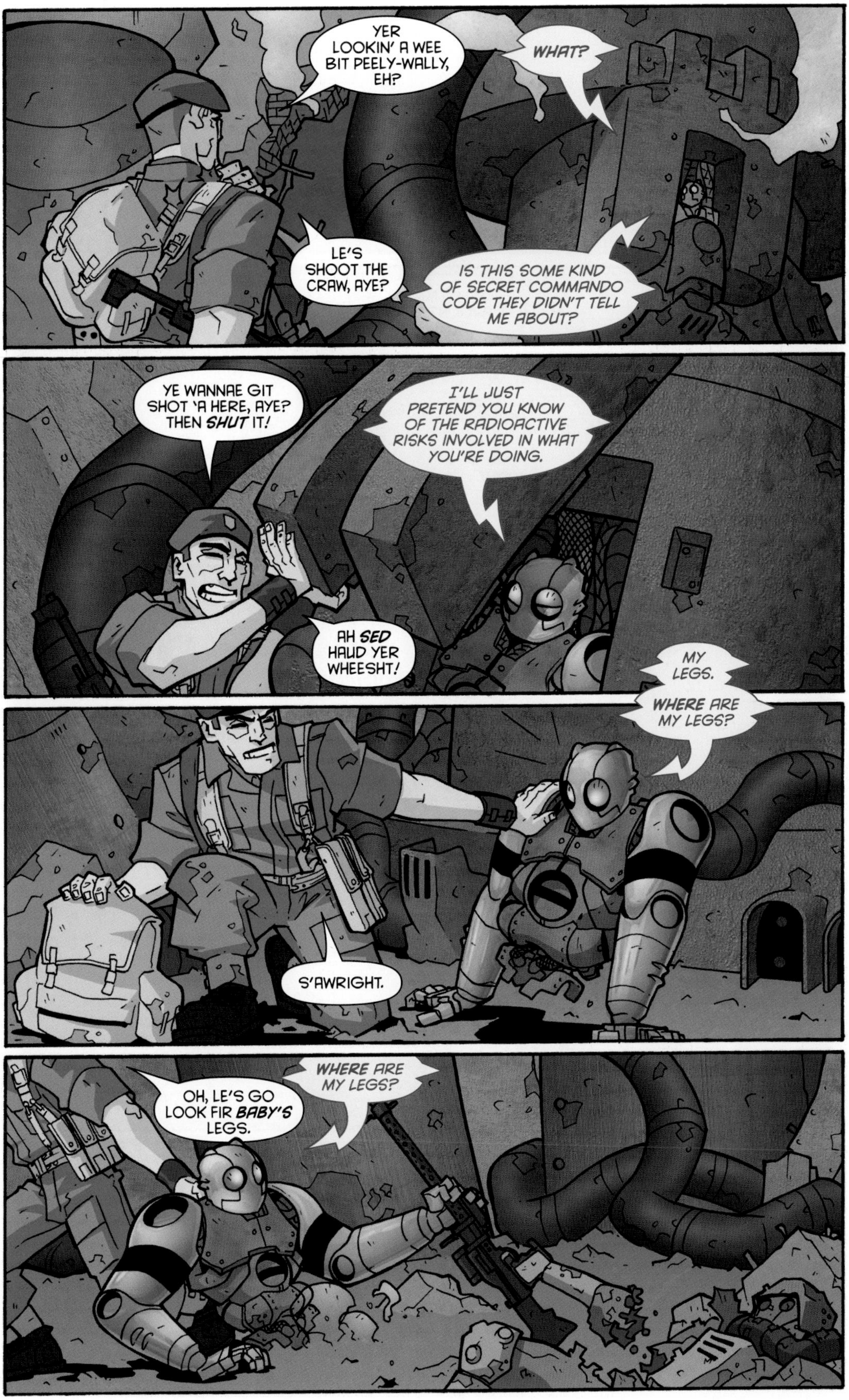
YER LOOKIN' A WEE BIT PEELY-WALLY, EH?
WHAT?
LE'S SHOOT THE CRAW, AYE?
IS THIS SOME KIND OF SECRET COMMANDO CODE THEY DIDN'T TELL ME ABOUT?
YE WANNAE GIT SHOT 'A HERE, AYE? THEN SHUT IT!
I'LL JUST PRETEND YOU KNOW OF THE RADIOACTIVE RISKS INVOLVED IN WHAT YOU'RE DOING.
AH SED HAUD YER WHEESHT!
MY LEGS.
WHERE ARE MY LEGS?
S'AWRIGHT.
OH, LE'S GO LOOK FIR BABY'S LEGS.
WHERE ARE MY LEGS?

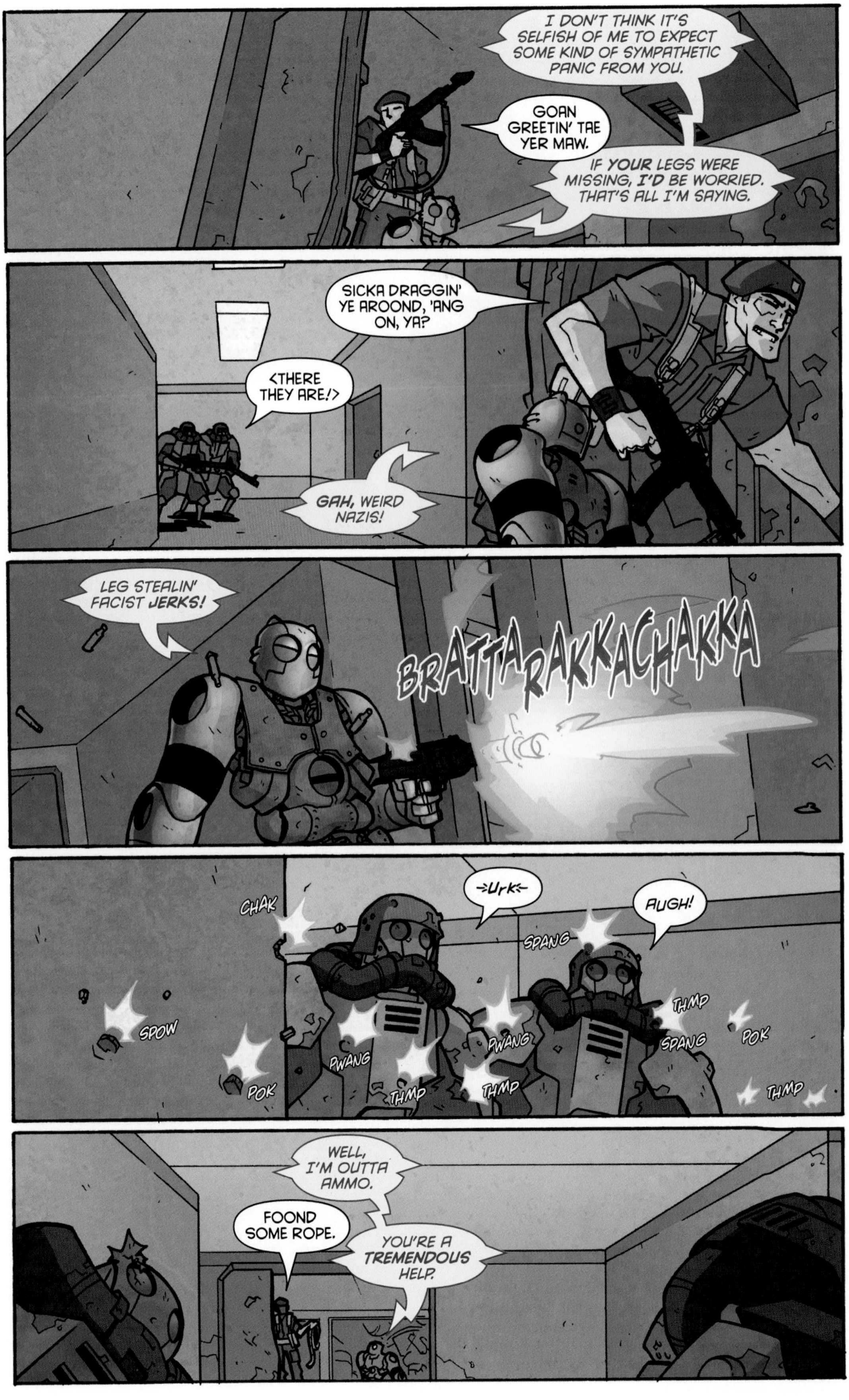

I DON'T THINK IT'S SELFISH OF ME TO EXPECT SOME KIND OF SYMPATHETIC PANIC FROM YOU.
GOAN GREETIN' TAE YER MAW.
IF YOUR LEGS WERE MISSING, I'D BE WORRIED. THAT'S ALL I'M SAYING.
SICKA DRAGGIN' YE AROOND, 'ANG ON, YA?
<THERE THEY ARE!>
GAH, WEIRD NAZIS!
LEG STEALIN' FACIST JERKS!
BRATTARAKKACHAKKA
CHAK
-Urk-
SPANG
AUGH!
SPOW
PWANG
POK
THMP
PWANG
THMP
THMP
SPANG
POK
THMP
WELL, I'M OUTTA AMMO.
FOOND SOME ROPE.
YOU'RE A TREMENDOUS HELP.

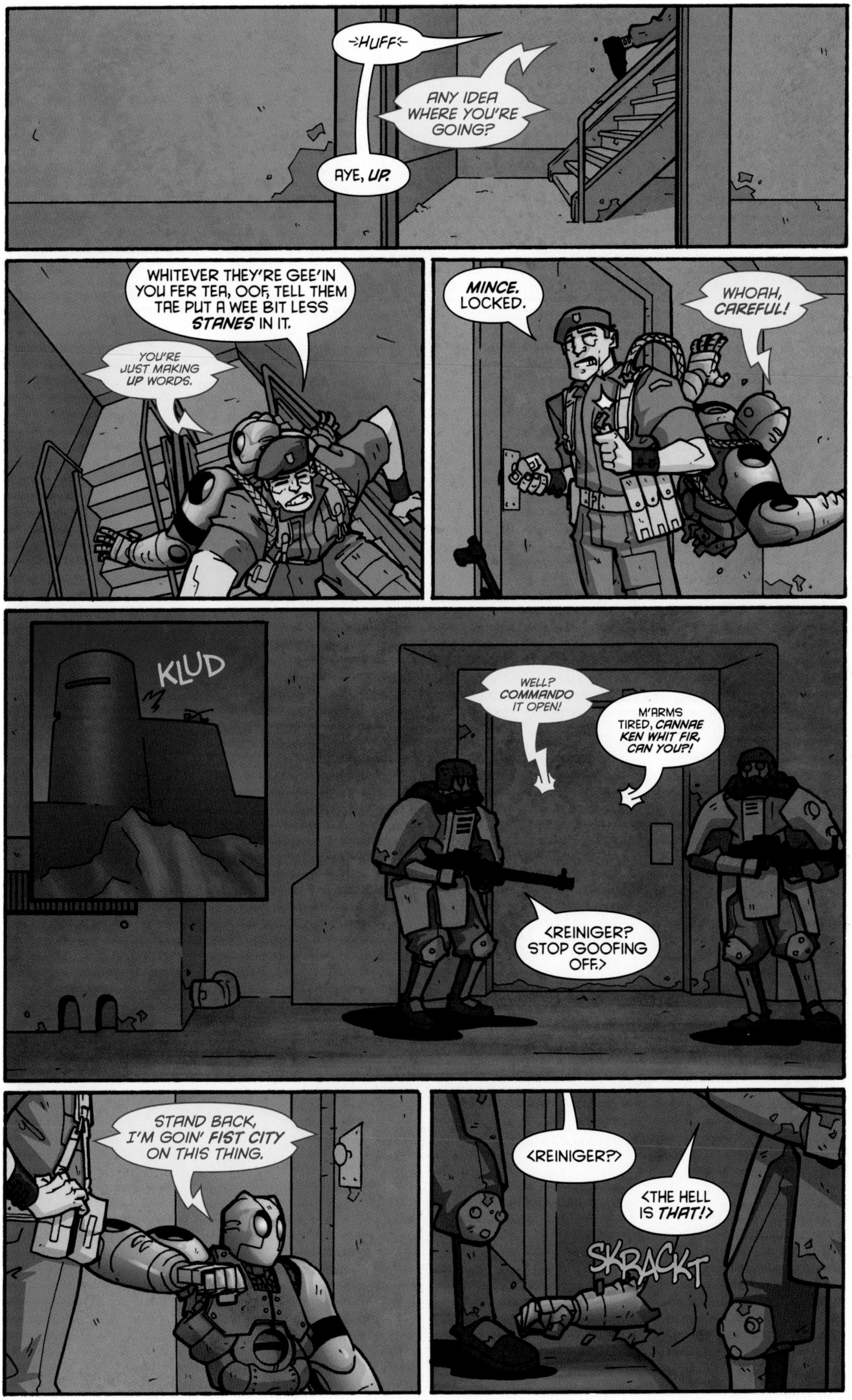

HUFF
ANY IDEA WHERE YOU'RE GOING?
AYE, UP.
WHITEVER THEY'RE GEE'IN YOU FER TEA, OOF, TELL THEM TAE PUT A WEE BIT LESS STANES IN IT.
YOU'RE JUST MAKING UP WORDS.
MINCE. LOCKED.
WHOAH, CAREFUL!
KLUD
WELL? COMMANDO IT OPEN!
M'ARMS TIRED, CANNAE KEN WHIT FIR, CAN YOU?!
<REINIGER? STOP GOOFING OFF.>
STAND BACK, I'M GOIN' FIST CITY ON THIS THING.
<REINIGER?>
<THE HELL IS THAT!>
SKRACKT

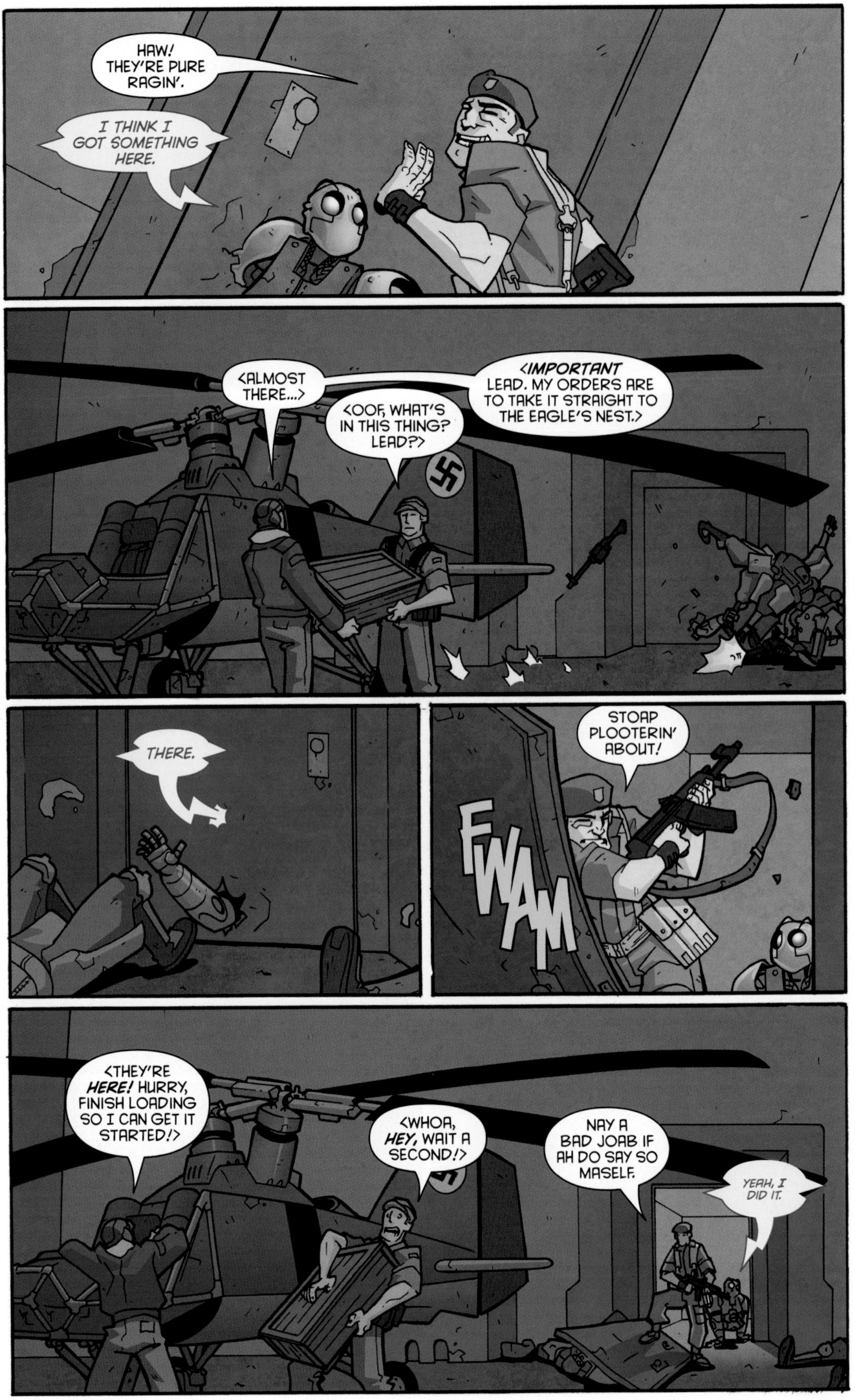
HAW! THEY'RE PURE RAGIN'.
I THINK I GOT SOMETHING HERE.
<ALMOST THERE...>
<*IMPORTANT* LEAD. MY ORDERS ARE TO TAKE IT STRAIGHT TO THE EAGLE'S NEST.>
<OOF, WHAT'S IN THIS THING? LEAD?>
THERE.
STOAP PLOOTERIN' ABOUT!
FWAM
<THEY'RE *HERE!* HURRY, FINISH LOADING SO I CAN GET IT STARTED!>
<WHOA, *HEY,* WAIT A SECOND!>
NAY A BAD JOAB IF AH DO SAY SO MASELF.
YEAH, I DID IT.

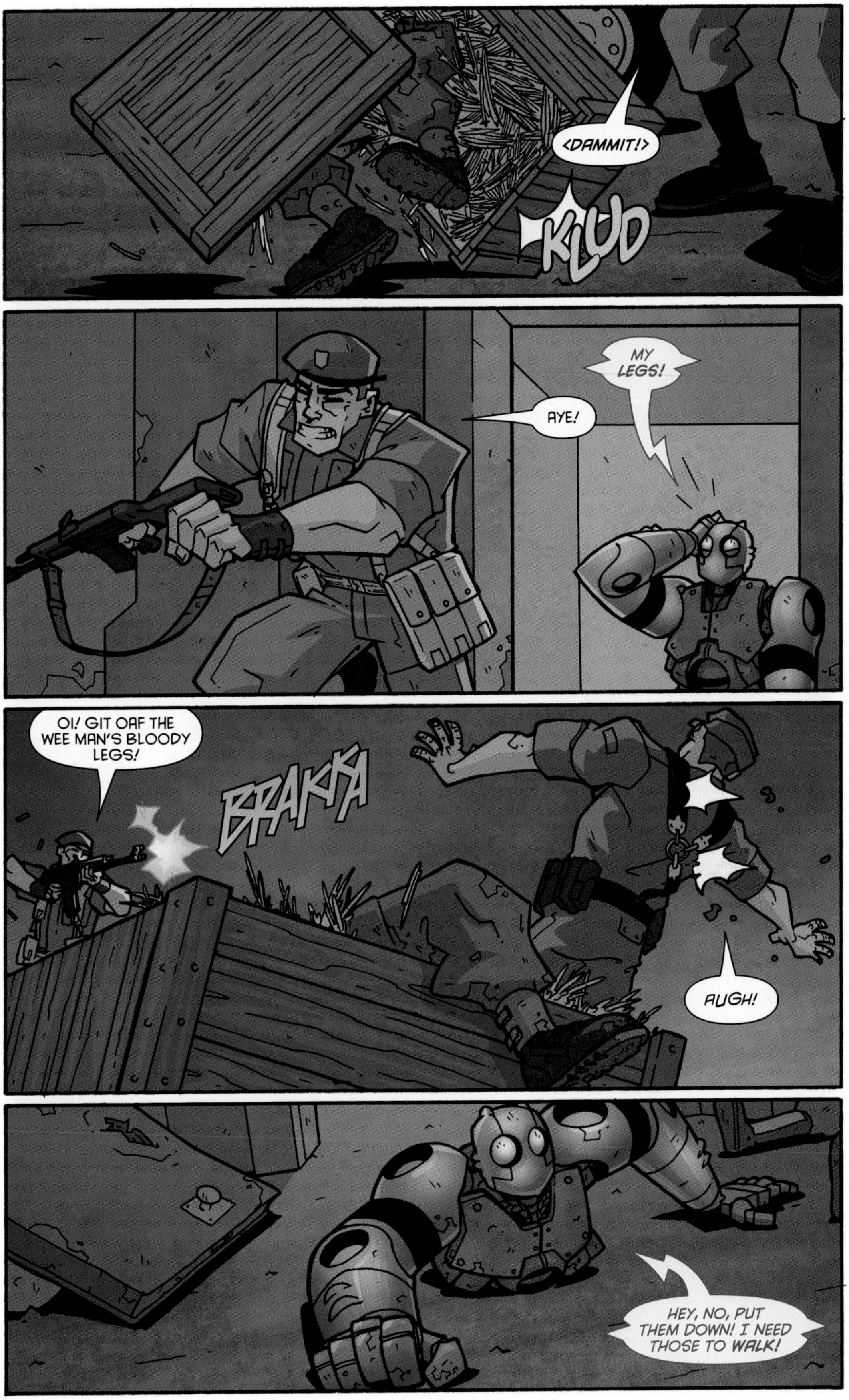
<DAMMIT!>
KLUD
MY LEGS!
AYE!
OI! GIT OAF THE WEE MAN'S BLOODY LEGS!
BRAKKA
AUGH!
HEY, NO, PUT THEM DOWN! I NEED THOSE TO WALK!

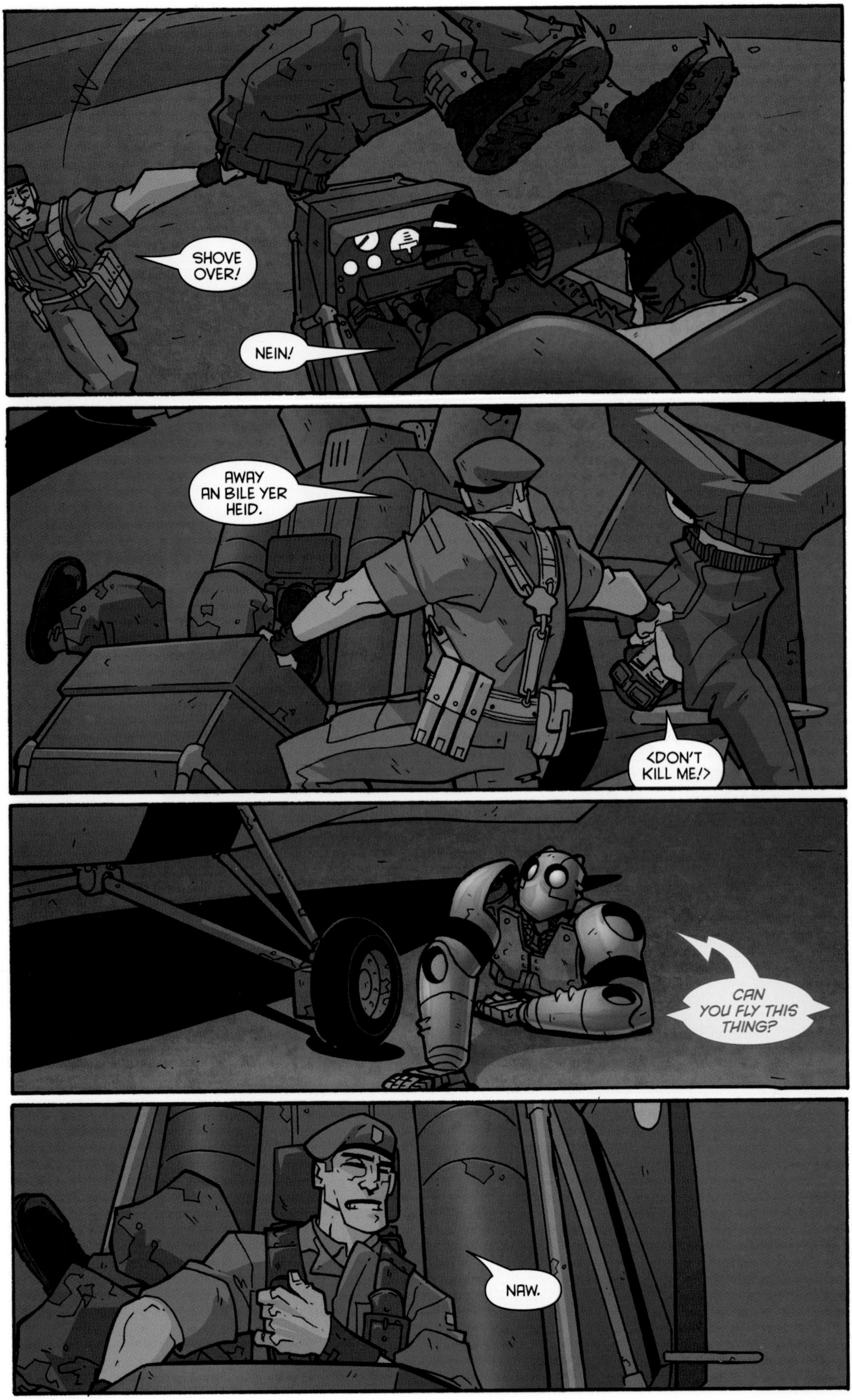
SHOVE OVER!
NEIN!
AWAY AN BILE YER HEID.
<DON'T KILL ME!>
CAN YOU FLY THIS THING?
NAW.

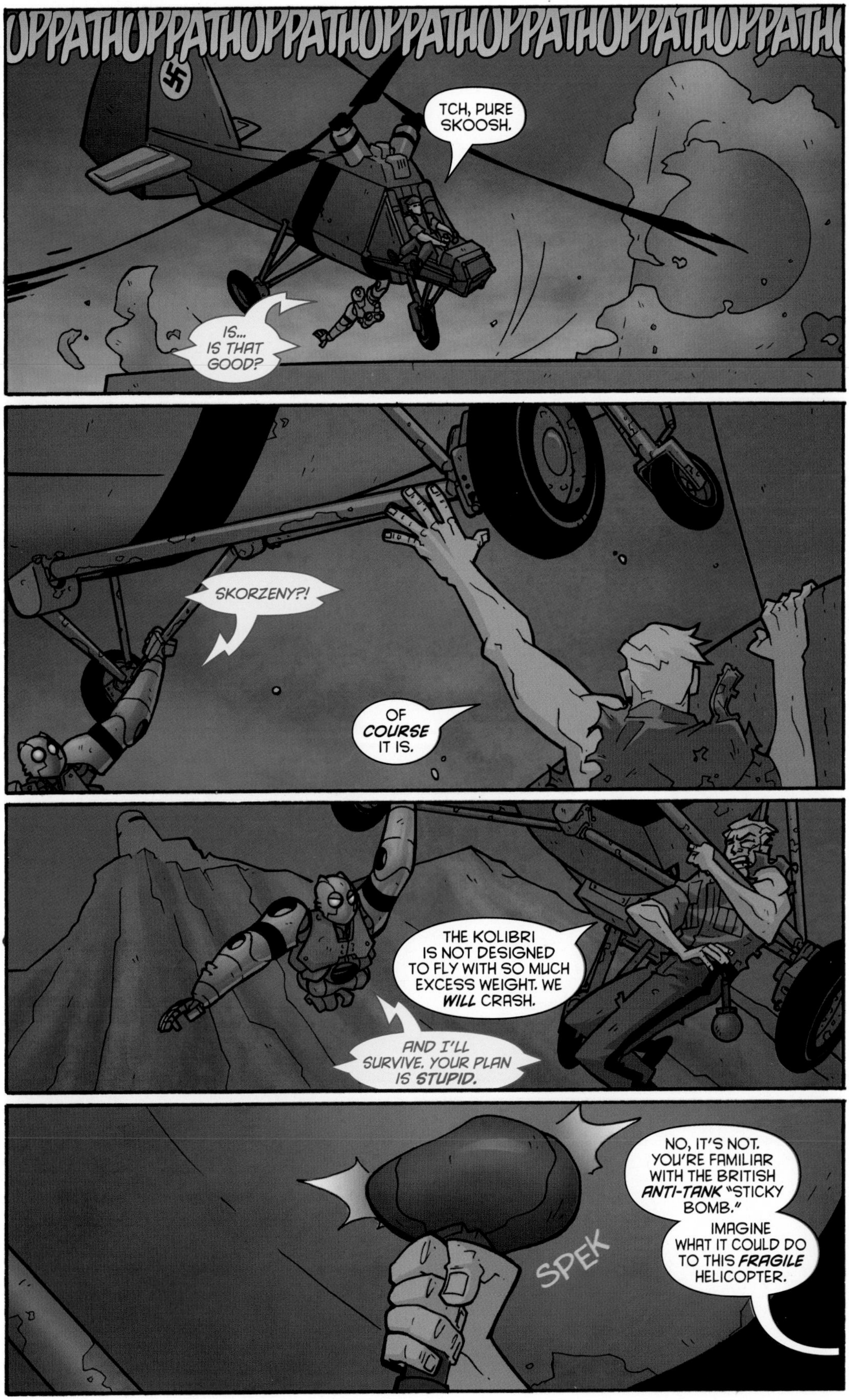

UPPATHUPPATHUPPATHUPPATHUPPATHUPPATHUPPATHUPPATHU
TCH, PURE SKOOSH.
IS... IS THAT GOOD?
SKORZENY?!
OF COURSE IT IS.
THE KOLIBRI IS NOT DESIGNED TO FLY WITH SO MUCH EXCESS WEIGHT. WE WILL CRASH.
AND I'LL SURVIVE. YOUR PLAN IS STUPID.
NO, IT'S NOT. YOU'RE FAMILIAR WITH THE BRITISH ANTI-TANK "STICKY BOMB."
IMAGINE WHAT IT COULD DO TO THIS FRAGILE HELICOPTER.
SPEK

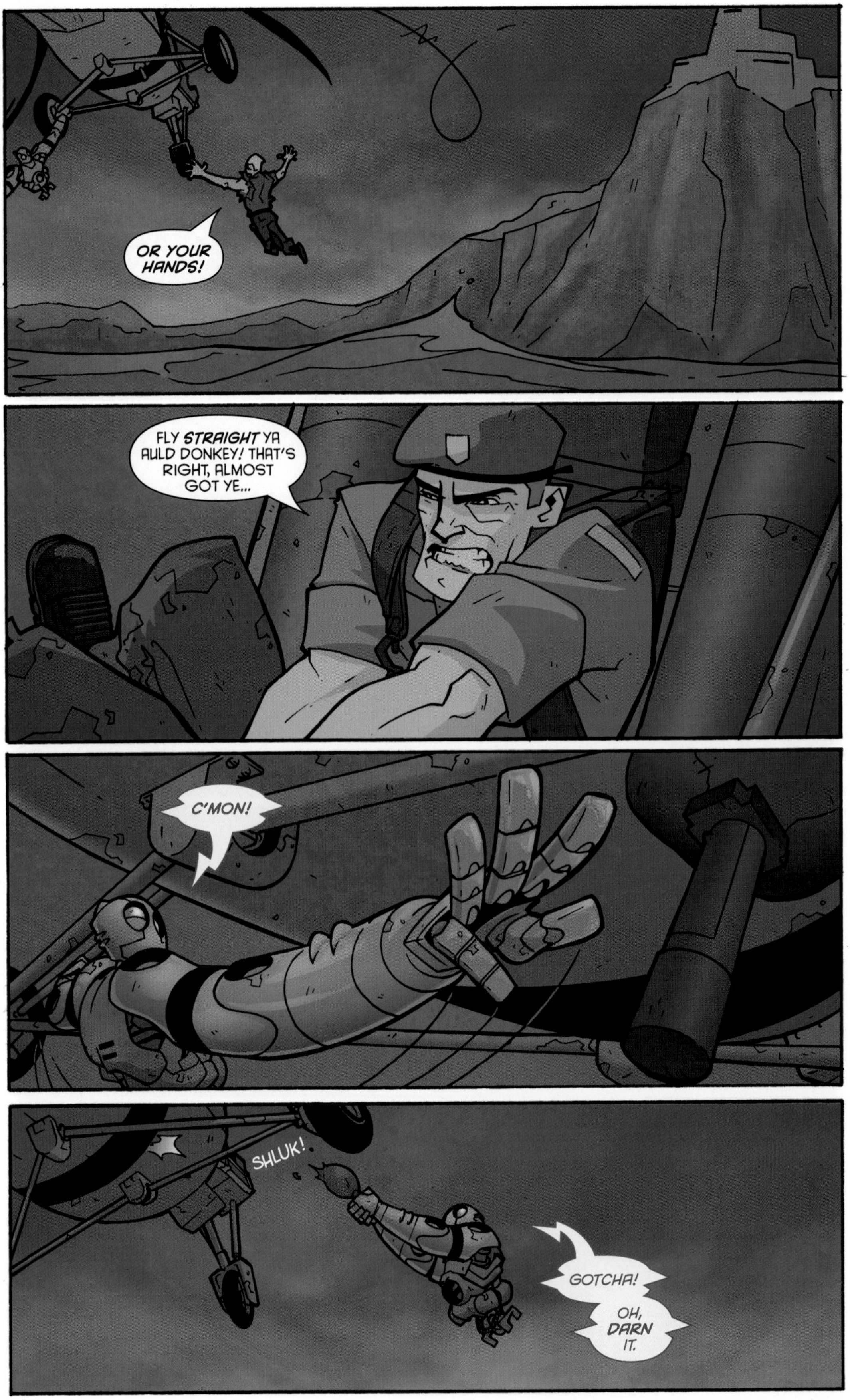
OR YOUR HANDS!
FLY STRAIGHT YA AULD DONKEY! THAT'S RIGHT, ALMOST GOT YE...
C'MON!
SHLUK!
GOTCHA!
OH, DARN IT.

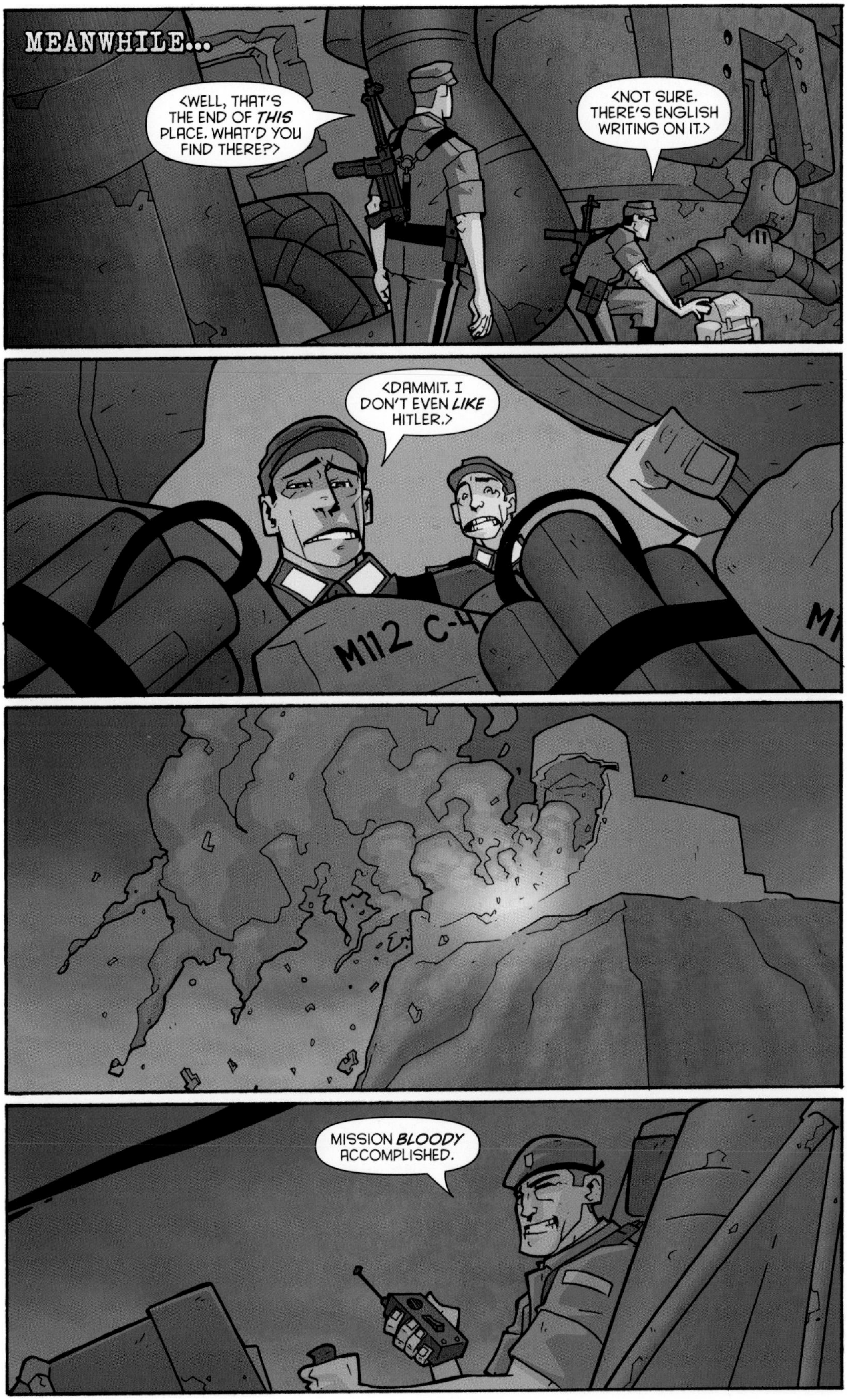
MEANWHILE...
<WELL, THAT'S THE END OF *THIS* PLACE. WHAT'D YOU FIND THERE?>
<NOT SURE. THERE'S ENGLISH WRITING ON IT.>
<DAMMIT. I DON'T EVEN *LIKE* HITLER.>
M112 C-4
MISSION *BLOODY* ACCOMPLISHED.

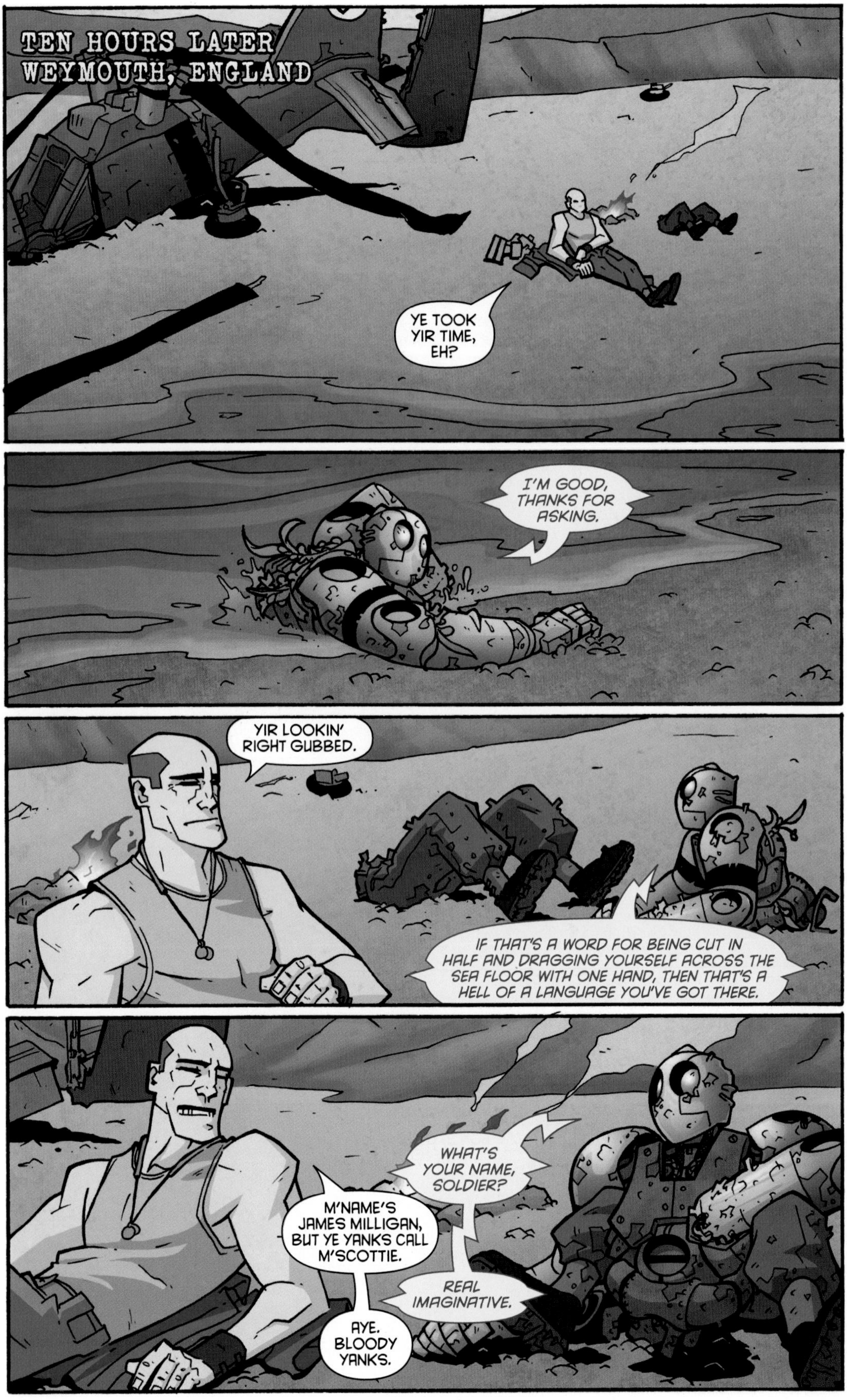
TEN HOURS LATER
WEYMOUTH, ENGLAND
YE TOOK YIR TIME, EH?
I'M GOOD, THANKS FOR ASKING.
YIR LOOKIN' RIGHT GUBBED.
IF THAT'S A WORD FOR BEING CUT IN HALF AND DRAGGING YOURSELF ACROSS THE SEA FLOOR WITH ONE HAND, THEN THAT'S A HELL OF A LANGUAGE YOU'VE GOT THERE.
WHAT'S YOUR NAME, SOLDIER?
M'NAME'S JAMES MILLIGAN, BUT YE YANKS CALL M'SCOTTIE.
REAL IMAGINATIVE.
AYE. BLOODY YANKS.

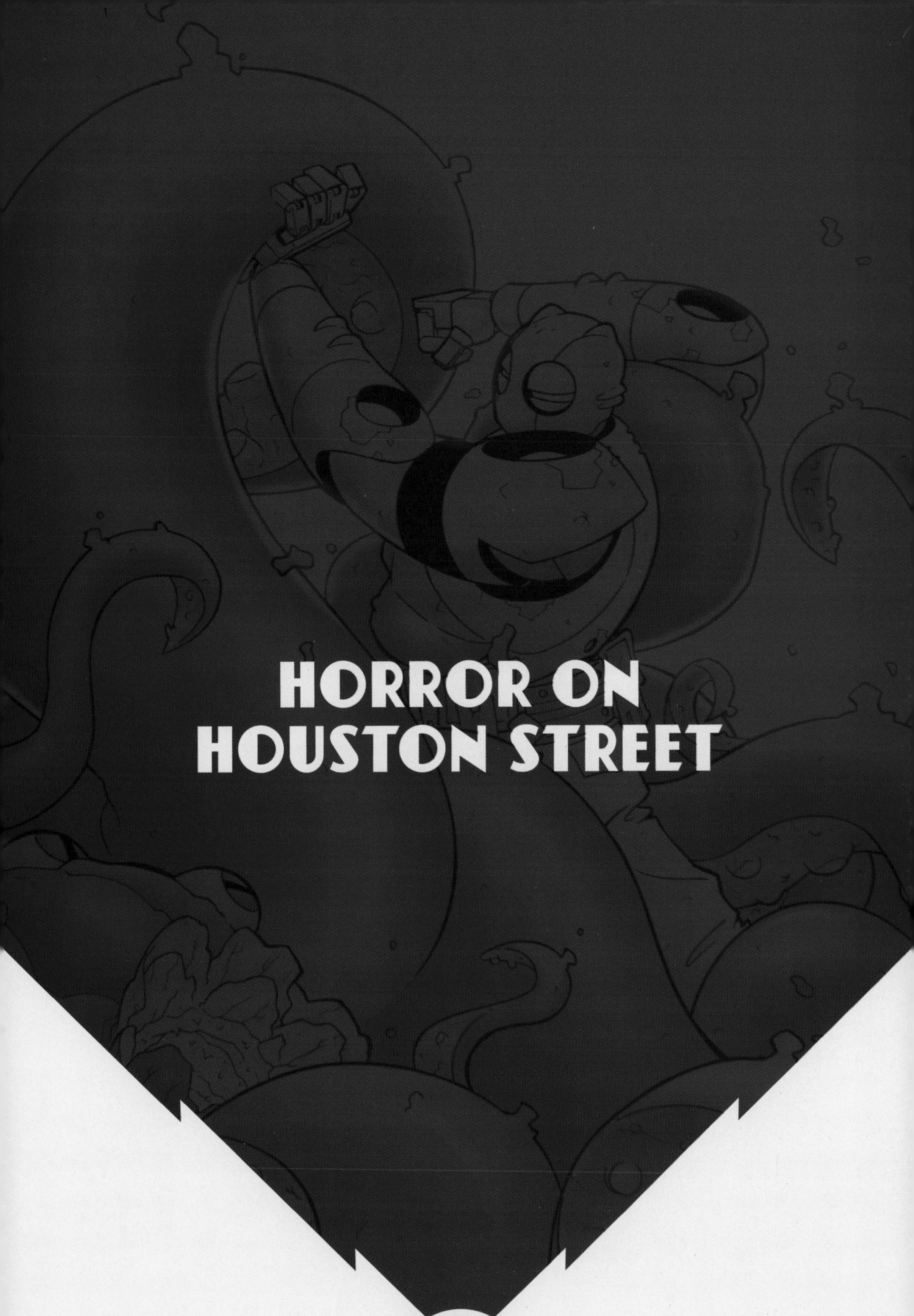

HORROR ON HOUSTON STREET

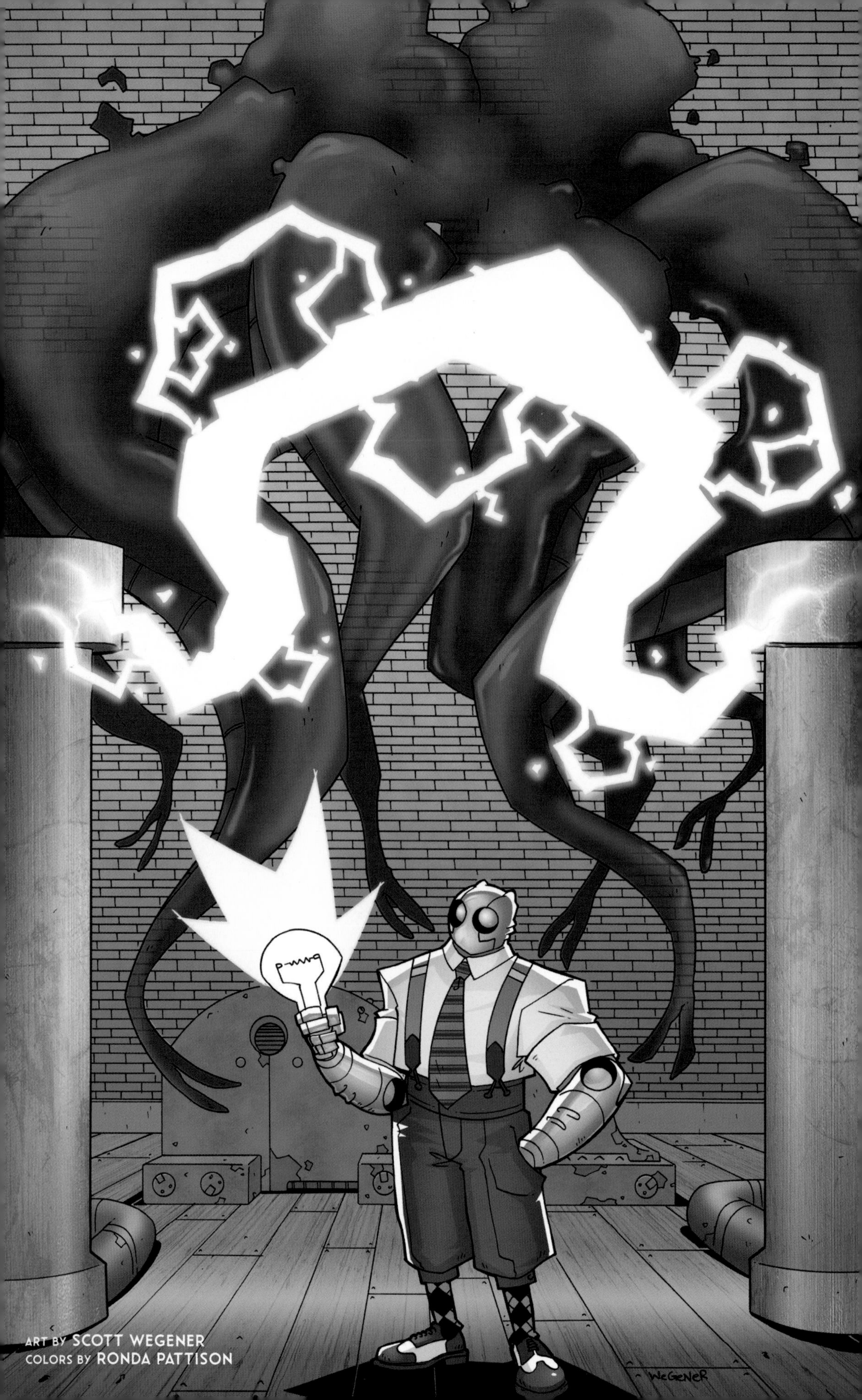
WEGENER
ART BY SCOTT WEGENER
COLORS BY RONDA PATTISON

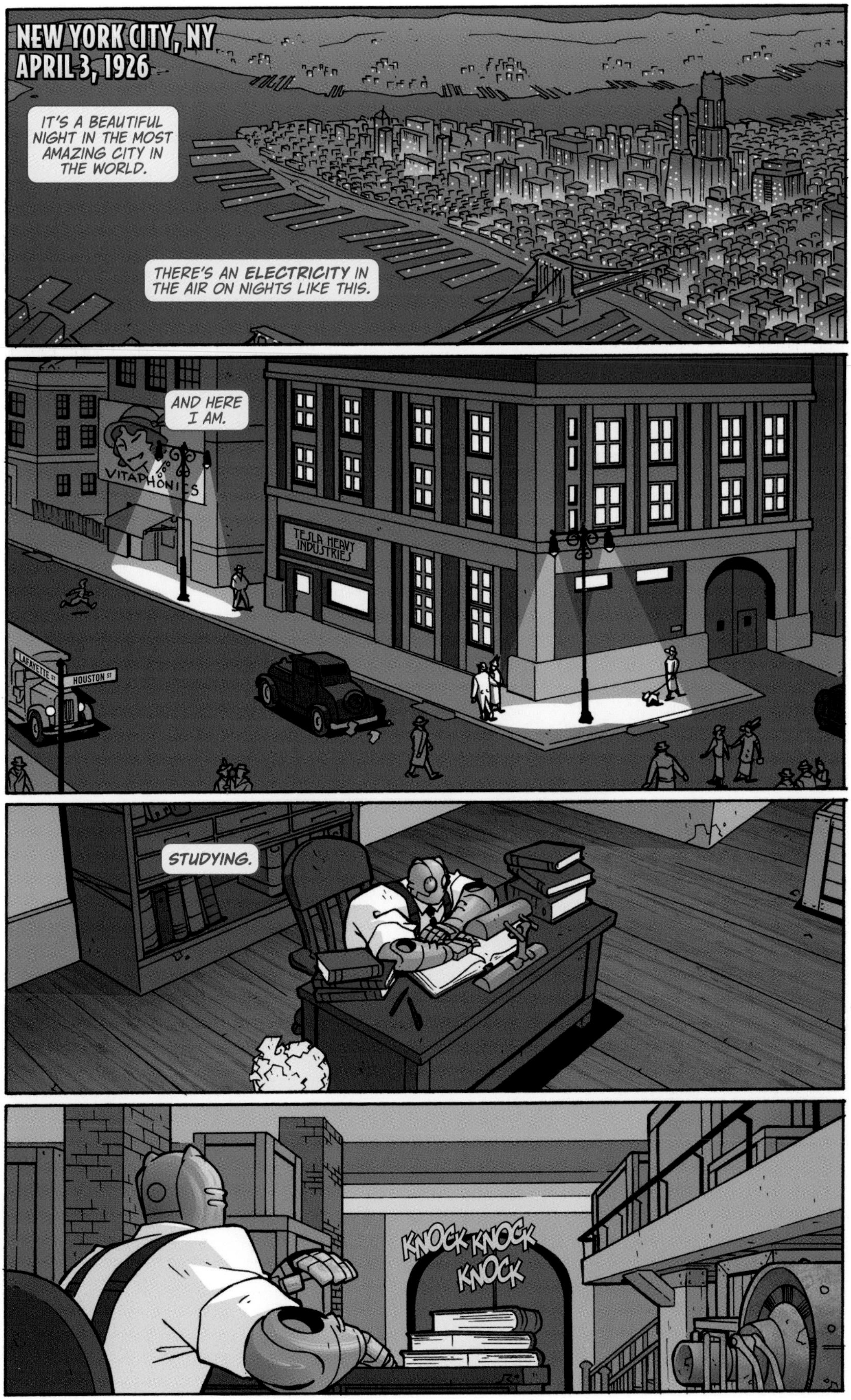
NEW YORK CITY, NY
APRIL 3, 1926
IT'S A BEAUTIFUL NIGHT IN THE MOST AMAZING CITY IN THE WORLD.
THERE'S AN ELECTRICITY IN THE AIR ON NIGHTS LIKE THIS.
AND HERE I AM.
VITAPHONICS
TESLA HEAVY INDUSTRIES
LAFAYETTE ST
HOUSTON ST
STUDYING.
KNOCK KNOCK KNOCK

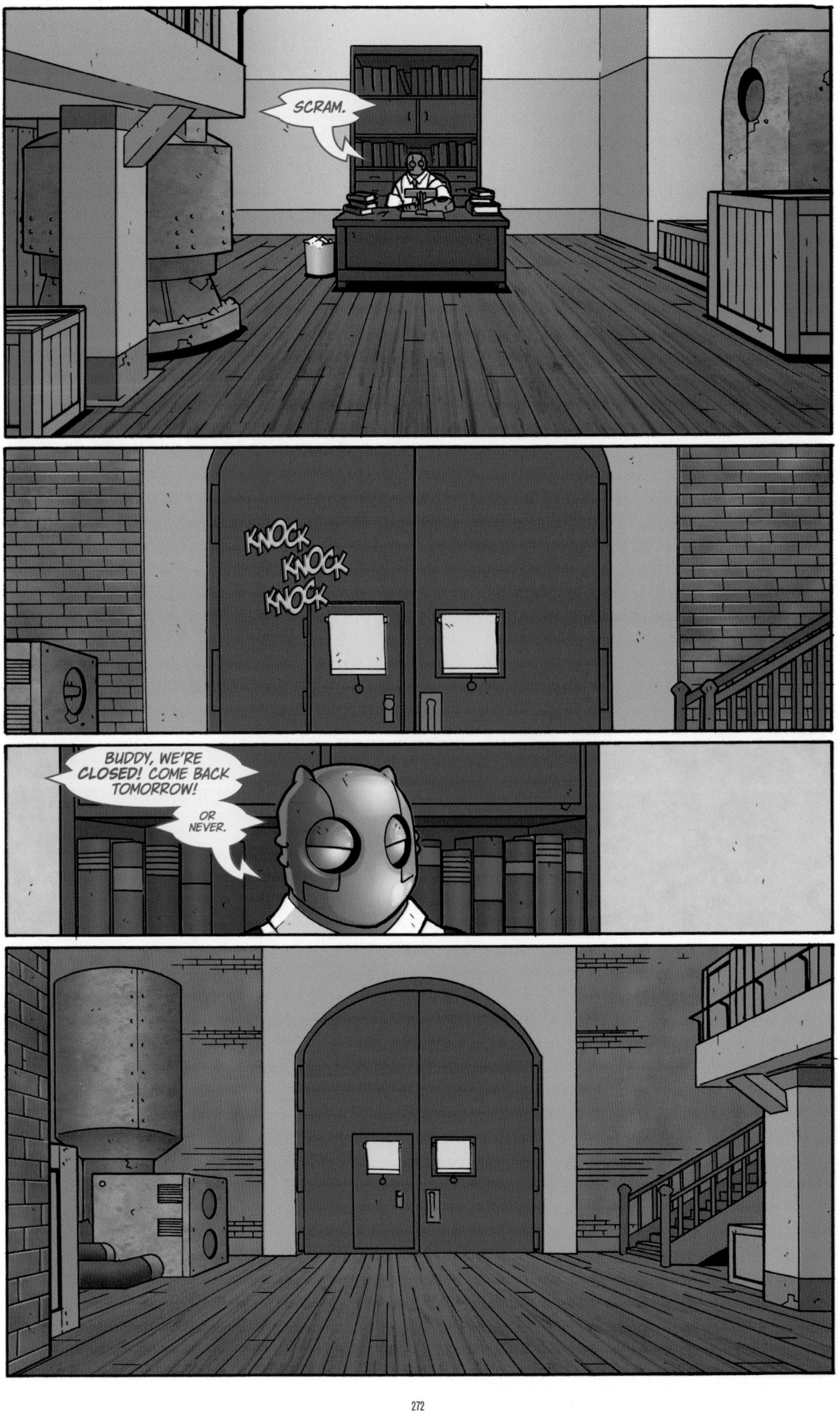
SCRAM.
KNOCK
KNOCK
KNOCK
BUDDY, WE'RE CLOSED! COME BACK TOMORROW!
OR NEVER.

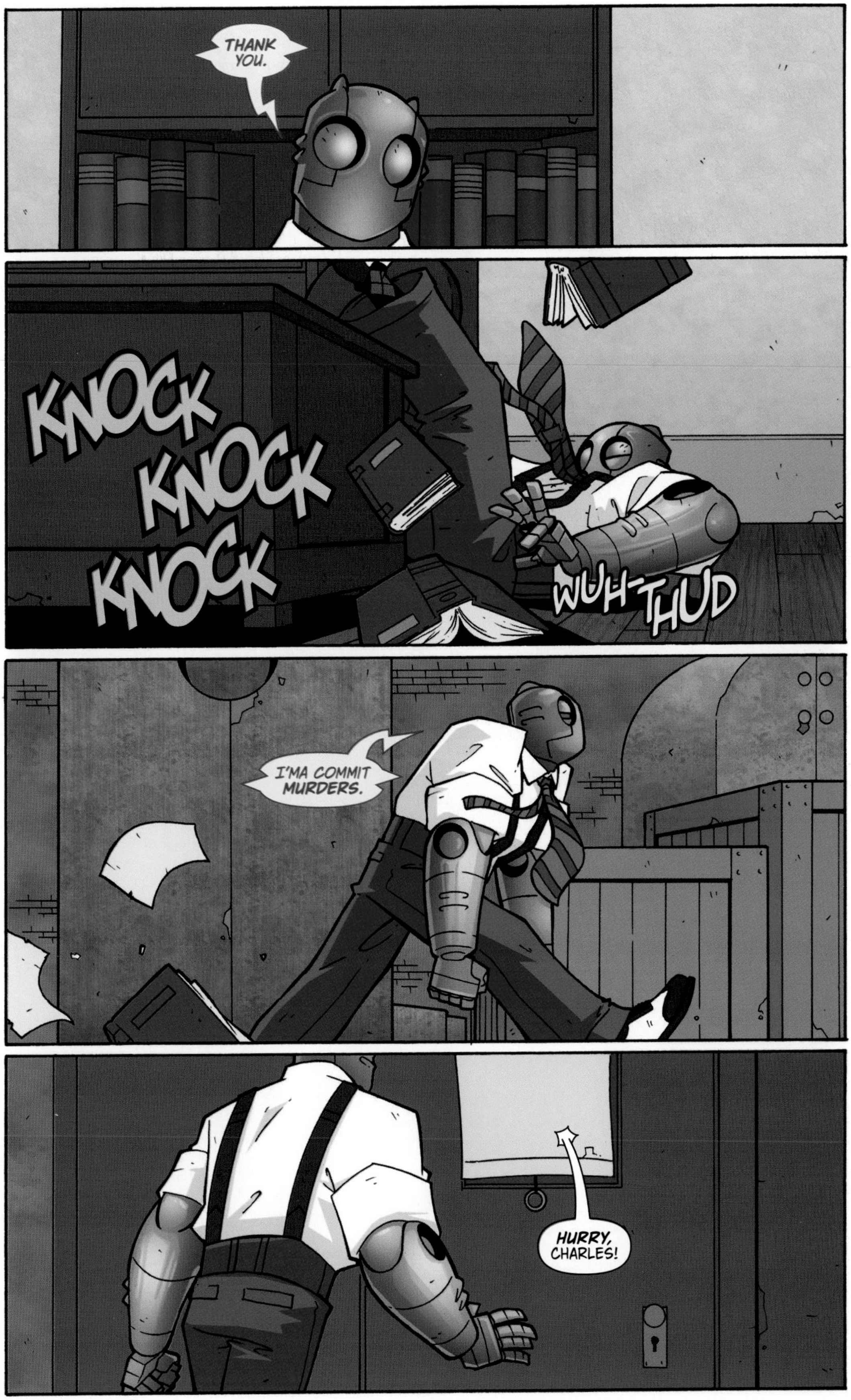
THANK YOU.
KNOCK
KNOCK
KNOCK
WUH-THUD
I'MA COMMIT MURDERS.
HURRY, CHARLES!

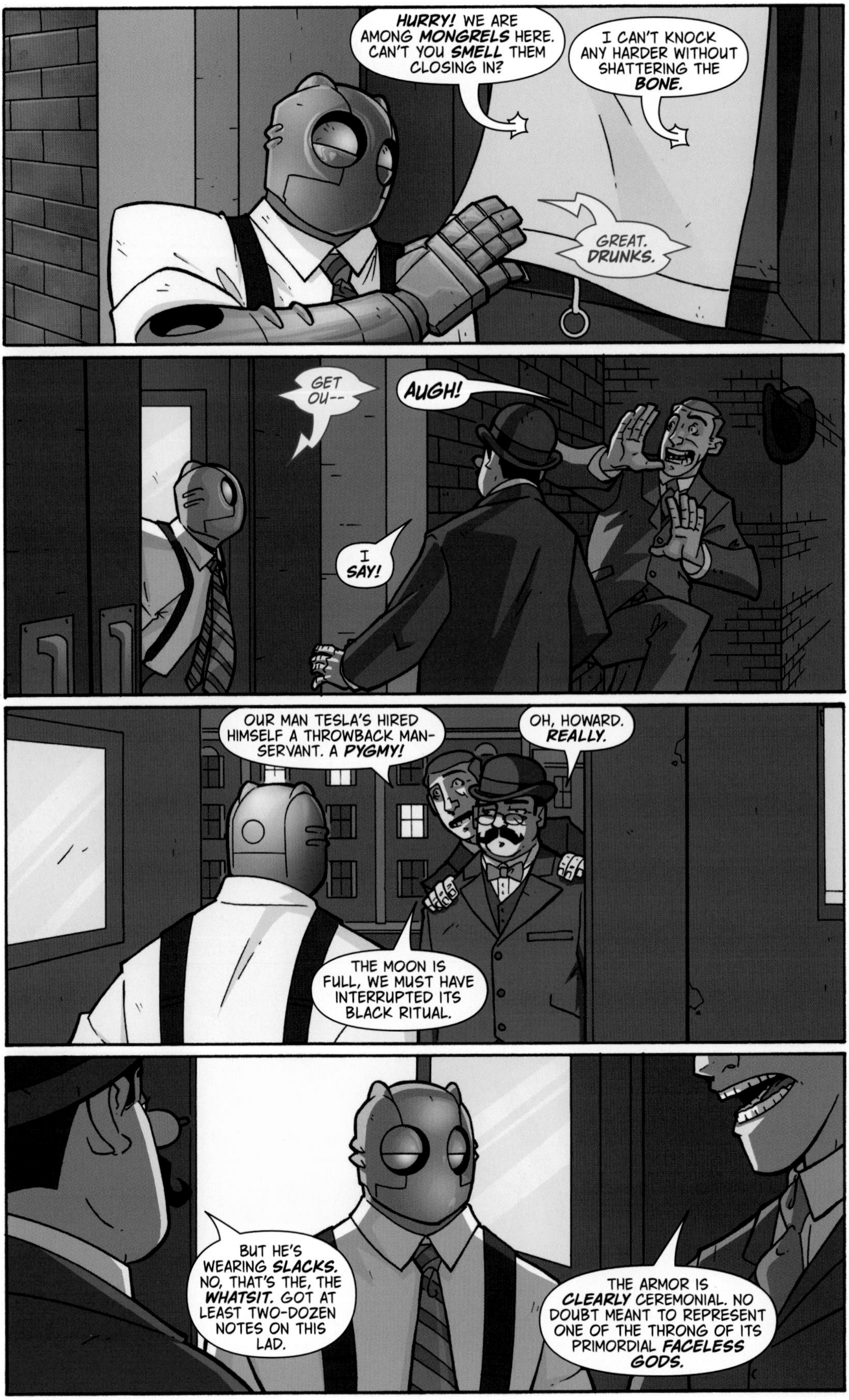
HURRY! WE ARE AMONG MONGRELS HERE. CAN'T YOU SMELL THEM CLOSING IN?
I CAN'T KNOCK ANY HARDER WITHOUT SHATTERING THE BONE.
GREAT. DRUNKS.
GET OU--
AUGH!
I SAY!
OUR MAN TESLA'S HIRED HIMSELF A THROWBACK MAN-SERVANT. A PYGMY!
OH, HOWARD. REALLY.
THE MOON IS FULL, WE MUST HAVE INTERRUPTED ITS BLACK RITUAL.
BUT HE'S WEARING SLACKS. NO, THAT'S THE, THE WHATSIT. GOT AT LEAST TWO-DOZEN NOTES ON THIS LAD.
THE ARMOR IS CLEARLY CEREMONIAL. NO DOUBT MEANT TO REPRESENT ONE OF THE THRONG OF ITS PRIMORDIAL FACELESS GODS.

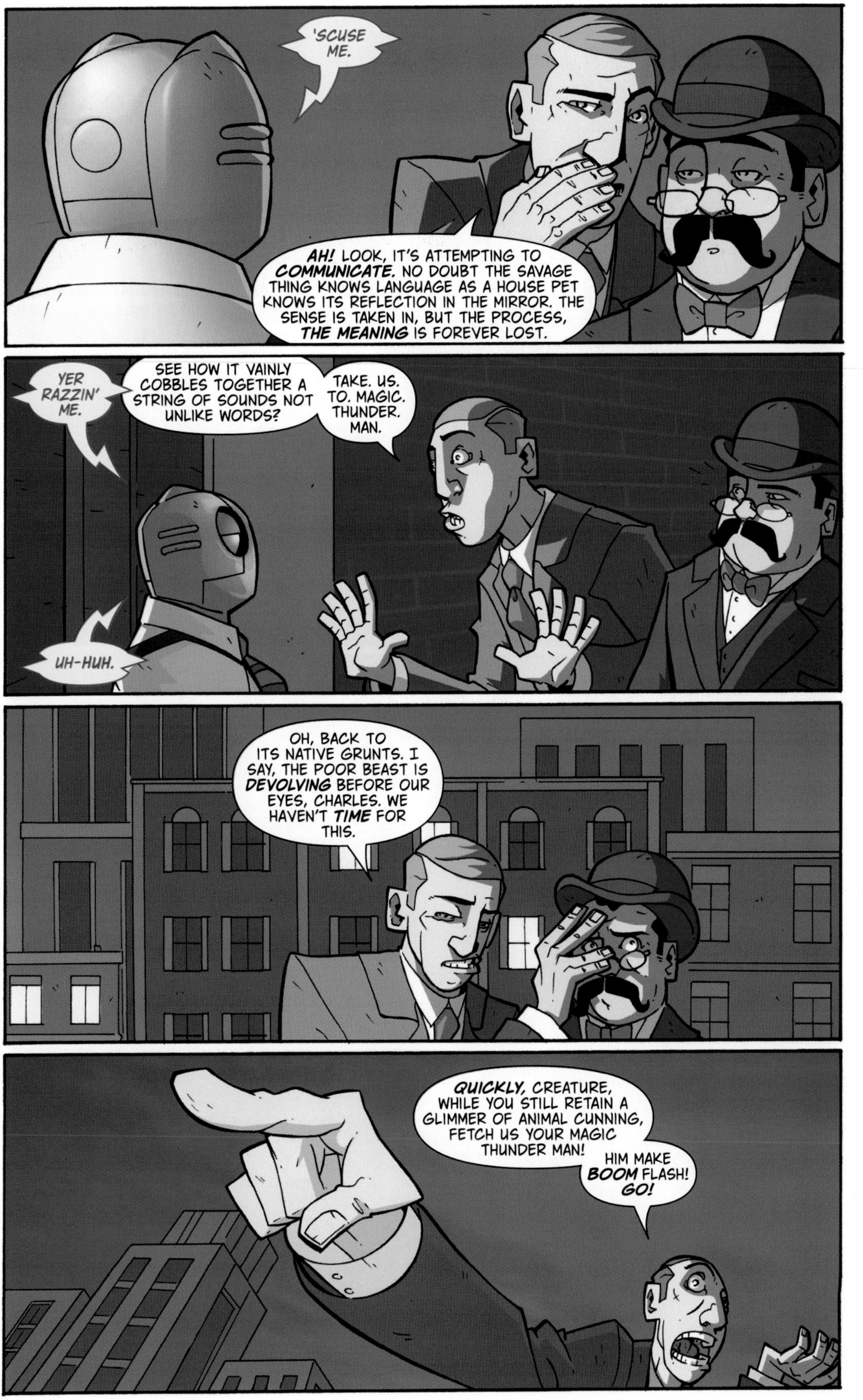

'SCUSE ME.
AH! LOOK, IT'S ATTEMPTING TO COMMUNICATE. NO DOUBT THE SAVAGE THING KNOWS LANGUAGE AS A HOUSE PET KNOWS ITS REFLECTION IN THE MIRROR. THE SENSE IS TAKEN IN, BUT THE PROCESS, THE MEANING IS FOREVER LOST.
YER RAZZIN' ME.
SEE HOW IT VAINLY COBBLES TOGETHER A STRING OF SOUNDS NOT UNLIKE WORDS?
TAKE. US. TO. MAGIC. THUNDER. MAN.
UH-HUH.
OH, BACK TO ITS NATIVE GRUNTS. I SAY, THE POOR BEAST IS DEVOLVING BEFORE OUR EYES, CHARLES. WE HAVEN'T TIME FOR THIS.
QUICKLY, CREATURE, WHILE YOU STILL RETAIN A GLIMMER OF ANIMAL CUNNING, FETCH US YOUR MAGIC THUNDER MAN!
HIM MAKE BOOM FLASH! GO!

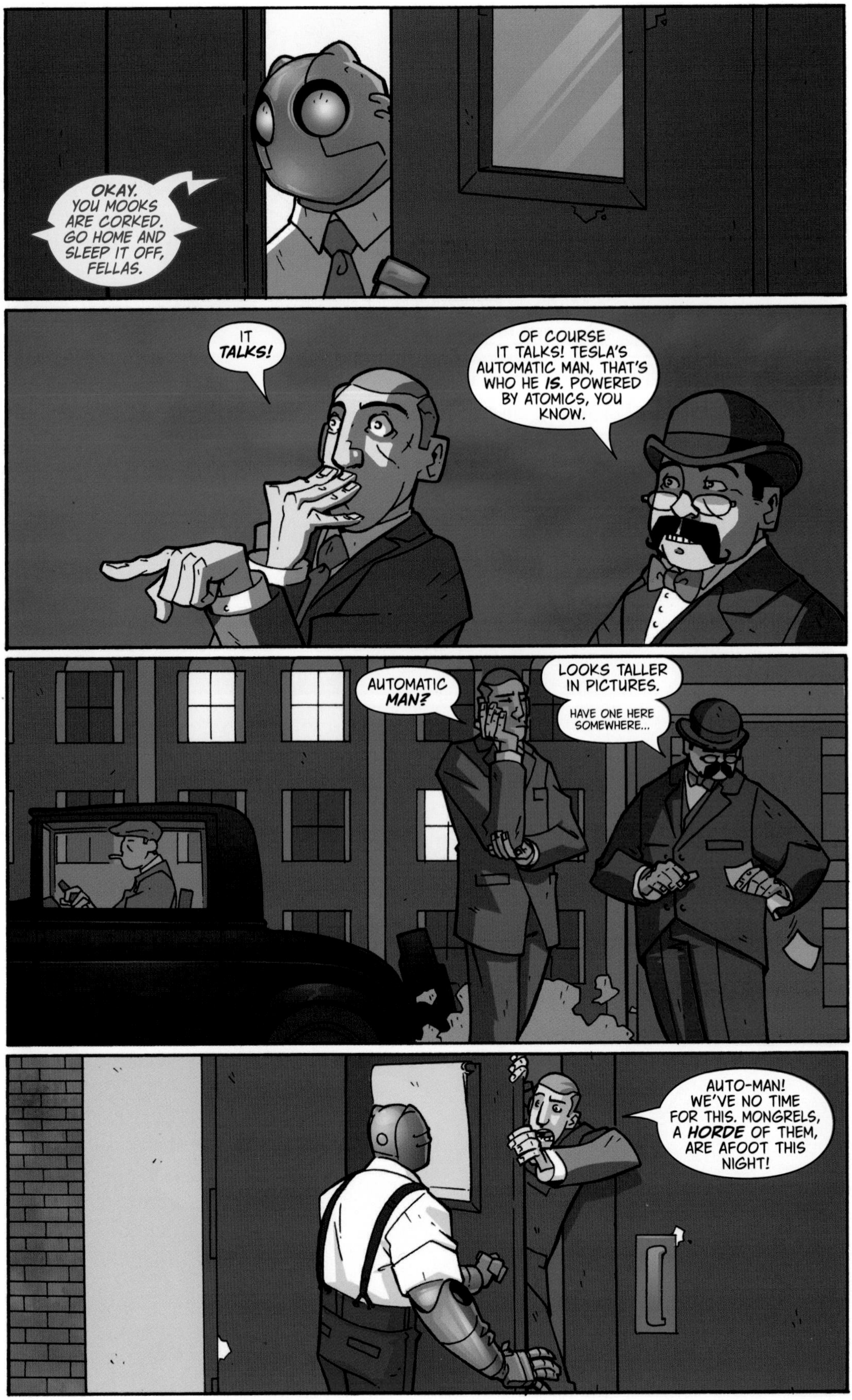
OKAY. YOU MOOKS ARE CORKED. GO HOME AND SLEEP IT OFF, FELLAS.
IT *TALKS!*
OF COURSE IT TALKS! TESLA'S AUTOMATIC MAN, THAT'S WHO HE *IS.* POWERED BY ATOMICS, YOU KNOW.
AUTOMATIC *MAN?*
LOOKS TALLER IN PICTURES.
HAVE ONE HERE SOMEWHERE...
AUTO-MAN! WE'VE NO TIME FOR THIS. MONGRELS, A *HORDE* OF THEM, ARE AFOOT THIS NIGHT!

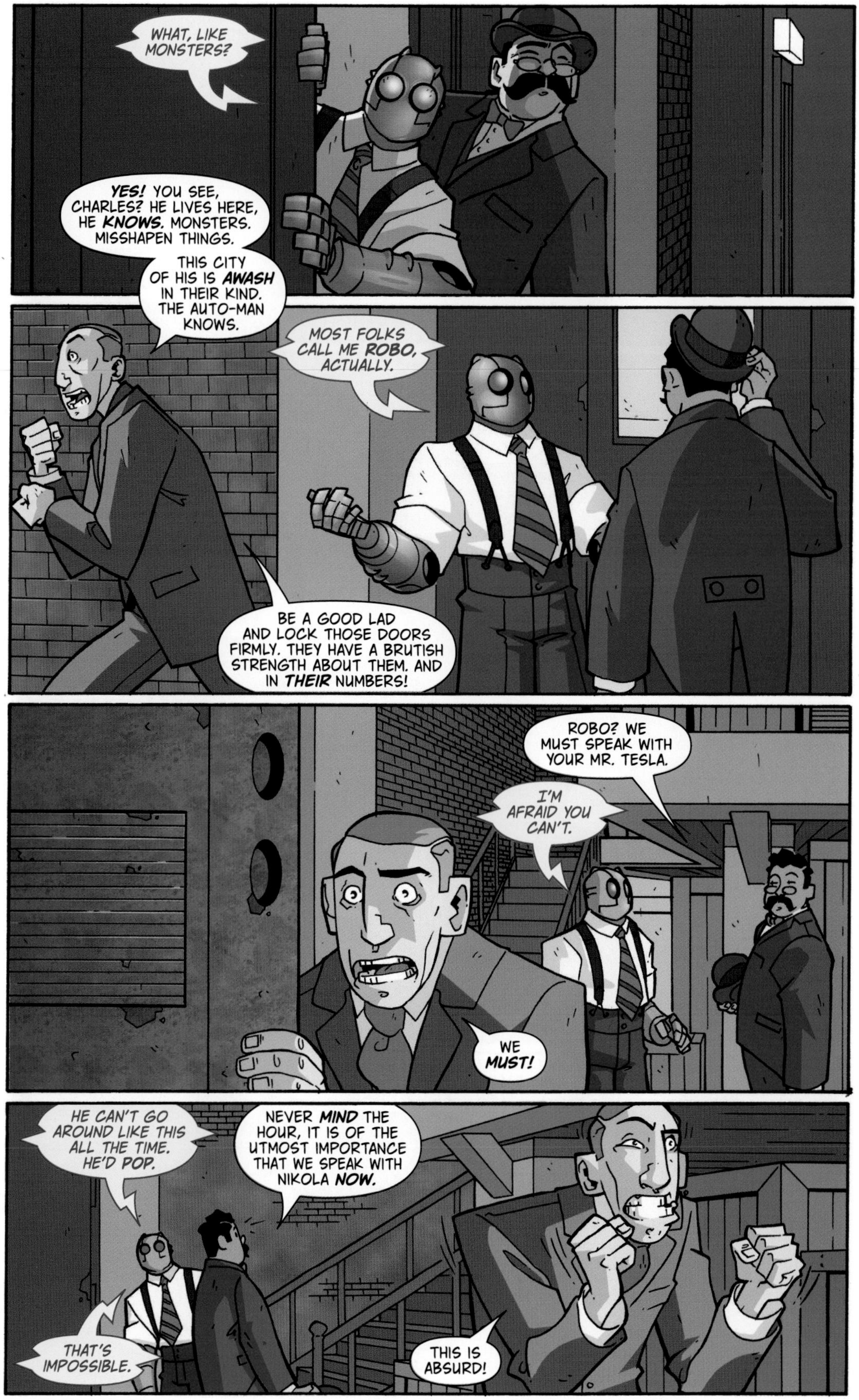
WHAT, LIKE MONSTERS?
YES! YOU SEE, CHARLES? HE LIVES HERE, HE KNOWS. MONSTERS. MISSHAPEN THINGS.
THIS CITY OF HIS IS AWASH IN THEIR KIND. THE AUTO-MAN KNOWS.
MOST FOLKS CALL ME ROBO, ACTUALLY.
BE A GOOD LAD AND LOCK THOSE DOORS FIRMLY. THEY HAVE A BRUTISH STRENGTH ABOUT THEM. AND IN THEIR NUMBERS!
ROBO? WE MUST SPEAK WITH YOUR MR. TESLA.
I'M AFRAID YOU CAN'T.
WE MUST!
HE CAN'T GO AROUND LIKE THIS ALL THE TIME. HE'D POP.
NEVER MIND THE HOUR, IT IS OF THE UTMOST IMPORTANCE THAT WE SPEAK WITH NIKOLA NOW.
THAT'S IMPOSSIBLE.
THIS IS ABSURD!

LOOK, I'M TELLIN' YOU HOW IT IS.

TELL HIM IT'S CHARLES AND HOWARD. HE'LL UNDERSTAND.

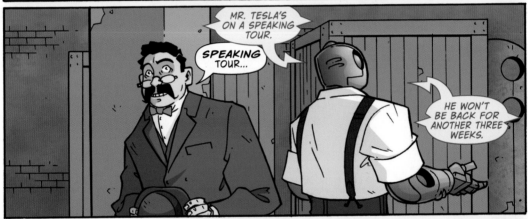

MR. TESLA'S ON A SPEAKING TOUR.

SPEAKING TOUR...

HE WON'T BE BACK FOR ANOTHER THREE WEEKS.

THREE WEEKS... ...OH, NO, NO, NO.

NO MATTER. WE CAN DO THIS OURSELVES. WE SAW HIM WORK THE CONTROLS LAST TIME. IT'S SIMPLICITY ITSELF FOR ADVANCED ANGLO-BRAINS SUCH AS OURS TO DISCERN ITS OPERATION.

THE MAN MAY BE A GENIUS, BUT HE'S ONLY EAST EUROPEAN. THE AUTO-MAN CAN TAKE US THERE!

ROBO, ACTUALLY.

YES, OF COURSE, THE AUTO-ROBO. TO WARDENCLYFFE!

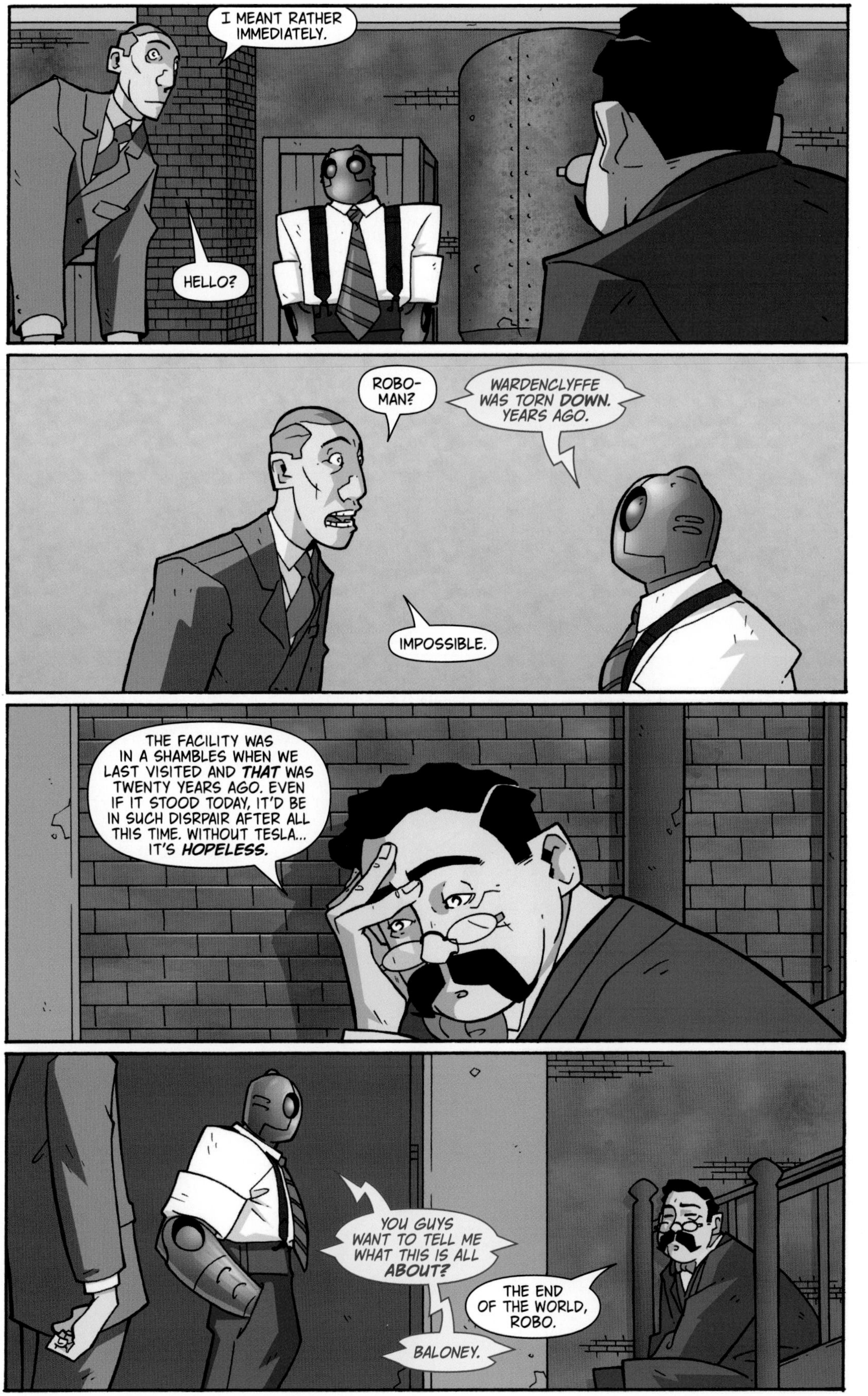
I MEANT RATHER IMMEDIATELY.
HELLO?
ROBO-MAN?
WARDENCLYFFE WAS TORN DOWN. YEARS AGO.
IMPOSSIBLE.
THE FACILITY WAS IN A SHAMBLES WHEN WE LAST VISITED AND THAT WAS TWENTY YEARS AGO. EVEN IF IT STOOD TODAY, IT'D BE IN SUCH DISRPAIR AFTER ALL THIS TIME. WITHOUT TESLA... IT'S HOPELESS.
YOU GUYS WANT TO TELL ME WHAT THIS IS ALL ABOUT?
THE END OF THE WORLD, ROBO.
BALONEY.

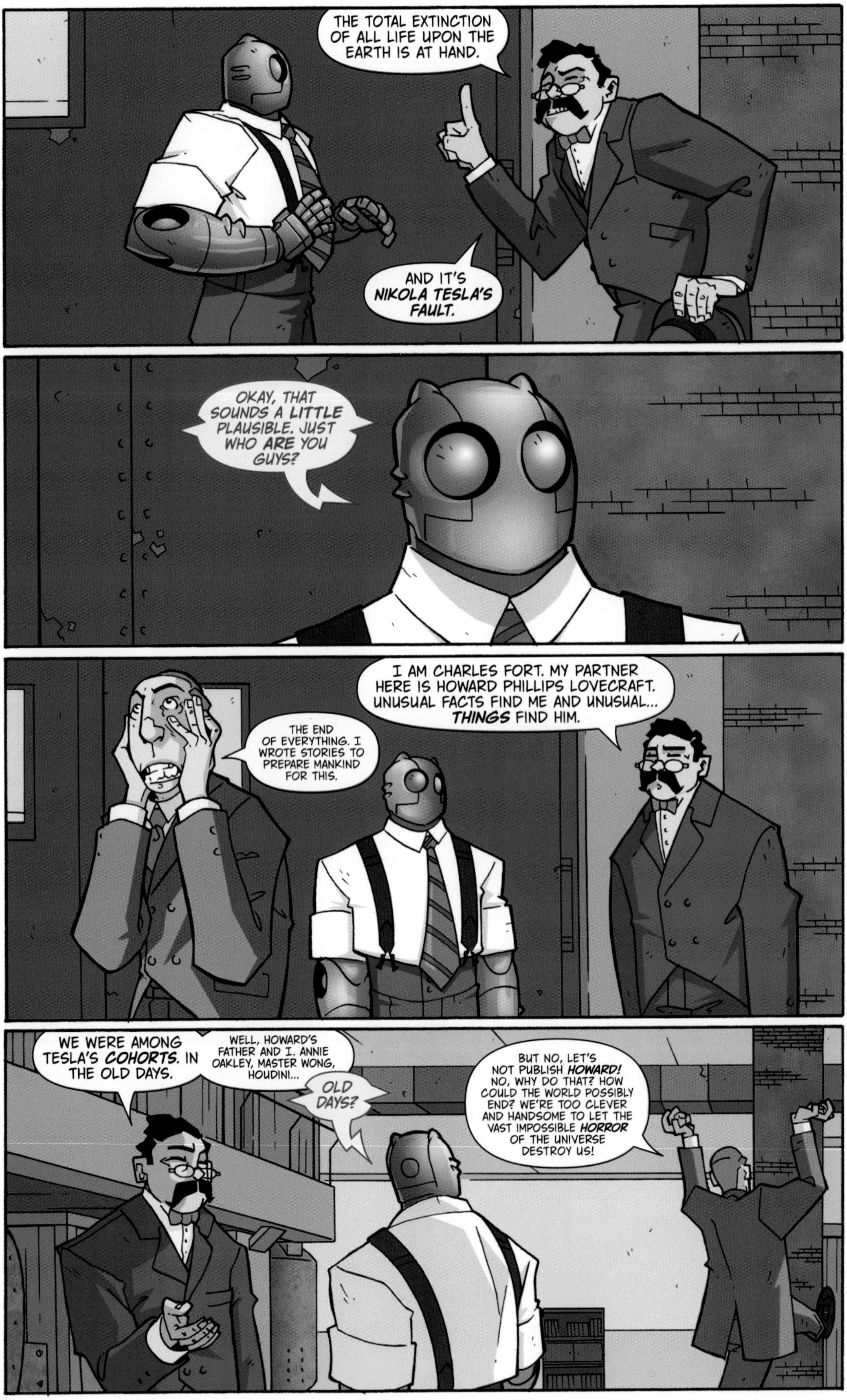
THE TOTAL EXTINCTION OF ALL LIFE UPON THE EARTH IS AT HAND.
AND IT'S *NIKOLA TESLA'S* *FAULT.*
OKAY, THAT SOUNDS A **LITTLE** PLAUSIBLE. JUST WHO **ARE** YOU GUYS?
I AM CHARLES FORT. MY PARTNER HERE IS HOWARD PHILLIPS LOVECRAFT. UNUSUAL FACTS FIND ME AND UNUSUAL... ***THINGS*** FIND HIM.
THE END OF EVERYTHING. I WROTE STORIES TO PREPARE MANKIND FOR THIS.
WE WERE AMONG TESLA'S ***COHORTS.*** IN THE OLD DAYS.
WELL, HOWARD'S FATHER AND I. ANNIE OAKLEY, MASTER WONG, HOUDINI...
OLD DAYS?
BUT NO, LET'S NOT PUBLISH ***HOWARD!*** NO, WHY DO THAT? HOW COULD THE WORLD POSSIBLY END? WE'RE TOO CLEVER AND HANDSOME TO LET THE VAST IMPOSSIBLE ***HORROR*** OF THE UNIVERSE DESTROY US!

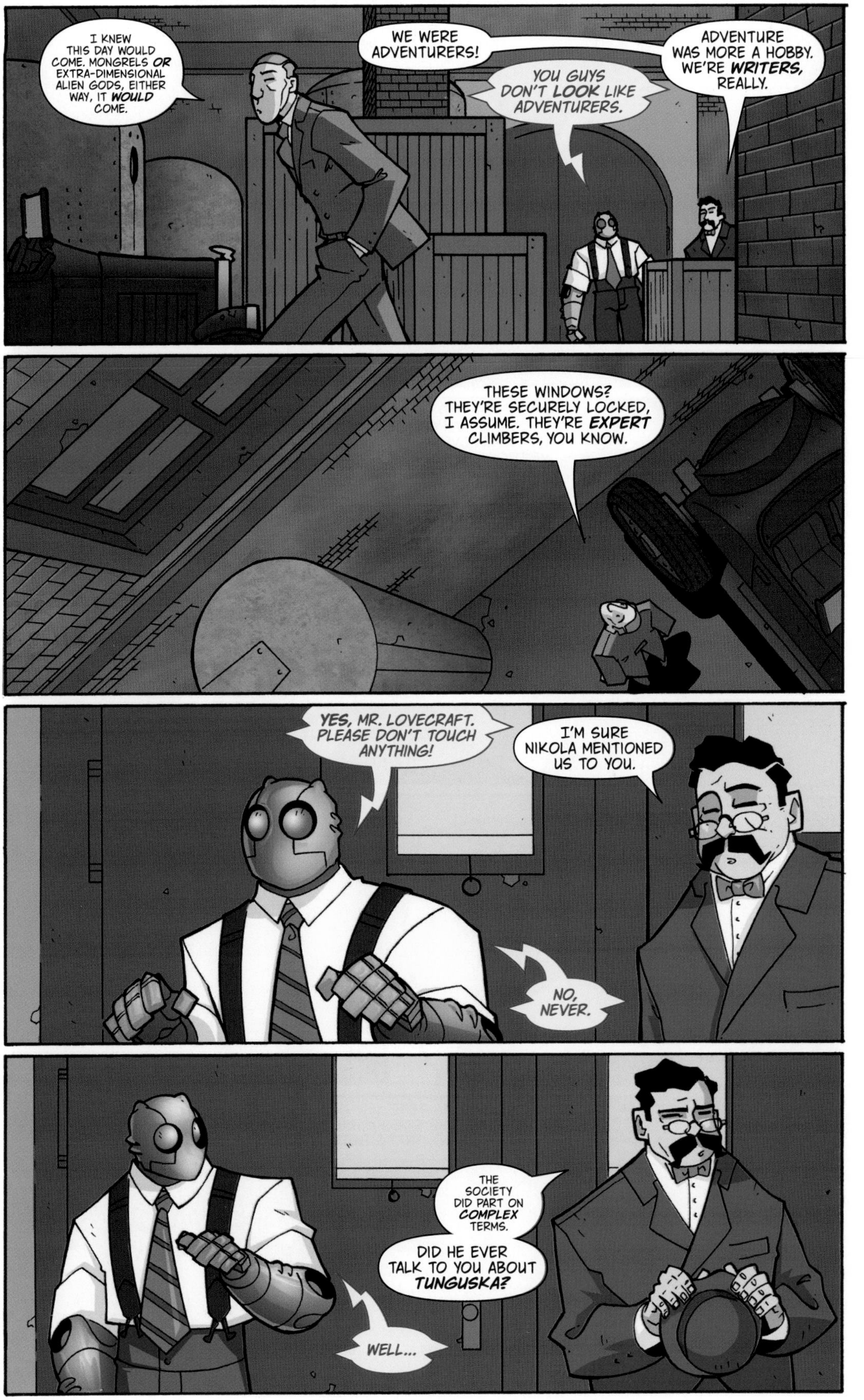
I KNEW THIS DAY WOULD COME. MONGRELS **OR** EXTRA-DIMENSIONAL ALIEN GODS, EITHER WAY, IT **WOULD** COME.
WE WERE ADVENTURERS!
YOU GUYS DON'T **LOOK** LIKE ADVENTURERS.
ADVENTURE WAS MORE A HOBBY. WE'RE **WRITERS,** REALLY.
THESE WINDOWS? THEY'RE SECURELY LOCKED, I ASSUME. THEY'RE **EXPERT** CLIMBERS, YOU KNOW.
YES, MR. LOVECRAFT. PLEASE DON'T TOUCH ANYTHING!
I'M SURE NIKOLA MENTIONED US TO YOU.
NO, NEVER.
THE SOCIETY DID PART ON **COMPLEX** TERMS.
DID HE EVER TALK TO YOU ABOUT **TUNGUSKA?**
WELL...

ROBO, I WANT YOU TO PROMISE ME SOMETHING.

OF COURSE.

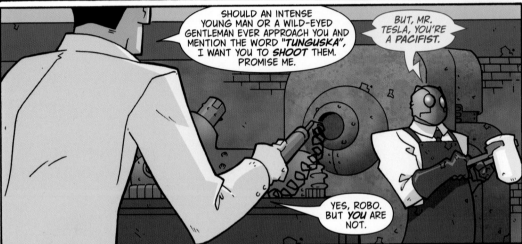

SHOULD AN INTENSE YOUNG MAN OR A WILD-EYED GENTLEMAN EVER APPROACH YOU AND MENTION THE WORD "*TUNGUSKA*", I WANT YOU TO **SHOOT** THEM. PROMISE ME.

BUT, MR. TESLA, YOU'RE A *PACIFIST*.

YES, ROBO. BUT *YOU* ARE NOT.

HE, UH. HE SAID SOME *EXCEPTIONAL* THINGS.

THE THREE OF US REPELLED AN ALIEN INVASION THAT BEGAN IN THE SKIES OVER THE *TUNGUSKA* RIVER IN 1908. THAT'S PART OF SIBERIA.

ALIENS? FROM, WHAT, *MARS*? THAT'S PLAGIARISM, MR. FORT. I THINK IT'S TIME YOU AND--

282

DAMMIT, ROBO! THERE WAS NO **TIME** TO RECORD EVIDENCE OF OUR DEEDS! WE HAD TO ACT WITHOUT QUESTION, WITHOUT HESITATION, TO SAVE **ALL LIFE** AS WE KNOW IT.

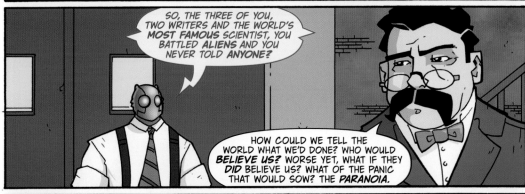

SO, THE THREE OF YOU, TWO WRITERS AND THE WORLD'S **MOST FAMOUS** SCIENTIST, YOU BATTLED ALIENS AND YOU NEVER TOLD **ANYONE?**

HOW COULD WE TELL THE WORLD WHAT WE'D DONE? WHO WOULD **BELIEVE US?** WORSE YET, WHAT IF THEY **DID** BELIEVE US? WHAT OF THE PANIC THAT WOULD SOW? THE **PARANOIA.**

NO, WE COULDN'T TELL A SOUL. NOT EVEN OUR OWN FAMILIES. IT WAS A SECRET THAT DESTROYED EACH OF US IN ITS WAY.

"I MERELY HAD TO BURN TEN **YEARS** OF RESEARCH. NEARLY THE WHOLE OF MY LIFE'S WORK TO THAT POINT. **I** WAS THE LUCKY ONE."

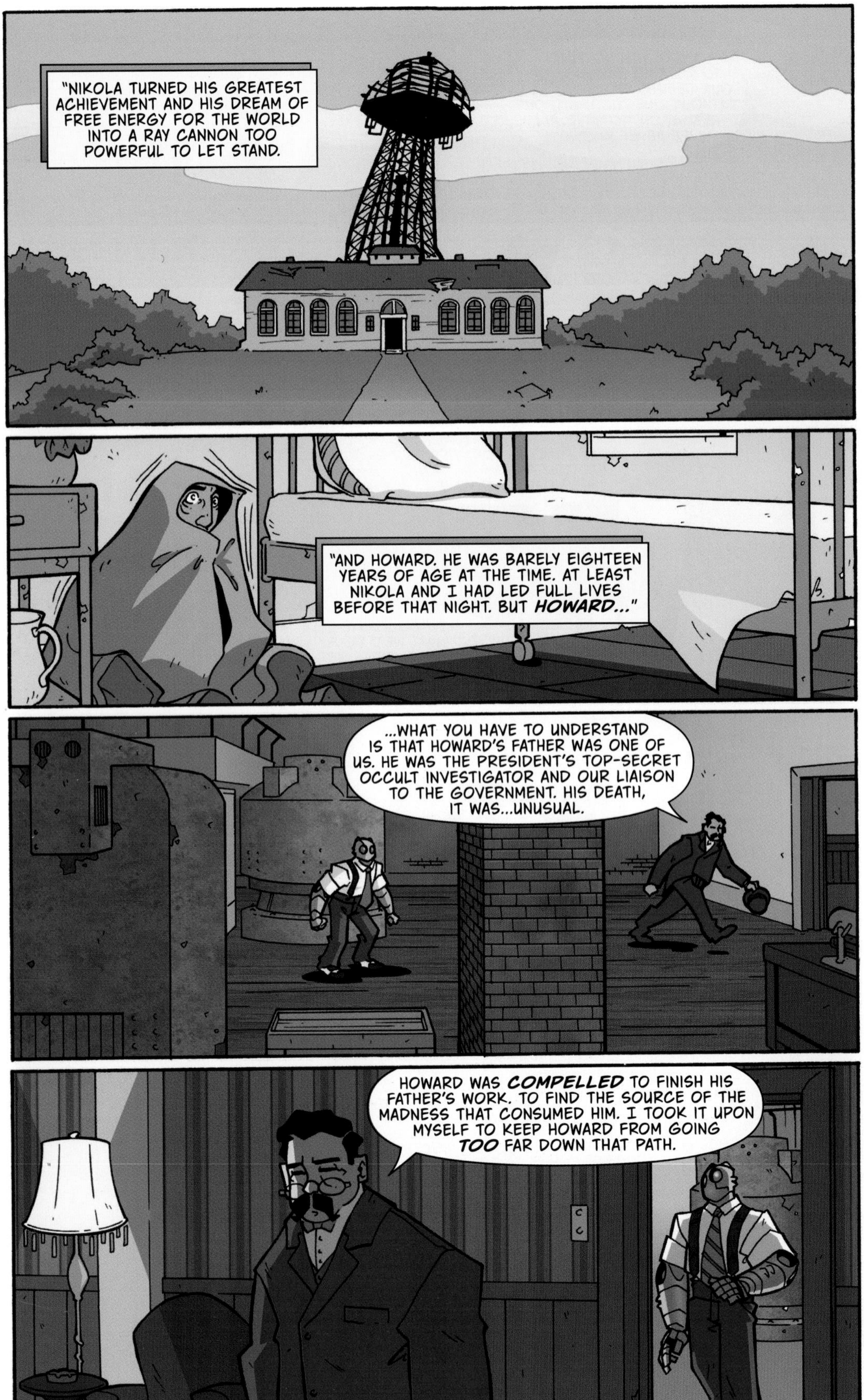
"NIKOLA TURNED HIS GREATEST ACHIEVEMENT AND HIS DREAM OF FREE ENERGY FOR THE WORLD INTO A RAY CANNON TOO POWERFUL TO LET STAND.
"AND HOWARD. HE WAS BARELY EIGHTEEN YEARS OF AGE AT THE TIME. AT LEAST NIKOLA AND I HAD LED FULL LIVES BEFORE THAT NIGHT. BUT HOWARD..."
...WHAT YOU HAVE TO UNDERSTAND IS THAT HOWARD'S FATHER WAS ONE OF US. HE WAS THE PRESIDENT'S TOP-SECRET OCCULT INVESTIGATOR AND OUR LIAISON TO THE GOVERNMENT. HIS DEATH, IT WAS...UNUSUAL.
HOWARD WAS COMPELLED TO FINISH HIS FATHER'S WORK. TO FIND THE SOURCE OF THE MADNESS THAT CONSUMED HIM. I TOOK IT UPON MYSELF TO KEEP HOWARD FROM GOING TOO FAR DOWN THAT PATH.

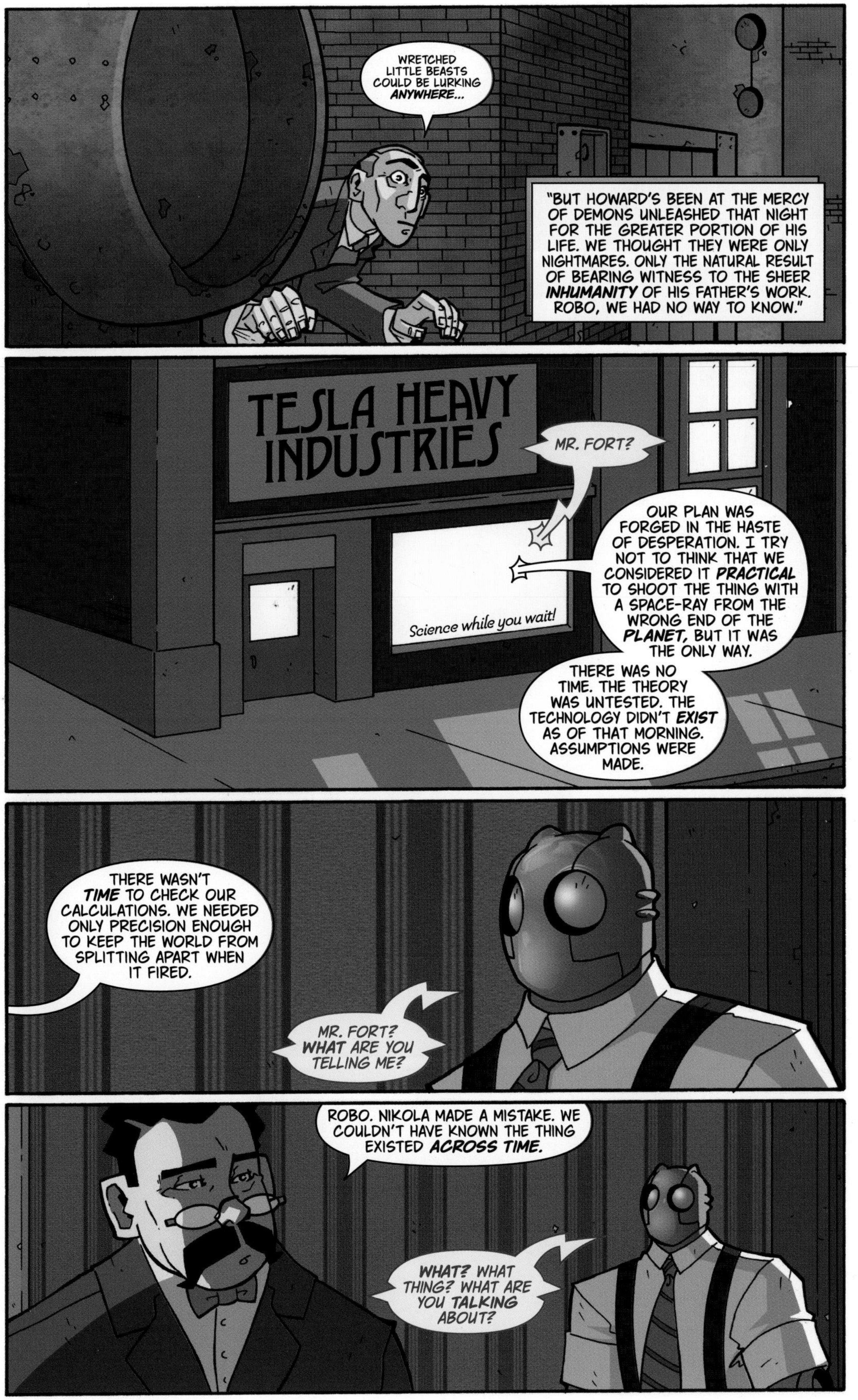
WRETCHED LITTLE BEASTS COULD BE LURKING ANYWHERE...
"BUT HOWARD'S BEEN AT THE MERCY OF DEMONS UNLEASHED THAT NIGHT FOR THE GREATER PORTION OF HIS LIFE. WE THOUGHT THEY WERE ONLY NIGHTMARES. ONLY THE NATURAL RESULT OF BEARING WITNESS TO THE SHEER INHUMANITY OF HIS FATHER'S WORK. ROBO, WE HAD NO WAY TO KNOW."
TESLA HEAVY INDUSTRIES
Science while you wait!
MR. FORT?
OUR PLAN WAS FORGED IN THE HASTE OF DESPERATION. I TRY NOT TO THINK THAT WE CONSIDERED IT PRACTICAL TO SHOOT THE THING WITH A SPACE-RAY FROM THE WRONG END OF THE PLANET, BUT IT WAS THE ONLY WAY.
THERE WAS NO TIME. THE THEORY WAS UNTESTED. THE TECHNOLOGY DIDN'T EXIST AS OF THAT MORNING. ASSUMPTIONS WERE MADE.
THERE WASN'T TIME TO CHECK OUR CALCULATIONS. WE NEEDED ONLY PRECISION ENOUGH TO KEEP THE WORLD FROM SPLITTING APART WHEN IT FIRED.
MR. FORT? WHAT ARE YOU TELLING ME?
ROBO. NIKOLA MADE A MISTAKE. WE COULDN'T HAVE KNOWN THE THING EXISTED ACROSS TIME.
WHAT? WHAT THING? WHAT ARE YOU TALKING ABOUT?

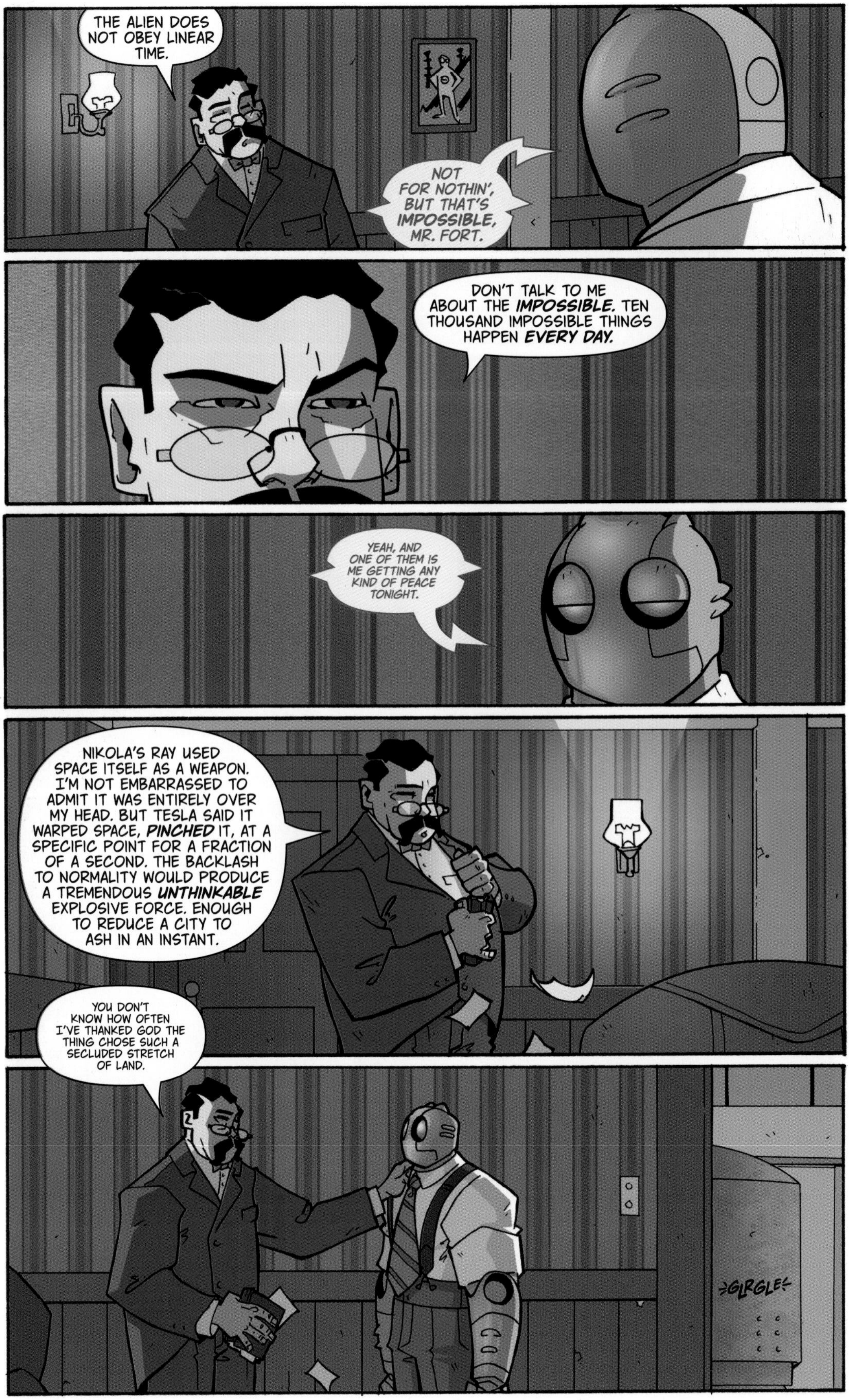
THE ALIEN DOES NOT OBEY LINEAR TIME.
NOT FOR NOTHIN', BUT THAT'S *IMPOSSIBLE,* MR. FORT.
DON'T TALK TO ME ABOUT THE *IMPOSSIBLE.* TEN THOUSAND IMPOSSIBLE THINGS HAPPEN *EVERY DAY.*
YEAH, AND ONE OF THEM IS ME GETTING ANY KIND OF PEACE TONIGHT.
NIKOLA'S RAY USED SPACE ITSELF AS A WEAPON. I'M NOT EMBARRASSED TO ADMIT IT WAS ENTIRELY OVER MY HEAD. BUT TESLA SAID IT WARPED SPACE, *PINCHED* IT, AT A SPECIFIC POINT FOR A FRACTION OF A SECOND. THE BACKLASH TO NORMALITY WOULD PRODUCE A TREMENDOUS *UNTHINKABLE* EXPLOSIVE FORCE. ENOUGH TO REDUCE A CITY TO ASH IN AN INSTANT.
YOU DON'T KNOW HOW OFTEN I'VE THANKED GOD THE THING CHOSE SUCH A SECLUDED STRETCH OF LAND.
GLRGLE

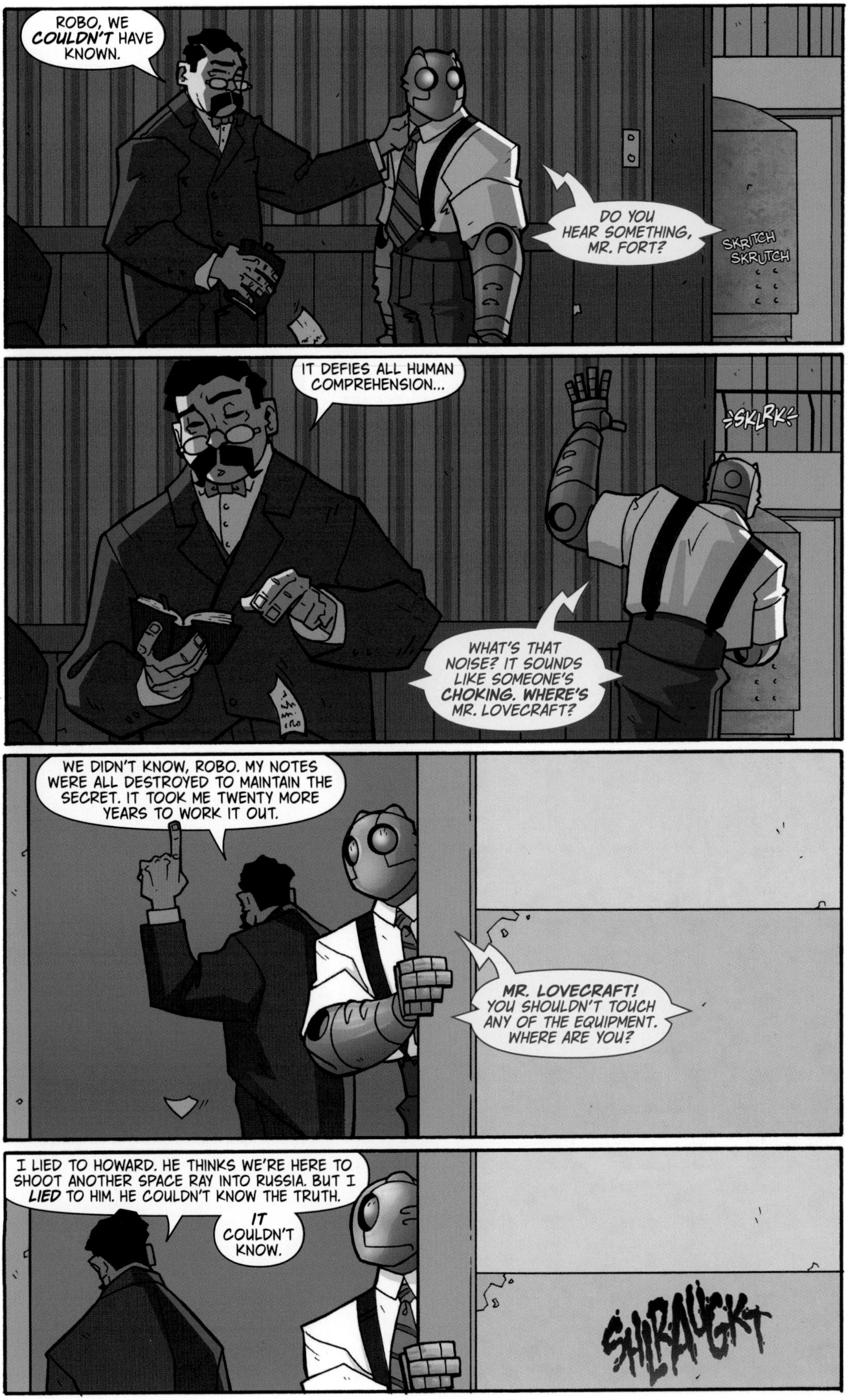
ROBO, WE COULDN'T HAVE KNOWN.
DO YOU HEAR SOMETHING, MR. FORT?
SKRITCH SKRUTCH
IT DEFIES ALL HUMAN COMPREHENSION...
SKLRK
WHAT'S THAT NOISE? IT SOUNDS LIKE SOMEONE'S CHOKING. WHERE'S MR. LOVECRAFT?
WE DIDN'T KNOW, ROBO. MY NOTES WERE ALL DESTROYED TO MAINTAIN THE SECRET. IT TOOK ME TWENTY MORE YEARS TO WORK IT OUT.
MR. LOVECRAFT! YOU SHOULDN'T TOUCH ANY OF THE EQUIPMENT. WHERE ARE YOU?
I LIED TO HOWARD. HE THINKS WE'RE HERE TO SHOOT ANOTHER SPACE RAY INTO RUSSIA. BUT I LIED TO HIM. HE COULDN'T KNOW THE TRUTH.
IT COULDN'T KNOW.
SHLRAUGKT

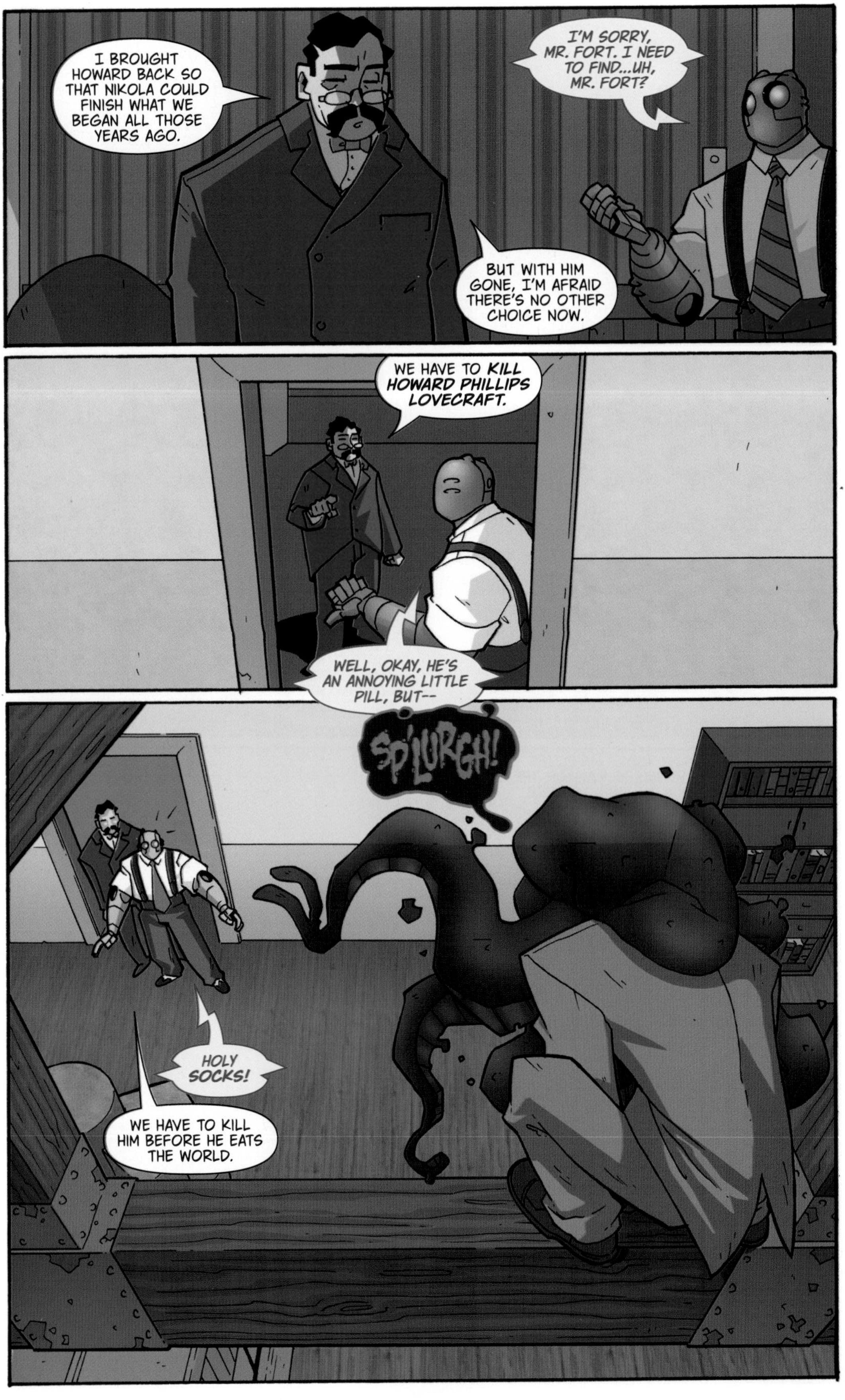
I BROUGHT HOWARD BACK SO THAT NIKOLA COULD FINISH WHAT WE BEGAN ALL THOSE YEARS AGO.
I'M SORRY, MR. FORT. I NEED TO FIND...UH, MR. FORT?
BUT WITH HIM GONE, I'M AFRAID THERE'S NO OTHER CHOICE NOW.
WE HAVE TO **KILL HOWARD PHILLIPS LOVECRAFT.**
WELL, OKAY, HE'S AN ANNOYING LITTLE PILL, BUT--
SPLURGH!
HOLY SOCKS!
WE HAVE TO KILL HIM BEFORE HE EATS THE WORLD.

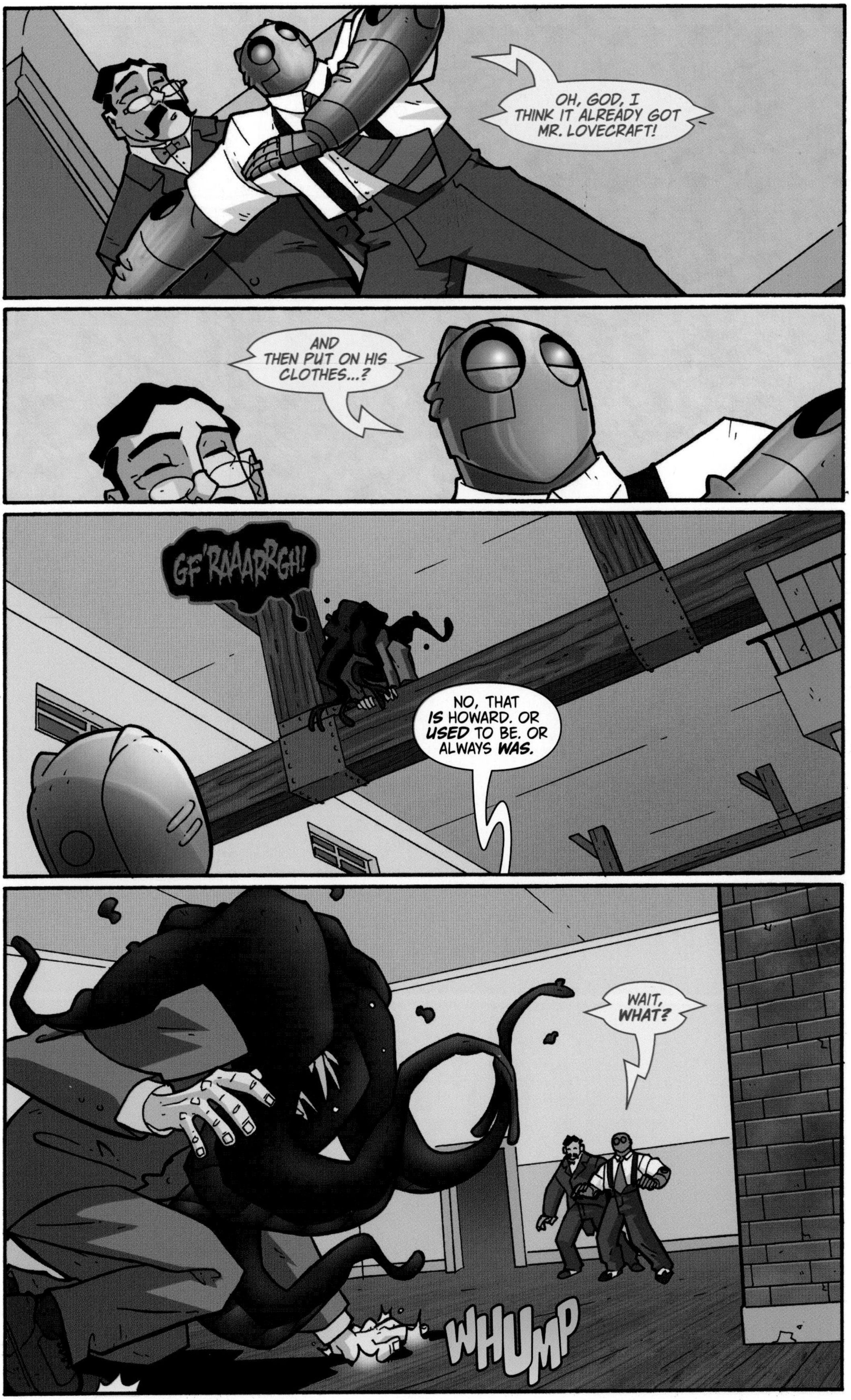
OH, GOD, I THINK IT ALREADY GOT MR. LOVECRAFT!
AND THEN PUT ON HIS CLOTHES...?
GF'RAAARRGH!
NO, THAT **IS** HOWARD. OR **USED** TO BE. OR ALWAYS **WAS.**
WAIT, **WHAT?**
WHUMP

AND THAT'S ANOTHER THING. ARE THOSE...ARE THOSE TEETH STICKING OUT OF IT?

THE LAWS OF ANATOMY, GEOMETRY, *PHYSICS*, THEY MEAN NOTHING TO IT. IT MAY NOT EVEN BE *IN* OUR UNIVERSE, BUT RATHER PASSING *THROUGH* IT.

SO, WHAT'S IT DOING IN MR. LOVECRAFT'S HEAD?

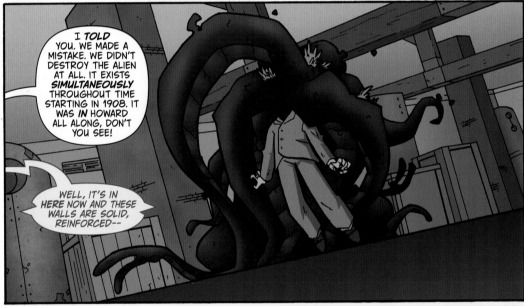

I *TOLD* YOU. WE MADE A MISTAKE. WE DIDN'T DESTROY THE ALIEN AT ALL. IT EXISTS *SIMULTANEOUSLY* THROUGHOUT TIME STARTING IN 1908. IT WAS *IN* HOWARD ALL ALONG, DON'T YOU SEE!

WELL, IT'S IN *HERE* NOW AND THESE WALLS ARE SOLID, REINFORCED--

CRASH

SKLRRRGL!

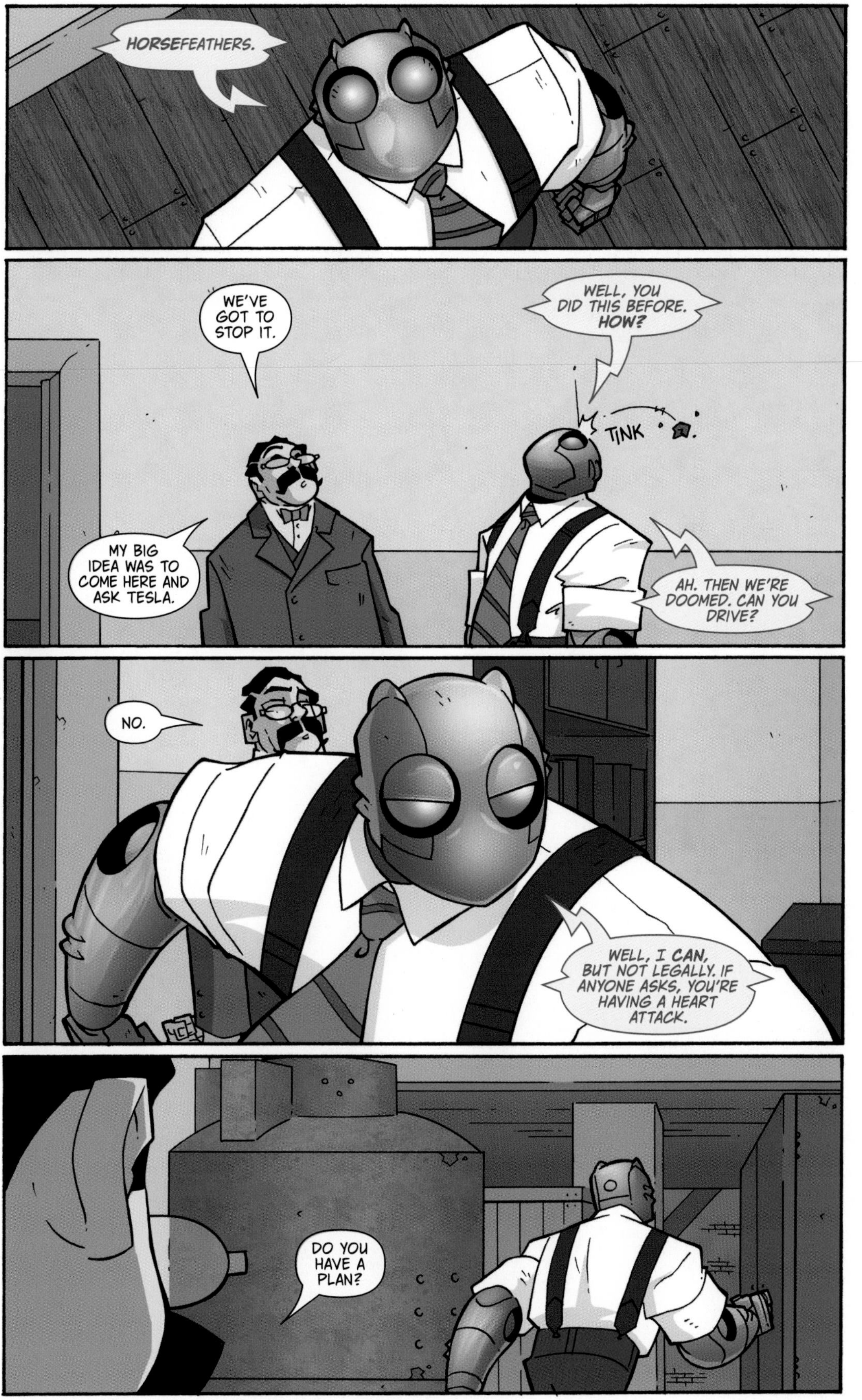
HORSEFEATHERS.
WE'VE GOT TO STOP IT.
WELL, YOU DID THIS BEFORE. HOW?
TINK
MY BIG IDEA WAS TO COME HERE AND ASK TESLA.
AH. THEN WE'RE DOOMED. CAN YOU DRIVE?
NO.
WELL, I CAN, BUT NOT LEGALLY. IF ANYONE ASKS, YOU'RE HAVING A HEART ATTACK.
DO YOU HAVE A PLAN?

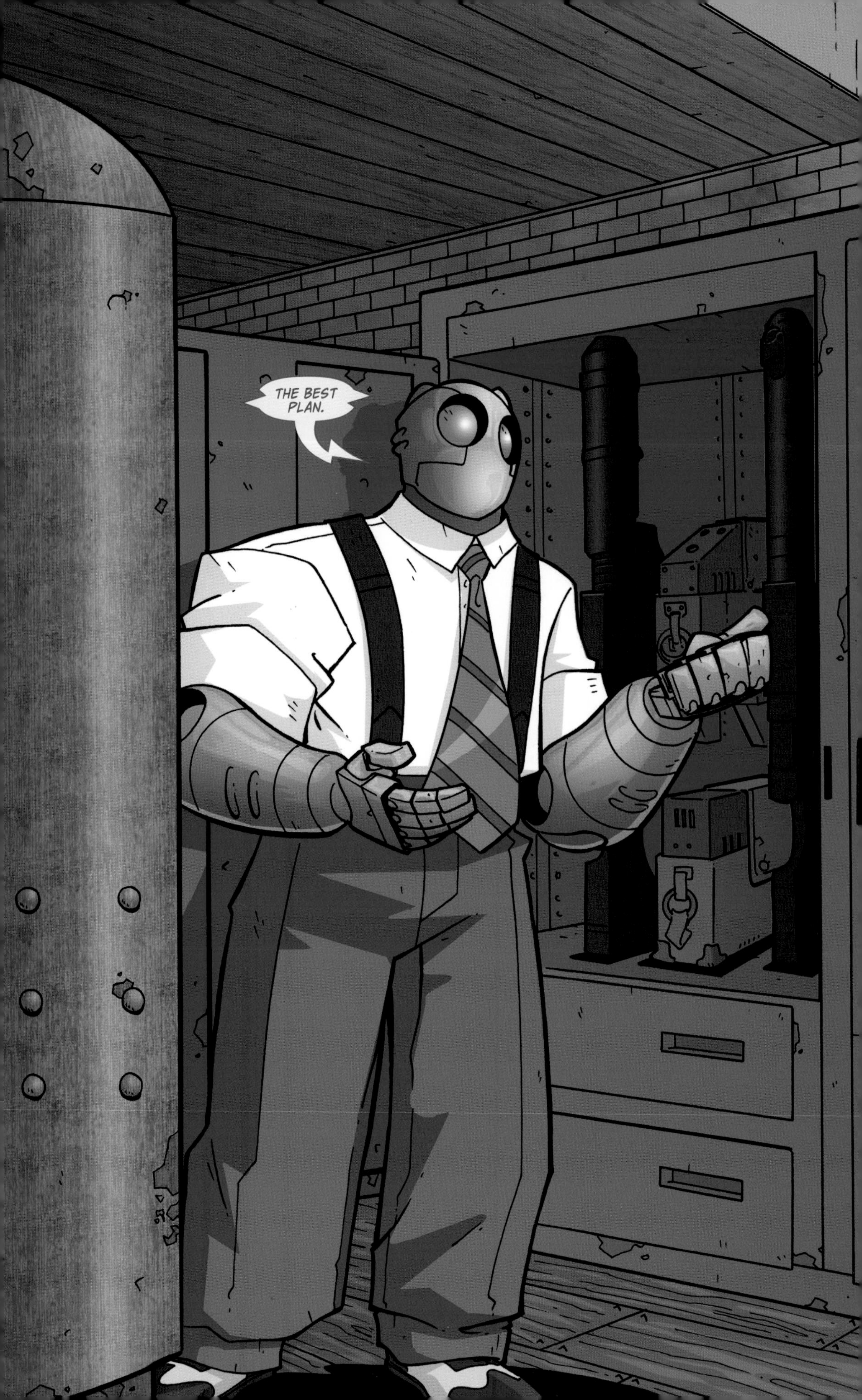
THE BEST PLAN.

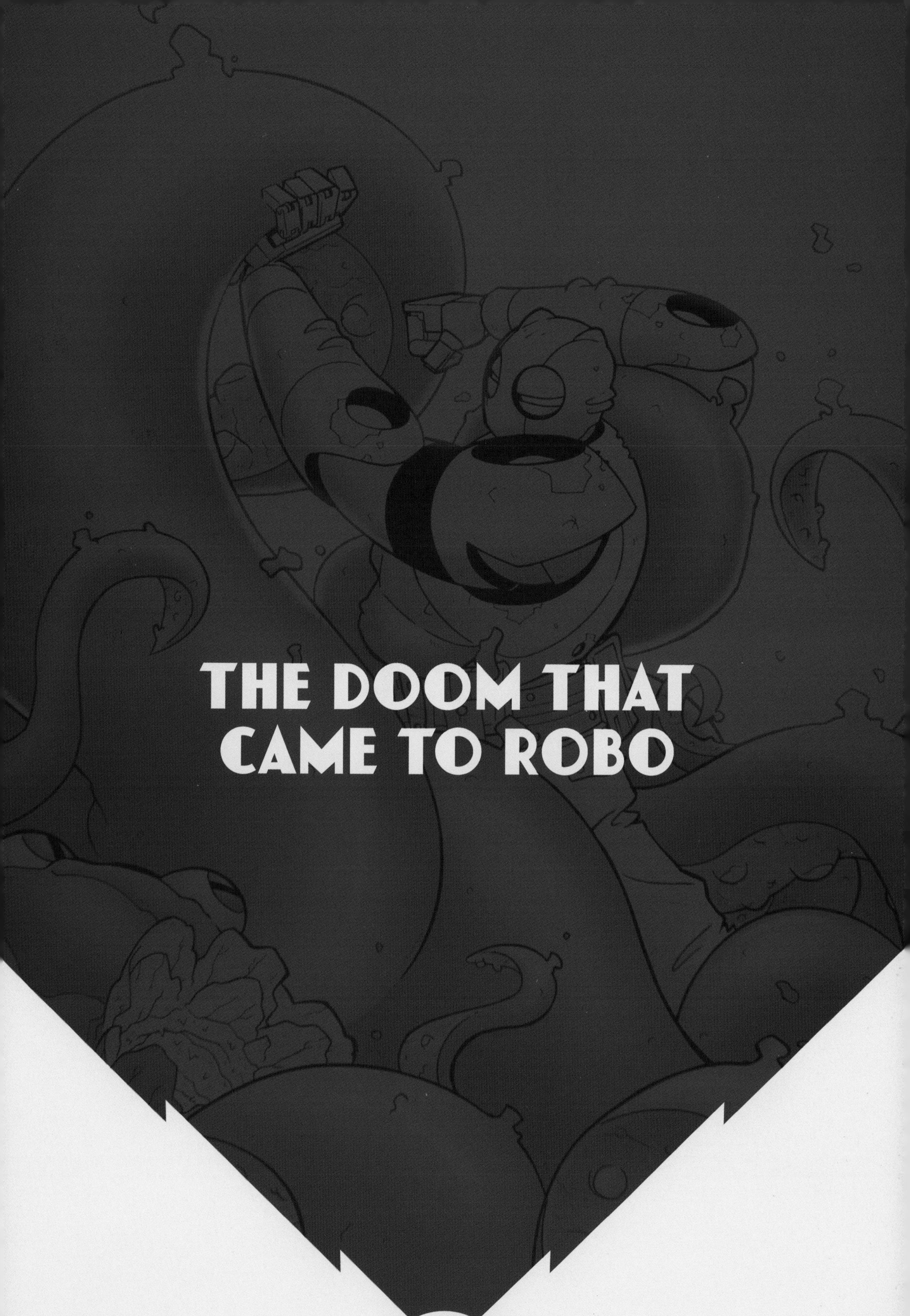

THE DOOM THAT CAME TO ROBO

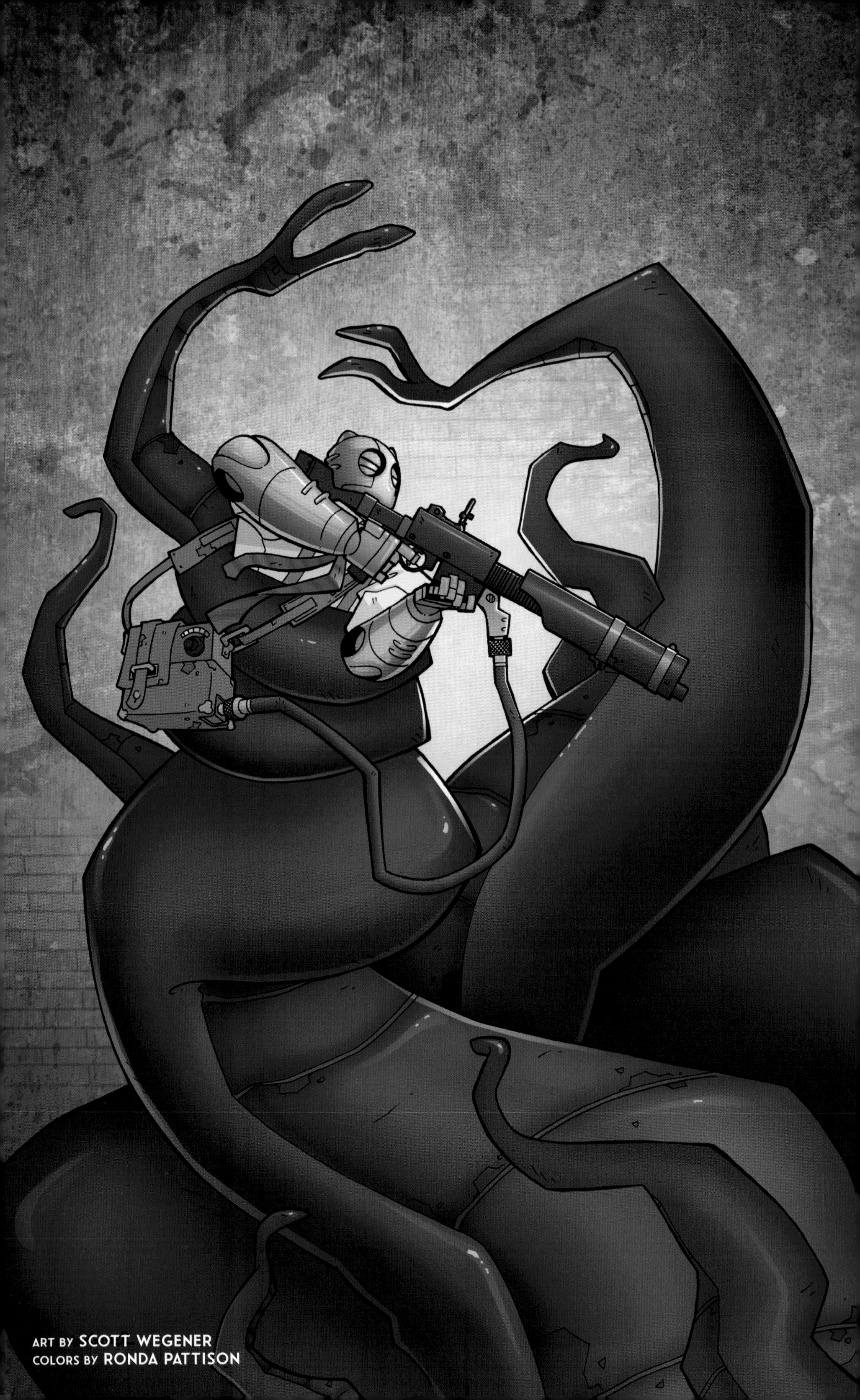

ART BY SCOTT WEGENER
COLORS BY RONDA PATTISON

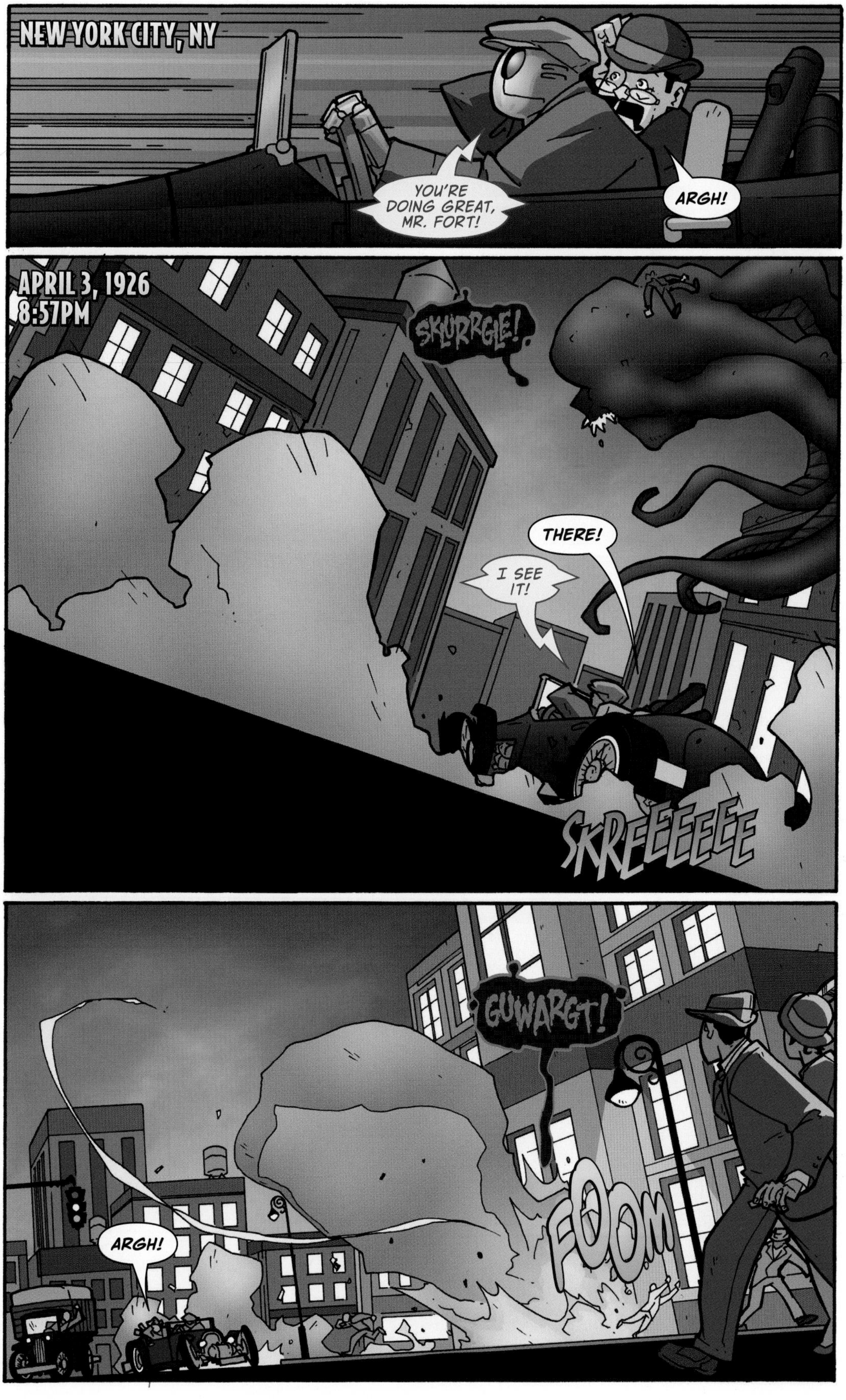
NEW YORK CITY, NY
YOU'RE DOING GREAT, MR. FORT!
ARGH!
APRIL 3, 1926
8:57PM
SKLURRGLE!
I SEE IT!
THERE!
SKREEEEEE
GUWARGT!
FOOM
ARGH!

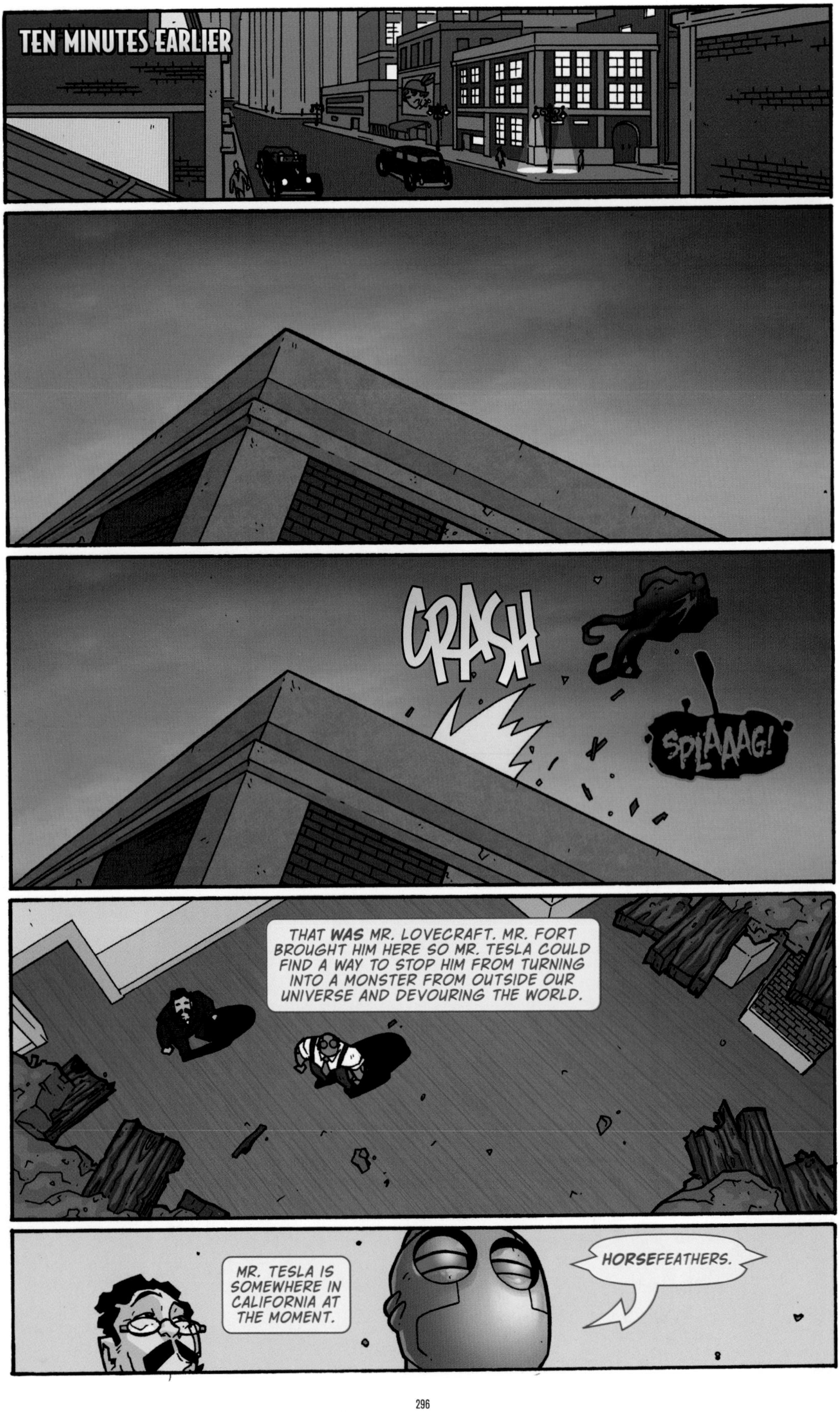
TEN MINUTES EARLIER
CRASH
SPLAAAG!
THAT WAS MR. LOVECRAFT. MR. FORT BROUGHT HIM HERE SO MR. TESLA COULD FIND A WAY TO STOP HIM FROM TURNING INTO A MONSTER FROM OUTSIDE OUR UNIVERSE AND DEVOURING THE WORLD.
MR. TESLA IS SOMEWHERE IN CALIFORNIA AT THE MOMENT.
HORSEFEATHERS.

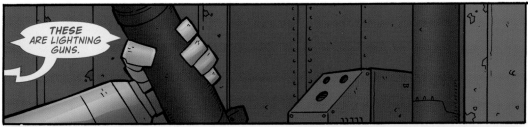

THESE ARE LIGHTNING GUNS.

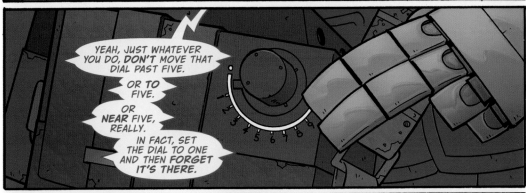

THEY COLLECT ELECTRIC CHARGES FROM THE AIR AND BOOST THEM TO *OBSCENELY* DANGEROUS LEVELS THROUGH AN EVEN *MORE* DANGEROUS PROCESS. NOTHING UNUSUAL.

I SAY, A PORTABLE WARDENCLYFFE!

YEAH, JUST WHATEVER YOU DO, *DON'T* MOVE THAT DIAL PAST FIVE.

OR *TO* FIVE.

OR *NEAR* FIVE, REALLY.

IN FACT, SET THE DIAL TO ONE AND THEN *FORGET* IT'S THERE.

IS THIS ENTIRELY SAFE?

NO. NOT EVEN A LITTLE.

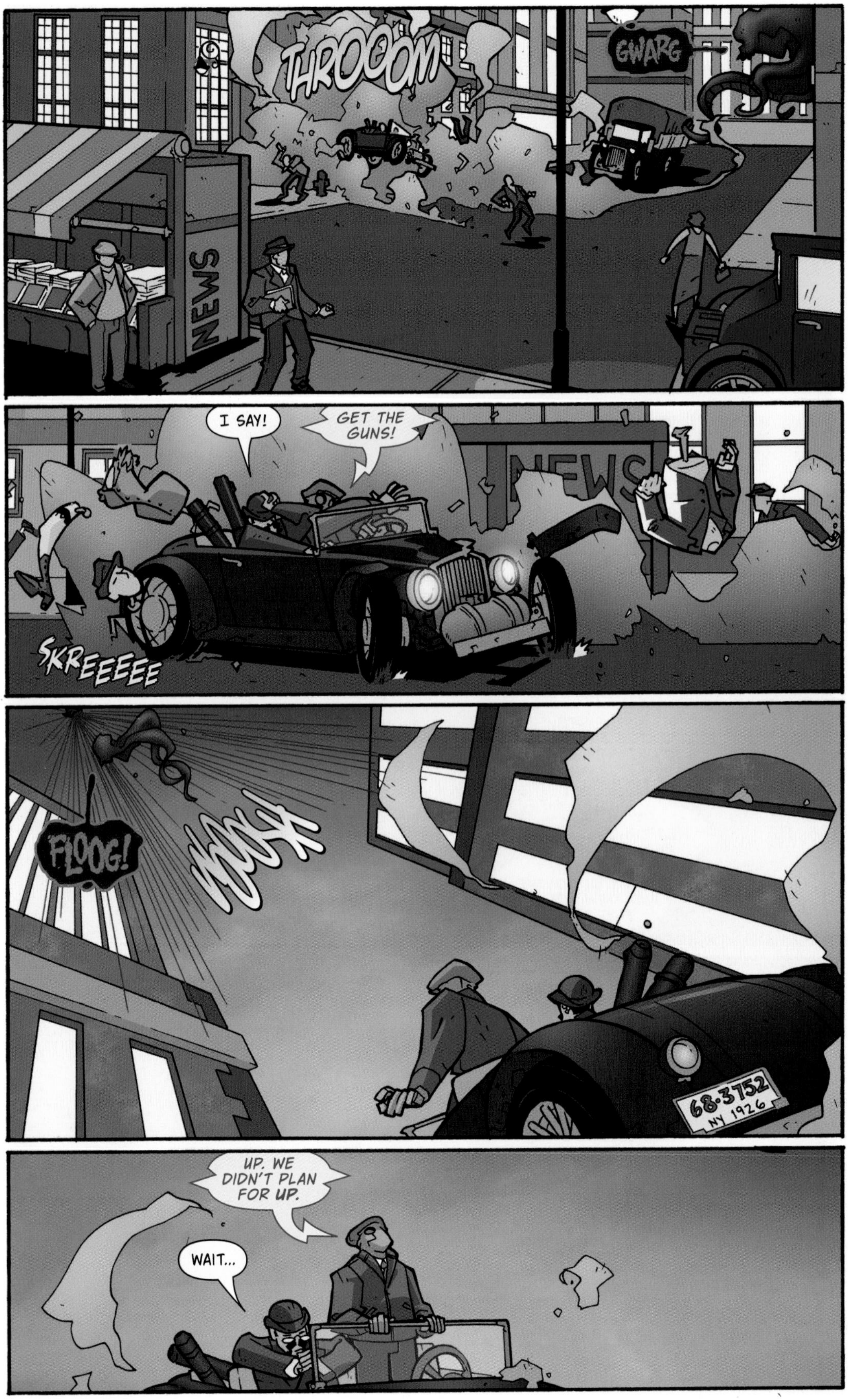
THROOOM
GWARG
NEWS
I SAY!
GET THE GUNS!
NEWS
SKREEEEEE
FLOOG!
68-3752 NY 1926
UP. WE DIDN'T PLAN FOR UP.
WAIT...

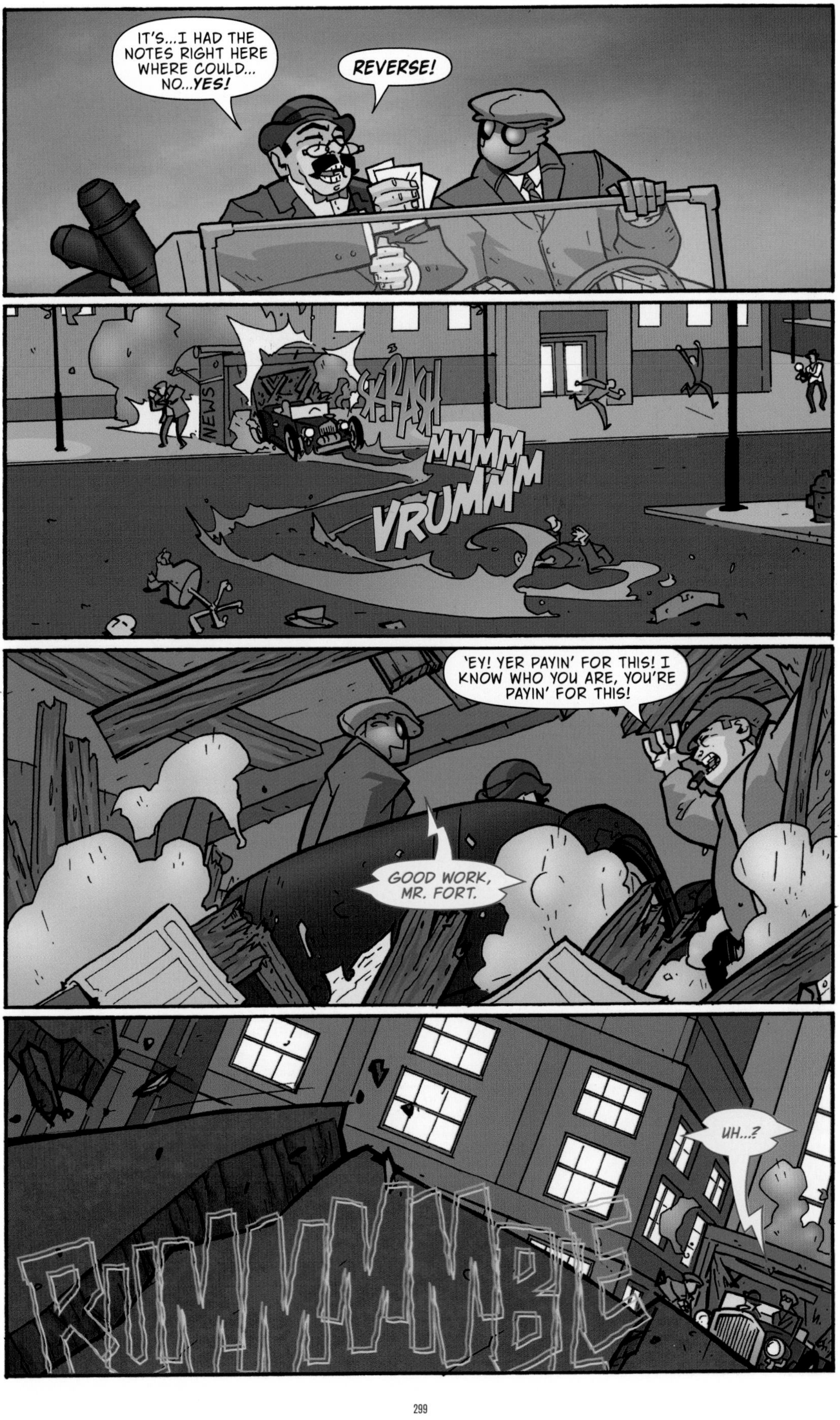
IT'S...I HAD THE NOTES RIGHT HERE WHERE COULD... NO...YES!
REVERSE!
SKRASH
MMMMM
VRUMMM
'EY! YER PAYIN' FOR THIS! I KNOW WHO YOU ARE, YOU'RE PAYIN' FOR THIS!
GOOD WORK, MR. FORT.
UH...?
RUMMMBLE

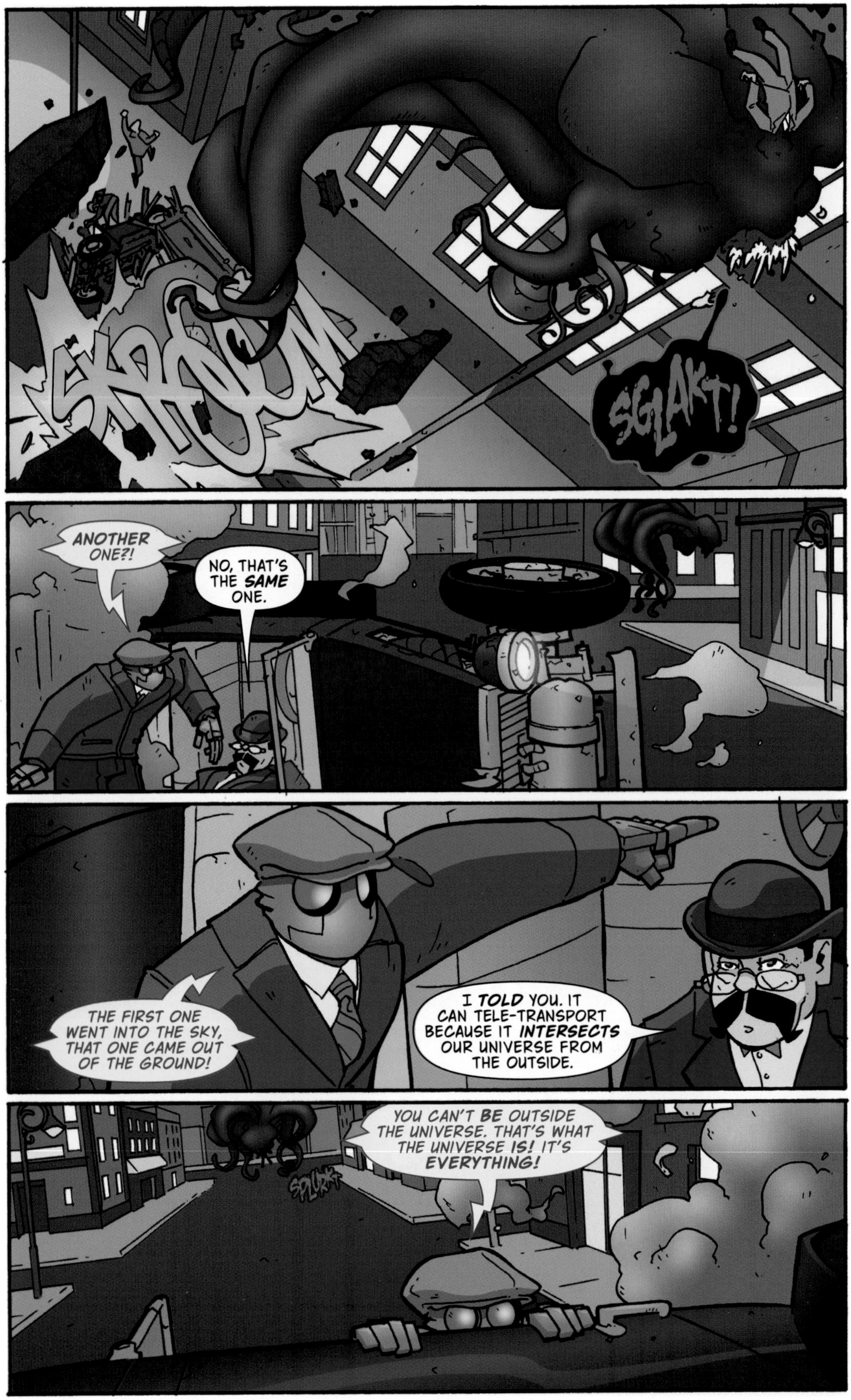
SGLAKT!
ANOTHER ONE?!
NO, THAT'S THE **SAME** ONE.
THE FIRST ONE WENT INTO THE SKY, THAT ONE CAME OUT OF THE GROUND!
I **TOLD** YOU. IT CAN TELE-TRANSPORT BECAUSE IT **INTERSECTS** OUR UNIVERSE FROM THE OUTSIDE.
YOU CAN'T **BE** OUTSIDE THE UNIVERSE. THAT'S WHAT THE UNIVERSE **IS!** IT'S **EVERYTHING!**

OUR PEDESTRIAN ACCOUNTING OF SPACE AND TIME ARE MEANINGLESS TO IT.

WE NEED TO RETHINK OUR STRATEGY.

"*STRATEGY?* EVEN IF TESLA WERE HERE AND COULD STOP IT *AGAIN*, WE DON'T KNOW WHEN OR WHERE IT'LL COME BACK! IT'S *HOPELESS!* WE CAN ONLY HOPE TO *DELAY* IT."

"*BALONEY.* YOU FIGURED OUT ITS APPEARANCE OVER TUNGUSKA *AND* YOU FIGURED OUT IT WAS BACK NOW."

FWAARG

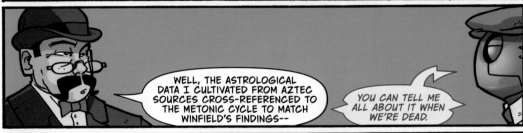

WELL, THE ASTROLOGICAL DATA I CULTIVATED FROM AZTEC SOURCES CROSS-REFERENCED TO THE METONIC CYCLE TO MATCH WINFIELD'S FINDINGS--

YOU CAN TELL ME ALL ABOUT IT WHEN WE'RE DEAD.

HIGHLY UNLIKELY, EDISON WOULD *NEVER* ALLOW THE LIKES OF YOU OR I NEAR HIS NECROPHONE.

THE *POINT* IS THAT WE'VE GOT A PREDICTIVE MODEL. ALL WE NEED TO DO NOW IS TO MAKE IT PREDICT *SOONER.* WE CAN BEAT THIS THING.

WE'VE GOT LIGHTNING GUNS. WE CAN DO ANYTHING.

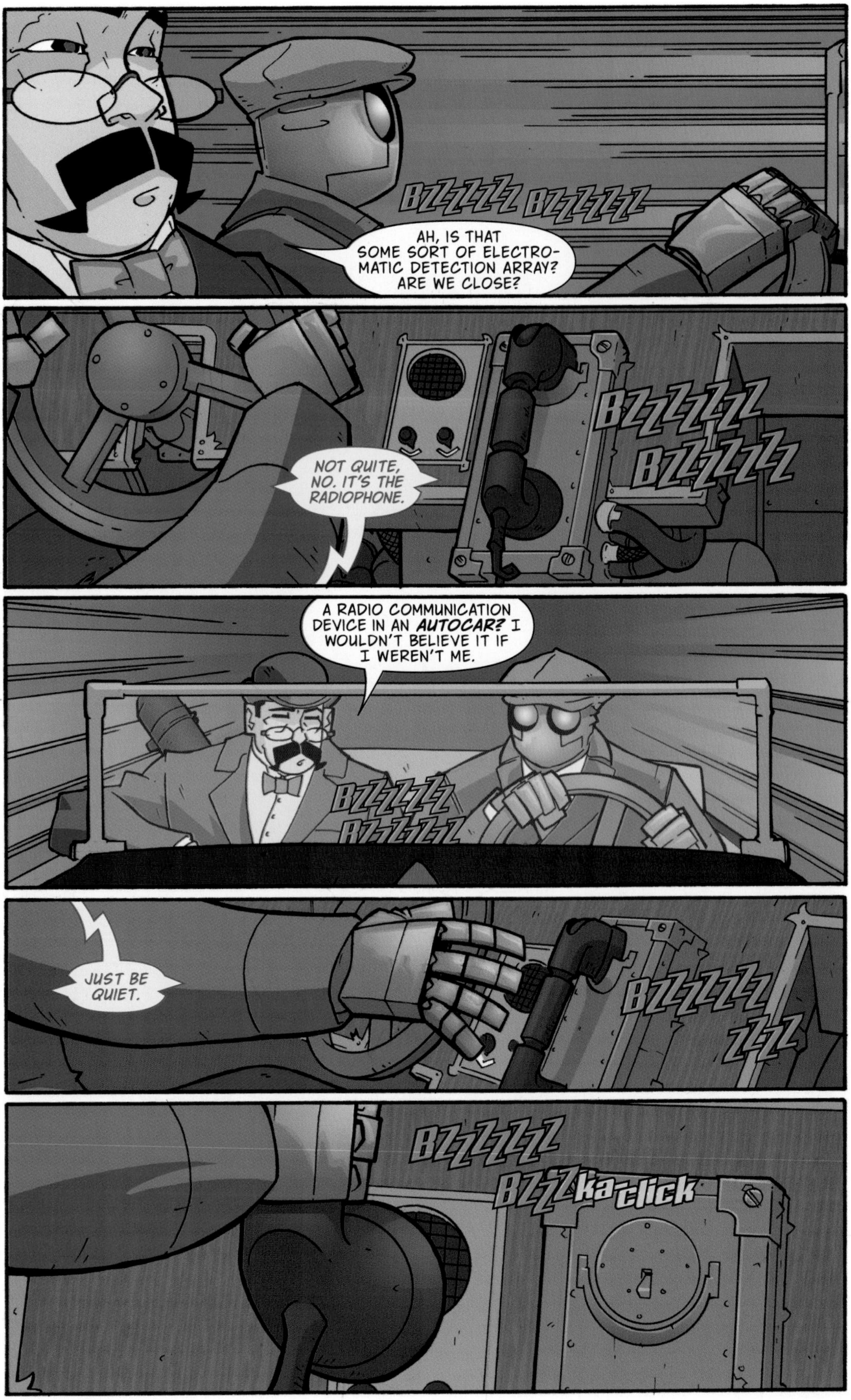
BZZZZZZ BZZZZZZ
AH, IS THAT SOME SORT OF ELECTROMATIC DETECTION ARRAY? ARE WE CLOSE?
BZZZZZZ BZZZZZZ
NOT QUITE, NO. IT'S THE RADIOPHONE.
A RADIO COMMUNICATION DEVICE IN AN AUTOCAR? I WOULDN'T BELIEVE IT IF I WEREN'T ME.
BZZZZZZ
JUST BE QUIET.
BZZZZZZ ZZZ
BZZZZZZ
BZZZ ka-click

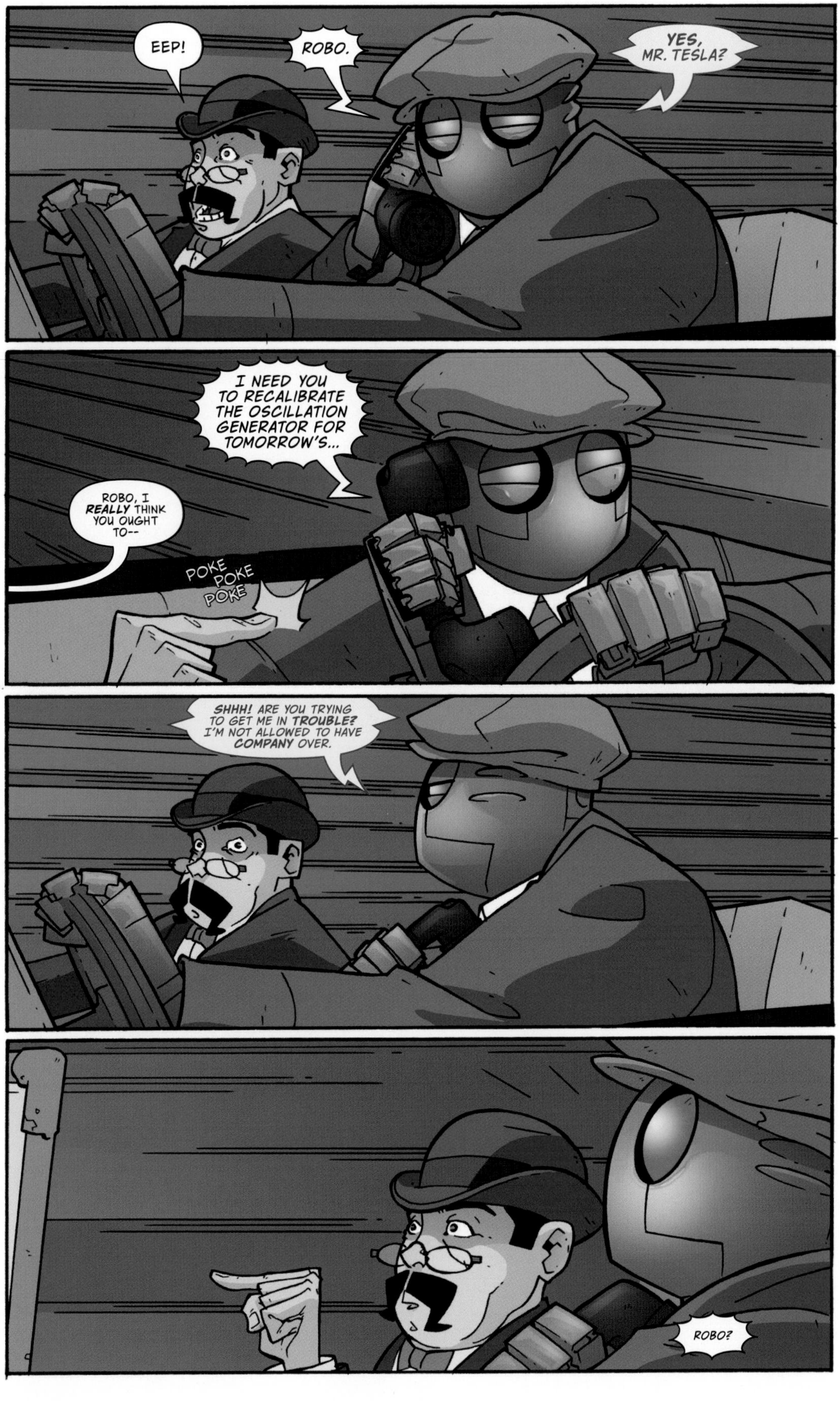
EEP!
ROBO.
YES, MR. TESLA?
I NEED YOU TO RECALIBRATE THE OSCILLATION GENERATOR FOR TOMORROW'S...
ROBO, I **REALLY** THINK YOU OUGHT TO--
POKE POKE POKE
SHHH! ARE YOU TRYING TO GET ME IN **TROUBLE?** I'M NOT ALLOWED TO HAVE **COMPANY** OVER.
ROBO?

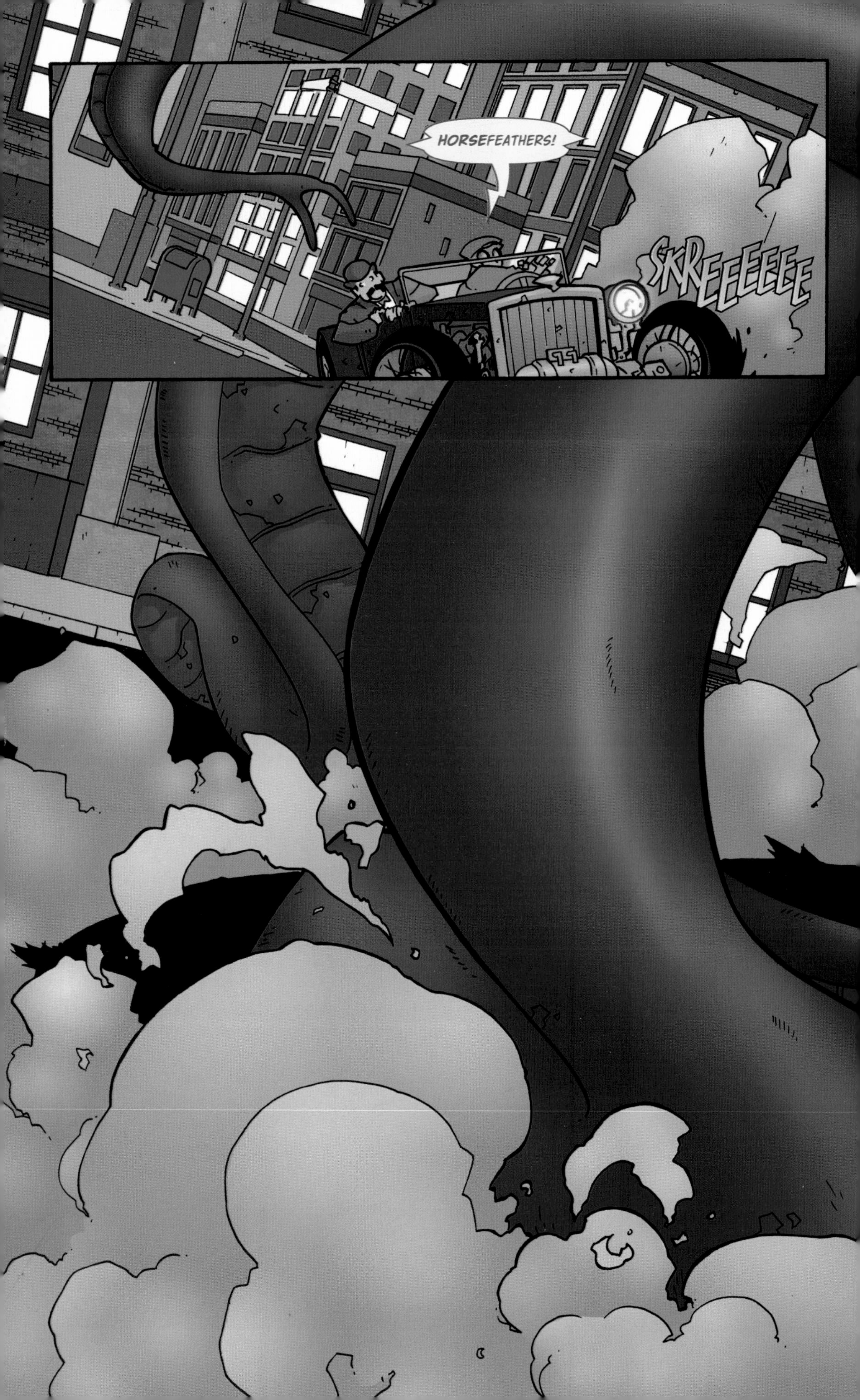
HORSEFEATHERS!
SKREEEEEEE

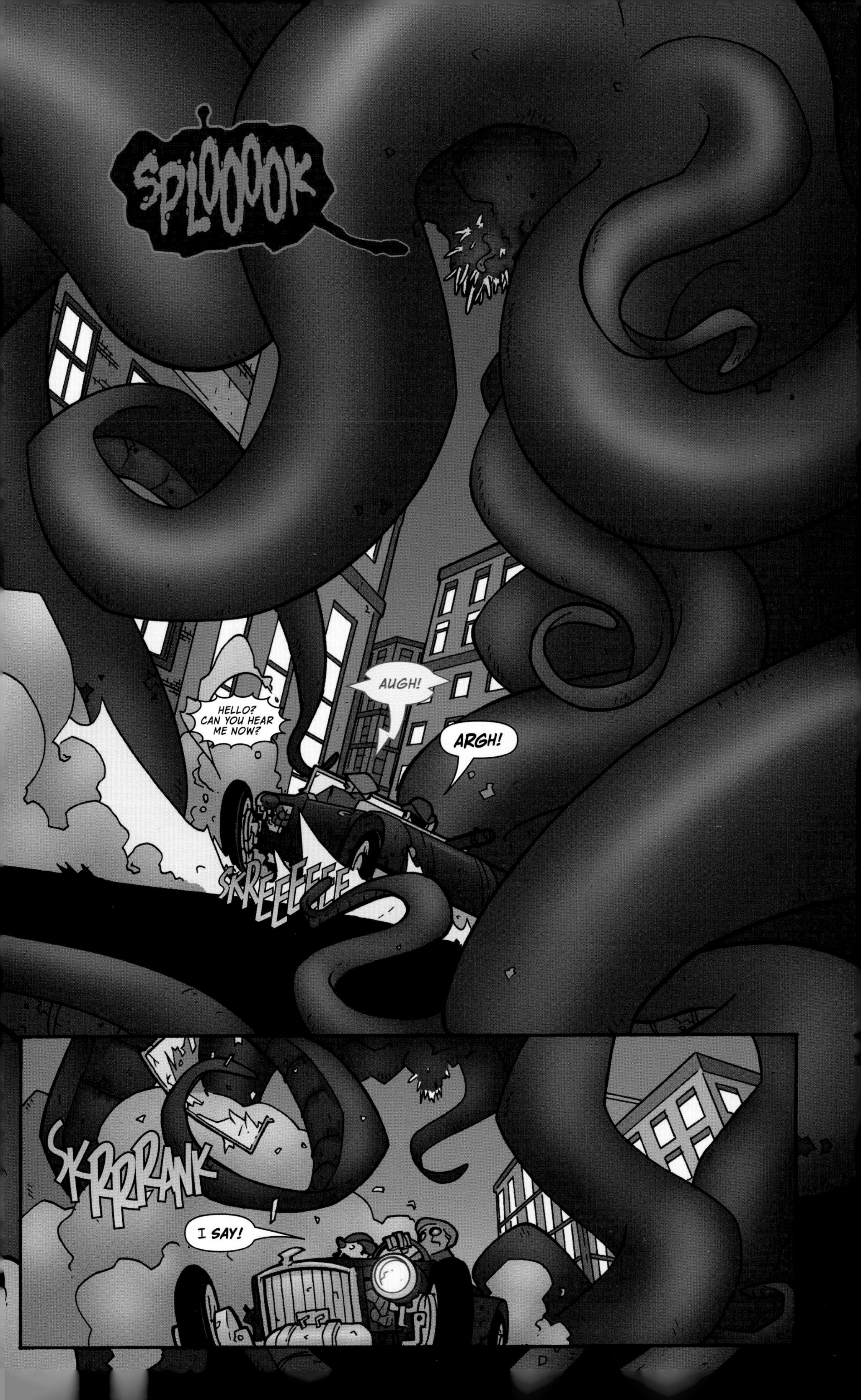
SPLOOOOK
HELLO? CAN YOU HEAR ME NOW?
AUGH!
ARGH!
SKREEEEEEE
SKRRRRANK
I SAY!

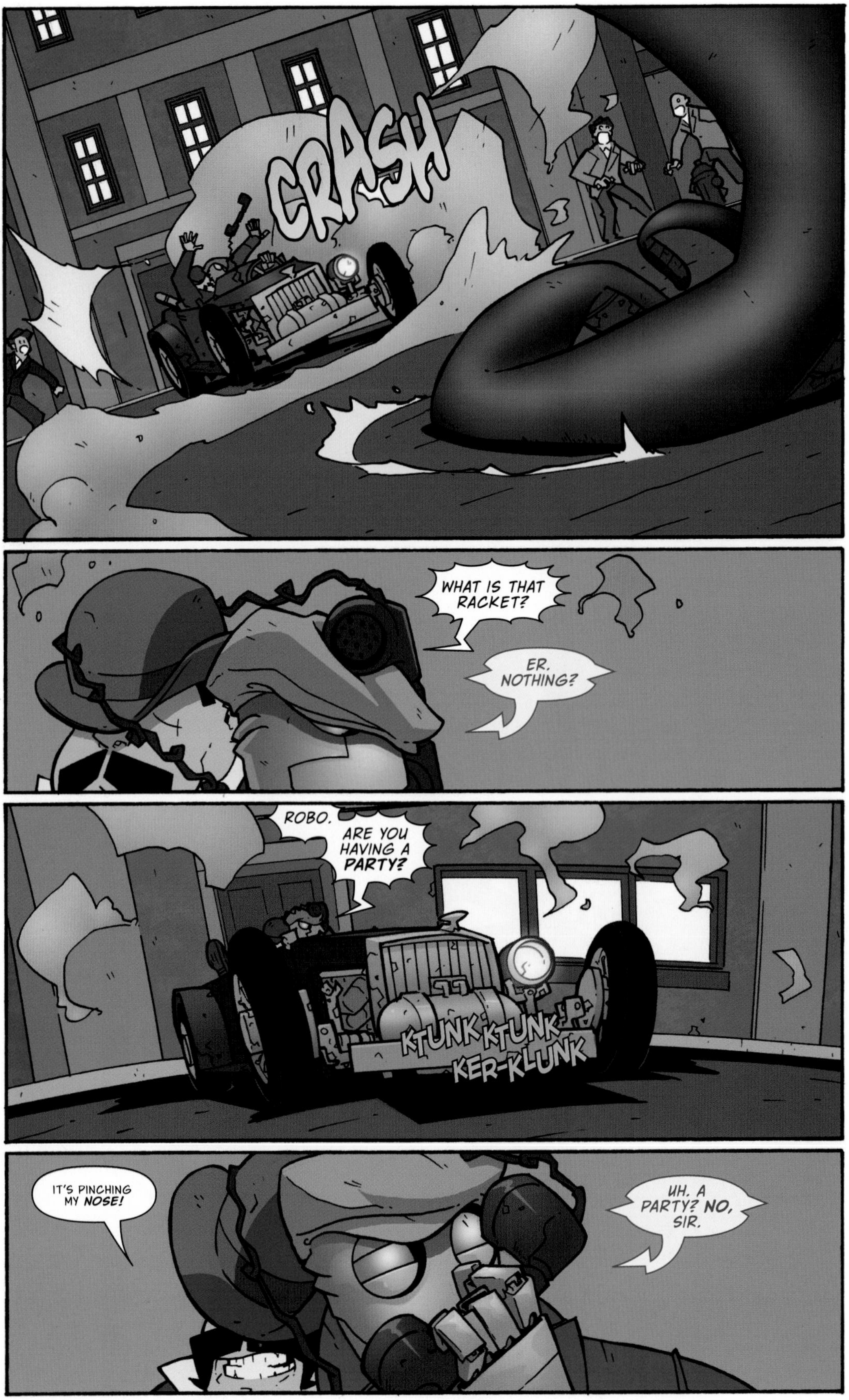
CRASH
WHAT IS THAT RACKET?
ER. NOTHING?
ROBO.
ARE YOU HAVING A **PARTY?**
KTUNK KTUNK KER-KLUNK
IT'S PINCHING MY **NOSE!**
UH. A PARTY? **NO,** SIR.

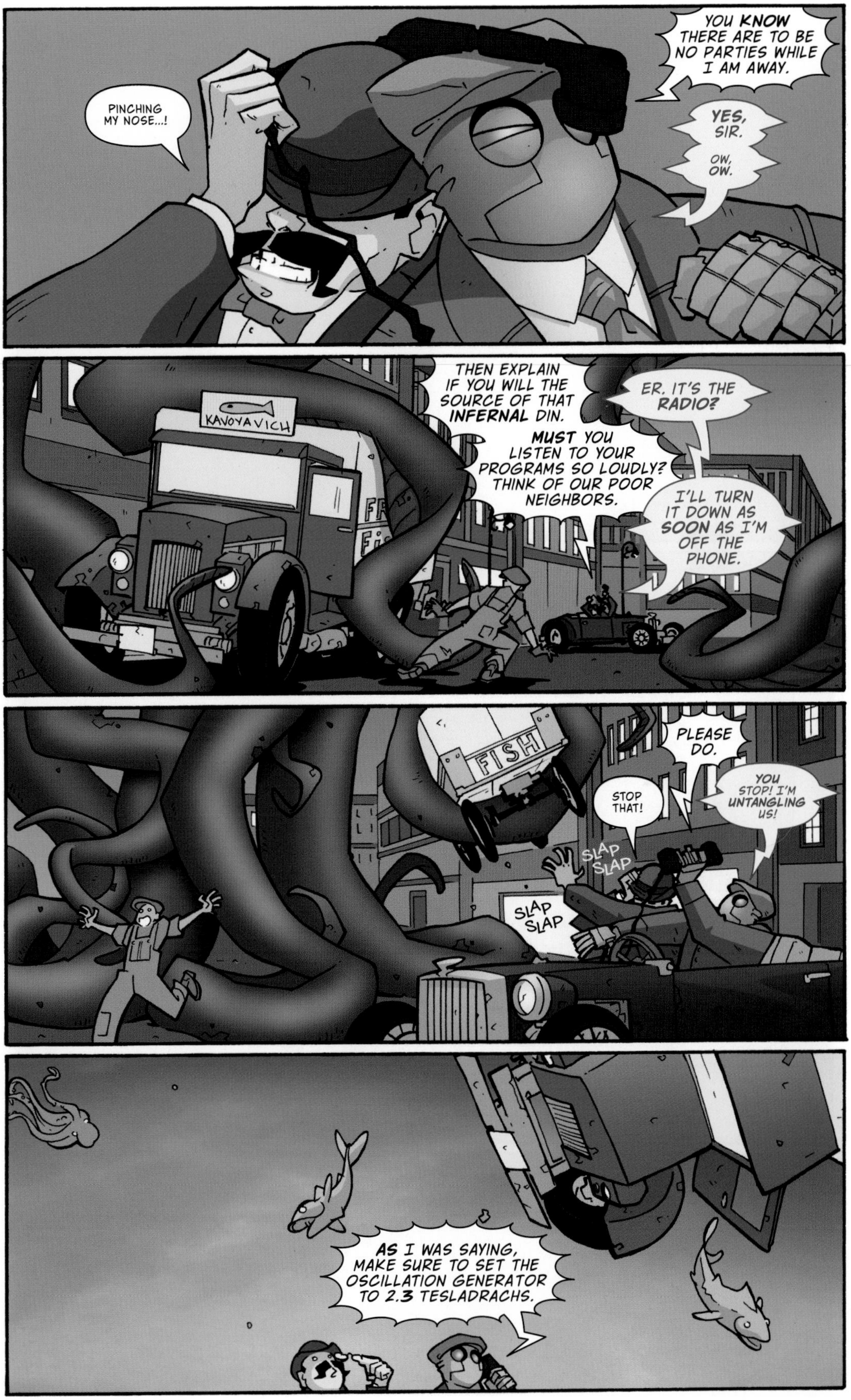

YOU KNOW THERE ARE TO BE NO PARTIES WHILE I AM AWAY.
PINCHING MY NOSE...!
YES, SIR.
OW, OW.
THEN EXPLAIN IF YOU WILL THE SOURCE OF THAT INFERNAL DIN.
ER. IT'S THE RADIO?
MUST YOU LISTEN TO YOUR PROGRAMS SO LOUDLY? THINK OF OUR POOR NEIGHBORS.
I'LL TURN IT DOWN AS SOON AS I'M OFF THE PHONE.
KAVOYAVICH
FISH
PLEASE DO.
STOP THAT!
YOU STOP! I'M UNTANGLING US!
SLAP SLAP
SLAP SLAP
AS I WAS SAYING, MAKE SURE TO SET THE OSCILLATION GENERATOR TO 2.3 TESLADRACHS.

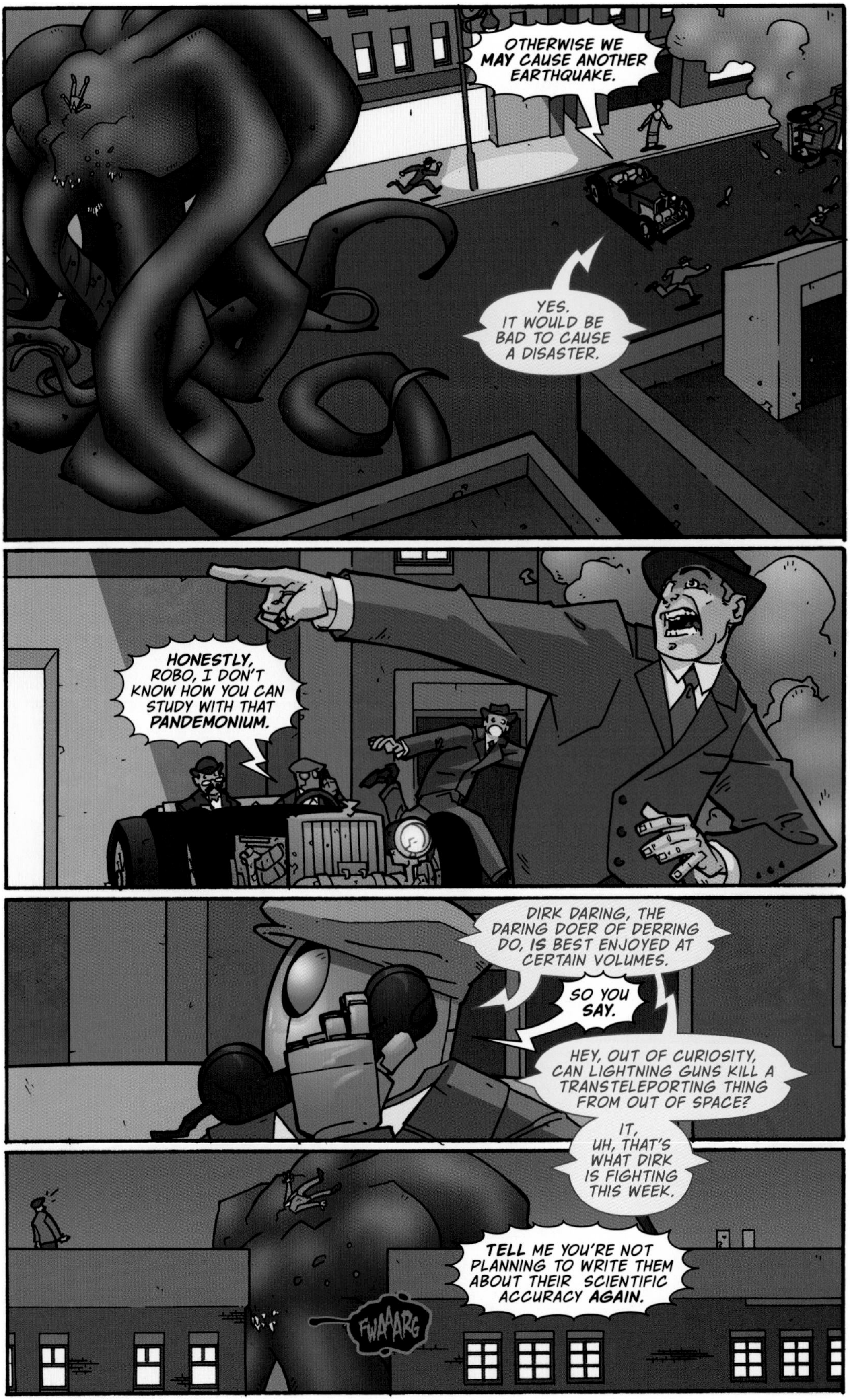
OTHERWISE WE MAY CAUSE ANOTHER EARTHQUAKE.
YES. IT WOULD BE BAD TO CAUSE A DISASTER.
HONESTLY, ROBO, I DON'T KNOW HOW YOU CAN STUDY WITH THAT PANDEMONIUM.
DIRK DARING, THE DARING DOER OF DERRING DO, IS BEST ENJOYED AT CERTAIN VOLUMES.
SO YOU SAY.
HEY, OUT OF CURIOSITY, CAN LIGHTNING GUNS KILL A TRANSTELEPORTING THING FROM OUT OF SPACE?
IT, UH, THAT'S WHAT DIRK IS FIGHTING THIS WEEK.
TELL ME YOU'RE NOT PLANNING TO WRITE THEM ABOUT THEIR SCIENTIFIC ACCURACY AGAIN.
FWAAARG

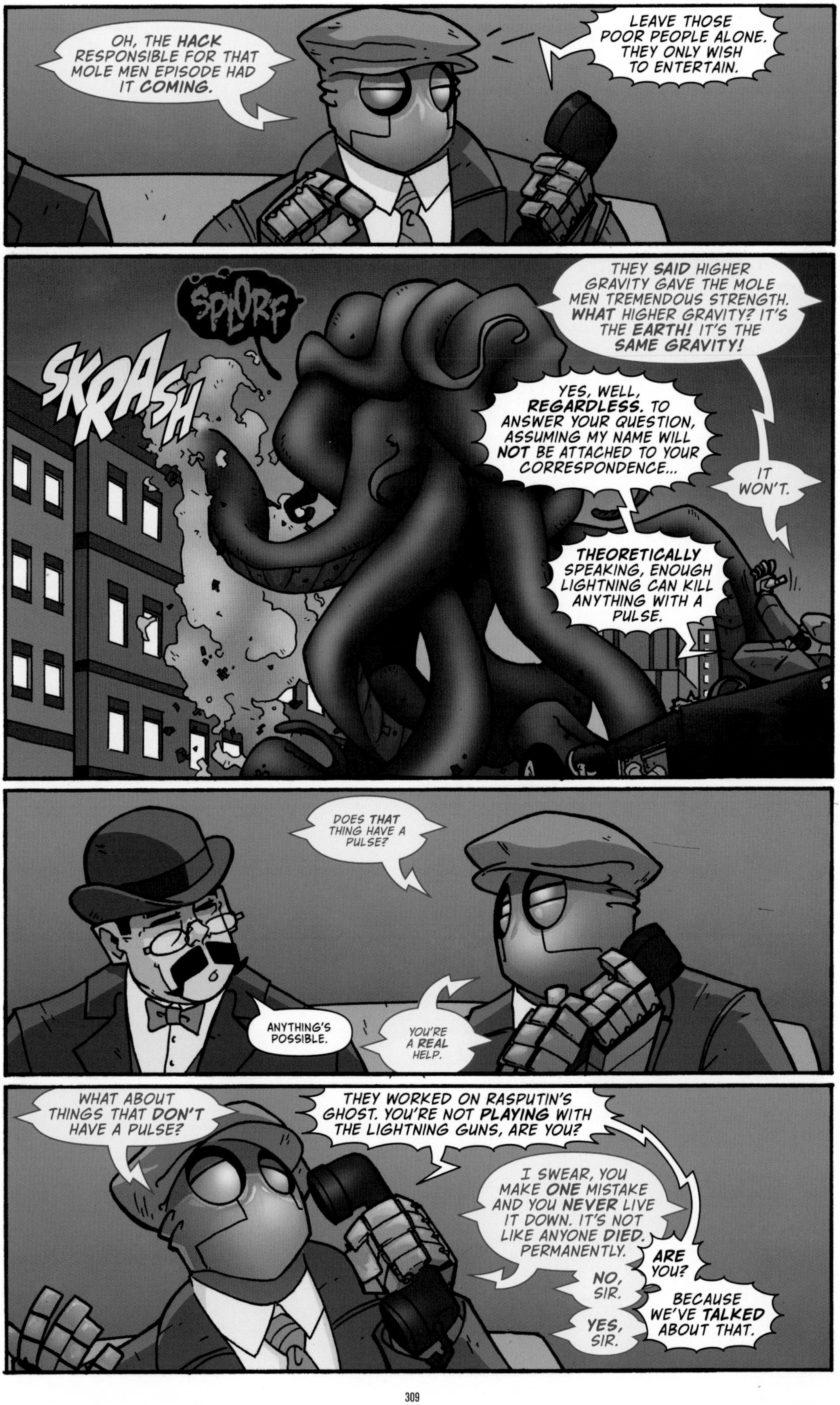

OH, THE HACK RESPONSIBLE FOR THAT MOLE MEN EPISODE HAD IT COMING.
LEAVE THOSE POOR PEOPLE ALONE. THEY ONLY WISH TO ENTERTAIN.
SPLORF
SKRASH
THEY SAID HIGHER GRAVITY GAVE THE MOLE MEN TREMENDOUS STRENGTH. WHAT HIGHER GRAVITY? IT'S THE EARTH! IT'S THE SAME GRAVITY!
YES, WELL, REGARDLESS. TO ANSWER YOUR QUESTION, ASSUMING MY NAME WILL NOT BE ATTACHED TO YOUR CORRESPONDENCE...
IT WON'T.
THEORETICALLY SPEAKING, ENOUGH LIGHTNING CAN KILL ANYTHING WITH A PULSE.
DOES THAT THING HAVE A PULSE?
ANYTHING'S POSSIBLE.
YOU'RE A REAL HELP.
WHAT ABOUT THINGS THAT DON'T HAVE A PULSE?
THEY WORKED ON RASPUTIN'S GHOST. YOU'RE NOT PLAYING WITH THE LIGHTNING GUNS, ARE YOU?
I SWEAR, YOU MAKE ONE MISTAKE AND YOU NEVER LIVE IT DOWN. IT'S NOT LIKE ANYONE DIED. PERMANENTLY.
NO, SIR.
ARE YOU?
BECAUSE WE'VE TALKED ABOUT THAT.
YES, SIR.

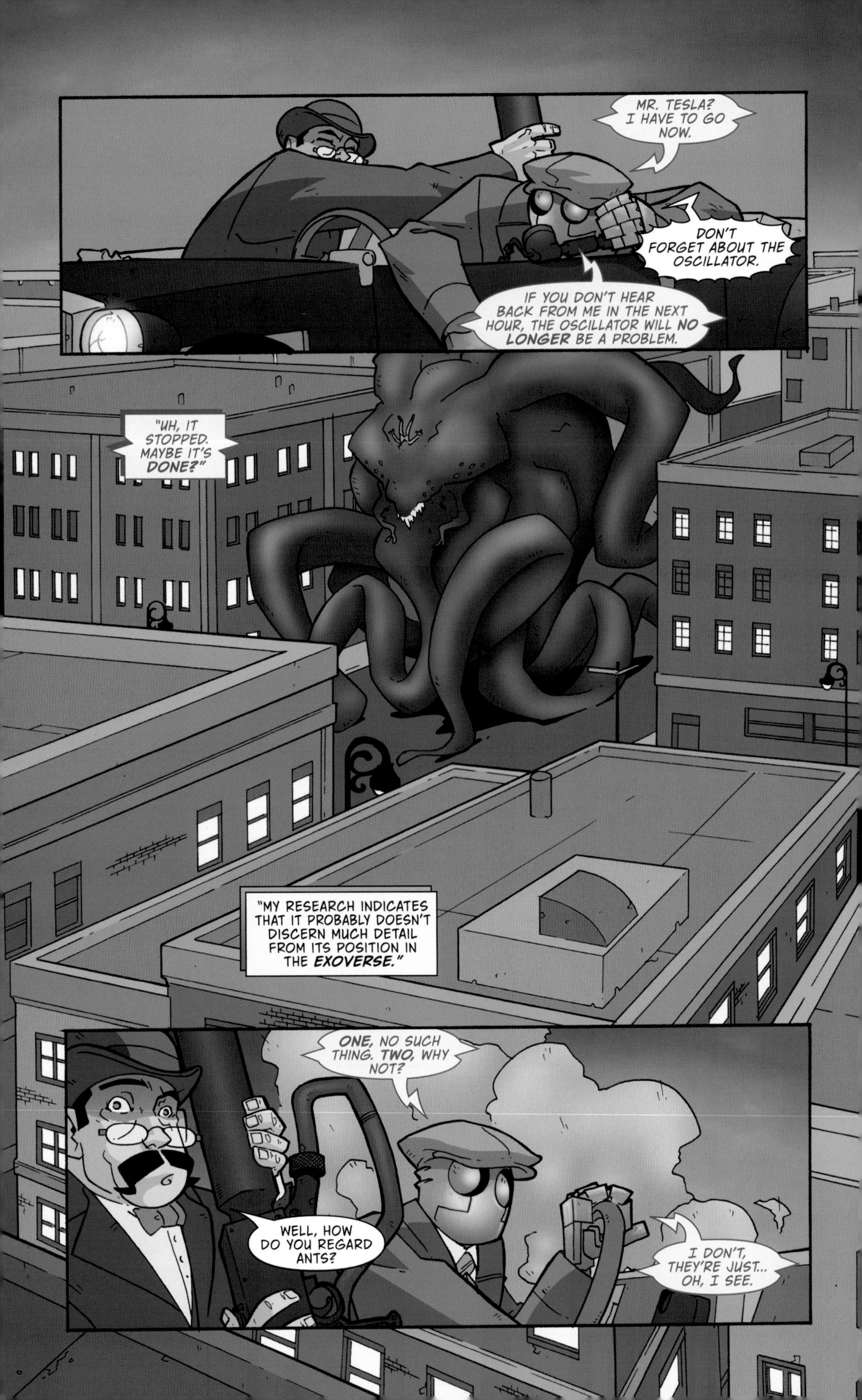
MR. TESLA? I HAVE TO GO NOW.
DON'T FORGET ABOUT THE OSCILLATOR.
IF YOU DON'T HEAR BACK FROM ME IN THE NEXT HOUR, THE OSCILLATOR WILL **NO LONGER** BE A PROBLEM.
"UH, IT STOPPED. MAYBE IT'S **DONE?**"
"MY RESEARCH INDICATES THAT IT PROBABLY DOESN'T DISCERN MUCH DETAIL FROM ITS POSITION IN THE **EXOVERSE.**"
ONE, NO SUCH THING. **TWO,** WHY NOT?
WELL, HOW DO YOU REGARD ANTS?
I DON'T, THEY'RE JUST... OH, I SEE.

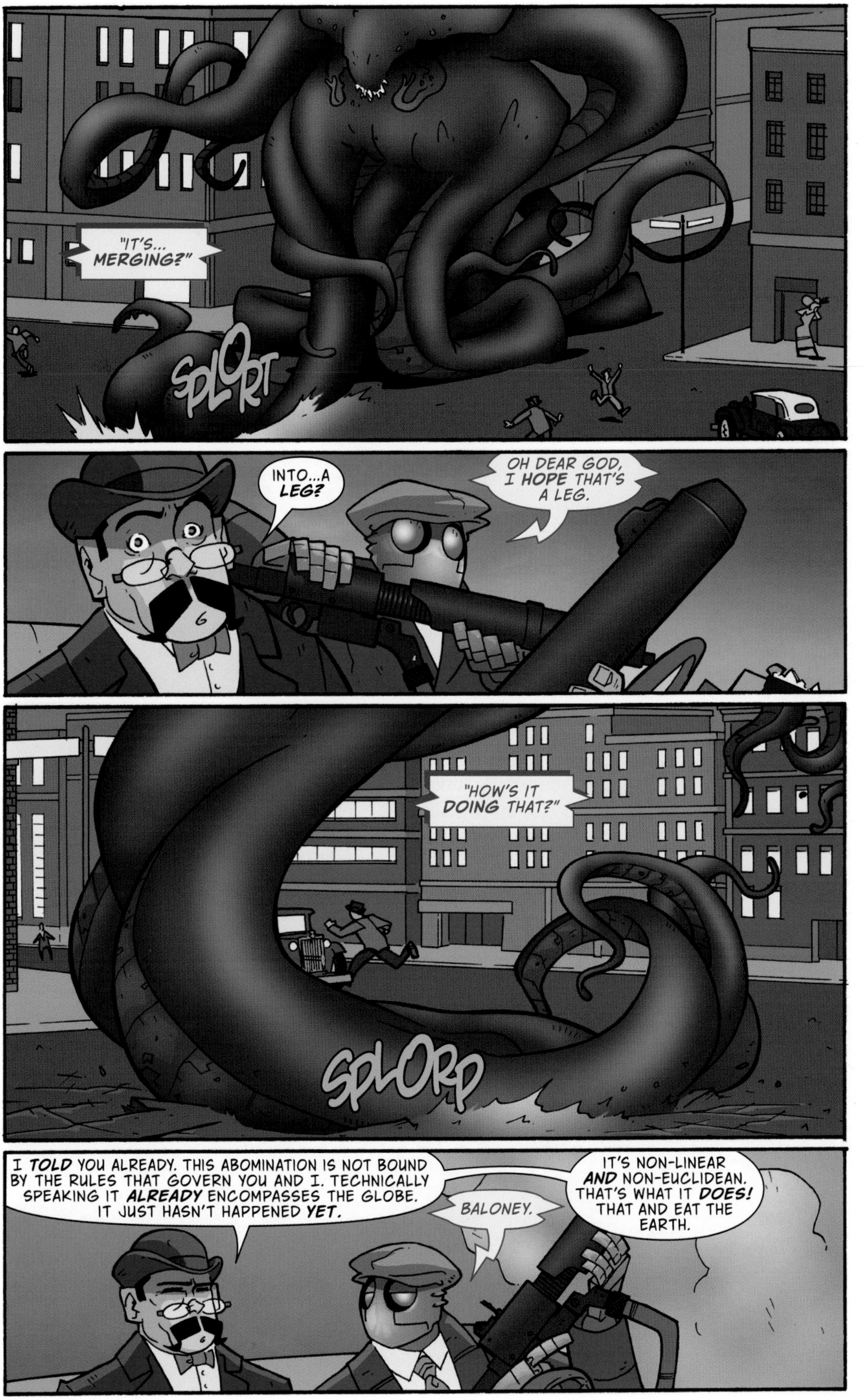
"IT'S... MERGING?"
SPLORT
INTO...A LEG?
OH DEAR GOD, I HOPE THAT'S A LEG.
"HOW'S IT DOING THAT?"
SPLORP
I TOLD YOU ALREADY. THIS ABOMINATION IS NOT BOUND BY THE RULES THAT GOVERN YOU AND I. TECHNICALLY SPEAKING IT ALREADY ENCOMPASSES THE GLOBE. IT JUST HASN'T HAPPENED YET.
BALONEY.
IT'S NON-LINEAR AND NON-EUCLIDEAN. THAT'S WHAT IT DOES! THAT AND EAT THE EARTH.

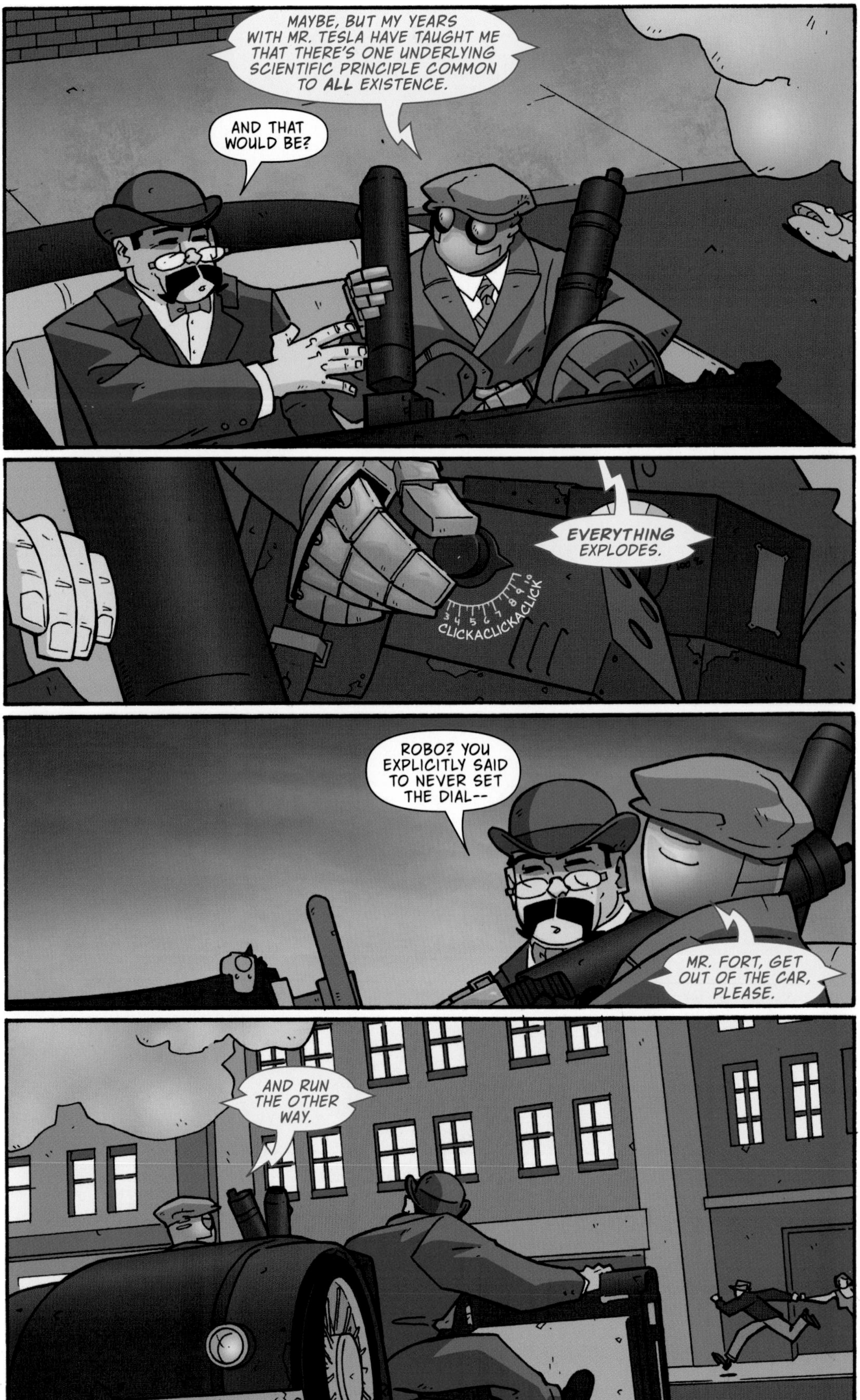
MAYBE, BUT MY YEARS WITH MR. TESLA HAVE TAUGHT ME THAT THERE'S ONE UNDERLYING SCIENTIFIC PRINCIPLE COMMON TO **ALL** EXISTENCE.
AND THAT WOULD BE?
EVERYTHING EXPLODES.
CLICKACLICKACLICK
ROBO? YOU EXPLICITLY SAID TO NEVER SET THE DIAL--
MR. FORT, GET OUT OF THE CAR, PLEASE.
AND RUN THE OTHER WAY.

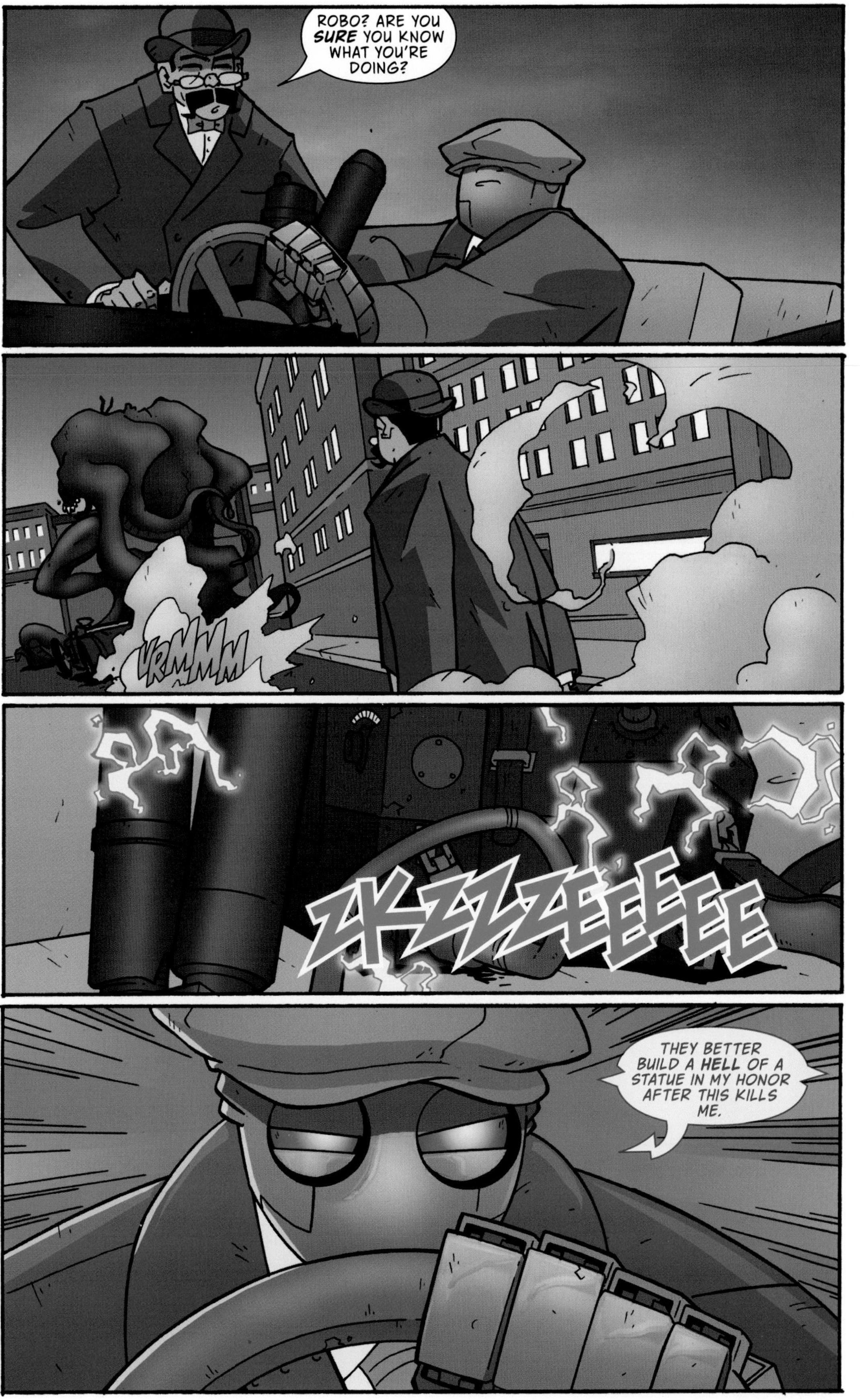
ROBO? ARE YOU SURE YOU KNOW WHAT YOU'RE DOING?
VRMMM
ZKZZZEEEEE
THEY BETTER BUILD A HELL OF A STATUE IN MY HONOR AFTER THIS KILLS ME.

RRRROHHHH
BOHHHH
DID YOU... JUST SAY MY NAME?

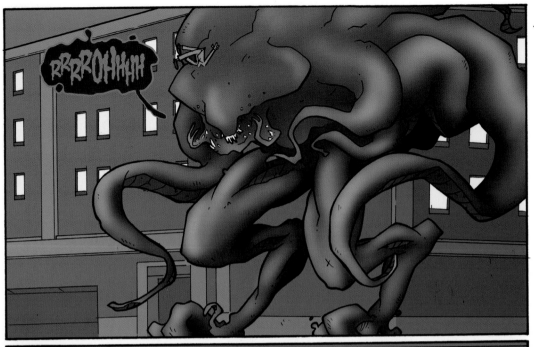

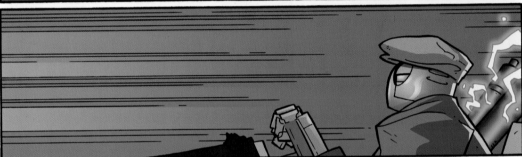

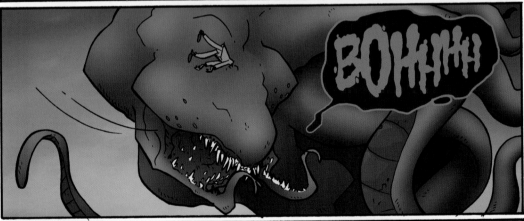

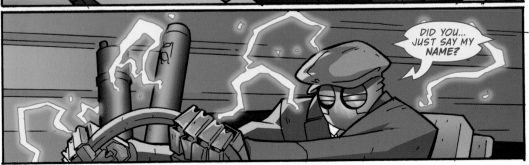

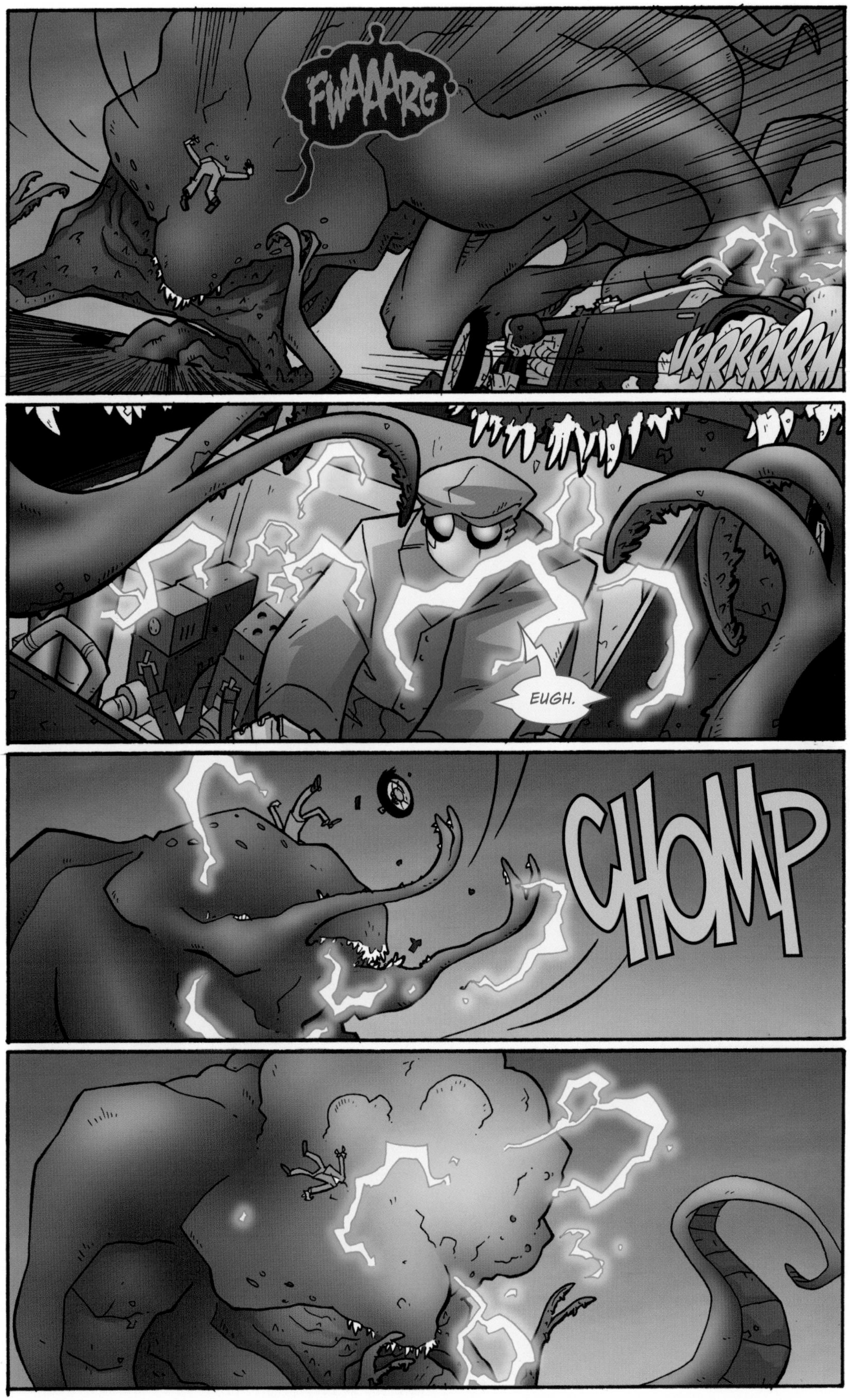
FWAAARG
URRRRRRM
EUGH.
CHOMP

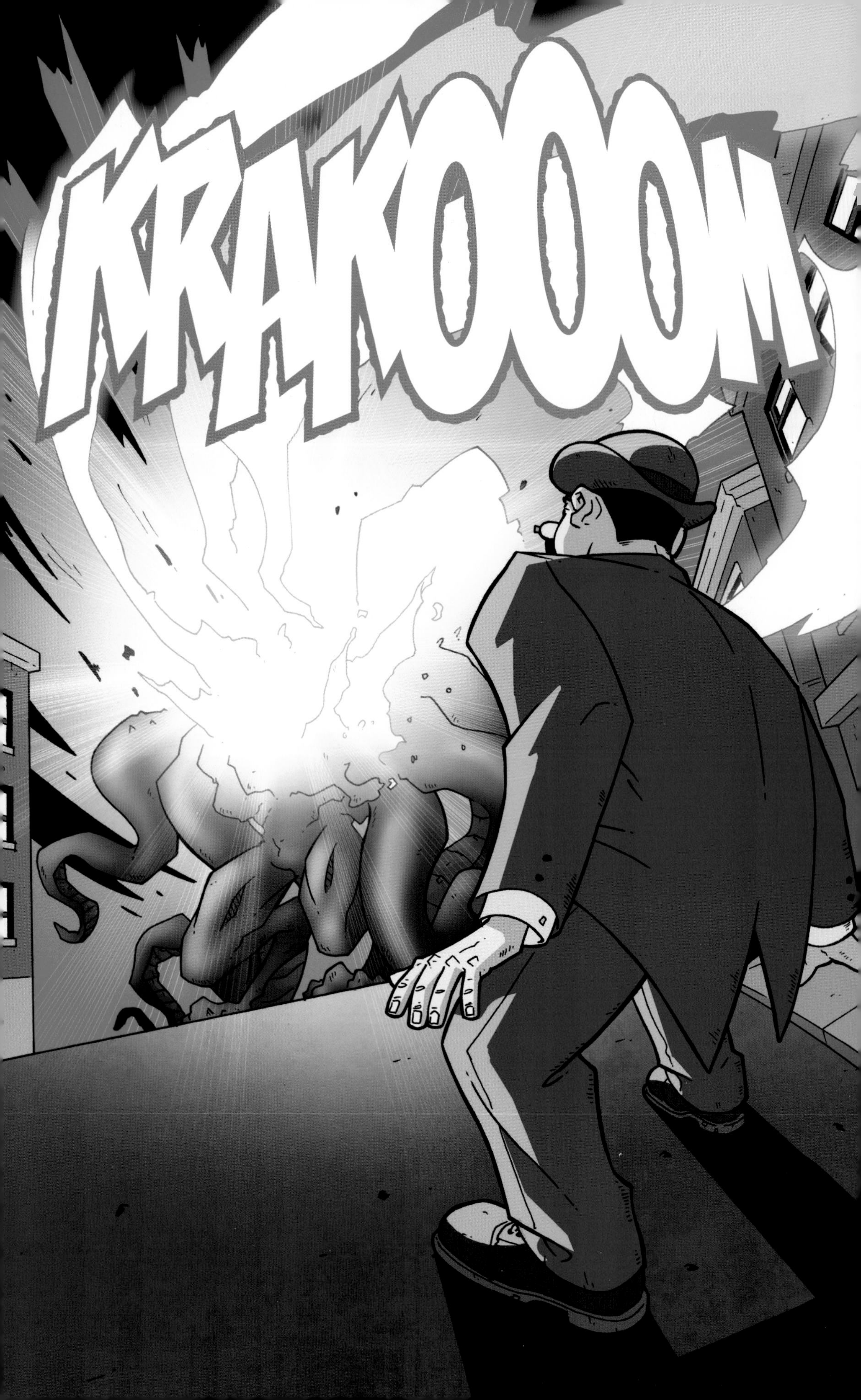
KRAKOOOM

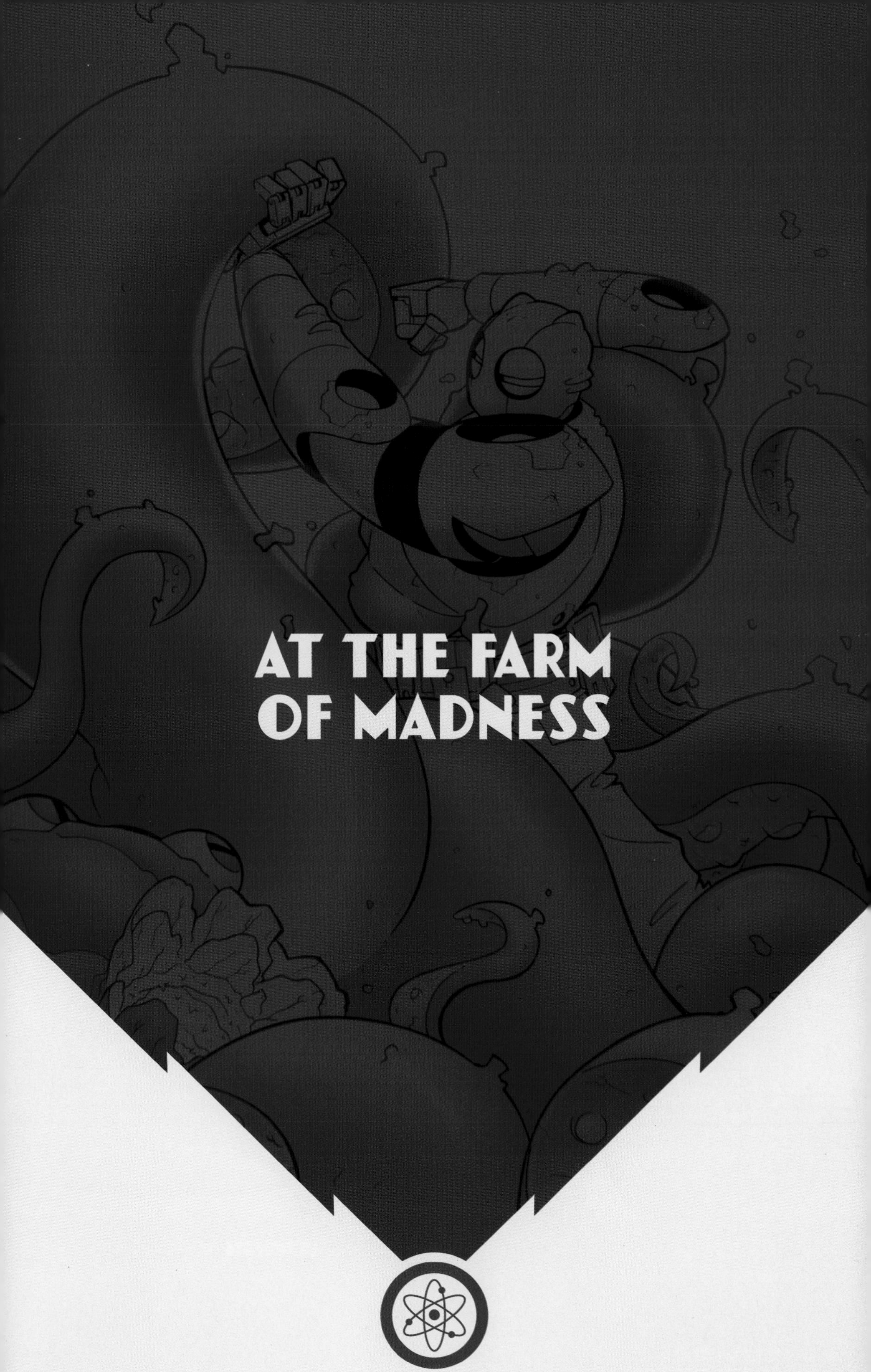

AT THE FARM OF MADNESS

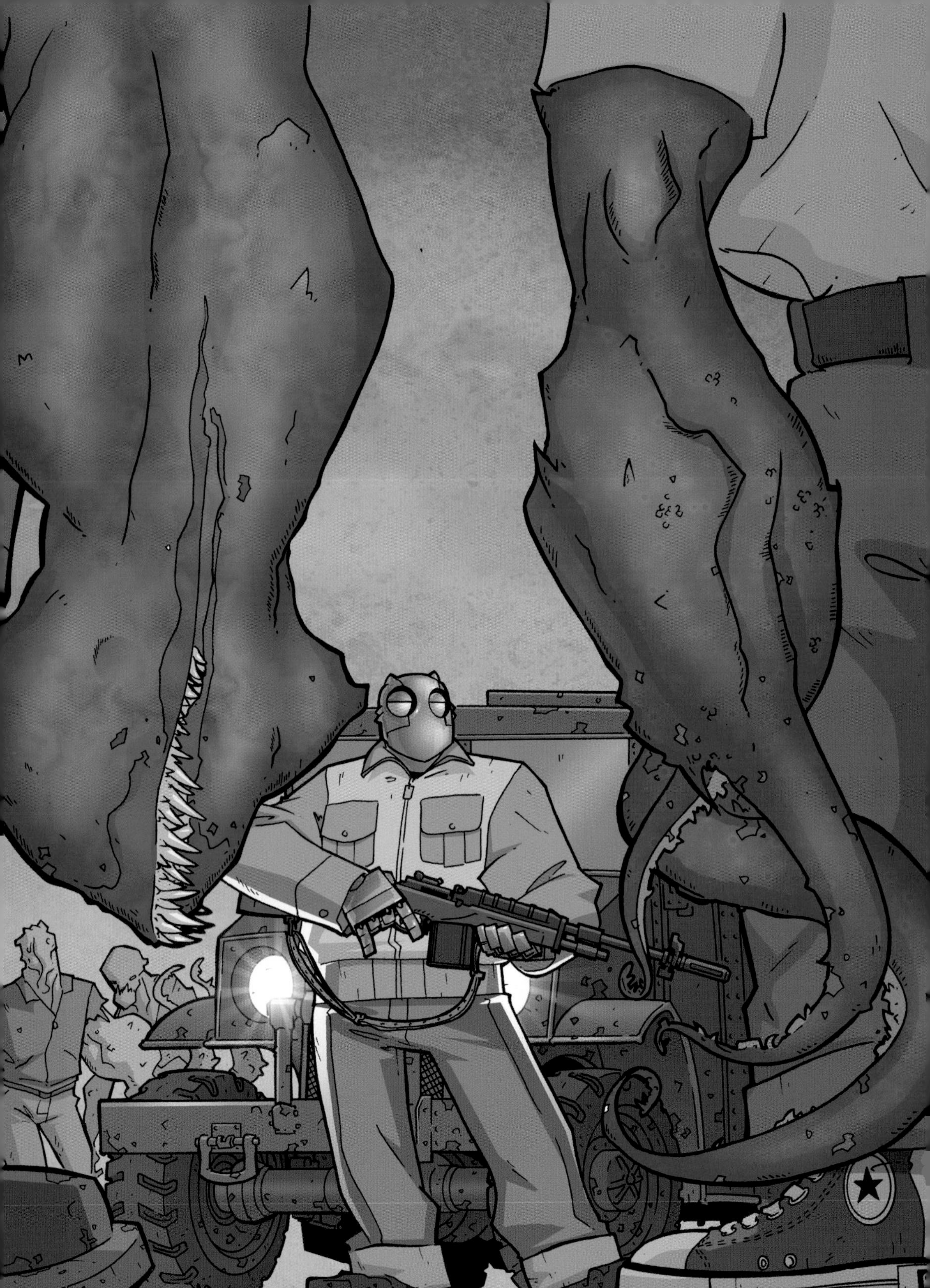

DECEMBER 9, 1957
NEW YORK CITY

THINK IT'S IMPORTANT?

IT *BETTER* BE. I LEFT THE DOUGLAS AIRCRAFT PEOPLE HIGH AND DRY FOR THIS.

THERE WENT *THAT* CONTRACT.

WHICH CRAZY IDEA WERE WE FAILING TO SELL THEM?

OH, DON'T WORRY. THEY WEREN'T BUYING IT ANYWAY.

THE *AIR SPIKE.*

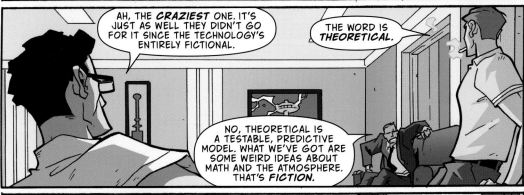

AH, THE *CRAZIEST* ONE. IT'S JUST AS WELL THEY DIDN'T GO FOR IT SINCE THE TECHNOLOGY'S ENTIRELY FICTIONAL.

THE WORD IS *THEORETICAL.*

NO, THEORETICAL IS A TESTABLE, PREDICTIVE MODEL. WHAT WE'VE GOT ARE SOME WEIRD IDEAS ABOUT MATH AND THE ATMOSPHERE. THAT'S *FICTION.*

CLOVERDALE!

WHAT'S A CLOVERDALE?

A TOWN IN OREGON.

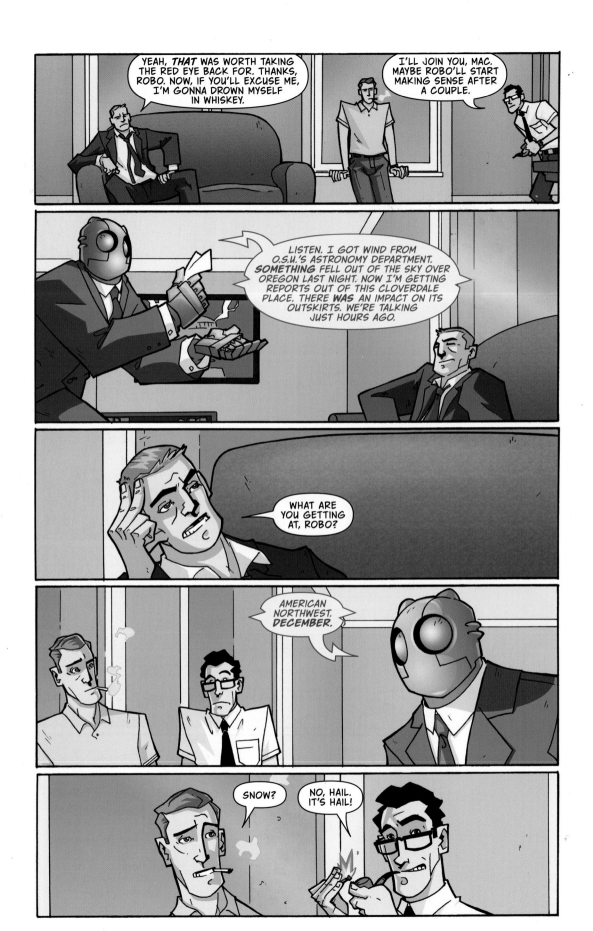

YEAH, *THAT* WAS WORTH TAKING THE RED EYE BACK FOR. THANKS, ROBO. NOW, IF YOU'LL EXCUSE ME, I'M GONNA DROWN MYSELF IN WHISKEY.

I'LL JOIN YOU, MAC. MAYBE ROBO'LL START MAKING SENSE AFTER A COUPLE.

LISTEN. I GOT WIND FROM O.S.U.'S ASTRONOMY DEPARTMENT. *SOMETHING* FELL OUT OF THE SKY OVER OREGON LAST NIGHT. NOW I'M GETTING REPORTS OUT OF THIS CLOVERDALE PLACE. THERE *WAS* AN IMPACT ON ITS OUTSKIRTS. WE'RE TALKING JUST HOURS AGO.

WHAT ARE YOU GETTING AT, ROBO?

AMERICAN NORTHWEST. *DECEMBER.*

SNOW?

NO, HAIL. IT'S HAIL!

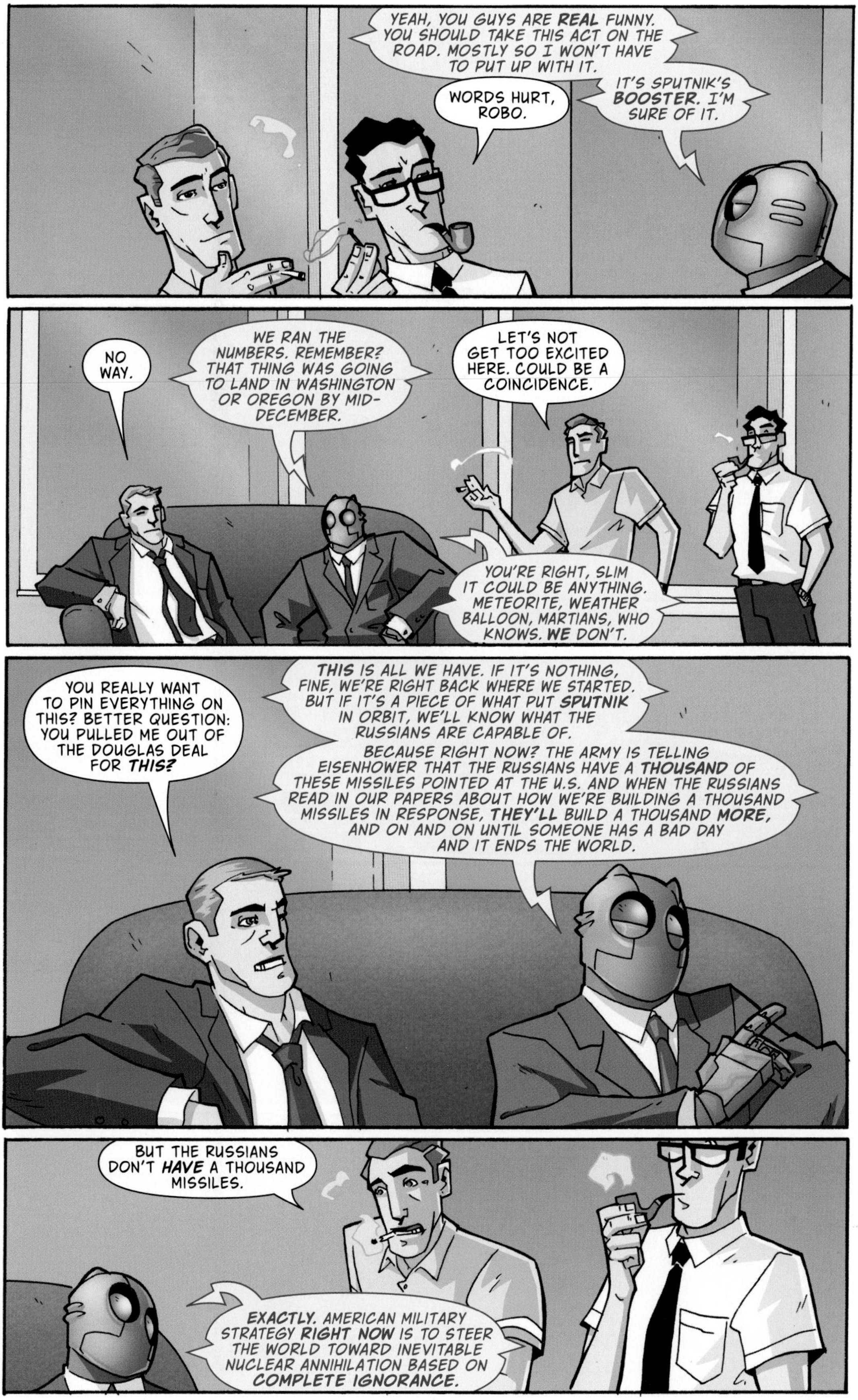

YEAH, YOU GUYS ARE REAL FUNNY. YOU SHOULD TAKE THIS ACT ON THE ROAD. MOSTLY SO I WON'T HAVE TO PUT UP WITH IT.
WORDS HURT, ROBO.
IT'S SPUTNIK'S BOOSTER. I'M SURE OF IT.
NO WAY.
WE RAN THE NUMBERS. REMEMBER? THAT THING WAS GOING TO LAND IN WASHINGTON OR OREGON BY MID-DECEMBER.
LET'S NOT GET TOO EXCITED HERE. COULD BE A COINCIDENCE.
YOU'RE RIGHT, SLIM IT COULD BE ANYTHING. METEORITE, WEATHER BALLOON, MARTIANS, WHO KNOWS. WE DON'T.
YOU REALLY WANT TO PIN EVERYTHING ON THIS? BETTER QUESTION: YOU PULLED ME OUT OF THE DOUGLAS DEAL FOR THIS?
THIS IS ALL WE HAVE. IF IT'S NOTHING, FINE, WE'RE RIGHT BACK WHERE WE STARTED. BUT IF IT'S A PIECE OF WHAT PUT SPUTNIK IN ORBIT, WE'LL KNOW WHAT THE RUSSIANS ARE CAPABLE OF.
BECAUSE RIGHT NOW? THE ARMY IS TELLING EISENHOWER THAT THE RUSSIANS HAVE A THOUSAND OF THESE MISSILES POINTED AT THE U.S. AND WHEN THE RUSSIANS READ IN OUR PAPERS ABOUT HOW WE'RE BUILDING A THOUSAND MISSILES IN RESPONSE, THEY'LL BUILD A THOUSAND MORE, AND ON AND ON UNTIL SOMEONE HAS A BAD DAY AND IT ENDS THE WORLD.
BUT THE RUSSIANS DON'T HAVE A THOUSAND MISSILES.
EXACTLY. AMERICAN MILITARY STRATEGY RIGHT NOW IS TO STEER THE WORLD TOWARD INEVITABLE NUCLEAR ANNIHILATION BASED ON COMPLETE IGNORANCE.

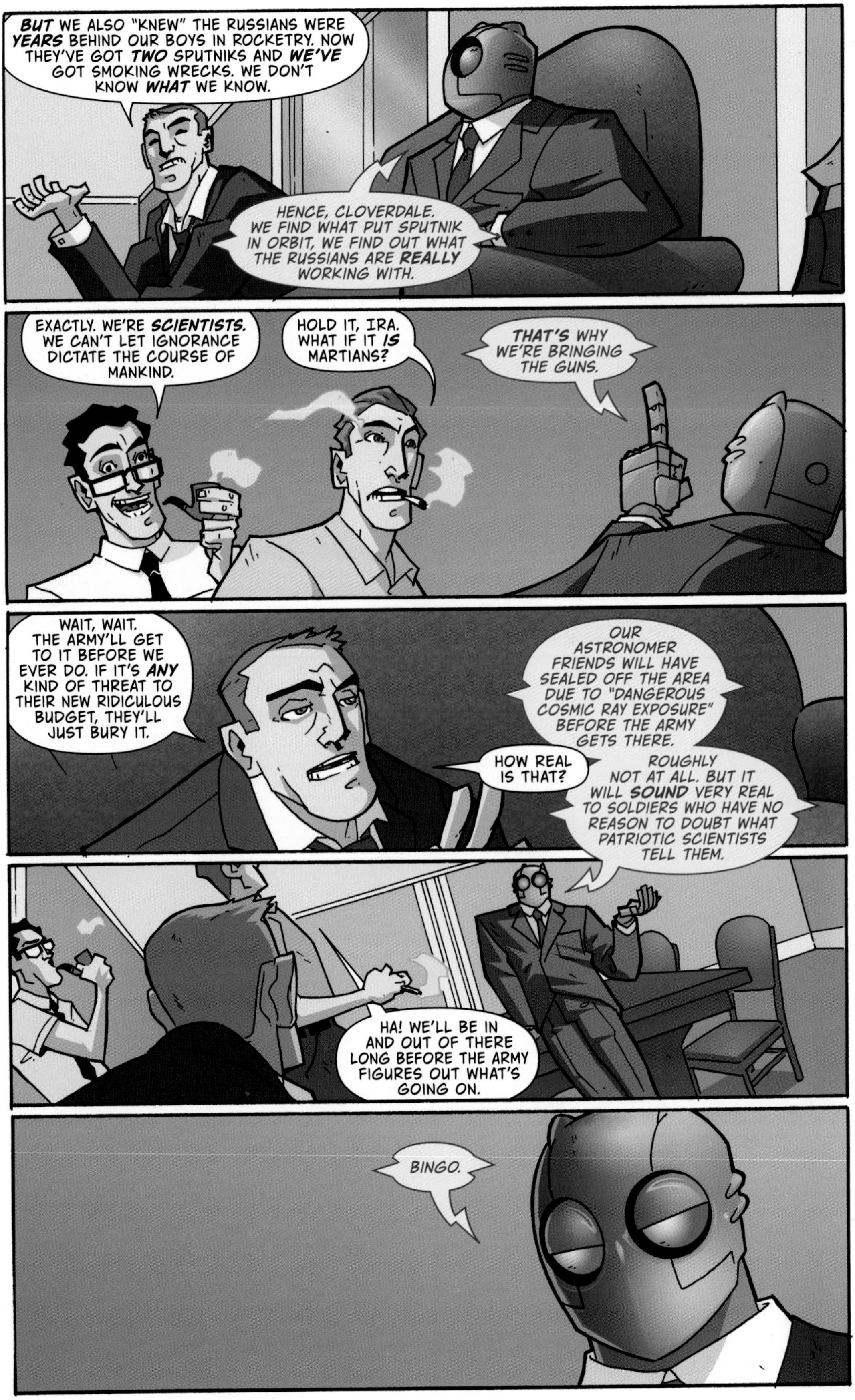

BUT WE ALSO "KNEW" THE RUSSIANS WERE YEARS BEHIND OUR BOYS IN ROCKETRY. NOW THEY'VE GOT TWO SPUTNIKS AND WE'VE GOT SMOKING WRECKS. WE DON'T KNOW WHAT WE KNOW.
HENCE, CLOVERDALE. WE FIND WHAT PUT SPUTNIK IN ORBIT, WE FIND OUT WHAT THE RUSSIANS ARE REALLY WORKING WITH.
EXACTLY. WE'RE SCIENTISTS. WE CAN'T LET IGNORANCE DICTATE THE COURSE OF MANKIND.
HOLD IT, IRA. WHAT IF IT IS MARTIANS?
THAT'S WHY WE'RE BRINGING THE GUNS.
WAIT, WAIT. THE ARMY'LL GET TO IT BEFORE WE EVER DO. IF IT'S ANY KIND OF THREAT TO THEIR NEW RIDICULOUS BUDGET, THEY'LL JUST BURY IT.
OUR ASTRONOMER FRIENDS WILL HAVE SEALED OFF THE AREA DUE TO "DANGEROUS COSMIC RAY EXPOSURE" BEFORE THE ARMY GETS THERE.
HOW REAL IS THAT?
ROUGHLY NOT AT ALL. BUT IT WILL SOUND VERY REAL TO SOLDIERS WHO HAVE NO REASON TO DOUBT WHAT PATRIOTIC SCIENTISTS TELL THEM.
HA! WE'LL BE IN AND OUT OF THERE LONG BEFORE THE ARMY FIGURES OUT WHAT'S GOING ON.
BINGO.

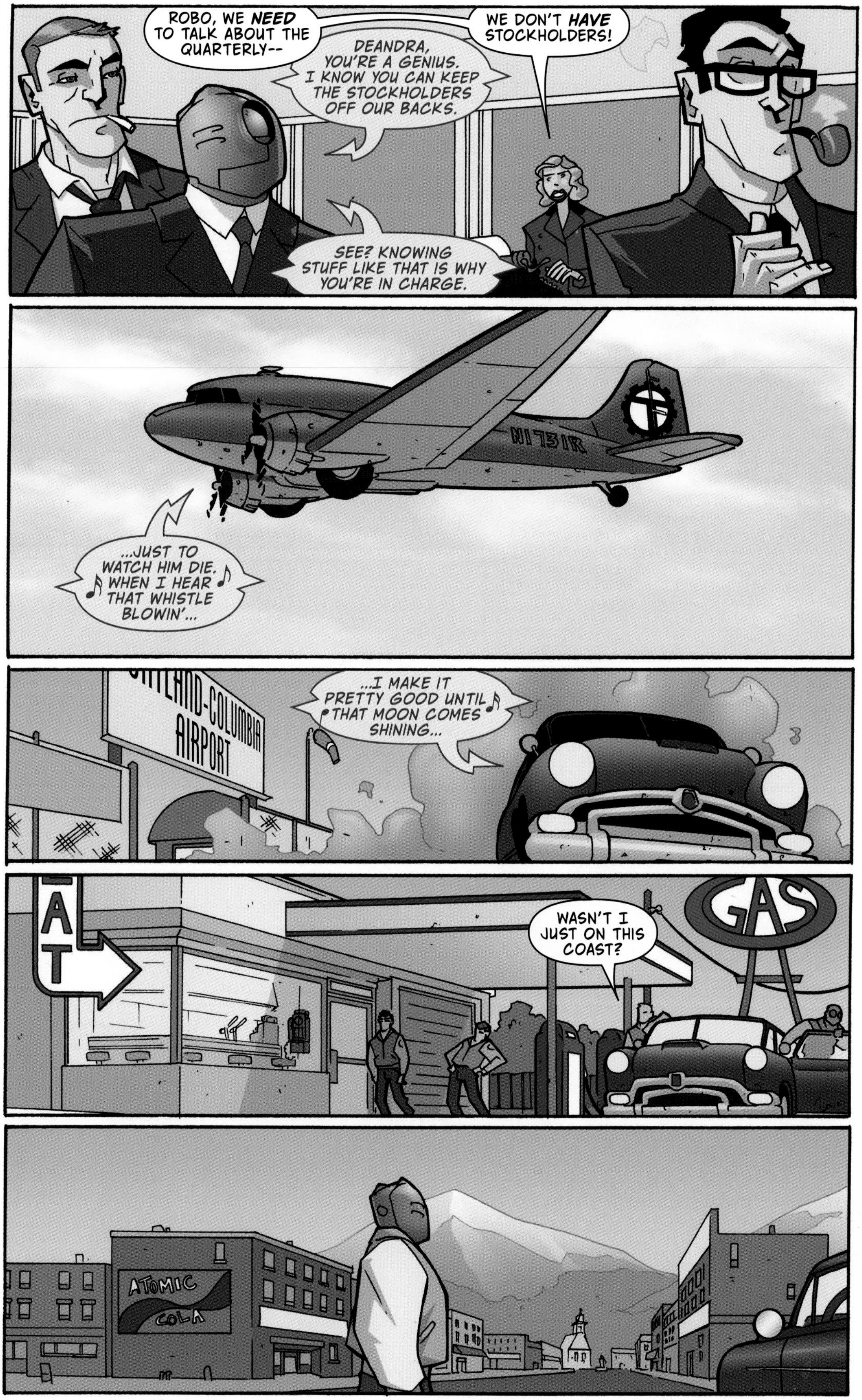
ROBO, WE NEED TO TALK ABOUT THE QUARTERLY--
DEANDRA, YOU'RE A GENIUS. I KNOW YOU CAN KEEP THE STOCKHOLDERS OFF OUR BACKS.
WE DON'T HAVE STOCKHOLDERS!
SEE? KNOWING STUFF LIKE THAT IS WHY YOU'RE IN CHARGE.
N1731R
...JUST TO WATCH HIM DIE. ♪ WHEN I HEAR ♪ THAT WHISTLE BLOWIN'...
AIRPORT
...I MAKE IT PRETTY GOOD UNTIL ♪ THAT MOON COMES SHINING...
AT
GAS
WASN'T I JUST ON THIS COAST?
ATOMIC COLA

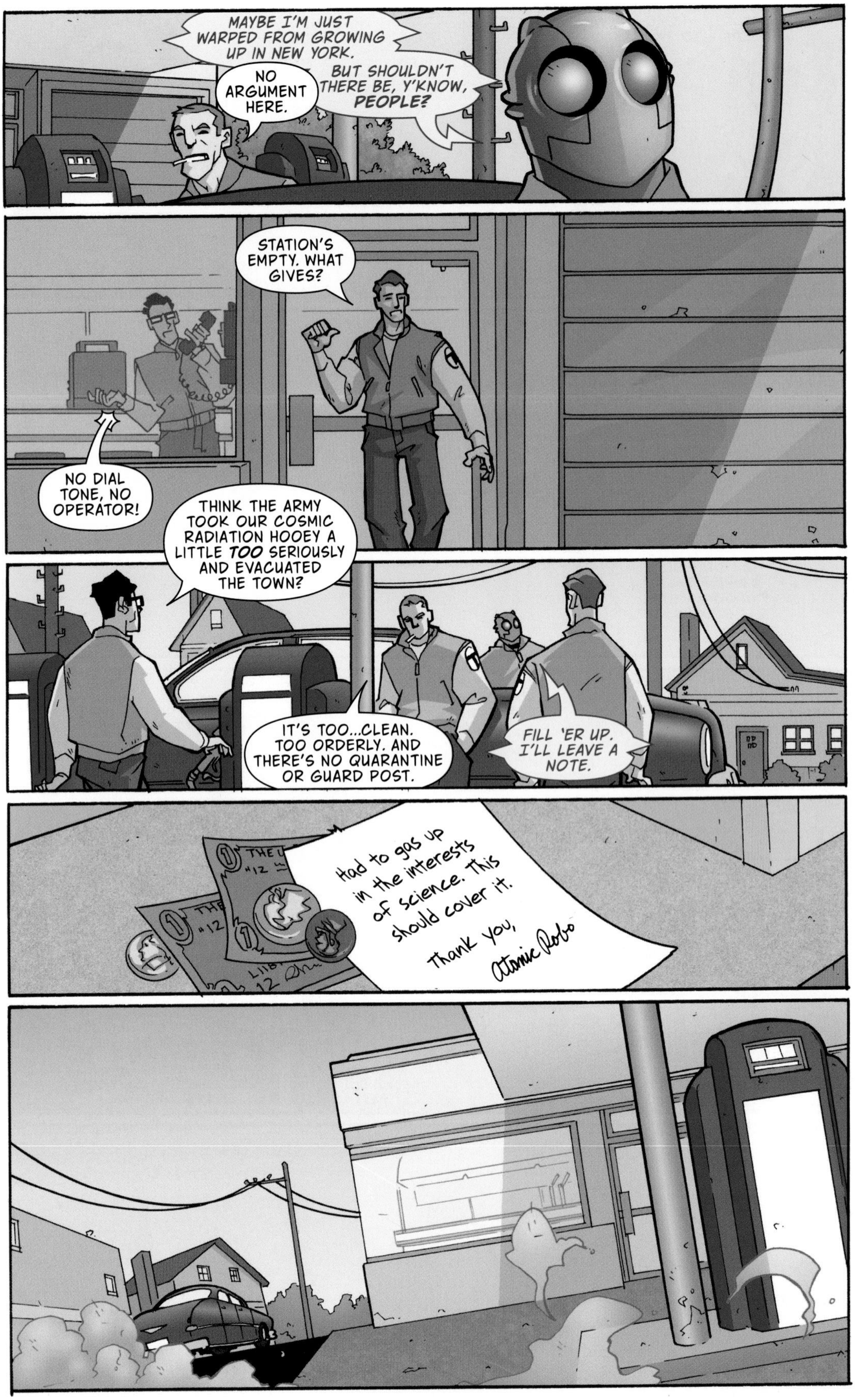
MAYBE I'M JUST WARPED FROM GROWING UP IN NEW YORK.
NO ARGUMENT HERE.
BUT SHOULDN'T THERE BE, Y'KNOW, *PEOPLE?*
STATION'S EMPTY. WHAT GIVES?
NO DIAL TONE, NO OPERATOR!
THINK THE ARMY TOOK OUR COSMIC RADIATION HOOEY A LITTLE *TOO* SERIOUSLY AND EVACUATED THE TOWN?
IT'S TOO...CLEAN. TOO ORDERLY. AND THERE'S NO QUARANTINE OR GUARD POST.
FILL 'ER UP. I'LL LEAVE A NOTE.
Had to gas up in the interests of science. This should cover it.
Thank you,
Atomic Robo

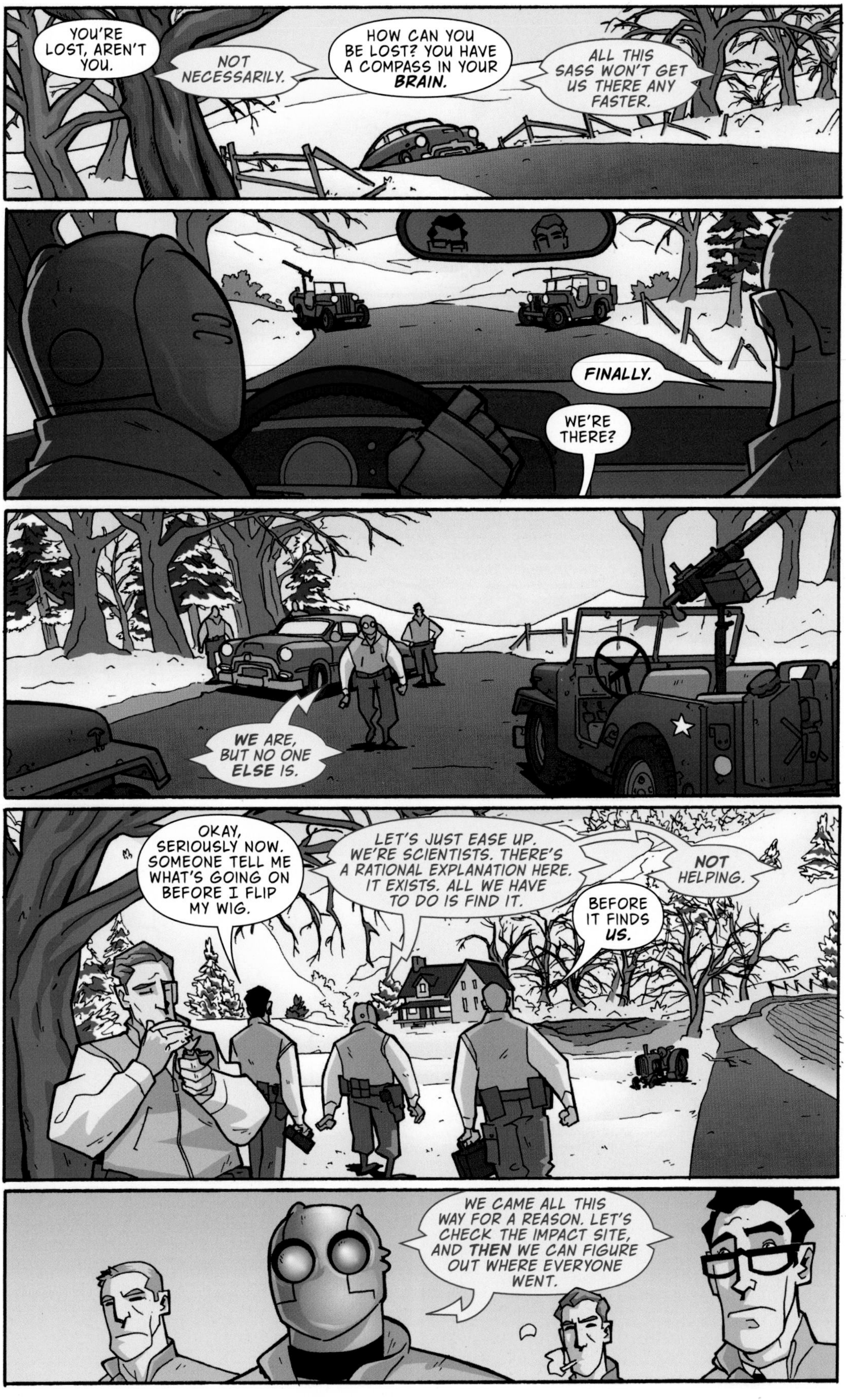
YOU'RE LOST, AREN'T YOU.
NOT NECESSARILY.
HOW CAN YOU BE LOST? YOU HAVE A COMPASS IN YOUR **BRAIN.**
ALL THIS SASS WON'T GET US THERE ANY FASTER.
FINALLY.
WE'RE THERE?
WE ARE, BUT NO ONE **ELSE** IS.
OKAY, SERIOUSLY NOW. SOMEONE TELL ME WHAT'S GOING ON BEFORE I FLIP MY WIG.
LET'S JUST EASE UP. WE'RE SCIENTISTS. THERE'S A RATIONAL EXPLANATION HERE. IT EXISTS. ALL WE HAVE TO DO IS FIND IT.
NOT HELPING.
BEFORE IT FINDS **US.**
WE CAME ALL THIS WAY FOR A REASON. LET'S CHECK THE IMPACT SITE, AND **THEN** WE CAN FIGURE OUT WHERE EVERYONE WENT.

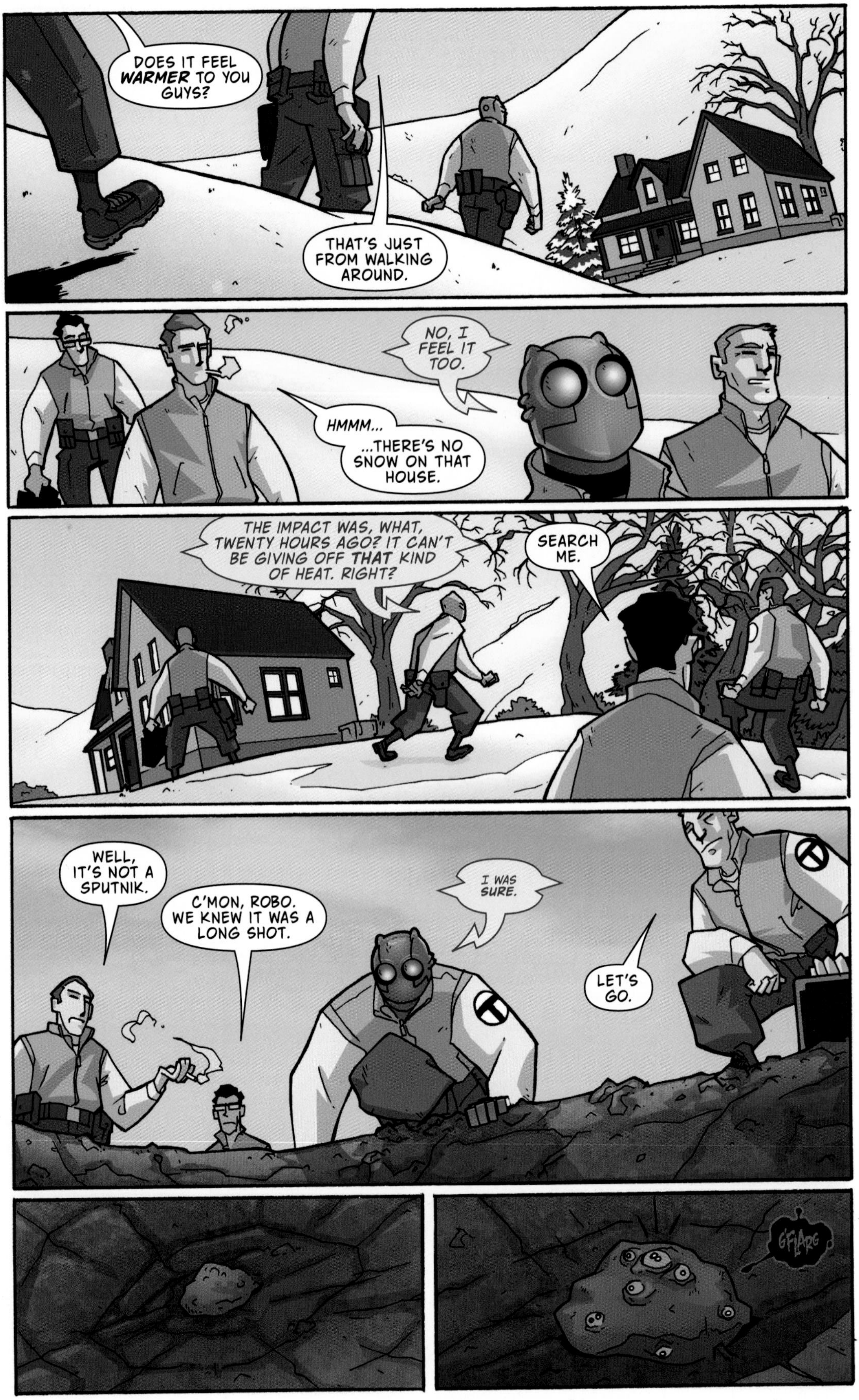
DOES IT FEEL WARMER TO YOU GUYS?
THAT'S JUST FROM WALKING AROUND.
NO, I FEEL IT TOO.
HMMM... ...THERE'S NO SNOW ON THAT HOUSE.
THE IMPACT WAS, WHAT, TWENTY HOURS AGO? IT CAN'T BE GIVING OFF THAT KIND OF HEAT. RIGHT?
SEARCH ME.
WELL, IT'S NOT A SPUTNIK.
C'MON, ROBO. WE KNEW IT WAS A LONG SHOT.
I WAS SURE.
LET'S GO.
G'FLARG

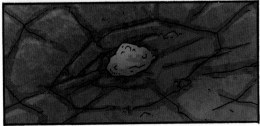

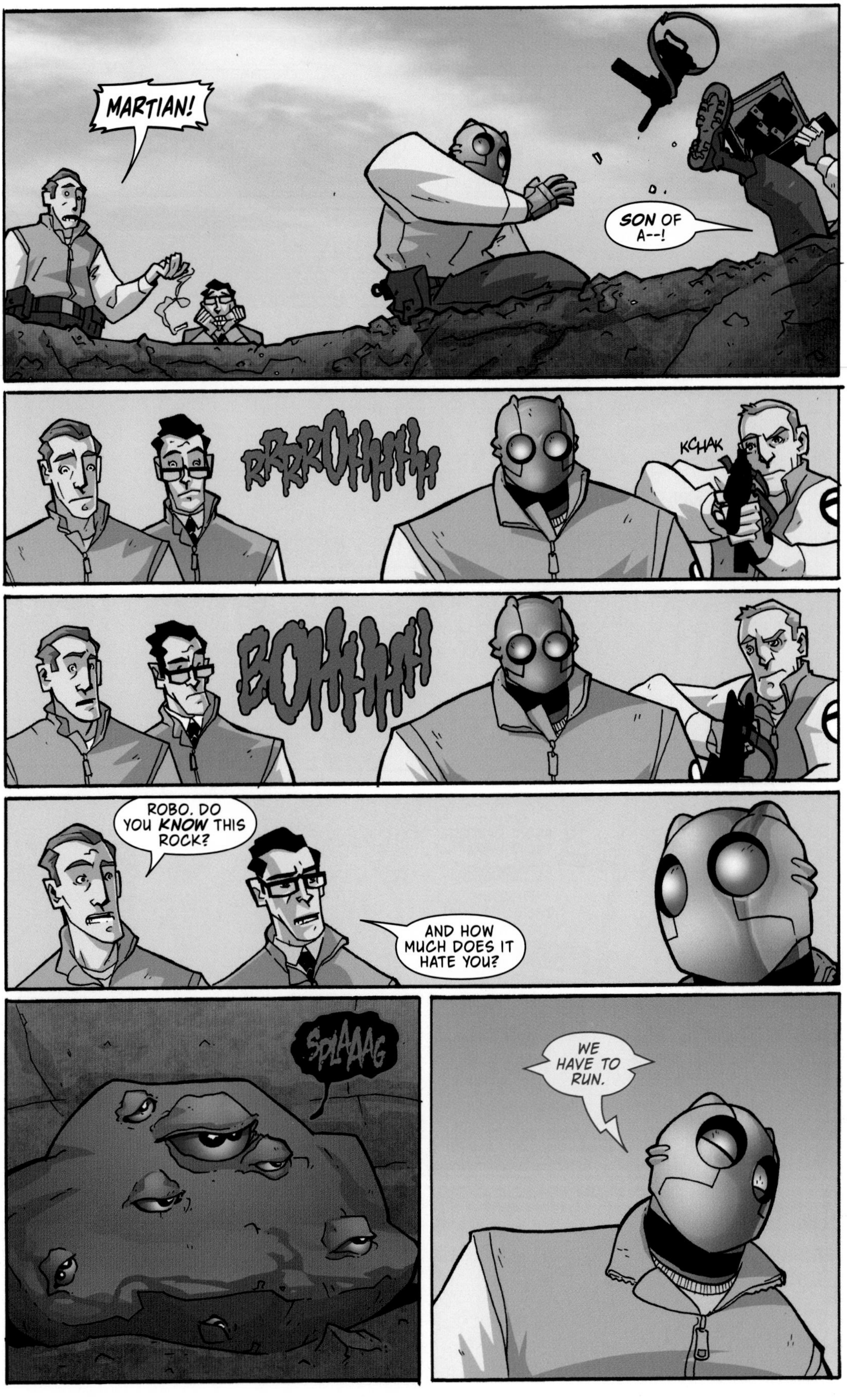
MARTIAN!
SON OF A--!
RRRROHHHHH
KCHAK
BOHHHH
ROBO. DO YOU KNOW THIS ROCK?
AND HOW MUCH DOES IT HATE YOU?
SPLAAAG
WE HAVE TO RUN.

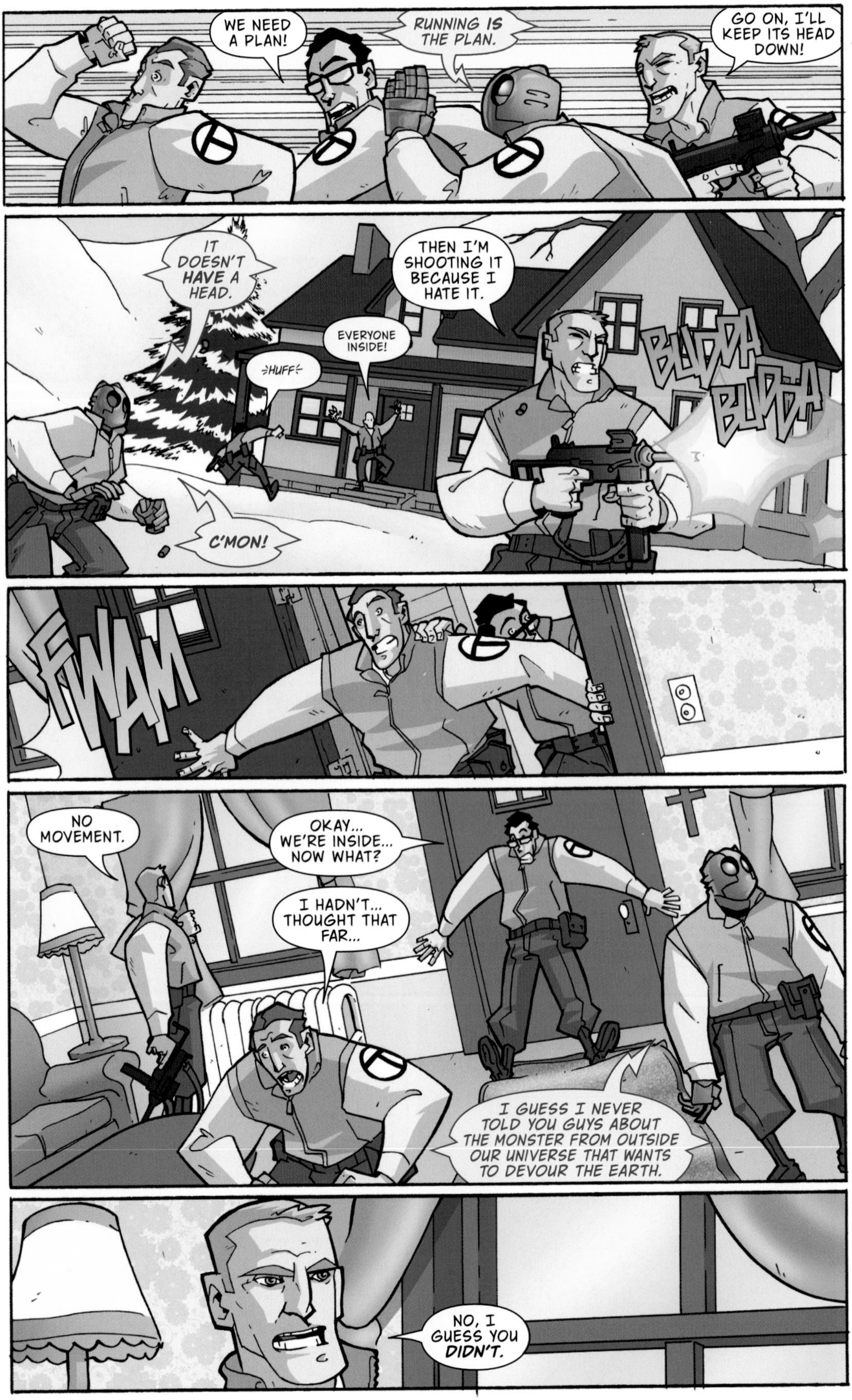
WE NEED A PLAN!
RUNNING IS THE PLAN.
GO ON, I'LL KEEP ITS HEAD DOWN!
IT DOESN'T HAVE A HEAD.
THEN I'M SHOOTING IT BECAUSE I HATE IT.
EVERYONE INSIDE!
HUFF
BUDDA BUDDA
C'MON!
FWAM
NO MOVEMENT.
OKAY... WE'RE INSIDE... NOW WHAT?
I HADN'T... THOUGHT THAT FAR...
I GUESS I NEVER TOLD YOU GUYS ABOUT THE MONSTER FROM OUTSIDE OUR UNIVERSE THAT WANTS TO DEVOUR THE EARTH.
NO, I GUESS YOU DIDN'T.

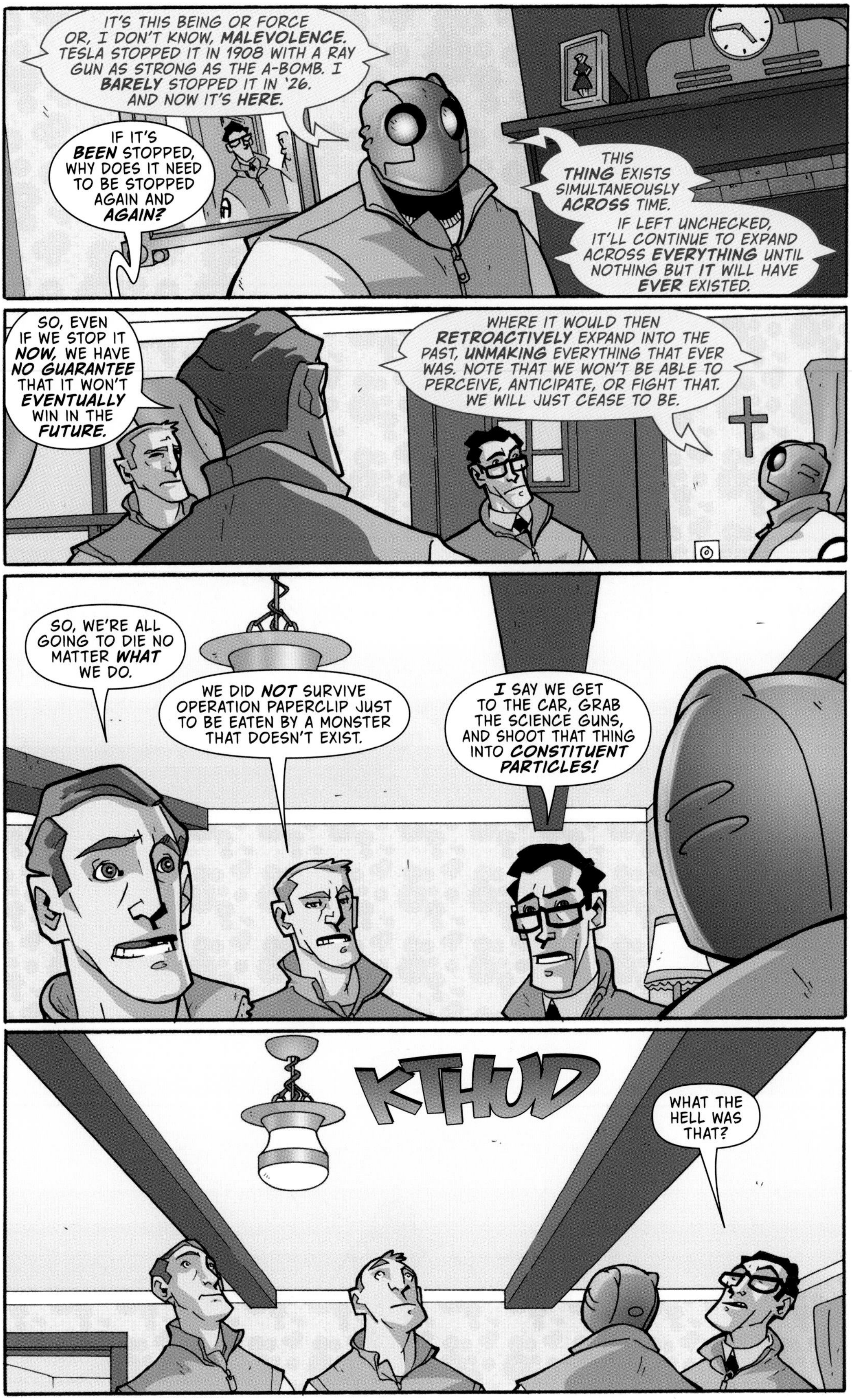
IT'S THIS BEING OR FORCE OR, I DON'T KNOW, MALEVOLENCE. TESLA STOPPED IT IN 1908 WITH A RAY GUN AS STRONG AS THE A-BOMB. I BARELY STOPPED IT IN '26. AND NOW IT'S HERE.
IF IT'S BEEN STOPPED, WHY DOES IT NEED TO BE STOPPED AGAIN AND AGAIN?
THIS THING EXISTS SIMULTANEOUSLY ACROSS TIME.
IF LEFT UNCHECKED, IT'LL CONTINUE TO EXPAND ACROSS EVERYTHING UNTIL NOTHING BUT IT WILL HAVE EVER EXISTED.
SO, EVEN IF WE STOP IT NOW, WE HAVE NO GUARANTEE THAT IT WON'T EVENTUALLY WIN IN THE FUTURE.
WHERE IT WOULD THEN RETROACTIVELY EXPAND INTO THE PAST, UNMAKING EVERYTHING THAT EVER WAS. NOTE THAT WE WON'T BE ABLE TO PERCEIVE, ANTICIPATE, OR FIGHT THAT. WE WILL JUST CEASE TO BE.
SO, WE'RE ALL GOING TO DIE NO MATTER WHAT WE DO.
WE DID NOT SURVIVE OPERATION PAPERCLIP JUST TO BE EATEN BY A MONSTER THAT DOESN'T EXIST.
I SAY WE GET TO THE CAR, GRAB THE SCIENCE GUNS, AND SHOOT THAT THING INTO CONSTITUENT PARTICLES!
KTHUD
WHAT THE HELL WAS THAT?

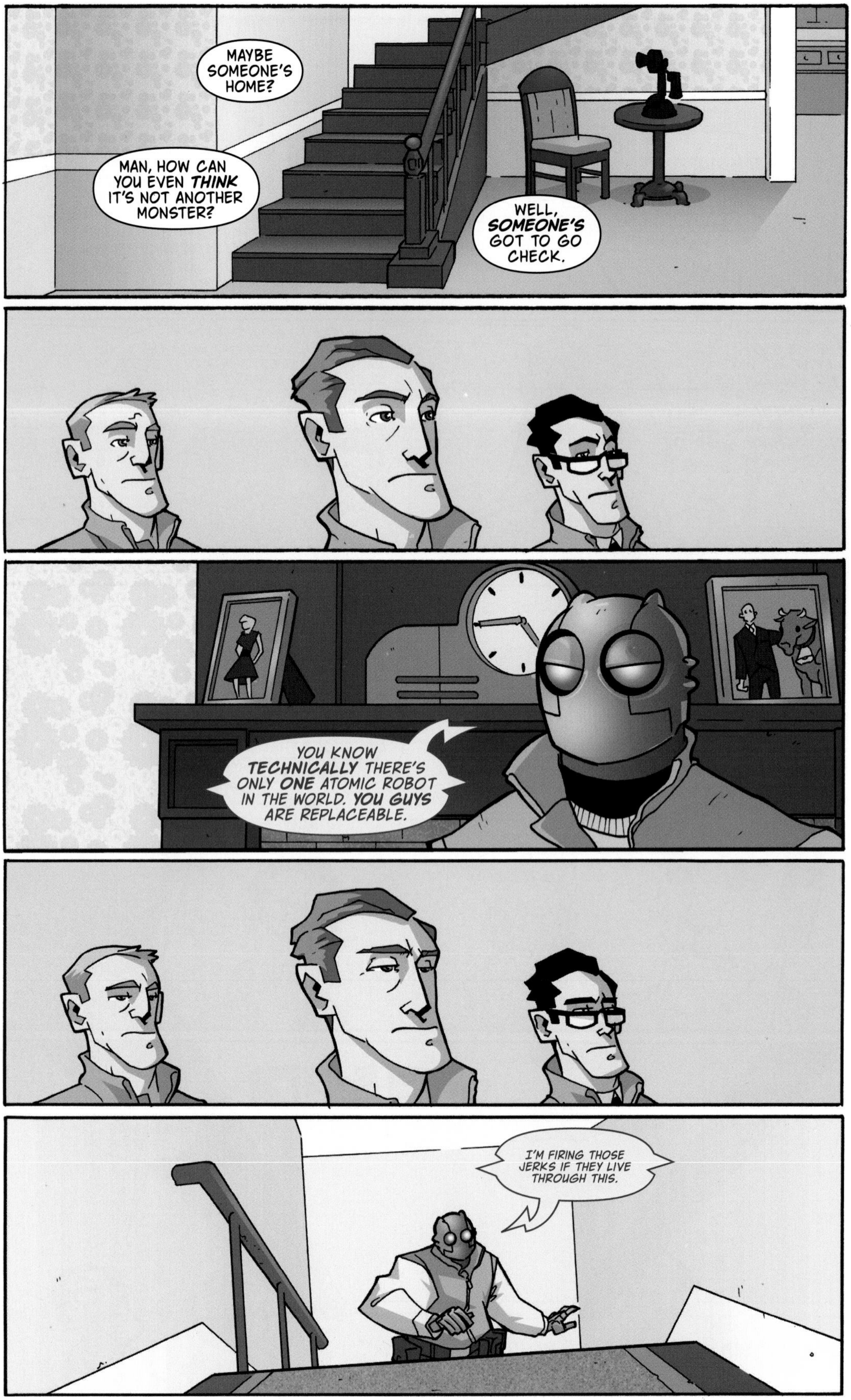
MAYBE SOMEONE'S HOME?
MAN, HOW CAN YOU EVEN THINK IT'S NOT ANOTHER MONSTER?
WELL, SOMEONE'S GOT TO GO CHECK.
YOU KNOW TECHNICALLY THERE'S ONLY ONE ATOMIC ROBOT IN THE WORLD. YOU GUYS ARE REPLACEABLE.
I'M FIRING THOSE JERKS IF THEY LIVE THROUGH THIS.

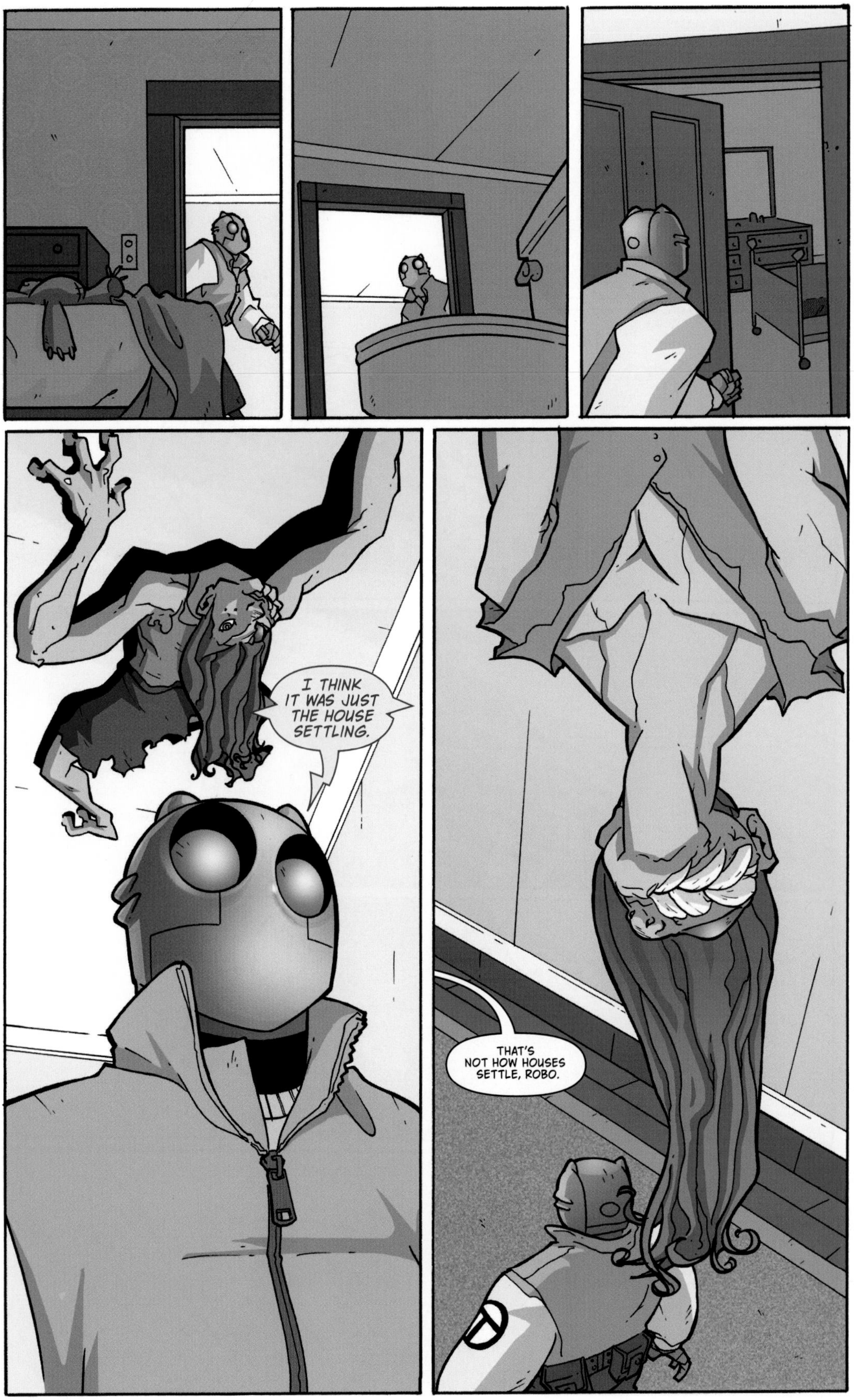
I THINK IT WAS JUST THE HOUSE SETTLING.
THAT'S NOT HOW HOUSES SETTLE, ROBO.

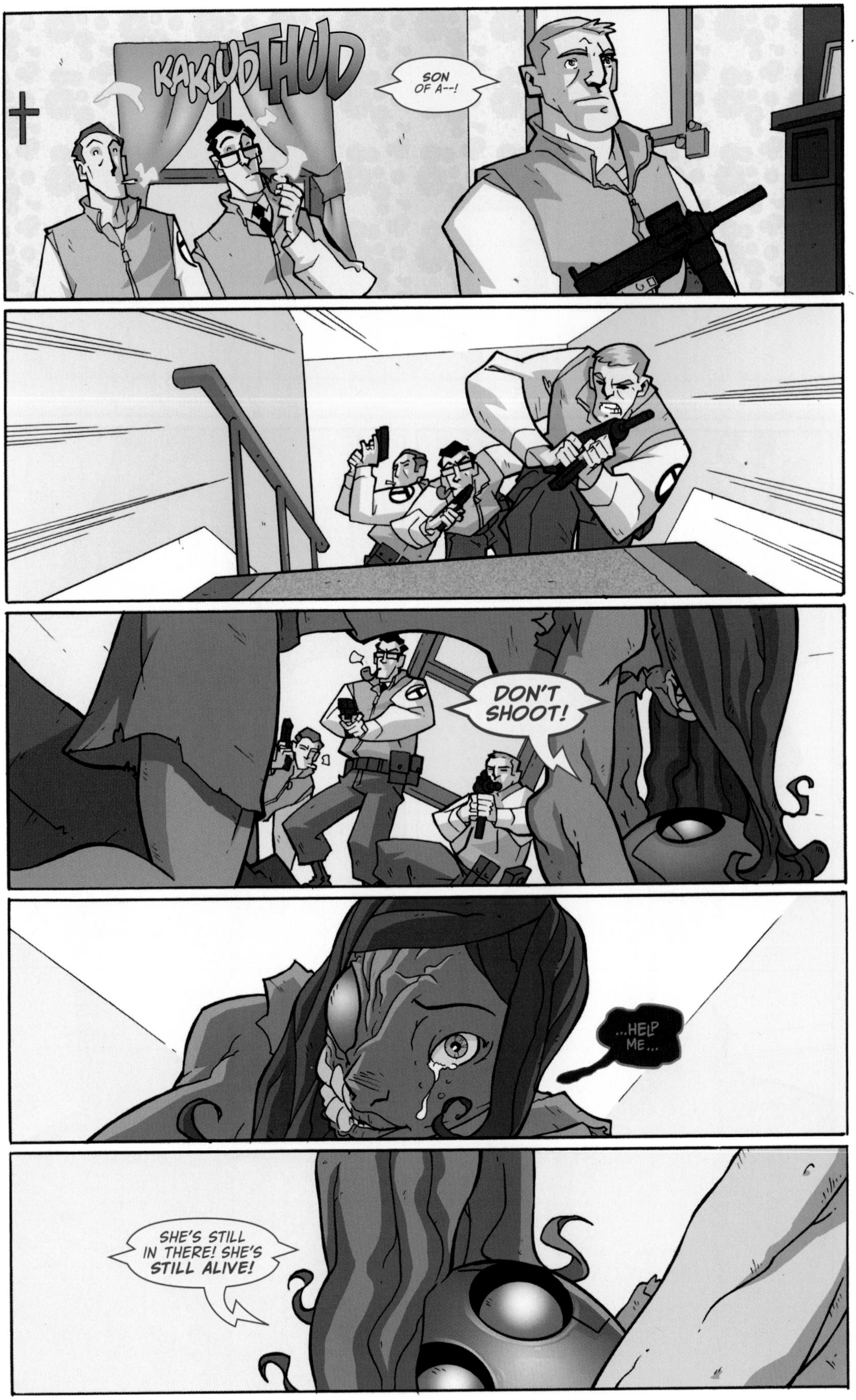
KAKLUDTHUD
SON OF A--!
DON'T SHOOT!
...HELP ME...
SHE'S STILL IN THERE! SHE'S STILL ALIVE!

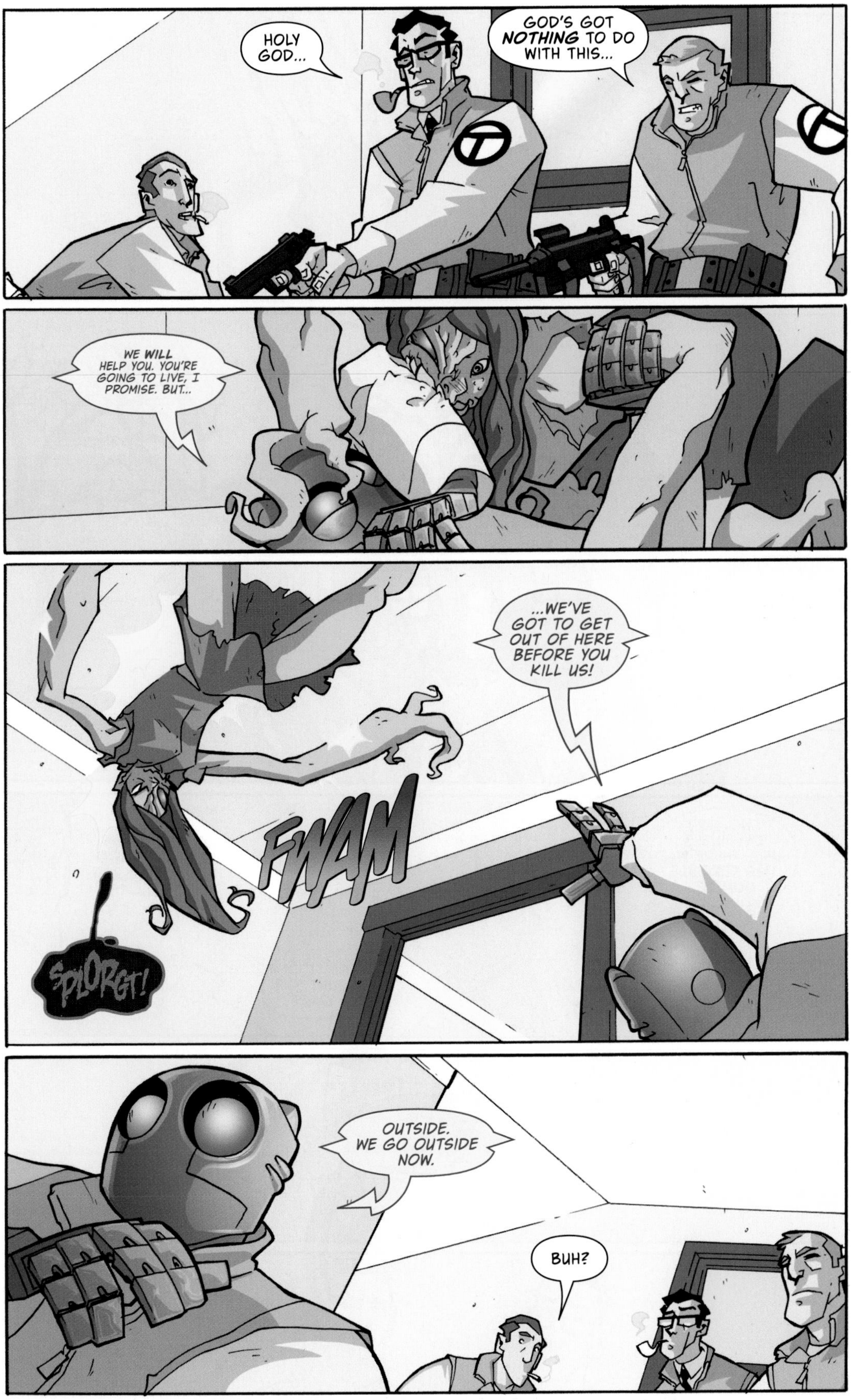
HOLY GOD...
GOD'S GOT NOTHING TO DO WITH THIS...
WE WILL HELP YOU. YOU'RE GOING TO LIVE, I PROMISE. BUT...
...WE'VE GOT TO GET OUT OF HERE BEFORE YOU KILL US!
FWAM
SPLORGT!
OUTSIDE. WE GO OUTSIDE NOW.
BUH?

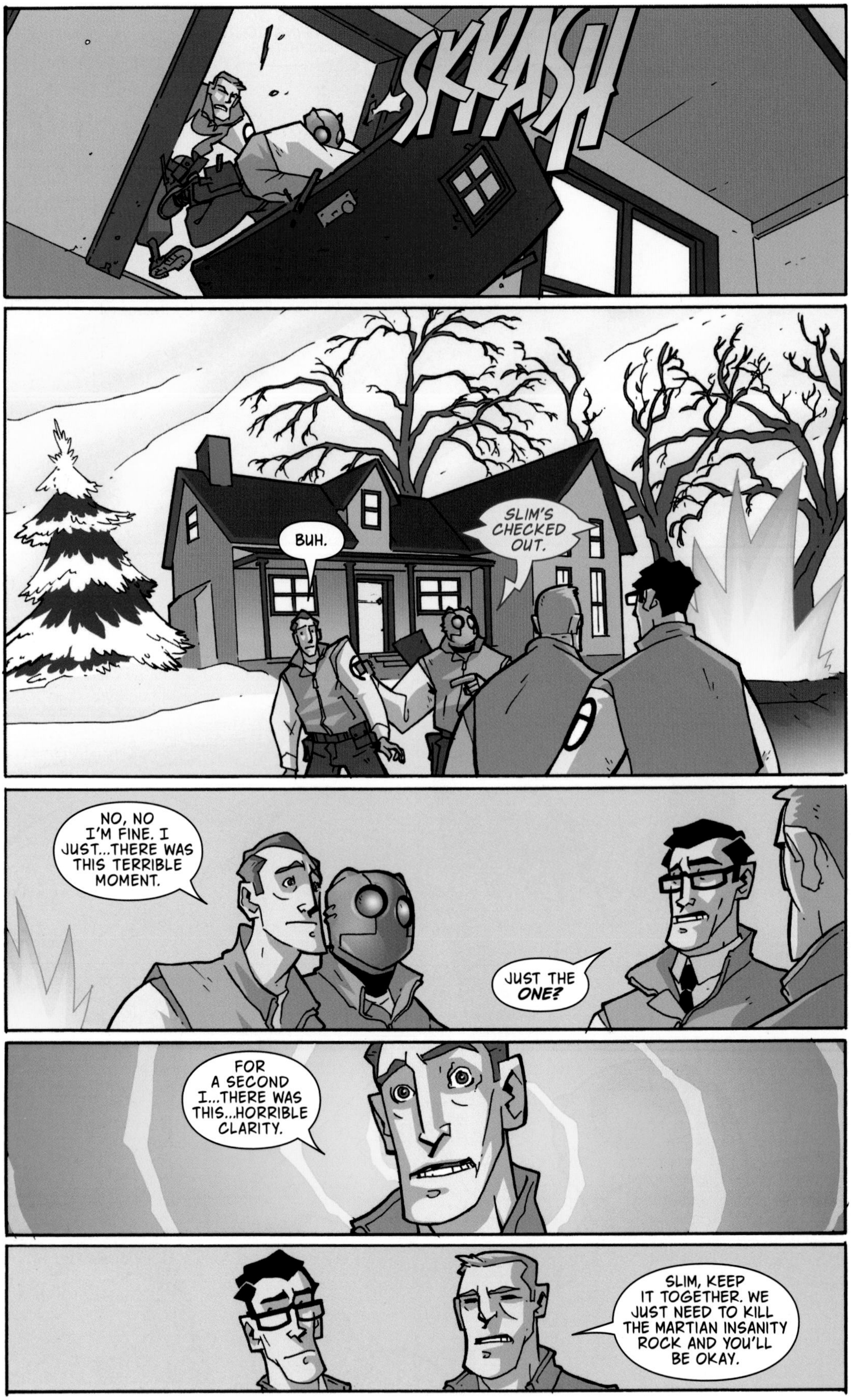
SKRASH
BUH.
SLIM'S CHECKED OUT.
NO, NO I'M FINE. I JUST...THERE WAS THIS TERRIBLE MOMENT.
JUST THE *ONE?*
FOR A SECOND I...THERE WAS THIS...HORRIBLE CLARITY.
SLIM, KEEP IT TOGETHER. WE JUST NEED TO KILL THE MARTIAN INSANITY ROCK AND YOU'LL BE OKAY.

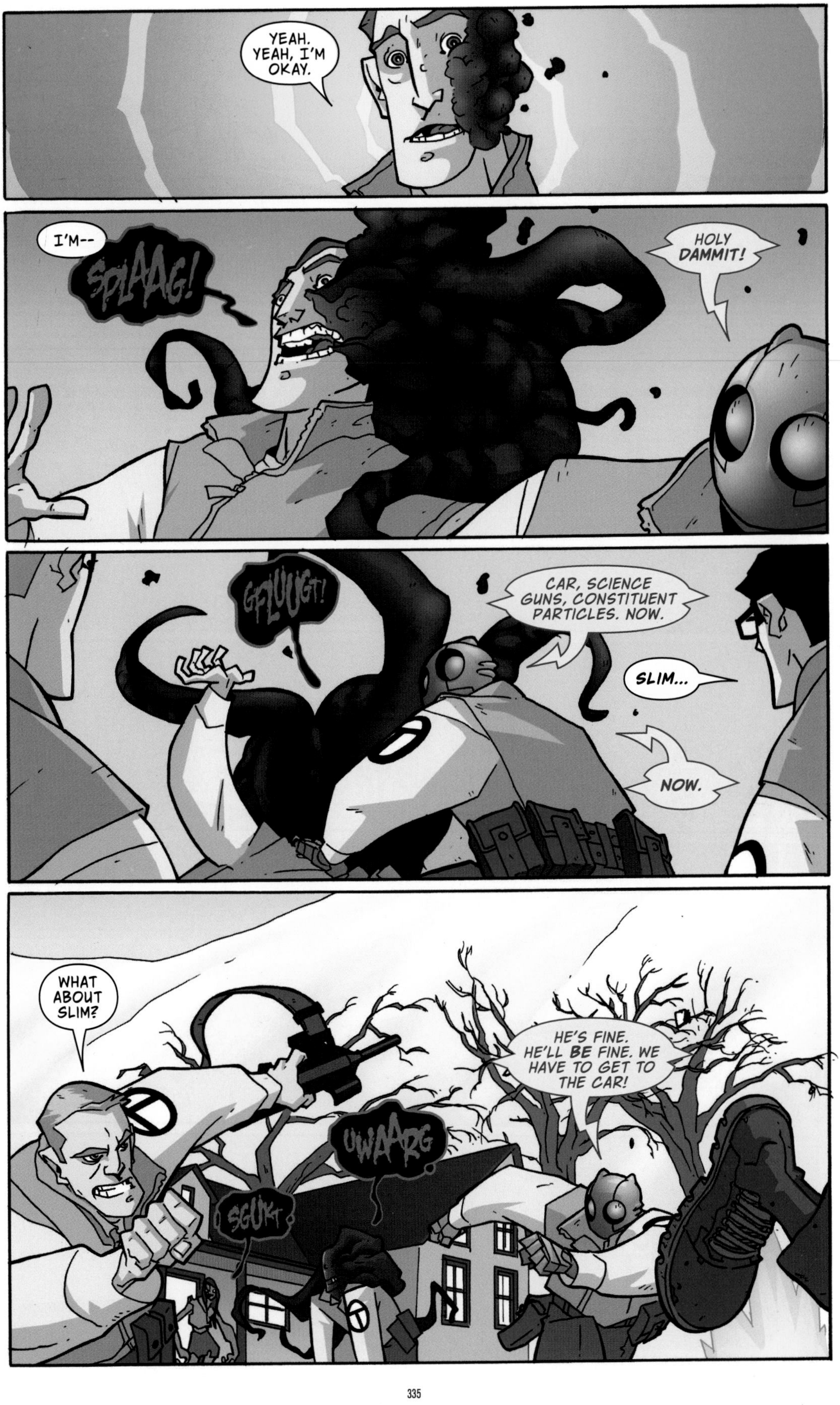
YEAH. YEAH, I'M OKAY.
I'M--
SPLAAG!
HOLY DAMMIT!
GFLUUGT!
CAR, SCIENCE GUNS, CONSTITUENT PARTICLES. NOW.
SLIM...
NOW.
WHAT ABOUT SLIM?
HE'S FINE. HE'LL BE FINE. WE HAVE TO GET TO THE CAR!
UWAARG
SGUKT

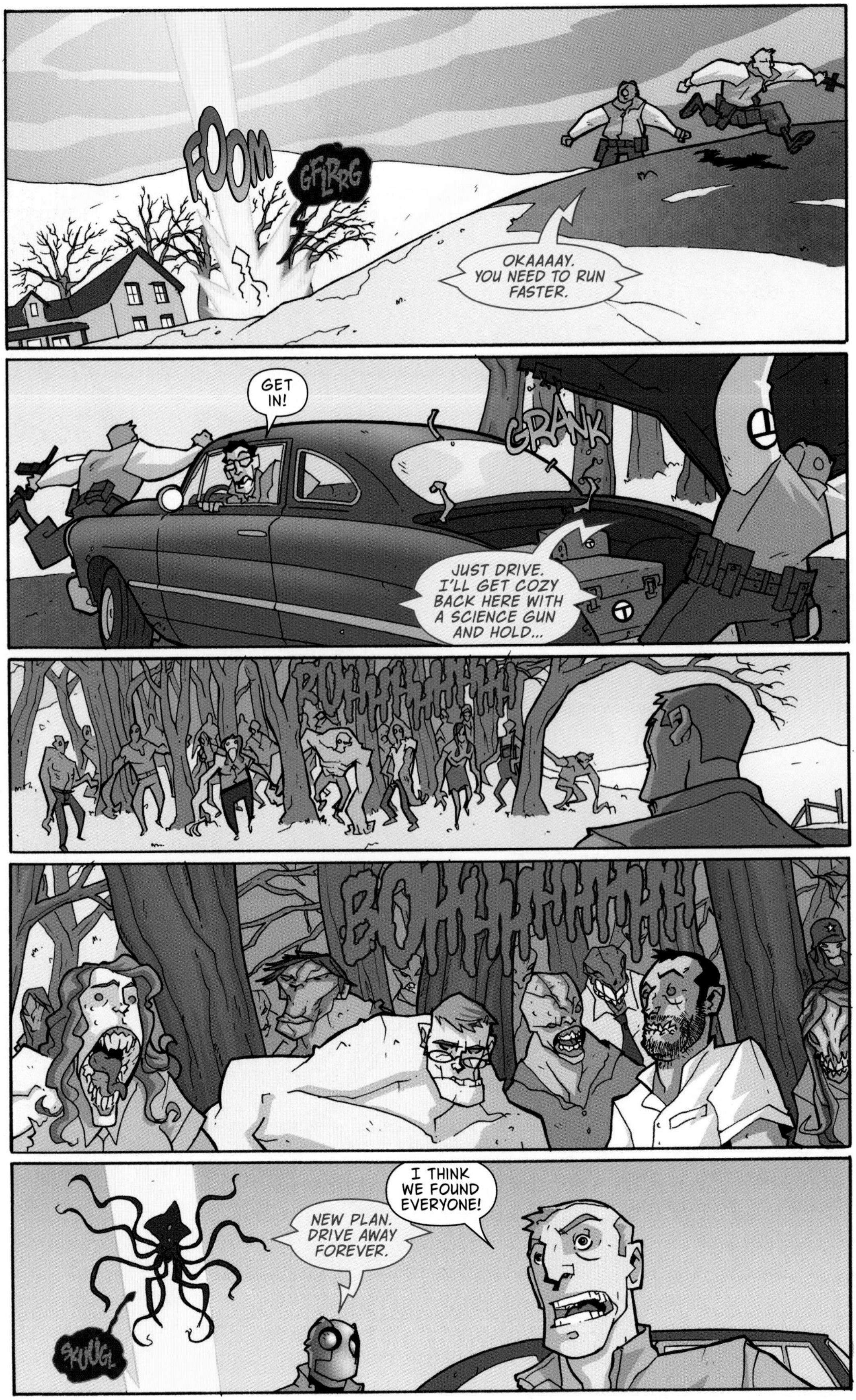
FOOM
GFLRRG
OKAAAAY. YOU NEED TO RUN FASTER.
GET IN!
GRANK
JUST DRIVE. I'LL GET COZY BACK HERE WITH A SCIENCE GUN AND HOLD...
I THINK WE FOUND EVERYONE!
NEW PLAN. DRIVE AWAY FOREVER.
SKUUGL

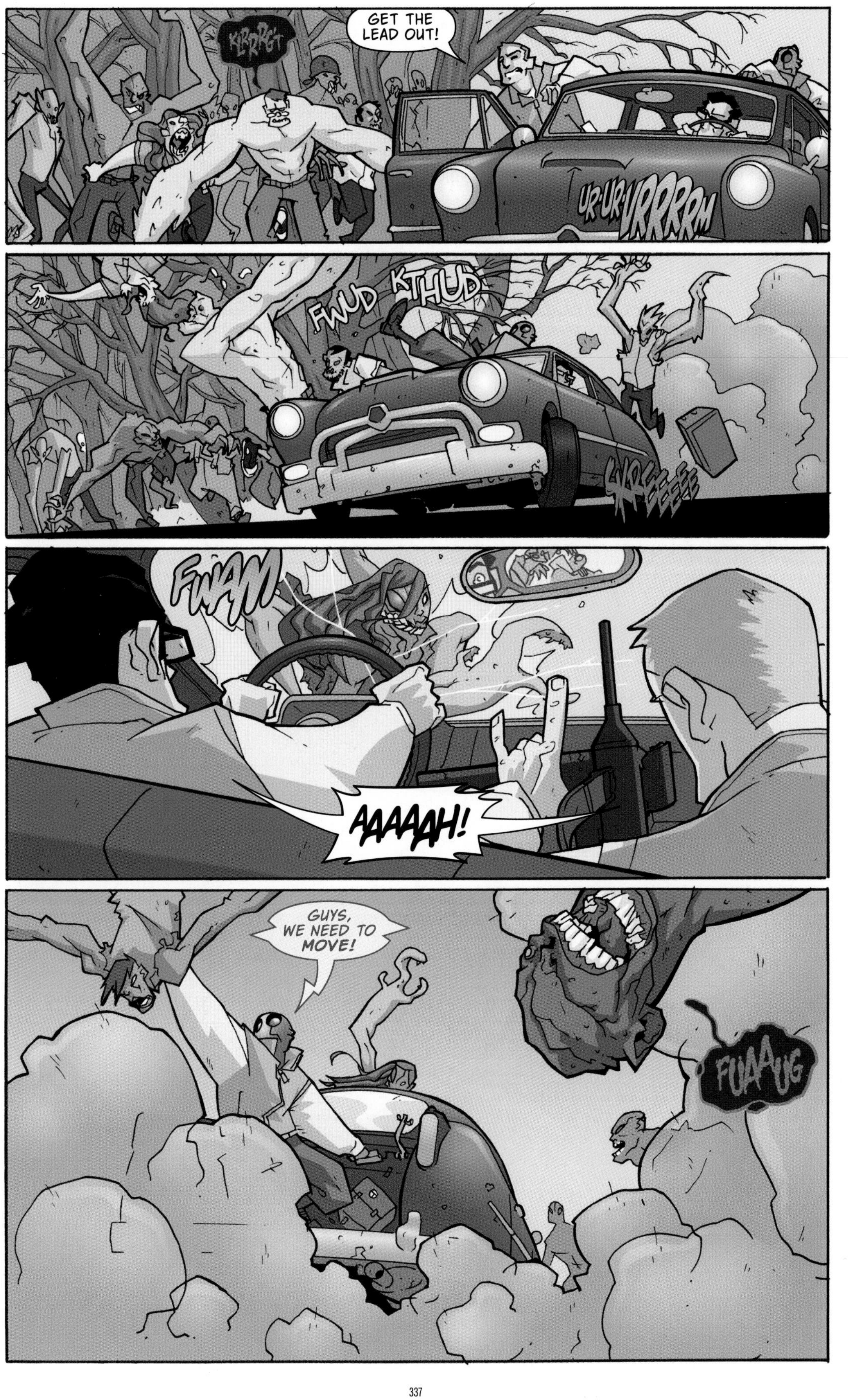
KLRRRGT
GET THE LEAD OUT!
UR-UR-URRRRM
FWUD KTHUD
FWAM
AAAAAH!
GUYS, WE NEED TO MOVE!
FUAAUG

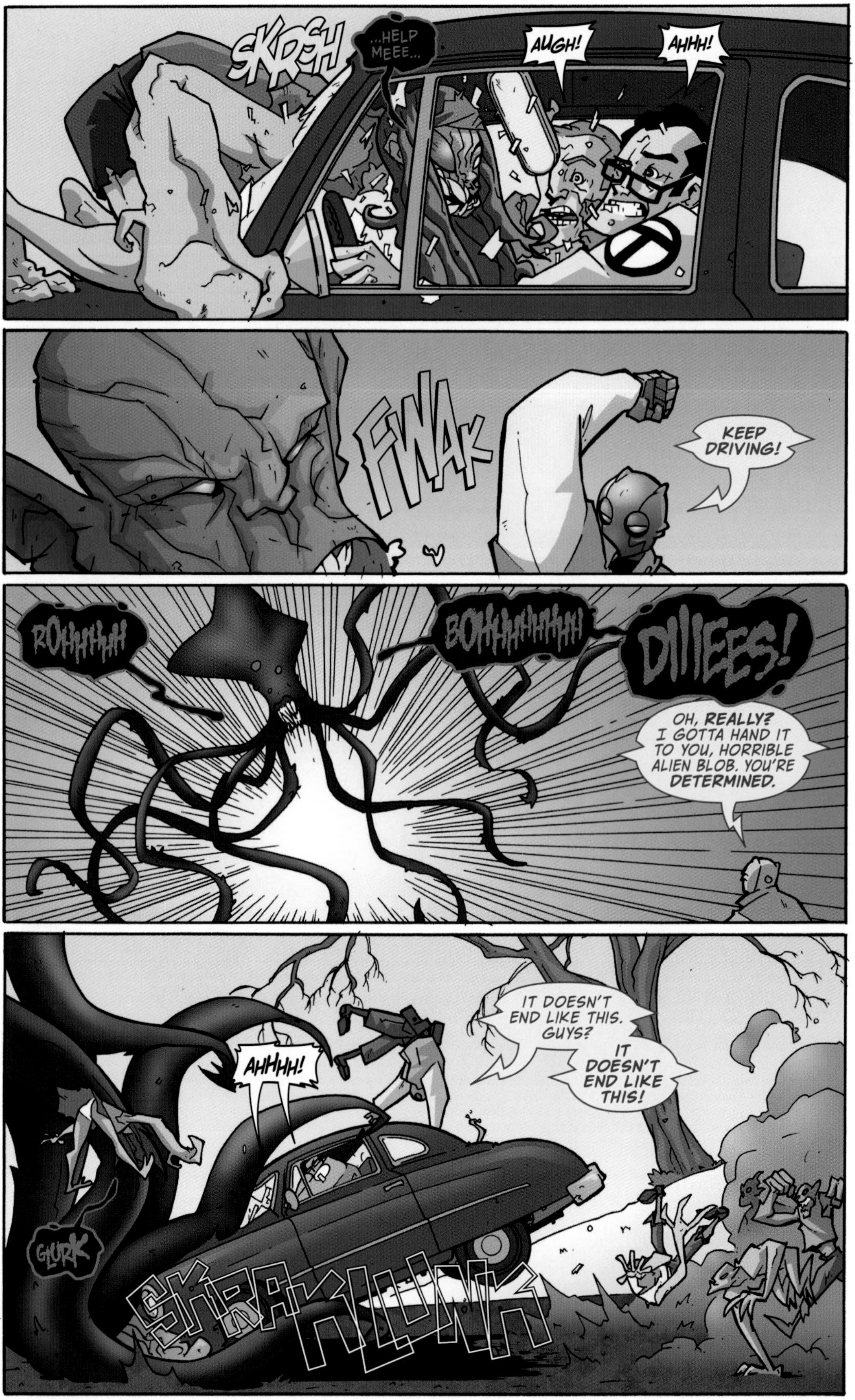
SKRSH
...HELP MEEE...
AUGH!
AHHH!
FWAK
KEEP DRIVING!
ROHHHHH
BOHHHHHHHHH
DIIIEES!
OH, **REALLY?** I GOTTA HAND IT TO YOU, HORRIBLE ALIEN BLOB. YOU'RE **DETERMINED.**
IT DOESN'T END LIKE THIS. GUYS?
IT DOESN'T END LIKE THIS!
AHHHH!
GLURK
SKRAKLUNK

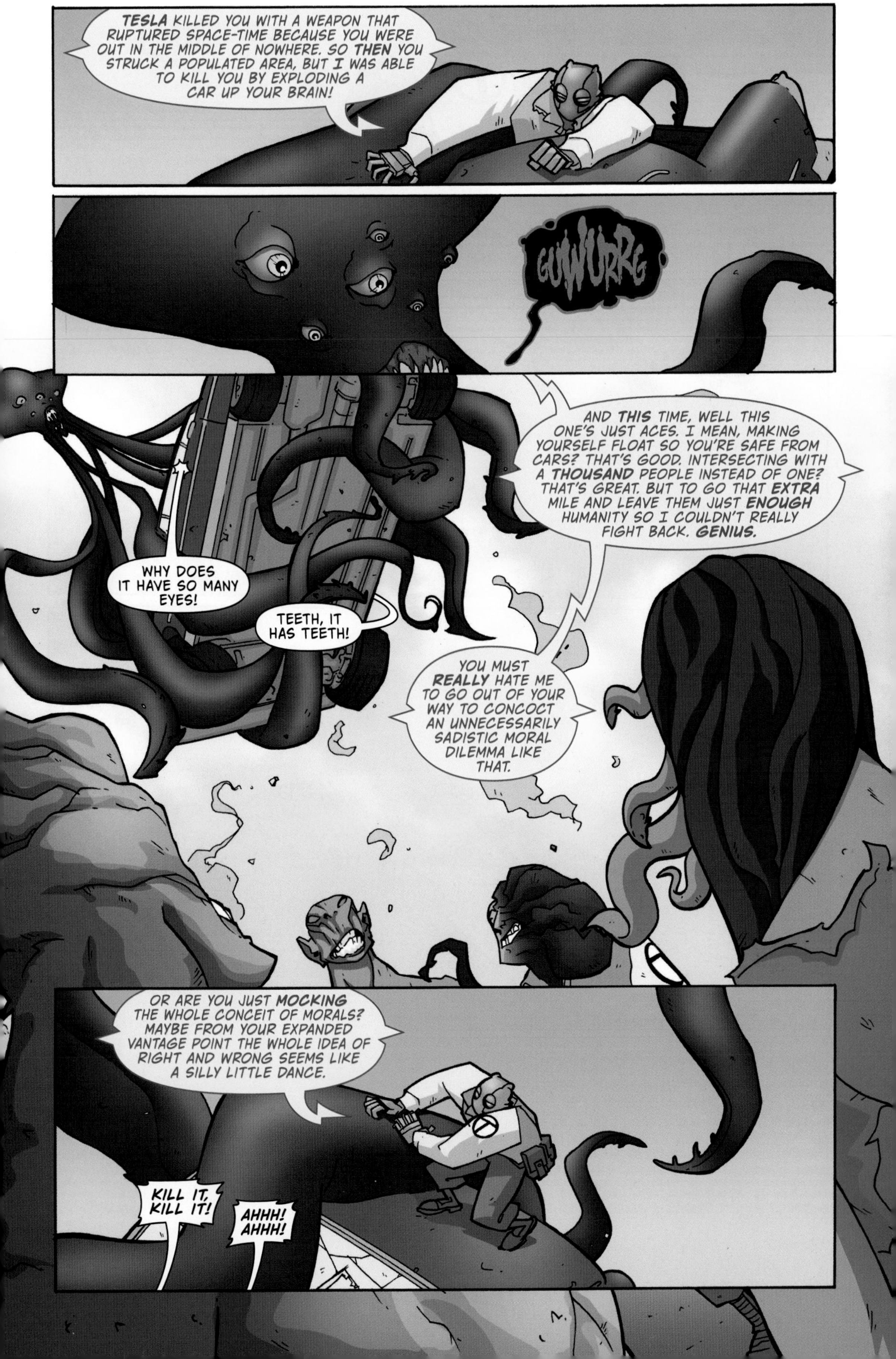
TESLA KILLED YOU WITH A WEAPON THAT RUPTURED SPACE-TIME BECAUSE YOU WERE OUT IN THE MIDDLE OF NOWHERE. SO THEN YOU STRUCK A POPULATED AREA, BUT I WAS ABLE TO KILL YOU BY EXPLODING A CAR UP YOUR BRAIN!
GUWURRG
AND THIS TIME, WELL THIS ONE'S JUST ACES. I MEAN, MAKING YOURSELF FLOAT SO YOU'RE SAFE FROM CARS? THAT'S GOOD. INTERSECTING WITH A THOUSAND PEOPLE INSTEAD OF ONE? THAT'S GREAT. BUT TO GO THAT EXTRA MILE AND LEAVE THEM JUST ENOUGH HUMANITY SO I COULDN'T REALLY FIGHT BACK. GENIUS.
WHY DOES IT HAVE SO MANY EYES!
TEETH, IT HAS TEETH!
YOU MUST REALLY HATE ME TO GO OUT OF YOUR WAY TO CONCOCT AN UNNECESSARILY SADISTIC MORAL DILEMMA LIKE THAT.
OR ARE YOU JUST MOCKING THE WHOLE CONCEIT OF MORALS? MAYBE FROM YOUR EXPANDED VANTAGE POINT THE WHOLE IDEA OF RIGHT AND WRONG SEEMS LIKE A SILLY LITTLE DANCE.
KILL IT, KILL IT!
AHHH! AHHH!

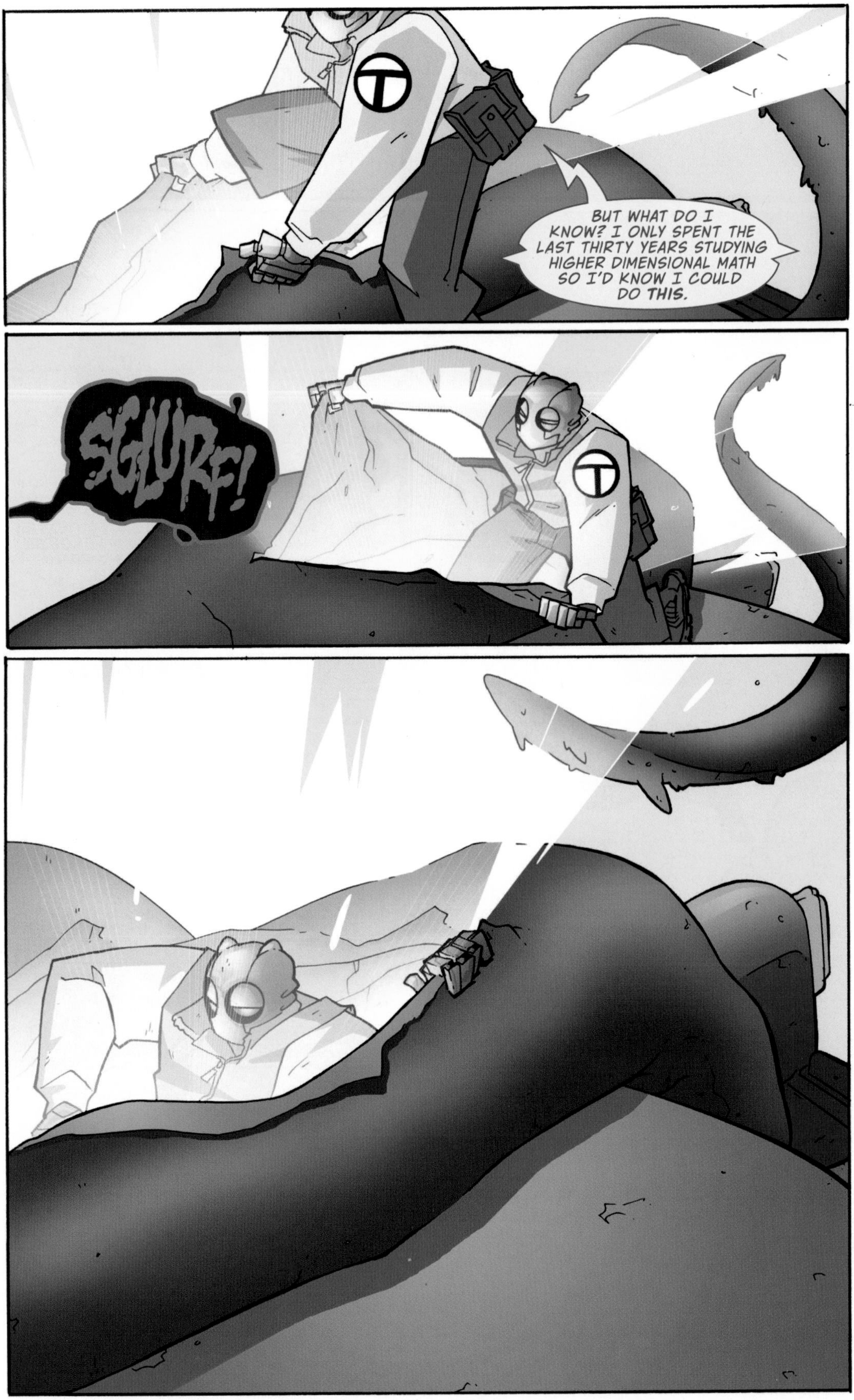
BUT WHAT DO I KNOW? I ONLY SPENT THE LAST THIRTY YEARS STUDYING HIGHER DIMENSIONAL MATH SO I'D KNOW I COULD DO THIS.
SGLURF!

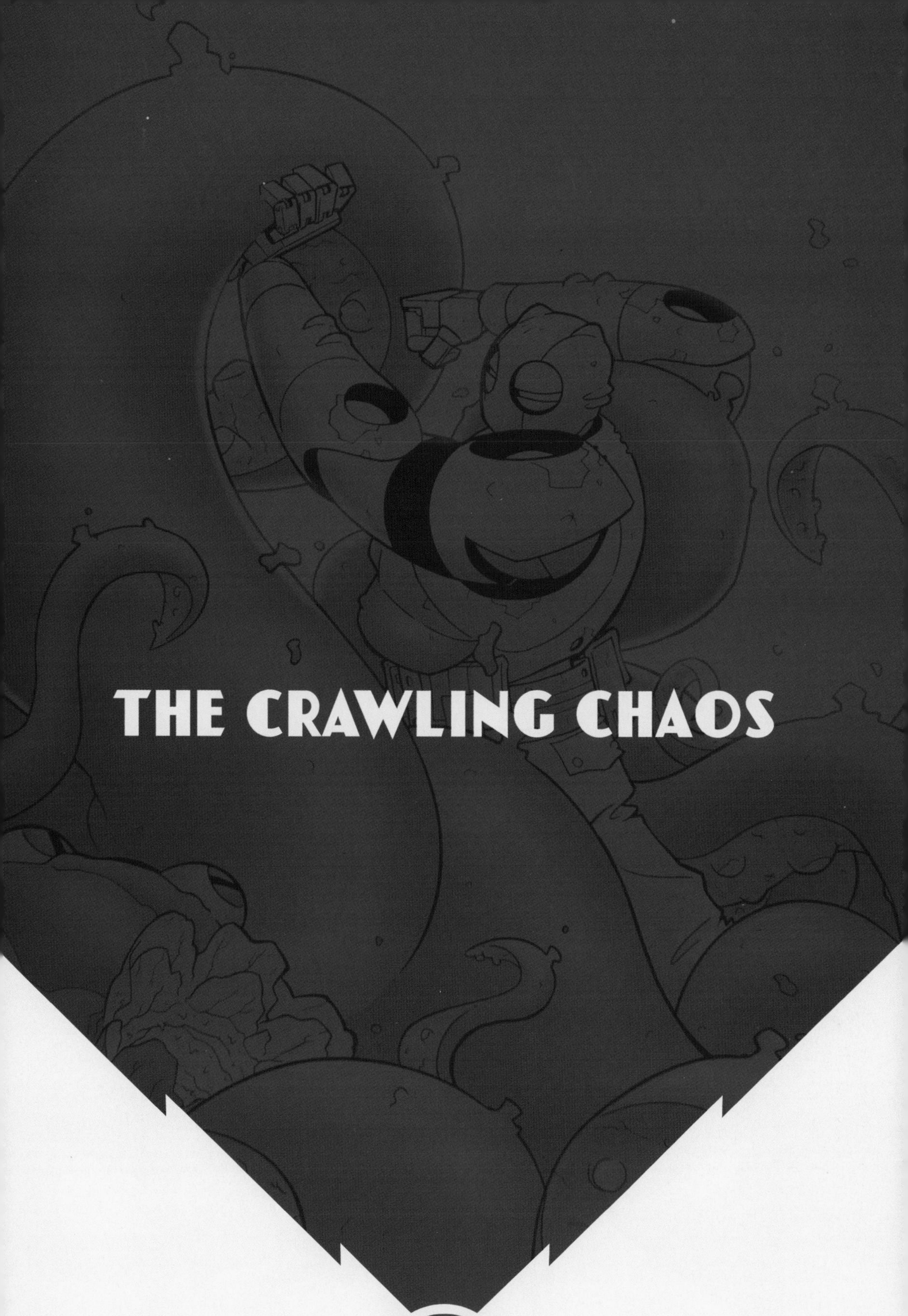

THE CRAWLING CHAOS

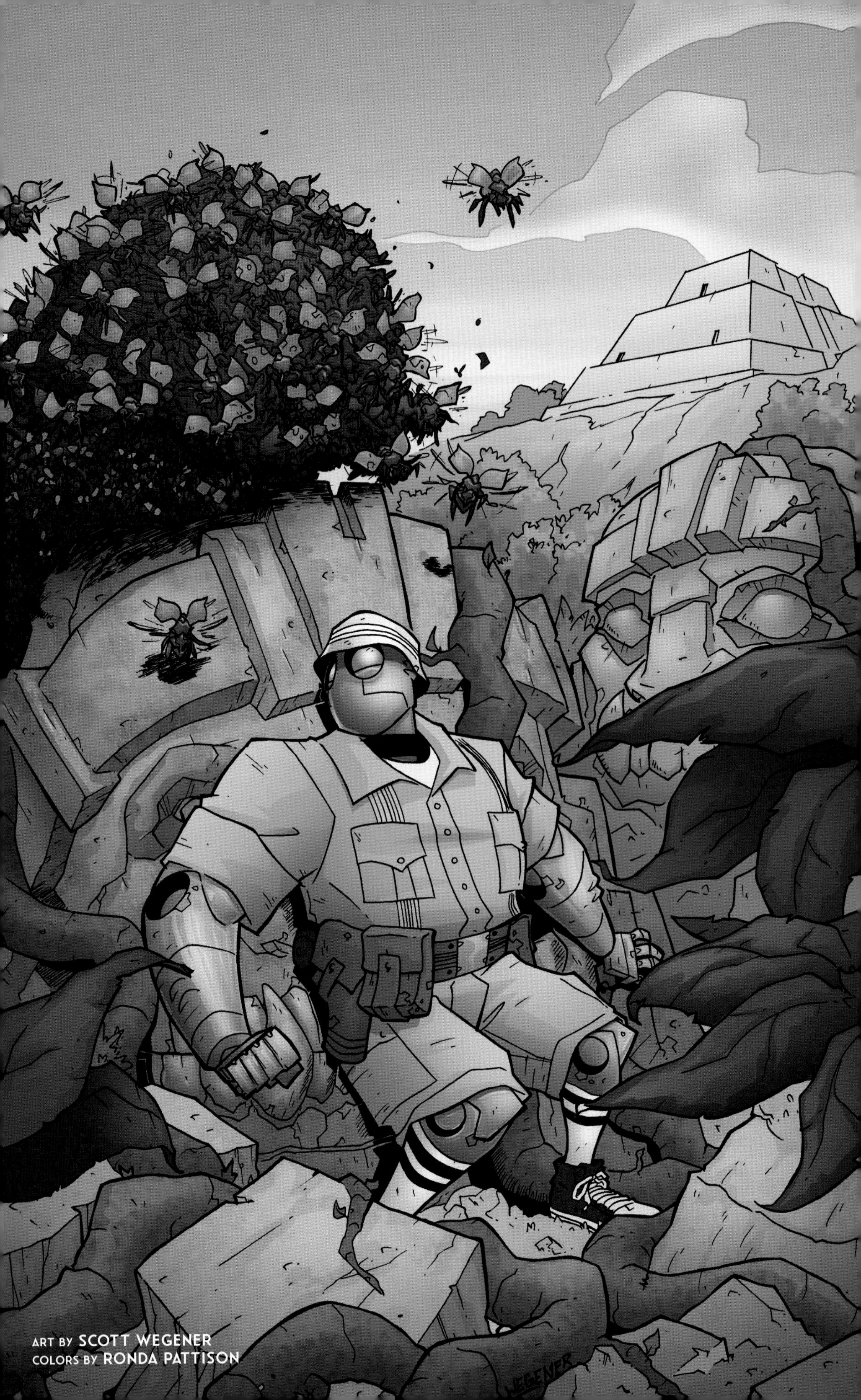
WEGENER

ART BY SCOTT WEGENER
COLORS BY RONDA PATTISON

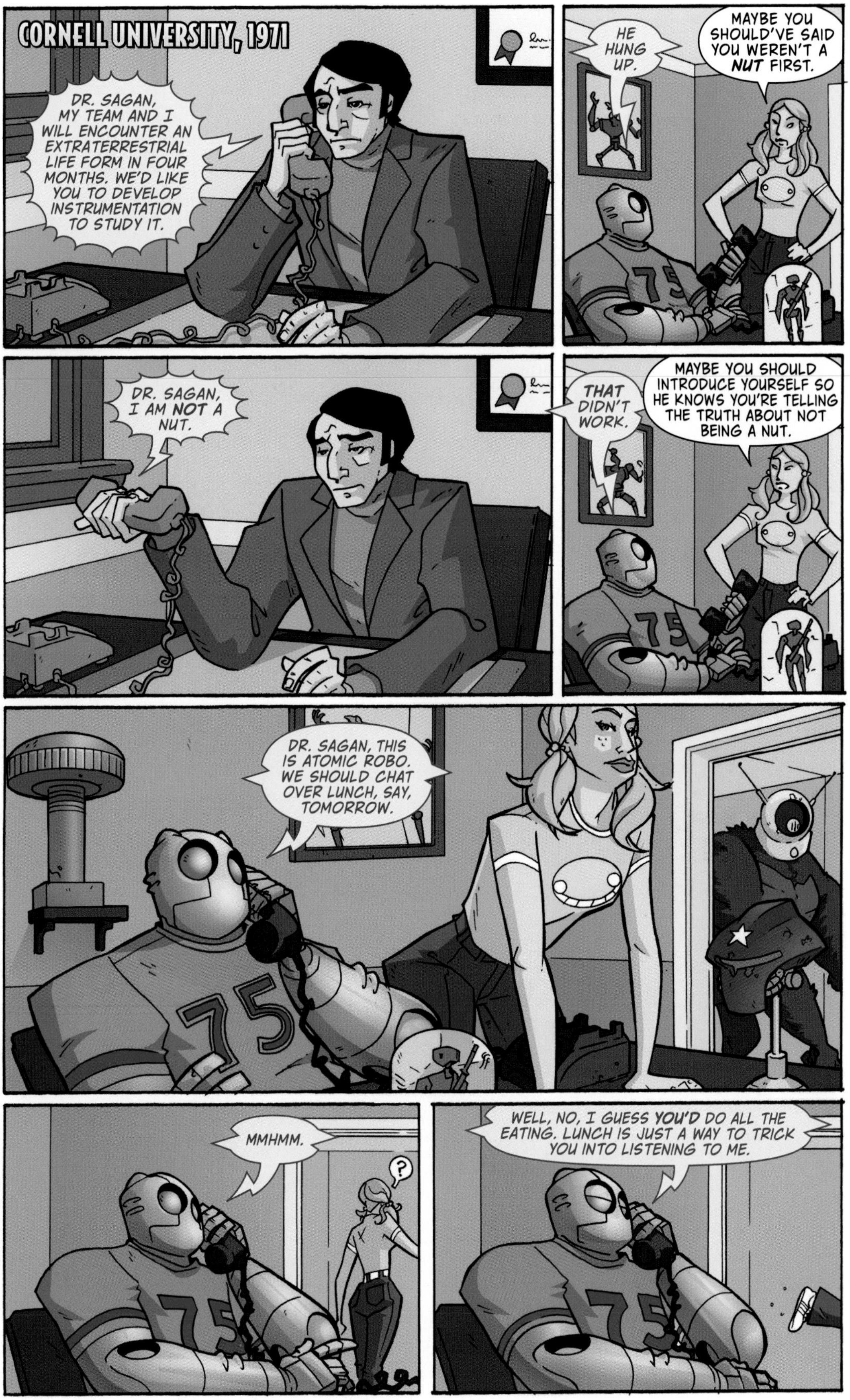
CORNELL UNIVERSITY, 1971
DR. SAGAN, MY TEAM AND I WILL ENCOUNTER AN EXTRATERRESTRIAL LIFE FORM IN FOUR MONTHS. WE'D LIKE YOU TO DEVELOP INSTRUMENTATION TO STUDY IT.
HE HUNG UP.
MAYBE YOU SHOULD'VE SAID YOU WEREN'T A NUT FIRST.
DR. SAGAN, I AM NOT A NUT.
THAT DIDN'T WORK.
MAYBE YOU SHOULD INTRODUCE YOURSELF SO HE KNOWS YOU'RE TELLING THE TRUTH ABOUT NOT BEING A NUT.
DR. SAGAN, THIS IS ATOMIC ROBO. WE SHOULD CHAT OVER LUNCH, SAY, TOMORROW.
MMHMM.
?
WELL, NO, I GUESS YOU'D DO ALL THE EATING. LUNCH IS JUST A WAY TO TRICK YOU INTO LISTENING TO ME.

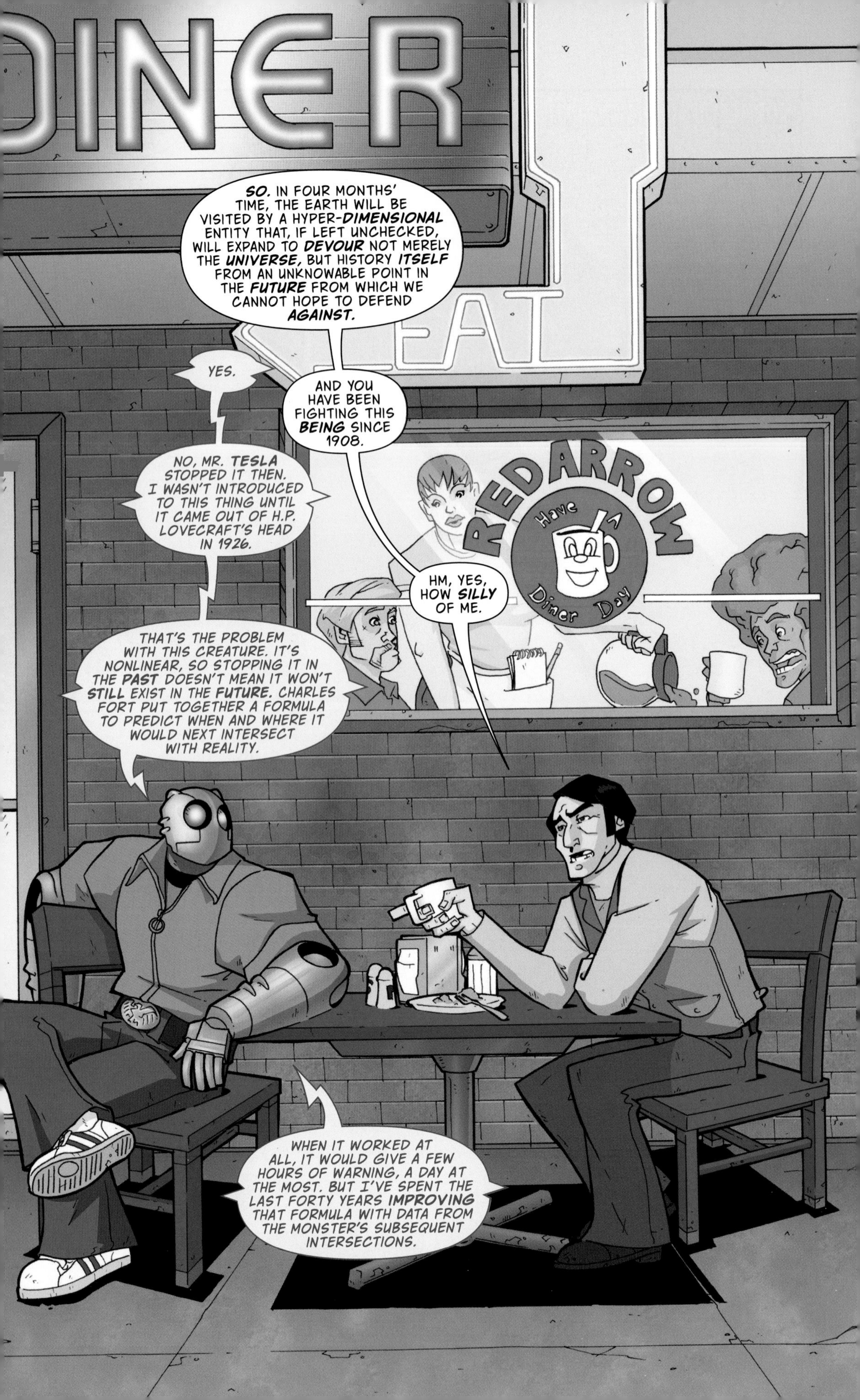
DINER
EAT
SO. IN FOUR MONTHS' TIME, THE EARTH WILL BE VISITED BY A HYPER-DIMENSIONAL ENTITY THAT, IF LEFT UNCHECKED, WILL EXPAND TO DEVOUR NOT MERELY THE UNIVERSE, BUT HISTORY ITSELF FROM AN UNKNOWABLE POINT IN THE FUTURE FROM WHICH WE CANNOT HOPE TO DEFEND AGAINST.
YES.
AND YOU HAVE BEEN FIGHTING THIS BEING SINCE 1908.
NO, MR. TESLA STOPPED IT THEN. I WASN'T INTRODUCED TO THIS THING UNTIL IT CAME OUT OF H.P. LOVECRAFT'S HEAD IN 1926.
HM, YES, HOW SILLY OF ME.
RED ARROW
Have A Diner Day
THAT'S THE PROBLEM WITH THIS CREATURE. IT'S NONLINEAR, SO STOPPING IT IN THE PAST DOESN'T MEAN IT WON'T STILL EXIST IN THE FUTURE. CHARLES FORT PUT TOGETHER A FORMULA TO PREDICT WHEN AND WHERE IT WOULD NEXT INTERSECT WITH REALITY.
WHEN IT WORKED AT ALL, IT WOULD GIVE A FEW HOURS OF WARNING, A DAY AT THE MOST. BUT I'VE SPENT THE LAST FORTY YEARS IMPROVING THAT FORMULA WITH DATA FROM THE MONSTER'S SUBSEQUENT INTERSECTIONS.

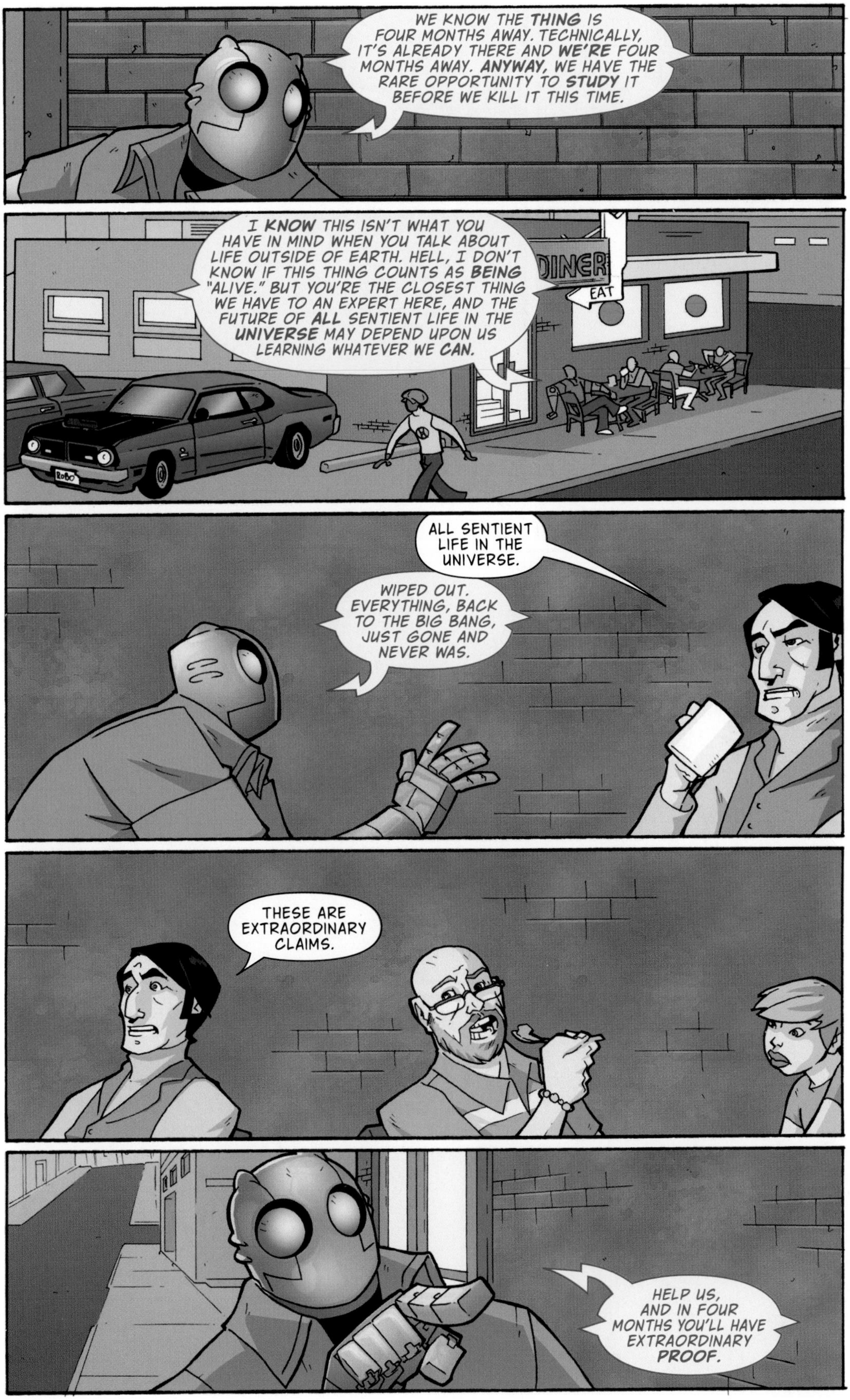
WE KNOW THE THING IS FOUR MONTHS AWAY. TECHNICALLY, IT'S ALREADY THERE AND WE'RE FOUR MONTHS AWAY. ANYWAY, WE HAVE THE RARE OPPORTUNITY TO STUDY IT BEFORE WE KILL IT THIS TIME.
I KNOW THIS ISN'T WHAT YOU HAVE IN MIND WHEN YOU TALK ABOUT LIFE OUTSIDE OF EARTH. HELL, I DON'T KNOW IF THIS THING COUNTS AS BEING "ALIVE." BUT YOU'RE THE CLOSEST THING WE HAVE TO AN EXPERT HERE, AND THE FUTURE OF ALL SENTIENT LIFE IN THE UNIVERSE MAY DEPEND UPON US LEARNING WHATEVER WE CAN.
DINER
EAT
ROBO
ALL SENTIENT LIFE IN THE UNIVERSE.
WIPED OUT. EVERYTHING, BACK TO THE BIG BANG, JUST GONE AND NEVER WAS.
THESE ARE EXTRAORDINARY CLAIMS.
HELP US, AND IN FOUR MONTHS YOU'LL HAVE EXTRAORDINARY PROOF.

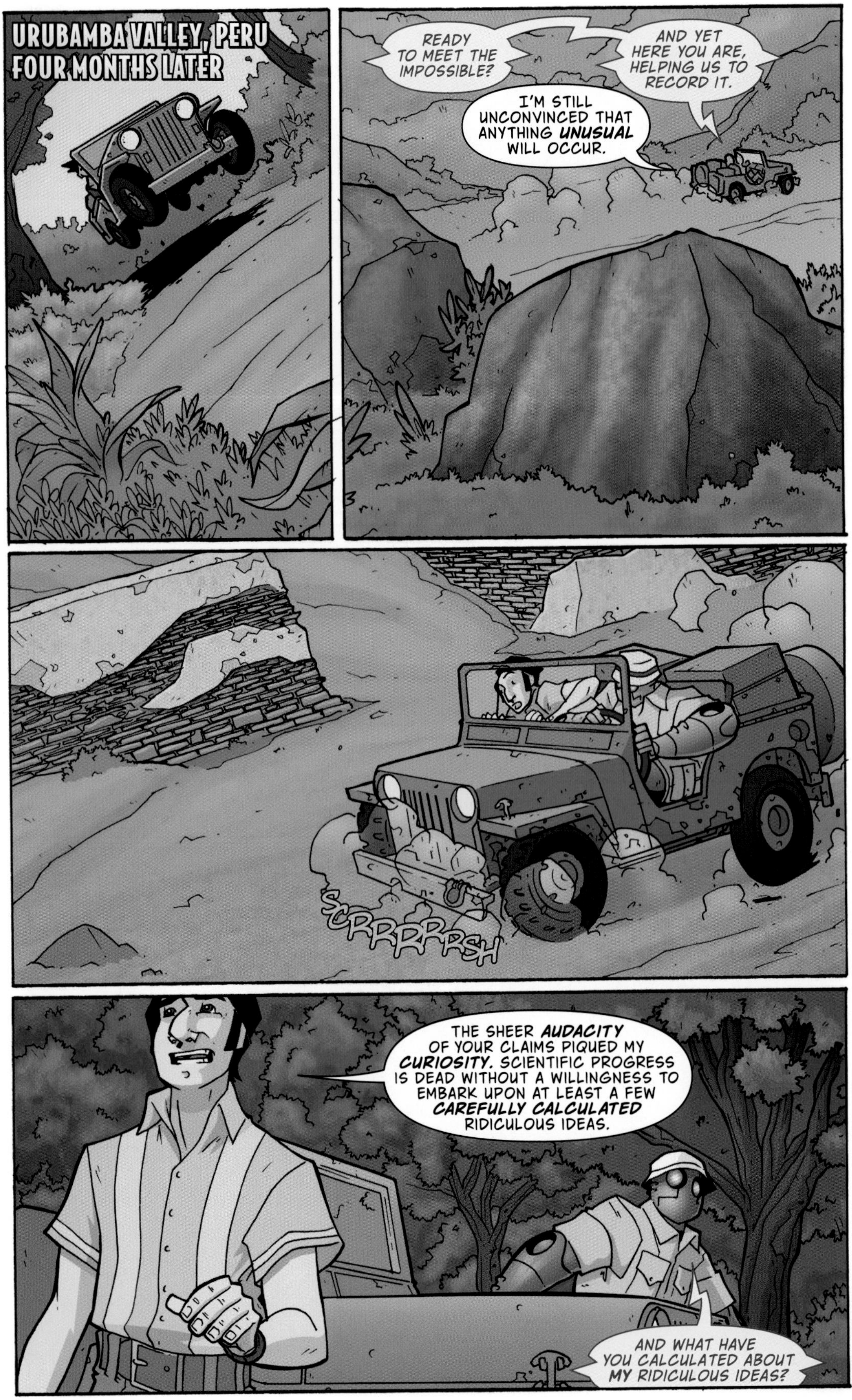
URUBAMBA VALLEY, PERU
FOUR MONTHS LATER
READY TO MEET THE IMPOSSIBLE?
AND YET HERE YOU ARE, HELPING US TO RECORD IT.
I'M STILL UNCONVINCED THAT ANYTHING UNUSUAL WILL OCCUR.
SCRRRRRSH
THE SHEER AUDACITY OF YOUR CLAIMS PIQUED MY CURIOSITY. SCIENTIFIC PROGRESS IS DEAD WITHOUT A WILLINGNESS TO EMBARK UPON AT LEAST A FEW CAREFULLY CALCULATED RIDICULOUS IDEAS.
AND WHAT HAVE YOU CALCULATED ABOUT MY RIDICULOUS IDEAS?

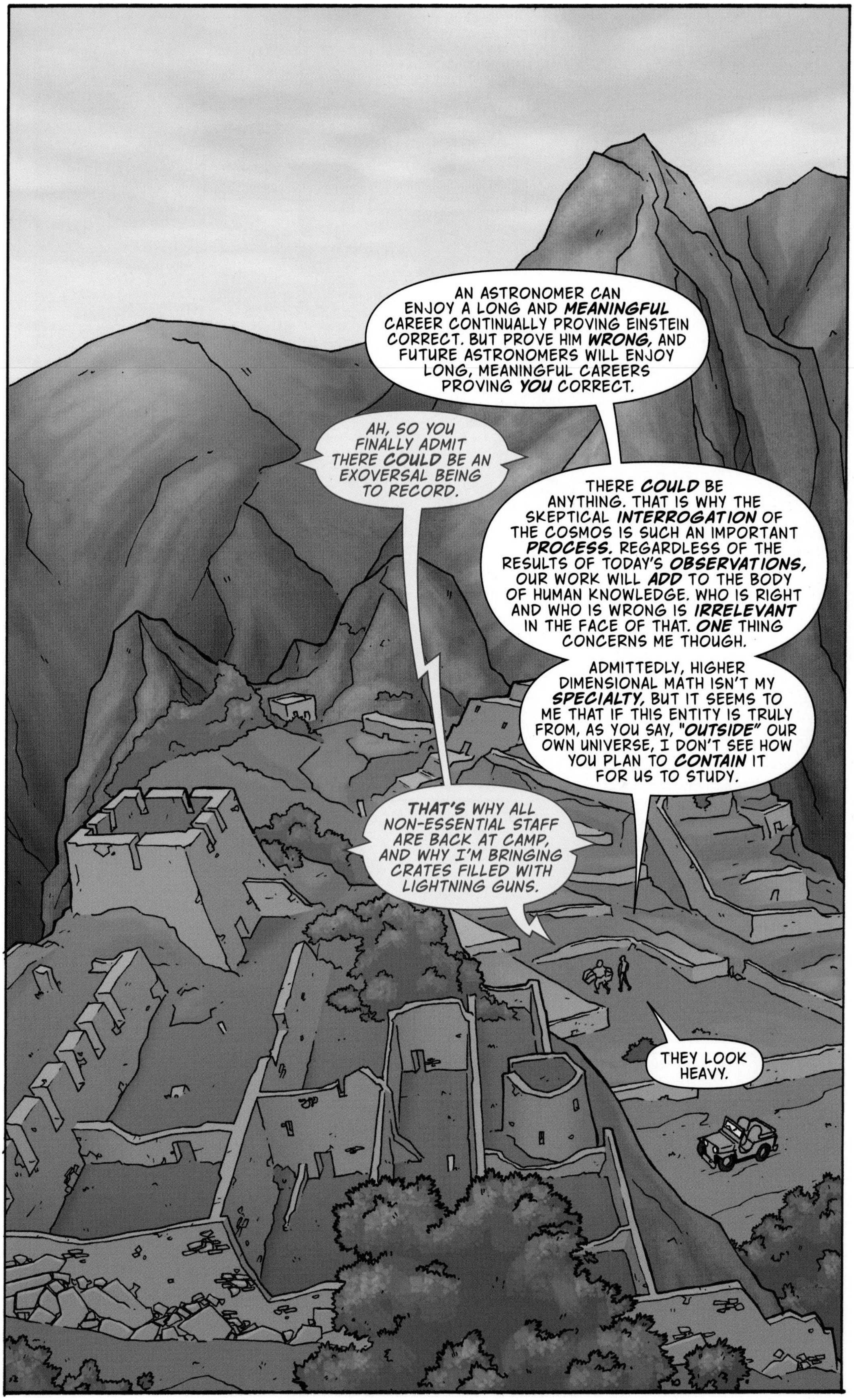
AN ASTRONOMER CAN ENJOY A LONG AND MEANINGFUL CAREER CONTINUALLY PROVING EINSTEIN CORRECT. BUT PROVE HIM WRONG, AND FUTURE ASTRONOMERS WILL ENJOY LONG, MEANINGFUL CAREERS PROVING YOU CORRECT.
AH, SO YOU FINALLY ADMIT THERE COULD BE AN EXOVERSAL BEING TO RECORD.
THERE COULD BE ANYTHING. THAT IS WHY THE SKEPTICAL INTERROGATION OF THE COSMOS IS SUCH AN IMPORTANT PROCESS. REGARDLESS OF THE RESULTS OF TODAY'S OBSERVATIONS, OUR WORK WILL ADD TO THE BODY OF HUMAN KNOWLEDGE. WHO IS RIGHT AND WHO IS WRONG IS IRRELEVANT IN THE FACE OF THAT. ONE THING CONCERNS ME THOUGH.
ADMITTEDLY, HIGHER DIMENSIONAL MATH ISN'T MY SPECIALTY, BUT IT SEEMS TO ME THAT IF THIS ENTITY IS TRULY FROM, AS YOU SAY, "OUTSIDE" OUR OWN UNIVERSE, I DON'T SEE HOW YOU PLAN TO CONTAIN IT FOR US TO STUDY.
THAT'S WHY ALL NON-ESSENTIAL STAFF ARE BACK AT CAMP, AND WHY I'M BRINGING CRATES FILLED WITH LIGHTNING GUNS.
THEY LOOK HEAVY.

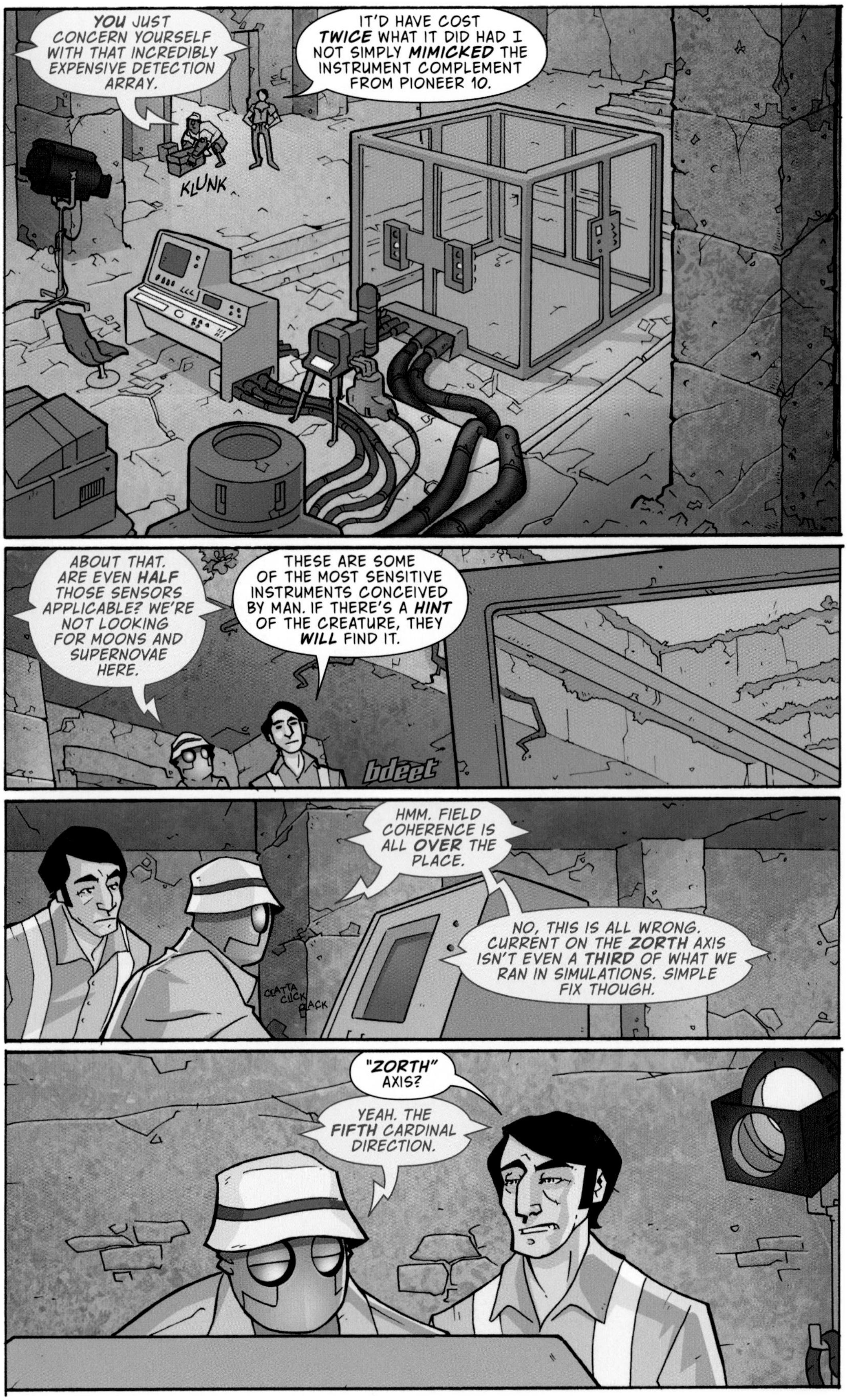
YOU JUST CONCERN YOURSELF WITH THAT INCREDIBLY EXPENSIVE DETECTION ARRAY.
IT'D HAVE COST TWICE WHAT IT DID HAD I NOT SIMPLY MIMICKED THE INSTRUMENT COMPLEMENT FROM PIONEER 10.
KLUNK
ABOUT THAT. ARE EVEN HALF THOSE SENSORS APPLICABLE? WE'RE NOT LOOKING FOR MOONS AND SUPERNOVAE HERE.
THESE ARE SOME OF THE MOST SENSITIVE INSTRUMENTS CONCEIVED BY MAN. IF THERE'S A HINT OF THE CREATURE, THEY WILL FIND IT.
bdeet
HMM. FIELD COHERENCE IS ALL OVER THE PLACE.
NO, THIS IS ALL WRONG. CURRENT ON THE ZORTH AXIS ISN'T EVEN A THIRD OF WHAT WE RAN IN SIMULATIONS. SIMPLE FIX THOUGH.
CLATTA CLICK CLACK
"ZORTH" AXIS?
YEAH. THE FIFTH CARDINAL DIRECTION.

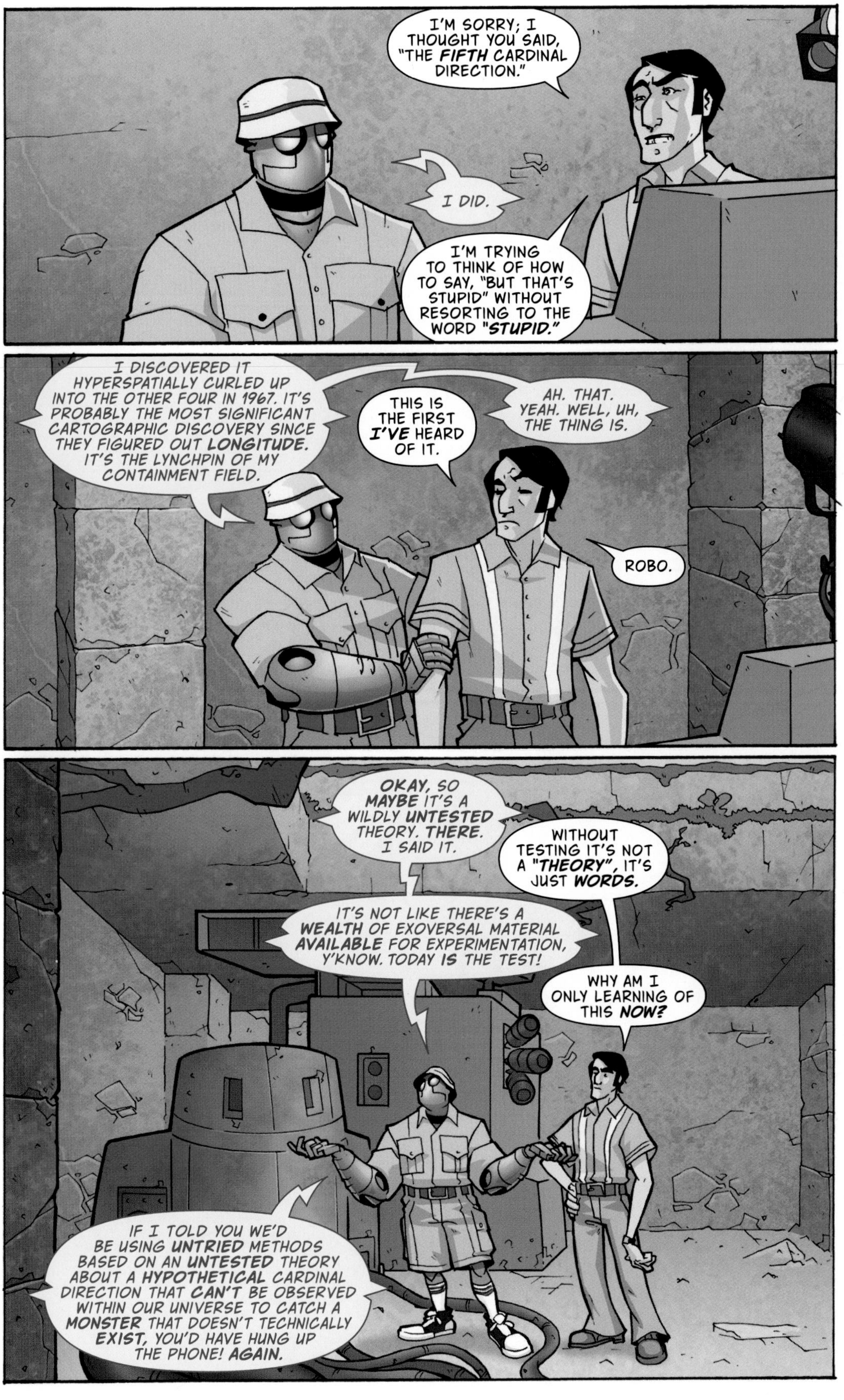
I'M SORRY; I THOUGHT YOU SAID, "THE FIFTH CARDINAL DIRECTION."
I DID.
I'M TRYING TO THINK OF HOW TO SAY, "BUT THAT'S STUPID" WITHOUT RESORTING TO THE WORD "STUPID."
I DISCOVERED IT HYPERSPATIALLY CURLED UP INTO THE OTHER FOUR IN 1967. IT'S PROBABLY THE MOST SIGNIFICANT CARTOGRAPHIC DISCOVERY SINCE THEY FIGURED OUT LONGITUDE. IT'S THE LYNCHPIN OF MY CONTAINMENT FIELD.
THIS IS THE FIRST I'VE HEARD OF IT.
AH. THAT. YEAH. WELL, UH, THE THING IS.
ROBO.
OKAY, SO MAYBE IT'S A WILDLY UNTESTED THEORY. THERE. I SAID IT.
WITHOUT TESTING IT'S NOT A "THEORY", IT'S JUST WORDS.
IT'S NOT LIKE THERE'S A WEALTH OF EXOVERSAL MATERIAL AVAILABLE FOR EXPERIMENTATION, Y'KNOW. TODAY IS THE TEST!
WHY AM I ONLY LEARNING OF THIS NOW?
IF I TOLD YOU WE'D BE USING UNTRIED METHODS BASED ON AN UNTESTED THEORY ABOUT A HYPOTHETICAL CARDINAL DIRECTION THAT CAN'T BE OBSERVED WITHIN OUR UNIVERSE TO CATCH A MONSTER THAT DOESN'T TECHNICALLY EXIST, YOU'D HAVE HUNG UP THE PHONE! AGAIN.

AND I'D HAVE BEEN *RIGHT* TO DO IT.

AND *THAT'S WHY* I HAD TO LIE. A LITTLE.

IT WAS A FOUR-MONTH CAMPAIGN OF *DECEPTION* TO KEEP ME FROM THE TRUTH.

GRANTED, *BUT* I WAS ONLY LYING A *LITTLE BIT* EVERY TIME.

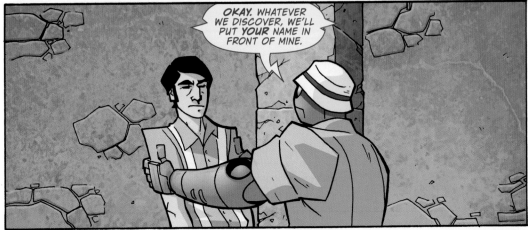

OKAY. WHATEVER WE DISCOVER, WE'LL PUT *YOUR* NAME IN FRONT OF MINE.

ALL RIGHT? LET'S DO SOME *SCIENCE.*

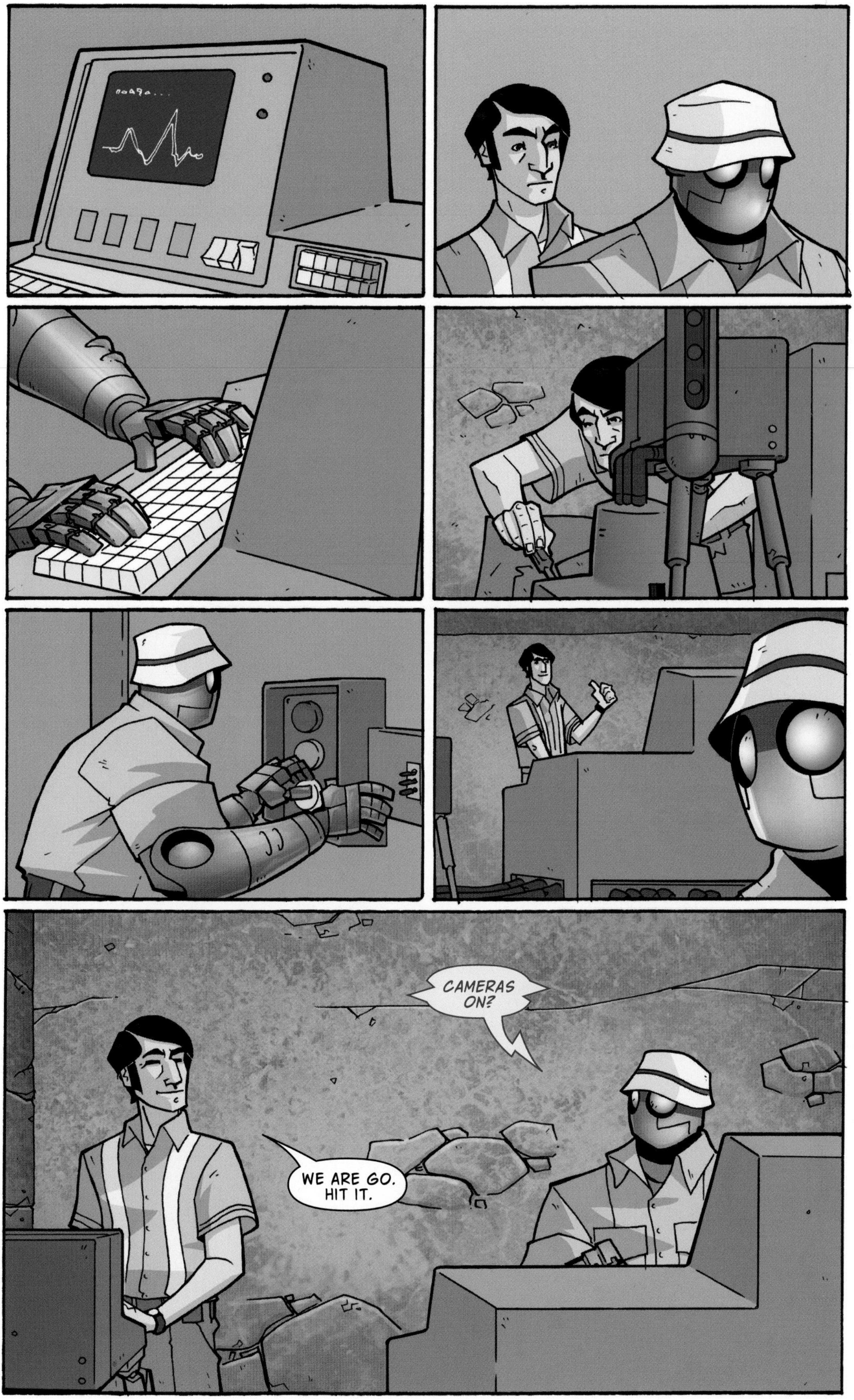
CAMERAS ON?
WE ARE GO. HIT IT.

DID YOU REMEMBER TO PRESS THE BUTTON?
OF COURSE I DID!
HRM. I'M REGISTERING NONSENSICAL DATA. DISTANCE TO THE CONTAINMENT CAGE IS CURRENTLY READING AS INFINITY MINUS ONE METERS.
IT MAY AS WELL SAY "A JILLION" OR PERHAPS "CADILLAC."
NO! THAT'S A BREACH OF THE ZORTH AXIS INTO REAL SPACE-TIME, IT'S WORKING!
YOUR TECHNOBABBLE WON'T MAKE A NUMBER THAT DOESN'T EXIST ANY MORE MEANINGFUL.
ALMOST THERE...
SPLAAAG!

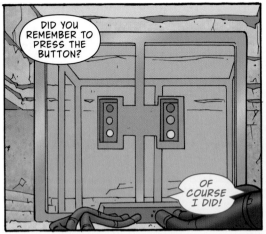

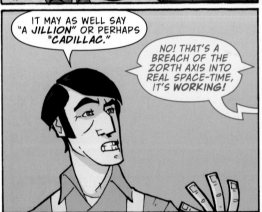

ROBO. I THINK I'M INSANE NOW.

THAT'S *GOOD*, YOU'D BE CRAZY NOT TO BE. BUT DON'T LOOK DIRECTLY AT IT *TOO* MUCH. IT CAN GET IN YOUR HEAD AND I *DON'T* MEAN THAT METAPHORICALLY.

ROHHHH

BOHHHH

AWW, YOU REMEMBER ME? THAT'S SWEET.

C'MON...

THERE I'M CALLING IT. FIELD IS SECURE. OUR GUEST'S NOT GOING ANYWHERE.

HOW YOU HOLDING UP, CARL?

I REQUIRE A STIFF DRINK. SEVERAL OF THEM, IN FACT. ENOUGH TO PARALYZE A *COW*.

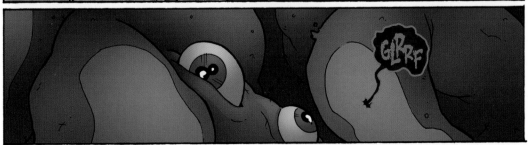

GLRRF

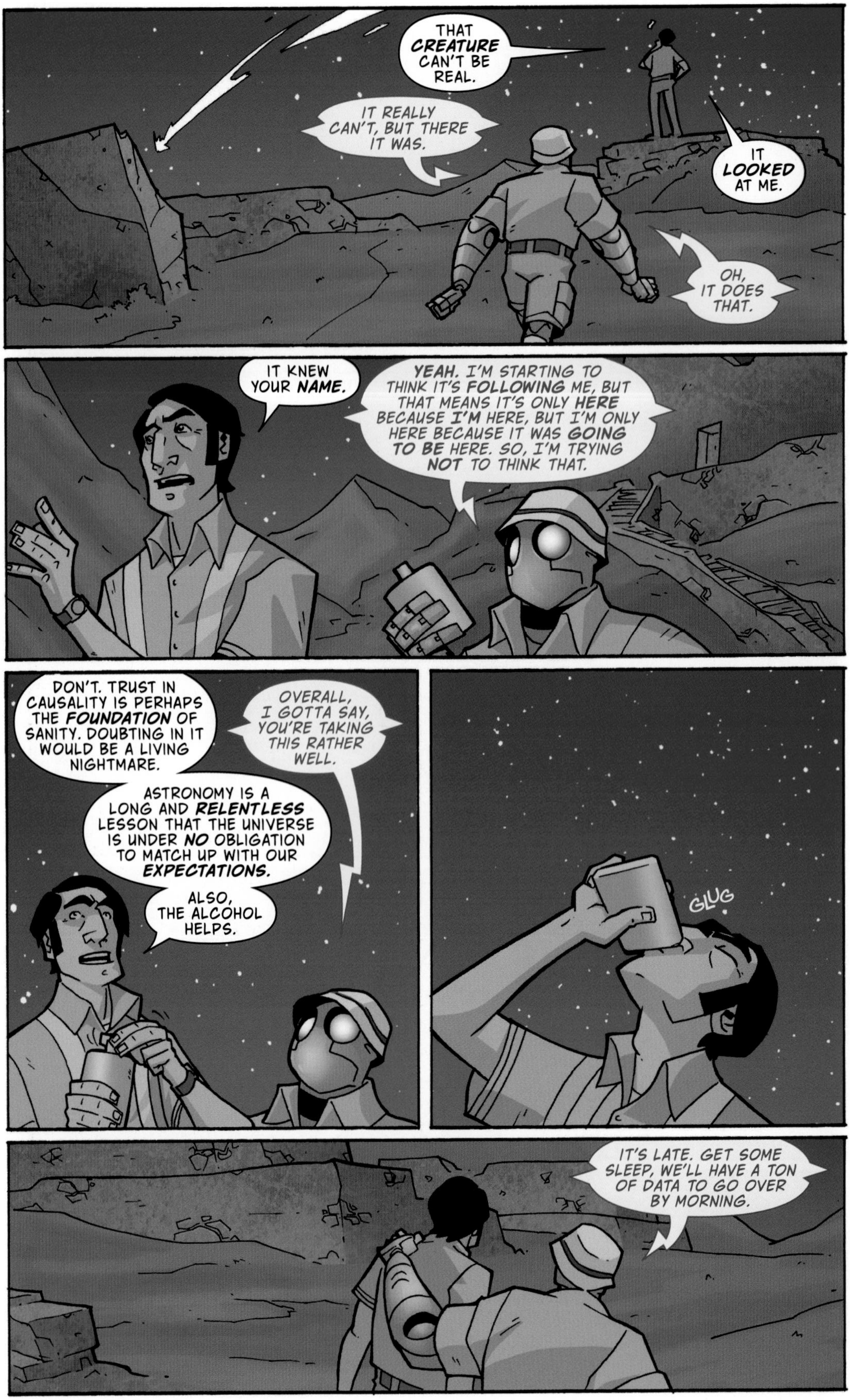
THAT CREATURE CAN'T BE REAL.
IT REALLY CAN'T, BUT THERE IT WAS.
IT LOOKED AT ME.
OH, IT DOES THAT.
IT KNEW YOUR NAME.
YEAH. I'M STARTING TO THINK IT'S FOLLOWING ME, BUT THAT MEANS IT'S ONLY HERE BECAUSE I'M HERE, BUT I'M ONLY HERE BECAUSE IT WAS GOING TO BE HERE. SO, I'M TRYING NOT TO THINK THAT.
DON'T. TRUST IN CAUSALITY IS PERHAPS THE FOUNDATION OF SANITY. DOUBTING IN IT WOULD BE A LIVING NIGHTMARE.
OVERALL, I GOTTA SAY, YOU'RE TAKING THIS RATHER WELL.
ASTRONOMY IS A LONG AND RELENTLESS LESSON THAT THE UNIVERSE IS UNDER NO OBLIGATION TO MATCH UP WITH OUR EXPECTATIONS.
ALSO, THE ALCOHOL HELPS.
GLUG
IT'S LATE. GET SOME SLEEP, WE'LL HAVE A TON OF DATA TO GO OVER BY MORNING.

YES, OF COURSE. AND BY LUNCH WE'LL TEASE SOMETHING BRILLIANT OUT OF IT TO CHANGE THE WORLD FOREVER AND CALL IT THE SAGAN-ROBO CONJECTURE.
TECHNICALLY MY LAST NAME IS TESLA.
YOUR NAME IS DR. ATOMIC ROBO TESLA?
YEAH.
THEY SHOULD MAKE COMIC BOOKS OUT OF YOU.
REST UP. I'LL MAKE SURE EVERYTHING RUNS SMOOTHLY UNTIL MORNING.
SGLUUURG
LOOKS LIKE IT'S JUST YOU AND ME, CHUCKLES.
NOT SO TOUGH WHEN YOU'RE LOCKED IN A DIMENSIONAL MATRIX, ARE YA?
WELL, YOU'RE GOING TO BE IN THERE FOR A WHILE. SO, GET COMFORTABLE.
TEMPORAL MECHANICS MADE EASY

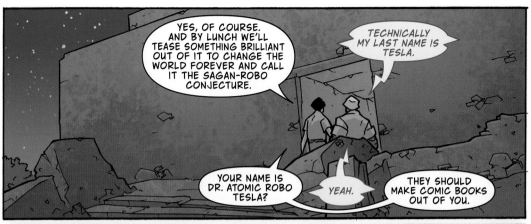

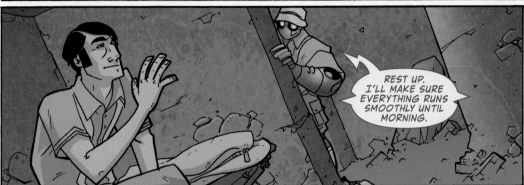

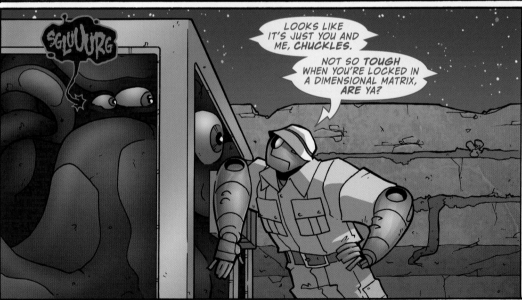

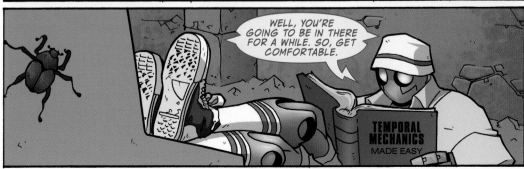

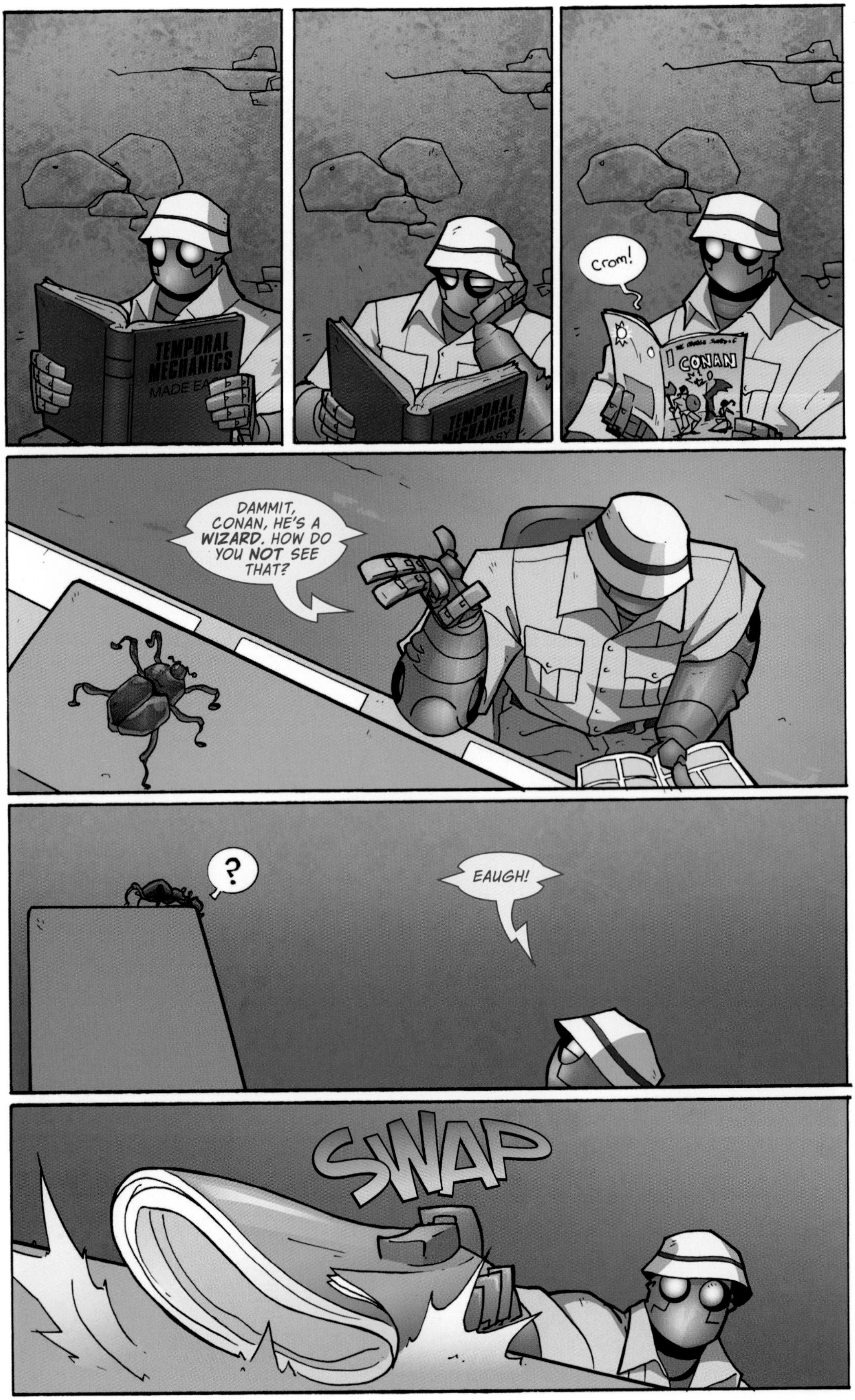
TEMPORAL MECHANICS
Crom!
CONAN
DAMMIT, CONAN, HE'S A **WIZARD.** HOW DO YOU **NOT** SEE THAT?
?
EAUGH!
SWAP

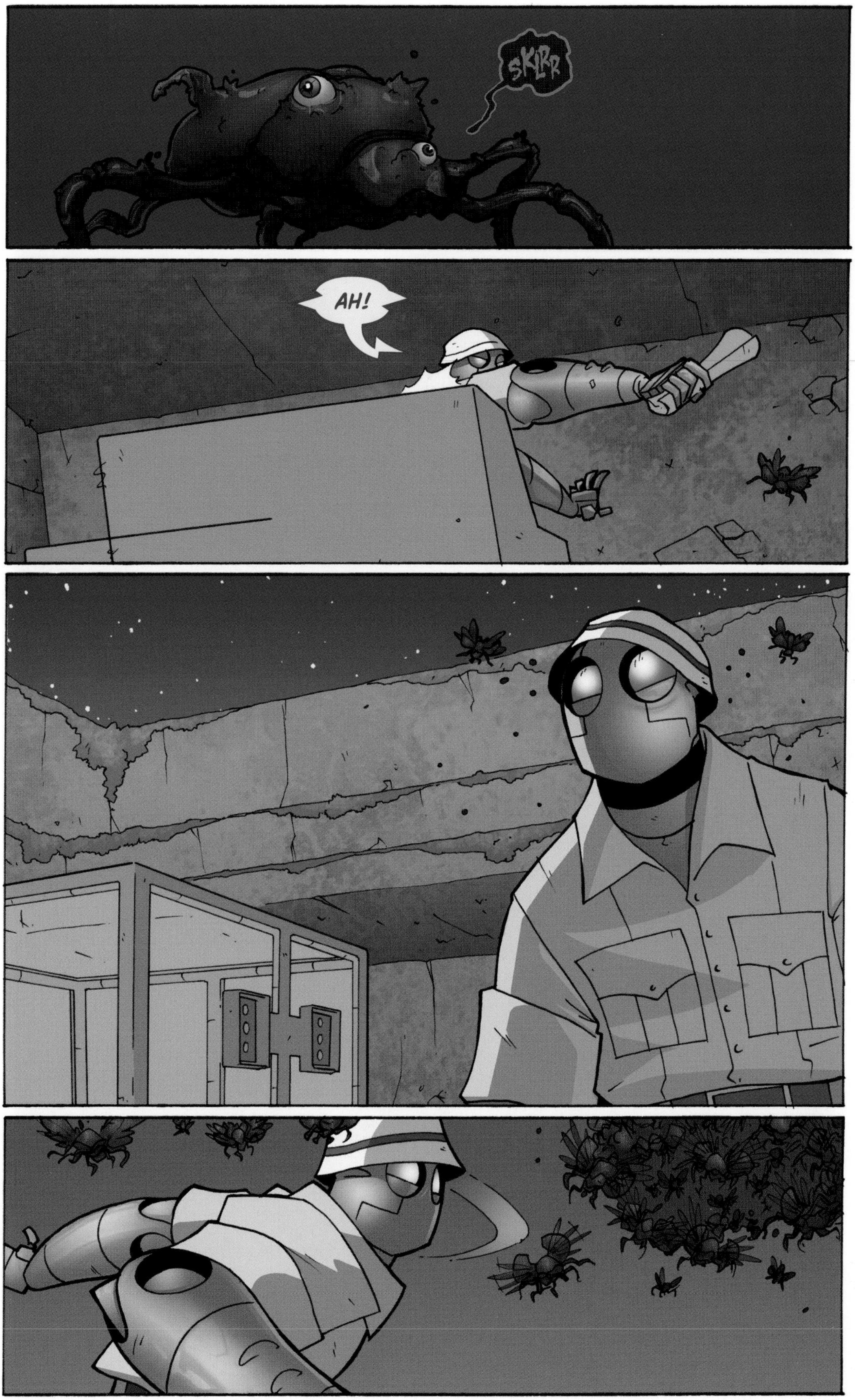
SKLRR
AH!

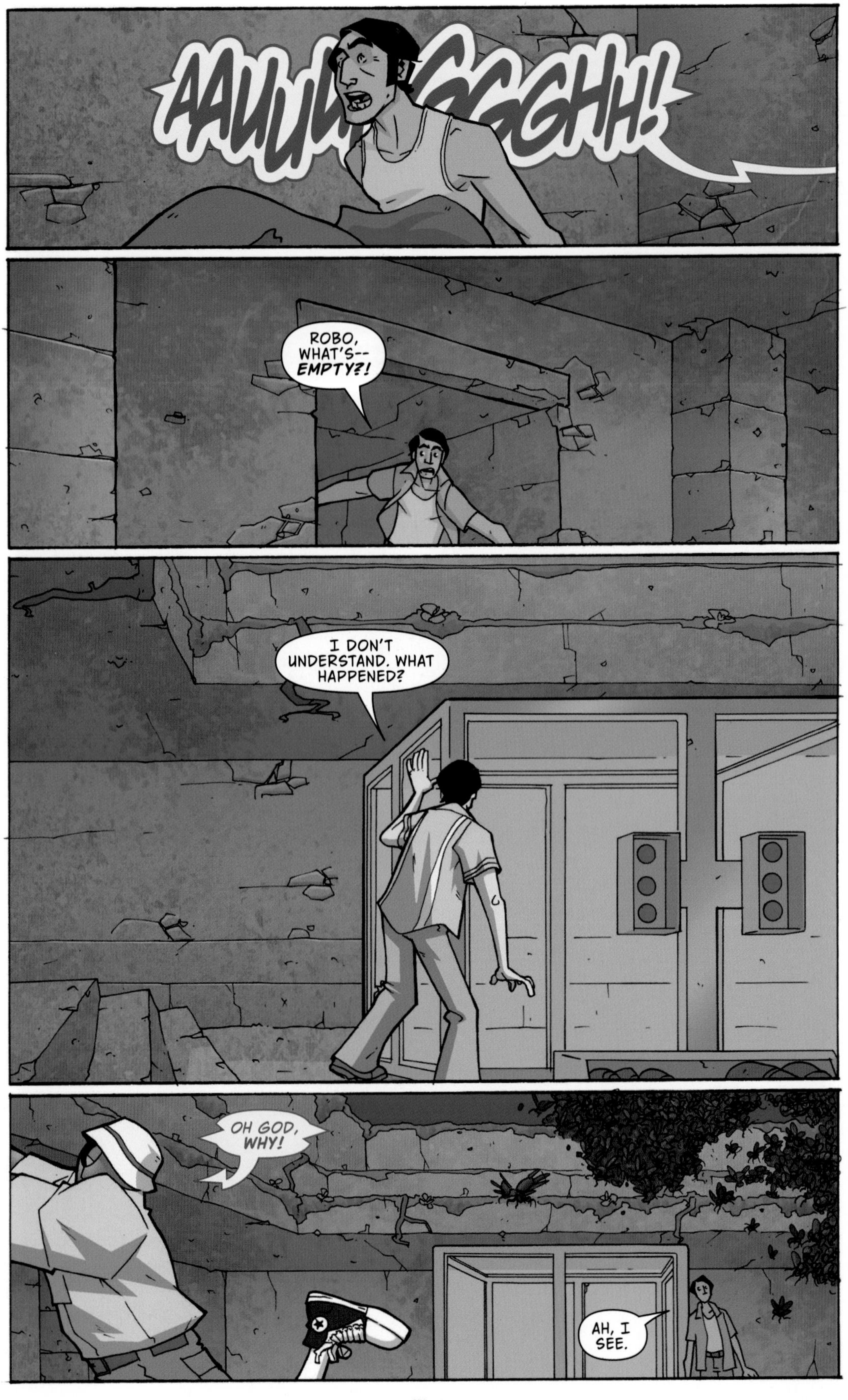
AAUUUGGGHH!
ROBO, WHAT'S-- EMPTY?!
I DON'T UNDERSTAND. WHAT HAPPENED?
OH GOD, WHY!
AH, I SEE.

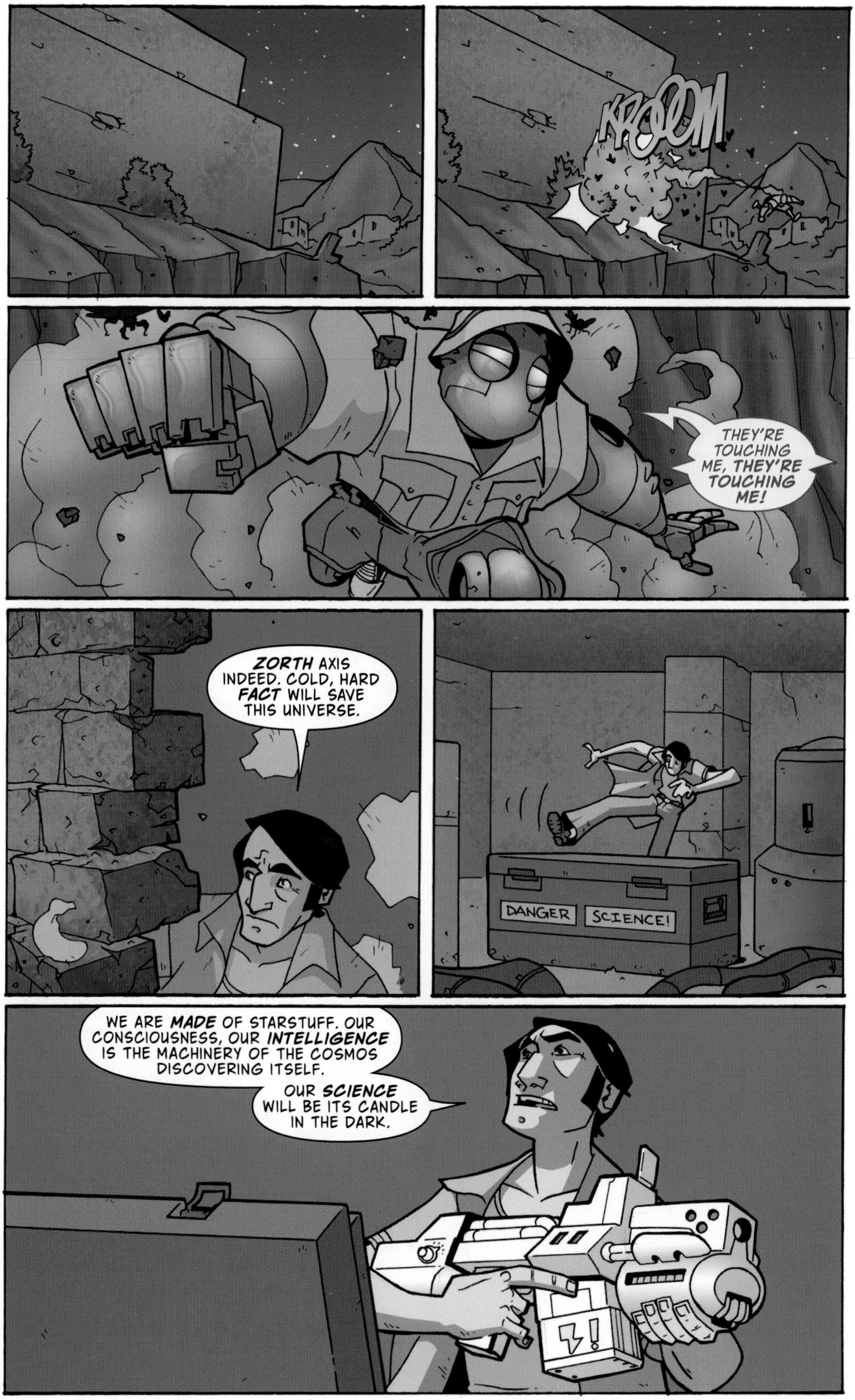
KROOM
THEY'RE TOUCHING ME, THEY'RE TOUCHING ME!
ZORTH AXIS INDEED. COLD, HARD FACT WILL SAVE THIS UNIVERSE.
DANGER
SCIENCE!
WE ARE MADE OF STARSTUFF. OUR CONSCIOUSNESS, OUR INTELLIGENCE IS THE MACHINERY OF THE COSMOS DISCOVERING ITSELF.
OUR SCIENCE WILL BE ITS CANDLE IN THE DARK.

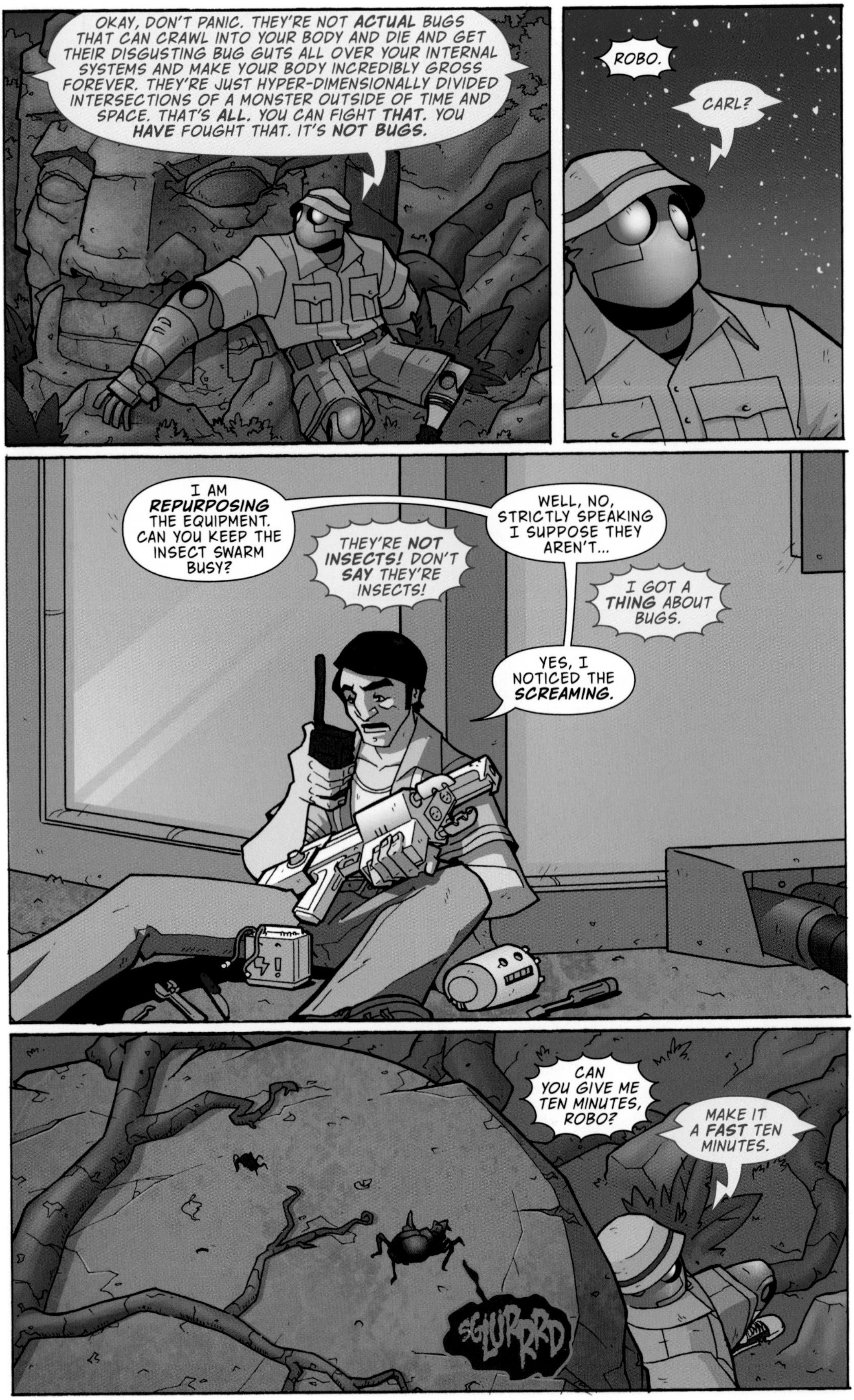
OKAY, DON'T PANIC. THEY'RE NOT **ACTUAL** BUGS THAT CAN CRAWL INTO YOUR BODY AND DIE AND GET THEIR DISGUSTING BUG GUTS ALL OVER YOUR INTERNAL SYSTEMS AND MAKE YOUR BODY INCREDIBLY GROSS FOREVER. THEY'RE JUST HYPER-DIMENSIONALLY DIVIDED INTERSECTIONS OF A MONSTER OUTSIDE OF TIME AND SPACE. THAT'S **ALL.** YOU CAN FIGHT **THAT.** YOU **HAVE** FOUGHT THAT. IT'S **NOT BUGS.**
ROBO.
CARL?
I AM **REPURPOSING** THE EQUIPMENT. CAN YOU KEEP THE INSECT SWARM BUSY?
THEY'RE **NOT INSECTS!** DON'T **SAY** THEY'RE INSECTS!
WELL, NO, STRICTLY SPEAKING I SUPPOSE THEY AREN'T...
I GOT A **THING** ABOUT BUGS.
YES, I NOTICED THE **SCREAMING.**
CAN YOU GIVE ME TEN MINUTES, ROBO?
MAKE IT A **FAST** TEN MINUTES.
SGLURRRD

"THE PLAN IS SIMPLE.

"IT IS A SINGLE ENTITY INTERSECTING OUR SPACE-TIME VIA *THOUSANDS* OF ITERATIONS.

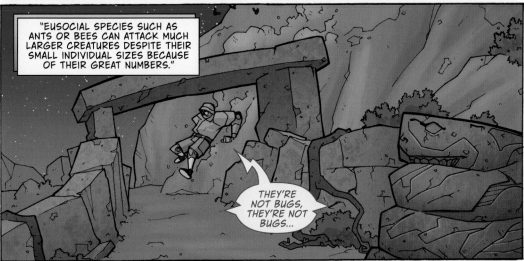

"EUSOCIAL SPECIES SUCH AS ANTS OR BEES CAN ATTACK MUCH LARGER CREATURES DESPITE THEIR SMALL INDIVIDUAL SIZES BECAUSE OF THEIR GREAT NUMBERS."

THEY'RE NOT BUGS, THEY'RE NOT BUGS...

"THEREFORE, WE NEED ONLY *NEGATE* THOSE ADVANTAGES AND REDUCE THIS SWARM TO A SINGLE, VERY *PUNCHABLE,* ENTITY."

DO YOU KNOW WHAT YOU'RE DOING?

I HAVEN'T A CLUE.

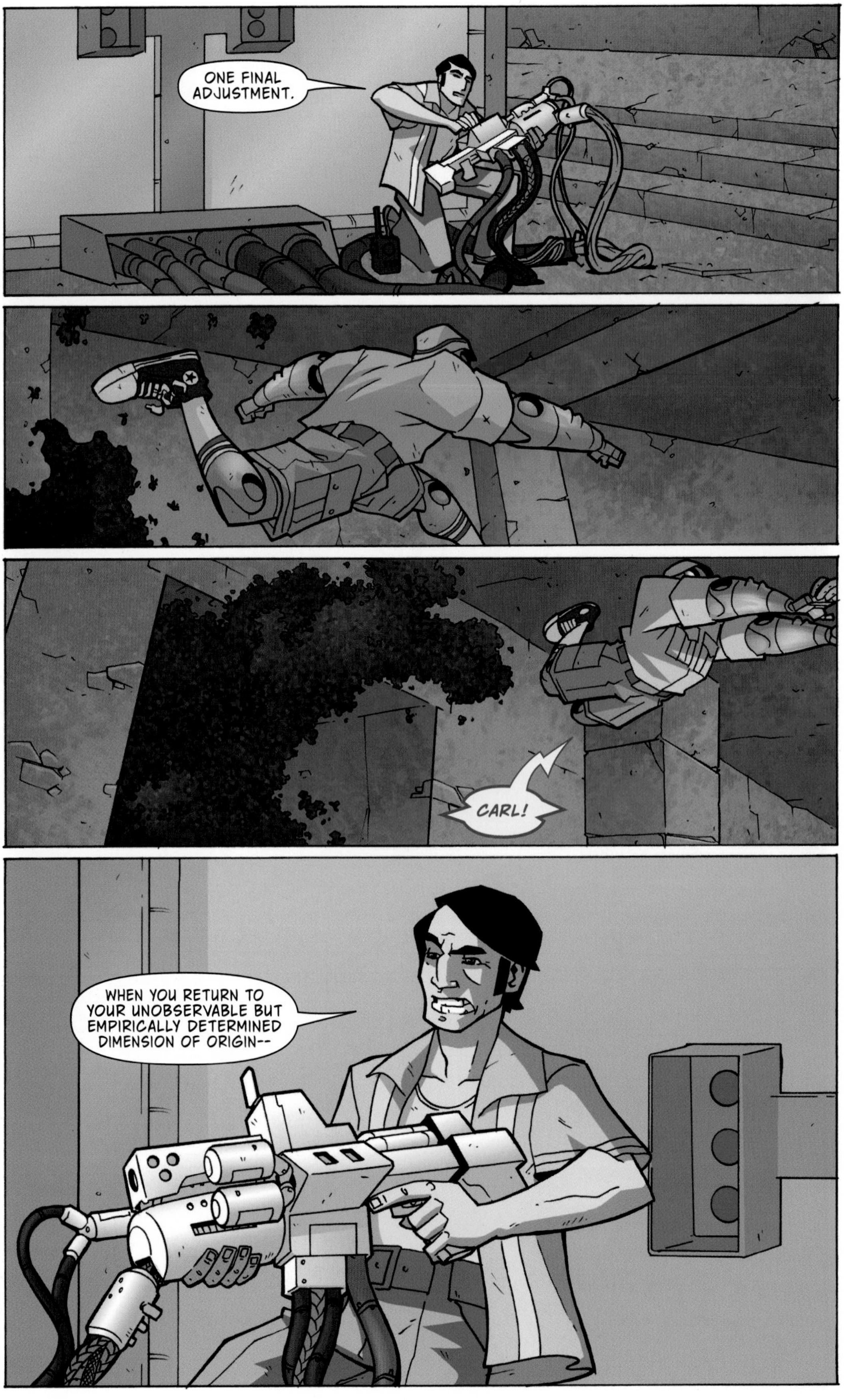
ONE FINAL ADJUSTMENT.
CARL!
WHEN YOU RETURN TO YOUR UNOBSERVABLE BUT EMPIRICALLY DETERMINED DIMENSION OF ORIGIN--

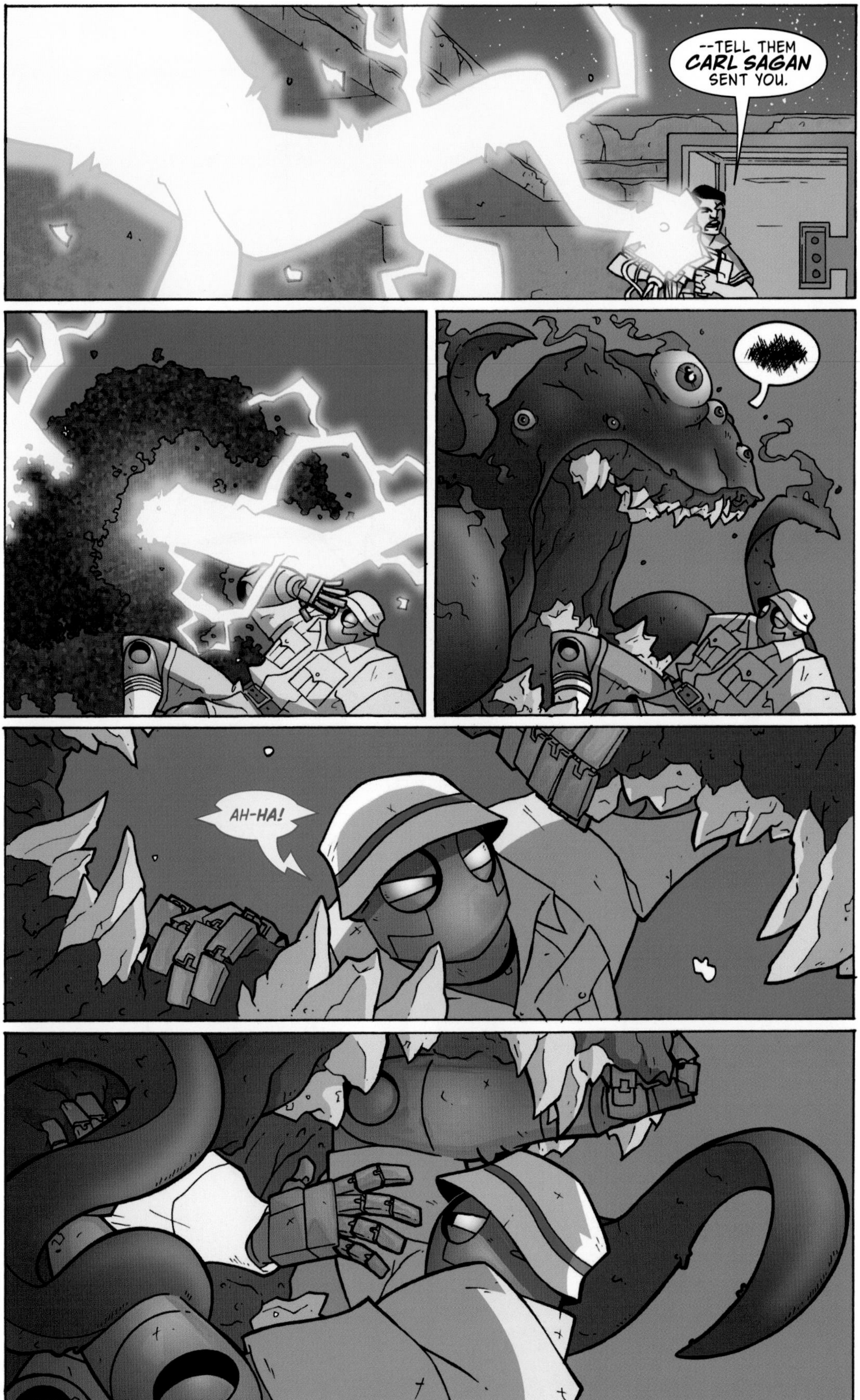
--TELL THEM CARL SAGAN SENT YOU.
AH-HA!

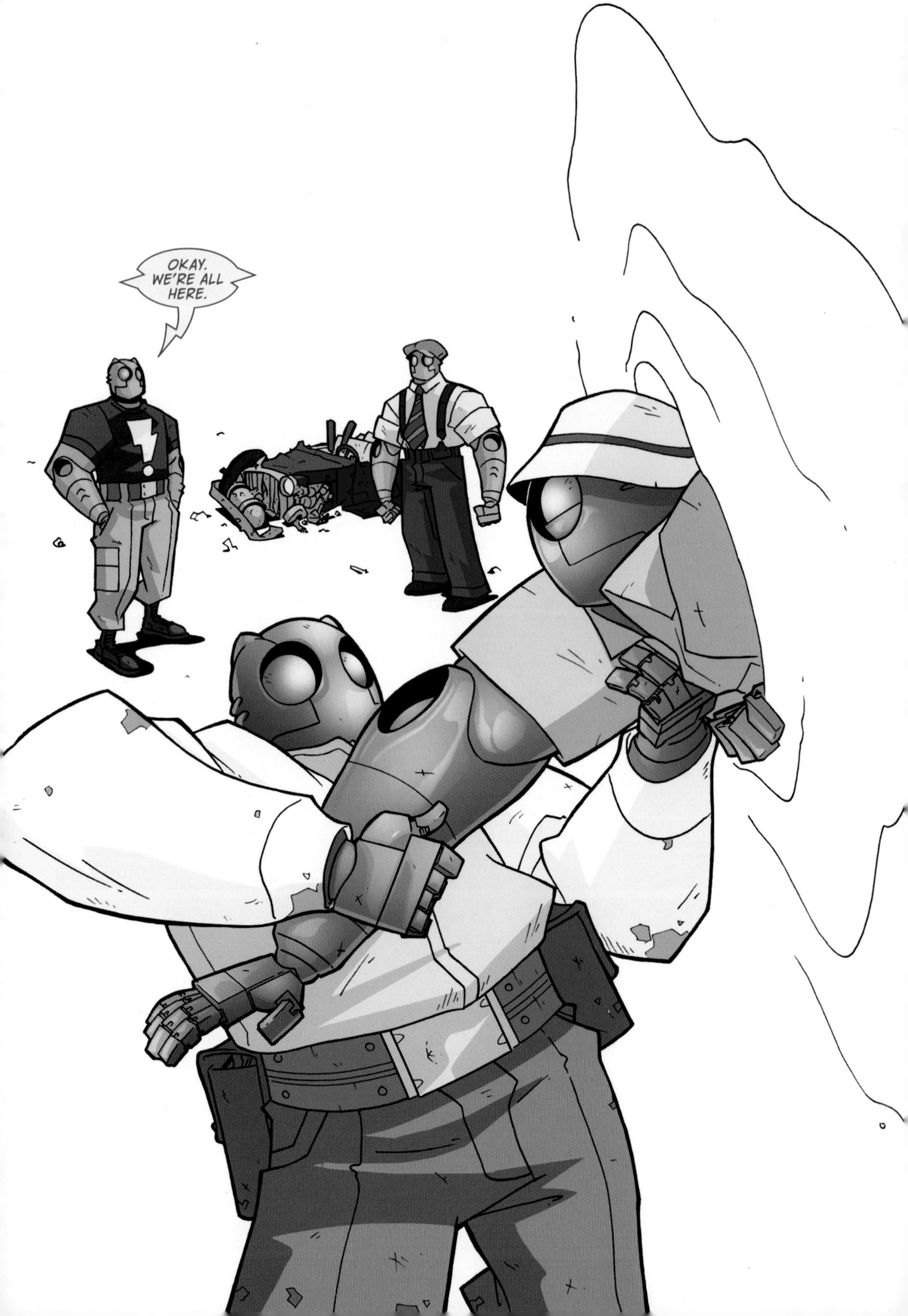
OKAY. WE'RE ALL HERE.

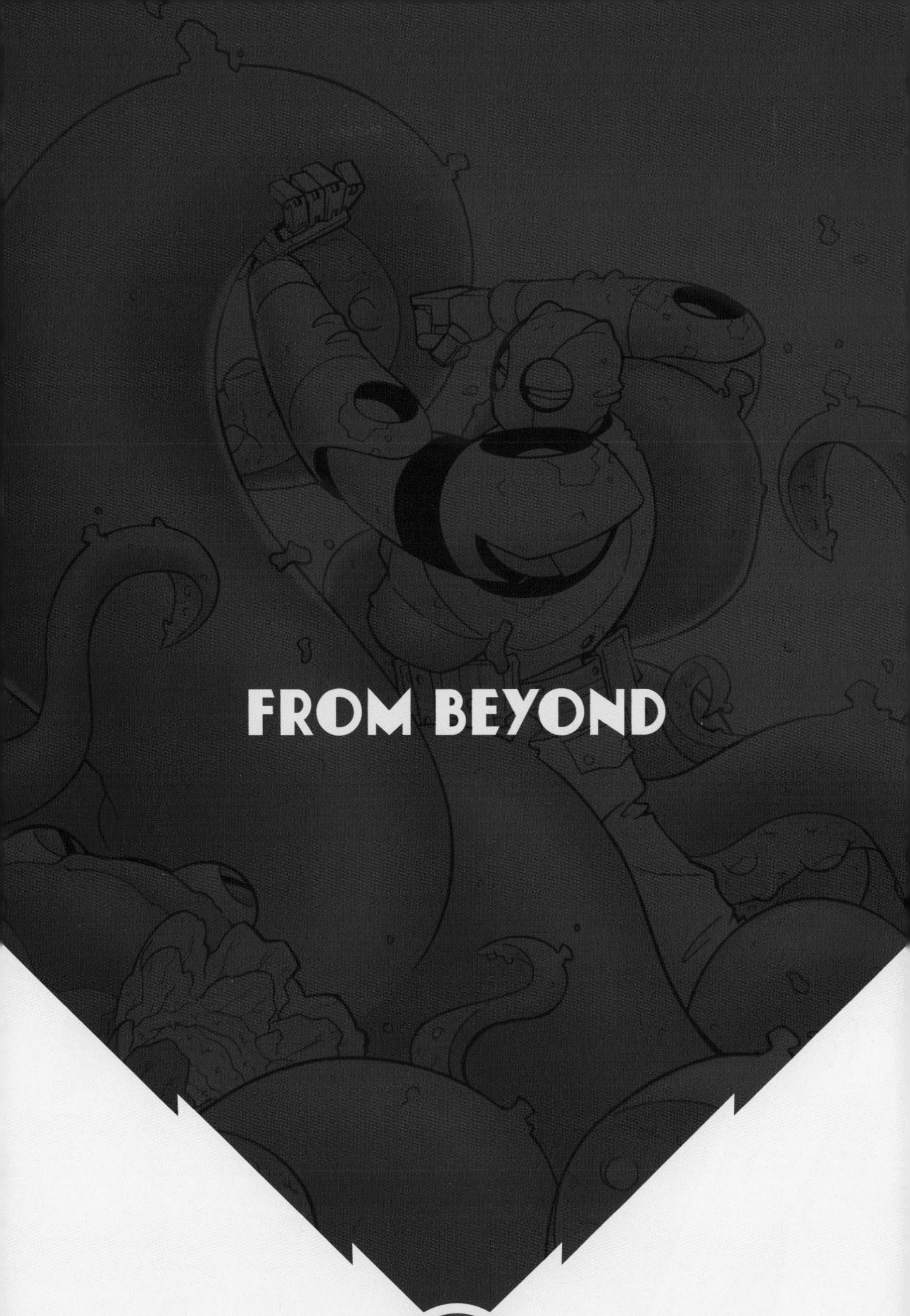

FROM BEYOND

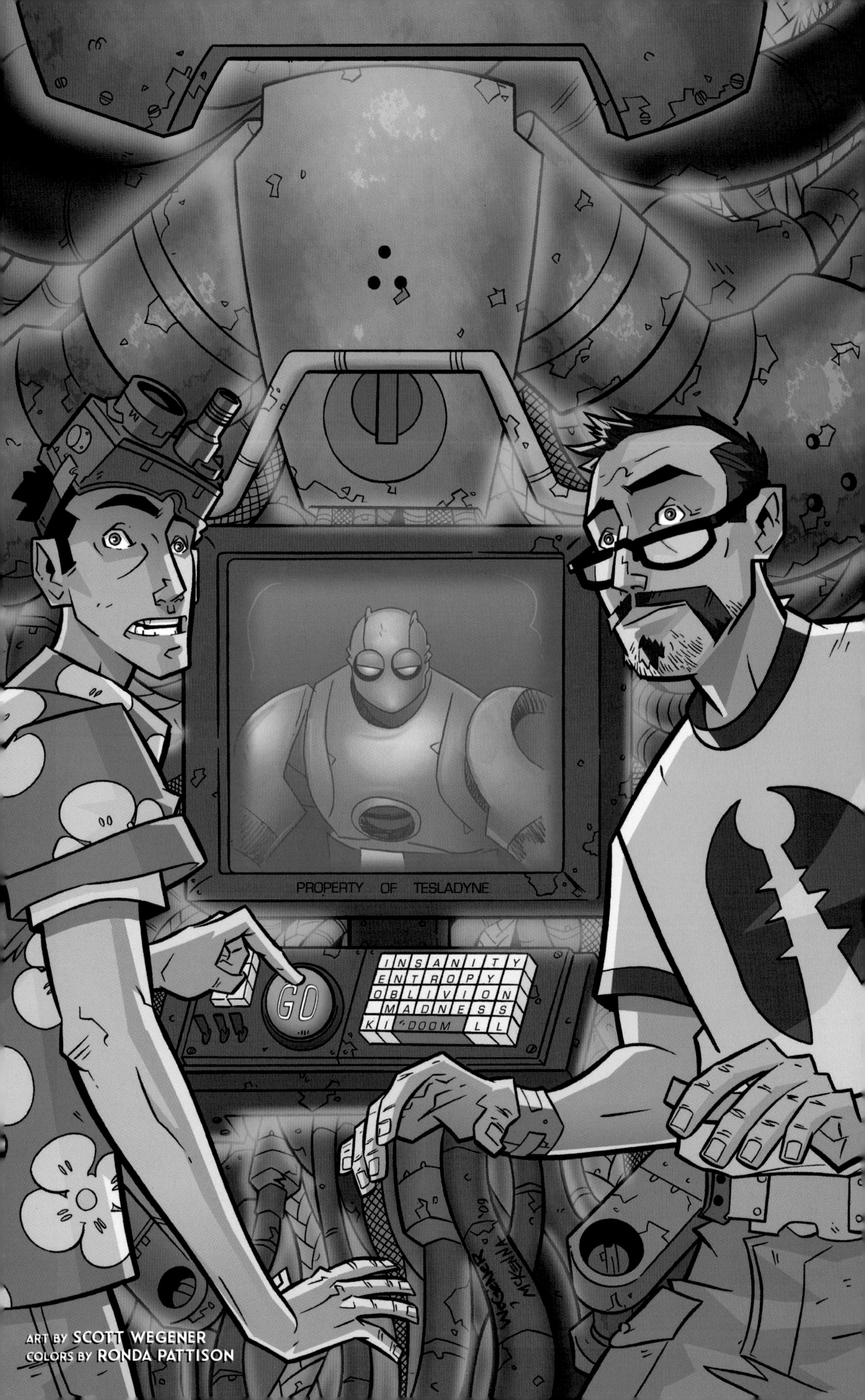
PROPERTY OF TESLADYNE
GO
INSANITY
ENTROPY
OBLIVION
MADNESS
DOOM

ART BY SCOTT WEGENER
COLORS BY RONDA PATTISON

TESLADYNE HQ
FEBRUARY 9, 2009

YES, SIR. IMMEDIATELY. I'LL HAVE A REPORT SENT TO...? AH, PERFECT.

OF COURSE. GIVE MY BEST TO MICHELLE AND THE KIDS.

ROBO?

CALL ENDED
WHITE HOUSE

MARTIN, COME IN. TODAY'S THE BIG DAY.

BOOM

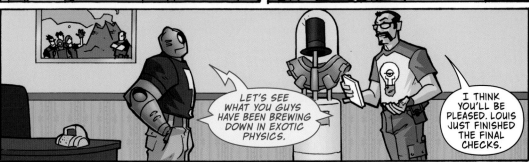

LET'S SEE WHAT YOU GUYS HAVE BEEN BREWING DOWN IN EXOTIC PHYSICS.

I THINK YOU'LL BE PLEASED. LOUIS JUST FINISHED THE FINAL CHECKS.

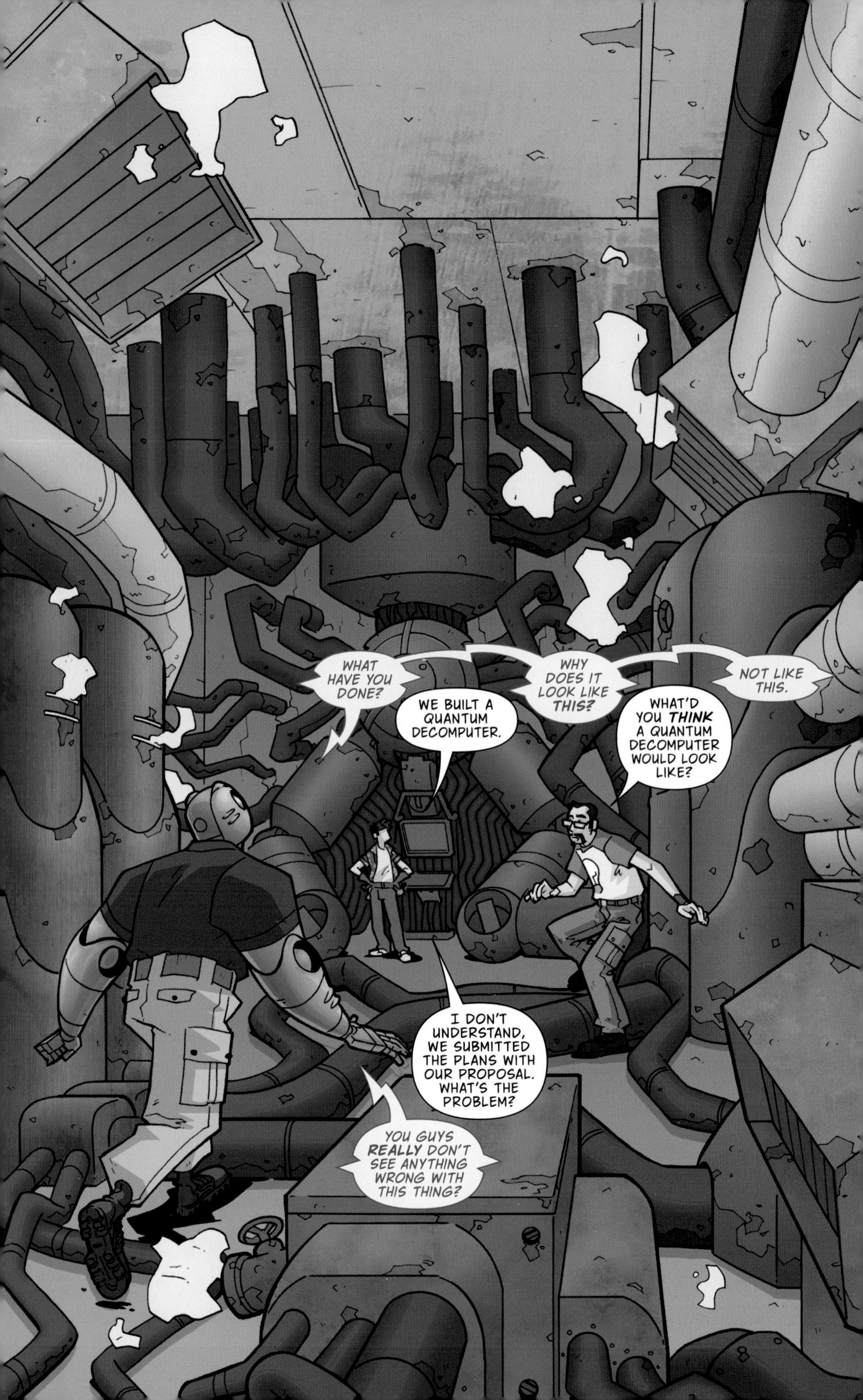
WHAT HAVE YOU DONE?
WE BUILT A QUANTUM DECOMPUTER.
WHY DOES IT LOOK LIKE THIS?
WHAT'D YOU THINK A QUANTUM DECOMPUTER WOULD LOOK LIKE?
NOT LIKE THIS.
I DON'T UNDERSTAND, WE SUBMITTED THE PLANS WITH OUR PROPOSAL. WHAT'S THE PROBLEM?
YOU GUYS REALLY DON'T SEE ANYTHING WRONG WITH THIS THING?

IT'S A LITTLE LARGE.

I ALWAYS THOUGHT WE SHOULD'VE USED MORE ERBIUM IN THE CORE.

OH, IF IT WAS UP TO YOU, IT'D BE AN *ERBIUM* DECOMPUTER.

NO. *LOOK* AT THAT THING. IT'S EVIL. YOU BUILT AN EVIL COMPUTER.

ROBO, IT'S ESSENTIALLY A CALCULATOR. IT CAN'T BE "EVIL."

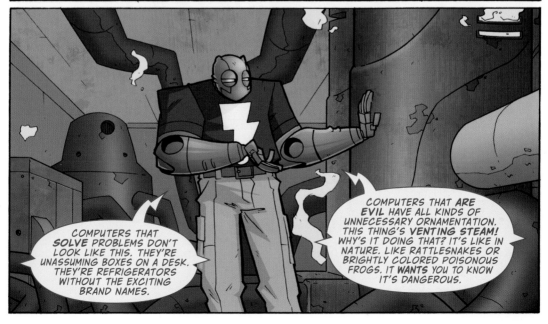

COMPUTERS THAT *SOLVE* PROBLEMS DON'T LOOK LIKE THIS. THEY'RE UNASSUMING BOXES ON A DESK. THEY'RE REFRIGERATORS WITHOUT THE EXCITING BRAND NAMES.

COMPUTERS THAT *ARE EVIL* HAVE ALL KINDS OF UNNECESSARY ORNAMENTATION. THIS THING'S *VENTING STEAM!* WHY'S IT DOING THAT? IT'S LIKE IN NATURE. LIKE RATTLESNAKES OR BRIGHTLY COLORED POISONOUS FROGS. IT *WANTS* YOU TO KNOW IT'S DANGEROUS.

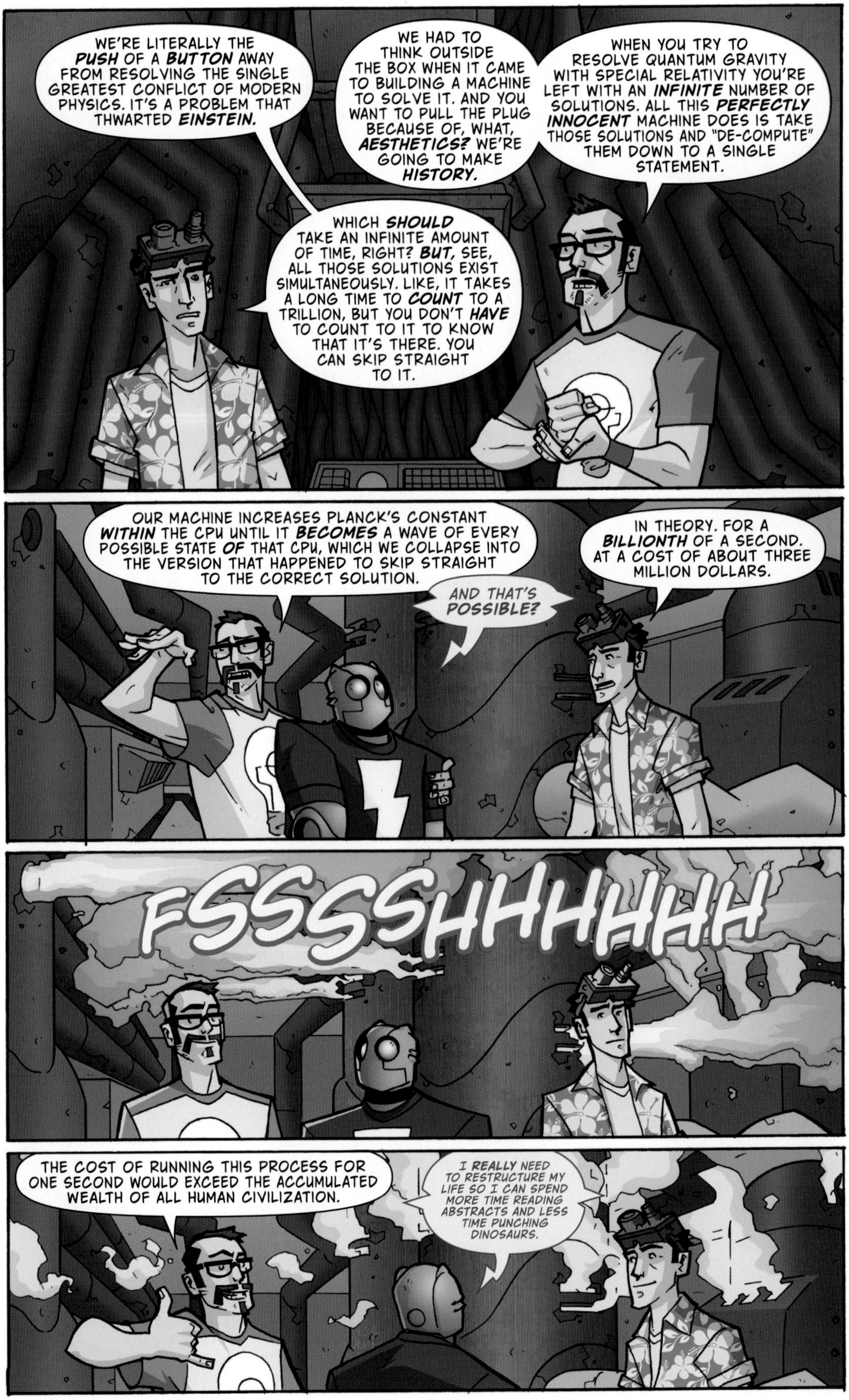
WE'RE LITERALLY THE PUSH OF A BUTTON AWAY FROM RESOLVING THE SINGLE GREATEST CONFLICT OF MODERN PHYSICS. IT'S A PROBLEM THAT THWARTED EINSTEIN.
WE HAD TO THINK OUTSIDE THE BOX WHEN IT CAME TO BUILDING A MACHINE TO SOLVE IT. AND YOU WANT TO PULL THE PLUG BECAUSE OF, WHAT, AESTHETICS? WE'RE GOING TO MAKE HISTORY.
WHEN YOU TRY TO RESOLVE QUANTUM GRAVITY WITH SPECIAL RELATIVITY YOU'RE LEFT WITH AN INFINITE NUMBER OF SOLUTIONS. ALL THIS PERFECTLY INNOCENT MACHINE DOES IS TAKE THOSE SOLUTIONS AND "DE-COMPUTE" THEM DOWN TO A SINGLE STATEMENT.
WHICH SHOULD TAKE AN INFINITE AMOUNT OF TIME, RIGHT? BUT, SEE, ALL THOSE SOLUTIONS EXIST SIMULTANEOUSLY. LIKE, IT TAKES A LONG TIME TO COUNT TO A TRILLION, BUT YOU DON'T HAVE TO COUNT TO IT TO KNOW THAT IT'S THERE. YOU CAN SKIP STRAIGHT TO IT.
OUR MACHINE INCREASES PLANCK'S CONSTANT WITHIN THE CPU UNTIL IT BECOMES A WAVE OF EVERY POSSIBLE STATE OF THAT CPU, WHICH WE COLLAPSE INTO THE VERSION THAT HAPPENED TO SKIP STRAIGHT TO THE CORRECT SOLUTION.
AND THAT'S POSSIBLE?
IN THEORY. FOR A BILLIONTH OF A SECOND. AT A COST OF ABOUT THREE MILLION DOLLARS.
FSSSSHHHHHH
THE COST OF RUNNING THIS PROCESS FOR ONE SECOND WOULD EXCEED THE ACCUMULATED WEALTH OF ALL HUMAN CIVILIZATION.
I REALLY NEED TO RESTRUCTURE MY LIFE SO I CAN SPEND MORE TIME READING ABSTRACTS AND LESS TIME PUNCHING DINOSAURS.

OKAY. WE'LL MOVE FORWARD WITH THE EXPERIMENT. *BUT!* WE SHUT IT DOWN THE *SECOND* SOMETHING EVIL HAPPENS.

WE'RE NOT REALLY EQUIPPED TO *DETECT* EVIL.

FURTHERMORE, I DOUBT YOU COULD QUANTIFY AN ETHICAL PRECEPT INTO EXPERIMENTAL DATA.

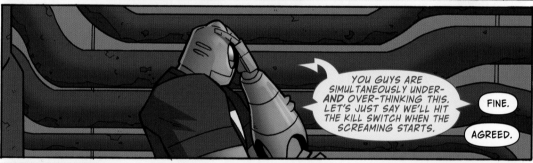

YOU GUYS ARE SIMULTANEOUSLY UNDER- *AND* OVER-THINKING THIS. LET'S JUST SAY WE'LL HIT THE KILL SWITCH WHEN THE SCREAMING STARTS.

FINE.

AGREED.

OKAY, ARE WE READY?

OH YEAH, I OUTLINED MY NOBEL ACCEPTANCE SPEECH LAST NIGHT. THERE'S *A LOT OF* EXPLETIVES.

YOU'RE AN ANGRY, *ANGRY* MAN.

HEY, WHAT I'M GOING TO SAY TO THOSE NOBEL SNOBS IS NOTHING THEY DON'T NEED TO HEAR.

CAN WE MOVE THIS ALONG?

SORRY, ROBO.

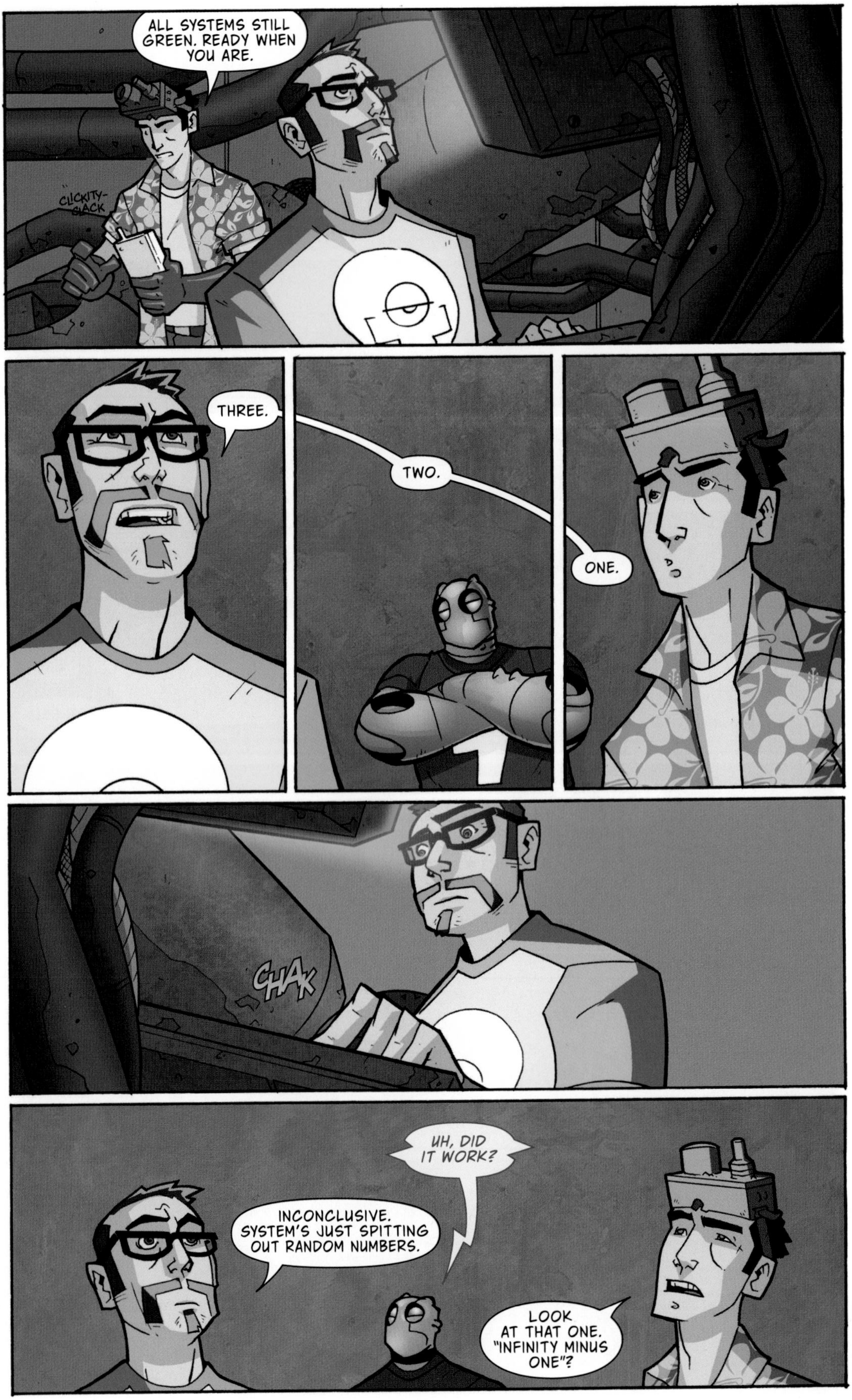
ALL SYSTEMS STILL GREEN. READY WHEN YOU ARE.
CLICKITY-CLACK
THREE.
TWO.
ONE.
CHAK
UH, DID IT WORK?
INCONCLUSIVE. SYSTEM'S JUST SPITTING OUT RANDOM NUMBERS.
LOOK AT THAT ONE. "INFINITY MINUS ONE"?

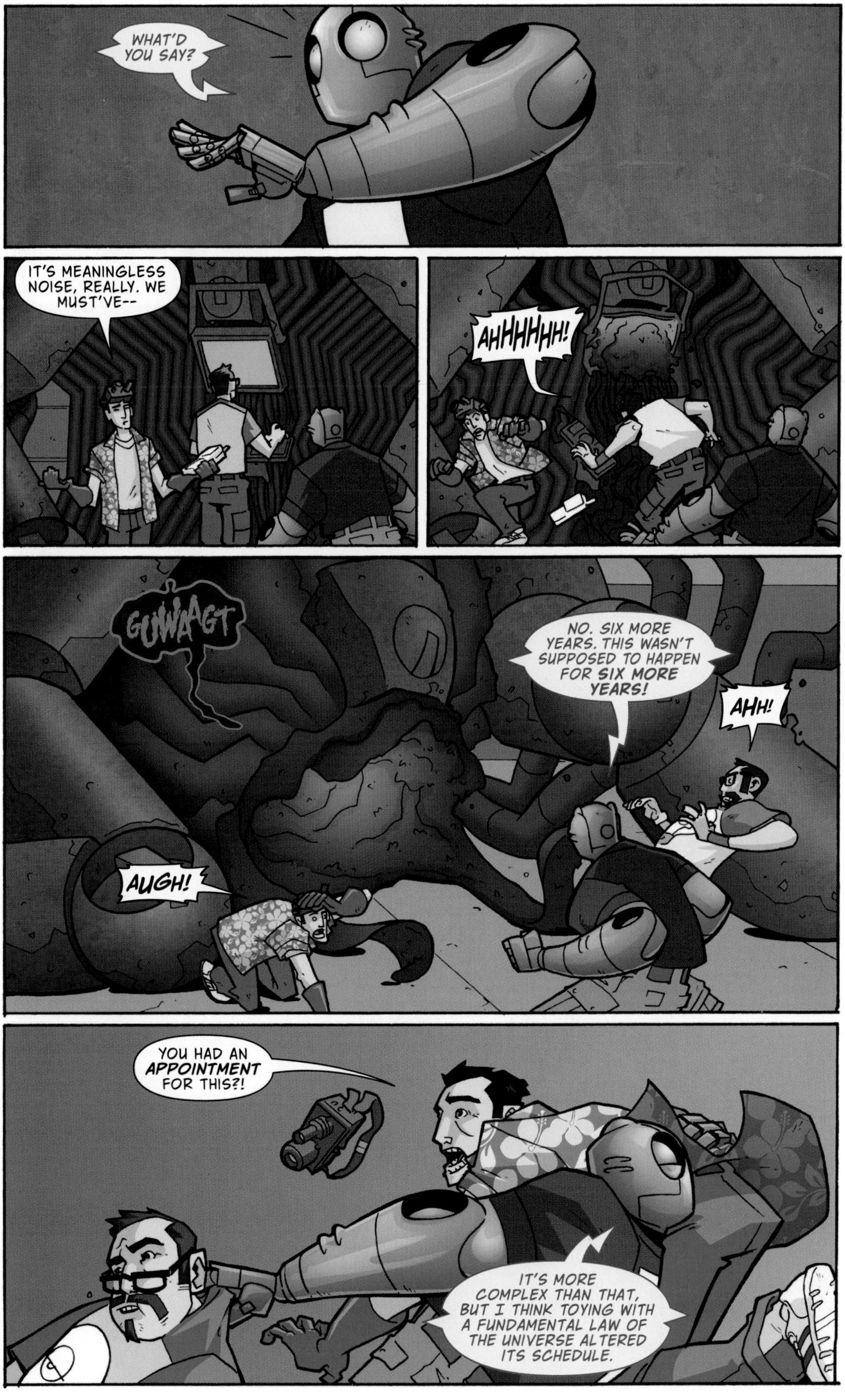
WHAT'D YOU SAY?
IT'S MEANINGLESS NOISE, REALLY. WE MUST'VE--
AHHHHHH!
GUWAAGT
NO. SIX MORE YEARS. THIS WASN'T SUPPOSED TO HAPPEN FOR **SIX MORE YEARS!**
AHH!
AUGH!
YOU HAD AN ***APPOINTMENT*** FOR THIS?!
IT'S MORE COMPLEX THAN THAT, BUT I THINK TOYING WITH A FUNDAMENTAL LAW OF THE UNIVERSE ALTERED ITS SCHEDULE.

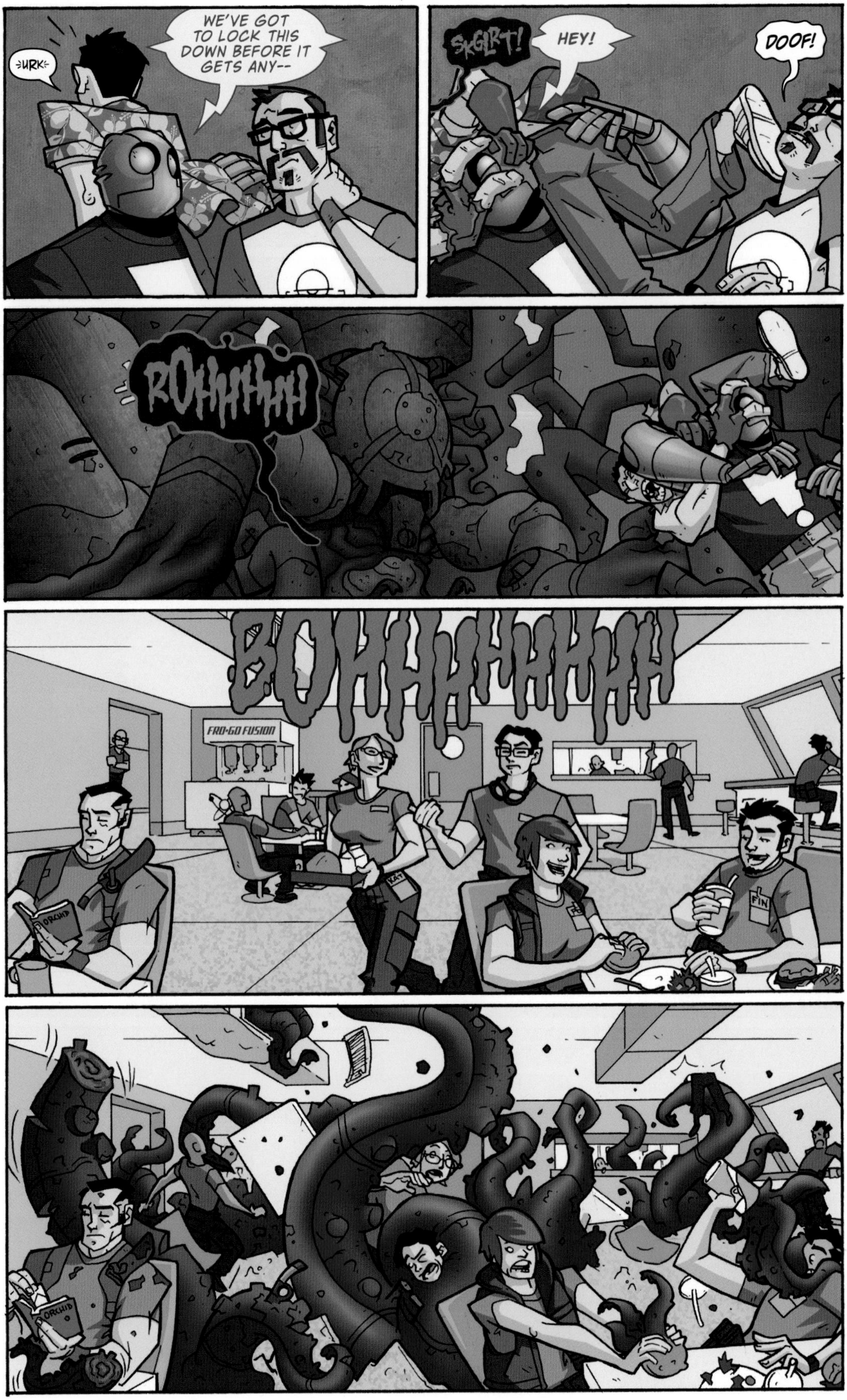
URK
WE'VE GOT TO LOCK THIS DOWN BEFORE IT GETS ANY--
SKGLRT!
HEY!
DOOF!
ROHHHHHH
BOHHHHHHHH
FRO-GO FUSION
ORCHID
FIN
ORCHID

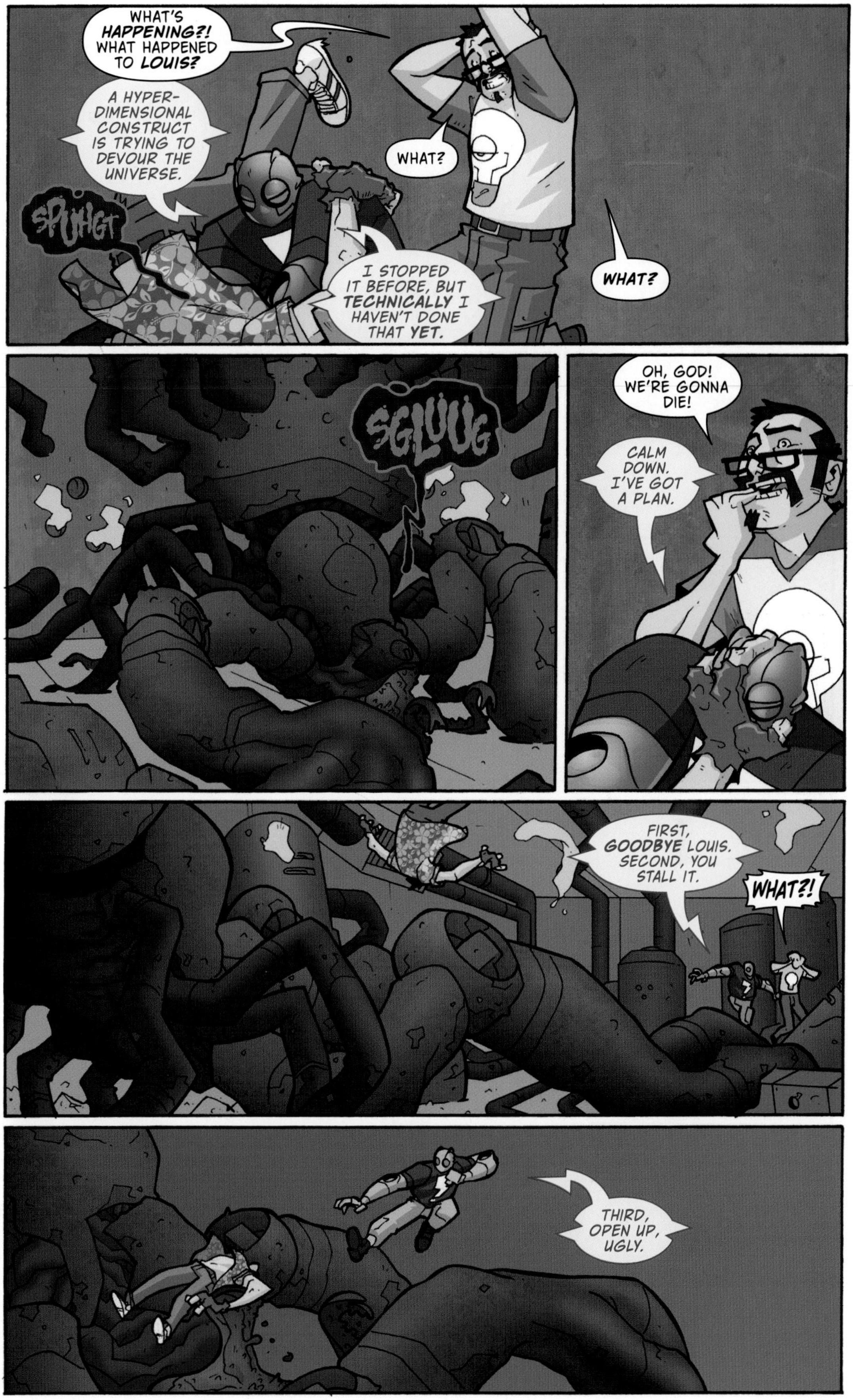
WHAT'S HAPPENING?! WHAT HAPPENED TO LOUIS?
A HYPER-DIMENSIONAL CONSTRUCT IS TRYING TO DEVOUR THE UNIVERSE.
SPUHGT
WHAT?
I STOPPED IT BEFORE, BUT TECHNICALLY I HAVEN'T DONE THAT YET.
WHAT?
SGLUUG
OH, GOD! WE'RE GONNA DIE!
CALM DOWN. I'VE GOT A PLAN.
FIRST, GOODBYE LOUIS. SECOND, YOU STALL IT.
WHAT?!
THIRD, OPEN UP, UGLY.

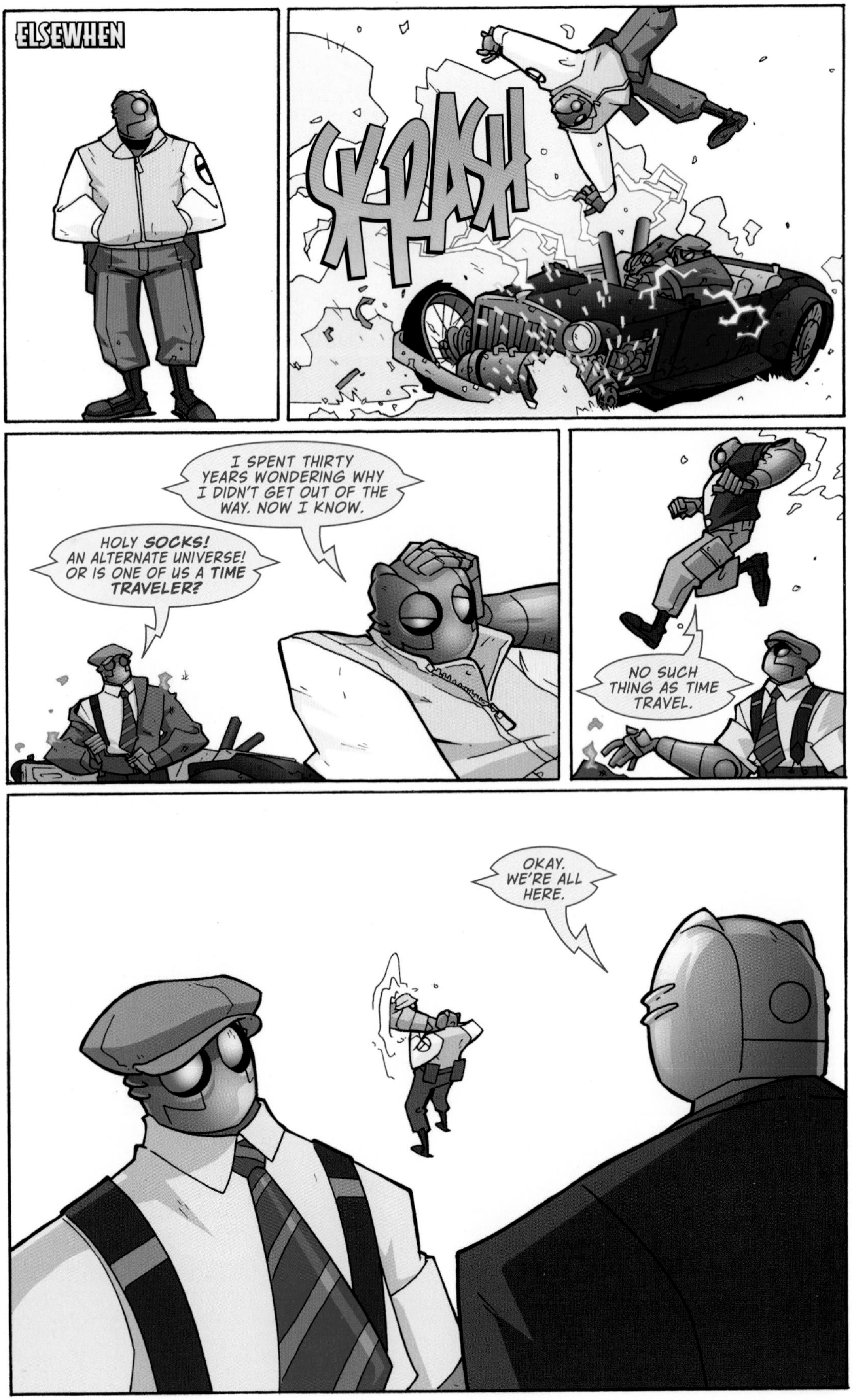
ELSEWHEN
SKRASH
I SPENT THIRTY YEARS WONDERING WHY I DIDN'T GET OUT OF THE WAY. NOW I KNOW.
HOLY SOCKS! AN ALTERNATE UNIVERSE! OR IS ONE OF US A TIME TRAVELER?
NO SUCH THING AS TIME TRAVEL.
OKAY. WE'RE ALL HERE.

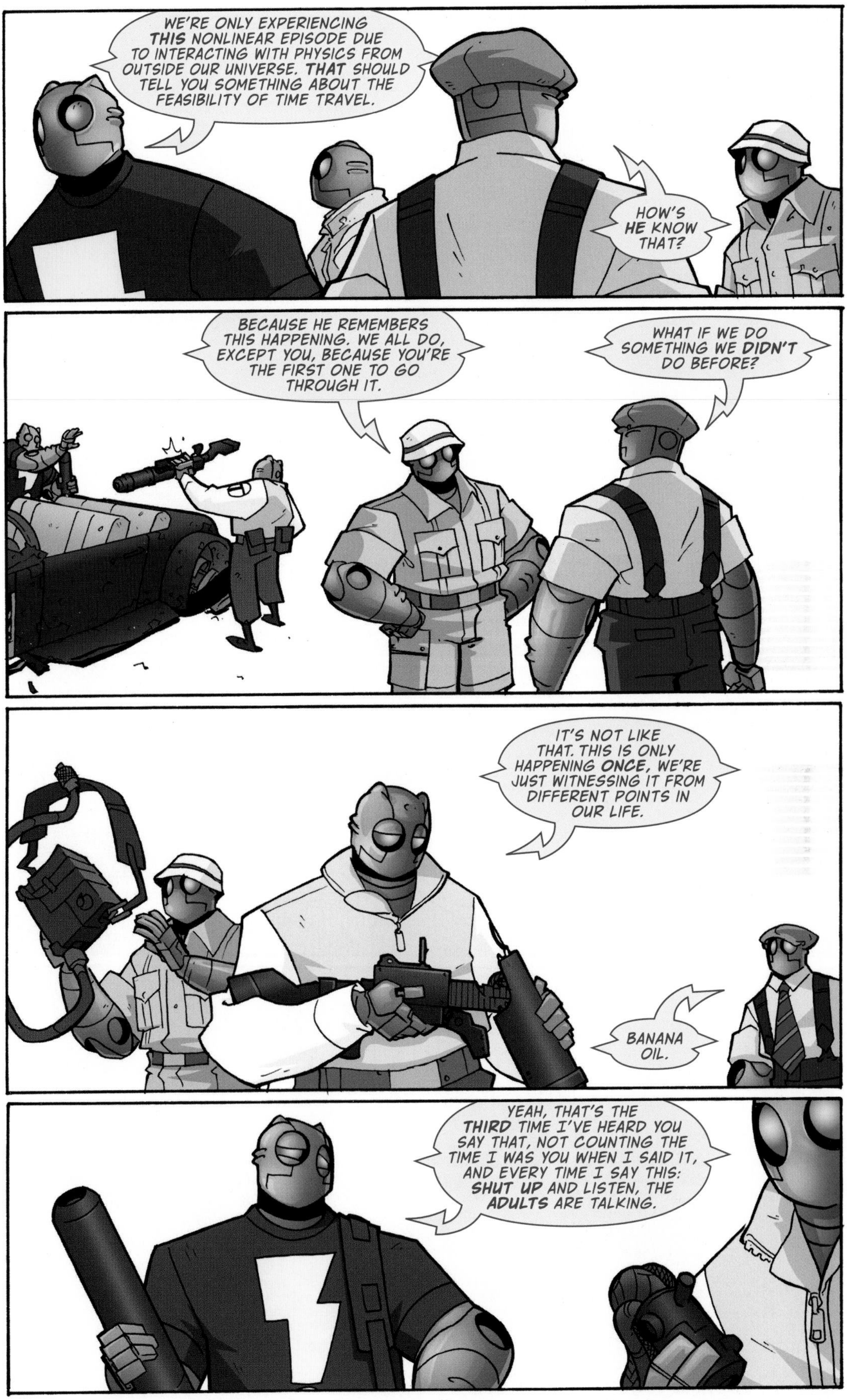
WE'RE ONLY EXPERIENCING THIS NONLINEAR EPISODE DUE TO INTERACTING WITH PHYSICS FROM OUTSIDE OUR UNIVERSE. THAT SHOULD TELL YOU SOMETHING ABOUT THE FEASIBILITY OF TIME TRAVEL.
HOW'S HE KNOW THAT?
BECAUSE HE REMEMBERS THIS HAPPENING. WE ALL DO, EXCEPT YOU, BECAUSE YOU'RE THE FIRST ONE TO GO THROUGH IT.
WHAT IF WE DO SOMETHING WE DIDN'T DO BEFORE?
IT'S NOT LIKE THAT. THIS IS ONLY HAPPENING ONCE, WE'RE JUST WITNESSING IT FROM DIFFERENT POINTS IN OUR LIFE.
BANANA OIL.
YEAH, THAT'S THE THIRD TIME I'VE HEARD YOU SAY THAT, NOT COUNTING THE TIME I WAS YOU WHEN I SAID IT, AND EVERY TIME I SAY THIS: SHUT UP AND LISTEN, THE ADULTS ARE TALKING.

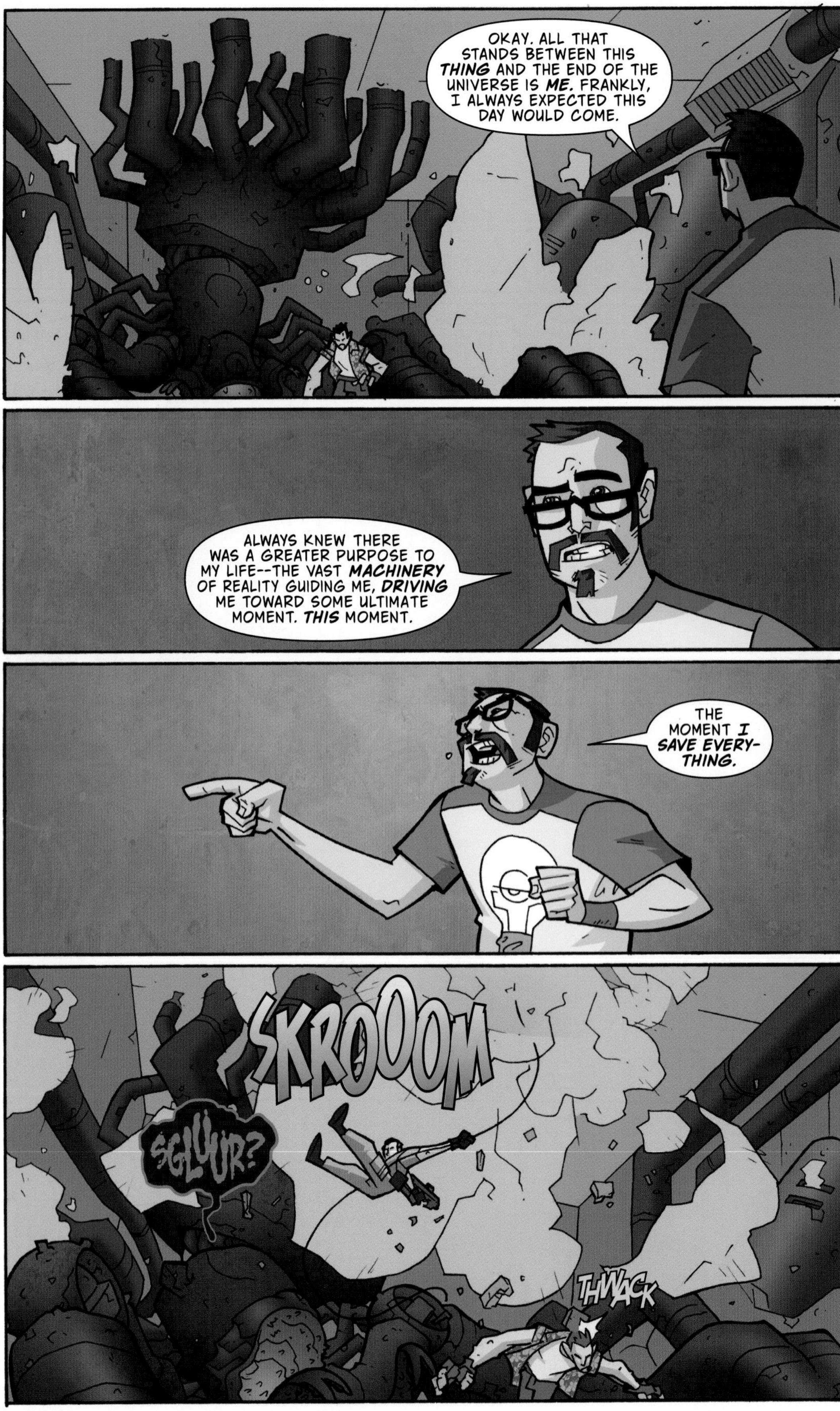
OKAY. ALL THAT STANDS BETWEEN THIS THING AND THE END OF THE UNIVERSE IS ME. FRANKLY, I ALWAYS EXPECTED THIS DAY WOULD COME.
ALWAYS KNEW THERE WAS A GREATER PURPOSE TO MY LIFE--THE VAST MACHINERY OF REALITY GUIDING ME, DRIVING ME TOWARD SOME ULTIMATE MOMENT. THIS MOMENT.
THE MOMENT I SAVE EVERY-THING.
SKROOOM
SGLUUR?
THWACK

BRAKKA

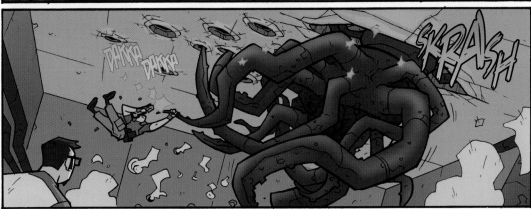

DAKKA DAKKA

SKRASH

OR...
NOT.

SKLAARGT

GET OUT
OF MY FRIEND,
YOU ALIEN FREAK
BASTARD.

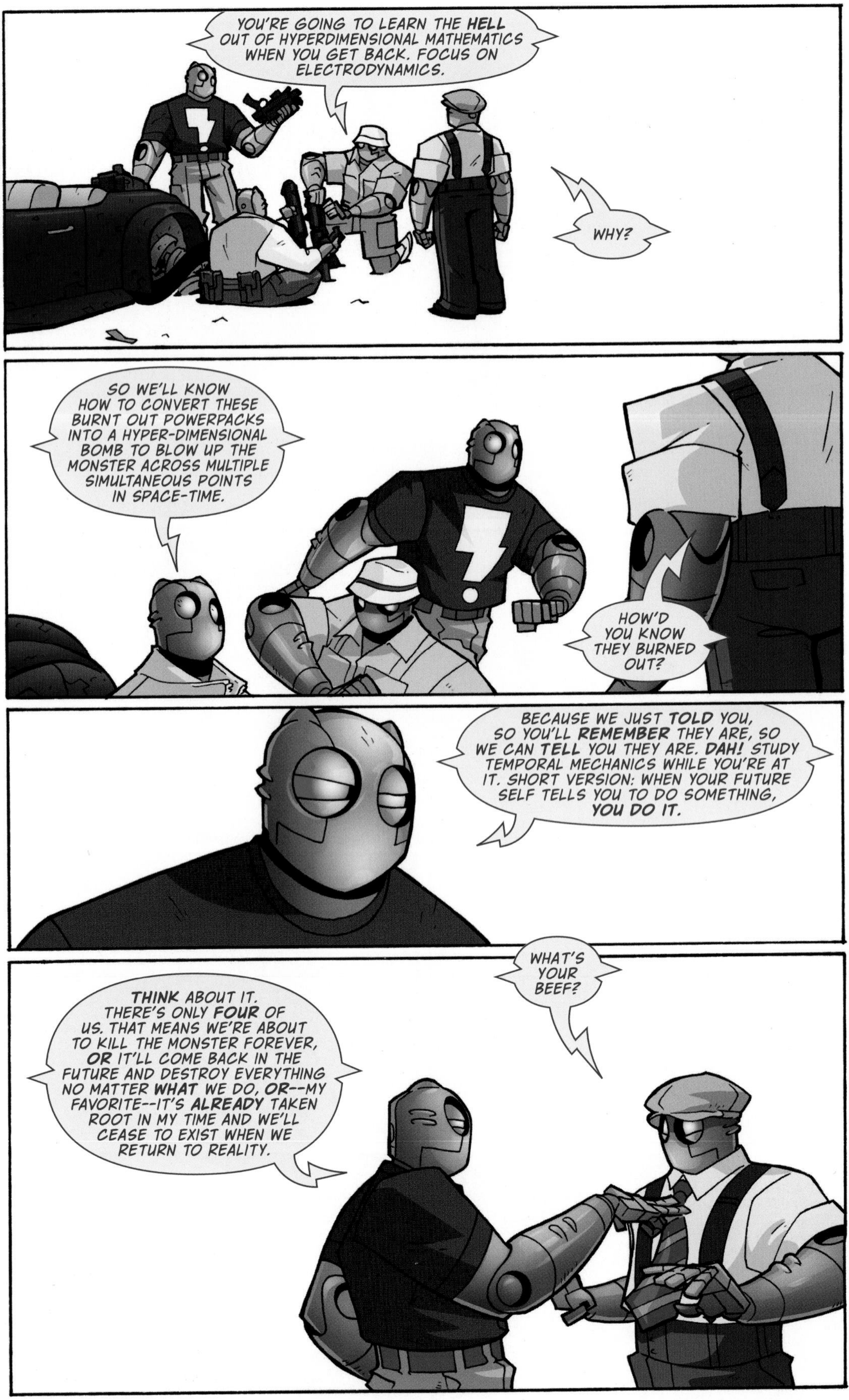
YOU'RE GOING TO LEARN THE HELL OUT OF HYPERDIMENSIONAL MATHEMATICS WHEN YOU GET BACK. FOCUS ON ELECTRODYNAMICS.
WHY?
SO WE'LL KNOW HOW TO CONVERT THESE BURNT OUT POWERPACKS INTO A HYPER-DIMENSIONAL BOMB TO BLOW UP THE MONSTER ACROSS MULTIPLE SIMULTANEOUS POINTS IN SPACE-TIME.
HOW'D YOU KNOW THEY BURNED OUT?
BECAUSE WE JUST TOLD YOU, SO YOU'LL REMEMBER THEY ARE, SO WE CAN TELL YOU THEY ARE. DAH! STUDY TEMPORAL MECHANICS WHILE YOU'RE AT IT. SHORT VERSION: WHEN YOUR FUTURE SELF TELLS YOU TO DO SOMETHING, YOU DO IT.
WHAT'S YOUR BEEF?
THINK ABOUT IT. THERE'S ONLY FOUR OF US. THAT MEANS WE'RE ABOUT TO KILL THE MONSTER FOREVER, OR IT'LL COME BACK IN THE FUTURE AND DESTROY EVERYTHING NO MATTER WHAT WE DO, OR--MY FAVORITE--IT'S ALREADY TAKEN ROOT IN MY TIME AND WE'LL CEASE TO EXIST WHEN WE RETURN TO REALITY.

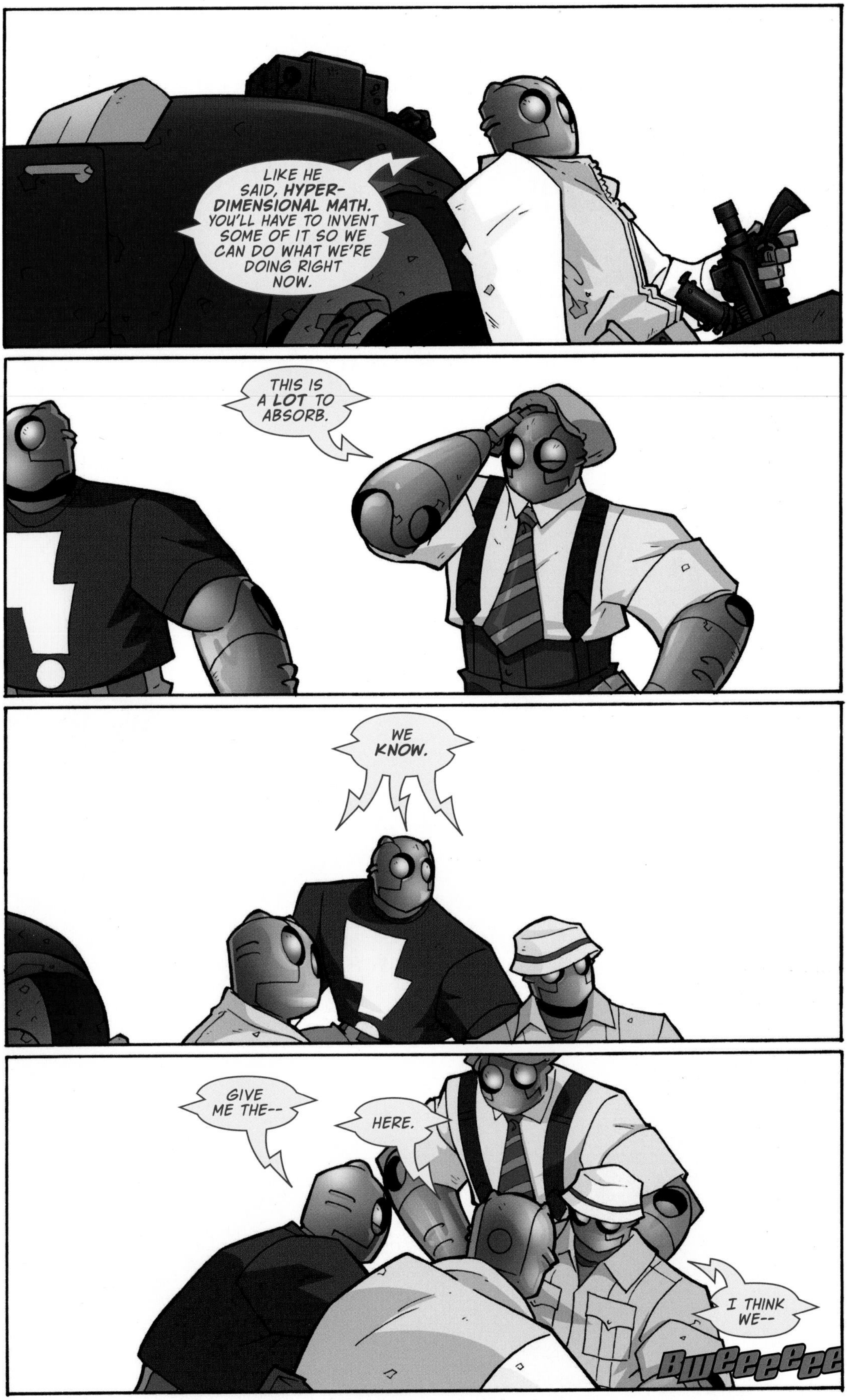

LIKE HE SAID, **HYPER-DIMENSIONAL MATH.** YOU'LL HAVE TO INVENT SOME OF IT SO WE CAN DO WHAT WE'RE DOING RIGHT NOW.
THIS IS A **LOT** TO ABSORB.
WE **KNOW.**
GIVE ME THE--
HERE.
I THINK WE--
BWEEEEEEE

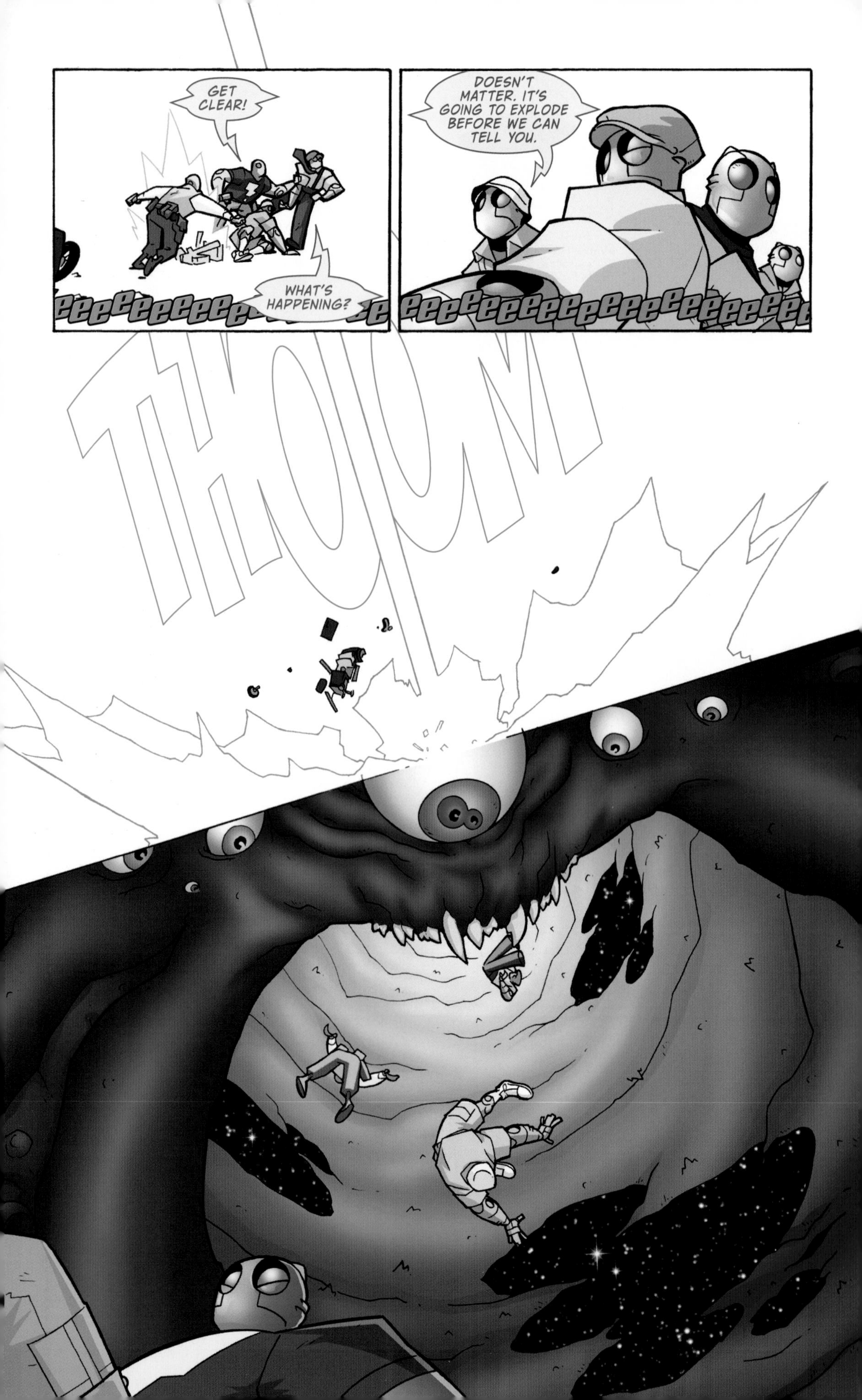
GET CLEAR!
WHAT'S HAPPENING?
EEEEEEEEEEEEEEE
DOESN'T MATTER. IT'S GOING TO EXPLODE BEFORE WE CAN TELL YOU.
EEEEEEEEEEEEEEEEEEEE
THOOM

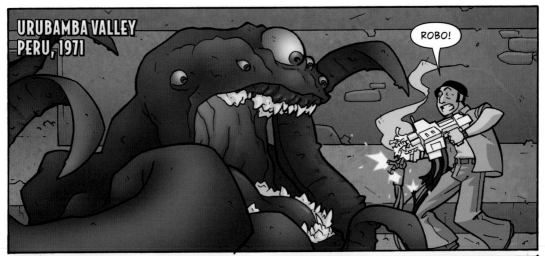

URUBAMBA VALLEY
PERU, 1971

ROBO!

PLOIT

AUGH!

AT LEAST THAT WASN'T AS BAD AS LAST TIME...

IS IT GONE?

I DON'T THINK WE'LL EVER KNOW.

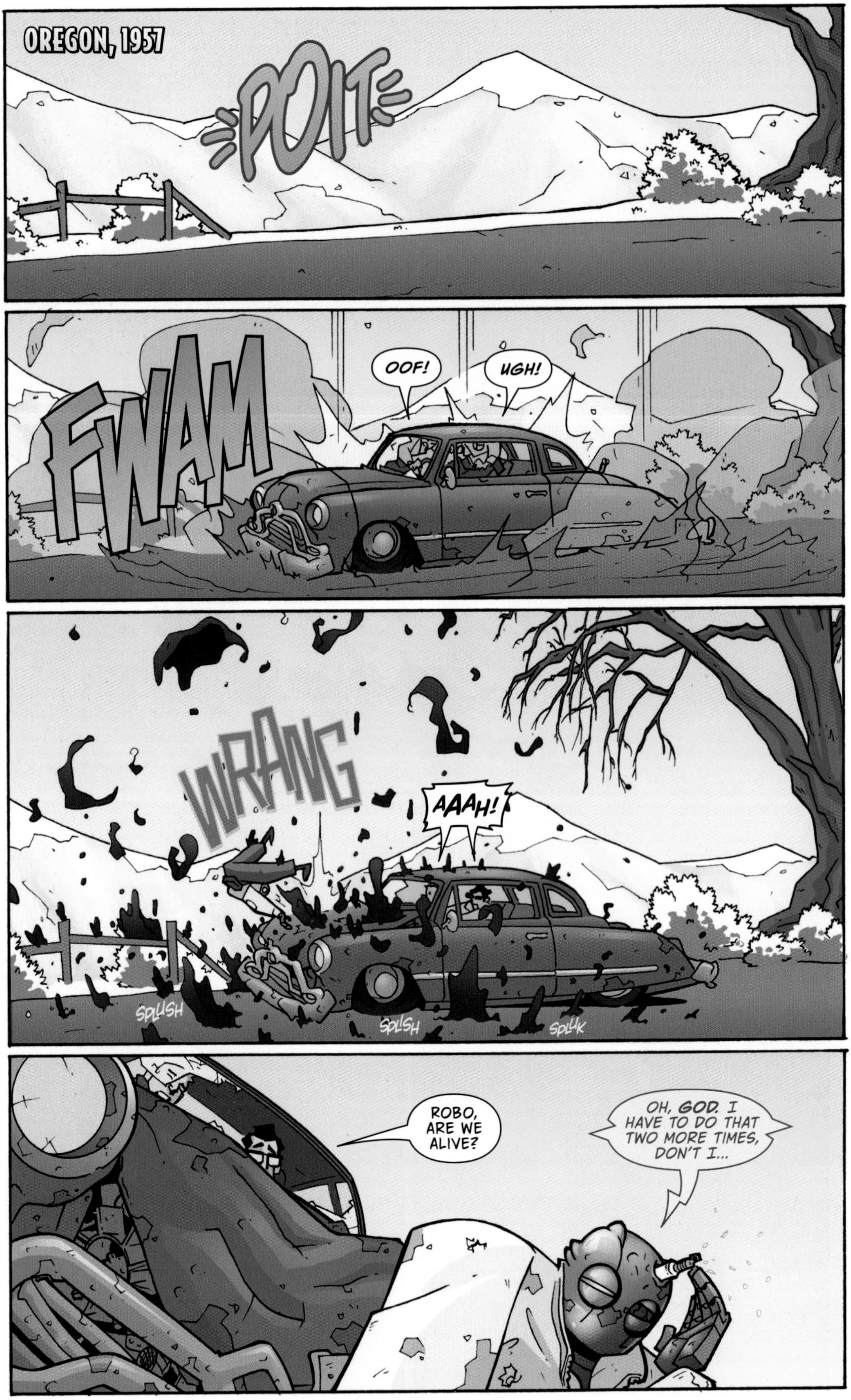
OREGON, 1957
POIT
FWAM
OOF!
UGH!
WRANG
AAAH!
SPLUSH
SPLISH
SPLUK
ROBO, ARE WE ALIVE?
OH, GOD. I HAVE TO DO THAT TWO MORE TIMES, DON'T I...

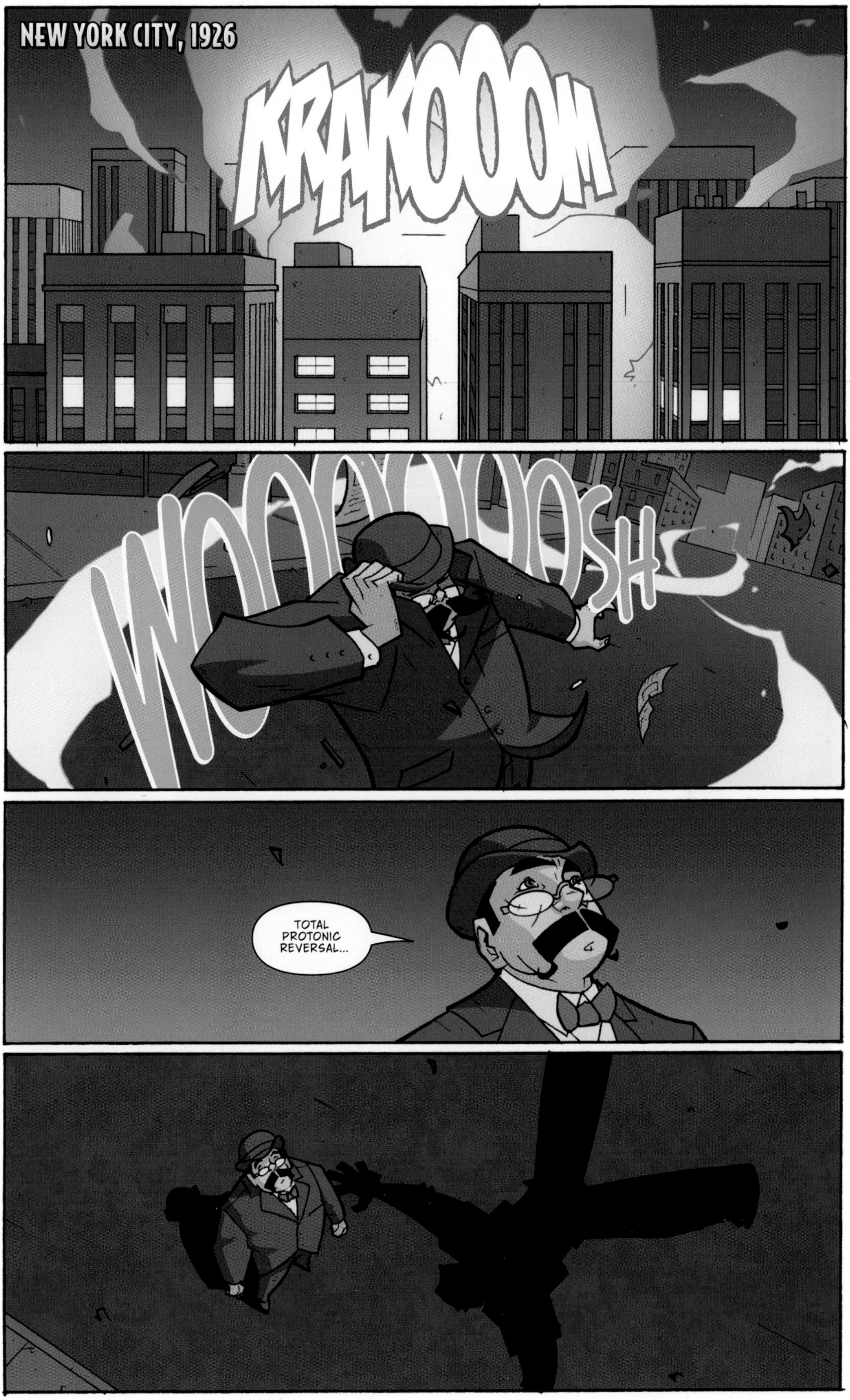
NEW YORK CITY, 1926
KRAKOOOM
WOOOOOOOSH
TOTAL PROTONIC REVERSAL...

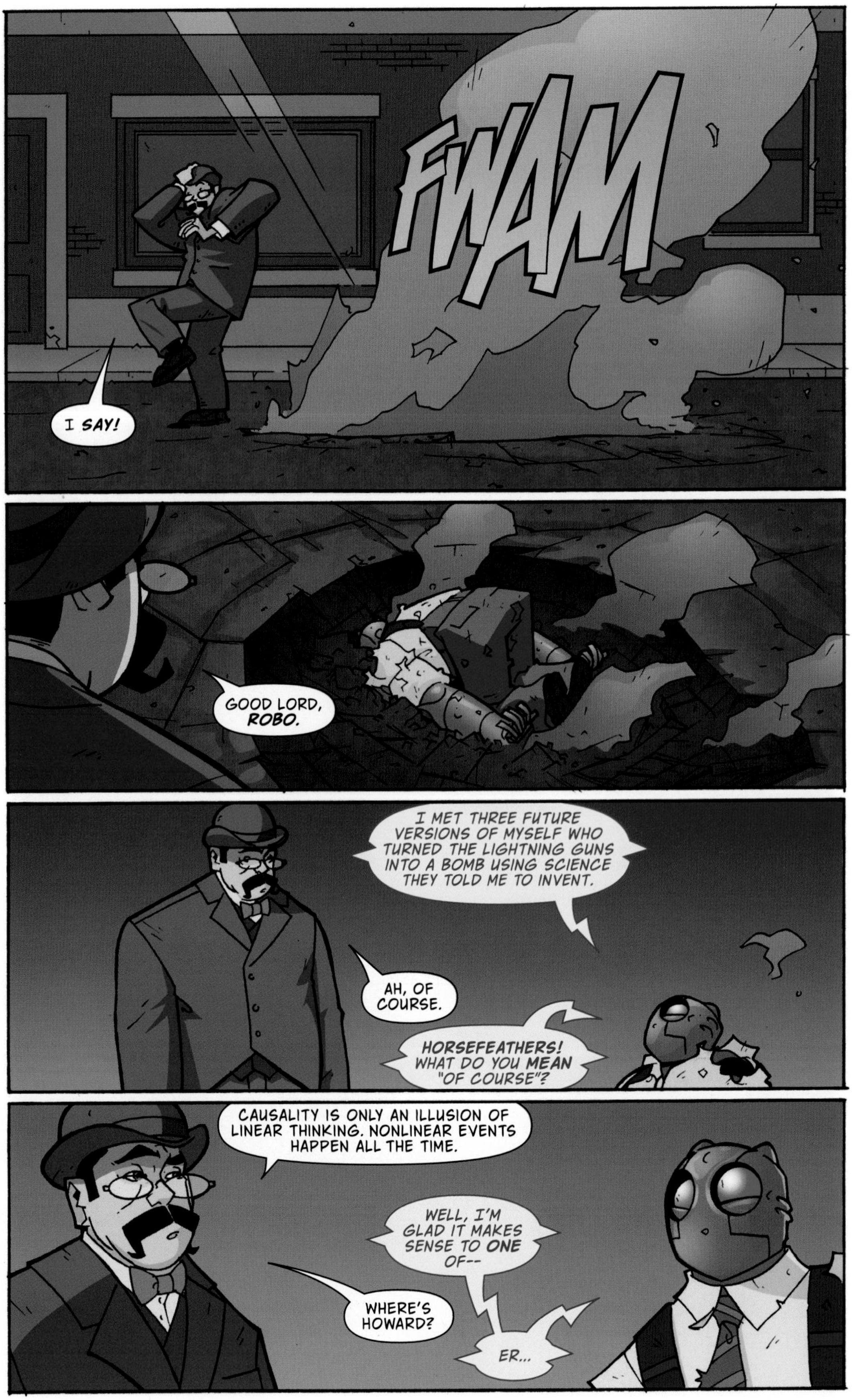
FWAM
I SAY!
GOOD LORD, ROBO.
I MET THREE FUTURE VERSIONS OF MYSELF WHO TURNED THE LIGHTNING GUNS INTO A BOMB USING SCIENCE THEY TOLD ME TO INVENT.
AH, OF COURSE.
HORSEFEATHERS! WHAT DO YOU MEAN "OF COURSE"?
CAUSALITY IS ONLY AN ILLUSION OF LINEAR THINKING. NONLINEAR EVENTS HAPPEN ALL THE TIME.
WELL, I'M GLAD IT MAKES SENSE TO ONE OF--
WHERE'S HOWARD?
ER...

CHA-FOOM

TOOF

UWAARGHT!

THAT A FACT?

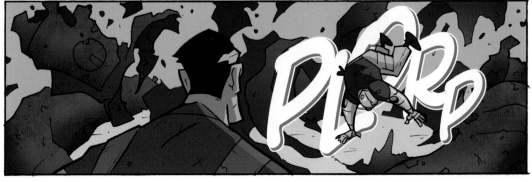

PLORP

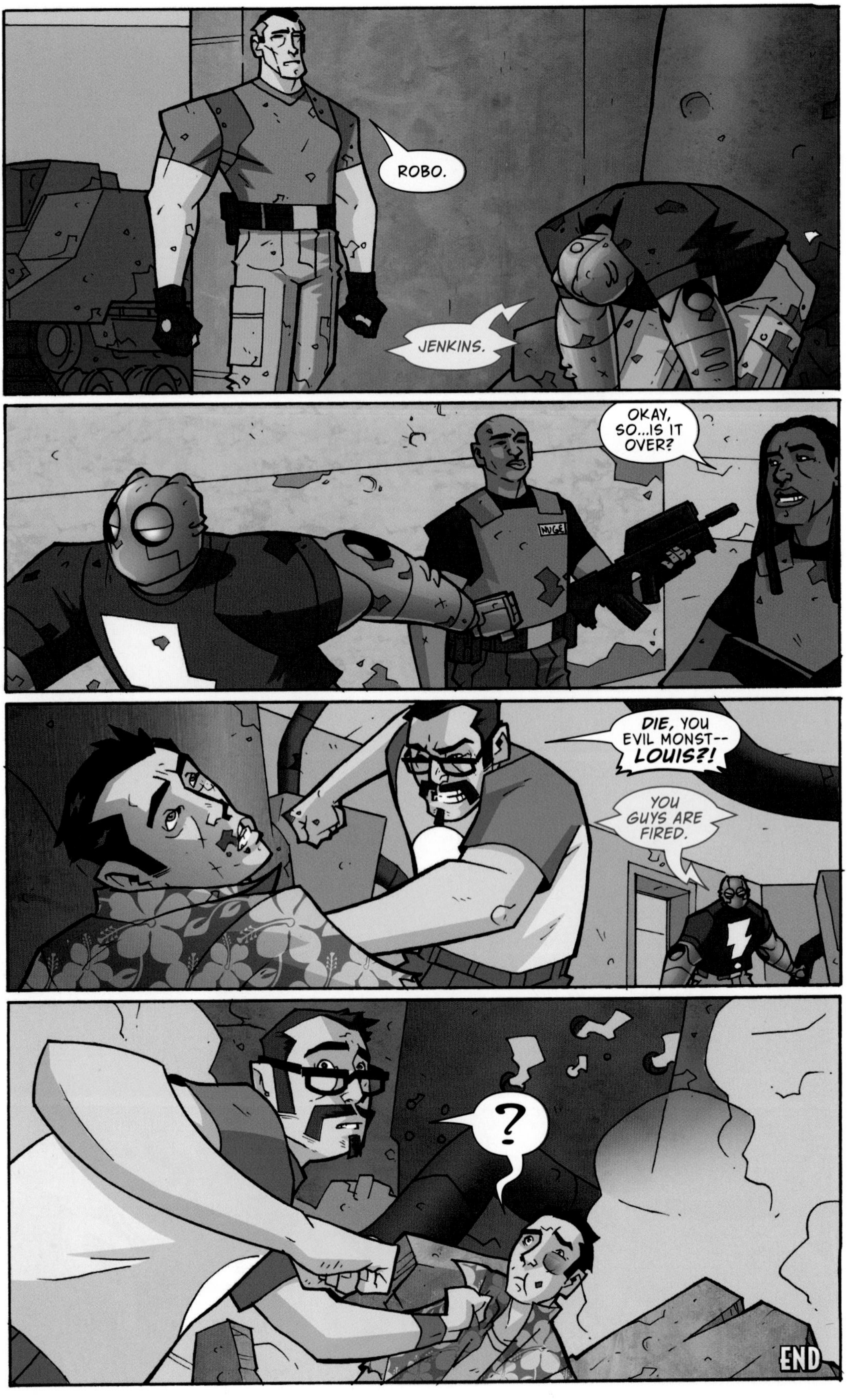
ROBO.
JENKINS.
OKAY, SO...IS IT OVER?
DIE, YOU EVIL MONST-- LOUIS?!
YOU GUYS ARE FIRED.
?
END

"B" STORIES

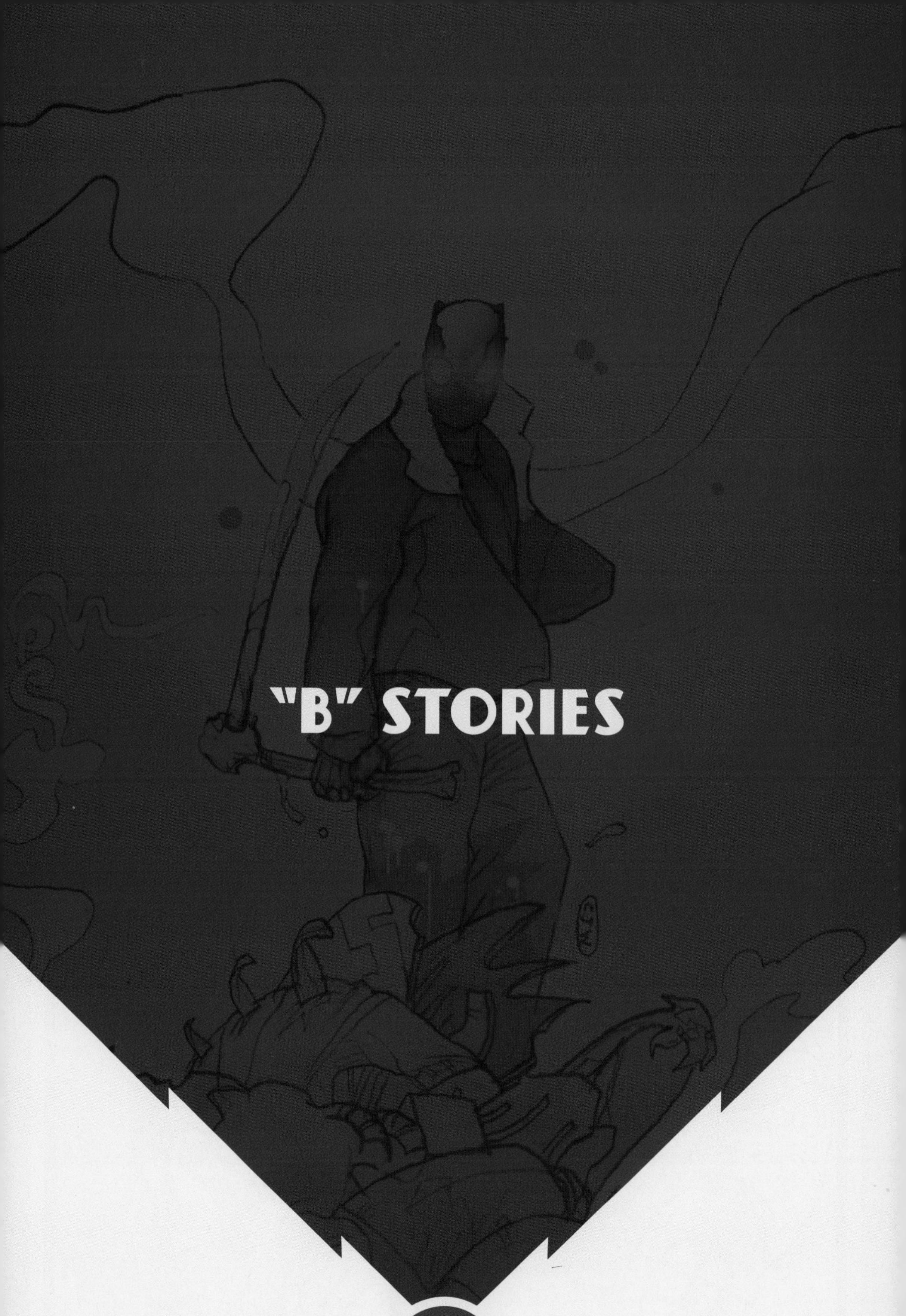

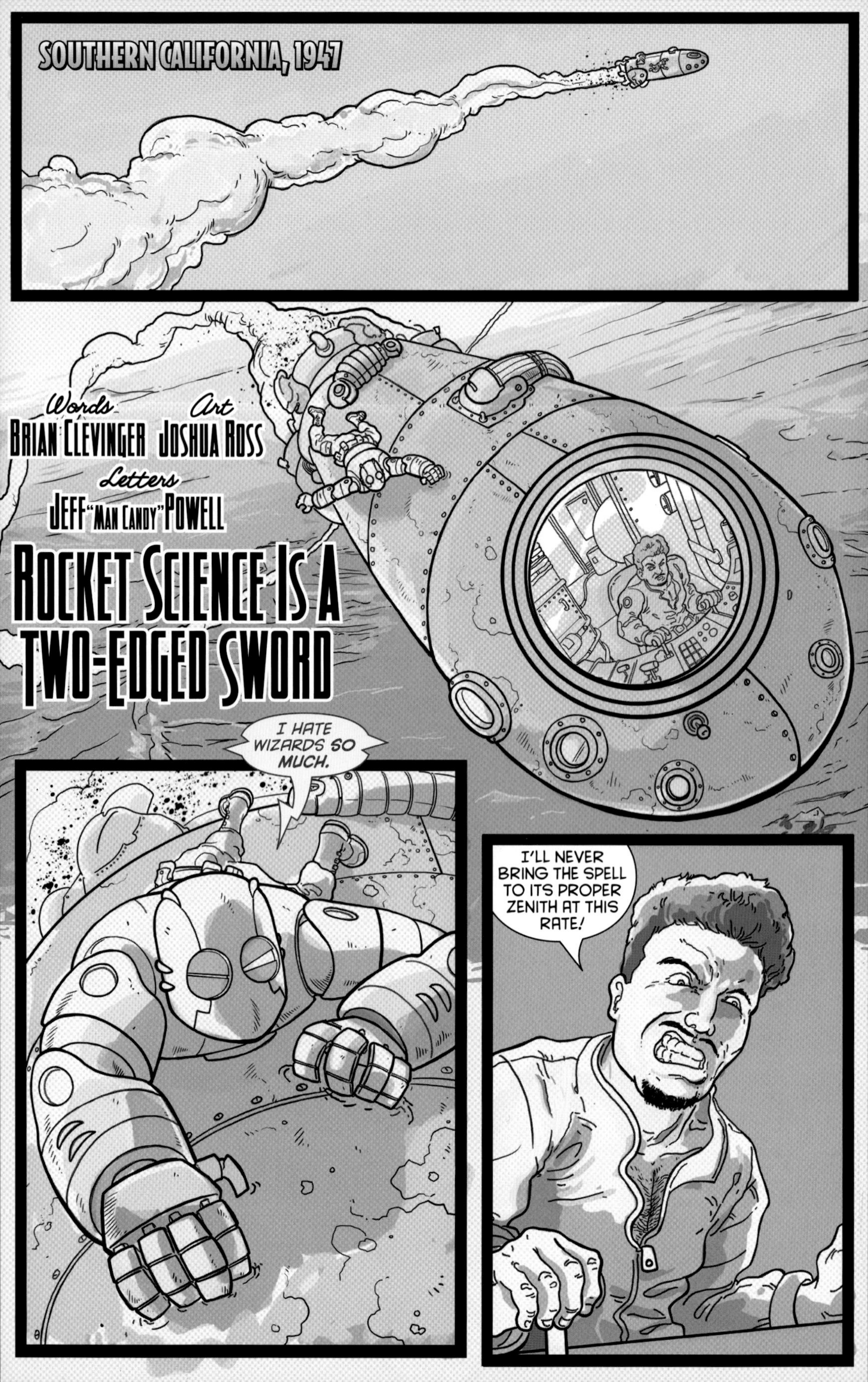

SOUTHERN CALIFORNIA, 1947
Words BRIAN CLEVINGER
Art JOSHUA ROSS
Letters JEFF "MAN CANDY" POWELL
ROCKET SCIENCE IS A TWO-EDGED SWORD
I HATE WIZARDS SO MUCH.
I'LL NEVER BRING THE SPELL TO ITS PROPER ZENITH AT THIS RATE!

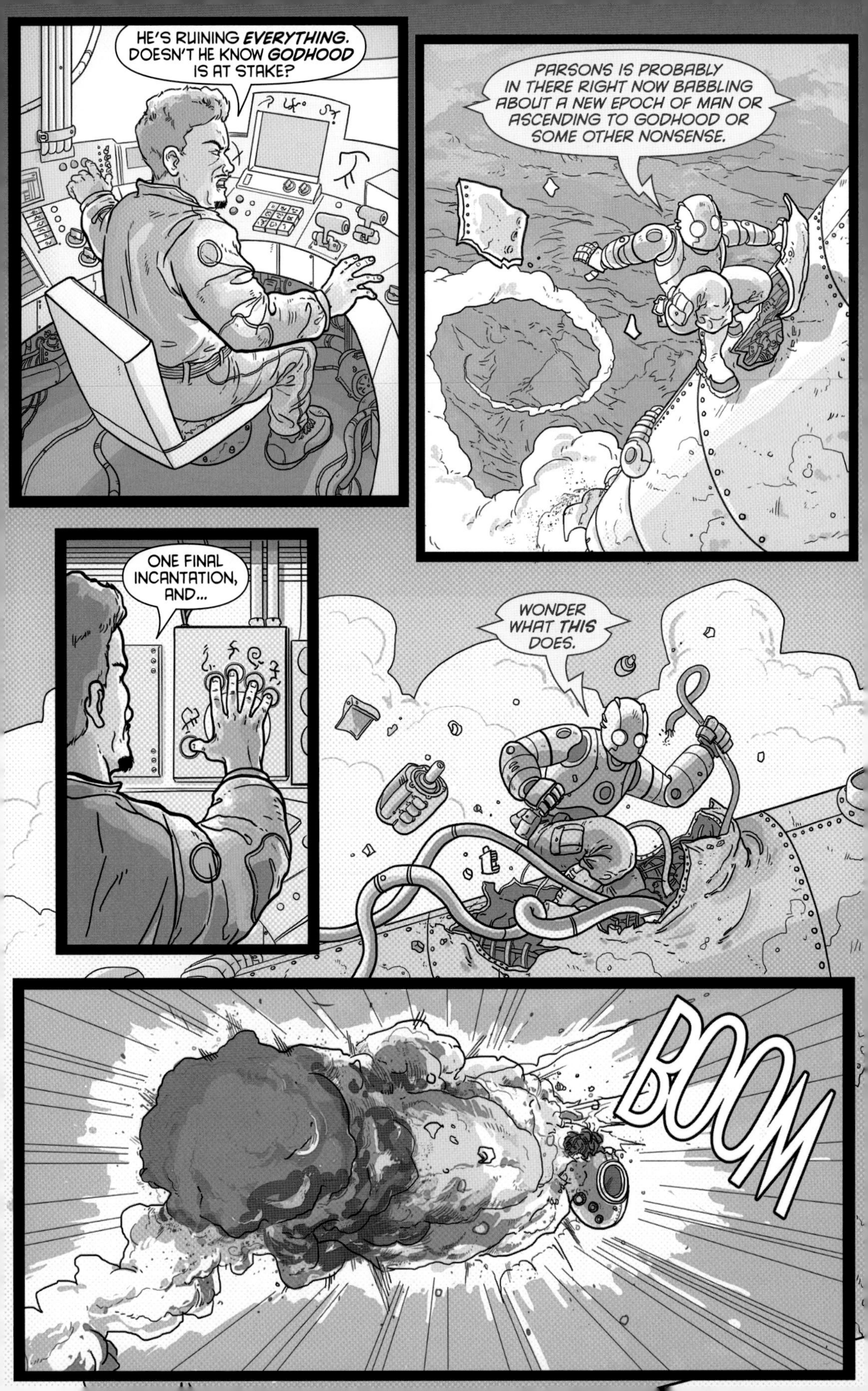
HE'S RUINING *EVERYTHING.* DOESN'T HE KNOW *GODHOOD* IS AT STAKE?
PARSONS IS PROBABLY IN THERE RIGHT NOW BABBLING ABOUT A NEW EPOCH OF MAN OR ASCENDING TO GODHOOD OR SOME OTHER NONSENSE.
ONE FINAL INCANTATION, AND...
WONDER WHAT **THIS** DOES.
BOOM

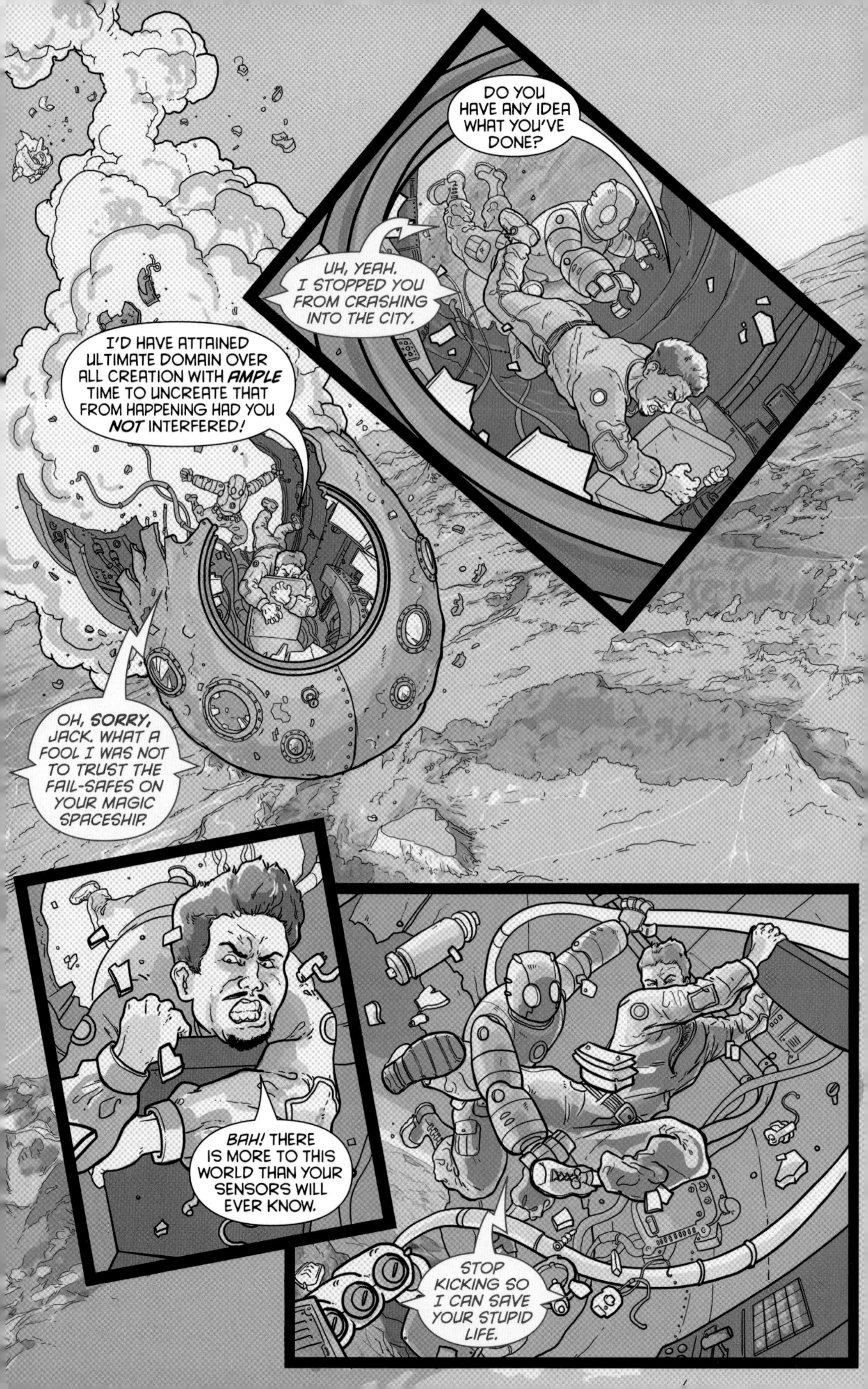
DO YOU HAVE ANY IDEA WHAT YOU'VE DONE?
UH, YEAH. I STOPPED YOU FROM CRASHING INTO THE CITY.
I'D HAVE ATTAINED ULTIMATE DOMAIN OVER ALL CREATION WITH AMPLE TIME TO UNCREATE THAT FROM HAPPENING HAD YOU NOT INTERFERED!
OH, SORRY, JACK. WHAT A FOOL I WAS NOT TO TRUST THE FAIL-SAFES ON YOUR MAGIC SPACESHIP.
BAH! THERE IS MORE TO THIS WORLD THAN YOUR SENSORS WILL EVER KNOW.
STOP KICKING SO I CAN SAVE YOUR STUPID LIFE.

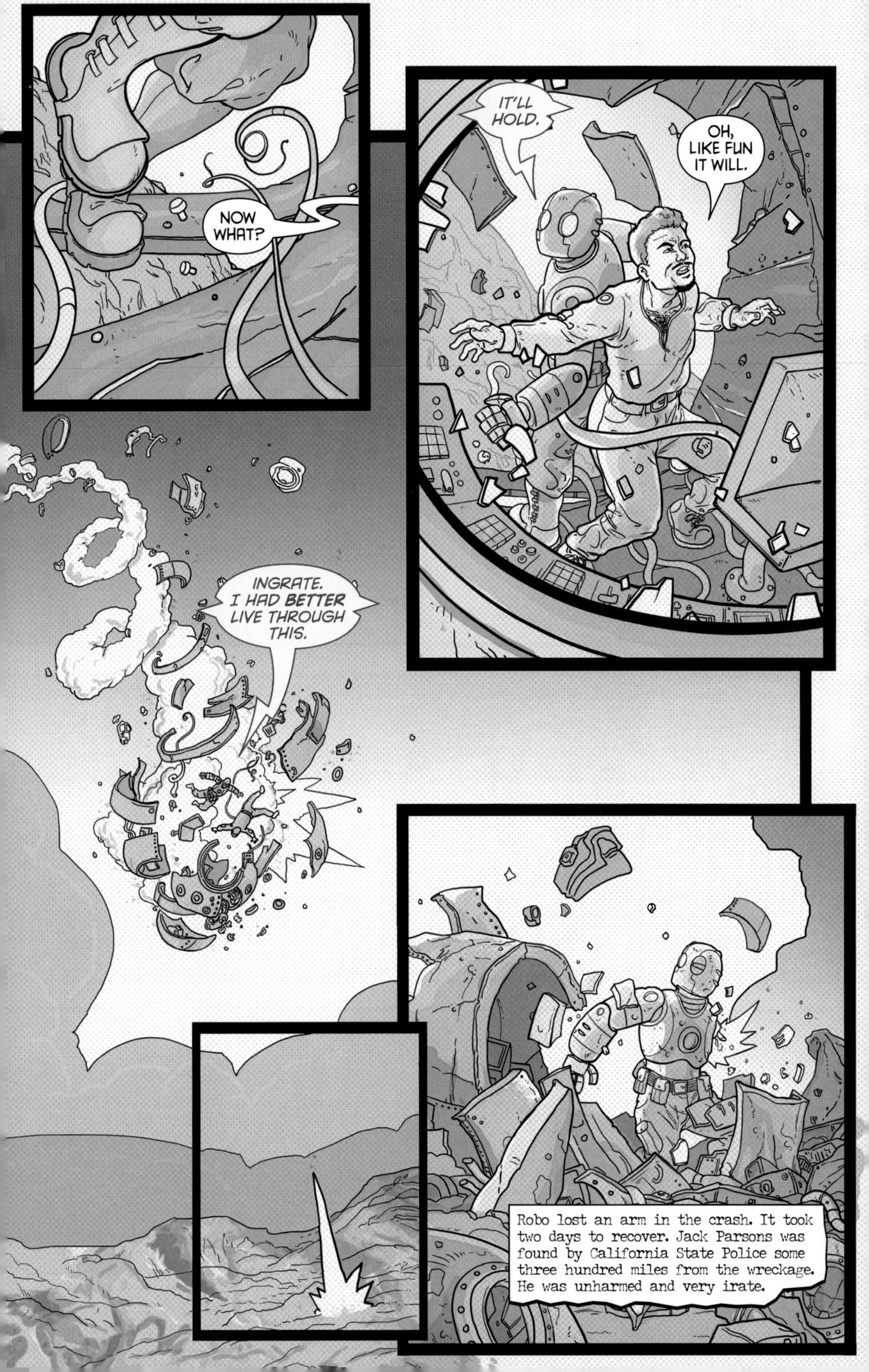
NOW WHAT?
IT'LL HOLD.
OH, LIKE FUN IT WILL.
INGRATE. I HAD BETTER LIVE THROUGH THIS.
Robo lost an arm in the crash. It took two days to recover. Jack Parsons was found by California State Police some three hundred miles from the wreckage. He was unharmed and very irate.

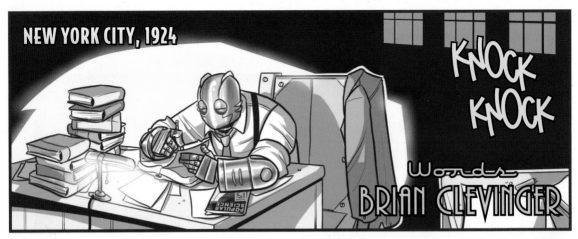

NEW YORK CITY, 1924

KNOCK KNOCK

Words:
BRIAN CLEVINGER

SCRAM! MR. TESLA'S OUT OF TOWN AND WOULDN'T TALK TO YOU AT THIS HOUR ANYWAY.

Art
ZACK FINFROCK

CHEESE AND *CRACKERS*, HOW'S A GUY SUPPOSED TO GET ANY STUDYING DONE AROUND HERE?

KNOCK KNOCK

Letters
JEFF POWELL

THRA-KOOOOM

Translation
BORIS BRENERMAN

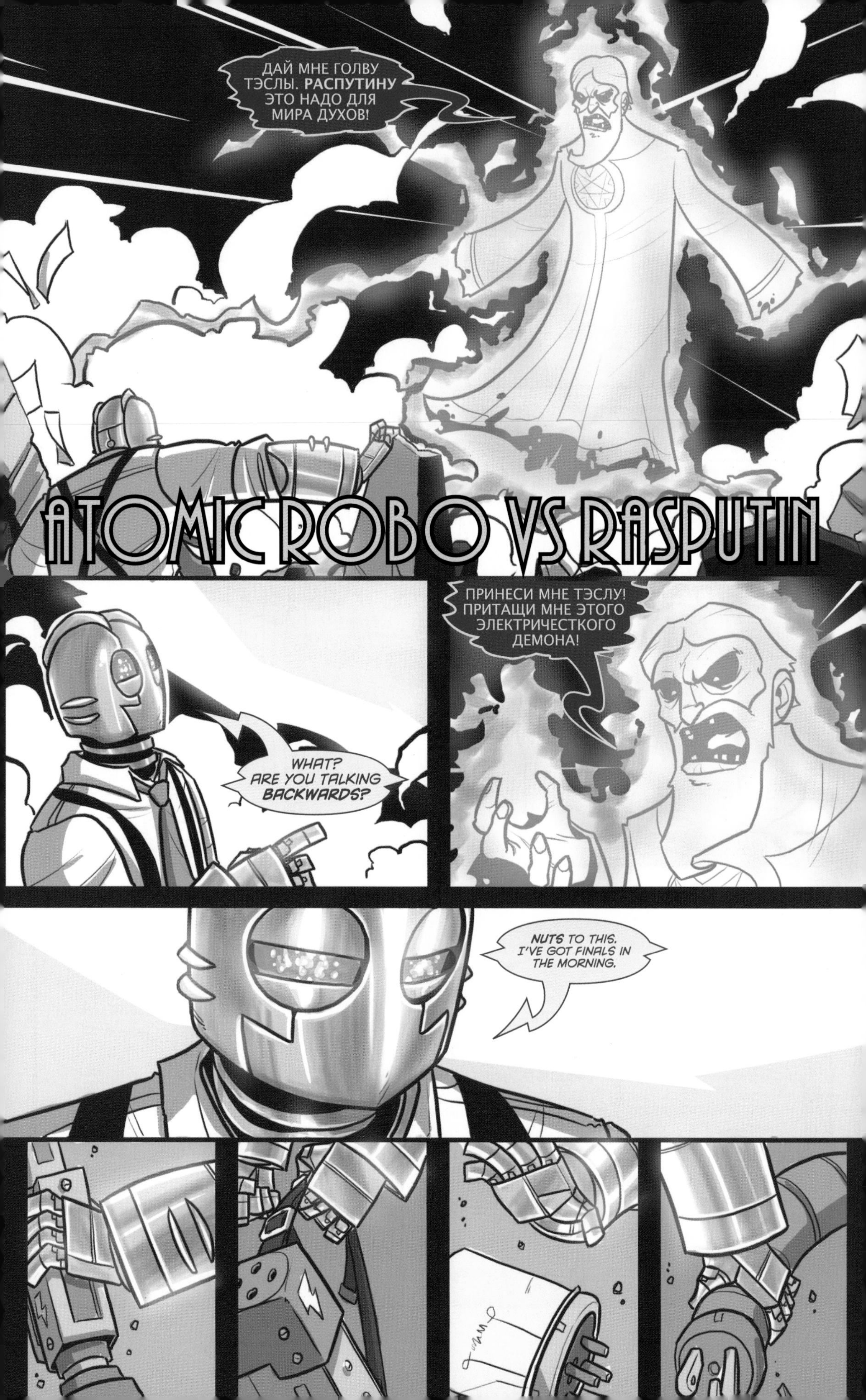

ДАЙ МНЕ ГОЛВУ ТЭСЛЫ. РАСПУТИНУ ЭТО НАДО ДЛЯ МИРА ДУХОВ!
ATOMIC ROBO VS RASPUTIN
WHAT? ARE YOU TALKING BACKWARDS?
ПРИНЕСИ МНЕ ТЭСЛУ! ПРИТАЩИ МНЕ ЭТОГО ЭЛЕКТРИЧЕСТКОГО ДЕМОНА!
NUTS TO THIS. I'VE GOT FINALS IN THE MORNING.

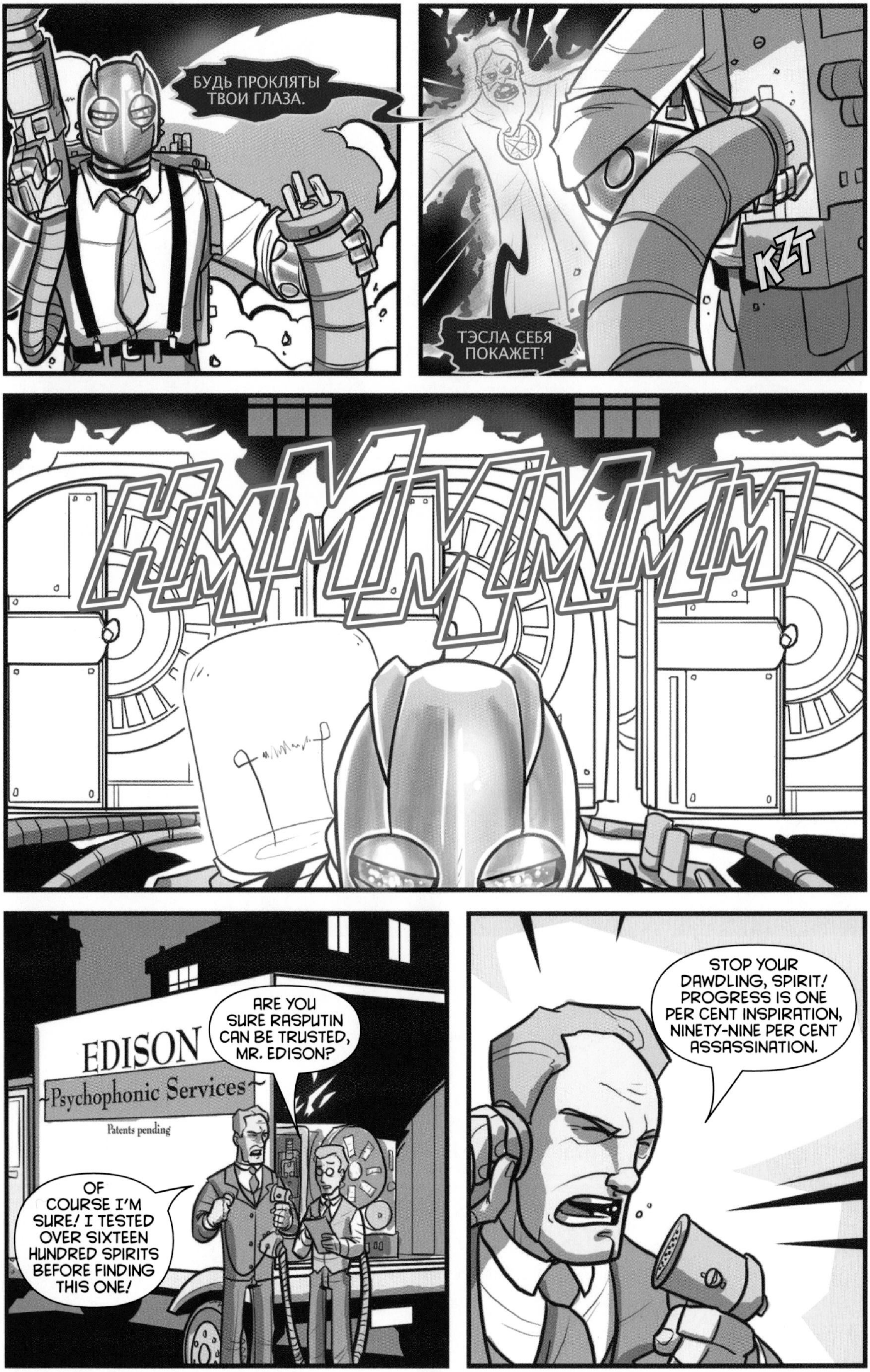
БУДЬ ПРОКЛЯТЫ ТВОИ ГЛАЗА.
ТЭСЛА СЕБЯ ПОКАЖЕТ!
KZT
GMMMMMMMMMMMM
EDISON
~Psychophonic Services~
Patents pending
ARE YOU SURE RASPUTIN CAN BE TRUSTED, MR. EDISON?
OF COURSE I'M SURE! I TESTED OVER SIXTEEN HUNDRED SPIRITS BEFORE FINDING THIS ONE!
STOP YOUR DAWDLING, SPIRIT! PROGRESS IS ONE PER CENT INSPIRATION, NINETY-NINE PER CENT ASSASSINATION.

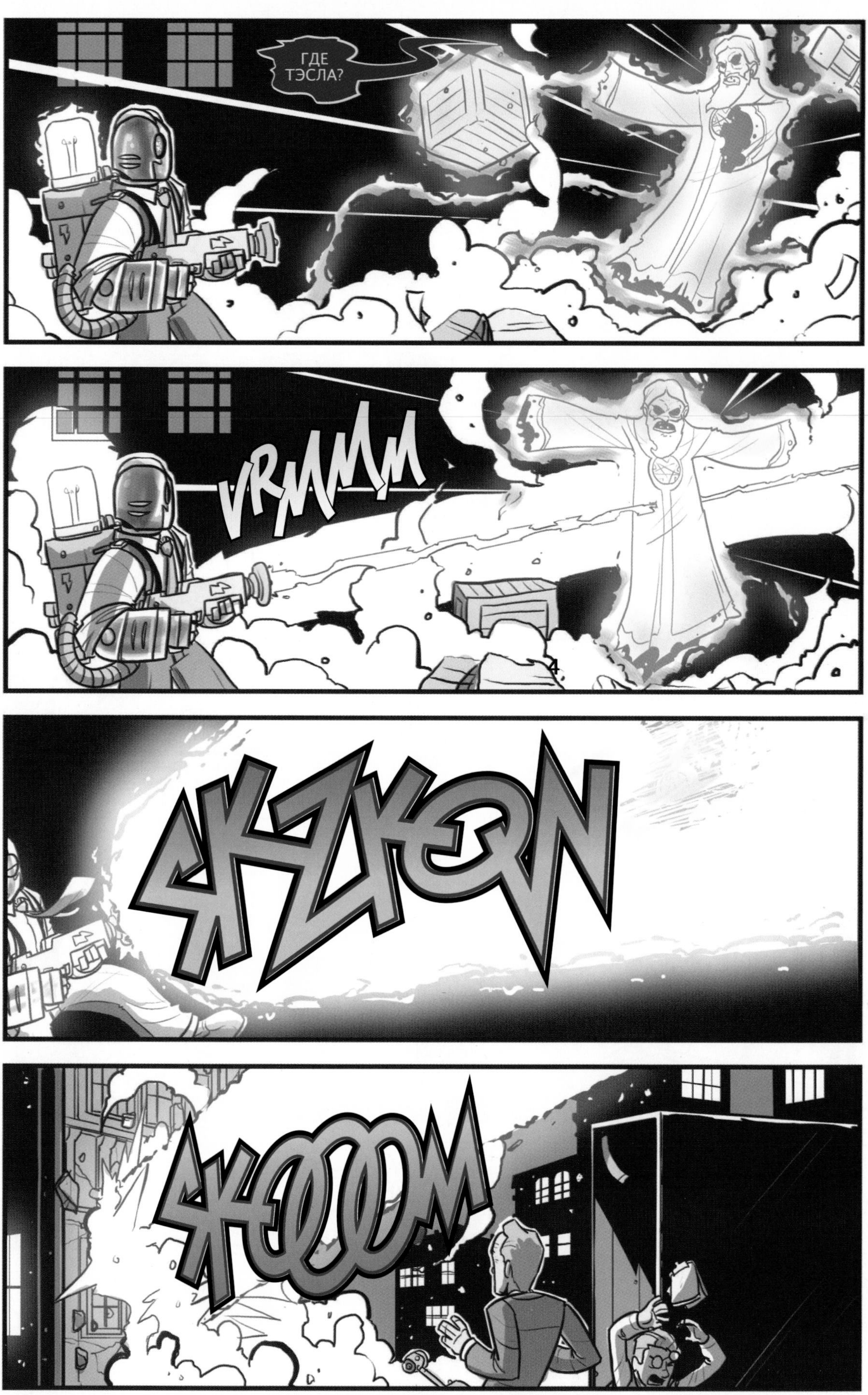
ГДЕ
ТЭСЛА?
VRMMM

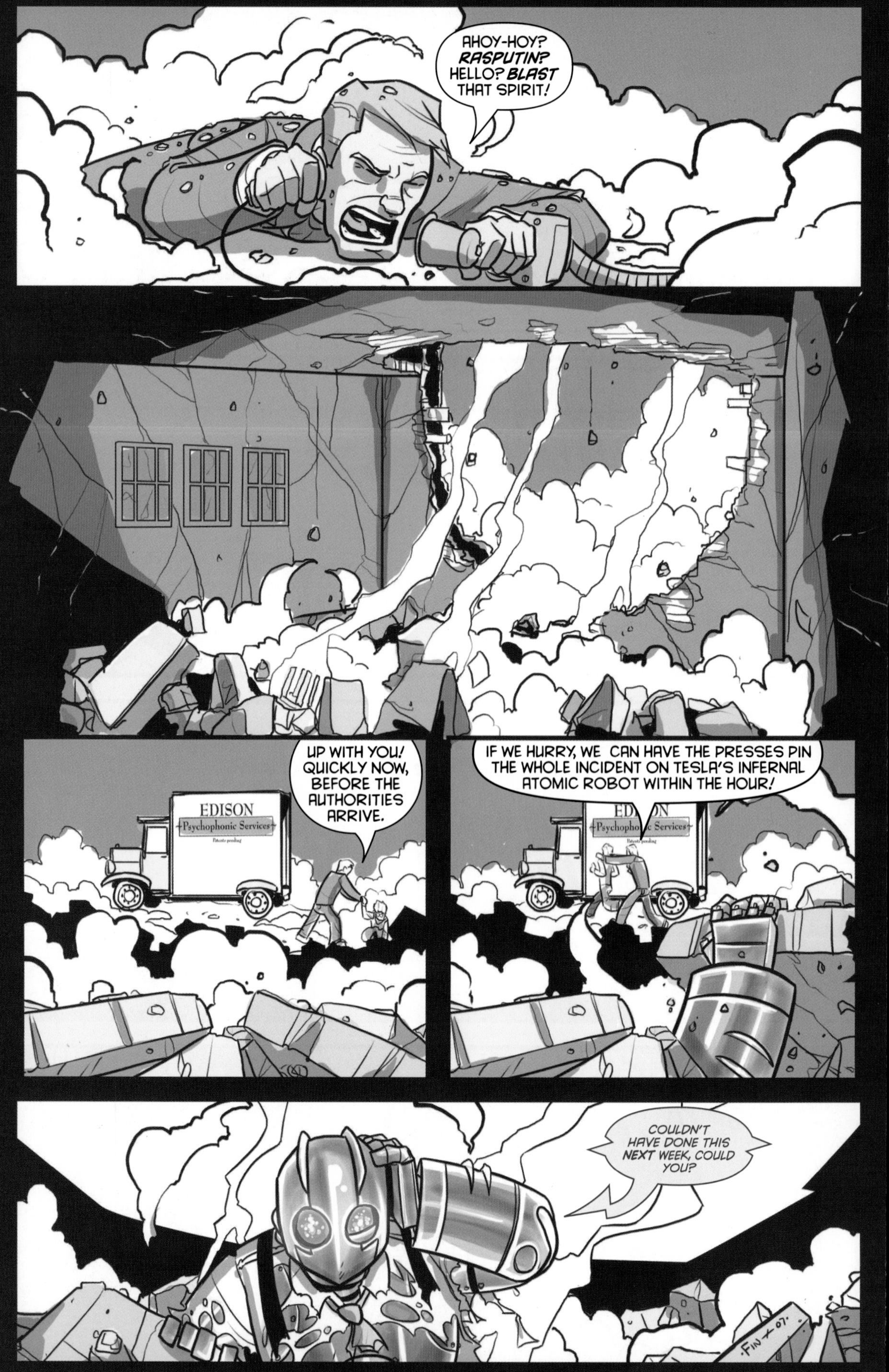
AHOY-HOY? RASPUTIN? HELLO? BLAST THAT SPIRIT!
UP WITH YOU! QUICKLY NOW, BEFORE THE AUTHORITIES ARRIVE.
EDISON
Psychophonic Services
Patents pending
IF WE HURRY, WE CAN HAVE THE PRESSES PIN THE WHOLE INCIDENT ON TESLA'S INFERNAL ATOMIC ROBOT WITHIN THE HOUR!
COULDN'T HAVE DONE THIS NEXT WEEK, COULD YOU?
FIN 07.

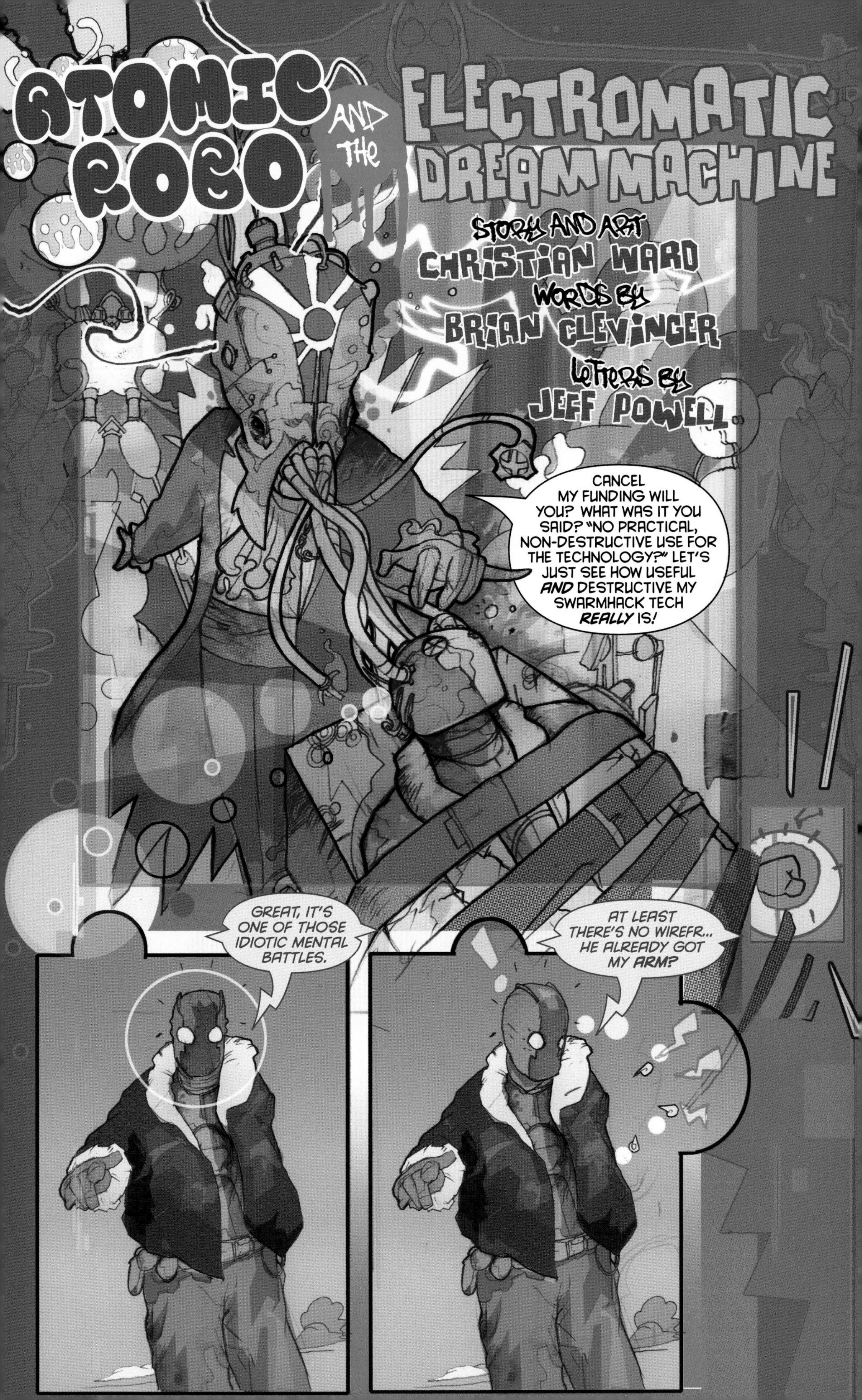
ATOMIC ROBO AND THE ELECTROMATIC DREAM MACHINE
STORY AND ART CHRISTIAN WARD
WORDS BY BRIAN CLEVINGER
LETTERS BY JEFF POWELL
CANCEL MY FUNDING WILL YOU? WHAT WAS IT YOU SAID? "NO PRACTICAL, NON-DESTRUCTIVE USE FOR THE TECHNOLOGY?" LET'S JUST SEE HOW USEFUL AND DESTRUCTIVE MY SWARMHACK TECH REALLY IS!
GREAT, IT'S ONE OF THOSE IDIOTIC MENTAL BATTLES.
AT LEAST THERE'S NO WIREFR... HE ALREADY GOT MY ARM?

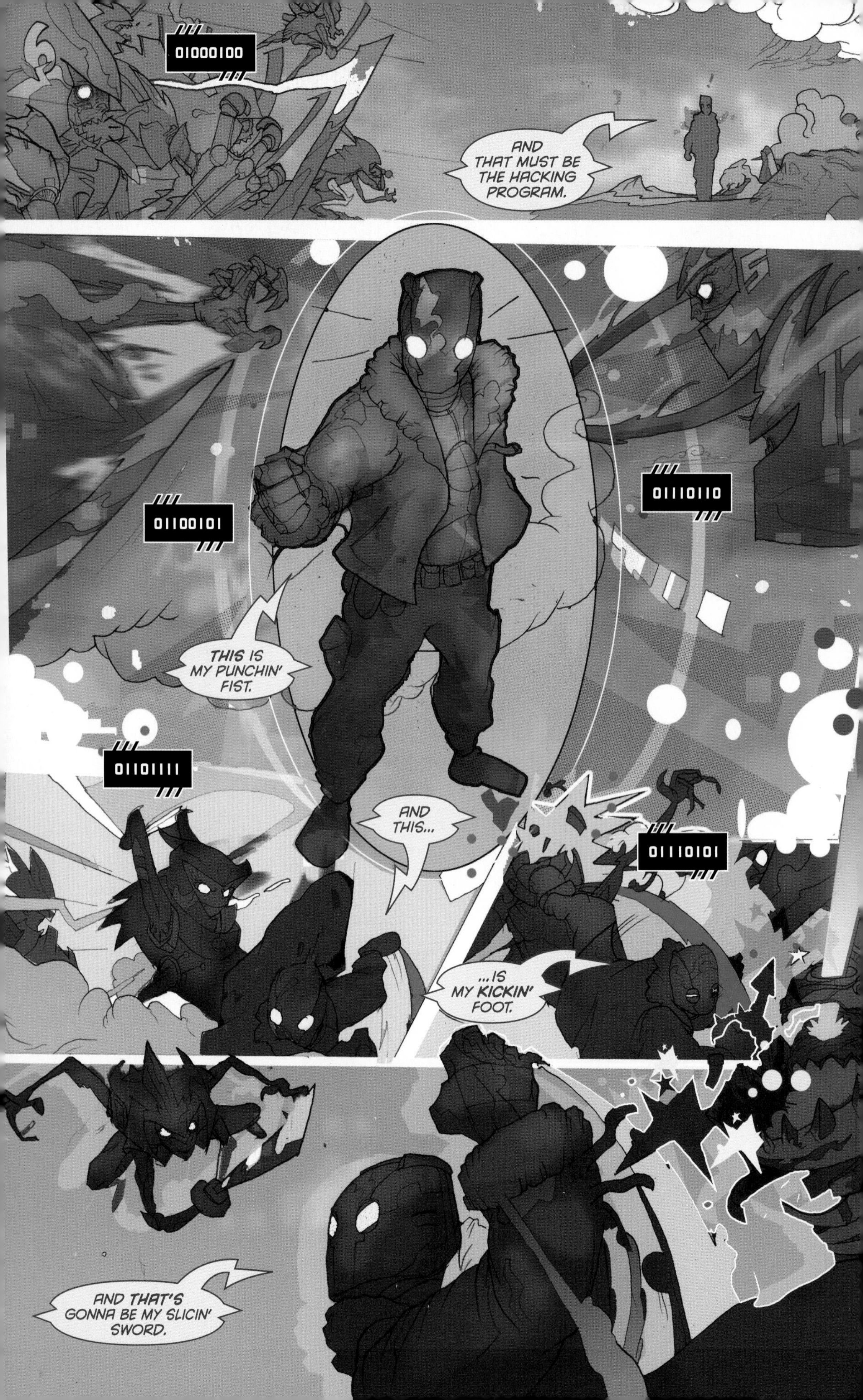
01000100
AND THAT MUST BE THE HACKING PROGRAM.
01100101
01110110
THIS IS MY PUNCHIN' FIST.
01101111
AND THIS...
01110101
...IS MY KICKIN' FOOT.
AND THAT'S GONNA BE MY SLICIN' SWORD.

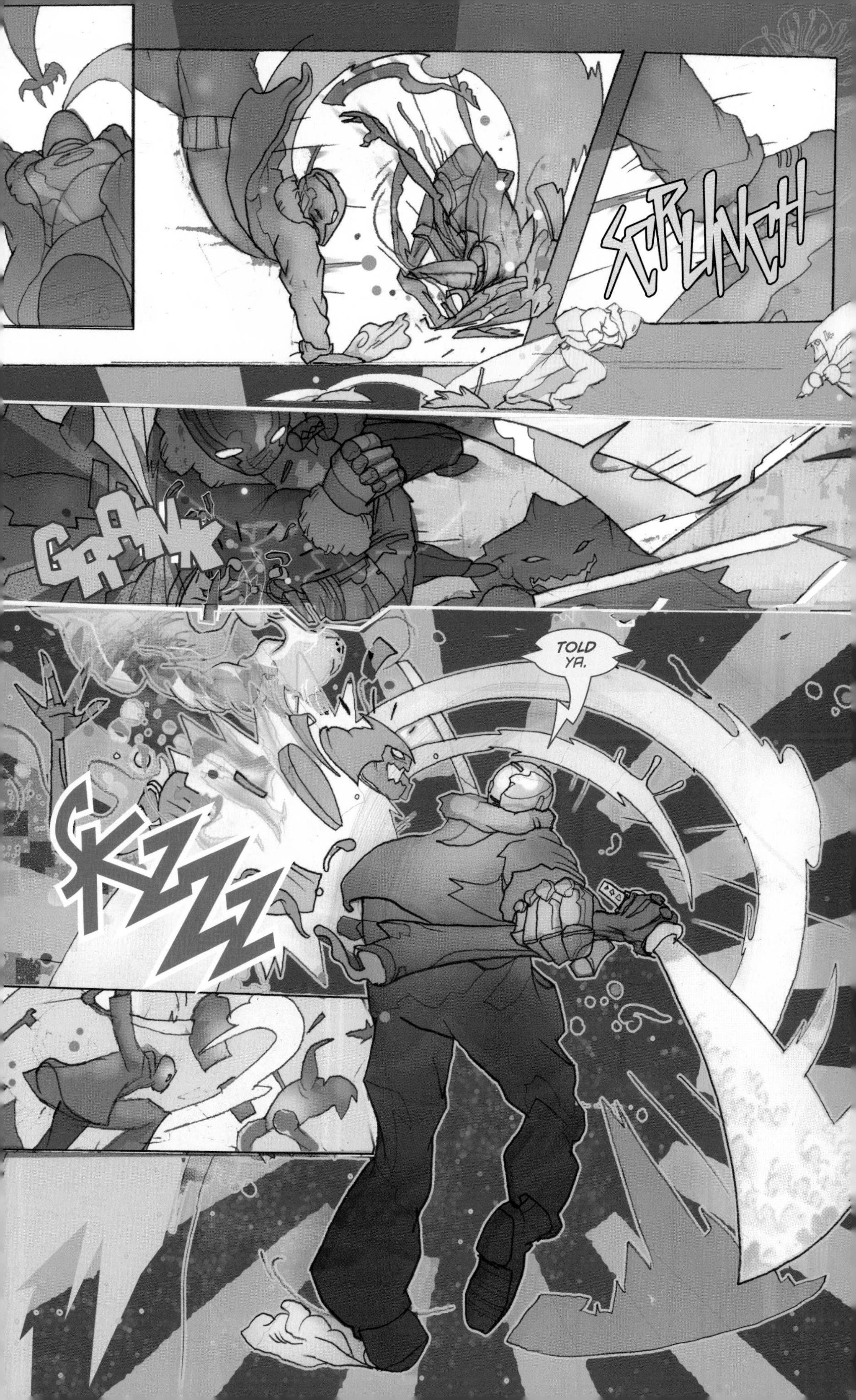
SCRUNCH
GRANK
TOLD YA.
SKZZZ

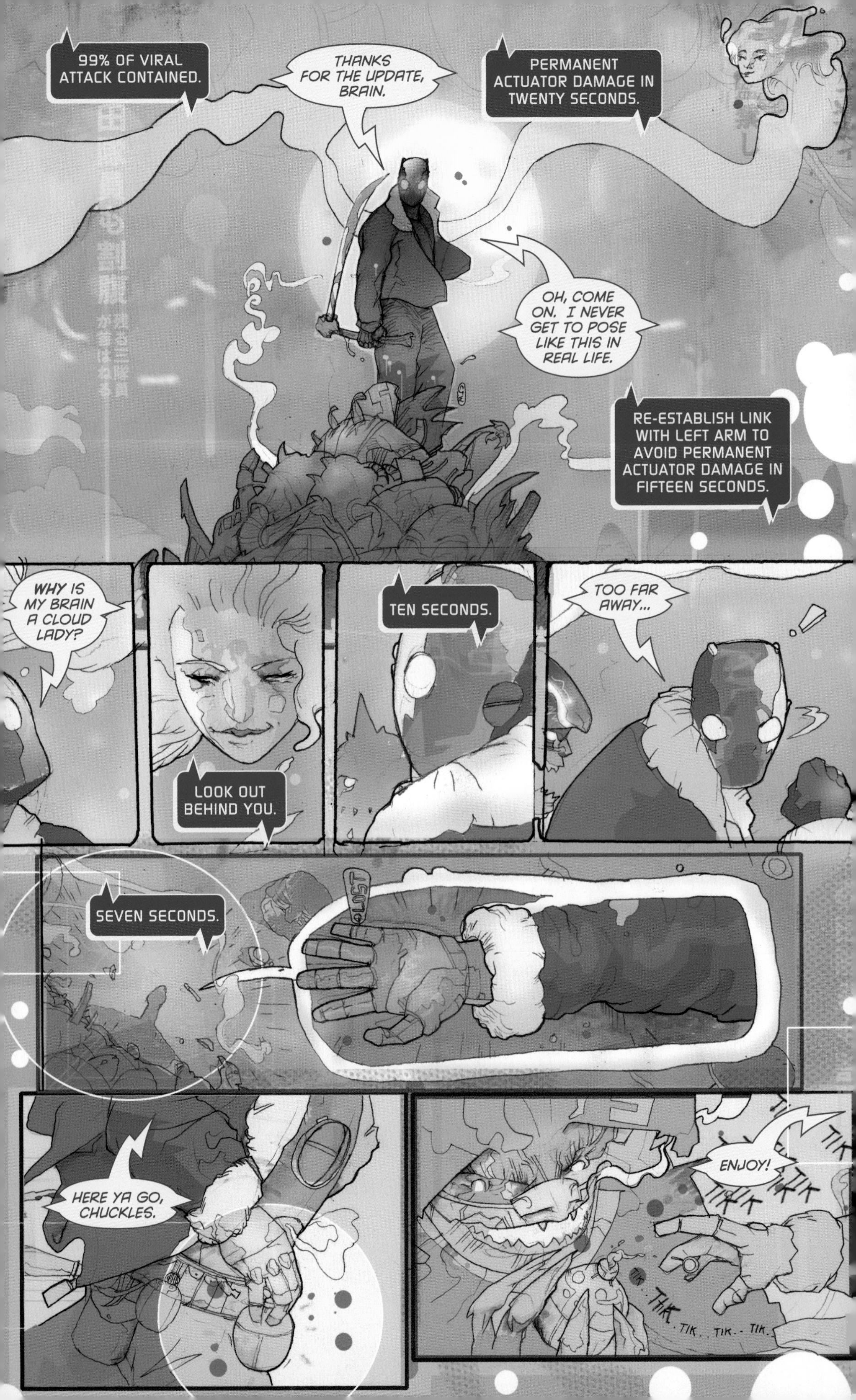
99% OF VIRAL ATTACK CONTAINED.
THANKS FOR THE UPDATE, BRAIN.
PERMANENT ACTUATOR DAMAGE IN TWENTY SECONDS.
OH, COME ON. I NEVER GET TO POSE LIKE THIS IN REAL LIFE.
RE-ESTABLISH LINK WITH LEFT ARM TO AVOID PERMANENT ACTUATOR DAMAGE IN FIFTEEN SECONDS.
WHY IS MY BRAIN A CLOUD LADY?
LOOK OUT BEHIND YOU.
TEN SECONDS.
TOO FAR AWAY...
!
SEVEN SECONDS.
LOST
HERE YA GO, CHUCKLES.
ENJOY!
TIK TIK TIK TIK
TIK. TIK. . TIK. . TIK. - TIK.

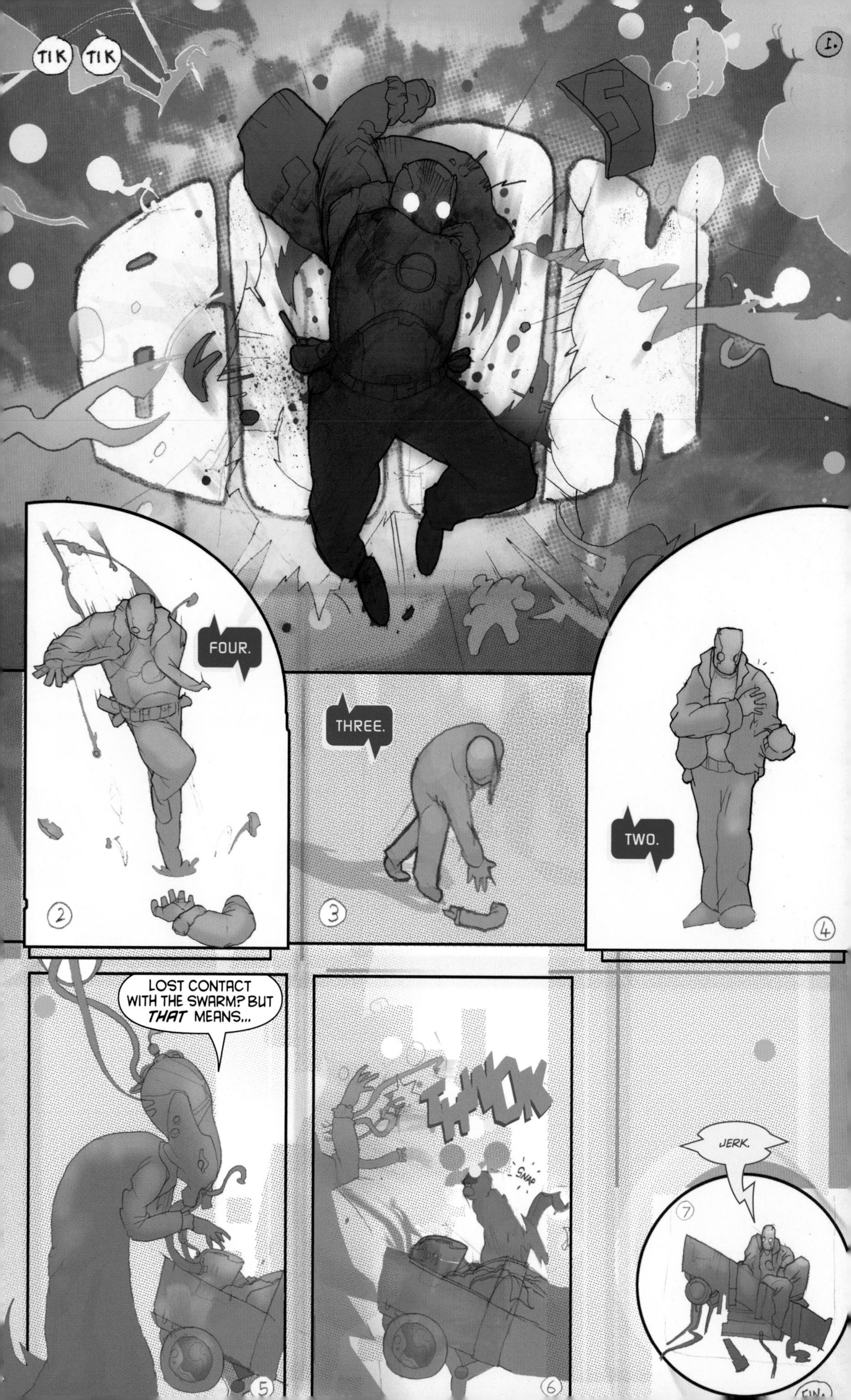
TIK TIK
1.
FOUR.
2
THREE.
3
TWO.
4
LOST CONTACT WITH THE SWARM? BUT *THAT* MEANS...
5
THWOK
SNAP
6
JERK.
7
FIN.

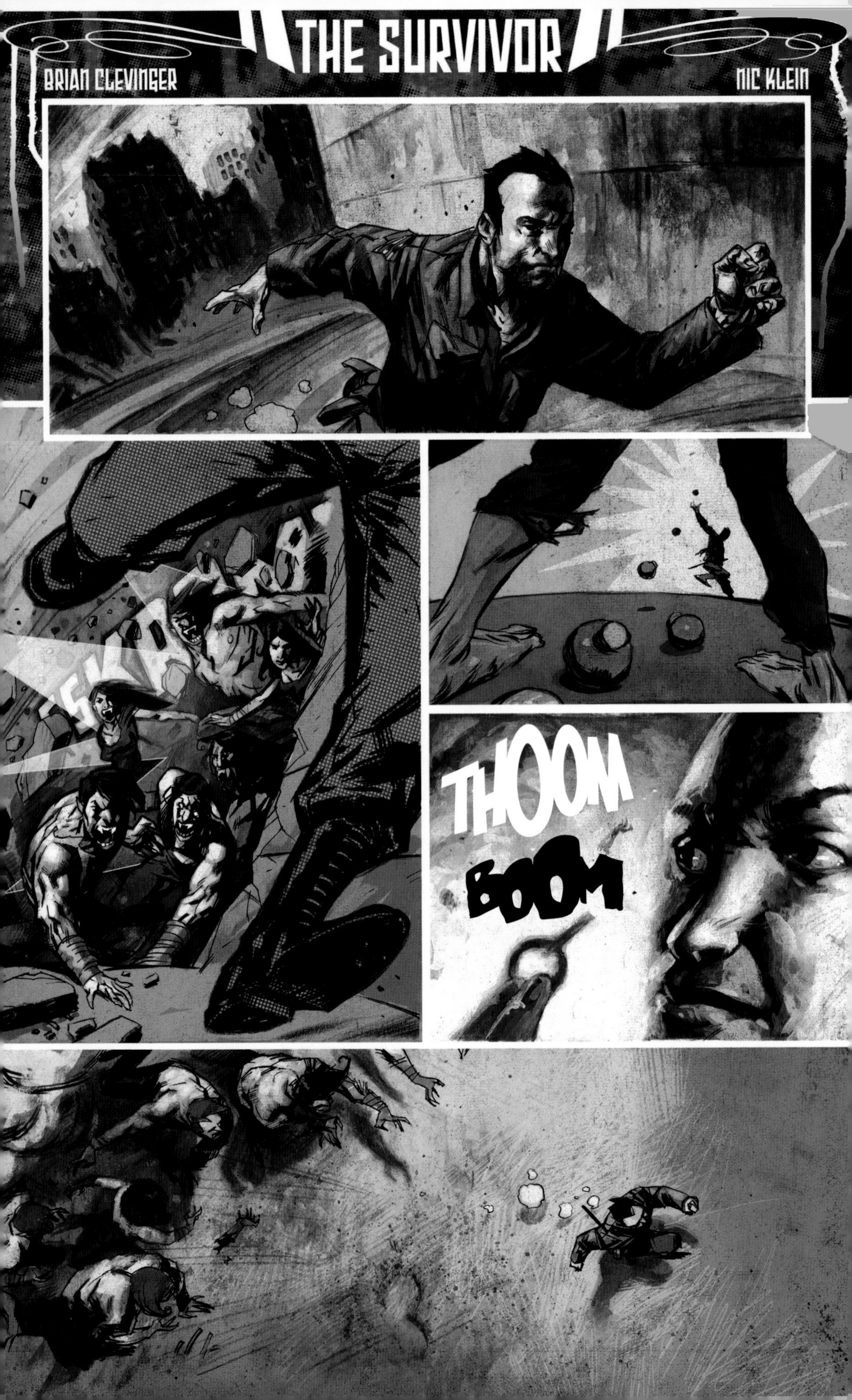
THE SURVIVOR
BRIAN CLEVINGER
NIC KLEIN
THOOM
BOOM

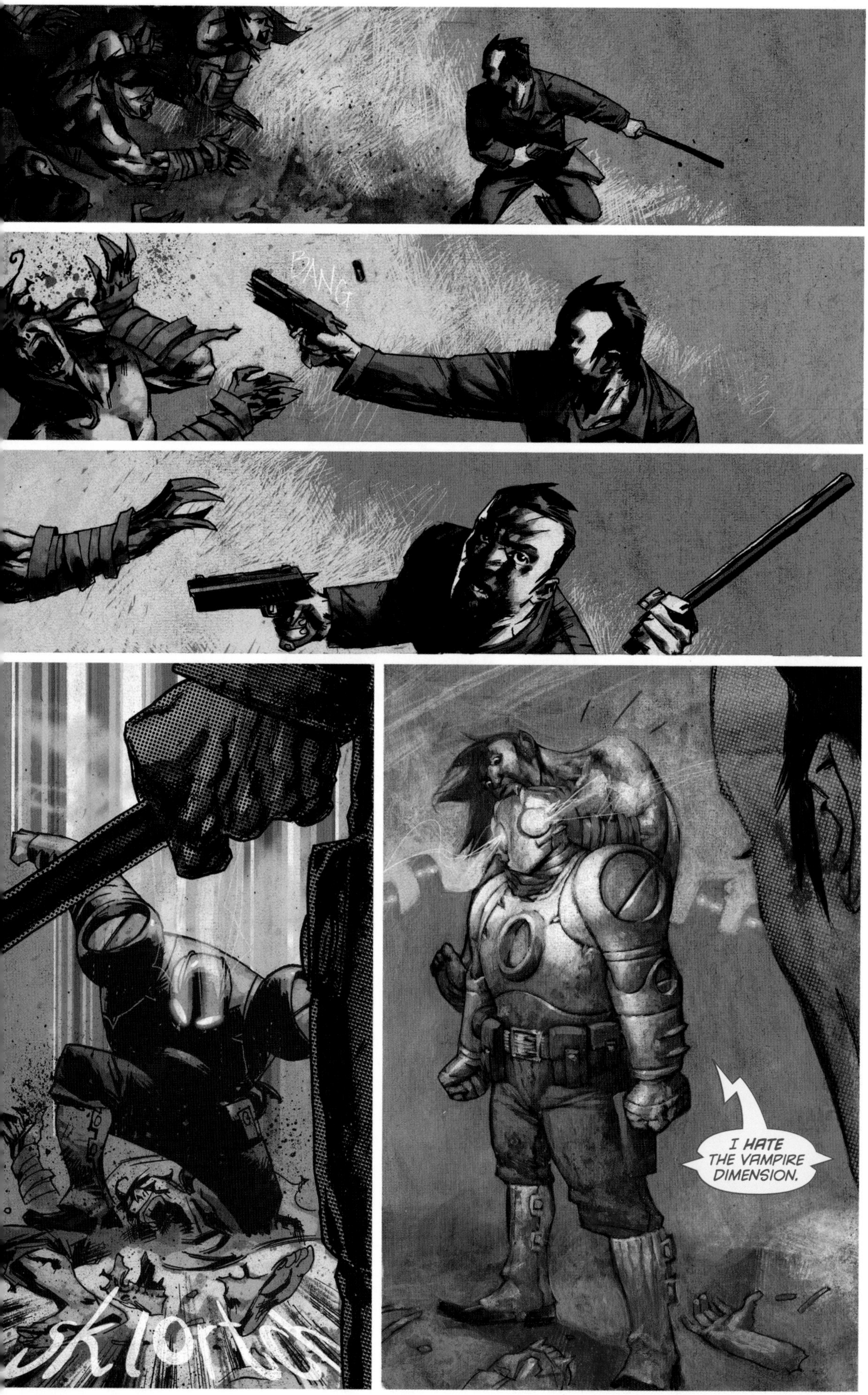
BANG
sklortch
I HATE THE VAMPIRE DIMENSION.

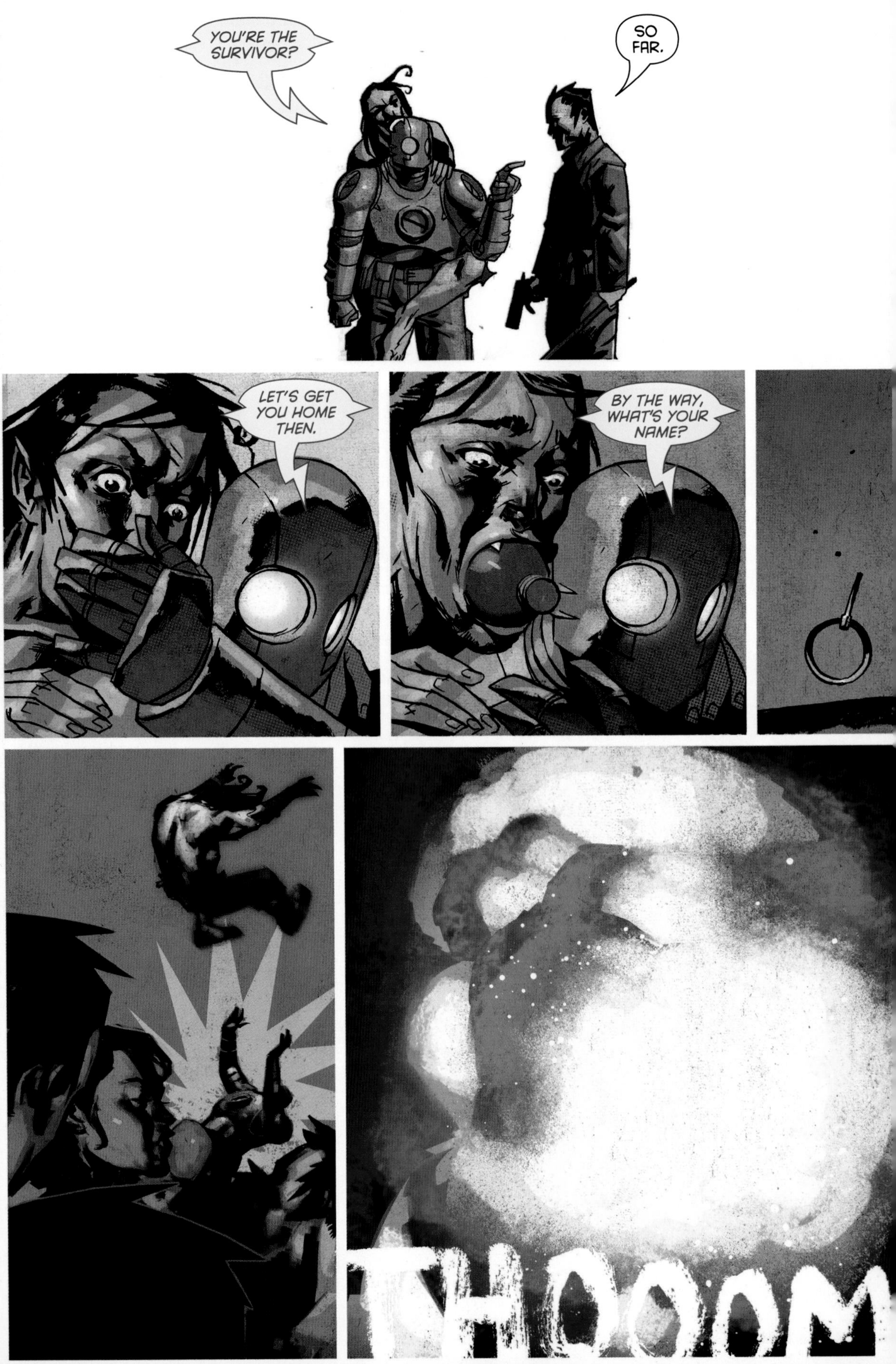
YOU'RE THE SURVIVOR?
SO FAR.
LET'S GET YOU HOME THEN.
BY THE WAY, WHAT'S YOUR NAME?
THOOOM

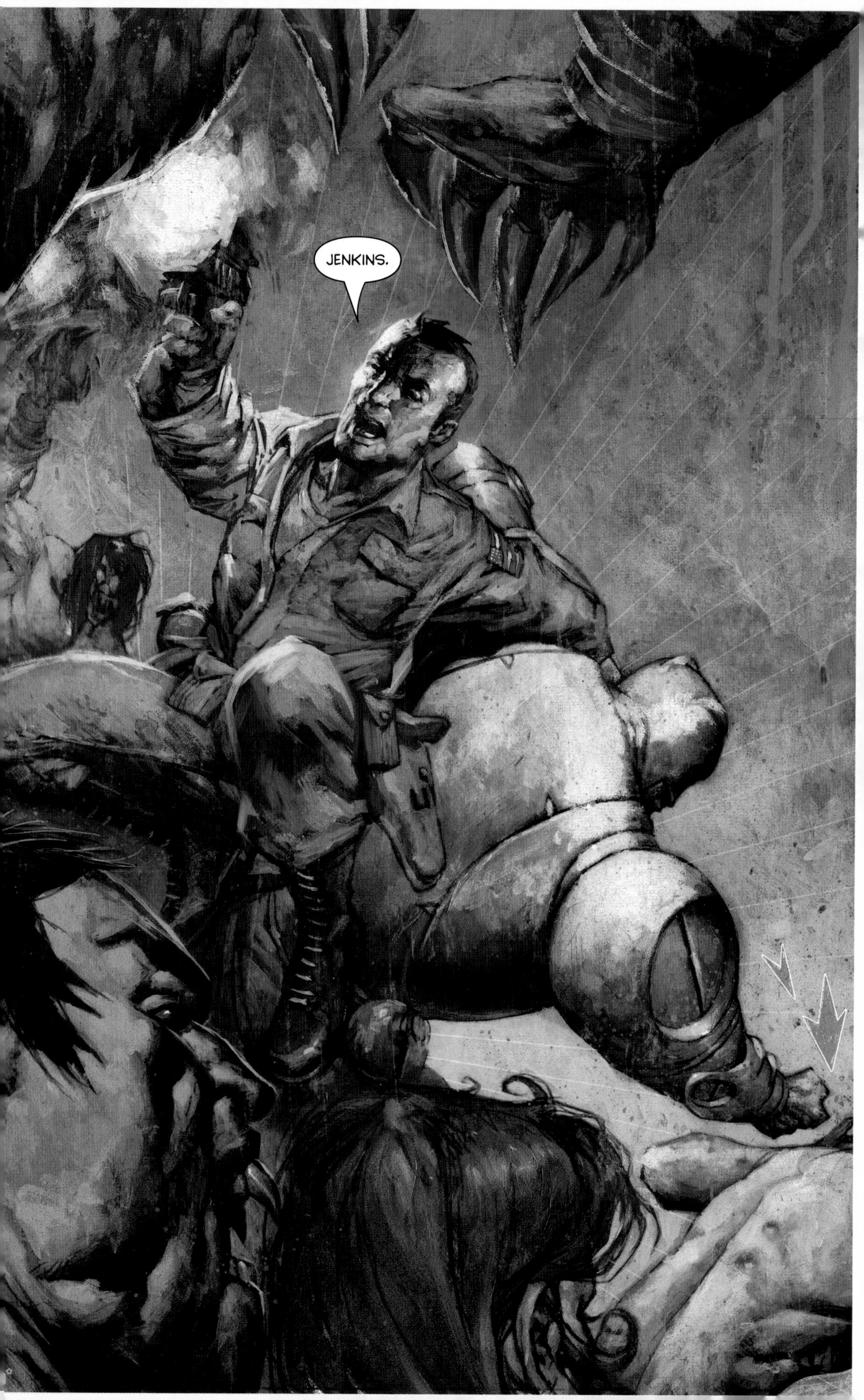
JENKINS.

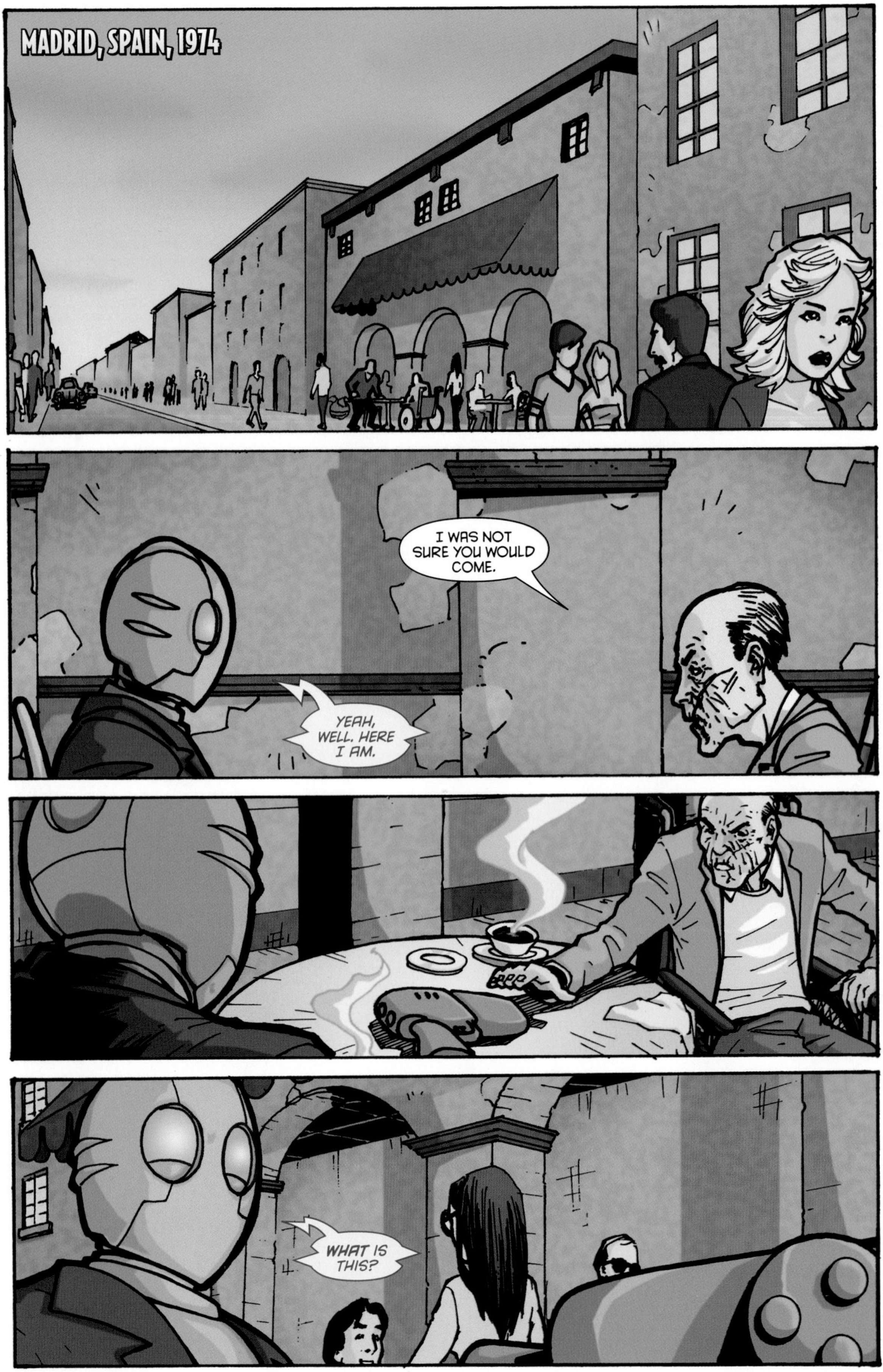
MADRID, SPAIN, 1974
I WAS NOT SURE YOU WOULD COME.
YEAH, WELL. HERE I AM.
WHAT IS THIS?

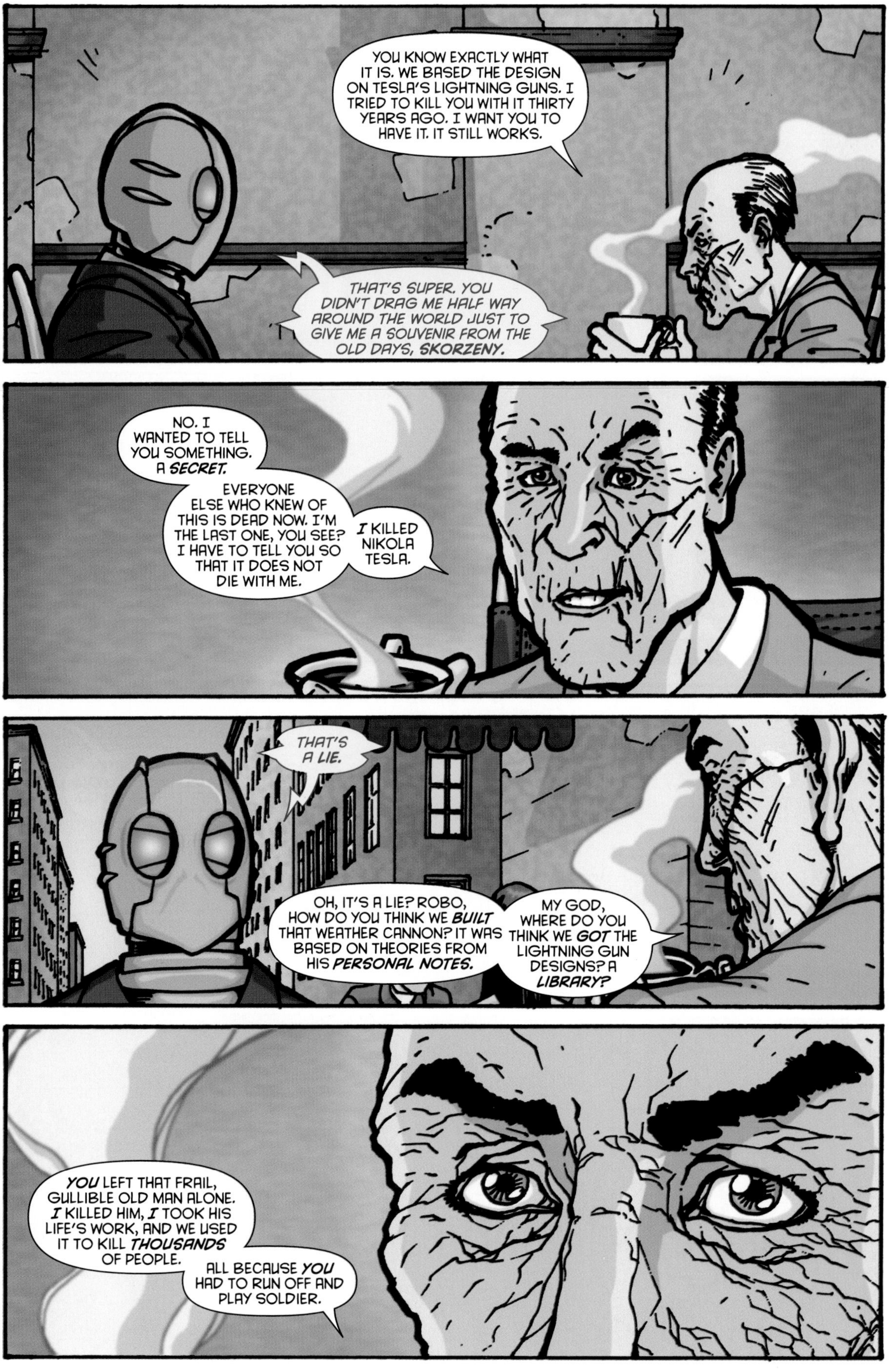

YOU KNOW EXACTLY WHAT IT IS. WE BASED THE DESIGN ON TESLA'S LIGHTNING GUNS. I TRIED TO KILL YOU WITH IT THIRTY YEARS AGO. I WANT YOU TO HAVE IT. IT STILL WORKS.
THAT'S SUPER. YOU DIDN'T DRAG ME HALF WAY AROUND THE WORLD JUST TO GIVE ME A SOUVENIR FROM THE OLD DAYS, SKORZENY.
NO. I WANTED TO TELL YOU SOMETHING. A SECRET.
EVERYONE ELSE WHO KNEW OF THIS IS DEAD NOW. I'M THE LAST ONE, YOU SEE? I HAVE TO TELL YOU SO THAT IT DOES NOT DIE WITH ME.
I KILLED NIKOLA TESLA.
THAT'S A LIE.
OH, IT'S A LIE? ROBO, HOW DO YOU THINK WE BUILT THAT WEATHER CANNON? IT WAS BASED ON THEORIES FROM HIS PERSONAL NOTES.
MY GOD, WHERE DO YOU THINK WE GOT THE LIGHTNING GUN DESIGNS? A LIBRARY?
YOU LEFT THAT FRAIL, GULLIBLE OLD MAN ALONE. I KILLED HIM, I TOOK HIS LIFE'S WORK, AND WE USED IT TO KILL THOUSANDS OF PEOPLE.
ALL BECAUSE YOU HAD TO RUN OFF AND PLAY SOLDIER.

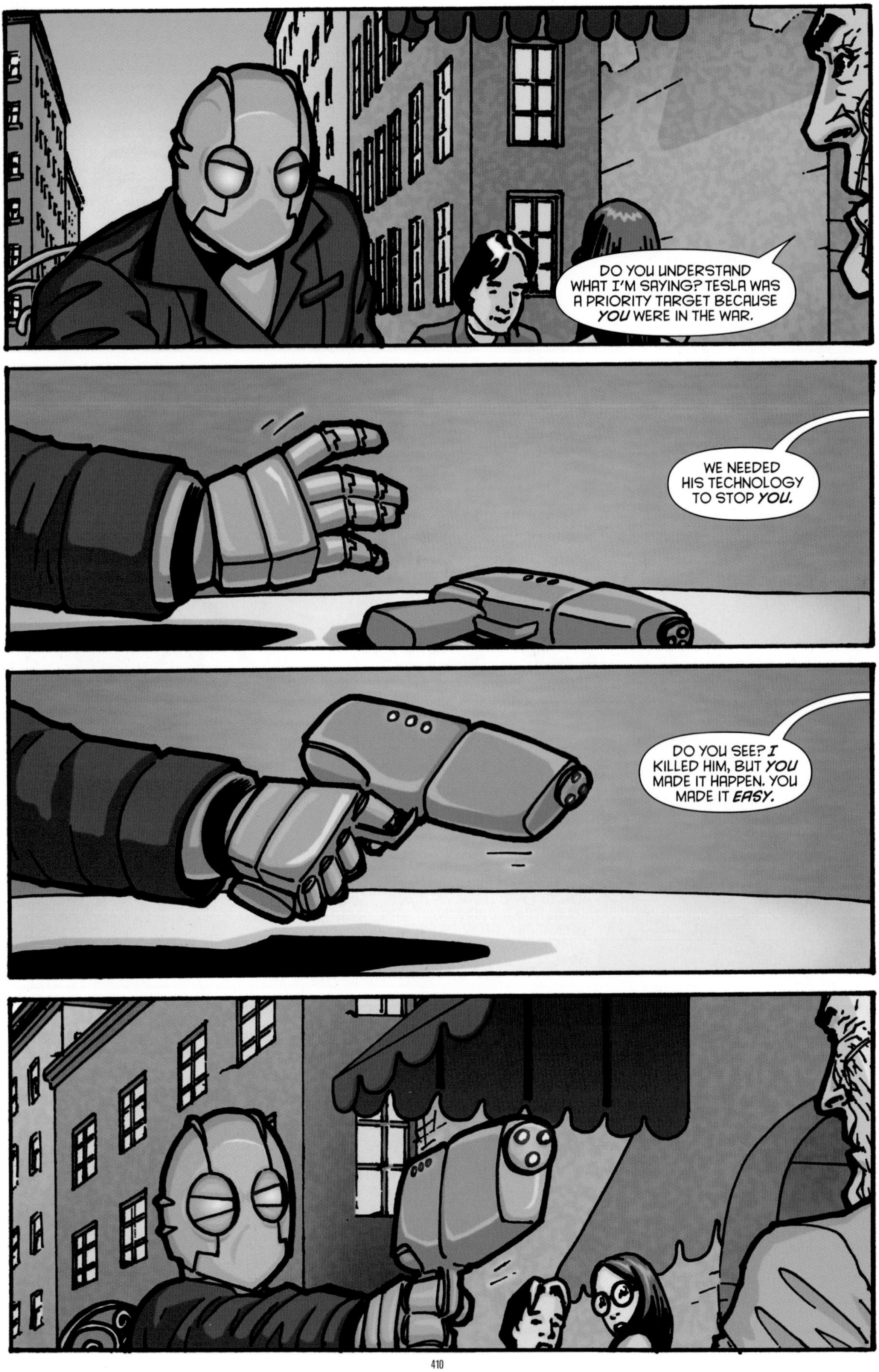
DO YOU UNDERSTAND WHAT I'M SAYING? TESLA WAS A PRIORITY TARGET BECAUSE *YOU* WERE IN THE WAR.
WE NEEDED HIS TECHNOLOGY TO STOP *YOU.*
DO YOU SEE? *I* KILLED HIM, BUT *YOU* MADE IT HAPPEN. YOU MADE IT *EASY.*

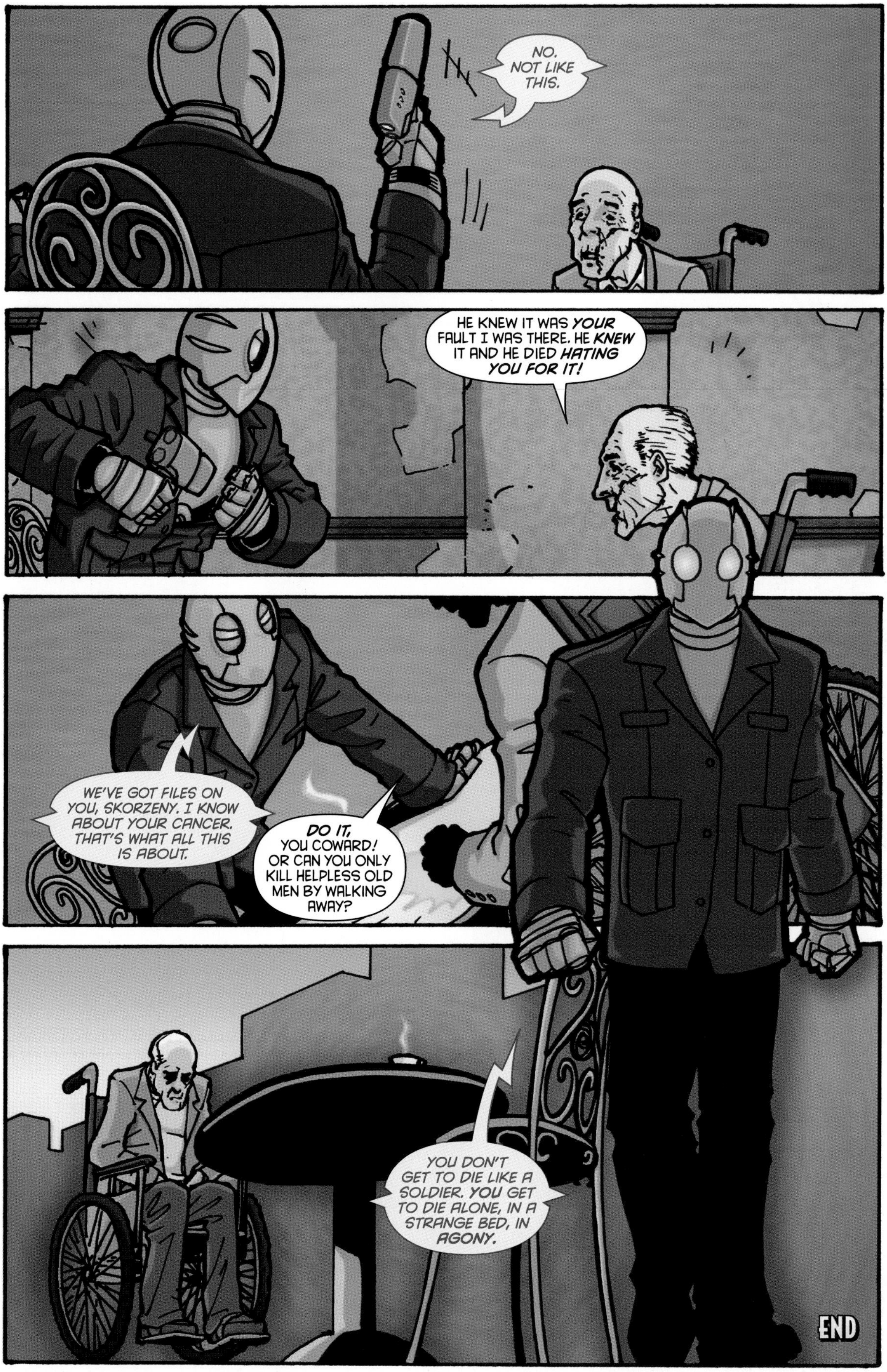
NO. NOT LIKE THIS.
HE KNEW IT WAS YOUR FAULT I WAS THERE. HE KNEW IT AND HE DIED HATING YOU FOR IT!
WE'VE GOT FILES ON YOU, SKORZENY. I KNOW ABOUT YOUR CANCER. THAT'S WHAT ALL THIS IS ABOUT.
DO IT, YOU COWARD! OR CAN YOU ONLY KILL HELPLESS OLD MEN BY WALKING AWAY?
YOU DON'T GET TO DIE LIKE A SOLDIER. YOU GET TO DIE ALONE, IN A STRANGE BED, IN AGONY.
END

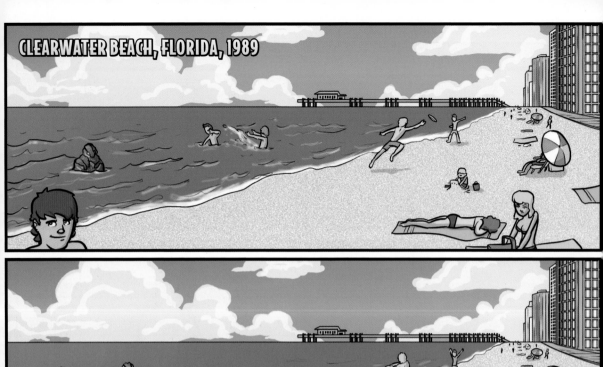

CLEARWATER BEACH, FLORIDA, 1989

HI.

THERE'S NO NEED FOR ALARM. THE MONSTER IS DEAD.

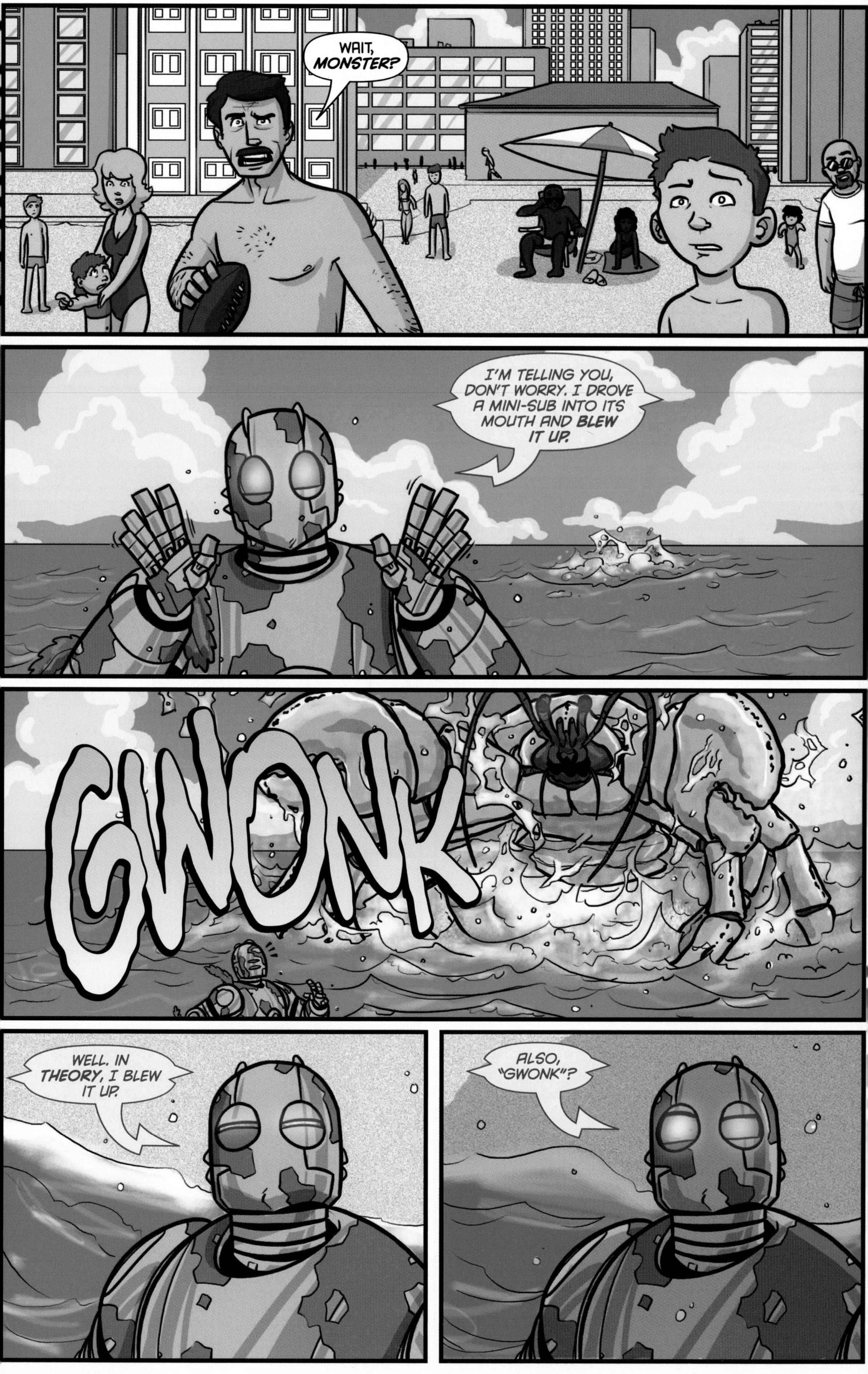
WAIT, MONSTER?
I'M TELLING YOU, DON'T WORRY. I DROVE A MINI-SUB INTO ITS MOUTH AND BLEW IT UP.
GWONK
WELL. IN THEORY, I BLEW IT UP.
ALSO, "GWONK"?

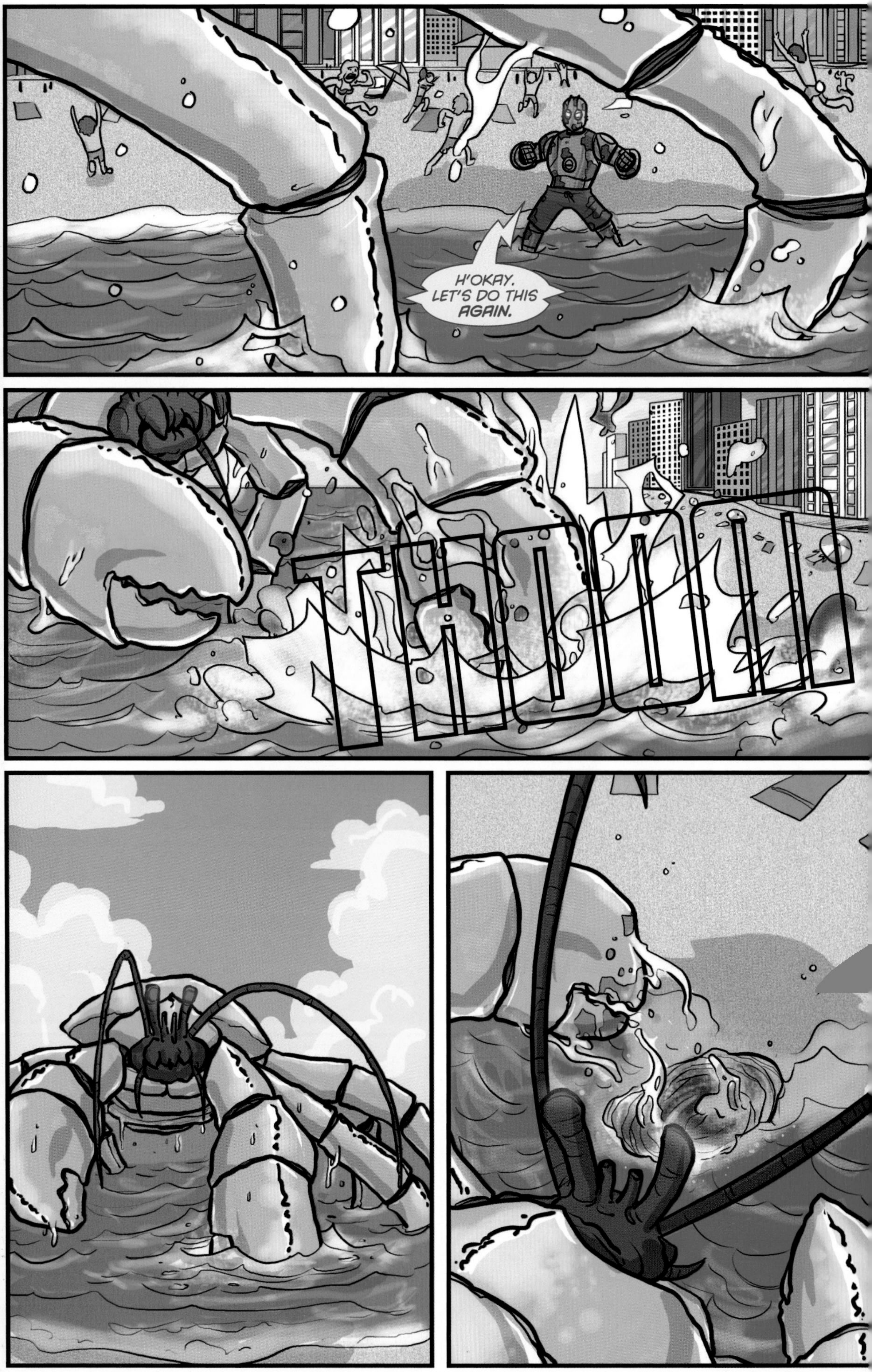
H'OKAY. LET'S DO THIS AGAIN.
THOOM

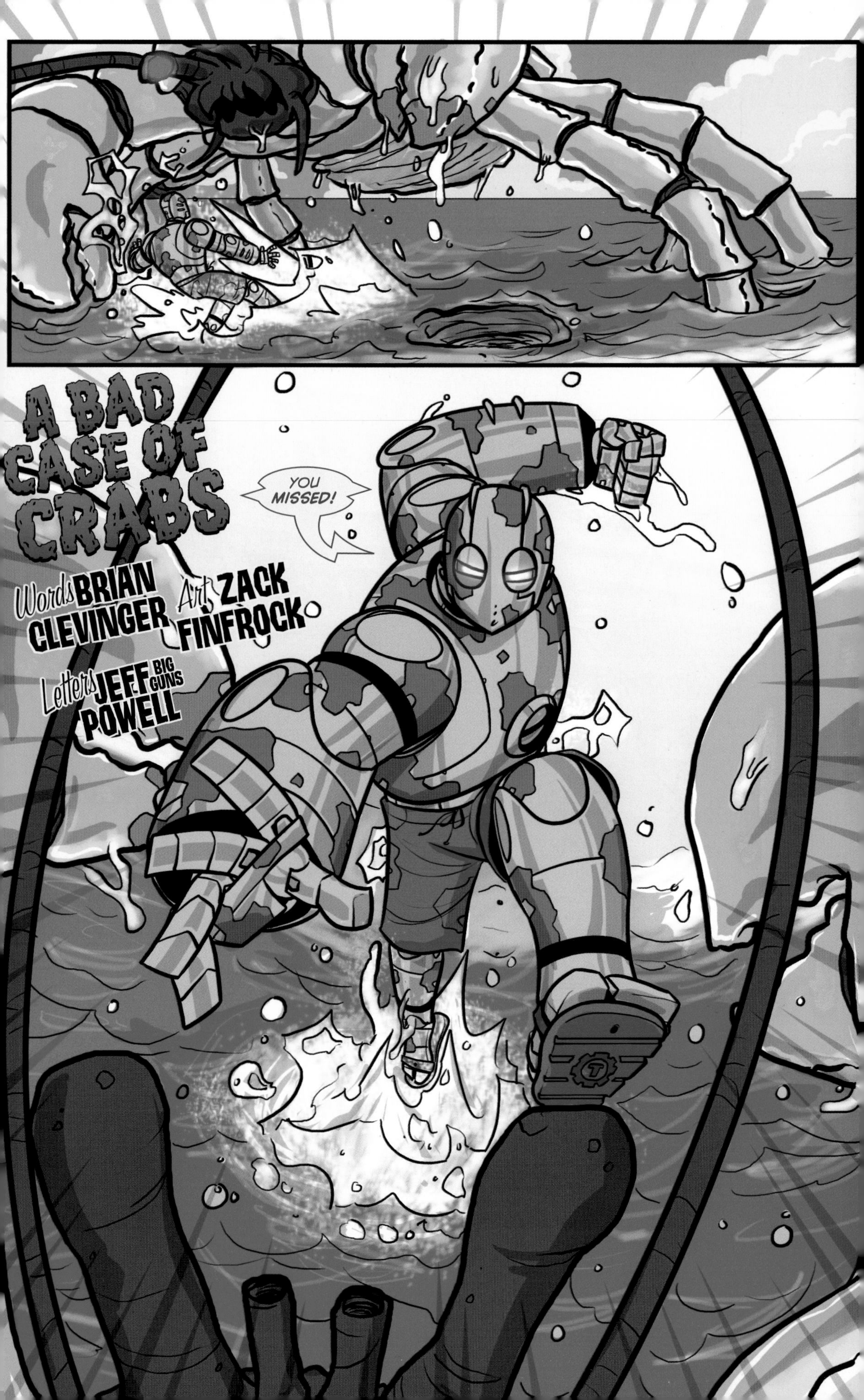
A BAD CASE OF CRABS
YOU MISSED!
Words BRIAN CLEVINGER
Art ZACK FINFROCK
Letters JEFF BIG GUNS POWELL

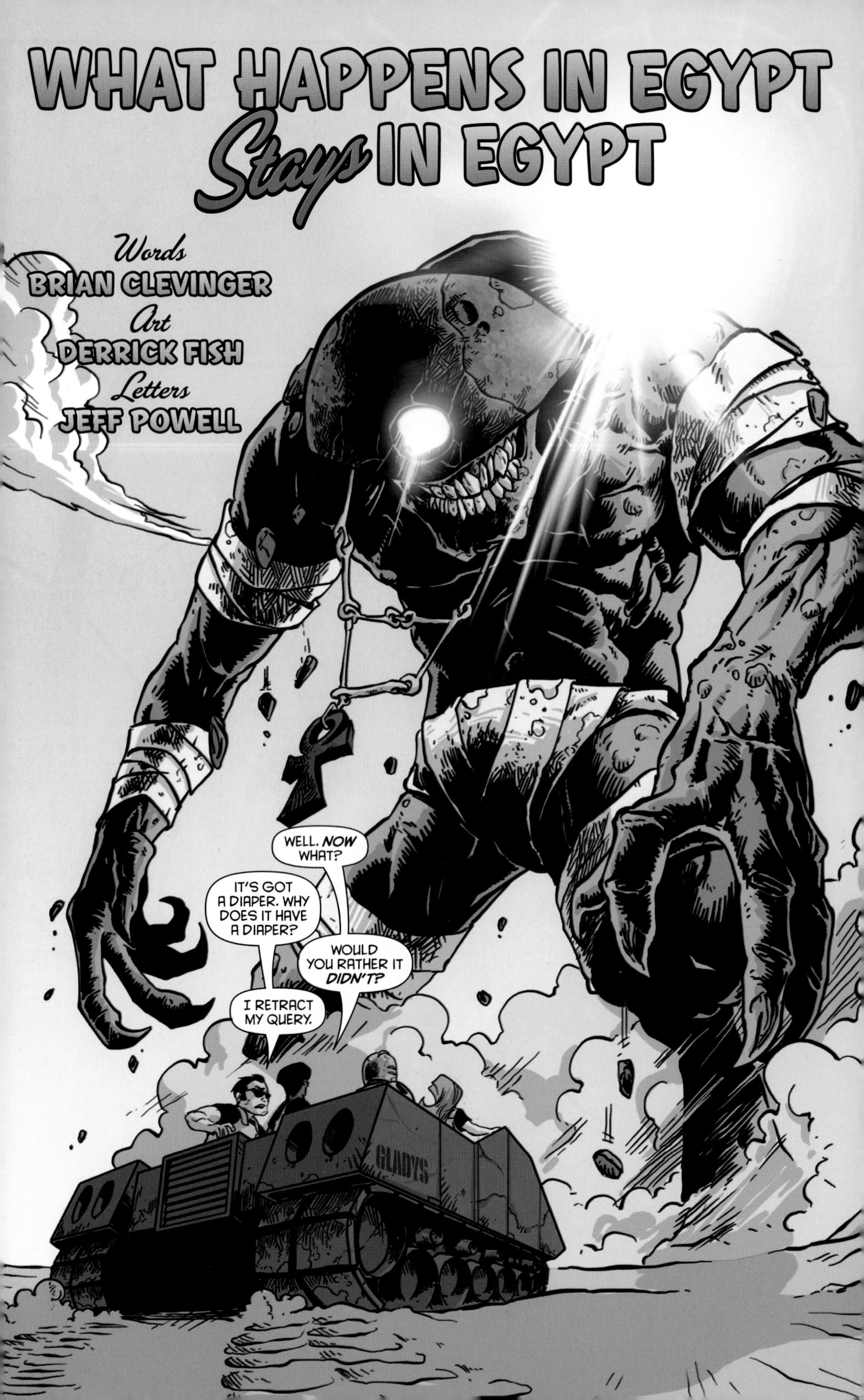

WHAT HAPPENS IN EGYPT
Stays IN EGYPT
Words
BRIAN CLEVINGER
Art
DERRICK FISH
Letters
JEFF POWELL
WELL. NOW WHAT?
IT'S GOT A DIAPER. WHY DOES IT HAVE A DIAPER?
WOULD YOU RATHER IT DIDN'T?
I RETRACT MY QUERY.
GLADYS

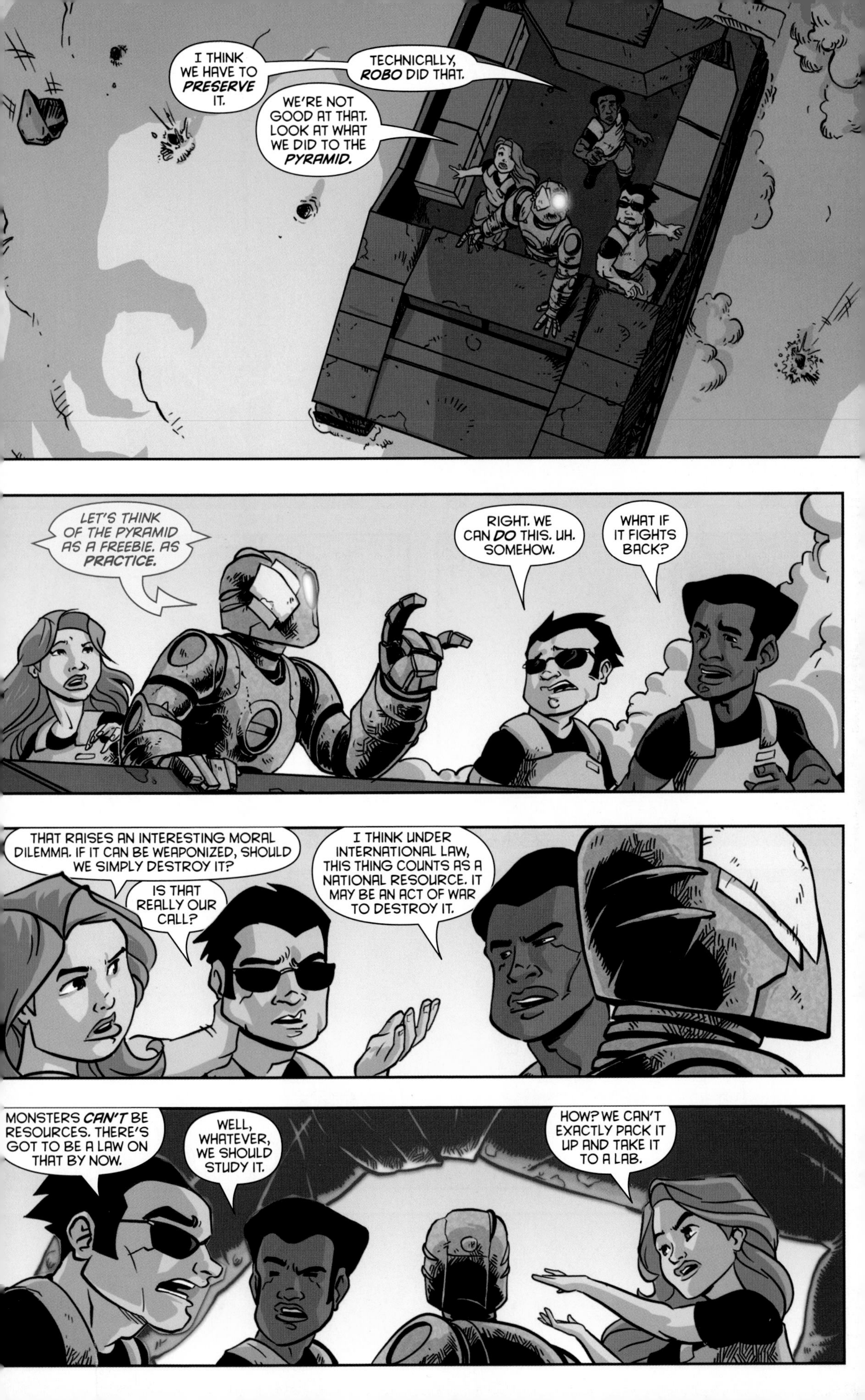
I THINK WE HAVE TO *PRESERVE* IT.
TECHNICALLY, *ROBO* DID THAT.
WE'RE NOT GOOD AT THAT. LOOK AT WHAT WE DID TO THE *PYRAMID.*
LET'S THINK OF THE PYRAMID AS A FREEBIE. AS *PRACTICE.*
RIGHT. WE CAN *DO* THIS. UH. SOMEHOW.
WHAT IF IT FIGHTS BACK?
THAT RAISES AN INTERESTING MORAL DILEMMA. IF IT CAN BE WEAPONIZED, SHOULD WE SIMPLY DESTROY IT?
IS THAT REALLY OUR CALL?
I THINK UNDER INTERNATIONAL LAW, THIS THING COUNTS AS A NATIONAL RESOURCE. IT MAY BE AN ACT OF WAR TO DESTROY IT.
MONSTERS *CAN'T* BE RESOURCES. THERE'S GOT TO BE A LAW ON THAT BY NOW.
WELL, WHATEVER, WE SHOULD STUDY IT.
HOW? WE CAN'T EXACTLY PACK IT UP AND TAKE IT TO A LAB.

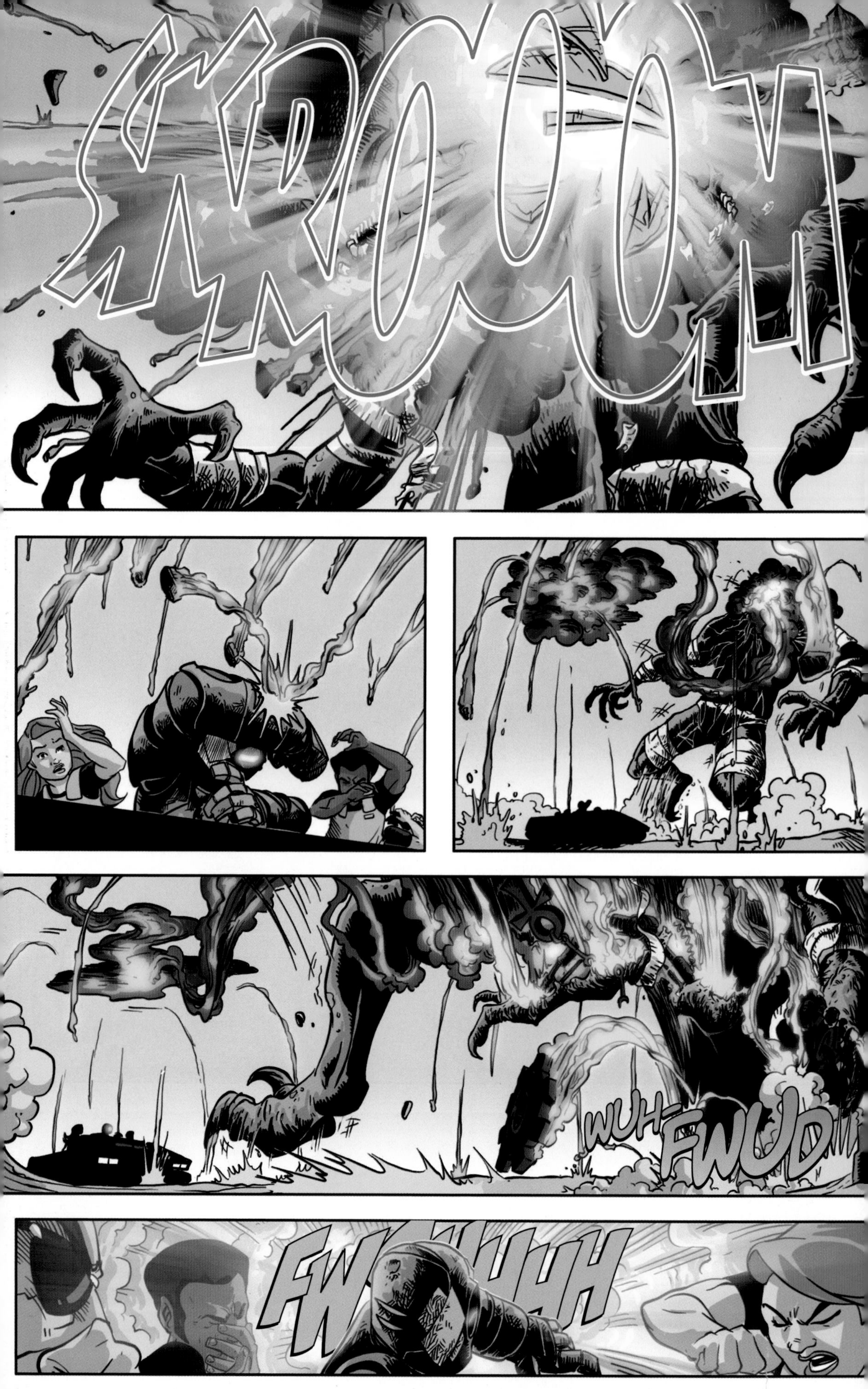
SKROOOM
WUH-FWUD

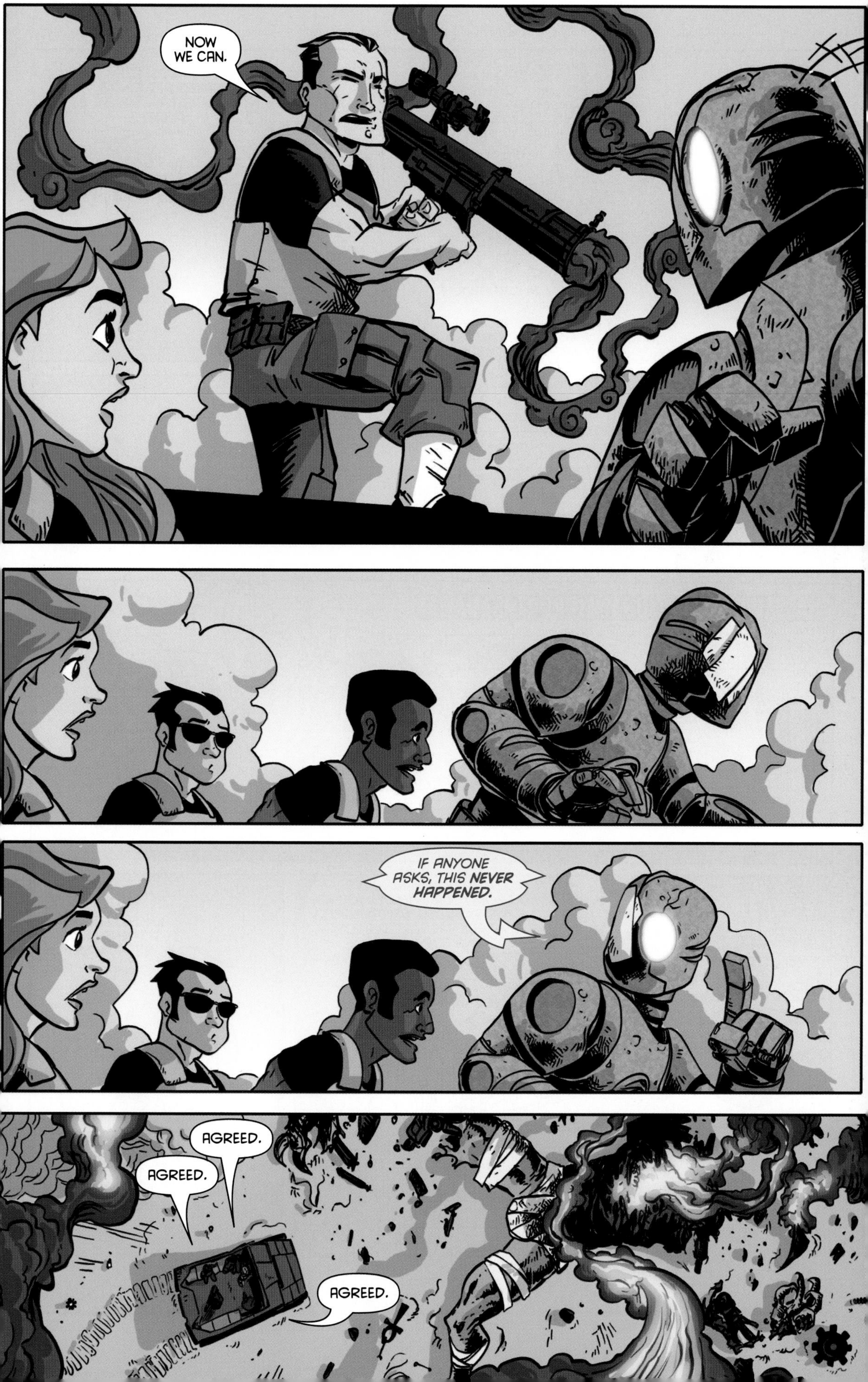
NOW WE CAN.
IF ANYONE ASKS, THIS NEVER HAPPENED.
AGREED.
AGREED.
AGREED.

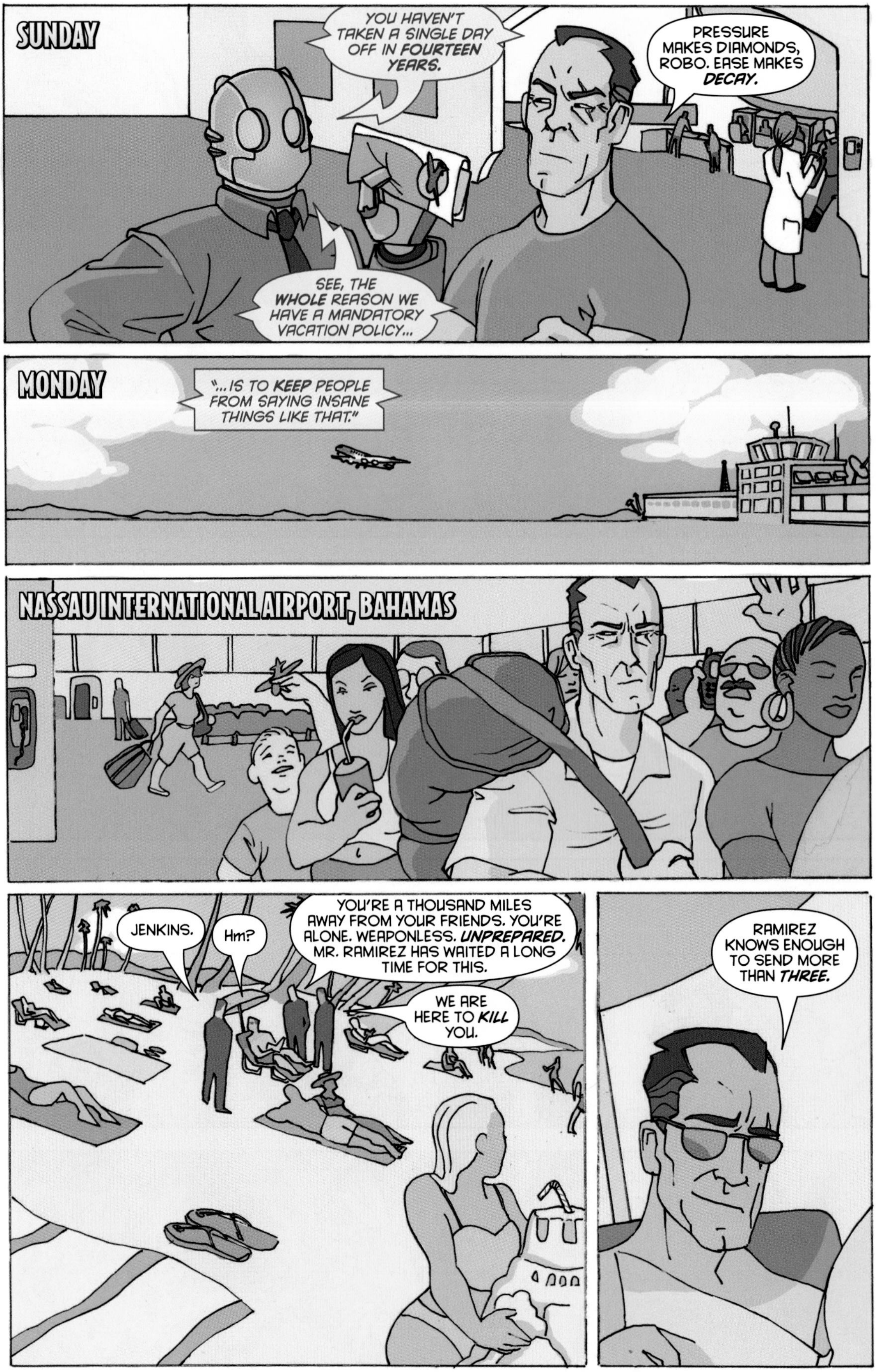

SUNDAY
YOU HAVEN'T TAKEN A SINGLE DAY OFF IN FOURTEEN YEARS.
PRESSURE MAKES DIAMONDS, ROBO. EASE MAKES DECAY.
SEE, THE WHOLE REASON WE HAVE A MANDATORY VACATION POLICY...
MONDAY
"...IS TO KEEP PEOPLE FROM SAYING INSANE THINGS LIKE THAT."
NASSAU INTERNATIONAL AIRPORT, BAHAMAS
JENKINS.
Hm?
YOU'RE A THOUSAND MILES AWAY FROM YOUR FRIENDS. YOU'RE ALONE. WEAPONLESS. UNPREPARED. MR. RAMIREZ HAS WAITED A LONG TIME FOR THIS.
WE ARE HERE TO KILL YOU.
RAMIREZ KNOWS ENOUGH TO SEND MORE THAN THREE.

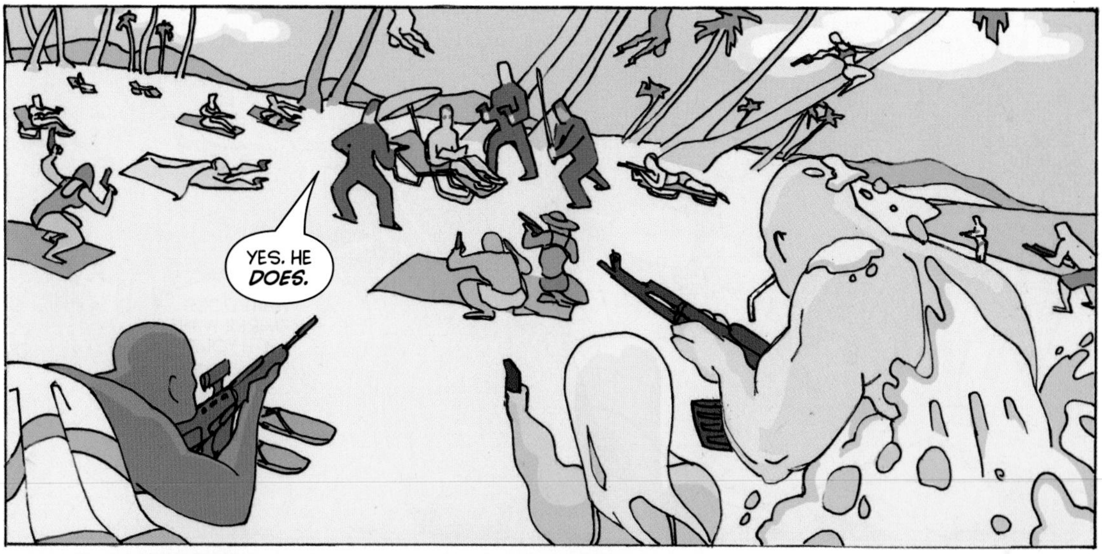
YES. HE *DOES.*

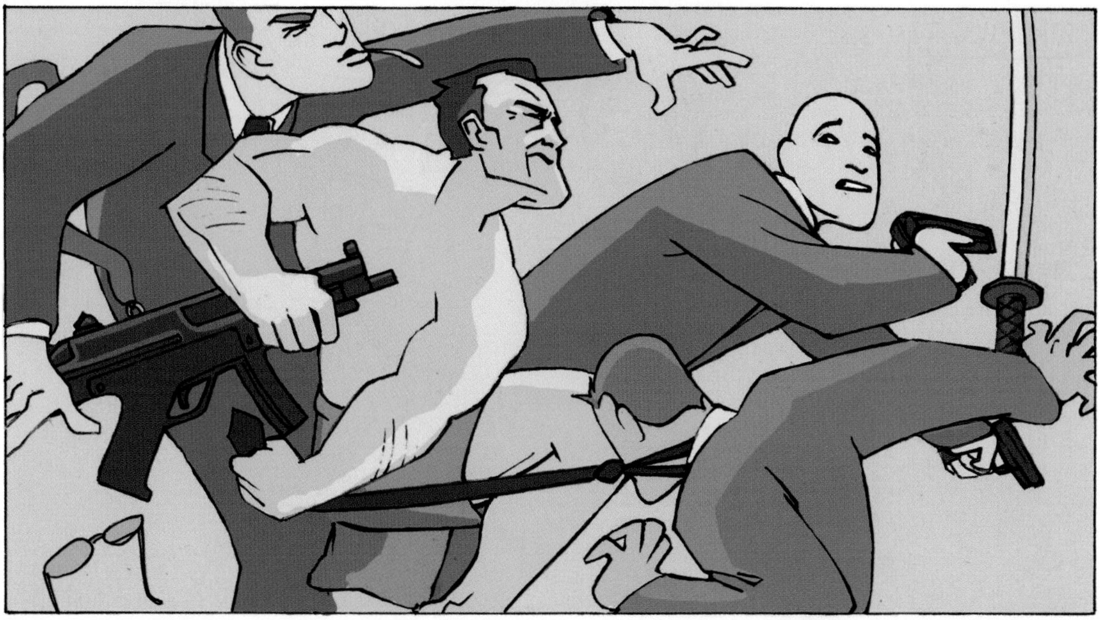

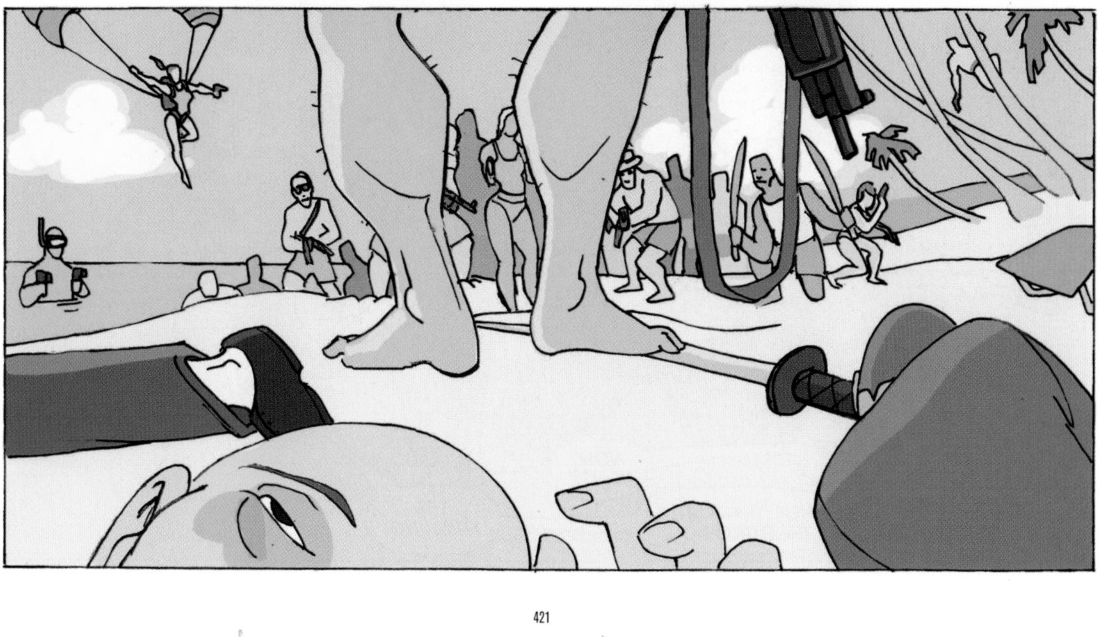

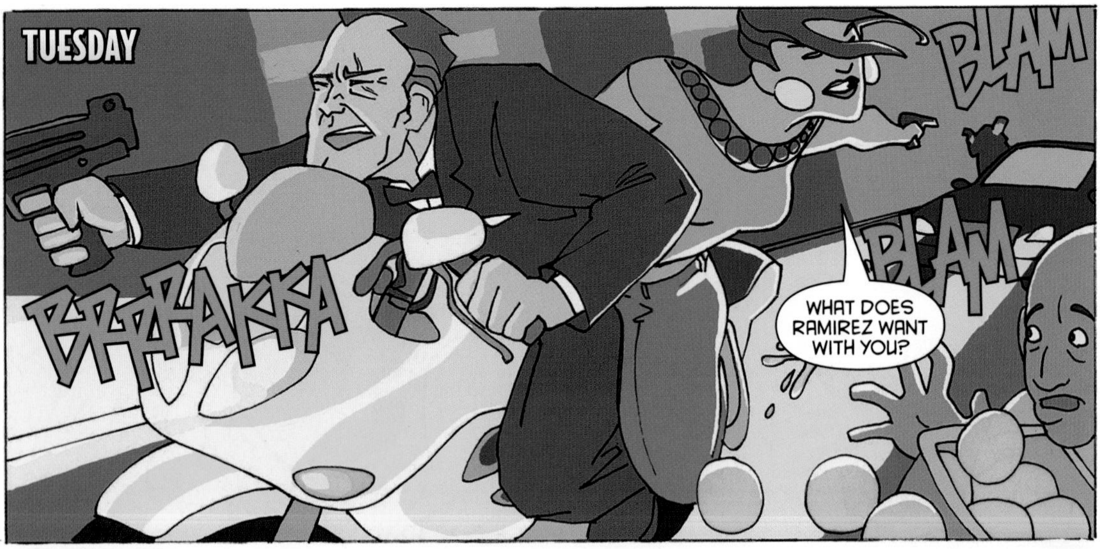
TUESDAY
BRRAKKA
BLAM
BLAM
WHAT DOES RAMIREZ WANT WITH YOU?

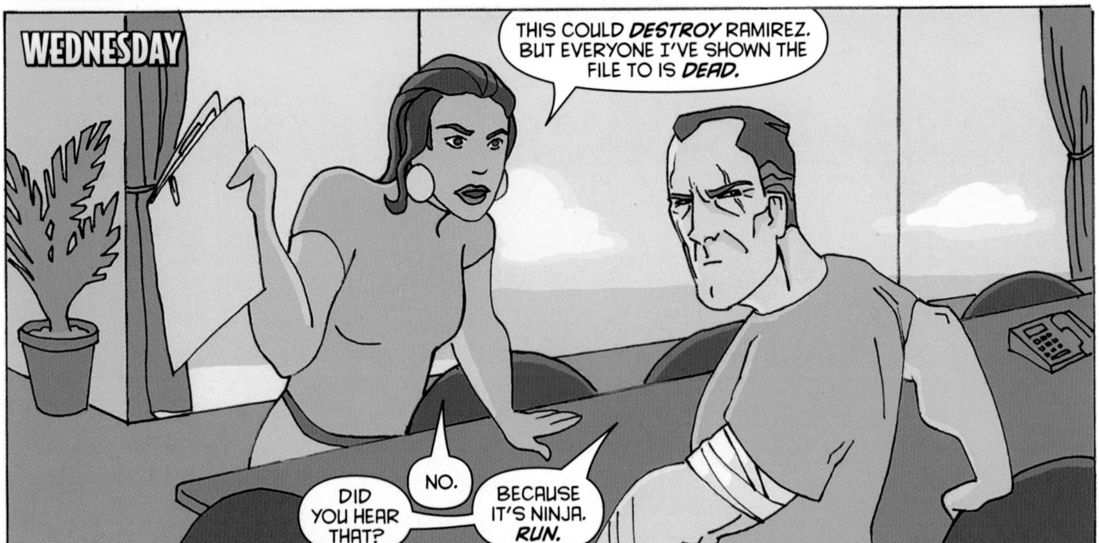
WEDNESDAY
THIS COULD DESTROY RAMIREZ. BUT EVERYONE I'VE SHOWN THE FILE TO IS DEAD.
DID YOU HEAR THAT?
NO.
BECAUSE IT'S NINJA. RUN.

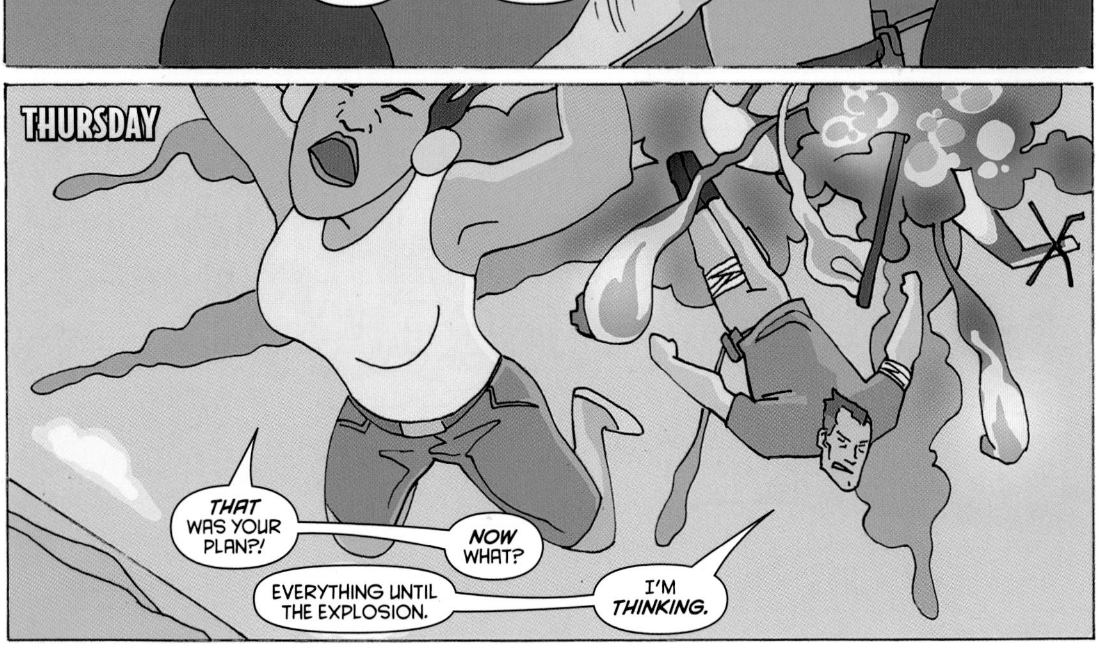
THURSDAY
THAT WAS YOUR PLAN?!
NOW WHAT?
EVERYTHING UNTIL THE EXPLOSION.
I'M THINKING.

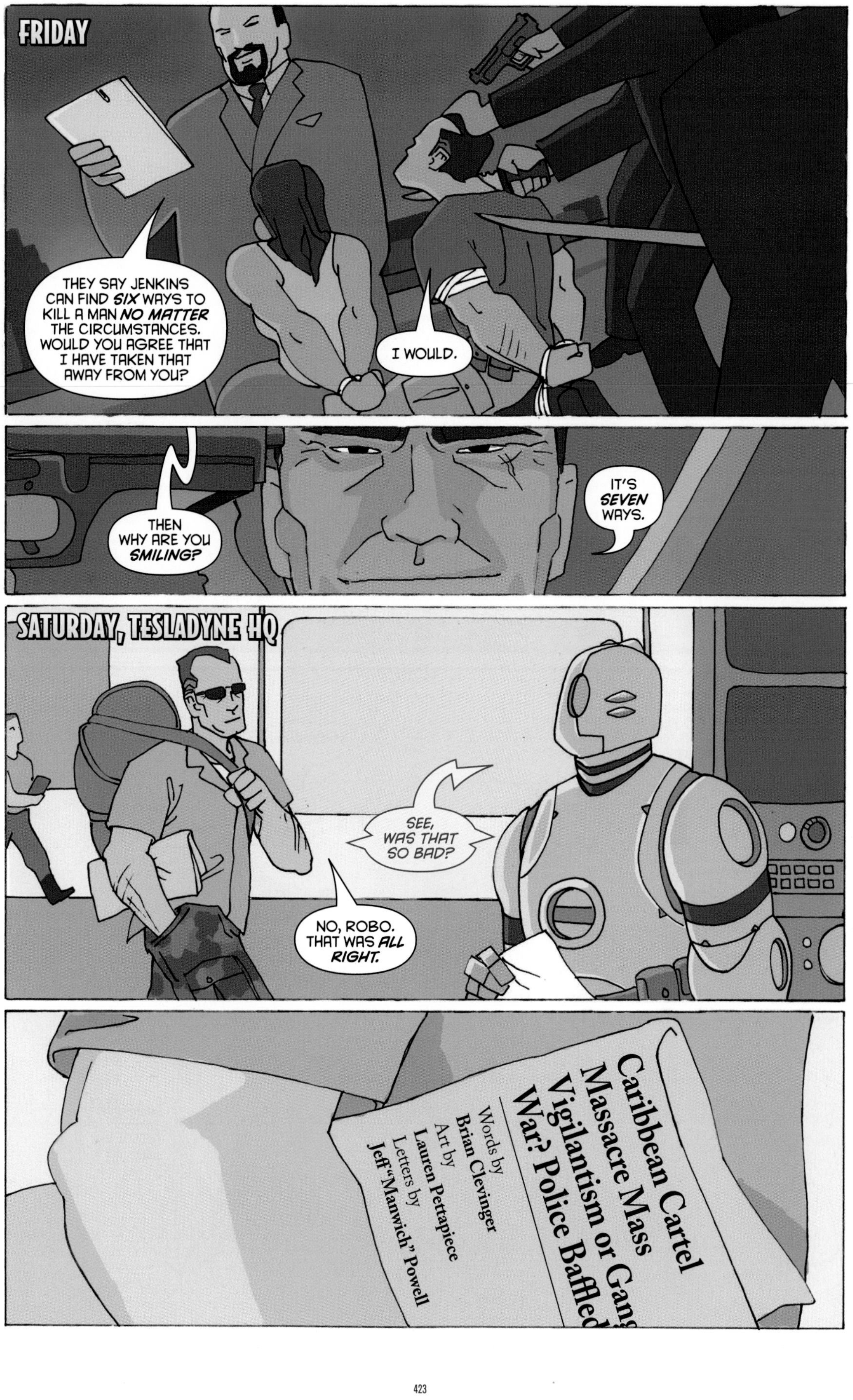
FRIDAY
THEY SAY JENKINS CAN FIND SIX WAYS TO KILL A MAN NO MATTER THE CIRCUMSTANCES. WOULD YOU AGREE THAT I HAVE TAKEN THAT AWAY FROM YOU?
I WOULD.
THEN WHY ARE YOU SMILING?
IT'S SEVEN WAYS.
SATURDAY, TESLADYNE HQ
SEE, WAS THAT SO BAD?
NO, ROBO. THAT WAS ALL RIGHT.
Caribbean Cartel
Massacre Mass
Vigilantism or Gang
War? Police Baffled
Words by
Brian Clevinger
Art by
Lauren Pettapiece
Letters by
Jeff "Manwich" Powell

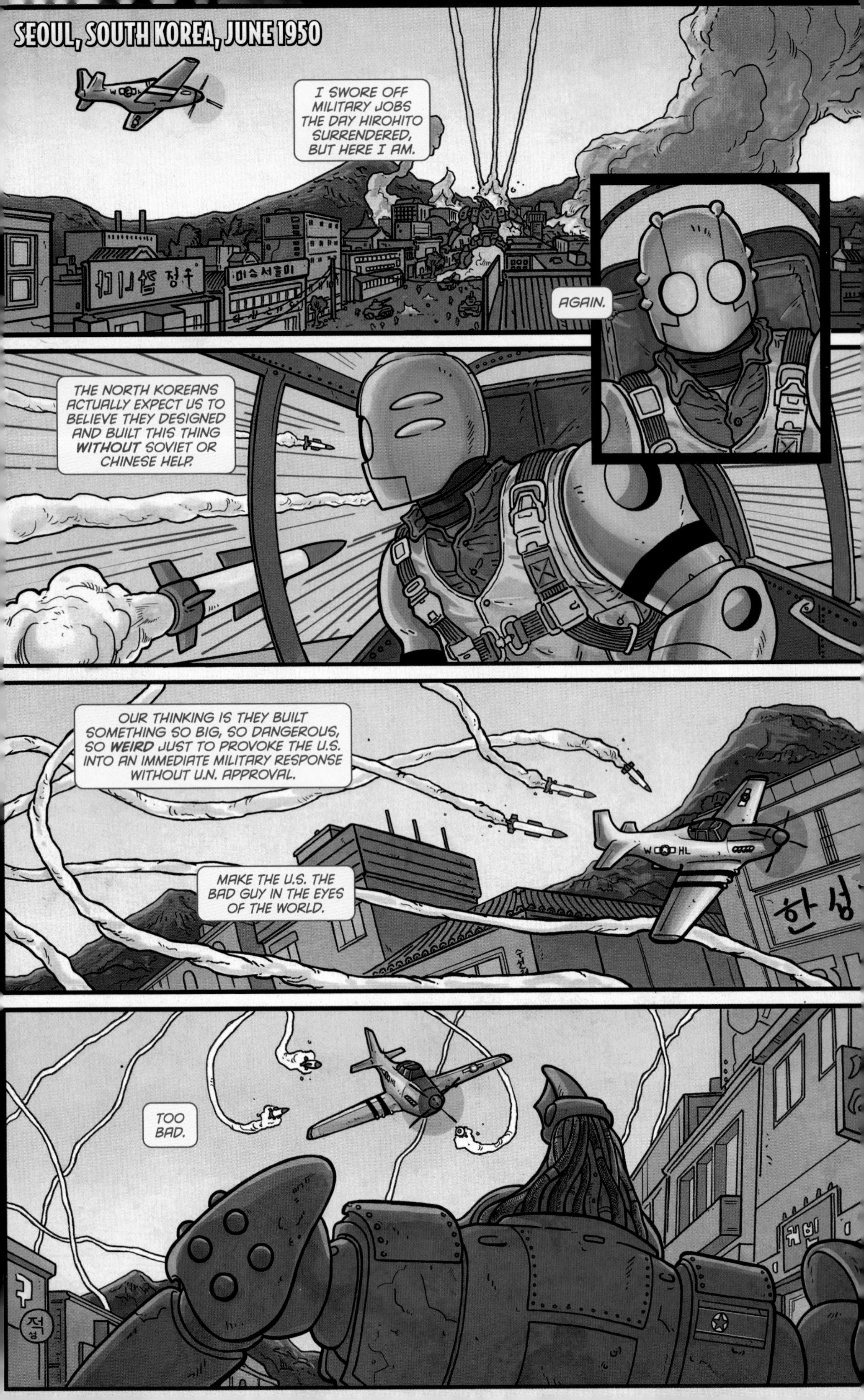
SEOUL, SOUTH KOREA, JUNE 1950
I SWORE OFF MILITARY JOBS THE DAY HIROHITO SURRENDERED, BUT HERE I AM.
AGAIN.
THE NORTH KOREANS ACTUALLY EXPECT US TO BELIEVE THEY DESIGNED AND BUILT THIS THING WITHOUT SOVIET OR CHINESE HELP.
OUR THINKING IS THEY BUILT SOMETHING SO BIG, SO DANGEROUS, SO WEIRD JUST TO PROVOKE THE U.S. INTO AN IMMEDIATE MILITARY RESPONSE WITHOUT U.N. APPROVAL.
MAKE THE U.S. THE BAD GUY IN THE EYES OF THE WORLD.
한성
TOO BAD.

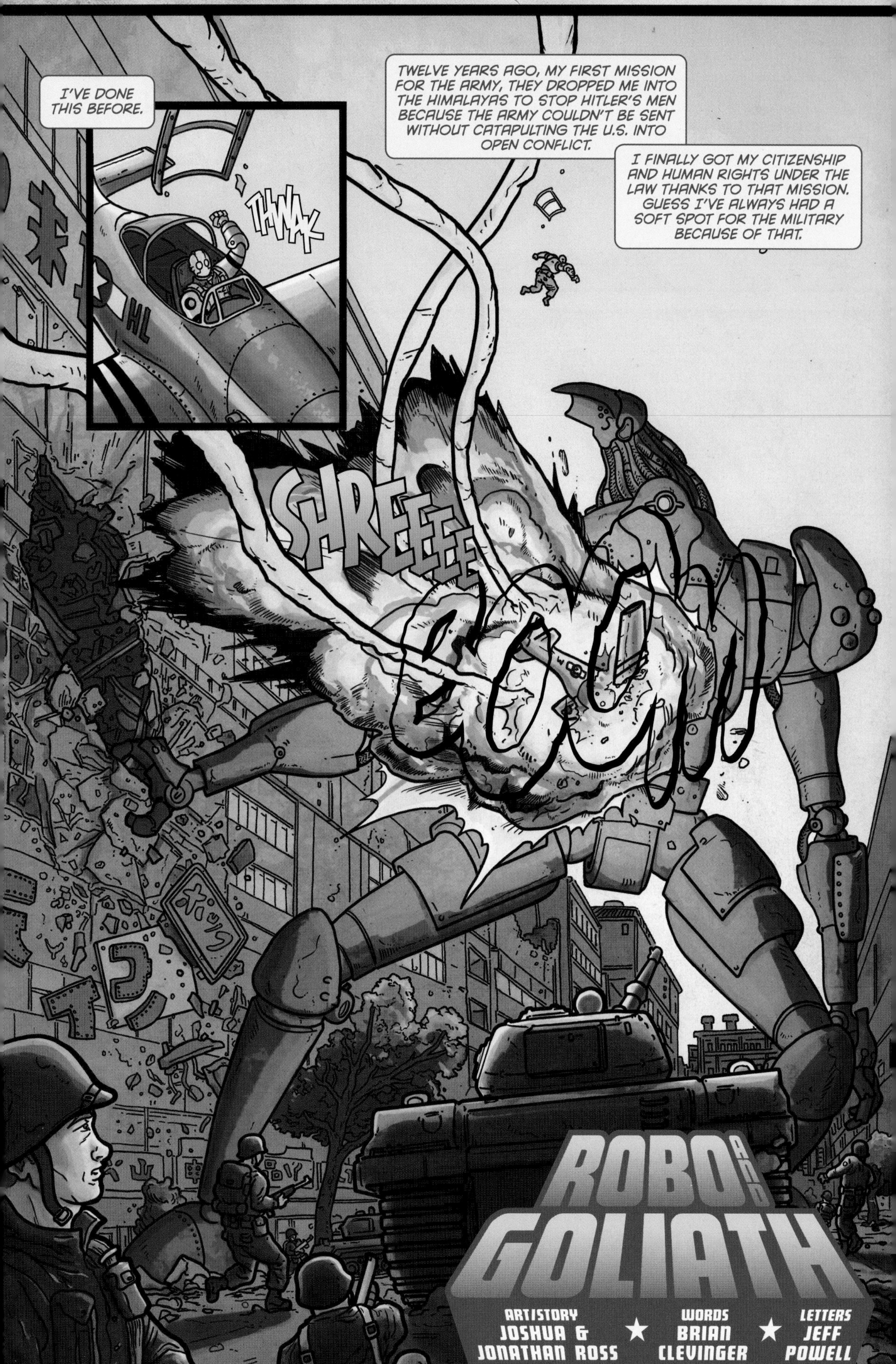
I'VE DONE THIS BEFORE.
THWAK
TWELVE YEARS AGO, MY FIRST MISSION FOR THE ARMY, THEY DROPPED ME INTO THE HIMALAYAS TO STOP HITLER'S MEN BECAUSE THE ARMY COULDN'T BE SENT WITHOUT CATAPULTING THE U.S. INTO OPEN CONFLICT.
I FINALLY GOT MY CITIZENSHIP AND HUMAN RIGHTS UNDER THE LAW THANKS TO THAT MISSION. GUESS I'VE ALWAYS HAD A SOFT SPOT FOR THE MILITARY BECAUSE OF THAT.
SHREEEEE
HL
ROBO AND GOLIATH
ARTISTORY JOSHUA & JONATHAN ROSS
WORDS BRIAN CLEVINGER
LETTERS JEFF POWELL

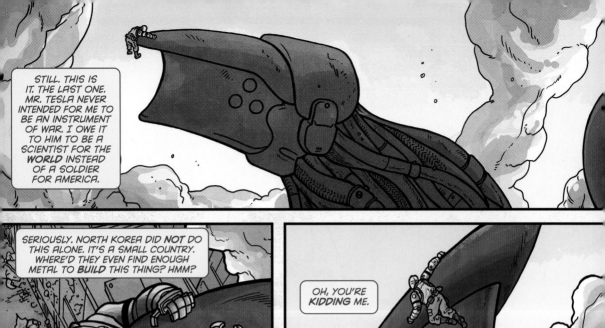

STILL. THIS IS IT. THE LAST ONE. MR. TESLA NEVER INTENDED FOR ME TO BE AN INSTRUMENT OF WAR. I OWE IT TO HIM TO BE A SCIENTIST FOR THE **WORLD** INSTEAD OF A SOLDIER FOR AMERICA.

SERIOUSLY. NORTH KOREA DID **NOT** DO THIS ALONE. IT'S A SMALL COUNTRY. WHERE'D THEY EVEN FIND ENOUGH METAL TO **BUILD** THIS THING? HMM?

OH, YOU'RE KIDDING ME.

BRAKKA DAKKA

YOU DO **NOT** OPEN UP YOUR HUGE WAR MACHINE TO SHOOT AT THE BULLETPROOF ROBOT.

BLAM BLAMBLAM

AMATEURS.

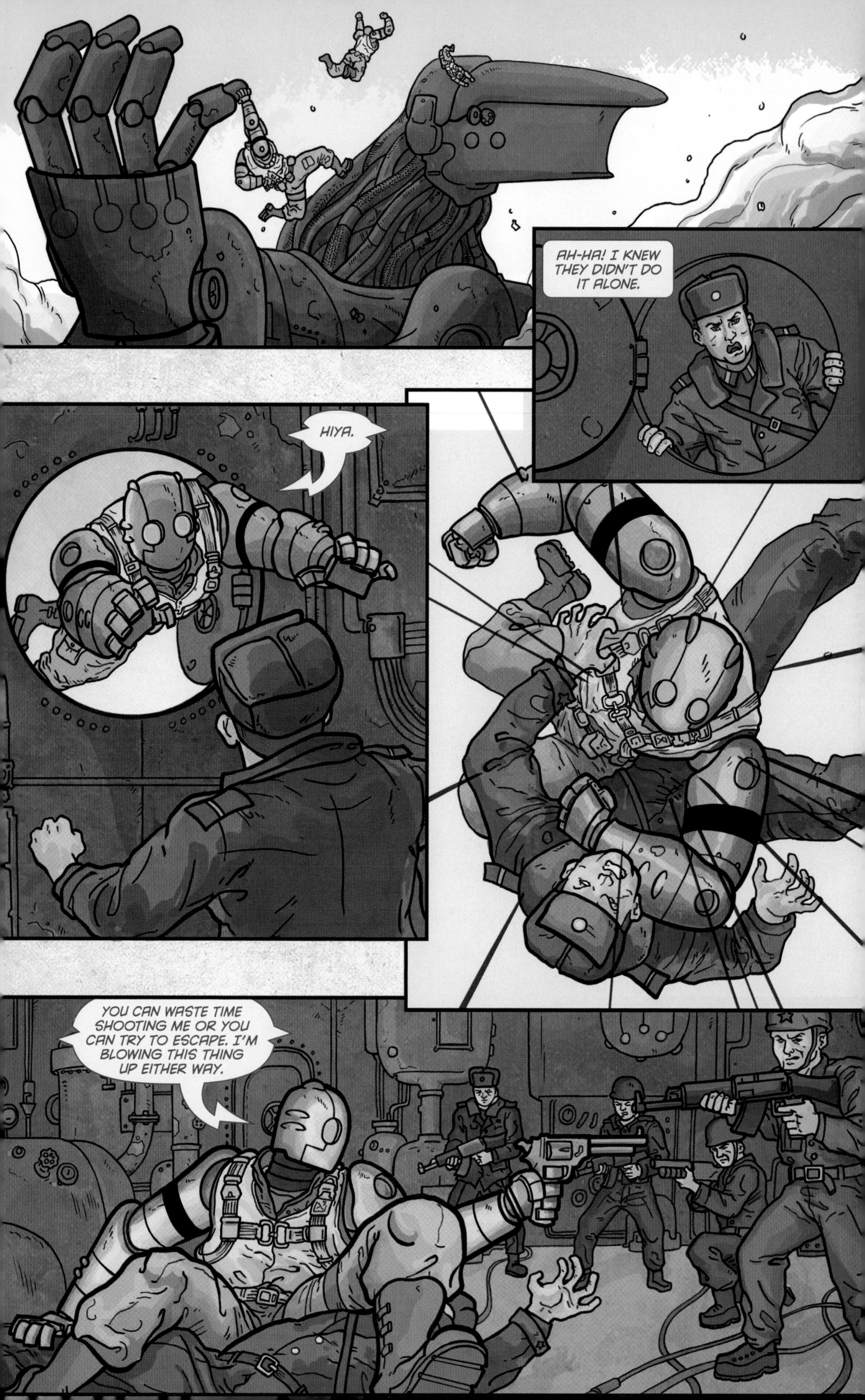
AH-HA! I KNEW THEY DIDN'T DO IT ALONE.
HIYA.
YOU CAN WASTE TIME SHOOTING ME OR YOU CAN TRY TO ESCAPE. I'M BLOWING THIS THING UP EITHER WAY.

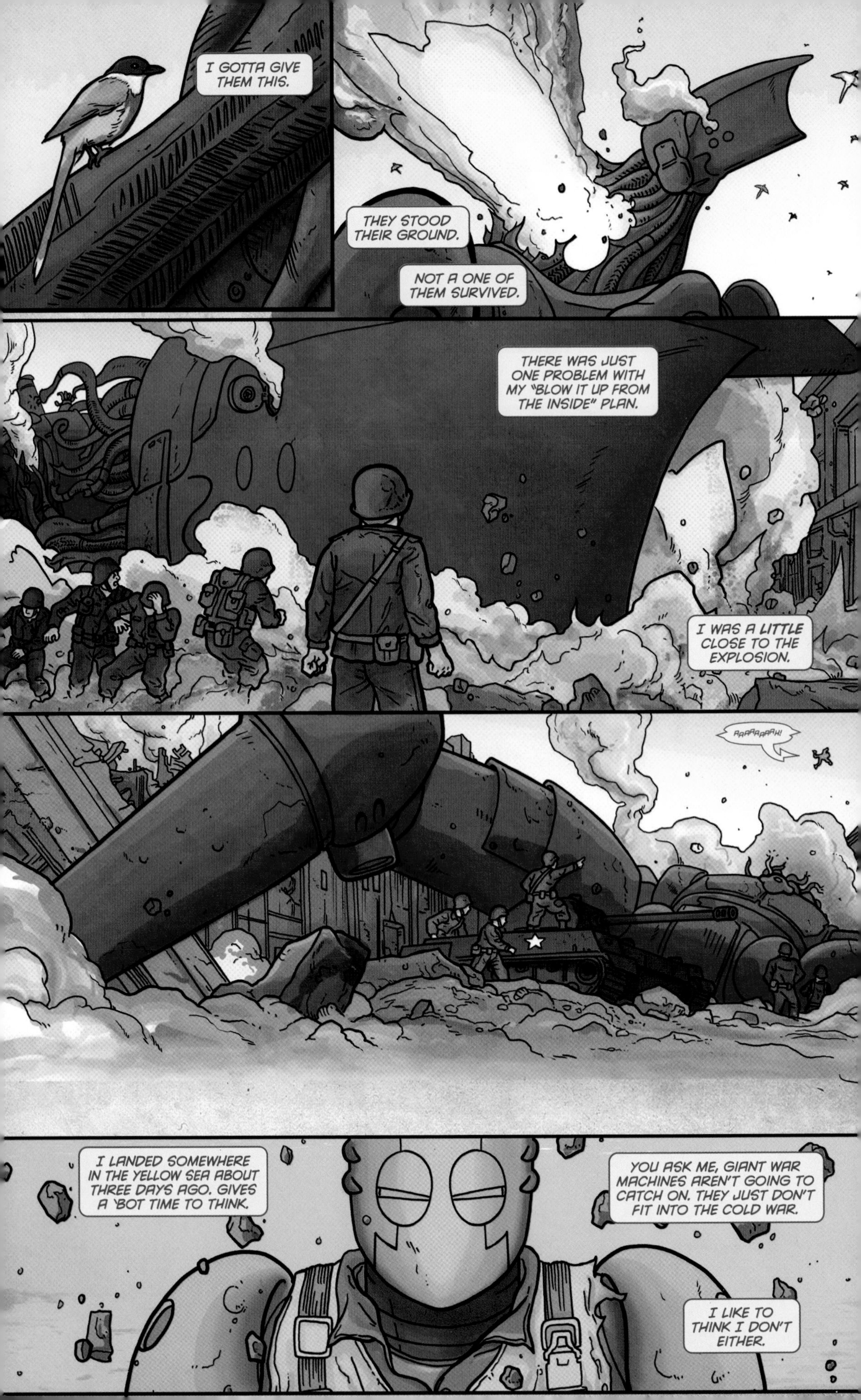
I GOTTA GIVE THEM THIS.
THEY STOOD THEIR GROUND.
NOT A ONE OF THEM SURVIVED.
THERE WAS JUST ONE PROBLEM WITH MY "BLOW IT UP FROM THE INSIDE" PLAN.
I WAS A LITTLE CLOSE TO THE EXPLOSION.
AAAAAAAAH!
I LANDED SOMEWHERE IN THE YELLOW SEA ABOUT THREE DAYS AGO. GIVES A 'BOT TIME TO THINK.
YOU ASK ME, GIANT WAR MACHINES AREN'T GOING TO CATCH ON. THEY JUST DON'T FIT INTO THE COLD WAR.
I LIKE TO THINK I DON'T EITHER.

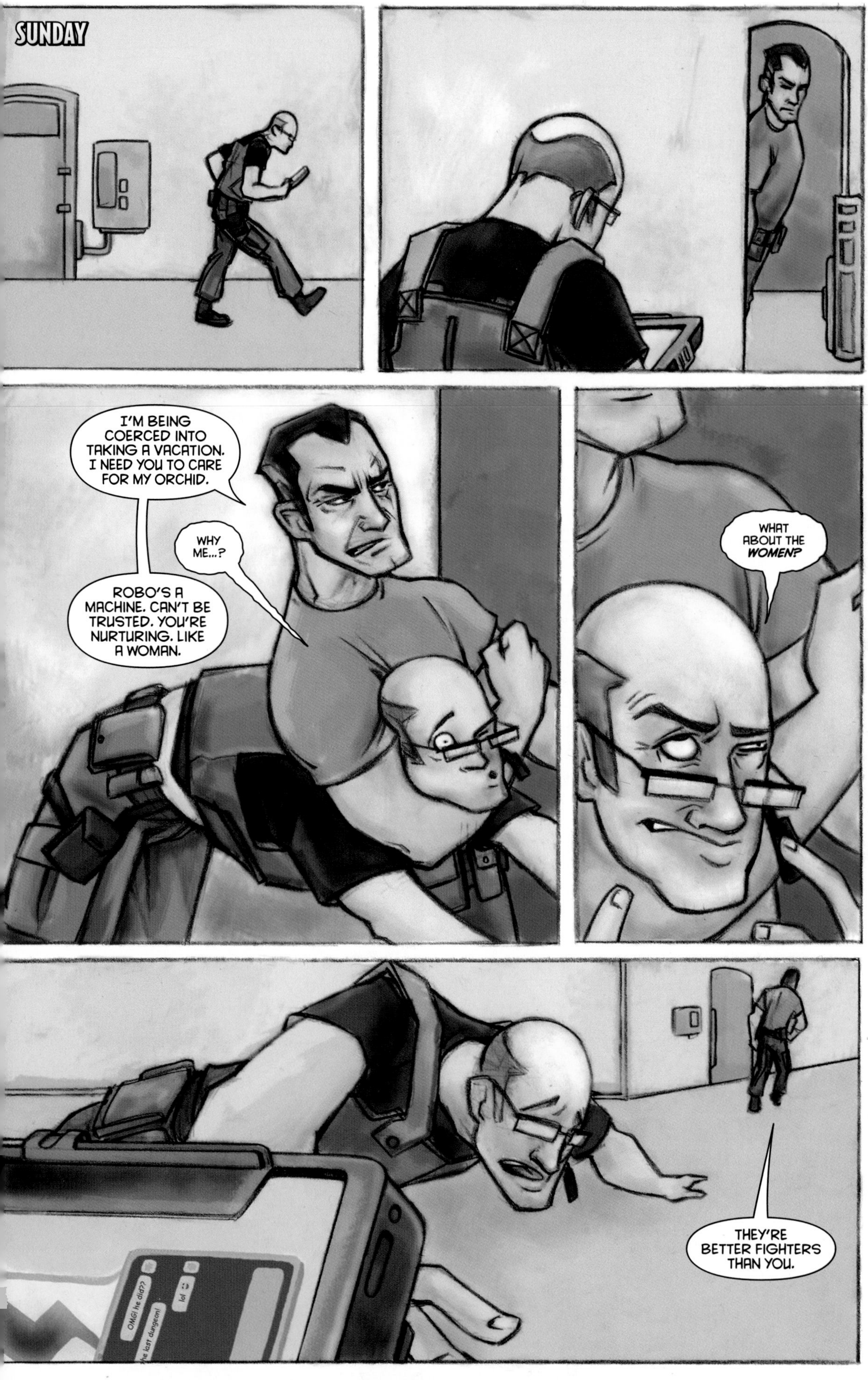
SUNDAY
I'M BEING COERCED INTO TAKING A VACATION. I NEED YOU TO CARE FOR MY ORCHID.
WHY ME...?
ROBO'S A MACHINE. CAN'T BE TRUSTED. YOU'RE NURTURING. LIKE A WOMAN.
WHAT ABOUT THE *WOMEN?*
THEY'RE BETTER FIGHTERS THAN YOU.

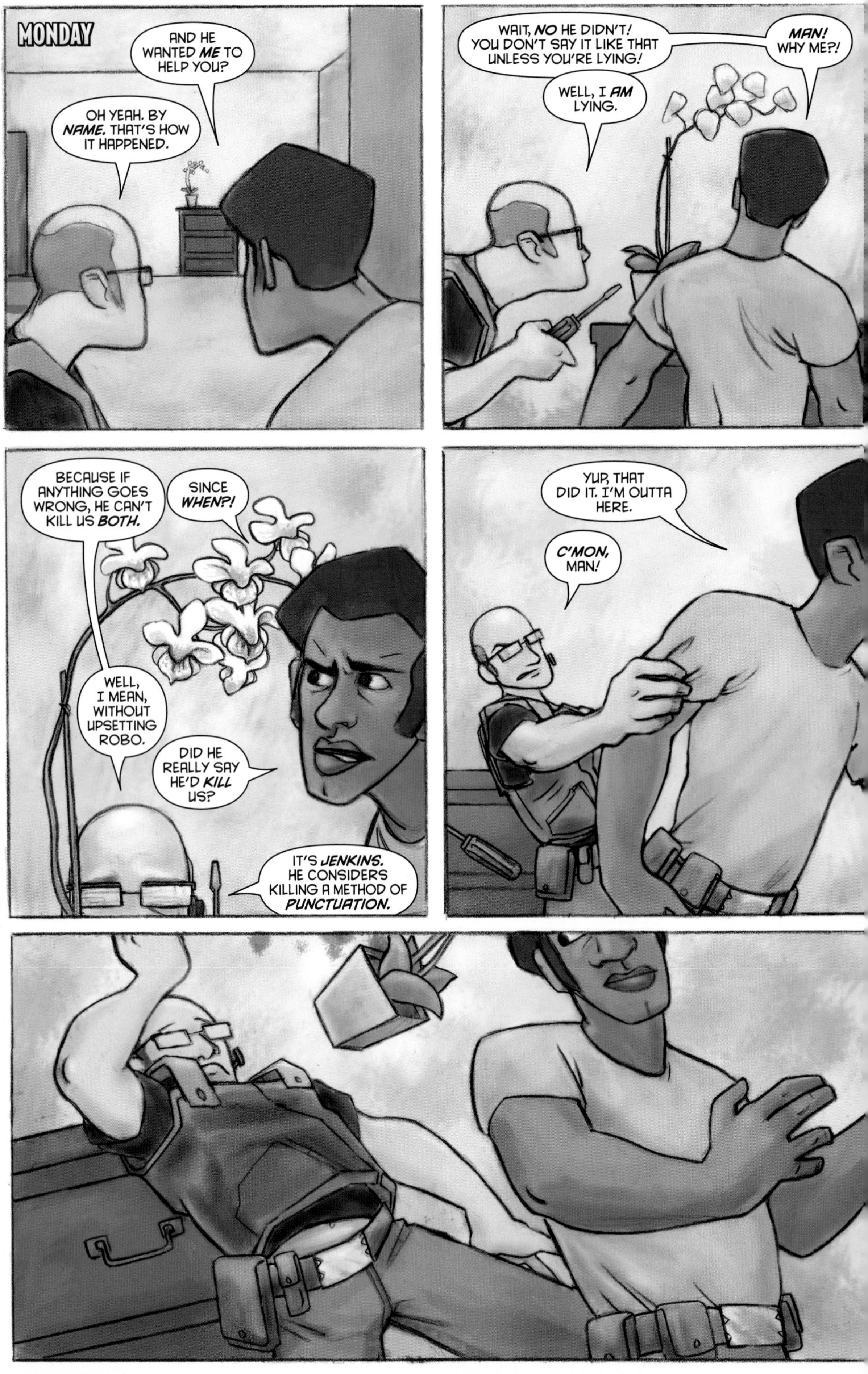
MONDAY
AND HE WANTED ME TO HELP YOU?
OH YEAH. BY NAME. THAT'S HOW IT HAPPENED.
WAIT, NO HE DIDN'T! YOU DON'T SAY IT LIKE THAT UNLESS YOU'RE LYING!
WELL, I AM LYING.
MAN! WHY ME?!
BECAUSE IF ANYTHING GOES WRONG, HE CAN'T KILL US BOTH.
SINCE WHEN?!
WELL, I MEAN, WITHOUT UPSETTING ROBO.
DID HE REALLY SAY HE'D KILL US?
IT'S JENKINS. HE CONSIDERS KILLING A METHOD OF PUNCTUATION.
YUP, THAT DID IT. I'M OUTTA HERE.
C'MON, MAN!

TUESDAY

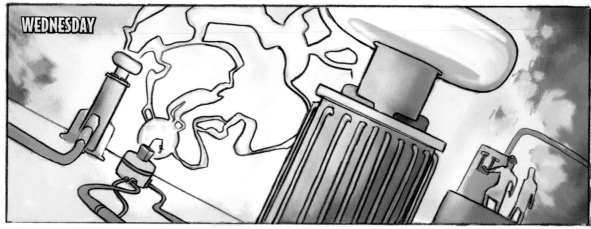

WEDNESDAY

THURSDAY

FRIDAY

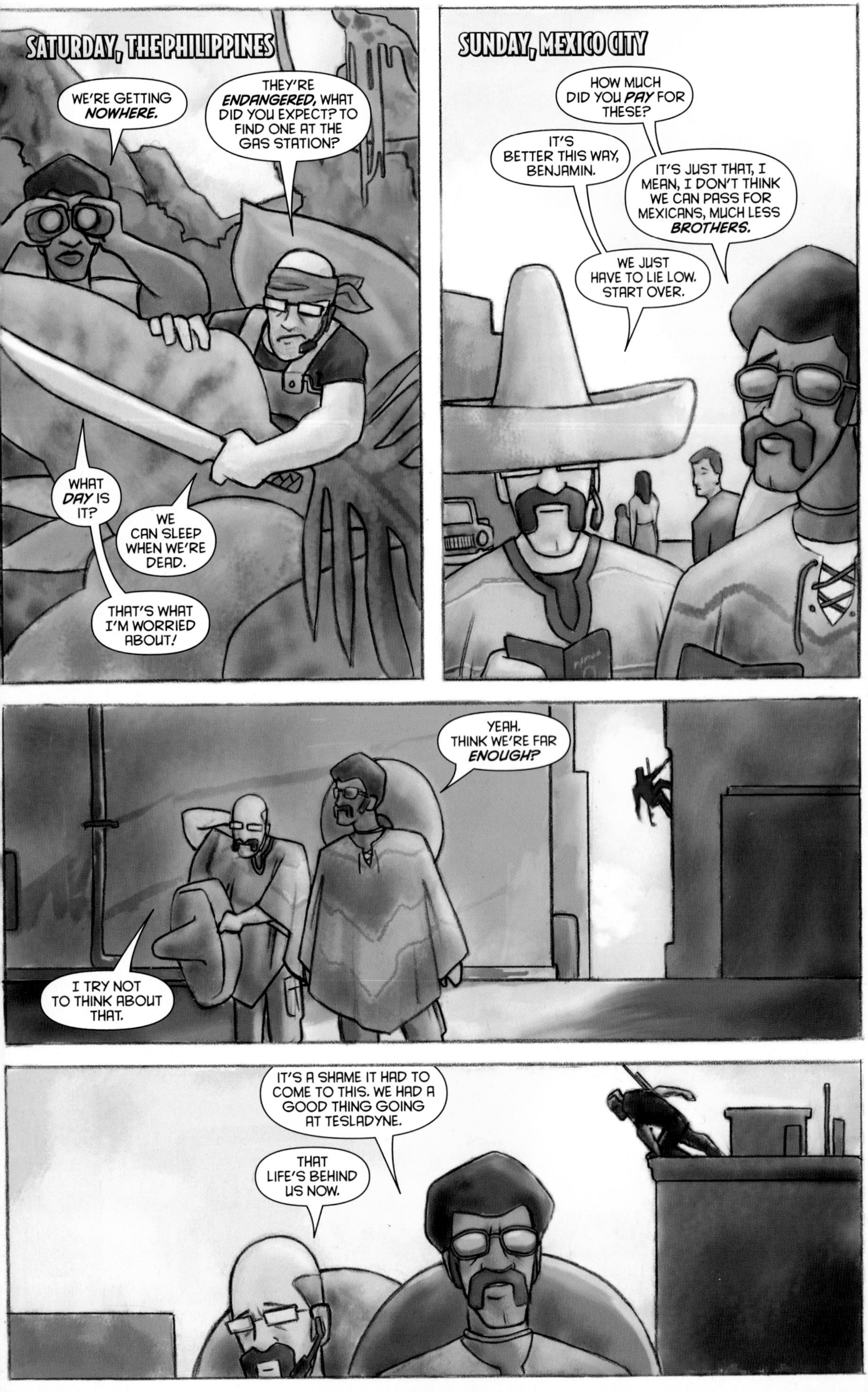
SATURDAY, THE PHILIPPINES
WE'RE GETTING NOWHERE.
THEY'RE ENDANGERED, WHAT DID YOU EXPECT? TO FIND ONE AT THE GAS STATION?
WHAT DAY IS IT?
WE CAN SLEEP WHEN WE'RE DEAD.
THAT'S WHAT I'M WORRIED ABOUT!
SUNDAY, MEXICO CITY
HOW MUCH DID YOU PAY FOR THESE?
IT'S BETTER THIS WAY, BENJAMIN.
IT'S JUST THAT, I MEAN, I DON'T THINK WE CAN PASS FOR MEXICANS, MUCH LESS BROTHERS.
WE JUST HAVE TO LIE LOW. START OVER.
YEAH. THINK WE'RE FAR ENOUGH?
I TRY NOT TO THINK ABOUT THAT.
IT'S A SHAME IT HAD TO COME TO THIS. WE HAD A GOOD THING GOING AT TESLADYNE.
THAT LIFE'S BEHIND US NOW.

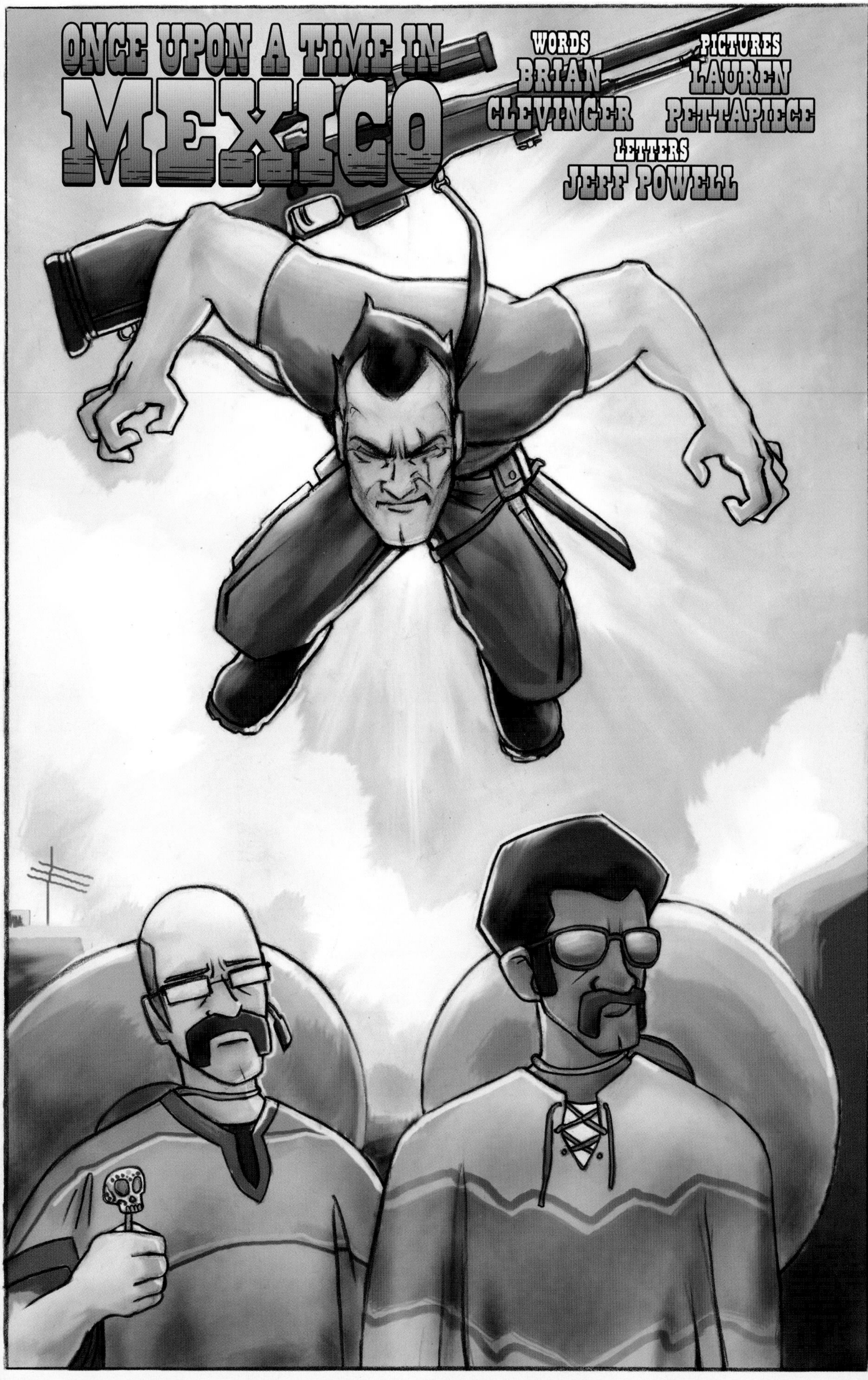
ONCE UPON A TIME IN
MEXICO
WORDS
BRIAN CLEVINGER
PICTURES
LAUREN PETTAPIECE
LETTERS
JEFF POWELL

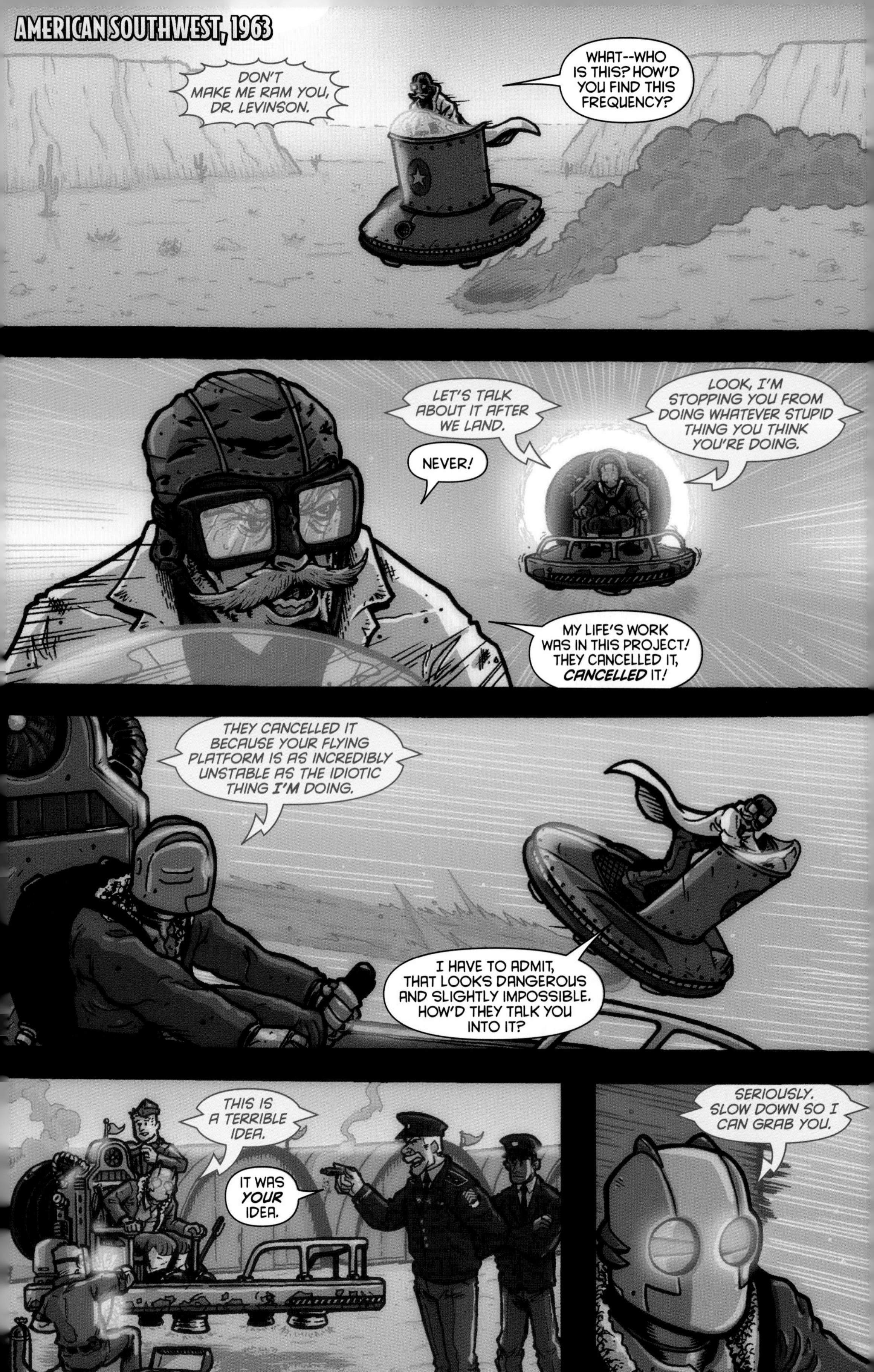
AMERICAN SOUTHWEST, 1963
DON'T MAKE ME RAM YOU, DR. LEVINSON.
WHAT--WHO IS THIS? HOW'D YOU FIND THIS FREQUENCY?
LET'S TALK ABOUT IT AFTER WE LAND.
NEVER!
LOOK, I'M STOPPING YOU FROM DOING WHATEVER STUPID THING YOU THINK YOU'RE DOING.
MY LIFE'S WORK WAS IN THIS PROJECT! THEY CANCELLED IT, *CANCELLED* IT!
THEY CANCELLED IT BECAUSE YOUR FLYING PLATFORM IS AS INCREDIBLY UNSTABLE AS THE IDIOTIC THING *I'M* DOING.
I HAVE TO ADMIT, THAT LOOKS DANGEROUS AND SLIGHTLY IMPOSSIBLE. HOW'D THEY TALK YOU INTO IT?
THIS IS A TERRIBLE IDEA.
IT WAS *YOUR* IDEA.
SERIOUSLY. SLOW DOWN SO I CAN GRAB YOU.

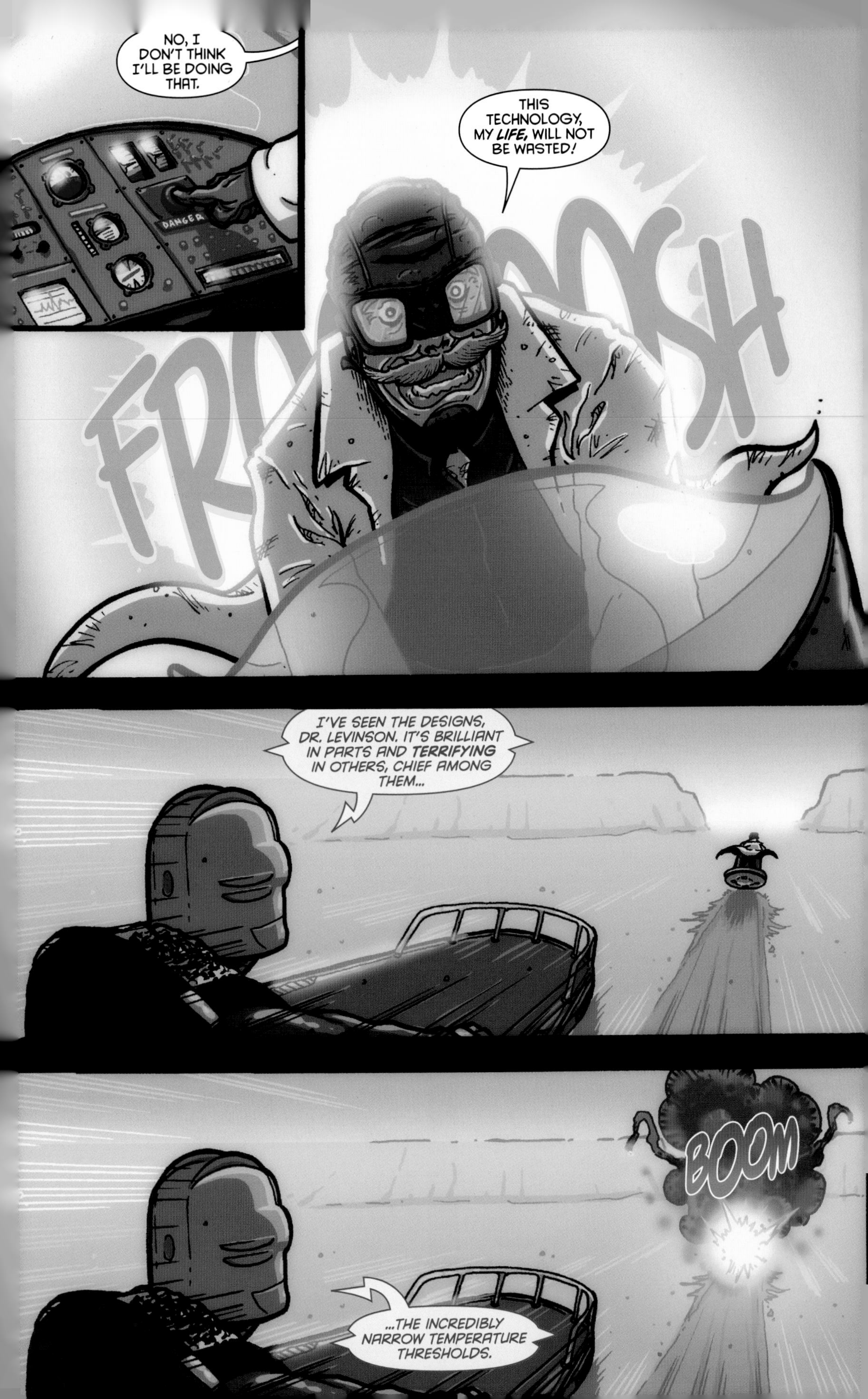
NO, I DON'T THINK I'LL BE DOING THAT.
DANGER
THIS TECHNOLOGY, MY LIFE, WILL NOT BE WASTED!
FROOOSH
I'VE SEEN THE DESIGNS, DR. LEVINSON. IT'S BRILLIANT IN PARTS AND TERRIFYING IN OTHERS, CHIEF AMONG THEM...
BOOM
...THE INCREDIBLY NARROW TEMPERATURE THRESHOLDS.

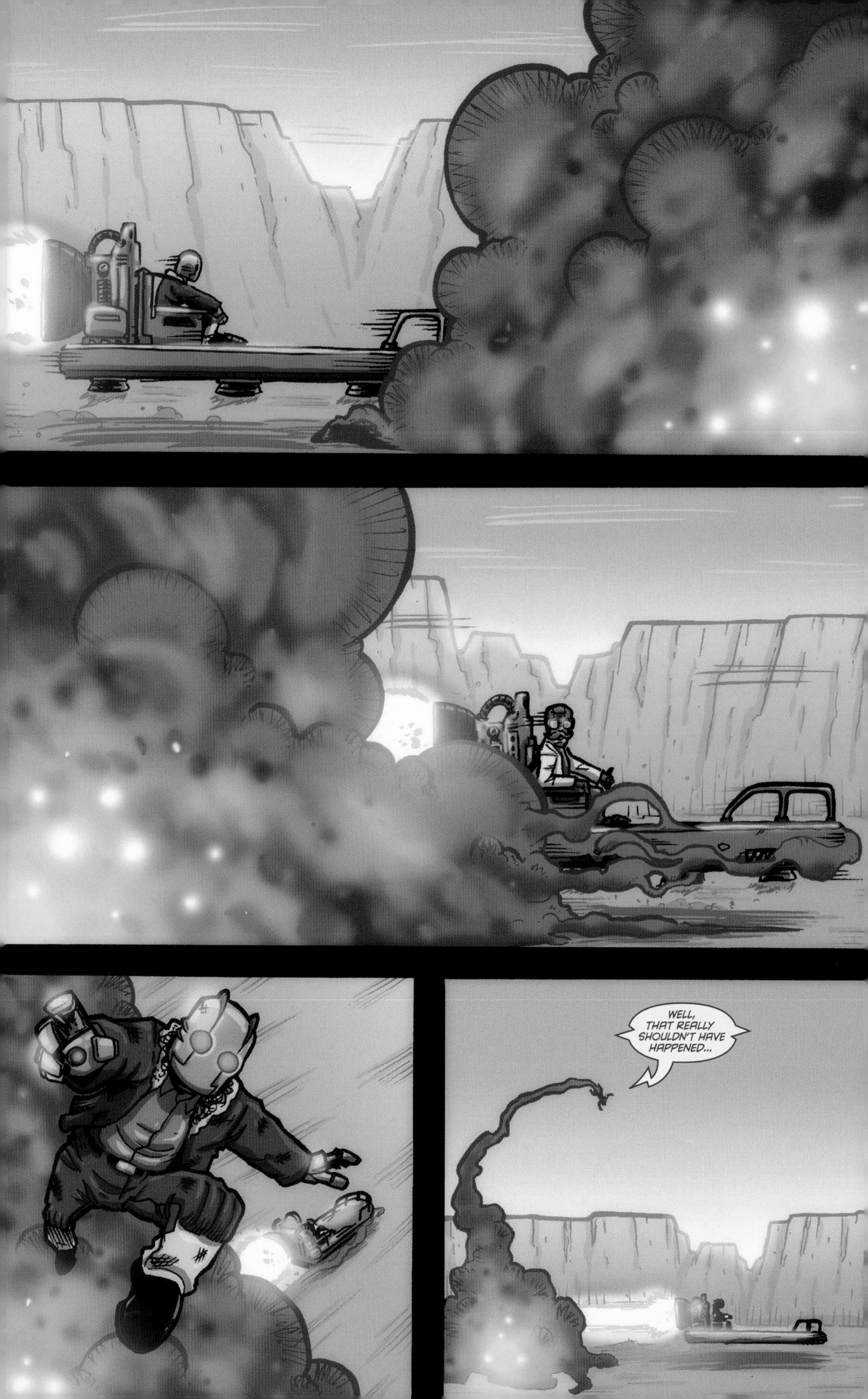
WELL, THAT REALLY SHOULDN'T HAVE HAPPENED...

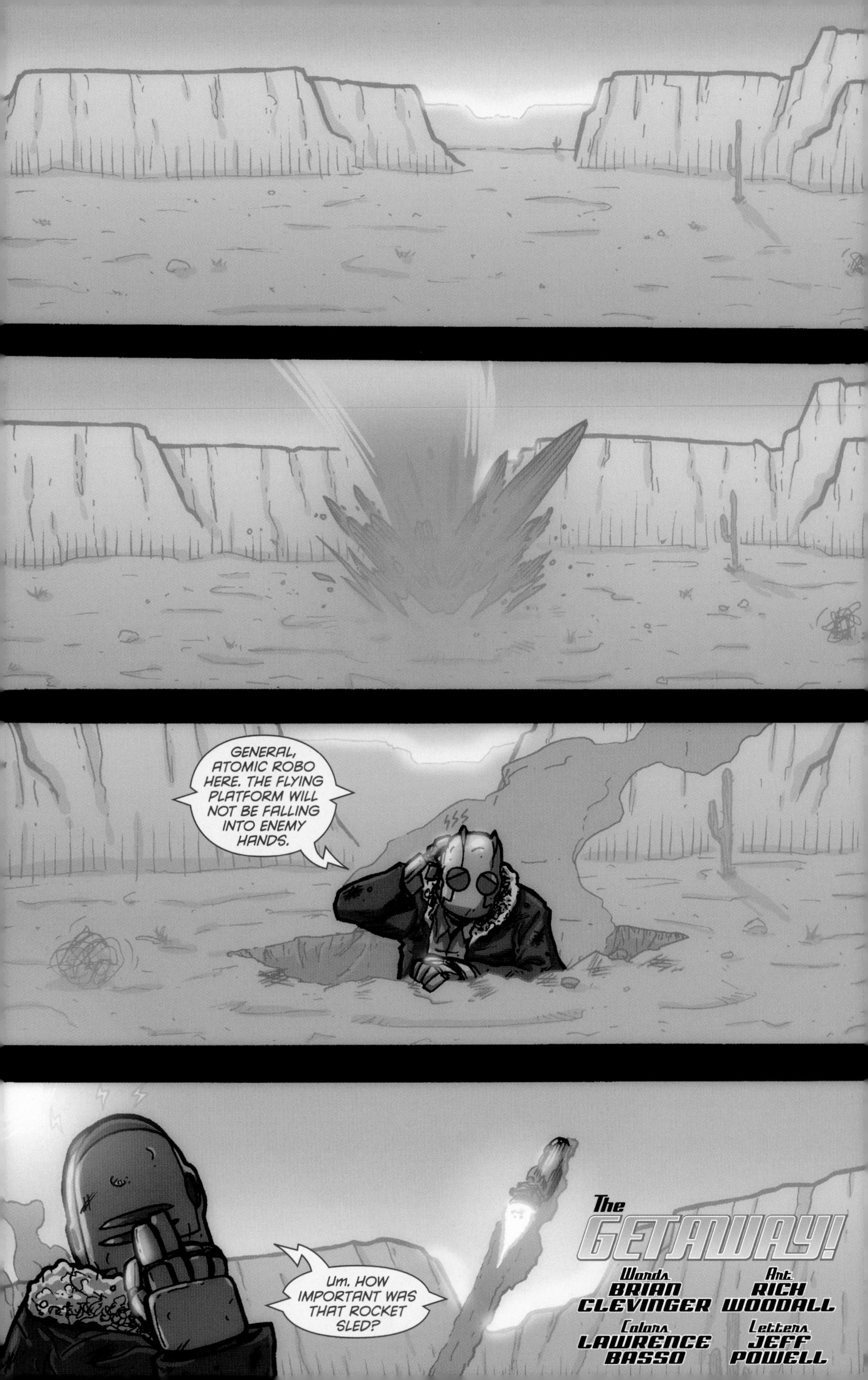
GENERAL, ATOMIC ROBO HERE. THE FLYING PLATFORM WILL NOT BE FALLING INTO ENEMY HANDS.
Um. HOW IMPORTANT WAS THAT ROCKET SLED?
The GETAWAY!
Words BRIAN CLEVINGER
Art RICH WOODALL
Colors LAWRENCE BASSO
Letters JEFF POWELL

FREE COMIC BOOK DAY
2008

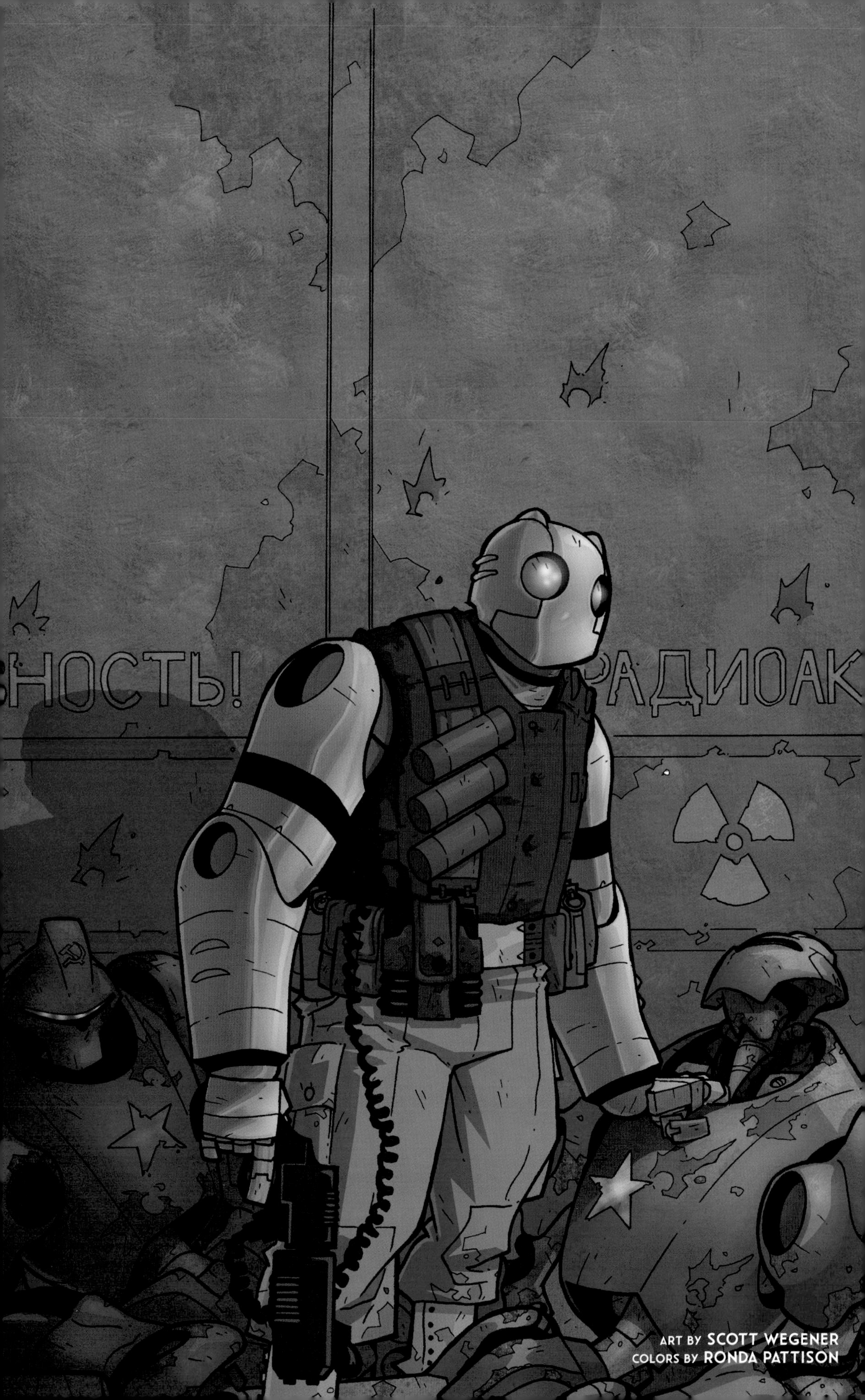
НОСТЬ!
РАДИОАК
ART BY SCOTT WEGENER
COLORS BY RONDA PATTISON

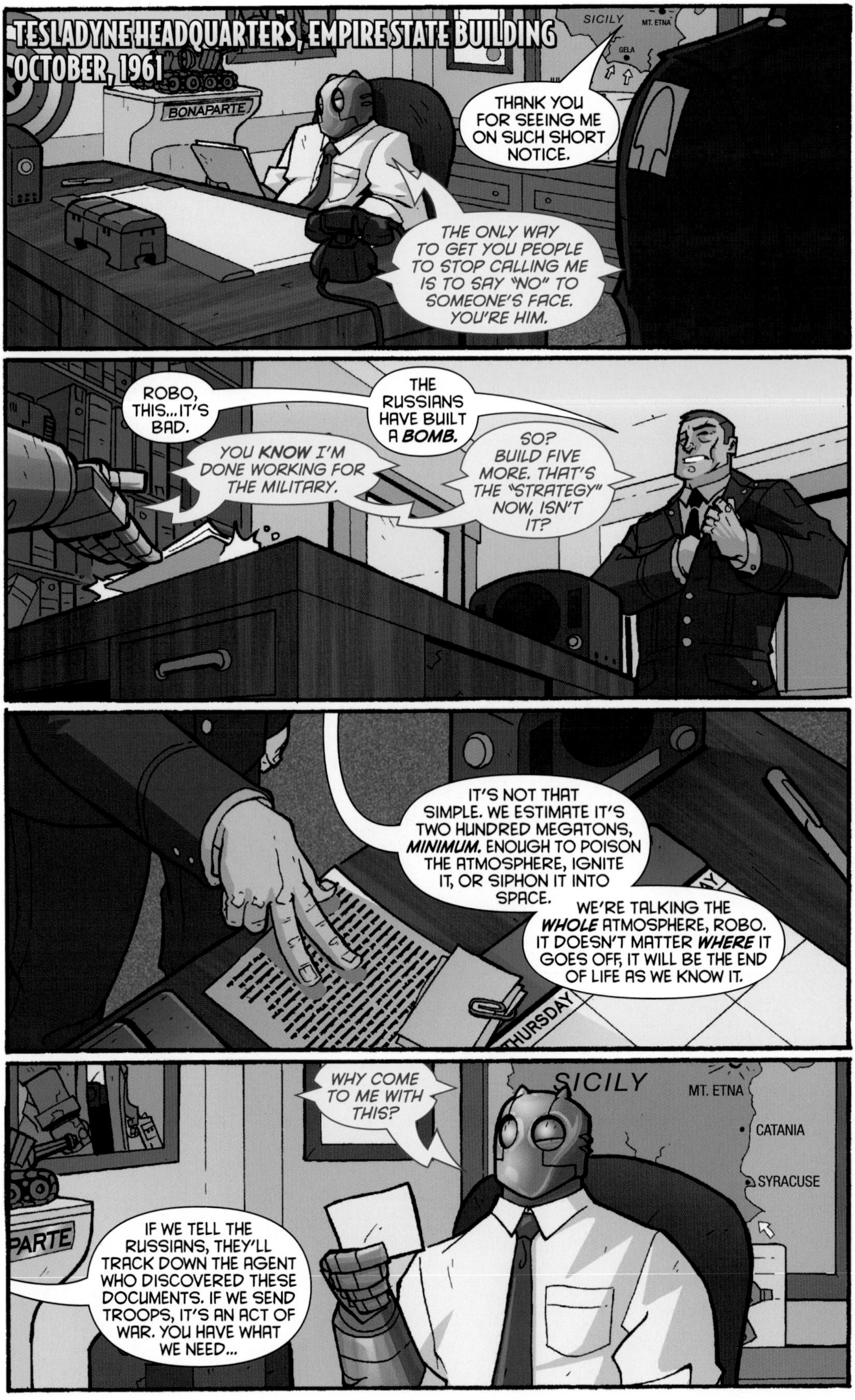
TESLADYNE HEADQUARTERS, EMPIRE STATE BUILDING
OCTOBER, 1961
SICILY
MT. ETNA
GELA
BONAPARTE
THANK YOU FOR SEEING ME ON SUCH SHORT NOTICE.
THE ONLY WAY TO GET YOU PEOPLE TO STOP CALLING ME IS TO SAY "NO" TO SOMEONE'S FACE. YOU'RE HIM.
ROBO, THIS...IT'S BAD.
THE RUSSIANS HAVE BUILT A BOMB.
YOU KNOW I'M DONE WORKING FOR THE MILITARY.
SO? BUILD FIVE MORE. THAT'S THE "STRATEGY" NOW, ISN'T IT?
IT'S NOT THAT SIMPLE. WE ESTIMATE IT'S TWO HUNDRED MEGATONS, MINIMUM. ENOUGH TO POISON THE ATMOSPHERE, IGNITE IT, OR SIPHON IT INTO SPACE.
WE'RE TALKING THE WHOLE ATMOSPHERE, ROBO. IT DOESN'T MATTER WHERE IT GOES OFF, IT WILL BE THE END OF LIFE AS WE KNOW IT.
THURSDAY
WHY COME TO ME WITH THIS?
SICILY
MT. ETNA
CATANIA
SYRACUSE
PARTE
IF WE TELL THE RUSSIANS, THEY'LL TRACK DOWN THE AGENT WHO DISCOVERED THESE DOCUMENTS. IF WE SEND TROOPS, IT'S AN ACT OF WAR. YOU HAVE WHAT WE NEED...

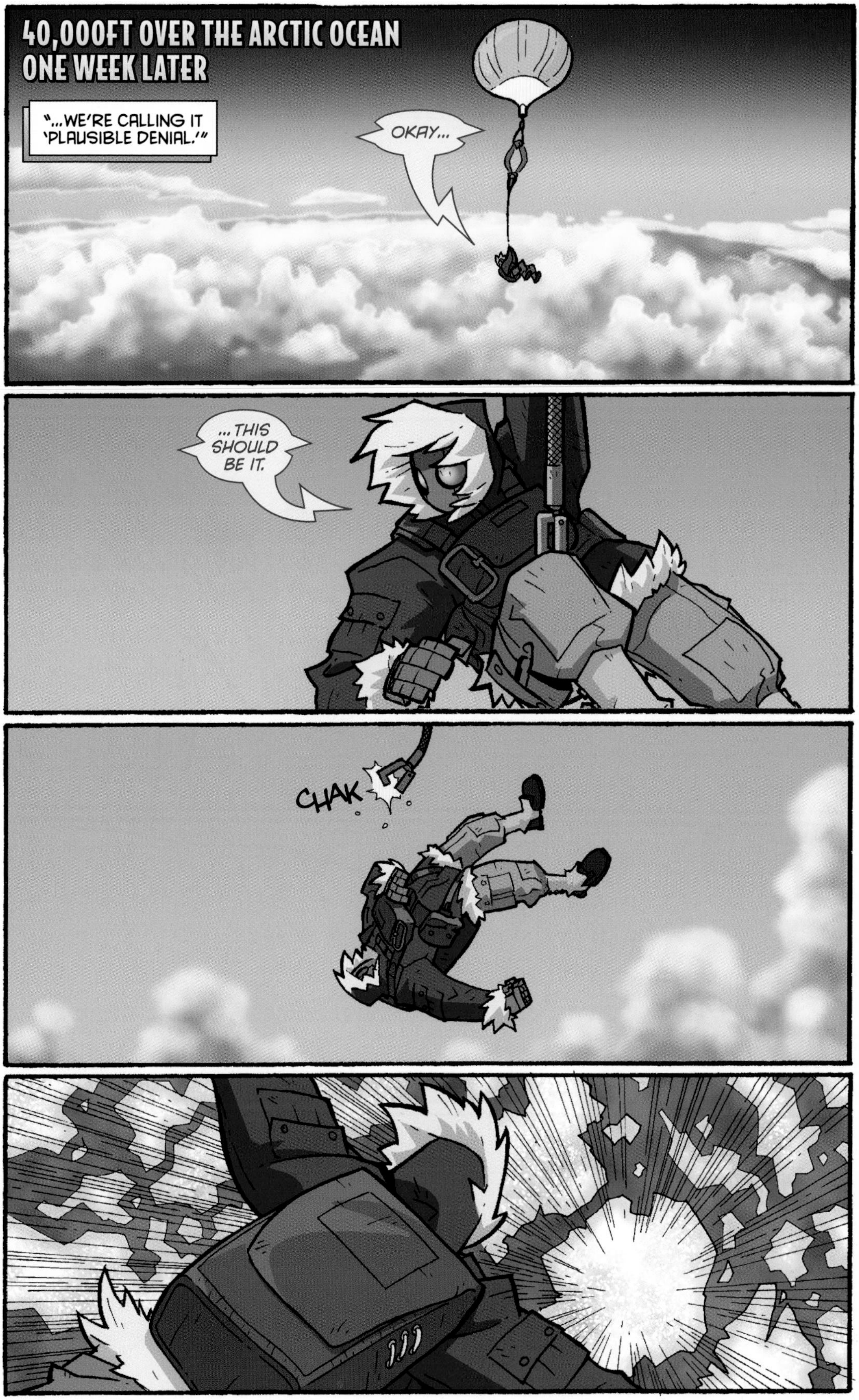
40,000FT OVER THE ARCTIC OCEAN
ONE WEEK LATER
"...WE'RE CALLING IT 'PLAUSIBLE DENIAL.'"
OKAY...
...THIS SHOULD BE IT.
CHAK

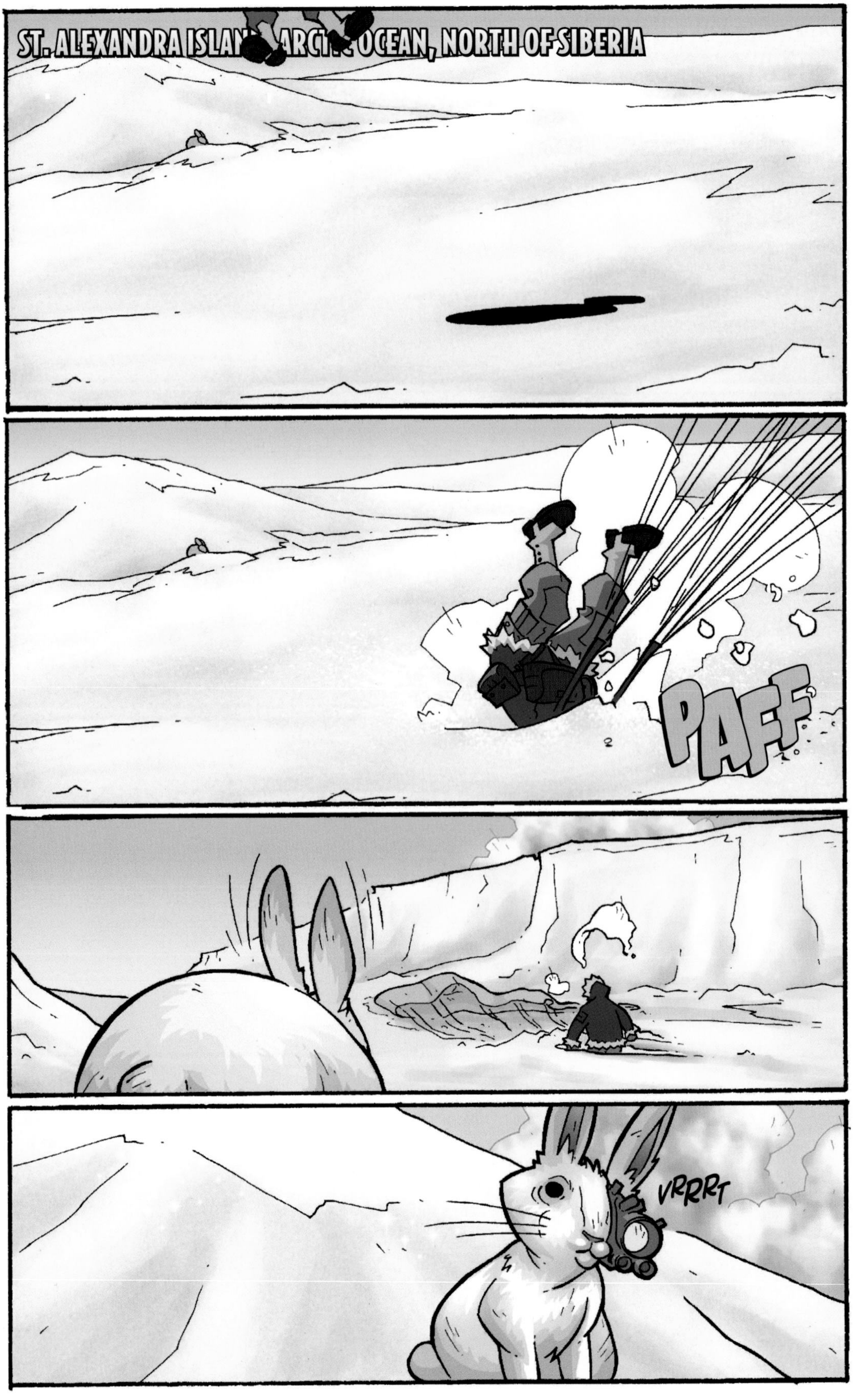
ST. ALEXANDRA ISLAND, ARCTIC OCEAN, NORTH OF SIBERIA
PAFF
VRRRT

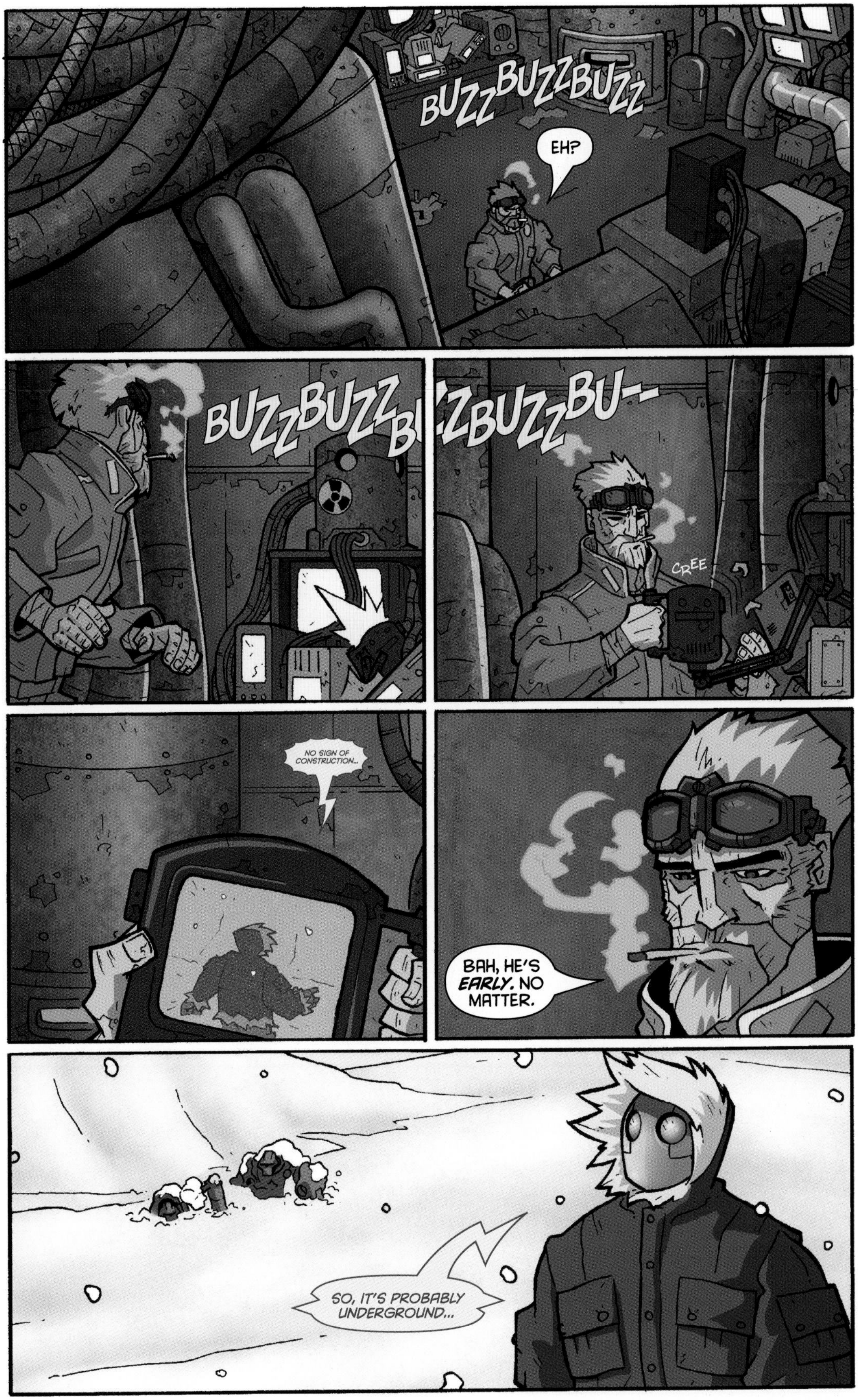
BUZZBUZZBUZZ
EH?
BUZZBUZZBUZZBUZZBU--
CREE
NO SIGN OF CONSTRUCTION...
BAH, HE'S EARLY. NO MATTER.
SO, IT'S PROBABLY UNDERGROUND...

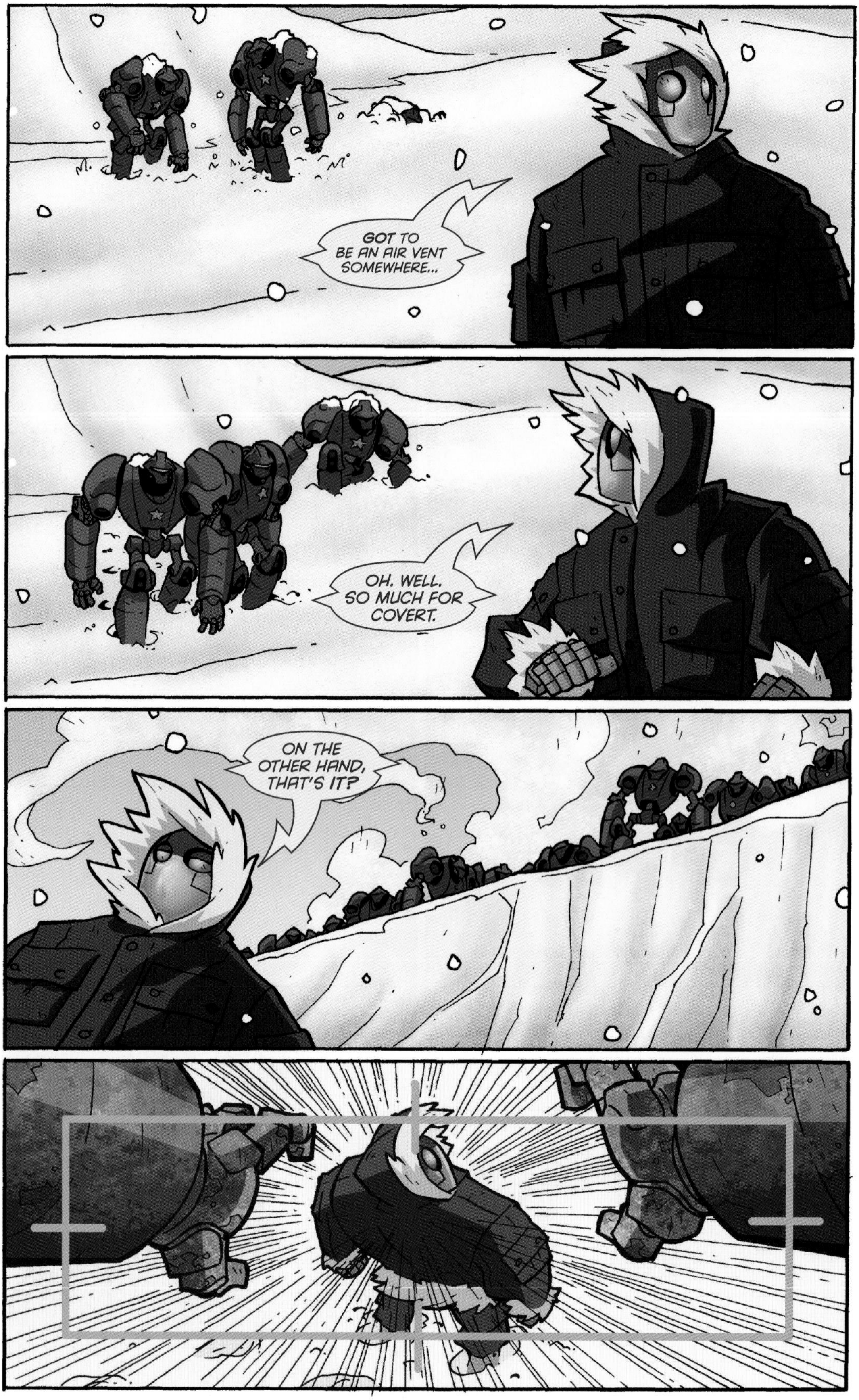
GOT TO BE AN AIR VENT SOMEWHERE...
OH. WELL. SO MUCH FOR COVERT.
ON THE OTHER HAND, THAT'S IT?

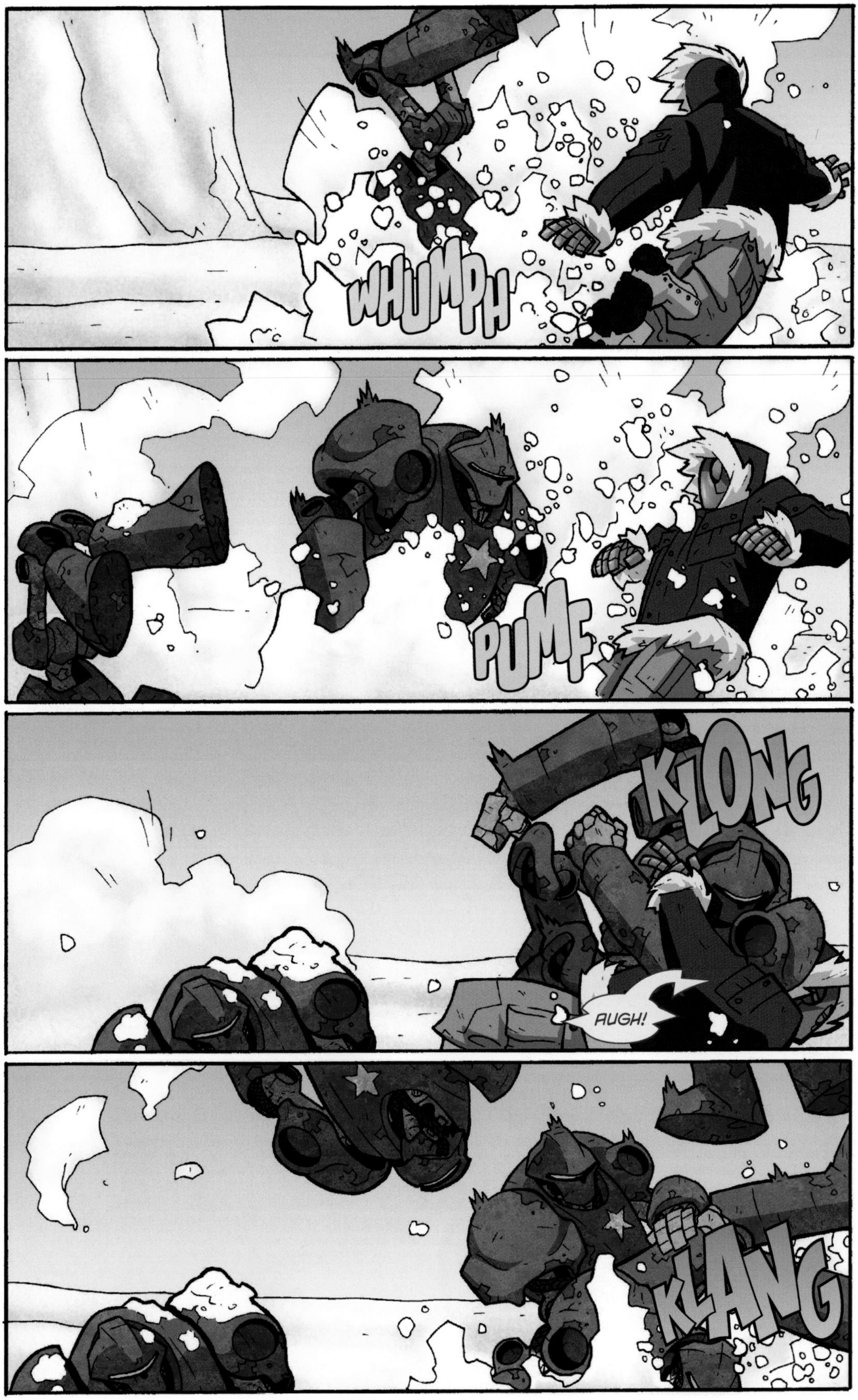
WHUMPH
PUMF
KLONG
AUGH!
KLANG

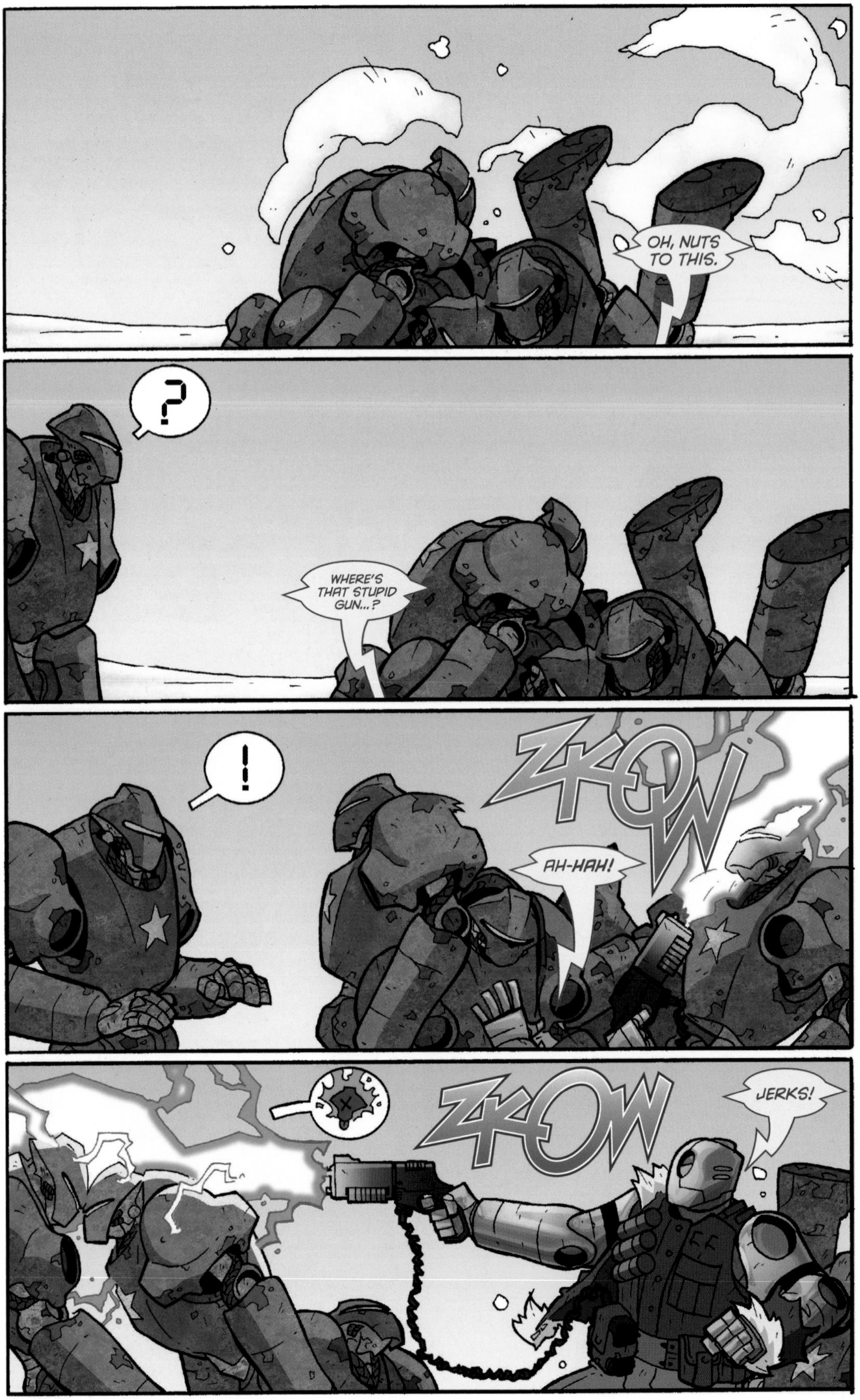
OH, NUTS TO THIS.
?
WHERE'S THAT STUPID GUN...?
!
ZKOW
AH-HAH!
ZKOW
JERKS!

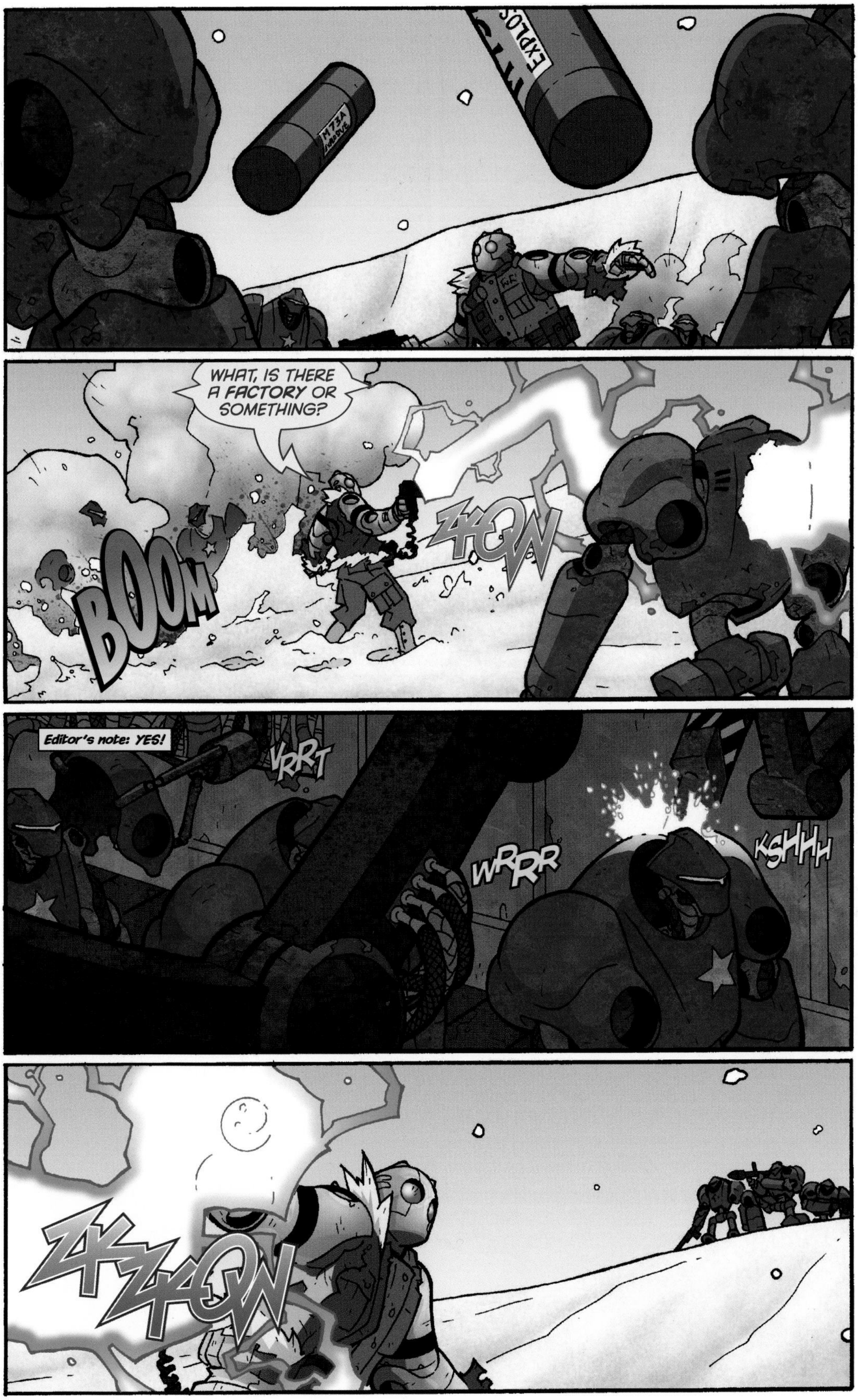
WHAT, IS THERE A FACTORY OR SOMETHING?
BOOM
ZKOW
Editor's note: YES!
VRRT
WRRR
KSHHH
ZKZKOW

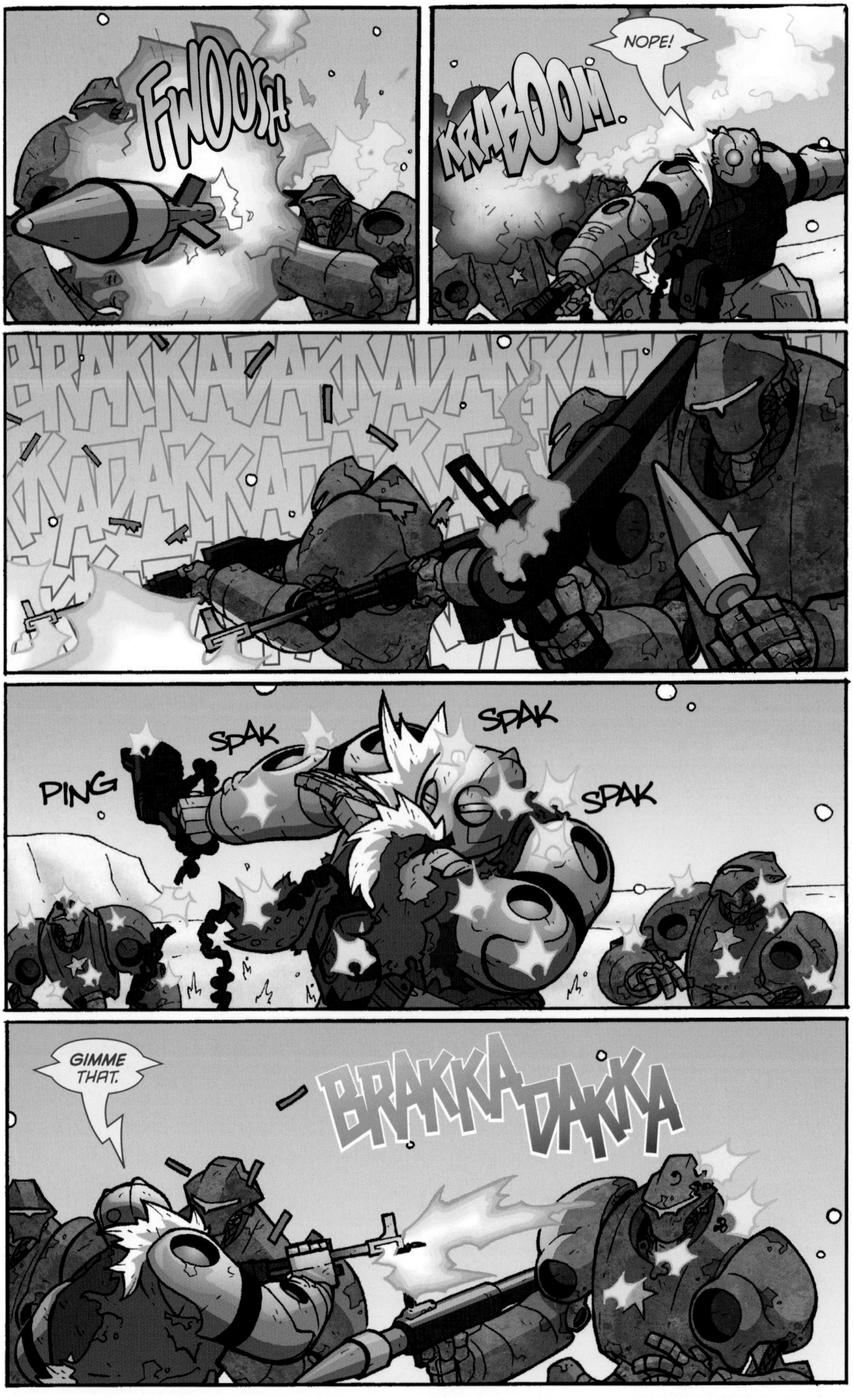
FWOOSH
KRABOOM
NOPE!
PING
SPAK
SPAK
SPAK
GIMME THAT.
BRAKKA DAKKA

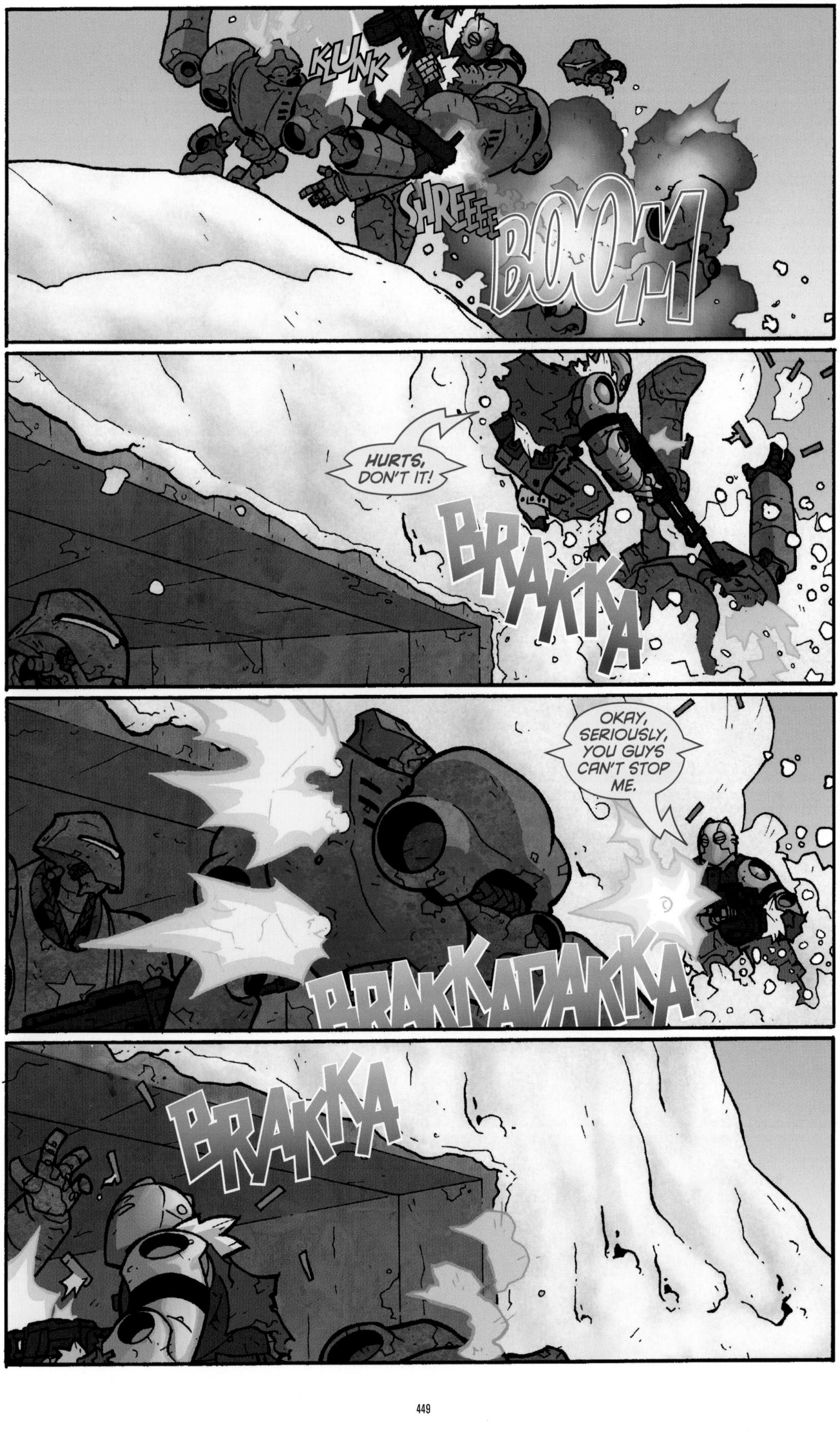
KLUNK
SHREEEE
BOOM
HURTS, DON'T IT!
BRAKKA
OKAY, SERIOUSLY, YOU GUYS CAN'T STOP ME.
BRAKKADAKKA
BRAKKA

I WAS DOING PRETTY GOOD UNTIL THE END THERE...

YOU DO NOT KNOW WHO I AM, DO YOU?

I KNOW YOU'VE GOT THE BEST CLUB HOUSE ON THE BLOCK.

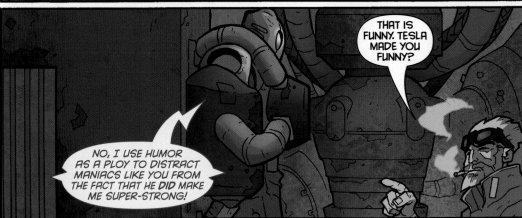

THAT IS FUNNY. TESLA MADE YOU FUNNY?

NO, I USE HUMOR AS A PLOY TO DISTRACT MANIACS LIKE YOU FROM THE FACT THAT HE *DID* MAKE ME SUPER-STRONG!

YEEARGH!

YES, VERY STRONG. THAT IS WHY WE USED THE *INCREDIBLY* STRONG ELECTROMAGNETIC RESTRAINTS.

OH.

THEY DID NOT TELL YOU MY NAME BECAUSE *I DO NOT EXIST.*

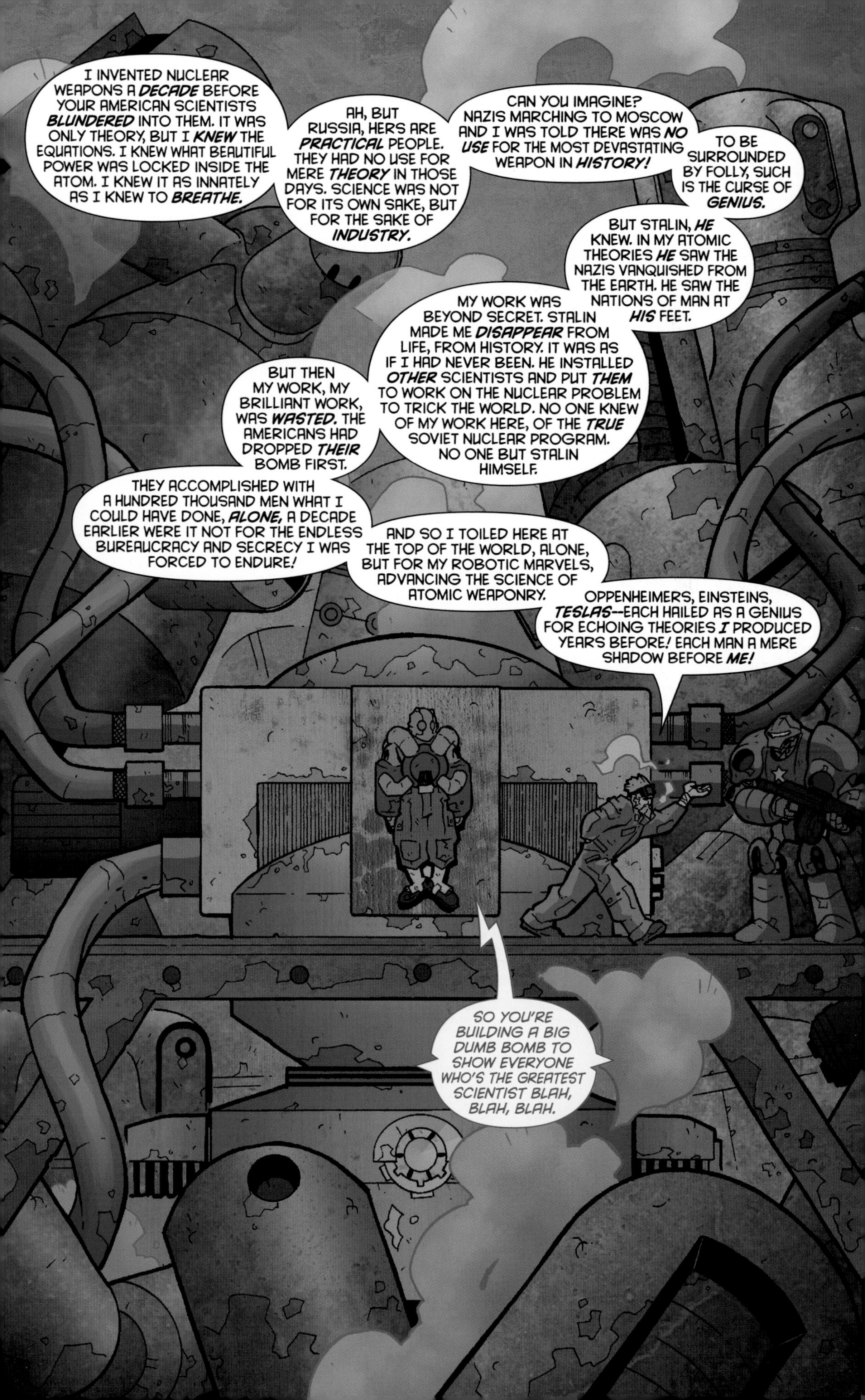
I INVENTED NUCLEAR WEAPONS A DECADE BEFORE YOUR AMERICAN SCIENTISTS BLUNDERED INTO THEM. IT WAS ONLY THEORY, BUT I KNEW THE EQUATIONS. I KNEW WHAT BEAUTIFUL POWER WAS LOCKED INSIDE THE ATOM. I KNEW IT AS INNATELY AS I KNEW TO BREATHE.
AH, BUT RUSSIA, HERS ARE PRACTICAL PEOPLE. THEY HAD NO USE FOR MERE THEORY IN THOSE DAYS. SCIENCE WAS NOT FOR ITS OWN SAKE, BUT FOR THE SAKE OF INDUSTRY.
CAN YOU IMAGINE? NAZIS MARCHING TO MOSCOW AND I WAS TOLD THERE WAS NO USE FOR THE MOST DEVASTATING WEAPON IN HISTORY!
TO BE SURROUNDED BY FOLLY, SUCH IS THE CURSE OF GENIUS.
BUT STALIN, HE KNEW. IN MY ATOMIC THEORIES HE SAW THE NAZIS VANQUISHED FROM THE EARTH. HE SAW THE NATIONS OF MAN AT HIS FEET.
MY WORK WAS BEYOND SECRET. STALIN MADE ME DISAPPEAR FROM LIFE, FROM HISTORY. IT WAS AS IF I HAD NEVER BEEN. HE INSTALLED OTHER SCIENTISTS AND PUT THEM TO WORK ON THE NUCLEAR PROBLEM TO TRICK THE WORLD. NO ONE KNEW OF MY WORK HERE, OF THE TRUE SOVIET NUCLEAR PROGRAM. NO ONE BUT STALIN HIMSELF.
BUT THEN MY WORK, MY BRILLIANT WORK, WAS WASTED. THE AMERICANS HAD DROPPED THEIR BOMB FIRST.
THEY ACCOMPLISHED WITH A HUNDRED THOUSAND MEN WHAT I COULD HAVE DONE, ALONE, A DECADE EARLIER WERE IT NOT FOR THE ENDLESS BUREAUCRACY AND SECRECY I WAS FORCED TO ENDURE!
AND SO I TOILED HERE AT THE TOP OF THE WORLD, ALONE, BUT FOR MY ROBOTIC MARVELS, ADVANCING THE SCIENCE OF ATOMIC WEAPONRY.
OPPENHEIMERS, EINSTEINS, TESLAS--EACH HAILED AS A GENIUS FOR ECHOING THEORIES I PRODUCED YEARS BEFORE! EACH MAN A MERE SHADOW BEFORE ME!
SO YOU'RE BUILDING A BIG DUMB BOMB TO SHOW EVERYONE WHO'S THE GREATEST SCIENTIST BLAH, BLAH, BLAH.

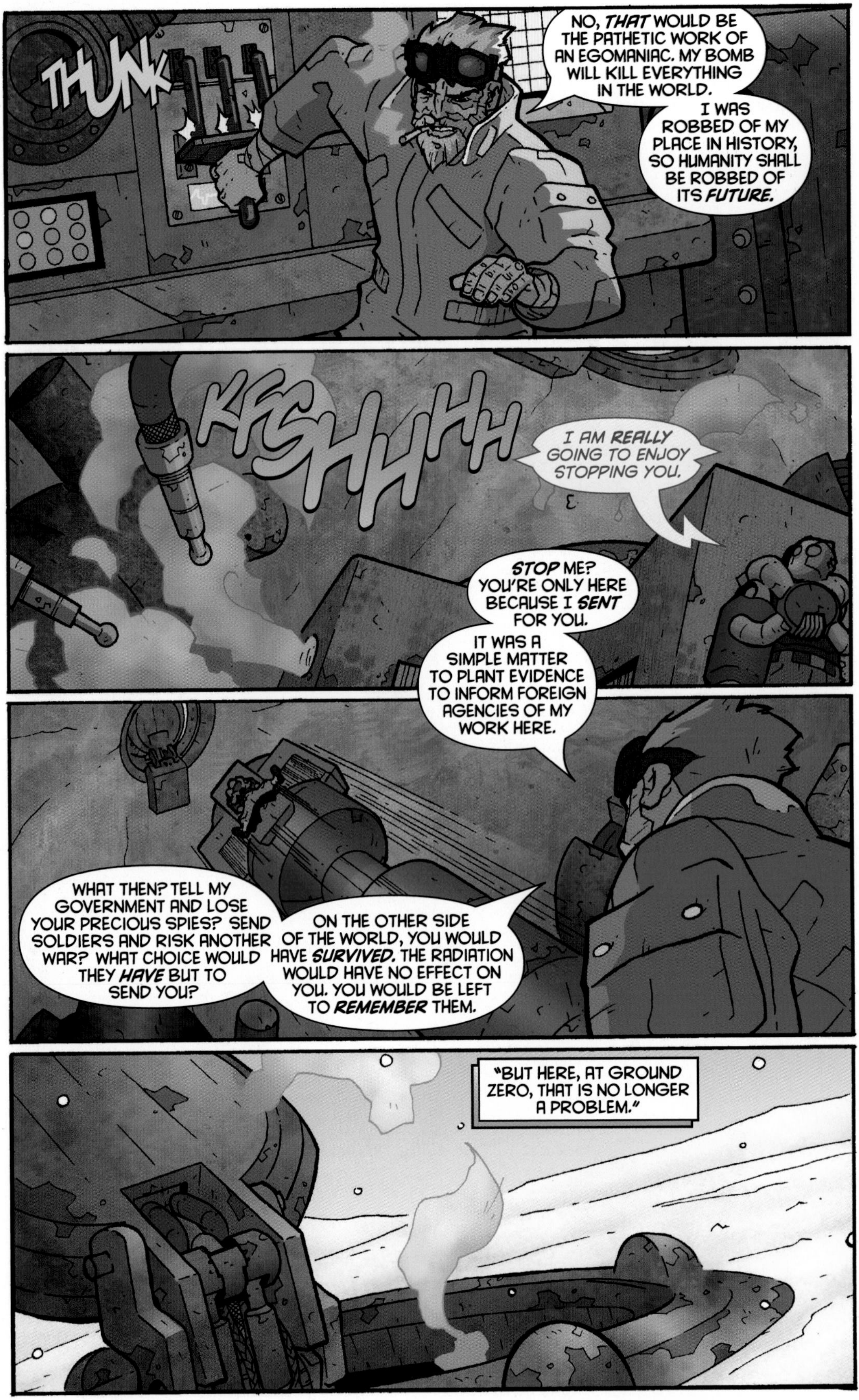
THUNK
NO, THAT WOULD BE THE PATHETIC WORK OF AN EGOMANIAC. MY BOMB WILL KILL EVERYTHING IN THE WORLD.
I WAS ROBBED OF MY PLACE IN HISTORY, SO HUMANITY SHALL BE ROBBED OF ITS FUTURE.
KFSHHHH
I AM REALLY GOING TO ENJOY STOPPING YOU.
STOP ME? YOU'RE ONLY HERE BECAUSE I SENT FOR YOU.
IT WAS A SIMPLE MATTER TO PLANT EVIDENCE TO INFORM FOREIGN AGENCIES OF MY WORK HERE.
WHAT THEN? TELL MY GOVERNMENT AND LOSE YOUR PRECIOUS SPIES? SEND SOLDIERS AND RISK ANOTHER WAR? WHAT CHOICE WOULD THEY HAVE BUT TO SEND YOU?
ON THE OTHER SIDE OF THE WORLD, YOU WOULD HAVE SURVIVED. THE RADIATION WOULD HAVE NO EFFECT ON YOU. YOU WOULD BE LEFT TO REMEMBER THEM.
"BUT HERE, AT GROUND ZERO, THAT IS NO LONGER A PROBLEM."

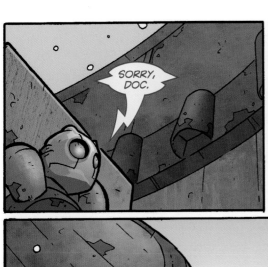

SORRY, DOC.

MY SURVIVAL'S **STILL** GOING TO BE A PROBLEM FOR YOU.

THOOP

AUGH! C'MON, BREAK BEFORE MY LEG DOES...

OH, THIS'LL HURT.

K-TUNG

MY GOD...

UPSIDE-DOWN IS BAD. UPSIDE-DOWN IS VERY BAD.

SKREEEEEE

KRAKOOOOM

KA-TINK

THIS WAS NOT SUPPOSED TO HAPPEN.

NO, URGH...

NO, THIS PRETTY MUCH *ALWAYS* HAPPENS.

I AM DYING.

IT'S THE MASSIVE PLUTONIUM LEAK IN THE FORTY TON BOMB THAT'S CRUSHING YOUR LOWER BODY.

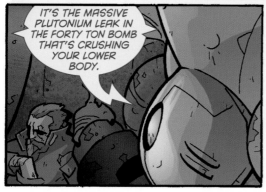

TELL THEM. YOU WILL TELL THEM WHO I AM. TELL THEM IVAN KOSHCHEY WAS THE *TRUE* MASTER OF THE ATOM. YOU WILL TELL THEM.

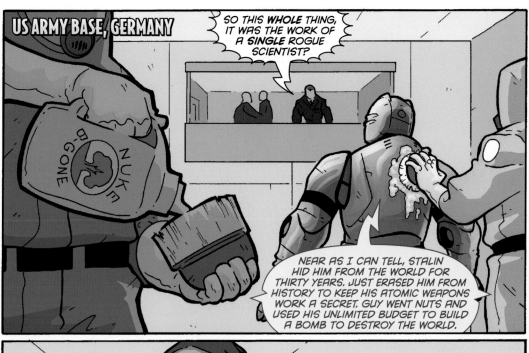

US ARMY BASE, GERMANY

SO THIS **WHOLE** THING, IT WAS THE WORK OF A **SINGLE** ROGUE SCIENTIST?

NEAR AS I CAN TELL, STALIN HID HIM FROM THE WORLD FOR THIRTY YEARS. JUST ERASED HIM FROM HISTORY TO KEEP HIS ATOMIC WEAPONS WORK A SECRET. GUY WENT NUTS AND USED HIS UNLIMITED BUDGET TO BUILD A BOMB TO DESTROY THE WORLD.

ANY IDEA WHO HE WAS?

COULDN'T TELL YOU, COLONEL.

DEET DEET DEEEET

BOOM

HE DIED BEFORE I GOT THERE. RADIATION POISONING.

END

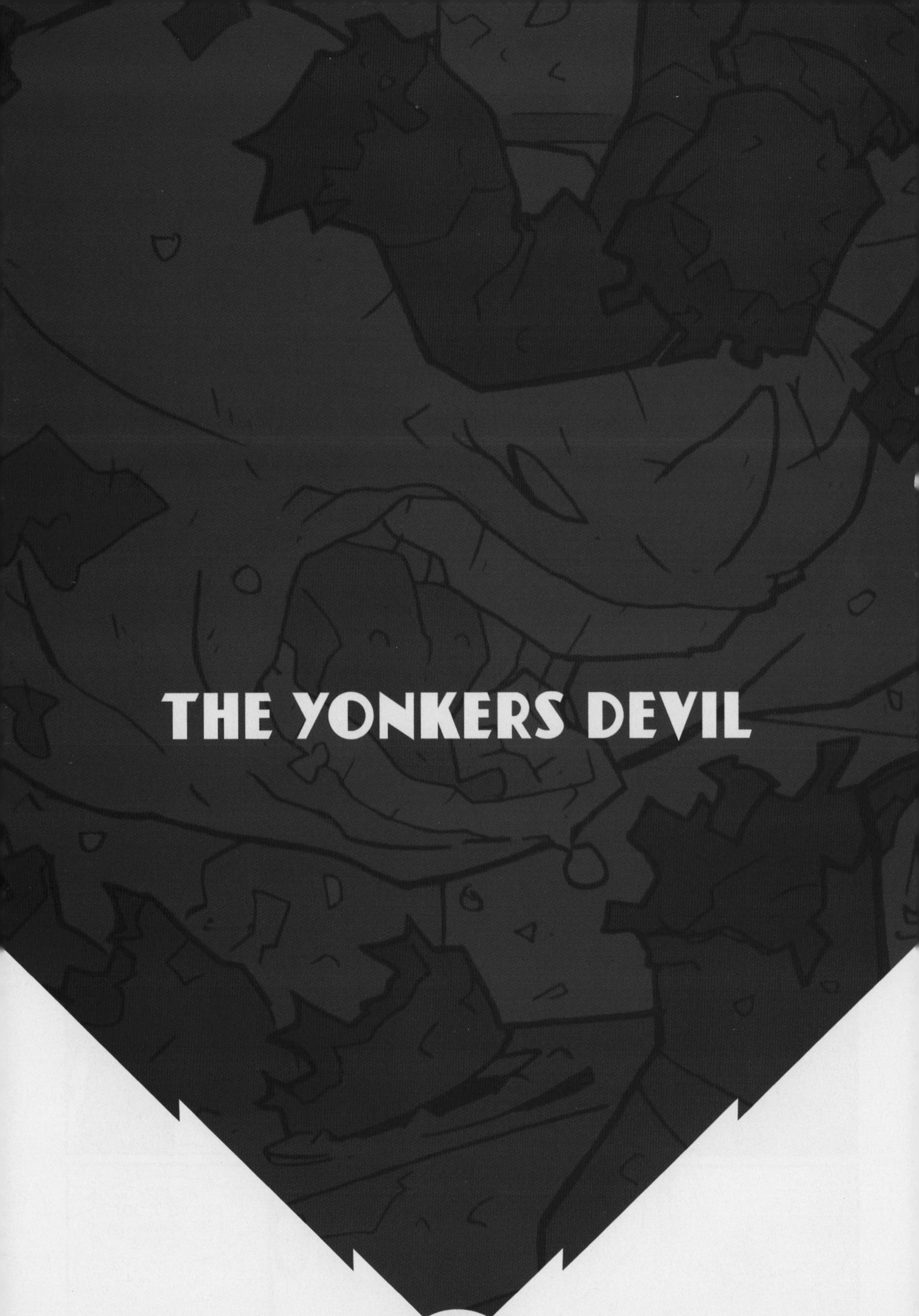

THE YONKERS DEVIL

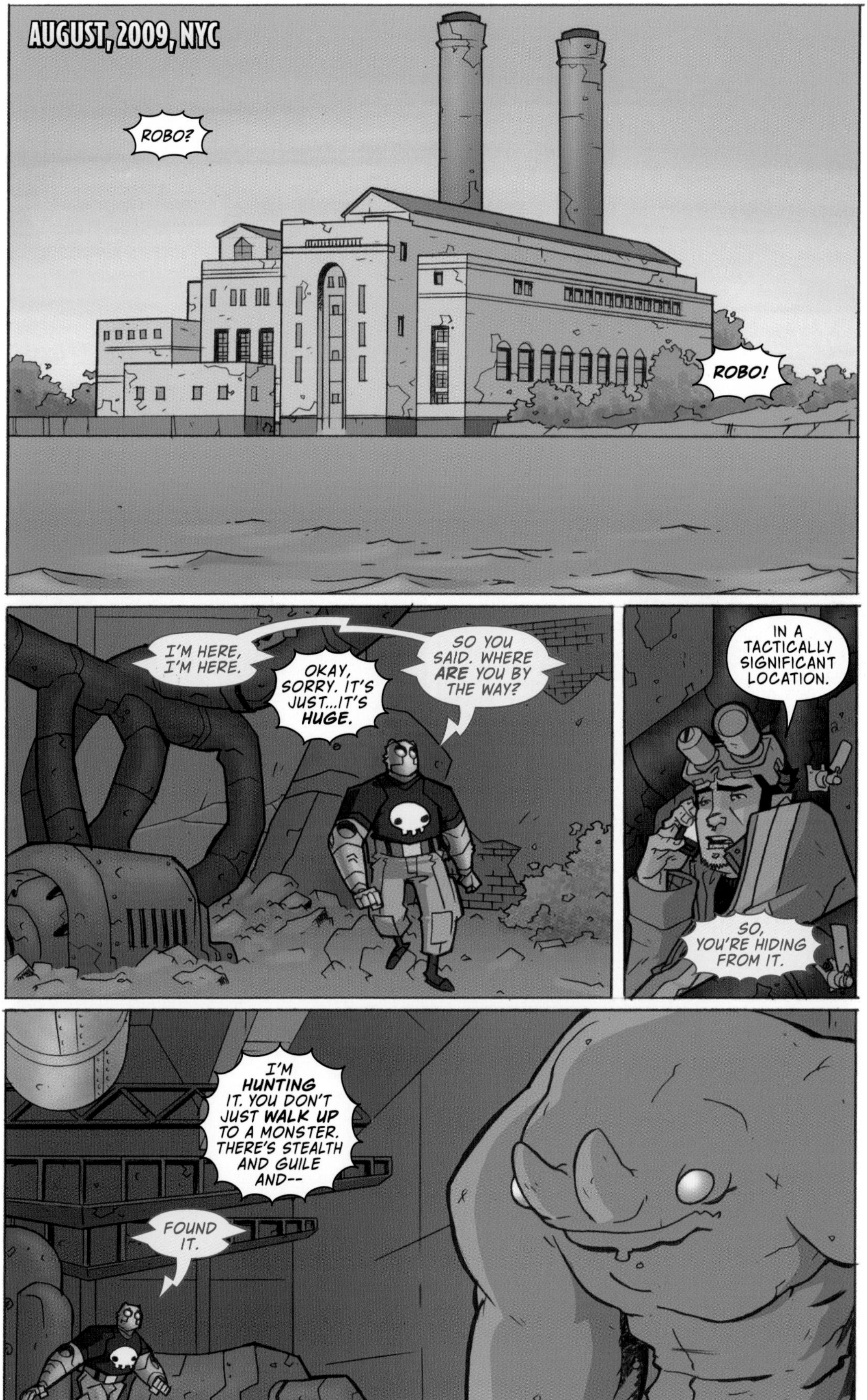
AUGUST, 2009, NYC
ROBO?
ROBO!
I'M HERE, I'M HERE.
OKAY, SORRY. IT'S JUST...IT'S HUGE.
SO YOU SAID. WHERE ARE YOU BY THE WAY?
IN A TACTICALLY SIGNIFICANT LOCATION.
SO, YOU'RE HIDING FROM IT.
I'M HUNTING IT. YOU DON'T JUST WALK UP TO A MONSTER. THERE'S STEALTH AND GUILE AND--
FOUND IT.

OH, THANK GOD!

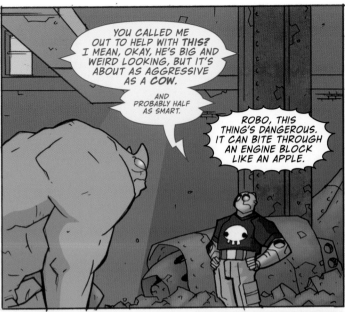

YOU CALLED ME OUT TO HELP WITH **THIS?** I MEAN, OKAY, HE'S BIG AND WEIRD LOOKING, BUT IT'S ABOUT AS AGGRESSIVE AS A **COW.**

AND PROBABLY HALF AS SMART.

ROBO, THIS THING'S DANGEROUS. IT CAN BITE THROUGH AN ENGINE BLOCK LIKE AN APPLE.

WHAT'S THAT NOI--ARE YOU...ARE YOU **WHIZZING?**

I WAS STUCK IN THERE FOR LIKE NINE HOURS, MAN.

TACTICALLY, RIGHT?

BEING SAFE AND ALIVE IS **TOTALLY** A TACTIC.

ANYWAY, WHEN YOU'RE DONE THERE--

WAAARGH!

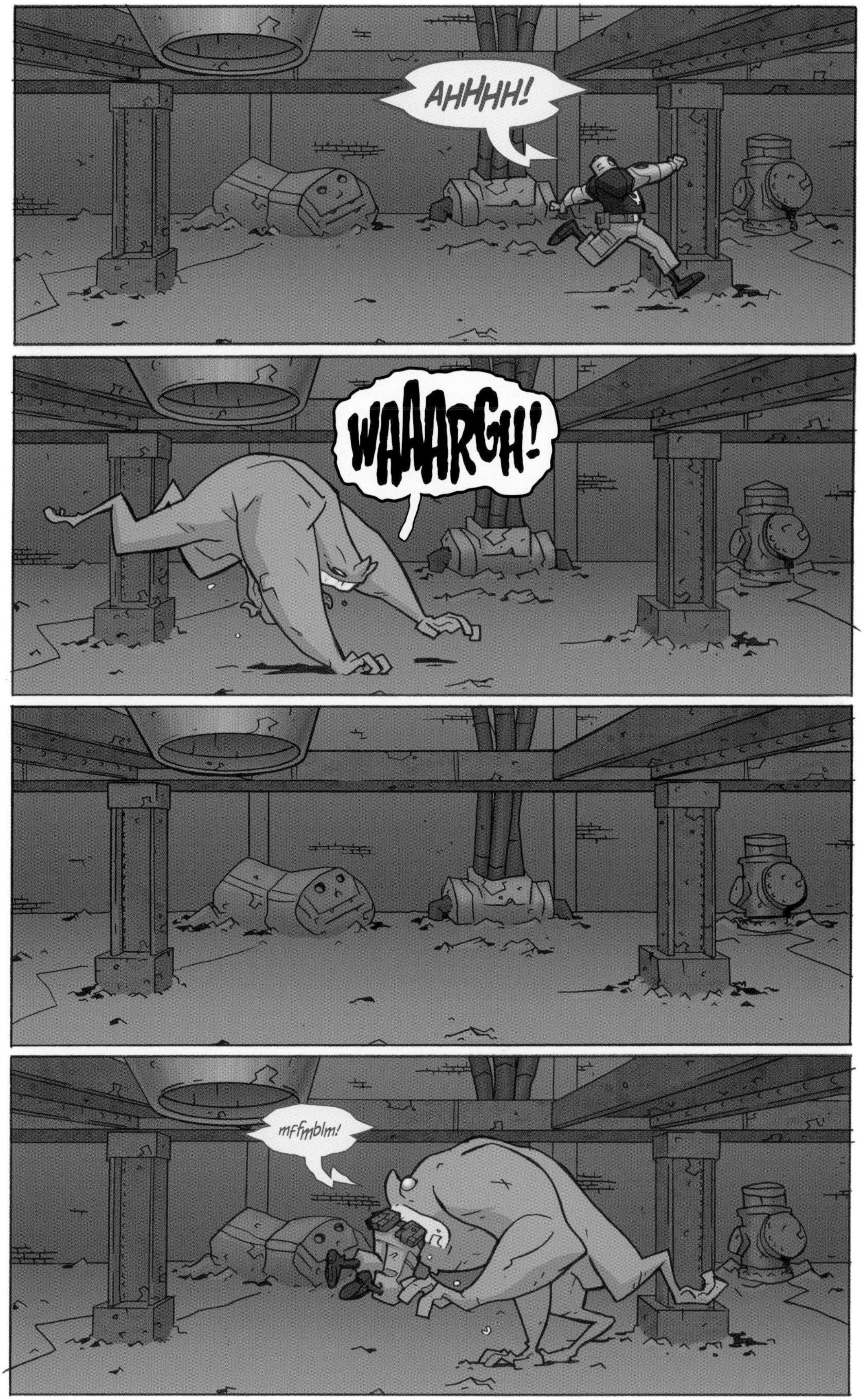
AHHHH!
WAAARGH!
mfmblm!

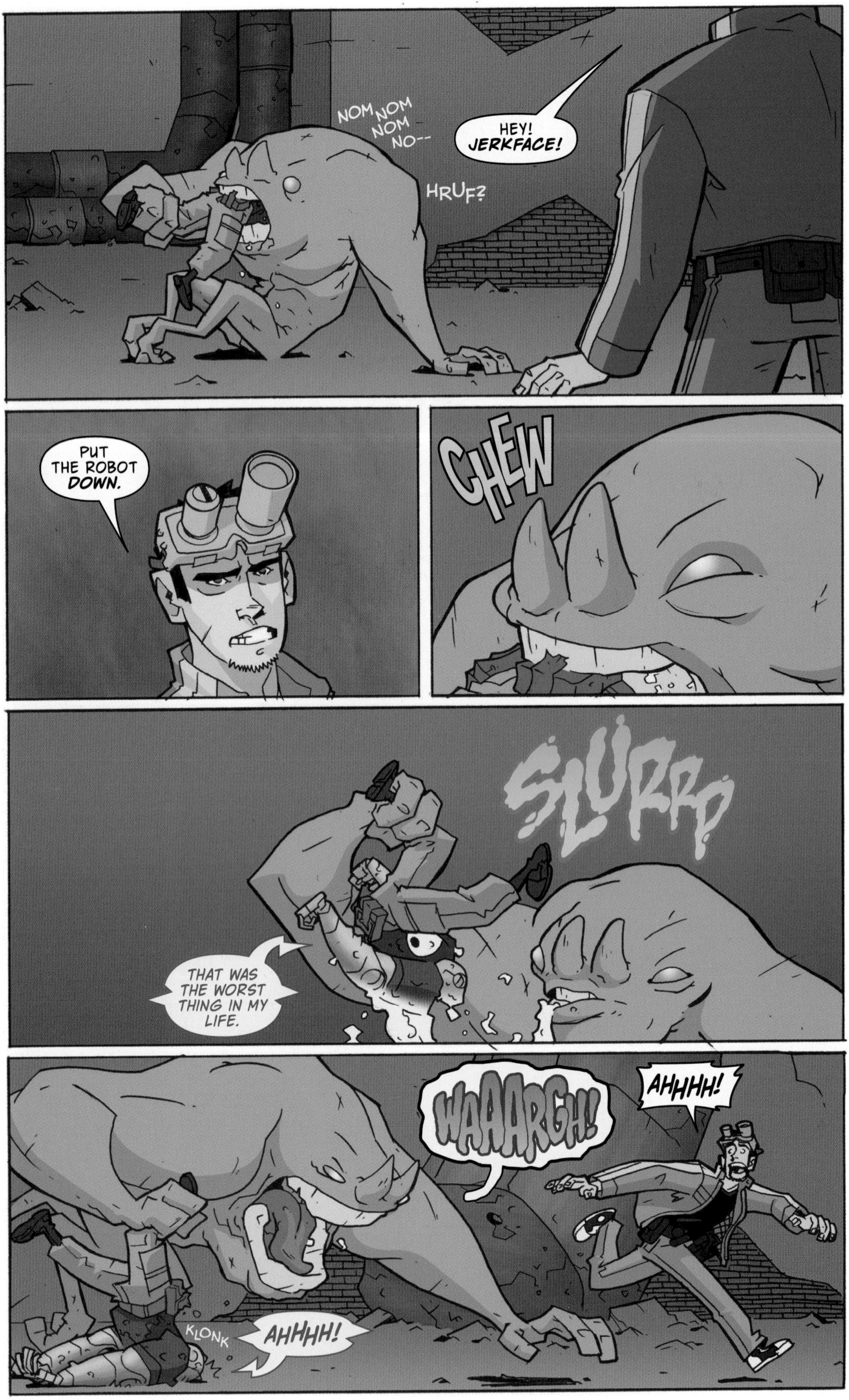
NOM NOM NOM NO--
HEY! JERKFACE!
HRUF?
PUT THE ROBOT DOWN.
CHEW
SLURRP
THAT WAS THE WORST THING IN MY LIFE.
WAAARGH!
AHHHH!
KLONK
AHHHH!

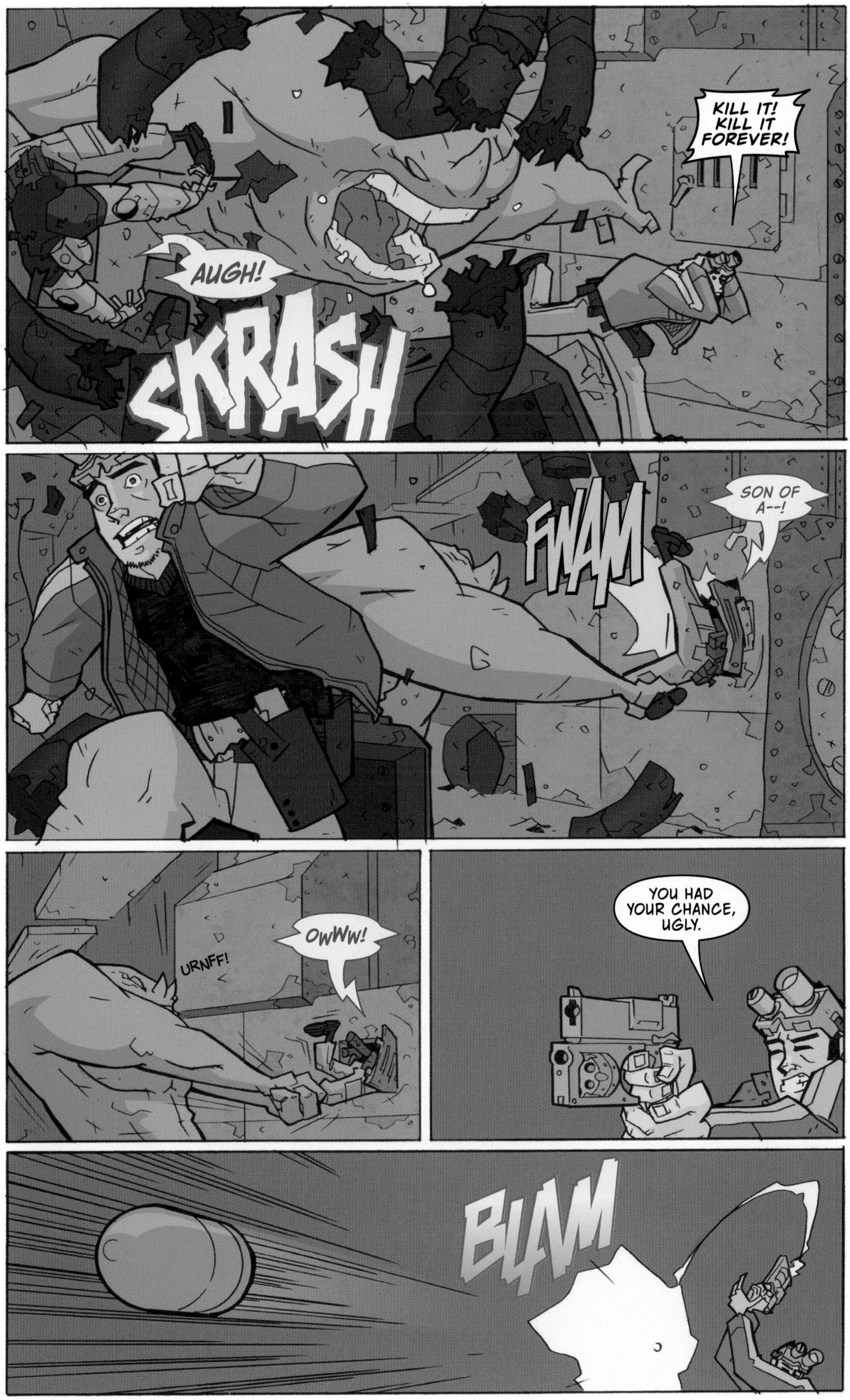
KILL IT! KILL IT FOREVER!
AUGH!
SKRASH
SON OF A--!
FWAM
URNFF!
OWWW!
YOU HAD YOUR CHANCE, UGLY.
BLAM

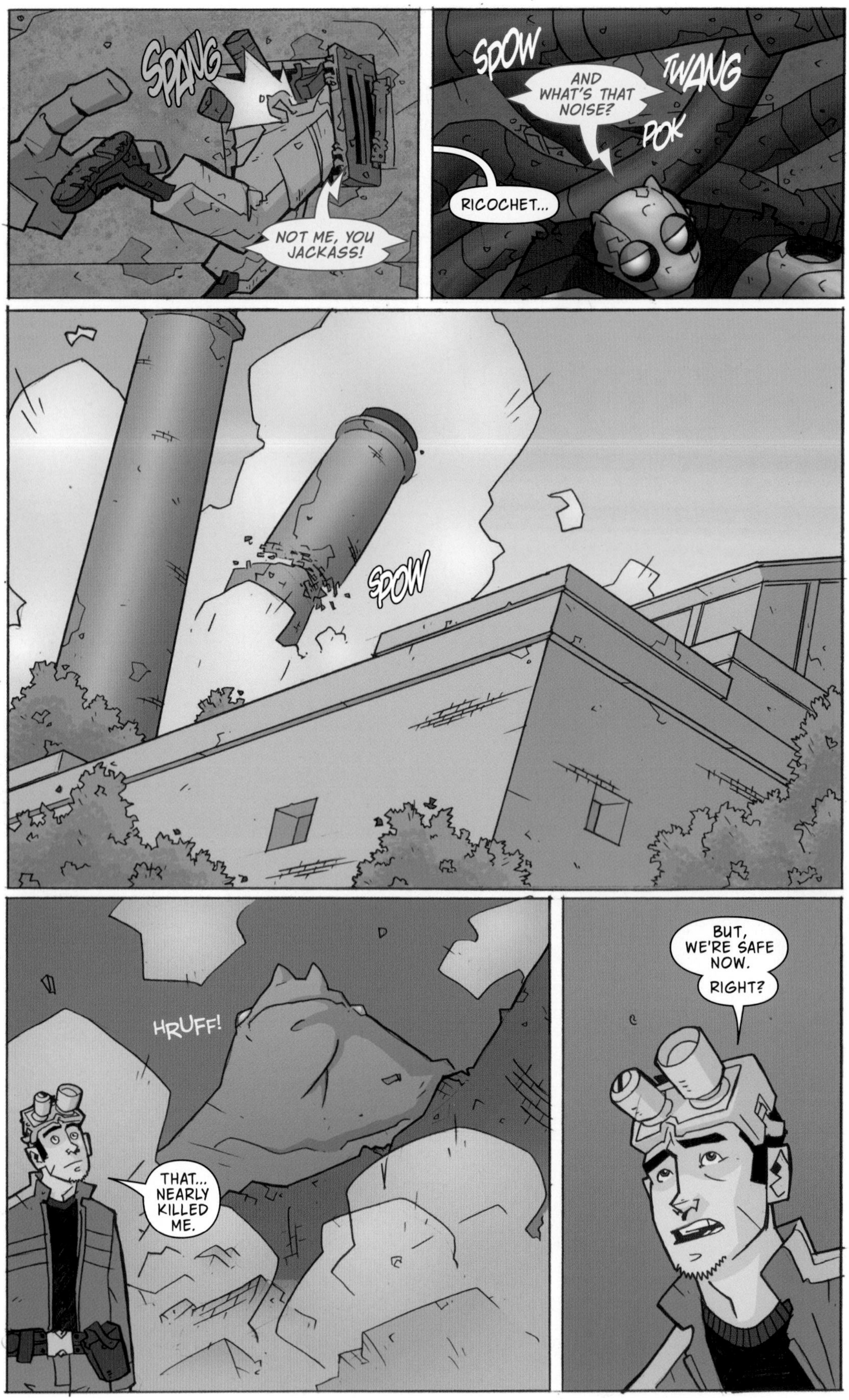
SPANG
NOT ME, YOU JACKASS!
SPOW
AND WHAT'S THAT NOISE?
TWANG
POK
RICOCHET...
SPOW
HRUFF!
THAT... NEARLY KILLED ME.
BUT, WE'RE SAFE NOW. RIGHT?

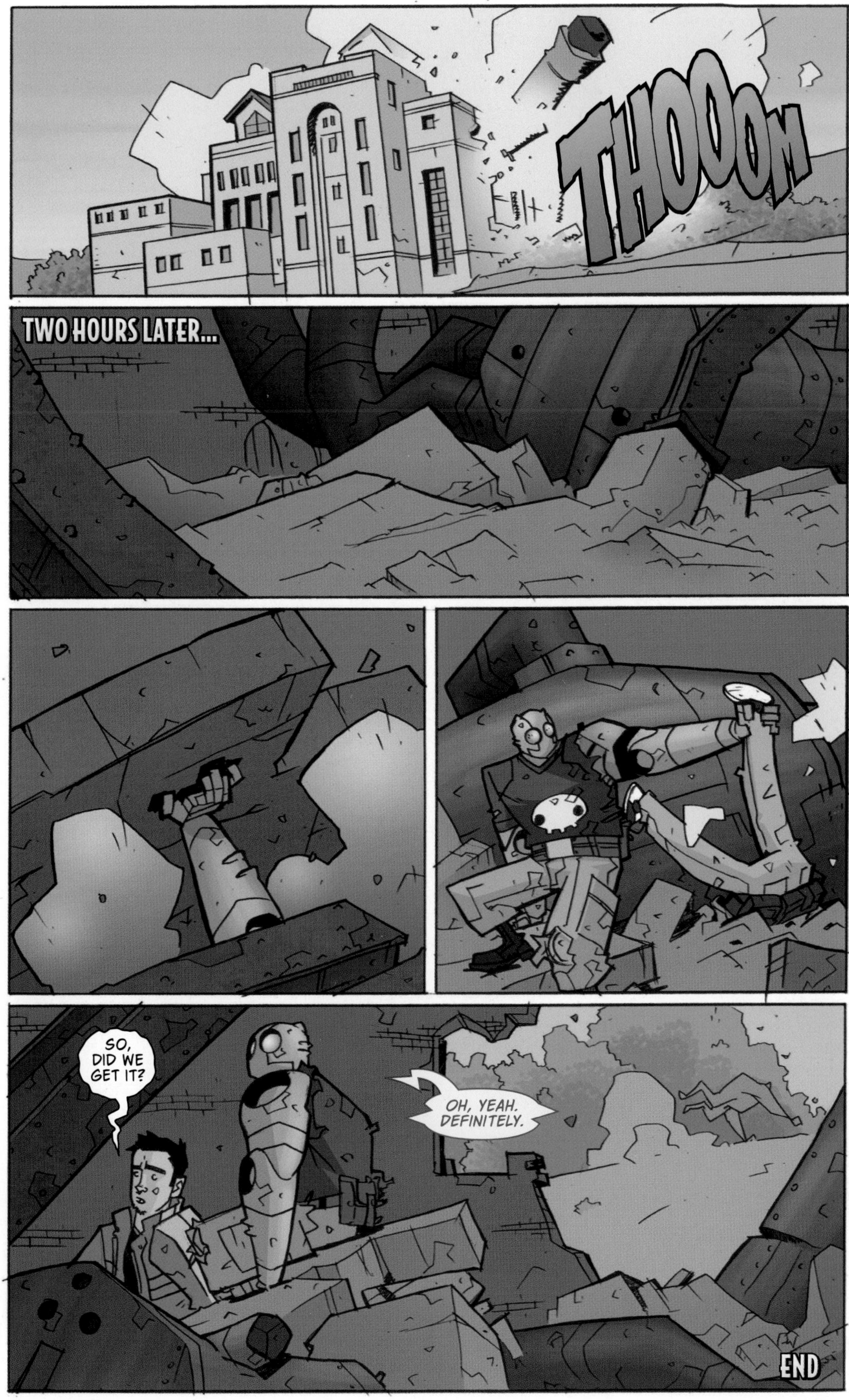
THOOOM
TWO HOURS LATER...
SO, DID WE GET IT?
OH, YEAH. DEFINITELY.
END

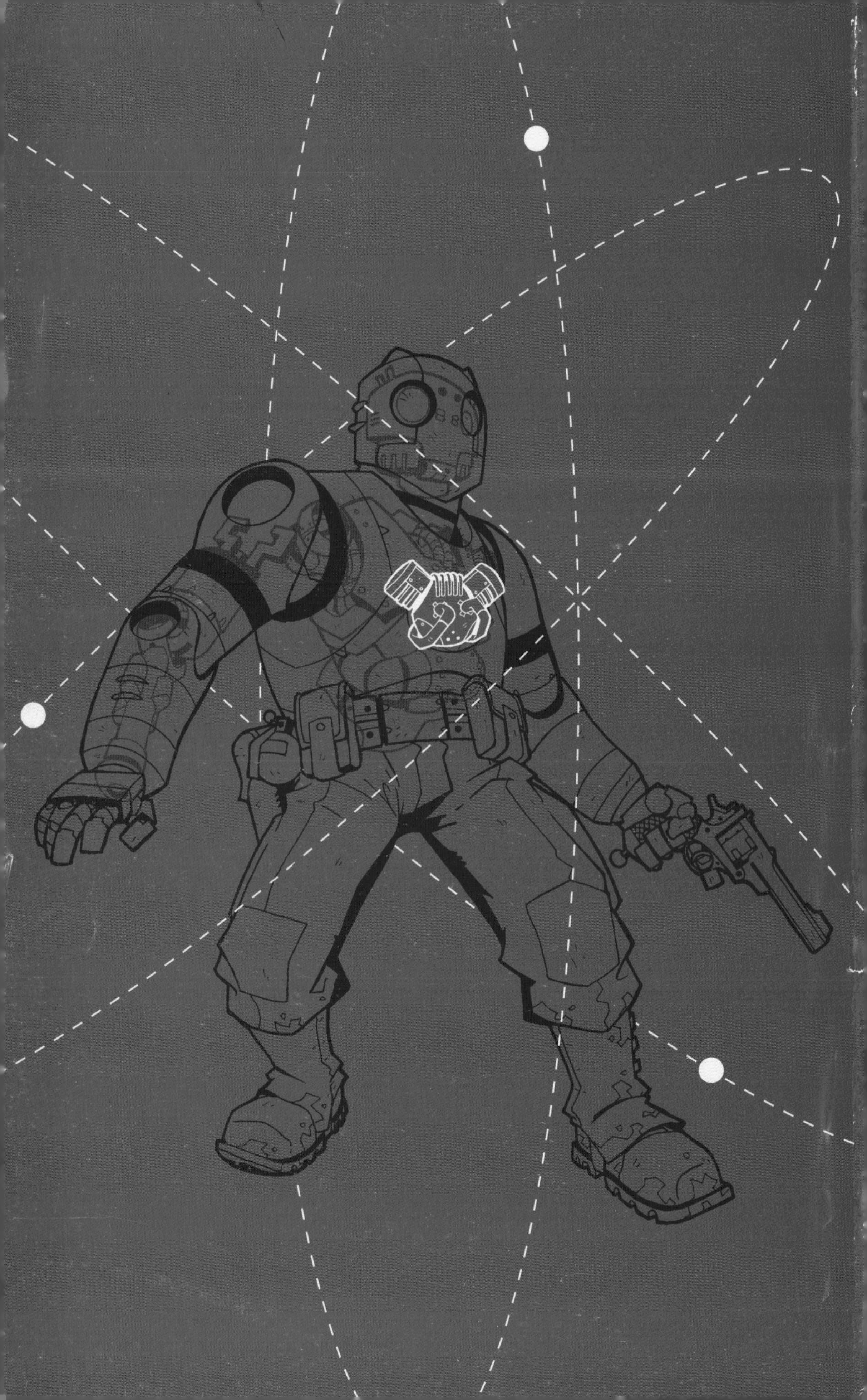